Praise for Lawrence Block and *Enough Rope*

"Raymond Chandler and Dashiell Hammett still cast long shadows across the mystery genre. If there is one crime writer currently capable of matching their legacies, it's Lawrence Block."

—*San Francisco Chronicle*

"True-blue mystery fans would be crazy to pass it up."

—*Kirkus Reviews*

"Lawrence Block combines three characteristics that rarely show up in the same crime writer: he's versatile, he's prolific, and he's damn good. . . . Offers an impressive testament to a modern master of crime fiction whose talent shines just as brightly in the short form as it does in the novel."

—*Booklist*

"Block's wit and propensity for jaunty protagonists are on full display here."

—*Fort Worth Star-Telegram*

"An invaluable addition."

—*Mystery Ink*

"Enough to tie up any Lawrence Block fan."

—Associated Press

"Block once again proves that he's imaginative, funny, insightful, wise about women, a clever and unpredictable plotter, a prodigious creator of memorable characters . . . and worth hating for all his talents."

—JanuaryMagazine.com

"[A] remarkable dark carnival. . . . Lawrence Block is the real thing, a living American writer necessary to know."

—*Buffalo News*

"This is a seminal collection of crime fiction."

—*Mystery Scene Magazine*

Athena Gassoumis

A Mystery Writers of America Grand Master, LAWRENCE BLOCK is a four-time winner of the Edgar Allan Poe and Shamus Awards, as well as a recipient of prizes in France, Germany, and Japan. The author of more than fifty books and numerous short stories, he is a devout New Yorker who spends much of his time traveling.

www.lawrenceblock.com

BOOKS BY LAWRENCE BLOCK

The Matthew Scudder Novels

The Sins of the Fathers • *Time to Murder and Create* • *In the Midst of Death* • *A Stab in the Dark* • *Eight Million Ways to Die* • *When the Sacred Ginmill Closes* • *Out on the Cutting Edge* • *A Ticket to the Boneyard* • *A Dance at the Slaughterhouse* • *A Walk Among the Tombstones* • *The Devil Knows You're Dead* • *A Long Line of Dead Men* • *Even the Wicked* • *Everybody Dies* • *Hope to Die*

The Bernie Rhodenbarr Mysteries

Burglars Can't Be Choosers • *The Burglar in the Closet* • *The Burglar Who Liked to Quote Kipling* • *The Burglar Who Studied Spinoza* • *The Burglar Who Painted Like Mondrian* • *The Burglar Who Traded Ted Williams* • *The Burglar Who Thought He Was Bogart* • *The Burglar in the Library* • *The Burglar in the Rye*

The Adventures of Evan Tanner

The Thief Who Couldn't Sleep • *The Canceled Czech* • *Tanner's Twelve Swingers* • *Two for Tanner* • *Tanner's Tiger* • *Here Comes a Hero* • *Me Tanner, You Jane* • *Tanner on Ice*

The Affairs of Chip Harrison

No Score • *Chip Harrison Scores Again* • *Make Out With Murder* • *The Topless Tulip Caper*

Other Novels

After the First Death • *Ariel* • *Coward's Kiss* • *Deadly Honeymoon* • *The Girl With the Long Green Heart* • *Hit List* • *Hit Man* • *Mona* • *Not Comin' Home to You* • *Random Walk* • *Ronald Rabbit Is a Dirty Old Man* • *The Specialists* • *Such Men Are Dangerous* • *The Triumph of Evil* • *You Could Call It Murder*

Collected Short Stories

Sometimes They Bite • *Like a Lamb to Slaughter* • *Some Days You Get the Bear* • *Ehrengraf for the Defense* • *One Night Stands* • *The Lost Cases of Ed London*

Anthologies

Death Cruise • *Master's Choice* • *Opening Shots* • *Master's Choice 2* • *Speaking of Lust* • *Speaking of Greed* • *Opening Shots 2*

Books for Writers

Writing the Novel from Plot to Print • *Telling Lies for Fun & Profit* • *Write for Your Life* • *Spider, Spin Me a Web*

Enough Rope

Lawrence Block

collected stories

DARK ALLEY
An *Imprint of* HarperCollins*Publishers*

This is for Marty Greenberg
and the Green Bay Packagers

This book is a work of fiction. The characters, incidents, and dialogue are drawn from the author's imagination and are not to be construed as real. Any resemblance to actual events or persons, living or dead, is entirely coincidental.

Portions of this book were originally published as *The Collected Mystery Stories* in Great Britain in 1999 by Orion, an imprint of Orion Books Ltd. A hardcover edition was published in 2002 by William Morrow, an imprint of HarperCollins Publishers.

First Dark Alley edition published 2003.

Designed by Nicola Ferguson

The Library of Congress has cataloged the hardcover edition as follows:

Block, Lawrence.
Enough rope : collected stories / Lawrence Block.—1st ed.
p. cm.
ISBN 0-06-018890-1 (hc)
1. Detective and mystery stories, American. I. Title.
PS3552.L63 A6 2002
813'.54—dc21 2001051821

ISBN 0-06-055967-5 (pbk.)

03 04 05 06 07 JTC/RRD 10 9 8 7 6 5 4 3 2 1

Contents

Short Stories

A Bad Night for Burglars, 3
A Blow for Freedom, 8
A Little Off the Top, 17
And Miles to Go Before I Sleep, 25
As Good as a Rest, 35
The Books Always Balance, 42
The Boy Who Disappeared Clouds, 48
Change of Life, 56
Cleveland in My Dreams, 65
Click!, 73
Collecting Ackermans, 80
The Dangerous Business, 95
Death Wish, 100
The Dettweiler Solution, 107
Funny You Should Ask, 117
The Gentle Way, 120
Going Through the Motions, 127
Good for the Soul, 137
Hilliard's Ceremony, 147
Hot Eyes, Cold Eyes, 164
How Would You Like It?, 170
If This Be Madness, 173
Leo Youngdahl, R.I.P., 177
Like a Bug on a Windshield, 182
Like a Dog in the Street, 194

The Most Unusual Snatch, 211
Nothing Short of Highway Robbery, 221
One Thousand Dollars a Word, 230
Passport in Order, 234
Someday I'll Plant More Walnut Trees, 240
Some Days You Get the Bear, 252
Something to Remember You By, 265
Some Things a Man Must Do, 271
Sometimes They Bite, 280
Strangers on a Handball Court, 290
That Kind of a Day, 298
This Crazy Business of Ours, 305
The Tulsa Experience, 315
Weekend Guests, 324
When This Man Dies, 328
With a Smile for the Ending, 335
You Could Call It Blackmail, 350

Chip Harrison

Death of the Mallory Queen, 361
As Dark as Christmas Gets, 372

Martin Ehrengraf

The Ehrengraf Defense, 393
The Ehrengraf Presumption, 400
The Ehrengraf Experience, 409
The Ehrengraf Appointment, 420
The Ehrengraf Riposte, 432
The Ehrengraf Obligation, 442
The Ehrengraf Alternative, 451
The Ehrengraf Nostrum, 462
The Ehrengraf Affirmation, 472
The Ehrengraf Reverse, 482

Bernie Rhodenbarr

Like a Thief in the Night, 499
The Burglar Who Dropped In on Elvis, 509
The Burglar Who Smelled Smoke, 520

Keller

Answers to Soldier, 539
Keller's Therapy, 551
Keller on the Spot, 571
Keller's Horoscope, 586
Keller's Designated Hitter, 613

Matthew Scudder

Out the Window, 633
A Candle for the Bag Lady, 657
By the Dawn's Early Light, 679
Batman's Helpers, 692
The Merciful Angel of Death, 703
The Night and the Music, 714
Looking for David, 716
Let's Get Lost, 727
A Moment of Wrong Thinking, 737

New Stories

Almost Perfect, 751
Headaches and Bad Dreams, 761
Hit the Ball, Drag Fred, 776
How Far It Could Go, 788
In for a Penny, 796
Like a Bone in the Throat, 801
Points, 819
Sweet Little Hands, 829
Terrible Tommy Terhune, 837
Three in the Side Pocket, 850
You Don't Even Feel It, 858

Two Old Stories

It Took You Long Enough, 873
You Can't Lose, 878

Introduction

"Eighty-four stories?" My friend gave me a look. "That's not a book," he said. "That's a skyscraper."

It's a handful, too, as you've no doubt already noticed yourself, and I'm conscious as I prepare these introductory remarks that I'm only making the damned thing longer with every word I write. This book was very nearly entitled *Long Story Short*, and it's been observed that when you utter the words "to make a long story short," it's already too late.

But I digress, and not for the first time. A short story collection seems to cry out for an introduction, especially when it's a huge doorstop of a thing like this one, and especially when it represents one person's entire output of short fiction over a career that began in (gulp!) 1957.

Well, virtually entire . . .

My earliest stories, collected a few years ago in a signed limited edition (*One Night Stands*, Crippen & Landru), have been purposely omitted. I don't think much of them—which puts me in the majority, I'd have to say—and, while I'm not unwilling for collectors and specialists to have them, they don't belong in this book. (I've made one exception, my first published story, called "You Can't Lose." It seemed worth including, if only as a curiosity.)

Two more recent shorter fictions, "Speaking of Lust" and "Speaking of Greed," have also been omitted. Each is the title novella in a volume of the Seven Deadly Sins anthology series, and when all seven novellas have been written and published, they'll be gathered into a single volume. I'm very fond of the two written to date—but they're long, running around 20,000 words each, and they don't belong here.

And, come to think of it, my episodic novel *Hit Man* is essentially a collection of ten short stories, and that constituted a quandary all its own. If I were to include them all, I'd be folding a full book into this one, and making people buy it a second time. If I left them all out, well, I'd be passing up the chance to include one story that was shortlisted for the Edgar Allan Poe Award and two others that won it outright. Some authors might be modest enough to omit such stories, and even to leave off mentioning the awards, but I am not of their number.

So I've compromised, and included those three of the ten, along with two more Keller stories—"Keller's Horoscope," extracted from the second Keller novel, *Hit List*, for publication in a German anthology, and "Keller's Designated Hitter," written for an anthology of baseball stories and otherwise unpublished. If there's a third book about Keller, perhaps it will be included. Then again, perhaps not. At any rate, it's here.

Once I'd selected the stories, I had to put them in order.

As far as I can see, there are three accepted ways to organize collections of short fiction. You can line them up in the order they were written, you can alphabetize them by title, or you can place them here and there like paintings in a gallery, trying to arrange them so that they'll complement one another.

The last is altogether beyond me—how the hell do I know in what order you'll enjoy coming upon these stories? And chronological order is out the question, because I couldn't possibly recall precisely when each story was written. Alphabetical order has always made perfect sense to me, it's so deliciously arbitrary and yet so marvelously unequivocal. How better to construct a sheer hodgepodge with the illusion of order?

But there's another variable to weigh in the balance, and that's that some of my stories are about series characters, and they really ought to be set off by themselves. And I do recall the order in which the series stories were written, and they really ought to be arranged in that order.

So here's the plan:

The stories which appeared in my three previously published collections, *Sometimes They Bite*, *Like a Lamb to Slaughter*, and *Some Days You Get the Bear*, appear first, in one great alphabetically ordered jumble.

The groups of stories which follow—about Martin Ehrengraf, Chip Harrison, Keller, Bernie Rhodenbarr, and Matthew Scudder—appear chronologically. Many of these showed up in the three above-named collections, but quite a few did not, and these are collected here for the first time: "The Ehrengraf Presumption," "The Ehrengraf Riposte," "The Ehrengraf Affirmation," and "The Ehrengraf Reverse"; "As Dark as Christmas Gets"; "Keller's Horoscope" and "Keller's Designated Hitter"; "The Burglar Who Smelled Smoke"; and "The Night and the Music," "Looking for David," "Let's Get Lost," and "A Moment of Wrong Thinking."

Next are twelve new non-series stories. (One of them, "It Took You Long Enough," was written thirty years ago and just now rediscovered.) And last and least is an old story, indeed a first story, "You Can't Lose," sold to *Manhunt* in the summer of 1957 and published in February 1958.

And is that it?

Well, I hope not. I still get an enormous amount of satisfaction out of writing short stories, and I still find things I haven't done and try to work out ways to do them.

There is one thing I've noticed over the years, and maybe it's worth comment. It is, simply, that the stories have grown longer over time. In the early days I had to work at it to stretch a story to 3,000 words—and that was when I had every incentive to write long, as every word I used meant another cent and a half in my pocket. Now, when I tend to get paid by the story rather than by the word, I have to work even harder to hold them to two to three times that length.

(The same's true for books, and you hear people blame computers for making it easier to go on and on. I thought that might be it, until I wrote *Tanner on Ice*, the first Tanner novel in twenty-eight years, and found it running half again as long as its predecessors. I couldn't blame a computer, either, as I wrote the thing with a ballpoint pen on a stack of legal pads.)

Not long ago I read a thoughtful and perceptive introduction to a collection called *Here's O'Hara*, by Albert Erskine, John O'Hara's longtime editor. He noted that the more recent stories were substantially longer than the earlier ones, and said that they were also better. He wouldn't be foolish enough to argue that they were better because they were longer, Erskine wrote, but thought it was fair to contend that they were longer because they were better.

I know that's true for O'Hara, and I'd like to think it's true of my work as well. And maybe it is, maybe I write longer these days because my characters and situations are more richly conceived, and I consequently have more to say about them.

Or perhaps I'm just turning into a wordy old bastard. Tell you what—you decide.

—Lawrence Block
Greenwich Village

Short Stories

A Bad Night for Burglars

The burglar, a slender and clean-cut chap just past thirty, was rifling a drawer in the bedside table when Archer Trebizond slipped into the bedroom. Trebizond's approach was as catfooted as if he himself were the burglar, a situation which was manifestly not the case. The burglar never did hear Trebizond, absorbed as he was in his perusal of the drawer's contents, and at length he sensed the other man's presence as a jungle beast senses the presence of a predator.

The analogy, let it be said, is scarcely accidental.

When the burglar turned his eyes on Archer Trebizond his heart fluttered and fluttered again, first at the mere fact of discovery, then at his own discovery of the gleaming revolver in Trebizond's hand. The revolver was pointed in his direction, and this the burglar found upsetting.

"Darn it all," said the burglar, approximately. "I could have sworn there was nobody home. I phoned, I rang the bell—"

"I just got here," Trebizond said.

"Just my luck. The whole week's been like that. I dented a fender on Tuesday afternoon, overturned my fish tank the night before last. An unbelievable mess all over the carpet, and I lost a mated pair of African mouthbreeders so rare they don't have a Latin name yet. I'd hate to tell you what I paid for them."

"Hard luck," Trebizond said.

"And just yesterday I was putting away a plate of fettucine and I bit the inside of my mouth. You ever done that? It's murder, and the worst part is you feel so stupid about it. And then you keep biting it over and over again because it sticks out while it's healing. At least I do." The burglar gulped a breath and ran a moist hand over a moister forehead. "And now this," he said.

"This could turn out to be worse than fenders and fish tanks," Trebizond said.

"Don't I know it. You know what I should have done? I should have spent the entire week in bed. I happen to know a safecracker who consults an astrologer before each and every job he pulls. If Jupiter's in the wrong place or Mars is squared with Uranus or something he won't go in. It sounds ridiculous, doesn't it? And yet it's eight years now since anybody put a handcuff on that man. Now who do you know who's gone eight years without getting arrested?"

"I've never been arrested," Trebizond said.

"Well, you're not a crook."

"I'm a businessman."

The burglar thought of something but let it pass. "I'm going to get the name of his astrologer," he said. "That's just what I'm going to do. Just as soon as I get out of here."

"If you get out of here," Trebizond said. "Alive," Trebizond said.

The burglar's jaw trembled just the slightest bit. Trebizond smiled, and from the burglar's point of view Trebizond's smile seemed to enlarge the black hole in the muzzle of the revolver.

"I wish you'd point that thing somewhere else," he said nervously.

"There's nothing else I want to shoot."

"You don't want to shoot me."

"Oh?"

"You don't even want to call the cops," the burglar went on. "It's really not necessary. I'm sure we can work things out between us, two civilized men coming to a civilized agreement. I've some money on me. I'm an openhanded sort and would be pleased to make a small contribution to your favorite charity, whatever it might be. We don't need policemen to intrude into the private affairs of gentlemen."

The burglar studied Trebizond carefully. This little speech had always gone over rather well in the past, especially with men of substance. It was hard to tell how it was going over now, or if it was going over at all. "In any event," he ended somewhat lamely, "you certainly don't want to shoot me."

"Why not?"

"Oh, blood on the carpet, for a starter. Messy, wouldn't you say? Your wife would be upset. Just ask her and she'll tell you shooting me would be a ghastly idea."

"She's not at home. She'll be out for the next hour or so."

"All the same, you might consider her point of view. And shooting me would be illegal, you know. Not to mention immoral."

"Not illegal," Trebizond remarked.

"I beg your pardon?"

"You're a burglar," Trebizond reminded him. "An unlawful intruder on my property. You have broken and entered. You have invaded the sanctity of my home. I can shoot you where you stand and not get so much as a parking ticket for my trouble."

"Of course you can shoot me in self-defense—"

"Are we on *Candid Camera*?"

"No, but—"

"Is Allen Funt lurking in the shadows?"

"No, but I—"

"In your back pocket. That metal thing. What is it?"

"Just a pry bar."

"Take it out," Trebizond said. "Hand it over. Indeed. A weapon if I ever saw one. I'd state that you attacked me with it and I fired in self-defense. It would be my word against yours, and yours would remain unvoiced since you would be dead. Whom do you suppose the police would believe?"

The burglar said nothing. Trebizond smiled a satisfied smile and put the pry bar in his own pocket. It was a piece of nicely shaped steel and it had a nice heft to it. Trebizond rather liked it.

"Why would you want to kill me?"

"Perhaps I've never killed anyone. Perhaps I'd like to satisfy my curiosity. Or perhaps I got to enjoy killing in the war and have been yearning for another crack at it. There are endless possibilities."

"But—"

"The point is," said Trebizond, "you might be useful to me in that manner. As it is, you're not useful to me at all. And stop hinting about my favorite charity or other euphemisms. I don't want your money. Look about you. I've ample money of my own—that should be obvious. If I were a poor man you wouldn't have breached my threshold. How much money are you talking about, anyway? A couple of hundred dollars?"

"Five hundred," the burglar said.

"A pittance."

"I suppose. There's more at home but you'd just call that a pittance too, wouldn't you?"

"Undoubtedly." Trebizond shifted the gun to his other hand. "I told you I was a businessman," he said. "Now if there were any way in which you could be more useful to me alive than dead—"

"You're a businessman and I'm a burglar," the burglar said, brightening.

"Indeed."

"So I could steal something for you. A painting? A competitor's trade secrets? I'm really very good at what I do, as a matter of fact, although you wouldn't guess it by my performance tonight. I'm not saying I could whisk the Mona Lisa out of the Louvre, but I'm pretty good at your basic hole-and-corner job of everyday burglary. Just give me an assignment and let me show my stuff."

"Hmmmm," said Archer Trebizond.

"Name it and I'll swipe it."

"Hmmmm."

"A car, a mink coat, a diamond bracelet, a Persian carpet, a first edition, bearer bonds, incriminating evidence, eighteen-and-a-half minutes of tape—"

"What was that last?"

"Just my little joke," said the burglar. "A coin collection, a stamp collection, psychiatric records, phonograph records, police records—"

"I get the point."

"I tend to prattle when I'm nervous."

"I've noticed."

"If you could point that thing elsewhere—"

Trebizond looked down at the gun in his hand. The gun continued to point at the burglar.

"No," Trebizond said, with evident sadness. "No, I'm afraid it won't work."

"Why not?"

"In the first place, there's nothing I really need or want. Could you steal me a woman's heart? Hardly. And more to the point, how could I trust you?"

"You could trust me," the burglar said. "You have my word on that."

"My point exactly. I'd have to take your word that your word is good, and where does that lead us? Down the proverbial garden path, I'm afraid. No, once I let you out from under my roof I've lost my advantage. Even if I have a gun trained on you, once you're in the open I can't shoot you with impunity. So I'm afraid—"

"No!"

Trebizond shrugged. "Well, really," he said. "What use are you? What are you good for besides being killed? Can you do anything besides steal, sir?"

"I can make license plates."

"Hardly a valuable talent."

"I know," said the burglar sadly. "I've often wondered why the state bothered to teach me such a pointless trade. There's not even much call for counterfeit license plates, and they've got a monopoly on making the legitimate ones. What else can I do? I must be able to do something. I could shine your shoes, I could polish your car—"

"What do you do when you're not stealing?"

"Hang around," said the burglar. "Go out with ladies. Feed my fish, when they're not all over my rug. Drive my car when I'm not mangling its fenders. Play a few games of chess, drink a can or two of beer, make myself a sandwich—"

"Are you any good?"

"At making sandwiches?"

"At chess."

"I'm not bad."

"I'm serious about this."

"I believe you are," the burglar said. "I'm not your average woodpusher, if that's what you want to know. I know the openings and I have a good sense of space. I don't have the patience for tournament play, but at the chess club downtown I win more games than I lose."

"You play at the club downtown?"

"Of course. I can't burgle seven nights a week, you know. Who could stand the pressure?"

"Then you *can* be of use to me," Trebizond said.

"You want to learn the game?"

"I know the game. I want you to play chess with me for an hour until my wife gets home. I'm bored, there's nothing in the house to read, I've never cared much for television, and it's hard for me to find an interesting opponent at the chess table."

"So you'll spare my life in order to play chess with me."

"That's right."

"Let me get this straight," the burglar said. "There's no catch to this, is there? I don't get shot if I lose the game or anything tricky like that, I hope."

"Certainly not. Chess is a game that ought to be above gimmickry."

"I couldn't agree more," said the burglar. He sighed a long sigh. "If I didn't play chess," he said, "you wouldn't have shot me, would you?"

"It's a question that occupies the mind, isn't it?"

"It is," said the burglar.

They played in the front room. The burglar drew the white pieces in the first game, opened King's Pawn, and played what turned out to be a reasonably imaginative version of the Ruy Lopez. At the sixteenth move Trebizond forced the exchange of knight for rook, and not too long afterward the burglar resigned.

In the second game the burglar played the black pieces and offered the Sicilian Defense. He played a variation that Trebizond wasn't familiar with. The game stayed remarkably even until in the end game the burglar succeeded in developing a passed pawn. When it was clear that he would be able to queen it, Trebizond tipped over his king, resigning.

"Nice game," the burglar offered.

"You play well."

"Thank you."

"Seems a pity that—"

His voice trailed off. The burglar shot him an inquiring look. "That I'm wasting myself as a common criminal? Is that what you were going to say?"

"Let it go," Trebizond said. "It doesn't matter."

They began setting up the pieces for the third game when a key slipped into a lock. The lock turned, the door opened, and Melissa Trebizond stepped into the foyer and through it to the living room.

Both men got to their feet. Mrs. Trebizond advanced, a vacant smile on her pretty face. "You found a new friend to play chess with. I'm happy for you."

Trebizond set his jaw. From his back pocket he drew the burglar's pry bar. It had an even nicer heft than he had thought "Melissa," he said, "I've no need to waste time with a recital of your sins. No doubt you know precisely why you deserve this."

She stared at him, obviously not having understood a word he had said to her, whereupon Archer Trebizond brought the pry bar down on the top of her skull. The first blow sent her to her knees. Quickly he struck her three more times, wielding the metal bar with all his strength, then turned to look into the wide eyes of the burglar.

"You've killed her," the burglar said.

"Nonsense," said Trebizond, taking the bright revolver from his pocket once again.

"Isn't she dead?"

"I hope and pray she is," Trebizond said, "but I haven't killed her. You've killed her."

"I don't understand."

"The police will understand," Trebizond said, and shot the burglar in the shoulder. Then he fired again, more satisfactorily this time, and the burglar sank to the floor with a hole in his heart.

Trebizond scooped the chess pieces into their box, swept up the board, and set about the business of arranging things. He suppressed an urge to whistle. He was, he decided, quite pleased with himself. Nothing was ever entirely useless, not to a man of resources. If fate sent you a lemon, you made lemonade.

A Blow for Freedom

The gun was smaller than Elliott remembered. At Kennedy, waiting for his bag to come up on the carousel, he'd been irritated with himself for buying the damned thing. For years now, ever since Pan Am had stranded him in Milan with the clothes he was wearing, he'd made an absolute point of never checking luggage. He'd flown to Miami with his favorite carry-on bag; returning, he'd checked the same bag, all because it now contained a Smith & Wesson revolver and a box of fifty .38-caliber shells.

At least he hadn't had to take a train. "Oh, for Christ's sake," he'd told Huebner, after they'd bought the gun together. "I'll have to take the train back, won't I? I can't get on the plane with a gun in my pocket."

"It's not recommended," Huebner had said. "But all you have to do is check your bag with the gun and shells in it."

"Isn't there a regulation against it?"

"Probably. There's rules against everything. All I know is, I do it all the time, and I never heard of anyone getting into any trouble over it. They scope the checked bags, or at least they're supposed to, but they're looking for bombs. There's nothing very dangerous about a gun locked away in the baggage compartment."

"Couldn't the shells explode?"

"In a fire, possibly. If the plane goes down in flames, the bullets may go off and put a hole in the side of your suitcase."

"I guess I'm being silly."

"Well, you're a New Yorker. You don't know a whole lot about guns."

"No." He'd hesitated. "Maybe I should have bought one of those plastic ones."

"The Glock?" Huebner smiled. "It's a nice weapon, and it's probably the one I'll buy next. But you couldn't carry it on a plane."

"But I thought—"

"You thought it would fool the scanners and metal detectors at airport security. It won't. That's hardly the point of it, a big gun like that. No, they replaced a lot of the metal with high-impact plastic to reduce the weight. It's supposed to lessen recoil slightly, too, but I don't know if it does. Personally, I like the looks of it. But it'll show up fine on a scanner if you put it in a carry-on bag, and it'll set off alarms if you walk it through a metal detector." He snorted. "Of course, that didn't keep some idiots from introducing bills banning it in the United States. Nobody in politics likes to let a fact stand in the way of a grandstand play."

His bag was one of the last ones up. Waiting for it, he worried that there was going to be trouble about the gun. When it came, he had to resist the urge to open the bag immediately and make sure the gun was still there. The bag felt light, and he decided some baggage handler had detected it and appropriated it for his own use.

Nervous, he thought. Scared it's there, scared it's not.

He took a cab home to his Manhattan apartment and left the bag unopened while he made himself a drink. Then he unpacked, and the gun was smaller than he remembered it. He picked it up and felt its weight, and that was greater than he recalled. And it was empty. It would be even heavier fully loaded.

After Huebner had helped him pick out the gun, they'd driven way out on Route 27, where treeless swamps extended for miles in every direction. Huebner pulled off the road a few yards from a wrecked car, its tires missing and most of its window glass gone.

"There's our target," he said. "You find a lot of cars abandoned along this stretch, but you don't want to start shooting up the newer ones."

"Because someone might come back for them?"

Huebner shook his head. "Because there might be a body in the trunk. This is where the drug dealers tend to drop off the unsuccessful competition, but no self-respecting drug dealer would be caught dead in a wreck like this one. You figure it'll be a big enough target for you?"

Embarrassingly enough, he missed the car altogether with his first shot. "You pulled up on it," Huebner told him. "Probably anticipating the recoil. Don't waste time worrying where the bullets are going yet. Just get used to pointing and firing."

And he got used to it. The recoil was considerable and so was the weight of the gun, but he did get used to both and began to be able to make the shots go where he wanted them to go. After Elliott had used up a full box of shells, Huebner got a pistol of his own from the glove compartment and put a few rounds into the fender of the ruined automobile. Huebner's gun was a nine-millimeter automatic with a clip that held twelve cartridges. It was much larger, noisier, and heavier than the .38, and it did far more damage to the target.

"Got a whole lot of stopping power," Huebner said. "Hit a man in the arm with this, you're likely to take him down. Here, try it. Strike a blow for freedom."

The recoil was greater than the .38's, but less so than he would have guessed. Elliott fired off several rounds, enjoying the sense of power. He returned the gun to Huebner, who emptied the clip into the old car.

Driving back, Elliott said, "A phrase you used: 'Strike a blow for freedom.' "

"Oh, you never heard that? I had an uncle used that expression every time he took a drink. They used to say that during Prohibition. You hoisted a few then in defiance of the law, you were striking a blow for freedom."

The gun, the first article Elliott unpacked, was the last he put away.

He couldn't think of what to do with it. Its purchase had seemed appropriate in Florida, where they seemed to have gun shops everywhere. You walked into one and walked out owning a weapon. There was even a town in central Georgia where they'd passed their own local version of gun control, an ordinance requiring the adult population to go about armed. There had never been any question of enforcing the law, he knew; it had been passed as a statement of local sentiment.

Here in New York, guns were less appropriate. They were illegal, to begin with. You could apply for a carry permit, but unless there was some genuine reason connected with your occupation, your application was virtually certain to be denied. Elliott worked in an office and never carried anything to it or from it but a briefcase filled with papers, nor did his work take him down streets any meaner than the one he lived on. As far as the law was concerned, he had no need for a gun.

Yet he owned one, legally or not. Its possession was at once unsettling and thrilling, like the occasional ounce or so of marijuana secreted in his various living quarters during his twenties. There was something exciting, something curiously estimable, about having that which was prohibited, and at the same time, there was a certain amount of danger connected with its possession.

There ought to be security as well, he thought. He'd bought the gun for his protection in a city that increasingly seemed incapable of protecting its own inhabitants. He turned the gun over, let the empty cylinder swing out, accustomed his fingers to the cool metal.

His apartment was on the twelfth floor of a prewar building. Three shifts of doormen guarded the lobby. No other building afforded access to any of his windows, and those near the fire escape were protected by locked window gates, the key to which hung out of reach on a nail. The door to the hallway had two deadbolt locks, each with its cylinder secured by an escutcheon plate. The door had a steel core and was further reinforced by a Fox police lock.

Elliott had never felt insecure in his apartment, nor were its security measures the result of his own paranoia. They had all been in place when he moved in. And they were standard for the building and the neighborhood.

He passed the gun from hand to hand, at once glad to have it and, like an impulse shopper, wondering why he'd bought it.

Where should he keep it?

The drawer of the nightstand suggested itself. He put the gun and the box of shells in it, closed the drawer, and went to take a shower.

It was almost a week before he looked at the gun again. He didn't mention it and rarely thought about it. News items would bring it to mind. A hardware-store owner in Rego Park killed his wife and small daughter with an unregistered handgun, then turned the weapon on himself; reading about it in the paper, Elliott thought of the revolver in his nightstand drawer. An honor student was slain in his bedroom by a stray shot from a high-powered assault rifle, and Elliott, watching TV, thought again of his gun.

On the Friday after his return, some item about the shooting of a drug dealer again directed his thoughts to the gun, and it occurred to him that he ought at least to load it. Suppose someone came crashing through his door or used some advance in criminal technology to cut the gates on his windows. If he were reaching hurriedly for a gun, it should be loaded.

He loaded all six chambers. He seemed to remember that you were supposed to leave one chamber empty as a safety measure. Otherwise, the gun might discharge if dropped. Cocking the weapon would presumably rotate the cylinder and ready it for shooting. Still, it wasn't going to fire itself just sitting in his nightstand drawer, was it, now? And if he reached for it, if he needed it in a hurry, he'd want it fully loaded.

If you had to shoot at someone, you didn't want to shoot once or twice and then stop. You wanted to empty the gun.

Had Huebner told him that? Or had someone said it in a movie or on television? It didn't matter, he decided. Either way, it was sound advice.

A few days later, he saw a movie in which the hero, a renegade cop up against an entrenched drug mob, slept with a gun under his pillow. It was a much larger gun than Elliott's, something like Huebner's big automatic.

"More gun than you really need in your situation," Huebner had told him. "And it's too big and too heavy. You want something you can slip into a pocket. A cannon like this, you'd need a whole shoulder rig or it'd pull at your suit coat something awful."

Not that he'd ever carry it.

That night, he got the gun out of the drawer and put it under his pillow. He thought of the princess who couldn't sleep with a pea under her mattress. He felt a little silly, and he felt, too, some of what he had felt playing with toy guns as a child.

He got the gun from under his pillow and put it back in the drawer, where it belonged. He lay for a long time, inhaling the smell of the gun, metal and machine oil, interesting and not unpleasant.

A masculine scent, he thought. Blend in a little leather and tobacco, maybe a little horseshit, and you've got something to slap on after a shave. Win the respect of your fellows and drive the women wild.

He never put the gun under his pillow again. But the linen held the scent of the gun, and even after he'd changed the sheets and pillowcases, he could detect the smell on the pillow.

It was not until the incident with the panhandler that he ever carried the gun outside the apartment.

There were panhandlers all over the place, had been for several years now. It seemed to Elliott that there were more of them every year, but he wasn't sure if that was really the case. They were of either sex and of every age and color, some of them proclaiming well-rehearsed speeches on subway cars, some standing mute in doorways and extending paper cups, some asking generally for spare change or specifically for money for food or for shelter or for wine.

Some of them, he knew, were homeless people, ground down by the system. Some belonged in mental institutions. Some were addicted to crack. Some were layabouts, earning more this way than they could at a menial job. Elliott couldn't tell which was which and wasn't sure how he felt about them, his emotions ranging from sympathy to irritation, depending on circumstances. Sometimes he gave money, sometimes he didn't. He had given up trying to devise a consistent policy and simply followed his impulse of the moment.

One evening, walking home from the bus stop, he encountered a panhandler who demanded money. "Come on," the man said. "Gimme a dollar."

Elliott started to walk past him, but the man moved to block his path. He was taller and heavier than Elliott, wearing a dirty army jacket, his face partly hidden behind a dense black beard. His eyes, slightly exophthalmic, were fierce.

"Didn't you hear me? Gimme a fuckin' dollar!"

Elliott reached into his pocket, came out with a handful of change. The man made a face at the coins Elliott placed in his hand, then evidently decided the donation was acceptable.

"Thank you kindly," he said. "Have a nice day."

Have a nice day, indeed. Elliott walked on home, nodded to the doorman, let himself into his apartment. It wasn't until he had engaged the locks that he realized his heart was pounding and his hands trembling.

He poured himself a drink. It helped, but it didn't change anything.

Had he been mugged? There was a thin line, he realized, and he wasn't sure if the man had crossed it. He had not been asking for money, he had been demanding it, and the absence of a specific threat did not mean there was no menace in the demand. Elliott, certainly, had given him money out of fear. He'd been intimidated. Unwilling to display his wallet, he'd fished out a batch of coins, including a couple of quarters and a subway token, currently valued at $1.15.

A small enough price, but that wasn't the point. The point was that he'd been made to pay it. *Stand and deliver,* the man might as well have said. Elliott had stood and delivered.

A block from his own door, for God's sake. A good street in a good neighborhood. Broad daylight.

And you couldn't even report it. Not that anyone reported anything anymore. A friend at work had reported a burglary only because you had to in order to collect on your insurance. The police, he'd said, had taken the report over the phone. "I'll send somebody if you want," the cop had said, "but I've got to tell you, it's a waste of your time and ours." Someone else had been robbed of his watch and wallet at gunpoint and had not bothered reporting the incident. "What's the point?" he'd said.

But even if there were a point, Elliott had nothing to report. A man had asked for money and he'd given it to him. They had a right to ask for money, some judge had ruled. They were exercising their First Amendment right of free speech. Never mind that there had been an unvoiced threat, that Elliott had paid the money out of intimidation. Never mind that it damn well felt like a mugging.

First Amendment rights. Maybe he ought to exercise his own rights under the Second Amendment—the right to bear arms.

That same evening, he took the gun from the drawer and tried it in various pockets—unloaded now. He tried tucking it into his belt, first in front, then behind, in the small of his back. He practiced reaching for it, drawing it. He felt foolish, and it was uncomfortable walking around with the gun in his belt like that.

It was comfortable in his right-hand jacket pocket, but the weight of it spoiled the line of the jacket. The pants pocket on the same side was better. He had reached into that pocket to produce the handful of change that had mollified the panhandler. Suppose he had come out with a gun instead?

"Thank you kindly. Have a nice day."

Later, after he'd eaten, he went to the video store on the next block to rent a movie for the evening. He was out the door before he realized he still had the gun in his pocket. It was still unloaded, the six shells lying where he had spilled them on his bed. He had reached for the keys to lock up and there was the gun.

He got the keys, locked up, and went out with the gun in his pocket.

The sensation of being on the street with a gun in his pocket was an interesting one. He felt as though he were keeping a secret from everyone he met, and that the secret empowered him. He spent longer than usual in the video store. Two fantasies came and went. In one, he held up the clerk, brandishing his empty gun and walking out with all the money in the register. In the other, someone else attempted to rob the place and Elliott drew his weapon and foiled the holdup.

Back home, he watched the movie, but his mind insisted on replaying the second fantasy. In one version, the holdup man spun toward him, gun in hand, and Elliott had to face him with an unloaded revolver.

When the movie ended, he reloaded the gun and put it back in the drawer.

The following evening, he carried the gun, loaded this time. The night after that was a Friday, and when he got home from the office, he put the gun in his pocket almost without thinking about it. He went out for a bite of dinner, then played cards at a friend's apartment a dozen blocks away. They played, as always, for low stakes, but Elliott was the big winner. Another player joked that he had better take a cab home.

"No need," he said. "I'm armed and dangerous."

He walked home, and on the way, he stopped at a bar and had a couple of beers. Some people at a table near where he stood were talking about a recent outrage, a young advertising executive in Greenwich Village shot dead while using a pay phone around the corner from his apartment. "I'll tell you something," one of the party said. "I'm about ready to start carrying a gun."

"You can't, legally," someone said.

"Screw legally."

"So a guy tries something and you shoot him and you're the one winds up in trouble."

"I'll tell you something," the man said. "I'd rather be judged by twelve than carried by six."

He carried the gun the whole weekend. It never left his pocket. He was at home much of the time, watching a ball game on television, catching up with his bookkeeping, but he left the house several times each day and always had the gun on his person.

He never drew it, but sometimes he would put his hand in his pocket and let his fingers curl around the butt of it. He found its presence increasingly reassuring. If anything happened, he was ready.

And he didn't have to worry about an accidental discharge. The chamber under the hammer was unloaded. He had worked all that out. If he dropped the gun, it wouldn't go off. But if he cocked it and worked the trigger, it would fire.

When he took his hand from his pocket and held it to his face, he could smell the odor of the gun on his fingers. He liked that.

By Monday morning, he had grown used to the gun. It seemed perfectly natural to carry it to the office.

On the way home, not that night but the following night, the same aggressive panhandler accosted him. His routine had not changed. "Come on," he said. "Gimme a dollar."

Elliott's hand was in his pocket, his fingers touching the cold metal.

"Not tonight," he said.

Maybe something showed in his eyes.

"Hey, that's cool," the panhandler said. "You have a good day just the same." And stepped out of his path.

A week or so after that, he was riding the subway, coming home late after dinner with married friends in Forest Hills. He had a paperback with him, but he couldn't concentrate on it, and he realized that the two young men across the car from him were looking him over, sizing him up. They were wearing untied basketball sneakers and warm-up jackets, and looked street smart and dangerous. He was wearing the suit he'd worn to the office and had a briefcase beside him; he looked prosperous and vulnerable.

The car was almost empty. There was a derelict sleeping a few yards away, a woman with a small child all the way down at the other end. One of the pair nudged the other, then turned his eyes toward Elliott again.

Elliott took the gun out of his pocket. He held it on his lap and let them see it, then put it back in his pocket.

The two of them got off at the next station, leaving Elliott to ride home alone.

When he got home, he took the gun from his pocket and set it on the nightstand. (He no longer bothered tucking it in the drawer.) He went into the bathroom and looked at himself in the mirror.

"Fucking thing saved my life," he said.

One night, he took a woman friend to dinner. Afterward, they went back to her place and wound up in bed. At one point, she got up to use the bathroom, and while she was up, she hung up her own clothing and went to put his pants on a hanger.

"These weigh a ton," she said. "What have you got in here?"

"See for yourself," he said. "But be careful."

"My God. Is it loaded?"

"They're not much good if they're not."

"My God."

He told her how he'd bought it in Florida, how it had now become second nature for him to carry it. "I'd feel naked without it," he said.

"Aren't you afraid you'll get into trouble?"

"I look at it this way," he told her. "I'd rather be judged by twelve than carried by six."

One night, two men cut across the avenue toward him while he was walking home from his Friday card game. Without hesitation, he drew the gun.

"Whoa!" the nearer of the two sang out. "Hey, it's cool, man. Thought you was somebody else, is all."

They veered off, gave him a wide berth.

Thought I was somebody else, he thought. Thought I was a victim, is what you thought.

There were stores around the city that sold police equipment. Books to study for the sergeant's exam. Copies of the latest revised penal code. A T-shirt that read N.Y.P.D. HOMICIDE SQUAD, OUR DAY BEGINS WHEN YOUR DAY ENDS.

He stopped in and didn't buy anything, then returned for a kit to clean his gun. He hadn't fired it yet, except in Florida, but it seemed as though he ought to clean it from time to time anyway. He took the kit home and unloaded the gun and cleaned it, working an oiled patch of cloth through the short barrel. When he was finished, he put everything away and reloaded the gun.

He liked the way it smelled, freshly cleaned with gun oil.

A week later, he returned and bought a bulletproof vest. They had two types, one significantly more expensive than the other. Both were made of Kevlar, whatever that was.

"Your more expensive one provides you with a little more protection," the proprietor explained. "Neither one's gonna stop a shot from an assault rifle. The real high-powered rounds; concrete don't stop 'em. This here, though, it provides the most protection available, plus it provides protection against a knife thrust. Neither one's a sure thing to stop a knife, but this here's reinforced."

He bought the better vest.

One night, lonely and sad, he unloaded the gun and put the barrel to his temple. His finger was inside the trigger guard, curled around the trigger.

You weren't supposed to dry-fire the gun. It was bad for the firing pin to squeeze off a shot when there was no cartridge in the chamber.

Quit fooling around, he told himself.

He cocked the gun, then took it away from his temple. He uncocked it, put the barrel in his mouth. That was how cops did it when they couldn't take it anymore. Eating your gun, they called it.

He didn't like the taste, the metal, the gun oil. Liked the smell but not the taste.

He loaded the gun and quit fooling around.

A little later, he went out. It was late, but he didn't feel like sitting around the apartment, and he knew he wouldn't be able to sleep. He wore the Kevlar vest—he wore it all the time lately—and, of course, he had the gun in his pocket.

He walked around, with no destination in mind. He stopped for a beer but drank only a few sips of it, then headed out to the street again. The moon came into view, and he wasn't surprised to note that it was full.

He had his hand in his pocket, touching the gun. When he breathed deeply, he could feel the vest drawn tight around his chest. He liked the sensation.

When he reached the park, he hesitated. Years ago, back when the city was safe, you knew not to walk in the park at night. It was dangerous even then. It could hardly be otherwise now, when every neighborhood was a jungle.

So? If anything happened, if anybody tried anything, he was ready.

A Little Off the Top

"Consider the gecko," the doctor said, with a gesture toward the wall at my left. There one of the tiny lizards clung effortlessly, as if painted. "Remarkable for its rather piercing cry, the undoubted source of its name. Remarkable as well for the suction cups at the tips of its fingers and toes, which devices enable it to scurry across the ceiling as readily as you or I might cross a floor. Now a Darwinian would point to the gecko and talk of evolution and mutation and fitness to survive, but can you honestly regard such an adaptation as the result of random chance? I prefer to see the fingerprints of the Creator in the fingertips of that saurian. It would take a God to create a gecko, and a whimsical fun-loving God at that. The only sort, really, in whom one would care to believe."

The doctor's name was Turnquist. He was an Englishman, an anomaly on an island where the planters were predominantly Dutch with a scattering of displaced French. He had just given me the best dinner I'd had since I left the States, a perfectly seasoned curried goat complemented by an even dozen side dishes and perhaps as many chutneys. Thus far in my travels I'd been exposed almost exclusively to Chinese cooks, and not one of them could have found work on Mott Street.

Dr. Turnquist's conversation was as stimulating as his cook's curry. He was dressed in white, but there his resemblance to Sidney Greenstreet ended. He was a short man and a slender one, with rather large and long-fingered hands, and as he sat with his hands poised on the white linen cloth, it struck me that there was about him a quality not dissimilar to the gecko. He might have been clinging to a wall, waiting for a foolish insect to venture too close.

There was a cut crystal bell beside his wineglass. He rang it, and almost immediately a young woman appeared in the kitchen doorway. "Bring the brandy," he told her, "and a pair of the medium-sized bell glasses."

She withdrew, returning moments later with a squat-bodied ship's decanter and a pair of glasses. "Very good, Leota," he said. "You may pour a glass for each of us."

She served me first, placing the glass on the tablecloth at my right, pouring a generous measure of cognac into it. I watched the procedure out of the corner of my eye. She was of medium height, slender but full-figured, with a rich brown skin and arresting cheekbones. Her scent was heavy and rich in the tropical air. My eyes followed her as she moved around the table and filled my host's glass. She left the bottle on the table. He said, "Thank you, Leota," and she crossed to the kitchen door.

My eyes returned to the doctor. He was holding his glass aloft. I raised mine. "Cheers," he said, and we drank.

The cognac was excellent and I said as much. "It's decent," he allowed. "Not the best the French ever managed, but good enough." His dry lizard eyes twinkled. "Is it the cognac you admired? Or the hand that poured it?"

"Your servant is a beautiful woman," I said, perhaps a little stiffly.

"She's a Tamil. They are an attractive race, most especially in the bloom of youth. And Leota is particularly attractive, even for a Tamil." His eyes considered me carefully. "You recently ended a marriage," he said.

"A relationship. We weren't actually married. We lived together."

"It was painful, I suppose."

I hesitated, then nodded.

"Then I daresay travel was the right prescription," the doctor said. "Your appetites are returning. You did justice to your dinner. You're able to appreciate a good cognac and a beautiful woman."

"One could hardly do otherwise. All three are quite superb."

He lifted his glass again, warmed its bowl in his palm, inhaled its bouquet, took a drop of the liquid on his tongue. His eyes closed briefly. For a moment I might have been alone in the high-ceilinged dining room.

His eyes snapped open. "Have you," he demanded, "ever had a cognac of the comet year?"

"I beg your pardon?"

"Eighteen thirty-five. Have you ever tasted an eighteen thirty-five cognac?"

"Not that I recall."

"Then you very likely have not, because you would recall it. Have you ever made love to a virgin? Let me rephrase that. Have you ever embraced a virgin of mixed ancestry, Tamil and Chinese and Scandinavian? You needn't answer. A rhetorical question, of course."

I took a small sip of cognac. It was really quite excellent.

"I could tell you a story," Dr. Turnquist said. "Of course you'd want to change the names if you ever decided to do anything with it. And you might take care to set it on some other island."

"I wouldn't have to name the island at all," I said.

"No," he said. "I don't suppose you would."

There were, it seemed, two brothers named Einhoorn. One, Piet, was a planter, with large and valuable holdings in the southern portion of the island. The other, Rolf, was a trader with offices in the capital city on the island's eastern rim. Both were quite prosperous, and each had survived the trauma of the island's metamorphosis from colony to independent nation.

Both had been married. Piet's wife had died years ago, while delivering a stillborn child. Rolf's wife deserted him at about the same time, leaving on a Europe-bound freighter with whose captain Rolf had traded for years. The ship still called at the island from time to time, and Rolf still did business with her captain. The woman was never a subject of conversation between them.

Although he saw them infrequently, Dr. Turnquist got along well enough with both of the Einhoorn brothers. He thought them coarse men. They both had a hearty appetite for the pleasures of the flesh, which he approved, but it seemed to him that they lacked refinement. Neither had the slightest taste for art, for music, for literature. Neither gave any evidence of having a spiritual dimension. Both delighted in making money, in drinking brandy, and embracing young women. Neither cared much for anything else.

One evening, Rolf, the trader, appeared at the doctor's door. The doctor had already finished his dinner. He was sitting on the enclosed veranda, sipping a postprandial brandy and reading, for the thousandth time, a sonnet of Wordsworth's, the one comparing the evening to a nun breathless with adoration. A felicitous phrase, he had thought for the thousandth time.

He set the book aside and put his guest in a wicker chair and poured him a brandy. Rolf drank it down, pronounced it acceptable, and demanded to know if the doctor had ever had an 1835 cognac. The doctor said that he had not.

"The comet year," Rolf said. "Halley's Comet. It came in eighteen thirty-five. It was important, the coming of the comet. The American writer, Mark Twain. You know him? He was born in that year."

"I would suppose he was not the only one."

"He thought it significant," Rolf Einhoorn said. "He said he was born when the comet came and would die when it reappeared. He believed this, I think. I don't know if it happened."

"Twain died in nineteen ten."

"Then perhaps he was right," the trader said, "because the comet comes every seventy-five years. I think it is every seventy-five years. It will be due again in a couple of years, and that is when I intended to drink the bottle."

"The bottle?"

"Of eighteen thirty-five cognac." Rolf rubbed his fleshy palms together. "I've had it for two years. It came off a Chinese ship. The man I bought it from didn't know what he had but he knew he had something. Cognac of the comet year is legendary, my dear Turnquist. I couldn't guess at its value. It is not like a wine, changing with the years, perhaps deteriorating beneath the cork. Brandies and whiskeys do not change once they have been bottled. They neither ripen nor decay. A man may spend a thousand pounds buying a rare wine at a London auction house only to find himself the owner of the world's most costly vinegar. But a cognac—it will no more spoil with age than gold will rust. And a cognac of eighteen thirty-five—"

"A famous cognac."

"A legend, as I've said." He put down his empty glass, folded his hands on his plump stomach. "And I shall never taste it."

The silence stretched. A fly buzzed against a lightbulb, then flew off. "Well, why not?" the doctor asked at length. "You haven't sworn off drinking. I don't suppose you've lost your corkscrew. What's the problem?"

"My brother is the problem."

"Piet?"

"Have I another brother? One is sufficient. He wants the cognac, the Comet Year cognac."

"I daresay he does. Who wouldn't? But why should you give it to him?"

"Because he has something I want."

"Oh?"

"You know his ward? She's called Freya."

"I've heard of her," the doctor said. "A half-caste, isn't she?"

"Her mother was half Tamil and half Chinese. Her father was a Norwegian seaman, captain of a freighter that docked here once and has never returned. You haven't seen Freya?"

"No."

"She is exquisite. Golden skin that glows as if lighted from within. A heart-shaped face, cheekbones to break your heart, and the most impossible blue eyes. A waist you could span with your hands. Breasts like, like—"

The man was breathless with adoration, Dr. Turnquist thought, though not like a nun. "How old is this goddess?" he asked.

"Fifteen," Rolf Einhoorn said. "Her mother died five years ago. Piet took her into his household, made a home for her. People credit him with an act of charity. My brother has never performed an act of charity in his life."

"He makes sexual use of her?"

"Not yet. The bastard's been *saving* her."

"Ah," said the doctor. "Even as you have been saving your cognac. Waiting, you might say, for the reappearance of the comet."

"Piet has been waiting for her sixteenth birthday. Then he will make her his mistress. But he wants my cognac."

"And you want—I've forgotten her name."

"Freya. He has offered a trade. Her virginity for my bottle."

"And you have accepted?"

"I have accepted."

The doctor raised his eyebrows.

"It seems unfair," Rolf said. The doctor noted a crafty light in his eyes. "Piet will have every drop of my precious cognac. He may drink it all in one night or stretch it out over a lifetime, and if he wishes he may shatter the bottle when he has drained it. And what will I have in return? One night with this beauty. Her maidenhead will be mine, but when I return her to him she will be a far cry from an empty bottle. She will be his to enjoy for as long as he wants her, and I will be left with the memory of her flesh and not even the memory of the cognac. Does it seem fair to you?"

"Can't you get out of the deal?"

"I could," Rolf said. "And yet there ought to be a better solution, don't you think? The little angel's birthday is two months from tomorrow. That is when the exchange will take place." He lowered his eyes deliberately. "Piet has seen my bottle. He has examined the seal."

"Ah."

"You are a clever man. A doctor, good with your hands. Perhaps there is a way to remove the contents from a sealed bottle, eh?"

"You would have to bring me the bottle," the doctor said, "and I should have to see what I could do."

Piet turned up later that week. Coincidentally, Dr. Turnquist was reading another sonnet of Wordsworth's at the moment of his arrival, the one about the world being too much with us. Old Wordsworth, he thought, had a knack.

Piet, not surprisingly, told essentially the same story as his brother. He spoke quite eloquently of the legendary perfection of the 1835 cognac, then spoke at least as eloquently of his ward. "She has spent five years under my roof," he said. "She is like a daughter to me."

"I'm sure."

"And now I've traded her to my *verdammte* brother for a bottle of brandy. Five years, doctor!"

"The brandy's been around for almost a century and a half. Five years seems a short time in comparison."

"You know what I mean," Piet said. "I wonder."

"What is it that you wonder?"

"I wonder what virginity is," Piet mused. "A virgin's embrace is nothing so special, is it? Ordinarily one wants one's partner to be schooled, able. With a virgin, one delights in her incompetence. What is so special, eh, about a tiny membrane?"

The doctor kept silent.

"You are a doctor," Piet Einhoorn said. "One hears tales, you know. Exotic bordellos whose madams sell a virginity ten times over, tightening the passage with alum, restoring the maidenhead. One hears these things and wonders what to believe."

"One cannot believe everything one hears."

"Oh," Piet said.

"Still, there is something that can be done. If the girl is a virgin in the first place."

"I have not had her, if that is what you are implying."

"I implied nothing. Even if she hasn't been with a man, she could have lost her hymen in any of a dozen ways. But if it's intact—"

"Yes?"

"You want to be with her once, is that right? You want to be the first man to have her."

"That is exactly what I want."

"If the hymen were surgically detached before the first intercourse, and if it were subsequently reattached *after* intercourse has taken place—"

"It is possible?"

"Bring the child," the doctor said. "Let me have a look at her, eh?"

Two days later Rolf returned to the doctor's house. This time his visit was expected. He carried a small leather satchel, from which he produced a bottle that fairly shouted its age. The doctor took it from him, held it to the light, examined its label and seal, turned it this way and that.

"This will take careful study," he announced.

"Can you do it?"

"Can I remove the contents without violating the seal? I think not. There is a trick of removing a tablecloth without disturbing the dishes and glasses resting atop it. One gives an abrupt all-out pull. That would not do in this case. But perhaps the seal can be removed and ultimately restored without its appearance being altered in any way." He set the bottle down. "Leave it with me. There is lead foil here which will not be readily removed, paper labels which might yield if the glue holding them can be softened. It is a Chinese puzzle, Einhoorn. Come back Saturday. If it can be done, it shall be done that day in front of your eyes."

"If my brother suspects—"

"If it cannot be done safely it will not be done at all. So he will suspect nothing. Oh, bring a bottle of the best cognac you can find, will you? We can't replace cognac of the comet year with rotgut, can we now?"

The following day it was Piet's turn. He brought with him not a leather satchel but an altogether more appealing cargo, the girl Freya.

She was, the doctor noted, quite spectacular. Rolf's cognac had looked like any other cognac, possessed of a good enough color and a perfect clarity but otherwise indistinguishable from any other amber liquid. Freya, her skin a good match for the cognac, looked like no other young woman the doctor had ever seen. Three races had blended themselves to perfection in her lithe person. Her skin was like hot velvet, while her eyes made one wonder why blue had ever been thought a cool color. And, thought Dr. Turnquist, a man could impale himself upon those cheekbones.

"I'll want to examine her," he told Piet. "Make yourself comfortable on the veranda."

In his surgery, Freya shucked off her clothing without a word, and without any trace of embarrassment. He placed her on his table, put her feet in the stirrups, and bent to his task. She was warm to the touch, he noted, and after a moment or two she began to move rhythmically beneath his fingers. He looked up from his work, met her eyes. She was smiling at him.

"Why, you little devil," he said.

He left her there, found Piet on the veranda. "You're very fortunate," he told the planter. "The membrane is intact. It hasn't yielded to horseback riding or an inquisitive finger."

"Have you detached it?"

"That will take some time. It's minor surgery, but I'd as soon sedate her all the same. It would be best if she didn't know the nature of the procedure, don't you think? So she can't say anything that might find its way to your brother's ear."

"Good thinking."

"Come back in the morning," the doctor told him. "Then you may enjoy her favors tomorrow night and bring her back to me the next morning for repair. Or restoration, if you prefer."

Piet came in the morning to reclaim his ward. As he led her to his car, the doctor thought not for the first time what a coarse, gross man the planter was.

Not that his brother was any better. Rolf arrived scarcely an hour after Piet had left—there was an element of French farce in the staging of this, the doctor remembered thinking—and the doctor led him into his study and showed him the bottle. Its neck was bare now, the wax and lead foil and paper labels carefully removed.

"Please notice," he said, "that the cork is quite dry. If this bottle held wine it would only be fit for pouring on a salad."

"But since it is brandy—"

"It is presumably in excellent condition. Still, if one attempts to remove this cork it will at once crumble into dust."

"Then—"

"Then we must be inventive," said the doctor. He brought forth an oversized hypodermic needle and plunged it in a single motion through the cork. As he drew back its plunger the syringe filled with the amber liquid.

"Brilliant," the trader said.

The doctor drew the syringe from the bottle, squirted its contents into a beaker, and repeated the process until the bottle was empty. Then he took the bottle that Rolf had brought—an excellent flask of twenty-year-old Napoleon brandy—and transferred its contents via the syringe into the ancient bottle. It was the work of another hour to replace the various sealing materials, and when he was done the bottle looked exactly as it had when the trader first obtained it from the Chinese seaman who'd been its previous owner.

"And now we'll employ a funnel," Dr. Turnquist said, "and pour your very old cognac into a much newer bottle, and let's not spill one precious drop, eh?" He sniffed appreciatively at the now empty beaker. "A rich bouquet. You'll postpone your enjoyment until the return of Halley's Comet?"

"Perhaps I'll have one glass ahead of schedule," Rolf Einhoorn said, grinning lewdly. "To toast Freya's sixteenth birthday."

The conversation took a similar turn when Piet collected his ward after the surgical restoration of her physical virginity. "I have had my cake," the planter said, smacking his lips like an animal. "And in less than a month's time I shall eat it, too. Or drink it, more precisely. I will be sipping cognac of the comet year while my fool of a brother makes do with—" And here he employed a Dutch phrase with which the doctor was not familiar, but which he later was able to translate loosely as *sloppy seconds*.

Piet left, taking Freya with him. The doctor stood for a moment at the front door, watching the car drive out of sight. Then he went looking for his volume of Wordsworth.

"It's a beautiful story," I told him. "A classic, really. I assume the exchange went according to plan? Freya spent the night of her sixteenth birthday with Rolf? And Piet had the brandy in exchange?"

"All went smoothly. As smooth as old cognac, as smooth as Freya's skin."

"Each had his cake," I said, "and each ate it, too. Or thought he did, which amounts to the same thing, doesn't it?"

"Does it?"

"I should think so. If you think you're drinking a legendary cognac, isn't that the same as drinking it? And if you think you're a woman's first lover, isn't that the same as actually being the first?"

"I would say it is *almost* the same." He smiled. "In addition, these brothers each enjoyed a third pleasure, and perhaps it was the most exquisite of all. Each had the satisfaction of having pulled something over on the other. So the whole arrangement could hardly have been more satisfactory."

"A beautiful story," I said again.

He leaned forward to pour a little more cognac into my glass. "I thought you would appreciate its subtleties," he said. "I sensed that about you. Of course, there's an element you haven't considered."

"Oh?"

"You raised a point. Is the illusion quite the same as the reality? Was Piet's experience in drinking the cognac identical to Rolf's?"

"Except insofar as one cognac was actually better or worse than the other."

"Ah," the doctor said. "Of course in this instance both drank the same cognac."

"Because they believed it to be the same?"

He shook his head impatiently. "Because it *was* the same," he said. "The identical brand of twenty-year-old Napoleon, and that's not as great a coincidence as it might appear, since it's the best brandy available on this island. It's the very same elixir you and I have been drinking this very evening."

"Piet and Rolf were both drinking it?"

"Of course."

"Then what happened to the real stuff?"

"I got it, of course," said the doctor. "It was easy to jab the hypodermic needle straight through the cork, since I'd already performed the procedure a matter of hours earlier. That part was easy enough. It was softening the wax without melting it altogether, and removing the lead foil without destroying it, that made open-heart surgery child's play by comparison."

"So you wound up with the Comet Year cognac."

"Quite," he said, smiling. And, as an afterthought, "And with the girl, needless to say."

"The girl?"

"Freya." He looked down into his glass. "A charming, marvelously exciting creature. Genetics can no more explain her perfection than can Darwin account for the gecko's fingertips. A benevolent Creator was at work there. I detached her hymen, had her during the night she spent here, then let her go off to lose her already-lost virginity to Piet. And then he brought her back for hymenal restoration, had me lock up the barn door, if you will, after I'd galloped off on the horse. And now Rolf has had her, gathering the dear thing's first fruits for the third time."

"Good Lord."

"Quite. Now if the illusion is identical to the reality, then Piet and Rolf have both gained everything and lost nothing. Whereas I have gained everything and lost nothing whether the illusion is equal to the reality or not. There are points here, I suspect, that a philosopher might profitably ponder. Philosophical implications aside, I thought you might enjoy the story."

"I love the story."

He smiled, enjoying my enjoyment. "It's getting late. A pity you can't meet Freya. I'm afraid my description has been woefully inadequate. But she's with Piet and he's never welcomed visitors. Still, if you don't mind, I think I'll send Leota to your room. I know you fancy her, and I saw the look she was giving you. She's not Freya, but I think you'll enjoy her acquaintance."

I muttered something appreciative.

"It's nothing," he said. "I wish, too, that I could let you have a taste of the Comet Year cognac. From the bouquet, it should turn out to be quite nice. It may not be all that superior to what we've been drinking, but think of the glamor that accompanies it."

"You haven't tasted it yet?"

He shook his head. "Those two brothers have probably finished their bottles by now. I shouldn't doubt it. But I think I'd rather hold out until the comet comes up again. If you're in this part of the world in a couple of years, you might want to stop in and watch the comet with me. I suppose one ought to be able to turn up a telescope somewhere, and we could raise a glass or two, don't you think?"

"I'm sure we could."

"Quite." He winked slowly, looking more than ever like an old gecko waiting for a fly. He lifted the crystal bell, rang. "Ah, Leota," he said, when the Tamil woman appeared. "My guest's the least bit tired. Perhaps you could show him to his room."

And Miles to Go Before I Sleep

When the bullets struck, my first thought was that someone had raced up behind me to give me an abrupt shove. An instant later I registered the sound of the gunshots, and then there was fire in my side, burning pain, and the impact had lifted me off my feet and sent me sprawling at the edge of the lawn in front of my house.

I noticed the smell of the grass. Fresh, cut the night before and with the dew still on it.

I can recall fragments of the ambulance ride as if it took place in some dim dream. I worried at the impropriety of running the siren so early in the morning.

They'll wake half the town, I thought.

Another time, I heard one of the white-coated attendants say something about a red blanket. My mind leaped to recall the blanket that lay on my bed when I was a boy almost forty years ago. It was plaid, mostly red with some green in it. Was that what they were talking about?

These bits of awareness came one after another, like fast cuts in a film. There was no sensation of time passing between them.

I was in a hospital room. The operating room, I suppose. I was spread out on a long white table while a masked and green-gowned doctor probed a wound in the left side of my chest. I must have been under anesthetic—there was a mask on my face with a tube connected to it. And I believe my eyes were closed. Nevertheless, I was aware of what was happening, and I could see.

I don't know how to explain this.

There was a sensation I was able to identify as pain, although it didn't actually hurt me. Then I felt as though my side were a bottle and a cork was being drawn from it. It popped free. The doctor held up a misshapen bullet for examination. I watched it fall in slow motion from his forceps, landing with a plinking sound in a metal pan.

"Other's too close to the heart," I heard him say. "Can't get a grip on it. Don't dare touch it, way it's positioned. Kill him if it moves."

Cut.

Same place, an indefinite period of time later. A nurse saying, "Oh, God, he's going," and then all of them talking at once.

Then I was out of my body.

It just happened, just like that. One moment I was in my dying body on the table and a moment later I was floating somewhere beneath the ceiling. I could look down and see myself on the table and the doctors and nurses standing around me.

I'm dead, I thought.

I was very busy trying to decide how I felt about it. It didn't hurt. I had always thought it would hurt, that it would be awful. But it wasn't so terrible.

So this is death, I thought.

And it was odd seeing myself, my body, lying there. I thought, you were a good body. I'm all right, I don't need you, but you were a good body.

Then I was gone from that room. There was a rush of light that became brighter and brighter, and I was sucked through a long tunnel at a furious speed, and then I was in a world of light and in the presence of a Being of light.

This is hard to explain.

I don't know if the Being was a man or a woman. Maybe it was both, maybe it changed back and forth. I don't know. He was all in white, and He was light and was surrounded by light.

And in the distance behind Him were my father and my mother and my grandparents. People who had gone before me, and they were holding out their hands to me and beaming at me with faces radiant with light and love.

I went to the Being, I was drawn to Him, and He held out His arm and said, "Behold your life."

And I looked, and I could behold my entire life. I don't know how to say what I saw. It was as if my whole life had happened at once and someone had taken a photograph of it and I was looking at that photograph. I could see in it everything that I remembered in my life and everything that I had forgotten, and it was all happening at once and I was seeing it happen. And I would see something bad that I'd done and think, I'm sorry about that. And I would see something good and be glad about it.

And at the end I woke and had breakfast and left the house to walk to work and a car passed by and a gun came out the window. There were two shots and I fell and the ambulance came and all the rest of it.

And I thought, Who killed me?

The Being said, "You must find out the answer."

I thought, I don't care, it doesn't matter.

He said, "You must go back and find the answer."

I thought, No, I don't want to go back.

All of the brilliant light began to fade. I reached out toward it because I didn't want to go back, I didn't want to be alive again. But it all continued to fade.

Then I was back in my body again.

"We almost lost you," the nurse said. Her smile was professional but the light in her eyes showed she meant it. "Your heart actually stopped on the operating table. You really had us scared there."

"I'm sorry," I said.

She thought that was funny. "The doctor was only able to remove one of the two bullets that were in you. So you've still got a chunk of lead in your chest. He sewed you up and put a drain in the wound, but obviously you won't be able to walk around like that. In fact it's important for you to lie absolutely still or the bullet might shift in position. It's right alongside your heart, you see."

It might shift even if I didn't move, I thought. But she knew better than to tell me that.

"In four or five days we'll have you scheduled for another operation," she went on. "By then the bullet may move of its own accord to a more accessible position. If not, there are surgical techniques that can be employed." She told me some of the extraordinary things surgeons could do. I didn't pay attention.

After she left the room, I rolled back and forth on the bed, shifting my body as jerkily as I could. But the bullet did not change its position in my chest.

I was afraid of that.

I stayed in the hospital that night. No one came to see me during visiting hours, and I thought that was strange. I asked the nurse and was told I was in intensive care and could not have visitors.

I lost control of myself. I shouted that she was crazy. How could I learn who did it if I couldn't see anyone?

"The police will see you as soon as it's allowed," she said. She was terribly earnest. "Believe me," she said, "it's for your own protection. They want to ask you a million questions, naturally, but it would be bad for your health to let you get all excited."

Silly bitch, I thought. And almost put the thought into words.

Then I remembered the picture of my life and the pleasant and unpleasant things I had done and how they all had looked in the picture.

I smiled. "Sorry I lost control," I said. "But if they didn't want me to get excited they shouldn't have given me such a beautiful nurse."

She went out beaming.

I didn't sleep. It did not seem to be necessary.

I lay in bed wondering who had killed me.

My wife? We'd married young, then grown apart. Of course she hadn't shot at me because she'd been in bed asleep when I left the house that morning. But she might have a lover. Or she could have hired someone to pull the trigger for her.

My partner? Monty and I had turned a handful of borrowed capital into a million-dollar business. But I was better than Monty at holding onto money. He spent it, gambled it away, paid it out in divorce settlements. Profits were off lately. Had he been helping himself to funds and cooking the books? And did he then decide to cover his thefts the easy way?

My girl? Peg had a decent apartment, a closet full of clothes. Not a bad deal. But for a while I'd let her think I'd divorce Julia when the kids were grown, and now she and I both knew better. She'd seemed to adjust to the situation, but had the resentment festered inside her?

My children?

The thought was painful. Mark had gone to work for me after college. The arrangement didn't last long. He'd been too headstrong, while I'd been unwilling to give him the responsibility he wanted. Now he was talking about going into business for himself. But he lacked the capital.

If I died, he'd have all he needed.

Debbie was married and expecting a child. First she'd lived with another young man, one of whom I hadn't approved, and then she'd married Scott, who was hard-working and earnest and ambitious. Was the marriage bad for her, and did she blame me for costing her the other boy? Or did Scott's ambition prompt him to make Debbie an heiress?

These were painful thoughts.

Someone else? But who and why?

Some days ago I'd cut off another motorist at a traffic circle. I remembered the sound of his horn, his face glimpsed in my rearview mirror, red, ferocious. Had he copied down my license plate, determined my address, lain in ambush to gun me down?

It made no sense. But it did not make sense for anyone to kill me.

Julia? Monty? Peg? Mark? Debbie? Scott?

A stranger?

I lay there wondering and did not truly care. Someone had killed me and I was supposed to be dead. But I was not permitted to be dead until I knew the answer to the question.

Maybe the police would find it for me.

They didn't.

I saw two policemen the following day. I was still in intensive care, still denied visitors, but an exception was made for the police. They were very courteous and spoke in hushed voices. They had no leads whatsoever in their investigation and just wanted to know if I could suggest a single possible suspect.

I told them I couldn't.

My nurse turned white as paper.

"You're not supposed to be out of bed! You're not even supposed to move! What do you think you're doing?"

I was up and dressed. There was no pain. As an experiment, I'd been palming the pain pills they issued me every four hours, hiding them in the bedclothes instead of swallowing them. As I'd anticipated, I did not feel any pain.

The area of the wound was numb, as though that part of me had been excised altogether. But nothing hurt. I could feel the slug that was still in me and could tell that it remained in position. It did not hurt me, however.

She went on jabbering away at me. I remembered the picture of my life and avoided giving her a sharp answer.

"I'm going home," I said.

"Don't talk nonsense."

"You have no authority over me," I told her. "I'm legally entitled to take responsibility for my own life."

"For your own death, you mean."

"If it comes to that. You can't hold me here against my will. You can't operate on me without my consent."

"If you don't have that operation, you'll die."

"Everyone dies."

"I don't understand," she said, and her eyes were wide and filled with sorrow, and my heart went out to her.

"Don't worry about me," I said gently. "I know what I'm doing. And there's nothing anyone can do."

"They wouldn't even let me see you," Julia was saying. "And now you're home."

"It was a fast recovery."

"Shouldn't you be in bed?"

"The exercise is supposed to be good for me," I said. I looked at her, and for a moment I saw her as she'd appeared in parts of the picture of my life. As a bride. As a young mother.

"You know, you're a beautiful woman," I said.

She colored.

"I suppose we got married too young," I said. "We each had a lot of growing to do. And the business took too much of my time over the years. And I'm afraid I haven't been a very good husband."

"You weren't so bad."

"I'm glad we got married," I said. "And I'm glad we stayed together. And that you were here for me to come home to."

She started to cry. I held her until she stopped. Then, her face to my chest, she said, "At the hospital, waiting, I realized for the first time what it would mean for me to lose you. I thought we'd stopped loving each other a long time ago. I know you've had other women. For that matter, I've had lovers from time to time. I don't know if you knew that."

"It's not important."

"No," she said, "it's not important. I'm glad we got married, darling. And I'm glad you're going to be all right."

Monty said, "You had everybody worried there, kid. But what do you think you're doing down here? You're supposed to be home in bed."

"I'm supposed to get exercise. Besides, if I don't come down here how do I know you won't steal the firm into bankruptcy?"

My tone was light, but he flushed deeply. "You just hit a nerve," he said.

"What's the matter?"

"When they were busy cutting the bullet out of you, all I could think was you'd die thinking I was a thief."

"I don't know what you're talking about."

He lowered his eyes. "I was borrowing partnership funds," he said. "I was in a bind because of my own stupidity and I didn't want to admit it to you, so I dipped into the till. It was a temporary thing, a case of the shorts. I got everything straightened out before that clown took a shot at you. They know who it was yet?"

"Not yet."

"The night before you were shot, I stayed late and covered things. I wasn't going to say anything, and then I wondered if you'd been suspicious, and I decided

I'd tell you about it first thing in the morning. Then it looked as though I wasn't going to get the chance. You didn't suspect anything?"

"I thought our cash position was light. But after all these years I certainly wasn't afraid of you stealing from me."

"All those years," he echoed, and I was seeing the picture of my life again. All the work Monty and I had put in side by side. The laughs we'd shared, the bad times we'd survived.

We looked at each other, and a great deal of feeling passed between us. Then he drew a breath and clapped me on the shoulder. "Well, that's enough about old times," he said gruffly. "Somebody's got to do a little work around here."

"I'm glad you're here," Peg said. "I couldn't even go to the hospital. All I could do was call every hour and ask anonymously for a report on your condition. Critical condition, that's what they said. Over and over."

"It must have been rough."

"It did something to me and for me," she said. "It made me realize that I've cheated myself out of a life. And I was the one who did it. You didn't do it to me."

"I told you I'd leave Julia."

"Oh, that was just a game we both played. I never really expected you to leave her. No, it's been my fault, dear. I settled into a nice secure life. But when you were on the critical list I decided my life was on the critical list, too, and that it was time I took some responsibility for it."

"Meaning?"

"Meaning it's good you came over tonight and not this afternoon, because you wouldn't have found me at home. I've got a job. It's not much, but it's enough to pay the rent. You see, I've decided it's time I started paying my own rent. In the fall I'll start night classes at the university."

"I see."

"You're not angry?"

"Angry? I'm happy for you."

"I don't regret what we've been to each other. I was a lost little girl with a screwed-up life and you made me feel loved and cared for. But I'm a big girl now. I'll still see you, if you want to see me, but from here on in I pay my own way."

"No more checks?"

"No more checks. I mean it."

I remembered some of our times together, seeing them as I had seen them in the picture of my life. I was filled with desire. I went and took her in my arms.

She said, "But is it safe? Won't it be dangerous for you?"

"The doctor said it'll do me good."

Her eyes sparkled. "Well, if it's just what the doctor ordered—" And she led me to the bedroom.

Afterward I wished I could have died in Peg's bed. Almost immediately I realized that would have been bad for her and bad for Julia.

Anyway, I hadn't yet done what I'd come back to do.

Later, while Julia slept, I lay awake in the darkness. I thought, This is crazy. I'm no detective. I'm a businessman. I died and You won't let me stay dead. Why can't I be dead?

I got out of bed, went downstairs, and laid out the cards for a game of solitaire. I toasted a slice of bread and made myself a cup of tea.

I won the game of solitaire. It was a hard variety, one I could normally win once in fifty or a hundred times.

I thought. It's not Julia, it's not Monty, it's not Peg. All of them have love for me.

I felt good about that.

But who killed me? Who was left of my list?

I didn't feel good about that.

The following morning I was finishing my breakfast when Mark rang the bell. Julia went to the door and let him in. He came into the kitchen and got himself a cup of coffee from the pot on the stove.

"I was at the hospital," he said. "Night and day, but they wouldn't let any of us see you. I was there."

"Your mother told me."

"Then I had to leave town the day before yesterday and I just got back this morning. I had to meet with some men." A smile flickered on his face. He looked just like his mother when he smiled.

"I've got the financing," he said. "I'm in business."

"That's wonderful."

"I know you wanted me to follow in your footseps, Dad. But I couldn't be happy having my future handed to me that way. I wanted to make it on my own."

"You're my son. I was the same myself."

"When I asked you for a loan—"

"I've been thinking about that," I said, remembering the scene as I'd witnessed it in the picture of my life. "I resented your independence and I envied your youth. I was wrong to turn you down."

"You were *right* to turn me down." That smile again, just like his mother. "I wanted to make it on my own, and then I turned around and asked for help from you. I'm just glad you knew better than to give me what I was weak enough to ask for. I realized that almost immediately, but I was too proud to say anything, and then some madman shot you and—well, I'm glad everything turned out all right, Dad."

"Yes," I said. "So am I."

Not Mark, then.

Not Debbie either. I always knew that, and knew it with utter certainty when she cried out "Oh, Daddy!" and rushed to me and threw herself into my arms. "I'm so glad," she kept saying. "I was so worried."

"Calm down," I told her. "I don't want my grandchild born with a nervous condition."

"Don't worry about your grandchild. Your grandchild's going to be just fine."

"And how about my daughter?"

"Your daughter's just fine. Do you want to know something? These past few days, wow, I've really learned a lot during these past few days."

"So have I."

"How close I am to you, for one thing. Waiting at the hospital, there was a time when I thought, God, he's gone. I just had this feeling. And then I shook my head and said, no, it was nonsense, you were all right. And you know what they told us afterward? Your heart stopped during the operation, and it must have happened right when I got that feeling. I *knew*, and then I knew again when it resumed beating."

When I looked at my son I saw his mother's smile. When I looked at Debbie I saw myself.

"And another thing I learned, and that's how much people need each other. People were so good to us! So many people called me, asked about you. Even Philip called, can you imagine? He just wanted to let me know that I should call on him if there was anything he could do."

"What could he possibly do?"

"I have no idea. It was funny hearing from him, though. I hadn't heard his voice since we were living together. But it was nice of him to call, wasn't it?"

I nodded. "It must have made you wonder what might have been."

"What it made me wonder was how I ever thought Philip and I were made for each other. Scott was with me every minute, you know, except when he went down to give blood for you—"

"He gave blood for me?"

"Didn't mother tell you? You and Scott are the same blood type. It's one of the rarer types and you both have it. Maybe that's why I fell in love with him."

"Not a bad reason."

"He was with me all the time, you know, and by the time you were out of danger I began to realize how close Scott and I have grown, how much I love him. And then when I heard Philip's voice I thought what kid stuff that relationship of ours had been. I know you never approved."

"It wasn't my business to approve or disapprove."

"Maybe not. But I know you approve of Scott, and that's important to me."

I went home.

I thought, What do You want from me? It's not my son-in-law. You don't try to kill a man and then donate blood for a transfusion. Nobody would do a thing like that.

The person I cut off at the traffic circle? But that was insane. And how would I know him anyway? I wouldn't know where to start looking for him.

Some other enemy? But I had no enemies.

Julia said, "The doctor called again. He still doesn't see how you could check yourself out of the hospital. But he called to say he wants to schedule you for surgery."

Not yet, I told her. Not until I'm ready.

"When will you be ready?"

When I feel right about it, I told her.

She called him back, relayed the message. "He's very nice," she reported. "He says any delay is hazardous, so you should let him schedule as soon as you possibly can. If you have something to attend to he says he can understand that, but try not to let it drag on too long."

I was glad he was a sympathetic and understanding man, and that she liked him. He might be a comfort to her later when she needed someone around to lean on.

Something clicked.

I called Debbie.

"Just the one telephone call," she said, puzzled. "He said he knew you never liked him but he always respected you and he knew what an influence you were in my life. And that I should feel free to call on him if I needed someone to turn to. It was nice of him, that's what I told myself at the time, but there was something creepy about the conversation."

And what had she told him?

"That it was nice to hear from him, and that, you know, my husband and I would be fine. Sort of stressing that I was married, but in a nice way. Why?"

The police were very dubious. Ancient history, they said. The boy had lived with my daughter a while ago, parted amicably, never made any trouble. Had he ever threatened me? Had we ever fought?

He's the one, I said. Watch him, I said. Keep an eye on him.

So they assigned men to watch Philip, and on the fourth day the surveillance paid off. They caught him tucking a bomb beneath the hood of a car. The car belonged to my son-in-law, Scott.

"He thought you were standing between them. When she said she was happily married, well, he shifted his sights to the husband."

There had always been something about Philip that I had not liked. Something creepy, as Debbie put it. Perhaps he'll get treatment now. In any event, he'll be unable to harm anyone.

Is that why I was permitted to return? So that I could prevent Philip from harming Scott?

Perhaps that was the purpose. The conversations with Julia, with Monty, with Peg, with Mark and Debbie, those were fringe benefits.

Or perhaps it was the other way around.

All right.

They've prepared me for surgery. The doctor, understanding as ever, called again. This time I let him schedule me, and I came here and let them prepare me. And I've prepared myself.

All right.

I'm ready now.

As Good as a Rest

Andrew says the whole point of a vacation is to change your perspective of the world. A change is as good as a rest, he says, and vacations are about change, not rest. If we just wanted a rest, he says, we could stop the mail and disconnect the phone and stay home: that would add up to more of a traditional rest than traipsing all over Europe. Sitting in front of the television set with your feet up, he says, is generally considered to be more restful than climbing the forty-two thousand steps to the top of Notre Dame.

Of course, there aren't forty-two thousand steps, but it did seem like it at the time. We were with the Dattners—by the time we got to Paris the four of us had already buddied up—and Harry kept wondering aloud why the genius who'd built the cathedral hadn't thought to put in an elevator. And Sue, who'd struck me earlier as unlikely to be afraid of anything, turned out to be petrified of heights. There are two staircases at Notre Dame, one going up and one coming down, and to get from one to the other you have to walk along this high ledge. It's really quite wide, even at its narrowest, and the view of the rooftops of Paris is magnificent, but all of this was wasted on Sue, who clung to the rear wall with her eyes clenched shut.

Andrew took her arm and walked her through it, while Harry and I looked out at the City of Light. "It's high open spaces that does it to her," he told me. "Yesterday, the Eiffel Tower, no problem, because the space was enclosed. But when it's open she starts getting afraid that she'll get sucked over the side or that she'll get this sudden impulse to jump, and, well, you see what it does to her."

While neither Andrew nor I have ever been troubled by heights, whether open or enclosed, the climb to the top of the cathedral wasn't the sort of thing we'd have done at home, especially since we'd already had a spectacular view of the city the day before from the Eiffel Tower. I'm not mad about walking up stairs, but it didn't occur to me to pass up the climb. For that matter, I'm not that mad about walking generally—Andrew says I won't go anywhere without a guaranteed parking space—but it seems to me that I walked from one end of Europe to the other, and didn't mind a bit.

When we weren't walking through streets or up staircases, we were parading through museums. That's hardly a departure for me, but for Andrew it is uncharacteristic behavior in the extreme. Boston's Museum of Fine Arts is one of the best in the country, and it's not twenty minutes from our house. We have a membership, and I go all the time, but it's almost impossible to get Andrew to go.

But in Paris he went to the Louvre, and the Rodin Museum, and that little museum in the sixteenth arrondissement with the most wonderful collection of Monets. And in London he led the way to the National Gallery and the National Portrait Gallery and the Victoria and Albert—and in Amsterdam he spent three hours in the Rijksmuseum and hurried us to the Van Gogh Museum first thing the next morning. By the time we got to Madrid, I was museumed out. I knew it was a sin to miss the Prado but I just couldn't face it, and I wound up walking around the city with Harry while my husband dragged Sue through galleries of El Grecos and Goyas and Velázquezes.

"Now that you've discovered museums," I told Andrew, "you may take a different view of the Museum of Fine Arts. There's a show of American landscape painters that'll still be running when we get back—I think you'll like it."

He assured me he was looking forward to it. But you know he never went. Museums are strictly a vacation pleasure for him. He doesn't even want to hear about them when he's at home.

For my part, you'd think I'd have learned by now not to buy clothes when we travel. Of course, it's impossible not to—there are some genuine bargains and some things you couldn't find at home—but I almost always wind up buying something that remains unworn in my closet forever after. It seems so right in some foreign capital, but once I get it home I realize it's not me at all, and so it lives out its days on a hanger, a source in turn of fond memories and faint guilt. It's not that I lose judgment when I travel, or become wildly impulsive. It's more that I become a slightly different person during the course of the trip and the clothes I buy for that person aren't always right for the person I am in Boston.

Oh, why am I nattering on like this? You don't have to look in my closet to see how travel changes a person. For heaven's sake, just look at the Dattners.

If we hadn't all been on vacation together, we would never have come to know Harry and Sue, let alone spend so much time with them. We would never have encountered them in the first place—day-to-day living would not have brought them to Boston, or us to Enid, Oklahoma. But even if they'd lived down the street from us, we would never have become close friends at home. To put it as simply as possible, they were not our kind of people.

The package tour we'd booked wasn't one of those escorted ventures in which your every minute is accounted for. It included our charter flights over and back, all our hotel accommodations, and our transportation from one city to the next. We "did" six countries in twenty-two days, but what we did in each, and where and with whom, was strictly up to us. We could have kept to ourselves altogether, and have often done so when traveling, but by the time we checked into our hotel in London the first day we'd made arrangements to join the Dattners that night for dinner, and before we knocked off our after-dinner brandies that night it had been tacitly agreed that we would be a foursome throughout the trip—unless, of course, it turned out that we tired of each other.

"They're a pair," Andrew said that first night, unknotting his tie and giving it a shake before hanging it over the doorknob. "That y'all-come-back accent of hers sounds like syrup flowing over corn cakes."

"She's a little flashy, too," I said. "But that sport jacket of his—"

"I know," Andrew said. "Somewhere, even as we speak, a horse is shivering, his blanket having been transformed into a jacket for Harry."

"And yet there's something about them, isn't there?"

"They're nice people," Andrew said. "Not our kind at all, but what does that matter? We're on a trip. We're ripe for a change . . ."

In Paris, after a night watching a floor show at what I'm sure was a rather disreputable little nightclub in Les Halles, I lay in bed while Andrew sat up smoking a last cigarette. "I'm glad we met the Dattners," he said. "This trip would be fun anyway, but they add to it. That joint tonight was a treat, and I'm sure we wouldn't have gone if it hadn't been for them. And do you know something? I don't think *they'd* have gone if it hadn't been for *us*."

"Where would we be without them?" I rolled onto my side. "I know where Sue would be without your helping hand. Up on top of Notre Dame, frozen with fear. Do you suppose that's how the gargoyles got there? Are they nothing but tourists turned to stone?"

"Then you'll never be a gargoyle. You were a long way from petrification whirling around the dance floor tonight."

"Harry's a good dancer. I didn't think he would be, but he's very light on his feet."

"The gun doesn't weigh him down, eh?"

I sat up. "I *thought* he was wearing a gun," I said. "How on earth does he get it past the airport scanners?"

"Undoubtedly by packing it in his luggage and checking it through. He wouldn't need it on the plane—not unless he was planning to divert the flight to Havana."

"I don't think they go to Havana anymore. Why would he need it *off* the plane? I suppose tonight he'd feel safer armed. That place was a bit on the rough side."

"He was carrying it at the Tower of London, and in and out of a slew of museums. In fact, I think he carries it all the time except on planes. Most likely he feels naked without it."

"I wonder if he sleeps with it."

"I think he sleeps with her."

"Well, I know *that*."

"To their mutual pleasure, I shouldn't wonder. Even as you and I."

"Ah," I said.

And, a bit later, he said, "You like them, don't you?"

"Well, of course I do. I don't want to pack them up and take them home to Boston with us, but—"

"You like *him.*"

"Harry? Oh, *I* see what you're getting at."

"Quite."

"And she's attractive, isn't she? You're attracted to her."

"At home I wouldn't look at her twice, but here—"

"Say no more. That's how I feel about him. That's exactly how I feel about him."

"Do you suppose we'll do anything about it?"

"I don't know. Do you suppose they're having this very conversation two floors below?"

"I wouldn't be surprised. If they *are* having this conversation, and if they had the same silent prelude to this conversation, they're probably feeling very good indeed."

"Mmmmm," I said dreamily. "Even as you and I."

I don't know if the Dattners had that conversation that particular evening, but they certainly had it somewhere along the way. The little tensions and energy currents between the four of us began to build until it seemed almost as though the air were crackling with electricity. More often than not we'd find ourselves pairing off on our walks, Andrew with Sue, Harry with me. I remember one moment when he took my hand crossing the street—I remember the instant but not the street, or even the city—and a little shiver went right through me.

By the time we were in Madrid, with Andrew and Sue trekking through the Prado while Harry and I ate garlicky shrimp and sipped a sweetish white wine in a little café on the Plaza Mayor, it was clear what was going to happen. We were almost ready to talk about it.

"I hope they're having a good time," I told Harry. "I just couldn't manage another museum."

"I'm glad we're out here instead," he said, with a wave at the plaza. "But I would have gone to the Prado if you went." And he reached out and covered my hand with his.

"Sue and Andy seem to be getting along pretty good," he said.

Andy! Had anyone else ever called my husband Andy?

"And you and me, we get along all right, don't we?"

"Yes," I said, giving his hand a little squeeze. "Yes, we do."

Andrew and I were up late that night, talking and talking. The next day we flew to Rome. We were all tired our first night there and ate at the restaurant in our hotel rather than venture forth. The food was good, but I wonder if any of us really tasted it.

Andrew insisted that we all drink *grappa* with our coffee. It turned out to be a rather nasty brandy, clear in color and quite powerful. The men had a second round of it. Sue and I had enough work finishing our first.

Harry held his glass aloft and proposed a toast. "To good friends," he said. "To close friendship with good people." And after everyone had taken a sip he said, "You know, in a couple of days we all go back to the lives we used to lead. Sue and I go back to Oklahoma, you two go back to Boston, Mass. Andy, you go back to your investments business and I'll be doin' what I do. And we got each other's addresses and phone, and we say we'll keep in touch, and maybe we will. But if we do or we don't, either way one thing's sure. The minute we get off that plane at JFK, that's when the carriage turns into a pumpkin and the horses go back to bein' mice. You know what I mean?"

Everyone did.

"Anyway," he said, "what me an' Sue were thinkin', we thought there's a whole lot of Rome, a mess of good restaurants, and things to see and places to go. We thought it's silly to have four people all do the same things and go the same places and miss out on all the rest. We thought, you know, after breakfast tomorrow, we'd split up and spend the day separate." He took a breath. "Like Sue and Andy'd team up for the day and, Elaine, you an' me'd be together."

"The way we did in Madrid," somebody said.

"Except I mean for the whole day," Harry said. A light film of perspiration gleamed on his forehead. I looked at his jacket and tried to decide if he was wearing his gun. I'd seen it on our afternoon in Madrid. His jacket had come open and I'd seen the gun, snug in his shoulder holster. "The whole day and then the evening, too. Dinner—and after."

There was a silence which I don't suppose could have lasted nearly as long as it seemed to. Then Andrew said he thought it was a good idea, and Sue agreed, and so did I.

Later, in our hotel room, Andrew assured me that we could back out. "I don't think they have any more experience with this than we do. You saw how nervous Harry was during his little speech. He'd probably be relieved to a certain degree if we did back out."

"Is that what you want to do?"

He thought for a moment. "For my part," he said, "I'd as soon go through with it."

"So would I. My only concern is if it made some difference between us afterward."

"I don't think it will. This is fantasy, you know. It's not the real world. We're not in Boston or Oklahoma. We're in Rome, and you know what they say. When in Rome, do as the Romans do."

"And is this what the Romans do?"

"It's probably what they do when they go to Stockholm," Andrew said.

In the morning, we joined the Dattners for breakfast. Afterward, without anything being said, we paired off as Harry had suggested the night before. He and I walked through a sun-drenched morning to the Spanish Steps, where I bought a bag of crumbs and fed the pigeons. After that—

Oh, what does it matter what came next, what particular tourist things we found to do that day? Suffice it to say that we went interesting places and saw rapturous sights, and everything we did and saw was heightened by anticipation of the evening ahead.

We ate lightly that night, and drank freely but not to excess. The trattoria where we dined wasn't far from our hotel and the night was clear and mild, so we walked back. Harry slipped an arm around my waist. I leaned a little against his shoulder. After we'd walked a way in silence, he said very softly, "Elaine, only if you want to."

"But I do," I heard myself say.

Then he took me in his arms and kissed me.

I ought to recall the night better than I do. We felt love and lust for each other, and sated both appetites. He was gentler than I might have guessed he'd be, and I more abandoned. I could probably remember precisely what happened if I put my mind to it, but I don't think I could make the memory seem real. Because it's as if it happened to someone else. It was vivid at the time, because at the time I truly was the person sharing her bed with Harry. But that person had no existence before or after that European vacation.

There was a moment when I looked up and saw one of Andrew's neckties hanging on the knob of the closet door. It struck me that I should have put the tie away, that it was out of place there. Then I told myself that the tie was where it ought to be, that it was Harry who didn't belong here. And finally I decided that both belonged, my husband's tie and my inappropriate Oklahoma lover. Now both belonged, but in the morning the necktie would remain and Harry would be gone.

As indeed he was. I awakened a little before dawn and was alone in the room. I went back to sleep, and when I next opened my eyes Andrew was in bed beside me. Had they met in the hallway? I wondered. Had they worked out the logistics of this passage in advance? I never asked. I still don't know.

Our last day in Rome, the Dattners went their way and we went ours. Andrew and I got to the Vatican, saw the Colosseum, and wandered here and there, stopping at sidewalk cafés for espresso. We hardly talked about the previous evening, beyond assuring each other that we had enjoyed it, that we were glad it had happened, and that our feelings for one another remained unchanged—deepened, if anything, by virtue of having shared this experience, if it could be said to have been shared.

We joined Harry and Sue for dinner. And in the morning we all rode out to the airport and boarded our flight to New York. I remember looking at the other passengers on the plane, few of whom I'd exchanged more than a couple of sentences with in the course of the past three weeks. There were almost certainly couples among them with whom we had more in common than we had with the Dattners. Had any of them had comparable flings in the course of the trip?

At JFK we all collected our luggage and went through customs and passport control. Then we were off to catch our connecting flight to Boston while Harry and Sue had a four-hour wait for their TWA flight to Tulsa. We said good-bye. The men shook hands while Sue and I embraced. Then Harry and I kissed, and Sue and Andrew kissed. That woman slept with my husband, I thought. And that man—I slept with him. I had the thought that, were I to continue thinking about it, I would start laughing.

Two hours later we were on the ground at Logan, and less than an hour after that we were in our own house.

That weekend Paul and Marilyn Welles came over for dinner and heard a play-by-play account of our three-week vacation—with the exception, of course, of that second-to-last night in Rome. Paul is a business associate of Andrew's and Marilyn is a woman not unlike me, and I wondered to myself what would happen if we four traded partners for an evening.

But it wouldn't happen and I certainly didn't want it to happen. I found Paul attractive and I know Andrew had always found Marilyn attractive. But such an incident among us wouldn't be appropriate, as it had somehow been appropriate with the Dattners.

I know Andrew was having much the same thoughts. We didn't discuss it afterward, but one knows . . .

I thought of all of this just last week. Andrew was in a bank in Skokie, Illinois, along with Paul Welles and two other men. One of the tellers managed to hit the silent alarm and the police arrived as they were on their way out. There was some shooting. Paul Welles was wounded superficially, as was one of the policemen. Another of the policemen was killed.

Andrew is quite certain he didn't hit anybody. He fired his gun a couple of times, but he's sure he didn't kill the police officer.

But when he got home we both kept thinking the same thing. It could have been Harry Dattner.

Not literally, because what would an Oklahoma state trooper be doing in Skokie, Illinois? But it might as easily have been the Skokie cop in Europe with us. And it might have been Andrew who shot him—or been shot by him, for that matter.

I don't know that I'm explaining this properly. It's all so incredible. That I should have slept with a policeman while my husband was with a policeman's wife. That we had ever become friendly with them in the first place. I have to remind myself, and keep reminding myself, that it all happened overseas. It happened in Europe, and it happened to four other people. We were not ourselves, and Sue and Harry were not themselves. It happened, you see, in another universe altogether, and so, really, it's as if it never happened at all.

The Books Always Balance

The first envelope arrived on a Tuesday. This marked it as slightly atypical from the start, as Myron Hettinger received very little mail at his office on Tuesdays. Letters mailed on Fridays arrived Monday morning, and letters mailed on Monday, unless dispatched rather early in the day, did not arrive until Wednesday, or at the earliest on Tuesday afternoon. This envelope, though, arrived Tuesday morning. John Palmer brought it into Myron Hettinger's office a few minutes past ten, along with the other mail. Like the other envelopes, it was unopened. Only Myron Hettinger opened Myron Hettinger's mail.

The rest of the mail, by and large, consisted of advertisements and solicitations of one sort or another. Myron Hettinger opened them in turn, studied them very briefly, tore them once in half and threw them into the wastebasket. When he came to this particular envelope, however, he paused momentarily.

He studied it. It bore his address. The address had been typed in a rather ordinary typeface. It bore, too, a Sunday evening postmark. It bore a four-cent stamp commemorating the one hundred fiftieth anniversary of the founding of a land grant college in the Midwest. It did not bear a return address or any other hint as to who had sent it or what might be contained therein.

Myron Hettinger opened the envelope. There was no letter inside. There was instead a photograph of two partially clad persons. One of them was a man who looked to be in his early fifties, balding, perhaps fifteen pounds overweight, with a narrow nose and rather thin lips. The man was with a woman who looked to be in her middle twenties, blonde, small-boned, smiling, and extraordinarily attractive. The man was Myron Hettinger, and the woman was Sheila Bix.

For somewhere between fifteen and thirty seconds, Myron Hettinger looked at the picture. Then he placed it upon the top of his desk and walked to the door of his office, which he locked. Then he returned to his desk, sat down in his straight-backed chair, and made sure that the envelope contained nothing but the photograph. After assuring himself of this, he tore the photograph twice in half, did as much with the envelope, placed the various scraps of paper and film in his ashtray, and set them aflame.

A less stable man might have ripped photo and envelope into an inestimable number of shreds, scattered the shreds to four or more winds, and crouched in mute terror behind his heavy desk. Myron Hettinger was stable. The photograph was not a threat but merely the promise of a threat, a portent of probable menace. Fear could wait until the threat itself came to the fore.

A more whimsical man might have pasted the photograph in his scrapbook, or might have saved it as a memory piece. Myron Hettinger was not whimsical; he had no scrapbook and kept no memorabilia.

The fire in the ashtray had a foul odor. After it ceased to burn, Myron Hettinger turned on the air conditioner.

The second envelope arrived two days later in Thursday morning's mail. Myron Hettinger had been expecting it, with neither bright anticipation nor with any real fear. He found it among a heavy stack of letters. The envelope was the same as the first. The address was the same, the typeface appeared to be the same, and the stamp, too, was identical with the stamp on the first envelope. The postmark was different, which was not surprising.

This envelope contained no photograph. Instead it contained an ordinary sheet of cheap stationery on which someone had typed the following message:

> Get one thousand dollars in ten and twenty dollar bills. Put them in a package and put the package in a locker in the Times Square station of the IRT. Put the key in an envelope and leave it at the desk of the Slocum Hotel addressed to Mr. Jordan. Do all this today or a photo will be sent to your wife. Do not go to the police. Do not hire a detective. Do not do anything stupid.

The final three sentences of the unsigned letter were quite unnecessary. Myron Hettinger had no intention of going to the police, or of engaging the services of a detective. Nor did he intend to do anything stupid.

After letter and envelope had been burned, after the air conditioner had cleared the small room of its odor, Myron Hettinger stood at his window, looking out at East Forty-third Street and thinking. The letter bothered him considerably more than the photograph had bothered him. It was a threat. It might conceivably intrude upon the balanced perfection of his life. This he couldn't tolerate.

Until the letter had arrived, Myron Hettinger's life had indeed been perfect. His work was perfect, to begin with. He was a certified public accountant, self-employed, and he earned a considerable amount of money every year by helping various persons and firms pay somewhat less in the way of taxes than they might have paid without his services. His marriage, too, was perfect. His wife, Eleanor, was two years his junior, kept his home as he wanted it kept, cooked perfect meals, kept him company when he wished her company, let him alone when he wished to be alone, kept her slightly prominent nose out of his private affairs and was the beneficiary of a trust fund which paid her in the neighborhood of twenty-five thousand dollars per year.

Finally, to complete this picture of perfection, Myron Hettinger had a perfect mistress. This woman, of course, was the woman pictured in the unpleasant photograph. Her name was Sheila Bix. She provided comfort, both physical and emotional, she was the essence of discretion, and her demands were minimal—rent for her apartment, a small sum for incidentals, and an occasional bonus for clothing.

A perfect career, a perfect wife, a perfect mistress. This blackmailer, this *Mr. Jordan*, now threatened all three components of Myron Hettinger's perfect life. If the damnable photograph got into Mrs. Hettinger's hands, she would divorce him. He was very certain of this. If the divorce were scandalous, as it well might be, his business would suffer. And if all of this happened, it was quite likely that, for one reason or another, he would wind up losing Sheila Bix as well.

Myron Hettinger closed his eyes and drummed his fingers upon his desk top. He did not want to hurt his business, did not want to lose his wife or mistress. His business satisfied him, as did Eleanor and Sheila. He did not *love* either Eleanor or Sheila, not any more than he *loved* his business. Love, after all, is an imperfect emotion. So is hate. Myron Hettinger did not hate this Mr. Jordan, much as he would have enjoyed seeing the man dead.

But what could he do?

There was, of course, one thing and only one thing that he could do. At noon he left his office, went to his bank, withdrew one thousand dollars in tens and twenties, packed them neatly in a cigar box, and deposited the box in a locker in the Times Square station of the IRT. He tucked the locker key into an envelope, addressed the envelope to the annoying Mr. Jordan, left the envelope at the desk of the Slocum Hotel, and returned to his office without eating lunch. Later in the day, perhaps because of Mr. Jordan or perhaps because of the missed meal, Myron Hettinger had a rather severe case of heartburn. He took bicarbonate of soda.

The third envelope arrived a week to the day after the second. Thereafter, for four weeks, Myron Hettinger received a similar envelope every Thursday morning. The letters within varied only slightly. Each letter asked for a thousand dollars. Each letter directed that he go through the rather complicated business of putting money in a locker and leaving the locker key at the hotel desk. The letters differed each from the other only as to the designated hotel.

Three times Myron Hettinger followed the instructions to the letter. Three times he went to his bank, then to the subway station, then to the appointed hotel, and finally back to his office. Each time he missed lunch, and each time, probably as a direct result, he had heartburn. Each time he remedied it with bicarbonate of soda.

Things were becoming routine.

Routine in and of itself was not unpleasant. Myron Hettinger preferred order. He even devoted a specific page of his personal books to his account with the intrusive Mr. Jordan, listing each thousand-dollar payment the day it was paid. There were two reasons for this. First of all, Myron Hettinger never let an expenditure go unrecorded. His books were always in order and they always balanced. And secondly, there was somewhere in the back of his mind the faint hope that these payments to Mr. Jordan could at least be deducted from his income taxes.

Aside from his Thursday ventures, Myron Hettinger's life stayed pretty much as it had been. He did his work properly, spent two evenings a week with Sheila Bix, and spent five evenings a week with his wife.

He did not mention the blackmail to his wife, of course. Not even an idiot could have done this. Nor did he mention it to Sheila Bix. It was Myron Hettinger's firm conviction that personal matters were best discussed with no one. He knew, and Mr. Jordan knew, and that already was too much. He had no intention of enlarging this circle of knowledgeable persons if he could possibly avoid it.

When the sixth of these letters arrived—the seventh envelope in all from Mr. Jordan—Myron Hettinger locked his office door, burned the letter, and sat at his desk in deep thought. He did not move from his chair for almost a full hour. He did not fidget with desk top gadgets. He did not doodle.

He thought.

This routine, he realized, could not possibly continue. While he might conceivably resign himself to suffering once a week from heartburn, he could not resign himself to the needless expenditure of one thousand dollars per week. One thousand dollars was not a tremendous amount of money to Myron Hettinger. Fifty-two thousand dollars was, and one did not need the mind of a certified public accountant to determine that weekly payments of one thousand dollars would run into precisely such a sum yearly. The payments, then, had to stop.

This could be accomplished in one of two ways. The blackmailer could be allowed to send his wretched photograph to Myron Hettinger's perfect wife, or he could be caused to stop his blackmailing. The first possibility seemed dreadful in its implications, as it had seemed before. The second seemed impossible.

He could, of course, appeal to his blackmailer's nobler instincts by including a plaintive letter with his payments. Yet this seemed potentially useless. Having no nobler instincts of his own, Myron Hettinger was understandably unwilling to attribute such instincts to the faceless Mr. Jordan.

What else?

Well, he could always kill Mr. Jordan.

This seemed to be the only solution, the only way to check this impossible outflow of cash. It also seemed rather difficult to bring off. It is hard to kill a man without knowing who he is, and Myron Hettinger had no way of finding out more about the impertinent Mr. Jordan. He could not lurk at the appointed hotel; Mr. Jordan, knowing him, could simply wait him out before putting in an appearance. Nor could he lurk near the subway locker, for the same reason.

And how on earth could you kill a man without either knowing him or meeting him?

Myron Hettinger's mind leaped back to an earlier thought, the thought of appealing to the man's nobler instincts through a letter. Then daylight dawned. He smiled the smile of a man who had solved a difficult problem through the application of sure and perfect reasoning.

That day, Myron Hettinger left his office at noon. He did not go to his bank, however. Instead he went to several places, among them a chemical supply house, a five-and-dime, and several drugstores. He was careful not to buy more than one item at any one place. We need not concern ourselves with the precise nature of his purchases. He was buying the ingredients for a bomb, and there is no point in telling the general public how to make bombs.

He made his bomb in the stall of a public lavatory, using as its container the same sort of cigar box in which he normally placed one thousand dollars in ten and twenty dollar bills. The principle of the bomb was simplicity itself. The working ingredient was nitroglycerine, a happily volatile substance which would explode upon the least provocation. A series of devices so arranged things that, were the cover of the cigar box to be lifted, enough hell would be raised to raise additional hell in the form of an explosion. If the box were not opened, but were dropped or banged, a similar explosion would occur. This last provision existed in the event that Mr. Jordan might suspect a bomb at the last moment and might drop the thing and run off. It also existed because Myron Hettinger could not avoid it. If you drop nitroglycerine, it explodes.

Once the bomb was made, Myron Hettinger did just what he always did. He went to the Times Square IRT station and deposited the bomb very gently in a locker. He took the key, inserted it in an envelope on which he had inscribed Mr. Jordan's name, and left the envelope at the desk of the Blackmore Hotel. Then he returned to his office. He was twenty minutes late this time.

He had difficulty keeping his mind on his work that afternoon. He managed to list the various expenses he had incurred in making the bomb on the sheet devoted to payments made to Mr. Jordan, and he smiled at the thought that he would be able to mark the account closed by morning. But he had trouble doing much else that day. Instead he sat and thought about the beauty of his solution.

The bomb would not fail. There was enough nitroglycerine in the cigar box to atomize not only Mr. Jordan but virtually anything within twenty yards of him, so the blackmailer could hardly hope to escape. There was the possibility—indeed, one might say the probability—that a great many persons other than Mr. Jordan might die. If the man was fool enough to open his parcel in the subway station, or if he was clumsy enough to drop it there, the carnage would be dreadful. If he took it home with him and opened it in the privacy of his own room or apartment, considerably less death and destruction seemed likely to occur.

But Myron Hettinger could not have cared less about how many persons Mr. Jordan carried with him to his grave. Men or women or children, he was sure he could remain totally unconcerned about their untimely deaths. If Mr. Jordan died, Myron Hettinger would survive. It was that simple.

At five o'clock, a great deal of work undone, Myron Hettinger got to his feet. He left his office and stood for a moment on the sidewalk, breathing stuffy air and considering his situation. He did not want to go home now, he decided. He had done something magnificent, he had solved an unsolvable problem, and he felt a need to celebrate.

An evening with Eleanor, while certainly comfortable, did not impress him as much of a celebration. An evening with Sheila Bix seemed far more along the lines of what he wanted. Yet he hated to break established routine. On Mondays and on Fridays he went to Sheila Bix's apartment. All other nights he went directly home.

Still, he had already broken one routine that day, the unhappy routine of payment. And why not do in another routine, if just for one night?

He called his wife from a pay phone. "I'll be staying in town for several hours," he said. "I didn't have a chance to call you earlier."

"You usually come home on Thursdays," she said.

"I know. Something's come up."

His wife did not question him, nor did she ask just what it was that had come up. She was the perfect wife. She told him that she loved him, which was quite probably true, and he told her that he loved her, which was most assuredly false. Then he replaced the receiver and stepped to the curb to hail a taxi. He told the driver to take him to an apartment building on West Seventy-third Street just a few doors from Central Park.

The building was an unassuming one, a remodeled brownstone with four apartments to the floor. Sheila's apartment, on the third floor, rented for only one hundred twenty dollars per month, a very modest rental for what the tabloids persist in referring to as a love nest. This economy pleased him, but then it was what one would expect from the perfect mistress.

There was no elevator. Myron Hettinger climbed two flights of stairs and stood slightly but not terribly out of breath in front of Sheila Bix's door. He knocked on the door and waited. The door was not answered. He rang the bell, something he rarely did. The door was still not answered.

Had this happened on a Monday or on a Friday, Myron Hettinger might have been understandably piqued. It had never happened on a Monday or on a Friday. Now, though, he was not annoyed. Since Sheila Bix had no way of knowing that he was coming, he could hardly expect her to be present.

He had a key, of course. When a man has the perfect mistress, or even an imperfect one, he owns a key to the apartment for which he pays the rent. He used this key, opened the door, and closed it behind him. He found a bottle of scotch and poured himself the drink which Sheila Bix poured for him every Monday and every Friday. He sat in a comfortable chair and sipped the drink, waiting for the arrival of Sheila Bix and dwelling both on the pleasant time he would have after she arrived and on the deep satisfaction to be derived from the death of the unfortunate Mr. Jordan.

It was twenty minutes to six when Myron Hettinger entered the comfortable, if inexpensive apartment, and poured himself a drink. It was twenty minutes after six when he heard footsteps on the stairs and then heard a key being fitted into a lock. He opened his mouth to let out a hello, then stopped. He would say nothing, he decided. And she would be surprised.

This happened.

The door opened. Sheila Bix, a blonde vision of loveliness, tripped merrily into the room with shining eyes and the lightest of feet. Her arms were extended somewhat oddly. This was understandable, for she was balancing a parcel upon her pretty head much in the manner of an apprentice model balancing a book as part of a lesson in poise.

It took precisely as long for Myron Hettinger to recognize the box upon her head as it took for Sheila Bix to recognize Myron Hettinger. Both reacted nicely. Myron Hettinger put two and two together with speed that made him a credit to his profession. Sheila Bix performed a similar feat, although she came up with a somewhat less perfect answer.

Myron Hettinger did several things. He tried to get out of the room. He tried to make the box stay where it was, poised precariously upon that pretty and treacherous head. And, finally, he made a desperate lunge to catch the box before it reached the floor, once Sheila Bix had done the inevitable, recoiling in horror and spilling the box from head through air.

His lunge was a good one. He left his chair in a single motion. His hands reached out, groping for the falling cigar box.

There was a very loud noise, but Myron Hettinger only heard the beginnings of it.

The Boy Who Disappeared Clouds

Jeremy's desk was at the left end of the fifth row. Alphabetical order had put him in precisely the desk he would have selected for himself, as far back as you could get without being in the last row. The last row was no good, because there were things you were called upon to do when you were in the last row. Sometimes papers were passed to the back of the room, for example, and the kids in the last row brought them forward to the teacher. In the fifth row you were spared all that.

And, because he was on the end, and the left end at that, he had the window to look out of. He looked out of it now, watching a car brake almost to a stop, then accelerate across the intersection. You were supposed to come to a full stop but hardly anybody ever did, not unless there were other cars or a crossing guard around. They probably figured nobody was looking, he thought, and he liked the idea that they were unaware that he was watching them.

He sensed that Ms. Winspear had left her desk and turned to see her standing a third of the way up the aisle. He faced forward, paying attention, and when her eyes reached his he looked a little off to the left.

When she returned to the front of the room and wrote on the blackboard, he shifted in his seat and looked out the window again. A woman was being pulled down the street by a large black and white dog. Jeremy watched until they turned a corner and moved out of sight, watched another car not quite stop for the stop sign, then raised his eyes to watch a cloud floating free and untouched in the open blue sky.

"Lots of kids look out the window," Cory Buckman said. "Sometimes I'll hear myself, standing in front of them and droning on and on, and I'll wonder why they're not all lined up at the windows with their noses pressed against the glass. Wouldn't you rather watch paint dry than hear me explain quadratic equations?"

"I used to know how to solve quadratic equations," Janice Winspear said, "and now I'm not even sure what they are. I know lots of kids look out the window. Jeremy's different."

"How?"

"Oh, I don't know." She took a sip of coffee, put her cup down. "You know what he is? He's a nice quiet boy."

"That has a ring to it. Page five of the *Daily News*: ' "He was always a nice quiet boy," the neighbors said. "Nobody ever dreamed he would do something like this." ' Is that the sort of thing you mean?"

"I don't think he's about to murder his parents in their beds, although I wouldn't be surprised if he wanted to."

"Oh?"

She nodded. "Jeremy's the youngest of four children. The father drinks and beats his wife and the abuse gets passed on down the line, some of it verbal and some of it physical. Jeremy's at the end of the line."

"And he gets beaten?"

"He came to school in the fall with his wrist in a cast. He said he fell and it's possible he did. But he fits the pattern of an abused child. And he doesn't have anything to balance the lack of affection in the home."

"How are his grades?"

"All right. He's bright enough to get C's and B's without paying attention. He never raises his hand. When I call on him he knows the answer—*if* he knows the question."

"How does he get along with the other kids?"

"They barely know he exists." She looked across the small table at Cory. "And that's in the sixth grade. Next year he'll be in junior high with classes twice the size of mine and a different teacher for every subject."

"And three years after that he'll be in senior high, where I can try teaching him quadratic equations. Unless he does something first to get himself locked up."

"I'm not afraid he'll get locked up, not really. I'm just afraid he'll get lost."

"How is he at sports?"

"Hopeless. The last one chosen for teams in gym class, and he doesn't stay around for after-school games."

"I don't blame him. Any other interests? A stamp collection? A chemistry set?"

"I don't think he could get to have anything in that house," she said. "I had his older brothers in my class over the years and they were monsters."

"Unlike our nice quiet boy."

"That's right. If he had anything they'd take it away from him. Or smash it."

"In that case," Cory said, "what you've got to give him is something nobody can take away. Why don't you teach him how to disappear clouds?"

"How to—?"

"Disappear clouds. Stare at them and make them disappear."

"Oh?" She arched an eyebrow. "You can do that?"

"Uh-huh. So can you, once you know how."

"Cory—"

He glanced at the check, counted out money to cover it. "Really," he said. "There's nothing to it. Anybody can do it."

"For a minute there," she said, "I thought you were serious."

"About the clouds? Of course I was serious."

"You can make clouds disappear."

"And so can you."

"By staring at them."

"Uh-huh."

"Well," she said, "let's see you do it."

He looked up. "Wrong kind of clouds," he announced.

"Oh, right. It figures."

"Have I ever lied to you? Those aren't individual clouds up there; that's just one big overcast mess blocking the sun."

"That's why we need you to work your magic, sir."

"Well, I'm only a journeyman magician. What you need are cumulus clouds, the puffy ones like balls of cotton. Not cumulonimbus, not the big rain clouds, and not the wispy cirrus clouds either, but the cumulus clouds."

"I know what cumulus clouds look like," she said. "It's not like quadratic equations, it stays with you. When the sky is full of cumulus clouds, what will your excuse be? Wrong phase of the moon?"

"I suppose everyone tells you this," he said, "but you're beautiful when you're skeptical."

She was sorting laundry when the phone rang. It was Cory Buckman. "Look out the window," he ordered. "Drop everything and look out the window."

She was holding the receiver in one hand and a pair of tennis shorts in the other, and she looked out the window without dropping either. "It's still there," she reported.

"What's still there?"

"Everything's still there."

"What did you see when you looked out the window?"

"The house across the street. A maple tree. My car."

"Janice, it's a beautiful day out there!"

"Oh. So it is."

"I'll pick you up in half an hour. We're going on a picnic."

"Oh, don't I wish I could. I've got—"

"What?"

"Laundry to sort, and I have to do my lesson plans for the week."

"Try to think in terms of crusty french bread, a good sharp cheese, a nice fruity zinfandel, and a flock of cumulus clouds overhead."

"Which you will cause to disappear?"

"We'll both make them disappear, and we'll work much the same magic upon the bread and the cheese and the wine."

"You said half an hour? Give me an hour."

"Split the difference. Forty-five minutes."

"Sold."

"You see that cloud? The one that's shaped like a camel?"

"More like a llama," she said.

"Watch."

She watched the cloud, thinking that he was really very sweet and very attractive, and that he didn't really need a lot of nonsense about disappearing clouds to lure her away from a Saturday afternoon of laundry and lesson plans. A grassy meadow, air fresh with spring, cows lowing off to the right, and—

A hole began to open in the center of the cloud. She stared, then glanced at him. His fine brow was tense, his mouth a thin line, his hands curled up into fists.

She looked at the cloud again. It was breaking up, collapsing into fragments.

"I don't believe this," she said.

He didn't reply. She watched, and the process of celestial disintegration continued. The hunks of cloud turned wispy and, even as she looked up at them, disappeared altogether. She turned to him, open-mouthed, and he sighed deeply and beamed at her.

"See?" he said. "Nothing to it."

"You cheated," she said.

"How?"

"You picked one you knew was going to disappear."

"How would I go about doing that?"

"I don't know. I'm not a meteorologist, I'm a sixth-grade teacher. Maybe you used math."

"Logarithms," he said. "Cumulus clouds are powerless against logarithms. You pick one."

"Huh?"

"You pick a cloud and I'll disappear it. But it has to be the right sort of cloud."

"Cumulus."

"Uh-huh. And solitary—"

"Wandering lonely as a cloud, for instance."

"Something like that. And not way off on the edge of the horizon. It doesn't have to be directly overhead, but it shouldn't be in the next county."

She picked a cloud. He stared at it and it disappeared.

She gaped at him. "You really did it."

"Well, I really stared at it and it really disappeared. You don't have to believe the two phenomena were connected."

"You made it disappear."

"If you say so."

"Could you teach my nice quiet boy? Could you teach Jeremy?"

"Nope. I don't teach sixth graders."

"But—"

"*You* teach him."

"But I don't know how to do it!"

"So I'll teach you," he said. "Look, Jan, it's not as remarkable as you think it is. Anybody can do it. It's about the easiest ESP ability to develop. Pick a cloud."

"You pick one for me."

"All right. That one right there, shaped like a loaf of white bread."

"Not like any loaf I ever saw." Why was she quibbling? "All right," she said. "I know which cloud you mean."

"Now let me tell you what you're going to do. You're going to stare at it and focus on it, and you're going to send energy from your Third Eye chakra, that's right here—" he touched his finger to a spot midway between her eyebrows "—and that energy is going to disperse the cloud. Take a couple of deep, deep breaths, in and out, and focus on the cloud, that's right, and talk to it in your mind. Say, 'Disappear, disappear.' That's right, keep breathing, focus your energies—"

He kept talking to her and she stared at the loaf-shaped cloud. *Disappear,* she told it. She thought about energy, which she didn't believe in, flowing from her Third Eye whatsit, which she didn't have.

The cloud began to get thin in the middle. *Disappear,* she thought savagely, squinting at it, and a hole appeared. Her heart leaped with exultation.

"Look!"

"You got it now," he told her. "Keep on going. Put it out of its misery."

When the cloud was gone (gone!) she sat for a moment staring at the spot in the sky where it had been, as if it might have left a hole there. "You did it," Cory said.

"Impossible."

"Okay."

"I couldn't have done that. You cheated, didn't you?"

"How?"

"You helped me. By sending your energies into the cloud or something. What's so funny?"

"You are. Five minutes ago you wouldn't believe that I could make clouds disappear, and now you figure I must have done this one, because otherwise you'd have to believe *you* did it, and you know it's impossible."

"Well, it is."

"If you say so."

She poured a glass of wine, sipped at it. "Clearly impossible," she said. "I did it, didn't I?"

"Did you?"

"I don't know. Can I do another?"

"It's not up to me. They're not my clouds."

"Can I do that one? It looks like—I don't know what it looks like. It looks like a cloud."

"That's what it looks like, all right."

"Well? Can I do the cloud-shaped one?"

She did, and caused it to vanish. This time she could tell that it was her energy that was making the cloud disperse. She could actually feel that something was happening, although she didn't know what it was and couldn't understand how it worked. She did a third cloud, dispatching it in short order, and when it fell to her withering gaze she felt a remarkable surge of triumph.

She also felt drained. "I've got a headache," she told Cory. "I suppose the sun and the wine would do it, but it doesn't feel like the usual sort of headache."

"You're using some mental muscles for the first time," he explained. "They say we only use a small percentage of the brain. When we learn to use a new part, it's a strain."

"So what I've got is brain fatigue."

"A light case thereof."

She cocked her head at him. "You think you know a person," she said archly, "and then you find he's got hitherto undreamt-of talents. What else can you do?"

"Oh, all sorts of things. Long division, for example. And I can make omelets."

"What other occult powers have you got?"

"Thousands, I suppose, but that's the only one I've ever developed. Oh, and sometimes I know when a phone's about to ring, but not always."

"When I'm in the tub," she said, "that's when my phone always rings. What a heavenly spot for a picnic, incidentally. And private, too. The ants didn't even find us here."

She closed her eyes and he kissed her. *I have psychic powers,* she thought. *I knew you were going to do that.*

She said, "I'll bet you can make inhibitions disappear, too. Can't you?"

He nodded. "First your inhibitions," he said. "Then your clothes."

The hardest part was waiting for the right sort of day. For a full week it rained. Then for two days the sky was bright and cloudless, and then it was utterly overcast. By the time the right sort of clouds were strewn across the afternoon sky, she had trouble trusting the memory of that Saturday afternoon. Had she really caused clouds to break up? Could she still do it? And could she teach her Jeremy, her nice quiet boy?

Toward the end of the last class period she walked to the rear of the room, moved over toward the windows. She had them writing an exercise in English composition, a paragraph on their favorite television program. They always loved to write about television, though not as much as they loved to watch it.

She watched over Jeremy's shoulder. His handwriting was very neat, very precise.

Softly she said, "I'd like you to stay for a few minutes after class, Jeremy." When he stiffened she added, "It's nothing to worry about."

But of course he would worry, she thought, returning to the front of the room. There was no way to stop his worrying. No matter, she told herself. She was going to give him a gift today, a gift of self-esteem that he badly needed. A few minutes of anxiety was a small price for such a gift.

And, when the room had cleared and the others had left, she went again to his desk. He looked up at her approach, not quite meeting her eyes. He had the sort of undefined pale countenance her southern relatives would call po-faced. But it was, she thought, a sweet face.

She crouched by the side of his desk. "Jeremy," she said, pointing, "do you see that cloud?"

He nodded.

"Oh, I don't know," she said, thinking aloud. "The glass might be a problem. You used to be able to open classroom windows, before everything got climate-controlled. Jeremy, come downstairs with me. I want to take you for a ride."

"A ride?"

"In my car," she said. And when they reached her car, a thought struck her. "Your mother won't worry, will she? If you're a half hour or so late getting home?"

"No," he said. "Nobody'll worry."

When she stopped the car, on a country road just past the northern belt of suburbs, the perfect cloud was hovering almost directly overhead. She opened the door for Jeremy and found a patch of soft grass for them both to sit on. "See that cloud?" she said, pointing. "Just watch what happens to it."

Sure, she thought. Nothing was going to happen and Jeremy was going to be convinced that his teacher was a certifiable madwoman. She breathed deeply, in and out, in and out. She stared hard at the center of the cloud and visualized her energy as a beam of white light running from her Third Eye chakra directly into the cloud's middle. *Disappear*, she thought. *Come on, you. Disappear.*

Nothing happened.

She thought, *Cory, damn you, if you set me up like this to make a fool of myself*— she pushed the thought aside and focused on the cloud. *Disappear, disappear*—

The cloud began to break up, crumbling into fragments. Relief flowed through her like an electric current. She set her jaw and concentrated, and in less than a minute not a trace of the cloud remained in the sky.

The other clouds around it were completely undisturbed.

She looked at Jeremy, whose expression was guarded. She asked him if he'd been watching the cloud. He said he had.

"What happened to it?" she asked.

"It broke up," he said. "It disappeared."

"I made it disappear," she said.

He didn't say anything.

"Oh, Jeremy," she said, taking his hand in both of hers, "Jeremy, it's easy! You can do it. You can make clouds disappear. I can teach you."

"I—"

"I can teach you," she said.

"I think he's got a natural talent for it," she told Cory.

"Sure," he said. "Everybody does."

"Well, maybe his strength is as the strength of ten because his heart is pure. Maybe he has the simple single-mindedness of a child. Whatever he's got, the clouds of America aren't safe with him on the loose."

"Hmmm," he said.

"What's the matter?"

"Nothing. I was just going to say not to expect miracles. You gave him a great gift, but that doesn't mean he's going to be elected class president or captain of the football team. He'll still be a basically shy boy with a basically difficult situation at home and not too much going for him in the rest of the world. Maybe he can disappear clouds, but that doesn't mean he can move mountains."

"Killjoy."

"I just—"

"He can do something rare and magical," she said, "and it's his secret, and it's something for him to cling to while he grows up and gets out of that horrible household. You should have seen his face when that very first cloud caved in and gave up the ghost. Cory, he looked transformed."

"And he's still a nice quiet boy?"

"He's a lovely boy," she said.

The window glass was no problem.

She'd thought it might be, that was why they'd gone all the way out into the country, but it turned out the glass was no problem at all. Whatever it was that got the cloud, it went right through the glass the same way your vision did.

She was in the front of the room now, thrusting a pointer at the pulled down map of the world, pointing out the oil-producing nations. He turned and looked out the window.

The clouds were the wrong kind.

A tree surgeon's pickup truck, its rear a jumble of sawn limbs, slowed almost to a stop, then moved on across the intersection. Jeremy looked down at the stop sign. A few days ago he'd spent most of math period trying to make the stop sign disappear, and there it was, same as ever, slowing the cars down but not quite bringing them to a halt. And that night he'd sat in his room trying to disappear a sneaker, and of course nothing had happened.

Because that wasn't how it worked. You couldn't take something and make it stop existing, any more than a magician could really make an object vanish. But clouds were masses of water vapor held together by—what? Some kind of energy, probably. And the energy that he sent out warred with the energy that held the water vapor particles together, and the particles went their separate ways, and that was the end of the cloud. The particles still existed but they were no longer gathered into a cloud.

So you couldn't make a rock disappear. Maybe, just maybe, if you got yourself tuned just right, you could make a rock crumble into a little pile of dust. He hadn't been able to manage that yet, and he didn't know if it was really possible, but he could see how it might be.

In the front of the room Ms. Winspear indicated oil-producing regions of the United States. She talked about the extraction of oil from shale, and he smiled at the mental picture of a rock crumbling to dust, with a little stream of oil flowing from it.

He looked out the window again. One of the bushes in the foundation planting across the street had dropped its leaves. The bushes on either side of it looked healthy, but the leaves of the one bush had turned yellow and fallen overnight.

Two days ago he'd looked long and hard at that bush. He wondered if it was dead, or if it had just sickened and lost its leaves. Maybe that was it, maybe they would grow back.

He rubbed his wrist. It had been out of the cast for months, it never bothered him, but in the past few days it had been hurting him some. As if he was feeling pain now that he hadn't allowed himself to feel when the wrist broke.

He was starting to feel all sorts of things.

Ms. Winspear asked a question, something about oil imports, and a hand went up in the fourth row. Of course, he thought. Tracy Morrow's hand always went up. She always knew the answer and she always raised her hand, the little snot.

For a moment the strength of his feeling surprised him. Then he took two deep breaths, in and out, in and out, and stared hard at the back of Tracy's head.

Just to see.

Change of Life

In a sense, what happened to Royce Arnstetter wasn't the most unusual thing in the world. What happened to him was that he got to be thirty-eight years old. That's something that happens to most people and it isn't usually much, just a little way station on the road of life, a milepost precisely halfway between thirty-two and forty-four, say.

Not the most significant milestone in the world for most of us either. Since the good Lord saw fit to equip the vast majority of us with ten fingers, we're apt to attach more significance to those birthdays that end with a nought. Oh, there are a few other biggies—eighteen, twenty-one, sixty-five—but usually it's hitting thirty or forty or fifty that makes a man stop and take stock of his life.

For Royce Arnstetter it was old number thirty-eight. The night before he'd gone to bed around ten o'clock—he just about always went to bed around ten o'clock—and his wife Essie said, "Well, when you wake up you'll be thirty-eight, Royce."

"Sure will," he said.

Whereupon she turned out the light and went back to the living room to watch a rerun of *Hee Haw* and Royce rolled over and went to sleep. Fell right off to sleep too. He never did have any trouble doing that.

Then just about exactly eight hours later he opened his eyes and he was thirty-eight years old. He got out of bed quietly, careful not to wake Essie, and he went into the bathroom and studied his face as a prelude to shaving it.

"Be double damned," he said. "Thirty-eight years old and my life's half over and I never yet did a single thing."

While it is given to relatively few men to know in advance the precise dates of their death, a perhaps surprising number of them think they know. Some work it out actuarially with slide rules. Some dream their obituaries and note the date on the newspaper. Others draw their conclusions by means of palmistry or phrenology or astrology or numerology or some such. (Royce's birthday, that we've been talking about, fell on the fourth of March that year, same as it did every year. That made him a Pisces, and he had Taurus rising, Moon in Leo, Venus in Capricorn, Mars in Taurus, and just a shade over three hundred dollars in the First National Bank of Schuyler County. He knew about the bank account but not about the astrology business. I'm just putting it in in case you care. He had lines on the palms of his hands and bumps on the top of his head, but he'd never taken any particular note of them, so I don't see why you and I have to.)

It's hard to say why Royce had decided he'd live to be seventy-six years old. The ages of his four grandparents at death added up to two hundred and ninety-seven, and if you divide that by four (which I just took the trouble to do for you) you come up with seventy-four and a quarter change. Royce's pa was still hale and hearty at sixty-three, and his ma had died some years back at fifty-one during an electric storm when a lightning-struck old silver maple fell on her car while she was in it.

Royce was an only child.

Point is, you can juggle numbers until you're blue in the face and get about everything but seventy-six in connection with Royce Arnstetter. Maybe he dreamed the number, or maybe he saw *The Music Man* and counted trombones, or maybe he was hung up on the Declaration of Independence.

Point is, it hardly matters why Royce had this idea in his head. But he had it, and he'd had it for as many years as he could remember. If you could divide seventy-six by three he might have had a bad morning some years earlier, and if he'd picked seventy-five or seventy-seven he might have skipped right on by the problem entirely, but he picked seventy-six and even Royce knew that half of seventy-six was thirty-eight, which was what he was.

He had what the French, who have a way with words, call an *idée fixe*. If you went and called it a fixed idea you wouldn't go far wrong. And you know what they say about the power of a fixed idea whose time has come.

Or maybe you don't, but it doesn't matter much. Let's get on back to Royce, still staring at himself in the mirror. What he did was fairly usual. He lathered up and started shaving.

But this time, when he had shaved precisely half of his face, one side of his neck and one cheek and one half of his chin and one half of his mustache, he plumb stopped and washed off the rest of the lather.

"Half done," he said, "and half to go."

He looked pretty silly, if you want to know.

Now I almost said earlier that the only thing noteworthy about the number thirty-eight, unless you happen to be Royce Arnstetter, is that it's the caliber of a gun. That would have had a nice ironical sound to it, at least the first time I ran it on by you, but the thing is it would be a fairly pointless observation. Only time Royce ever handled a pistol in his whole life was when he put in his six months in the National Guard so as not to go into the army, and what they had there was a forty-five automatic, and he never did fire it.

As far as owning guns, Royce had a pretty nice rimfire .22 rifle. It was a pretty fair piece of steel in its day and Royce's pa used to keep it around as a varmint gun. That was before Royce married Essie Handridge and took a place on the edge of town, and Royce used to sit up in his bedroom with the rifle and plink away at woodchucks and rabbits when they made a pass at his ma's snap beans and lettuce and such. He didn't often hit anything. It was his pa's gun, really, and it was only in Royce's keeping because his pa had taken to drinking some after Royce's ma got crushed by the silver maple. "Shot out a whole raft of windows last Friday and don't even recall it," Royce's pa said. "Now why don't you just hold onto this here for me? I got enough to worry about as it is."

Royce kept the gun in the closet. He didn't even keep any bullets for it, because what did he need with them?

The other gun was a Worthington twelve gauge, which is a shotgun of a more or less all-purpose nature. Royce's was double-barrel, side by side, and there was nothing automatic about it. After you fired off both shells you had to stop and open the gun and take out the old shells and slap in a couple of fresh ones. Once or twice a year Royce would go out the first day of small-game season and try to get himself a rabbit or a couple pheasant. Sometimes he did and sometimes not. And every now and then he'd try for a deer, but he never did get one of them. Deer have been thin in this part of the state since a few years after the war.

So basically Royce wasn't much for guns. What he really preferred was fishing, which was something he was tolerably good at. His pa was always a good fisherman and it was about the only thing the two of them enjoyed doing together. Royce wasn't enough of a nut to tie his own flies, which his pa had done now and then, but he could cast and he knew what bait to use for what fish and all the usual garbage fishermen have to know if they expect to do themselves any good. He knew all that stuff, Royce did, and he took double-good care of his fishing tackle and owned nothing but quality gear. Some of it was bought second-hand but it was all quality merchandise and he kept it in the best kind of shape.

But good as he was with a fishing rod and poor as he might be with a gun, it didn't make no nevermind, because how in blue hell are you going to walk into a bank and hold it up with a fly rod?

Be serious, will you now?

Well, Royce was there at twenty minutes past nine, which was eleven minutes after the bank opened, which in turn was nine minutes after it was supposed to open. It's not only the First National Bank of Schuyler County, it's the only bank, national or otherwise, in the county. So if Buford Washburn's a handful of minutes late opening up, nobody's about to take his business across the street, because across the street's nothing but Eddie Joe Tyler's sporting goods store. (Royce bought most of his fishing tackle from Eddie Joe, except for the Greenbriar reel he bought when they auctioned off George McEwan's leavings. His pa bought the Worthington shotgun years ago in Clay County off a man who advertised it in the Clay County *Weekly Republican*. I don't know what-all that has to do with anything, but the shotgun's important because Royce had it on his shoulder when he walked on into the bank.)

There was only the one teller behind the counter, but then there was only Royce to give her any business. Buford Washburn was at his desk along the side, and he got to his feet when he saw Royce. "Well, say there, Royce," he said.

"Say, Mr. Washburn," said Royce.

Buford sat back down again. He didn't stand more than he had to. He was maybe six, seven years older than Royce, but if he lived to be seventy-six it would be a miracle, being as his blood pressure was high as July corn and his belt measured fifty-two inches even if you soaked it in brine. Plus he drank. Never before dinner, but that leaves you a whole lot of hours if you're a night person.

The teller was Ruth Van Dine. Her ma wanted her to get braces when she was twelve, thirteen, but Ruth said she didn't care to. I'd have to call that a big mistake on her part. "Say there, Royce," she said. "What can I do for you?"

Now Royce shoved his savings passbook across the top of the counter. Don't ask me why he brought the blame thing. I couldn't tell you.

"Deposit?"

"Withdrawal."

"How much?"

Every dang old cent you got in this here bank was what he was going to say. But what came out of his mouth was, "Every dang old cent."

"Three hundred twelve dollars and forty-five cents? Plus I guess you got some extra interest coming which I'll figure out for you."

"Well—"

"Better make out a slip, Royce. Just on behind you?"

He turned to look for the withdrawal slips and there was Buford Washburn, also standing. "They off at the sawmill today, Royce? I didn't hear anything."

"No, I guess they're workin', Mr. Washburn. I guess I took the day."

"Can't blame you, beautiful day like this. What'd you do, go and get a little hunting in?"

"Not in March, Mr. Washburn."

"I don't guess nothing's in season this time of year."

"Not a thing. I was just gone take this here across to Eddie Joe. Needs a little gunsmithin'."

"Well, they say Eddie Joe knows his stuff."

"I guess he does, Mr. Washburn."

"Now this about drawing out all your money," Buford said. He fancied himself smoother than a bald tire at getting from small talk to business, Buford did. "I guess you got what they call an emergency."

"Somethin' like."

"Well now, maybe you want to do what most folks do, and that's leave a few dollars in to keep the account open. Just for convenience. Say ten dollars? Or just draw a round amount, say you draw your three hundred dollars. Or—" And he went through a whole routine about how Royce could take his old self a passbook loan and keep the account together and keep earning interest and all the rest of it, which I'm not going to spell out here for you.

Upshot of it was Royce wound up drawing three hundred dollars. Ruth Van Dine gave it to him in tens and twenties because he just stood there stiffer than new rope when she asked him how did he want it. Three times she asked him, and she's a girl no one ever had to tell to speak up, and each time it was like talking to a wall, so she counted out ten tens and ten twenties and gave it to him, along with his passbook. He thanked her and walked out with the passbook and money in one hand and the other holding the twelve gauge Worthington, which was still propped up on his shoulder.

Before he got back in his panel truck he said, "Half my life, Lord, half my dang life."

Then he got in the truck.

When he got back to his house he found Essie in the kitchen soaking the labels off some empty jam jars. She turned and saw him, then shut off the faucet and turned to look at him again. She said, "Why, Royce honey, what are you doing back here? Did you forget somethin'?"

"I didn't forget nothin'," he said. What he forgot was to hold up the bank like he'd set out to do, but he didn't mention that.

"You didn't get laid off," she said mournfully. (I didn't put in a question mark there because her voice didn't turn up at the end. She said it sort of like it would be O.K. if Royce did get laid off from the sawmill, being that the both of them could always go out in the backyard and eat dirt. She was always a comfort, Essie was.)

"Didn't go to work," Royce said. "Today's my dang birthday," Royce said.

" 'Course it is! Now I never wished you a happy birthday but you left 'fore I was out of bed. Well, happy birthday and many more. Thirty-nine years, land sakes."

"Thirty-*eight!*"

"What did I say? Why, I said thirty-*nine*. Would you believe that. I know it's thirty-eight, 'course I know that. Why are you carrying that gun, I guess there's rats in the garbage again."

"Half my life," Royce said.

"Is there?"

"Is there what?"

"Rats in the garbage again?"

"Now how in blue hell would I know is there rats in the garbage?"

"But you have that gun, Royce."

He discovered the gun, took it off his shoulder, and held it out in both hands, looking at it like it was the prettiest thing since a new calf.

"That's your shotgun," Essie said.

"Well, I guess I know that. Half my dang life."

"What about half your life?"

"My life's half gone," he said, "and what did I ever do with it, would you tell me that? Far as I ever been from home is Franklin County and I never stayed there overnight, just went and come back. Half my life and I never left the dang old state."

"I was thinkin' we might run out to Silver Dollar City this summer," Essie said. "It's like an old frontier city come to life or so they say. That's across the state line, come to think on it."

"Never been anyplace, never done any dang thing. Never had no woman but you."

"Well now."

"I'm gone to Paris," Royce said.

"What did you say?"

"I'm gone to Paris is what I said. I'm gone rob Buford Washburn's bank and I'm not even gone call him Mr. Washburn this time. Gone to Paris France, gone buy a Cadillac big as a train, gone do every dang thing I never did. Half my life, Essie."

Well, she frowned. You blame her? "Royce," she said, "you better lie down."

"Paris, France."

"What I'll do," she said, "I'll just call on over at Dr. LeBeau's. You lie down and put the fan on and I'll just finish with these here jars and then call the doctor. You know something? Just two more cases and we'll run out of your ma's plum preserves. Two cases of twenty-four jars to the case is forty-eight jars and we'll be out. Now I never thought we'd be out of them plums she put up but we'll be plumb out, won't we. Hear me talk, plumb out of plums, I did that without even thinking."

Essie wasn't normally quite this scatterbrained. Almost, but not quite. Thing is, she was concerned about Royce, being as he wasn't acting himself.

"Problem is getting in a rut," Royce said. He was talking to his own self now, not to Essie. "Problem is you leave yourself openings and you back down because it's the easy thing to do. Like in the bank."

"Royce, ain't you goin' to lay down?"

"Fillin' out a dang slip," Royce said.

"Royce? You know somethin'? You did the funniest thing this mornin', honey. You know what you did? You went and you only shaved the half of your face. You shaved the one half and you didn't shave the other half."

(Now this is something that both Ruth Van Dine and Buford Washburn had already observed, and truth to tell they had both called it to Royce's attention—in a friendly way, of course. I'd have mentioned it but I figured if I kept sliding in the same little piece of conversation over and over it'd be about as interesting for you as watching paint dry. But I had to mention when Essie said it out of respect, see, because it was the last words that woman ever got to speak, because right after she said it Royce stuck the shotgun right in her face and fired off one of the barrels. Don't ask me which one.)

"Now the only way to go is forward," Royce said. "Fix things so you got no bolt hole and you got to do what you got to do." He went to the cupboard, got a shotgun shell, broke open the gun, dug out the empty casing, popped in the new shell, and closed the gun up again.

On the way out of the door he looked at Essie and said, "You weren't so bad, I don't guess."

Well, Royce drove on back to the bank and parked directly in front of it, even though there's a sign says plainly not to, and he stepped on into that bank with the twelve-gauge clenched in his hand. It wasn't over his shoulder this time. He had his right hand wrapped around the barrel at the center of gravity or close to it. (It's not the worst way to carry a gun, though you'll never see it advocated during a gun safety drive.)

He was asked later if he felt remorse at that time about Essie. It was the sort of dumb question they ask you, and it was especially dumb in light of the fact that Royce probably didn't know what the hell remorse meant, but in plain truth he didn't. What he felt was in motion.

And in that sense he felt pretty fine. Because he'd been standing plumb still for thirty-eight years and never even knew it, and now he was in motion, and it hardly mattered where exactly he was going.

"I want every dang cent in this bank!" he sang out, and Buford Washburn just about popped a blood vessel in his right eye, and Ruth Van Dine stared, and old Miz Cristendahl who had made a trip to town just to get the interest credited to her account just stood there and closed her eyes so nothing bad would happen to her. (I guess it worked pretty good. That woman's still alive, and she was seventy-six years old when Calvin Coolidge didn't choose to run. All those Cristendahls live pretty close to forever. Good thing they're not much for breeding or the planet would be armpit deep in Cristendahls.)

"Now you give me every bit of that money," he said to Ruth. And he kept saying it, and she got rattled.

"I *can't*," she said finally, "because anyway it's not mine to give and I got no authority and besides there's another customer ahead of you. What you got to do is you got to speak to Mr. Buford Washburn."

And what Buford said was, "Now, Royce, say, Royce, you want to put down that gun."

"I'm gone to Paris, France, Mr. Washburn." You notice he forgot and went and called him Mr. Washburn. Old habits die hard.

"Royce, you still didn't finish your morning shave. What's got into you, boy?"

"I killed my wife, Mr. Washburn."

"Royce, why don't you just have a seat and I'll get you a cold glass of Royal Crown. Take my chair."

So Royce pointed the gun at him. "You better give me that money," he said, "or I could go and blow your dang head off your dumb shoulders."

"Boy, does your pappy have the slightest idea what you're up to?"

"I don't see what my pa's got to do with this."

"Because your pappy, he wouldn't take kindly to you carrying on this way, Royce. Now just sit down in my chair, you hear?"

At this point Royce was getting riled, plus he was feeling the frustration of it. Here he went and burned his britches by shooting Essie and where was he? Still trying to hold up a bank that wouldn't take him seriously. So what he did, he swung the gun around and shot out the plate-glass window. You wouldn't think the world would make that much noise in the course of coming to an end.

"Well, now you went and did it," Buford told him. "You got the slightest idea what a plate-glass window costs? Royce, boy, you went and bought yourself a peck of trouble."

So what Royce did, he shot Ruth Van Dine.

Now that doesn't sound like it makes a whole vast amount of sense, but Royce had his reasons, if you want to go and call them by that name. He couldn't kill Buford, according to his thinking, because Buford was the only one who could authorize giving him the money. And he didn't think to shoot Miz Cristendahl because he didn't notice her. (Maybe because she closed her eyes. Maybe those ostriches know what they're about. I'm not going to say they don't.)

On top of which Ruth was screaming a good bit and it was getting on Royce's nerves.

He wasn't any Dead-Eye Dick, as I may have pointed out before, and although he was standing right close to Ruth he didn't get a very good shot at her. A twelve gauge casts a pretty tight pattern as close as he was to her, with most of the charge going right over her head. There was enough left to do the job, but it was close for a while. Didn't kill her right off, left them plenty of time to rush her to Schuyler County Memorial and pop her into the operating room. It was six hours after that before she died, and there's some say better doctors could have saved her. That's a question I'll stay away from myself. It's said she'd of been a vegetable even if she lived, so maybe it's all for the best.

Well, that was about the size of it. Buford fainted, which was plain sensible on his part, and Miz Cristendahl stood around with her eyes shut and her fingers in her ears, and Royce Arnstetter went behind the counter and opened the cash drawer and started pulling out stacks of money. He got all the money on top of the counter. There wasn't a whole hell of a lot of it. He was looking for a bag to put it in when a couple of citizens rushed in to see what was going on.

He picked up the gun and then just threw it down in disgust because it was full of nothing but two spent shells. And he couldn't have reloaded if he'd thought of it because he never did bring along any extra shells when he left the house. Just the two that were loaded into the gun, and one of those took out the window and the other took out poor Ruth. He just threw the gun down and said a couple bad words and thought what a mess he'd made of everything, letting the first half of his life just dribble out and then screwing up the second half on the very first day of it.

He would of pleaded at the trial but he had this young court-appointed lawyer who wanted to do some showboating, and the upshot of it was he wound up drawing ninety-nine-to-life, which sounds backwards to me, as the average life runs out way in front of the ninety-nine mark, especially when you're thirty-eight to start with.

He's in the state prison now over to Millersport. It's not quite as far from his home as Franklin County where he went once, but he didn't get to stay overnight that time. He sure gets to stay overnight now.

Well, there's people to talk to and he's learning things. His pa's been to visit a few times. They don't have much to say to each other but when did they ever? They'll reminisce about times they went fishing. It's not so bad.

He thinks about Essie now and then. I don't know as you'd call it remorse though.

"Be here until the day I die," he said one day. And a fellow inmate sat him down and told him about parole and time off for good behavior and a host of other things, and this fellow worked it out with pencil and paper and told Royce he'd likely be breathing free air in something like thirty-three years.

"Means I'll have five left to myself," Royce said.

The fellow gave him this look.

"I'm fixin' to live until I'm seventy-six," Royce explained. "Thirty-eight now and thirty-three more in here is what? Seventy-one, isn't it? Seventy-six take away seventy-one and you get five, don't you? Five years left when I'm out of here." And he scratched his head and said, "Now what am I gone do with them five years?"

Well, I just guess he'll have to think of something.

Cleveland in My Dreams

"So," Loebner said. "You continue to have the dream."

"Every night."

"And it is always without variation yet? Perhaps you will tell me the dream again."

"Oh, God," said Hackett. "It's the same dream, all right? I get a phone call, I have to go to Cleveland, I drive there, I drive back. End of dream. What's the point of going through it every time we have a session? Unless you just can't remember the dream from one week to the next."

"That is interesting," Loebner said. "Why do you suppose I would forget your dream?"

Hackett groaned. You couldn't beat the bastards. If you landed a telling shot, they simply asked you what you meant by it. It was probably the first thing they taught them in shrink school, and possibly the only thing.

"Of course I remember your dream," Loebner went on smoothly. "But what is important is not my recollection of it but what it means to you, and if you recount it once more, in the fullest detail, perhaps you will find something new in it."

What was to be found in it? It was the ultimate boring dream, and it had been boring months ago when he dreamed it the first time. Nightly repetition had done nothing to enliven it. Still, it might give him the illusion that he was getting something out of the session. If he just sprawled on the couch for what was left of his fifty minutes, he ran the risk of falling asleep.

Perchance to dream.

"It's always the same dream," he said, "and it always starts the same way. I'm in bed and the phone rings. I answer it. A voice tells me I have to go to Cleveland right away."

"You recognize this voice?"

"I recognize it from other dreams. It's always the same voice. But it's not the voice of anyone I know, if that's what you mean."

"Interesting," Loebner said.

To you perhaps, thought Hackett. "I get up," he said. "I throw on some clothes. I don't bother to shave, I'm in too much of a hurry. It's very urgent that I go to Cleveland right away. I go down to the garage and unlock my car, and there's a briefcase on the front passenger seat. I have to deliver it to somebody in Cleveland.

"I get in the car and start driving. I take I-71 all the way. That's the best route, but even so it's just about two hundred fifty miles door to door. I push it a little and there's no traffic to speak of at that hour, but it's still close to four hours to get there."

"The voice on the phone has given you an address?"

"No, I just somehow know where I'm supposed to take the briefcase. Hell, I ought to know, I've been there every night for months. Maybe the first time I was given an address, it's hard to remember, but by now I know the route and I know the destination. I park in the driveway, I ring the bell, the door opens, a woman accepts the briefcase and thanks me—"

"A woman takes the briefcase from you?" Loebner said.

"Yes."

"What does this woman look like?"

"That's sort of vague. She just reaches out and takes the briefcase and thanks me. I'm not positive it's the same woman each time."

"But it is always a woman?"

"Yes."

"Why do you suppose that is?"

"I don't know. Maybe her husband's out, maybe he works nights."

"She is married, this woman?"

"I don't *know*," said Hackett. "I don't know anything about her. She opens the door, she takes the briefcase, she thanks me, and I get back in my car."

"You never enter the house? She does not offer you a cup of coffee?"

"I'm in too much of a hurry," Hackett said. "I have to get home. I get in the car, I backed out of the driveway, and I'm gone. It's another two hundred fifty miles to get home, and I'm dog-tired. I've already been driving four hours, but I push it, and I get home and go to bed."

"And then?"

"And then I barely get to sleep when the alarm rings and it's time to get up. I never get a decent night's sleep. I'm exhausted all the time, and my work's falling off and I'm losing weight, and sometimes I'm just about hallucinating at my desk, and I can't stand it, I just can't *stand* it."

"Yes," Loebner said. "Well, I see our hour is up."

"Now let us talk about this briefcase," Loebner said at their next meeting. "Have you ever tried to open it?"

"It's locked."

"Ah. And you do not have the key?"

"It has one of those three-number combination locks."

"And you do not know the combination?"

"Of course not. Anyway, I'm not supposed to open the briefcase. I'm just supposed to deliver it."

"What do you suppose is in the briefcase?"

"I don't know."

"But what do you suppose *might* be in it?"

"Beats me."

"State secrets, perhaps? Drugs? Cash?"

"For all I know it's dirty laundry," Hackett said. "I just have to deliver it to Cleveland."

"You always follow the same route?" Loebner said at their next session.

"Naturally," Hackett said. "There's really only one way to get to Cleveland. You take I-71 all the way."

"You are never tempted to vary the route?"

"I did once," Hackett remembered.

"Oh?"

"I took I-75 to Dayton, I-70 east to Columbus, and then I picked up I-71 and rode it the rest of the way. I wanted to do something different, but it was the same boring ride on the same boring kind of road, and what did I accomplish? It's thirty-five miles longer that way, so all I really did was add half an hour to the trip, and my head barely hit the pillow before it was time to get up for work."

"I see."

"So that was the end of that experiment," Hackett said. "Believe me, it's simpler if I just stick with I-71. I could drive that highway in my sleep."

Loebner was dead.

The call, from the psychiatrist's receptionist, shocked Hackett. For months he'd been seeing Loebner once a week, recounting his dream, waiting for some breakthrough that would relieve him of it. While he had just about given up anticipating that breakthrough, neither had he anticipated that Loebner would take himself abruptly out of the game.

He had to call back to ask how Loebner had died. "Oh, it was a heart attack," the woman told him. "He just passed away in his sleep. He went to sleep and never woke up."

Later, Hackett found himself entertaining a fantasy. Loebner, sleeping the big sleep, would take over the chore of dreaming Hackett's dream. The little psychiatrist could rise every night to convey the dreaded briefcase to Cleveland while Hackett slept dreamlessly.

It was such a seductive notion that he went to bed expecting it to happen. No sooner had he dozed off, though, than he was in the dream again, with the phone ringing and the voice at the other end telling him what he had to do.

"I wasn't going to continue with another psychiatrist," Hackett explained, "because I don't really think I was getting anywhere with Dr. Loebner. But I'm not getting anywhere on my own, either. Every night I dream this goddamned dream and it's ruining my health. I'm here because I don't know what else to do."

"Figures," said the new psychiatrist, whose name was Krull. "That's the only reason anybody goes to a shrink."

"I suppose you want to hear the dream."

"Not particularly," said Krull.

"You don't?"

"In my experience," Krull said, "there's nothing duller than somebody else's dream. But it's probably a good place to get started, so let's hear it."

While Hackett recounted the dream, sitting upright in a chair instead of lying on a couch, Krull fidgeted. This new shrink was a man about Hackett's age, and he was dressed casually in khakis and a polo shirt with a reptile on the pocket. He was clean-shaven and had a crew cut. Loebner had looked the way a psychiatrist was supposed to look.

"Well, what do you want to do now?" Hackett asked when he'd finished. "Should I try to figure out what the dream means or do you want to suggest what the dream might mean or what?"

"Who cares?"

Hackett stared at him.

"Really," Krull said, "do you honestly give a damn what your dream means?"

"Well, I—"

"I mean," said Krull, "what's the problem here? The problem's not that you're in love with your raincoat, the problem's not that they potty-trained you too early, the problem's not that you're repressing your secret desire to watch *My Little Margie* reruns. The problem is you're not getting any rest. Right?"

"Well, yes," Hackett said. "Right."

"You have this ditsy dream every night, huh?"

"Every night. Unless I take a sleeping pill, which I've done half a dozen times, but that's even worse in the long run. I don't really *feel* rested—I have a sort of hangover all day from the pill, and I find drugs a little worrisome, anyway."

"Mmmm," Krull said, clasping his hands behind his head and leaning back in his chair. "Let's see now. Is the dream scary? Filled with terror?"

"No."

"Painful? Harrowing?"

"No."

"So the only problem is exhaustion," Krull said.

"Yes."

"Exhaustion that's perfectly natural, because a man who drives five hundred miles every night when he's supposed to be resting is going to be beat to hell the next day. Does that pretty much say it?"

"Yes."

"Sure it does. You can't drive five hundred miles every night and feel good. But"—he leaned forward—"I'll bet you could drive half that distance, couldn't you?"

"What do you mean?"

"What I mean," said Krull, "is there's a simple way to solve your problem." He scribbled on a memo pad, tore off the top sheet, handed it to Hackett. "My home phone number," he said. "When the guy calls and tells you to go to Cleveland, what I want you to do is call me."

"Wait a minute," Hackett said. "I'm asleep while this is happening. How the hell can I call you?"

"In the *dream* you call me. I'll come over to your place, I'll get in the car with you, and we'll drive to Cleveland together. After you deliver the briefcase, you can just curl up in the backseat and I'll drive back. You ought to be able to get four hours' sleep on the way home, or close to it."

Hackett straightened up in his chair. "Let me see if I understand this," he said. "I get the call, and I turn around and call you, and the two of us drive to Cleveland together. I drive there, and you drive back, and I get to nap on the drive home."

"Right."

"You think that would work?"

"Why not?"

"It sounds crazy," Hackett said, "but I'll try it."

The following morning he called Krull. "I don't know how to thank you," he said.

"It worked?"

"Like a charm. I got the call, I called you, you came over, and off we went to Cleveland together. I drove there, you drove back, I got a solid three and a half hours in the backseat, and I feel like a new man. It's the craziest thing I ever heard of, but it worked."

"I thought it would," Krull said. "Just keep doing it every time you have the dream. Call me the end of the week and let me know if it's still working."

At the week's end, Hackett made the phone call. "It works better than ever," he said. "It's gotten so I'm not dreading that phone call either, because I know we'll have a good time on the road. The drive to Cleveland is a pleasure now that I've got you in the car to talk to, and the nap I get on the way home makes all the difference in the world. I can't thank you enough."

"That's terrific," Krull told him. "I wish all my patients were as easily satisfied."

And that was that. Every night Hackett had the dream, and every night he drove to Cleveland and let the psychiatrist take the wheel on the way home. They talked about all sorts of things on the way to Cleveland—girls, baseball, Kant's categorical imperative, and how to know when it was time to discard a disposable razor. Sometimes they talked about Hackett's personal life, and he felt he was getting a lot of insight from their conversations. He wondered if he ought to send Krull a check for services rendered and asked Krull the following night in the dream. The dream-Krull told him not to worry about it: "After all," he said, "you're paying for the gas."

Hackett's health improved. He was able to concentrate better, and the improvement showed in his work. His love life improved as well, after having virtually ceased to exist. He felt reborn, and he was beginning to love his life.

Then he ran into Feverell.

"My God," he said. "Mike Feverell."

"Hello, George."

"How've you been, Mike? Lord, it's been years, hasn't it? You look—"

"I look like hell," Feverell said. "Don't I?"

"I wasn't going to say that."

"You weren't? I don't know why not, because it's the truth. I look terrible and I know it."

"How's your health, Mike?"

"My health? That's what's ridiculous. My health is fine, perfectly fine. I don't know how much longer I can go on before I just plain drop dead, but in the meantime my health is a hundred percent."

"What's wrong?"

"Oh, it's too stupid to talk about."

"Oh?"

"It's this recurring dream," Feverell said. "I have the same dream every goddamned night, and it's driving me nuts."

The room seemed to fill up with light. Hackett took his friend's arm. "Let's get a couple of beers," he said, "and you can tell me all about your dream."

"It's stupid," Feverell said. "It's an adolescent sex fantasy. I'm almost ashamed to talk about it, but the thing is I can't seem to do anything about it."

"Tell me."

"Well, it's the same every night," Feverell said. "I go to sleep and the doorbell rings. I get up, put on a robe, answer the door, and there are three beautiful women there. They want to come in, and they want to have a party."

"A party?"

"What they want," said Feverell, "is for me to make love to them."

"And?"

"And I do."

"It sounds," said Hackett, "like a wonderful dream. It sounds like a dream people would pay money to have."

"You'd think that, wouldn't you?"

"What's the problem?"

"The problem," said Feverell, "is that it's too much. I make love to all three of them and I'm exhausted, drained, an empty shell, and no sooner do I drift off to sleep than the alarm clock's ringing and it's time to get up. I'm too old for three women in one night, and these aren't hasty encounters. It takes the whole night to satisfy them all, and I've got no strength left for the rest of my life."

"Interesting," said Hackett, in a manner not altogether unlike the late Dr. Loebner's. "Tell me, are they always the same women?"

Feverell shook his head. "If they were," he said, "it'd be a cinch, because I wouldn't keep getting turned on. But every night it's three brand-new ladies, and the only common denominator is that they're all gorgeous. Tall ones, short ones, light ones, dark ones. Blondes, brunettes, redheads. Even a bald one the other night."

"That must have been interesting."

"It was damned interesting," Feverell said, "but who needs it? Too much is still too much. I can't resist them, I can't turn them down, but I'll tell you, I shudder when the doorbell rings." He sighed. "I suppose it relates to being divorced a little over a year and some kind of performance anxiety, something like that. Or do you suppose there's a deeper cause?"

"Who cares?"

Feverell stared at him.

"Really," said Hackett. "What's the difference why you're having the dream? The *dream* is the problem, isn't it?"

"Well, yeah, I guess so. But—"

"As a matter of fact," Hackett went on, "the dream isn't the problem either. The problem is that there are too many women in it."

"Well—"

"If there were just one woman," Hackett said, "you'd do just fine, wouldn't you?"

"I suppose so—but there's always three, and no matter how much I want to I can't seem to tell two of them to go away. I don't want to hurt their feelings, see, and it'd be impossible to choose among them anyway—"

"Suppose you only had to make love to one of them," Hackett said. "Could you handle that?"

"Sure, but—"

"And then you could get plenty of sleep after she left."

"I guess so, but—"

"And you'd be rested in the morning. In fact, after a dream like that you'd probably feel like a million dollars, wouldn't you?"

"What are you getting at, George?"

"Simple," said Hackett. "Simplest thing in the world."

He got out a business card and scribbled on the back. "My home phone number," he said, thrusting the card at Feverell. "Go ahead, take it."

"What am I supposed to do with this?"

"Memorize it," Hackett said, "and when the doorbell rings tonight, call me."

"What do you mean, call you? I'm supposed to get up out of a sound sleep and call you? And then what happens? Is it like AA or something—you come over and we have coffee and you talk me out of dreaming?"

Hackett shook his head. "You don't get up," he said. "In the *dream* you call me. You call me, and then you go open the door and let the girls in."

"What's the point of that?"

"The point is that I've got a friend, a psychiatrist as it happens, a very nice clean-cut type of guy. You'll call me, and I'll call him, and the two of us'll come over to your place."

"You're going to schlepp some shrink to my house in the middle of the night?"

"This is in the dream," Hackett told him. "We'll come over, and you'll make love to one of the girls, whichever one you choose, and I'll take one, and my friend'll take one. And after you're done with your girl you can go to sleep, and you'll be perfectly well rested in the morning. And we can do this every night you have the dream. All you have to do is call me and we'll show up and help you out."

Feverell stared at him. "If only it would work."

"It will."

"There was a Chinese girl the other night who was just plain out of this world," Feverell said. "But I couldn't really relax and enjoy her, because the Jamaican and the Norwegian girls were in the other room and, well—"

Hackett clapped his friend on the shoulder. "Call me," he said. "Your troubles are over."

The following morning, on his way to work, Hackett gave himself up to a feeling of supreme well-being. He had repaid Krull's kindness to him in the best way possible, by passing on the favor to another. At his desk that morning, he waited for the phone to ring with a report from Feverell.

But Feverell didn't call. Not that morning, not the next morning, not all week. And something kept Hackett from calling Feverell.

Until finally he ran into him on the street during the noon hour—and Feverell looked *terrible!* Bags under his eyes, deeper than ever. Sallow skin, trembling hands. "Mike!" he said. "Mike, are you all right?"

"Do I look all right?"

"No, you don't," Hackett said honestly. "You look awful."

"Well, I *feel* awful," Feverell said savagely. "And I don't feel a whole lot better for being told how terrible I look, but thanks all the same."

"Mike, what's wrong?"

"What's wrong? You know damned well what's wrong. It's this dream I've been having. I told you the whole story. Or did it slip your mind?"

Hackett sighed. "You're still having the dream?"

"Of course I'm still having the dream."

"Mike," Hackett said, "when the doorbell rings, before you do anything else, you were going to call me, remember?"

"Of course I remember."

"So?"

"So I've called you. Every night I call you, for all the good it does."

"You do?"

"Of course I do, every goddamned night."

"And then I come over? And I bring my friend?"

"Oh, right," said Feverell. "Your famous friend, the clean-cut psychiatrist. Whom I've yet to meet, because he doesn't come over and neither do you. Every night I call you, and every night you hang up on me."

"I hang up on you?" Hackett stared. "Why would I do a thing like that?"

"I don't know," said Feverell. "I don't have the slightest idea. But every night I call you and you don't even let me get a word in edgewise. 'I'm sorry,' you say, 'but I can't talk to you now, I'm on my way to Cleveland.' Cleveland yet! And you hang up on me!"

Click!

It was late afternoon by the time Dandridge got back to the lodge. The mountain air was as crisp as the fallen leaves that crunched under his heavy boots. He turned for a last look at the western sky, then hurried up the steps and into the massive building. In his room he paused only long enough to drop his gear onto a chair and hang his bright orange cap on a peg. Then he strode to the lobby and through it to the taproom.

He bellied up to the bar, a big, thick-bodied man. "Afternoon, Eddie," he said to the barman. "The usual poison."

Dandridge's usual poison was sour mash whiskey. The barman poured a generous double into a tumbler and stood, bottle in hand, while Dandridge knocked the drink back in a single swallow. "First of the day," he announced, "and God willing it won't be the last."

Both the Lord and the barman were willing. This time Eddie added ice and a splash of soda. Dandridge accepted the drink, took a small sip of it, nodded his approval, and turned to regard the only other man present at the bar, a smaller, less obtrusive man who regarded Dandridge in turn.

"Afternoon," Dandridge said.

"Good afternoon," said the other man. He was smoking a filtered cigarette and drinking a vodka martini. He looked Dandridge over thoroughly, from the rugged face weathered by sun and wind down over the heavy red and black checked jacket and wool pants to the knee-high leather boots. "If I were to guess," the man said, "I'd say you've been out hunting."

Dandridge smiled. "Well, you'd be right," he said. "In a manner of speaking."

" 'In a manner of speaking,' " the smaller man echoed. "I like the phrase. I'd guess further that you had a good day."

"A damn good day. Hard not to on a day like this. When it's this kind of a day, the air just the right temperature and so fresh you know it was just made this morning, and the sun comes through the trees and casts a dappled pattern on the ground, and you've got a spring in your step that makes you positive you're younger than the calendar tells you, well hell, sir, you could never set eyes on bird or beast and you'd still have to call it a good day."

"You speak like a poet."

"Afraid I'm nothing of the sort. I'm in insurance, fire and casualty and the like, and let me tell you there's nothing the least bit poetic about it. But when I get out here the woods and the mountains do their best to make a poet out of me."

The smaller man smiled, raised his glass, took a small sip. "I would guess," he said, "that today wasn't a day in which you failed to—how did you put it? To set eyes on bird or beast."

"No, you'd be right. I had good hunting."

"Then let me congratulate you," the man said. He raised his glass to Dandridge, who raised his in return.

"Dandridge," said Dandridge. "Homer Dandridge."

"Roger Krull," said the other man.

"A pleasure, Mr. Krull."

"My pleasure, Mr. Dandridge."

They drank, and both of their glasses stood empty. Dandridge motioned to the barman, his hand indicating both glasses. "On me," he said. "Mr. Krull, would I be wrong in guessing you're a hunter yourself?"

"In a manner of speaking."

"Oh?"

Krull glanced down into his newly freshened drink. "I've hunted for years," he said. "And I still hunt. I haven't given it up, not by any means. But—"

"It's not the same, is it?"

Krull looked up. "That's absolutely right," he said. "How did you know?"

"Go on," Dandridge urged. "Tell me how it's different."

Krull thought a moment. "I don't know exactly," he said. "Of course the novelty's gone, but hell, the novelty wore off years ago. The thing about any first-time thrill is it's only really present the first time, and eventually it's all gone. But there's something else. The stalking is still exciting, the pursuit, all of that, and there's still that instant of triumph when the prey is in your sights, and then the gun bucks, and then—"

"Yes?"

"Then you stand there, deafened for a moment by the roar of the gun, and you watch your prey gather and fall, and then—" He shrugged heavily. "Then it's a letdown. It even feels like—"

"Yes? Go on, Mr. Krull. Go on, sir."

"Well, I hope you won't take offense," Krull said. "It feels like a waste, a waste of life. Here I've taken life away from another creature, but I don't own that life. It's just . . . gone."

Dandridge was silent for a moment. He sipped his drink, made circles on the bar with the glass. He said, "You didn't feel this way in the past, I take it."

"No, not at all. The kill was always thrilling and there were no negative feelings accompanying it. But in the past year, maybe even the past two years, it's all been changing. What used to be a thrill is hollow now." The smaller man reached for his own glass. "I'm sorry I mentioned this," he said. "Sorry as hell. Here you had a good day and I have to bring you down with all this nonsense."

"Not at all, Mr. Krull. Not at all, sir. Eddie, fill these up again, will you? That's a good fellow." Dandridge planted a large hand on the top of the bar. "Don't regret what you've said, Mr. Krull. Be glad of it. I'm glad you spoke up and I'm glad I was here to hear you."

"You are?"

"Absolutely." Dandridge ran a hand through his wiry gray hair. "Mr. Krull—or if I may call you Roger?"

"By all means, Homer."

"Roger, I daresay I've been hunting more years than you have. Believe me, the feelings you've just expressed so eloquently are not foreign to me. I went through precisely what you're going through now. I came very close to giving it up, all of it."

"And then the feelings passed?"

"No," Dandridge said. "No, Roger. They did not."

"Then—"

Dandridge smiled hugely. "I'll tell you what I did," he said. "I didn't give it up. I thought of doing that because I grew to hate killing, but the idea of missing the woods and the mountains galled me. Oh, you can go walking in the woods without hunting, but that's not the same thing. The pleasure of the stalk, the pursuit, the matching of human wit and intelligence against the instincts and cunning of game—that's what makes hunting what it is for me, Roger."

"Yes," Krull murmured. "Certainly."

"So what I did," Dandridge said, "was change my style. No more bang-bang."

"I beg your pardon?"

"No more bang-bang," Dandridge said, gesturing. "Now it's click-click instead." And when Krull frowned uncomprehendingly, the big man put his hands in front of his face and mimed the operation of a camera. "Click!" he said.

Light dawned. "Oh," said Krull.

"Exactly."

"Not with a bang but a click."

"Nicely put."

"Photography."

"Let's not say photography," Dandridge demurred. "Let us say hunting with a camera."

"Hunting with a camera."

Dandridge nodded. "So you see now why I said I was a hunter in a manner of speaking. Many people would not call me a hunter. They would say I was a photographer of animals in the wild, while I consider myself a hunter who simply employs a camera instead of a gun."

Krull took his time digesting this. "I understand the distinction," he said.

"I felt that you would."

"The act of taking the picture is equivalent to making the kill. It's how you take the trophy, but you don't go out because you want a picture of an elk any more than a man hunts because he wants to put meat on the table."

"You do understand, Mr. Krull." The glasses, it was noticed, were once more empty. "Eddie!"

"My turn this time, Eddie," said Roger Krull. He waited until the drinks were poured and tasted. Then he said, "Do you get the same thrill, Homer?"

"Roger, I get twice the thrill. Another old hunter name of Hemingway said a moral act is one that makes you feel good afterward. Well, if that's the case, then hunting with a gun became immoral for me a couple of years back. Hunting with a camera has all the thrills and excitement of gun hunting without the letdown that comes when you realize you've caused pain and death to an innocent creature. If I want meat on the table I'll buy it, Roger. I don't have to kill a deer to prove to myself I'm a man."

"I'll certainly go along with that, Homer."

"Here, let me show you something." Dandridge produced his wallet, drew out a sheaf of color snapshots. "I don't normally do this," he confided. "I could wind up being every bit as much of a bore as those pests who show you pictures of their grandchildren. But I get the feeling you're interested."

"You're damned right I'm interested, Homer."

"Well, now," Dandridge said. "All right, we'll lead off with something big. This here is a Kodiak bear. I went up to Alaska to get him, hired a guide, tracked the son of a bitch halfway across the state until I got close enough for this one. That's not taken with a telephoto lens, incidentally. I actually got in close and took that one."

"You hire guides and backpack and everything."

"Oh, the whole works, Roger. I'm telling you, it's the same sport right up to the moment of truth. Then I take a picture instead of a life. I take more risks now than I did when I carried a gun through the woods. I never would have stood that close to the bear in order to shoot him. Hell, you can drop them from a quarter of a mile if you want, but I got right in close to take his picture. If he'd have charged—"

They reached for their drinks.

"I'll just show you a few more of these," Dandridge said. "You'll notice some of them aren't game animals, strictly speaking. Of course when you hunt with a camera you're not limited to what the law says is game, and the seasons don't apply. An endangered species doesn't shrink because I take its photograph. I can shoot does, I can photograph in or out of season, anything I want. The fact of the matter is that I prefer to go after trophy animals in season because that makes more of a game out of it, but sometimes it's as much of a challenge to try for a particular songbird that's hard to get up close to. That's a scarlet tanager there, it's a bird that lives in deep woods and spooks easy. Of course I had to use a telephoto lens to get anything worth looking at but it's still considered something of an accomplishment. I got a thrill out of that shot, Roger. Now no one would shoot a little bird like that, nobody would want to, but when you hunt with a camera it's another story entirely, and I don't mind telling you I got a thrill out of that shot."

"I can believe it."

"Now here's a couple of mountain goats, that was quite a trip I had after them, and this antelope, oh, there's a heck of a story goes with this one—"

It was a good hour later when Homer Dandridge returned the photographs to his wallet. "Here I went and talked your ear off," he said apologetically, but Roger Krull insisted quite sincerely that he had been fascinated throughout.

"I wonder," he said. "I just wonder."

"If it would work for you or not?"

Krull nodded. "Of course I had a camera years ago," he said, "but I never had much interest in it. I couldn't tell you how long it's been since I took a photograph of anything."

"Never had the slightest interest in it myself," Dandridge said. "Until I substituted click for bang, that is."

"No more bang-bang. Click-click instead. I don't know, Homer. I suppose you've got all sorts of elaborate equipment, fancy cameras, all the rest. It'd take me a year and a day to learn how to load one of those things."

"They're easier than you think," Dandridge said. "As a matter of fact, I've got some reasonably fancy gear. Hell, you wouldn't believe the money I used to spend on guns. Or I guess you would if you're a hunter yourself. Well, it's not surprising that I spend money the same way on cameras. I've got a new Japanese model that I'm just getting the hang of, and I've got my eyes on a lens for it that's going to cost me more than a whole camera ought to cost, and the next step's developing my own pictures and I don't suppose that's very far off. Just around the corner, I suspect. In another few months I'll likely have my own darkroom in the basement and be up to my elbows in chemicals."

"That's what I thought. I don't know if I'd want to get into all that."

"But that's the whole thing, Roger. You don't have to. Look, I don't know what your first hunting experience was like, but I remember mine. I was fourteen years old and I was out in a field down near the railroad tracks with an old rimfire twenty-two rifle, and I shot a squirrel out of an oak tree. Just a poor raggedy squirrel that I plinked with a broken-down rifle, and that's as big a hunting thrill as I guess I ever had. Now I'd guess your first experience wasn't a hell of a lot different."

"Not a whole hell of a lot, no."

"Well, when I put down the gun and took up the camera, the camera I took up was a little Instamatic that cost under twenty dollars. And I'll tell you a thing. The picture I took with that little camera was at least as much of a thrill as I get with my Japanese job."

"You can get decent pictures that way?"

"You can get perfect pictures that way," Dandridge said. "If I had any sense I'd still use the Instamatic, but as you go along you want to try getting fancy. And anyway, it hardly matters how good the pictures are. You don't want to sell 'em to *Field and Stream*, do you?"

"Of course not."

"Hell, no. You want to find out if you can go on having the sheer joy and excitement of hunting without having the guilt and sorrow of killing. That's it in a nutshell, right?"

"That's it."

"So pick up a cheap camera and find out."

"By God," said Roger Krull, "that's just what I'll do. There's a drugstore in town that'll have cameras. I'll go there first thing in the morning."

"Do it, Roger."

"Homer, I intend to. Oh, I'm a little dubious about it. I've got to admit as much. But what have I got to lose?"

"That calls for a drink," said Homer Dandridge.

Dandridge was out in the woods early the next morning. His head was clear and his hand steady, as was always the case on hunting trips. In the city he drank moderately, and his rare overindulgences were followed by mind-shattering hangovers. On hunting trips he drank heavily every evening and never had the whisper of a hangover. The fresh air, he thought, probably had something to do with it, and so too did the way the excitement of the chase sent the blood singing in his veins.

He had another good day, shooting several rolls of film, and by the time he returned to the lodge he was ready for that first double shot of sour mash whiskey, and ready too for the good company of Roger Krull. Dandridge was not by nature a proselytizer, and in casual conversations with other hunters he rarely let on that he employed a camera instead of a gun. But Krull had been an obvious candidate for conversation, and now Dandridge was excited at the thought that he had been instrumental in leading another man from bang-bang, as it were, to click-click.

Again he stowed his cap and gear and hurried to the taproom. But this time Krull was not there waiting for him, and Dandridge was disappointed. He drowned his disappointment with a drink, his usual straight double, and then he settled down and sipped a second drink on the rocks with a splash of soda. He had almost finished the drink when Roger Krull made his appearance.

"Well, Roger!" he said. "How did it go?"

"Spent the whole day at it."

"And?"

Roger Krull shrugged. "Hate to say it," he said. He took a roll of film from his jacket pocket, weighed it in his hand. "Didn't work for me," he said.

"Oh," Dandridge said.

"I envy you, Homer. I had my doubts last night and I had them this morning, but I went out and got myself a camera and gave it a try. I honestly thought it might be exciting after all. The pursuit and everything, and no death at the end of it."

"And it didn't work."

"No, it didn't. I'll tell you something. I'd like myself better if it had. But for one reason or another it isn't hunting for me without the bang-bang part. Just squeezing the shutter on a camera isn't the same as squeezing a trigger. Some primitive streak, I suppose. I stopped enjoying killing a while ago but it's just not hunting without it."

"Hell," Dandridge said. "I don't know what to say."

And that was true for both of them. They suddenly found themselves with nothing at all to say and the silence was awkward. "Well, I'm damned glad I tried it all the same," Krull said. "I really enjoyed talking with you last night. You're a hell of a guy, Homer."

"You're all right yourself, Roger."

"Take care of yourself, you hear?"

"You too," Dandridge said. "Say, don't you want this?" He indicated the roll of film, which Krull had left on top of the bar.

"What for?"

"Might get it developed, see how your pictures turned out."

"I don't really care how they turned out, Homer."

"Well—"

"Keep it," Krull said.

Dandridge picked up the film, looked at it for a moment, then dropped it in his pocket. He wondered if Roger Krull had even bothered to purchase a camera at all. Men sometimes came to momentous decisions under the heady influence of alcohol and changed their minds the following morning. Krull might have decided that hunting with a camera made as much sense as taking portrait photographs with a shotgun, and then might have gone through the charade with the film to keep up appearances. Not that Krull had seemed like the sort to go through that kind of nonsense, but people did strange things sometimes.

Psychology was another hobby of Homer Dandridge's.

Well, it was easy enough to find out, he decided. All he had to do was include Krull's film with his own when he sent it off to be developed. It would be interesting to see if there were any pictures on it, and if so it would be even more interesting to see what animals Krull had snapped and how well he had done.

When the pictures came back Homer Dandridge was very confused indeed.

Oh, there were pictures, all right. An even dozen of them, and they had all come out successfully. They did not have the contrast and brightness of the pictures Dandridge took with his expensive Japanese camera, but they were certainly clear enough, and they revealed that Roger Krull had a good intuitive sense of composition.

But they had not been taken in the woods. They had been taken in a city, and their subjects were not animals or birds at all.

They were people. Ten men and two women, captured in various candid poses as they went about their business in a city.

It took Dandridge a moment. Then his jaw fell and a chill raced through him. God!

He examined the pictures again, thinking that there ought to be something he should do, deciding that there was not. The name Roger Krull was almost certainly an alias. And even if it was not, what could he say? What could he do?

He wasn't even certain in what city the twelve pictures had been taken. And he didn't recognize any of the men or women in them.

Not then. A week later, when they started turning up in the newspaper, then he recognized them.

Collecting Ackermans

On an otherwise unremarkable October afternoon, Florence Ackerman's doorbell sounded. Miss Ackerman, who had been watching a game show on television and clucking at the mental lethargy of the panelists, walked over to the intercom control and demanded to know who was there.

"Western Union," a male voice announced.

Miss Ackerman repeated the clucking sound she had most recently aimed at Charles Nelson Reilly. She clucked this time at people who lost their keys and rang other tenants' bells in order to gain admittance to the building. She clucked at would-be muggers and rapists who might pass themselves off as messengers or deliverymen for an opportunity to lurk in the hallways and stairwell. In years past this building had had a doorman, but the new landlord had curtailed services, aiming to reduce his overhead and antagonize long-standing tenants at the same time.

"Telegram for Miz Ackerman," the voice added.

And was it indeed a telegram? It was possible, Miss Ackerman acknowledged. People were forever dying and other people were apt to communicate such data by means of a telegram. It was easier to buzz whoever it was inside than to brood about it. The door to her own apartment would remain locked, needless to say, and the other tenants could look out for themselves. Florence Ackerman had been looking out for her own self for her whole life and the rest of the planet could go and do the same.

She pressed the buzzer, then went to the door and put her eye to the peephole. She was a small birdlike woman and she had to come up onto her toes to see through the peephole, but she stayed on her toes until her caller came into view. He was a youngish man and he wore a large pair of mirrored sunglasses. Besides obscuring much of his face, the sunglasses kept Miss Ackerman from noticing much about the rest of his appearance. Her attention was inescapably drawn to the twin images of her own peephole reflected in the lenses.

The young man, unaware that he was being watched, rapped on the door with his knuckles. "Telegram," he said.

"Slide it under the door."

"You have to sign for it."

"That's ridiculous," Miss Ackerman said. "One never has to sign for a telegram. As a matter of fact they're generally phoned in nowadays."

"This one you got to sign for."

Miss Ackerman's face, by no means dull to begin with, sharpened. She who had been the scourge of several generations of fourth-grade pupils was not to be intimidated by a pair of mirrored sunglasses. "Slide it under the door," she demanded. "Then I'll open the door and sign your book." If there was indeed anything to be slid beneath the door, she thought, and she rather doubted that there was.

"I can't."

"Oh?"

"It's a singin' telegram. Singin' telegram for Miz Ackerman, what it says here."

"And you're to sing it to me?"

"Yeah."

"Then sing it."

"Lady, are you kiddin'? I'm gonna sing a telegram through a closed door? Like forget it."

Miss Ackerman made the clucking noise again. "I don't believe you have a telegram for me," she said. "Western Union suspended their singing telegram service some time ago. I remember reading an article to that effect in the *Times.*" She did not bother to add that the likelihood of anyone's ever sending a singing telegram to her was several degrees short of infinitesimal.

"All I know is I'm supposed to sing this, but if you don't want to open the door—"

"I wouldn't dream of opening my door."

"—then the hell with you, Miz Ackerman. No disrespect intended, but I'll just tell 'em I sang it to you and who cares what you say."

"You're not even a good liar, young man. I'm calling the police now. I advise you to be well out of the neighborhood by the time they arrive."

"You know what you can do," the young man said, but in apparent contradiction to his words he went on to tell Miss Ackerman what she could do. While we needn't concern ourselves with his suggestion, let it be noted that Miss Ackerman could not possibly have followed it, nor, given her character and temperament, would she have been likely at all to make the attempt.

Neither did she call the police. People who say "I am calling the police now" hardly ever do. Miss Ackerman did think of calling her local precinct but decided it would be a waste of time. In all likelihood the young man, whatever his game, was already on his way, never to return. And Miss Ackerman recalled a time two years previously, just a few months after her retirement, when she returned from an afternoon chamber music concert to find her apartment burglarized and several hundred dollars' worth of articles missing. She had called the police, naively assuming there was a point to such a course of action, and she'd only managed to spend several hours of her time making out reports and listing serial numbers, and a sympathetic detective had as much as told her nothing would come of the effort.

Actually, calling the police wouldn't really have done her any good this time, either.

Miss Ackerman returned to her chair and, without too much difficulty, picked up the threads of the game show. She did not for a moment wonder who might have sent her a singing telegram, knowing with cool certainty that no one had done so, that there had been no telegram, that the young man had intended rape or robbery or some other unpleasantness that would have made her life substantially worse than it already was. That robbers and rapists and such abounded was no news to Miss Ackerman. She had lived all her life in New York and took in her stride the possibility of such mistreatment, even as residents of California take in their stride the possibility of an earthquake, even as farmers on the Vesuvian slopes acknowledge that it is in the nature of volcanoes periodically to erupt. Miss Ackerman sat in her chair, leaving it to make a cup of tea, returning to it teacup in hand, and concentrated on her television program.

The following afternoon, as she wheeled her little cart of groceries around the corner, a pair of wiry hands seized her without ceremony and yanked her into the narrow passageway between a pair of brick buildings. A gloved hand covered her mouth, the fingers digging into her cheek.

She heard a voice at her ear: "Happy birthday to you, you old hairbag, happy birthday to you." Then she felt a sharp pain in her chest, and then she felt nothing, ever.

"Retired schoolteacher," Freitag said. "On her way home with her groceries. Hell of a thing, huh? Knifed for what she had in her purse, and what could she have, anyway? Livin' on Social Security and a pension and the way inflation eats you up nowadays she wouldn't of had much on her. Why stick a knife in a little old lady like her, huh? He didn't have to kill her."

"Maybe she screamed," Ken Poolings suggested. "And he got panicky."

"Nobody heard a scream. Not that it proves anything either way." They were back at the station house and Jack Freitag was drinking lukewarm coffee out of a Styrofoam container. But for the Styrofoam the beverage would have been utterly tasteless. "Ackerman, Ackerman, Ackerman. It's hell the way these parasites prey on old folks. It's the judges who have to answer for it. They put the creeps back on the street. What they ought to do is kill the little bastards, but that's not humane. Sticking a knife in a little old lady, that's humane. Ackerman, Ackerman. Why does that name do something to me?"

"She was a teacher. Maybe you were in one of her classes."

Freitag shook his head. "I grew up in Chelsea. West Twenty-fourth Street. Miss Ackerman taught all her life here in Washington Heights just three blocks from the place where she lived. And she didn't even have to leave the neighborhood to get herself killed. Ackerman. Oh, I know what it was. Remember three or maybe it was four days ago, this faggot in the West Village? Brought some other faggot home with him and got hisself killed for his troubles? They found him all tied up with things carved in him. It was all over page three of the *Daily News*. Ritual murder, sadist cult, sex perversion, blah blah blah. His name was Ackerman."

"Which one?"

"The dead one. They didn't pick up the guy who did it yet. I don't know if they got a make or not."

"Does it make any difference?"

"Not to me it don't." Freitag finished his coffee, threw his empty container at the green metal wastebasket, then watched as it circled the rim and fell on the floor. "The Knicks stink this year," he said. "But you don't care about basketball, do you?"

"Hockey's my game."

"Hockey," Freitag said. "Well, the Rangers stink, too. Only they stink on ice." He leaned back in his chair and laughed at his own wit and stopped thinking of two murder victims who both happened to be named Ackerman.

Mildred Ackerman lay on her back. Her skin was slick with perspiration, her limbs heavy with spent passion. The man who was lying beside her stirred, placed a hand upon her flesh and began to stroke her. "Oh, Bill," she said. "That feels so nice. I love the way you touch me."

The man went on stroking her.

"You have the nicest touch. Firm but gentle. I sensed that about you when I saw you." She opened her eyes, turned to face him. "Do you believe in intuition, Bill? I do. I think it's possible to know a great deal about someone just on the basis of your intuitive feelings."

"And what did you sense about me?"

"That you would be strong but gentle. That we'd be very good together. It was good for you, wasn't it?"

"Couldn't you tell?"

Millie giggled.

"So you're divorced," he said.

"Uh-huh. You? I'll bet you're married, aren't you? It doesn't bother me if you are."

"I'm not. How long ago were you divorced?"

"It's almost five years now. It'll be exactly five years in January. That's since we split, but then it was another six months before the divorce went through. Why?"

"And Ackerman was your husband's name?"

"Yeah. Wallace Ackerman."

"No kids?"

"No, I wanted to but he didn't."

"A lot of women take their maiden names back after a divorce."

She laughed aloud. "They don't have a maiden name like I did. You wouldn't believe the name I was born with."

"Try me."

"Plonk. Millie Plonk. I think I married Wally just to get rid of it. I mean Mildred's bad enough, but Plonk? Like forget it. I don't think you even told me your last name."

"Didn't I?" The hand moved distractingly over Millie's abdomen. "So you decided to go on being an Ackerman, huh?"

"Sure. Why not?"

"Why not indeed."

"It's not a bad name."

"Mmmm," the man said. "This is a nice place you got here, incidentally. Been living here long?"

"Ever since the divorce. It's a little small. Just a studio."

"But it's a good-sized studio, and you must have a terrific view. Your window looks out on the river, doesn't it?"

"Oh, sure. And you know, eighteen flights up, it's gotta be a pretty decent view."

"It bothers some people to live that high up in the air."

"Never bothered me."

"Eighteen floors," the man said. "If a person went out that window there wouldn't be much left of her, would there?"

"Jeez, don't even talk like that."

"You couldn't have an autopsy, could you? Couldn't determine whether she was alive or dead when she went out the window."

"Come on, Bill. That's creepy."

"Your ex-husband living in New York?"

"Wally? I think I heard something about him moving out to the West Coast, but to be honest I don't know if he's alive or dead."

"Hmmm."

"And who cares? You ask the damnedest questions, Bill."

"Do I?"

"Uh-huh. But you got the nicest hands in the world, I swear to God. You touch me so nice. And your eyes, you've got beautiful eyes. I guess you've heard that before?"

"Not really."

"Well, how could anybody tell? Those crazy glasses you wear, a person tries to look into your eyes and she's looking into a couple of mirrors. It's a sin having such beautiful eyes and hiding them."

"Eighteen floors, that's quite a drop."

"Huh?"

"Nothing," he said, and smiled. "Just thinking out loud."

Freitag looked up when his partner entered the room. "You look a little green in the face," he said. "Something the matter?"

"Oh, I was just looking at the *Post* and there's this story that's enough to make you sick. This guy out in Sheepshead Bay, and he's a policeman, too."

"What are you talking about?"

Poolings shrugged. "It's nothing that doesn't happen every couple of months. This policeman, he was depressed or he had a fight with his wife or something, I don't know what. So he shot her dead, and then he had two kids, a boy and a girl, and he shot them to death in their sleep and then he went and ate his gun. Blew his brains out."

"Jesus."

"You just wonder what goes through a guy's mind that he does something like that. Does he just go completely crazy or what? I can't understand a person who does something like that."

"I can't understand people, period. Was this somebody you knew?"

"No, he lives in Sheepshead Bay. *Lived* in Sheepshead Bay. Anyway, he wasn't with the department. He was a Transit Authority cop."

"Anybody spends all his time in the subways, it's got to take its toll. Has to drive you crazy sooner or later."

"I guess."

Freitag plucked a cigarette from the pack in his shirt pocket, tapped it on the top of his desk, held it between his thumb and forefinger, frowned at it, and returned it to the pack. He was trying to cut back to a pack a day and was not having much success. "Maybe he was trying to quit smoking," he suggested. "Maybe it was making him nervous and he just couldn't stand it anymore."

"That seems a little far-fetched, doesn't it?"

"Does it? Does it really?" Freitag got the cigarette out again, put it in his mouth, lit it. "It don't sound all that far-fetched to me. What was this guy's name, anyway?"

"The TA cop? Hell, I don't know. Why?"

"I might know him. I know a lot of transit cops."

"It's in the *Post*. Bluestein's reading it."

"I don't suppose it matters, anyway. There's a ton of transit cops and I don't know that many of them. Anyway, the ones I know aren't crazy."

"I didn't even notice his name," Poolings said. "Let me just go take a look. Maybe *I* know him, as far as that goes."

Poolings went out, returning moments later with a troubled look on his face. Freitag looked questioningly at him.

"Rudy Ackerman," he said.

"Nobody I know. Hey."

"Yeah, right. Another Ackerman."

"That's three Ackermans, Ken."

"It's six Ackermans if you count the wife and kids."

"Yeah, but three incidents. I mean it's no coincidence that this TA cop and his wife and kids all had the same last name, but when you add in the schoolteacher and the faggot, then you got a coincidence."

"It's a common name."

"Is it? How common, Ken?" Freitag leaned forward, stubbed out his cigarette, picked up a Manhattan telephone directory and flipped it open. "Ackerman, Ackerman," he said, turning pages. "Here we are. Yeah, it's common. There's close to two columns of Ackermans in Manhattan alone. And then there's some that spell it with two *n*'s. I wonder."

"You wonder what?"

"If there's a connection."

Poolings sat on the edge of Freitag's desk. "How could there be a connection?"

"Damned if I know."

"There couldn't, Jack."

"An old schoolteacher gets stabbed by a mugger in Washington Heights. A faggot picks up the wrong kind of rough trade and gets tied up and tortured to death. And a TA cop goes berserk and kills his wife and kids and himself. No connection."

"Except for them all having the same last name."

"Yeah. And the two of us just happened to notice that because we investigated the one killing and read about the other two."

"Right."

"So maybe nobody else even knows that there were three homicides involving Ackermans. Maybe you and me are the only people in the city who happened to notice this little coincidence."

"So?"

"So maybe there's something we didn't notice," Freitag said. He got to his feet. "Maybe there have been more than three. Maybe if we pull a printout of deaths over the past few weeks we're going to find Ackermans scattered all over it."

"Are you serious, Jack?"

"Sounds crazy, don't it?"

"Yeah, that's how it sounds, all right."

"If there's just the three it don't prove a thing, right? I mean, it's a common name and you got lots of people dying violently in New York City. When you have eight million people in a city it's no big surprise that you average three or four murders a day. The rate's not even so high compared to other cities. With three or four homicides a day, well, when you got three Ackermans over a couple of weeks, that's not too crazy all by itself to be pure coincidence, right?"

"Right."

"Suppose it turns out there's more than the three."

"You've got a hunch, Jack. Haven't you?"

Freitag nodded. "That's what I got, all right. A hunch. Let's just see if I'm nuts or not. Let's find out."

"A fifth of Courvoisier, V.S.O.P." Mel Ackerman used a stepladder to reach the bottle. "Here we are, sir. Now will there be anything else?"

"All the money in the register," the man said.

Ackerman's heart turned over. He saw the gun in the man's hand and his own hands trembled so violently that he almost dropped the bottle of cognac. "Jesus," he said. "Could you point that somewhere else? I get very nervous."

"The money," the man said.

"Yeah, right. I wish you guys would pick on somebody else once in a while. This makes the fourth time I been held up in the past two years. You'd think I'd be used to it by now, wouldn't you? Listen, I'm insured, I don't care about the money, just be careful with the gun, huh? There's not much money in the register but you're welcome to every penny I got." He punched the No Sale key and scooped up bills, emptying all of the compartments. Beneath the removable tray he had several hundred dollars in large bills, but he didn't intend to call them to the robber's attention. Sometimes a gunman made you take out the tray and hand over everything. Other times the man would take what you gave him and be anxious to get the hell out. Mel Ackerman didn't much care either way. Just so he got out of this alive, just so the maniac would take the money and leave without firing his gun.

"Four times in two years," Ackerman said, talking as he emptied the register, taking note of the holdup man's physical appearance as he did so. Tall but not too tall, young, probably still in his twenties. White. Good build. No beard, no mustache. Big mirrored sunglasses that hid a lot of his face.

"Here we go," Ackerman said, handing over the bills. "No muss, no fuss. You want me to lie down behind the counter while you go on your way?"

"What for?"

"Beats me. The last guy that held me up, he told me so I did it. Maybe he got the idea from a television program or something. Don't forget the brandy."

"I don't drink."

"You just come to liquor stores to rob 'em, huh?" Mel was beginning to relax now. "This is the only way we get your business, is that right?"

"I've never held up a liquor store before."

"So you had to start with me? To what do I owe the honor?"

"Your name."

"My name?"

"You're Melvin Ackerman, aren't you?"

"So?"

"So this is what you get," the man said, and shot Mel Ackerman three times in the chest.

"It's crazy," Freitag said. "What it is is crazy. Twenty-two people named Ackerman died in the past month. Listen to this. Arnold Ackerman, fifty-six years of age, lived in Flushing. Jumped or fell in front of the E train."

"Or was pushed."

"Or was pushed," Freitag agreed. "Wilma Ackerman, sixty-two years old, lived in Flatbush. Heart attack. Mildred Ackerman, thirty-six, East Eighty-seventh Street, fell from an eighteenth-story window. Rudolph Ackerman, that's the Transit Authority cop, killed his wife and kids and shot himself. Florence Ackerman was stabbed, Samuel Ackerman fell down a flight of stairs, Lucy Ackerman took an overdose of sleeping pills, Walter P. Ackerman was electrocuted when a radio fell in the bathtub with him, Melvin Ackerman's the one who just got shot in a holdup—" Freitag spread his hands. "It's unbelievable. And it's completely crazy."

"Some of the deaths must be natural," Poolings said. "Here's one. Sarah Ackerman, seventy-eight years old, spent two months as a terminal cancer patient at St. Vincent's and finally died last week. Now that has to be coincidental."

"Uh-huh. Unless somebody slipped onto the ward and held a pillow over her face because he didn't happen to like her last name."

"That seems pretty far-fetched, Jack."

"Far-fetched? Is it any more far-fetched than the rest of it? Is it any crazier than the way all these other Ackermans got it? Some nut case is running around killing people who have nothing in common but their last names. There's no way they're related, you know. Some of these Ackermans are Jewish and some are gentiles. It's one of those names that can be either. Hell, this guy Wilson Ackerman was black. So it's not somebody with a grudge against a particular family. It's somebody who has a thing about the name, but why?"

"Maybe somebody's collecting Ambroses," Poolings suggested.

"Huh? Where'd you get Ambrose?"

"Oh, it's something I read once," Poolings said. "This writer Charles Fort used to write about freaky things that happen, and one thing he wrote was that a guy named Ambrose had walked around the corner and disappeared, and the writer Ambrose Bierce had disappeared in Mexico, and he said maybe somebody was collecting Ambroses."

"That's ridiculous."

"Yeah. But what I meant—"

"Maybe somebody's collecting Ackermans."

"Right."

"Killing them. Killing everybody with that last name and doing it differently each time. Every mass murderer I ever heard of had a murder method he was nuts about and used it over and over, but this guy never does it the same way twice. We got—what is it, twenty-two deaths here? Even if some of them just happened, there's no question that at least fifteen out of twenty-two have to be the work of this nut, whoever he is. He's going to a lot of trouble to keep this operation of his from looking like what it is. Most of these killings look like suicide or accidental death, and the others were set up to look like isolated homicides in the course of a robbery or whatever. That's how he managed to knock off this many Ackermans before anybody suspected anything. Ken, what gets me is the question of why. Why is he doing this?"

"He must be crazy."

"Of course he's crazy, but being crazy don't mean you don't have reasons for what you do. It's just that they're crazy reasons. What kind of reasons could he have?"

"Revenge."

"Against all the Ackermans in the world?"

Poolings shrugged. "What else? Maybe somebody named Ackerman did him dirty once upon a time and he wants to get even with all the Ackermans in the world. I don't see what difference it makes as far as catching him is concerned, and once we catch him the easiest way to find out the reason is to ask him."

"*If* we catch him."

"Sooner or later we'll catch him, Jack."

"Either that or the city'll run out of Ackermans. Maybe *his* name is Ackerman."

"How do you figure that?"

"Getting even with his father, hating himself, *I* don't know. You want to start looking somewhere, it's gotta be easier to start with people named Ackerman than with people not named Ackerman."

"Even so there's a hell of a lot of Ackermans. It's going to be some job checking them all out. There's got to be a few hundred in the five boroughs, plus God knows how many who don't have telephones. And if the guy we're looking for is a drifter living in a dump of a hotel somewhere, there's no way to find him, and that's if he's even using his name in the first place, which he probably isn't, considering the way he feels about the name."

Freitag lit a cigarette. "Maybe he *likes* the name," he said. "Maybe he wants to be the only one left with it."

"You really think we should check all the Ackermans?"

"Well, the job gets easier every day, Ken. 'Cause every day there's fewer Ackermans to check on."

"God."

"Yeah."

"Do we just do this ourselves, Jack?"

"I don't see how we can. We better take it upstairs and let the brass figure out what to do with it. You know what's gonna happen."

"What?"

"It's gonna get in the papers."

"Oh, God."

"Yeah." Freitag drew on his cigarette, coughed, cursed, and took another drag anyway. "The newspapers. At which point all the Ackermans left in the city start panicking, and so does everybody else, and don't ask me what our crazy does because I don't have any idea. Well, it'll be somebody else's worry." He got to his feet. "And that's what we need—for it to be somebody else's worry. Let's take this to the lieutenant right now and let him figure out what to do with it."

The pink rubber ball came bouncing crazily down the driveway toward the street. The street was a quiet suburban cul-de-sac in a recently developed neighborhood on Staten Island. The house was a three-bedroom expandable colonial ranchette. The driveway was concrete, with the footprints of a largish dog evident in two of its squares. The small boy who came bouncing crazily after the rubber ball was towheaded and azure-eyed and, when a rangy young man emerged from behind the barberry hedge and speared the ball one-handed, seemed suitably amazed.

"Gotcha," the man said, and flipped the ball underhand to the small boy, who missed it, but picked it up on the second bounce.

"Hi," the boy said.

"Hi yourself."

"Thanks," the boy said, and looked at the pink rubber ball in his hand. "It was gonna go in the street."

"Sure looked that way."

"I'm not supposed to go in the street. On account of the cars."

"Makes sense."

"But sometimes the dumb ball goes in the street anyhow, and then what am I supposed to do?"

"It's a problem," the man agreed, reaching over to rumple the boy's straw-colored hair. "How old are you, my good young man?"

"Five and a half."

"That's a good age."

"Goin' on six."

"A logical assumption."

"Those are funny glasses you got on."

"These?" The man took them off, looked at them for a moment, then put them on. "Mirrors," he said.

"Yeah, I know. They're funny."

"They are indeed. What's your name?"

"Mark."

"I bet I know your last name."

"Oh, yeah?"

"I bet it's Ackerman."

"How'd you know?" The boy wrinkled up his face in a frown. "Aw, I bet you know my daddy."

"We're old friends. Is he home?"

"You silly. He's workin'."

"I should have guessed as much. What else would Hale Ackerman be doing on such a beautiful sunshiny day, hmmmm? How about your mommy? She home?"

"Yeah. She's watchin' the teevee."

"And you're playing in the driveway."

"Yeah."

The man rumpled the boy's hair again. Pitching his voice theatrically low, he said, "It's a tough business, son, but that doesn't mean it's a *heartless* business. Keep that in mind."

"Huh?"

"Nothing. A pleasure meeting you, Mark, me lad. Tell your parents they're lucky to have you. Luckier than they'll ever have to know."

"Whatcha mean?"

"Nothing," the man said agreeably. "Now I have to walk all the way back to the ferry slip and take the dumb old boat all the way back to Manhattan and then I have to go to . . ." he consulted a slip of paper from his pocket ". . . to Seaman Avenue way the hell up in Washington Heights. Pardon me. Way the *heck* up in Washington Heights. Let's just hope *they* don't turn out to have a charming kid."

"You're funny."

"You bet," the man said.

"Police protection," the lieutenant was saying. He was a beefy man with an abundance of jaw. He had not been born looking particularly happy, and years of police work had drawn deep lines of disappointment around his eyes and mouth. "That's the first step, but how do you even go about offering it? There's a couple of hundred people named Ackerman in the five boroughs and one's as likely to be a target as the next one. And we don't know who the hell we're protecting 'em *from.* We don't know if this is one maniac or a platoon of them. Meaning we have to take every dead Ackerman on this list and backtrack, looking for some common element, which since we haven't been looking for it all along we're about as likely to find it as a virgin on Eighth Avenue. Twenty-two years ago I coulda gone with the police or the fire department and I couldn't make up my mind. You know what I did? I tossed a goddam coin. It hadda come up heads."

"As far as protecting these people—"

"As far as protecting 'em, how do you do that without you let out the story? And when the story gets out it's all over the papers, and suppose you're a guy named Ackerman and you find out some moron just declared war on your last name?"

"I suppose you get out of town."

"Maybe you get out of town, and maybe you have a heart attack, and maybe you call the mayor's office and yell a lot, and maybe you sit in your apartment with a loaded gun and shoot the mailman when he does something you figure is suspicious. And maybe if you're some *other* lunatic you read the story and it's like tellin' a kid don't put beans up your nose, so you go out and join in the Ackerman hunt yourself. Or if you're another kind of lunatic which we're all of us familiar with you call up the police and confess. Just to give the nice cops something to do."

A cop groaned.

"Yeah," the lieutenant said. "That about sums it up. So the one thing you don't want is for this to get in the papers, but—"

"But it's too late for that," said a voice from the doorway. And a uniformed patrolman entered the office holding a fresh copy of the *New York Post.* "Either somebody told them or they went and put two and two together."

"I coulda been a fireman," the lieutenant said. "I woulda got to slide down the pole and wear one of those hats and everything, but instead the goddam coin had to come up heads."

The young man paid the cashier and carried his tray of food across the lunchroom to a long table at the rear. A half dozen people were already sitting there. The young man joined them, ate his macaroni and cheese, sipped his coffee, and listened as they discussed the Ackerman murders.

"I think it's a cult thing," one girl was saying. "They have this sort of thing all the time out in California, like surfing and est and all those West Coast trips. In order to be a member you have to kill somebody named Ackerman."

"That's a theory," a bearded young man said. "Personally, I'd guess the whole business is more logically motivated than that. It looks to me like a chain murder."

Someone wanted to know what that was.

"A chain murder," the bearded man said. "Our murderer has a strong motive to kill a certain individual whose name happens to be Ackerman. Only problem is his motive is so strong that he'd be suspected immediately. So instead he kills a whole slew of Ackermans and the one particular victim he has a reason to kill is no more than one face in a crowd. So his motive gets lost in the shuffle." The speaker smiled. "Happens all the time in mystery stories. Now it's happening in real life. Not the first time life imitates art."

"Too logical," a young woman objected. "Besides, all these murders had different methods and a lot of them were disguised so as not to look like murders at all. A chain murderer wouldn't want to operate that way, would he?"

"He might. If he was very, very clever—"

"But he'd be too clever for his own good, don't you think? No, I think he had a grudge against one Ackerman and decided to exterminate the whole tribe. Like Hitler and the Jews."

The conversation went on in this fashion, with the young man who was eating macaroni and cheese contributing nothing at all to it. Gradually the talk trailed off and so indeed did the people at the table, until only the young man and the girl next to whom he'd seated himself remained. She took a sip of coffee, drew on her cigarette, and smiled at him. "You didn't say anything," she said. "About the Ackerman murders."

"No," he agreed. "People certainly had some interesting ideas."

"And what did you think?"

"I think I'm happy my name isn't Ackerman."

"What is it?"

"Bill. Bill Trenholme."

"I'm Emily Kuystendahl."

"Emily," he said. "Pretty name."

"Thank you. What *do* you think? Really?"

"Really?"

"Uh-huh."

"Well," he said, "I don't think much of the theories everybody was coming up with. Chain murders and cult homicide and all the rest of it. I have a theory of my own, but of course that's all it is. Just a theory."

"I'd really like to hear it."

"You would?"

"Definitely."

Their eyes met and wordless messages were exchanged. He smiled and she smiled in reply. "Well," he said, after a moment. "First of all, I think it was just one guy. Not a group of killers. From the way it was timed. And because he keeps changing the murder method I think he wanted to keep what he was doing undiscovered as long as possible."

"That makes sense. But why?"

"I think it was a source of fun for him."

"A source of fun?"

The man nodded. "This is just hypothesis," he said, "but let's suppose he just killed a person once for the sheer hell of it. To find out what it felt like, say. To enlarge his area of personal experience."

"God."

"Can you accept that hypothetically?"

"I guess so. Sure."

"Okay. Now we can suppose further that he liked it, got some kind of a kick out of it. Otherwise he wouldn't have wanted to continue. There's certainly precedent for it. Not all the homicidal maniacs down through history have been driven men. Some of them have just gotten a kick out of it so they kept right on doing it."

"That gives me the shivers."

"It's a frightening concept," he agreed. "But let's suppose that the first person this clown killed was named Ackerman, and that he wanted to go on killing people and he wanted to make a game out of it. So he—"

"A game!"

"Sure, why not? He could just keep on with it, having his weird jollies and seeing how long it would take for the police and the press to figure out what was going on. There are a lot of Ackermans. It's a common name, but not so common that a pattern wouldn't begin to emerge sooner or later. Think how many Smiths there are in the city, for instance. I don't suppose police in the different boroughs coordinate their activities so closely, and I guess the Bureau of Vital Statistics doesn't bother to note if a lot of fatalities have the same last name, so it's a question of how long it takes for the pattern to emerge in and of itself. Well, it's done so now, and what does the score stand at now? Twenty-seven?"

"That's what the paper said, I think."

"It's quite a total when you stop and think of it. And there may have been a few Ackermans not accounted for. A body or two in the river, for instance."

"You make it sound—"

"Yes?"

"I don't know. It gives me the willies to think about it. Will he just keep on now? Until they catch him?"

"You think they'll catch him?"

"Well, sooner or later, won't they? The Ackermans know to be careful now and the police will have stakeouts. Is that what they call it? Stakeouts?"

"That's what they call it on television."

"Don't you think they'll catch him?"

The young man thought it over. "I'm sure they'll catch him," he said, "*if* he keeps it up."

"You mean he might stop?"

"I would. If I were him."

"If you were him. What a thought!"

"Just projecting a little. But to continue with it, if I were this creep, I'd leave the rest of the world's Ackermans alone from here on in."

"Because it would be too dangerous?"

"Because it wouldn't be any fun for me."

"Fun!"

"Oh, come on," he said, smiling. "Once you get past the evilness of it, which I grant you is overwhelming, can't you see how it would be fun for a demented mind? But try not to think of him as fundamentally cruel. Think of him as someone responding to a challenge. Well, now the police and the newspapers and the Ackermans themselves know what's going on, so at this point it's not a game anymore. The game's over and if he were to go on with it he'd just be conducting a personal war of extermination. And if he doesn't really have any genuine grudge against Ackermans, well, I say he'd let them alone."

She looked at him and her eyes were thoughtful. "Then he might just stop altogether."

"Sure."

"And get away with it?"

"I suppose. Unless they pick him up for killing somebody else." Her eyes widened and he grinned. "Oh, really, Emily, you can't expect him to stop this new hobby of his entirely, can you? Not if he's been having so much fun at it? I don't think killers like that ever stop, not once it gets in their blood. They don't stop until the long arm of the law catches up with them."

"The way you said that."

"Pardon me?"

" 'The long arm of the law.' As if it's sort of a joke."

"Well, when you see how this character operated, he does make the law look like something of a joke, doesn't he?"

"I guess he does."

He smiled, got to his feet. "Getting close in here. Which way are you headed? I'll walk you home."

"Well, I have to go uptown—"

"Then that's the way I'm headed."

"And if I had to go downtown?"

"Then I'd have urgent business in that direction, Emily."

On the street she said, "But what do you suppose he'll do? Assuming you're right that he'll stop killing Ackermans but he'll go on killing. Will he just pick out innocent victims at random?"

"Not if he's a compulsive type, and he certainly looks like one to me. No, I guess he'd just pick out another whole category of people."

"Another last name? Just sifting through the telephone directory and seeing what strikes his fancy? God, that's a terrifying idea. I'll tell you something, I'm glad my name's not such a common one. There aren't enough Kuystendahls in the world to make it very interesting for him."

"Or Trenholmes. But there are plenty of Emilys, aren't there?"

"Huh?"

"Well, he doesn't have to pick his next victims by last name. In fact, he'd probably avoid that because the police would pick up on something like that in a minute after this business with the Ackermans. He could establish some other kind of category. Men with beards, say. Oldsmobile owners."

"Oh, my God."

"People wearing brown shoes. Bourbon drinkers. Or, uh, girls named Emily."

"That's not funny, Bill."

"Well, no reason why it would have to be Emily. Any first name—that's the whole point, the random nature of it. He could pick guys named Bill, as far as that goes. Either way it would probably take the police a while to tip to it, don't you think?"

"I don't know."

"You upset, Emily?"

"Not upset, exactly."

"You certainly don't have anything to worry about," he said, and slipped an arm protectively around her waist. "I'll take good care of you, baby."

"Oh, will you?"

"Count on it."

They walked together in silence for a while and after a few moments she relaxed in his embrace. As they waited for a light to change he said, "Collecting Emilys."

"Pardon?"

"Just talking to myself," he said. "Nothing important."

The Dangerous Business

When she heard his car in the driveway she hurried at once to the door and opened it. Her first glimpse of his face told her all she wanted to know. She'd grown used to that expression over the years, the glow of elation underladen with exhaustion, the whole look foreshadowing the depression that would surely settle on him in an hour or a day or a week.

How many times had he come home to her like this? How many times had she rushed to the door to meet him?

And how could he go on doing this, year after year after year?

She could see, as he walked toward her now, just how much this latest piece of work had taken out of him. It had drawn new lines on his face. Yet, when he smiled at her, she could see too the young man she had married so many years ago.

Almost thirty years, and she treasured all those years, every last one of them. But what a price he'd paid for them! Thirty years in a dangerous, draining business, thirty years spent in the company of violent men, criminals, killers. Men whose names were familiar to her, men like Johnny Speed and Bart Callan, men he had used (or been used by) on and off throughout his career. And other men he would work with once and never again.

"It's finished," she said.

"All wrapped up." His smile widened. "You can always tell, can't you?"

"Well, after all these years. How did it go?"

"Not bad. It's gone better, but at least it's finished and I got out of it alive. I'll say this for it, it's thirsty work."

"Martini?"

"What else?"

She made a pitcher of them. They always had one drink apiece before dinner, but on the completion of a job he needed more of a release than came with one martini. They would drain the pitcher, with most of the martinis going to him, and dinner would be light, and before long they would be in bed.

She stirred at the thought. He would want her tonight, he would need her. Their pleasure in each other was as vital as ever after almost thirty years, if less frequently taken, and they both lived for nights like this one.

She handed him his drink, held her own aloft. "Well," she said.

"Here's to crime," he said. Predictably.

She drank without hesitating, but later that evening she said, "You know, I like our toast less and less these days."

"Well, get a new toaster. We can afford it. They have models now that do four slices of bread at a time."

"I mean *Here's to crime*. You knew what I meant."

"Of course I knew what you meant. I don't know that I like it much myself. *Here's to crime*. Force of habit, I guess."

"It takes so much out of you, darling. I wish—"

"What?"

She lowered her eyes. "That you could do something else."

"Might as well wish for wings."

"You're really that completely locked in?"

"Of course I am, baby. Now how many times have we been over this? I've been doing this my whole life. I have contacts, I have a certain reputation, there are some people who are kind enough to think I'm good at what I do—"

"You'd be good at anything you did."

"That's a loyal wife talking."

"It's still true."

He put his hand on hers. "Maybe. Sometimes I like to think so. And other times it seems to me that I was always cut out for this line of work. Crime and violence and sudden death."

"You're such a gentle, gentle man."

"Don't let the word get out, huh? Not that anyone would be likely to believe you."

"Oh, baby—"

"It's not such a bad life, kid. And I'm too old to change now. Isn't it funny how I get older all the time and you stay the same? It's my bedtime already, an old man like me."

"Some old man. But I guess you're tired."

"I said bedtime. I didn't say anything about being tired."

But in the days that followed she knew just how tired he was, and there was a brooding quality to his exhaustion that frightened her. Often at such times he liked to get away, and they would flee the city and spend a couple of weeks unwinding in unfamiliar terrain. This time, when his depression failed to pass, she suggested that they go away for a while. But he didn't want to go anywhere. He didn't even want to leave the house, and he passed the daytime hours sitting in front of the television set or turning the pages of books and magazines. Not *watching* the television, not *reading* the books and magazines.

At one point she thought he might want to talk about his work. In their first years together he had been excited about what he did, and at times she had felt herself a participant. But with the passage of time and with his growing discontent about his profession he tended to keep more and more of it to himself. In a sense she was grateful; it alienated her, the corruption and violence, the wanton killing, and it was easier for her to love him if she let herself dissociate the man from his work. And yet she wondered if this didn't make the burden on his shoulders that much heavier for the lack of anyone to share it.

So she made an effort. "You've hardly talked about it," she said one afternoon. "It went well, you said."

"Well enough. Won't make us rich, but it went quite smoothly. Hit a couple of snags along the way but nothing serious."

"Who was in this one? Johnny Speed?"

"No."

"Callan?"

"I don't think I'm going to be able to use Callan anymore. No, none of the regulars came into it this time. Let's say I put it together with a cast of unknowns. And there was nobody in it I'd care to work with again." He chuckled mirthlessly. "Hardly anybody got out of it alive, as a matter of fact."

"Then it was very violent."

"You might say that."

"I thought so. I can tell, you know."

"You've said that before. It's hard to believe, but I guess I believe you."

"If there were just a way to avoid the violence, the awful bloodshed—"

He shook his head. "Part of the game."

"I know, but—"

"Part of the game."

She let it go.

His mood lifted, of course. The depression had been deeper than usual and had lasted longer than usual, but it was not nearly so deep or so enduring as some he—and she—had been forced to live through in the past. Some years previously drinking had become a problem. Alcoholism was virtually an occupational illness in his profession, and of course it made efficient functioning impossible.

He'd gone on the wagon for several years, then found he was able to drink normally again. A single martini before the evening meal, a pitcher of them at the conclusion of a job, an occasional beer with lunch when he was resting up between jobs. But drinking never became a problem again, and she thanked God for that, even as she prayed to God that he could get into a line of work that didn't take so much out of him.

She raised the subject again one evening. He'd begun to talk about going back to work, not right away but before too long, and she wondered how he could face it so soon.

"You don't have to work so much," she said. "The kids are grown and gone. You and I have everything we want and money in the bank. You don't have to drive yourself."

"It's not a matter of driving myself. I can't sit idle too long. It gets to me."

"I know, but—"

"Rather wear out than rust out. Trite but true."

"Couldn't you try something else some of the time? Couldn't you try doing what you really want to do?"

He looked at her for a long moment, then turned his eyes aside and gazed off into space. Or, perhaps, into time.

"I've tried that," he said at length.

"I didn't know that."

"I didn't really want to talk about it. It didn't work out." Now he turned to face her again, and the expression on his face was enough to break her heart. "Maybe there was once something else I wanted to do. Maybe at some stage in my life I had the potential to do other things, to be somebody other than the man I turned into."

But I love the man you turned into, she thought. *I love the man you are, the man you've always been.*

"I may have the dreams," he said. "But that's all they ever were, baby. Dreams. You know what happens to dreams when you wake up. They go where smoke goes, into the air. Maybe I was born to do what I do. Maybe I just trained myself and wound up painting myself into a corner. But I'm an old man now—"

"You are like hell an old man!"

"—and it's all I know how to do and all I even seem to want to do. I've spent my whole life with crooks and grifters and strong-arm men, and I'll spend the rest of it with the same awful types, and yes, there'll be violence, but I guess I can go on living with that."

He smiled suddenly, and not merely with his mouth. "It's not so bad," he said. "It's depressing when I think of what might have been, but the hell with that, kid. I'm doing what I was cut out for. That's a hard thing to admit to yourself and it hurts, I'll say it hurts, but once you make yourself believe it, then it becomes a liberating thing."

She thought for a moment. "Yes," she said. "Yes, I suppose that's true."

And so she was prepared a week later when he told her he was ready to go back to work. He'd been restless for a day or two, pacing back and forth across the living-room rug, jotting incomprehensible notes on long yellow pads of paper, even mumbling and muttering to himself. Then on Monday morning he looked at her over the brim of his second cup of coffee and told her.

"Well, the signs were there," she said. "You're sure you don't want more time off?"

"Positive."

"And you know what you want to do?"

"Uh-huh. I'm going to use Johnny again."

"Johnny Speed. How many times have you used him?"

"I don't know. Too many, I guess. He's got a lot of miles on the clock but I guess he's good for another go-round."

"How long do you think it'll take?"

"Couple of weeks."

"Be careful."

He looked at her. "Oh, come on," he said. "The violence never touches me, baby. You know that."

"Oh, but it does."

"Come off it."

"It's a dangerous business."

"Dangerous business," he said, tasting the phrase. "I kind of like that."

"Well, it is."

"I like the phrase," he said. "I don't know that it fits my life—"

"I think it does."

"—but it certainly fits the current project. *Dangerous Business. A Dangerous Business.* Which do you prefer?"

"I don't know. *The Dangerous Business*?"

"You know, that's best of all. *The Dangerous Business.* I think I'm going to use it."

"Don't you have to make sure nobody's used it already?"

"Doesn't matter. There's no such thing as copyright on titles. I thought you knew that."

"I must have forgotten."

"*The Dangerous Business.* A Johnny Speed Mystery. Yes, by God, I'm going to use it. It has a nice ring to it and it fits the plot I've got in mind."

"It fits, all right," she said. But he was caught up in the book he'd start that morning and didn't even notice the tone of her voice.

Death Wish

The cop saw the car stop on the bridge but didn't pay any particular attention to it. People were apt to pull over to the side in the middle of the span, especially late at night when the traffic was thin and they could stop for a moment without somebody's horn stabbing them in the back. The bridge was a graceful steel parabola over the deep channel of river that cut the city neatly in two, and the center of the bridge provided the best view of the city, with the old downtown buildings clustered together on the right, the flour mills downriver on the left, the gentle skyline, the gulls maneuvering over the river. The bridge was the best place to see it all. It wasn't private enough for the teenagers, who were given to long-term parking and preferred drive-in movie theaters or stretches of road along the north bank of the river, but sightseers stopped often, took in the view for a few moments, and then continued across.

Suicides liked the bridge, too. The cop didn't think of that at first, not until he saw the man emerge from the car, and walk slowly to the footpath at the edge, and place a hand tentatively upon the rail. There was something in his stance, something in the pose of the solitary figure upon the empty bridge in the after-midnight gloom, something about the grayness of the night, the way the fog was coming off the river. The cop looked at him and cursed and wondered if he could get to him in time.

He walked toward the man, headed over the bridge on the footpath. He didn't want to shout or blow his whistle at him because he knew what shock or surprise could do to a potential jumper. Once he saw the man's hands tense on the rail, his feet lifting up on the toes. At that moment he almost cried out, almost broke into a run, but then the man's feet came back into position, his hands loosened their grip, and he took out a cigarette and lit it. Then the cop knew he had time. They always smoked that last cigarette all the way down before they went over the edge.

When the cop was within ten yards of him the man turned, started slightly, then nodded in resignation. He appeared to be somewhere in his middle thirties, tall, with a long narrow face and deep-set eyes topped with thick black eyebrows.

"Nice night," the cop said.

"Yes."

"Having a look at the sights?"

"That's right."

"Saw you out here, thought I'd come out and have a talk with you. It can get lonely this hour at night." The cop patted his pockets, passed over his cigarettes. "Say, you don't happen to have a spare cigarette on you, do you? I must have run out."

The man gave him a cigarette. It was a filter, and the cop normally smoked nothing but regulars, but he wasn't about to complain. He thanked the man, accepted a light, thanked him again, and stood beside him, hands on the rail, leaning out over the water and looking at the city and the river.

"Looks pretty from here," he said.

"Does it?"

"Sure, I'd say so. Makes a man feel at peace with himself."

"It hasn't had that effect on me," the man said. "I was thinking about, oh, the ways a man could find peace for himself."

"I guess the best way is just to go on plugging away at life," the cop said. "Things generally have a way of straightening themselves out, sooner or later. Some of the time they take awhile, and I guess they don't look too good, but they work out."

"You really believe that?"

"Sure."

"With the things you see in your job?"

"Even with all of it," the cop said. "It's a tough world, but that's nothing new. It's the best we've got, the way I figure it. You're sure not going to find a better one at the bottom of a river."

The man said nothing for a long time, then he pitched his cigarette over the rail. He and the cop stood watching it as it shed sparks on the way down, then heard the tiny hiss as it met the water.

"It didn't make much of a splash," the man said.

"No."

"Few of us do," the man said. He paused for a moment, then turned to face the cop. "My name's Edward Wright," he added. The cop gave his own name. "I don't think I would have done it," the man went on. "Not tonight."

"No sense taking chances, is there?"

"I guess not."

"You're taking a chance yourself, aren't you? Coming out here, standing at the edge, thinking it over. Anyone who does that long enough, sooner or later gets a little too nervous and goes over the edge. He doesn't really want to and he's sorry long before he hits the water, but it's too late; he took too many chances and it's over for him. Tempt fate too much and fate gets you."

"I suppose you're right."

"Something in particular bothering you?"

"Not . . . anything special, no."

"Have you been seeing a doctor?"

"Off and on."

"That can help, you know."

"So they say."

"Want to go grab a cup of coffee?"

The man opened his mouth, started to say something, then changed his mind. He lit another cigarette and blew out a cloud of smoke, watching the way the wind dispersed it. "I'll be all right now," he said.

"Sure?"

"I'll go home, get some sleep. I haven't been sleeping so well, not since my wife—"

"Oh," the cop said.

"She died. She was all I had and, well, she died."

The cop put a hand on his shoulder. "You'll get over it, Mr. Wright. You just have to hold on, that's all. Hold on, and sooner or later you'll get over it. Maybe you think you can't live through it, nothing will be the same, but— "

"I know."

"You sure you don't want a cup of coffee?"

"No, I'd better get home," the man said. "I'm sorry to cause trouble. I'll try to relax, I'll be all right."

The cop watched him drive away and wondered whether he should have taken him in. No point, he decided. You went crazy enough hauling in every attempted suicide, and this one hadn't actually attempted anything, he had merely thought about it. Too, if you started picking up everyone who contemplated suicide you'd have your hands full.

He headed back for the other side of the bridge. When he reached his post he decided he should make a note of it, anyway, so he hauled out his pencil and his notebook and wrote down the name, *Edward Wright*. So he would remember what the name meant, he added *Big Eyebrows, Wife Dead, Contemplated Jumping.*

The psychiatrist stroked his pointed beard and looked over at the patient on the couch. The importance of beard and couch, as he had told his wife many times, lay in their property for enabling his patients to see him as a function of such outward symbols rather than as an individual, thus facilitating transference. His wife hated the beard and felt he used the couch for amorous dalliance. It was true, he thought, that he and his plump blonde receptionist had on a few occasions occupied the couch together. A few memorable occasions, he amended, and he closed his eyes, savoring the memory of the delicious way he and Hannah had gone through Krafft-Ebing together, page by delirious page.

Reluctantly, he dragged himself back to his current patient. ". . . no longer seems worth living," the man said. "I drag myself through life a day at a time."

"We all live our lives a day at a time," the psychiatrist commented.

"But is it always an ordeal?"

"No."

"I almost killed myself last night. No, the night before last. I almost jumped from the Morrissey Bridge."

"And?"

"A policeman came along. I wouldn't have jumped anyway."

"Why not?"

"I don't know."

The interplay went on, the endless dialogue of patient and doctor. Sometimes the doctor could go through the whole hour without thinking at all, making automatic responses, reacting as he always did, but not really hearing a word that was said to him. *I wonder,* he thought, *whether I do these people any good at all. Perhaps they only wish to talk and need only the illusion of a listener. Perhaps the en-*

tire profession is no more than an intellectual confidence game. If I were a priest, he thought wistfully, *I could go to my bishop when struck by doubts of faith, but psychiatrists do not have bishops. The only trouble with the profession is the unfortunate absence of an orderly hierarchy. Absolute religions could not be so democratically organized.*

He listened, next, to a dream. Almost all of his patients delighted in telling him their dreams, a source of unending frustration to the psychiatrist, who never in his life remembered having a dream of his own. From time to time he fantasized that it was all a gigantic put-on, that there were really no dreams at all. He listened to this dream with academic interest, glancing now and then at his watch, wishing the fifty-minute hour would end. The dream, he knew, indicated a diminishing enthusiasm for life, a development of the death wish, and a desire for suicide that was being tentatively held in check by fear and moral training. He wondered how long his patient would be able to refrain from taking his own life. In the three weeks he had been coming for therapy, he had seemed to be making only negative progress.

Another dream. The psychiatrist closed his eyes, sighed, and ceased listening. Five more minutes, he told himself. Five more minutes and then this idiot would leave, and perhaps he could persuade plump blonde Hannah to do some further experimentation with him. There was a case of Stekel's he had read just the other night that sounded delicious.

The doctor looked up at the man, took in the heavy eyebrows, the deep-set eyes, the expression of guilt and fear. "I have to have my stomach pumped, Doctor," the man said. "Can you do it here or do we have to go to a hospital?"

"What's the matter with you?"

"Pills."

"What sort? Sleeping pills? Is that what you mean?"

"Yes."

"What sort? And how many did you take?"

The man explained the content of the pills and said that he had taken twenty. "Ten is a lethal dose," the doctor said. "How long ago did you take them?"

"Half an hour. No, less than that. Maybe twenty minutes."

"And then you decided not to act like a damned fool, eh? I gather you didn't fall asleep. Twenty minutes? Why wait this long?"

"I tried to make myself throw up."

"Couldn't do it? Well, we'll try the stomach pump," the doctor said. The operation of the pump was unpleasant, the analysis of the stomach's contents even less pleasant. The pumping had been in plenty of time, the doctor discovered. The pills had not yet been absorbed to any great degree by the bloodstream.

"You'll live," he said finally.

"Thank you, Doctor."

"Don't thank me. I'll have to report this, you know."

"I wish you wouldn't. I'm . . . I'm under a psychiatrist's care. It was more an accident than anything else, really."

"Twenty pills?" The doctor shrugged. "You'd better pay me now," he said. "I hate to send bills to potential suicides. It's risky."

"This is a fine shotgun for the price," the clerk said. "Now, if you want to get fancy, you can get yourself a weapon with a lot more range and accuracy. For just a few dollars more—"

"No, this will be satisfactory. And I'll need a box of shells."

The clerk put the box on the counter. "Or three boxes for—"

"Just the one."

"Sure thing," the clerk said. He drew the registry ledger from beneath the counter, opened it, set it on the top of the counter. "You'll have to sign right there," he said, "to keep the state happy." He checked the signature when the man had finished writing. "Now I'm supposed to see some identification, Mr. Wright. Just a driver's license if you've got it handy." He checked the license, compared the signatures, jotted down the license number, and nodded, satisfied.

"Thank you," said the man, when he had received his change. "Thank you very much."

"Thank *you*, Mr. Wright. I think you'll get a lot of use out of that gun."

"I'm sure I will."

At nine o'clock that night Edward Wright heard his back doorbell ring. He walked downstairs, glass in hand, finished his drink, and went to the door. He was a tall man, with sunken eyes topped by thick black eyebrows. He looked outside, recognized his visitor, hesitated only momentarily, and opened the door.

His visitor poked a shotgun into Edward Wright's abdomen.

"Mark—"

"Invite me in," the man said. "It's cold out here."

"Mark, I don't—"

"Inside."

In the living room Edward Wright stared into the mouth of the shotgun and knew that he was going to die.

"You killed her, Ed," the visitor said. "She wanted a divorce. You couldn't stand that, could you? I told her not to tell you. I told her it was dangerous, that you were nothing but an animal. I told her to run away with me and forget you but she wanted to do the decent thing and you killed her."

"You're crazy!"

"You made it good, didn't you? Made it look like an accident. How did you do it? You'd better tell me, or this gun goes off."

"I hit her."

"You hit her and killed her? Just like that?"

Wright swallowed. He looked at the gun, then at the man. "I hit her a few times. Quite a few times. Then I threw her down the cellar stairs. You can't go to the police with this, you know. They can't prove it and they wouldn't believe it."

"We won't go to the police," the man said. "I didn't go to them at the beginning. They didn't know of a motive for you, did they? I could have told them a motive, but I didn't go, Edward. Sit down at your desk, Edward. Now. That's right. Take out a sheet of paper and a pen. You'd better do as I say, Edward. There's a message I want you to write."

"You can't—"

"Write *I can't stand it any longer. This time I won't fail,* and sign your name."

"I won't do it."

"Yes, you will, Edward." He pressed the gun against the back of Edward Wright's shaking head.

"You wouldn't do it," Wright said.

"But I would."

"You'll hang for it, Mark. You won't get away with it."

"Suicide, Edward."

"No one would believe I would commit suicide, note or no note. They won't believe it."

"Just write the note, Edward. Then I'll give you the gun and leave you with your conscience. I definitely know what you'll do."

"You—"

"Just write the note. I don't want to kill you, Edward. I want you to write the note as a starter, and then I'll leave you here."

Wright did not exactly believe him, but the shotgun poised against the back of his head left him little choice. He wrote the note, signed his name.

"Turn around, Edward."

He turned, stared. The man looked very different. He had put on false eyebrows and a wig, and he had done something to his eyes, put makeup around them.

"Do you know who I look like now, Edward?"

"No."

"I look like *you,* Edward. Not exactly like you, of course. Not close enough to fool people who know you, but we're both about the same height and build. Add the character tags, the eyebrows and the hair and the hollow eyes, and put them on a man who introduces himself as Edward Wright and carries identification in that name, and what have you got? You've got a good imitation of you, Edward."

"You've been impersonating me."

"Yes, Edward."

"But why?"

"Character development," the man said. "You just told me you're not the suicidal type and no one will believe it when you kill yourself. However, you'd be surprised at your recent actions, Edward. There's a policeman who had to talk you out of jumping off the Morrissey Bridge. There's the psychiatrist who has been treating you for suicidal depression, complete with some classic dreams and fantasies. And there's the doctor who had to pump your stomach this afternoon." He prodded Edward's stomach with the gun.

"Pump my—"

"Yes, your stomach. A most unpleasant procedure, Edward. Do you see what I've gone through on your account? Sheer torture. You know, I was worried that my wig might slip during the ordeal, but these new epoxy resins are extraordinary. They say you can even wear a wig swimming, or in the shower." He rubbed one of the false eyebrows with his forefinger. "See how it stays on? And very lifelike, don't you think?"

Edward didn't say anything.

"All those things you've been doing, Edward. Funny you can't recall them. Do you remember buying this shotgun, Edward?"

"I—"

"You did, you know. Not an hour ago, you went into a store and bought this gun and a box of shells. Had to sign for it. Had to show your driver's license, too."

"How did you get my license?"

"I didn't. I created it." The man chuckled. "It wouldn't fool a policeman, but no policeman ever saw it. It certainly fooled the clerk, though. He copied that number very carefully. So you must have bought that gun after all, Edward."

The man ran his fingers through his wig. "Remarkably lifelike," he said again. "If I ever go bald, I'll have to get myself one of these." He laughed. "Not the suicidal type? Edward, this past week you've been the most suicidal man in town. Look at all the people who will swear to it."

"What about my friends? The people at the office?"

"They'll all help it along. Whenever a man commits suicide, his friends start to remember how moody he's been lately. Everybody always wants to get into the act, you know. I'm sure you've been acting very shocked and distraught over her death. You'd have to play the part, wouldn't you? Ah, you never should have killed her, Edward. I loved her, even if you didn't. You should have let her go, Edward."

Wright was sweating. "You said you weren't going to murder me. You said you would leave me alone with the gun—"

"Don't believe everything you hear," the man said, and very quickly, very deftly, he jabbed the gun barrel into Wright's mouth and pulled the trigger. Afterward he arranged things neatly enough, removed one of Wright's shoes, positioned his foot so that it appeared he had triggered the shotgun with his big toe. Then he wiped his own prints from the gun and managed to get Wright's prints all over the weapon. He left the note on top of the desk, slipped the psychiatrist's business card into Wright's wallet, stuffed the bill of sale for the gun into Wright's pocket.

"You shouldn't have killed her," he said to Wright's corpse. Then, smiling privately, he slipped out the back door and walked off into the night.

The Dettweiler Solution

Sometimes you just can't win for losing. Business was so bad over at Dettweiler Bros. Fine Fashions for Men that Seth Dettweiler went on back to the store one Thursday night and poured out a five-gallon can of lead-free gasoline where he figured as it would do the most good. He lit a fresh Philip Morris King Size and balanced it on the edge of the counter so as it would burn for a couple of minutes and then get unbalanced enough to drop into the pool of gasoline. Then he got into an Oldsmobile that was about five days clear of a repossession notice and drove on home.

You couldn't have had a better fire dropping napalm on a paper mill. Time it was done you could sift those ashes and not find so much as a collar button. It was far and away the most spectacularly total fire Schuyler County had ever seen, so much so that Maybrook Fidelity Insurance would have been a little tentative about settling a claim under ordinary circumstances. But the way things stood there wasn't the slightest suspicion of arson, because what kind of a dimwitted hulk goes and burns down his business establishment a full week after his fire insurance has lapsed?

No fooling.

See, it was Seth's brother Porter who took care of paying bills and such, and a little over a month ago the fire-insurance payment had been due, and Porter looked at the bill and at the bank balance and back and forth for a while and then he put the bill in a drawer. Two weeks later there was a reminder notice, and two weeks after that there was a notice that the grace period had expired and the insurance was no longer in force, and then a week after that there was one pluperfect hell of a bonfire.

Seth and Porter had always got on pretty good. (They took after each other quite a bit, folks said. Especially Porter.) Seth was forty-two years of age, and he had that long Dettweiler face topping a jutting Van Dine jaw. (Their mother was a Van Dine hailing from just the other side of Oak Falls.) Porter was thirty-nine, equipped with the same style face and jaw. They both had black hair that lay flat on their heads like shoe polish put on in slapdash fashion. Seth had more hair left than Porter, in spite of being the older brother by three years. I could describe them in greater detail, right down to scars and warts and sundry distinguishing marks, but it's my guess that you'd enjoy reading all that about as much as I'd enjoy writing it, which is to say less than somewhat. So let's get on with it.

I was saying they got on pretty good, rarely raising their voices one to the other, rarely disagreeing seriously about anything much. Now the fire didn't entirely change the habits of a lifetime but you couldn't honestly say that it did anything to improve their relationship. You'd have to allow that it caused a definite strain.

"What I can't understand," Seth said, "is how anybody who is fool enough to let fire insurance lapse can be an even greater fool by not telling his brother about it. That in a nutshell is what I can't understand."

"What beats *me*," Porter said, "is how the same person who has the nerve to fire a place of business for the insurance also does so without consulting his partner, especially when his partner just happens to be his brother."

"Allus I was trying to do," said Seth, "was save you from the criminal culpability of being an accessory before, to, and after the fact, plus figuring you might be too chickenhearted to go along with it."

"Allus *I* was trying to do," said Porter, "was save you from worrying about financial matters you would be powerless to contend with, plus figuring it would just be an occasion for me to hear further from you on the subject of those bow ties."

"Well, you did buy one powerful lot of bow ties."

"I knew it."

"Something like a Pullman car full of bow ties, and it's not like every man and boy in Schuyler County's been getting this mad passion for bow ties of late."

"I just knew it."

"I wasn't the one brought up the subject, but since you went and mentioned those bow ties—"

"Maybe I should of mentioned the spats," Porter said.

"Oh, I don't want to hear about spats."

"No more than I wanted to hear about bow ties. Did we sell one single damn pair of spats?"

"We did."

"We did?"

"Feller bought one about fifteen months back. Had Maryland plates on his car, as I recall. Said he always wanted spats and didn't know they still made 'em."

"Well, selling one pair out of a gross isn't too bad."

"Now you leave off," Seth said.

"And you leave off of bow ties?"

"I guess."

"Anyway, the bow ties and the spats all burned up in the same damn fire," Porter said.

"You know what they say about ill winds," Seth said. "I guess there's a particle of truth in it, what they say."

While it didn't do the Dettweiler brothers much good to discuss spats and bow ties, it didn't solve their problems to leave off mentioning spats and bow ties. By the time they finished their conversation all they were back to was square one, and the view from that spot wasn't the world's best.

The only solution was bankruptcy, and it didn't look to be all that much of a solution.

"I don't mind going bankrupt," one of the brothers said. (I think it was Seth.

Makes no nevermind, actually. Seth, Porter, it's all the same who said it.) "I don't mind going bankrupt, but I sure do hate the thought of being broke."

"Me too," said the other brother. (Porter, probably.)

"I've thought about bankruptcy from time to time."

"Me too."

"But there's a time and a place for bankruptcy."

"Well, the place is all right. No better place for bankruptcy than Schuyler County."

"That's true enough," said Seth. (Unless it was Porter.) "But this is surely not the time. Time to go bankrupt is in good times when you got a lot of money on hand. Only the damnedest kind of fool goes bankrupt when he's stony broke busted and there's a depression going on."

What they were both thinking on during this conversation was a fellow name of Joe Bob Rathburton who was in the construction business over to the other end of Schuyler County. I myself don't know of a man in this part of the state with enough intelligence to bail out a leaky rowboat who doesn't respect Joe Bob Rathburton to hell and back as a man with good business sense. It was about two years ago that Joe Bob went bankrupt and he did it the right way. First of all he did it coming off the best year's worth of business he'd ever done in his life. Then what he did was he paid off the car and the house and the boat and put them all in his wife's name. (His wife was Mabel Washburn, but no relation to the Washburns who have the Schuyler County First National Bank. That's another family entirely.)

Once that was done, Joe Bob took out every loan and raised every dollar he possibly could, and he turned all that capital into green folding cash and sealed it in quart Mason jars which he buried out back of an old pear tree that's sixty-plus years old and still bears fruit like crazy. And then he declared bankruptcy and sat back in his Mission rocker with a beer and a cigar and a real big-tooth smile.

"If I could think of anything worth doing," Porter Dettweiler said one night, "why, I guess I'd just go ahead and do it."

"Can't argue with that," Seth said.

"But I can't," Porter said.

"Nor I either."

"You might pass that old jug over here for a moment."

"Soon as I pour a tad for myself, if you've no objection."

"None whatsoever," said Porter.

They were over at Porter's place on the evening when this particular conversation occurred. They had taken to spending most of their evenings at Porter's on account of Seth had a wife at home, plus a daughter named Rachel who'd been working at the Ben Franklin store ever since dropping out of the junior college over at Monroe Center. Seth didn't have but the one daughter. Porter had two sons and a daughter, but they were all living with Porter's ex-wife, who had divorced him two years back and moved clear to Georgia. They were living in Valdosta now, as far as Porter knew. Least that was where he sent the check every month.

"Alimony jail," said Porter.

"How's that?"

"What I said was alimony jail. Where you go when you quit paying on your alimony."

"They got a special jug set aside for men don't pay their alimony?"

"Just an expression. I guess they put you into whatever jug's the handiest. All I got to do is quit sendin' Gert her checks and let her have them cart me away. Get my three meals a day and a roof over my head and the whole world could quit nagging me night and day for money I haven't got."

"You could never stand it. Bein' in a jail day in and day out, night in and night out."

"I know it," Porter said unhappily. "There anything left in that there jug, on the subject of jugs?"

"Some. Anyway, you haven't paid Gert a penny in how long? Three months?"

"Call it five."

"And she ain't throwed you in jail yet. Least you haven't got her close to hand so's she can talk money to you."

"Linda Mae givin' you trouble?"

"She did. Keeps a civil tongue since I beat up on her the last time."

"Lord knew what he was doin'," Porter said, "makin' men stronger than women. You ever give any thought to what life would be like if wives could beat up on their husbands instead of the other way around?"

"Now I don't even want to think about that," Seth said.

You'll notice nobody was mentioning spats or bow ties. Even with the jug of corn getting discernibly lighter every time it passed from one set of hands to the other, these two subjects did not come up. Neither did anyone speak of the shortsightedness of failing to keep up fire insurance or the myopia of incinerating a building without ascertaining that such insurance was in force. Tempers had cooled with the ashes of Dettweiler Bros. Fine Fashions for Men, and once again Seth and Porter were on the best of terms.

Which just makes what happened thereafter all the more tragic.

"What I think I got," Porter said, "is no way to turn."

(This wasn't the same evening, but if you put the two evenings side by side under a microscope you'd be hard pressed to tell them apart each from the other. They were at Porter's little house over alongside the tracks of the old spur off the Wyandotte & Southern, which I couldn't tell you the last time there was a train on that spur, and they had their feet up and their shoes off, and there was a jug of corn in the picture. Most of their evenings had come to take on this particular shade.)

"Couldn't get work if I wanted to," Porter said, "which I don't, and if I did I couldn't make enough to matter, and my debts is up to my ears and rising steady."

"It doesn't look to be gettin' better," Seth said. "On the other hand, how can it get worse?"

"I keep thinking the same."

"And?"

"And it keeps getting worse."

"I guess you know what you're talkin' about," Seth said. He scratched his bulldog chin, which hadn't been in the same room with a razor in more than a day or two. "What I been thinkin' about," he said, "is killin' myself."

"You been thinking of that?"

"Sure have."

"I think on it from time to time myself," Porter admitted. "Mostly nights when I can't sleep. It can be a powerful comfort around about three in the morning. You think of all the different ways and the next thing you know you're asleep. Beats the stuffing out of counting sheep jumping fences. You seen one sheep you seen 'em all is always been my thoughts on the subject, whereas there's any number of ways of doing away with yourself."

"I'd take a certain satisfaction in it," Seth said, more or less warming to the subject. "What I'd leave is this note tellin' Linda Mae how her and Rachel'll be taken care of with the insurance, just to get the bitch's hopes up, and then she can find out for her own self that I cashed in that insurance back in January to make the payment on the Oldsmobile. You know it's pure uncut hell gettin' along without an automobile now."

"You don't have to tell me."

"Just put a rope around my neck," said Seth, smothering a hiccup, "and my damn troubles'll be over."

"And mine in the bargain," Porter said.

"By you doin' your own self in?"

"Be no need," Porter said, "if you did *yourself* in."

"How you figure that?"

"What I figure is a hundred thousand dollars," Porter said. "Lord love a duck, if I had a hundred thousand dollars I could declare bankruptcy and live like a king!"

Seth looked at him, got up, walked over to him, and took the jug away from him. He took a swig and socked the cork in place, but kept hold of the jug.

"Brother," he said, "I just guess you've had enough of this here."

"What makes you say that, brother?"

"Me killin' myself and you gettin' rich, you don't make sense. What you think you're talkin' about, anyhow?"

"Insurance," Porter said. "Insurance, that's what I think I'm talking about. Insurance."

Porter explained the whole thing. It seems there was this life insurance policy their father had taken out on them when they weren't but boys. Face amount of a hundred thousand dollars, double indemnity for accidental death. It was payable to him while they were alive, but upon his death the beneficiary changed. If Porter was to die the money went to Seth. And vice versa.

"And you knew about this all along?"

"Sure did," Porter said.

"And never cashed it in? Not the policy on me and not the policy on you?"

"Couldn't cash 'em in," Porter said. "I guess I woulda if I coulda, but I couldn't so I didn't."

"And you didn't let these here policies lapse?" Seth said. "On account of occasionally a person can be just the least bit absentminded and forget about keeping a policy in force. That's been known to happen," Seth said, looking off to one side, "in matters relating to fire insurance, for example, and I just thought to mention it."

(I have the feeling he wasn't the only one to worry on that score. You may have had similar thoughts yourself, figuring you know how the story's going to end, what with the insurance not valid and all. Set your mind at rest. If that was the way it had happened I'd never be taking the trouble to write it up for you. I got to select stories with some satisfaction in them if I'm going to stand a chance of selling them to the magazine, and I hope you don't figure I'm sitting here poking away at this typewriter for the sheer physical pleasure of it. If I just want to exercise my fingers I'll send them walking through the Yellow Pages if it's all the same to you.)

"Couldn't let 'em lapse," Porter said. "They're all paid up. What you call twenty-payment life, meaning you pay it in for twenty years and then you got it free and clear. And the way Pa did it, you can't borrow on it or nothing. All you can do is wait and see who dies."

"Well, I'll be."

"Except we don't have to wait to see who dies."

"Why, I guess not. I just guess a man can take matters into his own hands if he's of a mind to."

"He surely can," Porter said.

"Man wants to kill himself, that's what he can go and do."

"No law against it," Porter said.

Now you know and I know that that last is not strictly true. There's a definite no-question law against suicide in our state, and most likely in yours as well. It's harder to make it stand up than a calf with four broken legs, however, and I don't recall that anyone hereabouts was ever prosecuted for it, or likely will be. It does make you wonder some what they had in mind writing that particular law into the books.

"I'll just have another taste of that there corn," Porter said, "and why don't you have a pull on the jug your own self? You have any idea just when you might go and do it?"

"I'm studying on it," Seth said.

"There's a lot to be said for doing something soon as a man's mind's made up on the subject. Not to be hurrying you or anything of the sort, but they say that he who hesitates is last." Porter scratched his chin. "Or some such," he said.

"I just might do it tonight."

"By God," Porter said.

"Get the damn thing over with. Glory Hallelujah and my troubles is over."

"And so is mine," said Porter.

"You'll be in the money then," said Seth, "and I'll be in the boneyard, and both of us is free and clear. You can just buy me a decent funeral and then go bankrupt in style."

"Give you Johnny Millbourne's number-one funeral," Porter promised. "Brass-bound casket and all. I mean, price is no object if I'm going bankrupt anyway. Let old Johnny swing for the money."

"You a damn good man, brother."

"You the best man in the world, brother."

The jug passed back and forth a couple more times. At one point Seth announced that he was ready, and he was halfway out the door before he recollected that his car had been repossessed, which interfered with his plans to drive it off a cliff. He came back in and sat down again and had another drink on the strength of it all, and then suddenly he sat forward and stared hard at Porter.

"This policy thing," he said.

"What about it?"

"It's on both of us, is what you said."

"If I said it then must be it's the truth."

"Well then," Seth said, and sat back, arms folded on his chest.

"Well then what?"

"Well then if *you* was to kill yourself, then *I'd* get the money and *you'd* get the funeral."

"I don't see what you're getting at," Porter said slowly.

"Seems to me either one of us can go and do it," Seth said. "And here's the two of us just takin' it for granted that I'm to be the one to go and do it, and I think we should think on that a little more thoroughly."

"Why, being as you're older, Seth."

"What's that to do with anything?"

"Why, you got less years to give up."

"Still be givin' up all that's left. Older or younger don't cut no ice."

Porter thought about it. "After all," he said, "it was your idea."

"That don't cut ice neither. I could mention I got a wife and child."

"I could mention I got a wife and three children."

"Ex-wife."

"All the same."

"Let's face it," Seth said. "Gert and your three don't add up to anything and neither do Linda Mae and Rachel."

"Got to agree," Porter said.

"So."

"One thing. You being the one who put us in this mess, what with firing the store, it just seems you might be the one to get us out of it."

"You bein' the one let the insurance lapse through your own stupidity, you could get us out of this mess through insurance, thus evenin' things up again."

"Now talkin' about stupidity—"

"Yes, talkin' about stupidity—"

"Spats!"

"Bow ties, damn you! *Bow ties!*"

You might have known it would come to that.

Now I've told you Seth and Porter generally got along pretty well and here's further evidence of it. Confronted by such a stalemate, a good many people would have wrote off the whole affair and decided not to take the suicide route at all. But not even spats and bow ties could deflect Seth and Porter from the road they'd figured out as the most logical to pursue.

So what they did, one of them tossed a coin, and the other one called it while it was in the air, and they let it hit the floor and roll, and I don't recollect whether it was heads or tails, or who tossed and who called—what's significant is that Seth won.

"Well now," Seth said. "I feel I been reprieved. Just let me have that coin. I want to keep it for a luck charm."

"Two out of three."

"We already said once is as good as a million," Seth said, "so you just forget that two-out-of-three business. You got a week like we agreed but if I was you I'd get it over soon as I could."

"I got a week," Porter said.

"You'll get the brassbound casket and everything, and you can have Minnie Lucy Boxwood sing at your funeral if you want. Expense don't matter at all. What's your favorite song?"

"I suppose 'Your Cheatin' Heart.' "

"Minnie Lucy does that real pretty."

"I guess she does."

"Now you be sure and make it accidental," Seth said. "Two hundred thousand dollars goes just about twice as far as one hundred thousand dollars. Won't cost you a thing to make it accidental, just like we talked about it. What I would do is borrow Fritz Chenoweth's half-ton pickup and go up on the old Harburton Road where it takes that curve. Have yourself a belly full of corn and just keep goin' straight when the road doesn't. Lord knows I almost did that myself enough times without tryin'. Had two wheels over the edge less'n a month ago."

"That close?"

"That close."

"I'll be doggone," Porter said.

Thing is, Seth went on home after he failed to convince Porter to do it right away, and that was when things began to fall into the muck. Because Porter started thinking things over. I have a hunch it would have worked about the same way if Porter had won the flip, with Seth thinking things over. They were a whole lot alike, those two. Like two peas in a pod.

What occurred to Porter was would Seth have gone through with it if he lost, and what Porter decided was that he wouldn't. Not that there was any way for him to prove it one way or the other, but when you can't prove something you generally tend to decide on believing in what you want to believe, and Porter Dettweiler was no exception. Seth, he decided, would not have killed himself and didn't never have no intention of killing himself, which meant that for Porter to go through with killing his own self amounted to nothing more than damned foolishness.

Now it's hard to say just when he figured out what to do, but it was in the next two days, because on the third day he went over and borrowed that pickup off Fritz Chenoweth. "I got the back all loaded down with a couple sacks of concrete mix and a keg of nails and I don't know what all," Fritz said. "You want to unload it back of my smaller barn if you need the room."

"Oh, that's all right," Porter told him. "I guess I'll just leave it loaded and be grateful for the traction."

"Well, you keep it overnight if you have a mind," Fritz said.

"I just might do that," Porter said, and he went over to Seth's house. "Let's you and me go for a ride," he told Seth. "Something we was talking about the other night, and I went and got me a new slant on it which the two of us ought to discuss before things go wrong altogether."

"Be right with you," Seth said, "soon as I finish this sandwich."

"Oh, just bring it along."

"I guess," said Seth.

No sooner was the pickup truck backed down and out of the driveway than Porter said, "Now will you just have a look over there, brother."

"How's that?" said Seth, and turned his head obligingly to the right, whereupon Porter gave him a good lick upside the head with a monkey wrench he'd brought along expressly for that purpose. He got him right where you have a soft spot if you're a little baby. (You also have a soft spot there if someone gets you just right with a monkey wrench.) Seth made a little sound which amounted to no more than letting his breath out, and then he went out like an icebox light when you have closed the door on it.

Now as to whether or not Seth was dead at this point I could not honestly tell you, unless I were to make up an answer knowing how slim is the likelihood of anyone presuming to contradict me. But the plain fact is that he might have been dead and he might not and even Seth could not have told you, being at the very least stone-unconscious at the time.

What Porter did was drive up the old Harburton Road, I guess figuring that he might as well stick to as much of the original plan as possible. There's a particular place where the road does a reasonably convincing imitation of a fishhook, and that spot's been described as Schuyler County's best natural brake on the population explosion since they stamped out the typhoid. A whole lot of folks fail to make that curve every year, most of them young ones with plenty of breeding years left in them. Now and then there's a movement to put up a guard rail, but the ecology people are against it so it never gets anywhere.

If you miss that curve, the next land you touch is a good five hundred feet closer to sea level.

So Porter pulls over to the side of the road and then he gets out of the car and maneuvers Seth (or Seth's body, whichever the case may have been) so as he's behind the wheel. Then he stands alongside the car working the gas pedal with one hand and the steering wheel with the other and putting the fool truck in gear and doing this and that and the other thing so he can run the truck up to the edge and over, and thinking hard every minute about those two hundred thousand pretty green dollars that are destined to make his bankruptcy considerably easier to contend with.

Well, I told you right off that sometimes you can't win for losing, which was the case for Porter and Seth both, and another way of putting it is to say that when everything goes wrong there's nothing goes right. Here's what happened. Porter slipped on a piece of loose gravel while he was pushing, and the truck had to go on its own, and where it went was halfway and no further, with its back wheel hung up on a hunk of tree limb or some such and its two front wheels hanging out over nothing and its motor stalled out deader'n a smoked fish.

Porter said himself a whole mess of bad words. Then he wasted considerable time shoving the back of that truck, forgetting it was in gear and not about to budge. Then he remembered and said a few more bad words and put the thing in neutral, which involved a long reach across Seth to get to the floor shift and a lot of coordination to manipulate it and the clutch pedal at the same time. Then Porter got out of the truck and gave the door a slam, and just about then a beat-up old Chevy with Indiana plates pulls up and this fellow leaps out screaming that he's got a tow rope and he'll pull the truck to safety.

You can't hardly blame Porter for the rest of it. He wasn't the type to be great at contingency planning anyhow, and who could allow for something like this? What he did, he gave this great sob and just plain hurled himself at the back of that truck, it being in neutral now, and the truck went sailing like a kite in a tornado, and Porter, well, what he did was follow right along after it. It wasn't part of his plan but he just had himself too much momentum to manage any last-minute change of direction.

According to the fellow from Indiana, who it turned out was a veterinarian from Bloomington, Porter fell far enough to get off a couple of genuinely rank words on the way down. Last words or not, you sure wouldn't go and engrave them on any tombstone.

Speaking of which, he has the last word in tombstones, Vermont granite and all, and his brother Seth has one just like it. They had a double-barreled funeral, the best Johnny Millbourne had to offer, and they each of them reposed in a brass-bound casket, the top-of-the-line model. Minnie Lucy Boxwood sang "Your Cheatin' Heart," which was Porter's favorite song, plus she sang Seth's favorite, which was "Old Buttermilk Sky," plus she also sang free gratis "My Buddy" as a testament to brotherly love.

And Linda Mae and Rachel got themselves two hundred thousand dollars from the insurance company, which is what Gert and her kids in Valdosta, Georgia, also got. And Seth and Porter have an end to their miseries, which was all they really wanted before they got their heads turned around at the idea of all that money.

The only thing funnier than how things don't work out is how they do.

Funny You Should Ask

On what a less original writer might deign to describe as a fateful day, young Robert Tillinghast approached the proprietor of a shop called Earth Forms. "Actually," he said, "I don't think I can buy anything today, but there's a question I'd like to ask you. It's been on my mind for the longest time. I was looking at those recycled jeans over by the far wall."

"I'll be getting a hundred pair in Monday afternoon," the proprietor said.

"Is that right?"

"It certainly is."

"A hundred pair," Robert marveled. "That's certainly quite a lot."

"It's the minimum order."

"Is that a fact? And they'll all be the same quality and condition as the ones you have on display over on the far wall?"

"Absolutely. Of course, I won't know what sizes I'll be getting."

"I guess that's just a matter of chance."

"It is. But they'll all be first-quality name brands, and they'll all be in good condition, broken in but not broken to bits. That's a sort of an expression I made up to describe them."

"I like it," said Robert, not too sincerely. "You know, there's a question that's been nagging at my mind for the longest time. Now you get six dollars a pair for the recycled jeans, is that right?" It was. "And it probably wouldn't be out of line to guess that they cost you about half that amount?" The proprietor, after a moment's reflection, agreed that it wouldn't be far out of line to make that estimate.

"Well, that's the whole thing," Robert said. "You notice the jeans I'm wearing?"

The proprietor glanced at them. They were nothing remarkable, a pair of oft-washed Lee Riders that were just beginning to go thin at the knees. "Very nice," the man said. "I'd get six dollars for them without a whole lot of trouble."

"But I wouldn't want to sell them."

"And of course not. Why should you? They're just getting to the comfortable stage."

"Exactly!" Robert grew intense, and his eyes bulged slightly. This was apt to happen when he grew intense, although he didn't know it, never having seen himself at such times. "Exactly," he repeated. "The recycled jeans you see in the shops, this shop and other shops, are just at the point where they're breaking in right. They're never really worn out. Unless you only put the better pairs on display?"

"No, they're all like that."

"That's what everybody says." Robert had had much the same conversation before in the course of his travels. "All top quality, all in excellent condition, and all in the same stage of wear."

"So?"

"So," Robert said in triumph, "who throws them out?"

"Oh."

"The company that sells them. Where do they get them from?"

"You know," the proprietor said, "it's funny you should ask. The same question's occurred to me. People buy these jeans because this is the way they want 'em. But who in the world sells them?"

"That's what I'd like to know. Not that it would do me any good to have the answer, but the question preys on my mind."

"Who sells them? I could understand about young children's jeans that kids would outgrow them, but what about the adult sizes? Unless kids grow up and don't want to wear jeans anymore."

"I'll be wearing jeans as long as I live," Robert said recklessly. "I'll never get too old for jeans."

The proprietor seemed not to have heard. "Now maybe it's different out in the farm country," he said. "I buy these jeans from a firm in Rockford, Illinois—"

"I've heard of the firm," Robert said. "They seem to be the only people supplying recycled jeans."

"Only one I know of. Now maybe things are different in their area and people like brand-new jeans and once they break in somewhat they think of them as worn out. That's possible, don't you suppose?"

"I guess it's possible."

"Because it's the only explanation I can think of. After all, what could they afford to pay for the jeans? A dollar a pair? A dollar and a half at the outside? Who would sell 'em good-condition jeans for that amount of money?" The man shook his head. "Funny you should ask a question that I've asked myself so many times and never put into words."

"That Rockford firm," Robert said. "That's another thing I don't understand. Why would they develop a sideline business like recycled jeans?"

"Well, you never know about that," the man said. "Diversification is the keynote of American business these days. Take me, for example. I started out selling flowerpots, and now I sell flowerpots and guitar strings and recapped tires and recycled jeans. Now there are people who would call that an unusual combination."

"I suppose there are," said Robert.

An obsession of the sort that gripped Robert is a curious thing. After a certain amount of time it is either metamorphosized into neurosis or it is tamed, surfacing periodically as a vehicle for casual conversation. Young Robert Tillinghast, neurotic enough in other respects, suppressed his curiosity on the subject of recycled jeans and only raised the question at times when it seemed particularly apropos.

And it did seem apropos often enough. Robert was touring the country, depending for his locomotion upon the kindness of passing motorists. As charitable as his hosts were, they were apt to insist upon a quid pro quo of conversation, and Robert had learned to converse extemporaneously upon a variety of subjects. One of these was that of recycled blue jeans, a subject close at once to his heart and his skin, and Robert's own jeans often served as the lead-in to this line of conversation, being either funky and mellow or altogether disreputable, depending upon one's point of view, which in turn largely depended (it must be said) upon one's age.

One day in West Virginia, on that stretch of Interstate 79 leading from Morgantown down to Charleston, Robert thumbed a ride with a man who, though not many years older than himself, drove a late-model Cadillac. Robert, his backpack in the backseat and his body in the front, could not have been more pleased. He had come to feel that hitching a ride in an expensive car endowed one with all the privileges of ownership without the nuisance of making the payments.

Then, as the car cruised southward, Robert noticed that the driver was glancing repeatedly at his, which is to say Robert's, legs. Covert glances at that, sidelong and meaningful. Robert sighed inwardly. This, too, was part of the game, and had ceased to shock him. But he had so been looking forward to riding in this car and now he would have to get out.

The driver said, "Just admiring your jeans."

"I guess they're just beginning to break in," Robert said, relaxing now. "I've certainly had them a while."

"Well, they look just right now. Got a lot of wear left in them."

"I guess they'll last for years," Robert said. "With the proper treatment. You know, that brings up something I've been wondering about for a long time." And he went into his routine, which had become rather a little set piece by this time, ending with the question that had plagued him from the start. "So where on earth does that Rockford company get all these jeans? Who provides them?"

"Funny you should ask," the young man said. "I don't suppose you noticed my license plates before you got in?" Robert admitted he hadn't. "Few people do," the young man said. "Land of Lincoln is the slogan on them, and they're from Illinois. And I'm from Rockford. As a matter of fact, I'm with that very company."

"But that's incredible! For the longest time I've wanted to know the answers to my questions, and now at long last—" He broke off. "Why are we leaving the Interstate?"

"Bypass some traffic approaching Charleston. There's construction ahead and it can be a real bottleneck. Yes, I'm with the company."

"In sales, I suppose? Servicing accounts? You certainly have enough accounts. Why, it seems every store in the country buys recycled jeans from you people."

"Our distribution is rather good," the young man said, "and our sales force does a good job. But I'm in Acquisitions, myself. I go out and round up the jeans. Then in Rockford they're washed to clean and sterilize them, patched if they need it and—"

"You're actually in Acquisitions?"

"That's a fact."

"Well, this *is* my lucky day," Robert exclaimed. "You're just the man to give me all the answers. Where do you get the jeans? Who sells them to you? What do you pay for them? What sort of person sells perfectly good jeans?"

"That's a whole lot of questions at once."

Robert laughed, happy with himself, his host, and the world. "I just don't know where to start and it's got me rattled. Say, this bypass is a small road, isn't it? I guess not many people know about it and that's why there's no other traffic on it. Poor saps'll all get tangled in traffic going into Charleston."

"We'll miss all that."

"That's good luck. Let's see, where can I begin? All right, here's the big question and I've always been puzzled by this one. What's a company like yours doing in the recycled jeans business?"

"Well," said the young man, "diversification is the keynote of American business these days."

"But a company like yours," Robert said. "Rockford Dog Food, Inc. How did you ever think to get into the business in the first place?"

"Funny you should ask," said the young man, braking the car smoothly to a stop.

The Gentle Way

I was at the animal shelter over an hour that morning before I found the lamb. She was right out in plain sight in the middle of the barnyard, but the routine called for me to run through the inside chores before taking care of the outside animals. I arrived at the shelter around seven, so I had two hours to get things in shape before Will Haggerty arrived at nine to open up for business.

First on the list that morning was the oven. Will and I had had to put down a dog the night before, a rangy Doberman with an unbreakable vicious streak. The dog had come to us two months ago, less than a month after I started working there. He'd been a beloved family pet for a year and a half before almost taking an arm off a seven-year-old neighbor boy. Two hours after that the Dobe was in a cage at the far end of the shelter. "Please try and find a good home for Rex," the owners begged us. "Maybe a farm, someplace where he has room to run."

Will had said all the right things and they left, smiling bravely. When they were gone Will sighed and went back to look at the dog and talk to him. He turned to me. "We could put a fifty-dollar adoption tag on him and move him out of here in a week, Eddie, but I won't do it. A farm—now this is just what your average farmer needs, isn't it? Good old Rex is a killer. He'd rip up cats and chickens. Give him room to run and he'd go after sheep and calves. No Dobe is worth a damn unless he's trained by an expert and the best experts won't get a hundred percent success. Train one right and he's still no family pet. He'll be a good guard dog, a good attack dog, but who wants to live with one of those? I know people who swear by them, but I never yet met a Dobe I could trust."

"So what happens now?"

"We tag the cage 'Not For Adoption' and give the poor beast food and water. Maybe I'll turn up a trainer who wants to take a chance on him, but frankly I doubt it. Rex here is just too old and too mean. It's not teaching him new tricks but making him forget the ones he already knows, and that's a whole lot easier said than done."

Rex was the first animal we had to put away since I went to work for Will. There must have been a dozen people who walked past the cage and asked to adopt him. Some of them wanted to give him a try even after they heard why he wasn't available. We wouldn't let him go. Will worked with him a few times and only confirmed what he already knew. The dog was vicious, and his first taste of blood had finished him; but we kept him around for weeks even after we knew what we had to do.

We were standing in front of the Doberman's cage when Will dropped a big hand on my shoulder and shook his head sadly. "No sense putting it off anymore," he said. "That cage is no place for him and there's no other place he can go. Might as well get it over."

"You want me to help?"

"He's a big old boy and it'd be easier with two of us, but I'm not going to tell you to. God knows I got no stomach for it myself."

I said I'd stick around.

He got a pistol and loaded it with tranquilizer darts, then filled a hypodermic syringe with morphine. We walked back to Rex's cage and Will kept the pistol out of sight at his side until Rex was facing the other way. He raised the gun and fired quickly, planting two darts an inch apart in the big dog's shoulder. Rex dropped like a stone.

Will crawled into the cage and hunkered down next to him. He had the needle poised but hesitated. The tranquilizer darts would keep the dog unconscious for fifteen or twenty minutes. The morphine would kill. There were tears flowing down Will Haggerty's weathered face. I tried to look away but couldn't, and I watched him find a vein and fill the comatose dog with a lethal dose of morphine.

We put him in the wheelbarrow and took him inside. The other animals seemed restless, but that may have been my imagination. I had opened the lid of the incinerator while Will was preparing the morphine. The two of us got the dead dog out of the wheelbarrow and into the big metal box. I closed the lid and Will threw the switch without hesitation. Then we turned away and walked into another room.

We had used the oven before. We would pick up dogs on the street, dogs run down in traffic. Or dogs would die at home and people would bring us their bodies for disposal. Twice in the time I'd been there we'd had auto victims who were alive when we found them but could not possibly be saved. Those had received morphine shots and gone into the incinerator, but that had been very different. Rex was a beautiful animal in splendid health and it went against the grain to kill him.

"I hate it," Will had told me. "There's nothing worse. I'll keep an animal forever if there's any chance of placing him. There are those in this business who burn half the dogs they get and sell the others to research labs. I never yet let one go for research and never will. And I never yet burned one that I had the slightest hope for."

I opened the oven and swept out a little pile of powdery white ash, unable to believe that nothing more remained of the Doberman. I was glad when the job was done and the oven closed. It was a relief to get busy with the routine work of feeding and watering the dogs and cats, cleaning cages, sweeping up.

Then I went out to the barnyard and found the dead lamb.

The shelter is in the middle of the city, a drab, gray, hopeless part of a generally hopeless town. The barnyard covers about a quarter of an acre girdled by eight feet of cyclone fencing. We keep farm animals there; chickens, ducks and geese, ponies and pigs and sheep. Some had been pets that outgrew their welcome. Others were injured animals we had patched up. Some of them came through cruelty cases we prosecuted, on the rare occasions when Will managed to get a court order divesting the owner of his charges. Supermarkets brought us their distressed produce as feed, and a farmer who owed Will a favor had sent over a load of hay a couple of weeks ago. The barnyard was open to the public during normal business hours, and kids from all over the city would come in and play with the animals.

In theory, the barnyard exists to generate goodwill for the shelter operation. The stray-dog contract with the city is a virtual guarantee of Will's operating expenses. I hadn't worked for him a week, however, before I knew that was just an excuse. He loved to walk among his animals, loved to slip a sugar cube to a pony, scratch a pig's back with a long stick, or just stand chewing a dead cigar and watching the ducks and geese.

The lamb had been born at the shelter shortly after I started working there. Ewes often need assistance at lambing time, and Will had delivered her while I stood around feeling nervous. We named the lamb Fluff, which was accurate if unimaginative, and she was predictably the hit of the barnyard. Everybody loved her—except for the person who killed her.

He had used a knife, and he had used it over and over again. The ground was littered with bloody patches of wool. I took one look and was violently ill, something that hadn't happened since the days of college beer parties. I stood there for what must have been a long time. Then I went inside and called Will.

"You'd better come down here," I said. "Somebody killed Fluff."

When he got here we put her in the oven and he threw the switch. We made coffee and sat in the office letting it get cold on the desk in front of us. It was past nine and time to open the front doors, but neither of us was in a hurry.

After a while he said, "Well, we haven't had one of these for six months. I suppose we were overdue."

"This has happened before?"

He looked at me. "I keep forgetting how young you are."

"What's that supposed to mean?"

"It may have sounded nastier than I meant it. I guess I'm feeling nasty, that's all. Yes, it's happened before, and it will happen again. Kids. They come over the fence and kill something."

"Why?"

"Because they want to. Because they'd like to kill a person but they're not ready for that yet, so they practice on an animal that never knew there was evil on earth. One time, two years ago, a batch of them killed fifteen chickens, the whole flock. Chopped their heads off. Left everything else alone, just killed the chickens. The police asked them why and they said it was fun watching them run around headless. *It was fun.*"

I didn't say anything.

"It's always kids, Eddie. Rotten kids from rotten homes. The police pick them up, but they're children, so they run them through juvenile court and it shakes up the kids and terrifies the parents. The kids are released in their parents' custody and maybe the parents pay a fine and the kids learn a lesson. They learn not to break into this particular barnyard and not to kill these particular animals." He took the cellophane from a cigar and rolled it between his palms. "Some of the time I don't call the police. There's a gentler way to go about it and it works better in the long run. I'd rather do it that way this time, but I'd need your help."

"How do you mean?"

"Catch him ourselves." He took his time lighting the cigar. "They always try it again. We can stake out the place as easily as the cops can, and when we take him we can operate more flexibly than they can. There's a method I've worked out. It lets them understand our operation, gives them a better perspective."

"I think I understand."

"But it means staying up all night for the next night or two, so it's a question of whether you want to give up the time."

"Sure."

"Won't be more than two nights, I would say. He'll be back."

"How do you know there's just one of them?"

"Because there was only one dead animal, son. If you got two there's going to be a minimum of two dead animals. Everybody has to have a turn. It always seems to work that way, anyhow."

We staked out the place that night and the night after. We took turns sleeping during daylight hours, and we were both planted behind cover in the barnyard all through the dark hours. The killer stayed away two nights running. We decided to give it three more tries, but one was all we needed.

Around one in the morning of the third night we heard someone at the fence. I could just make out a shape in the darkness. He would climb halfway up the fence, then hesitate and drop back to the ground. He seemed to be trying to get up the courage to climb all the way over.

I had a tranquilizer dart pistol and I was dying to try dropping him then and there while he was outlined against the fence. I was afraid he would sense our presence and be warned off, but I forced myself to wait. Finally he climbed all the way up, poised there on the balls of his tennis shoes, and jumped toward us.

We had our flashlights on him before he hit the ground, big five-cell jobs that threw a blinding beam.

"Hold it right there," Will boomed out, striding toward him. He had a dart pistol in his right hand and was holding it out in front of the flashlight so that the boy could see it. All it could shoot were the trank darts, but you couldn't tell that by looking at it.

Either the kid panicked or he figured nobody would shoot him for climbing a barnyard fence. He was quick as a snake. He got three-quarters of the way up the fence when Will put a dart into his shoulder, and he hit the ground the way Rex had hit the floor of his cage.

Will hoisted him easily onto his shoulder and toted him into the office. We turned on a desk lamp and propped the kid in a chair. He was about thirteen or fourteen, skinny, with a mop of lifeless black hair. In the pockets of his jeans we found three clasp knives and a switchblade, and on his belt he had a hunting knife in a sheath. There were stains in the hunting knife's blood groove, and in one of the clasp knives we found bits of bloody wool.

"Just follow my play, Eddie," Will told me. "There's a technique I worked out and you'll see how it goes."

We keep milk in a little fridge, mostly for the cats and puppies. Will poured out a glass of it and put it on the desk. The kid opened his eyes after about twelve minutes. His face was deadly pale and his blue eyes burned in the white face.

Will said, "How you feeling? Never run, son, when someone holds a gun on you. There's milk in front of you. You look a little peaked and it'll do you good."

"I don't want any milk."

"Well, it's there if you change your mind. I guess you wanted to have a look at our animals. Just your hard luck you picked tonight." He reached over and rumpled the boy's hair affectionately. "See, there was a gang of troublemakers here a few nights ago. We know who they are, we had trouble with them before. They hang out in Sayreville over to the north. They broke in the other night and killed a poor little lamb."

I was watching the kid's face. His mind wasn't all that quick and it dawned on him rather slowly that we didn't know he was Fluff's killer.

"But it's one thing to know who they are and another thing to prove it," Will went on. "So we thought we'd try catching them in the act. You just happened to drop in at the wrong time. I thought you were too young to be one of them, but when you started to bolt I couldn't take chances. That was a tranquilizer dart, by the way. We use it on animals that are impossible to control."

Like the kid himself, I thought, but Will was talking to him now in the gentle voice he uses on high-strung dogs and spooked ponies, showing him the pistol and the darts and explaining how they work.

"I guess those punks won't be here tonight after all," Will said. "You wouldn't believe what they did to a poor innocent creature. Well, they'll be back sooner or later, and when they do return we'll get them."

"What will happen to them then?" the kid asked.

"A whole lot more than they counted on, son. First off the cops will take them in the back room and pound hell out of them—kill a cop or an animal in this town and the police tend to throw the book away—but those kids won't have a mark on them. Then they'll sit in jail until their case comes up, and then they'll be in a reformatory for a minimum of three years. And I wouldn't want to tell you what happens to them in reform school. Let's just say it won't be a Sunday school picnic and let it go at that."

"Well, I guess they deserve it," the kid said.

"You bet they do."

"Anybody who'd do a thing like that," the kid added.

Will heaved a sigh. "Well, now that you're here, son, maybe we can make it up to you for scaring you like that. How about a guided tour of the place? Give you some kind of an idea of the operation we're running here."

I don't know whether the kid was enthusiastic about the idea or whether he just had the sense to give that impression. Either way, he tagged along as we led him all through the place, inside and out. We showed him around the barnyard, pointed out Fluff's mother, talked about how Fluff had been born. We showed him the dog and cat cages and the small animal section with mice and hamsters and gerbils. He was full of questions and Will gave him detailed answers.

It wasn't hard to see what Will was doing. First, we were making it obvious that we knew a decent kid like him couldn't possibly be an animal killer. We let him know that we suspected somebody else for the act and that he was home free. We reinforced things by telling him his act would have earned him precisely the sort of treatment it *should* have earned him—a good beating and a stiff sentence. Then, while all that soaked in, we made him feel a part of the animal shelter instead of an enemy.

It looked good, but I had my doubts. The kid was having too much fun making the most of the situation. He was going to go home convinced we were a couple of damn fools who couldn't recognize a villain when he almost literally fell into our laps. Still, I didn't see how we could get worse results than the police got by following the book—and Will had done this before, so I wasn't going to give him an argument.

"And this here is the incinerator," Will said finally.

"For garbage?"

"Used to be. But there's an ordinance against burning garbage within city limits, on account of the air pollution. What we use it for is disposal of dead animals." He hung his head. "Poor little Fluff went in here. All that was left of her was enough ashes to fill an envelope—a small one at that."

The kid was impressed. "How long does it take?"

"No time at all. She heats up to something like three thousand degrees Fahrenheit and nothing lasts long at that temperature." Will unhooked the cover, raised it up. "You're just about tall enough to see in there. Enough room for two or three big dogs at a time."

"I'll say."

"You could pretty near fit a pony in there."

"You sure could," the kid said. He thought for a moment, still staring down into the oven. "What would happen if you put an animal in there while it was still alive?"

"Now there's an interesting question," Will allowed. "Of course I would never do that to an animal."

"Of course not."

"Because it would be cruel."

"Sure, but I was just wondering."

"But a dirty little lamb-killing brat like you," he said, talking and moving at the same time, gripping the boy by the scruff of the neck and the seat of the pants and heaving him in one motion into the incinerator, "a brat like you is another story entirely."

The lid was closing before the kid even thought to scream. When it slammed shut and Will hooked the catch, you could barely hear the boy's voice. You could tell that he was yelling in terror, and there were also sounds of him kicking at the walls. Of course the big metal box didn't budge an inch.

"If that isn't brilliant," I said.

"I was wondering if you knew what I was leading up to."

"I didn't. I followed the psychology but didn't think it would really work. But this is just perfect."

"I'm glad you think so."

"Just perfect. Why, after the scare he's getting right now, he'll never want to look at another animal."

"The scare?" Will's face had a look on it I had never seen before. "You think all this is to *scare* him?"

He reached over and threw the switch.

Going Through the Motions

On the way home I had picked up a sack of burgers and fries at the fast-food place near the Interstate off-ramp. I popped a beer, but before I got it poured or the meal eaten I checked my phone answering machine. There was a message from Anson Pollard asking me to call him right away. His voice didn't sound right, and there was something familiar in what was wrong with it.

I ate a hamburger and drank half a beer, then made the call. He said, "Thank God, Lou. Can you come over here?"

"What's the matter?"

"Come over and I'll tell you."

I went back to the kitchen table, unwrapped a second hamburger, then wrapped it up again. I bagged the food and put it in the fridge, poured the beer down the sink.

The streetlights came on while I was driving across town to his place. No question, the days were getting longer. Not much left of spring. I switched on my headlights and thought how fast the years were starting to go, and how Anson's voice hadn't sounded right.

I parked at the head of his big circular driveway. My engine went on coughing for ten or twenty seconds after I cut the ignition. It'll do that, and the kid at the garage can't seem to figure out what to do about it. I'd had to buy my own car after the last election, and this had been as good as I could afford. Of course it didn't settle into that coughing routine until I'd owned it a month, and now it wouldn't quit.

Anson had the door open before I got to it. "Lou," he said, and gripped me by the shoulders.

He was only a year older than me, which made him forty-two, but he was showing all those years and more. He was balding and carried too much weight, but that wasn't what did it. His whole face was drawn and desperate, and I put that together with his tone of voice and knew what I'd been reminded of over the phone. He'd sounded the same way three years ago when Paula died.

"What's the matter, Anse?"

He shook his head. "Come inside," he said. I followed him to the room where he kept the liquor. Without asking he poured us each a full measure of straight bourbon. I didn't much want a drink but I took it and held onto it while he drank his all the way down. He shuddered, then took a deep breath and let it out slowly.

"Beth's been kidnapped," he said.

"When?"

"This afternoon. She left school at the usual time. She never got home. This was in the mailbox when I got home. It hadn't gone through the mails. They just stuck it in the box."

I removed a sheet of paper from the envelope he handed me, unfolded it.

Words cut from a newspaper, fastened in place with rubber cement. I brought the paper close to my face and sniffed at it.

He asked me what I was doing. "Sometimes you can tell by the smell when the thing was prepared. The solvent evaporates, so if you can still smell it it's recent."

"Does it matter when they prepared the note?"

"Probably not. Force of habit, I guess." I'd been sheriff for three terms before Wallace Hines rode into office on the governor's coattails. Old habits die hard.

"I just can't understand it," he was saying. "She knew not to get in a stranger's car. I don't know how many times I told her."

"I used to talk about that at school assemblies, Anse. 'Don't go with strangers. Don't accept food or candy from people you don't know. Cross at corners. Don't ever play in an old icebox.' Lord, all the things you have to tell them."

"I can't understand it."

"How old is Bethie?" I'd almost said was, caught myself in time. That would have crushed him. The idea that she might already be dead was one neither of us would voice. It hung in the room like a silent third party to the conversation.

"She's nine. Ten in August. Lou, she's all I've got in the world, all that's left to me of Paula. Lou, I've got to get her back."

I looked at the note again. "Says a quarter of a million dollars," I said.

"I know."

"Have you got it?"

"I can raise it. I'll go talk to Jim McVeigh at the bank tomorrow. He doesn't have to know what I need it for. I've borrowed large sums in cash before on a signature loan, for a real estate deal or something like that. He won't ask too many questions."

"Says old bills, out of sequence. Nothing larger than a twenty. He'll fill an order like that and think it's for real estate?"

He poured himself another drink. I still hadn't touched mine. "Maybe he'll figure it out," he allowed. "He still won't ask questions. And he won't carry tales, either."

"Well, you're a good customer down there. And a major stockholder, aren't you?"

"I have some shares, yes."

I looked at the note, then at him. "Says no police and no FBI," I said. "What do you think about that?"

"That's what I was going to ask you."

"Well, you might want to call Wally Hines. They tell me he's the sheriff."

"You don't think much of Hines."

"Not a whole lot," I admitted, "but I'm prejudiced on the subject. He doesn't run the department the way I did. Well, I didn't do things the way my predecessor did, either. Old Bill Hurley. He probably didn't think much of me, old Hurley."

"Should I call Hines?"

"I wouldn't. It says here they'll kill her if you do. I don't know that they're watching the house, but it wouldn't be hard for them to know if the sheriff's office came in on the operation." I shrugged. "I don't know what Hines could do, to tell you the truth. You want to pay the ransom?"

"Of course I do."

"Hines could maybe set up a stakeout, catch the kidnapper when he picks up the ransom. But they generally don't release the victim until after they get away clean with the ransom." If ever, I thought. "Now as far as the FBI is concerned, they know their job. They can look at the note and figure out what newspaper the words came from, where the paper was purchased, the envelope, all of that. They'll dust for fingerprints and find mine and yours, but I don't guess the kidnapper's were on here in the first place. What you might want to do, you might want to call the Bureau as soon as you get Bethie back. They've got the machinery and the know-how to nail those boys afterward."

"But you wouldn't call them until then?"

"I wouldn't," I said. "Not that I'm going to tell you what to do or not to do, but I wouldn't do it myself. Not if it were my little girl."

We talked about some things. He poured another drink and I finally got around to sipping at the one he'd poured me when I first walked in. We'd been in that same room three years ago, drinking the same brand of whiskey. He'd managed to hold himself together through Paula's funeral, and after everybody else cleared out and Bethie was asleep he and I settled in with a couple of bottles. Tonight I would take it easy on the booze, but that night three years ago I'd matched him drink for drink.

Out of the blue he said, "She could have been, you know." I missed the connection. "Could have been your little girl," he explained. "Bethie could have. If you'd have married Paula."

"If your grandmother had wheels she'd be a tea cart."

" 'But she'd still be your grandmother.' Isn't that what we used to say? You could have married Paula."

"She had too much sense for that." Though the cards might have played that way, if Anson Pollard hadn't come along. Now Paula was three years dead, dead of anaphylactic shock from a bee sting, if you can believe it. And the woman I'd married, and a far cry from Paula she was, had left me and gone to California. I heard someone say that the Lord took the United States by the state of Maine and lifted, so that everything loose wound up in Southern California. Well, she was and she did, and now Anse and I were a couple of solitary birds going long in the tooth. Take away thirty pounds and a few million dollars and a nine-year-old girl with freckles and you'd be hard-pressed to tell us apart.

Take away a nine-year-old girl with freckles. Somebody'd done just that.

"You'll see me through this," he said. "Won't you, Lou?"

"If it's what you want."

"I wish to hell you were still sheriff. The voters of this county never had any sense."

"Maybe it's better that I'm not. This way I'm just a private citizen, nobody for the kidnappers to get excited about."

"I want you to work for me after this is over."

"Well, now."

"We can work out the details later. By God, I should have hired you the minute the election results came in. I figured we knew each other too well, we'd been through too much together. But you can do better working for me than you're doing now, and I can use you, I know I can. We'll talk about it later."

"We'll see."

"Lou, we'll get her back, won't we?"

"Sure we will, Anse. Of course we will."

Well, you have to go through the motions. There was no phone call that night. If the victim's alive they generally make a call and let you hear their voice. On tape, maybe, but reading that day's newspaper so you can place the recording in time. Any proof they can give you that the person's alive makes it that much more certain you'll pay the ransom.

Of course nothing's hard and fast. Kidnapping's an amateur crime and every fool who tries it has to make up his own rules. So it didn't necessarily prove anything that there was no call.

I hung around, waiting it out with him. He hit the bourbon pretty hard but he was always a man who could take on a heavy load without showing it much. Somewhere along the way I went into the kitchen and made a pot of coffee.

A little past midnight I said, "I don't guess there's going to be a call tonight, Anse. I'm gonna head for home."

He wanted me to stay over. He had reasons—in case there was a call in the middle of the night, in case something called for action. I told him he had my number and he could call me at any hour. What we both knew is his real reason was he didn't want to be alone there, and I thought about staying with him and decided I didn't want to. The hours were just taking too long to go by, and I didn't figure I'd get a good night's sleep under his roof.

I drove right on home. I kept it under the speed limit because I didn't want one of Wally Hines's eager beavers coming up behind me with the siren wailing. They'll do that now. We hardly ever gave out tickets to local people when I was running the show, just a warning and a soft one at that. We saved the tickets for the leadfoot tourists. Well, another man's apt to have his own way of doing things.

In my own house I popped a beer and ate my leftover hamburger. It was cold with the grease congealed on it but I was hungry enough to get it down. I could have had something out of Anse's refrigerator but I hadn't been hungry while I was there.

I sat in a chair and put on Johnny Carson but didn't even try to pay attention. I thought how little Bethie was dead and buried somewhere that nobody would likely ever find her. Because that was the way it read, even if it wasn't what Anse and I dared to say to each other. I sat there and thought how Paula was dead of a bee sting and my wife was on the other side of the continent and now Bethie. Thoughts swirled around in my head like water going down a bathtub drain.

I was up a long while. The television was still on when they were playing the "Star-Spangled Banner," and I might as well have been watching programs in Japanese for all the sense they made to me.

Somewhere down the line I went to bed.

I was eating a sweet roll and drinking a cup of coffee when he called. There'd been a phone call just moments earlier from the kidnapper, he told me, his voice hoarse with the strain of it all.

"He whispered. I was half asleep, I could barely make out what he was saying. I was afraid to ask him to repeat anything. I was just afraid, Lou."

"You get everything?"

"I think so. I have to buy a special suitcase, I have to pack it a certain way and chuck it into a culvert at a certain time." He mentioned some of the specifics. I was only half listening. Then he said, "I asked them to let me talk to Bethie."

"And?"

"It was as if he didn't even hear me. He just went on telling me things, and I asked him again and he hung up."

She was dead and in the ground, I thought.

I said, "He probably made the call from a pay phone. Most likely they're keeping her at a farmhouse somewhere and he wouldn't want to chance a trace on the call. He wouldn't have her along to let her talk, he wouldn't want to take the chance. And he'd speed up the conversation to keep it from being traced at all."

"I thought of that, Lou. I just wished I could have heard her voice."

He'd never hear her voice again, I thought. My mind filled with an image of a child's broken body on a patch of ground, and a big man a few yards from her, holding a shovel, digging. I blinked my eyes, trying to chase the image, but it just went and hovered there on the edge of thought.

"You'll hear it soon enough," I said. "You'll have her back soon."

"Can you come over, Lou?"

"Hell, I'm on my way."

I poured what was left of my coffee down the sink. I took the sweet roll with me, ate it on the way to the car. The sun was up but there was no warmth in it yet.

In the picture I'd had, with the child's corpse and the man digging, a light rain had been falling. But there'd been no rain yesterday and it didn't look likely today. A man's mind'll do tricky things, fill in details on its own. A scene like that, gloomy and all, it seems like there ought to be rain. So the mind just sketches it in.

On the way to the bank he said, "Lou, I want to hire you."

"Well, I don't know," I said. "I guess we can talk about it after Bethie's back and all this is over, but I'm not even sure I want to stay around town, Anse. I've been talking with some people down in Florida and there might be something for me down there."

"I can do better for you than some crackers down in Florida," he said gruffly. "But I'm not talking about that, I'm talking about now. I want to hire you to help me get Bethie back."

I shook my head. "You can't pay me for that, Anson."

"Why the hell not?"

"Because I won't take the money. Did you even think I would?"

"No. I guess I just wish you would. I'm going to have to lean on you some, Lou. It seems a lot to ask as a favor."

"It's not such a much," I said. "All I'll be doing is standing alongside you and backing you up." Going through the motions with you, I thought.

I waited in the car while he went into the bank. I might have played the radio but he'd taken the keys with him. Force of habit, I guess. I just sat and waited.

He didn't have the money when he came out. "Jim has to make a call or two to get that much cash together," he explained. "It'll be ready by two this afternoon."

"Did he want to know what it was for?"

"I told him I had a chance to purchase an Impressionist painting from a collector who'd had financial reverses. The painting's provenance was clear but the sale had to be a secret and the payment had to be in cash for tax purposes."

"That's a better story than a real estate deal."

He managed a smile. "It seemed more imaginative. He didn't question it. We'd better buy that suitcase."

We parked in front of a luggage and leather goods store on Grandview Avenue. I remembered they'd had a holdup there while I was sheriff. The proprietor had been shot in the shoulder but had recovered well enough. I went in with him and Anson bought a plaid canvas suitcase. The whisperer had described the bag very precisely.

"He's a fussy son of a bitch," I said. "Maybe he's got an outfit he wants it to match."

Anse paid cash for the bag. On the drive back to his house I said, "What you were saying yesterday, Anse, that Bethie could have been mine. She's spit and image of you. You'd hardly guess she was Paula's child."

"She has her mother's softness, though."

A child's crumpled body, a man turning shovelfuls of earth, a light rain falling. I kept putting the rain into that picture. A mind's a damn stubborn thing.

"Maybe she does," I said. "But one look at her and you know she's her father's daughter."

His hands tightened on the steering wheel. I pictured Paula in my mind, and then Bethie. Then my own wife, for some reason, but it was a little harder to bring her image into focus.

Until it was time to go to the bank we sat around waiting for the phone to ring. The whisperer had told Anse there wouldn't be any more calls, but what guarantee was that?

He mostly talked about Paula, maybe to keep from talking about Bethie. It bothered me some, the turn the conversation was taking, but I don't guess I let it show.

When the phone finally did ring it was McVeigh at the bank, saying the money was ready. Anse took the new plaid suitcase and got in his car, and I followed him down there in my own car. He parked in the bank's lot. I found a spot on the street. It was a little close to a fireplug, but I was behind the wheel with the motor running and didn't figure I had much to worry about from Wally's boys in blue.

He was in the bank a long time. I kept looking at my watch and every few hours another minute would pass. Then he came out of the bank's front door and the suitcase looked heavier than when he'd gone in there. He came straight to the car and went around to the back. I'd left the trunk unlocked and he tossed the suitcase inside and slammed it shut.

He got in beside me and I drove. "I feel like a bank robber," he said. "I come out with the money and you've got the motor running."

My car picked that moment to backfire. "Some getaway car," I said.

I kept an eye on the rearview mirror. I'd suggested taking my car just in case anybody was watching him. McVeigh might have acted on suspicions, I'd told Anse, and might say something to law enforcement people without saying anything to us. It wouldn't do to be tailed to the overpass where the exchange was supposed to take place. If the kidnappers spotted a tail they might panic and kill Bethie.

Of course I didn't believe for a moment she was still alive. But you play these things by the book. What else can you do?

No one was following us. I cut the engine when we got to the designated spot. It was an overpass, and a good spot for a drop. A person could be waiting below, hidden from view, and he could pick up the suitcase and get out of there on foot and nobody up above could do anything about it.

The engine coughed and coughed and sputtered and finally cut out. Anse told me I ought to get it fixed. I didn't bother saying that nobody seemed to be able to fix it. "Just sit here," I told him. "I'll take care of it."

I got out of the car, went around to the trunk. He was watching as I carried the plaid suitcase and sent it sailing over the rail. I heard the car door open, and then he was standing beside me, trying to see where it had landed. I pointed to the spot but he couldn't see it, and I'm not sure there was anything to see.

"I can't look down from heights," he said.

"Nothing to look at anyway."

We got back in the car. I dropped him at the bank, and on the way there he asked if the kidnappers would keep their end of the bargain. "They said she'd be delivered to the house within the next four hours," he said. "But would they take the chance of delivering her to the house?"

"Probably not," I told him. "Easiest thing would be to drive her into the middle of one town or another and just let her out of the car. Somebody'll find her and call you right off. Bethie knows her phone number, doesn't she?"

"Of course she does."

"Best thing is for you to be at home and wait for a call."

"You'll come over, Lou, won't you?"

I said I would. He went to get his car from the lot and I drove to my house to check the mail. It didn't take me too long to get to his place, and we sat around waiting for a call I knew would never come.

Because it was pretty clear somebody local had taken her. An out-of-towner wouldn't have known what a perfect spot that overpass was for dropping a suitcase of ransom money. An out-of-towner wouldn't have sent Anse to a specific luggage shop to buy a specific suitcase. An out-of-towner probably wouldn't have known how to spot Bethie Pollard in the first place.

And a local person wouldn't dare leave her alive, because she was old enough and bright enough to tell people who had taken her. It stood to reason that she'd been killed right away, as soon as she'd been snatched, and that her corpse had been covered with fresh earth before the ransom note had been delivered to Anson's mailbox.

After I don't know how long he said, "I don't like it, Lou. We should have heard something by now."

"Could be they're playing it cagey."

"What do you mean?"

"Could be they're watching that dropped suitcase, waiting to make sure it's not staked out."

He started. "Staked out?"

"Well, say you'd gone and alerted the Bureau. What they might have done is staked out the area of the drop and just watched and waited to see who picked up the suitcase. Now a kidnapper might decide to play it just as cagey his own self. Maybe they'll wait twenty-four hours before they make their move."

"God."

"Or maybe they picked it up before it so much as bounced, say, but they want to hold onto Bethie long enough to be sure the bills aren't in sequence and there's no electronic bug in the suitcase."

"Or maybe they're not going to release her, Lou."

"You don't want to think about that, Anse."

"No," he said. "I don't want to think about it."

He started in on the bourbon then, and I was relieved to see him do it. I figured he needed it. To tell the truth, I had a thirst for it myself right about then. The plain fact is that sitting and waiting is the hardest thing I know about, especially when you're waiting for something that's not going to happen.

I was about ready to make an excuse and go on home when the doorbell rang. "Maybe that's her now," he said. "Maybe they waited until dark." But there was a hollow tone in his voice, as if to say he didn't believe it himself.

"I'll get it," I told him. "You stay where you are."

There were two men at the door. They were almost my height, dressed alike in business suits, and holding guns, nasty little black things. First thought I had was they were robbers, and what crossed my mind was how bad Anse's luck had turned.

Then one of them said, "FBI," and showed me an ID I didn't have time to read. "Let's go inside," he said, and we did.

Anse had a glass in his hand. His face didn't look a whole lot different from before. If he was surprised he didn't much show it.

One of them said, "Mr. Pollard? We kept the drop site under careful observation for three full hours. In that time no one approached the suitcase. The only persons entering the culvert were two boys approximately ten years old, and they never went near the suitcase."

"Ten years old," Anse said.

"After three hours Agent Boudreau and I went down into the culvert and examined the suitcase. The only contents were dummy packages like this one." He showed a banded stack of bills, then riffled it to reveal that only the top and bottom were currency. The rest of the stack consisted of newspaper cut the size of bills.

"I guess your stakeout wasn't such a much," I said. "Anse, why didn't you tell me you decided to call the Bureau after all?"

"Jim McVeigh called them," he said. "They were there when I went to get the money. I didn't know anything about it until then."

"Well, either we beat 'em to the drop site or they don't know much about staking a place out. You get people who aren't local and it's easy for them to make a mistake, I guess. The kidnappers just went and switched suitcases on you. You saw a suitcase still lying in the weeds and you figured nobody'd come by yet, but it looks like you were wrong." I took a breath and let it out slow. "Maybe they saw you there after they told Anse not to go to the cops. Maybe that's why Bethie's not home yet."

"That's not why," one of them said. Boudreau, I guess his name was. "We were there to see you fling that case over the railing. I had it under observation through high-powered field glasses from the moment it landed and I didn't take my eyes off it until we went and had a look at it."

Must have been tiring, I thought, staring through binoculars for three full hours.

"Nobody touched the suitcase," the other one said. "There was a rip in the side from when it landed. It was the same suitcase."

"That proves a lot, a rip in the side of a suitcase."

"There was a switch," Boudreau said. "You made it. You had a second suitcase in the trunk of your car, underneath the blankets and junk you carry around. Mr. Pollard here put the suitcase full of money in your trunk. Then you got the other case out of the trunk and threw it over the side."

"Her father taught her not to go with strangers," the other said. I never did get his name. "But you weren't a stranger, were you? You were a friend of the family. The sheriff, the man who lectured on safety procedures. She got in your car without a second thought, didn't she?"

"Anse," I said, "tell them they're crazy, will you?"

He didn't say anything.

Boudreau said, "We found the money, Mr. Pollard. That's what took so long. We wanted to find it before confronting him. He'd taken up some floorboards and stashed the money under them, still in the suitcase it was packed in. We didn't turn up any evidence of your daughter's presence. He may never have taken her anywhere near his house."

"This is all crazy," I said, but it was as if they didn't hear me.

"We think he killed her immediately upon picking her up," Boudreau went on. "He'd have to do that. She knew him, after all. His only chance to get away with it lay in murdering her."

My mind filled with that picture again. Bethie's crumpled body lying on the ground in that patch of woods the other side of Little Cross Creek. And a big man turning the damp earth with a spade. I could feel a soreness in my shoulders from the digging.

I should have dug that hole the day before. Having to do it with Bethie lying there, that was a misery. Better by far to have it dug ahead of time and just drop her in and shovel on the lid, but you can't plan everything right.

Not that I ever had much chance of getting away with it, now that I looked at it straight on. I'd had this picture of myself down in the Florida sun with more money than God's rich uncle, but I don't guess I ever really thought it would happen that way. I suppose all I wanted was to take a few things away from Anson Pollard.

I sort of tuned out for a while there. Then one of them—I'm not even sure which one—was reading me my rights. I just stood there, not looking at anybody, least of all at Anse. And not listening too close to what they were saying.

Then they were asking me where the body was, and talking about checking the stores to find out when I'd bought the duplicate suitcase, and asking other questions that would build the case against me. I sort of pulled myself together and said that somebody was evidently trying real hard to frame me and I couldn't understand why but in the meantime I wasn't going to answer any questions without a lawyer present.

Not that I expected it would do me much good. But you have to make an effort, you have to play the hand out. What else can you do? You go through the motions, that's all.

Good for the Soul

In the morning, Warren Cuttleton left his furnished room on West Eighty-third Street and walked over to Broadway. It was a clear day, cool, but not cold, bright but not dazzling. At the corner, Mr. Cuttleton bought a copy of the *Daily Mirror* from the blind newsdealer who sold him a paper every morning and who, contrary to established stereotype, recognized him by neither voice nor step. He took his paper to the cafeteria where he always ate breakfast, kept it tucked tidily under his arm while he bought a sweet roll and a cup of coffee, and sat down alone at a small table to eat the roll, drink the coffee, and read the *Daily Mirror* cover to cover.

When he reached page three, he stopped eating the roll and set the coffee aside. He read a story about a woman who had been killed the evening before in Central Park. The woman, named Margaret Waldek, had worked as a nurse's aide at Flower Fifth Avenue Hospital. At midnight her shift had ended. On her way home through the park, someone had thrown her down, assaulted her, and stabbed her far too many times in the chest and abdomen. There was a long and rather colorful story to this effect, coupled with a moderately grisly picture of the late Margaret Waldek. Warren Cuttleton read the story and looked at the grisly picture.

And remembered.

The memory rushed upon him with the speed of a rumor. A walk through the park. The night air. A knife—long, cold—in one hand. The knife's handle moist with his own urgent perspiration. The waiting, alone in the cold. Footsteps, then coming closer, and his own movement off the path and into the shadows, and the woman in view. And the awful fury of his attack, the fear and pain in the woman's face, her screams in his ears. And the knife, going up and coming down, rising and descending. The screams peaking and abruptly ending. The blood.

He was dizzy. He looked at his hand, expecting to see a knife glistening there. He was holding two thirds of a sweet roll. His fingers opened. The roll dropped a few inches to the tabletop. He thought that he was going to be sick, but this did not happen.

"Oh, God," he said, very softly. No one seemed to hear him. He said it again, somewhat louder, and lit a cigarette with trembling hands. He tried to blow out the match and kept missing it. He dropped the match to the floor and stepped on it and took a very large breath.

He had killed a woman. No one he knew, no one he had ever seen before. He was a word in headlines—fiend, attacker, killer. He was a murderer, and the police would find him and make him confess, and there would be a trial and a conviction and an appeal and a denial and a cell and a long walk and an electrical jolt and then, mercifully, nothing at all.

He closed his eyes. His hands curled up into fists, and he pressed his fists against his temples and took furious breaths. Why had he done it? What was wrong with him? Why, why, why had he killed?

Why would *anyone* kill?

He sat at his table until he had smoked three cigarettes, lighting each new one from the butt of the one preceding it. When the last cigarette was quite finished he got up from the table and went to the phone booth. He dropped a dime and dialed a number and waited until someone answered the phone.

"Cuttleton," he said. "I won't be in today. Not feeling well."

One of the office girls had taken the call. She said that it was too bad and she hoped Mr. Cuttleton would be feeling better. He thanked her and rang off.

Not feeling well! He had never called in sick in the twenty-three years he had worked at the Bardell Company, except for two times when he had been running a fever. They would believe him, of course. He did not lie and did not cheat and his employers knew this. But it bothered him to lie to them.

But then it was no lie, he thought. He was not feeling well, not feeling well at all.

On the way back to his room he bought the *Daily News* and the *Herald Tribune* and the *Times*. The *News* gave him no trouble, as it too had the story of the Waldek murder on page three, and ran a similar picture and a similar text. It was harder to find the stories in the *Times* and the *Herald Tribune*; both of those papers buried the murder story deep in the second section, as if it were trivial. He could not understand that.

That evening he bought the *Journal American* and the *World Telegram* and the *Post*. The *Post* ran an interview with Margaret Waldek's half sister, a very sad interview indeed. Warren Cuttleton wept as he read it, shedding tears in equal measure for Margaret Waldek and for himself.

At seven o'clock, he told himself that he was surely doomed. He had killed and he would be killed in return.

At nine o'clock, he thought that he might get away with it. He gathered from the newspaper stories that the police had no substantial clues. Fingerprints were not mentioned, but he knew for a fact that his own fingerprints were not on file anywhere. He had never been fingerprinted. So, unless someone had seen him, the police would have no way to connect him with the murder. And he could not remember having been seen by anyone.

He went to bed at midnight. He slept fitfully, reliving every unpleasant detail of the night before—the footsteps, the attack, the knife, the blood, his flight from the park. He awoke for the last time at seven o'clock, woke at the peak of a nightmare with sweat streaming from every pore.

Surely there was no escape if he dreamed those dreams night after endless night. He was no psychopath; right and wrong had a great deal of personal meaning to him. Redemption in the embrace of an electrified chair seemed the least horrible of all possible punishments. He no longer wanted to get away with the murder. He wanted to get away *from* it.

He went outside and bought a paper. There had been no developments in the case. He read an interview in the *Mirror* with Margaret Waldek's little niece, and it made him cry.

He had never been to the police station before. It stood only a few blocks from his rooming house but he had never passed it, and he had to look up its address in the telephone directory. When he got there he stumbled around aimlessly looking for someone in a little authority. He finally located the desk sergeant and explained that he wanted to see someone about the Waldek killing.

"Waldek," the desk sergeant said.

"The woman in the park."

"Oh. Information?"

"Yes," Mr. Cuttleton said.

He waited on a wooden bench while the desk sergeant called upstairs to find out who had the Waldek thing. Then the desk sergeant told him to go upstairs where he would see a Sergeant Rooker. He did this.

Rooker was a young man with a thoughtful face. He said yes, he was in charge of the Waldek killing, and just to start things off, could he have name and address and some other details?

Warren Cuttleton gave him all the details he wanted. Rooker wrote them all down with a ballpoint pen on a sheet of yellow foolscap. Then he looked up thoughtfully.

"Well, that's out of the way," he said. "Now what have you got for us?"

"Myself," Mr. Cuttleton said. And when Sergeant Rooker frowned curiously he explained, "I did it. I killed that woman, that Margaret Waldek, I did it."

Sergeant Rooker and another policeman took him into a private room and asked him a great many questions. He explained everything exactly as he remembered it, from beginning to end. He told them the whole story, trying his best to avoid breaking down at the more horrible parts. He only broke down twice. He did not cry at those times, but his chest filled and his throat closed and he found it temporarily impossible to go on.

Questions—

"Where did you get the knife?"

"A store. A five-and-ten."

"Where?"

"On Columbus Avenue."

"Remember the store?"

He remembered the counter, a salesman, remembered paying for the knife and carrying it away. He did not remember which store it had been.

"Why did you do it?"

"I don't know."

"Why the Waldek woman?"

"She just . . . came along."

"Why did you attack her?"

"I wanted to. Something . . . came over me. Some need, I didn't understand it then, I don't understand it now. Compulsion. I just had to do it!"

"Why kill her?"

"It happened that way. I killed her, the knife, up, down. That was why I bought the knife. To kill her."

"You planned it?"

"Just . . . hazily."

"Where's the knife?"

"Gone. Away. Down a sewer."

"What sewer?"

"I don't remember. Somewhere."

"You got blood on your clothes. You must have, she bled like a flood. Your clothes at home?"

"I got rid of them."

"Where? Down a sewer?"

"Look, Ray, you don't third-degree a guy when he's trying to confess something."

"I'm sorry. Cuttleton, are the clothes around your building?"

He had vague memories, something about burning. "An incinerator," he said.

"The incinerator in your building?"

"No. Some other building, there isn't any incinerator where I live. I went home and changed, I remember it, and I bundled up the clothes and ran into another building and put everything in an incinerator and ran back to my room. I washed. There was blood under my fingernails, I remember it."

They had him take off his shirt. They looked at his arms and his chest and his face and his neck.

"No scratches," Sergeant Rooker said. "Not a mark, and she had stuff under her nails, from scratching."

"Ray, she could have scratched herself."

"Mmmm. Or he mends quick. Come on, Cuttleton."

They went to a room, fingerprinted him, took his picture, and booked him on suspicion of murder. Sergeant Rooker told him that he could call a lawyer if he wanted one. He did not know any lawyers. There had been a lawyer who had notarized a paper for him once, long ago, but he did not remember the man's name.

They took him to a cell. He went inside, and they closed the door and locked it. He sat down on a stool and smoked a cigarette. His hands did not shake now for the first time in almost twenty-seven hours.

Four hours later Sergeant Rooker and the other policeman came into his cell. Rooker said, "You didn't kill that woman, Mr. Cuttleton. Now why did you tell us you did?"

He stared at them.

"First, you had an alibi and you didn't mention it. You went to a double feature at Loew's Eighty-third, the cashier recognized you from a picture and remembered you bought a ticket at nine-thirty. An usher also recognized you and remembers you tripped on your way to the men's room and he had to give you a hand, and that was after midnight. You went straight to your room, one of the women lives downstairs remembers that. The fellow down the hall from you swears you were in your room by one and never left it and the lights were out fifteen minutes after you got there. Now why in the name of heaven did you tell us you killed that woman?"

This was incredible. He did not remember any movies. He did not remember buying a ticket, or tripping on the way to the men's room. Nothing like that. He remembered only the lurking and the footsteps and the attack, the knife and the screams, the knife down a sewer and the clothes in some incinerator and washing away the blood.

"More. We got what must be the killer. A man named Alex Kanster, convicted on two counts of attempted assault. We picked him up on a routine check and found a bloody knife under his pillow and his face torn and scratched, and I'll give three-to-one he's confessed by now, and he killed the Waldek woman and you didn't, so why the confession? Why give us trouble? Why lie?"

"I don't lie," Mr. Cuttleton said.

Rooker opened his mouth and closed it. The other policeman said, "Ray, I've got an idea. Get someone who knows how to administer a polygraph thing."

He was very confused. They led him to another room and strapped him to an odd machine with a graph, and they asked him questions. What was his name? How old was he? Where did he work? Did he kill the Waldek woman? How much was four and four? Where did he buy the knife? What was his middle name? Where did he put his clothes?

"Nothing," the other policeman said. "No reaction. See? He *believes* it, Ray."

"Maybe he just doesn't react to this. It doesn't work on everybody."

"So ask him to lie."

"Mr. Cuttleton," Sergeant Rooker said, "I'm going to ask you how much four and three is. I want you to answer six. Just answer six."

"But it's seven."

"Say six anyway, Mr. Cuttleton."

"Oh."

"How much is four and three?"

"Six."

He reacted, and heavily. "What it is," the other cop explained, "is he believes this, Ray. He didn't mean to make trouble, he believes it, true or not. You know what an imagination does, how witnesses swear to lies because they remember things wrong. He read the story and he believed it all from the start."

They talked to him for a long time, Rooker and the other policeman, explaining every last bit of it. They told him he felt guilty, he had some repression deep down in his sad soul, and this made him believe that he had killed Mrs. Waldek when, in fact, he had not. For a long time he thought that they were crazy, but in time they proved to him that it was quite impossible for him to have done what he said he had done. It could not have happened that way, and they proved it, and there was no argument he could advance to tear down the proof they offered him. He had to believe it.

Well!

He believed them, he knew they were right and he—his memory—was wrong. This did not change the fact that he remembered the killing. Every detail was still quite clear in his mind. This meant, obviously, that he was insane.

"Right about now," Sergeant Rooker said, perceptively, "you probably think you're crazy. Don't worry about it, Mr. Cuttleton. This confession urge isn't as uncommon as you might think. Every publicized killing brings us a dozen confessions, with some of them dead sure they really did it. You have the urge to kill locked up inside somewhere, you feel guilty about it, so you confess to what you maybe wanted to do deep in your mind but would never really do. We get this all the time. Not many of them are as sure of it as you, as clear on everything. The lie detector is what got to me. But don't worry about being crazy, it's nothing you can't control. Just don't sweat it."

"Psychological," the other policeman said.

"You'll probably have this bit again," Rooker went on. "Don't let it get to you. Just ride it out and remember you couldn't possibly kill anybody and you'll get through all right. But no more confessions. Okay?"

For a time he felt like a stupid child. Then he felt relieved, tremendously relieved. There would be no electrified chair. There would be no perpetual burden of guilt.

That night he slept. No dreams.

That was March. Four months later, in July, it happened again. He awoke, he went downstairs, he walked to the corner, he bought the *Daily Mirror*, he sat down at a table with his sweet roll and his coffee, he opened the paper to page three, and he read about a schoolgirl, fourteen, who had walked home the night before in Astoria and who had not reached her home because some man had dragged her into an alley and had slashed her throat open with a straight razor. There was a grisly picture of the girl's body, her throat cut from ear to ear.

Memory, like a stroke of white lightning across a flat black sky. Memory, illuminating all.

He remembered the razor in his hand, the girl struggling in his grasp. He remembered the soft feel of her frightened young flesh, the moans she made, the incredible supply of blood that poured forth from her wounded throat.

The memory was so real that it was several moments before he remembered that his rush of awful memory was not a new phenomenon. He recalled that other memory, in March, and remembered it again. That had been false. This, obviously, was false as well.

But it could not be false. He *remembered* it. Every detail, so clear, so crystal clear.

He fought with himself, telling himself that Sergeant Rooker had told him to expect a repeat performance of this false-confession impulse. But logic can have little effect upon the certain mind. If one holds a rose in one's hand, and feels that rose, and smells the sweetness of it, and is hurt by the prick of its thorns, all the rational thought in creation will not serve to sway one's conviction that this rose is a reality. And a rose in memory is as unshakable as a rose in hand.

Warren Cuttleton went to work that day. It did him no good, and did his employers no good either, since he could not begin to concentrate on the papers on his desk. He could only think of the foul killing of Sandra Gitler. He knew that he could not possibly have killed the girl. He knew, too, that he had done so.

An office girl asked him if he was feeling well, he looked all concerned and unhappy and everything. A partner in the firm asked him if he had had a physical checkup recently. At five o'clock he went home. He had to fight with himself to stay away from the police station, but he stayed away.

The dreams were very vivid. He awoke again and again. Once he cried out. In the morning, when he gave up the attempt to sleep, his sheets were wet with his perspiration. It had soaked through to the mattress. He took a long shivering shower and dressed. He went downstairs, and he walked to the police station.

Last time, he had confessed. They had proved him innocent. It seemed impossible that they could have been wrong, just as it seemed impossible that he could have killed Sandra Gitler, but perhaps Sergeant Rooker could lay the girl's ghost for him. The confession, the proof of his own real innocence—then he could sleep at night once again.

He did not stop to talk to the desk sergeant. He went directly upstairs and found Rooker, who blinked at him.

"Warren Cuttleton," Sergeant Rooker said. "A confession?"

"I tried not to come. Yesterday, I remembered killing the girl in Queens. I know I did it, and I know I couldn't have done it, but—"

"You're sure you did it."

"Yes."

Sergeant Rooker understood. He led Cuttleton to a room, not a cell, and told him to stay there for a moment. He came back a few moments later.

"I called Queens Homicide," he said. "Found out a few things about the murder, some things that didn't get into the paper. Do you remember carving something into the girl's belly?"

He remembered. The razor, slicing through her bare flesh, carving something.

"What did you carve, Mr. Cuttleton?"

"I . . . I can't remember, exactly."

"You carved *I love you.* Do you remember?"

Yes, he remembered. Carving *I love you,* carving those three words into that tender flesh, proving that his horrid act was an act of love as well as an act of destruction. Oh, he remembered. It was clear in his mind, like a well-washed window.

"Mr. Cuttleton. Mr. Cuttleton, that wasn't what was carved in the girl. Mr. Cuttleton, the words were unprintable, the first word was unprintable, the second word was *you.* Not *I love you,* something else. That was why they kept it out of the papers, that and to keep off false confessions which is, believe me, a good idea.

Your memory picked up on that the minute I said it, like the power of suggestion. It didn't happen, just like you never touched that girl, but something got triggered in your head so you snapped it up and remembered it like you remembered everything you read in the paper, the same thing."

For several moments he sat looking at his fingernails while Sergeant Rooker sat looking at him. Then he said, slowly, "I knew all along I couldn't have done it. But that didn't help."

"I see."

"I had to prove it. You can't remember something, every last bit of it, and then just tell yourself that you're crazy. That it simply did not happen. I couldn't sleep."

"Well."

"I had dreams. Reliving the whole thing in my dreams, like last time. I knew I shouldn't come here, that it's wasting your time. There's knowing and knowing, Sergeant."

"And you had to have it proved to you."

He nodded miserably. Sergeant Rooker told him it was nothing to sweat about, that it took some police time but that the police really had more time than some people thought, though they had less time than some other people thought, and that Mr. Cuttleton could come to him anytime he had something to confess.

"Straight to me," Sergeant Rooker said. "That makes it easier, because I understand you, what you go through, and some of the other boys who aren't familiar might not understand."

He thanked Sergeant Rooker and shook hands with him. He walked out of the station, striding along like an ancient mariner who had just had an albatross removed from his shoulders. He slept that night, dreamlessly.

It happened again in August. A woman strangled to death in her apartment on West Twenty-seventh Street, strangled with a piece of electrical wire. He remembered buying an extension cord the day before for just that purpose.

This time he went to Rooker immediately. It was no problem at all. The police had caught the killer just minutes after the late editions of the morning papers had been locked up and printed. The janitor did it, the janitor of the woman's building. They caught him and he confessed.

On a clear afternoon that followed on the heels of a rainy morning in late September, Warren Cuttleton came home from the Bardell office and stopped at a Chinese laundry to pick up his shirts. He carried his shirts around the corner to a drugstore on Amsterdam Avenue and bought a tin of aspirin tablets. On the way back to his rooming house he passed—or started to pass—a small hardware store.

Something happened.

He walked into the store in robotish fashion, as though some alien had taken over control of his body, borrowing it for the time being. He waited patiently while the clerk finished selling a can of putty to a flat-nosed man. Then he bought an ice pick.

He went back to his room. He unpacked his shirts—six of them, white, stiffly starched, each with the same conservative collar, each bought at the same small haberdashery—and he packed them away in his dresser. He took two of the aspirin tablets and put the tin in the top drawer of the dresser. He held the ice pick between his hands and rubbed his hands over it, feeling the smoothness of the wooden handle and stroking the cool steel of the blade. He touched the tip of his thumb with the point of the blade and felt how deliciously sharp it was.

He put the ice pick in his pocket. He sat down and smoked a cigarette, slowly, and then he went downstairs and walked over to Broadway. At Eighty-sixth Street he went downstairs into the IRT station, dropped a token, passed through the turnstile. He took a train uptown to Washington Heights. He left the train, walked to a small park. He stood in the park for fifteen minutes, waiting.

He left the park. The air was chillier now and the sky was quite dark. He went to a restaurant, a small diner on Dyckman Avenue. He ordered the chopped sirloin, very well done, with french-fried potatoes and a cup of coffee. He enjoyed his meal very much.

In the men's room at the diner he took the ice pick from his pocket and caressed it once again. So very sharp, so very strong. He smiled at the ice pick and kissed the tip of it with his lips parted so as to avoid pricking himself. So very sharp, so very cool.

He paid his check and tipped the counterman and left the diner. Night now, cold enough to freeze the edge of thought. He walked through lonely streets. He found an alleyway. He waited, silent and still.

Time.

His eyes stayed on the mouth of the alley. People passed—boys, girls, men, women. He did not move from his position. He was waiting. In time the right person would come. In time the streets would be clear except for that one person, and the time would be right, and it would happen. He would act. He would act fast.

He heard high heels tapping in staccato rhythm, approaching him. He heard nothing else, no cars, no alien feet. Slowly, cautiously, he made his way toward the mouth of the alley. His eyes found the source of the tapping. A woman, a young woman, a pretty young woman with a curving body and a mass of jet-black hair and a raw red mouth. A pretty woman, his woman, the right woman, this one, yes, now!

She moved within reach, her high-heeled shoes never altering the rhythm of their tapping. He moved in liquid perfection. One arm reached out, and a hand fastened upon her face and covered her raw red mouth. The other arm snaked around her waist and tugged at her. She was off-balance, she stumbled after him, she disappeared with him into the mouth of the alley.

She might have screamed, but he banged her head on the cement floor of the alley and her eyes went glassy. She started to scream later, but he got a hand over her mouth and cut off the scream. She did not manage to bite him. He was careful.

Then, while she struggled, he drove the point of the ice pick precisely into her heart.

He left her there, dead and turning cold. He dropped the ice pick into a sewer. He found the subway arcade and rode the IRT back to where he had come from, went to his room, washed hands and face, got into bed, and slept. He slept very well and did not dream, not at all.

When he woke up in the morning at his usual time he felt as he always felt, cool and fresh and ready for the day's work. He showered and he dressed and he went downstairs, and he bought a copy of the *Daily Mirror* from the blind newsdealer.

He read the item. A young exotic dancer named Mona More had been attacked in Washington Heights and had been stabbed to death with an ice pick.

He remembered. In an instant it all came back, the girl's body, the ice pick, murder—

He gritted his teeth together until they ached. The realism of it all! He wondered if a psychiatrist could do anything about it. But psychiatrists were so painfully expensive, and he had his own psychiatrist, his personal and no-charge psychiatrist, his Sergeant Rooker.

But he remembered it! Everything, buying the ice pick, throwing the girl down, stabbing her—

He took a very deep breath. It was time to be methodical about this, he realized. He went to the telephone and called his office. "Cuttleton here," he said. "I'll be late today, an hour or so. A doctor's appointment. I'll be in as soon as I can."

"It's nothing serious?"

"Oh, no," he said. "Nothing serious." And, really, he wasn't lying. After all, Sergeant Rooker did function as his personal psychiatrist, and a psychiatrist was a doctor. And he did have an appointment, a standing appointment, for Sergeant Rooker had told him to come in whenever something like this happened. And it was nothing serious, that too was true, because he knew that he was really very innocent no matter how sure his memory made him of his guilt.

Rooker almost smiled at him. "Well, look who's here," he said. "I should have figured, Mr. Cuttleton. It's your kind of crime, isn't it? A woman assaulted and killed, that's your trademark, right?"

Warren Cuttleton could not quite smile. "I . . . the More girl. Mona More."

"Don't those strippers have wild names? Mona More. As in Mon Amour. That's French."

"It is?"

Sergeant Rooker nodded. "And you did it," he said. "That's the story?"

"I know I couldn't have, but—"

"You ought to quit reading the papers," Sergeant Rooker said. "Come on, let's get it out of your system."

They went to the room. Mr. Cuttleton sat in a straight-backed chair. Sergeant Rooker closed the door and stood at the desk. He said, "You killed the woman, didn't you? Where did you get the ice pick?"

"A hardware store."

"Any special one?"

"It was on Amsterdam Avenue."

"Why an ice pick?"

"It excited me, the handle was smooth and strong, and the blade was so sharp."

"Where's the ice pick now?"

"I threw it in a sewer."

"Well, that's no switch. There must have been a lot of blood, stabbing her with an ice pick. Loads of blood?"

"Yes."

"Your clothes get soaked with it?"

"Yes." He remembered how the blood had been all over his clothes, how he had had to hurry home and hope no one would see him.

"And the clothes?"

"In the incinerator."

"Not in your building, though."

"No. No, I changed in my building and ran to some other building, I don't remember where, and threw the clothes down the incinerator."

Sergeant Rooker slapped his hand down on the desk. "This is getting too easy," he said. "Or I'm getting too good at it. The stripper was stabbed in the heart with an ice pick. A tiny wound and it caused death just about instantly. Not a drop of blood. Dead bodies don't bleed, and wounds like that don't let go with much blood anyhow, so your story falls apart like wet tissue. Feel better?"

Warren Cuttleton nodded slowly. "But it seemed so horribly real," he said.

"It always does." Sergeant Rooker shook his head. "You poor son of a gun," he said. "I wonder how long this is going to keep up." He grinned wryly. "Much more of this and one of us is going to snap."

Hilliard's Ceremony

The old man sat on a low three-legged stool in the courtyard. He had removed his caftan and sandals. Hilliard had thought he'd be wearing a loincloth beneath the caftan, but in fact the old man was wearing a pair of boxer shorts, light blue in color. The incongruity struck Hilliard for a moment, but it did not linger; he had already learned that incongruity was to be expected in West Africa. Hilliard, nominally a cultural attaché, was in fact a coordinator of intelligence-gathering in the region, running a loose string of part-time agents and trying to make sense of their reports. Incongruity was his stock-in-trade.

He watched as two women—girls, really—dipped sponges in a large jar of water and sluiced the old man down with them. One knelt to wash the old fellow's feet with near-biblical ardor. When she had finished she stood up, and her companion indicated to the old man that he should lean forward with his head between his knees. When he was arranged to her satisfaction she upended the clay jar and poured the remaining water over his head. He remained motionless, allowing the water to drain from him onto the hard-packed dirt floor.

"They are washing him," Atuele said. "For the ceremony. Now he will go into a room and light a candle and observe its flame. Then he will have his ceremony."

Hilliard waited for Donnelly to say something, but his companion was silent. Hilliard said, "What's the ceremony for?"

Atuele smiled. He had a well-shaped oval head, regular features, an impish white-toothed grin. He had one white grandparent, and was dark enough to be regarded as a black man in America. Here in Togo, where mixed blood was a rarity, he looked to be of another race altogether.

"The ceremony," he said, "is to save his life. Did you see his eyes?"

"Yes."

"The whites are yellow. There is no life in them. His skin has an ashen cast to it. He has a stone in his liver. Without a ceremony, it will kill him in a month. Perhaps sooner. Perhaps a week, perhaps a matter of days."

"Shouldn't he be—"

"Yes?"

"In a hospital, I was going to say."

Atuele took a cigarette from the pack Donnelly had given him earlier. He inhaled deeply, exhaled slowly, watching the smoke rise. Tall poles supported a thatch woven of palm fronds, and the three of them sat in its shade. Atuele stared, seemingly fascinated, as the smoke rose up into the thatch.

"American cigarettes," he said. "The best, eh?"

"The best," Hilliard agreed.

"He came from the hospital. He was there a week. More, ten days. They ran tests, they took pictures, they put his blood under a microscope. They said they could do nothing for him." He puffed on his cigarette. "So," he said, "he comes here."

"And you can save him?"

"We will see. A stone in the liver—without a ceremony it is certain he will die. With a ceremony?" The smiled flashed. "We will see."

The ceremony was doubly surprising. Hilliard was surprised that he was allowed to witness it, and surprised that its trappings were so mundane, its ritual so matter-of-fact. He had expected drums, and dancers with their eyes rolling in their heads, and a masked witch doctor stamping on the ground and shaking his dreadlocks at unseen spirits. But there were no drums and no dancers, and Atuele was a far cry from the stereotypical witch doctor. He wore no mask, his hair was cropped close to his skull, and he never raised his voice or shook a fist at the skies.

At the far end of the walled compound, perhaps twenty yards from where they had been sitting, there was a small area reserved for ceremonies, its perimeter outlined by whitewashed stones. Within it, the old man knelt before a carved wooden altar. He was dressed again, but in a pure white caftan, not his original garment. Atuele, too, had changed to a white caftan, but his had gold piping on the shoulders and down the front.

To one side, two men and a woman, Africans in Western dress, stood at rapt attention. "His relatives," Donnelly whispered. Alongside Atuele stood the two girls who had washed the old man. They were also dressed in white, and their feet were bare. One of them, Hilliard noticed, had her toenails painted a vivid scarlet.

She was holding an orange and a knife. The knife looked to be ordinary kitchen cutlery, the sort of thing you'd use to bone a roast. Or to quarter an orange, which was what Atuele had the old man do with it. Having done so, he placed the four sections of fruit upon the altar, whereupon Atuele lit the four white candles that stood upon the altar, two at either end. Hilliard noticed that he employed the same disposable lighter he'd used earlier to light his American cigarette.

Next the girl with the red toenails covered the old man's head with a white handkerchief. Then the other girl, who had been holding a white chicken, handed the bird to Atuele. The chicken—pure white, with a red comb—struggled at first, and tried to flap a wing. Atuele said something to it and it calmed down. He placed it on the altar and placed the old man's hands on top of the bird.

"A lot of the ceremonies involve a chicken," Donnelly whispered.

No one moved. The old man, his head bent, the handkerchief covering his head, rested his hands upon the white chicken. The chicken remained perfectly still and did not let out a peep. The girl, the old man's relatives, all stood still and silent. Then the old man let out a sigh and Hilliard sensed that something had happened.

Atuele bent over the altar and drew the chicken out from under the man's grasp. The chicken remained curiously docile. Atuele straightened up, holding the bird in both hands, then inclined his head and seemed to be whispering into its ear. Did chickens have ears? Hilliard wasn't sure, but evidently the message got through, because the bird's response was immediate and dramatic. Its head fell forward, limp, apparently lifeless.

"It's dead," Donnelly said.

"How—"

"I've seen him do this before. I don't know what it is he says. I think he tells them to die. Of course, he doesn't speak English to them."

"What does he speak? Chicken?"

"Ewé, I suppose." He pronounced it *Eh-veh*. "Or some tribal dialect. Anyway, the chicken's dead."

Maybe he's hypnotized it, Hilliard thought. A moment later he had to discard the notion when Atuele took up the knife and severed the chicken's head. No blood spurted. Indeed, Atuele had to give the bird a good shake in order to get some of its blood to dribble out onto the dirt in front of the altar. If Atuele had hypnotized the bird, he'd hypnotized its bloodstream, too.

Atuele handed the bird to one of the girls. She walked off with it. He leaned forward and snatched the handkerchief from the old man's head. He said something, presumably in Ewé, and the old man stood up. Atuele gathered up the sections of orange and gave one each to the old man and his relatives. All, without hesitation, commenced eating the fruit.

The old man embraced one of his male relatives, stepped back, let out a rich laugh, then embraced the other man and the woman in turn. He held himself differently now, Hilliard noticed. And his eyes were clear. Still—

Atuele took Hilliard and Donnelly by the arm and led them back into the shade. He motioned them to their chairs, and a male servant came and poured out three glasses of palm wine. "He is well," Atuele announced. "The stone has passed from his liver into the liver of the chicken. He is lively now, see how he walks with a light step. In an hour he will lie down and sleep the clock around. Tomorrow he will feel fine. He is healed."

"And the chicken?"

"The chicken is dead, of course."

"What will happen to the chicken?"

"What should happen to a dead chicken? The women will cook him." He smiled. "Togo is not a rich country, you know. We cannot be throwing away perfectly good chickens. Of course, the liver will not be eaten."

"Because there is a stone in it."

"Exactly."

"I should have asked," Hilliard said, "to see the chicken cut open. To examine the liver."

"And if there wasn't a stone in it? Alan, you saw the old man, you shook his hand and looked him in the eye. He had eyes like egg yolks when he walked in there. His shoulders were slumped, his gut sagged. When Atuele was done with him he was a new man."

"Power of suggestion."

"Maybe."

"What else?"

Donnelly started to say something, held off while the waiter set drinks and a bowl of crisp banana chips before them. They were at the Hotel de la Paix in Lomé, the capital and the only real city in Togo. Atuele's hamlet, twenty minutes distant in Donnelly's Renault, seemed a world away.

"You know," Donnelly said, "he has an interesting story. His father's father was German. Of course, the whole place was a German colony until the First World War. Togoland, they called it."

"I know."

"Then the French took it over, and now of course it's independent." Donnelly glanced involuntarily at the wall, where the ruler's portrait was to be seen. It was a rare public room in Togo that did not display the portrait. A large part of

Hilliard's job lay in obtaining foreknowledge of the inevitable coup that would one day dislodge all those portraits from all those walls. It would not happen soon, he had decided, and whenever it did happen, it would come as a surprise to businessmen like Donnelly, as well as to everyone like Hilliard whose job it was to predict such things.

"Atuele was brought up Christian," Donnelly went on. "A modern family, Western dress, a good education at church schools. Further education at the Sorbonne."

"In Paris?"

"Last I looked. You're surprised? He graduated from there and studied medicine in Germany. Frankfurt, I think it was."

"The man's a physician?"

"He left after two years. He became disenchanted with Western medicine. Nothing but drugs and surgery, according to him, treating the symptoms and overlooking the underlying problem. The way he tells it, a spirit came to him one night and told him his path called for a return to the old ways."

"A spirit," Hilliard said.

"Right. He quit med school, flew home, and looked for people to study with. Apprenticed himself to the best herbalist he could find. Then went upcountry and spent months with several of the top shamans. He'd already begun coming into his powers back in Germany, and they increased dramatically once he channeled his energies in the right direction."

Donnelly went on, telling Atuele's story. How he'd gathered a few dozen people around him; they served him, and he saw to their welfare. How several of his brothers and sisters had followed him back to the old ways, much to the despair of their parents.

"There are shamans behind every bush in this country," Donnelly said. "Witch doctors, charlatans. Even in the Moslem north they're thicker than flies. Down here, where the prevailing religion is animist, they're all over the place. But most of them are a joke. This guy's the real tinsel."

"A stone in the liver," Hilliard said. "What do you suppose that means, anyway? I've heard of kidney stones, gallstones. What the hell is a stone in the liver?"

"What's the difference? Maybe the old guy had some calcification of the liver. Cirrhosis, say."

"And Atuele cured cirrhosis by giving it to the chicken?"

Donnelly smiled gently. "Atuele wouldn't say he cured it. He might say that he got a spirit to move the stone from the man to the chicken."

"A spirit again."

"He works with spirits. They do his bidding."

Hilliard looked at his friend. "I'm not sure what happened back there," he said, "but I can live without knowing. I was in Botswana before they sent me here, and in Chad before that. You see things, and you hear of things. But what I'd really like to know is how seriously you take this guy."

"Pretty seriously."

"Why? I mean, I'm willing to believe he cures people, including some specimens the doctors have given up on. Powers of the mind and all that, and if he wants to think it's spirits, and if his clients believe it, that's fine for them. But you're saying it's more than that, aren't you?"

"Uh-huh."

"Why?"

Donnelly drank his drink. "They say seeing is believing," he said, "but that's crap. This afternoon didn't make a believer out of you, and why should it? But think what an impact it must have had on the old man."

"What's your point?"

"I had a ceremony," Donnelly said. "Nine, ten months ago, just before the July rains. Atuele summoned a spirit and ordered it to enter into me." He smiled almost apologetically. "It worked," he said.

The Hilliards' dinner was guinea fowl with a rice stuffing, accompanied by sautéed green beans and a salad. Hilliard wished his wife would get their cook to prepare some of the native specialties. The hotels and all of the better restaurants served a watered-down French cuisine, but he'd eaten a fiery stew at an unassuming place down the street from the embassy that made him want more. Marilyn had passed on his request to the cook, and reported that the woman did not seem to know how to cook Togolese dishes.

"She said they're very common anyway," she told him. "Not to Western tastes. You wouldn't like them, she said."

"But I do like them. We already know that much."

"I'm just telling you what she said."

They ate on the screened patio, with moths buzzing against the screens. Hilliard wondered what moths had done ages ago, before electric lights, before candles, before human campfires. What did their phototropism do for them when the only lights at night were the stars?

"I had lunch with Donnelly," he said. "I never did get back to the office. He dragged me out of town to see a witch doctor with a college education."

"Oh?"

He described Atuele briefly, and the ritual they had witnessed. "I don't know if he was really cured," he concluded, "or what was wrong with him in the first place, but the change in him was pretty dramatic."

"He was probably the witch doctor's uncle."

"I never thought of that."

"More likely he believed he was sick, and the witch doctor got him to believe himself well. You know how superstitious they are in places like this."

"I guess the chicken was superstitious, too."

She rang for the serving girl, told her to bring more iced tea. To Hilliard she said, "I don't suppose you'd have to study at the Sorbonne to learn how to kill a chicken."

He laughed. The girl brought the tea. Hilliard normally drank his unsweetened, but tonight he added two spoons of sugar. He'd been doing this lately. Because life needs a little sweetness, he told himself.

He did not say anything to Marilyn about Donnelly's ceremony.

"I wasn't getting anywhere," Donnelly had explained. "I was the kind of guy never got fired and never got promoted. What I was, I was never a take-charge kind of a guy."

"That's not how you seem."

The smile again. "Alan, you never knew me before my ceremony. That's the whole point. I'm changed."

"A new man."

"You could say that."

"Tell me about it," he'd said, and Donnelly had done just that. Reluctantly, he'd let it drop to Atuele that he'd been overlooked for promotion. Before he knew what was happening, he was admitting things to the shaman he'd never even admitted to himself. That he was ineffectual. That something always held him back. That his timing was off, that he never did the right thing or said the right thing, that when the going got tough he invariably shot himself in the foot.

"He told me I was afflicted," Donnelly recalled. "That there was an imbalance that ought to be set right. That I needed a spirit."

"And what happened?"

Donnelly shook his head. "I can't really talk about that," he said.

"You're not allowed? If you talk about it your wish won't come true?"

"Nothing like that. I mean I literally cannot talk about it. I can't fit words to the tune. I don't know exactly what happened."

"Well, what did you do? You put your hands on a chicken and the poor thing couldn't peck straight anymore?"

"Nothing like that."

"Then what? I'm not making fun of you, I'm just trying to get the picture. What happened?"

"There was a ceremony," Donnelly said. "Lots of people, lots of dancing and drumming. He gave me an herbal preparation that I had to swallow."

"Uh-huh."

"It didn't get me high, if that's what you're thinking. It tasted like grass. Not dope, not that kind of grass. The kind cows eat. It tasted like lawn clippings that had started to compost."

"Yum."

"It wasn't that terrible, but not your standard gourmet treat, either. I didn't get a buzz from it. At least I don't think I did. Later on I was dancing, and I think I went into a trance."

"Really."

"And there was a ritual in which I had to break an egg into a clean white cotton handkerchief, and Atuele rubbed the yolk of the egg into my hair."

"It sounds like a conditioning treatment."

"I know. Then they took me into one of the huts and let me go to sleep. I was exhausted, and I slept like a corpse for two or three hours. And then I woke up."

"And?"

"And I went home."

"That's all?"

"And I've never been the same again."

Hilliard looked at him. "You're serious."

"Utterly."

"What happened?"

"I don't know what happened. But something happened. I was different. I acted differently and people reacted to me differently. I had confidence. I commanded respect. I—"

"*Wizard of Oz* stuff," Hilliard said. "All he could give you was what you had all along, but the mumbo jumbo made you think you had confidence, and therefore you had it."

But Donnelly was shaking his head. "There's no way I can expect you to believe this," he said, "because seeing isn't believing, and neither is hearing. Let me tell you how I experienced it, all right?"

"By all means."

"I woke up the next morning and nothing was different, I felt the same, except I'd slept very deeply and felt refreshed. But I also felt like an idiot, because I'd danced around like a savage and paid five hundred dollars for the privilege, and—"

"Five hundred dollars!"

"Yes, and—"

"Is that what it costs?"

"It varies, but it's never cheap. It's a lot higher relatively for the Togolese who must make up ninety-five percent of his regular clients. I'm sure that old man this afternoon must have paid a hundred dollars, and likely more. What do you give your house servants, twenty-five bucks a month? Believe me, it's less of a sacrifice for me to come up with five hundred dollars than for a native to part with several months' wages."

"It still seems high."

"It seemed high the morning after, take my word for it. I felt bloody stupid. I blamed myself six ways and backwards—for falling for it in the first place, and for not getting anything out of it, as if there was something there to be gotten and it was my fault it hadn't worked. And then, it must have been ten days later and I'd put the whole thing out of my mind, and I was in a meeting with my then-boss and that old bastard Kostler. Do you know him?"

"No."

"Consider yourself lucky. I was in there, and Kostler was kicking our brains in, really killing us. And something clicked in. I felt the presence of a power within me that had not been there before. I took a breath, and I literally felt the energy shift in the room, the whole balance among the three of us. And I started talking, and the words were just *there*, Alan. I could have charmed the birds out of the trees, I could have talked a dog off a meat wagon."

"You were on," Hilliard suggested. "Everybody has days like that, when the edges just line up for you. I had it one night playing pool at the Harcourt Club in Nairobi. I couldn't miss a shot. Bank shots, combinations—everything worked. And the next day I was the same klutz I'd always been."

"But I wasn't," Donnelly said. "I had something extra, something I hadn't had before, and it didn't go away the next day or the next week or the next month. It can't go away now. It's not a lucky charm, something you could pick up downtown at the fetish market. It's a part of who I am, but it's a part that never existed before I ate Atuele's lawn clippings and had an egg rubbed in my scalp."

Hilliard thought about this. "You don't think it's all in your mind, then," he said.

"I think it's all in my self. I think, if you will, that my self has been enlarged by the addition of a spirit that wasn't there before, and that this spirit has incorporated itself into my being, and—" He broke off abruptly, gave his head a shake. "Do you know something? I don't know what I believe, or what happened, or how or why, either. I know that a month after my ceremony I got a five-thousand-dollar raise without asking for it, which makes Atuele look like a damned good investment. I've had two raises since then, and a promotion to the second desk in the Transcorporate Division. And they're right to promote me, Alan. Before they were carrying me. Now I'm worth every penny they pay me."

After dinner Hilliard and his wife watched a movie on the VCR. He couldn't keep his mind on it. All he could think about was what he had seen in Atuele's compound, and what Donnelly had told him at the hotel bar.

In the shower, he tried to picture the ceremony Donnelly had described. The roar of the shower became the relentless drumming of a quartet of grinning sweating half-naked blacks.

He dried off, made himself a drink, carried it into the air-conditioned bedroom. The lights were out and his wife was already sleeping, or putting on a good act. He got into bed and sipped his drink in the darkness. His heart welled up with the mixture of tenderness and desire that she always inspired in him. He set down his drink half-finished and laid a hand on her exposed shoulder.

His hand moved on her body. For a while she made no response, although he knew she was awake. Then she sighed and rolled over and he moved to take her.

Afterward he kissed her and told her that he loved her.

"It's late," she said. "I have an early day tomorrow."

She rolled over and lay as she had lain when he came into the room. He sat up and took his drink from the nightstand. The ice had melted but the whiskey was cool. He sipped the drink slowly, but when the glass was empty he was still not sleepy. He thought of fixing himself another but he didn't want to risk disturbing her.

He had the urge to put his hand on her bare shoulder again, not as a sexual overture but just to touch her. But he did not do this. He sat up, his hand at his side. After a while he lay down and put his head on the pillow, and after a while he slept.

Two days later he lunched with Donnelly at the native restaurant. Hilliard had chicken with yams with some sort of red sauce. It brought tears to his eyes and beaded his forehead with sweat. It was, he decided, even better than the stew he'd had there earlier.

To Donnelly he said, "The thing is, my life works fine just as it is. I'm happily married, I love my wife, and I'm doing well at the embassy. So why would I want a ceremony?"

"Obviously you don't."

"But the thing is I do, and I couldn't tell you why. Silly, isn't it?"

"You could talk with Atuele," Donnelly offered.

"Talk with him?"

"He may tell you you don't need a ceremony. One woman came to him with a list of symptoms a yard long. She was all primed to pay a fortune and be ordered to smear herself with palm oil and dance naked in the jungle. Atuele told her to cut back on starches and take a lot of vitamin C." Donnelly poured the last of his beer into his glass. "I thought I'd take a run out there this afternoon myself," he said. "Do you want to come along and talk with him?"

"I'm actually a very happy man," he told Atuele. "I love my job, I love my wife, we have a pleasant, well-run home—"

Atuele listened in silence. He was smoking one of the cigarettes Hilliard had brought him. Donnelly had said it was customary to bring a gift, so Hilliard had picked up a carton of Pall Malls. For his part, Donnelly had brought along a liter of good scotch.

When Hilliard had run out of things to say, Atuele finished his cigarette and put it out. He gazed at Hilliard. "You are walking on the beach," he said suddenly, "and you stop and turn around, and what do you see?"

What kind of nonsense was this? Hilliard tried to think of an answer. His own voice, unbidden, said: "I have left no footprints."

And, quite unaccountably, he burst into tears.

He sobbed shamelessly for ten minutes. At last he stopped and looked across at Atuele, who had smoked half of another cigarette. "You ought to have a ceremony," Atuele said.

"Yes."

"The price will be four hundred dollars U.S. You can manage this?"

"Yes."

"Friday night. Come here before sundown."

"I will. Uh. Is it all right to eat first? Or should I skip lunch that day?"

"If you do not eat you will be hungry."

"I see. Uh, what should I wear?"

"What you wish. Perhaps not a jacket, not a tie. You will want to be comfortable."

"Casual clothes, then."

"Casual," Atuele said, enjoying the word. "Casual, casual. Yes, casual clothes. We are casual here."

"Friday night," Hilliard said. "How long do these things last?"

"Figure midnight, but it could go later."

"That long."

"Or you could be home by ten. It's hard to say."

Hilliard was silent for a moment. Then he said, "I don't think I would want Marilyn to know about this."

"She's not going to hear it from me, Alan."

"I'll say there's an affair at the Gambian embassy."

"Won't she want to go?"

"God, have you ever been to anything at the Gambian embassy? No, she won't want to go." He looked out the car window. "I could tell her. It's not that I have to ask her permission to do anything. It's just—"

"Say no more," said Donnelly. "I was married once."

The lie was inconvenient in one respect. In order to appear suitably dressed for the mythical Gambian party, Hilliard left his house in black tie. At Donnelly's office he changed into khakis and a white safari shirt and a pair of rope sandals.

"Casual," Donnelly said, approvingly.

They took two cars and parked side by side at the entrance to Atuele's compound. Inside, rows of benches were set up to accommodate perhaps three dozen Africans, ranging from very young to very old. Children were free to run around and play in the dirt, although most of them sat attentively beside their parents. Most of the Africans wore traditional garb, and all but a few were barefoot.

To the side of the benches ranged half a dozen mismatched armchairs with cushioned bottoms. Two of these were occupied by a pair of sharp-featured angular ladies who could have been sisters. They spoke to each other in what sounded a little like German and a little like Dutch. Hilliard guessed that they were Belgian, and that the language was Flemish. A third chair held a fat red-faced Australian whose name was Farquahar. Hilliard and Donnelly each took a chair. The sixth chair remained vacant.

At the front, off to one side, six drummers had already begun playing. The rhythm they laid down was quite complicated, and unvarying. Hilliard watched them for a while, then looked over at Atuele, who was sitting in an armchair and chatting with a black woman in a white robe. He was smoking a cigarette.

"For a spiritual guy," Hilliard said, "he sure smokes a lot."

"He has a taste for good scotch, too," Farquahar said. "Puts a lot of it away, though you won't see him drink tonight. Says alcohol and tobacco help keep him grounded."

"You've been here before?"

"Oh, I'm an old hand," Farquahar said. "I'm here every month or so. Don't always have a personal ceremony, but I come just the same. He's one of a kind, is our Atuele."

"Really."

"How old do you think he is?"

Hilliard hadn't really thought about it. It was hard to tell with Africans. "I don't know," he said. "Twenty-eight?"

"You'd say that, wouldn't you? He's my age exactly and I'm forty-two. And he drinks like a fish and smokes like a chimney. Makes you think, doesn't it?"

One of the girls who'd assisted at the old man's ceremony collected money from Hilliard and Donnelly and the Belgian ladies. Then Atuele came over and gave each of the four a dose of an herbal preparation. Farquahar, who was not having a ceremony this evening, did not get an herb to eat. Hilliard's portion was a lump the size of a pigeon's egg, and it did taste much as Donnelly had described it. Lawn clippings left in a pile for a few days, with an aftertaste of something else. Dirt, say.

He sat with it on his tongue like a communion wafer, wondering if he was supposed to chew it. Tasty, he thought, and he considered voicing the thought to either Donnelly or Farquahar, but something told him not to say anything to anyone from this point on but to be silent and let this happen, whatever it was. He chewed the stuff and swallowed it, and if anything the taste got worse the more you chewed it, but he had no trouble getting it down.

He waited for it to hit him.

Nothing happened. Meanwhile, though, the drumming was beginning to have an effect on a couple of the women in the crowd. Several of them had risen from the benches and were standing near the drummers, shuffling their feet to the intricate beat.

Then one of them went into an altered state. It happened quite suddenly. Her movements became jerky, almost spastic, and her eyes rolled up into her head, and she danced with great authority, her whole body taken over by the dance. She made her way throughout the assembly, pausing now and then in front of someone. The person approached would extend a hand, palm up, and she would slap palms forcefully before dancing on.

The people whose palms were slapped mostly stayed where they were and went on as before, but periodically the slappee would be immediately taken over by whatever was in possession of the dancer. Then he or she—it was mostly women, but not exclusively so—he or she would rise and go through the same sort of fitful gyrations as the original dancer, and would soon be approaching others and slapping their palms.

Like vampires making new vampires, Hilliard thought.

One woman, eyes rolling, brow dripping sweat, danced over to the row of armchairs. Hilliard at once hoped and feared he'd get his palm slapped. Instead it was Donnelly she approached, Donnelly whose palm received her slap. Hilliard fancied that electricity flowed from the woman into the man beside him, but Donnelly did not react. He went on sitting there.

Meanwhile, Atuele had taken one of the Belgian women over to the drummers. He had her holding a white metal basin on top of her head. A group of Africans were dancing around her, dancing *at* her, it seemed to Hilliard. The woman just stood there balancing the dishpan on her head and looking uncomfortable about it.

Her companion, Hilliard saw, was dancing by herself, shuffling her feet.

Another dancer approached. She went down the row, a dynamo of whatever energy the dance generated, and she slapped palms with Donnelly, with Hilliard, with Farquahar. Donnelly received the slap as he'd received the first. Hilliard felt something, felt energy leap from the dancer into his hand and up his arm. It was like getting an electrical shock, and yet it wasn't.

Donnelly was on his feet now. He was not dancing like the Africans, he was sort of stomping in a rhythm all his own, and Hilliard looked at him and thought how irremediably white the man was.

What, he wondered, was he doing here? What were any of them doing here? Besides having a grand cross-cultural experience, something to wow them with next time he got Stateside, what in God's name was he doing here?

Farquahar was up, dancing. Bouncing around like a man possessed, or at least like a man determined to appear possessed. The bastard hadn't even paid for a private ceremony and here he was caught up in something, or at any rate uninhibited enough to pretend to be, while Hilliard himself was sitting here, unaffected by the gloppy lawn clippings, unaffected by the slapped palm, unaffected by the goddamned drums, unaffected by any damn thing, and four hundred dollars poorer for it.

Wasn't he supposed to have a private ceremony, a ritual all his own? Wasn't something supposed to happen? Maybe Atuele had forgotten him. Or maybe, because he had come here without a goal, he was not supposed to get anything. Maybe it was a great joke.

He got up and looked around for Atuele. A man danced over, behaving just as weirdly as the women, and slapped Hilliard's palm, then held out his own palm. Hilliard slapped him back. The man danced away.

Hilliard, feeling foolish, began to shuffle his feet.

A little after midnight Hilliard had the thought that it was time to go home. He had danced for a while—he had no idea how long—and then he had returned to his chair. He had been sitting there lost in thought ever since. He could not recall what he had been thinking about, any more than he could remember a dream once he'd fully awakened from it.

He looked around. The drummers were still at it. They had been playing without interruption for five hours. A few people were dancing, but none were twitching as if possessed. The ones who had done that had not seemed to remain in trance for very long. They would go around slapping palms and spreading energy for ten frenzied minutes or so; then someone would lead them away, and later they'd return, dressed in clean white robes and much subdued.

The Belgian women were nowhere to be seen. Donnelly, too, was missing. Farquahar was up front chatting with Atuele. Both men were smoking, and drinking what Hilliard assumed was whiskey.

Time to go.

He got to his feet, swayed, before catching his balance. What was protocol? Did you shake hands with your host, thank your hostess? He took a last look around, then walked off toward where they'd left the cars.

Donnelly's car was gone. Hilliard's evening clothes were in the backseat of his own car. Marilyn would be sleeping, it was pointless to change, but he did so anyway, stowing his khakis and safari shirt in the trunk. It wasn't until he was putting on his socks and black pumps that he realized his sandals were missing. Evidently he'd kicked them off earlier. He couldn't recall doing it, but he must have.

He didn't go back for them.

In the morning he waited for Marilyn to ask about the party. He had a response ready but was never called upon to deliver it. She went out for a tennis date right after breakfast, and she never did ask him about his evening.

They played bridge the following night with a British couple. The husband was some sort of paper shuffler, the wife an avid amateur astrologer who, unless she was playing cards, became quite boring on the subject.

Sunday was quiet. Hilliard drank a bit more than usual Sunday night, and he thought of telling his wife how he'd actually spent Friday evening. The impulse was not a terribly urgent one and he had the good sense to suppress it.

Monday he lunched with Donnelly.

"Well, it was an experience," he said.

"It always is."

"I'm not sorry I went."

"I'm not surprised," Donnelly said. "You went really deep, didn't you?"

"Deep? What do you mean?"

"Your trance. Or don't you even know you were in one?"

"I wasn't."

Donnelly laughed. "I wish I had a film of you dancing," he said. "I wondered if you were even aware of how caught up you were in it."

"I remember dancing. I wasn't leaping around like an acrobat or anything. Was I?"

"No, but you were . . . what's the word I want?"

"I don't know."

"Abandoned," Donnelly said. "You were dancing with abandon."

"That's hard to believe."

"And then you sat down and stared at nothing at all for hours on end."

"Maybe I fell asleep."

"You were in a trance, Alan."

"It didn't feel like a trance."

"Yes it did. That's what a trance feels like. It can be disappointing, because it feels like a normal state while it's going on, but it isn't."

He nodded, but he didn't speak right away. Then he said, "I thought I'd get something special for my money. An egg to rub into my scalp or something. A pot to hold on my head. A private ceremony—"

"The herb was your private ceremony."

"What did it do? Drug me so that I went into the trance-that-didn't-feel-like-a-trance? Farquahar got the same thing for free."

"The herb contained your spirit, or allowed the spirit to enter into you. Or whatever. I'm not too clear on how it works."

"So I've got a spirit in me now?"

"That's the theory."

"I don't feel different."

"You probably won't. And then one day something will click in, and you'll realize that you're different, that you've changed."

"Changed how?"

"I don't know. Look, maybe nothing will happen and you're out whatever it was. Four hundred dollars?"

"That's right. How about you? What did it cost you?"

"A thousand."

"My God."

"It was five hundred the first time, three hundred the second, and this time it was an even thousand. I don't know how he sets the prices. Maybe a spirit tells him what to charge."

"Maybe if I'd paid more—" Hilliard began, and then he caught himself and started laughing. "Did you hear that? My God, I'm the original con man's dream. No sooner do I decide I've wasted my money than I start wondering if I shouldn't have wasted a little more of it."

"Give it a while," Donnelly said. "Maybe you didn't waste it. Wait and see."

Nothing was changed. Hilliard went to his office, did his work, lived his life. Evenings he went to diplomatic functions or played cards or, more often, sat home watching films with Marilyn.

On one such evening, almost a month after his ceremony, Hilliard frowned at his dish of *poulet rôti avec pommes frites et haricots verts.* "I'll be a minute," he told his wife, and he got up and went into the kitchen.

The cook was a tall woman, taller than Hilliard. She had glossy black skin and a full figure. Her cheekbones were high, her smile blinding.

"Liné," he said, "I'd like you to try something different for tomorrow night's dinner."

"Dinner is not good?"

"Dinner is fine," he said, "but it's not very interesting, is it? I would like you to prepare Togolese dishes for us."

"Ah," she said, and flashed her smile. "You would not like them."

"I would like them very much."

"No," she assured him. "Americans not like Togolese food. Is very simple and common, not good. I know what you like. I cook in the hotels, I cook for American people, for French people, for Nor, Nor—"

"Norwegian," he supplied.

"For Norjian people, yes. I know what you like."

"No," he said with conviction. "*I* know what I like, Liné, and I like Togolese dishes very much. I like chicken and yams with red sauce, and I like Togolese stew, I like them very hot and spicy, very fiery."

She looked at him, and it seemed to him that she had never actually looked at him before. She extended the tip of her tongue and ran it across her upper lip. She said, "You want this tomorrow?"

"Yes, please."

"Real Togolese food," she said, and all at once her smile came, but now it was in her eyes as well. "Oh, I cook you some meal, boss! You see!"

That night, showering, he felt different. He couldn't define the difference but it was palpable.

He dried off and went to the bedroom. Marilyn was already asleep, lying on her side facing away from him. He got into bed and felt himself fill with desire for her.

He put a hand on her shoulder.

She rolled over to face him, as if she'd been waiting for his touch. He began to make love to her and her response had an intensity it had never had before. She cried out at climax.

"My God," she said afterward. She was propped up on one arm and her face was glowing. "What was that all about?"

"It's the Togolese food," he told her.

"But that's tomorrow night. If she actually cooks it."

"She'll cook it. And it's the expectation of the Togolese food. It heats the blood."

"Something sure did," she said.

She turned over and went to sleep. Moments later, so did Hilliard.

In the middle of the night he came half-awake. He realized that Marilyn had shifted closer to him in sleep, and that she had thrown an arm across his body. He liked the feeling. He closed his eyes and drifted off again.

The following evening Liné laid on a feast. She had produced a beef stew with yams and served it on a bed of some grain he'd never had before. It was not quite like anything he'd eaten at the native restaurant, and it was hotter than anything he'd ever eaten anywhere, but with all the flavors in good proportion. Midway through the meal Liné came out to the patio and beamed when they praised the food.

"I cook terrific every night now," she said. "You see!"

When the serving girl cleared the dishes, her little breast brushed Hilliard's arm. He could have sworn it was deliberate. Later, when she brought the coffee, she grinned at him as if they shared a secret. He glanced at Marilyn, but if she caught it she gave no indication.

Later, they watched *Dr. Zhivago* on the VCR. Midway through it Marilyn got up from her chair and sat next to him on the couch. "This is the most romantic movie ever made," she told him. "It makes me want to cuddle."

"It's the spicy food," he said, slipping an arm around her.

"No, it's the movie," she said. She stroked his cheek, breathed kisses against the side of his neck. "Now *this*," she said, dropping a hand into his lap, "*this*," she said, fondling him, "*this* is an effect of the spicy food."

"I see the difference."

"I thought you would," she said.

"Good morning, Peggy," he said to Hank Suydam's secretary.

"Why, good morning, Mr. Hilliard," she said, a hitherto unseen light dancing in her brown eyes.

"Alan," he said.

"Alan," she said archly. "Good morning, Alan."

He called Donnelly, arranging to meet him for lunch. "And you can pay for lunch," Donnelly said.

"I was planning on it," he said, "but how did you know that?"

"Because it clicked in and you're eager to express your gratitude. I know it happened, I can hear it in your voice. How do you feel?"

"How do you think I feel?"

He hung up and started to go through the stack of letters on his desk. After a few minutes he realized he was grinning hugely. He got up and closed his office door.

Then, tentatively, he began to do a little dance.

Hot Eyes, Cold Eyes

Some days were easy. She would go to work and return home without once feeling the invasion of men's eyes. She might take her lunch and eat it in the park. She might stop on the way home at the library for a book, at the deli for a barbequed chicken, at the cleaner's, at the drugstore. On those days she could move coolly and crisply through space and time, untouched by the stares of men.

Doubtless they looked at her on those days, as on the more difficult days. She was the sort men looked at, and she had learned that early on—when her legs first began to lengthen and take shape, when her breasts began to bud. Later, as the legs grew longer and the breasts fuller, and as her face lost its youthful plumpness and was sculpted by time into beauty, the stares increased. She was attractive, she was beautiful, she was—curious phrase—easy on the eyes. So men looked at her, and on the easy days she didn't seem to notice, didn't let their rude stares penetrate the invisible shield that guarded her.

But this was not one of those days.

It started in the morning. She was waiting for the bus when she first felt the heat of a man's eyes upon her. At first she willed herself to ignore the feeling, wished the bus would come and whisk her away from it, but the bus did not come and she could not ignore what she felt and, inevitably, she turned from the street to look at the source of the feeling.

There was a man leaning against a red brick building not twenty yards from her. He was perhaps thirty-five, unshaven, and his clothes looked as though he'd slept in them. When she turned to glance at him his lips curled slightly, and his eyes, red-rimmed and glassy, moved first to her face, then drifted insolently the length of her body. She could feel their heat; it leaped from the eyes to her breasts and loins like an electric charge bridging a gap.

He placed his hand deliberately upon his crotch and rubbed himself. His smile widened.

She turned from him, drew a breath, let it out, wished the bus would come. Even now, with her back to him, she could feel the embrace of his eyes. They were like hot hands upon her buttocks and the backs of her thighs.

The bus came, neither early nor late, and she mounted the steps and dropped her fare in the box. The usual driver, a middle-aged fatherly type, gave her his usual smile and wished her the usual good morning. His eyes were an innocent watery blue behind thick-lensed spectacles.

Was it only her imagination that his eyes swept her body all the while? But she could feel them on her breasts, could feel too her own nipples hardening in response to their palpable touch.

She walked the length of the aisle to the first available seat. Male eyes tracked her every step of the way.

The day went on like that. This did not surprise her, although she had hoped it would be otherwise, had prayed during the bus ride that eyes would cease to bother her when she left the bus. She had learned, though, that once a day began in this fashion its pattern was set, unchangeable.

Was it something she did? Did she invite their hungry stares? She certainly didn't do anything with the intention of provoking male lust. Her dress was conservative enough, her makeup subtle and unremarkable. Did she swing her hips when she walked? Did she wet her lips and pout like a sullen sexpot? She was positive she did nothing of the sort, and it often seemed to her that she could cloak herself in a nun's habit and the results would be the same. Men's eyes would lift the black skirts and strip away the veil.

At the office building where she worked, the elevator starter glanced at her legs, then favored her with a knowing, wet-lipped smile. One of the office boys, a rabbity youth with unfortunate skin, stared at her breasts, then flushed scarlet when she caught him at it. Two older men gazed at her from the water cooler. One leaned over to murmur something to the other. They both chuckled and went on looking at her.

She went to her desk and tried to concentrate on her work. It was difficult, because intermittently she felt eyes brushing her body, moving across her like searchlight beams scanning the yard in a prison movie. There were moments when she wanted to scream, moments when she wanted to spin around in her chair and hurl something. But she remained in control of herself and did none of these things. She had survived days of this sort often enough in the past. She would survive this one as well.

The weather was good, but today she spent her lunch hour at her desk rather than risk the park. Several times during the afternoon the sensation of being watched was unbearable and she retreated to the ladies' room. She endured the final hours a minute at a time, and finally it was five o'clock and she straightened her desk and left.

The descent on the elevator was unbearable. She bore it. The bus ride home, the walk from the bus stop to her apartment building, were unendurable. She endured them.

In her apartment, with the door locked and bolted, she stripped off her clothes and hurled them into a corner of the room as if they were unclean, as if the day had irrevocably soiled them. She stayed a long while under the shower, washed her hair, blow-dried it, then returned to her bedroom and stood nude before the full-length mirror on the closet door. She studied herself at some length, and intermittently her hands would move to cup a breast or trace the swell of a thigh, not to arouse but to assess, to chart the dimensions of her physical self.

And now? A meal alone? A few hours with a book? A lazy night in front of the television set?

She closed her eyes, and at once she felt other eyes upon her, felt them as she had been feeling them all day. She knew that she was alone, that now no one was watching her, but this knowledge did nothing to dispel the feeling.

She sighed.

She would not, could not, stay home tonight.

When she left the building, stepping out into the cool of dusk, her appearance was very different. Her tawny hair, which she'd worn pinned up earlier, hung free. Her makeup was overdone, with an excess of mascara and a deep blush of rouge in the hollows of her cheeks. During the day she'd worn no scent beyond a touch of Jean Naté applied after her morning shower; now she'd dashed on an abundance of the perfume she wore only on nights like this one, a strident scent redolent of musk. Her dress was close-fitting and revealing, the skirt slit Oriental-fashion high on one thigh, the neckline low to display her décolletage. She strode purposefully on her high-heeled shoes, her buttocks swaying as she walked.

She looked sluttish and she knew it, and gloried in the knowledge. She'd checked the mirror carefully before leaving the apartment and she had liked what she saw. Now, walking down the street with her handbag bouncing against her swinging hip, she could feel the heat building up within her flesh. She could also feel the eyes of the men she passed, men who sat on stoops or loitered in doorways, men walking with purpose who stopped for a glance in her direction. But there was a difference. Now she relished those glances. She fed on the heat in those eyes, and the fire within herself burned hotter in response.

A car slowed. The driver leaned across the seat, called to her. She missed the words but felt the touch of his eyes. A pulse throbbed insistently throughout her entire body now. She was frightened—of her own feelings, of the real dangers she faced—but at the same time she was alive, gloriously alive, as she had not been in far too long. Before she had walked through the day. Now the blood was singing in her veins.

She passed several bars before finding the cocktail lounge she wanted. The interior was dimly lit, the floor soft with carpeting. An overactive air conditioner had lowered the temperature to an almost uncomfortable level. She walked bravely into the room. There were several empty tables along the wall but she passed them by, walking her swivel-hipped walk to the bar and taking a stool at the far end.

The cold air was stimulating against her warm skin. The bartender gave her a minute, then ambled over and leaned against the bar in front of her. He looked at once knowing and disinterested, his heavy lids shading his dark brown eyes and giving them a sleepy look.

"Stinger," she said.

While he was building the drink she drew her handbag into her lap and groped within it for her billfold. She found a ten and set it on top of the bar, then fumbled reflexively within her bag for another moment, checking its contents. The bartender placed the drink on the bar in front of her, took her money, returned with her change. She looked at her drink, then at her reflection in the back bar mirror.

Men were watching her.

She could tell, she could always tell. Their gazes fell on her and warmed the skin where they touched her. Odd, she thought, how the same sensation that had been so disturbing and unpleasant all day long was so desirable and exciting now.

She raised her glass, sipped her drink. The combined flavor of cognac and crème de menthe was at once warm and cold upon her lips and tongue. She swallowed, sipped again.

"That a stinger?"

He was at her elbow and she flicked her eyes in his direction while continuing to face forward. A small man, stockily built, balding, tanned, with a dusting of freckles across his high forehead. He wore a navy blue Quiana shirt open at the throat, and his dark chest hair was beginning to go gray.

"Drink up," he suggested. "Let me buy you another."

She turned now, looked levelly at him. He had small eyes. Their whites showed a tracery of blue veins at their outer corners. The irises were a very dark brown, an unreadable color, and the black pupils, hugely dilated in the bar's dim interior, covered most of the irises.

"I haven't seen you here," he said, hoisting himself onto the seat beside her. "I usually drop in around this time, have a couple, see my friends. Not new in the neighborhood, are you?"

Calculating eyes, she thought. Curiously passionless eyes, for all their cool intensity. Worst of all, they were small eyes, almost beady eyes.

"I don't want company," she said.

"Hey, how do you know you don't like me if you don't give me a chance?" He was grinning, but there was no humor in it. "You don't even know my name, lady. How can you despise a total stranger?"

"Please leave me alone."

"What are you, Greta Garbo?" He got up from his stool, took a half step away from her, gave her a glare and a curled lip. "You want to drink alone," he said, "why don't you just buy a bottle and take it home with you? You can take it to bed and suck on it, honey."

He had ruined the bar for her. She scooped up her change, left her drink unfinished. Two blocks down and one block over she found a second cocktail lounge virtually indistinguishable from the first one. Perhaps the lighting was a little softer, the background music the slightest bit lower in pitch. Again she passed up the row of tables and seated herself at the bar. Again she ordered a stinger and let it rest on the bar top for a moment before taking the first exquisite sip.

Again she felt male eyes upon her, and again they gave her the same hot-cold sensation as the combination of brandy and crème de menthe.

This time when a man approached her she sensed his presence for a long moment before he spoke. She studied him out of the corner of her eye. He was tall and lean, she noted, and there was a self-contained air about him, a sense of considerable self-assurance. She wanted to turn, to look directly into his eyes, but instead she raised her glass to her lips and waited for him to make a move.

"You're a few minutes late," he said.

She turned, looked at him. There was a weathered, raw-boned look to him that matched the western-style clothes he wore—the faded chambray shirt, the skin-tight denim jeans. Without glancing down she knew he'd be wearing boots and that they would be good ones.

"I'm late?"

He nodded. "I've been waiting for you for close to an hour. Of course it wasn't until you walked in that I knew it was you I was waiting for, but one look was all it took. My name's Harley."

She made up a name. He seemed satisfied with it, using it when he asked her if he could buy her a drink.

"I'm not done with this one yet," she said.

"Then why don't you just finish it and come for a walk in the moonlight?"

"Where would we walk?"

"My apartment's just a block and a half from here."

"You don't waste time."

"I told you I waited close to an hour for you. I figure the rest of the evening's too precious to waste."

She had been unwilling to look directly into his eyes but she did so now and she was not disappointed. His eyes were large and well-spaced, blue in color, a light blue of a shade that often struck her as cold and forbidding. But his eyes were anything but cold. On the contrary, they burned with passionate intensity.

She knew, looking into them, that he was a dangerous man. He was strong, he was direct, and he was dangerous. She could tell all this in a few seconds, merely by meeting his relentless gaze.

Well, that was fine. Danger, after all, was an inextricable part of it.

She pushed her glass aside, scooped up her change. "I don't really want the rest of this," she said.

"I didn't think you did. I think I know what you really want."

"I think you probably do."

He took her arm, tucked it under his own. They left the lounge, and on the way out she could feel other eyes on her, envious eyes. She drew closer to him and swung her hips so that her buttocks bumped into his lean flank. Her purse slapped against her other hip. Then they were out the door and heading down the street.

She felt excitement mixed with fear, an emotional combination not unlike her stinger. The fear, like the danger, was part of it.

His apartment consisted of two sparsely furnished rooms three flights up from street level. They walked wordlessly to the bedroom and undressed. She laid her clothes across a wooden chair, set her handbag on the floor at the side of the platform bed. She got onto the bed and he joined her and they embraced. He smelled faintly of leather and tobacco and male perspiration, and even with her eyes shut she could see his blue eyes burning in the darkness.

She wasn't surprised when his hands gripped her shoulders and eased her downward on the bed. She had been expecting this and welcomed it. She swung her head, letting her long hair brush across his flat abdomen, and then she moved to accept him. He tangled his fingers in her hair, hurting her in a not unpleasant way. She inhaled his musk as her mouth embraced him, and in her own fashion she matched his strength with strength of her own, teasing, taunting, heightening his passion and then cooling it down just short of culmination. His breathing grew ragged and muscles worked in his legs and abdomen.

At length he let go of her hair. She moved upward on the bed to join him and he rolled her over onto her back and covered her, his mouth seeking hers, his flesh burying itself in her flesh. She locked her thighs around his hips. He pounded at her loins, hammering her, hurting her with the brute force of his masculinity.

How strong he was, and how insistent. Once again she thought what a dangerous man he was, and what a dangerous game she was playing. The thought served only to spur her own passion on, to build her fire higher and hotter.

She felt her body preparing itself for orgasm, felt the urge growing to abandon herself, to lose control utterly. But a portion of herself remained remote, aloof, and she let her arm hang over the side of the bed and reached for her purse, groped within it.

And found the knife.

Now she could relax, now she could give up, now she could surrender to what she felt. She opened her eyes, stared upward. His own eyes were closed as he thrust furiously at her. *Open your eyes,* she urged him silently. Open them, open them, look at me—

And it seemed that his eyes did open to meet hers, even as they climaxed together, even as she centered the knife over his back and plunged it unerringly into his heart.

Afterward, in her own apartment, she put his eyes in the box with the others.

How Would You Like It?

I suppose it really started for me when I saw the man whipping his horse. He was a hansom cabdriver, dressed up like the chimney sweep in *Mary Poppins* with a top hat and a cutaway tailcoat, and I saw him on Central Park South, where the horse-drawn rigs queue up waiting for tourists who want a ride in the park. His horse was a swaybacked old gelding with a noble face, and it did something to me to see the way that driver used the whip. He didn't have to hit the horse like that.

I found a policeman and started to tell him about it, but it was clear he didn't want to hear it. He explained to me that I would have to go to the station house and file a complaint, and he said it in such a way as to discourage me from bothering. I don't really blame the cop. With crack dealers on every block and crimes against people and property at an all-time high and climbing, I suppose crimes against animals have to receive low priority.

But I couldn't forget about it.

I had already had my consciousness raised on the subject of animal rights. There was a campaign a few years ago to stop one of the cosmetic companies from testing their products on rabbits. They were blinding thousands of innocent rabbits every year, not with the goal of curing cancer but just because it was the cheapest way to safety-test their mascara and eyeliner.

I would have liked to sit down with the head of that company. "How would you like it?" I would have asked him. "How would you like having chemicals painted on your eyes to make you blind?"

All I did was sign a petition, like millions of other Americans, and I understand that it worked, that the company has gone out of the business of blinding bunnies. Sometimes, when we all get together, we can make a difference.

Sometimes we can make a difference all by ourselves.

Which brings me back to the subject of the horse and his driver. I found myself returning to Central Park South over the next several days and keeping tabs on that fellow. I thought perhaps I had just caught him on a bad day, but it became clear that it was standard procedure for him to use the whip that way. I went up to him and said something finally, and he turned positively red with anger. I thought for a moment he was going to use the whip on me, and I frankly would have liked to see him try it, but he only turned his anger on the poor horse, whipping him more brutally than ever and looking at me as if daring me to do something about it.

I just walked away.

That afternoon I went to a shop in Greenwich Village where they sell extremely odd paraphernalia to what I can only suppose are extremely odd people. They have handcuffs and studded wrist bands and all sorts of curious leather goods. Sadie Mae's Leather Goods, they call themselves. You get the picture.

I bought a ten-foot whip of plaited bullhide, and I took it back to Central Park

South with me. I waited in the shadows until that driver finished for the day, and I followed him home.

You can kill a man with a whip. Take my word for it.

Well, I have to tell you that I never expected to do anything like that again. I can't say I felt bad about what I'd done. The brute only got what he deserved. But I didn't think of myself as the champion of all the abused animals of New York. I was just someone who had seen his duty and had done it. It wasn't pleasant, flogging a man to death with a bullwhip, but I have to admit there was something almost shamefully exhilarating about it.

A week later, and just around the corner from my own apartment, I saw a man kicking his dog.

It was a sweet dog, too, a little beagle as cute as Snoopy. You couldn't imagine he might have done anything to justify such abuse. Some dogs have a mean streak, but there's never any real meanness in a hound. And this awful man was hauling off and savaging the animal with vicious kicks.

Why do something like that? Why have a dog in the first place if you don't feel kindly toward it? I said something to that effect, and the man told me to mind my own business.

Well, I tried to put it out of my mind, but it seemed as though I couldn't go for a walk without running into the fellow, and he always seemed to be walking the little beagle. He didn't kick him all the time—you'd kill a dog in short order if you did that regularly. But he was always cruel to the animal, yanking hard on the chain, cursing with genuine malice, and making it very clear that he hated it.

And then I saw him kick it again. Actually it wasn't the kick that did it for me, it was the way the poor dog cringed when the man drew back his foot. It made it so clear that he was used to this sort of treatment, that he knew what to expect.

So I went to a shoe store on Broadway in the teens where they have a good line of work shoes, and I bought a pair of steel-toed boots of the kind construction workers wear. I was wearing them the next time I saw my neighbor walking his dog, and I followed him home and rang his bell.

It would have been quicker and easier, I'm sure, if I'd had some training in karate. But even an untrained kick has a lot of authority to it when you're wearing steel-toed footwear. A couple of kicks in his legs and he fell down and couldn't get up, and a couple of kicks in the ribs took the fight out of him, and a couple of kicks in the head made it absolutely certain he would never harm another of God's helpless creatures.

It's cruelty that bothers me, cruelty and wanton indifference to another creature's pain. Some people are thoughtless, but when the inhumanity of their actions is pointed out to them they're able to understand and are willing to change.

For example, a young woman in my building had a mixed-breed dog that barked all day in her absence. She didn't know this because the dog never started barking until she'd left for work. When I explained that the poor fellow couldn't bear to be alone, that it made him horribly anxious, she went to the animal shelter and adopted the cutest little part Sheltie to keep him company. You never hear a peep out of either of those dogs now, and it does me good to see them on the street when she walks them, both of them obviously happy and well cared for.

And another time I met a man carrying a litter of newborn kittens in a sack. He was on his way to the river and intended to drown them, not out of cruelty but because he thought it was the most humane way to dispose of kittens he could not provide a home for. I explained to him that it was cruel to the mother cat to take her kittens away before she'd weaned them, and that when the time came he could simply take the unwanted kittens to the animal shelter; if they failed to find homes for them, at least their deaths would be easy and painless. More to the point, I told him where he could get the mother cat spayed inexpensively, so that he would not have to deal with this sad business again.

He was grateful. You see, he wasn't a cruel man, not by any means. He just didn't know any better.

Other people just don't want to learn.

Just yesterday, for example, I was in the hardware store over on Second Avenue. A well-dressed young woman was selecting rolls of flypaper and those awful Roach Motel devices.

"Excuse me," I said, "but are you certain you want to purchase those items? They aren't even very efficient, and you wind up spending a lot of money to kill very few insects."

She was looking at me oddly, the way you look at a crank, and I should have known I was just wasting my breath. But something made me go on.

"With the Roach Motels," I said, "they don't really kill the creatures at all, you know. They just immobilize them. Their feet are stuck, and they stand in place wiggling their antennae until I suppose they starve to death. I mean, how would you like it?"

"You're kidding," she said. "Right?"

"I'm just pointing out that the product you've selected is neither efficient nor humane," I said.

"So?" she said. "I mean, they're cockroaches. If they don't like it let them stay the hell out of my apartment." She shook her head, impatient. "I can't believe I'm having this conversation. My place is swarming with roaches and I run into a nut who's worried about hurting their feelings."

I wasn't worried about any such thing. And I didn't care if she killed roaches. I understand the necessity of that sort of thing. I just don't see the need for cruelty. But I knew better than to say anything more to her. It's useful to talk to some people. With others, it's like trying to blow out a lightbulb.

So I picked up a half-dozen tubes of Super Glue and followed her home.

If This Be Madness

St. Anthony's wasn't a bad place at all. There were bars on the windows, of course, and one couldn't come and go as one pleased, but it might have been a lot worse. I had always thought of insane asylums as something rather grim. The fictional treatment of such institutions leaves a good deal to be desired. Sadistic orderlies, medieval outlook, all of that. It wasn't like that, though.

I had a room to myself, with a window facing out on the main grounds. There were a great many elms on the property, plus some lovely shrubs which I would be hard-pressed to name. When I was alone I would watch the groundskeeper go back and forth across the wide lawn behind a big power mower. But of course I didn't spend all of my time in the room—or cell, if you prefer it. There was a certain amount of social intercourse—gab sessions with the other patients, interminable Ping-Pong matches, all of that. And the occupational therapy which was a major concern at St. Anthony's. I made these foolish little ceramic tile plates, and I wove baskets, and I made potholders. I suppose this was of some value. The simple idea of concentrating very intently on something which is essentially trivial must have some therapeutic value in cases of this nature—perhaps the same value that hobbies have for sane men.

Perhaps you're wondering why I was in St. Anthony's. A simple explanation. One cloudless day in September I left my office a few minutes after noon and went to my bank, where I cashed a check for two thousand dollars. I asked for—and received—two hundred crisp new ten-dollar bills. Then I walked aimlessly for two blocks until I came to a moderately busy street corner. Euclid and Paine, as I remember, but it's really immaterial.

There I sold the bills. I stopped passers-by and offered the bills at fifty cents apiece, or traded them for cigarettes, or gave them away in return for a kind word. I recall paying one man fifteen dollars for his necktie, and it was spotted at that. Not surprisingly, a great many persons refused to have anything to do with me. I suspect they thought the bills were counterfeit.

In less than a half hour I was arrested. The police, too, thought the bills were counterfeit. They were not. When the police led me off to the patrol car I laughed uproariously and hurled the ten-dollar bills into the air. The sight of the officers of the law chasing after these fresh new bills was quite comic, and I laughed long and loud.

In jail, I stared around blindly and refused to speak to people. Mary appeared in short order with a doctor and a lawyer in tow. She cried a great deal into a lovely linen handkerchief, but I could tell easily how much she was enjoying her new role. It was a marvelous experiment in martyrdom for her—loving wife of a man who has just managed to flip his lid. She played it to the hilt.

When I saw her, I emerged at once from my lethargy. I banged hysterically on the bars of the cell and called her the foulest names imaginable. She burst into tears and they led her away. Someone gave me a shot of something—a tranquilizer, I suspect. Then I slept.

I did not go to St. Anthony's then. I remained in jail for three days—under observation, as it were—and then I began to return to my senses. Reality returned. I was quite baffled about the entire experience. I asked guards where I was, and why. My memory was very hazy. I could recall bits and pieces of what had happened but it made no sense to me.

There were several conferences with the prison psychiatrist. I told him how I had been working very hard, how I had been under quite a strain. This made considerable sense to him. My "sale" of the ten-dollar bills was an obvious reaction of the strain of work, a symbolic rejection of the fruits of my labors. I was fighting against overwork by ridding myself of the profits of that work. We talked it all out, and he took elaborate notes, and that was that. Since I had done nothing specifically illegal, there were no charges to worry about. I was released.

Two months thereafter, I picked up my typewriter and hurled it through my office window. It plummeted to the street below, narrowly missing the bald head of a Salvation Army trumpet player. I heaved an ashtray after the typewriter, tossed my pen out the window, pulled off my necktie and hurled it out. I went to the window and was about to leap out after my typewriter and necktie and ashtray and pen when three of my employees took hold of me and restrained me, at which point I went joyously berserk.

I struck my secretary—a fine woman, loyal and efficient to the core—in the teeth, chipping one incisor rather badly. I kicked the office boy in the shin and belted my partner in the belly. I was wild, and quite difficult to subdue.

Shortly thereafter, I was in a room at St. Anthony's.

As I have said, it was not an unpleasant place at all. At times I quite enjoyed it. There was the utter freedom from responsibility, and a person who has not spent time in a sanitarium of one sort or another could not possibly appreciate the enormity of this freedom. It was not merely that there was nothing that I had to *do*. It goes considerably deeper than that.

Perhaps I can explain. I could *be* whomever I wished to be. There was no need to put up any sort of front whatsoever. There was no necessity for common courtesy or civility. If one wished to tell a nurse to go to the devil, one went ahead and did so. If one wished for any reason at all to urinate upon the floor, one went ahead and did so. One needed to make no discernible effort to appear sane. If I had been sane, after all, I would not have been there in the first place.

Every Wednesday, Mary visited me. This in itself was enough reason to fall in love with St. Anthony's. Not because she visited me once a week, but because for six days out of every seven I was spared her company. I have spent forty-four years on this planet, and for twenty-one of them I have been married to Mary, and her companionship has grown increasingly less tolerable over the years. Once, several years ago, I looked into the possibility of divorcing her. The cost would have been exorbitant. According to the lawyer I consulted, she would have wound up with house and car and the bulk of my worldly goods, plus monthly alimony sufficient to keep me permanently destitute. So we were never divorced.

As I said, she visited me every Wednesday. I was quite peaceable at those times; indeed, I was peaceable throughout my stay at St. Anthony's, aside from some minor displays of temper. But my hostility toward her showed through, I'm afraid. Periodically I displayed some paranoid tendencies, accusing her of having me committed for one nefarious motive or other, calling her to task for imagined affairs with my friends (as if any of them would want to bed down with the sloppy old bitch) and otherwise being happily nasty to her. But she kept returning, every Wednesday, like the worst of all possible pennies.

The sessions with my psychiatrist (not mine specifically, but the resident psychiatrist who had charge of my case) were not at all bad. He was a very bright man and quite interested in his work, and I enjoyed spending time with him. For the most part I was quite rational in our discussions. He avoided deep analysis—there was no time for it, really, as he had a tremendous workload as it was—and concentrated instead in trying to determine just what was causing my nervous breakdowns and just how they could be best controlled. We worked things out rather well. I made discernible progress, with just a few minor lapses from time to time. We investigated the causes of my hostility toward Mary. We talked at length.

I remember very clearly the day they released me from St. Anthony's. I was not pronounced cured—that's a rather difficult word to apply in cases of this particular nature. They said that I was readjusted, or something of the nature, and that I was in condition to rejoin society. Their terminology was a bit more involved than all that. I don't recall the precise words and phrases, but that's the gist of it.

That day, the air was cool and the sky was filled with clouds. There was a pleasant breeze blowing. Mary came to pick me up. She was noticeably nervous, perhaps afraid of me, but I was quite docile and perfectly friendly toward her. I took her arm. We walked out of the door to the car. I got behind the wheel—that gave her pause, as I think she would have preferred to do the driving just then. I drove, however. I drove the car out through the main gate and headed toward our home.

"Oh, darling," she said. "You're all better now, aren't you?"

"I'm fine," I said.

I was released five months ago. At first it was far more difficult on the outside than it had been within St. Anthony's heavy stone walls. People did not know how to speak with me. They seemed afraid that I might go berserk at any moment. They wanted to talk normally with me, yet they did not know how to refer to my "trouble." It was all quite humorous.

People warmed to me, yet at the same time they never entirely relaxed with me. While I was normal in most respects, certain mannerisms of mine were unnerving, to say the least. At times, for instance, I was observed mumbling incoherently to myself. At other times I answered questions before they were asked of me, or ignored questions entirely. Once, at a party, I walked over to the hi-fi, removed a record from the turntable, sailed it out of an open window, and put another record on. These periodic practices of mine were bizarre, and they set people on edge, yet they caused no one any real harm.

The general attitude seemed to be this—I was a little touched, but I was not dangerous, and I seemed to be getting better with the passage of time. Most important, I was able to function in the world at large. I was able to earn a living. I was able to live in peace and harmony with my wife and my friends. I might be quite mad, but it hurt no one.

Saturday night Mary and I are invited to a party. We will go to the home of some dear friends whom we have known for at least fifteen years. There will be eight or ten other couples there, all of them friends of a similar vintage.

It's time, now. This will be it.

You must realize that it was very difficult at first. The affair with the ten-dollar bills, for example—I'm essentially frugal, and such behavior went very much against the grain. The time when I hurled the typewriter out of the window was even harder. I did not want to hurt my secretary, of whom I have always been very fond, nor did I want to strike all those other people. But I did very well, I think. Very well indeed.

Saturday night, at the party, I will be quite uncommunicative. I will sit in a chair by the fireside and nurse a single drink for an hour or two, and when people talk to me I will stare myopically at them and will not answer them. I will make little involuntary facial movements, nervous twitches of one sort or another.

Then I will rise abruptly and hurl my glass into the mirror over the fireplace, hard enough to shatter either the glass or the mirror or both. Someone will come over in an attempt to subdue me. Whoever it is, I will strike him or her with all my might. Then, cursing violently, I will hurry to the side of the hearth and will pick up the heavy cast-iron poker.

I will smash Mary's head with it.

The happy thing is that there will be no nonsense about a trial. Temporary insanity may be difficult to plead in some cases, but it should hardly be a problem when the murderer has a past record of psychic instability. I have been in the hospital for a nervous breakdown. I have spent considerable time in a mental institution. The course is quite obvious—I shall be arrested and shall be sent forthwith to St. Anthony's.

I suspect they'll keep me there for a year or so. This time, of course, I can let them cure me completely. Why not? I don't intend to kill anyone else, so there's nothing to set up. All I have to do is make gradual progress until such time as they pronounce me fit to return to the world at large. But when that happens, Mary will not be there to meet me at the gate. Mary will be quite dead.

Already I can feel the excitement building within me. The tension, the thrill of it all. I can feel myself shifting over into the role of the madman, preparing for the supreme moment. Then the glass crashing into the mirror, and my body moving in perfect synchronization, and the poker in my hand, and Mary's skull crushed like an eggshell.

You may think I'm quite mad. That's the beauty of it—that's what everyone thinks, you see.

Leo Youngdahl, R.I.P.

Dear Larry,

I'm not sure if there's a story in this or not.

It happened about a year ago, at a time when I was living in New Hope, Pennsylvania, with a man named Evans Wheeler. New Hope is a small town with a reputation as an artists' colony. There is a theater there. At the time Evans was its assistant manager. I was doing some promotional work for the theater, which is how we originally met, and I was also briefly managing a spectacularly unsuccessful art gallery.

One afternoon in the late summer I returned to the apartment we shared. Evans was reading a magazine and drinking a beer. "There's a letter for you on the table," he said. "From your mother."

He must have assumed this from the postmark. The envelope was addressed in my mother's hand, but he wouldn't have recognized it as we never wrote each other. The city where she lives, and where I was born, is only an inexpensive telephone call away from New Hope. (In other respects, of course, it is much further removed.) My mother and I would speak once or twice a week over the phone.

I remember taking my time opening the envelope. There was a single sheet of blank typing paper inside, folded to enclose a small newspaper clipping. This was an obituary notice, and I read it through twice without having the vaguest idea why it had been sent to me. I even turned it over but the reverse held nothing but a portion of a department store ad. I turned the clipping for a third look and the name, "Youngdahl, Leo," suddenly registered, and I gave a shrill yelp of laughter that ended as abruptly as it had begun.

Evans said, "What's so funny?"

"Leo Youngdahl died."

"I didn't even know he was sick."

I started to laugh again. I really couldn't help it.

"All right, give. Who the hell is Leo Youngdahl? And why is his death so hysterical?"

"It's not really funny. And I don't know exactly who he is. Was. He was a man, he lived in Bethel. As far as I know, I only met him once. That was six years ago at my father's funeral."

"Oh, that explains it."

"Pardon?"

"I never felt more like a straight man in my life. 'You say you met him at your father's funeral, Gracie?' "

"There's really nothing to it," I said. "It's a sort of a family joke. It would take forever to explain and it wouldn't be funny to anyone else."

"Try me."

"It really wouldn't be funny."

"Oh, for Christ's sake," he said. "You're really too much, you know that?"

"I just meant—"

"I think I'll get out of the house for a while."

"Hey, you're really steamed."

"Not exactly that."

"Come on, sit down. I'll get you another beer. Or would you rather have some scotch, because I think I will."

"All right."

I made him a drink and got him back in his chair. Then I said, "I honestly don't think this is something you want to hear, but God knows it's nothing to start a fight over. It was just an incident, or rather a couple of incidents. It must have been ten years ago. I was home from school for I think it was Christmas—"

"You said six years ago, and at your father's funeral."

"I was starting at the beginning."

"That's supposed to be the best place."

"Yes, so I've been told. Are you sure you really want to hear this?"

"I'm positive I want to hear it. I won't interrupt."

"Well, it was nine or ten years ago, and it was definitely Christmas vacation. We were all over at Uncle Ed and Aunt Min's house. The whole family, on my mother's side, that is. A couple sets of aunts and uncles and the various children, and my grandmother. It wasn't Christmas dinner but a family dinner during that particular week."

"I get the picture."

"Well, as usual there were three or four separate conversations going on, and occasionally one of them would get prominent and the others would merge with it, the way conversations seem to go at family dinners."

"I've been to family dinners."

"And I don't know who brought it up, or in what connection, but at some point or the other the name Leo Youngdahl was mentioned."

"And everybody broke up."

"No, everybody did not break up, damn it. Suddenly I'm the straight man and I'm beginning to see why you objected to the role. If you don't want to hear this—"

"I'm sorry. The name Leo Youngdahl came up."

"And my father said, 'Wait a minute, I think he's dead.' "

"But he wasn't?"

"My father said he was dead, and somebody else said they were sure he was alive, and in no time at all this was the main subject of conversation at the table. As you can see, nobody knew Mr. Youngdahl terribly well, not enough to say with real certainty whether he was alive or dead. It seems ridiculous now, but there was quite a debate on the subject, and then my cousin Jeremy stood up and said there was obviously only one way to settle it. I believe you met Jeremy."

"The family faggot? No, I never met him, although you keep thinking I did. I've heard enough about him, but no, I never met him."

"Well, he's gay, but that hardly enters into it. When this happened he was in high school, and if he was gay then nobody knew it at the time. I don't think Jeremy knew it at the time."

"I'm sure he had fun finding out."

"He didn't have any gay mannerisms then. Not that he does now, in the sense of being effeminate, but he can come on a little nellie now and then. I suppose that's a learned attitude, wouldn't you think?"

"I'm sure I wouldn't know, sweetie."

"What he did have, even as a kid, was a very arch sense of humor. There's a Dutch expression, *kochloffel*, which means cooking spoon, in the sense of someone who's always stirring things up. Jeremy was a *kochloffel*. I forget who it was who used to call him that."

"I'm not sure it matters."

"I'm sure it doesn't. Anyway, Jeremy the *kochloffel* went over to the phone and got out the phone book and proceeded to look up Leo Youngdahl in the listings, and announced that he was listed. Of course the faction who said he was dead, including my father, started to say that a listing didn't prove anything, that he could have died since the book came out, or that his wife might have kept the listing active under his name, which was evidently common practice. But Jeremy didn't even wait out the objections, he just started dialing, and when someone answered he said, 'Is Leo Youngdahl there?' And whoever it was said that he was indeed there, and asked who was calling, and Jeremy said, 'Oh, it doesn't matter, I was just checking, and please give Leo my best wishes.' Then he hung up, and everybody laughed and made various speculations as to the reaction that exchange must have caused at the Youngdahl household, and there the matter stood, because the subject was settled and Leo Youngdahl was alive and well."

Evans looked at me and asked if that was the whole story, and how my father's funeral entered into it.

I said, "No, it's not the whole story. I'm going to have another drink. Do you want one?"

He didn't. I made myself one and came back into the room. "My father's funeral," I said. "I don't want to go into all of it now, but it was a very bad time for me. I'm sure it usually is. In this case there were complicating factors, including the fact that I was away from home when he died. It happened suddenly and I felt guilty about not being there. What happened was he had a heart attack and died about fifteen hours later, and I was in New York and was spending the night with a man and they couldn't reach me by phone, and—"

"Look, why don't you sit down."

"No, I'd rather stand. Let's just say I was guilty and let it go at that. *Feeling* guilty. I wish you would stop it with those wise Freudian nods."

"Oh, for God's sake."

"I'm sorry. Where was I? Another thing, it was my first real experience with death. Both of my grandfathers had died when I was too young to understand what was going on. This was the first death I related to personally as an adult.

"The point of this is that we were all at the funeral parlor the day before the funeral—actually it was the night before—and there was this endless stream of people paying condolence calls. My mother and brother and I had to sit there forever while half the town came up to take our hands and tell us how sorry they were and what a wonderful man my father was. I didn't recognize more than half of them. Bethel's not that large, but my father was a rather prominent man—"

"So you've told me."

"You're a son of a bitch. Have I told you that?"

"Hey!"

"Oh, I'm sorry. But just let me get this over with. Finally one of these strangers took my mother's hand and said, 'Edna, I'm terribly sorry,' or whatever the hell he said, and then he turned his head toward me—I was sitting next to her between her and Gordon—and said, 'I don't think you know me, my name is Leo Youngdahl,' and I cracked up completely."

"You cried? Yes, I can see that, hearing the name and all—"

"No, no, no! You're missing the whole point. I cracked up, I *laughed*!"

"Oh."

"It was such incredible comic relief. The only thing on earth the name Leo Youngdahl meant to me was Jeremy phoning to find out if he was alive or dead, and now meeting him for the first time and at my father's funeral. I have never laughed so uncontrollably in my life."

"What did he do?"

"That's just it. *He never knew I was laughing.* Nobody ever knew, because my mother did the most positively brilliant thing anybody ever did in their lives. *She* knew I was laughing, and she knew why, but without the slightest hesitation she put her arm around me and drew me down and said, 'Don't cry, baby, don't cry, it's all right,' and I finally got hold of myself enough to turn off the laughter and turn it into the falsest tears I've ever shed, and by the time I picked my face up Leo Youngdahl was gone and I was able to handle myself. I went downstairs and washed my face and settled myself down, and after that I was all right."

I lit a cigarette, and Evans said something or other, but I wasn't done yet. That might have been the end of the story. But I sometimes have difficulty determining where to end a story.

"Later that night the parade ended and we went home. Mother and Gordon and I had coffee, and neither of us mentioned the incident in front of Gordon. I don't know why. I told him the next day and he couldn't get over how it had happened right next to him and he had missed it, and we both went on and on about how incredibly poised she had been. I don't know how you develop that kind of social grace under pressure.

"After Gordon went to bed, I thanked her for covering for me and we talked about the whole thing and laughed about it. Then she said, 'You know, that's just the kind of thing your dad would have loved. He would have loved it.' And then her face changed, and she said, 'And I can never tell him about it, oh God, I can never tell him anything again,' and *she* cried. We both cried, and just remembering it—"

"Come here, baby."

"No. The last time I talked to him was three days before he died. Over the phone, and we quarreled. I don't remember what about. Oh, I *do* remember. It doesn't matter."

"Of course not."

"We quarreled, and then they tried to reach me to tell me he was dying, and they couldn't and then he was dead and there were all those things I couldn't tell him. And now Leo Youngdahl is dead. I can't even remember what he looked like."

"Come on, let's get out of here. Let's go over to Sully's and I'll buy you a drink."

"No, you go."

"I'll stay with you."

"No, *you* go. I want a little time alone. I'm a mess. I'll meet you over there in a little while. You said Sully's?"

"Sure."

And so that's the story, if indeed it is a story. I thought about sending a contribution to the American Cancer Society in Leo Youngdahl's memory. I never did. I often conceive gestures of that sort but rarely carry them out.

There's nothing more to it, except to say that within two weeks of that conversation Evans Wheeler packed his things and moved out. There is no earthly way to attribute his departure to that particular conversation. Nor is there any earthly way I can be convinced that the two events are unrelated.

I still have Leo Youngdahl's obituary notice around somewhere. At least I think I do. I certainly don't remember ever throwing it away.

As always,
Jill

Like a Bug on a Windshield

There are two Rodeway Inns in Indianapolis, but Waldron only knew the one on West Southern Avenue, near the airport. He made it a point to break trips there if he could do so without going out of his way or messing up his schedule. There were eight or ten motels around the country that were favorites of his, some of them chain affiliates, a couple of them independents. A Days Inn south of Tulsa, for example, was right across the street from a particularly good restaurant. A Quality Court outside of Jacksonville had friendly staff and big cakes of soap in the bathroom. Sometimes he didn't know exactly why a motel was on his list, and he thought that it might be habit, like the brand of cigarettes he smoked, and that habit in turn might be largely a matter of convenience. Easier to buy Camels every time than to stand around deciding what you felt like smoking. Easier to listen to WJJD out of Chicago until the signal faded, then dial on down to KOMA in Omaha, than to hunt around and try to guess what kind of music you wanted to hear and where you were likely to find it.

It was more than habit, though, that made him stop at the Indianapolis Rodeway when he was in the neighborhood. They made it nice for a trucker without running a place that felt like a truck stop. There was a separate lot for the big rigs, of course, but there was also a twenty-four-hour check-in area around back just for truckers, with a couple of old boys sitting around in chairs and country music playing on the radio. The coffee was always hot and always free, and it was real coffee out of a Silex, not the brown dishwater the machines dispensed.

Inside, the rooms were large and clean and the beds comfortable. There was a huge indoor pool with Jacuzzi and sauna. A good bar, an okay restaurant—and, before you hit the road again, there was more free coffee at the truckers' room in back.

Sometimes a guy could get lucky at the bar or around the pool. If not, well, there was free HBO on the color television and direct-dial phones to call home on. You wouldn't drive five hundred miles out of your way, but it was worth planning your trip to stop there.

He walked into the Rodeway truckers' room around nine on a hot July night. The room was air-conditioned but the door was always open, so the air-conditioning didn't make much difference. Lundy rocked back in his chair and looked up at him. "Hey, boy," Lundy said. "Where you *been*?"

"Drivin'," he said, giving the ritual response to the ritual question.

"Yeah, I guess. You look about as gray as this desk. Get yourself a cup of coffee, I think you need it."

"What I need is about four ounces of bourbon and half an hour in the Jacuzzi."

"And two hours with the very best TWA has to offer," Lundy said. "What we all need, but meantime grab some coffee."

"I guess," Waldron said, and poured himself a cup. He blew on the surface to cool it and glanced around the room. Besides Lundy, a chirpy little man with wire-rimmed glasses and a built-up shoe, there were three truckers in the room. Two, like Waldron, were drinking coffee out of Styrofoam cups. The third man was drinking Hudepohl beer out of the can.

Waldron filled out the registration card, paid with his Visa card, pocketed his room key and receipt. Then he sat down and took another sip of his coffee.

"The way some people drive," he said.

There were murmurs of agreement.

"About forty miles out of here," he said, "I'm on the Interstate—what's the matter with me, I can't even think of the goddamned number—"

"Easy, boy."

"Yeah, easy." He took a breath, sipped at his coffee, blew at the surface. It was cool enough to drink, but blowing on it was reflexive, habitual. "Two kids in a Toyota. I thought at first it was two guys, but it was a guy and a girl. I'm going about five miles over the limit, not pushing it, and they pass me on a slight uphill and then they cut in tight. I gotta step on my brake or I'm gonna walk right up their back bumper."

"These people don't know how to drive," one of the coffee drinkers said. "I don't know where they get their licenses."

"Through the mails," the beer drinker said. "Out of the Monkey Ward catalog."

"So I tapped the horn," Waldron said. "Just a tap, you know? And the guy was driving, he taps back."

"Honks his horn."

"Right. And slows down. Sixty-two, sixty, fifty-eight, he's dying out there in front of me. So I wait, and I flip the brights on and off to signal him, and then I go around him and wait until I'm plenty far ahead of him before I move back in."

"And he passes you again," said the other coffee drinker, speaking for the first time.

"How'd you know?"

"He cut in sharp again?"

Waldron nodded. "I guess I was expecting it once he moved out to pass me. I eased up on the gas, and when he cut in I had to touch the brake, but it wasn't close, and this time I didn't bother hitting the horn."

"I'da used the horn," the beer drinker said. "I'da *stood up* on the horn."

"Then he slowed down again," the second coffee drinker said. "Am I right?"

"What are these guys, friends of yours?"

"They slow down again?"

"To a crawl. And then I *did* use the horn, and the girl turned around and gave me the finger." He drank the rest of the coffee. "And I got angry," he said. "I pulled out. I put the pedal on the floor and I moved out in front of them—and this time they're not gonna let me pass, you know, they're gonna pace me, fast when I speed up, slow when I lay off. And they're looking up at me, and they're laughing, and she's leaning across his lap and she's got her blouse or the front of her dress, whatever it is, she's got it pushed down, you know, like I've never seen it before and my eyeballs are gonna go out on stalks—"

"Like in a cartoon."

"Right. And I thought, You idiots, because all I had to do, you know, was turn the wheel. Because where are they gonna go? The shoulder? They won't have time to get there. I'll run right over them, I'll smear 'em like a bug on the windshield. Splat, and they're gone."

"I like that," Lundy said.

Waldron took a breath. "I almost did it," he said.

"How much is almost?"

"I could feel it in my hands," he said. He held them out in front of him, shaped to grip a steering wheel. "I could feel the thought going into my hands, to turn that wheel and flatten them. I could see it all happening. I had the picture in my mind, and I was seeing myself driving away from them, just driving off, and they're wrecked and burning."

Lundy whistled.

"And I had the thought, That's murder! And the thought like registered, but I was still going to do it, the hell with it. My hands"—he flexed his fingers—"my hands were ready to move on the wheel, and then it was gone."

"The Toyota was gone?"

"The *thought* was gone. I hit the brake and I got behind them and a rest area came up and I took it, fast. I pulled in and cut the engine and had a smoke. I was all alone there. It was empty and I was thinking that maybe they'd come back and pull into the rest area, too, and if they did I was gonna take him on with a tire iron. There's one I keep in the front seat with me and I actually got it down from the rig and walked around with it in one hand, smoking a cigarette and swinging the tire iron just so I'll be ready."

"You see 'em again?"

"No. They were just a couple of kids clowning around, probably working themselves up. Now they'll get into the backseat and have themselves a workout."

"I don't envy them," Lundy said. "Not in the backseat of an effing Toyota."

"What they don't know," said Waldron, "is how close they came to being dead."

They were all looking up at him. The second coffee drinker, a dark-haired man with deep-set brown eyes, smiled. "You really think it was close?"

"I told you, I almost—"

"So how close is almost? You thought about it and then you didn't do it."

"I thought about making it with Jane Fonda," Lundy said, "but then I didn't do it."

"I was going to do it," Waldron said.

"And then you didn't."

"And then I didn't." He shook a cigarette out of his pack and picked up Lundy's Zippo and lit it. "I don't know where the anger came from. I was angry enough to kill. Why? Because the girl shot me a bone? Because she waggled her—?"

"Because you were afraid," the first coffee drinker suggested.

"Afraid of what? I got eighteen wheels under me, I'm hauling building materials, how'm I afraid of a Toyota? It's not my ass if I hit them." He took the cigarette out of his mouth and looked at it. "But you're right," he said. "I was scared I'd hit them and kill them, and that turned into anger, and I almost *did* kill them."

"Maybe you should have," someone said. Waldron was still looking at his cigarette, not noticing who was speaking. "Whole road's full of amateurs and people thinking they're funny. Maybe you got to teach 'em a lesson."

"Swat 'em," someone else said. "Like you said, bug on the windshield."

" 'I'm just a bug on the windshield of life,' " Lundy sang in a tuneless falsetto whine. "Now who was it sang that or did I just make it up?" Dolly Parton, the beer drinker suggested. "Now wouldn't I just love to be a bug on her windshield?" Lundy said.

Waldron picked up his bag and went to look for his room.

Eight, ten weeks later, he was eating eggs and scrapple in a diner on Route 1 outside of Bordentown, New Jersey. The diner was called the Super Chief and was designed to look like a diesel locomotive and painted with aluminum paint. Waldron was reading a paper someone else had left in the booth. He almost missed the story, but then he saw it.

A camper had plunged through a guardrail and off an embankment on a branch of the Interstate near Gatlinburg, Tennessee. The driver, an instructor at Ozark Community College in Pine Bluff, Arkansas, had survived with massive chest and leg injuries. His wife and infant son had died in the crash.

According to the driver, an eighteen-wheeler had come up "out of nowhere" and shoved the little RV off the road. "It's like he was a snowplow," he said, "and he was clearing us out of the way."

Like a bug on a windshield, thought Waldron.

He read the story again, closed the paper. His hand was shaking as he picked up his cup of coffee. He put the cup down, took a few deep breaths, then picked up the cup again without trembling.

He pictured them in the truckers' room at the Rodeway, Lundy rocking back in his chair with his feet up, built-up shoe and all. The beer drinker, the two coffee drinkers. Had he even heard their names? He couldn't remember, nor could he keep their images in focus in his memory. But he could hear their voices. And he could hear his own, suggesting an act not unlike the one he had just read about.

My God, had he given someone an idea?

He sipped his coffee, left the rest of his food untouched on the plate. Scrapple was a favorite of his and you could only find it in and around Philadelphia, and they did it right here, fried it crisp and served it with maple syrup, but he was letting the grease congeal around it now. That one coffee drinker, the one with the deep-set eyes, was he the one who'd spoken the words, but he remembered the anger in them, and something else, too, something like a blood lust.

Of course, the teacher could have dreamed the part about the eighteen-wheeler. Could have gone to sleep at the wheel and made up a story to keep him from seeing he'd driven off the road and killed his own family. Pin it on the Phantom Trucker and keep the blame off your own self.

Probably how it happened.

Still, from that morning on, Waldron kept an eye on the papers.

"Hey, boy," Lundy said. "Where *you* been?"

It was a cold December afternoon, overcast, with a raw wind blowing out of the northwest. The daylight ran out early this time of year but there were hours of it left. Waldron had broken his trip early just to stop at the Rodeway.

"Been up and down the Seaboard," he said. "Mostly. Hauling a lot of loads in and out of Baltimore." Of course there'd been some cross-country trips, too, but he'd managed to miss Indianapolis each time, once or twice distorting his schedule as much to avoid Indy as he'd fooled with it today to get here.

"Been a while," Lundy said.

"Six months."

"That long?"

"July, last I was here."

"Makes five months, don't it?"

"Well, early July. Say five and a half."

"Say a year and a half if you want. Your wife asks, I'll swear you was never here at all. Get some coffee, boy."

There was another trucker sitting with a cup of coffee, a bearded longhair with a fringed buckskin jacket, and he'd laughed at Lundy's remark. Waldron poured himself a cup of coffee and sat down with it, sitting quietly, listening to the radio and the two men's light banter. When the fellow in buckskin left, Waldron leaned forward.

"The last time I was here," he said.

"July, if we take your word for it."

"I was wired that night, I'd had a clown playing tag with me on the road."

"If you say so."

"There were three truckers in here plus yourself. One was drinking beer and the other two were drinking coffee."

Lundy looked at him.

"What I need to know," Waldron said, "is their names."

"You must be kidding."

"It wouldn't be hard to find out. You'd have the registrations. I checked the date, it was the ninth of July."

"Wait a minute." Lundy rocked his chair back and put both feet on the metal desk. Waldron glanced at the built-up shoe. "A night in July," Lundy said. "What in hell happened?"

"You must remember. I almost had an accident with a wise-ass, cut me off, played tag, made a game of it. I was saying how angry I was, how I wanted to kill him."

"So?"

"I wanted to kill him with the truck."

"So?"

"Don't you remember? Something I said, you made a song out of it. I said I could have killed him like a bug on the windshield."

"Now I remember," Lundy said, showing interest. "Just a bug on the windshield of life, that's the song that came to me, I couldn't get it out of my head for the next ten or twelve days. Now I'll be stuck with it for the *next* ten or twelve days, like as not. Don't tell me you want to haul my ass down to Nashville and make me a star."

"What I want," Waldron said evenly, "is for you to check the registrations and figure out who was in the room that night."

"Why?"

"Because somebody's doing it."

Lundy looked at him.

"Killing people. With trucks."

"Killing people with trucks? Killing drivers or owners or what?"

"Using trucks as murder weapons," Waldron said. On the radio, David Allen Coe insisted he was an outlaw like Waylon and Willie. "Running people off the road. Flyswatting 'em."

"How d'you know all this?"

"Look," Waldron said. He took an envelope from his pocket, unfolded it, and spread newspaper clippings on the top of Lundy's desk. Without removing his feet from the desk, Lundy leaned forward to scan the clips. "These are from all over," he said after a moment.

"I know."

"Any of these here could be an accident."

"Then somebody's leaving the scene of a lot of accidents. Last I heard, there was a law against it."

"Could be a whole lot of different accidents."

"It could," Waldron admitted. "But I don't believe it. It's murder and it's one man doing it and I know who he is."

"Who?"

"At least I think I know."

"You gonna tell me or is it a secret?"

"Not the beer drinker," Waldron said. "One of the two fellows who were drinking coffee."

"Narrows it down. Not too many old boys drive trucks and drink coffee."

"I can almost picture him. Deep-set eyes, dark hair, sort of a dark complexion. He had a way of speaking. I can about hear his voice."

"What makes you think he's the one?"

"I don't know. You want to get those registrations?"

He didn't, and Waldron had to talk him into it. Then there were three check-ins, one right after the other, and two of the men lingered with their coffee. When they left, Lundy heaved a sigh and told Waldron to mind the store. He limped off and came back ten minutes later with a stack of index cards.

"July the ninth," he announced, sinking into his chair and slapping the cards onto the desk. "You want to deal those, we can play some Five Hundred Rummy. You got enough cards for it."

Not quite. There were forty-three registrations that had come through the truckers' check-in room for that date. Just over half were names that one of the two men recognized and could rule out as the possible identity of the dark-eyed coffee drinker. But there were still twenty possibles, names that meant nothing to either man—and Lundy explained that their man might not have filled in a card.

"He could of shared a room and the other man registered," he said, "or he could have just come by for the coffee and the company. There's old boys every night that pull in for half an hour and the free coffee, or maybe they're taking a meal break and they come around back to say hello. So what you got, you got it narrowed down to twenty, but he might not be one of the twenty anyway. You get tired of driving a truck, boy, you can get a job with Sherlock Holmes. Get you the cap and the pipe, nobody'll know the difference."

Waldron was going through the cards, reading the names and addresses.

"Looking through a stack of cards for a man who maybe isn't there in the first place and who probably didn't do anything anyway. And what are you gonna do if you find him?"

"I don't know."

"Where's it your business, come to that?"

Waldron didn't say anything at first. Then he said, "I gave him the idea."

"With what you said? Bug on the windshield?"

"That's right."

"Oh, that's crazy," Lundy said. "Where you been, boy? I hear that same kind of talk four days out of seven. Guy walks in, hot about some fool who almost made him lose it, next thing you know he's saying how instead of driving off the road, next time he'll drive right *through* the mother. Even if somebody's doin' this"—he tapped Waldron's clippings—"which I don't think they are, there's no way it's you gave him the idea. My old man, he'd wash his car and then it'd rain and he'd swear it was him brought the rain on. You're startin' to remind me of him, you know that?"

"I can picture him," Waldron said. "Sitting up behind the wheel, a light rain coming down, the windshield wipers working at the low speed. And he's smiling."

"And about to run some sucker off the road."

"I can just see it so clear. This one time"—he sorted through the newspaper clippings—"downstate Illinois, this sportscar. Witness said a truck just ran right *over* it."

"Like steppin' on it," Lundy said thoughtfully.

"And when I think about it—"

"You don't know it's on purpose," Lundy said. "All the pills some of you old boys take. And you don't know it's one man doing it, and you don't know it's him, and you don't know who he is anyway. And you don't know you gave him the idea, and if there's a God or not you ain't It, so why are you makin' yourself crazy over it?"

"Well, you got a point," Waldron said.

He went to his room, showered, put on swim trunks, and picked up a towel. He went back and forth from the sauna to the pool and into the Jacuzzi and back into the pool again. He swam some laps, then stretched out on a chaise next to the pool. He listened, eyes closed, while a man with a soft hill-country accent was trying to teach his young son to swim. Then he must have dozed off, and when he opened his eyes he was alone in the pool area. He returned to his room, showered, shaved, put on fresh clothes, and went to the bar.

It was a nice room—low lighting, comfortable chairs, and bar stools. Some decorator had tricked it out with a library motif, and there were bookshelves here and there with real books in them. At least Waldron supposed they were real books. He'd never seen anyone reading one of them.

He settled in at the bar with bourbon and dry-roast peanuts from the dish on the bartop. An hour later he was in a conversation, and thirty minutes after that he was back in his room, bedded down with an old girl named Claire who said she was assistant manager of the gift shop at the airport. She was partial to truckers, she told him. She'd even married one, and although it hadn't worked out they remained good friends. "Man drives for a living, chances are he's thoughtful and considerate and sure of himself, you know what I mean?"

Waldron saw those deep-set brown eyes looking over the steering wheel. And that slow smile.

After that he seemed to catch a lot of cross-country hauling and he stopped pretty regularly at the Rodeway. It was convenient enough, and the Jacuzzi was a big attraction during the winter months. It really took the road tension out of you.

Claire was an attraction, too. He didn't see her every visit, but if the hour was right he sometimes gave her a call and they sometimes got together. She'd come by for a drink or a swim, and one night he put on a jacket and took her to dinner in town at the King Cole.

She knew he was married and felt neither jealousy nor guilt about it. "Me and my ex," she said, "it wasn't what he did on the road that broke us up. It was what he didn't do when he was home."

It was mid-March when he finally found the man. And it was nowhere near Indianapolis.

It was a truck stop just east of Tucumcari, New Mexico, and he'd had no intention of stopping there. He'd had breakfast a while back in a Tex-Mex diner midway between Gallup and Albuquerque, and by the time he hit Tucumcari his gut was rumbling and he was ready for an unscheduled pit stop. He picked a place he'd never stopped at. If it had a name he didn't know what it was. The signs said nothing but DIESEL FUEL and TRUCKERS WELCOME. He clambered down from the cab and used the john, then went in for a cup of coffee he didn't particularly want.

And saw the man right away.

He'd been able to picture the eyes and the smile, and a pair of hands on a wheel. Now the image enlarged to include a round, close-cropped head with a receding hairline, a bulldog jaw, a massive pair of shoulders. The man sat on a stool at the counter, drinking coffee and reading a magazine, and Waldron just stood for a moment, looking at him.

There was a point where he almost turned and walked out. It passed, and instead he took the adjoining stool and ordered coffee. When the girl brought it, he let it sit there. Beside him, the man with the deep-set eyes was reading an article about bonefishing in the Florida Keys.

"Nice day out there," Waldron said.

The man raised his eyes, nodded.

"I think I met you sometime last summer. Indianapolis, the Rodeway Inn."

"I've been there."

"I met you in Lundy's room in the back. There were three men there besides Lundy. One of them was drinking a can of Hudepohl."

"You got a memory," the man said.

"Well, the night stuck in my mind. I had a close one out on the highway, I came in jawing about it. A jerk in a car playing tag with me and I came in mad enough to talk about running him off the road, killing him."

"I remember that night," the man said, and he smiled the way Waldron remembered. "Now I remember you."

Waldron sipped his coffee.

" 'Like a bug on a windshield,' " the man said. "I remember you saying that. Next little while, every time some insect went and gummed up the glass, it came to me, you saying that. You ever find them?"

"Find who?"

"Whoever was playing tag with you."

"I never looked for them."

"You were mad enough to," the man said. "That night you were."

"I got over it."

"Well, people get over things."

There was a whole unspoken conversation going on and Waldron wanted to cut through and get to it. "Who I been looking for," he said, "is I been looking for you."

"Oh?"

"I get things in my mind I can't get rid of," Waldron said. "I'll get a thought working and I won't be able to let go of it for a hundred miles. And my stomach's been turning on me."

"You lost me on a curve there."

"What we talked about. What I said that night, just running my mouth, and you picked up on it." Waldron's hands worked, forming into fists, opening again. "I read the papers," he said. "I find stories, I clip them out of the papers." He met the man's eyes. "I know what you're doing," he said.

"Oh?"

"And I gave you the idea," he said.

"You think so, huh?"

"The thought keeps coming to me," Waldron said. "I can't shake it off. I drop it and it comes back."

"You want the rest of that coffee?" Waldron looked at his cup, put it down unfinished. "C'mon then," the man said, and put money on the counter to cover both their checks.

Waldron kept his newspaper clippings in a manila envelope in the zippered side pocket of his bag. The bag rode on the floor of the cab in front of the passenger seat. They were standing beside the cab now, facing away from the sun. The man was going through some of the clippings and Waldron was holding the rest of them.

"You must read a lot of papers," the man said.

Waldron didn't say anything.

"You think I been killing people. With my truck."

"I thought so, all these months."

"And now?"

"I still think so."

"You think I did all these here. And you think you started it all by getting mad at some fool driver in Indiana."

Waldron felt the sun on the back of his neck. The world had gone silent and all he could hear was his own breathing.

Then the man said, "This here one was mine. Little panel truck, electrical contractor or some damn thing. Rode him right off a mountain. I didn't figure he'd walk away from it, but then I didn't stay around to find out, you know, and I don't get around to reading the papers much." He put the clipping on the pile. "A few of these are mine," he said.

Waldron felt a pressure in his chest, as if his heart had turned to iron and was being drawn by a magnet.

"But most of these," the man went on, "the hell, I'd have to work night and day doing nothing else. I mean, figure it out, huh? Some of these are accidents, just like they're written up."

"And the rest?"

"The rest are a whole lot of guys like you and me taking a whack at somebody once in a while. You think it's one man doing all of it and you said something to get him started, hell, put your mind to rest. I did it a couple of times before you ever said a word. And I wasn't the first trucker ever thought of it, or the first ever did it."

"Why?"

"Why do it?"

Waldron nodded.

"Sometimes to teach some son of a bitch a lesson. Sometimes to get the anger out. And sometimes—look, you ever go hunting?"

"Years ago, with my old man."

"You remember what it felt like?"

"Just that I was scared all the time," Waldron said, remembering. "That I'd do something wrong, miss a shot or make noise or something, and my dad would get mad at me."

"So you never got to like it."

"No."

"Well, it's like hunting," the man said. "Seeing if you can do it. And there's you and him, and it's like you're dancing, and then he's gone and you're all that's left. It's like a bullfight, it's like shooting a bird on the wing. There's something about it that's beautiful."

Waldron couldn't speak.

"It's just a once-in-a-while thing," the man said. "It's a way to have fun, that's all. It's no big deal."

He drove all day, eastbound on 66, his mind churning and his stomach a wreck. He stopped often for coffee, sitting by himself, avoiding conversations with other drivers. Any of them could be a murderer, he thought, and once he fancied that they were all murderers, unpunished killers racing back and forth across the country, running down anyone who got in their way.

He knew he ought to eat, and twice he ordered food only to leave it untouched on his plate. He drank coffee and smoked cigarettes and just kept going.

At a diner somewhere he reached for a newspaper someone else had left behind. Then he changed his mind and drew away from it. When he returned to his truck he took the manila envelope of newspaper clippings from his bag and dropped it into a trash can. He wouldn't clip any more stories, he knew, and for the next little while he wouldn't even read the papers. Because he'd only be looking for stories he didn't want to find.

He kept driving. He thought about stopping when the sky darkened but he decided against it. Sleep just seemed out of the question. Being off the highway for longer than it took to gulp a cup of coffee seemed impossible. He played the radio once or twice but turned it off almost immediately; the country music he normally liked just didn't sound right to him. At one point he switched on the CB—he hardly ever listened to it these days, and now the chatter that came over it sounded like a mockery. They were out there killing people for sport, he thought, and they were chatting away in that hokey slang and he couldn't stand it . . .

Four in the morning, or close to it, he was on a chunk of Interstate in Missouri or maybe Iowa—he wasn't too sure where he was, his mind was running all over the place. The median strip was broad here and you couldn't see the lights of cars in the other lane. The traffic was virtually nonexistent—it was like he was the only driver on the road, a trucker's Flying Dutchman or something out of a Dave Dudley song, doomed to ride empty highways until the end of time.

Crazy.

There were lights in his mirror. High beams, somebody coming up fast. He moved to his right, hugging the shoulder.

The other vehicle moved out and hovered alongside him. For a mindless instant he had the thought that it was the man with the deep-set eyes, the killer come to kill him. But this wasn't even a truck, this was a car, and it was just sort of dipsy-doodling along next to Waldron. Waldron wondered what was the matter with the damn fool.

Then the car passed him in a quick burst of speed and Waldron saw what it was.

The guy was drunk.

He got past Waldron's rig, cut in abruptly, then almost drove off the road before he got the wheel straightened out again. He couldn't keep the car in line, he kept wandering off to the left or the right, he was all over the road.

A fucking menace, Waldron thought.

He took his own foot off the gas and let the car pull away from him, watching the taillights get smaller in the distance. Only when the car was out of sight did Waldron bring his truck back up to running speed.

His mind wandered then, drifting along some byway, and he came back into present time to note that he was driving faster than usual, pushing past the speed limit. He found he was still doing it even after he noticed it.

Why?

When the taillights came into view, he realized what he'd subconsciously been doing all along. He was looking for the drunk driver, and there he was. He recognized the taillights. Even if he hadn't, he'd recognize the way the car swung from side to side, raising gravel on the shoulder, then wandering way over into the left-hand lane and back again.

Drivers like that were dangerous. They killed people every day and the cops couldn't keep the bastards off the roads. Look at this crazy son of a bitch, look at him, for God sake, he was all over the place, he was sure to kill himself if he didn't kill someone else first.

Downhill stretch coming up. Waldron was loaded up with kitchen appliances, just a hair under his maximum gross weight. Give him a stretch of downhill loaded like that, hell, wasn't anyone could run away from him going downhill.

He looked at the weaving car in front of him. Nobody else out in front, nobody in his mirror. Something quickened in his chest. He got a flash of deep-set eyes and a knowing smile.

He put the gas pedal on the floor.

Like a Dog in the Street

The capture of the man called Anselmo amounted to the gathering together of innumerable threads, many of them wispy and frail. For almost two years the terrorist had been the target of massive manhunt operations launched by not one but over a dozen nations. The one valid photograph of him, its focus blurred and indistinct, had been reproduced and broadcast throughout the world; his features—the jagged and irregular yellow teeth, the too-small upturned nose, the underslung jaw, the bushy eyebrows grown together into a single thick, dark line—were as familiar to the general public as they were to counterintelligence professionals and Interpol agents.

Bit by bit, little by little, the threads began to link up. In a cafe in a working-class neighborhood in Milan, two men sat sipping espresso laced with anisette. They spoke of an interregional soccer match, and of the possibility of work stoppage by the truck dispatchers. Then their voices dropped, and one spoke quickly and quietly of Anselmo while the other took careful note of every word.

In a suburb of Asunción, a portly gentleman wearing the uniform of a brigadier general in the Paraguayan army shared the front seat of a four-year-old Chevrolet Impala with a slender young man wearing the uniform of a chauffeur. The general talked while the chauffeur listened. While Anselmo was not mentioned by name, he was the subject of the conversation. At its conclusion the chauffeur gave the general an envelope containing currency in the amount of two thousand German marks. Three hours later the chauffeur—who was not a chauffeur—was on a plane for Mexico City. The following afternoon the general—who was not really a general—was dead of what the attending physician diagnosed as a massive myocardial infarction.

In Paris, in the ninth arrondissement, three security officers, one of them French, entered an apartment which had been under surveillance for several weeks. It proved to be empty. Surveillance was continued but no one returned to the apartment during the course of the following month. A thoroughgoing analysis of various papers and detritus found in the apartment was relayed in due course to authorities in London and Tel Aviv.

In West Berlin, a man and woman, both in their twenties, both blond and fair-skinned and blue-eyed and looking enough alike to be brother and sister, made the acquaintance of a dark-haired and full-bodied young woman at a cabaret called Justine's. The three shared a bottle of sparkling Burgundy, then repaired to a small apartment on the Bergenstrasse where they shared several marijuana cigarettes, half a bottle of Almspach brandy, and a bed. The blond couple did certain things which the dark-haired young woman found quite painful, but she gave every appearance of enjoying the activity. Later, when she appeared to be asleep, the blond man and woman talked at some length. The dark-haired young woman, who was in fact awake throughout this conversation, was still awake later on when the other two lay sprawled beside her, snoring lustily. She dressed and left quickly, pausing only long enough to slit their throats with a kitchen knife. Her flight to Beirut landed shortly before two in the afternoon, and within an hour after that she was talking with a middle-aged Armenian gentleman in the back room of a travel agency.

Bits and pieces. Threads, frail threads, coming together to form a net . . .

And throughout it all the man called Anselmo remained as active as ever. A Pan Am flight bound for Belgrade blew up in the air over Austria. A telephone call claiming credit for the deed on behalf of the Popular Front for Croatian Autonomy was logged at the airline's New York offices scant minutes before an explosion shredded the jetliner.

A week earlier, rumors had begun drifting around that Anselmo was working with the Croats.

In Jerusalem, less than a quarter of a mile from the Wailing Wall, four gunmen burst into a Sephardic synagogue during morning services. They shot and killed twenty-eight members of the congregation before they themselves were rooted out and shot down by police officers. The dead gunmen proved to be members of a leftist movement aimed at securing the independence of Puerto Rico from the United States. But why should Puerto Rican extremists be mounting a terrorist operation against Israel?

The common denominator was Anselmo.

An embassy in Washington. A police barracks in Strabane, in Northern Ireland. A labor union in Buenos Aires.

Anselmo.

Assassinations. The Spanish ambassador to Sweden shot down in the streets of Stockholm. The sister-in-law of the premier of Iraq. The Research and Development head of a multinational oil company. A British journalist. An Indonesian general. An African head of state.

Anselmo.

Hijacking and kidnapping. Ransom demands. Outrages.

Anselmo. Always Anselmo.

Of course it was not always his hand on the trigger. When the Puerto Rican gunmen shot up the Jerusalem synagogue, Anselmo was playing solitaire in a dimly lit basement room in Pretoria. When a firebomb roasted the Iraqi premier's sister-in-law, Anselmo was flashing a savage yellow smile in Bolivia. It was not Anselmo's hand that forced a dagger between the ribs of General Suprandoro in Jakarta; the hand belonged to a nubile young lady from Thailand, but it was Anselmo who had given her her instructions, Anselmo who had decreed that Suprandoro must die and who had staged and scripted his death.

Bits and pieces. A couple of words scrawled on the back of an envelope. A scrap of conversation overheard. Bits, pieces, scraps. Threads, if you will.

Threads braided together can make strong rope. Strands of interwoven rope comprise a net.

When the net dropped around Anselmo, Nahum Grodin held its ends in his knobby hands.

It was early summer. For three days a dry wind had been blowing relentlessly. The town of Al-dhareesh, a small Arab settlement on the West Bank of the Jordan, yielded to the wind as to a conquering army. The women tended their cooking fires. Men sat at small tables in their courtyards sipping cups of sweet black coffee. The yellow dogs that ran through the narrow streets seemed to stay more in the shadows than was their custom, scurrying from doorway to doorway, keeping their distance from passing humans.

"Even the dogs feel it," Nahum Grodin said. His Hebrew bore Russian and Polish overtones. "Look at them. The way they slink around."

"The wind," Gershon Meir said.

"Anselmo."

"The wind," Meir insisted. A sabra, he had the unromantic outlook of the native-born. He was Grodin's immediate subordinate in the counter-terror division of Shin Bet, and the older man knew there was no difference in the keenness both felt at the prospect of springing a trap upon Anselmo. But Grodin felt it all in the air while Meir felt nothing but the dry wind off the desert.

"The same wind blows over the whole country," Grodin said. "And yet it's different here. The way those damned yellow dogs stay in the shadows."

"You make too much of the Arabs' mongrel dogs."

"And their children?"

"What children?"

"Aha!" Grodin extended a forefinger. "The dogs keep to the shadows. The children stay in their huts and avoid the streets altogether. Don't tell me, my friend, that the wind is enough to keep children from their play."

"So the townspeople know he's here. They shelter him. That's nothing new."

"A few know he's here. The ones planning the raid across the Jordan, perhaps a handful of others. The rest are like the dogs and the children. They sense something in the air."

Gershon Meir looked at his superior officer. He considered the set of his jaw, the reined excitement that glinted in his pale blue eyes. "Something in the air," he said.

"Yes. You feel something yourself, Gershon. Admit it."

"I feel too damned much caffeine in my blood. That last cup of coffee was a mistake."

"You feel more than caffeine."

Meir shrugged but said nothing.

"He's here, Gershon."

"Yes, I think he is. But we have been so close to him so many times—"

"This time we have him."

"When he's behind bars, that's when I'll say we have him."

"Or when he's dead."

Again the younger man looked at Grodin, a sharp look this time. Grodin's right hand, knuckles swollen with arthritis, rested on the butt of his holstered machine pistol.

"Or when he's dead," Gershon Meir agreed.

Whether it was merely the wind or something special in the air, the man called Anselmo felt it, too. He set down his little cup of coffee—it was sweeter than he liked it—and worried his chin with the tips of his fingers. With no apparent concern he studied the five men in the room with him. They were local Arabs ranging in age from sixteen to twenty-eight. Anselmo had met one of them before in Beirut and knew two of the others by reputation. The remaining two were unequivocally guaranteed by their comrades. Anselmo did not specifically trust them—he had never in his life placed full trust in another human being—but neither did he specifically distrust them. They were village Arabs, politically unsophisticated and mentally uncomplicated, desperate young men who would perform any act and undertake any risk. Anselmo had known and used just that sort of man throughout the world. He could not have functioned without such men.

Something in the air . . .

He went to a window, inched the burlap curtain aside with the edge of his palm. He saw nothing remarkable, yet a special perception more reliable than eyesight told him the town was swarming with Israelis. He did not have to see them to be certain of their presence.

He turned, considered his five companions. They were to cross the river that night. By dawn they would have established their position. A school bus loaded with between fifty and sixty retarded childen would slow down before making a left turn at the corner where Anselmo and his men would be posted. It would be child's play—he bared his teeth in a smile at the phrase—child's play to shoot the tires out of the bus. In a matter of minutes all of the Jewish children and their driver would be dead at the side of the road. In a few more minutes Anselmo and the Arabs would have scattered and made good their escape.

A perfect act of terror, mindless, meaningless, unquestionably dramatic. The Jews would retaliate, of course, and of course their retaliation would find the wrong target, and the situation would deteriorate. And in the overall scheme of things—

But was there an overall scheme of things? At times, most often late at night just before his mind slipped over the edge into sleep, then Anselmo could see the outline of some sort of master plan, some way in which all the component parts of terror which he juggled moved together to make a new world. The image of the plan hovered at such times right at the perimeter of his inner vision, trembling at the edge of thought. He could almost see it, as one can almost see God in a haze of opium.

The rest of the time he saw no master plan and had no need to search for one. The existential act of terror, theatrical as thunder, seemed to him to be a perfectly satisfactory end in itself. Let the children bleed at the roadside. Let the plane explode overhead. Let the rifle crack.

Let the world take note.

He turned once more to the window but left the curtain in place, merely testing the texture of the burlap with his fingertips. Out there in the darkness. Troops, police officers. Should he wait in the shadows for them to pass? No, he decided quickly. The village was small and they could search it house by house with little difficulty. He could pass as an Arab—he was garbed as one now—but if he was the man they were looking for they would know him when they saw him.

He could send these five out, sacrifice them to suicidal combat while he made good his own escape. It would be a small sacrifice. They were unimportant, expendable; he was Anselmo. But if the Jews had encircled the town a diversion would have little effect.

He snapped his head back, thrust his chin forward. A sudden gesture. Time was his enemy, only drawing the net tighter around him. The longer he delayed, the greater his vulnerability. Better a bad decision than no decision at all.

"Wait here for me," he told his men, his Arabic low and guttural. "I would see how the wind blows."

He began to open the door, disturbing the rest of a scrawny long-muzzled dog. The animal whined softly and took itself off to the side. Anselmo slipped through the open door and let it close behind him.

The moon overhead was just past fullness. There were no clouds to block it. The dry wind had blown them all away days ago. Anselmo reached through his loose clothing, touched the Walther automatic on his hip, the long-bladed hunting knife in a sheath strapped to his thigh, the smaller knife fastened with tape to the inside of his left forearm. Around his waist an oilcloth money belt rested next to his skin. It held four passports in as many names and a few thousand dollars in the currencies of half a dozen countries. Anselmo could travel readily, crossing borders as another man would cross the street. If only he could first get out of Al-dhareesh.

He moved quickly and sinuously, keeping to the shadows, letting his eyes and ears perform a quick reconnaissance before moving onward. Twice he spotted armed uniformed men and withdrew before he was seen, changing direction, scurrying through a yard and down an alleyway.

They were everywhere.

Just as he caught sight of still another Israeli patrol on a street corner, gunfire broke out a few hundred yards to his left. There was a ragged volley of pistol fire answered by several bursts from what he identified as an Uzi machine pistol. Then silence.

His five men, he thought. Caught in the house or on the street in front of it, and if he'd stayed there he'd have been caught with them. From the sound of it, they hadn't made much trouble. His lip curled and a spot of red danced in his forebrain. He only hoped the five had been shot dead so that they couldn't inform the Jews of his own presence.

As if they had to. As if the bastards didn't already know . . .

A three-man patrol turned into the street a dozen houses to Anselmo's left. One of the men kicked at the earth as he walked and the dust billowed around his feet in the moonlight. Anselmo cursed the men and the moonlight and circled around the side of a house and slipped away from the men.

But there was no way out. All the streets were blocked. Once Anselmo drew his Walther and took deliberate aim at a pair of uniformed men. They were within easy range and his finger trembled on the trigger. It would be so nice to kill them, but where was the profit in it? Their companions would be on him in an instant.

If you teach a rat to solve mazes, presenting it over a period of months with mazes of increasing difficulty and finally placing it in a maze which is truly unsolvable, the rat will do a curious thing. He will scurry about in an attempt to solve the maze, becoming increasingly inefficient in his efforts, and ultimately he will sit down in a corner and devour his own feet.

There was no way out of Al-dhareesh and the Israelis were closing in, searching the village house by house, moving ever nearer to Anselmo, cutting down his space. He tucked himself into a corner where a four-foot wall of sun-baked earth butted against the wall of a house. He sat on his haunches and pressed himself into the shadows.

Footsteps—

A dog scampered along close to the wall, found Anselmo, whimpered. The same dog he'd disturbed on leaving the house? Not likely, he thought. The town was full of these craven whining beasts. This one poked its nose into Anselmo's side and whimpered again. The sound was one the terrorist did not care for. He laid a hand on the back of the dog's skull, gentling it. The whimpering continued at a slightly lower pitch. With his free hand, Anselmo drew the hunting knife from the sheath on his thigh. While he went on rubbing the back of the dog's head he found the spot between the ribs. The animal had almost ceased to whimper when he sent the blade home, finding the heart directly, making the kill in silence. He wiped the blade in the dog's fur and returned it to its sheath.

A calm descended with the death of the dog. Anselmo licked a finger, held it overhead. Had the wind ceased to blow? It seemed to him that it had. He took a deep breath, released it slowly, got to his feet.

He walked not in the shadows but down the precise middle of the narrow street. When the two men stepped into view ahead of him he did not turn aside or bolt for cover. His hand quivered, itching to reach for the Walther, but the calm which had come upon him enabled him to master this urge.

He threw his hands high overhead. In reasonably good Hebrew he sang out, "I am your prisoner!" And he drew his lips back, exposing his bad teeth in a terrible grin.

Both men trained their guns on him. He had faced guns innumerable times in the past and did not find them intimidating. But one of the men held his Uzi as if he was about to fire it. Moonlight glinted on the gun barrel. Anselmo, still grinning, waited for a burst of fire and an explosion in his chest.

It never came.

The two men sat in folding chairs and watched their prisoner through a one-way mirror. His cell was as small and bare as the room from which they watched him. He sat on a narrow iron bedstead and stroked his chin with the tips of his fingers. Now and then his gaze passed over the mirror.

"You'd swear he can see us," Gershon Meir said.

"He knows we're here."

"I suppose he must. The devil's cool, isn't he? Do you think he'll talk?"

Nahum Grodin shook his head.

"He could tell us a great deal."

"He'll never tell us a thing. Why should he? The man's comfortable. He was comfortable dressed as an Arab and now he's as comfortable dressed as a prisoner."

Anselmo had been disarmed, of course, and relieved of his loose-fitting Arab clothing. Now he wore the standard clothing issued to prisoners—trousers and a short-sleeved shirt of gray denim, cloth slippers. The trousers were of course beltless and the slippers had no laces.

Grodin said, "He could be made to talk. No, *nahr,* I don't mean torture. You watch too many films. Pentothal, if they'd let me use it. Although I suspect his resistance is high. He has such enormous confidence."

"The way he smiled when he surrendered to us."

"Yes."

"For a moment I thought—"

"Yes?"

"That you were going to shoot him, Nahum."

"I very nearly did."

"You suspected a trap? I suppose—"

"No." Grodin interlaced his fingers, cracked his knuckles. Several of the joints throbbed slightly. "No," he said, "I knew it was no trick. The man is a pragmatist. He knew he was trapped. He surrendered to save his skin."

"And you thought to shoot him anyway?"

"I should have done it, Gershon. I should have shot him. Something made me hesitate. And you know the saying. He who hesitates and so forth, and I hesitated and was lost. I was not lost but the opportunity was. I should have shot him at once. Without hesitating, without thinking, without anything but an ounce of pressure on the trigger and a few punctuation marks for the night."

Gershon studied the man they were discussing. He had removed one of the slippers and was picking at his feet. Gershon wanted to look away but watched, fascinated. "You want him dead," he said.

"Of course."

"We're a progressive nation. We don't put them to death anymore. Life imprisonment's supposed to be punishment enough. You don't agree?"

"No."

"You like the eye-for-eye stuff, huh?"

" '*And you shall return eye for eye, tooth for tooth, hand for hand, foot for foot, burning for burning.*' It's not a terrible idea, you know. I would not be so quick to dismiss it out of hand."

"Revenge."

"Or retribution, more accurately. You can't have revenge, my friend. Not in this sort of case. The man's crimes are too enormous for his own personal death to balance them out. But that is not why I wish I'd killed him."

"Then I don't understand."

Nahum Grodin aimed a forefinger at the glass. "Look," he said. "What do you see?"

"A piggish lout picking his feet."

"You see a prisoner."

"Of course. I don't understand what you're getting at, Nahum."

"You think you see a prisoner. But he is not our prisoner, Gershon."

"Oh?"

"We are his prisoners."

"I do not follow that at all."

"No?" The older man massaged the knuckle of his right index finger. It was that finger, he thought, which had hesitated upon the trigger of the Uzi. And now it throbbed and ached. Arthritis? Or the punishment it deserved for its hesitation?

"Nahum—"

"We are at his mercy," Grodin said crisply. "He's our captive. His comrades will try to bring about his release. As long as he is our prisoner he is a sword pointed at our throats."

"That's far-fetched."

"Do you really think so?" Nahum Grodin sighed. "I wish we were not so civilized as to have abolished capital punishment. And at this particular moment I wish we were a police state and this vermin could be officially described as having been shot while attempting to escape. We could take him outside right now, you and I, and he could attempt to escape."

Gershon shuddered. "We could not do that."

"No," Grodin agreed. "No, we could not do that. But I could have gunned him down when I had the chance. Did you ever see a mad dog? When I was a boy in Lublin, Gershon, I saw one running wild. They don't really foam at the mouth, you know. But I seem to remember that dog having a foamy mouth. And a policeman shot him down. I remember that he held his pistol in both hands, held it out in front of him with both arms fully extended. Do you suppose I actually saw the beast shot down or that the memory is in part composed of what I was told? I could swear I actually saw the act. I can see it now in my mind, the policeman with his legs braced and his two arms held out in front of him. And the dog charging. I wonder if that incident might have had anything to do with this profession I seem to have chosen."

"Do you think it did?"

"I'll leave that to the psychiatrists to decide." Grodin smiled, then let the smile fade. "I should have shot this one down like a dog in the street," he said. "When I had the chance."

"How is he dangerous in a cell?"

"And how long will he remain in that cell?" Grodin sighed. "He is a leader. He has a leader's magnetism. The world is full of lunatics to whom this man is special. They'll demand his release. They'll hijack a plane, kidnap a politician, hold schoolchildren for ransom."

"We have never paid ransom."

"No."

"They've made such demands before. We've never released a terrorist in response to extortion."

"Not yet we haven't."

Both men fell silent. On the other side of the one-way mirror, the man called Anselmo had ceased picking his toes. Now he stripped to his underwear and seated himself on the bare tiled floor of his cell. His fingers interlaced behind his head, he began doing sit-ups. Muscles worked in his flat abdomen and his thin corded thighs as he raised and lowered the upper portion of his body. He exercised rhythmically, pausing after each series of five sit-ups, then springing to his feet after he had completed six such series. Having done so, he paused deliberately to flash his teeth at the one-way mirror.

"Look at that," Gershon Meir said. "Like an animal."

Nahum Grodin's right forefinger resumed aching.

Grodin was right, of course. Revolutionaries throughout the world had very strong reasons for wishing to see Anselmo released from his cell. In various corners of the globe, desperate men plotted desperate acts to achieve this end.

The first attempts were not successful. Less than a week after Anselmo was taken, four men and two women stormed a building in Geneva where high-level international disarmament talks were being conducted. Two of the men were shot, one fatally. One of the women had her arm broken in a struggle with a guard. The rest were captured. In the course of interrogation, Swiss authorities determined that the exercise had had as its object the release of Anselmo. The two women and one of the men were West German anarchists. The other three men, including the one who was shot dead, were Basque separatists.

A matter of days after this incident, guerrillas in Uruguay stopped a limousine carrying the Israeli ambassador to a reception in the heart of Montevideo. Security police were following the ambassador's limousine at the time, and the gun battle which ensued claimed the lives of all seven guerrillas, three security policemen, the ambassador, his chauffeur, and four presumably innocent bystanders. While the purpose of the attempted kidnapping was impossible to determine, persistent rumors linked the action to Anselmo.

Within the week, Eritrean revolutionaries succeeded in skyjacking an El Al 747 en route from New York to Tel Aviv. The jet with 144 passengers and crew members was diverted to the capital of an African nation where it overshot the runway, crashed, and was consumed in flames. A handful of passengers survived. The remaining passengers, along with all crew members and the eight or ten Eritreans, were all killed.

Palestinians seized another plane, this one an Air France jetliner. The plane was landed successfully in Libya and demands presented which called for the release of Anselmo and a dozen or so other terrorists then held by the Israelis. The demands were rejected out of hand. After several deadlines had come and gone, the terrorists began executing hostages, ultimately blowing up the plane with the remaining hostages aboard. According to some reports, the terrorists were taken into custody by Libyan authorities; according to other reports they were given token reprimands and released.

After the affair in Libya, both sides felt they had managed to establish something. The Israelis felt they had proved conclusively that they would not be blackmailed. The loosely knit group who aimed to free Anselmo felt just as strongly that they had demonstrated their resolve to free him—no matter what risks they were forced to run, no matter how many lives, their own or others, they had to sacrifice.

"If there were two Henry Clays," said the bearer of that name after a bitterly disappointing loss of the presidency, "then one of them would make the other president of the United States of America."

It is unlikely that Anselmo knew the story. He cared nothing for the past, read nothing but current newspapers. But as he exercised in his cell his thoughts often echoed those of Henry Clay.

If there were only two Anselmos, one could surely spring the other from this cursed jail.

But it didn't require a second Anselmo, as it turned out. All it took was a nuclear bomb.

The bomb itself was stolen from a NATO installation forty miles from Antwerp. A theft of this sort is perhaps the most difficult way of obtaining such a weapon. Nuclear technology is such that anyone with a good grounding in college-level science can put together a rudimentary atomic bomb in his own basement workshop, given access to the essential elements. Security precautions being what they are, it is worlds easier to steal the component parts of a bomb than the assembled bomb itself. But in this case it was necessary not merely to have a bomb but to let the world know that one had a bomb. Hence the theft via a daring and dramatic dead-of-night raid. While media publicity was kept to a minimum, people whose job it was to know such things knew overnight that a bomb had been stolen, and that the thieves had in all likelihood been members of the Peridot Gang.

The Peridot Gang was based in Paris, although its membership was international in nature. The gang was organized to practice terrorism in the Anselmo mode. Its politics were of the left, but very little ideology lay beneath the commitment to extremist activism. Security personnel throughout Europe and the Middle East shuddered at the thought of a nuclear device in the hands of the Peridots. Clearly they had not stolen the bomb for the sheer fun of it. Clearly they intended to make use of it, and clearly they were capable of almost any outrage.

Removing the bomb from the Belgian NATO installation had been reasonably difficult. In comparison, disassembling it and smuggling it into the United States, then transporting it into New York City and reassembling it and finally installing it in the interfaith meditation chamber of the United Nations—all of that was simplicity itself.

Once the meditation chamber had been secured, a Peridot emissary presented a full complement of demands. Several of these had to do with guaranteeing the eventual safety of gang members at the time of their withdrawal from the chamber, the UN building, and New York itself. Another, directed at the General Assembly of the United Nations, called for changes in international policy toward insurgent movements and revolutionary organizations. Various individual member nations were called upon to liberate specific political prisoners, including several dozen persons belonging to or allied with the Peridot organization. Specifically, the government of Israel was instructed to grant liberty to the man called Anselmo.

Any attempt to seize the bomb would be met by its detonation. Any effort to evacuate the United Nations building or New York itself would similarly prompt the Peridots to set the bomb off. If all demands were not met within ten days of their publication, the bomb would go off.

Authorities differed in their estimates of the bomb's lethal range. But the lowest estimate of probable deaths was in excess of one million.

Throughout the world, those governments blackmailed by the Peridots faced up to reality. One after the other they made arrangements to do what they could not avoid doing. Whatever their avowed policy toward extortion, however great their reluctance to liberate terrorists, they could not avoid recognizing a fairly simple fact: they had no choice.

Anselmo could not resist a smile when the two men came into the room. How nice, he thought, that it was these two who came to him. They had captured him in the first place, they had attempted to interrogate him time and time again, and now they were on hand to make arrangements for his release. It seemed to him that there was something fitting in all of this.

"Well," he said. "I guess I won't be with you much longer, eh?"

"Not much longer," the older man said.

"When do you release me?"

"The day after tomorrow. In the morning. You are to be turned over to Palestinians at the Syrian border. A private jet will fly you to one of the North African countries, either Algeria or Libya. I don't have the details. I don't believe they have been finalized as yet."

"It hardly matters."

The younger of the Israelis, dark-eyed and olive-skinned, cleared his throat. "You won't want to leave here in prison clothes," he said. "We can give you what you wore when you were captured or you may have western dress. It's your choice."

"You are very accommodating," Anselmo told him.

The man's face colored. "The choice is yours."

"It's of no importance to me."

"Then you'll walk out as you walked in."

"It doesn't matter what I wear." He touched his gray denim clothing. "Just so it's not this." And he favored them with a smile again.

The older man unclasped a small black bag, drew out a hypodermic needle. Anselmo raised his eyebrows. "Pentothal," the man said.

"You could have used it before."

"It was against policy."

"And has your policy changed?"

"Obviously."

"A great deal has changed," the younger man added. "A package bill passed the Knesset last evening. There was a special session called for the purpose. The death penalty has been restored."

"Ah."

"For certain crimes only. Crimes of political terrorism. Any terrorists captured alive will be brought to trial within three days after capture. If convicted, sentence will be carried out within twenty-four hours after it has been pronounced."

"Was there much opposition to this bill?"

"There was considerable debate. But when it came to a vote the margin was overwhelming for passage."

Anselmo considered this in the abstract. "It seems to me that it is an intelligent bill," he said at length. "I inspired it, eh?"

"You might say that."

"So you will avoid this sort of situation in the future. But of course there is a loss all the same. No doubt that explains the debate. You will not look good to the rest of the world, executing prisoners so quickly after capture. There will be talk of kangaroo courts, star chamber hearings, that sort of thing." He flashed his teeth. "But what choice did you have? None."

"There's another change that did not require legislation," the older man said. "An unofficial change of policy for troops and police officers. We will have slower reflexes when it comes to noticing that a man is attempting to surrender."

Anselmo laughed aloud at the phrasing. "Slower reflexes! You mean you will shoot first and ask questions later."

"Something along those lines."

"Also an intelligent policy. I shall make my own plans accordingly. But I don't think it will do you very much good, you know."

The man shrugged. The hypodermic needle looked small in his big gnarled hand. "The pentothal," he said. "Will it be necessary to restrain you? Or will you cooperate?"

"Why should I require restraint? We are both professionals, after all. I'll cooperate."

"That simplifies things."

Anselmo extended his arm. The younger man took him by the wrist while the other one readied the needle. "This won't do you any good either," Anselmo said conversationally. "I've had pentothal before. It's not effective on me."

"We'll have to establish that for ourselves."

"As you will."

"At least you'll get a pleasant nap out of it."

"I never have trouble sleeping," Anselmo said. "I sleep like a baby."

He didn't fight the drug but went with the flow as it circulated in his bloodstream. His consciousness went off to the side somewhere. There was orchestral music interwoven with a thunderstorm. The bolts of lightning, vivid against an indigo background, were extraordinarily beautiful.

Then he was awake, aware of his surroundings, aware that the two men were speaking but unable to make sense of their conversation. When full acuity returned he gave no sign of it at first, hoping to overhear something of importance, but their conversation held nothing of interest to him. After a few minutes he stirred himself and opened his eyes.

"Well?" he demanded. "Did I tell you any vital secrets?"

The older one shook his head.

"I told you as much."

"So you did. You'll forgive our not taking your word, I hope."

Anselmo laughed aloud. "You have humor, old one. It's almost a pity we're enemies. Tell me your name."

"What does it matter?"

"It doesn't."

"Nahum Grodin."

Anselmo repeated the name aloud. "When you captured me," he said. "In that filthy Arab town."

"Al-dhareesh."

"Al-dhareesh. Yes. When I surrendered, you know, I thought for a long moment that you were going to gun me down. That wind that blew endlessly, and the moon glinting off your pistol, and something in the air. Something in the way you were standing. I thought you were going to shoot me."

"I very nearly did."

"Yes, so I thought." Anselmo laughed suddenly. "And now you must wish that you did, eh? Hesitation, that's what kills men, Grodin. Better the wrong choice than no choice at all. You should have shot me."

"Yes."

"Next time you'll know better, Grodin."

"Next time?"

"Oh, there will be a next time for us, old one. And next time you won't hesitate to fire, but then next time I'll know better than to surrender. Eh?"

"I almost shot you."

"I sensed it."

"Like a dog."

"A dog?" Anselmo thought of the dogs in the Arab town, the one he'd disturbed when he opened the door, the whining one he'd killed. His hand remembered the feel of the animal's skull and the brief tremor that passed through the beast when the long knife went home. It was difficult now to recall just why he had knifed the dog. He supposed he must have done it to prevent the animal's whimpering from drawing attention, but was that really the reason? The act itself had been so reflexive that one could scarcely determine its motive.

As if it mattered.

Outside, the sunlight was blinding. Gershon Meir took a pair of sunglasses from his breast pocket and put them on. Nahum Grodin squinted against the light. He never wore sunglasses and didn't mind the glare. And the sun warmed his bones, eased the ache in his joints.

"The day after tomorrow," Gershon Meir said. "I'll be glad to see the last of him."

"Will you?"

"Yes. I hate having to release him but sometimes I think I hate speaking with him even more."

"I know what you mean."

They walked through the streets in a comfortable silence. After a few blocks the younger man said, "I had the oddest feeling earlier. Just for a moment."

"Oh?"

"When you gave him the pentothal. For an instant I was afraid you were going to kill him."

"With pentothal?"

"I thought you might inject an air bubble into a vein. Anything along those lines. It would have been easy enough."

"Perhaps. I don't know that I'd be able to find a vein that easily, actually. I'm hardly a doctor. A subcutaneous injection of pentothal, that's within my capabilities, but I might not be so good at squirting air into a vein. But do you think for a moment I'd be mad enough to kill him?"

"It was a feeling, not a thought."

"I'd delight in killing him," Grodin said. "But I'd hate to wipe out New York in the process."

"They might not detonate the bomb just for Anselmo. They want to get the other prisoners out, and they want their other demands. If you told them Anselmo had died a natural death they might swallow it and pretend to believe it."

"You think we should call their bluff that way?"

"No. They're lunatics. Who knows what they might do?"

"Exactly," Grodin said.

"It was just a feeling, that's all."

And a little further on: "Nahum? It's a curious thing. When you and Anselmo talk I might as well not be in the room."

"I don't take your meaning, Gershon."

"There's a current that runs between the two of you. I feel utterly excluded from the company. The two of you, you seem to understand each other."

"That's interesting. You think I understand Anselmo? I don't begin to understand him. You know, I didn't expect to gain any real information from him while he was under the pentothal. But I did hope to get some insight into what motivated the man. And he gave me nothing. He likes to see blood spill, he likes loud noises. You know what Bakunin said?"

"I don't even know who Bakunin was. A Russian?"

"A Russian. 'The urge to destroy is a creative urge,' that's what he said. Perhaps the context in which he said it mitigates the line somewhat. I wouldn't know. Anselmo is an embodiment of that philosophy. He only wishes to destroy. No. Gershon, I do not understand him."

"But there is a sympathy between the two of you. I'm not putting it well, I know, but there is something."

Grodin did not reply immediately. Finally he said, "The man says we'll meet again. He's wrong."

Yet they might have met again on the day that Anselmo was released. Grodin and his assistant were on hand. They watched from a distance while the terrorist was escorted from his cell to an armored car for transport to the Syrian lines, and Grodin had been assigned to oversee security procedures lest some zealot shoot Anselmo down as he emerged from the prison. They followed the armored car in a vehicle of their own, Meir driving, Grodin at his side. The ceremony at the Syrian border, by means of which custody of Anselmo was transferred from his Israeli guards to a group of Palestinian commandos, was indescribably tense; nevertheless it was concluded without a hitch.

Just before he entered the waiting car, Anselmo turned for a last look across the border. His eyes darted around as if seeking a specific target. Then he thrust out his jaw and drew back his lips, baring his jagged teeth in a final hideous smile. He gave his head a toss and ducked down into the car. The door swung shut. Moments later the car sped toward Damascus.

"Quite a performance," Gershon Meir said.

"He's an actor. Everything is performance for him. His whole life is theater."

"He was looking for you."

"I think not."

"He was looking for someone. For whom else would he look?"

Grodin gave his head an impatient shake. His assistant looked as though he would have liked to continue the conversation, but recognized the gesture and let it drop.

On the long drive back Nahum Grodin leaned back in his seat and closed his eyes. It seemed to him that he dreamed without quite losing consciousness. After perhaps half an hour he opened his blue eyes and straightened up in his seat.

"Where is he now?" he wondered aloud. "Damascus? Or is his plane already in the air?"

"I'd guess he's still on the ground."

"No matter. How do you feel, Gershon? Letting such a one out of our hands? Forget revenge. Think of the ability he has to work with disparate groups of lunatics. He takes partisans of one mad cause and puts them to work on behalf of another equally insane movement. He coordinates the actions of extremists who have nothing else in common. And his touch is like nobody else's. This latest devilment at the United Nations—it is almost impossible to believe that someone other than Anselmo planned it. In fact I would not be surprised to learn that he had hatched the concept some time ago to be held at the ready in the event that he should ever be captured."

"I wonder if that could be true."

"It's not impossible, is it? And we had to let him go."

"We'll never have to do that again."

"No," Grodin agreed. "One good thing's come of this. The new law is not perfect, God knows. Instant trials and speedy hangings are not what democracies ought to aspire to. But it is comforting to know that we will not be in this position again. Gershon?"

"Yes?"

"Stop the car, please. Pull off on the shoulder."

"Is something wrong?"

"No. But there is something I've decided to tell you. Good, and turn off the engine. We'll be here a few moments." Grodin squeezed his eyes shut, put his hand to his forehead. Without opening his eyes he said, "Anselmo said he and I would meet again. I told you the other day that he was wrong."

"I remember."

"He'll never return to Israel, you see. He'll meet his friends, if one calls such people friends, and he'll go wherever he has it in mind to go. And in two weeks or a month or possibly as much as two months he will experience a certain amount of nervousness. He may be mentally depressed, he may grow anxious and irritable. It's quite possible that he'll pay no attention to these signs because they may not be very much out of the ordinary. His life is disorganized, chaotic, enervating, so this state I've discussed may be no departure from the normal course of things."

"I don't understand, Nahum."

"Then after a day or so these symptoms will be more pronounced," Grodin went on. "He may run a fever. His appetite will wane. He'll grow quite nervous. He may talk a great deal, might even become something of a chatterbox. You recall that he said he sleeps like a baby. Well, he may experience insomnia.

"Then after a couple of days things will take a turn for the worse." Grodin took a pinseal billfold from his pocket, drew out an unfolded sheet of paper. "Here's a description from a medical encyclopedia. 'The agitation of the sufferer now becomes greatly increased and the countenance now exhibits anxiety and terror. There is marked embarrassment of the breathing, but the most striking and terrible features of this stage are the effects produced by attempts to swallow fluids. The patient suffers from thirst and desires eagerly to drink, but on making the effort is seized with a violent suffocative paroxysm which continues for several seconds and is succeeded by a feeling of intense alarm and distress. Indeed the very thought of drinking suffices to bring on a choking paroxysm, as does also the sound of running water.

" 'The patient is extremely sensitive to any kind of external impression—a bright light, a loud noise, a breath of cool air—anything of this sort may bring on a seizure. There also occur general convulsions and occasionally a condition of tetanic spasm. These various paroxysms increase in frequency and severity with the advance of the disease.' "

"Disease?" Gershon Meir frowned. "I don't understand, Nahum. What disease? What are you driving at?"

Grodin went on reading. " 'The individual experiences alternate intervals of comparative quiet in which there is intense anxiety and more or less constant difficulty in respiration accompanied by a peculiar sonorous exhalation which has suggested the notion that the patient barks like a dog. In many instances—' "

"A dog!"

" 'In many instances there are intermittent fits of maniacal excitement. During all this stage of the disease the patient is tormented with a viscid secretion accumulating in his mouth. From dread of swallowing this he constantly spits about himself. He may also make snapping movements of the jaws as if attempting to bite. These are actually a manifestation of the spasmodic action which affects the muscles in general. There is no great amount of fever, but the patient will be constipated, his flow of urine will be diminished, and he will often feel sexual excitement.

" 'After two or three days of suffering of the most terrible description the patient succumbs, with death taking place either in a paroxysm of choking or from exhaustion. The duration of the disease from the first declaration of symptoms is generally from three to five days.' "

Grodin refolded the paper, returned it to his wallet. "Rabies," he said quietly. "Hydrophobia. Its incubation period is less than a week in dogs and other lower mammals. In humans it generally takes a month to erupt. It works faster in small children, I understand. And if the bite is in the head or neck the incubation period is speeded up."

"Can't it be cured? I thought—"

"The Pasteur shots. A series of about a dozen painful injections. I believe the vaccine is introduced by a needle into the stomach. And there are other less arduous methods of vaccination if the particular strain of rabies virus can be determined. But they have to be employed immediately. Once the incubation period is complete, once the symptoms manifest themselves, then death is inevitable."

"God."

"By the time Anselmo has the slightest idea what's wrong with him—"

"It will be too late."

"Exactly," Grodin said.

"When you gave him the pentothal—"

"Yes. There was more than pentothal in the needle."

"I sensed something."

"So you said."

"But I never would have guessed—"

"No. Of course not."

Gershon Meir shuddered. "When he realizes what you did to him and how you did it—"

"Then what?" Grodin spread his hands. "Could he be more utterly our enemy than he is already? And I honestly don't think he'll guess how he was tricked. He'll most likely suppose he was exposed to rabies from an animal source. I understand you can get it from inhaling the vapors of the dung of rabid bats. Perhaps he'll hide out in a bat-infested cave and blame the bats for his illness. But it doesn't matter, Gershon. Let him know what I did to him. I almost hope he guesses, for all the good it will do him."

"God."

"I just wanted to tell you," Grodin said, his voice calmer now. "There's poetry to it, don't you think? He's walking around now like a time bomb. He could get the Pasteur shots and save himself, but he doesn't know that, and by the time he does—"

"God."

"Start the car, eh? We'd better be getting back." And the older man straightened up in his seat and rubbed the throbbing knuckles of his right hand. They ached, but all the same he was smiling.

The Most Unusual Snatch

They grabbed Carole Butler a few minutes before midnight just a block and a half from her own front door. It never would have happened if her father had let her take the car. But she was six months shy of eighteen, and the law said you had to be eighteen to drive at night, and her father was a great believer in the law. So she had taken the bus, got off two blocks from her house, and walked half a block before a tall thin man with his hat down over his eyes appeared suddenly and asked her the time.

She was about to tell him to go buy his own watch when an arm came around her from behind and a damp cloth fastened over her mouth and nose. It smelled like a hospital room.

She heard voices, faintly, as if from far away. "Not too long, you don't want to kill her."

"What's the difference? Kill her now or kill her later, she's just as dead."

"You kill her now and she can't make the phone call."

There was more, but she didn't hear it. The chloroform did its work and she sagged, limp, unconscious.

At first, when she came to, groggy and weak and sick to her stomach, she thought she had been taken to a hospital. Then she realized it was just the smell of the chloroform. Her head seemed awash in the stuff. She breathed steadily, in and out, in and out, stayed where she was, and didn't open her eyes.

She heard the same two voices she had heard before. One was assuring the other that everything would go right on schedule, that they couldn't miss. "Seventy-five thou," he said several times. "Wait another hour, let him sweat a little. Then call him and tell him it'll cost him seventy-five thou to see his darling daughter again. That's all we tell him, just that we got her, and the price. Then we let him stew in it for another two hours."

"Why drag it out?"

"Because it has to drag until morning anyway. He's not going to have that kind of bread around the house. He'll have to go on the send for it, and that means nine o'clock when the banks open. Give him the whole message right away and he'll have too much time to get nervous and call copper. But space it out just right and we'll have him on the string until morning, and then he can go straight to the bank and get the money ready."

Carole opened her eyes slowly, carefully. The one who was doing most of the talking was the same tall thin man who had asked her the time. He was less than beautiful, she noticed. His nose was lopsided, angling off to the left as though it had been broken and improperly reset. His chin was scarcely there at all. He ought to wear a goatee, she thought. He would still be no thing of beauty, but it might help.

The other one was shorter, heavier, and younger, no more than ten years older than Carole. He had wide shoulders, close-set eyes, and a generally stupid face, but he wasn't altogether bad-looking. Not bad at all she told herself. Between the two of them, they seemed to have kidnapped her. She wanted to laugh out loud.

"Better cool it," the younger one said. "Looks like she's coming out of it."

She picked up her cue, making a great show of blinking her eyes vacantly and yawning and stretching. Stretching was difficult, as she seemed to be tied to a chair. It was an odd sensation. She had never been tied up before, and she didn't care for it.

"Hey," she said, "where am I?"

She could have answered the question herself. She was, to judge from appearances, in an especially squalid shack. The shack itself was fairly close to a highway, judging from the traffic noises. If she had to guess, she would place the location somewhere below the southern edge of the city, probably a few hundred yards off

Highway 130 near the river. There were plenty of empty fishing shacks there, she remembered, and it was a fair bet that this was one of them.

"Now just take it easy, Carole," the thin man said. "You take it easy and nothing's going to happen to you."

"You kidnapped me."

"You just take it easy and—"

She squealed with joy. "This is too much! You've actually kidnapped me. Oh, this is wild! Did you call my old man yet?"

"No."

"Will you let me listen when you do?" She started to giggle. "I'd give anything to see his face when you tell him. He'll split. He'll just fall apart."

They were both staring at her, open-mouthed. The younger man said, "You sound happy about it."

"Happy? Of course I'm happy. This is the most exciting thing that ever happened to me!"

"But your father—"

"I hope you gouge him good," she went on. "He's the cheapest old man on earth. He wouldn't pay a nickel to see a man go over the Falls. How much are you going to ask?"

"Never mind," the thin man said.

"I just hope it's enough. He can afford plenty."

The thin man grinned. "How does seventy-five thousand dollars strike you?"

"Not enough. He can afford more than that," she said. "He's very rich, but you wouldn't know it the way he hangs onto his money."

"Seventy-five thou is pretty rich."

She shook her head. "Not for him. He could afford plenty more."

"It's not what he can afford, it's what he can raise in a hurry. We don't want to drag this out for days. We want it over by morning."

She thought for a minute. "Well, it's your funeral," she said pertly.

The shorter man approached her. "What do you mean by that?"

"Forget it, Ray," his partner said.

"No, I want to find out. What did you mean by that, honey?"

She looked up at them. "Well, I don't want to tell you your business," she said slowly. "I mean, you're the kidnappers. You're the ones who are taking all the chances. I mean, if you get caught they can really give you a hard time, can't they?"

"The chair," the thin man said.

"That's what I thought, so I don't want to tell you how to do all this, but there was something that occurred to me."

"Let's hear it."

"Well, first of all, I don't think it's a good idea to wait for morning. You wouldn't know it, of course, but he doesn't have to wait until the banks open. He's a doctor, and I know he gets paid in cash a lot of the time—cash that never goes to the bank, never gets entered in the books. It goes straight into the safe in the basement and stays there."

"Taxes—"

"Something like that. Anyway, I heard him telling somebody that he never has less than a hundred thousand dollars in that safe. So you wouldn't have to wait until the banks open, and you wouldn't have to settle for seventy-five thousand either. You could ask for an even hundred thousand and get it easy."

The two kidnappers looked at her, at each other, then at her again.

"I mean," she said, "I'm only trying to be helpful."

"You must hate him something awful, kid."

"Now you're catching on."

"Doesn't he treat you right?"

"All his money," she said, "and I don't even get my own car. I had to take the bus tonight; otherwise you wouldn't have got me the way you did, so it's his fault I was kidnapped. Why shouldn't he pay a bundle?"

"This is some kid, Howie," the younger man said.

Howie nodded. "You sure about the hundred thousand?"

"He'll probably try to stall, tell us he needs time to raise the dough."

"So tell him you know about the safe."

"Maybe he—"

"And that way he won't call the police," she went on. "Because of not paying taxes on the money and all that. He won't want that to come out into the open, so he'll pay."

"It's like you planned this job yourself, baby," Ray said.

"I almost did."

"Huh?"

"I used to think what a gas it would be if I got kidnapped. What a fit the old man would throw and everything." She giggled. "But I never really thought it would happen. It's too perfect."

"I think I'll make that call now," Howie said. "I'll be back in maybe half an hour. Ray here'll take good care of you, kitten." He nodded and was gone.

She had expected that Howie would make the call and was glad it had turned out that way. Ray seemed to be the easier of the two to get along with. It wasn't just that he was younger and better-looking. He was also, as far as she could tell, more good-natured and a whole lot less intelligent.

"Who would have figured it?" he said now. "I mean, you go and pull a snatch, you don't expect anybody to be so cooperative."

"Have you ever done this before, Ray?"

"No."

"It must be scary."

"Aw, I guess it's easy enough. More money than a bank job and a whole lot less risk. The only hard part is when the mark—your old man, that is—delivers the money. You have to get the dough without being spotted. Outside of that, it's no sweat at all."

"And afterward?"

"Huh?"

The palms of her hands were moist with sweat. She said, "What happens afterward? Will you let me go, Ray?"

"Oh, sure."

"You won't kill me?"

"Oh, don't be silly," he said.

She knew exactly what he meant. He meant, Let's not talk about it, doll, but of course we'll kill you. What else?

"I'm more fun when I'm alive," she said.

"I'll bet you are."

"You better believe it."

He came closer to her. She straightened her shoulders to emphasize her youthful curves and watched his eyes move over her body.

"That's a pretty sweater," he said. "You look real good in a sweater. I'll bet a guy could have a whole lot of fun with you, baby."

"I'm more fun," she said, "when I'm not tied up. Howie won't be back for a half hour. But I don't guess that would worry you."

"Not a bit."

She sat perfectly still while he untied her. Then she got slowly to her feet. Her legs were cramped and her fingers tingled a little from the limited circulation. Ray took her in his arms and kissed her, then took a black automatic from his pocket and placed it on the table.

"Now don't get any idea about making a grab for the gun," he said. "You'd only get hurt, you know."

Later he insisted on tying her up again.

"But I won't try anything," she protested. "Honest, Ray. You know I wouldn't try anything. I want everything to go off just right."

"Howie wouldn't like it," he said doggedly, and that was all there was to it.

"But don't make it too tight," she begged. "It hurts."

He didn't make it too tight.

When Howie came back he was smiling broadly. He closed the door and locked it and lit a cigarette. "Like a charm," he said through a cloud of smoke. "Went like a charm. You're okay, honey girl."

"What did he say?"

"Got hysterical first of all. Kept telling me not to hurt you, that he'd pay if only we'd release you. He kept saying how much he loved you and all."

She started to laugh. "Oh, beautiful!"

"And you were right about the safe. He started to blubber that he couldn't possibly raise a hundred thousand on short notice. Then I hit him with the safe, said I knew he kept plenty of dough right there in his own basement, and that really got to him. He went all to pieces. I think you could have knocked him over with a lettuce leaf when he heard that."

"And he'll pay up?"

"No trouble at all, and if it's all cash he's been salting away that's the best news yet: no serial numbers copied down, no big bills, no runs of new bills in sequence. That means we don't have to wholesale the kidnap dough to one of the Eastern mobs for forty cents on the dollar. We wind up with a hundred thousand, and we wind up clean."

"And he'll be scared to go to the police afterward," Carole put in. "Did you set up the delivery of the money?"

"No. I said I'd call in an hour. I may cut it to a half hour though. I think we've got him where we want him. This is going so smooth it scares me. I want it over and done with, nice and easy."

She was silent for a moment. Howie wanted it over and done with, undoubtedly wanted no loose ends. Inevitably he was going to think of her, Carole Butler, as an obvious loose end, which meant that he would probably want to tie her off, and the black automatic on the table was just the thing to do the job. She stared at the gun, imagined the sound of it, the impact of the bullet in her flesh. She was terrified, but she made sure none of this showed in her face or in her voice.

Casually she asked, "About the money—how are you going to pick it up?"

"That's the only part that worries me."

"I don't think he'll call the police. Not my old man. Frankly, I don't think he'd have the guts. But if he did, that would be the time when they'd try to catch you, wouldn't it?"

"That's the general idea."

She thought for a moment. "If we were anywhere near the south end of town, I know a perfect spot—but I suppose we're miles from there."

"What's the spot?"

She told him about it—the overpass on Route 130 at the approach to the turnpike. They could have her father drive onto the pike, toss the money over the side of the overpass when he reached it, and they could be waiting down below to pick it up. Any cops who were with him would be stuck up there on the turnpike and they could get away clean.

"It's not bad," Ray said.

"It's perfect," Howie added. "You thought that up all by yourself?"

"Well, I got the idea from a really super-duper movie—"

"I think it's worth doing it that way." Howie sighed. "I was going to get fancy, have him walk to a garbage can, stick it inside, then cut out. Then we go in and get it out of the can. But suppose the cops had the whole place staked out?" He smiled. "You've got a good head on your shoulders, kitten. It's a shame—"

"What's a shame?"

"That you're not part of the gang, the way your mind works. You'd be real good at it."

That, she knew, was not really what he'd meant. It's a shame we have to kill you anyway, he meant. You're a smart kid, and even a pretty kid, but all the same you're going to get a bullet between the eyes, and it's a shame.

She pictured her father, waiting by the telephone. If he called the police, she knew it would be all over for her, and he might very well call them. But if she could stop him, if she could make sure that he let the delivery of the ransom money go according to plan, then maybe she would have a chance. It wouldn't be the best chance in the world, but anything was better than nothing at all.

When Howie said he was going to make the second phone call she asked him to take her along. "Let me talk to him," she begged. "I want to hear his voice. I want to hear him in a panic. He's always so cool about everything, so smug and superior. I want to see what he sounds like when he gets in a sweat."

"I don't know—"

"I'll convince him that you're desperate and dangerous," she continued. "I'll tell him—" she managed to giggle "—that I know you'll kill me if he doesn't cooperate, but that I'm sure you'll let me go straight home just as soon as the ransom is paid as long as he keeps the police out of it."

"Well, I don't know. It sounds good, but—"

"It's a good idea, Howie," Ray said. "That way he knows we've got her and he knows she's still alive. I think the kid knows what she's talking about."

It took a little talking, but finally Howie was convinced of the wisdom of the move. Ray untied her and the three of them got into Howie's car and drove down the road to a pay phone. Howie made the call and talked for a few minutes, explaining how and where the ransom was to be delivered. Then he gave the phone to Carole.

"Oh, Daddy," she sobbed. "Oh, Daddy, I'm scared! Daddy, do just what they tell you. There are four of them and they're desperate, and I'm scared of them. Please pay them, Daddy. The woman said if the police were brought in she'd cut my throat with a knife. She said she'd cut me and kill me, Daddy, and I'm so scared of them—"

Back in the cabin, as Howie tied her in the chair, he asked, "What was all that gas about four of us? And the bit about the woman?"

"I just thought it sounded dramatic."

"It was dramatic as a nine-alarm fire, but why bother?"

"Well," she said, "the bigger the gang is, the more dangerous it sounds and if he reports it later, let the police go looking for three men and a woman. That way you'll have even less trouble getting away clear. And of course I'll give them four phony descriptions, just to make it easier for you."

She hoped that would soak in. She could only give the phony descriptions if she were left alive, and she hoped that much penetrated.

It was around three-thirty in the morning when Howie left for the ransom. "I should be about an hour," he said. "If I'm not back in that time, then things are bad. Then we've got trouble."

"What do I do then?" Ray asked.

"You know what to do."

"I mean, how do I get out of here? We've only got the one car, and you'll be in it."

"So beat it on foot, or stay right where you are. You don't have to worry about me cracking. The only way they'll get me is dead, and if I'm dead you won't have to worry about them finding out where we've got her tucked away. Just take care of the chick and get out on foot."

"Nothing's going to go wrong."

"I think you're right. I think this is smooth as silk, but anything to be sure. You got your gun?"

"On the table."

"Ought to keep it on you."

"Well, maybe."

"Remember," Howie said, "you can figure on me getting back in an hour at the outside. Probably be no more than half of that, but an hour is tops. So long."

"Good luck," Carole called after him.

Howie stopped and looked at her. He had a very strange expression on his face. "Yeah," he said finally. "Luck. Sure, thanks."

When Howie was gone, Ray said, "You never should have made the phone call. I mean, I think it was a good idea and all, but that way Howie tied you up, see, and he tied you tight. Me, I would have tied you loose, see, but he doesn't think the same way." He considered things. "In a way," he went on, "Howie is what you might call a funny guy. Everything has to go just right, know what I mean? He doesn't like to leave a thing to chance."

"Could you untie me?"

"Well, I don't know if I should."

"At least make this looser? It's got my fingers numb already. It hurts pretty bad, Ray. Please?"

"Well, I suppose so." He untied her. As soon as she was loose he moved to the table, scooped up the gun, wedged it beneath the waistband of his trousers.

He likes me, she thought. He even wants me to be comfortable and he doesn't particularly want to kill me, but he doesn't trust me. He's too nervous to trust anybody.

"Could I have a cigarette?" she asked.

"Huh? Oh, sure." He gave her one, lit it for her. They smoked together for several minutes in silence. It isn't going to work, she thought, not the way things are going. She had him believing her, but that didn't seem to be enough. Howie was the brains and the boss, and what Howie said went, and Howie would say to kill her. She wondered which one of them would use the gun on her.

"Uh, Carole—"

"What?"

"Oh, nothing. Just forget it."

He wanted her to bring it up, she knew. So she said, "Listen, Ray, let me tell you something. I like you a lot, but to tell you the truth I'm scared of Howie."

"You are?"

"I've been playing it straight with you, and I think you've been straight with me. Ray, you've got the brains to realize you'll be much better off if you let me go." He doesn't, she thought, have any brains at all, but flattery never hurt. "But Howie is different from you and me. He's not—well, normal. I know he wants to kill me."

"Oh, now—"

"I mean it, Ray." She clutched his arm. "If I live, Dad won't report it. He can't afford to. But if you kill me—"

"Yeah, I know."

"Suppose you let me go."

"Afterward?"

She shook her head. "No, now, before Howie comes back. He won't care by then, he'll have the money. You can just let me go, and then the two of you will take the money and get out of town. Nobody will ever know a thing. I'll tell Dad the two of you released me and he'll be so glad to get me back and so scared of the tax men he'll never say a word. You could let me go, Ray, couldn't you? Before Howie gets back?"

He thought it over for a long time, and she could see he wanted to. But he said, "I don't know, Howie would take me apart—"

"Say I grabbed something and hit you, and managed to knock you out. Tell him he tied the ropes wrong and I slipped loose and got you from behind. He'll be mad, maybe, but what will he care? As long as you have the money—"

"He won't believe you hit me."

"Suppose I did hit you? Not hard, but enough to leave a mark so you could point to it for proof."

He grinned suddenly. "Sure, Carole, you've been good to me. The first time, when he made that first phone call, you were real good. I'll tell you something, the idea of killing you bothers me. And you're right about Howie. Here, belt me one behind the ear. Make it a good one, but not too hard, okay?" And he handed her the gun.

He looked completely astonished when she shot him. He just didn't believe it. She reversed the gun in her hand, curled her index finger around the trigger, and pointed the gun straight at his heart. His eyes bugged out and his mouth dropped open, and he just stared at her, not saying anything at all. She shot him twice in the center of the chest and watched him fall slowly, incredibly, to the floor, dead.

When Howie's car pulled up she was ready. She crouched by the doorway, gun in hand, waiting. The car door flew open and she heard his footsteps on the gravel path. He pulled the door open, calling out jubilantly that it had gone like clockwork, just like clockwork, then he caught sight of Ray's corpse on the floor and did a fantastic double take. When he saw her and the gun, he started to say something, but she emptied the gun into him, four bullets, one after the other, and all of them hit him and they worked; he fell; he died.

She got the bag of money out of his hand before he could bleed on it.

The rest wasn't too difficult. She took the rope with which she'd been tied and rubbed it back and forth on the chair leg until it finally frayed through. Behind the cabin she found a toolshed. She used a shovel, dug a shallow pit, dropped the money into it, filled in the hole. She carried the gun down to the water's edge, wiped it free of fingerprints, and heaved it into the creek.

Finally, when just the right amount of time had passed, she walked out to the highway and kept going until she found a telephone, a highway emergency booth.

"Just stay right where you are," her father said. "Don't call the police. I'll come for you."

"Hurry. Daddy. I'm so scared."

He picked her up. She was shaking, and he held her in his arms and soothed her.

"I was so frightened," she said. "And then when the one man came back with the ransom money, the other man took out a gun and shot him and the third man, and then the man who did the shooting, he and the woman ran away in their other car. I was sure they were going to kill me but the man said not to bother, the gun was empty and it didn't matter now. The woman wanted to kill me with the knife but she didn't. I was sure she would. Oh, Daddy—"

"It's all right now," he said. "Everything's going to be all right."

She showed him the cabin and the two dead men and the rope. "It took me forever to get out of it," she said. "But I saw in the movies how you can work your way out, and I wasn't tied too tight, so I managed to do it."

"You're a brave girl, Carole."

On the way home he said, "I'm not going to call the police, Carole. I don't want to subject you to a lot of horrible questioning. Sooner or later they'll find those two in the cabin, but that has nothing to do with us. They'll just find two dead criminals, and the world's better off without them." He thought for a moment. "Besides," he added, "I'm sure I'd have a hard time explaining where I got that money."

"Did they get very much?"

"Only ten thousand dollars," he said.

"I thought they asked for more."

"Well, after I explained that I didn't have anything like that around the house they listened to reason."

"I see," she said.

You old liar, she thought, it was a hundred thousand dollars, and I know it. And it's mine now. Mine.

"Ten thousand dollars is a lot of money," she said. "I mean, it's a lot for you to lose."

"It doesn't matter."

"If you called the police, maybe they could get it back."

He shuddered visibly, and she held back laughter. "It doesn't matter," he said. "All that matters is that we got you back safe and sound. That's more important than all the money in the world."

"Oh, Daddy," she said, hugging him, "oh, I love you, I love you so much!"

Nothing Short of Highway Robbery

I eased up on the gas pedal a few hundred yards ahead of the service station. I was putting the brakes on when my brother Newton opened his eyes and straightened up in his seat.

"We haven't got but a gallon of gas left if we got that much," I told him. "And there's nothing out ahead of us but a hundred miles of sand and a whole lot of cactus, and I already seen enough cactus to last me a spell."

He smothered a yawn with the back of his hand. "Guess I went and fell asleep," he said.

"Guess you did."

He yawned again while a fellow a few years older'n us came off of the front porch of the house and walked our way, moving slow, taking his time. He was wearing a broad-brimmed white hat against the sun and a pair of bib overalls. The house wasn't much, a one-story clapboard structure with a flat roof. The garage alongside it must have been built at the same time and designed by the same man.

He came around to my side and I told him to fill the tank. "Regular," I said.

He shook his head. "High-test is all I got," he said. "That be all right?"

I nodded and he went around the car and commenced unscrewing the gas cap. "Only carries high-test," I said, not wildly happy about it.

"It'll burn as good as the regular, Vern."

"I guess I know that. I guess I know it's another five cents a gallon or another dollar bill on a tankful of gas, and don't you just bet that's why he does it that way? Because what the hell can you do if you want regular? This bird's the only game in town."

"Well, I don't guess a dollar'll break us, Vern."

I said I guessed not and I took a look around. The pump wasn't so far to the rear that I couldn't get a look at it, and when I did I saw the price per gallon, and it wasn't just an extra nickel that old boy was taking from us. His high-test was priced a good twelve cents a gallon over everybody else's high-test.

I pointed this out to my brother and did some quick sums in my head. Twelve cents plus a nickel times, say, twenty gallons was three dollars and forty cents. I said, "Damn, Newton, you know how I hate being played for a fool."

"Well, maybe he's got his higher costs and all. Being out in the middle of nowhere and all, little town like this."

"Town? Where's the town at? Where we are ain't nothing but a wide place in the road."

And that was really all it was. Not even a crossroads, just the frame house and the garage alongside it, and on the other side of the road a cafe with a sign advertising home-cooked food and package goods. A couple cars over by the garage, two of them with their hoods up and various parts missing from them. Another car parked over by the cafe.

"Newt," I said, "you ever see a softer place'n this?"

"Don't even think about it."

"Not thinking about a thing. Just mentioning."

"We don't bother with nickels and dimes no more, Vernon. We agreed on that. By tonight we'll be in Silver City. Johnny Mack Lee's already there and first thing in the morning we'll be taking that bank off slicker'n a bald tire. You know all that."

"I know."

"So don't be exercising your mind over nickels and dimes."

"Oh, I know it," I said. "Only we could use some kind of money pretty soon. What have we got left? Hundred dollars?"

"Little better than that."

"Not much better, though."

"Well, tomorrow's payday," Newt said.

I knew he was right but it's a habit a man gets into, looking at a place and figuring how he would go about taking it off. Me and Newt, we always had a feeling for places like filling stations and liquor stores and 7-Eleven stores and like that. You just take 'em off nice and easy, you get in and get out and a man can make a living that way. Like the saying goes, it don't pay much but it's regular.

But then the time came that we did a one-to-five over to the state pen and it was an education. We both of us came out of there knowing the right people and the right way to operate. One thing we swore was to swear off nickels and dimes. The man who pulls quick-dollar stickups like that, he works ten times as often and takes twenty times the risks of the man who takes his time setting up a big job and scoring it. I remember Johnny Mack Lee saying it takes no more work to knock over a bank than a bakery and the difference is dollars to doughnuts.

I looked up and saw the dude with the hat poking around under the hood. "What's he doing now, Newt? Prospecting for more gold?"

"Checking the oil, I guess."

"Hope we don't need none," I said. " 'Cause you just know he's gotta be charging two dollars a quart for it."

Well, we didn't need any oil. And you had to admit he did a good job of checking under there, topping up the battery terminals and all. Then he came around and leaned against the car door.

"Oil's okay," he said. "You sure took a long drink of gas. Good you had enough to get here. And this here's the last station for a whole lot of highway."

"Well," I said. "How much do we owe you?"

He named a figure. High as it was, it came as no surprise to me since I'd already turned and read it off of the pump. Then as I was reaching in my pocket he said, "I guess you know about that fan clutch, don't you?"

"Fan clutch?"

He gave a long slow nod. "I suppose you got a few miles left in it," he said. "Thing is, it could go any minute. You want to step out of the car for a moment I can show you what I'm talking about."

Well, I got out, and Newt got out his side, and we went and joined this bird and peeked under the hood. He reached behind the radiator and took ahold of some damned thing or other and showed us how it was wobbling. "The fan clutch," he said. "You ever replace this here since you owned the car?"

Newt looked at me and I looked back at him. All either of us ever knew about a car is starting it and stopping it and the like. As a boy Newt was awful good at starting them without keys. You know how kids are.

"Now if this goes," he went on, "then there goes your water pump. Probably do a good job on your radiator at the same time. You might want to wait and have your own mechanic take care of it for you. The way it is, though, I wouldn't want to be driving too fast or too far with it. 'Course if you hold it down to forty miles an hour and stop from time to time so's the heat won't build up—"

His voice trailed off. Me and Newt looked at each other again. Newt asked some more about the fan clutch and the dude wobbled it again and told us more about what it did, which we pretended to pay attention to and nodded like it made sense to us.

"This fan clutch," Newt said. "What's it run to replace it?"

"Around thirty, thirty-five dollars. Depends on the model and who does the work for you, things like that."

"Take very long?"

"Maybe twenty minutes."

"Could you do it for us?"

The dude considered, cleared his throat, spat in the dirt. "Could," he allowed. "If I got the part. Let me just go and check."

When he walked off I said, "Brother, what's the odds that he's got that part?"

"No bet a-tall. You figure there's something wrong with our fan clutch?"

"Who knows?"

"Yeah," Newt said. "Can't figure on him being a crook and just spending his life out here in the middle of nowhere, but then you got to consider the price he gets for the gas and all. He hasn't had a customer since we pulled in, you know. Maybe he gets one car a day and tries to make a living off it."

"So tell him what to do with his fan clutch."

"Then again, Vern, maybe all he is in the world is a good mechanic trying to do us a service. Suppose we cut out of here and fifty miles down the road our fan clutch up and kicks our water pump through our radiator or whatever the hell it is. By God, Vernon, if we don't get to Silver City tonight Johnny Mack Lee's going to be vexed with us."

"That's a fact. But thirty-five dollars for a fan clutch sure eats a hole in our capital, and suppose we finally get to Silver City and find out Johnny Mack Lee got out the wrong side of bed and slipped on a banana peel or something? Meaning if we get there and there's no job and we're stuck in the middle of nowhere, then what do we do?"

"Well, I guess it's better'n being stuck in the desert."

"I guess."

Of course he had just the part he needed. You had to wonder how a little gas station like that would happen to carry a full line of fan clutches, which I never even heard of that particular part before, but when I said as much to Newt he shrugged and said maybe an out-of-the-way place like that was likely to carry a big stock because he was too far from civilization to order parts when the need for them arose.

"The thing is," he said, "all up and down the line you can read all of this either way. Either we're being taken or we're being done a favor for, and there's no way to know for sure."

While he set about doing whatever he had to do with the fan clutch, we took his advice and went across the street for some coffee. "Woman who runs the place is a pretty fair cook," he said. "I take all my meals there my own self."

"Takes all his meals here," I said to Newt. "Hell, she's got him where he's got us. He don't want to eat here, he can walk sixty miles to a place more to his liking."

The car that had been parked at the cafe was gone now and we were the only customers. The woman in charge was too thin and rawboned to serve as an advertisement for her own cooking. She had her faded blonde hair tied up in a red kerchief and she was perched on a stool smoking a cigarette and studying a *True Confessions* magazine. We each of us ordered apple pie at a dollar a wedge and coffee at thirty-five cents a cup. While we were eating a car pulled up and a man wearing a suit and tie bought a pack of cigarettes from her. He put down a dollar bill and didn't get back but two dimes change.

"I think I know why that old boy across the street charges so much," Newt said softly. "He needs to get top dollar if he's gonna pay for his meals here."

"She does charge the earth."

"You happen to note the liquor prices? She gets seven dollars for a bottle of Ancient Age bourbon. And that's not for a quart, either. That's for a fifth."

I nodded slowly. I said, "I just wonder where they keep all that money."

"Brother, we don't even want to think on that."

"Never hurt a man to think."

"These days it's all credit cards anyways. The tourist trade is nothing but credit cards and his regular customers most likely run a monthly tab and give him a check for it."

"We'll be paying cash."

"Well, it's a bit hard to establish credit in our line of work."

"Must be other people pays him cash. And the food and liquor over here, that's gotta be all cash, or most all cash."

"And how much does it generally come to in a day? Be sensible. As little business as they're doing—"

"I already thought of that. Same time, though, look how far they are from wherever they do their banking."

"So?"

"So they wouldn't be banking the day's receipts every night. More likely they drive in and make their deposits once a week, maybe even once every two weeks."

Newt thought about that. "Likely you're right," he allowed. "Still, we're just talking small change."

"Oh, I know."

But when we paid for our pie and coffee Newton gave the old girl a smile and told her how we sure had enjoyed the pie, which we hadn't all that much, and how her husband was doing a real good job on our car over across the street.

"Oh, he does real good work," she said.

"What he's doing for us," Newt said, "he's replacing our fan clutch. I guess you probably get a lot of people here needing new fan clutches."

"I wouldn't know about that," she said. "Thing is I don't know much about cars. He's the mechanic and I'm the cook is how we divvy things up."

"Sounds like a good system," Newt told her.

On the way across the street Newt separated two twenties from our bankroll and tucked them into his shirt pocket. Then I reminded him about the gas and he added a third twenty. He gave the rest of our stake a quick count and shook his head in annoyance. "We're getting pretty close to the bone," he said. "Johnny Mack Lee better be where's he's supposed to be."

"He's always been reliable."

"That's God's truth. And the bank, it better be the piece of cake he says it is."

"I just hope."

"Twenty thousand a man is how he has it figured. Plus he says it could run three times that. I sure wouldn't complain if it did, brother."

I said I wouldn't either. "It does make it silly to even think about nickels and dimes," I said.

"Just what I was telling you."

"I was never thinking about it, really. Not in the sense of doing it. Just mental exercise, keeps the brain in order."

He gave me a brotherly punch in the shoulder and we laughed together some. Then we went on to where the dude in the big hat was playing with our car. He gave us a big smile and held out a piece of metal for us to admire. "Your old fan clutch," he said, which I had more or less figured. "Take hold of this part. That's it, right there. Now try to turn it."

I tried to turn it and it was hard to turn. He had Newt do the same thing. "Tight," Newt said.

"Lucky you got this far with it," he said, and clucked his tongue and shook his head and heaved the old fan clutch onto a heap of old metallic junk.

I stood there wondering if a fan clutch was supposed to turn hard or easy or not at all, and if that was our original fan clutch or a piece of junk he kept around for this particular purpose, and I knew my brother Newton was wondering just the same thing. I wished they could have taught us something useful in the state pen, something that might have come in handy in later life, something like your basic auto mechanics course. But they had me melting my flesh off my bones in the prison laundry and they had Newt sewing mail sacks, which there isn't much call for in civilian life, being the state penal system has an official monopoly on the business.

Meanwhile Newt had the three twenties out of his shirt pocket and was standing there straightening them out and lining up their edges. "Let's see now," he said. "That's sixteen and change for the gas, and you said thirty to thirty-five for the fan clutch, so what's that all come to?"

It turned out that it came to just under eighty-five dollars.

The fan clutch, it seemed, had run higher than he'd thought it would. Forty-two fifty was what it came to, and that was for the part exclusive of labor. Labor tacked another twelve dollars onto our tab. And while he'd been working there under the hood, our friend had found a few things that simply needed attending to. Our fan belt, for example, was clearly on its last legs and ready to pop any minute. He showed it to us and you could see how worn it was, all frayed and just a thread or two away from popping.

So he had replaced it, and he'd replaced our radiator hoses at the same time. He fished around in his junkpile and came up with a pair of radiator hoses which he said had come off our car. The rubber was old and stiff with little cracks in the surface, and it sure smelled like something awful.

I studied the hoses and agreed they were in terrible shape. "So you just went ahead and replaced them on your own," I said.

"Well," he said, "I didn't want to bother you while you were eating."

"That was considerate," Newt said.

"I figured you fellows would want it seen to. You blow a fan belt or a hose out there, well, it's a long walk back, you know. 'Course I realize you didn't authorize me to do the work, so if you actually want me to take the new ones off and put the old back on—"

Of course there was no question of doing that. Newt looked at me for a minute and I looked back at him and he took out our roll, which I don't guess you could call a roll anymore from the size of it, and he peeled off another twenty and a ten and added them to the three twenties from his shirt pocket. He held the money in his hand and looked at it and then at the dude, then back at the money, then back at the dude again. You could see he was doing heavy thinking, and I had an idea where his thoughts were leading.

Finally he took in a whole lot of air and let it out in a rush and said, "Well, hell, I guess it's worth it if it leaves us with a car in good condition. Last thing either of us wants is any damn trouble with the damn car and I guess it's worth it. This fixes us up, right? Now we're in good shape with nothing to worry about, right?"

"Well," the dude said.

We looked at him.

"There is a thing I noticed."

"Oh?"

"If you'll just look right here," he said. "See how the rubber grommet's gone on the top of your shock absorber mounting, that's what called it to my attention. Now you see your car's right above the hydraulic lift, that's cause I had it up before to take a look at your shocks. Now let me just raise it up again and I can point out to you what's wrong."

Well, he pressed a switch or some such to send the car up off the ground, and then he pointed here and there underneath it to show us where the shocks were shot and something was cutting into something else and about to commence bending the frame.

"If you got the time you ought to let me take care of that for you," he said. "Because if you don't get it seen to you wind up with frame damage and your whole front end goes on you, and then where are you?"

He let us take a long look at the underside of the car. There was no question that something was pressing on something and cutting into it. What the hell it all added up to was beyond me.

"Just let me talk to my brother a minute," Newt said to him, and he took hold of my arm and we walked around the side.

"Well," he said, "what do you think? It looks like this old boy here is sticking it in pretty deep."

"It does at that. But that fan belt was shot and those hoses was the next thing to petrified."

"True."

"If they was our fan belt and hoses in the first place and not some junk he had around."

"I had that very thought, Vern."

"Now as for the shock absorbers—"

"Something sure don't look altogether perfect underneath that car. Something's sure cutting into something."

"I know it. But maybe he just went and got a file or some such thing and did some cutting himself."

"In other words, either he's a con man or he's a saint."

"Except we know he ain't a saint, not at the price he gets for gasoline, and not telling us how he eats all his meals across the road and all the time his own wife's running it."

"So what do we do? You want to go on to Silver City on those shocks? I don't even know if we got enough money to cover putting shocks on, far as that goes."

We walked around to the front and asked the price of the shocks. He worked it all out with pencil and paper and came up with a figure of forty-five dollars, including the parts and the labor and the tax and all. Newt and I went into another huddle and he counted his money and I went through my own pockets and came up with a couple of dollars, and it worked out that we could pay what we owed and get the shocks and come up with three dollars to bless ourselves with.

So I looked at Newt and he looked back at me and gave a great shrug of his shoulders. Close as we are we can say a lot without speaking.

We told the dude to go ahead and do the work.

While he installed the shocks, me and Newt went across the road and had us a couple of chicken-fried steaks. They wasn't bad at all even if the price was on the high side. We washed the steaks down with a beer apiece and then each of us had a cup of that coffee. I guess there's been times I had better coffee.

"I'd say you fellows sure were lucky you stopped here," the woman said.

"It's our lucky day, all right," Newt said. While he paid her I looked over the paperback books and magazines. Some of them looked to be old and secondhand but they weren't none of them reduced in price on account of it, and this didn't surprise me much.

What also didn't surprise us was when we got back to find the shocks installed and our friend with his big hat off and scratching his mop of hair and telling us how the rear shocks was in even worse shape than the front ones. He went and ran the car up in the air again to show us more things that didn't mean much to us.

Newton said, "Well, sir, my brother and I, we talked it over. We figure we been neglecting this here automobile and we really ought to do right by it. If those rear shocks is bad, well, let's just get 'em the hell off of there and new ones on. And while we're here I'm just about positive we're due for an oil change."

"And I'll replace the oil filter while I'm at it."

"You do that," Newt told him. "And I guess you'll find other things that can do with a bit of fixing. Now we haven't got all the time in the world or all the money in the world either, but I guess we got us a pair of hours to spare, and we consider ourselves lucky having the good fortune to run up against a mechanic who knows which end of the wrench is which. So what we'll do, we'll just find us a patch of shade to set in and you check that car over and find things to do to her. Only things that need doing, but I guess you'd be the best judge of that."

Well, I'll tell you he found things to fix. Now and then a car would roll on in and he'd have to go and sell somebody a tank of gas, but we sure got the lion's share of his time. He replaced the air filter, he cleaned the carburetor, he changed the oil and replaced the oil filter, he tuned the engine and drained and flushed the radiator and filled her with fresh coolant, he gave us new plugs and points, he did this and that and every damn thing he could think of, and I guess the only parts of that car he didn't replace were ones he didn't have replacement parts for.

Through it all Newt and I sat in a patch of shade and sipped Cokes out of the bottle. Every now and then that bird would come over and tell us what else he found that he ought to be doing, and we'd look at each other and shrug our shoulders and say for him to go ahead and do what had to be done.

"Amazing what was wrong with that car of ours," Newt said to me. "Here I thought it rode pretty good."

"Hell, I pulled in here wanting nothing in the world but a tank of gas. Maybe a quart of oil, and oil was the one thing in the world we didn't need, or it looks like."

"Should ride a whole lot better once he's done with it."

"Well I guess it should. Man's building a whole new car around the cigarette lighter."

"And the clock. Nothing wrong with that clock, outside of it loses a few minutes a day."

"Lord," Newt said, "don't you be telling him about those few minutes the clock loses. We won't never get out of here."

That dude took the two hours we gave him and about twelve minutes besides, and then he came on over into the shade and presented us with his bill. It was all neatly itemized, everything listed in the right place and all of it added up, and the figure in the bottom right-hand corner with the circle around it read $277.45.

"That there is quite a number," I said.

He put the big hat on the back of his head and ran his hand over his forehead. "Whole lot of work involved," he said. "When you take into account all of those parts and all that labor."

"Oh, that's for certain," Newt said. "And I can see they all been taken into account, all right."

"That's clear as black and white," I said. "One thing, you couldn't call this a nickel-and-dime figure."

"That you couldn't," Newton said. "Well, sir, let me just go and get some money from the car. Vern?"

We walked over to the car together. "Funny how things work out," Vern said. "I swear people get forced into things, I just swear to hell and gone they do. What did either of us want beside a tank of gas?"

"Just a tank of gas is all."

"And here we are," he said. He opened the door on the passenger side, waited for a pickup truck to pass going west to east, then popped the glove compartment. He took the .38 for himself and gave me the .32 revolver. "I'll just settle up with our good buddy here," he said, loud enough for the good buddy in question to hear him. "Meanwhile, why don't you just step across the street and pick us up something to drink later on this evening? You never know, might turn out to be a long ways between liquor stores."

I went and gave him a little punch in the upper arm. He laughed the way he does and I put the .32 in my pocket and trotted on across the road to the cafe.

One Thousand Dollars a Word

The editor's name was Warren Jukes. He was a lean sharp-featured man with slender long-fingered hands and a narrow line for a mouth. His black hair was going attractively gray on top and at the temples. As usual, he wore a stylish three-piece suit. As usual, Trevathan felt logy and unkempt in comparison, like a bear having trouble shaking off the torpor of hibernation.

"Sit down, Jim," Jukes said. "Always a pleasure. Don't tell me you're bringing in another manuscript already? It never ceases to amaze me the way you keep grinding them out. Where do you get your ideas, anyway? But I guess you're tired of that question after all these years."

He was indeed, and that was not the only thing of which James Trevathan was heartily tired. But all he said was, "No, Warren. I haven't written another story."

"Oh?"

"I wanted to talk with you about the last one."

"But we talked about it yesterday," Jukes said, puzzled. "Over the telephone. I said it was fine and I was happy to have it for the magazine. What's the title, anyway? It was a play on words, but I can't remember it offhand."

" 'A Stitch in Crime,' " Trevathan said.

"Right, that's it. Good title, good story, and all of it wrapped up in your solid professional prose. What's the problem?"

"Money," Trevathan said.

"A severe case of the shorts, huh?" The editor smiled. "Well, I'll be putting a voucher through this afternoon. You'll have the check early next week. I'm afraid that's the best I can do, Jimbo. The corporate machinery can only go so fast."

"It's not the time," Trevathan said. "It's the amount. What are you paying for the story, Warren?"

"Why, the usual. How long was it? Three thousand words, wasn't it?"

"Thirty-five hundred."

"So what does that come to? Thirty-five hundred at a nickel a word is what? One seventy-five, right?"

"That's right, yes."

"So you'll have a check in that amount early next week, as soon as possible, and if you want I'll ring you when I have it in hand and you can come over and pick it up. Save waiting a couple of days for the neither-rain-nor-snow people to get it from my desk to yours."

"It's not enough."

"Beg your pardon?"

"The price," Trevathan said. He was having trouble with this conversation. He'd written a script for it in his mind on the way to Jukes's office, and he'd been infinitely more articulate then than now. "I should get more money," he managed. "A nickel a word is . . . Warren, that's no money at all."

"It's what we pay, Jim. It's what we've always paid."

"Exactly."

"So?"

"Do you know how long I've been writing for you people, Warren?"

"Quite a few years."

"Twenty years, Warren."

"Really?"

"I sold a story called 'Hanging by a Thread' to you twenty years ago last month. It ran twenty-two hundred words and you paid me a hundred and ten bucks for it."

"Well, there you go," Jukes said.

"I've been working twenty years, Warren, and I'm getting the same money now that I got then. Everything's gone up except my income. When I wrote my first story for you I could take one of those nickels that a word of mine brought and buy a candy bar with it. Have you bought a candy bar recently, Warren?"

Jukes touched his belt buckle. "If I went and bought candy bars," he said, "my clothes wouldn't fit me."

"Candy bars are forty cents. Some of them cost thirty-five. And I still get a nickel a word. But let's forget candy bars."

"Fine with me, Jim."

"Let's talk about the magazine. When you bought 'Hanging by a Thread,' what did the magazine sell for on the stands?"

"Thirty-five cents, I guess."

"Wrong. Twenty-five. About six months later you went to thirty-five. Then you went to fifty, and after that sixty and then seventy-five. And what does the magazine sell for now?"

"A dollar a copy."

"And you still pay your authors a nickel a word. That's really wealth beyond the dreams of avarice, isn't it, Warren?"

Jukes sighed heavily, propped his elbows on his desk top, tented his fingertips. "Jim," he said, dropping his voice in pitch, "there are things you're forgetting. The magazine's no more profitable than it was twenty years ago. In fact we're working closer now than we did then. Do you know anything about the price of paper? It makes candy look pretty stable by comparison. I could talk for hours on the subject of the price of paper. Not to mention all the other printing costs, and shipping costs and more other costs than I want to mention or you want to hear about. You look at that buck-a-copy price and you think we're flying high, but it's not like that at all. We were doing better way back then. Every single cost of ours has gone through the roof."

"Except the basic one."

"How's that?"

"The price you pay for material. That's what your readers are buying from you, you know. Stories. Plots and characters. Prose and dialogue. Words. And you pay the same for them as you did twenty years ago. It's the only cost that's stayed the same."

Jukes took a pipe apart and began running a pipe cleaner through the stem. Trevathan started talking about his own costs—his rent, the price of food. When he paused for breath Warren Jukes said, "Supply and demand, Jim."

"What's that?"

"Supply and demand. Do you think it's hard for me to fill the magazine at a nickel a word? See that pile of scripts over there? That's what this morning's mail brought. Nine out of ten of those stories are from new writers who'd write for nothing if it got them into print. The other ten percent is from pros who are damned glad when they see that nickel-a-word check instead of getting their stories mailed back to them. You know, I buy just about everything you write for us, Jim. One reason is I like your work, but that's not the only reason. You've been with us for twenty years and we like to do business with our old friends. But you evidently want me to raise your word rate, and we don't pay more than five cents a word to anybody, because in the first place we haven't got any surplus in the budget and in the second place we damn well don't *have* to pay more than that. So before I raise your rate, old friend, I'll give your stories back to you. Because I don't have any choice."

Trevathan sat and digested this for a few moments. He thought of some things to say but left them unsaid. He might have asked Jukes how the editor's own salary had fluctuated over the years, but what was the point of that? He could write for a nickel a word or he could not write for them at all. That was the final word on the subject.

"Jim? Shall I put through a voucher or do you want 'A Stitch in Crime' back?"

"What would I do with it? No, I'll take the nickel a word, Warren."

"If there was a way I could make it more—"

"I understand."

"You guys should have got yourselves a union years ago. Give you a little collective muscle. Or you could try writing something else. We're in a squeeze, you know, and if we were forced to pay more for material we'd probably have to fold the magazine altogether. But there are other fields where the pay is better."

"I've been doing this for twenty years, Warren. It's all I know. My God, I've got a reputation in the field, I've got an established name—"

"Sure. That's why I'm always happy to have you in the magazine. As long as I do the editing, Jimbo, and as long as you grind out the copy, I'll be glad to buy your yarns."

"At a nickel a word."

"Well—"

"Nothing personal, Warren. I'm just a little bitter. That's all."

"Hey, think nothing of it." Jukes got to his feet, came around from behind his desk. "So you got something off your chest, and we cleared the air a little. Now you know where you stand. Now you can go on home and knock off something sensational and get it to me, and if it's up to your usual professional standard you'll have another check coming your way. That's the way to double the old income, you know. Just double the old production."

"Good idea," Trevathan said.

"Of course it is. And maybe you can try something for another market while you're at it. It's not too late to branch out, Jim. God knows I don't want to lose you, but if you're having trouble getting by on what we can pay you, well—"

"It's a thought," Trevathan said.

Five cents a *word.*

Trevathan sat at his battered Underwood and stared at a blank sheet of paper. The paper had gone up a dollar a ream in the past year, and he could swear they'd cheapened the quality in the process. Everything cost more, he thought, except his own well-chosen words. They were still trading steadily at a nickel apiece.

Not too late to branch out, Jukes had told him. But that was a sight easier to say than to do. He'd tried writing for other kinds of markets, but detective stories were the only kind he'd ever had any luck with. His mind didn't seem to produce viable fictional ideas in other areas. When he'd tried writing longer works, novels, he'd always gotten hopelessly bogged down. He was a short-story writer, recognized and frequently anthologized, and he was prolific enough to keep himself alive that way, but—

But he was sick of living marginally, sick of grinding out story after story. And heartily sick of going through life on a nickel a word.

What would a decent word rate be?

Well, if they paid him twenty-five cents a word, then he'd at least be keeping pace with the price of a candy bar. Of course after twenty years you wanted to do a little better than stay even. Say they paid him a dollar a word. There were writers who earned that much. Hell, there were writers who earned a good deal more than that, writers whose books wound up on best-seller lists, writers who got six-figure prices for screenplays, writers who wrote themselves rich.

One thousand dollars a word.

The phrase popped into his mind, stunning in its simplicity, and before he was aware of it his fingers had typed the words on the page before him. He sat and looked at it, then worked the carriage return lever and typed the phrase again.

One thousand dollars a word.

He studied what he had typed, his mind racing on ahead, playing with ideas, shaking itself loose from its usual stereotyped thought patterns. Well, why not? Why shouldn't he earn a thousand dollars a word? Why not branch out into a new field?

Why not?

He took the sheet from the typewriter, crumpled it into a ball, pegged it in the general direction of the wastebasket. He rolled a new sheet in its place and sat looking at its blankness, waiting, thinking. Finally, word by halting word, he began to type.

Trevathan rarely rewrote his short stories. At a nickel a word he could not afford to. Furthermore, he had acquired a facility over the years which enabled him to turn out acceptable copy in first draft. Now, however, he was trying something altogether new and different, and so he felt the need to take his time getting it precisely right. Time and again he yanked false starts from the typewriter, crumpled them, hurled them at the wastebasket.

Until finally he had something he liked.

He read it through for the fourth or fifth time, then took it from the typewriter and read it again. It did the job, he decided. It was concise and clear and very much to the point.

He reached for the phone. When he'd gotten through to Jukes he said, "Warren? I've decided to take your advice."

"Wrote another story for us? Glad to hear it."

"No," he said, "another piece of advice you gave me. I'm branching out in a new direction."

"Well, I think that's terrific," Jukes said. "I really mean it. Getting to work on something big? A novel?"

"No, a short piece."

"But in a more remunerative area?"

"Definitely. I'm expecting to net a thousand dollars a word for what I'm doing this afternoon."

"A thousand—" Warren Jukes let out a laugh, making a sound similar to the yelp of a startled terrier. "Well, I don't know what you're up to, Jim, but let me wish you the best of luck with it. I'll tell you one thing. I'm damned glad you haven't lost your sense of humor."

Trevathan looked again at what he'd written. *"I've got a gun. Please fill this paper sack with thirty thousand dollars in used tens and twenties and fifties or I'll be forced to blow your stupid head off."*

"Oh, I've still got my sense of humor," he said. "Know what I'm going to do, Warren? I'm going to laugh all the way to the bank."

Passport in Order

Marcia stood up, yawned, and crushed out a cigarette in the round glass ashtray. "It's late," she said. "I should be getting home. How I hate to leave you!"

"You said it was his poker night."

"It is, but he might call me. Sometimes, too, he loses a lot of money in a hurry and comes home early, and in a foul mood, naturally." She sighed, turned to look at him. "I wish it didn't have to be secretive like this—hotel rooms, motels."

"It can't stay this way much longer."

"Why not?"

Bruce Farr ran a hand through his wavy hair, groped for a cigarette, and lit it. "Inventory is scheduled in a month," he said. "It won't be ten minutes before they discover I'm into them up to the eyes. They're a big firm, but a quarter of a million dollars worth of jewelry can't be eased out of the vaults without someone noticing it sooner or later."

"Did you take that much?"

He grinned. "That much," he said, "a little at a time. I picked pieces no one would ever look for, but the inventory will show them gone. I made out beautifully on the sale, honey; peddled some of the goods outright and borrowed on the rest. Got a little better than a hundred thousand dollars, safely stowed away."

"All that money," she said. She pursed her lips as if to whistle. "A hundred thousand—"

"Plus change." His smile spread and she thought how pleased he was with himself. Then he became serious. "Close to half the retail value. It went pretty well, Marcia, but we can't sit on it. We have to get out, out of the country."

"I know, but I'm afraid," Marcia said.

"They won't get us. Once we're out of the country, we don't have a thing to worry about. There are countries where you can buy yourself citizenship for a few thousand U.S. dollars, and beat extradition forever. They can't get us."

She was silent for a moment. When he took her hand and asked her what was wrong, she turned away, then met his eyes. "I'm not that worried about the police. If you say we can get away with it, well, I believe you."

"Then what's scaring you?"

"It's Ray," she said, and dropped her eyes. "Ray, my sweet loving husband. He'll find us, darling. I know he will. He'll find us, and he won't care whether we're citizens of Patagonia or Cambodia or wherever we go. He won't try to extradite us. He'll—" her voice broke, "he'll kill us," she finished.

"How can he find us? And what makes you think—"

She was shaking her head. "You don't know him."

"I don't particularly want to. Honey—"

"You don't know him," she repeated. "I do. I wish I didn't, I wish I'd never met him. I'm one of his possessions, I belong to him, and he wouldn't let me get away from him, not in a million years. He knows all kinds of people, terrible people. Criminals, gangsters." She gnawed her lip. "Why do you think I never left him? Why do you think I stay with him? Because I know what would happen if I didn't. He'd find me, one way or another, and he'd kill me, and—"

She broke. His arms went around her and held her, comforted her.

"I'm not giving you up," he said, "and he won't kill us. He won't kill either of us."

"You don't know him." Panic rose in her voice. "He's vicious, ruthless. He—"

"Suppose we kill him first, Marcia?"

He had to go over it with her a long time before she would even listen to him. They had to leave the country anyway. Neither of them was ready to spend a lifetime, or part of it, in jail. Once they were out they could stay out. So why not burn an extra bridge on the way? If Ray was really a threat to them, why not put him all the way out of the picture?

"Besides," he told her, "I'd like to see him dead. I really would. For months now you've been mine, yet you always have to go home to him."

"I'll have to think about it," she said.

"You wouldn't have to do a thing, baby. I'd take care of everything."

She nodded, got to her feet. "I never thought of—murder," she said. "Is this how murders happen? When ordinary people get caught up over their heads? Is that how it starts?"

"We're not ordinary people, Marcia. We're special. And we're not in over our heads. It'll work."

"I'll think about it," she said. "I'll—I'll think about it."

Marcia called Bruce two days later. She said, "Do you remember what we were talking about? We don't have a month anymore."

"What do you mean?"

"Ray surprised me last night. He showed me a pair of airline tickets for Paris. We're set to fly in ten days. Our passports are still in order from last year's trip. I couldn't stand another trip with him, dear. I couldn't live through it."

"Did you think about—"

"Yes, but this is no time to talk about it," she said. "I think I can get away tonight."

"Where and when?"

She named a time and place. When she placed the receiver back in its cradle she was surprised that her hand did not tremble. So easy, she thought. She was deciding a man's fate, planning the end of a man's life, and her hand was as steady as a surgeon's. It astonished her that questions of life and death could be so easily resolved.

She was a few minutes late that night. Bruce was waiting for her in front of a tavern on Randolph Avenue. As she approached, he stepped forward and took her arm.

"We can't talk here," he said. "I don't think we should chance being seen together. We can drive around. My car's across the street."

He took Claibourne Drive out to the east end of town. She lit a cigarette with the dashboard lighter and smoked in silence. He asked her what she had decided.

"I tried not to think about it," she told him. "Then last night he sprang this jaunt on me, this European tour. He's planning on spending three weeks over there. I don't think I could endure it."

"So?"

"Well, I got this wild idea. I thought about what you said, about—about killing him . . ."

"Yes?"

She drew a breath, let it out slowly. "I think you're right. We have to kill him. I'd never rest if I knew he was after us. I'd wake up terrified in the middle of the night. I know I would. So would you."

He didn't say anything. His eyes were on hers and he clasped her hands.

"I guess I'm a worrier. I'd worry about the police, too. Even if we managed to do what you said, to buy our way out of extradition. The things you read, I don't know. I'd hate to feel like a hunted animal for the rest of my life. I'd rather have the police hunting me than Ray, but even so, I don't think I'd like it."

"So?"

She lit another cigarette. "It's probably silly," she said. "I thought there might be a way to keep them from looking for you, and to get rid of him at the same time. Last night it occurred to me that you're about his build. About six-one, aren't you?"

"Just about."

"That's what I thought. You're younger, and you're much better looking than he is, but you're both about the same height and weight. And I thought—Oh, this is silly!"

"Keep going."

"Oh, this is the kind of crazy thing you see on television. I don't know what kind of a mind I must have to think of it. But I thought that you could leave a note. You'd go to sleep at your house, then get up in the middle of the night and leave a long note explaining how you stole jewelry from your company and lost the money gambling and kept stealing more money and getting in deeper and deeper until there's no way out. And that you're doing the only thing you can do, that you've decided, well, to commit suicide."

"I thing I'm beginning to get it."

Her eyes lowered. "It doesn't make any sense, does it?"

"It sure does. You're about as crazy as a fox. Then we kill Ray and make it appear to be me."

She nodded. "I thought of a way we could do it. I can't believe it's really me saying all of this! I thought we could do it that same night. You would come over to the house and I would let you in. We could get Ray in his sleep. Press a pillow over his face or something like that. I don't know. Then we could load him into your car and drive somewhere and . . ."

"And put him over a cliff." His eyes were filled with frank admiration. "Beautiful, just beautiful."

"Do you really think so?"

"It couldn't be better. They'll have a perfect note, in my handwriting. They'll have my car over a cliff and a burned body in it. And they'll have a good motive for suicide. You're a wonder, honey."

She managed a smile. "Then your company won't be hunting you, will they?"

"Not me or their money. *Gambled every penny away*—that'll throw 'em a curve. I haven't bet more than two bucks on a horse in my life. But your sweetheart of a husband will be gone, and somebody might start wondering where he is. Oh, wait a minute . . ."

"What?"

"This gets better the more I think about it. He'll take my place in the car and I'll take his on that plane to Europe. We're the same build, his passport is in good order, and the reservations are all made. We'll use those tickets to take the Grand Tour, except that we won't come back. Or if we do, we'll wind up in some other city where nobody knows us, baby. We'll have every bridge burned the minute we cross over. When are you scheduled to take that trip?"

She closed her eyes, thought it through. "A week from Friday," she said. "We fly to New York in the morning, and then on to Paris the next afternoon."

"Perfect. You can expect company Thursday night. Slip downstairs after he goes to bed and let me into the house. I'll have the note written. We'll take care of him and go straight to the airport. We won't even have to come back to the house."

"The money?"

"I'll have it with me. You can do your packing Thursday so we'll have everything ready, passports and all." He shook his head in disbelief. "I always knew you were wonderful, Marcia. I didn't realize you were a genius."

"You really think it will work?"

He kissed her and she clung to him. He kissed her again, then grinned down at her. "I don't see how it can miss," he said.

The days crawled. They couldn't risk seeing each other until Thursday night, but Bruce assured Marcia that it wouldn't be long.

But it was long. Although she found herself far calmer than she had dared to expect, Marcia was still anxious, nervous about the way it might go.

Oh, it was long, very long. Bruce called Wednesday afternoon to make final plans. They arranged a signaling system. When Ray was sleeping soundly, she would slip out of bed and go downstairs. She would dial his phone number. He would have the note written, the money stowed in the trunk of his car. As soon as she called he would drive over to her house, and she would be waiting downstairs to let him in.

"Don't worry about what happens then," he said. "I'll take care of the details."

That night and the following day consumed at least a month of subjective time for her. She called him, finally, at twenty minutes of three Friday morning. He answered at once.

"I thought you weren't going to call at all," he said.

"He was up late, but he's asleep now."

"I'll be right over."

She waited downstairs at the front door, heard his car pull to a stop, had the door open for him before he could knock. He stepped quickly inside and closed the door.

"All set," he said. "The note, everything."

"The money?"

"It's in the trunk, in an attaché case, packed to the brim."

"Fine," she said. "It's been fun, darling."

But Bruce never heard the last sentence. Just as her lips framed the words, a form moved behind him and a leather-covered sap arced downward, catching him deftly and decisively behind the right ear. He fell like a stone and never made a sound.

Ray Danahy straightened up. "Out cold," he said. "Neat and sweet. Take a look outside and check the traffic. This is no time for nosy neighbors."

She opened the door, stepped outside. The night was properly dark and silent. She filled her lungs gratefully with fresh air.

Ray said, "Pull his car into the driveway alongside the house. Wait a sec, I think he's got the keys on him." He bent over Farr, dug a set of car keys out of his pocket. "Go ahead," he said.

She brought the car to the side door. Ray appeared in the doorway with Bruce's inert form over one shoulder. He dumped him onto the backseat and walked around the car to get behind the wheel.

"Take our buggy," he told Marcia. "Follow me, but not too close. I'm taking Route Thirty-two north of town. There's a good drop about a mile and a half past the county line."

"Not too good a drop, I hope," she said. "He could be burned beyond recognition."

"No such thing. Dental x-rays—they can't miss. It's a good thing he didn't have the brains to think of that."

"He wasn't very long on brains," she said.

"*Isn't*," he corrected. "He's not dead yet."

She followed Ray, lagging about a block and a half behind him. At the site he had chosen, she stood by while he took the money from the trunk and checked Farr's pockets to make sure he wasn't carrying anything that might tip anybody off. Ray propped him behind the wheel, put the car in neutral, braced Farr's foot on the gas pedal. Farr was just beginning to stir.

"Good-bye, Brucie," Marcia said. "You don't know what a bore you were."

Ray reached inside and popped the car into gear, then jumped aside. The heavy car hurtled through an ineffective guard rail, hung momentarily in the air, then began the long fast fall. First, there was the noise of the impact. Then there was another loud noise, an explosion, and the vehicle burst into flames.

They drove slowly away, the suitcase full of money between them on the seat of their car. "Scratch one fool," Ray said pleasantly. "We've got two hours to catch our flight to New York, then on to Paris."

"Paris," she sighed. "Not on a shoestring, the way we did it last time. This time we'll do it in style."

She looked down at her hands, her steady hands. How surprisingly calm she was, she thought, and a slow smile spread over her face.

Someday I'll Plant More Walnut Trees

There is a silence that is just stillness, just the absence of sound, and there is a deeper silence that is more than that. It is the antithesis, the aggressive opposite, of sound. It is to sound as antimatter is to matter, an auditory black hole that reaches out to swallow up and nullify the sounds of others.

My mother can give off such a silence. She is a master at it. That morning at breakfast she was thus silent, silent as she cooked eggs and made coffee, silent while I spooned baby oatmeal into Livia's little mouth, silent while Dan fed himself and while he smoked the day's first cigarette along with his coffee. He had his own silence, sitting there behind his newspaper, but all it did was insulate him. It couldn't reach out beyond that paper shield to snatch other sounds out of the air.

He finished and put out his cigarette, folded his paper. He said it was supposed to be hot today, with rain forecast for late afternoon. He patted Livia's head, and with his forefinger drew aside a strand of hair that had fallen across her forehead.

I can see that now, his hand so gentle, and her beaming up at him, wide-eyed, gurgling.

Then he turned to me, and with the same finger and the same softness he reached to touch the side of my face. I did not draw away. His finger touched me, ever so lightly, and then he reached to draw me into the circle of his arms. I smelled his shirt, freshly washed and sun-dried, and under it the clean male scent of him.

We looked at each other, both of us silent, the whole room silent. And then Livia cooed and he smiled quickly and chucked me under the chin and left. I heard the screen door slam, and then the sounds of the car as he drove to town. When I could not hear it anymore I went over to the radio and switched it on. They were playing a Tammy Wynette song. "Stand by your man," Tammy urged, and my mother's silence swallowed up the words.

While the radio played unheard I changed Livia and put her in for her nap. I came back to the kitchen and cleared the table. My mother waved a hand at the air in front of her face.

"He smokes," I said.

"I didn't say anything," she said.

We did the dishes together. There is a dishwasher but we never use it for the breakfast dishes. She prefers to run it only once a day, after the evening meal. It could hold all the day's dishes, they would not amount to more than one load in the machine, but she does not like to let the breakfast and lunch dishes stand. It seems wasteful to me, of time and effort, and even of water, although our well furnishes more than we ever need. But it is her house, after all, and her dishwasher, and hers the decision as to when it is to be used.

Silently she washed the dishes, silently I wiped them. As I reached to stack plates in a cupboard I caught her looking at me. Her eyes were on my cheek, and I could feel her gaze right where I had felt Dan's finger. His touch had been light. Hers was firmer.

I said, "It's nothing."

"All right."

"Dammit, Mama!"

"I didn't say anything, Tildie."

I was named Matilda for my father's mother. I never knew her, she died before I was born, before my parents met. I was never called Matilda. It was the name on my college diploma, on my driver's license, on Livia's birth certificate, but no one ever used it.

"He can't help it," I said. "It's not his fault."

Her silence devoured my words. On the radio Tammy Wynette sang a song about divorce, spelling out the word. Why were they playing all her records this morning? Was it her birthday? Or an anniversary of some failed romance?

"It's not," I said. I moved to her right so that I could talk to her good ear. "It's a pattern. His father was abusive to his mother. Dan grew up around that. His father drank and was free with his hands. Dan swore he would never be like that, but patterns like that are almost impossible to throw off. It's what he knows, can you understand that? On a deep level, deeper than intellect, bone deep, that's how he knows to behave as a man, as a husband."

"He marked your face. He hasn't done that before, Tildie."

My hand flew to the spot. "You knew that—"

"Sounds travel. Even with my door closed, even with my good ear on the pillow. I've heard things."

"You never said anything."

"I didn't say anything today," she reminded me.

"He can't help it," I said. "You have to understand that. Didn't you see him this morning?"

"I saw him."

"It hurts him more than it hurts me. And it's my fault as much as it's his."

"For allowing it?"

"For provoking him."

She looked at me. Her eyes are a pale blue, like mine, and at times there is accusation in them. My gaze must have the same quality. I have been told that it is penetrating. "Don't look at me like that," my husband has said, raising a hand as much to ward off my gaze as to threaten me. "Damn you, don't you look at me like that!"

Like what? I'd wondered. How was I looking at him? What was I doing wrong?

"I do provoke him," I told her. "I make him hit me."

"How?"

"By saying the wrong thing."

"What sort of thing?"

"Things that upset him."

"And then he has to hit you, Tildie? Because of what you say?"

"It's a *pattern*," I said. "It's the way he grew up. Men who drink have sons who drink. Men who beat their wives have sons who beat their wives. It's passed on over the generations like a genetic illness. Mama, Dan's a good man. You see how he is with Livia, how he loves her, how she loves him."

"Yes."

"And he loves me, Mama. Don't you think it tears him up when something like this happens? Don't you think it eats at him?"

"It must."

"It does!" I thought how he'd cried last night, how he'd held me and touched the mark on my cheek and cried. "And we're going to try to do something about it," I said. "To break the pattern. There's a clinic in Fulton City where you can go for counseling. It's not expensive, either."

"And you're going?"

"We've talked about it. We're considering it."

She looked at me and I made myself meet her eyes. After a moment she looked away. "Well, you would know more about this sort of thing than I do," she said. "You went to college, you studied, you learned things."

I studied art history. I can tell you about the Italian Renaissance, although I have already forgotten much of what I learned. I took one psychology course in my freshman year and we observed the behavior of white rats in mazes.

"Mama," I said, "I know you disapprove."

"Oh, no," she said. "Tildie, that's not so."

"It's not?"

She shook her head. "I just hurt for you," she said. "That's all."

We live on 220 acres, only a third of them level. The farm has been in our family since the land was cleared early in the last century. It has been years since we farmed it. The MacNaughtons run sheep in our north pastures, and Mr. Parkhill leases forty acres, planting alfalfa one year and field corn the next. Mama has some bank stock and some utilities, and the dividends plus what she's paid for the land rent are enough to keep her. There's no mortgage on the land and the taxes have stayed low. And she has a big kitchen garden. We eat out of it all summer long and put up enough in the fall to carry us through the winter.

Dan studied comparative lit while I studied art history. He got a master's and did half the course work for a doctorate and then knew he couldn't do it anymore. He got a job driving a taxi and I worked waiting tables at Paddy Mac's, where we used to come for beer and hamburgers when we were students. When I got pregnant with Livia he didn't want me on my feet all day but we couldn't make ends meet on his earnings as a cabdriver. Rents were high in that city, and everything cost a fortune.

And we both loved country living, and knew the city was no place to bring up Livia. So we moved here, and Dan got work right away with a construction company in Caldwell. That's the nearest town, just six miles from us on country roads, and Fulton City is only twenty-two miles.

After that conversation with Mama I went outside and walked back beyond the garden and the pear and apple orchard. There's a stream runs diagonally across our land, and just beyond it is the spot I always liked the best, where the walnut trees are. We have a whole grove of black walnuts, twenty-six trees in all. I know because Dan counted them. He was trying to estimate what they'd bring.

Walnut is valuable. People will pay thousands of dollars for a mature tree. They make veneer from it, because it's too costly to use as solid wood.

"We ought to sell these off," Dan said. "Your mama's got an untapped resource here. Somebody could come in, cut 'em down, and steal 'em. Like poachers in Kenya, killing the elephants for their ivory."

"No one's going to come onto our land."

"You never know. Anyway, it's a waste. You can't even see this spot from the house. And nobody does anything with the nuts."

When I was a girl my mama and I used to gather the walnuts after they fell in early autumn. Thousands fell from the trees. We would just gather a basketful and crack them with a hammer and pick the meat out. My hands always got black from the husks and stayed that way for weeks.

We only did this a few times. It was after Daddy left, but while Grandma Yount was still alive. I don't remember Grandma bothering with the walnuts, but she did lots of other things. When the cherries came in we would all pick them and she would bake pies and put up jars of the rest, and she'd boil the pits to clean them and sew scraps of cloth to make beanbags. There are still beanbags in the attic that Grandma Yount made. I'd brought one down for Livia and fancied I could still smell cherries through the cloth.

"We could harvest the walnuts," I told Dan. "If you want."

"What for? You can't get anything for them. Too much trouble to open and hardly any meat in them. I'd sooner harvest the trees."

"Mama likes having them here."

"They're worth a fortune. And they're a renewable resource. You could cut them and plant more and someday they'd put your grandchildren through college."

"You don't need to cut them to plant more. There's other land we could use."

"No point planting more if you're not going to cut these, is there? What do we need them for?"

"What do our grandchildren need college for?"

"What's that supposed to mean?"

"Nothing," I'd said, backing away.

And hours later he'd taken it up again. "You meant I wasted my education," he said. "That's what you meant by that crack, isn't it?"

"No."

"Then what did you mean? What do I need a master's for to hammer a nail? That's what you meant."

"It's not, but evidently that's how you'd rather hear it."

He hit me for that. I guess I had it coming. I don't know if I deserved it, I don't know if a woman deserves to get hit, but I guess I provoked it. Something makes me say things I shouldn't, things he'll take amiss. I don't know why.

Except I do know why, and I'd walked out of the kitchen and across to the walnut grove to keep from talking about it to Mama. Because he had his pattern and I had mine.

His was what he'd learned from his daddy, which was to abuse a woman, to slap her, to strike her with his fists. And mine was a pattern I'd learned from my mama, which was to make a man leave you, to taunt him with your mouth until one day he put his clothes in a suitcase and walked out the door.

In the mornings it tore at me to hear the screen door slam. Because I thought, Tildie, one day you'll hear that sound and it'll be for the last time. One day you'll do what your mother managed to do, and he'll do like your father did and you'll never see him again. And Livia will grow up as you did, in a house with her mother and her grandmother, and she'll have cherry-pit beanbags to play with and she'll pick the meat out of black walnuts, but what will she do for a daddy? And what will you do for a man?

All the rest of that week he never raised his hand to me. One night Mama stayed with Livia while Dan and I went to a movie in Fulton City. Afterward we went to a place that reminded us both of Paddy Mac's, and we drank beer and got silly. Driving home, we rolled down the car windows and sang songs at the top of our lungs. By the time we got home the beer had worn off but we were still happy and we hurried upstairs to our room.

Mama didn't say anything next morning but I caught her looking at me and knew she'd heard the old iron bedstead. I thought, *You hear a lot, even with your good ear pressed against the pillow.* Well, if she had to hear the fighting, let her hear the loving, too.

She could have heard the bed that night, too, although it was a quieter and gentler lovemaking than the night before. There were no knowing glances the next day, but after the screen door closed behind Dan and after Livia was in for her nap, there was a nice easiness between us as we stood side by side doing the breakfast dishes.

Afterward she said, "I'm so glad you're back home, Tildie."

"So you don't have to do the dishes all by yourself."

She smiled. "I knew you'd be back," she said.

"Did you? I wonder if I knew. I don't think so. I thought I wanted to live in a city, or in a college town. I thought I wanted to be a professor's wife and have earnest conversations about literature and politics and art. I guess I was just a country girl all along."

"You always loved it here," she said. "Of course it will be yours when I'm gone, and I had it in mind that you'd come back to it then. But I hoped you wouldn't wait that long."

She had never left. She and her mother lived here, and when she married my father he just moved in. It's a big old house, with different wings added over the years. He moved in, and then he left, and she just stayed on.

I remembered something. "I don't know if I thought I'd live here again," I said, "but I always thought I would die here." She looked at me, and I said, "Not so much die here as be buried here. When we buried Grandma I thought, *Well, this is where they'll bury me someday*. And I always thought that."

Grandma Yount's grave is on our land, just to the east of the pear and apple orchard. There are graves there dating back to when our people first lived here. The two children Mama lost are laid to rest there, and Grandma Yount's mother, and a great many children. It wasn't that long ago that people would have four or five children to raise one. You can't read what's cut into most of the stones, it's worn away with time, and it wears faster now that we have the acid rain, but the stones are there, the graves are there, and I always knew I'd be there, too.

"Well, I'll be there, too," Mama said. "But not too soon, I hope."

"No, not soon at all," I said. "Let's live a long time. Let's be old ladies together."

I thought it was a sweet conversation, a beautiful conversation. But when I told Dan about it we wound up fighting.

"When she goes," he said, "that's when those walnuts go to market."

"That's all you can think about," I said. "Turning a beautiful grove into dollars."

"That timber's money in the bank," he said, "except it's not in the bank because anybody could come in and haul it out of there behind our backs."

"Nobody's going to do that."

"And other things could happen. It's no good for a tree to let it grow beyond its prime. Insects can get it, or disease. There's one tree already that was struck by lightning."

"It didn't hurt it much."

"When they're my trees," he said, "they're coming down."

"They won't be your trees."

"What's that supposed to mean?"

"Mama's not leaving the place to you, Dan."

"I thought what's mine is yours and what's yours is mine."

"I love those trees," I said. "I'm not going to see them cut." His face darkened, and a muscle worked in his jaw. This was a warning sign, and I knew it as such, but I was stuck in a pattern, God help me, and I couldn't leave it alone. "First you'd sell off the timber," I said, "and then you'd sell off the acreage."

"I wouldn't do that."

"Why? Your daddy did."

Dan grew up on a farm that came down through his father's father. Unable to make a living farming, first his grandfather and then his father had sold off parcels of land little by little, whittling away at their holdings and each time reducing the potential income of what remained. After Dan's mother died his father had stopped farming altogether and drank full time, and the farm was auctioned for back taxes while Dan was still in high school.

I knew what it would do to him and yet I threw that in his face all the same. I couldn't seem to help it, any more than he could help what followed.

At breakfast the next day the silence made me want to scream. Dan read the paper while he ate, then hurried out the door without a word. I couldn't hear the screen door when it banged shut or the car engine when it started up. Mama's silence—and his, and mine—drowned out everything else.

I thought I'd burst when we were doing the dishes. She didn't say a word and neither did I. Afterward she turned to me and said, "I didn't go to college so I don't know about patterns, or what you do and what it makes him do."

The *quattrocento* and rats in a maze, that's all I learned in college. What I know about patterns and family violence I learned watching *Oprah* and *Phil Donahue*, and she watched the same programs I did. ("He blacked your eye and broke your nose. He kicked you in the stomach while you were pregnant. How can you stay with a brute like this?" "But I love him, Geraldo. And I know he loves me.")

"I just know one thing," she said. "It won't get better. And it will get worse."

"No."

"Yes. And you know it, Tildie."

"No."

He hadn't blacked my eye or broken my nose, but he had hammered my face with his fists and it was swollen and discolored. He hadn't kicked me in the stomach but he had shoved me from him. I had been clinging to his arm. That was stupid, I knew better than to do that, it drove him crazy to have me hang on him like that. He had shoved me and I'd gone sprawling, wrenching my leg when I fell on it. My knee ached now, and the muscles in the front of that thigh were sore. And my rib cage was sore where he'd punched me.

But I love him, Geraldo, Oprah, Phil. And I know he loves me.

That night he didn't come home.

I couldn't sit still, couldn't catch my breath. Livia caught my anxiety and wouldn't sleep, couldn't sleep. I held her in my arms and paced the floor in front of the television set. Back and forth, back and forth.

At midnight finally I put her in her crib and she slept. Mama was playing solitaire at the pine table. Only the top is pine, the base is maple. An antique, Dan pronounced it when he first saw it, and better than the ones in the shops. I suppose he had it priced in his mind, along with the walnut trees.

I pointed out a move. Mama said, "I know about that. I just haven't decided whether I want to do it, that's all." But she always says that. I don't believe she saw it.

At one I heard our car turn off the road and onto the gravel. She heard it, too, and gathered up the cards and said she was tired now, she'd just turn in. She was out of the room and up the stairs before he came in the door.

He was drunk. He lurched into the room, his shirt open halfway to his waist, his eyes unfocused. He said, "Oh, Jesus, Tildie, what's happening to us?"

"Shhh," I said. "You'll wake the baby."

"I'm sorry, Tildie," he said. "I'm sorry, I'm so goddam sorry."

Going up the stairs, he spun away from me and staggered into the railing. It held. I got him upstairs and into our room, but he passed out the minute he lay down on our bed. I got his shoes off, and his shirt and pants, and let him sleep in his socks and underwear.

In the morning he was still sleeping when I got up to take care of Livia. Mama had his breakfast on the table, his coffee poured, the newspaper at his place. He rushed through the kitchen without a word to anybody, tore out the door, and was gone. I moved toward the door but Mama was in my path.

I cried, "Mama, he's leaving! He'll never be back!"

She glanced meaningfully at Livia. I stepped back, lowered my voice. "He's leaving," I said, helpless. He had started the car, he was driving away. "I'll never see him again."

"He'll be back."

"Just like my daddy," I said. "Livvy, your father's gone, we'll never see him again."

"Stop that," Mama said. "You don't know how much sticks in their minds. You mind what you say in front of her."

"But it's true."

"It's not," she said. "You won't lose him that easy. He'll be back."

In the afternoon I took Livia with me while I picked pole beans and summer squash. Then we went back to the pear and apple orchard and played in the shade. After a while I took her over to Grandma Yount's grave. We'll all be here someday, I wanted to say, your grandma and your daddy and your mama, too. And you'll be here when your time comes. This is our land, this is where we all end up.

I might have said this, it wouldn't hurt for her to hear it, but for what Mama said. I guess it's true you don't know what sticks in their minds, or what they'll make of it.

She liked it out there, Livia did. She crawled right up to Grandma Yount's stone and ran her hand over it. You'd have thought she was trying to read it that way, like a blind person with Braille.

He didn't come home for dinner. It was going on ten when I heard the car on the gravel. Mama and I were watching television. I got up and went into the kitchen to be there when he came in.

He was sober. He stood in the doorway and looked at me. Every emotion a man could have was there on his face.

"Look at you," he said. "I did that to you."

My face was worse than the day before. Bruises and swellings are like that, taking their time to ripen.

"You missed dinner," I said, "but I saved some for you. I'll heat up a plate for you."

"I already ate. Tildie, I don't know what to say."

"You don't have to say anything."

"No," he said. "That's not right. We have to talk."

We slipped up to our room, leaving Mama to the television set. With our door closed we talked about the patterns we were caught in and how we seemed to have no control, like actors in a play with all their lines written for them by someone else. We could improvise, we could invent movements and gestures, we could read our lines in any of a number of ways, but the script was all written down and we couldn't get away from it.

I mentioned counseling. He said, "I called that place in Fulton City. I wouldn't tell them my name. Can you feature that? I called them for help but I was too ashamed to tell them my name."

"What did they say?"

"They would want to see us once a week as a couple, and each of us individually once a week. Total price for the three sessions would be eighty dollars."

"For how long?"

"I asked. They couldn't say. They said it's not the sort of change you can expect to make overnight."

I said, "Eighty dollars a week. We can't afford that."

"I had the feeling they might reduce it some."

"Did you make an appointment?"

"No. I thought I'd call tomorrow."

"I don't want to cut the trees," I said. He looked at me. "To pay for it. I don't want to cut Mama's walnut trees."

"Tildie, who brought up the damn trees?"

"We could sell the table," I said.

"What are you talking about?"

"In the kitchen. The pine-top table, didn't you say it was an antique? We could sell that."

"Why would I want to sell the table?"

"You want to sell those trees bad enough. You as much as said that as soon as my mama dies you'll be out back with a chain saw."

"Don't start with me," he said. "Don't you start with me, Tildie."

"Or what? Or you'll hit me? Oh, God, Dan, what are we doing? Fighting over how to pay for the counseling to keep from fighting. Dan, what's the matter with us?"

I went to embrace him but he backed away from me. "Honey," he said, "we better be real careful with this. They were telling me about escalating patterns of violence. I'm afraid of what could happen. I'm going to do what they said to do."

"What's that?"

"I want to pack some things," he said. "That's what I came home to do. There's that Welcome Inn Motel outside of Caldwell, they say it's not so bad and I believe they have weekly rates."

"No," I said. "No."

"They said it's best. Especially if we're going to start counseling, because that brings everything up and out into the open, and it threatens the part of us that wants to be in this pattern. Tildie, from what they said it'd be dangerous for us to be together right now."

"You can't leave," I said.

"I wouldn't be five miles away. I'd be coming for dinner some nights, we'd be going to a movie now and then. It's not like—"

"We can't afford it," I said. "Dan, how can we afford it? Eighty dollars a week for the counseling and God knows how much for the motel, and you'd be having most of your meals out, and how can we afford it? You've got a decent job but you don't make that kind of money."

His eyes hardened but he breathed in and out, in and out, and said, "Tildie, just talking like this is a strain, don't you see that? We can afford it, we'll find a way to afford it. Tildie, don't grab on to my arm like that, you know what it does to me. Tildie, stop it, will you for God's sake stop it?"

I put my arms around my own self and hugged myself. I was shaking. My hands just wanted to take hold of his arm. What was so bad about holding on to your husband's arm? What was wrong with that?

"Don't go," I said.

"I have to."

"Not now. It's late, they won't have any rooms left anyhow. Wait until morning. Can't you wait until morning?"

"I was just going to get some of my things and go."

"Go in the morning. Don't you want to see Livvy before you go? She's your daughter, don't you want to say good-bye to her?"

"I'm not leaving, Tildie. I'm just staying a few miles from here so we'll have a chance to keep from destroying ourselves. My God, Tildie, I don't want to leave you. That's the whole point, don't you see that?"

"Stay until morning," I said. "Please?"

"And will we go through this again in the morning?"

"No," I said. "I promise."

We were both restless, but then we made love and that settled him, and soon he was sleeping. I couldn't sleep, though. I lay there for a time, and then I put a robe on and went down to the kitchen and sat there for a long time, thinking of patterns, thinking of ways to escape them. And then I went back up the stairs to the bedroom again.

I was in the kitchen the next morning before Livia woke up. I was there when Mama came down, and her eyes widened at the sight of me. She started to say something but then I guess she saw something in my eyes and she stayed silent.

I said, "Mama, we have to call the police. You'll mind the baby when they come for me. Will you do that?"

"Oh, Tildie," she said.

I led her up the stairs again and into our bedroom. Dan lay facedown, the way he always slept. I drew the sheet down and showed her where I'd stabbed him, slipping the kitchen knife between two ribs and into the heart. The knife lay on the table beside the bed. I had wiped the blood from it. There had not been very much blood to wipe.

"He was going to leave," I said, "and I couldn't bear it, Mama. And I thought, Now he won't leave, now he'll never leave me. I thought, This is a way to break the pattern. Isn't that crazy, Mama? It doesn't make any sense, does it?"

"My poor Tildie."

"Do you want to know something? I feel safe now, Mama. He won't hit me anymore and I never have to worry about him leaving me. He can't leave me, can he?" Something caught in my throat. "Oh, and he'll never hold me again, either. In the circle of his arms."

I broke then, and it was Mama who held me, stroking my forehead, soothing me. I was all right then, and I stood up straight and told her she had better call the police.

"Livia'll be up any minute now," she said. "I think she's awake, I think I heard her fussing a minute ago. Change her and bring her down and feed her her breakfast."

"And then?"

"And then put her in for her nap."

After I put Livia back in her crib for her nap Mama told me that we weren't going to call the police. "Now that you're back where you belong," she said, "I'm not about to see them take you away. Your baby needs her mama and I need you, too."

"But Dan—"

"Bring the big wheelbarrow around to the kitchen door. Between the two of us we can get him down the stairs. We'll dig his grave in the back, we'll bury him here on our land. People won't suspect anything. They'll just think he went off, the way men do."

"The way my daddy did," I said.

Somehow we got him down the stairs and out through the kitchen. The hardest part was getting him into the old wheelbarrow. I checked Livia and made sure she was sleeping soundly, and then we took turns with the barrow, wheeling it out beyond the kitchen garden.

"What I keep thinking," I said, "is at least I broke the pattern."

She didn't say anything, and what she didn't say became one of her famous silences, sucking up all the sound around us. The barrow's wheel squeaked, the birds sang in the trees, but now I couldn't hear any of that.

Suddenly she said, "Patterns." Then she didn't say anything more, and I tried to hear the squeak of the wheel.

Then she said, "He never would have left you. If he left he'd only come back again. And he never would have quit hitting you. And each time would be a little worse than the last."

"It's not always like it is on *Oprah*, Mama."

"There's things you don't know," she said.

"Like what?"

The squeaking of the wheel, the song of birds. She said, "You know how I lost the hearing in the one ear?"

"You had an infection."

"That's what I always told you. It's not true. Your daddy cupped his hands and boxed my ears. He deafened me on the one side. I was lucky, nothing happened to the other ear. I still hear as good as ever out of it."

"I don't believe it," I said.

"It's the truth, Tildie."

"Daddy never hit you."

"Your daddy hit me all the time," she said. "All the time. He used his hands, he used his feet. He used his belt."

I felt a tightening in my throat. "I don't remember," I said.

"You didn't know. You were little. What do you think Livia knows? What do you think she'll remember?"

We walked on a ways. I said, "I just remember the two of you hollering. I thought you hollered and finally he left. That's what I always thought."

"That's what I let you think. It's what I wanted you to think. I had a broken jaw, I had broken ribs, I had to keep telling the doctor I was clumsy, I kept falling down. He believed me, too. I guess he had lots of women told him the same thing." We switched, and I took over the wheelbarrow. She said, "Dan would have done the same to you, if you hadn't done what you did."

"He wanted to stop."

"They can't stop, Tildie. No, not that way. To your left."

"Aren't we going to bury him alongside Grandma Yount?"

"No," she said. "That's too near the house. We'll dig his grave across the stream, where the walnut grove is."

"It's beautiful there."

"You always liked it."

"So did Dan," I said. I felt so funny, so light-headed. My world was turned upside down and yet it felt safe, it felt solid. I thought how Dan had itched to cut down those walnut trees. Now he'd lie forever at their feet, and I could come back here whenever I wanted to feel close to him.

"But he'll be lonely here," I said. "Won't he? Mama, won't he?"

The walnut trees lose their leaves early in the fall, and they put on less of a color show than the other hardwoods. But I like to come to the grove even when the trees are bare. Sometimes I bring Livia. More often I come by myself.

I always liked it here. I love our whole 220 acres, every square foot of it, but this is my favorite place, among these trees. I like it even better than the graveyard over by the pear and apple orchard. Where the graves have stones, and where the women and children of our family are buried.

Some Days You Get the Bear

Beside him, the girl issued a soft grunt of contentment and burrowed closer under the covers. Her name was Karin, with the accent on the second syllable, and she worked for a manufacturer of floor coverings, doing something unfathomable with a computer. They'd had three dates, each consisting of dinner and a screening. On their first two dates he'd left her at her door and gone home to write his review of the film they'd just seen. Tonight she'd invited him in.

And here he was, happily exhausted at her side, breathing her smell, warmed by her body heat. Perhaps this will work, he thought, and closed his eyes, and felt himself drifting.

Only to snap abruptly awake not ten minutes later. He lay still at first, listening to her measured breathing, and then he slipped slowly out of the bed, careful not to awaken her.

She lived in one room, an L-shaped studio in a high rise on West Eighty-ninth Street. He gathered his clothes and dressed in darkness, tiptoed across the uncarpeted parquet floor.

There were five locks on her door. He unfastened them all, and when he tried the door it wouldn't open. Evidently she'd left one or more of them unlocked; thus, meddling with all five, he'd locked some even as he was unlocking the others. When this sort of dilemma was presented as a logic problem, to be attacked with pencil and paper, he knew better than to attempt its solution. Now, when he had to work upon real locks in darkness and in silence, with a sleeping woman not ten yards away, the whole thing was ridiculous.

"Paul?"

"I'm sorry," he said. "I didn't mean to wake you."

"Where are you going? I was planning to offer you breakfast in the morning. Among other things."

"I've got work to do first thing in the morning," he told her. "I'd really better get on home. But these locks—"

"I know," she said. "It's a Roach Motel I'm running here. You get in, but you can't get out." And, grinning, she slipped past him, turned this lock and that one, and let him out.

He hailed a taxi on Broadway, rode downtown to the Village. His apartment was a full floor of a brownstone on Bank Street. He had moved into it when he first came to New York and had never left it. It had been his before he was married and remained his after the divorce. "This is the one thing I'll miss," Phyllis had said.

"What about the screenings?"

"To tell you the truth," she said, "I've pretty much lost my taste for movies."

He occasionally wondered if that would ever happen to him. He contributed a column of film reviews to two monthly magazines; because the publications were mutually noncompetitive, he was able to use his own name on both columns. The columns themselves differed considerably in tone and content. For one magazine he tended to write longer and more thoughtful reviews, and leaned toward films with intellectual content and artistic pretension. His reviews for the other magazine tended to be briefer, chattier, and centered more upon the question of whether a film would be fun to see than if seeing it would make you a more worthwhile human being. In neither column, however, did he ever find himself writing something he did not believe to be the truth.

Nor had he lost his taste for movies. There were times, surely, when his perception of a movie was colored for the worse by his having seen it on a day when he wasn't in the mood for it. But this didn't happen that often, because he was usually in the mood for almost any movie. And screenings, whether in a small upstairs room somewhere in midtown or at a huge Broadway theater, were unquestionably the best way to see a film. The print was always perfect, the projectionist always kept his mind on what he was doing, and the audience, while occasionally jaded, was nevertheless respectful, attentive, and silent. Every now and then Paul took a busman's holiday and paid his way into a movie house, and the difference was astounding. Sometimes he had to change his seat three or four times to escape from imbeciles explaining the story line to their idiot companions; other times, especially at films with an enthusiastic teenage following, the audience seemed to have more dialogue than the actors.

Sometimes he thought that he enjoyed his work so much he'd gladly do it for free. Happily, he didn't have to. His two columns brought him a living, given that his expenses were low. Two years ago his building went co-op and he'd used his savings for the down payment. The mortgage payment and monthly maintenance charges were quite within his means. He didn't own a car, had no aged or infirm relatives to support, and had been blissfully spared a taste for cocaine, high-stakes gambling, and the high life. He preferred cheap ethnic restaurants, California zinfandel, safari jackets, and blue jeans. His income supported this sort of lifestyle quite admirably.

And, as the years went by, more opportunities for fame and fortune presented themselves. *The New York Times Book Review* wanted 750 words from him on a new book on the films of King Vidor. A local cable show had booked him half a dozen times to do capsule reviews, and there was talk of giving him a regular ten-minute slot. Last semester he'd taught a class, "Appreciating the Silent Film," at the New School for Social Research; this had increased his income by fifteen hundred dollars and he'd slept with two of his students, a thirty-three-year-old restless housewife from Jamaica Heights and a thirty-eight-year-old single mother who lived with her single child in three very small rooms on East Ninth Street.

Now, home again, he shucked his clothes and showered. He dried off and turned down his bed. It was a queen-size platform bed, with storage drawers underneath it and a bookcase headboard, and he made it every morning. During his marriage he and Phyllis generally left the bed unmade, but the day after she moved out he made the bed, and he'd persisted with this discipline ever since. It was, he'd thought, a way to guard against becoming one of those seedy old bachelors you saw in British spy films, shuffling about in slippers and feeding shillings to the gas heater.

He got into bed, settled his head on the pillow, closed his eyes. He thought about the film he'd seen that night, and about the Ethiopian restaurant at which they'd dined afterward. Whenever a country had a famine, some of its citizenry escaped to the United States and opened a restaurant. First the Bangladeshi, now the Ethiopians. Who, he wondered, was next?

He thought about Karin—whose name, he suddenly realized, rhymed with Marin County, north of San Francisco. He'd first encountered Marin County in print and had assumed it was pronounced with the accent on the first syllable, and he had accordingly mispronounced it for some time until Phyllis had taken it upon herself to correct him. He'd had no opportunity to make the same mistake with Karin; he had met her in the flesh, so to speak, before he knew how her name was spelled, and thus—

No, he thought. This wasn't going to work. What was he trying to prove? Who (or, more grammatically, whom) was he kidding?

He got out of bed. He went to the closet and took the bear down from the top shelf. "Well, what the hell," he said to the bear. (If you could sleep with a bear, you could scarcely draw the line at talking to it.) "Here we go again, fella," he said.

He got into bed again and took the bear in his arms. He closed his eyes. He slept.

The whole thing had taken him by surprise. It was not as though he had intentionally set out one day to buy himself a stuffed animal as a nocturnal companion. He supposed there were grown men who did this, and he supposed there was nothing necessarily wrong with their so doing, but that was not what had happened. Not at all.

He had bought the bear for a girl. Sibbie was her name, short for Sybil, and she was a sweet and fresh young thing just a couple of years out of Skidmore, a junior assistant production person at one of the TV nets. She was probably a little young for him, but not *that* young, and she seemed to like screenings and ethnic restaurants and guys who favored blue jeans and safari jackets.

For a couple of months they'd been seeing each other once or twice a week. Often, but not always, they went to a screening. Sometimes he stayed over at her place just off Gramercy Park. Now and then she stayed over at his place on Bank Street.

It was at her apartment that she'd talked about her stuffed animals. How she'd slept with a whole menagerie of them as a child, and how she'd continued to do so all through high school. How, when she'd gone off to college, her mother had exhorted her to put away childish things. How she had valiantly and selflessly packed up all her beloved plush pets and donated them to some worthy organization that recycled toys to poor children. How she'd held back only one animal, her beloved bear Bartholomew, intending to take him along to Skidmore. But at the last minute she'd been embarrassed ("Em*bear*assed?" Paul wondered) to pack him, afraid of how her roommates might react, and when she got home for Thanksgiving break she discovered that her mother had given the bear away, claiming that she'd thought that was what Sibbie had wanted her to do.

"So I started sleeping with boys," Sibbie explained. "I thought, 'All right, bitch, I'll just show you,' and I became, well, not promiscuous exactly, but not antimiscuous either."

"All for want of a bear."

"Exactly," she'd said. "So do you see what that makes you? You're just a big old bear substitute."

The next day, though, he found himself oddly touched by her story. There was hurt there, for all the brittle patter, and when he passed the Gingerbread House the next afternoon and saw the bear in the window he never even hesitated. It cost more than he would have guessed, and more than he really felt inclined to spend on what was a sort of half-joke, but they took credit cards, and they took his.

The next night they spent together he almost gave her the bear, but he didn't want the gift to follow that quickly upon their conversation. Better to let her think her story had lingered in his consciousness awhile before he'd acted on it. He'd wait another few days and say something like, "You know, that story you told me, I couldn't get it out of my mind. What I decided, I decided you need a bear." And so they'd spent that night in his bed, with only each other for company, while the bear spent the night a few yards away on the closet shelf.

He next saw her five days later, and he'd have given her the bear then but they wound up at her apartment, and of course he hadn't dragged the creature along to the Woody Allen screening, or to the Thai restaurant. A week later, just to set the stage, he'd made his bed that morning with the bear in it, its head resting on the middle pillow, its fat little arms outside the bedcovers.

"Oh, it's a *bear*!" she would say. And he would say, "The thing is, I've got a no-bears clause in my lease. Do you think you could give it a good home?"

Except it didn't work that way. They had dinner, they saw a movie, and then when he suggested they repair to his place she said, "Could we go someplace for a drink, Paul? There's a conversation we really ought to have."

The conversation was all one-sided. He sat there, holding but not sipping his glass of wine, while she explained that she'd been seeing someone else once or twice a week, since theirs had not been designed to be an exclusive relationship, and that the other person she was seeing, well, it seemed to be getting serious, see, and it had reached the point where she didn't feel it was appropriate for her to be seeing other people. Such as Paul, for example.

It was, he had to admit, not a bad kissoff, as kissoffs go. And he'd expected the relationship to end sooner or later, and probably sooner.

But he hadn't expected it to end quite yet. Not with a bear in his bed.

He put her in a cab, and then he put himself in a cab, and he went home and there was the bear. Now what? Send her the bear? No, the hell with that; she'd be convinced he'd bought it *after* she dumped him, and the last thing he wanted her to think was that he was the kind of dimwit who would do something like that.

The bear went back into the closet.

And stayed there.

It was surprisingly hard to give the bear away. It was not, after all, like a box of candy or a bottle of cologne. You could not give a stuffed bear to just anyone. The recipient had to be the right sort of person, and the gift had to be given at the right stage of the relationship. And many of his relationships, it must be said, did not survive long enough to reach the bear-giving stage.

Once he had almost made a grave mistake. He had been dating a rather abrasive woman named Claudia, a librarian who ran a research facility for a Wall Street firm, and one night she was grousing about her ex-husband. "He didn't want a wife," she said. "He wanted a daughter, he wanted a child. And that's how he treated me. I'm surprised he didn't buy me Barbie dolls and teddy bears."

And he'd come within an inch of giving her the bear! That, he realized at once, would have been the worst possible thing he could have done. And he realized, too, that he didn't really want to spend any more time with Claudia. He couldn't say exactly why, but he didn't really feel good about the idea of having a relationship with the sort of woman you couldn't give a bear to.

There was one of those cardboard signs over the cash register of a hardware store on Hudson Street. SOME DAYS YOU GET THE BEAR, it said. SOME DAYS THE BEAR GETS YOU.

He discovered an addendum: Sooner or later, you sleep with the bear.

It happened finally on an otherwise unremarkable day. He'd spent the whole day working on a review of a biography (*Sydney Greenstreet: The Untold Story*), having a lot of trouble getting it the way he wanted it. He had dinner alone at the

Greek place down the street and rented the video of *Casablanca*, sipping jug wine and reciting the lines along with the actors. The wine and the film ran out together.

He got undressed and went to bed. He lay there, waiting for sleep to come, and what came instead was the thought that he was, all things considered, the loneliest and most miserable son of a bitch he knew.

He sat up, astonished. The thought was manifestly untrue. He liked his life, he had plenty of companionship whenever he wanted it, and he could name any number of sons of bitches who were ever so much lonelier and more miserable than he. A wine thought, he told himself. *In vino stupiditas.* He dismissed the thought, but sleep remained elusive. He tossed around until something sent him to the closet. And there, waiting patiently after all these months, was the bear.

"Hey, there," he said. "Time to round up the usual suspects. Can't sleep either, can you, big fellow?"

He took the bear and got back into bed with it. He felt a little foolish, but he also felt oddly comforted. And he felt a little foolish *about* feeling comforted, but that didn't banish the comfort.

With his eyes closed, he saw Bogart clap Claude Rains on the back. "This could be the start of a beautiful friendship," Bogart said.

And, before he could begin to figure it all out, Paul fell asleep.

Every night since, with only a handful of exceptions, he had slept with the bear.

Otherwise he slept poorly. On a couple of occasions he had stayed overnight with a woman, and he had learned not to do this. He had explained to one woman (the single mother on East Ninth Street, as a matter of fact) that he had this quirk, that he couldn't fall fully asleep if another person was present.

"That's more than a quirk," she'd told him. "Not to be obnoxious about it, but that sounds pretty neurotic, Paul."

"I know," he'd said. "I'm working on it in therapy."

Which was quite untrue. He wasn't in therapy. He had indeed thought of checking in with his old therapist and examining the whole question of the bear, but he couldn't see the point. It was like the old Smith-and-Dale routine: "Doctor, it hurts when I do this." "So don't do that!" If it meant a sleepless night to go to bed without the bear, then don't go to bed without the bear!

A year ago he'd gone up to Albany to participate in an Orson Welles symposium. They put him up at the Ramada for two nights, and after the first sleepless night he actually thought of running out to a store and buying another bear. Of course he didn't, but after the second night he wished he had. There was, thank God, no third night; as soon as the program ended he glanced at the honorarium check to make sure the amount was right, grabbed his suitcase, and caught the Amtrak train back to the city, where he slept for twelve solid hours with the bear in his arms.

And, several months later when he flew out to the Palo Alto Film Festival, the bear rode along at the bottom of his duffel bag. He felt ridiculous about it, and every morning he stowed the bear in his luggage, afraid that the chambermaids might catch on otherwise. But he slept nights.

The morning after the night with Karin, he got up, made the bed, and returned the bear to the closet. As he did so, for the first time he felt a distinct if momentary pang. He closed the door, hesitated, then opened it. The bear sat uncomplaining on its shelf. He closed the door again.

This was not, he told himself, some Stephen King movie, with the bear possessed of some diabolical soul, screaming to be let out of the closet. He could imagine such a film, he could just about sit down and write it. The bear would see itself as a rival for Paul's affections, it would be jealous of the women in his life, and it would find some bearish way to kill them off. Hugging them to death, say. And in the end Paul would go to jail for the murders, and his chief concern would be the prospect of spending life in prison without the possibility of either parole or a good night's sleep. And the cop, or perhaps the prosecuting attorney, would take the bear and toss it in the closet, and then one night, purely on a whim, would take it to bed.

And the last shot would be an ECU of the bear, and you'd swear it was smiling.

No, scratch that. Neither he nor the bear inhabited a Stephen King universe, for which he gave thanks. The bear was not alive. He could not even delude himself that it had been made by some craftsman whose subtle energies were locked in the bear, turning it into more than the inanimate object it appeared to be. It had been made, according to its tag, in Korea, at a factory, by workers who couldn't have cared less whether they were knocking out bears or bow ties or badminton sets. If he happened to sleep better with it in his bed, if he indeed took comfort in its presence, that was his eccentricity, and a remarkably harmless one at that. The bear was no more than an inanimate participant in it all.

Two days later he made the bed and tucked the bear under the covers, its head on a pillow, its arms outside the blankets.

Not, he told himself, because he fancied that the bear didn't like it in the closet. But because it seemed somehow inappropriate to banish the thing with daylight. It was more than inappropriate. It was dishonest. Why, when people all over America were emerging from their closets, should the bear be tucked into one?

He had breakfast, watched *Donahue,* went to work. Paid some bills, replied to some correspondence, labored over some revisions on an essay requested by an academic quarterly. He made another pot of coffee, and while it was brewing he went into the bedroom to get something, and there was the bear.

"Hang in there," he said.

He found he was dating less.

This was not strictly true. He no less frequently took a companion to a screening, but more and more of these companions tended to be platonic. Former lovers with whom he'd remained friendly. Women to whom he was not attracted physically. Male friends, colleagues.

He wondered if he was losing interest in sex. This didn't seem to be the case. When he was with a woman, his lovemaking was as ardent as ever. Of course, he never spent the night, and he had ceased to bring women back to his own apartment, but it seemed to him that he took as much pleasure as ever in the physical embrace. He didn't seek it as often, wasn't as obsessed with it, but couldn't that just represent the belated onset of maturity? If he was at last placing sex in its proper proportion, surely that was not cause for alarm, was it?

In February, another film festival.

This one was in Burkina Faso. He received the invitation in early December. He was to be a judge, and would receive a decent honorarium and all expenses, including first-class travel on Air Afrique. This last gave him his first clue as to where Burkina Faso was. He had never previously heard of it, but now guessed it was in Africa.

A phone call unearthed more information. Burkina Faso had earlier been Upper Volta. Its postage stamps, of which his childhood collection had held a handful, bore the name Haute-Volta; the place had been a French colony, and French remained the prevailing language, along with various tribal dialects. The country was in West Africa, north of the Equator but south of the Sahel. The annual film festival, of which this year's would be the third, had not yet established itself as terribly important cinematically, but the Burkina Fasians (or whatever you called them) had already proved to be extremely gracious hosts, and the climate in February was ever more hospitable than New York's. "Marisa went last year," a friend told him, "and she hasn't left off talking about it yet. Not to be missed. *Emphatically* not to be missed."

But how to bring the bear?

He obtained a visa, he got a shot for yellow fever (providing ten years of immunity; he could go to no end of horrid places before the shot need be renewed) and began taking chloroquine as a malaria preventative. He went to Banana Republic and bought clothing he was assured would be appropriate. He made a couple of phone calls and landed a sweet assignment, thirty-five hundred words plus photos for an airline in-flight magazine. The airline in question didn't fly to Burkina Faso, or anywhere near it, but they wanted the story all the same.

But he couldn't take the bear. He had visions of uniformed Africans going through his luggage, holding the bear aloft and jabbering, demanding to know what it was and why he was bringing it in. He saw himself, flushing crimson, surrounded by other festival-goers, all either staring at him or pointedly *not* staring at him. He could imagine Cary Grant, say, or Michael Caine, playing a scene like that and coming out of it rather well. He could not envision himself coming out of it well at all.

Nor did he have room for a stuffed animal that measured twenty-seven inches end to end. He intended to make do with carry-on luggage, not much wanting to entrust his possessions to the care of Air Afrique, and if he took the bear he would have to check a bag. If they did not lose it in the first leg of the flight, from New York to Dakar, surely it would vanish somewhere between Dakar and Ouagadougou, Burkina Faso's unpronounceable capital.

He went to a doctor and secured a prescription for Seconal. He flew to Dakar, and on to Ouagadougou. The bear stayed at home.

The customs check upon arrival was cursory at best. He was given VIP treatment, escorted through customs by a giant of a woman who so intimidated the functionaries that he was not even called upon to open his bag. He could have brought the bear, he could have brought a couple of Uzis and a grenade launcher, and no one would have been the wiser.

The Seconal, the bear substitute, was a total loss. His only prior experience with sleeping pills was when he was given one the night before an appendectomy. The damned pill had kept him up all night, and he learned later that this was known as a paradoxical effect, and that it happened with some people. It still happened years later, he discovered. He supposed it might be possible to override the paradoxical effect by increasing the dosage, but the Burkina Fasians were liberal suppliers of wine and stronger drinks, and the local beer was better than he would ever have guessed it might be, and he knew about the synergy of alcohol and barbiturates. Enough film stars had been done in by the combination; there was no need for a reviewer to join their company.

He might not have slept anyway, he told himself, even with the bear. There were two distractions, a romance with a Polish actress who spoke no more English than he spoke Polish ("The Polish starlet," he would tell friends back home. "Advancing her career by sleeping with a writer.") and a case of dysentery, evidently endemic in Burkina Faso, that was enough to wake a bear from hibernation.

"They didn't paw through my bag at Oogabooga," he told the bear upon his return, "but they sure did a number at JFK. I don't know what they think anybody could bring back from Burkina Faso. There's nothing there. I bought a couple of strands of trading beads and a mask that should look good on the wall, if I can find the right spot for it. But just picture that clown at Customs yanking you out of the suitcase!"

They might have cut the bear open. They did things like that, and he supposed they had to. People smuggled things all the time, drugs and diamonds and state secrets and God knew what else. A hardened smuggler would hardly forbear (for-*bear*!) to use a doll or a stuffed animal to conceal contraband. And a bear that had been cut open and probed could, he supposed, be stitched back together, and be none the worse for wear.

Still, something within him recoiled at the thought.

One night he dreamed about the bear.

He rarely dreamed, and what dreams he had were fragmentary and hazy. This one, though, was linear, and remarkably detailed. It played on his mind's retina like a movie on a screen. In fact dreaming it was not unlike watching a movie, one in which he was also a participant.

The story line fell somewhere between *Pygmalion* and "The Frog Prince." The bear, he was given to understand, was enchanted, under a spell. If the bear could win the unconditional love of a human being it would cast off its ursine form and emerge as the ideal partner of the person who loved it. And so he gave his heart to the bear, and fell asleep clutching it, and woke up with his arms around the woman of his, well, dreams.

Then he woke up in fact, and it was a bear he was clutching so desperately. Thank God, he thought.

Because it had been a nightmare. Because he didn't want the bear to transform itself into anything, not even the woman of his dreams.

He rose, made the bed, tucked the bear in. And chucked the bear under its chin.

"Don't ever change," he told it.

The woman was exotic. She'd been born in Ceylon, her mother a Sinhalese, her father an Englishman. She had grown up in London, went to college in California, and had lately moved to New York. She had high cheekbones, almond-shaped eyes, a sinuous figure, and a general appearance that could have been described as Nonspecific Ethnic. Whatever restaurant Paul took her to, she looked as though she belonged there. Her name was Sindra.

They met at a lecture at NYU, where he talked about Hitchcock's use of comic relief and where she asked the only really provocative question. Afterward, he invited her to a screening. They had four dates, and he found that her enthusiasm for film matched his own. So, more often than not, did her taste and her opinions.

Four times at the evening's end she went home alone in a taxi. At first he was just as glad, but by the fourth time his desire for her was stronger than his inclination to end the evening alone. He found himself leaning in the window of her cab, asking her if she wouldn't like a little company.

"Oh, I would," she assured him. "But not tonight, Paul."

Not tonight, darling, I've got a . . . what? A headache, a husband? What?

He called her the next morning, asked her out to yet another screening two days hence. The movie first, then a Togolese restaurant. The food was succulent, and fiery hot. "I guess there's a famine in Togo," he told her. "I hadn't heard about it."

"It's hard to keep up. This food's delicious."

"It is, isn't it?" His hand covered hers. "I'm having a wonderful time. I don't want the night to end."

"Neither do I."

"Shall I come up to your place?"

"It would be so much nicer to go to yours."

They cabbed to Bank Street. The bear, of course, was in the bed. He settled Sindra with a drink and went to stow the bear in the closet, but Sindra tagged after him. "Oh, a teddy bear!" she cried, before he could think what to do.

"My daughter's," he said.

"I didn't even know you had a daughter. How old is she?"

"Seven."

"I thought you'd been divorced longer than that."

"What did I say, seven? I meant eleven."

"What's her name?"

"Doesn't have one."

"Your daughter doesn't have a name?"

"I thought you meant the bear. My daughter's name is uh Paula."

"Apolla? The feminine of Apollo?"

"That's right."

"It's an unusual name. I like it. Was it your idea or your wife's?"

Christ! "Mine."

"And the bear doesn't have a name?"

"Not yet," he said. "I just bought it for her recently, and she sleeps with it when she stays over. I sleep in the living room."

"Yes, I should think so. Do you have any pictures?"

"Of the bear? I'm sorry, of course you meant of my daughter."

"Quite," she said. "I already know what the bear looks like."

"Right."

"Do you?"

"Shit."

"I beg your—"

"Oh, the hell with it," he said. "I don't have a daughter, the marriage was childless. I sleep with the bear myself. The whole story's too stupid to go into, but if I don't have the bear in bed with me I don't sleep well. Believe me, I know how ridiculous that sounds."

Something glinted in her dark almond eyes. "I think it sounds sweet," she said.

He felt curiously close to tears. "I've never told anyone," he said. "It's all so silly, but—"

"It's not silly. And you never named the bear?"

"No. It's always been just The Bear."

"It? Is it a boy bear or a girl bear?"

"I don't know."

"May I see it? No clothing, so there's no help there. Just a yellow ribbon at the throat, and that's a sexually neutral color, isn't it? And of course it's not anatomically correct, in the manner of those nasty dolls they're selling for children who haven't the ingenuity to play doctor." She sighed. "It would appear your bear is androgynous."

"We, on the other hand," he said, "are not."

"No," she said. "We're not, are we?"

The bear remained in the bed with them. It was absurd to make love in the bear's company, but it would have been more absurd to banish the thing to the closet.

No matter; they soon became sufficiently aware of one another as to be quite unaware of the bear.

Then two heartbeats returning to normal, and the air cool on sweat-dampened skin. A few words, a few phrases. Drowsiness. He lay on his side, the bear in his arms. She twined herself around him.

Sleep, blissful sleep.

He woke, clutching the bear but unclutched in return. The bed was full of her scent. She, however, was gone. Sometime during the night she had risen and dressed and departed.

He called her just before noon. "I can't possibly tell you," he said, "how much I enjoyed being with you last night."

"It was wonderful."

"I woke up wanting you. But you were gone."

"I couldn't sleep."

"I never heard you leave."

"I didn't want to disturb you. You were sleeping like a baby."

"Hugging my bear."

"You looked so sweet," she said.

"Sindra, I'd like to see you. Are you free tonight?"

There was a pause, time enough for him to begin to regret having asked. "Let me call you after lunch," she said.

A colleague had just published an insufferably smug piece on Godard in a quarterly with a circulation in the dozens. He was reading it and clucking his tongue at it when she called. "I'm going to have to work late," she said.

"Oh."

"But you could come over to my place around nine-thirty or ten, if that's not too late. We could order a pizza. And pretend there's a famine in Italy."

"Actually, I believe they've been having a drought."

She gave him the address. "I hope you'll come," she said, "but you may not want to."

"Of course I want to."

"The thing is," she said, "you're not the only one with a nocturnal eccentricity."

He tried to think what he had done that might have been characterized as eccentric, and tried to guess what eccentricity she might be about to confess. Whips and chains? Rubber attire? Enemas?

"Oh," he said, light dawning. "You mean the bear."

"I also sleep with an animal, Paul. And sleep poorly without it."

His heart cast down its battlements and surrendered. "I should have known," he said. "Sindra, we were made for each other. What kind of animal?"

"A snake."

"A snake," he echoed, and laughed. "Well, that's more exotic than a bear, isn't it? Although I suppose they're more frequently encountered than bears in Sri Lanka. Do you know something? I don't think I've ever even seen a stuffed snake."

"Paul, I—"

"Squirrels, raccoons, beavers, all of those. Little cuddly furry creatures. And bears, of course. But—"

"Paul, it's not a stuffed snake."

"Oh."

"It's a living snake. I got it in California, I had the deuce of a time shipping it when I moved. It's a python."

"A python," he said.

"A reticulated python."

"Well, if you were going to have a python," he said, "you would certainly want to have it reticulated."

"That refers to its markings. It's twelve feet long, Paul, although in time it will grow to be considerably larger. It eats mice, but it doesn't eat very often or very much. It sleeps in my bed, it wraps itself around me. For warmth, I'm sure, although it seems to me that there's love in its embrace. But I may very well be imagining that."

"Uh," he said.

"You're the first person I've ever told. Oh, my friends in L.A. knew I had a snake, but that was before I started sleeping with it. I never had that intention when I bought it. But then one night it crawled into the bed. And I felt truly safe for the first time in my life."

An army of questions besieged his mind. He picked one. "Does it have a name?"

"Its name is Sunset. I bought it in a pet shop on Sunset Boulevard. They specialize in reptiles."

"Sunset," he said. "That's not bad. I mean, there but for the grace of God goes Harbor Freeway. Is Sunset a boy snake or a girl snake? Or aren't pythons anatomically correct?"

"The pet-shop owner assured me Sunset was female. I haven't figured out how to tell. Paul, if the whole thing puts you off, well, I can understand that."

"It doesn't."

"If it disgusts you, or if it just seems too weird by half."

"Well, it seems weird," he allowed. "You said nine-thirty, didn't you? Nine-thirty or ten?"

"You still want to come?"

"Absolutely. And we'll call out for a pizza. Will they toss in a side order of mice?"

She laughed. "I fed her just this morning. She won't be hungry for days."

"Thank God. And Sindra? Will it be all right if I stay over? I guess what I'm asking is should I bring the bear?"

"Oh, yes," she said. "By all means bring the bear."

Something to Remember You By

He picked her up at her dorm. She was out in front with her suitcases and her duffel bag and he pulled up right on time and helped her load everything. She got in front with him and he waited until she had fastened her seat belt before pulling away from the curb.

"I'll be glad to get home," she said. "I didn't think I was going to live through finals."

"Well, you made it."

"Uh-huh. This is a nice car. What is it, a Plymouth?"

"That's right."

"Almost new, too."

"Two years old. Three in a couple of months when the new cars come out."

"That's still pretty new. Does the radio work?"

He turned it on. "Find something you like," he said.

"You're driving. What kind of music do you like?"

"It doesn't matter."

She found a country station and asked if that was all right. He said it was. "I'll probably just fall asleep anyway," she said. "I was up most of the night. Will that bother you?"

"If you fall asleep? Why should it?"

"I won't be much company."

"That's okay," he said.

When they got out onto the interstate she let her eyes close and slumped a little in her seat. The car rode comfortably and she thought how lucky she was to be in it. She'd put a notice up on the bulletin board outside the cafeteria, RIDE WANTED TO CHICAGO END OF TERM, and just when she was beginning to think no one would respond he had called. All she had to do was pay half the gas money and she had her ride.

She drifted then, and her mind wandered up one path and down another, and then she came to with a start when he turned off the radio in the middle of a song. She opened her eyes and saw that it was getting dark out. And they had left the interstate.

"I was sleeping," she said.

"Like a log. Where do you suppose that expression comes from?"

"I don't know. I never thought about it. Where are we?"

"On our way to Chicago."

"What happened to the interstate?"

"It was putting me to sleep," he said. "Too much traffic, too little scenery. Too many troopers, too. It's the end of the month and they've all got their quotas to make."

"Oh."

"I like back roads better," he said. "Especially at night. You're not afraid, are you?"

"Why should I be afraid?"

"I just wondered if you were. Some people get agoraphobic, and just being out in wide open spaces bothers them."

"Not me."

"I guess you're not scared of anything, huh?"

She looked at him. His eyes were on the road, his hands steady on the wheel. "What's that supposed to mean?"

"Nothing in particular. It's pretty daring of you, though, when you stop to think of it."

"What is?"

"Being here. In this car, out in the middle of nowhere with someone you don't know from Adam."

"You're a college student," she said.

"Am I? You don't know that for sure. I said I was, that's all. I'm the right age, more or less, but that doesn't make me a student."

"You've got a KU decal on your window."

"You don't have to pay tuition to get one." She tried to look at him, but his face was hard to read in the dim light. "You were the one who put the notice up," he reminded her. "I called you. I gave you a name and said I was a student and I'd be heading for Chicago when the term ended, but I never gave you my phone number or told you where I lived. Did you check up on me at all, find out if there was a student registered under the name I gave you?"

"Hey, cut it out," she said.

"Cut what out?"

"Cut out trying to freak me out."

"You're not scared, are you?"

"No, but—"

"But you're wondering if maybe you should be. You're in a car with someone you don't know on a lonely road you don't know either, and you're starting to realize that you don't have much control over the situation. In fact you don't really have any control at all, do you?"

"Stop it."

"Okay," he said. "Hey, I'm sorry. I didn't mean to upset you."

"I'm not upset."

"Well, whatever. I'm a psych major and sometimes I tend to get into head games. It's nothing serious, but if I increased your anxiety level I want to apologize."

"It's all right."

"I'm forgiven?"

"There's nothing to forgive."

"Fair enough," he said. He yawned.

"Are you tired? Do you want me to drive?"

"No, I'm fine," he said. "And I'm the kind of control freak who uses up twice as much energy when somebody else is driving."

"My dad's like that."

"I guess lots of men are. Could you do me a favor? Could you get me something from the glove compartment?"

"What?"

"Right next to the flashlight there. That leather pouch. Could you hand it to me?"

It was a black leather pouch with a drawstring. She gave it to him and he weighed it in his hand. "What do you suppose is in this?" he asked her.

"I have no idea."

"Not even a far-fetched one? Take a guess."

"I couldn't."

"Drugs, do you suppose?"

"Maybe."

"Not drugs," he said. "I don't use drugs. Don't approve of them."

"Good."

He reached to set the pouch on top of the dashboard. "You were scared before," he said.

"A little."

"But not anymore."

"No."

"Why not?"

"Well, because—"

"When you stop to think about it," he said, "nothing's changed. The situation's the same as it was. You're alone with a stranger in a dangerous place, and you don't know anything about the man you're with, and what could you do if I tried something? You've got a purse. Do you happen to have a gun in it?"

"Of course not."

"Don't say it that way. Lots of people have guns. But not you, evidently. How about some chemical Mace? Paralyze attackers with no loss of life. Got any of that stuff?"

"You know I don't."

"How would I know that? It's not as though I searched your purse. But I'm willing to take your word for it. No gun and no Mace. What else? A nail file? Some pepper to throw in my eyes?"

"I have an emery board."

"That's something. You could sort of saw me in half with it, I suppose, but it'd take a long time. You're really essentially defenseless, though, aren't you?"

"Stop it."

"It's true, though, isn't it? If I tried something—"

"What do you mean, tried something?"

"Want me to come right out and say it, huh? Okay. I could stop the car and overpower you and rape you and you couldn't do a thing about it, could you?"

"I could put up a fight."

"What would that get you? I'd just have to hurt you and that would take the fight right out of you. You'd be better off giving in from the start and hoping I'd take it easy on you."

"Look," she said, "cut it out, huh?"

"Cut what out?"

"You know damn well what you should cut out. Quit doing a number on my mind."

"It's getting to you, isn't it?"

"Look, I told you—"

"I know what you told me. Maybe you ought to consider the possibility that I don't much care what you want."

"I don't like this," she said. "I just want to get out, okay? Just stop the car and let me out."

"Are you sure you want me to stop the car?"

"I—"

"Of course it's not a good idea to get out while we're sailing along at fifty miles an hour, but you're safe as long as the car's moving, aren't you? If I was going to do anything, I'd really have to stop the car first."

"Why would you want to—"

"To rape you? I'm a man and you're a woman. An attractive one, too. Isn't that enough of a reason?"

"Is it?"

"I don't know," he said. "What do you think?"

"I think you're not being very nice."

"No," he agreed, "I guess I'm not. You're really scared now, aren't you?"

"Stop it."

"Why do you have so much trouble answering that question? 'Cut it *out*. *Stop* it.' What's such a big deal about admitting that you're scared?"

"I don't know."

"You *are* scared, though. Aren't you?"

"You're trying to scare me."

"Uh-huh, and it seems to be working. You're terrified, aren't you? I guess you have a right to be. I mean, there's a very good chance that you're going to be raped. At least you think there is, and all on the basis of a brief conversation. You're beginning to see just how powerless you are. I could do whatever I want with you and you couldn't do a thing about it."

"You'd be punished," she said.

"They wouldn't know who to punish."

"I could tell them."

"You don't even know my name."

"You're a student."

"Are you sure of that?"

"I could describe you," she said. "I could describe the car, I could give them the license number."

"Maybe it's stolen."

"I bet it's not. I could work with a police artist, I could have him make up a sketch of you. You really wouldn't get away with it."

"Hmmmm," he said. "I guess you're right."

"So there's no point in doing anything, and you can stop playing mind games, okay?"

"You could describe me," he said. "I guess I'd have to kill you."

"Don't even say that."

"Why not? That's the best policy anyway, and it's part of the fun, isn't it? If it weren't so much fun there wouldn't be so many people doing it, would there?"

"Stop."

" 'Stop, stop, stop.' You don't look very strong. I bet you'd be easy to kill."

"Why kill me?"

"Why not?"

"The police would be after you. People don't get away with murder."

"Are you kidding? People get away with murder every day. And they wouldn't have any idea who to look for."

"You'd leave evidence behind. They have these new techniques, matching the DNA."

"Maybe I'll practice safe sex."

"Even so, there's always physical evidence."

"They could use it to convict me after they caught me, but it wouldn't help them catch me. And I don't intend to be caught. They haven't caught me so far."

"What?"

"Did you think you were the first?"

She closed her eyes and tried to breathe evenly, regularly. Her heart was racing. Evenly she said, "All right, you've got me frightened. I suppose that's what you wanted."

"It's part of it."

"Are you satisfied now?"

"Oh, I wouldn't say I was satisfied," he said. "I wouldn't use that word. I won't be satisfied until I've got you raped and strangled and lying in a ditch. And incidentally there's not a lot of physical evidence unless they find you fairly quickly, and I'm pretty good at hiding things. They may not find you for months."

"Oh, don't do this to me—"

"By then you'll be nothing but a memory to me," he said. "That's all I'll have of you, that and your little finger."

"My little finger?"

"The little finger of your left hand." He shrugged. "I'm the kind of sentimental fool who likes to take a souvenir. I won't cut it off until afterward. You won't feel a thing."

"My God," she said. "You're crazy."

"Do you really think so? Maybe this is just a joke."

"It's not a funny one."

"We could argue the point. But if it's not a joke, if I'm serious, does that necessarily mean I'm crazy? And what act would serve to identify me as crazy? Am I crazy if I rape you? Crazy if I kill you? Or only crazy if I cut off your finger?"

"Don't do this."

"I don't see anything fundamentally wacko in wanting a souvenir. Something to remember you by. Remember the song?"

"Please. Please."

"Now I'll ask you a question I asked you before. What do you think's in the pouch?"

"The pouch?"

He took it from the dashboard, held it in the palm of his hand. "Guess the contents," he said, "and you win the prize. What's in the bag?"

"Oh, God. I'm going to be sick."

"Want to see for yourself?"

She shrank from it.

"Suit yourself," he said, returning it to the dashboard. "Because of our conversation, because of a chance remark about little fingers, you've jumped to the conclusion that the pouch contains something grisly. It could be full of cowrie shells, or horse chestnuts, or jelly beans, but that's not what you think, is it? I think it's time to stop and pull off the road, don't you think?"

"No!"

"You want me to keep driving?"

"Yes."

"Then take off your sweater." She stared at him. "Your choice," he said. "Take off the sweater or I put on the brakes. Come on. Take it off."

"Why are you making me do this?"

"The same reason some people make other people dig their own graves. It saves time and effort. First unhook your seat belt, make it easier for yourself. Oh, very pretty, very pretty. You're terrified now, aren't you? Say it."

"I'm terrified."

"You're scared to death. Say it."

"I'm scared to death."

"And now I think it's time to find a parking place."

"*No!*" she cried. Her foot found his and pressed the accelerator flat against the floorboards, while her hand wrenched the wheel hard to the right. The car took flight. Then there was impact, and then there was noise, and then there was nothing.

She came to suddenly, abruptly. She had a headache and she'd hurt her shoulder badly and she could taste blood in the back of her throat. But she was alive. God, she was alive!

The car was upside down, its top crushed. And he was behind the wheel, his head bent at an impossible angle. Blood trailed from the corner of one eye, and more blood leaked from between his lips. His eyes were wide open, staring, and rolled up in their sockets.

The passenger door wouldn't open. She had to roll down the window and wriggle out through it. She felt faint when she stood up, and she had to hold on to the side of the car for support. She looked in the window she had just crawled through, and there, within reach, was the leather drawstring pouch.

She had not willed her foot to press down on the gas pedal, or her hand to yank the steering wheel. She did not now will her hand to reach through the window and extract the leather pouch. It did so of its own accord.

You don't have to open it, she told herself.

She took a breath. *Yes you do,* she thought, and loosened the drawstring.

Inside, she found a small bottle of aspirin, a package of cheese-and-peanut-butter crackers, a small tin of nonprescription stay-awake pills, a bank-wrapped roll of quarters, and a nail clipper. She looked at all of this and shook her head.

But he'd made her take her sweater off. And it was still off, she was bare to the waist.

She couldn't find her sweater, couldn't guess where it had landed after the car flipped and bounced around. She tried one of the rear doors and managed to open it. When she did so the dome light went on, which made it easier for her to see what she was doing.

She found a sweatshirt in one of her bags and put it on. She found her purse—it had somehow ended up in the backseat—and she set that aside. And something made her open one of his bags and go through it, not certain what she was looking for.

She had to go through a second bag before she found it. A three-blade pocketknife with a simulated stag handle.

She cut off the little finger of his left hand. This was harder than it sounded, but she kept at it, and she seemed to have all the time in the world. Not a single car had passed on that desolate road.

When she was done she closed his knife and put it in her purse. She dumped everything else from the drawstring pouch, put the finger inside it, and tucked the pouch into her purse. Then, her purse on her shoulder, she made her way to the road and began walking along it, toward whatever came next.

Some Things a Man Must Do

Just a few minutes before twelve on one of the best Sunday nights of the summer, a clear and fresh-aired and moonlit night, Thomas M. "Lucky Tom" Carroll collected his black snap-brim hat from the hat-check girl at Cleo's Club on Broderick Avenue. He tipped the girl a crisp dollar bill, winked briskly at her, and headed out the front door. He was fifty-two, looked forty-five, felt thirty-nine. He flipped his expensive cigar into the gutter and strolled to the Cleo's Club parking lot next door, where his very expensive, very large car waited in the parking space reserved for it.

When he had settled himself behind the wheel with the key fitted snugly in the ignition, he suddenly felt that he might not be alone.

Hearing a clicking sound directly behind him, Carroll stiffened, and then the little man in the backseat shot him six times in the back of the head. While the shots echoed deafeningly, the little man opened the car door, jammed his gun into the pocket of his suit jacket, and scurried off down the street as fast as he could, which was not terribly fast at all. He peeled his white gloves from his tiny hands, and managed to slow down a bit. Holding the white gloves in one hand, he looked rather like the White Rabbit rushing frenetically to keep his appointment with the Duchess.

Finney and Mattera caught the squeal. The scene was packed with onlookers, but Finney and Mattera didn't share their overwhelming interest in the spectacle. They came, they looked, they confirmed there were no eyewitnesses to question, and they went over to the White Tower for coffee. Let the lab boys sweat it out all night, searching through a coal mine for a black cat that wasn't there. Fingerprints? Evidence? Clues? A waste of time.

"Figure the touch man is on a plane by now," Finney said. "Be on the West Coast before the body's cold."

"Uh-huh."

"So Lucky Tom finally bought it. Nice of him to pick a decent night for it. You hate to leave the station house when it's raining. But a night like this, I don't mind it at all."

"It's a pleasure to get out."

"It is at that," said Finney. He stirred his coffee thoughtfully, wondering as he did so if there were a way of stirring your coffee without seeming thoughtful about it. "I wonder," he said, "why anyone would want to kill him."

"Good question. After all, what did he ever do? Strong-arm robbery, assault, aggravated assault, assault with a deadly weapon, extortion, three murders we knew of and none we could prove—"

"Just trivial things," said Finney.

"Undercover owner of Cleo's Club, operator of three illegal gambling establishments—"

"Four."

"Four? I only knew three." Mattera finished his coffee. "Loan-shark setup, number-two man in Barry Beyer's organization, not too much else. We did have a rape complaint maybe eight years ago—"

"A solid citizen."

"The best."

"A civic leader."

"None other."

"It was sure one peach of a professional touch," Finney said. "Six shots fired point-blank. Revenge, huh?"

"Something like that."

"No bad blood coming up between Beyer and Archie Moscow?"

"Haven't heard a word. They've been all peace and quiet for years. Two mobs carve up the city instead of each other. No bad blood spilled in the streets of our fair city. Instead of killing each other they cool it, and rob the public."

"True public spirit," said Finney. "The reign of law and order. It makes one proud to serve the cause of law and order in this monument to American civic pride."

"Shut up," Mattera said.

Approximately two days and three hours later, three men walked out the front door at 815 Cameron Street. The establishment they left didn't have an official name, but every cabdriver in town knew it. Good taste precludes a precise description of the principal business activity conducted therein; suffice it to say that seven attractive young ladies lived there, and that it was neither a nurses' residence nor a college dormitory.

The three men headed for their car. They had parked it next to a fire hydrant, supremely confident that no police officer who noted its license number would have the temerity to hang a parking ticket on the windshield. The three men were trusted employees of Mr. Archer Moscow. They had come to collect the week's receipts, and, incidentally, to act as a sort of quality-control inspection team.

As they reached the street, a battered ten-year-old convertible drew up slowly alongside them. The driver, alone in the car, leaned across the front seat and shot the center man in the chest with a sawed-off shotgun. Then he quickly scooped an automatic pistol from the seat and used it to shoot the other two men, three times each. He did all of this very quickly, and all three men were very dead before they hit the sidewalk.

The man stomped on the accelerator pedal and the car leaped forward as if startled. The convertible took the corner on two wheels and as suddenly slowed its speed to twenty-five miles an hour. The little man drove four blocks, parked the car, and raised the convertible top. He disassembled the sawed-off shotgun and packed it away in his thin black attaché case with the automatic, removed the jumper wire from the ignition switch, and left the car. Once outside the car he removed his white gloves and put them, too, inside the attaché case. His own car was parked right around the corner. He put the attaché case into his trunk, got into his car, and went home.

Finney and Mattera got the squeal again, only this time it was a pain in the neck, good weather notwithstanding. This time there were eyewitnesses, and sometimes eyewitnesses can be a pain in the neck, and this was one of those times. One of the eyewitnesses reported that the killer had been on foot, but this was a minority opinion. All of the other witnesses agreed there had been a murder car.

One said that it was a convertible, another that it was a sedan, and a third that it was a panel truck. There were two other minority opinions as well. One witness said there had been three killers. Another said one. The rest agreed on two, and Finney and Mattera figured three sounded reasonable, since two guns had been used, and someone had to drive the car, whatever kind of car it was. Then they asked the witnesses if they would be able to identify the killer or killers, and all of the witnesses suddenly remembered that this was a gangster murder, and what was apt to happen to eyewitnesses who remembered what killers looked like, and they all agreed, strange as it may seem, that they had not gotten a good look at the killers at all.

Finney had to ask the stupid questions, and Mattera had to write down the stupid answers, and it was an hour before they got over to the White Tower.

"Eyewitnesses," said Finney, "are notoriously unreliable."

"Eyewitnesses are a pain in the neck."

"True. Three more solid citizens—"

"Three of Archie Moscow's solid citizens this time—Joe Dant and Third-Time Charlie Weiss and Big Nose Murchison. How would you like to have a name like Big Nose Murchison?"

"He doesn't even have a nose now," said Finney. "And couldn't smell much if he did."

"How do you figure it?"

"Well, as they said on Pearl Harbor Day—"

"Uh-huh."

"This do look like war, sir."

"Mmmmm," said Mattera. "Doesn't make sense, does it? You would think we would have heard something. That's usually the nice thing about being a cop. You get to hear things, things the average citizen may not know about. You don't always get to do anything about what you hear, but you hear about it. We're only in this business because it gives us the feeling of being on the inside."

"I thought it was for the free coffee," said the counterman. They drank, pretending not to hear him.

"We're going to look real bad, you know," Finney said. "If Moscow and Beyer have a big hate going, they're going to spill a lot of blood, and the chance of solving any of those jobs isn't worth pondering." He broke off suddenly, pleased with himself. He was fairly certain he had never used "pondering" in conversation before.

"And," he went on, "with various killers flying in and out of town and leaving us with a file of unsolved homicides, the newspapers may start hinting that we are not the best police force in the world."

"Everybody knows we're the best money can buy," said Mattera.

"Isn't it the truth," said Finney.

"And what bothers me most," said Mattera, "is the innocent men who will die in a war like this. Men like Big Nose, for example."

"Pillars of the community."

"We'll miss them," said Mattera.

The following afternoon, Mr. Archer Moscow used his untapped private line to call the untapped private line of Mr. Barry Beyer. "You had no call to do that," he said.

"To do what?"

"Dant and Third-Time and Big Nose," said Moscow. "You know I didn't have a thing to do with Lucky Tom. You got no call for revenge."

"Who was it hit Lucky Tom?"

"How should I know?"

"Well," said Beyer, reasonably, "then how should I know who hit Dant and Third-Time and Big Nose?"

There was a long silent moment. "We've been friends a long time," Moscow said. "We have kept things cool, and we have all done very nicely that way—with no guns, and no blasting a bunch of guys out of revenge for something which we never did to Lucky Tom in the first place."

"If I thought you hit Lucky Tom—"

"The bum," said Moscow, "was not worth killing."

"If I thought you did it," Beyer went on, "I wouldn't go and shoot up a batch of punks like Dant and Third-Time and Big Nose. You know what I'd do?"

"What?"

"I'd go straight to the top," said Beyer. "I'd kill you, you bum!"

"That's no way to talk, Barry."

"You had no call to kill Lucky Tom. So maybe he was holding out a little in Ward Three, it don't make no difference."

"You had no call to kill those three boys."

"You don't know what killing is, bum."

"Yeah?" Moscow challenged.

"Yeah!"

That night, a gentleman named Mr. Roswell "Greasy" Spune turned his key in his ignition and was immediately blown from this world into the next. The little man with the small hands and the white gloves watched from a tavern across the street. Mr. Spune was a bagman for Barry Beyer's organization. Less than two hours after Mr. Spune's abrupt demise, six of Barry Beyer's boys hijacked an ambulance from the hospital garage. Five sat in back, and the sixth, garbed in white, drove the sporty vehicle through town with the pedal on the floor and the siren wide open. "This takes me back," one of them was heard to say. "This is the way it used to be before the world went soft in the belly. This is what you would call doing things with a little class."

The ambulance pulled up in front of a West Side tavern where the Moscow gang hung out. The ambulance tailgate burst open, and the five brave men and true emerged with submachine guns and commenced blasting away. Eight of Archie Moscow's staunchest associates died in the fray, and only one of the boys from the ambulance crew was killed in return.

Moscow retaliated the next day, shooting up two Beyer-operated card games, knocking off two small-time dope peddlers, and gunning down a Beyer lieutenant as he emerged from his bank at two-thirty in the afternoon. The gunman who accomplished this last feat then raced down an alleyway into the waiting arms of a rookie patrolman, who promptly shot him dead. The kid had been on the force only three months and was sure he would be up on departmental charges for forgetting to fire two warning shots into the air. Instead he got an on-the-spot promotion to detective junior grade.

By the second week of the war, the pace began to slow down. Pillars of both mobs were beginning to realize that a state of war demanded wartime security measures. One could not wander about without a second thought as in times of peace. One could not visit a meeting or a nightclub or a gaming house or a girlfriend without posting a guard, or even several guards. In short, one had to be very careful.

Even so, not everyone was careful enough. Muggsy Lopez turned up in the trunk of his car wearing a necktie of piano wire. Look-See Logan was found in his own kidney-shaped swimming pool with his hands and feet tied together and a few quarts of chlorinated water in his lungs. Benny Benedetto looked under the hood of his brand-new car, found a bomb wired to the ignition, removed it gingerly and dismantled it efficiently, and climbed behind the steering wheel clucking his tongue at the perfidy of his fellow man. But he completely missed the bomb wired to the gas pedal. It didn't miss him; they picked him up with a mop.

The newspapers screamed. The city fathers screamed. The police commissioner screamed. Finney and Mattera worked double-duty and tried to explain to their wives that this was war. Their wives screamed.

It was war for three solid months. It blew hot and cold, and there would be rumors of high-level conferences, of face-to-face meets between Archer Moscow and Barry Beyer, cautious summit meetings held on neutral ground. Then, for a week, the killings would cease, and the word would go out that a truce had been called. Then someone would be gunned down or stabbed or blown to bits, and the war would start all over again.

At the end of the third month there was supposed to be another truce in progress, but by now no one was taking truce talk too seriously. There had not been a known homicide in five days. The count now stood at eighty-three dead, several more wounded, five in jail, and two missing in action. The casualties were almost perfectly balanced between the two mobs. Forty of Beyer's men were dead, forty-three Moscow men were in their graves, and each gang had one man missing.

That night, as usual, Finney and Mattera prowled the uneasy streets in an unmarked squad car. Only this particular night was different. This night they caught the little man.

Mattera was the one who spotted him. He noticed someone sitting in a car on Pickering Road, with the lights out and the motor running. His first thought was that it was high school kids necking, but there was only one person there, and the person seemed to be doing something, so Mattera slowed to a stop and killed the lights.

The little man straightened up finally. He opened the car door, stepped out, and saw Finney and Mattera standing in front of him with drawn revolvers.

"Oh, my," said the little man.

Finney moved past him, checked the car. "Cute job," he said. "He's got this little gun lashed to the steering column, and there's a wire hooked around the trigger and connected to the gas pedal. You step on the gas and the gun goes off and gets you right in the chest. I read about a bit like that down in Texas. Very professional."

Mattera looked at the little man and shook his head. "Professional," he said. "A little old guy with glasses. Who belongs to the car, friend?"

"Ears Carradine," said the little man.

"One of Moscow's boys," Finney said. "You work for Barry Beyer, friend?"

The little man's jaw dropped. "Oh, goodness, no," he said. His voice was high-pitched, reedy. "Oh, certainly not."

"Who do you work for?"

"Aberdeen Pharmaceutical Supply," the little man said. "I'm a research chemist."

"You're a *what*?"

The little man took off his gloves and wrung them sadly in his hands. "Oh, this won't do at all," he said unhappily. "I suppose I'll have to tell you everything now, won't I?"

Finney allowed that this sounded like a good idea. The little man suggested they sit in the squad car. They did, one on either side of him.

"My name is Edward Fitch," the little man said. "Of course, there's no reason on earth why you should have heard of me, but you may recall my son. His name was Richard Fitch. I called him Dick, of course, because Rich Fitch would not have done at all. I'm sure you can appreciate that readily enough."

"Get to the point," Mattera said.

"Well," said Mr. Fitch, "is his name familiar?"

It wasn't.

"He killed himself in August," Mr. Fitch said. "Hanged himself, you may recall, with the cord from his electric razor. I gave him that razor, actually. A birthday present, oh, several years ago."

"Now I remember," Finney said.

"I didn't know at the time just why he had killed himself," Mr. Fitch went on. "It seemed an odd thing to do. And then I learned that he had lost an inordinate amount of money gambling—"

"Inordinate," Finney said, choked with admiration.

"Indeed," said Mr. Fitch. "As much as five thousand dollars, if I'm not mistaken. He didn't have the money. He was trying to raise it, but evidently the sum increased day by day. Interest, so to speak."

"So to speak," echoed Finney.

"He felt the situation was hopeless, which was inaccurate, but understandable in one so young, so he took his own life." Mr. Fitch paused significantly. "The man to whom he owed the money," he said, "and who was charging him appalling interest, and who had won the money in an unfair gambling match, was Thomas M. Carroll."

Finney's jaw dropped. Mattera said, "You mean Lucky Tom—"

"Yes," said Mr. Fitch. For a moment he did not say anything more. Then, sheepishly, he raised his head and managed a tiny smile. "The more I learned about the man, the more I saw there were no legal means of bringing him to justice, and it became quite clear to me that I had to kill him. So I—"

"You killed Lucky Tom Carroll."

"Yes, I—"

"Six times. In the back of the head."

"I wanted to make it look like a professional killing," Mr. Fitch said. "I felt it wouldn't do to get caught."

"And then Beyer hit back the next night," Finney said, "and from there on it was war."

"Well, not exactly. There are some things a man must do," Mr. Fitch said. "They don't seem to fit into the law, I know. But—but they do seem right, you see. After I'd killed Mr. Carroll I realized everyone would assume it had been a revenge killing. A gangland slaying, the papers called it. I thought how very nice it would be if the two gangs really grew mad at one another. I couldn't kill them all myself, of course, but once things were set properly in motion—"

"You just went on killing," Mattera said.

"Like a one-man army," Finney said.

"Not exactly," said Mr. Fitch. "Of course I killed those three men on Cameron Street, and bombed that Mr. Spune's car, but then I just permitted nature to take its course. Now and then things would quiet down and I had to take an active hand, yet I didn't really do all that much of the killing."

"How much?"

Mr. Fitch sighed.

"How many did you kill, Mr. Fitch?"

"Fifteen. I don't really like killing, you know."

"If you liked it, you'd be pretty dangerous, Mr. Fitch. Fifteen?"

"Tonight would have been the sixteenth," Mr. Fitch said.

For a while no one said anything. Finney lit a cigarette, gave one to Mattera, and offered one to Mr. Fitch. Mr. Fitch explained that he didn't smoke. Finney started to say something and changed his mind.

Mattera said, "Not to be nasty, Mr. Fitch, but just what were you looking to accomplish?"

"I should think that's patently obvious," Mr. Fitch said gently. "I wanted to wipe out these criminal gangs, these mobs."

"Wipe them out," Finney said.

"You know, let them kill each other off."

"Kill each other off." He nodded.

"That's correct."

"And you thought that would work, Mr. Fitch?"

Mr. Fitch looked surprised. "But it is working, isn't it?"

"Uh—"

"I'm reminded of the anarchists around the turn of the century," said Mr. Fitch. "Of course, they were an unpleasant sort of men, but they had an interesting theory. They felt that if enough kings were assassinated, sooner or later no one would care to be king."

"That's an interesting theory," Finney said.

"So they went about killing kings. There aren't many kings these days," Mr. Fitch said quietly. "When you think about it, there are rather few of them about. Oh, I'm certain there are other explanations, but still—"

"I guess it's something to think about," Mattera said.

"It is," said Finney. "Mr. Fitch, what happens when you run through all the gangsters in town?"

"I suppose I would go on to another town."

"Another town?"

"I seem to have a calling for this sort of work," Mr. Fitch said. "But that's all over now, isn't it? You've arrested me, and there will have to be a trial, of course. What do you suppose they'll do to me?"

"They ought to give you a medal," said Mattera.

"Or put up a statue of you in front of City Hall," said Finney.

"I'm serious—"

"So are we, Mr. Fitch."

They fell silent again. Mattera thought about all the criminals who had been immune three months ago and who were now dead, and how much nicer a place it was without them. Finney tried to figure out how many kings there were. Not many, he decided, and the ones that were left didn't really do anything.

"I suppose you'll want to take me to jail now," said Mr. Fitch.

Mattera cleared his throat. "I'd better explain something to you, Mr. Fitch," he said. "A police officer is a very busy man. He can't waste his time with a lot of kooky stories that he might hear. Finney and I, uh, have crooks to catch. Things like that."

"What Mattera means, Mr. Fitch, is a nice old guy like you ought to run home to bed. We enjoy talking to you, and I really admire the way you speak, but Mattera and I, we're busy, see. We've got an inordinate lot of crooks to catch . . ." There! ". . . and you ought to go on home, so to speak."

"Oh," said Mr. Fitch. "Oh. Oh, bless you!"

They watched him scurry away, and they smoked more cigarettes, and remained silent for a very long time. After a while Mattera said, "A job like this, you got to do something crazy once in a while."

"Sure."

"I never did anything this crazy before. You?"

"No."

"That nutty little guy. How long do you figure he'll get away with it?"

"Who knows?"

"Fifteen so far. Fifteen—"

"Uh-huh. And close to seventy others that they did themselves."

A light went on across the street. A door opened, and a man walked toward his car. The man had ears like an elephant. "Ears Carradine," Mattera said. "Better get him before he gets into the car."

"You tell him."

"Hell, you're closer."

Carradine stopped to light a cigarette. He shook out the match and flung it aside.

"I had him nailed to the wall on an aggravated-assault thing a few years back," Finney said. "I had three witnesses that pinned him good—and not a breath of doubt."

"Witnesses."

"Two of them changed their minds and one disappeared. Never turned up."

"You better tell him," Mattera said.

"Funny the way that little guy had that car gimmicked. Read about it in the paper, you know, but I never saw anything like it before. Cute, though."

"He's getting in the car," Mattera said.

"You would wonder if a thing like that would work, wouldn't you?"

"You would at that. You should have told him, but it's that kind of a crazy night, isn't it?"

"He might see it himself."

"He might."

He didn't. They heard the ignition, and then the single shot, and Ears Carradine slumped over the wheel.

Mattera started up the squad car and pulled away from the curb. "How about that," he said. "It worked like a charm."

"Sixteen," said Finney.

Sometimes They Bite

Mowbray had been fishing the lake for better than two hours before he encountered the heavy-set man. The lake was supposed to be full of largemouth bass and that was what he was after. He was using spinning gear, working a variety of plugs and spoons and jigs and plastic worms in all of the spots where a lunker largemouth was likely to be biding his time. He was a good fisherman, adept at dropping his lure right where he wanted it, just alongside a weedbed or at the edge of subsurface structure. And the lures he was using were ideal for late fall bass. He had everything going for him, he thought, but a fish on the end of his line.

He would fish a particular spot for a while, then move off to his right a little ways, as much for something to do as because he expected the bass to be more co-operative in another location. He was gradually working his way around the western rim of the lake when he stepped from behind some brush into a clearing and saw the other man no more than a dozen yards away.

The man was tall, several inches taller than Mowbray, very broad in the shoulders and trim in the hips and at the waist. He wore a fairly new pair of blue jeans and a poplin windbreaker over a navy flannel shirt. His boots looked identical to Mowbray's, and Mowbray guessed they'd been purchased from the same mail-order outfit in Maine. His gear was a baitcasting outfit, and Mowbray followed his line out with his eyes and saw a red bobber sitting on the water's surface some thirty yards out.

The man's chestnut hair was just barely touched with gray. He had a neatly trimmed mustache and the shadowy beard of someone who had arisen early in the morning. The skin on his hands and face suggested he spent much of his time out of doors. He was certainly around Mowbray's age, which was forty-four, but he was in much better shape than Mowbray was, in better shape, truth to tell, than Mowbray had ever been. Mowbray at once admired and envied him.

The man had nodded at Mowbray's approach, and Mowbray nodded in return, not speaking first because he was the invader. Then the man said, "Afternoon. Having any luck?"

"Not a nibble."

"Been fishing long?"

"A couple of hours," Mowbray said. "Must have worked my way halfway around the lake, as much to keep moving as anything else. If there's a largemouth in the whole lake you couldn't prove it by me."

The man chuckled. "Oh, there's bass here, all right. It's a fine lake for bass, and a whole lot of other fish as well."

"Maybe I'm using the wrong lures."

The big man shook his head. "Doubtful. They'll bite anything when their dander is up. I think a largemouth would hit a shoelace if he was in the mood, and when he's sulky he wouldn't take your bait if you threw it in the water with no hook or line attached to it. That's just the way they are. Sometimes they bite and sometimes they don't."

"That's the truth." He nodded in the direction of the floating red bobber. "I don't suppose you're after bass yourself?"

"Not rigged up like this. No, I've been trying to get myself a couple of crappies." He pointed over his shoulder with his thumb, indicating where a campfire was laid. "I've got the skillet and the oil, I've got the meal to roll 'em in and I've got the fire all laid just waiting for the match. Now all I need is the fish."

"No luck?"

"No more than you're having."

"Which isn't a whole lot," Mowbray said. "You from around here?"

"No. Been through here a good many times, however. I've fished this lake now and again and had good luck more often than not."

"Well," Mowbray said. The man's company was invigorating, but there was a strict code of etiquette governing meetings of this nature. "I think I'll head on around the next bend. It's probably pointless but I'd like to get a plug in the water."

"You never can tell if it's pointless, can you? Any minute the wind can change or the temperature can drop a few degrees and the fish can change their behavior completely. That's what keeps us coming out here year after year, I'd say. The wonderful unpredictability of the whole affair. Say, don't go and take a hike on my account."

"Are you sure?"

The big man nodded, hitched at his trousers. "You can wet a line here as good as further down the bank. Your casting for bass won't make a lot of difference as to whether or not a crappie or a sunnie takes a shine to the shiner on my hook. And, to tell you the truth, I'd be just as glad for the company."

"So would I," Mowbray said, gratefully. "If you're sure you don't mind."

"I wouldn't have said boo if I did."

Mowbray set his aluminum tackle box on the ground, knelt beside it, and rigged his line. He tied on a spoon plug, then got to his feet and dug out a pack of cigarettes from the breast pocket of his corduroy shirt. He said, "Smoke?"

"Gave 'em up a while back. But thanks all the same."

Mowbray smoked his cigarette about halfway down, then dropped the butt and ground it underfoot. He stepped to the water's edge, took a minute or so to read the surface of the lake, then cast his plug a good distance out. For the next fifteen minutes or so the two men fished in companionable silence. Mowbray had no strikes but expected none and was resigned to it. He was enjoying himself just the same.

"Nibble," the big man announced. A minute or two went by and he began reeling in. "And a nibble's the extent of it," he said. "I'd better check and see if he left me anything."

The minnow had been bitten neatly in two. The big man had hooked him through the lips and now his tail was missing. His fingers very deft, the man slipped the shiner off the hook and substituted a live one from his bait pail. Seconds later the new minnow was in the water and the red bobber floated on the surface.

"I wonder what did that," Mowbray said.

"Hard to say. Crawdad, most likely. Something ornery."

"I was thinking that a nibble was a good sign, might mean the fish were going to start playing along with us. But if it's just a crawdad I don't suppose it means very much."

"I wouldn't think so."

"I was wondering," Mowbray said. "You'd think if there's bass in this lake you'd be after them instead of crappies."

"I suppose most people figure that way."

"None of my business, of course."

"Oh, that's all right. Hardly a sensitive subject. Happens I like the taste of little panfish better than the larger fish. I'm not a sport fisherman at heart, I'm afraid. I get a kick out of catching 'em, but my main interest is how they're going to taste when I've fried 'em up in the pan. A meat fisherman is what they call my kind, and the sporting fraternity mostly says the phrase with a certain amount of contempt." He exposed large white teeth in a sudden grin. "If they fished as often as I do, they'd probably lose some of their taste for the sporting aspect of it. I fish more days than I don't, you see. I retired ten years ago, had a retail business and sold it not too long after my wife died. We were never able to have any children so there was just myself and I wound up with enough capital to keep me without working if I didn't mind living simply. And I not only don't mind it, I prefer it."

"You're young to be retired."

"I'm fifty-five. I was forty-five when I retired, which may be on the young side, but I was ready for it."

"You look at least ten years younger than you are."

"If that's a fact, I guess retirement agrees with me. Anyway, all I really do is travel around and fish for my supper. And I'd rather catch small fish. I did the other kind of fishing and tired of it in no time at all. The way I see it, I never want to catch more fish than I intend to eat. If I kill something, it goes in that copper skillet over there. Or else I shouldn't have killed it in the first place."

Mowbray was silent for a moment, unsure what to say. Finally he said, "Well, I guess I just haven't evolved to that stage yet. I have to admit I still get a kick out of fishing, whether I eat what I catch or not. I usually eat them but that's not the most important part of it to me. But then I don't go out every other day like yourself. A couple times a year is as much as I can manage."

"Look at us talking," the man said, "and here you're not catching bass while I'm busy not catching crappie. We might as well announce that we're fishing for whales for all the difference it makes."

A little while later Mowbray retrieved his line and changed lures again, then lit another cigarette. The sun was almost gone. It had vanished behind the tree line and was probably close to the horizon by now. The air was definitely growing cooler. Another hour or so would be the extent of his fishing for the day. Then it would be time to head back to the motel and some cocktails and a steak and baked potato at the restaurant down the road. And then an evening of bourbon and water in front of the motel room's television set, lying on the bed with his feet up and the glass at his elbow and a cigarette burning in the ashtray.

The whole picture was so attractive that he was almost willing to skip the last hour's fishing. But the pleasure of the first sip of the first martini would lose nothing for being deferred an hour, and the pleasure of the big man's company was worth another hour of his time.

And then, a little while later, the big man said, "I have an unusual question to ask you."

"Ask away."

"Have you ever killed a man?"

It was an unusual question, and Mowbray took a few extra seconds to think it over. "Well," he said at length, "I guess I have. The odds are pretty good that I have."

"You killed someone without knowing it?"

"That must have sounded odd. You see, I was in the artillery in Korea. Heavy weapons. We never saw what we were shooting at and never knew just what our shells were doing. I was in action for better than a year, stuffing shells down the throat of one big mother of a gun, and I'd hate to think that in all that time we never hit what we aimed at. So I must have killed men, but I don't suppose that's what you're driving at."

"I mean up close. And not in the service, that's a different proposition entirely."

"Never."

"I was in the service myself. An earlier war than yours, and I was on a supply ship and never heard a shot fired in anger. But about four years ago I killed a man." His hand dropped briefly to the sheath knife at his belt. "With this."

Mowbray didn't know what to say. He busied himself taking up the slack in his line and waited for the man to continue.

"I was fishing," the big man said. "All by myself, which is my usual custom. Saltwater though, not fresh like this. I was over in North Carolina on the Outer Banks. Know the place?" Mowbray shook his head. "A chain of barrier islands a good distance out from the mainland. Very remote. Damn fine fishing and not much else. A lot of people fish off the piers or go out on boats, but I was surfcasting. You can do about as well that way as often as not, and that way I figured to build a fire right there on the beach and cook my catch and eat it on the spot. I'd gathered up the driftwood and laid the fire before I wet a line, same as I did today. That's my usual custom. I had done the same thing the day before and I caught myself half a dozen Norfolk spot in no time at all, almost before I could properly say I'd been out fishing. But this particular day I didn't have any luck at all in three hours, which shows that saltwater fish are as unpredictable as the freshwater kind. You done much saltwater fishing?"

"Hardly any."

"I enjoy it about as much as freshwater, and I enjoyed that day on the Banks even without getting a nibble. The sun was warm and there was a light breeze blowing off the ocean and you couldn't have asked for a better day. The next best thing to fishing and catching fish is fishing and not catching 'em, which is a thought we can both console ourselves with after today's run of luck."

"I'll have to remember that one."

"Well, I was having a good enough time even if it looked as though I'd wind up buying my dinner, and then I sensed a fellow coming up behind me. He must have come over the dunes because he was never in my field of vision. I knew he was there—just an instinct, I suppose—and I sent my eyes as far around as they'd go without moving my head, and he wasn't in sight." The big man paused, sighed. "You know," he said, "if the offer still holds, I believe I'll have one of those cigarettes of yours after all."

"You're welcome to one," Mowbray said, "but I hate to start you off on the habit again. Are you sure you want one?"

The wide grin came again. "I quit smoking about the same time I quit work. I may have had a dozen cigarettes since then, spaced over the ten-year span. Not enough to call a habit."

"Then I can't feel guilty about it." Mowbray shook the pack until a cigarette popped up, then extended it to his companion. After the man helped himself Mowbray took one as well, and lit them both with his lighter.

"Nothing like an interval of a year or so between cigarettes to improve their taste," the big man said. He inhaled a lungful of smoke, pursed his lips to expel it in a stream. "I'll tell you," he said, "I really want to tell you this story if you don't mind hearing it. It's one I don't tell often, but I feel a need to get it out from time to time. It may not leave you thinking very highly of me but we're strangers, never saw each other before and as likely will never see each other again. Do you mind listening?"

Mowbray was frankly fascinated and admitted as much.

"Well, there I was knowing I had someone standing behind me. And certain he was up to no good, because no one comes up behind you quiet like that and stands there out of sight with the intention of doing you a favor. I was holding onto my rod, and before I turned around I propped it in the sand butt end down, the way people will do when they're fishing on a beach. Then I waited a minute, and then I turned around as if not expecting to find anyone there, and there he was, of course.

"He was a young fellow, probably no more than twenty-five. But he wasn't a hippie. No beard, and his hair was no longer than yours or mine. It did look greasy, though, and he didn't look too clean in general. Wore a light blue T-shirt and a pair of white duck pants. Funny how I remember what he wore but I can see him clear as day in my mind. Thin lips, sort of a wedge-shaped head, eyes that didn't line up quite right with each other, as though they had minds of their own. Some active pimples and the scars of old ones. He wasn't a prize.

"He had a gun in his hand. What you'd call a belly gun, a little .32-caliber Smith & Wesson with a two-inch barrel. Not good for a single damned thing but killing men at close range, which I'd say is all he ever wanted it for. Of course I didn't know the maker or caliber at the time. I'm not much for guns myself.

"He must have been standing less than two yards away from me. I wouldn't say it took too much instinct to have known he was there, not as close as he was."

The man drew deeply on the cigarette. His eyes narrowed in recollection, and Mowbray saw a short vertical line appear, running from the middle of his forehead almost to the bridge of his nose. Then he blew out smoke and his face relaxed and the line was gone.

"Well, we were all alone on that beach," the man continued. "No one within sight in either direction, no boats in close offshore, no one around to lend a helping hand. Just this young fellow with a gun in his hand and me with my hands empty. I began to regret sticking the rod in the sand. I'd done it to have both hands free, but I thought it might be useful to swing at him and try whipping the gun out of his hand.

"He said, 'All right, old man. Take your wallet out of your pocket nice and easy.'

He was a Northerner, going by his accent, but the younger people don't have too much of an accent wherever they're from. Television, I suppose, is the cause of it. Makes the whole world smaller.

"Now I looked at those eyes, and at the way he was holding that gun, and I knew he wasn't going to take the wallet and wave bye-bye at me. He was going to kill me. In fact, if I hadn't turned around when I did he might well have shot me in the back. Unless he was the sort who liked to watch a person's face when he did it. There are people like that, I understand."

Mowbray felt a chill. The man's voice was so matter-of-fact, while his words were the stuff nightmares are made of.

"Well, I went into my pocket with my left hand. There was no wallet there. It was in the glove compartment of my car, parked off the road in back of the sand dunes. But I reached in my pocket to keep his eyes on my left hand, and then I brought the hand out empty and went for the gun with it, and at the same time I was bringing my knife out of the sheath with my right hand. I dropped my shoulder and came in low, and either I must have moved quick or all the drugs he'd taken over the years had slowed him some, but I swung that gun hand of his up and sent the gun sailing, and at the same time I got my knife into him and laid him wide open."

He drew the knife from its sheath. It was a filleting knife, with a natural wood handle and a thin, slightly curved blade about seven inches long. "This was the knife," he said. "It's a Rapala, made in Finland, and you can't beat it for being stainless steel and yet taking and holding an edge. I use it for filleting and everything else connected with fishing. But you've probably got one just like it yourself."

Mowbray shook his head. "I use a folding knife," he said.

"You ought to get one of these. Can't beat 'em. And they're handy when company comes calling, believe me. I'll tell you, I opened this youngster up the way you open a fish to clean him. Came in low in the abdomen and swept up clear to the bottom of the rib cage, and you'd have thought you were cutting butter as easy as it was." He slid the knife easily back into its sheath.

Mowbray felt a chill. The other man had finished his cigarette, and Mowbray put out his own and immediately selected a fresh one from his pack. He started to return the pack to his pocket, then thought to offer it to the other man.

"Not just now. Try me in nine or ten months, though."

"I'll do that."

The man grinned his wide grin. Then his face went quickly serious. "Well, that young fellow fell down," he said. "Fell right on his back and lay there all opened up. He was moaning and bleeding and I don't know what else. I don't recall his words, his speech was disjointed, but what he wanted was for me to get him to a doctor.

"Now the nearest doctor was in Manteo. I happened to know this, and I was near Rodanthe which is a good twenty miles from Manteo if not more. I saw how he was cut and I couldn't imagine his living through a half-hour ride in a car. In fact if there'd been a doctor six feet away from us I seriously doubt he could have done the boy any good. I'm no doctor myself, but I have to say it was pretty clear to me that boy was dying.

"And if I tried to get him to a doctor, I'd be ruining the interior of my car for all practical purposes, and making a lot of trouble for myself in the bargain. I didn't expect anybody would seriously try to pin a murder charge on me. It stood to reason that fellow had a criminal record that would reach clear to the mainland and back, and I've never had worse than a traffic ticket and few enough of those. And the gun had his prints on it and none of my own. But I'd have to answer a few million questions and hang around for at least a week and doubtless longer for a coroner's inquest, and it all amounted to a lot of aggravation for no purpose, since he was dying anyway.

"And I'll tell you something else. It wouldn't have been worth the trouble even to save him, because what in the world was he but a robbing, murdering snake? Why, if they stitched him up he'd be on the street again as soon as he was healthy and he'd kill someone else in no appreciable time at all. No, I didn't mind the idea of him dying." His eyes engaged Mowbray's. "What would you have done?"

Mowbray thought about it. "I don't know," he said. "I honestly can't say. Same as you, probably."

"He was in horrible pain. I saw him lying there, and I looked around again to assure myself we were alone, and we were. I thought that I could grab my pole and frying pan and my few other bits of gear and be in my car in two or three minutes, not leaving a thing behind that could be traced to me. I'd camped out the night before in a tent and sleeping bag and wasn't registered in any motel or campground. In other words I could be away from the Outer Banks entirely in half an hour, with nothing to connect me to the area, much less to the man on the sand. I hadn't even bought gas with a credit card. I was free and clear if I just got up and left. All I had to do was leave this young fellow to a horribly slow and painful death." His eyes locked with Mowbray's again, with an intensity that was difficult to bear. "Or," he said, his voice lower and softer, "or I could make things easier for him."

"Oh."

"Yes. And that's just what I did. I took and slipped the knife right into his heart. He went instantly. The life slipped right out of his eyes and the tension out of his face and he was gone. And that made it murder."

"Yes, of course."

"Of course," the man echoed. "It might have been an act of mercy, but legally it transformed an act of self-defense into an unquestionable act of criminal homicide." He breathed deeply. "Think I was wrong to do it?"

"No," Mowbray said.

"Do the same thing yourself?"

"I honestly don't know. I hope I would, if the alternative was leaving him to suffer."

"Well, it's what I did. So I've not only killed a man, I've literally murdered a man. I left him under about a foot of sand at the edge of the dunes. I don't know when the body was discovered. I'm sure it didn't take too long. Those sands shift back and forth all the time. There was no identification on him, but the police could have labeled him from his prints, because an upstanding young man like him would have had his prints on file. Nothing on his person at all except for about fifty dollars in cash, which destroys the theory that he was robbing me in order to provide himself with that night's dinner." His face relaxed in a half-smile. "I took the money," he said. "Didn't see as he had any need for it, and I doubted he had much of a real claim to it, as far as that goes."

"So you not only killed a man but made a profit on it."

"I did at that. Well, I left the Banks that evening. Drove on inland a good distance, put up for the night in a motel just outside of Fayetteville. I never did look back, never did find out if and when they found him. It'd be on the books as an unsolved homicide if they did. Oh, and I took his gun and flung it halfway to Bermuda. And he didn't have a car for me to worry about. I suppose he thumbed a ride or came on foot, or else he parked too far away to matter." Another smile. "Now you know my secret," he said.

"Maybe you ought to leave out place names," Mowbray said.

"Why do that?"

"You don't want to give that much information to a stranger."

"You may be right, but I can only tell a story in my own way. I know what's going through your mind right now."

"You do?"

"Want me to tell you? You're wondering if what I told you is true or not. You figure if it happened I probably wouldn't tell you, and yet it sounds pretty believable in itself. And you halfway hope it's the truth and halfway hope it isn't. Am I close?"

"Very close," Mowbray admitted.

"Well, I'll tell you something that'll tip the balance. You'll really want to believe it's all a pack of lies." He lowered his eyes. "The fact of the matter is you'll lose any respect you may have had for me when you hear the next."

"Then why tell me?"

"Because I feel the need."

"I don't know if I want to hear this," Mowbray said.

"I want you to. No fish and it's getting dark and you're probably anxious to get back to wherever you're staying and have a drink and a meal. Well, this won't take long." He had been reeling in his line. Now the operation was concluded, and he set the rod deliberately on the grass at his feet. Straightening up, he said, "I told you before about my attitude toward fish. Not killing what I'm not going to eat. And there this young man was, all laid open, internal organs exposed—"

"Stop."

"I don't know what you'd call it, curiosity or compulsion or some primitive streak. I couldn't say. But what I did, I cut off a small piece of his liver before I buried him. Then after he was under the sand I lit my cookfire and—well, no need to go into detail."

Thank God for that, Mowbray thought. For small favors. He looked at his hands. The left one was trembling. The right, the one gripping his spinning rod, was white at the knuckles, and the tips of his fingers ached from gripping the butt of the rod so tightly.

"Murder, cannibalism, and robbing the dead. That's quite a string for a man who never got worse than a traffic ticket. And all three in considerably less than an hour."

"Please," Mowbray said. His voice was thin and high-pitched. "Please don't tell me any more."

"Nothing more to tell."

Mowbray took a deep breath, held it. This man was either lying or telling the truth, Mowbray thought, and in either case he was quite obviously an extremely unusual person. At the very least.

"You shouldn't tell that story to strangers," he said after a moment. "True or false, you shouldn't tell it."

"I now and then feel the need."

"Of course, it's all to the good that I *am* a stranger. After all, I don't know anything about you, not even your name."

"It's Tolliver."

"Or where you live, or—"

"Wallace P. Tolliver. I was in the retail hardware business in Oak Falls, Missouri. That's not far from Joplin."

"Don't tell me anything more," Mowbray said desperately. "I wish you hadn't told me what you did."

"I had to," the big man said. The smile flashed again. "I've told that story three times before today. You're the fourth man ever to hear it."

Mowbray said nothing.

"Three times. Always to strangers who happen to turn up while I'm fishing. Always on long lazy afternoons, those afternoons when the fish just don't bite no matter what you do."

Mowbray began to do several things. He began to step backward, and he began to release his tight hold on his fishing rod, and he began to extend his left arm protectively in front of him.

But the filleting knife had already cleared its sheath.

Strangers on a Handball Court

We met for the first time on a handball court in Sheridan Park. It was a Saturday morning in early summer with the sky free of clouds and the sun warm but not yet unbearable. He was alone on the court when I got there and I stood for a few moments watching him warm up, slamming the little ball viciously against the imperturbable backstop.

He didn't look my way, although he must have known I was watching him. When he paused for a moment I said, "A game?"

He looked my way. "Why not?"

I suppose we played for two hours, perhaps a little longer. I've no idea how many games we played. I was several years younger, weighed considerably less, and topped him by four or five inches.

He won every game.

When we broke, the sun was high in the sky and considerably hotter than it had been when we started. We had both been sweating freely and we stood together, rubbing our faces and chests with our towels. "Good workout," he said. "There's nothing like it."

"I hope you at least got some decent exercise out of it," I said apologetically. "I certainly didn't make it much of a contest."

"Oh, don't bother yourself about that," he said, and flashed a shark's smile. "Tell you the truth, I like to win. On and off the court. And I certainly got a workout out of you."

I laughed. "As a matter of fact, I managed to work up a thirst. How about a couple of beers? On me, in exchange for the handball lesson."

He grinned. "Why not?"

We didn't talk much until we were settled in a booth at the Hofbrau House. Generations of collegians had carved combinations of Greek letters into the top of our sturdy oak table. I was in the middle of another apology for my athletic inadequacy when he set his stein down atop Zeta Beta Tau and shook a cigarette out of his pack. "Listen," he said, "forget it. What the hell, maybe you're lucky in love."

I let out a bark of mirthless laughter. "If this is luck," I said, "I'd hate to see misfortune."

"Problems?"

"You might say so."

"Well, if it's something you'd rather not talk about—"

I shook my head. "It's not that—it might even do me good to talk about it—but it would bore the daylights out of you. It's hardly an original problem. The world is overflowing these days with men in the very same leaky boat."

"Oh?"

"I've got a girl," I said. "I love her and she loves me. But I'm afraid I'm going to lose her."

He frowned, thinking about it. "You're married," he said.

"No."

"She's married."

I shook my head. "No, we're both single. She wants to get married."

"But you don't want to marry her."

"There's nothing I want more than to marry her and spend the rest of my life with her."

His frown deepened. "Wait a minute," he said. "Let me think. You're both single, you both want to get married, but there's a problem. All I can think of is she's your sister, but I can't believe that's it, especially since you said it's a common problem. I'll tell you, I think my brain's tired from too much time in the sun. What's the problem?"

"I'm divorced."

"So who isn't? I'm divorced and I'm remarried. Unless it's a religious thing. I bet that's what it is."

"No."

"Well, don't keep me guessing, fella. I already gave up once, remember?"

"The problem is my ex-wife," I said. "The judge gave her everything I had but the clothes I was wearing at the time of the trial. With the alimony I have to pay her, I'm living in a furnished room and cooking on a hotplate. I can't afford to get married, and my girl wants to get married—and sooner or later she's going to get tired of spending her time with a guy who can never afford to take her anyplace decent." I shrugged. "Well," I said, "you get the picture."

"Boy, do I get the picture."

"As I said, it's not a very original problem."

"You don't know the half of it." He signaled the waiter for two more beers, and when they arrived he lit another cigarette and took a long swallow of his beer. "It's really something," he said. "Meeting like this. I already told you I got an ex-wife of my own."

"These days almost everybody does."

"That's the truth. I must have had a better lawyer than you did, but I still got burned pretty bad. She got the house, she got the Cadillac and just about everything else she wanted. And now she gets fifty cents out of every dollar I make. She's got no kids, she's got no responsibilities, but she gets fifty cents out of every dollar I earn and the government gets another thirty or forty cents. What does that leave me?"

"Not a whole lot."

"You better believe it. As it happens I make a good living. Even with what she and the government take I manage to live pretty decently. But do you know what it does to me, paying her all that money every month? I hate that woman's guts and she lives like a queen at my expense."

I took a long drink of beer. "I guess our problems aren't all that different."

"And a lot of men can say the same thing. Millions of them. A word of advice, friend. What you should do if you marry your girlfriend—"

"I can't marry her."

"But if you go ahead and marry her anyway. Just make sure you do what I did before I married my second wife. It goes against the grain to do it because when you're about to marry someone you're completely in love and you're sure it's going to last forever. But make a prenuptial agreement. Have it all signed and witnessed before the marriage ceremony, and have it specify that if there's a divorce she does not get one dime, she gets zip. You follow me? Get yourself a decent lawyer so he'll draw up something that will stand up, and get her to sign it, which she most likely will because she'll be so starry-eyed about getting married. Then you'll have nothing to worry about. If the marriage is peaches and cream forever, which I hope it is, then you've wasted a couple of hundred dollars on a lawyer and that's no big deal. But if anything goes wrong with the marriage, you're in the catbird seat."

I looked at him for a long moment. "It makes sense," I said.

"That's what I did. Now my second wife and I, we get along pretty good. She's young, she's beautiful, she's good company, I figure I got a pretty good deal. We have our bad times, but they're nothing two people can't live with. And the thing is, she's not tempted by the idea of divorcing me, because she knows what she'll come out with if she does. Zeeee-ro."

"If I ever get married again," I said, "I'll take your advice."

"I hope so."

"But it'll never happen," I said. "Not with my ex-wife bleeding me to death. You know, I'm almost ashamed to say this, but what the hell, we're strangers, we don't really know each other, so I'll admit it. I have fantasies of killing her. Stabbing her, shooting her, tying her to a railroad track and letting a train solve my problem for me."

"Friend, you are not alone. The world is full of men who dream about killing their ex-wives."

"Of course I'd never do it. Because if anything ever happened to that woman, the police would come straight to me."

"Same here. If I ever put my ex in the ground, there'd be a cop knocking on my door before the body was cold. Of course that particular body was *born* cold, if you know what I mean."

"I know what you mean," I said. This time I signaled for more beer, and we fell silent until it was on the table in front of us. Then, in a confessional tone, I said, "I'll tell you something. I would do it. If I weren't afraid of getting caught, I would literally do it. I'd kill her."

"I'd kill mine."

"I mean it. There's no other way out for me. I'm in love and I want to get married and I can't. My back is to the proverbial wall. I'd do it."

He didn't even hesitate. "So would I."

"Really?"

"Sure. You could say it's just money, and that's most of it, but there's more to it than that. I hate that woman. I hate the fact that she's made a complete fool out of me. If I could get away with it, they'd be breaking ground in her cemetery plot any day now." He shook his head. "*Her* cemetery plot," he said bitterly. "It was originally our plot, but the judge gave her the whole thing. Not that I have any overwhelming urge to be buried next to her, but it's the principle of the thing."

"If only we could get away with it," I said. And, while the sentence hung in the air like an off-speed curveball, I reached for my beer.

Of course a lightbulb did not actually form above the man's head—that only happens in comic strips—but the expression on his jowly face was so eloquent that I must admit I looked up expecting to see the lightbulb. This, clearly, was a man who had just Had An Idea.

He didn't share it immediately. Instead he took a few minutes to work it out in his mind while I worked on my beer. When I saw that he was ready to speak I put my stein down.

"I don't know you," he said.

I allowed that this was true.

"And you don't know me. I don't know your name, even your first name."

"It's—"

He showed me a palm. "Don't tell me. I don't want to know. Don't you see what we are? We're strangers."

"I guess we are."

"We played handball for a couple of hours. But no one even knows we played handball together. We're having a couple of beers together, but only the waiter knows that and he won't remember it, and anyway no one would ever think to ask him. Don't you see the position we're in? We each have someone we want dead. Don't you understand?"

"I'm not sure."

"I saw a movie years ago. Two strangers meet on a train and—I wish I could remember the title."

"*Strangers on a Train*?"

"That sounds about right. Anyway, they get to talking, tell each other their problems, and decide to do each other's murder. Do you get my drift?"

"I'm beginning to."

"You've got an ex-wife, and I've got an ex-wife. You said you'd commit murder if you had a chance to get away with it, and *I'd* commit murder if I had a chance to get away with it. And all we have to do to get away with it is switch victims." He leaned forward and dropped his voice to an urgent whisper. There was no one near us, but the occasion seemed to demand low voices. "Nothing could be simpler, friend. *You* kill *my* ex-wife. *I* kill *your* ex-wife. And we're both home free."

My eyes widened. "That's brilliant," I whispered back. "It's absolutely brilliant."

"You'd have thought of it yourself in another minute," he said modestly. "The conversation was headed in that direction."

"Just brilliant," I said.

We sat that way for a moment, our elbows on the table, our heads separated by only a few inches, basking in the glow generated by his brilliant idea. Then he said, "One big hurdle. One of us has to go first."

"I'll go first," I offered. "After all, it was your idea. It's only fair that I go first."

"But suppose you went first and I tried to weasel out after you'd done your part?"

"Oh, you wouldn't do that."

"Damn right I wouldn't, friend. But you can't be sure of it, not sure enough to take the short straw voluntarily." He reached into his pocket and produced a shiny quarter. "Call it," he said, tossing it into the air.

"Heads," I said. I always call heads. Just about everyone always calls heads.

The coin landed on the table, spun for a dramatic length of time, then came to rest between Sigma Nu and Delta Kappa Epsilon.

Tails.

I managed to see Vivian for a half hour that afternoon. After the usual complement of urgent kisses I said, "I'm hopeful. About us, I mean. About our future."

"Really?"

"Really. I have the feeling things are going to work out."

"Oh, darling," she said.

The following Saturday dawned bright and clear. By arrangement we met on the handball court, but this time we played only half a dozen games before calling it a day. And after we had toweled off and put on shirts, we went to a different bar and had but a single beer apiece.

"Wednesday or Thursday night," he said. "Wednesday I'll be playing poker. It's my regular game and it'll last until two or three in the morning. It always does, and I'll make certain that this is no exception. On Thursday, my wife and I are invited to a dinner party and we'll be playing bridge afterward. That won't last past midnight, so Wednesday would be better—"

"Wednesday's fine with me."

"She lives alone and she's almost always home by ten. As a matter of fact she rarely leaves the house. I don't blame her, it's a beautiful house." He pursed his lips. "But forget that. The earlier in the evening you do the job, the better it is for me—in case doctors really can determine time of death—"

"I'll call the police."

"How's that?"

"After she's dead I'll give the police an anonymous phone call, tip them off. That way they'll discover the body while you're still at the poker game. That lets you out completely."

He nodded approval. "That's damned intelligent," he said. "You know something? I'm thrilled you and I ran into each other. I don't know your name and I don't want to know your name, but I sure like your style. Wednesday night?"

"Wednesday night," I agreed. "You'll hear it on the news Thursday morning, and by then your troubles will be over."

"Fantastic," he said. "Oh, one other thing." He flashed the shark's smile. "If she suffers," he said, "that's perfectly all right with me."

She didn't suffer.

I did it with a knife. I told her I was a burglar and that she wouldn't be hurt if she cooperated. It was not the first lie I ever told in my life. She cooperated, and when her attention was elsewhere I stabbed her in the heart. She died with an expression of extreme puzzlement on her none-too-pretty face, but she didn't suffer, and that's something.

Once she was dead I went on playing the part of the burglar. I ransacked the house, throwing books from their shelves and turning drawers over and generally making a dreadful mess. I found quite a bit of jewelry, which I ultimately put down a sewer, and I found several hundred dollars in cash, which I did not.

After I'd dropped the knife down another sewer and the white cotton gloves down yet a third sewer, I called the police. I said I'd heard sounds of a struggle coming from a particular house, and I supplied the address. I said that two men had rushed from the house and had driven away in a dark car. No, I could not identify the car further. No, I had not seen the license plate. No, I did not care to give my name.

The following day I spoke to Vivian briefly on the telephone. "Things are going well," I said.

"I'm so glad, darling."

"Things are going to work out for us," I said.

"You're wonderful. You know that, don't you? Absolutely wonderful."

On Saturday we played a mere three games of handball. He won the first, as usual, but astonishingly I beat him in the second game, my first victory over him, and I went on to beat him again in the third. It was then that he suggested that we call it a day. Perhaps he simply felt off his game, or wanted to reduce the chances of someone's noticing the two of us together. On the other hand, he had said at our first meeting that he liked to win. Conversely, one might suppose that he didn't like to lose.

Over a couple of beers he said, "Well, you did it. I knew you'd do it and at the same time I couldn't actually believe you would. Know what I mean?"

"I think so."

"The police didn't even hassle me. They checked my alibi, of course—they're not idiots. But they didn't dig too deep because they seemed so certain it was a burglary. I'll tell you something, it was such a perfectly faked burglary that I even began to get the feeling that that was what happened. Just a coincidence, like. You chickened out and a burglar just happened to do the job."

"Maybe that's what happened," I suggested.

He looked at me, then grinned slyly. "You're one hell of a guy," he said. "Cool as a cucumber, aren't you? Tell me something. What was it like, killing her?"

"You'll find out soon enough."

"Hell of a guy. You realize something? You have the advantage over me. You know my name. From the newspapers. And I still don't know yours."

"You'll know it soon enough," I said with a smile. "From the newspapers."

"Fair enough."

I gave him a slip of paper. Like the one he'd given me, it had an address block-printed in pencil. "Wednesday would be ideal," I said. "If you don't mind missing your poker game."

"I wouldn't have to miss it, would I? I'd just get there late. The poker game gives me an excuse to get out of my house, but if I'm an hour late getting there my wife'll never know the difference. And even if she knew I wasn't where I was supposed to be, so what? What's she gonna do, divorce me and cut herself out of my money? Not likely."

"I'll be having dinner with a client," I said. "Then he and I will be going directly to a business meeting. I'll be tied up until fairly late in the evening—eleven o'clock, maybe midnight."

"I'd like to do it around eight," he said. "That's when I normally leave for the poker game. I can do it and be drawing to an inside straight by nine o'clock. How does that sound?"

I allowed that it sounded good to me.

"I guess I'll make it another fake burglary," he said. "Ransack the place, use a knife. Let them think it's the same crazy burglar striking again. Or doesn't that sound good to you?"

"It might tend to link us," I said.

"Oh."

"Maybe you could make it look like a sex crime. Rape and murder. That way the police would never draw any connection between the two killings."

"Brilliant," he said. He really seemed to admire me now that I'd committed a murder and won two games of handball from him.

"You wouldn't actually have to rape her. Just rip her clothing and set the scene properly."

"Is she attractive?" I admitted that she was, after a fashion. "I've always sort of had fantasies about rape," he said, carefully avoiding my eyes as he spoke. "She'll be home at eight o'clock?"

"She'll be home."

"And alone?"

"Absolutely."

He folded the slip of paper, put it into his wallet, dropped bills from his wallet on the table, swallowed what remained of his beer, and got to his feet. "It's in the bag," he said. "Your troubles are over."

"Our troubles are over," I told Vivian.

"Oh, darling," she said. "I can hardly believe it. You're the most wonderful man in the world."

"And a sensational handball player," I said.

I left my house Wednesday night at half past seven. I drove a few blocks to a drugstore and bought a couple of magazines, then went to a men's shop next door and looked at sport shirts. The two shirts I liked weren't in stock in my size. The clerk offered to order them for me but I thought it over and told him not to bother. "I like them," I said, "but I'm not absolutely crazy about them."

I returned to my house. My handball partner's car was parked diagonally across the street. I parked my own car in the driveway and used my key to let myself in the front door. From the doorway I cleared my throat, and he spun around to face me, his eyes bulging out of his head.

I pointed to the body on the couch. "Is she dead?"

"Stone dead. She fought and I hit her too hard . . ." He flushed a deep red, then he blinked. "But what are you doing here? Don't you remember how we planned it? I don't understand why you came here tonight of all nights."

"I came here because I live here," I said. "George, I'd love to explain but there's no time. I wish there *were* time but there isn't."

I took the revolver from my pocket and shot him in the face.

"The police were very understanding," I told Vivian. "They seem to think the shock of his ex-wife's death unbalanced him. They theorize that he was driving by when he saw me leave my house. Maybe he saw Margaret at the door saying good-bye to me. He parked, perhaps with no clear intention, then went to the door. When she opened the door, he was overcome with desire. By the time I came back and let myself in and shot him it was too late. The damage had been done."

"Poor George."

"And poor Margaret."

She put her hand on mine. "They brought it on themselves," she said. "If George hadn't insisted on that vicious prenuptial agreement we could have had a properly civilized divorce like everybody else."

"And if Margaret had agreed to a properly civilized divorce she'd be alive today."

"We only did what we had to do," Vivian said. "It was a shame about his ex-wife, but I don't suppose there was any way around it."

"At least she didn't suffer."

"That's important," she said. "And you know what they say—you can't break an egg without making omelets."

"That's what they say," I agreed. We embraced, and some moments later we disembraced. "We'll have to give one another rather a wide berth for a month or two," I said. "After all, I killed your husband just as he finished killing my wife. If we should be seen in public, tongues would wag. In a month or so you'll sell your house and leave town. A few weeks after that I'll do the same. Then we can get married and live happily ever after, but in the meantime we'd best be very cautious."

"You're right," she said. "There was a movie like that, except nobody got killed in it. But there were these two people in a small town who were having an affair, and when they met in public they had to pretend they were strangers. I wish I could remember the title."

"*Strangers When We Meet*?"

"That sounds about right."

That Kind of a Day

Traynor got the call at a quarter to nine. The girl on the line was named Linda Haber and she was a secretary—the secretary—at Hofert & Jordan. The boss had been shot, she kept saying. It took Traynor close to five minutes to find out who she was and where she was and to tell her to sit down and stay put. She was still babbling hysterically when he hung up on her and pulled Phil Grey away from a cup of coffee. He said, "Homicide, downtown and west. Let's go."

Hofert & Jordan had two and a half rooms of office space in a squat redbrick building on Woodlawn near Marsh. There was a *No Smoking* sign in the elevator. Grey smoked anyway. Traynor kept his hands in his pockets and waited for the car to get to the fourth floor. The doors opened and a white-faced girl rushed up and asked them if they were the police. Grey said they were. The girl looked grateful.

"Right this way," she said. "Oh, it's so awful!"

They entered an anteroom, with two offices leading from it. One door was marked *David Hofert*, another marked *James Jordan*. They went through the door marked *James Jordan*. Linda Haber was trembling. Grey took her by an arm and eased her toward a chair. Traynor studied the scene.

There was an old oak desk with papers strewn over it; some papers had spilled down onto the floor. There was a gun on the floor a little to the left of the desk, and somewhat farther to that side of the desk there was a man lying facedown in a pool of partially dried blood, some of which had spattered onto the papers.

Traynor said, "Mr. Jordan?"

"Mr. Hofert," the Haber girl said. "Is he—" She didn't finish the question. Her face paled and then she fainted.

Some lab people came and took pictures, noted measurements, and made chalk marks. They had Hofert's body out of the building in less than half an hour. Grey and Traynor worked as a team, crisp and smooth and efficient. Traynor questioned the secretary when she came to, then had the medical examiner give her a sedative and commissioned a patrolman to drive her home. Grey routed the night elevator operator out of bed and asked him some questions. Traynor called the man who did the legal work for Hofert & Jordan. Grey got a prelim report from the M.E., pending autopsy results. Traynor bought two cups of coffee from a machine in the lobby and brought them upstairs. The coffee tasted of cardboard, from the containers.

"Almost too easy," Traynor said. "Too simple."

Grey nodded.

"At six forty-five last night the Haber kid went home. Jordan and Hofert were both here. Jordan stayed until eight. From six at night until eight in the morning nobody can get in or out of the building without signing the register, and the stairs are locked off at the second-floor landing. You have to sign and you have to use the elevator. Jordan signed out at eight. Hofert never signed out; he was dead."

"What was the time of death?"

"That fits, too. A rough estimate is twelve to fourteen hours. One bullet was in the chest a little below the heart. It took him a little while to die. Say five minutes, not much more than that. Enough time to lose a lot of blood."

"So if he got shot between seven and eight—"

"That's about it. No robbery motive. He has a full wallet on him. No suicide. He was standing up when he got shot, standing and facing the desk, Jordan's desk. The Haber girl couldn't have killed him. She left better than an hour before Jordan did and the sheet bears her out on that."

"Motive?"

Traynor put his coffee on the desk. "Maybe they hated each other," he said. "A little two-man operation jobbing office supplies. The lawyer says they didn't make much and they didn't lose much either. Partners for six years. Jordan's forty-four, Hofert was two years older. The secretary said they argued a lot."

"Everybody argues."

"They argued more. Especially yesterday, according to the secretary. There's a money motive, too. Partnership insurance."

Grey looked puzzled.

"Twin policies paid for out of partnership funds. Each partner is insured, with the face amount payable to the survivor if one of them dies."

"Why?"

"That's what I asked the lawyer. Look, suppose you and I are in business together. Then suppose you die—"

"Thanks."

"—and your wife inherits your share. She can't take a hand in the running of the business. After I pay myself a salary there's not much left in the way of profits for her. What she wants is the cash and what I want is full control of the business. Lots of friction."

"Maybe I'd better live," Grey said.

Traynor ignored him. "The insurance smooths things out. If you die, the insurance company pays me whatever the policy is. Then I have to use the money to buy your share of the business from your widow. She has the cash she needs, and I get the whole business without any cost to me. That way everybody's happy."

"Except me."

"Hofert and Jordan had partnership insurance," Traynor said. "Two policies, each with a face amount of a hundred grand. That's motive and means and opportunity, so pat it's hard to believe. I don't know what we're waiting around here for."

They didn't wait long. Half an hour later they picked up James Jordan at his home on Pattison. They asked him how come he hadn't gone to his office. He said he'd worked late the night before and wasn't feeling too well. They asked him why he had killed his partner. He stared at them and told them he didn't understand what they were talking about. They took him downtown and booked him for murder.

Hofert's widow lived in a ranch house just across the city line. The two kids were in school when Traynor and Grey got there. Mrs. Hofert was worried when she saw them. They told her as gently as you can tell a wife that someone has murdered her husband. A doctor came from down the block to give her a hypo, and an hour later she said she was ready to talk to them. She wasn't, really, but they didn't want to wait. It was a neat case, the kind you wrap up fast.

"That poor, poor man," she said. "He worked so hard. He worked and he worried and he wanted so very much to get ahead. He put his blood into that business. And now he's gone and nothing's left."

Grey started to light a cigarette, then changed his mind. Mrs. Hofert was crying quietly. Nobody said anything for a few minutes.

"I hardly ever saw him," she said. "Isn't that something? I hardly ever got to see him and now he's gone. So much work. And it wasn't for himself, nothing was ever for himself. He wanted money for us. For me, for the boys. As if we needed it. All we ever needed was him and now he's gone—"

Later, calmer, she said, "And he didn't leave us a thing. He was a gambler, Dave was. Oh, not cards or dice—not that kind of a gambler—stocks, the stock market. He made a decent living but that wasn't enough because he wanted more, he wanted a lot of money, and he tried to make it fast. He wanted to take risks in the business, to borrow money and expand. He had dreams. He always complained that Jim wouldn't let him build the business, that Jim was too conservative. So he took chances in the market, and at first he did all right, I think. He told me he did, and then everything fell in for him and . . . Oh, I don't understand anything!"

On the way downtown, Grey said, "Try it this way. Hofert went into Jordan's office last night. They'd been arguing off and on all day. He wanted to draw more money out of the company, or to borrow and expand, or anything. He was in terrible shape financially. The house was mortgaged to the roof. He'd already cashed in his personal insurance policies. He was in trouble, desperate. They argued again. Maybe he even threw a punch. The office was a mess, they could have been fighting a little. Then Jordan took out a gun and shot him. Right?"

"That's the only way it plays."

"Let's talk to Jordan again," Grey said.

They double-teamed Jordan and kept questions looping in at him until he had admitted almost everything. He admitted ownership of the gun, said he had bought it two years ago and had kept it in his desk ever since. He admitted quarreling with Hofert that afternoon and said that Hofert kept provoking arguments. He confirmed the secretary's statement about the time of her departure and the fact that he and Hofert had stayed alone in the office.

He denied killing Hofert.

"Why? Why would I do it?"

"You were fighting with him. Maybe he swung at you—"

"Dave? You're crazy. Why should he hit me?"

"Maybe he hated you. Maybe you hated each other. You shot him, panicked, and left. You couldn't face his corpse in the morning and you stayed home in bed until we came here for you."

"But I—"

"You stood to gain complete control of the business with him dead. All the profits instead of half, and no partner to get in your hair."

"Profits!" Jordan was shouting now. "I have enough! I have plenty!" He caught his breath, slowed down. "I'm a bachelor, I live alone, I save my money. Check my bank account. What do I want with blood money?"

"Hofert was dead weight. He was in hock up to his ears and he was giving you a bad time. You didn't plan on killing him, Jordan. You did it on the spur of the moment. He provoked it. And—"

"I did not kill David Hofert!"

"You admit it's your gun."

"Yes, damn it, it is my gun. I never fired it in my life. I never pointed it at anything. It was in my desk, in case I ever needed it—"

"And last night you needed it."

"No."

"Last night—"

"Last night I finished my work and went home," Jordan said. "I went home, I was tired, I had a headache. Dave stayed in the office. I told him I might not be in the next morning. 'Take it easy,' he said. That was the last thing he said to me. 'Take it easy.' "

Traynor and Grey looked at each other.

"He was alive when I left him."

"Then who killed him, Jordan? Who lured him into *your* office and took *your* gun and shot him in the chest and—"

They kept up the questions, kept hammering away like a properly efficient team. They got nowhere. Jordan never contradicted himself and never made very much sense. They kicked his story apart and he stayed with it anyway. After fifteen more minutes of getting nowhere they took him back to his cell and locked him away. Traynor stopped to stare at him, at the small round face peering out through the bars of the cage. Jordan looked trapped.

Two hours later, Traynor pushed a pile of papers to one side of his desk, eased his chair back, and stood up. Grey asked him where he was going. "Out," Traynor told him.

"He said that Jim Jordan was trying to ruin him," Mrs. Hofert said. "I always felt . . . well, Dave felt persecuted sometimes. He had so many big plans that came to nothing. He thought the world was ganging up on him. I never believed that Jim would actually—"

"We think it happened during an argument," Traynor told her. "Jordan got excited, didn't know exactly what he was doing. If he had planned to murder your husband he would have picked a brighter way to do it. But in the heat of an argument things happen in a hurry."

"The heat of an argument." She sat for a long time looking at nothing at all. Then she said, "I believe everything has a pattern, Mr. Traynor. Do you believe that?"

Traynor didn't answer.

"Dave's life—and his death, trying, struggling, working so very hard, and getting every bad break there was. Getting bad breaks *because* he tried so hard, because he wasn't prudent about money. And then having everything build to a climax with everything going wrong at once. And the tragic ending, dying at what he could only have thought of as the worst possible moment. You see, all he wanted to do was provide for me and for the boys. He was . . . he was the kind of man who would have thought it a triumph to die well insured." More long silence. "And not even that. A year ago, six months ago, all his policies were paid up. Then, as things went wrong, he cashed the policies to get money to recoup his losses, and lost that, too. And then the final irony of dying without anything to leave us but a legacy of debts. Do you see the pattern, Mr. Traynor?"

"I think so," Traynor said.

He got very busy then. He went to the lawyer he had spoken to earlier, went alone without Grey. He asked the lawyer some questions, went to an insurance man and asked more questions. He called the Haber girl, and with her he went over the few hours prior to Hofert's death. He got the autopsy results, the lab photos, the lab report. He went to the Hofert & Jordan office and stood in the room where Hofert had died, visualizing everything, running it through in his mind.

It was pushing six o'clock. He picked up a phone, called headquarters, and got through to Grey. "Don't leave yet," he said. "I'll be right over. Stay put."

"You got something?"

"Yes," he said.

They were in a small cubbyhole office off the main room. Grey sat at a desk. Traynor stood up and did a lot of pacing.

"There were no fingerprints on the gun," he said.

"So? Jordan wiped it."

"Why?"

"Why? If you shot somebody, would you leave prints on the gun?"

Traynor walked over to the door, turned, came halfway back. "If I was going to wipe prints off a gun I would also do something about setting up an alibi," he said. "The way we've got it figured, Jordan killed strictly on impulse and reacted like a scared rabbit. He went for his gun, shot Hofert, ran out of the building, and went home and stayed there shaking. He didn't sponge up blood, he didn't try to lug Hofert out of his office, didn't do a thing to disguise the killing. He left the gun right there, didn't try any of the tricks a panicky killer might try. But he wiped the prints off the gun."

"He must have been half out of his mind."

"It still doesn't add. There's another way, though, that does."

"Go on."

"Suppose you're Hofert. Now—"

"Why do we always have to suppose I'm the dead one?"

"Shut up," Traynor said. "Suppose you're David Hofert. You're deep in debt and you can't see your way clear. You look at yourself in the mirror and figure you're a failure. You want money for your wife, security for your kids. But you haven't got a penny, your insurance policies have lapsed, and your whole world is caving in on you. You're frantic."

"I don't—"

"Wait. You've always been a little paranoid. Now you think the whole world is after you and your partner is purposely trying to make things rough for you. You'd like to go and jump off a bridge, but that wouldn't get you anywhere. If you died in an accident, at least your wife and kids would get the hundred grand, the insurance dough which Jordan would turn over to them for your share of the business. Suicide voids that policy. If you kill yourself, they wind up with nothing."

Grey was nodding slowly now.

"But if your partner kills you—"

"What happens then?"

"It's a cute deal," Traynor said. "I went over it twice, with the lawyer and with the agent who wrote the policies. Now, each man is insured for a hundred grand, with that amount payable to the other or the other's heirs. If Jordan kills Hofert, he can't collect. You can't profit legally through the commission of a felony. But the insurance company still has to pay off. If the policy's paid up, and if it's been in force over two years, the company has to make it good. They can't hand the dough to Jordan if he's the killer, but they have to pay somebody."

"Who? I don't understand you."

"The dead man's estate. Hofert's estate. It can't go to Jordan because he's the murderer, and it can't go to Jordan's heirs because he never has legal title to it to pass on. And the company can't keep it, so it can only go to Hofert's wife and kids."

Grey hesitated, then nodded.

"That's the only way Hofert's family ever gets a dime. They get that hundred thousand as insurance on Hofert's life, and they collect another hundred thousand when Jordan goes to the chair for murder, and they have at least half the business as well. All Hofert has to do is find a way to kill himself and make it look like murder, and he sends all that dough to them and has the satisfaction of sticking Jordan with a murder rap. We get the other kind all the time, the murders that are faked to look like suicides. This one went the opposite way."

"How did he do it?"

"The easiest way in the world," Traynor said. "He covered all bets, gave Jordan motive and means and opportunity. He argued with him all day in front of the secretary. He fixed it so that he and Jordan were alone in the office. When Jordan left, he went into Jordan's office and got Jordan's gun. He messed up the place to stage a struggle. He wrapped the gun in a tissue or something to keep his prints off it. He stood in front of the desk, off to the side, and he angled the shot so that it would look as though he'd been shot by somebody behind the desk. He shot himself in a spot that would be sure to kill him but that would leave him a minute or two of life to drop the gun in a convenient spot. That may have been accidental; maybe he aimed for the heart and missed. We'll never know."

"What does the lab say?"

Traynor shrugged. "Maybe and maybe no, as far as they're concerned. It could have been that way—that's as much as they can say, and that's enough. The paraffin test didn't show that Hofert had fired a gun, but it wouldn't, not if he had a tissue or a handkerchief around his hand. There were tissues on the floor, and a lot of papers that he could have used. The bullet trajectory fits well enough. It's something you don't think of right off the bat. The way Hofert had it planned, we weren't supposed to think of it at all. And it almost worked. It almost had Jordan nailed."

"Now what?"

Traynor looked at him. "Now we tell Jordan to relax," he said. "And after the inquest calls it suicide, we let him go—very simple."

"No," Grey said. "I don't believe it."

"Why not?"

"Because it's crazy. You don't kill yourself to stick somebody for murder. It's too damned iffy, anyway. Why did Jordan stay home that morning?"

"He was feeling sick."

"Sure. He didn't come in, he didn't even call his office. You can make a suicide theory out of it. You can also read it as a very clear-cut murder, and that's the way I'd read it. You want to let Jordan off and take a couple hundred thousand away from Hofert's wife. Is that right?"

"Yes." Traynor looked at the floor. "And you want to see Jordan in the chair for this one."

"That's the way it reads to me."

"Well, I won't go along with that, Phil."

"And I won't buy suicide. You fought this one because it was too simple, and now you've got us stuck with two answers, one easy and one tough, and I like the easy one and you like the tough one. I hope to hell Jordan confesses and makes it easy for us."

"He won't," Traynor said. "He's innocent."

"How sure are you?"

"Positive."

"That's how sure I am he's guilty. What do we do if he doesn't confess, if he sticks to his story and the lab can't cut it any finer for us? What do we do? Toss a coin?"

No one said anything for a few minutes. Traynor looked at his watch. Grey lit a cigarette.

Traynor said, "I don't buy murder."

"I don't buy suicide."

"He won't confess, Phil. And we'll never know. If Jordan goes on trial he'll get off because I'll hand my angle to his lawyer. He'll beat it. But we'll never know, not really. You'll always think he's guilty and I'll always think he isn't, and we'll never know."

"Maybe we ought to toss that coin."

"If we did," Traynor said, "it would stand on end. It's been that kind of a day."

This Crazy Business of Ours

The elevator, swift and silent as a garotte, whisked the young man eighteen stories skyward to Wilson Colliard's penthouse. The doors opened to reveal Colliard himself. He wore a cashmere smoking jacket the color of vintage port. His flannel slacks and broadcloth shirt were a matching oyster white. They could have been chosen to match his hair, which had been expensively barbered in a leonine mane. His eyes, beneath sharply defined white brows, were as blue and as bottomless as the Caribbean, upon the shores of which he had acquired his radiant tan. He wore doeskin slippers upon his small feet and a smile upon his thinnish lips, and in his right hand he held an automatic pistol of German origin, the precise manufacturer and caliber of which need not concern us.

"My abject apologies," Colliard said. "Of course you're Michael Haig. I regret the gun, Mr. Haig, even as I regret the necessity for it. It's inconsistent greeting a guest with gun in hand and bidding him welcome, but I assure you that you are welcome indeed. Come in, come in. Ah, yes." The doors swept silently shut behind Haig. "This thing," Colliard said distastefully, looking down at the gun in his hand. "But of course you understand."

"Of course, Mr. Colliard."

"This crazy business of ours. Always the chance, isn't there, that you might turn out to be other than the admiring youngster you're purported to be. And surely there's a tradition of that sort of thing, isn't there? Just look at the Old West. Young gunfighter out to make a name for himself, so he goes up against the old gunfighter. Quickest way to acquire a reputation, isn't it? Why, it's a veritable cliché in the world of western movies, and I daresay they do the same thing in gangster films and who knows what else. Now I don't for the moment think that's your game, you see, but I've learned over the years never to take an unnecessary chance. And I've learned that most chances *are* unnecessary. So if you don't mind a frisk—"

"Of course not."

"You'll have to assume an undignified posture, I'm afraid. Over that way, if you don't mind. Now reach forward with both hands and touch the wall. Excellent. Now walk backwards a step and another step, that's right, very good, yes. You'll hardly make any abrupt moves now, will you? Undignified, as I said, but utilitarian beyond doubt."

The old man's hand moved expertly over the young man's body, patting and brushing here and there, making quite certain that no weapon was concealed beneath the dark pinstripe suit, no gun wedged under the waistband of the trousers, no knife strapped to calf or forearm. The search was quick but quite thorough, and at its conclusion Wilson Colliard sighed with satisfaction and returned his own weapon to a shoulder holster where it reposed without marring in the least the smooth lines of the smoking jacket. "There we are," he said. "Once again, my apologies. Now all that's out of the way and I have the opportunity to make you welcome. I have a very nice cocktail sherry which I think you might like. It's bone dry with a very nutty taste to it. Or perhaps you might care for something stronger?"

"The sherry sounds fine."

Colliard led his guest through rooms furnished as impeccably as he himself was dressed. He seated Michael Haig in one of a pair of green leather tub chairs on opposite sides of a small marble cocktail table. While he set about filling two glasses from a cutglass decanter, the younger man gazed out the window.

"Quite a view," he said.

"Central Park does look best when you're a good ways above it. But then so many things do. It's a great pleasure for me, sitting at this window."

"I can imagine."

"You can see for miles on a clear day. Pity there aren't more of them. When I was your age the air was clearer, but then at your age I could never have afforded an apartment anything like this one." The older man took a chair for himself, placed the two glasses of sherry on the table. "Well, well," he said. "So you're Michael Haig. The most promising young assassin in a great many years."

"You honor me."

"I merely echo what I've been given to understand. Your reputation precedes you."

"If I have a reputation, I'm sure it's a modest one. But you, sir. You're a legend."

"That union leader was one of yours, wasn't he? Head of the rubber workers or whatever he was? Nice bit of business the way you managed that decoy operation. And then you had to shoot downhill at a moving target. Very interesting the way you put all of that together."

Haig bared his bright white teeth in a smile that gave his otherwise unremarkable face a foxlike cast. "I patterned that piece of work on a job that went down twenty years ago. An Ecuadorian minister of foreign affairs, I think it was."

"Ah."

"One of yours, I think."

"Ah."

"Imitation, I assure you, is definitely the sincerest form of flattery in this case. If I do have a reputation, sir, I owe not a little of it to you."

"How kind of you to say so," Colliard said. His fingers curled around the stem of his glass. "The occasion would seem to call for a toast, but what sort of toast? No point in honoring the memory of those we've put in the ground. They're dead and gone. I never think about them. I've found it's best not to."

"I agree."

"We could drink to reputations and to legends."

"Fine."

"Or we could just drink to the line of work we're in. It's a crazy business, Lord knows, but it has its points."

They raised their glasses and drank.

"When I was young," Colliard was saying, "I drank whiskey on occasion. A highball or two in the evening, say. And I often had a martini before dinner. Not when I was working, of course. I've never had alcohol in any form when I was on a job. But between jobs I'd have spirits now and then. But I stopped that altogether."

"Why was that?"

"I decided that they are damaging. I'm not talking about what they might do to one's liver so much as what they do to one's brain. I think they dull one's edge like a file drawn across a knife blade. Wine's another matter entirely. In moderation, of course."

"Of course."

"But I'm rambling, Michael. You don't want to hear all of this. I've been talking for an hour now."

"And I've been hanging on every word, sir. This is the sort of thing I want to hear."

"You're just taking this all in and filing it all away, aren't you?"

"Yes, I am," Haig admitted. "Everything you can tell me about the way you operate and . . . and even the way you live, your whole style. If there were fan clubs in our profession I guess I'd be the president of yours."

"You flatter me."

"It's not flattery, sir. And it's not entirely unselfish, believe me." Haig lowered his eyes. He had long lashes, the older man noted, and his hands, one of them now in repose upon the little marble table, were possessed of a certain sensitivity. The fellow had no flair, but then he was young, unfinished. He himself had been relatively undefined at that age.

"I know I can learn from you," Michael Haig went on. "I've already learned a good deal from you, you know. Oh, it's hard to separate hard fact from legend, but I've picked up a lot from what I've heard about your career. Even though we've never met before, what I've known about you has helped form my whole attitude toward our profession."

"Really."

"Yes. Some months ago I had a problem, or at least it seemed like a problem to me. The, uh, the target was a woman."

"The client's wife?"

"Yes. You don't know the case?"

Colliard smiled, shook his head. "It's almost always the client's wife," he said. "But do continue. I gather this was the first time you had a woman for a target?"

"Yes, it was."

"And I gather further that it bothered you?"

Haig frowned at the question. "I *think* it bothered me," he said. "The idea of it seemed to bother me. I certainly wasn't afraid that I couldn't do it. If you pull a trigger, why should it matter to you what's standing in front of you? But, oh, I had difficulty with self-image, I guess you might say. It's one thing putting the touch to some powerful man who ought to be able to look out for himself and another thing entirely doing the same to a defenseless woman."

"The weaker sex," Colliard murmured.

"But then I asked myself, 'What about Wilson Colliard? How would he feel about a situation like this?' And that straightened me out, because I knew you'd killed women in your career, and I suppose what I told myself was that if it was all right for you to do, well, it was all right for me."

"And you went ahead and fulfilled the assignment."

"Yes."

"With no difficulty?"

"None." Michael Haig smiled, and Colliard felt there was pride in the smile. Proud as a puppy, he thought, and every bit as eager. "I killed her with a knife," he said. "Made it look like a burglary."

"And it felt no different than if she had been a man?"

"No different at all. There was that thrilling moment when I did it, that sensation that's always there, but it was no different from the way it always was."

Then a shadow flickered on the younger's man face, and Colliard, amused, left him wondering for a moment before rescuing him. "Yes," he said, "that little shiver of delight and triumph and something more. It's always there for me, too, Michael. In case you were wondering."

"I was, sir."

"The best people always get a thrill out of it, Michael. We don't do it for the thrill, of course. We do it for the money. But there's a touch of excitement in the act and it would be puerile to deny it. Don't bother worrying about it."

"I don't know that I was worried, exactly. But thank you, sir."

Colliard smiled. Now of whom did this young man remind him? The eagerness, the sincerity—God, the almost painful sincerity. It all held a sense of recognition, but recognition of whom? His own younger self? The son he had never sired? Those were the standard echoes one got, weren't they?

Yet he didn't really think he'd been very much like Michael Haig in his own younger days, not really. Had there been a veteran hand at the game whom he'd idolized? Certainly not. Could he ever, at his most callow, have been capable of playing the role Haig was playing in this conversation? No. God, no.

Nor would he have wanted a son like this youth, or indeed any sort of son at all. Women were a pleasure, certainly, like good food and good wine, like anything beautiful and luxurious and costly. But they were to be enjoyed and discarded. One didn't want to *own* one, and one surely wouldn't care to breed with them, to produce offspring, to litter the landscape with Xerox copies of oneself.

And yet he could not deny that he was enjoying this afternoon. The younger man's company was refreshing in its way, there was no denying that, and the idolatry he provided was pleasant food for the ego.

And it was not as if he had any pressing engagements.

"So you'd like to hear me talk about . . . what? My life and times? My distinguished career?"

"I'd like that very much."

"Anecdotes and bits of advice? The perspective gained through years at the top of this crazy business? All that sort of thing?"

"All of that. And anything else you'd care to tell me."

Wilson Colliard considered for a moment, then rose to his feet. "I'm going to smoke a cigar," he announced. "I allow myself one or two a day. They're Havanas, not terribly hard to get if you know someone. I acquired a taste for them, oh, it must be twenty years ago. I did a job of work down there, you see. But I suppose you know the story."

"I don't, and I'd love to hear it."

"Perhaps you will. Perhaps you will, Michael. But first may I bring a cigar for you?"

Michael Haig accepted the cigar. Somehow this did not surprise Wilson Colliard in the least.

As the afternoon wore on, Colliard found himself increasingly at ease in the role of reminiscent sage. Never before had he trotted out his memories like this for the entertainment and education of another. Oh, in recent years he had become increasingly inclined to sit at this window and look back over the years, but this had heretofore been a silent and solitary pursuit. It was quite a different matter to be giving voice to one's memories and to have another person on hand, worshipful and attentive, to utter appropriate syllables and draw out one's own recollections. Why, he was telling young Haig things he hadn't even bothered to think about in years, and in so doing he was making mental connections and developing perceptions he'd never had before.

With the cigars extinguished and fresh glasses of sherry poured, Colliard leaned back and said, "Now how far are we with our Assassin's Credo, Michael? Point the first—minimize risk. And point the second—seize the moment, strike while the iron is hot, all those banalities. Is that all we've established so far? It's certainly taken me a great many words to hammer out those two points. You know, I think the third principle is more important than either of them."

"And what is that, sir?"

"Look to your reputation."

"Ah."

"Reputation," Colliard said. "It's all one has going for oneself in this business, Michael. We have no bankable assets, you and I. We have only our reputations. And what reputations we possess are underground matters. We can't hire public relations men or press agents to give us standing. We have to depend wholly upon word of mouth. We must make ourselves known to those who might be inclined to engage our services, and they have to be supremely confident of our skill, our reliability, our discretion."

"Yes."

"We are paid in advance, Michael. Our clients must be able to take it for granted that once a fee has been passed to us the target is as good as dead. And, because the client himself is a party to criminal homicide, he must be assured that whatever fate befalls the assassin, the client will not be publicly involved. Skill, reliability, discretion. Reputation, Michael. It's everything to us."

They were silent for a moment. Wilson Colliard aimed his eyes out the window at the expanse of green far below. But his gaze was not focused on the park. He was looking off into the middle distance, seeing across time.

Tentatively Haig said, "I suppose if a man does good work, sooner or later he develops a good reputation."

"Sooner or later."

"You make it sound as though there's a better way to go about it."

"Oh, there is," Colliard agreed. "Sometimes circumstances are such that you can be your own advertising man, your own press agent, your own public relations bureau. Now and then you will find yourself with the opportunity to act with a certain flair that captures the public imagination so dramatically, so vividly, that it will go on to serve as the very cornerstone of your professional reputation for the remainder of your life. When such a chance comes to you, Michael, you have to take hold of it."

"I think—"

"Yes?"

"I think I know the case you mean, sir."

"It's quite possible that you do."

"I was wondering if you would mention it. I almost brought it up myself. I don't know how many times I've heard the story. It's at the very heart of the legend of Wilson Colliard."

"Indeed. 'The Legend of Wilson Colliard.' "

"But you *are* a legend, sir. And the story—I hope you'll tell me just what did and didn't happen. I've heard several versions and it's hard to know where the truth leaves off."

Colliard smiled indulgently. "Suppose you tell me what you've heard. If I'm to tell you the truth it wouldn't hurt me to know first how the legend goes. If the legend's better than the truth I'd probably be well advised to leave well enough alone."

"Well, from what I've heard, you accepted two assignments at about the same time. A businessman in New Jersey, I believe in Camden—"

"Trenton, actually," Colliard said. "Not that it makes any substantial difference. Neither city has ever been possessed of anything you might be inclined to call charm. Of course, this was some time ago and the urban blight was less pronounced then, but even so, both Trenton and Camden were towns no one ever went to without a good reason. My client manufactured bicycle tires. The business is long gone now, of course. I believe some bicycle manufacturer bought up the firm and absorbed it. My client's name—well, names don't really matter, do they?"

"And he wanted you to murder his wife."

"Indeed he did. Men so often do. If they want their mistresses killed they're apt to perform the deed on their own, but they call a professional when they want an instant divorce."

"And before you could conclude the assignment, a woman hired you to kill her husband."

"It's an interesting thing," Colliard said. "When a woman wants her husband done away with she's very much apt to hire help, but what's odd is she more often than not engages the services of a rank amateur. The newspapers are full of that sort of thing. Typically the woman works it all out with her lover, who's likely to be some rough-diamond type out of a James M. Cain novel. And the paramour knows someone who went to jail once for passing bad checks, and the bad-check artist knows somebody who served time for assault, and ultimately an exceedingly sloppy operation is mounted, and either the woman is swindled out of a couple of thousand dollars by a man who hasn't the slightest intention of killing anybody or else the husband is indeed killed and the police have everybody in custody before the body's had time to go cold. Interesting how often women operate in that fashion."

"Well, after you'd accepted both assignments, and of course you'd been paid in front by both clients—"

"A matter of personal policy."

"—Then you discovered that your two clients were husband and wife, and each had engaged you to murder the other."

"And what did I do?"

"According to what I've heard, the husband hired you first, and so the first thing you did was murder the wife."

Wilson Colliard nodded, smiling gently at a memory. "The husband had to go to Chicago on business. We scheduled the affair for that time. I called him at his hotel there to make very certain that he was indeed out of town. Then I went to his home. He and his wife shared an enormous Victorian pile of a house in the heart of Trenton. It was still a decent neighborhood at the time. By now the old house has probably been partitioned into a half dozen apartments. But that's off the point, isn't it? I went there and did what I was supposed to do. Made it look like a burglary, left some signs of forced entry, overturned dresser drawers, and added a few professional flourishes. I killed the bitch with a knife from her very own kitchen. I thought that was a nice touch."

"And of course the police figured it as a burglary."

"Of course they did. A burglary for gain followed by a murder on impulse. There was never the slightest suspicion of my client. He was rid of a wife and home free."

The younger man was breathing more quickly and his face was slightly flushed. "And then," he said.

"Yes?"

"Then you killed him."

"Indeed. Why would I do a thing like that?"

"Because the wife had hired you and once you accepted a fee the target was as good as dead. Of course you didn't have to kill the man. The only person who knew you'd been hired to kill him was the woman who hired you, and she was already dead. You could have kept the fee she paid you and done nothing to earn it and no one would ever have known the difference. But you were true to the ethics of the profession, true to your own personal ethics, and so you killed him all the same."

"I waited almost a month," Colliard said: "I didn't want his death to look like murder, and I didn't even want it to take place in Trenton, so I waited until he made another trip, this time a short one to Philadelphia. I followed him there, stole a car off the street, dogged his footsteps until they led off a curb, and then performed vehicular homicide. He turned in my direction just as the car was about to remove him from this life, and do you know, I can still see the expression on his face. I don't know whether he recognized my face through the windshield or whether he simply recognized that he was about to be struck down and killed. Facial expressions at such times are distressingly ambiguous, you see. Be that as it may, the car did the job and I had no trouble making a clean getaway."

"So it really happened that way," Haig said, eyes shining. "And then your reputation was made. Everyone knew that when Colliard took an assignment the target was a dead man."

"Yes. They all knew."

"So the legend is true."

"The Legend of Wilson Colliard," Colliard intoned. "It is an effective legend, isn't it? And now do you see what I meant when I said a man can see to the growth of his own reputation?"

"I certainly do. But isn't it really just a question of being true to your professional standards and ethics? Oh, I can see how you must have functioned as your own press agent and all that, because you would have had to be the source of the legend. Only the man and the woman knew they'd hired you, and even they didn't know that you were hired by both of them, so the story could never have gotten out if you hadn't done something to spread it in the first place. But as far as what you did, well, that was a matter of behaving professionally."

"Do you think so?" Colliard raised his prominent white eyebrows. "Don't you think it might have been more professional to keep the woman's fee and not kill her husband? After all, she was in the grave and was thus certain to remain silent. The only reason to kill her husband was for publicity purposes. Otherwise, Michael, I'd have been better advised to adhere to the first principle of minimizing risk. But by performing the second murder I assured myself of a reputation."

"Of course," Haig said. "You're absolutely right. I should have realized that."

Colliard made a tent of his fingertips. "Ah, Michael," he said, "there's more to it than you could possibly realize. It's interesting that the legend is incomplete. You know, I think this is really one of those rare occasions wherein the truth is more dramatic than the legend."

"How do you mean?"

"This crazy business of ours. Wheels within wheels, complexities underlying complexities. I wonder, Michael, if you have a sufficiently Byzantine mind to distinguish yourself in your chosen profession."

"I don't understand."

"The woman never hired me."

Michael Haig stared.

"Never hired me, never knew of my existence as far as I know. She and I didn't set eyes one upon the other until the night I stuck a carbon-steel Sabatier chef's knife between her ribs. For all I know the poor woman adored her husband and never would have harmed him for the world."

"But—"

"So I killed her and went on my way, Michael, and then about a month later I happened to be in Philadelphia for reasons I can't at the moment recall, not that they matter, and whom did I chance to see emerging from Bookbinder's after a presumably satisfying lunch than the Bicycle Tire King of Trenton. Do you know, the mind is capable of extraordinary quantum leaps. All at once I saw the whole thing plain, saw just the shape the entire legend would take. All I had to do was kill the fool and my place in my profession was assured. It was the sort of thing people would talk about forever, and everything they said could only redound to my benefit. I followed him, I stole a car, and—" he spread his hands "—and the rest is history. Or legend, if you prefer."

"That's . . . that's incredible."

"I saw an opportunity and I grasped it before it could get away."

"You just killed him for—"

"For the benefit that could not help but accrue to my reputation. Killed him without a fee, you might say, but there's no question but that his death paid me more handsomely in the long run than any murder I ever undertook for immediate gain. Overnight I became the standard of the profession. I stood head and shoulders above the competition as far as potential clients were concerned. I had an edge over men with infinitely more distinguished careers, men who had far more years in the business than I. And what gave me this advantage? An elementary hit-and-run killing of a former client, an act that but for the ensuing publicity would have been pointless beyond belief. Remarkable, isn't it?"

"It's better than the legend," Michael Haig said. There was a film of perspiration on his upper lip and he wiped at it with his forefinger. "Better than the legend. If people knew what you actually did—"

"I think it's ever so much better that they don't, Michael. Oh, if I were to write memoirs for posthumous publication it's the sort of material I'd be inclined to include, but I'm not the sort to write my memoirs, I'm afraid. No, I think I'd rather let the legend go on as it stands. It wouldn't do me much good if my public knew that Wilson Colliard was a man who once killed one of his clients for no reason at all. My reputation has been carefully designed to build a client's confidence and that's the sort of revelation that might have the opposite effect entirely."

"I don't know what to say."

"Then don't say anything at all," Colliard advised. "But let me just pour us each one final tot of sherry."

"I've had quite a bit already."

"It's very light stuff," Colliard said. "One more won't hurt you." And, returning with the filled glasses, he added, "We ought to drink to legends. May the truth never interfere with them."

The younger man took a sip. Then, when he saw his host toss off his drink in a single swallow, he imitated his example and drank off the rest of his own sherry. Wilson Colliard nodded, satisfied with the way things had gone. He could scarcely recall a more pleasant afternoon.

"Minimize your risks," he said. "Seize the moment. And look to your professional reputation."

"The three points of the Assassin's Credo," Haig said.

"Three of the four points."

"Oh?" The younger man grinned in anticipation. "You mean there's a fourth point?"

"Oh, yes." Colliard studied him, paying close attention to his guest's eyes. "A fourth point."

"Are you going to tell me what it is?"

"Squash the competition."

"Oh?"

"When it's convenient," Colliard said. "And when it's useful. There's no point doing anything about the bunglers. But when someone turns up who's talented and resourceful and not without a sense of the dramatic, and when you have the opportunity to wipe him out, why, it's just good business to do so. There are only so many really top jobs available every year, you know, and one doesn't want them spread too thin. Of course when you eliminate a competitor you don't noise it around. That sort of thing's kept secret. But there have been eight times over the years when I've had a chance to put the fourth principle into play."

"And you've seized the opportunity?"

"I could hardly do otherwise, could I?" Colliard smiled. "You're number nine, Michael. That last glass of sherry had poison in it, I'm afraid. You can probably feel the numbness spreading. It already shows in your eyes. No, don't even try to get up. You won't be able to accomplish anything. Don't blame yourself. You were doomed from the start, poor boy. I shouldn't have agreed to see you this afternoon if I hadn't decided to, uh, purge you from the ranks."

The younger man's face was a study in horror. Colliard eyed him equably. Already he was beginning to feel that familiar sensation, the excitement, the thrill.

"You were quite good," he said charitably. "For as long as you lasted you were quite good indeed. Otherwise I'd not have bothered with you. Oh, Michael, it's a crazy business, isn't it? Believe me, lad, you're lucky to be getting out of it."

The Tulsa Experience

They were teasing me Friday at the office. Sharon told me to be sure and send her a postcard, the way she always does, and I said what I always say, that I'd be back before the postcard reached her. And Warren asked which airline I was flying, and when I told him he very solemnly pulled out a quarter and handed it to me, telling me to buy some flight insurance and put him down as beneficiary.

Lee said, "Where's it going to be this time, Dennis? Acapulco? Macao? The south of France?"

"Tulsa," I said.

"Tulsa," he said. "Would that be Tulsa, Spain, on the Costa Brava? Or do you mean Tulsa, Nepal, gateway to the Himalayas?"

"This will come as a shock to you," I said, "but it's Tulsa, Oklahoma."

"Tulsa, Oklahoma," he marveled. "So the Gold Dust Twins are going to glamorous Tulsa, Oklahoma. I suppose Harry is up to it, but are you sure your heart can handle the excitement?"

"I'll try to pace myself," I said.

Harry and I are not twins, Gold Dust or otherwise. He's my brother, two years older than I, and aside from our vacations we actually see very little of each other.

Harry, who has never married, still lives in the row house in Woodside where we grew up. After college he helped in the store and took over the business when Dad retired. The house was left to both of us when our parents died, but we worked out a way for him to buy my share.

I was married for several years, but I've been divorced for longer than I was married, and I doubt I'll marry again. I have a nice apartment on East Eighty-third Street. It's small but it suits me, and it's rent-controlled. Work is a short bus ride away, a walk in good weather.

I had taken the bus that morning, although the weather was nice, because I had my suitcase with me. I worked right through lunch hour and then took the rest of the afternoon off and caught a cab to the airport. I got there over an hour before flight time and Harry was already there, his bag checked. "Well," he said, punching me affectionately on the shoulder. "You ready for the Tulsa experience, Denny?"

"I sure am," I said.

I've been at Langford Corporation for almost seventeen years. I had another job for a year and a half when I first got out of college, and then I came to Langford, and I've been with the company ever since. So for the past five years I've been entitled to four weeks of paid vacation a year. I take a week in the spring, a week in the summer, a week in the fall, and a week in the winter, and Harry arranges to close his store during those weeks. When we first started doing this he let his employees take over, but that didn't work out so well, and it's simpler and easier just to lock the doors for a week.

And that's really about the only time we see each other. Each season we pick a city, somewhere right here in the United States, and we take rooms in a nice hotel and make sure we experience the place to the hilt.

Boston was the third city we visited together, or maybe it was the fourth. I could stop and figure it out, but it doesn't matter; the point is that there was one of those multiscreen presentations in a theater near Quincy Market, giving you the history of the city and an armchair tour of the area. *The Boston Experience*, they called it, and ever since we've used that phrase to describe our travels to one another. After Boston we had the Atlanta experience. Now we were going to have the Tulsa experience, and three months ago, give or take a week, we were having the San Diego experience.

I can understand why Lee teases me. I have never been to London or Paris or Rome, and I don't know that I'll ever get out of this country at all. We've talked about it, Harry and I, but whenever it comes time to plan a trip we always wind up choosing an American city. I guess it's not glamorous, and maybe we're missing something, but we always have a great time, so why change?

Founded in 1879, Tulsa has a population of 360,919, and is the second-largest city in Oklahoma. (Oklahoma City, the capital, is larger by about forty thousand; we have not yet had the Oklahoma City experience.) Tulsa is 750 feet above sea level, located in the heart of a major oil- and gas-producing area. More than six hundred energy-oriented firms employ upward of thirty thousand people.

We reviewed this and other facts about Tulsa during our flight. Harry had done the planning, so he had the guidebooks, and we read passages aloud to one another. We both ordered martinis when the stewardess came around with the drinks cart. Harry's not a big drinker, and I hardly drink at all except when we travel. But the drinks are free in first class and it seems silly not to have one.

We always fly first class. The seats are more comfortable and they treat you with special care. It costs more, of course, and it may not really be worth the difference, but it helps make the trip special. And we can afford it. I earn a decent salary, and Harry has always done well with the store, and neither of us is given to high living. Harry has always lived alone, as I believe I mentioned, and my own marriage was childless, and my wife has long since remarried so I don't have any alimony to pay. That makes it easy enough for us to fly first class and stay at a good hotel and eat in the best restaurants. We don't throw money around like drunken sailors, or even like Tulsa oilmen, but we treat ourselves well.

There was an in-flight movie, but we didn't bother watching it. It was more interesting to read the guidebooks and discuss which attractions appealed and which we thought we could safely pass up. The average person would probably think that a week would be more than time enough to experience everything a city like Tulsa has to offer, but he would be very much mistaken.

You've probably heard jokes about Philadelphia, for example. That they had a contest, and first prize was a week in Philadelphia while second prize was two weeks. Well, we've had the Philadelphia experience, and a week was nowhere near enough to experience the city to the fullest. We did well, we went just about everywhere we really wanted to go, but there were still quite a few attractions we had to pass up with some regret.

The flight was enjoyable. Harry had the aisle seat this time, so he got to flirt a little with the stewardess. For my part, I was able to look out the window during our approach to Tulsa. It was still light out, but even on night flights I get a kick out of seeing the lights of the city below, as if they're all lit up just to welcome the two of us.

They delivered our rental car just minutes after our bags came off the luggage carousel. The car was a full-size Olds with a plush velour interior, very quiet and luxurious. Back home I don't even own a car, and all Harry has is the six-year-old panel truck with the name of the store painted on its sides. We could have managed just as well with a subcompact, but if you shop around you can usually get a really nice car for only a few dollars more. We'd had a great deal on a Lincoln Town Car in Denver, with free mileage and no charge for the full insurance coverage, for example.

We stayed downtown at the Westin on Second Street. Harry had booked us adjoining rooms on the luxury level. A double room or even a small suite would have been a lot less expensive, but we both like our privacy, as much as we enjoy being together on our vacations. And, as you probably have gathered by now, we don't stint on these trips. If we have one rule, it's to treat ourselves to what we want.

We made it an early night, unpacking, getting settled, and orienting ourselves in the hotel. First thing after breakfast the next day we took a Gray Line bus tour of Tulsa, which is what we always do when we can. It gives you a wonderful overview of the city and you don't have to find your own way around. You get to drive past some attractions that you might not be interested enough to see if they required a special trip, but that are certainly worth viewing through the window of the bus. And you pick up a familiarity with the place that makes it a lot easier to get around during the remainder of the stay. Harry and I are both sold on bus tours, and it's disappointing when a city doesn't have them.

The tour was a good one, and it took most of the morning. After lunch we went to the Thomas Gilcrease Institute of American History and Art. They have a wonderful collection of western art, with works by Remington, Moran, Charles Russell, and a great many others. The collection of Indian artifacts was also outstanding, but we spent so much time looking at the paintings that we didn't really have time to do the Indian collection justice.

"We'll get back during the week," Harry said.

We had dinner at a really nice restaurant just a short walk from our hotel. The menu was northern Italian, and they made their own pasta. We took a long walk afterward. When we got back to the hotel Harry wanted to have a swim in the pool, but I was ready to call it a night. I've found it's important to not try to do too much, especially the first couple of days. I took a long soak in the tub, watched a movie on HBO, and made an early night of it.

They brought in Tulsa's first oil well in 1901, and Tulsa invited oilmen to "come and make your homes in a beautiful little city that is high and dry, peaceful and orderly, where there are good churches, stores, schools, and banks, and where our ordinances prevent the desolation of our homes and property by oil wells."

Sunday morning we went to services at Boston Avenue United Methodist Church, which had been pointed out to us on the Gray Line tour. Neither Harry nor I go to church as an ordinary thing, and we weren't raised as Methodists to begin with, but that's the whole point of vacation, to get away from the workaday world and experience something different. Why, I hardly ever go to museums in New York, where we have some of the best in the world, but when I am in another city I can't get enough of them.

That afternoon, though, we tried a different sort of cultural experience and drove over to Bell's Amusement Park. They had a big old wooden roller coaster, three water slides, a log ride, and a sky ride and a pair of miniature golf courses. It was a little cold for the water slides but we did everything else, laughing and shouting and shoving each other like children. Harry threw darts at balloons until he won a stuffed panda, and then he gave it to the first little girl he saw.

"Now in the future," he told her, "don't you take pandas from strange men." And we laughed, and her mother and father laughed, and we went off to play miniature golf one more time.

There was a restaurant called Louisiane that we'd seen a few blocks from the church, and where we were planning to go for dinner. But after we got back to the hotel we arranged to meet in the bar downstairs, and when I got there Harry was knee-deep in conversation with a handsome woman with short dark hair and a full figure. He introduced her as Margaret Cummings, up from Fort Worth for the weekend.

I joined them for a quick drink, and then Harry took me aside and asked if I'd mind if he took Margaret to dinner. "I was talking to her at the pool last night," he said, "and the thing is, she's going back home tomorrow." I told him don't be silly, of course I didn't mind, and wished him luck.

So I ate right there in the hotel myself, and had a fine meal, and then went for a little walk after dinner. At breakfast the next day Harry grinned and said he'd had some fun with Margaret, and she'd given him her address and phone in case he ever got to Fort Worth. We've been to Dallas, and enjoyed that very much, and made a visit or two to Fort Worth at that time, taking in the Amon Carter Museum and some other attractions, so I doubt we'll be ready for the Fort Worth experience for quite a while yet.

"I was sorry to leave you stranded," Harry said, but I told him not to be silly. "You never know," I said. "Maybe we'll both get lucky here in Tulsa."

We started off the morning with an industrial tour of the Frankoma pottery. We both love industrial tours, and take advantage of them every chance we get. One of the highlights of the St. Louis experience was a tour of the Anheuser-Busch brewery, and we followed it up a day later with a half-hour tour of Bardenheier's Wine Cellars, followed by a half hour of wine-tasting. They didn't give you anything to drink at Frankoma, but it was very interesting to see how they made the pottery. Afterward they encouraged you to buy pottery in their shop, and they had some nice things for sale, but we didn't buy anything.

We almost never do. The National Park Service has a motto—"Take only snapshots, leave only footprints." (A side trip to Olympic National Park was one of the highlights of the Seattle experience.) We go them one better by not even taking snapshots. My apartment's too small to clutter it up with souvenirs, and Harry has the same attitude toward souvenirs, even though he has more than enough room for them at the house in Woodside.

As it is, I pick up one souvenir from every trip, a T-shirt with the name of the city we went to. My favorite so far is a fuchsia one from Indianapolis, with crossed black-and-white checkerboard racing flags on it to represent the Indianapolis 500. Most of the Tulsa T-shirts picture an oil well, and Thursday I finally picked out an especially nice one.

But I'm getting ahead of myself, aren't I?

Monday afternoon we went to the Tulsa Garden Center, and spent several hours there and nearby at the Park Department Conservatory. Tuesday we started out at the Historical Society Museum, then went to a synagogue to see the Gerson and Rebecca Fenster Gallery of Jewish Art, the largest collection of Judaica in the Southwest. From there we went to Oral Roberts University for a brief campus tour, and picked up tickets for a chamber music concert to be held the following evening.

We went to our rooms for a nap before dinner, arranging to meet in the cocktail lounge. This time I got there before Harry did, and I got into a conversation with a pretty young woman named Lylah. We were hitting it off pretty well, and then Harry joined us, and before you knew it a friend of Lylah's named Mary Eileen came by and made it a foursome. We had two rounds of drinks at a table and Harry said he hoped the two of them would join us for dinner.

Lylah and Mary Eileen exchanged glances, and then Mary Eileen said, "Why should a couple of nice fellows like you waste your money on dinner?"

Well, I won't say I was shocked, because I had the feeling that they were unusually quick to get friendly. Besides, this sort of thing has happened before. The Chicago experience, for example, included a couple of young ladies whose interest in us was purely professional, but we sure had a good time all the same.

The upshot of this was that Lylah came up to my room, and Mary Eileen went with Harry. I had some fun with Lylah, and she seemed happy with the hundred dollars I gave her. On her way out she gave me an engraved business card with just her first name and her phone number on it. Mary Eileen gave Harry one just like it, except with a different name, of course. They both had the same phone number.

"Take only snapshots," Harry said, tearing Mary Eileen's card in two. "Leave only footprints." And I did the same with Lylah's card. It wasn't likely we'd ever be back in Tulsa, and we wouldn't want to see those girls more than once this trip. The Gilcrease Institute might be worth a second visit, but not Lylah and Mary Eileen.

Wednesday we left town right after breakfast and drove fifty-five miles north to Bartlesville, where the founder of a big oil company set up a wildlife preserve with herds of bison, longhorn cattle, and all sorts of wild animals. We stayed right in the Olds and drove around, viewing them from the car. The complex includes a museum, and the western art and Plains Indian artifacts were magnificent, and just wonderfully displayed. They also had what was described as one of the finest collections of Colt weapons in the country, and I could believe it.

We wound up spending the whole day in Bartlesville, because there were other interesting attractions besides Woolaroc. We saw an exact replica of the state's first commercial drilling rig, we saw an exhibit on the development and uses of petroleum, and we saw a tower designed by Frank Lloyd Wright. North of Bartlesville in Dewey we paid a visit to the Tom Mix Museum and saw original costumes and cowboy gear from his movies along with film stills and other interesting items.

We finally got around to having dinner at Louisiane that night and just got to the concert on time at Oral Roberts. Afterward we roamed around the campus a bit, then took a lazy drive around Tulsa, just looking at people. There was a shopping mall Harry wanted to check out, but it was late by the time we got out of the concert so we decided we'd save that for tomorrow.

"We'll do some field work tomorrow afternoon and evening," Harry said, "and I figure Friday night we'll go for it."

I said that was fine with me. He'd been doing all the planning, and the Tulsa experience had been really fine so far.

When I had time to myself I'd read about Tulsa in the guidebook, or in some of the tourist brochures in the hotel room. I liked to pick up whatever information I could.

With the completion of the Arkansas River Navigation System, Tulsa has gained itself a water route to both the Great Lakes and the Gulf of Mexico. The port of Catoosa, three miles from Tulsa itself on Verdigris River, stands at the headwaters of the waterway and is presently America's westernmost inland water port.

Now you might think that a fact like that wouldn't stay with me, but it's funny how much of what we do and see and learn on these vacation trips remains in memory. It's a real education.

Thursday morning we went straight to the Philbrook Art Center after breakfast. It's set on over twenty acres and surrounded by gardens, and the collections ranged from Italian Renaissance paintings to Southeast Asian tradeware. It took the whole morning to do the place justice.

"I like Tulsa," I told Harry. "I really like it."

After lunch for a change of pace we went to the zoo in Mohawk Park. The performing elephants were the highlight, but just walking around and seeing the animals was enjoyable, too. Then toward the later part of the afternoon we went to that shopping mall and wandered around, and that was when I bought my souvenir T-shirt, a nice blue one with an oil well, of course, and the slogan "Progress and Culture." Harry thought it was a dopey slogan, but I liked the shirt. I still like it. The funny thing is nobody ever sees my T-shirts, because I wear a dress shirt and tie to the office every day, and even on weekends I'm afraid I'm not the T-shirt type. I wear them as undershirts beneath my dress shirts, or I'll wear them around the apartment, or to sleep in. I like having them, though, and you could say I'm developing quite a little collection, adding a new one every three months.

The Indianapolis shirt is my favorite so far, but I believe I mentioned that before.

We drove around Thursday night. We checked out the University of Tulsa campus and cruised around Mohawk Park. I was really glad we had the big car instead of an economy compact. I think it makes a difference.

I didn't sleep well Thursday night, and Harry said he was restless himself. We both had the impulse to skip the activity he had planned, but we stuck with it and

I'm glad we did. We drove ten miles south of the city to the Allen Ranch, where we were booked for a half-day trail ride on horseback through some really pretty country. Neither of us is much of a rider, but we've been on horseback on other vacations, and the horses they give you are always gentle and well trained. I knew I'd be sore for the next week or so, but it seemed like a small price to pay. We had a really good time, and the weather was perfect for it, too.

I showered as soon as we got back, and then I went downstairs for a whirlpool and sauna. That wouldn't do anything about the saddle sores, but it took some of the ache out of muscles that don't get much use back in New York.

Then I took a long nap and left a call so I'd be up in time for dinner. Dinner was just a light bite at a coffee shop because we were both keyed up and a big meal wouldn't have been a good idea even if we'd been in the mood for it.

We went to the shopping mall and prowled around there for a while, but we didn't find what we were looking for. Then we drove to the hospital and waited in the parking lot for twenty minutes or so without any success. We went back to the University of Tulsa campus and came very close there, but we aborted the mission at the last minute and drove to a supermarket we had researched the day before.

We parked where we could watch people entering and leaving. We were there twenty minutes or so when Harry nudged my arm and pointed to a woman getting out of a Japanese compact. We watched as she walked past us and into the market. I nodded, smiling.

"Bingo," he said.

He parked our car right next to her. She wasn't in there long, maybe another ten minutes, and she came out carrying her groceries in a plastic bag.

Harry had the window rolled down, and he called her over. "Miss," he said, "maybe you can help me. Would you know where this address is?"

She came over for a look. I was by the side of the car and I stepped up behind her and got her in a chokehold and clapped my other hand over her mouth so she couldn't make a sound. I dragged her into the shadows and kept the pressure on her throat and Harry got out of the car and hurried over and hit her three times, once in the solar plexus and twice in the pit of the stomach.

We'd bought supplies yesterday, including a roll of tape. She was pretty much unconscious from the chokehold so it was easy to tape her mouth shut and get her hands behind her back and tape her wrists together. Harry opened the back door and I got in back with her and he got behind the wheel and drove. I had her groceries in the back of the car with me, and her purse.

Harry headed for Mohawk Park and we drove right out onto the golf course. She came to in the car but she was all trussed up and there wasn't a thing she could do. When he stopped the car we dragged her outside and got her clothes off, and we took turns having fun with her. We both had a really wonderful time with her, we really did.

Finally Harry asked me if I was done and I had to say I was, and he told me in that case to go ahead and finish up. I told him it was his turn, but then he reminded me that he had done the nurse in San Diego. Don't ask me how I'd managed to forget that.

So it was my turn after all, and I got the belt out of my pants and strangled her with it. Then I took her arms and Harry took her legs and we carried her off the fairway and left her deep in the rough. You'd have to hook your tee shot real bad to get anywhere near her.

We threw her purse in a Dumpster outside a restaurant on Lewis Avenue. There was a Goodwill Industries collection box a few blocks away, and that's where we left her clothes. I would have liked to keep something, an intimate garment of some sort, but we never did that. *Take no snapshots, leave no footprints*—that's the National Park Service motto as we've adapted it for our own use.

I'd bought a Dustbuster the day before and I used it to go over the interior of the Olds very thoroughly. They'd vacuum the car after we turned it in, but you don't want to leave anything to chance. The Dustbuster went in another Dumpster, along with the roll of tape. And her bag of groceries, except for a box of Wheat Thins. I was pretty hungry, so I took those back and ate them in the room.

Saturday we pretty much took it easy. I went back for a second visit to the Gilcrease Institute but Harry passed that up and hung around the hotel pool instead. We were planning on another concert that evening but we spent a long time over dinner and wound up taking in a movie instead. Then back to the hotel for a quick brandy in the bar, and then up to bed.

And Sunday morning we flew back to New York.

Monday morning I was at my desk by nine, which was more than some of my fellow workers could claim. Sharon said she hadn't received my postcard, and as always I told her to keep watching the mailbox. Of course I hadn't sent one. Warren breezed in at a quarter to ten and said he guessed he'd wasted another twenty-five cents on flight insurance. I told him he could try again in August. "I'll have to," he said. "I can't quit now, I've got too much money invested."

Lee asked me where I'd be going in August. "Baghdad? Timbuktu? Or someplace really exotic, like Newark?"

I'm not sure. Buffalo, possibly. I'd like to see Niagara Falls. Or maybe Minneapolis–St. Paul. It's the right time of year for either of those cities. It's my turn to plan the trip, so I'll take my time and make the right decision.

In the meantime I go to my office every morning and read guidebooks evenings and weekends. Sometimes when I sit at my desk I'll think about the T-shirt I'm wearing, invisible under my dress shirt. I'll remember which one it is, and I'll take a moment to relive the Denver experience, or the Baltimore experience, or the Tulsa experience. Depending on what shirt I'm wearing.

Lee can tease me all he wants. I don't mind. Tulsa was *wonderful*.

Weekend Guests

We hadn't been in the house more than five minutes when Pete called. We were in the living room and I was trying to get Roz to calm down when the phone rang. I put her on the couch and went over to answer it.

"I can't talk to you," I told him. "We just this minute walked in and we got a little shock. It seems we had company."

"What do you mean?"

"I mean somebody came calling while we were spending the weekend at the lake. Forced the front door and turned the place upside down. Everything's a mess and Roz is hysterical and I'm not too happy myself."

"That's terrible, Eddie. They get much?"

"I don't even know what's missing. I told you, we just walked in. I have to run around now and start taking inventory and they left such a mess I don't even know where to start. You know, drawers upside down, that kind of thing."

"That's terrible, it really is. Look, you got things to do and I don't want to keep you. I just called to check that we're set for tonight."

I glanced over at the couch. "She's pretty shaky," I said, "but what the hell, she can always stay with friends if it bothers her to stay here alone."

"How about if I pick you up around nine-thirty?"

"Fine," I said. "I'll be waiting."

I was waiting out in front when he drove up in a large white panel truck. He pulled over to the curb and I opened the door and swung up onto the seat beside him.

"Well, you look real good," he said. "A few days in the sun didn't hurt you any. Roz all brown and beautiful?"

"She got a burn the first day and after that she kept out of the sun. Me, I never burn. I just lie there and soak it up like a storage battery or something. We had a great time, but what a shock to come home to the house and find some yo-yos turned the place inside out."

"They make much of a score?"

I shrugged. "They didn't get much cash because I never keep cash around the house. I generally have a couple of hundred dollars down at the bottom of my tobacco humidor and it's still there. Let's see. They took Roz's jewelry, except for what she had with her, and how much jewelry do you take to the lake? The insurance floater covers her jewelry up to ten thousand dollars, and I'd guess what she lost was probably worth two to three times that. So in that sense we took a beating, but on the other hand I didn't pay anywhere near fair market value for her stuff, so it's not that bad."

"Still, those were pieces she was crazy about. They get those ruby earrings?"

"Yeah, they went."

"That's a hell of a thing."

"She's not happy about it, I'll say that much. What else? Her full-length mink's in storage so they didn't get that, but she had some other furs in the closet that I don't know why she didn't put in storage, and of course they're gone now. They left the TV-stereo unit. You know the set, it's a big console unit, and for once I'm glad I bought it that way instead of picking up separate components, because evidently they decided it would be too much of a hassle to cart it out. But they took a couple of radios and a typewriter and little odds and ends like that."

"Hardly worth the trouble, it sounds like to me. What can you get for a secondhand radio?"

"Not much, I wouldn't think. Isn't that our turn coming up?"

"Uh-huh. So the jewelry was the main thing, right?"

I nodded. "They took a lot of stuff. They took one of my sport jackets, can you imagine that? I guess the son of a bitch saw something he liked and it was the right size for him."

"That's amazing. Which jacket?"

"The Black Watch plaid. The damn thing's three years old and I was frankly a little sick of it, but I'm positive it was hanging in the closet when we left, so I guess some penny-ante burglar doesn't care if he's wearing the latest styles or not."

"Amazing. You call the police?"

"I had no choice, Pete. I'll tell you something, the worst part of all this isn't what you lose when they rob you. It's the ordeal you wind up putting yourself through. We walked in there tired out from all that driving and the place looked like a cyclone hit it, and I called the fellow who takes care of my insurance and he told me I had to report the burglary to the police. He said nothing would be recovered but unless the incident's officially reported the company won't honor a claim. So we had these two plainclothes bulls over for half the afternoon, and Roz was shaky anyway and the cops knew they had to go through the motions but also knew it was a waste of time, and they're asking me like do I have the serial number from the typewriter, and who keeps track of that crap?"

"Nobody."

"Of course not. Even if you wrote it down you'd never remember where you put it."

"Or the crooks would steal the notebook along with the typewriter."

"Exactly. So they're asking me this garbage because it's their job, and in spite of myself I'm feeling guilty that I didn't know the serial number, and they're asking about the bill of sale for this thing or that thing, and who's got copies of things like that? Watch out, there's a kid on a bicycle."

"I see him, Eddie. You're jumpy as hell, you know that?"

"I'm sorry."

"I know not to run over kids on bicycles and I knew it was our turn coming up. It's not as if I never drove a truck before."

I put a hand on his arm. "Sorry," I said. "I *am* jumpy as hell and I'm sorry. Those cops, I finally told them enough was enough, and I poured drinks all around and everybody relaxed. They said off the record I could forget about seeing any of the stuff again, which I already knew, and I let them finish their drinks and got them the hell out of there. And I took Roz upstairs and got a handful of Valium into her."

"Not a whole handful, I hope."

"Maybe two pills."

"That's better."

"And I had one more drink for myself and then I put the plug in the jug because I didn't want to get loopy, not going out tonight. I almost called you and canceled out and opened the bottle again, but I figured that would be stupid."

"You sure?" He looked at me. "I could turn the car around, you know. There's other nights."

"Keep driving."

"You're absolutely sure?"

"Absolutely. But can you imagine guys like that?"

"You mean the cops?"

"No, I don't mean the cops. They're just doing their job. I mean the guys who ripped us off."

He laughed. "Maybe they're just doing their jobs, too, Eddie."

"That's some job, robbing people's homes. Can you imagine doing that?"

"No."

"Roz kept saying how she's always felt so safe and secure where we are, a good neighborhood and all, and how can she feel that way now? Well, that's nonsense, she'll get used to it again, but I know what she means."

"It's such an invasion of privacy."

"That's exactly what it is. People in her living space, you know what I mean? People in her house, getting dirt on her carpets, going through her things, sticking their noses into her private life. An invasion of privacy, that's exactly what it is. And for what, will you tell me that?"

"For ten cents on the dollar, and that's if they're lucky."

"If they get that much it's a lot. If they net two grand out of everything they took off us it's a hell of a lot, and in the process they gave us a bad day and put us to a lot of trouble and I don't know what it's going to cost to replace everything and clean up the mess they made. Going into people's houses like that, and that's nothing—suppose we were home?"

"Well, they probably were careful to make sure you weren't."

"Yeah, but if they're sloppy enough to rob us in the first place, how careful do they figure to be?"

We kicked it around some more. By the time we got to the gate I was feeling a whole lot calmer. I guess it helped to talk about it, and Pete was always easy to talk to.

He pulled the truck to a stop and I got out and opened the padlock and unfastened the chain, then swung the gate open. After the truck was through I closed the gate and locked it again. Then I climbed back into the truck and Pete cut across the lot to the warehouse.

"No trouble with the key, Eddie?"

"None."

"Good. What'd they do at your place, kick the door in?"

"Forced the lock with a crowbar, something like that."

"Slobs, it sounds like."

"Yeah, that's what they were. Slobs."

He maneuvered the truck, parking it with its back doors up against the loading dock. I climbed down and opened them, and while I was standing there the automatic door on the loading dock swung up. I had a bad second or two then, as if there'd be men with guns up on the dock, but of course it was empty. A second or two later the night watchman appeared through a door a dozen yards to our left. He gave us a wave, then took a drink of something from a brown paper bag.

Pete got out of the truck and we went over to the old man. "Thought I'd run the door open for you," he said. "Have a little something?"

He offered the paper bag to us. We declined without asking what it was and he took another little sip for himself. "You boys'll treat me right," he said. "Won't you, now?"

"No worries, Pops."

"You didn't have no trouble with that key, did you?"

"On the gate? No, it was a perfect fit."

"Now when you go out you'll break the chain so they won't know you had no key, right?"

"Takes too much time, Pops. Nobody's gonna suspect you and if they do they can't prove anything."

"They're gonna ask me questions," he whined.

"That's how you'll be earning your money. And they'll ask you questions whatever we do with the lock."

He wasn't crazy about it, but another sip from his bottle eased his mind some. "Guess you know what you're doing," he said. "Now be sure and tie me tight but not too tight, if you know what I mean. And I don't know about tape on my mouth."

"Well, that's up to you, Pops."

He decided on the tape after all. Pete got a roll of it from the truck, along with a coil of clothesline, and the three of us went inside. While Pete tied the old fellow up I got started stacking the color TVs in the truck. I made sure I arranged them compactly because I wanted to fit in as many as the truck would hold. It's not going to be a cinch, replacing all the jewelry Roz lost.

When This Man Dies

The night before the first letter came, he had Speckled Band in the feature at Saratoga. The horse went off at nine-to-two from the number one pole and Edgar Kraft had two hundred dollars on him, half to win and half to place. Speckled Band went to the front and stayed there. The odds-on favorite, a four-year-old named Sheila's Kid, challenged around the clubhouse turn and got hung up on the outside. Kraft was counting his money. In the stretch, Speckled Band broke stride, galloped home madly, was summarily disqualified, and placed fourth. Kraft tore up his tickets and went home.

So he was in no mood for jokes that morning. He opened five of the six letters that came in the morning mail, and all five were bills, none of which he had any prospect of paying in the immediate future. He put them in a drawer in his desk. There were already several bills in that drawer. He opened the final letter and was at first relieved to discover that it was not a bill, not a notice of payment due, not a threat to repossess car or furniture. It was, instead, a very simple message typed in the center of a large sheet of plain typing paper.

First a name:

Mr. Joseph H. Neimann

And below that:

When This Man Dies
You Will Receive
Five Hundred Dollars

He was in no mood for jokes. Trotters that lead all the way and then break in the stretch do not contribute to a man's sense of humor. He looked at the sheet of paper, turned it over to see if there was anything further on its reverse, turned it over again to read the message once more, picked up the envelope, saw nothing on it but his own name and a local postmark, said something unprintable about some idiots and their idea of a joke, and tore everything up and threw it away, message and envelope and all.

In the course of the next week he thought about the letter once, maybe twice. No more than that. He had problems of his own. He had never heard of anyone named Joseph H. Neimann and entertained no hopes of receiving five hundred dollars in the event of the man's death. He did not mention the cryptic message to his wife. When the man from Superior Finance called to ask him if he had any hopes of meeting his note on time, he did not say anything about the legacy that Mr. Neimann meant to leave him.

He went on doing his work from one day to the next, working with the quiet desperation of a man who knows his income, while better than nothing, will never quite get around to equaling his expenditures. He went to the track twice, won thirty dollars one night, lost twenty-three the next. He came quite close to forgetting entirely about Mr. Joseph H. Neimann and the mysterious correspondent.

Then the second letter came. He opened it mechanically, unfolded a large sheet of plain white paper. Ten fresh fifty-dollar bills fluttered down upon the top of his desk. In the center of the sheet of paper someone had typed:

Thank You

Edgar Kraft did not make the connection immediately. He tried to think what he might have done that would merit anyone's thanks, not to mention anyone's five hundred dollars. It took him a moment, and then he recalled that other letter and rushed out of his office and down the street to a drugstore. He bought a morning paper, turned to the obituaries.

Joseph Henry Neimann, 67, of 413 Park Place, had died the previous afternoon in County Hospital after an illness of several months' duration. He left a widow, three children, and four grandchildren. Funeral services would be private, flowers were please to be omitted.

He put three hundred dollars in his checking account and two hundred dollars in his wallet. He made his payment on the car, paid his rent, cleared up a handful of small bills. The mess in his desk drawer was substantially less baleful, although by no means completely cleared up. He still owed money, but he owed less now than before the timely death of Joseph Henry Neimann. The man from Superior Finance had been appeased by a partial payment; he would stop making a nuisance of himself, at least for the time being.

That night, Kraft took his wife to the track. He even let her make a couple of impossible hunch bets. He lost forty dollars and it hardly bothered him at all.

When the next letter came he did not tear it up. He recognized the typing on the envelope, and he turned it over in his hands for a few moments before opening it, like a child with a wrapped present. He was somewhat more apprehensive than child with present, however; he couldn't help feeling that the mysterious benefactor would want something in return for his five hundred dollars.

He opened the letter. No demands, however. Just the usual sheet of plain paper, with another name typed in its center:

Mr. Raymond Andersen

And below that:

When This Man Dies
You Will Receive
Seven Hundred Fifty Dollars.

For the next few days he kept telling himself that he did not wish anything unpleasant for Mr. Raymond Andersen. He didn't know the man, he had never heard of him, and he was not the sort to wish death upon some total stranger. And yet—

Each morning he bought a paper and turned at once to the death notices, searching almost against his will for the name of Mr. Raymond Andersen. *I don't wish him harm,* he would think each time. But seven hundred fifty dollars was a happy sum. If something were going to happen to Mr. Raymond Andersen, he might as well profit by it. It wasn't as though he was doing anything to cause Andersen's death. He was even unwilling to wish for it. But if something happened . . .

Something happened. Five days after the letter came, he found Andersen's obituary in the morning paper. Andersen was an old man, a very old man, and he had died in his bed at a home for the aged after a long illness. His heart jumped when he read the notice with a combination of excitement and guilt. But what was there to feel guilty about? He hadn't done anything. And death, for a sick old man like Raymond Andersen, was more a cause for relief than grief, more a blessing than a tragedy.

But why would anyone want to pay him seven hundred fifty dollars?

Nevertheless, someone did. The letter came the following morning, after a wretched night during which Kraft tossed and turned and batted two possibilities back and forth—that the letter would come and that it would not. It did come, and it brought the promised seven hundred fifty dollars in fifties and hundreds. And the same message:

Thank You

For what? He had not the slightest idea. But he looked at the two-word message again before putting it carefully away.

You're welcome, he thought. *You're entirely welcome.*

For two weeks no letter came. He kept waiting for the mail, kept hoping for another windfall like the two that had come so far. There were times when he would sit at his desk for twenty or thirty minutes at a time, staring off into space and thinking about the letters and the money. He would have done better keeping his mind on his work, but this was not easy. His job brought him five thousand dollars a year, and for that sum he had to work forty to fifty hours a week. His anonymous pen pal had thus far brought him a quarter as much as he earned in a year, and he had done nothing at all for the money.

The seven-fifty had helped, but he was still in hot water. On a sudden female whim his wife had had the living room recarpeted. The rent was due. There was another payment due on the car. He had one very good night at the track, but a few other visits took back his winnings and more.

And then the letter came, along with a circular inviting him to buy a dehumidifier for his basement and an appeal for funds from some dubious charity. He swept circular and appeal into his wastebasket and tore open the plain white envelope. The message was the usual sort:

Mr. Claude Pierce

And below the name:

When This Man Dies
You Will Receive
One Thousand Dollars.

Kraft's hands were shaking slightly as he put the envelope and letter away in his desk. One thousand dollars—the price had gone up again, this time to a fairly staggering figure. Mr. Claude Pierce. Did he know anyone named Claude Pierce? He did not. Was Claude Pierce sick? Was he a lonely old man, dying somewhere of a terminal illness?

Kraft hoped so. He hated himself for the wish, but he could not smother it. He hoped Claude Pierce was dying.

This time he did a little research. He thumbed through the phone book until he found a listing for a Claude Pierce on Honeydale Drive. He closed the book then and tried to put the whole business out of his mind, an enterprise foredoomed to failure. Finally he gave up, looked up the listing once more, looked at the man's name, and thought that this man was going to die. It was inevitable, wasn't it? They sent him some man's name in the mail, and then the man died, and then Edgar Kraft was paid. Obviously, Claude Pierce was a doomed man.

He called Pierce's number. A woman answered, and Kraft asked if Mr. Pierce was in.

"Mr. Pierce is in the hospital," the woman said. "Who's calling, please?"

"Thank you," Kraft said.

Of course, he thought. They, whoever they were, simply found people in hospitals who were about to die, and they paid money to Edgar Kraft when the inevitable occurred, and that was all. The why of it was impenetrable. But so few things made sense in Kraft's life that he did not want to question the whole affair too closely. Perhaps his unknown correspondent was like that lunatic on television who gave away a million dollars every week. If someone wanted to give Kraft money, Kraft wouldn't argue with him.

That afternoon he called the hospital. Claude Pierce had been admitted two days ago for major surgery, a nurse told Kraft. His condition was listed as *good*.

Well, he would have a relapse, Kraft thought. He was doomed—the letter writer had ordained his death. He felt momentarily sorry for Claude Pierce, and then he turned his attention to the entries at Saratoga. There was a horse named Orange Pips which Kraft had been watching for some time. The horse had a good post now, and if he was ever going to win, this was the time.

Kraft went to the track. Orange Pips ran out of the money. In the morning Kraft failed to find Pierce's obituary. When he called the hospital, the nurse told him that Pierce was recovering very nicely.

Impossible, Kraft thought.

For three weeks Claude Pierce lay in his hospital bed, and for three weeks Edgar Kraft followed his condition with more interest than Pierce's doctor could have displayed. Once Pierce took a turn for the worse and slipped into a coma. The nurse's voice was grave over the phone, and Kraft bowed his head, resigned to the inevitable. A day later Pierce had rallied remarkably. The nurse sounded positively cheerful, and Kraft fought off a sudden wave of rage that threatened to overwhelm him.

From that point on, Pierce improved steadily. He was released, finally, a whole man again, and Kraft could not understand quite what had happened. Something had gone wrong. When Pierce died, he was to receive a thousand dollars. Pierce had been sick, Pierce had been close to death, and then, inexplicably, Pierce had been snatched from the very jaws of death, with a thousand dollars simultaneously snatched from Edgar Kraft.

He waited for another letter. No letter came.

With the rent two weeks overdue, with a payment on the car past due, with the man from Superior Finance calling him far too often, Kraft's mind began to work against him. *When this man dies,* the letter had said. There had been no strings attached, no time limit on Pierce's death. After all, Pierce could not live forever. No one did. And whenever Pierce did happen to draw his last breath, he would get that thousand dollars.

Suppose something happened to Pierce—

He thought it over against his own will. It would not be hard, he kept telling himself. No one knew that he had any interest whatsoever in Claude Pierce. If he picked his time well, if he did the dirty business and got it done with and hurried off into the night, no one would know. The police would never think of him in the same breath with Claude Pierce, if police were in the habit of thinking in breaths. He did not know Pierce, he had no obvious motive for killing Pierce, and—

He couldn't do it, he told himself. He simply could not do it. He was no killer. And something as senseless as this, something so thoroughly absurd, was unthinkable.

He would manage without the thousand dollars. Somehow, he would live without the money. True, he had already spent it a dozen times over in his mind. True, he had been counting and recounting it when Pierce lay in a coma. But he would get along without it. What else could he do?

The next morning headlines shrieked Pierce's name at Edgar Kraft. The previous night someone had broken into the Pierce home on Honeydale Drive and had knifed Claude Pierce in his bed. The murderer had escaped unseen. No possible motive for the slaying of Pierce could be established. The police were baffled.

Kraft got slightly sick to his stomach as he read the story. His first reaction was a pure and simple onrush of unbearable guilt, as though he had been the man with the knife, as though he himself had broken in during the night to stab silently and flee promptly, mission accomplished. He could not shake this guilt away. He knew well enough that he had done nothing, that he had killed no one. But he had conceived of the act, he had willed that it be done, and he could not escape the feeling that he was a murderer, at heart if not in fact.

His blood money came on schedule. One thousand dollars, ten fresh hundreds this time. And the message. *Thank you.*

Don't thank me, he thought, holding the bills in his hand, holding them tenderly. Don't thank me!

Mr. Leon Dennison

When This Man Dies
You Will Receive
Fifteen Hundred Dollars.

Kraft did not keep the letter. He was breathing heavily when he read it, his heart pounding. He read it twice through, and then he took it and the envelope it had come in, and all the other letters and envelopes that he had so carefully saved, and he tore them all into little bits and flushed them down the toilet.

He had a headache. He took aspirin; but it did not help his headache at all. He sat at his desk and did no work until lunchtime. He went to the luncheonette around the corner and ate lunch without tasting his food. During the afternoon he found that, for the first time, he could not make heads or tails out of the list of entries at Saratoga. He couldn't concentrate on a thing, and he left the office early and took a long walk.

Mr. Leon Dennison.

Dennison lived in an apartment on Cadbury Avenue. No one answered his phone. Dennison was an attorney, and he had an office listing. When Kraft called it a secretary answered and told him that Mr. Dennison was in conference. Would he care to leave his name?

When this man dies.

But Dennison would not die, he thought. Not in a hospital bed, at any rate. Dennison was perfectly all right, he was at work and the person who had written all those letters knew very well that Dennison was all right, that he was not sick.

Fifteen hundred dollars.

But how, he wondered. He did not own a gun and had not the slightest idea how to get one. A knife? Someone had used a knife on Claude Pierce, he remembered. And a knife would probably not be hard to get his hands on. But a knife seemed somehow unnatural to him.

How, then? By automobile? He could do it that way, he could lie in wait for Dennison and run him down in his car. It would not be difficult, and it would probably be certain enough. Still, the police were supposed to be able to find hit-and-run drivers fairly easily. There was something about paint scrapings, or blood on your own bumper or something. He didn't know the details, but they always did seem to catch hit-and-run drivers.

Forget it, he told himself. You are not a killer.

He didn't forget it. For two days he tried to think of other things and failed miserably. He thought about Dennison, and he thought about fifteen hundred dollars and he thought about murder.

When this man dies—

One time he got up early in the morning and drove to Cadbury Avenue. He watched Leon Dennison's apartment, and he saw Dennison emerge, and when Dennison crossed the street toward his parked car Kraft settled his own foot on the accelerator and ached to put the pedal on the floor and send the car hurtling toward Leon Dennison. But he didn't do it. He waited.

So clever. Suppose he were caught in the act? Nothing linked him with the person who wrote him the letters. He hadn't even kept the letters, but even if he had, they were untraceable.

Fifteen hundred dollars—

On a Thursday afternoon he called his wife and told her he was going directly to Saratoga. She complained mechanically before bowing to the inevitable. He drove to Cadbury Avenue and parked his car. When the doorman slipped down to the corner for a cup of coffee, Kraft ducked into the building and found Leon Dennison's apartment. The door was locked, but he managed to spring the lock with the blade of a penknife. He was sweating freely as he worked on the lock, expecting every moment someone to come up behind him and lay a hand on his shoulder. The lock gave, and he went inside and closed it after him.

But something happened the moment he entered the apartment. All the fear, all the anxiety, all of this suddenly left Edgar Kraft. He was mysteriously calm now. Everything was prearranged, he told himself. Joseph H. Neimann had been doomed, and Raymond Andersen had been doomed, and Claude Pierce had been doomed, and each of them had died. Now Leon Dennison was similarly doomed, and he too would die.

It seemed very simple. And Edgar Kraft himself was nothing but a part of this grand design, nothing but a cog in a gigantic machine. He would do his part without worrying about it. Everything could only go according to plan.

Everything did. He waited three hours for Leon Dennison to come home, waited in calm silence. When a key turned in the lock, he stepped swiftly and noiselessly to the side of the door, a fireplace andiron held high overhead. The door opened and Leon Dennison entered, quite alone.

The andiron descended.

Leon Dennison fell without a murmur. He collapsed, lay still. The andiron rose and fell twice more, just for insurance, and Leon Dennison never moved and never uttered a sound. Kraft had only to wipe off the andiron and a few other surfaces to eliminate any fingerprints he might have left behind. He left the building by the service entrance. No one saw him.

He waited all that night for the rush of guilt. He was surprised when it failed to come. But he had already been a murderer—by wishing for Andersen's death, by planning Pierce's murder. The simple translation of his impulses from thought to deed was no impetus for further guilt.

There was no letter the next day. The following morning the usual envelope was waiting for him. It was quite bulky; it was filled with fifteen hundred-dollar bills.

The note was different. It said *Thank You*, of course. But beneath that there was another line:

How Do You Like Your New Job?

With a Smile for the Ending

I had one degree from Trinity, and one was enough, and I'd had enough of Dublin, too. It is a fine city, a perfect city, but there are only certain persons that can live there. An artist will love the town, a priest will bless it, and a clerk will live in it as well as elsewhere. But I had too little of faith and of talent and too much of a hunger for the world to be priest or artist or pen warden. I might have become a drunkard, for Dublin's a right city for a drinking man, but I've no more talent for drinking than for deception—yet another lesson I learned at Trinity, and equally a bargain. (Tell your story, Joseph Cameron Bane would say. Clear your throat and get on with it.)

I had family in Boston. They welcomed me cautiously and pointed me toward New York. A small but pretentious publishing house hired me; they leaned toward foreign editors and needed someone to balance off their flock of Englishmen. Four months was enough, of the job and of the city. A good place for a young man on the way up, but no town at all for a pilgrim.

He advertised for a companion. I answered his ad and half a dozen others, and when he replied I saw his name and took the job at once. I had lived with his books for years: *The Wind at Morning, Cabot's House, Ruthpen Hallburton, Lips That Could Kiss*, others, others. I had loved his words when I was a boy in Ennis, knowing no more than to read what reached me, and I loved them still at Trinity where one was supposed to care only for more fashionable authors. He had written a great many books over a great many years, all of them set in the same small American town. Ten years ago he'd stopped writing and never said why. When I read his name at the bottom of the letter I realized, though it had never occurred to me before, that I had somehow assumed him dead for some years.

We traded letters. I went to his home for an interview, rode the train there and watched the scenery change until I was in the country he had written about. I walked from the railway station carrying both suitcases, having gambled he'd want me to stay. His housekeeper met me at the door. I stepped inside, feeling as though I'd dreamed the room, the house. The woman took me to him, and I saw that he was older than I'd supposed him, and next saw that he was not. He appeared older because he was dying. "You're Riordan," he said. "How'd you come up? Train?"

"Yes, sir."

"Pete run you up?" I looked blank, I'm sure. He said that Pete was the town's cabdriver, and I explained that I'd walked.

"Oh? Could have taken a taxi."

"I like to walk."

"Mmmmm," he said. He offered me a drink. I refused, but he had one. "Why do you want to waste time watching a man die?" he demanded. "Not morbid curiosity, I'm sure. Want me to teach you how to be a writer?"

"No, sir."

"Want to do my biography? I'm dull and out of fashion, but some fool might want to read about me."

"No, I'm not a writer."

"Then why are you here, boy?"

He asked this reasonably, and I thought about the question before I answered it. "I like your books," I said finally.

"You think they're good? Worthwhile? Literature?"

"I just like them."

"What's your favorite?"

"I've never kept score," I answered.

He laughed, happy with the answer, and I was hired.

There was very little to do that could be called work. Now and then there would be a task too heavy for Mrs. Dettweiler, and I'd do that for her. There were occasional errands to run, letters to answer. When the weather turned colder he'd have me make up the fire for him in the living room. When he had a place to go, I'd drive him; this happened less often as time passed, as the disease grew in him.

And so, in terms of the time allotted to various tasks, my job was much as its title implied. I was his companion. I listened when he spoke, talked when he wanted conversation, and was silent when silence was indicated. There would be a time, his doctor told me, when I would have more to do, unless Mr. Bane would permit a nurse. I knew he would not, any more than he'd allow himself to die anywhere but in his home. There would be morphine shots for me to give him, because sooner or later the oral drug would become ineffective. In time he would be confined, first to his home and then to his room and at last to his bed, all a gradual preparation for the ultimate confinement.

"And maybe you ought to watch his drinking," the doctor told me. "He's been hitting it pretty heavy."

This last I tried once and no more. I said something foolish, that he'd had enough, that he ought to take it with a little water; I don't remember the words, only the stupidity of them, viewed in retrospect.

"I did not hire a damned warden," he said. "You wouldn't have thought of this yourself, Tim. Was this Harold Keeton's idea?"

"Well, yes."

"Harold Keeton is an excellent doctor," he said. "But only a doctor, and not a minister. He knows that doctors are supposed to tell their patients to cut down on smoking and drinking, and he plays his part. There is no reason for me to limit my drinking, Tim. There is nothing wrong with my liver or with my kidneys. The only thing wrong with me, Tim, is that I have cancer.

"I have cancer, and I'm dying of it. I intend to die as well as I possibly can. I intend to think and feel and act as I please, and go out with a smile for the ending. I intend, among other things, to drink what I want when I want it. I do not intend to get drunk, nor do I intend to be entirely sober if I can avoid it. Do you understand?"

"Yes, Mr. Bane."

"Good. Get the chessboard."

For a change, I won a game.

The morning after Rachel Avery was found dead in her bathtub I came downstairs to find him at the breakfast table. He had not slept well, and this showed in his eyes and at the corners of his mouth.

"We'll go into town today," he said.

"It snowed during the night, and you're tired. If you catch cold, and you probably will, you'll be stuck in bed for weeks." This sort of argument he would accept. "Why do you want to go to town, sir?"

"To hear what people say."

"Oh? What do you mean?"

"Because Rachel's husband killed her, Tim. Rachel should never have married Dean Avery. He's a man with the soul of an adding machine, but Rachel was poetry and music. He put her in his house and wanted to own her, but it was never in her to be true, to him or to another. She flew freely and sang magnificently, and he killed her.

"I want to learn just how he did it, and decide what to do about it. Perhaps you'll go to town without me. You notice things well enough. You sense more than I'd guessed you might, as though you know the people."

"You wrote them well."

This amused him. "Never mind," he said. "Make a nuisance of yourself if you have to, but see what you can learn. I have to find out how to manage all of this properly. I know a great deal, but not quite enough."

Before I left I asked him how he could be so sure. He said, "I know the town and the people. I knew Rachel Avery and Dean Avery. I knew her mother very well, and I knew his parents. I knew they should not have married, and that things would go wrong for them, and I am entirely certain that she was killed and that he killed her. Can you understand that?"

"I don't think so," I replied. But I took the car into town, bought a few paperbound books at the drugstore, had an unnecessary haircut at the barber's, went from here to there and back again, and then drove home to tell him what I had learned.

"There was a coroner's inquest this morning," I said. "Death by drowning induced as a result of electrical shock, accidental in origin. The funeral is tomorrow."

"Go on, Tim."

"Dean Avery was in Harmony Falls yesterday when they finally reached him and told him what had happened. He was completely torn up, they said. He drove to Harmony Falls the day before yesterday and stayed overnight."

"And he was with people all the while?"

"No one said."

"They wouldn't have checked," he said. "No need, not when it's so obviously an accident. You'll go to the funeral tomorrow."

"Why?"

"Because I can't go myself."

"And I'm to study him and study everyone else? Should I take notes?"

He laughed, then chopped off the laughter sharply. "I don't think you'd have to. I didn't mean that you would go in my place solely to observe, Tim, though that's part of it. But I would want to be there because I feel I ought to be there, so you'll be my deputy."

I had no answer to this. He asked me to build up the fire, and I did. I heard the newspaper boy and went for the paper. The town having no newspaper of its own, the paper he took was from the nearest city, and of course there was nothing in it on Rachel Avery. Usually he read it carefully. Now he skimmed it as if hunting something, then set it aside.

"I didn't think you knew her that well," I said.

"I did and I didn't. There are things I do not understand, Tim; people to whom I've barely spoken, yet whom I seem to know intimately. Knowledge has so many levels."

"You never really stopped writing about Beveridge." This was his fictional name for the town. "You just stopped putting it on paper."

He looked up, surprised, considering the thought with his head cocked like a wren's. "That's far more true than you could possibly know," he said.

He ate a good dinner and seemed to enjoy it. Over coffee I started aimless conversations but he let them die out. Then I said, "Mr. Bane, why can't it be an accident? The radio fell into the tub and shocked her and she drowned."

I thought at first he hadn't heard, or was pretending as much; this last is a special privilege of the old and the ill. Then he said, "Of course, you have to have facts. What should my intuition mean to you? And it would mean less, I suppose, if I assured you that Rachel Avery could not possibly be the type to play the radio while bathing?"

My face must have showed how much I thought of that. "Very well," he said. "We shall have facts. The water in the tub was running when the body was found. It was running, then, both before and after the radio fell into the tub, which means that Rachel Avery had the radio turned on while the tub was running, which is plainly senseless. She wouldn't be able to hear it well, would she? Also, she was adjusting the dial and knocked it into the tub with her.

"She would not have played the radio at all during her bath—this I simply *know*. She would not have attempted to turn on the radio until her bath was drawn, because no one would. And she would not have tried tuning the set while the water was running because that is sheerly pointless. Now doesn't that begin to make a slight bit of sense to you, Tim?"

They put her into the ground on a cold gray afternoon. I was part of a large crowd at the funeral parlor and a smaller one at the cemetery. There was a minister instead of a priest, and the service was not the one with which I was familiar, yet after a moment all of it ceased to be foreign to me. And then I knew. It was Emily Talstead's funeral from *Cabot's House*, except that Emily's death had justice to it, and even a measure of mercy, and this gray afternoon held neither.

In that funeral parlor I was the deputy of Joseph Cameron Bane. I viewed Rachel's small body and thought that all caskets should be closed, no matter how precise the mortician's art. We should not force ourselves to look upon our dead. I gave small words of comfort to Dean Avery and avoided his eyes while I did so. I sat in a wooden chair while the minister spoke of horrible tragedy and the unknowable wisdom of the Lord, and I was filled with a sense of loss that was complete in itself.

I shared someone's car to the cemetery. At graveside, with a wind blowing that chilled the edge of thought, I let the gloom slip free as a body into an envelope of earth, and I did what I'd come to do; I looked into the face of Dean Avery.

He was a tall man, thick in the shoulders, broad in the forehead, his hair swept straight back without a part, forming upon his head like a crown. I watched his eyes when he did not know that anyone watched him, and I watched the curl of his lip and the way he placed his feet and what he did with his hands. Before long I knew he mourned her not at all, and soon after that I knew the old man was right. He had killed her as sure as the wind blew.

They would have given me a ride back to his house, but I slipped away when the service ended, and spent time walking around, back and forth. By the time I was back at her grave, it had already been filled in. I wondered at the men who do such work, if they feel a thing at all. I turned from her grave and walked back through the town to Bane's house.

I found him in the kitchen with coffee and toast. I sat with him and told him about it, quickly, and he made me go back over all of it in detail so that he could feel he had been there himself. We sat in silence awhile, and then went to the living room. I built up the fire and we sat before it.

"You know now," he said. I nodded, for I did; I'd seen for myself, and knew it and felt it. "Knowing is most of it," he said. "Computers can never replace us, you know. They need facts, information. What's the term? Data. They need data. But sometimes men can make connections across gaps, without data. You see?"

"Yes."

"So we know." He drank, put down his glass. "But now we have to have our data. First the conclusion, and then backward to the proof."

My eyes asked the question.

"Because it all must round itself out," he said, answering the question without my giving voice to it. "This man killed and seems to have gotten away with it. This cannot be."

"Should we call the police?"

"Of course not. There's nothing to say to them, and no reason they should listen." He closed his eyes briefly, opened them. "We know what he did. We ought to know how, and why. Tell me the men at the funeral, Tim, as many as you remember."

"I don't remember much before the cemetery. I paid them little attention."

"At the cemetery, then. That's the important question, anyway."

I pictured it again in my mind and named the ones I knew. He listened very carefully. "Now there are others who might have been there," he said, "some of whom you may not know, and some you may not remember. Think, now, and tell me if any of these were there."

He named names, five of them, and it was my turn to listen. Two were strangers to me and I could not say if I'd seen them. One I remembered had been there, two others had not.

"Get a pencil and paper," he told me. "Write these names down. Robert Hardesty, Hal Kasper, Roy Teale, Thurman Goodin. Those will do for now."

The first two had been at the funeral, and at the cemetery. The other two had not.

"I don't understand," I said.

"She had a lover, of course. That was why he killed her. Robert Hardesty and Hal Kasper should not have been at the funeral, or at least not at the cemetery. I don't believe they're close to her family or his. Thurman Goodin and Roy Teale should have been at the funeral, at the least, and probably should have been at the cemetery. Now a dead woman's secret love may do what you would not expect him to do. He may stay away from a funeral he would otherwise be expected to attend, for fear of giving himself away, or he might attend a funeral where his presence would not otherwise be required, out of love or respect or no more than morbid yearning. We have four men, two who should have been present and were not, and two who should not have been present but were. No certainty, and nothing you might call data, but I've a feeling one of those four was Rachel Avery's lover."

"And?"

"Find out which one," he said.

"Why would we want to know that?"

"One must know a great many unimportant things in order to know those few things which are important." He poured himself more bourbon and drank some of it off. "Do you read detective stories? They always work with bits and pieces, like a jigsaw puzzle, find out trivia until it all fits together."

"And what might this fit into?"

"A shape. How, why, when."

I wanted to ask more, but he said he was tired and wanted to lie down. He must have been exhausted. He had me help him upstairs, change clothes, and into bed.

I knew Hal Kasper enough to speak to, so it was his shop I started in that night. He had a cigar store near the railroad terminal and sold magazines, paperbound books, candies, and stationery. You could place a bet on a horse there, I'd heard. He was thin, with prominent features—large hollow eyes, a long, slim nose, a large mouth with big gray-white teeth in it. Thirty-five or forty, with a childless wife whom I'd never met, I thought him an odd choice for a lover, but I knew enough to realize that women did not follow logic's rules when they committed adultery.

He had been at the funeral. Joseph Cameron Bane had found this a little remarkable. He had no family ties on either side with Rachel or Dean Avery. He was below them socially, and not connected through his business. Nor was he an automatic funeral-goer. There were such in the town, I'd been told, as there are in every town; they go to funerals as they turn on a television set or eavesdrop on a conversation, for entertainment and for lack of better to do. But he was not that sort.

"Hi, Irish," he said. "How's the old man?"

I thumbed a magazine. "Asleep," I said.

"Hitting the sauce pretty good lately?"

"I wouldn't say so, no."

"Well, he's got a right." He came out from behind the counter, walked over to me. "Saw you this afternoon. I didn't know you knew her. Or just getting material for that book of yours?"

Everyone assumed I was going to write a novel set in the town, and that this was what had led me to live with Mr. Bane. This would have made as much sense as visiting Denmark in order to rewrite *Hamlet.* I'd stopped denying it. It seemed useless.

"You knew her?" I asked.

"Oh, sure. You know me, Irish. I know everybody. King Farouk, Princess Grace—" He laughed shortly. "Sure, I knew her, a lot better than you'd guess."

I thought I'd learn something, but as I watched his face I saw his large mouth quiver with the beginnings of a leer, and then watched the light die in his eyes and the smile fade from his lips as he remembered that she was dead, cold and in the ground, and not fit to leer over or lust after. He looked ever so slightly ashamed of himself.

"A long time ago," he said, his voice pitched lower now. "Oh, a couple of years. Before she got married, well, she was a pretty wild kid in those days. Not wild like you might think; I mean, she was free, you understand?" He groped with his hands, long-fingered, lean. "She did what she wanted to do. I happened to be there. I was a guy she wanted to be with. Not for too long, but it was honey-sweet while it lasted. This is one fine way to be talking, isn't it? They say she went quick, though; didn't feel anything, but what a stupid way, what a crazy stupid way."

So it was not Hal Kasper who had loved her; not recently, at least. When I told all this to Joseph Cameron Bane he nodded several times and thought for some moments before he spoke.

"Ever widening circles, Tim," he said. "Throw a stone into a still pool and watch the circles spread. Now don't you see her more clearly? You wouldn't call Kasper a sentimental man, or a particularly sensitive man. He's neither of those things. Yet he felt that sense of loss, and that need to pay his last respects. There's purpose in funerals, you know, purpose and value. I used to think they were barbaric. I know better now. He had to talk about her, and had also to be embarrassed by what he'd said. Interesting."

"Why do we have to know all this?"

"Beginning to bother you, Tim?"

"Some."

" 'Because I am involved with mankind,' " he quoted.

"You'll learn more tomorrow, I think. Get the chessboard."

I did learn more the next day. I learned first to forget about Roy Teale. I had not recognized his name, but when I found him I saw that he was a man who had been at the funeral, as he might have been expected to be. I also learned, in the barbershop, that he was carrying on a truly passionate love affair, but with his own wife. He sat in a chair and grinned while two of the men ragged him about it.

I left, knowing what I had come to learn; if I'd stayed much longer I'd have had to get another haircut, and I scarcely needed one. I'd taken the car into town that day. It was colder than usual, and the snow was deep. I got into the car and drove to Thurman Goodin's service station. Mr. Bane usually had me fill the car at the station a few blocks to the north, but I did want to see Goodin. He and Robert Hardesty were the only names left on our list. If neither had been the woman's lover, then we were back where we'd started.

A high school boy worked afternoons and evenings for Goodin, but the boy had not come yet, and Thurman Goodin came out to the pump himself. While the tank filled he came over to the side of the car and rested against the door. His face needed shaving. He leaned his long hard body against the car door and said it had been a long time since he'd put any gas into the car.

"Mr. Bane doesn't get out much anymore," I said, "and I mostly walk except when the weather's bad."

"Then I'm glad for the bad weather." He lit a cigarette, and inhaled deeply. "Anyway, this buggy usually tanks up over to Kelsey's place. You had better than half a tankful; you could have made it over there without running dry, you know."

I gave him a blank look, then turned it around by saying, "I'm sorry, I didn't hear you. I was thinking about that woman who was killed."

I almost jumped at the sight of his face. A nerve twitched involuntarily, a thing he could not have controlled, but he might have covered up the other telltale signs. His eyes gave him away, and his hands, and the movements of his mouth.

"You mean Mrs. Avery," he said.

His wife was her cousin, Mr. Bane had told me. So he should have been at her funeral, and now should have been calling her Rachel or Rachel Avery. I wanted to get away from him!

"I was at the funeral," I said.

"Funerals," he said. "I got a business to run. Listen, I'll tell you something. Everybody dies. Fast or slow, old or young, it don't make a bit of difference. That's two twenty-seven for the gas."

He took three dollars and went into the station. He came back with the change and I took it from him. My hand shook slightly. I dropped a dime.

"Everybody gets it sooner or later," he said. "Why knock yourself out about it?"

When I told all this to Joseph Cameron Bane he leaned back in his chair with a sparkle in his eyes and the ghost of a smile on his pale lips. "So it's Thurman Goodin," he said. "I knew his father rather well. But I knew everybody's father, Tim, so that's not too important, is it? Tell me what you know."

"Sir?"

"Project, extend, extrapolate. What do you know about Goodin? What did he tell you? Put more pieces into the puzzle, Tim."

I said, "Well, he was her lover, of course. Not for very long, but for some space of time. It was nothing of long standing, and yet some of the glow had worn off."

"Go on, Tim."

"I'd say he made overtures for form's sake and was surprised when she responded. He was excited at the beginning, and then he began to be frightened of it all. Oh, this is silly, I'm making it all up—"

"You're doing fine, boy."

"He seemed glad she was dead. No, I'm putting it badly. He seemed relieved, and guilty about feeling relieved. Now he's safe. She died accidentally, and no one will ever find him out, and he can savor his memories without shivering in the night."

"Yes." He poured bourbon into his glass, emptying the bottle. Soon he would ask me to bring him another. "I agree," he said, and sipped at his whiskey almost daintily.

"Now what do we do?"

"What do you think we do, Tim?"

I thought about this. I said we might check with persons in Harmony Falls and trace Dean Avery's movements there. Or, knowing her lover's name, knowing so much that no one else knew, we might go to the police. We had no evidence, but the police could turn up evidence better than we, and do more with it once they had it.

He looked into the fire. When he did speak, I thought at first that he was talking entirely to himself and not to me at all. "And splash her name all over the earth," he said, "and raise up obscene court trials and filth in the newspapers, and pit lawyers against one another, and either hang him or jail him or free him. Ruin Thurman Goodin's marriage, and ruin Rachel Avery's memory."

"I don't think I understand."

He spun quickly around. His eyes glittered. "Don't you? Tim, Timothy, don't you truthfully understand?" He hesitated, groped for a phrase, then stopped and looked pointedly at his empty glass. I found a fresh bottle in the cupboard, opened it, handed it to him. He poured a drink but did not drink it.

He said, "My books always sold well, you know. But I had bad press. The small town papers were always kind, but the real critics . . . I was always being charged with sentimentality. They used words like *cloying* and *sugary* and *unrealistic*." I started to say something but he silenced me with an upraised palm. "Please, don't leap to my defense. I'm making a point now, not lamenting a misspent literary youth. Do you know why I stopped writing? I don't think I've ever told anyone. There's never been a reason to tell. I stopped, oh, not because critics were unkind, not because sales were disappointing. I stopped because I discovered that the critics, bless them, were quite right."

"That's not true!"

"But it is, Tim. I never wrote what you could honestly call sentimental slop, but everything always came out right, every book always had a happy ending. I simply *wanted* it to happen that way, I wanted things to work out as they *ought* to work out. Do you see? Oh, I let my people stay in character, that was easy enough. I was a good plot man and could bring that off well enough, weaving intricate webs that led inexorably to the silver lining in every last one of the blacker clouds. The people stayed true but the books became untrue, do you see? Always the happy ending, always the death of truth."

"In *Cabot's House* you had an unhappy ending."

"Not so. In *Cabot's House* I had death for an ending, but a death is not always an occasion for sorrow. Perhaps you're too young to know that, or to feel it within. You'll learn it soon enough. But to return to the point, I saw that my books were false. Good pictures of this town, of some people who lived either in it or in my mind or in both, but false portraits of life. I wrote a book, then, or tried to; an honest one, with loose *threads* at the end and—what was that precious line of Salinger's? Yes. With a touch of squalor, with love and squalor. I couldn't finish it. I hated it."

He picked up the glass, set it down again, the whiskey untouched. "Do you see? I'm an old man and a fool. I like things to come out right—neat and clean and sugary, wrapped with a bow, and a smile for the ending. No police, no trials, no public washing of soiled underwear. I think we are close enough now. I think we have enough of it." He picked up his glass once more and this time drained it. "Get the chessboard."

I got the board. We played, and he won, and my mind spent more of its time with other pawns than the ones we played with now. The image grew on me. I saw them all, Rachel Avery, Dean Avery, Thurman Goodin, carved of wood and all of a shade, either black or white; weighted with lead, and bottomed with a circlet of felt, green felt, and moved around by our hands upon a mirthless board.

"You're afraid of this," he said once. "Why?"

"Meddling, perhaps. Playing the divinity. I don't know, Mr. Bane. Something that feels wrong, that's all."

"Paddy from the peat bog, you've not lost your sense of the miraculous, have you? Wee folk, and gold at the rainbow's end, and things that go bump in the night, and man a stranger and afraid in someone else's world. Don't move there, Tim, your queen's *en prise*, you'll lose her."

We played three games. Then he straightened up abruptly and said, "I don't have the voice to mimic, I've barely any voice at all, and your brogue's too thick for it. Go up to the third floor, would you, and in the room all the way back, there's a closet with an infernal machine on its shelf—a tape recorder. I bought it with the idea that it might make writing simpler. Didn't work at all; I had to see the words in front of me to make them real. I couldn't sit like a fool talking at a machine. But I had fun with the thing. Get it for me, Tim, please."

It was where he'd said, in a box carpeted with dust. I brought it to him, and we went into the kitchen. There was a telephone there. First he tested the recorder, explaining that the tape was old and might not work properly. He turned it on and said, "Now is the time for all good men to come to the aid of the party. The quick brown fox jumped over the lazy dog." Then he winked at me and said, "Just like a typewriter; it's easiest to resort to formula when you want to say something meaningless, Tim. Most people have trouble talking when they have nothing to say. Though it rarely stops them, does it? Let's see how this sounds."

He played it back and asked me if the voice sounded like his own. I assured him it did. "No one ever hears his own voice when he speaks," he said. "I didn't realize I sounded that old. Odd."

He sent me for bourbon. He drank a bit, then had me get him the phone book. He looked up a number, read it to himself a time or two, then turned his attention again to the recorder.

"We ought to plug it into the telephone," he said.

"What for, sir?"

"You'll see. If you connect them lawfully, they beep every fifteen seconds, so that the other party knows what you're about, which hardly seems sensible. Know anything about these gadgets?"

"Nothing," I replied.

He finished the glass of whiskey. "Now what if I just hold the little microphone to the phone like this? Between my ear and the phone, hmm? Some distortion? Oh, won't matter, won't matter at all."

He dialed a number. The conversation, as much as I heard of it, went something like this:

"Hello, Mr. Taylor? No, wait a moment, let me see. Is this four-two-one-five? Oh, good. The Avery residence? Is Mrs. Avery in? I don't . . . Who'm I talking with, please? . . . Good. When do you expect your wife, Mr. Avery? . . . Oh, my! . . . Yes, I see, I see. Why, I'm terribly sorry to hear that, surely . . . Tragic. Well, I hate to bother you with this, Mr. Avery. Really, it's nothing . . . Well, I'm Paul Wellings of Wellings and Doyle Travel Agency . . . Yes, that's right, but I wish . . . Certainly. Your wife wanted us to book a trip to Puerto Rico for the two of you and . . . Oh? A surprise, probably . . . Yes, of course, I'll cancel everything. This is frightful. Yes, and I'm sorry for disturbing you at this—"

There was a little more, but not very much. He rang off, a bitter smile on his pale face, his eyes quite a bit brighter now than usual. "A touch of macabre poetry," he said. "Let him think she was planning to run off with Goodin. He's a cold one, though. So calm, and making me go on and on, however awkward it all was. And now it's all ready on the tape. But how can I manage this way?"

He picked up a phone and called another number. "Jay? This is Cam. Say, I know it's late, but is your tape recorder handy? Well, I'd wanted to do some dictation and mine's burned out a connection or something. Oh, just some work I'm doing. No, I haven't mentioned it, I know. It's something different. If anything ever comes of it, then I'll have something to tell you. But is it all right if I send Tim around for your infernal machine? Good, and you're a prince, Jay."

So he sent me to pick up a second recorder from Jason Falk. When I brought it to him, he positioned the two machines side by side on the table and nodded. "I hate deception," he said, "yet it seems to have its place in the scheme of things. I'll need half an hour or so alone, Tim. I hate to chase you away, but I have to play with these toys of mine."

I didn't mind. I was glad to be away from him for a few moments, for he was upsetting me more than I wanted to admit. There was something bad in the air that night, and more than my Irish soul was telling me so. Joseph Cameron Bane was playing God. He was manipulating people, toying with them. *Writing* them, and with no books to put them in.

It was too cold for walking. I got into the car and drove around the streets of the town, then out of the town and off on a winding road that went up into the hills beyond the town's edge. The snow was deep but no fresh snow was falling, and the moon was close to full and the sky cluttered with stars. I stopped the car and got out of it and took a long look back at the town below, his town. I thought it would be good right now to be a drinking man and warm myself from a bottle and walk in the night and pause now and then to gaze at the town below.

"You were gone long," he said.

"I got lost. It took time to find my way back."

"Tim, this still bothers you, doesn't it? Of course it does. Listen to me. I am going to put some people into motion, that is all. I am going to let some men talk to one another, and I am going to write their lines for them. Do you understand? Their opening lines. They wouldn't do it themselves. They wouldn't start it. I'll start it, and then they'll help it play itself out."

He was right, of course. Avery could not be allowed to get away with murder, nor should the dead woman's sins be placed on public display for all to stare at. "Now listen to this," he said, bright-eyed again. "I'm proud of myself, frankly."

He dialed a number, then poised his index finger above one of the buttons on the recorder. He was huddled over the table so that the telephone mouthpiece was just a few inches from the recorder's speaker. The phone was answered, and he pressed a button and I heard Dean Avery's voice. "Goodin?"

A pause. Then, "This is Dean Avery. I know all about it, Goodin. You and my wife. You and Rachel. I know all about it. And now she's dead. An accident. Think about it, Goodin. You'll have to think about it."

He replaced the receiver.

"How did you . . ."

He looked at my gaping mouth and laughed aloud at me. "Just careful editing," he said. "Playing from one machine to the next, back and forth, a word here, a phrase there, all interwoven and put together. Even the inflection can be changed by raising or lowering the volume as you bounce from one machine to the other. Isn't it startling? I told you I have fun with this machine. I never got anything written on it, but I had a good time fooling around with it."

"All those phrases—you even had his name."

"It was *good* of you to call. And the tail syllable of some other word, *happen*, I think. The two cropped out and spliced together and tossed back and forth until they fit well enough. I was busy while you were gone, Tim. It wasn't simple to get it all right."

"Now what happens?"

"Goodin calls Avery."

"How do you know?"

"Oh, Tim! I'll call Goodin and tell him how my car's broken down, or that he's won a football pool, or something inane, and do the same thing with his voice. And call Avery for him, and accuse him of the murder. That's all. They'll take it from there. I expect Avery will crack. If I get enough words to play with, I can have Goodin outline the whole murder, how it happened, everything."

His fingers drummed the table top. "Avery might kill himself," he said. "The killers always do in that woman's stories about the little Belgian detective. They excuse themselves and blow their brains out in a gentlemanly manner. There might be a confrontation between the two. I'm not sure."

"Will it wait until morning?"

"I thought I'd call Goodin now."

He was plainly exhausted. It was too late for him to be awake, but the excitement kept him from feeling the fatigue. I hated playing nursemaid. I let him drink too much every day, let him die as he wished, but it was not good for him to wear himself out this way.

"Goodin will be shaken by the call," I told him. "You'll probably have trouble getting him to talk. He may have closed the station for the night."

"I'll call and find out," he said.

He called, the recorder at the ready, and the phone rang and went unanswered. He wanted to wait up and try again, but I made him give it up and wait until the next day. I put him to bed and went downstairs and straightened up the kitchen. There was a half inch of whiskey in a bottle, and I poured it into a glass and drank it, a thing I rarely do. It warmed me and I'd needed warming. I went upstairs and to bed, and still had trouble sleeping.

There were dreams, and bad ones, dreams that woke me and sat me upright with a shapeless wisp of horror falling off like smoke. I slept badly and woke early. I was downstairs while he slept. While I ate toast and drank tea, Mrs. Dettweiler worried aloud about him. "You've got him all worked up," she said. "He shouldn't get like that. A sick man like him, he should rest, he should be calm."

"He wants the excitement. And it's not my doing."

"As sick as he is . . ."

"He's dying, and has a right to do it his own way."

"Some way to talk!"

"It's his way."

"There's a difference."

The radio was playing, tuned to a station in Harmony Falls. Our town had one FM station but the radio did not get FM. Mrs. Dettweiler always played a radio unless Mr. Bane was in the room, in which case he generally told her to turn it off. When she was upstairs in her own room, the television was always on, unless she was praying or sleeping. I listened to it now and thought that he might have used it for his taping and editing and splicing. If you wished to disguise your voice, you might do it that way. If Dean Avery had never heard Thurman Goodin's voice, or not well enough to recognize it, you could work it well enough that way. With all those words and phrases at your disposal . . .

Halfway through the newscast they read an item from our town, read just a brief news story, and I spilled my tea all over the kitchen table. The cup fell to the floor and broke in half.

"Why, for goodness . . ."

I turned off the radio, thought better, and reached to pull its plug. He never turned it on, hated it, but it might occur to him to tape from it, and I didn't want that. Not yet.

"Keep that thing off," I said. "Don't let him hear it, and don't tell him anything. If he tries to play the radio, say it's not working."

"I don't . . ."

"Just do as you're told!" I said. She went white and nodded mutely, and I hurried out of the house and drove into town. On the way I noticed that I held the steering wheel so tightly my fingers had gone numb. I couldn't help it. I'd have taken a drink then if there'd been one about. I'd have drunk kerosene, or perfume—anything at all.

I went to the drugstore and to the barbershop, and heard the same story in both places, and walked around a bit to relax, the last with little success. I left the car where I'd parked it and walked back to his house and breathed cold air and gritted my teeth against more than the cold. I did not even realize until much later that it was fairly stupid to leave the car. It seemed quite natural at the time.

He was up by the time I reached the house, wearing robe and slippers, seated at the table with telephone and tape recorder. "Where'd you go?" he wanted to know. "I can't reach Thurman Goodin. Nobody answers his phone."

"Nobody will."

"I've half a mind to try him at home."

"Don't bother."

"No? Why not?" And then, for the first time, he saw my face. His own paled. "Heavens, Tim, what's the matter?"

All the way back, through snow and cold air, I'd looked for a way to tell him—a proper way. There was none. Halfway home I'd thought that perhaps Providence might let him die before I had to tell him, but that could only have happened in one of his novels, not in this world.

So I said, "Dean Avery's dead. It happened last night; he's dead."

"Great God in heaven!" His face was white, his eyes horribly wide. "How? Suicide?"

"No."

"How?" he asked insistently.

"It was meant to look like suicide. Thurman Goodin killed him. Broke into his house in the middle of the night. He was going to knock him out and poke his head in the oven and put the gas on. He knocked him cold all right, but Avery came to on the way to the oven. There was a row and Thurman Goodin beat him over the head with some tool he'd brought along. I believe it was a tire iron. Beat his brains in, but all the noise woke a few of the neighbors and they grabbed Goodin on his way out the door. Two of them caught him and managed to hold him until the police came, and of course he told them everything."

I expected Bane to interrupt, but he waited without a word. I said, "Rachel Avery wanted him to run away with her. She couldn't stand staying with her husband, she wanted to go to some big city, try the sweet life. He told the police he tried to stop seeing her. She threatened him, that she would tell her husband, that she would tell his wife. So he went to her one afternoon and knocked her unconscious, took off her clothes, and put her in the bathtub. She was still alive then. He dropped the radio into the tub to give her a shock, then unplugged it and checked to see if she was dead. She wasn't so he held her head under water until she drowned, and then he plugged the radio into the socket again and left.

"And last night he found out that Avery knew about it, about the murder and the affair and all. So of course he had to kill Avery. He thought he might get away with it if he made it look like suicide, that Avery was depressed over his wife's death and went on to take his own life. I don't think it would have washed. I don't know much about it, but aren't the police more apt to examine a suicide rather carefully? They might see the marks on the head. Perhaps not. I don't really know. They've put Goodin in jail in Harmony Falls, and with two bloody murders like that, he's sure to hang." And then, because I felt even worse about it all than I'd known, "So it all comes out even, after all, the way you wanted it, the loose ends tied up in a bow."

"Good heavens!"

"I'm sorry." And I was, as soon as I'd said the words.

I don't think he heard me. "I am a bad writer and a bad man," he said, and not to me at all, and perhaps not even to himself but to whatever he talked to when the need came. "I thought I created them, I thought I knew them, I thought they all belonged to me."

So I went upstairs and packed my bags and walked all the way to the station. It was a bad time to leave him and a heartless way to do it, but staying would have been worse, even impossible. He was dying, and I couldn't have changed that, nor made the going much easier for him. I walked to the station and took the first train out and ended up here in Los Angeles, working for another foolish little man who likes to hire foreigners, doing the same sort of nothing I'd done in New York, but doing it at least in a warmer climate.

Last month I read he'd died. I thought I might cry but didn't. A week ago I reread one of his books, *Lips That Could Kiss.* I discovered that I did not like it at all, and then I did cry. For Rachel Avery, for Joseph Cameron Bane. For me.

You Could Call It Blackmail

He was in the garden when the phone rang. It rang several times before he remembered that Marjorie had taken Lisa to her piano lesson. He walked unhurriedly back to the house, expecting the caller to hang up before he reached the telephone, but it was still ringing when he got to it.

"David? This is Ellie."

"What's the matter?"

"Why?"

"Your voice. Is something wrong?"

"Everything's fine. No, everything's not fine."

"Ellie?"

"I'd like to see you. Could we meet for lunch?"

"Yes, of course. Just let me think. Today is what? Monday. I'm supposed to come into the city the day after tomorrow to have lunch with someone at Simon and Schuster. I hope I remember her name before I see her. I'm sure I could get out of it."

"No, don't do that. It doesn't have to be lunch. If we could meet for a drink?"

"Sure. Not that it would be any problem to cancel lunch. Let me think. There's an Italian place called the Grand Ticino on Thompson off Bleecker. It's always quiet during the day. I must be the only person who goes there, and I don't get there more than once or twice a year."

"How do you spell it?"

He spelled it. "Two o'clock Wednesday? I'll call what's-her-name and move lunch back to noon."

"Two is fine. I hope you remember her name."

"Penny Tobias. I just did."

The luncheon with Penny Tobias did not go well. Its unstated purpose was clear to both parties in advance; Simon & Schuster was interested in enticing David Barr away from his present publishers, while he in turn was not entirely averse to being enticed. Things would have gone well enough if he hadn't had Ellie Kilberg on his mind. But ever since her call he had been writing any number of mental drafts of the conversation they would have, and he couldn't stop doing this while Penelope Tobias stuffed fettuccine into herself and rattled on about the glories of the S & S spring list. He wasn't genuinely unpleasant, but he was certainly inattentive and was positive it showed.

A few minutes after one she broke a long silence by signaling abruptly for the check. "I certainly don't want to keep you," she said.

"Penny, I'm sorry as hell."

"Oh? Whatever for?"

"My manners. I have to meet an old friend in a little while and I guess it's bothering me more than I thought it would."

"You mean it's not me? Here I was all set to switch to a new brand of mouthwash."

He was twenty minutes early for his meeting with Ellie. The waiter, an elderly man with stooped shoulders, astonished him by greeting him by name.

"Mr. Barr, we never see you no more."

"I live up in Connecticut now."

"All alone, Mr. Barr?"

"A lady's meeting me for cocktails, but I'm very early and I don't think I can hold out until she gets here. I think an extra dry martini with a twist."

He made the drink last. At five minutes of two the only other customers settled their bill and left, and perhaps a minute later Ellie appeared. He got to his feet while the waiter bustled about seating her. Her eyes had the brittle sparkle of an amphetamine high.

She said, "If that's a martini I think I want one."

He ordered drinks for both of them. Until the waiter brought them she asked questions about Marjorie and Lisa and his work. Then she raised her glass, looked at it for a moment, and drained it in three quick swallows.

"I should have told him to wait," he said. " 'Keep the meter running and I'll be ready in a minute.' I don't think I ever saw you drink like that."

"Probably not."

"Want another?"

"No. I wanted that one a lot, but it's all I want for the time being." She opened her purse and found a pack of cigarettes. It was empty, and she crumpled it fiercely and put it down beside the ashtray.

"There's a machine in front," he said. "I'll get them for you."

He returned with a pack of Parliaments and opened them for her, then held a match. Her hand closed on his wrist as she got the cigarette lit. She let go, inhaled, blew out smoke, looked at him and away and at him again.

"Okay," she said.

He didn't say anything.

"I thought of writing Dear Abby, but she would just refer me to my priest, minister, or rabbi. And I don't *have* a priest, minister, or rabbi. You were the only person I could think of."

"Must be my clerical image."

"It's that you're a friend of mine and a friend of Bert's. More than that. He and I have a lot of friends in common, but you were his friend before I married him, and you and I—"

"Were very good friends once upon a time."

"I think I *will* have another drink. This is turning out to be harder than I thought." When the drinks came she took a small sip and placed her glass on the tablecloth. She helped herself to a second cigarette and let him light it for her.

She said, "For the past two days I've been trying to figure out how to start this conversation. I'm no closer now than I was at the beginning. I love Bert very much. We have a good marriage."

"I've always thought so."

"Have you?"

"Yes. I don't think I know two people who like each other's company as much. You both certainly give that impression."

"It's not a pose. It's very real." She lowered her eyes, worried the rim of the ashtray with the tip of her cigarette. "We have a problem. Or I have a problem. That's obvious, I didn't drag you here to discuss how perfectly happy I am."

"No."

"How well do you know Bert?"

"Well, that's a tough question. I've known him for, what, twenty years? We were in college together. He was a sophomore when I was a freshman, although I'm a month older. So I guess I've known him longer than anyone else I'm really friendly with now."

"But."

"Right: but. But he's the most guarded man I ever met, so in a sense I don't know him very well at all. Ellie, about two months ago I met a guy in a bar in Weston. He'd just got off the train and he was going to have one quick one before he went home to his wife, and the two of us wound up drinking and talking until close to midnight. I never saw him before and I'll never see him again. I don't remember his name. If he even told me his name. But I knew that son of a bitch more intimately than I ever got to know Bert Kilberg."

"He keeps himself very much to himself."

"Yes."

"David? This is what I want to ask you. How would he react if I had an affair?"

"You mean if he found out about it."

"Well, yes."

"Because I don't know why he'd have to know. Are you seeing somebody?"

"Oh, no."

"But you're thinking about it."

"I seem to feel the need."

He nodded. "Most people do," he said. "Sooner or later."

She excused herself to go to the ladies' room, first asking him to order another round of drinks. When she returned they were already on the table. "Scotch and water," he said. "I decided to switch to something less toxic and I thought you might be inclined to keep me company."

"Meaning don't let the lady get smashed. For which I'll surely thank you later. This is a nice place, although I don't see how they can afford to stay open. How come you never brought me here?"

"I only bring married ladies here."

"Is that the truth? It's a good answer, anyway. David, I think I need an affair. But I hate keeping secrets from him. I know I'd have the urge to tell him."

"Well, then, let me just tell you something." He leaned forward. "Every time you get that urge, you just step on it full force. You squelch it. If you absolutely can't help yourself, write it out on a sheet of paper and burn it and flush the ashes down the toilet. Because all you can accomplish by telling him is to create purposeless headaches for two people and possibly three. Or four, if the guy you pick is married. And he should be."

"Why do you say that?"

"Because, my dear, cheating is safer when there are two of you doing it. You've both got the same thing to lose. And it's more comfortable, it puts you both on common ground." He laughed shortly. "In other words, when you want to have an affair go pick out a married man, and there's something Dear Abby'll never tell you."

"Wherever would I find one?"

"Oh, that wouldn't be a problem. Married men are looking for it a lot more earnestly than single ones. With your looks you wouldn't have any trouble." Lightly he said, "You could always pick an old flame. For nostalgia, if nothing else."

"You're a very sweet man, David."

There was an awkward moment which they both attempted to cover by reaching for their drinks. Then she said, "He's not married."

"Who's not?"

"The man I'm sleeping with."

"Oh. Then this should-I-or-shouldn't-I wasn't as hypothetical as it sounded."

She shook her head. "I wasn't going to tell you but it doesn't make much sense not to. It's been going on for a little over a month. He's eight years younger than I am, he's not married, and the two of us have nothing whatsoever in common. His only strong point is that he makes me feel excited and exciting."

"Uh-huh."

"But I don't love him. I'm in bed next to him afterward and look at him and wish it was Bert next to me."

"Where did you find him? I'm assuming it's no one I know."

"It's not. I met him at Berlitz. He's my instructor."

"Berlitz? Oh, you're taking Spanish or something. I think Marjorie mentioned it."

"German. He was born in Germany and he looks like the really vicious blond captain in all the war movies. And I'm the girl who wouldn't buy a Volkswagen. Oh, hell. For the past month I haven't been able to figure out whether I'm wildly happy or wildly miserable. I don't know why I dragged you here, David, but I guess I just had to talk to someone. And you were elected."

They continued talking through another round of drinks. Then he put her in a cab, returned to the bar for one last drink, and took a cab of his own to Grand Central and caught the 4:17. "It was one of those endless lunches," he told Marjorie, "and I don't think it accomplished a thing. I behaved like a Dale Carnegie dropout."

He called his agent, catching her just before she left the office. He said, "Mary, I think we can forget all about Mr. Simon and Mr. Schuster." He gave her a brief version of the lunch, omitting mention of the reasons for his inattentiveness.

"Well, I always knew you were a bad judge of your own work, Dave. I thought it just applied to fiction, but evidently it's the same in other areas. Penny Tobias thinks you're sensational."

"You're kidding."

"She called me around one-thirty. She said now she knows why your books are so perceptive, you're the most sensitive person she ever met and she really hopes we can work something out because she personally would be so proud to publish you."

"Well, I'll be damned."

"I'm going to dine out on this story, Dave."

"Change one thing when you do, huh? Penny called you at *four*-thirty, right after she got back from lunch."

"Oh, dear," said Mary Fradin. "Davey was a bad boy."

Something was bothering him, and it was several days before he managed to figure out what it was. Then he waited until Marjorie was out of the house and dialed the Kilberg apartment. When Ellie answered he said, "This is David, but if you're not alone I'll be a wrong number."

"I'm alone. What is it?"

"Well, a couple of things. First of all, it's occurred to me that you might be having second thoughts about telling me as much as you did, and I hope you won't. Nothing we talked about will ever go any further."

"Oh, I know that."

"The other thing is silly but I'm going to mention it anyway because it's been bothering me. It occurs to me that this kraut might get to be a problem. This is probably not going to happen, and you can chalk it up to an overactive imagination, but just promise me one thing. If it looks as though he's going to cause you any trouble at all I want you to call me. Don't go to Bert and don't try to handle things yourself. Just call me."

"What kind of trouble?"

"Any kind."

"You're very sweet, but nothing like that is going to happen."

"I know it isn't. Now say you promise."

"It's silly. *All right.* I promise."

During the next two months David Barr saw Bert Kilberg twice on business matters and spoke to him perhaps a half dozen times over the telephone. He had wondered how this new knowledge of his friend would affect their relationship, and he was pleased to discover that it made no difference.

One Saturday evening he and Marjorie drove into New York to have dinner and see a show with Bert and Ellie. The secret he and Ellie shared did not seem to have changed the dynamics of the relationship among the four of them. He felt somewhat closer to Ellie for it, but he didn't think any of that showed on the surface.

Bert did not know that he and Ellie had been lovers years before she married Bert. It was possible that Marjorie had inferred as much, but if so she had kept her thoughts to herself.

Then one afternoon the telephone rang while he was working in his study. A little later Marjorie told him it had been Ellie. "I'm supposed to give you her fondest regards," she said. "She said it twice, as a matter of fact, so I suppose she really means it. It's funny."

"What is?"

"She called for my Stroganoff recipe, and I'm positive I gave it to her when they were here in December."

Within the hour he invented a pretext to drive into town. He called her from the drugstore.

He said, "Was that a signal? Or have I been reading too many spy novels?"

"I'm just keeping a promise."

"That's what I was afraid of. How bad is it?"

"Oh, it's pretty bad, David. I guess my judgment leaves something to be desired. From now on I'll ask you to pick my lovers for me."

"There's a title that goes with the duty and I'm not crazy about it. But tell me what he's pulled."

"Well, he's a bastard. He got very possessive for a starter. A lot of romantic nonsense, and I swear I did nothing to encourage it. He wanted me to leave Bert and run off with him. The fool. As if I would."

"And?"

"And then he turned on me. He started calling me at home, which I'd told him several times he was absolutely never to do. Then he, uh, began asking for small loans. Ten dollars, twenty dollars. Then he said he needed five hundred dollars, and of course I told him no, and I also told him I didn't think we should see each other anymore."

"Well, you were right about that."

"And now he's trying to blackmail me. I don't know if you'd call it blackmail from a legal point of view because he hasn't exactly made any threats. But just this morning he called and said that if I wouldn't lend him some money, then perhaps Bert would give him a loan. Needless to say he and Bert have never met, so my interpretation is that it's blackmail."

"I think you could call it blackmail. That was this morning?"

"Yes. I don't remember what I told him. But he called back less than an hour later with a whole song and dance about how he loves me and we should run off together. I'm scared of what he might do next. I think I would have called you even if you hadn't said what you did, because I wouldn't know who else to call and I just can't handle this one myself. But how did you know this would happen?"

"It was just a hunch. Let me think a minute. What's this bastard's name?"

"Klaus Eberhard."

"And his address?" She gave it to him and he wrote it down. "All right. Now this is important. Did you ever say anything to him about me? Anything at all?"

"No. I'm positive I never did. I never talked to him about anything, really. We just—"

"You just studied bedroom Deutsch, right. Call him up right now and tell him you'll meet him at his place tomorrow afternoon at three. Can you do that?"

"I never want to see him again, David."

"You'll never have to. I'll keep the appointment for you."

"I don't want you paying him."

"Don't worry about it. Just make the call. I'm in a phone booth, I'll give you my number and you can call me back and tell me the appointment's set."

He got to New York shortly after noon the next day. He stopped at a restaurant near Grand Central but when he looked at the menu he realized he was too edgy to eat anything. He had a drink but decided not to have a second one.

In a shop on Madison Avenue he bought a black hat with a very short brim. In a drugstore a few blocks further along Madison he bought two flashlight batteries and put one in either pocket of his suit jacket. Then he walked for a while, writing and rewriting scenes in his mind.

At half past two he got out of a cab at the corner of Eighty-eighth and York and walked to the address Ellie had given him. He rang a variety of bells until some obliging tenant buzzed him through the front door. He walked up two flights of stairs and knocked on Klaus Eberhard's door. It was opened by a man about thirty with pale blond hair and an open, engaging face. He was at least four inches taller than David Barr and weighed about the same. He wore an Italian knit sport shirt and tailored denim slacks, and he looked more like a ski instructor than an S.S. captain.

"Eberhard?"

"Yes, I am Eberhard." His English was just barely accented. "How may I help you?"

"Klaus Eberhard?"

"But yes."

He put his hands in his pockets and closed his fingers around the flashlight batteries. "You'd better close the door," he said, stepping around Eberhard and into the apartment. "I have a message from Mrs. Kilberg and we don't want the neighbors tuning in."

Eberhard closed the door and put the chain bolt on. As he was turning around again, Barr hit him on the side of the jaw with all his strength. The German fell back against the door and Barr waded in after him, striking him repeatedly in the face and chest. The weight of the batteries increased the effect of the blows immeasurably. He could hear ribs give way as he battered them, and when he landed a punch to Eberhard's nose there was an immediate geyser of blood.

He stepped back at last and Eberhard slid to the floor. Barr stood over him. He pitched his voice low and put the rasp of the New York streets into it. He said, "Now listen good, you son of a bitch. You are gonna stay away from Mrs. Kilberg. You are never gonna call her or see her or nothing. You spot her on the street, you better get your ass out of the way in a big hurry, because next time I kill you. This time I just send you to the hospital, but next time I kill you."

Eberhard couldn't get any words out. His lips moved but no sound was forthcoming.

"You get the message?" He drew back his foot. "Answer me."

"Do not hurt me."

"You understand what I been tellin' you?"

"I understand. Chust don't hurt me."

"I got paid to break your arm. I'll make it a clean break."

The German was beyond resistance. He lay there, his head propped oddly against the door, while Barr placed a foot on his upper arm. Then he gripped the younger man's wrist and pulled up against the elbow joint until he heard a snapping sound. Klaus Eberhard gave a short grunt and passed out.

On the street Barr walked two blocks until he came to a trash can. He deposited the two flashlight batteries and the hat and walked over to First Avenue to find a bar. He had two double scotches, tossing them off one after the other, then ordered a tall scotch and water. He drank about half of it before going to the men's room.

He was not sick to his stomach. He'd expected nausea, only hoping to control it until he was finished with Eberhard, but all he felt now was an unfamiliar sense of exhilaration and a bit of pain in his hands. The knuckles of his right hand were badly skinned. He washed his hands and decided he could explain the damage as having been caused by a fall.

He returned to the bar and finished his drink. Then he went to the telephone and dialed her number.

He said, "You can forget that son of a bitch. You won't hear from him again."

"What happened?"

"I'll probably tell you sometime. But not now. Just forget he ever existed. He'll stay clear of you, and I wouldn't be surprised if he leaves town."

"I hope you didn't give him any money."

"Put your mind at rest."

There was a pause. "I don't know what to say."

"You don't have to say anything."

"I suppose 'Thank you' would be a good place to start, but it seems inadequate. However—"

"Don't say anything." He breathed in and out. The feeling of exhilaration was still present. "Ellie? I'll be in the city again on Tuesday. I'd like you to meet me for lunch."

"Something you don't want to say on the phone?"

"Just a social lunch," he said.

She was silent for a moment. Then she said, "All right. It's such a complicated world, isn't it? Where shall I meet you?"

"How about the same place as last time? The Grand Ticino?"

"Of course. That's where you take married women, isn't it?"

"Is noon a good time for you?"

"Such a complicated world. Yes, noon is fine."

"Noon Tuesday at the Grand Ticino," he said. "I'll see you then."

He had another drink and took a cab to the train station. He had some time to kill before his train left. He bought a magazine and sat in the main waiting room until his train was ready for boarding.

On the train, half an hour out of New York, he found himself wondering whether he had unconsciously planned the end of it as well. It seemed to him that he had not known he was going to make a lunch date with her, and yet it also seemed to him that he must have known. Had he designed the whole episode with Eberhard with just that end in mind?

He thought it over and decided it didn't really matter.

When he got back home Marjorie asked him how the meeting had gone. "Went very well," he said. "If they do make the movie they want me for the screenplay. That's a big if, of course. I have to go in Tuesday for a conference with the director, and then we sit around and wait for the studio to say yes or no. But this afternoon was productive. I know I made a real impression on Eberhard."

"That's wonderful."

"Yes, you'd have been proud of me," said David Barr.

Chip Harrison

Death of the Mallory Queen

"I am going to be murdered," Mavis Mallory said, "and I want you to do something about it."

Haig did something, all right. He spun around in his swivel chair and stared into the fish tank. There's a whole roomful of tanks on the top floor, and other aquariums, which he wishes I would call aquaria, scattered throughout the house.

(Well, not the whole house. The whole house is a carriage house on West Twentieth Street, and on the top two floors live Leo Haig and Wong Fat and more tropical fish than you could shake a jar of tubifex worms at, but the lower two floors are still occupied by Madam Juana and her girls. How do you say *filles de joie* in Spanish, anyway? Never mind. If all of this sounds a little like a cut-rate, low-rent version of Nero Wolfe's establishment on West Thirty-fifth Street, the similarity is not accidental. Haig, you see, was a lifelong reader of detective fiction, and a penny-ante breeder of tropical fish until a legacy made him financially independent. And he was a special fan of the Wolfe canon, and he thinks that Wolfe really exists, and that if he, Leo Haig, does a good enough job with the cases that come his way, sooner or later he might get invited to dine at the master's table.)

"Mr. Haig—"

"*Huff,*" Haig said.

Except that he didn't exactly *say* huff. He *went* huff. He's been reading books lately by Sondra Ray and Leonard Orr and Phil Laut, books on rebirthing and physical immortality, and the gist of it seems to be that if you do enough deep circular breathing and clear out your limiting deathist thoughts, you can live forever. I don't know how he's doing with his deathist thoughts, but he's been breathing up a storm lately, as if air were going to be rationed any moment and he wants to get the jump on it.

He huffed again and studied the rasboras, which were the fish that were to-and-froing it in the ten-gallon tank behind his desk. Their little gills never stopped working, so I figured they'd live forever, too, unless their deathist thoughts were lurking to do them in. Haig gave another huff and turned around to look at our client.

She was worth looking at. Tall, willowy, richly curved, with a mane of incredible red hair. Last August I went up to Vermont, toward the end of the month, and all the trees were green except here and there you'd see one in the midst of all that green that had been touched by an early frost and turned an absolutely flaming scarlet, and that was the color of Mavis Mallory's hair. Haig's been quoting a lot of lines lately about the rich abundance of the universe we live in, especially when I suggest he's spending too much on fish and equipment, and looking at our client I had to agree with him. We live in an abundant world, all right.

"Murdered," he said.

She nodded.

"By whom?"

"I don't know."

"For what reason?"

"I don't know."

"And you want me to prevent it."

"No."

His eyes widened. "I beg your pardon?"

"How could you prevent it?" She wrinkled her nose at him. "I understand you're a genius, but what defense could you provide against a determined killer? You're not exactly the physical type."

Haig, who has been described as looking like a basketball with an Afro, huffed in reply. "My own efforts are largely in the cerebral sphere," he admitted. "But my associate, Mr. Harrison, is physically resourceful as well, and—" he made a tent of his fingertips "—still, your point is well taken. Neither Mr. Harrison nor I are bodyguards. If you wish a bodyguard, there are larger agencies which—"

But she was shaking her head. "A waste of time," she said. "The whole Secret Service can't protect a president from a lone deranged assassin. If I'm destined to be murdered, I'm willing to accede to my destiny."

"Huff," Haig huffed.

"What I want you to do," she said, "and Mr. Harrison, of course, except that he's so young I feel odd calling him by his last name." She smiled winningly at me. "Unless you object to the familiarity?"

"Call me Chip," I said.

"I'm delighted. And you must call me Mavis."

"Huff."

"Who wants to murder you?" I asked.

"Oh, dear," she said. "It sometimes seems to me that everyone does. It's been four years since I took over as publisher of *Mallory's Mystery Magazine* upon my father's death, and you'd be amazed how many enemies you can make in a business like this."

Haig asked if she could name some of them.

"Well, there's Abner Jenks. He'd been editor for years and thought he'd have a freer hand with my father out of the picture. When I reshuffled the corporate structure and created Mavis Publications, Inc., I found out he'd been taking kickbacks from authors and agents in return for buying their stories. I got rid of him and took over the editorial duties myself."

"And what became of Jenks?"

"I pay him fifty cents a manuscript to read slush pile submissions. And he picks up some freelance work for other magazines as well, and he has plenty of time to work on his own historical novel about the Venerable Bede. Actually," she said, "he ought to be grateful to me."

"Indeed," Haig said.

"And there's Darrell Crenna. He's the owner of Mysterious Ink, the mystery bookshop on upper Madison Avenue. He wanted Dorothea Trill, the Englishwoman who writes those marvelous gardening mysteries, to do a signing at his store. In fact he'd advertised the appearance, and I had to remind him that Miss Trill's contract with Mavis Publications forbids her from making any appearances in the States without our authorization."

"Which you refused to give."

"I felt it would cheapen the value of Dorothea's personal appearances to have her make too many of them. After all, Crenna talked an author out of giving a story to *Mallory's* on the same grounds, so you could say he was merely hoist with his own petard. Or strangled by his own clematis vine, like the woman in Dorothea's latest." Her face clouded. "I hope I haven't spoiled the ending for you?"

"I've already read it," Haig said.

"I'm glad of that. Or I should have to add you to the list of persons with a motive for murdering me, shouldn't I? Let me see now. Lotte Benzler belongs on the list. You must know her shop. The Murder Store?"

Haig knew it well, and said so. "And I trust you've supplied Ms. Benzler with an equally strong motive? Kept an author from her door? Refused her permission to reprint a story from *Mallory's* in one of the anthologies she edits?"

"Actually," our client said, "I fear I did something rather more dramatic than that. You know Bart Halloran?"

"The creator of Rocky Sledge, who's so hard-boiled he makes Mike Hammer seem poached? I've read him, of course, but I don't know him."

"Poor Lotte came to know him very well," Mavis Mallory purred, "and then I met dear Bart, and then it was I who came to know him very well." She sighed. "I don't think Lotte has ever forgiven me. All's fair in love and publishing, but some people don't seem to realize it."

"So there are three people with a motive for murdering you."

"Oh, I'm sure there are more than three. Let's not forget Bart, shall we? He was able to shrug it off when I dropped him, but he took it harder when his latest got a bad review in *Mallory's*. But I thought *Kiss My Gat* was a bad book, and why should I say otherwise?" She sighed again. "Poor Bart," she said. "I understand his sales are slipping. Still, he's still a name, isn't he? And he'll be there Friday night."

"Indeed?" Haig raised his eyebrows. He's been practicing in front of the mirror, trying to raise just one eyebrow, but so far he hasn't got the knack of it. "And just where will Mr. Halloran be Friday night?"

"Where they'll all be," Mavis Mallory said. "At Town Hall, for the panel discussion and reception to celebrate the twenty-fifth anniversary of *Mallory's Mystery Magazine.* Do you know, I believe everyone with a motive to murder me will be gathered together in one room?" She shivered happily. "What more could a mystery fan ask for?"

"Don't attend," Haig said.

"Don't be ridiculous," she told him. "I'm Mavis Mallory of Mavis Publications. I *am Mallory's*—in fact I've been called the Mallory Queen. I'll be chairing the panel discussion and hosting the celebration. How could I possibly fail to be present?"

"Then get bodyguards."

"They'd put such a damper on the festivities. And I already told you they'd be powerless against a determined killer."

"Miss Mallory—"

"And please don't tell me to wear a bulletproof vest. They haven't yet designed one that flatters the full-figured woman."

I swallowed, reminded again that we live in an abundant universe. "You'll be killed," Haig said flatly.

"Yes," said our client, "I rather suspect I shall. I'm paying you a five thousand dollar retainer now, in cash, because you might have a problem cashing a check if I were killed before it cleared. And I've added a codicil to my will calling for payment to you of an additional twenty thousand dollars upon your solving the circumstances of my death. And I do trust you and Chip will attend the reception Friday night? Even if I'm not killed, it should be an interesting evening."

"I have read of a tribe of Africans," Haig said dreamily, "who know for certain that gunshot wounds are fatal. When one of their number is wounded by gunfire, he falls immediately to the ground and lies still, waiting for death. He does this even if he's only been nicked in the finger, and, by the following morning, death will have inevitably claimed him."

"That's interesting," I said. "Has it got anything to do with the Mallory Queen?"

"It has everything to do with her. The woman—" he huffed again, and I don't think it had much to do with circular breathing "—the damnable woman is convinced she will be murdered. It would profoundly disappoint her to be proved wrong. She *wants* to be murdered, Chip, and her thoughts are creative, even as yours and mine. In all likelihood she will die on Friday night. She would have it no other way."

"If she stayed home," I said. "If she hired bodyguards—"

"She will do neither. But it would not matter if she did. The woman is entirely under the influence of her own death urge. Her death urge is stronger than her life urge. How could she live in such circumstances?"

"If that's how you feel, why did you take her money?"

"Because all abundance is a gift from the universe," he said loftily. "Further, she engaged us not to protect her but to avenge her, to solve her murder. I am perfectly willing to undertake to do that." *Huff.* "You'll attend the reception Friday night, of course."

"To watch our client get the axe?"

"Or the dart from the blowpipe, or the poisoned cocktail, or the bullet, or the bite from the coral snake, or what you will. Perhaps you'll see something that will enable us to solve her murder on the spot and earn the balance of our fee."

"Won't you be there? I thought you'd planned to go."

"I had," he said. "But that was before Miss Mallory transformed the occasion from pleasure to business. Nero Wolfe never leaves his house on business, and I think the practice a sound one. You will attend in my stead, Chip. You will be my eyes and my legs. *Huff.*"

I was still saying things like *Yes, but* when he swept out of the room and left for an appointment with his rebirther. Once a week he goes all the way up to Washington Heights, where a woman named Lori Schneiderman gets sixty dollars for letting him stretch out on her floor and watching him breathe. It seems to me that for that kind of money he could do his huffing in a bed at the Plaza Hotel, but what do I know?

He'd left a page full of scribbling on his desk and I cleared it off to keep any future clients from spotting it. *I, Leo, am safe and immortal right now,* he'd written five times. *You, Leo, are safe and immortal right now,* he'd written another five times. *Leo is safe and immortal right now,* he'd written a final five times. This was how he was working through his unconscious death urge and strengthening his life urge. I tell you, a person has to go through a lot of crap if he wants to live forever.

Friday night found me at Town Hall, predictably enough. I wore my suit for the occasion and got there early enough to snag a seat down front, where I could keep a private eye on things.

There were plenty of things to keep an eye on. The audience swarmed with readers and writers of mystery and detective fiction, and if you want an idea of who was in the house, just write out a list of your twenty-five favorite authors and be sure that seventeen or eighteen of them were in the house. I saw some familiar faces, a woman who'd had a long run as the imperiled heroine of a Broadway suspense melodrama, a man who'd played a police detective for three years on network television, and others whom I recognized from films or television but couldn't place out of context.

On stage, our client Mavis Mallory occupied the moderator's chair. She was wearing a strapless and backless floor-length black dress, and in combination with her creamy skin and fiery hair, its effect was dramatic. If I could have changed one thing it would have been the color of the dress. I suppose Haig would have said it was the color of her unconscious death urge.

Her panelists were arranged in a semicircle around her. I recognized some but not others, but before I could extend my knowledge through subtle investigative technique, the entire panel was introduced. The members included Darrell Crenna of Mysterious Ink and Lotte Benzler of The Murder Store. The two sat on either side of our client, and I just hoped she'd be safe from the daggers they were looking at each other.

Rocky Sledge's creator, dressed in his standard outfit of chinos and a T-shirt with the sleeve rolled to contain a pack of unfiltered Camels, was introduced as Bartholomew Halloran. "Make that Bart," he snapped. *If you know what's good for you,* he might have added.

Halloran was sitting at Mavis Mallory's left. A tall and very slender woman with elaborately coiffed hair and a lorgnette sat between him and Darrell Crenna. She turned out to be Dorothea Trill, the Englishwoman who wrote gardening mysteries. I always figured the chief gardening mystery was what to do with all the zucchini. Miss Trill seemed a little looped, but maybe it was the lorgnette.

On our client's other side, next to Lotte Benzler, sat a man named Austin Porterfield. He was a Distinguished Professor of English Literature at New York University, and he'd recently published a rather learned obituary of the mystery story in the *New York Review of Books.* According to him, mystery fiction had drawn its strength over the years from the broad base of its popular appeal. Now other genres had more readers, and thus mystery writers were missing the mark. If they wanted to be artistically important, he advised them, then get busy producing Harlequin romances and books about nurses and stewardesses.

On Mr. Porterfield's other side was Janice Cowan, perhaps the most prominent book editor in the mystery field. For years she had moved from one important publishing house to another, and at each of them she had her own private imprint. "A Jan Cowan Novel of Suspense" was a good guarantee of literary excellence, whoever happened to be Miss Cowan's employer that year.

After the last of the panelists had been introduced, a thin, weedy man in a dark suit passed quickly among the group with a beverage tray, then scurried off the stage. Mavis Mallory took a sip of her drink, something colorless in a stemmed glass, and leaned toward the microphone. "What Happens Next?" she intoned. "That's the title of our little discussion tonight, and it's a suitable title for a discussion on this occasion. A credo of *Mallory's Mystery Magazine* has always been that our sort of fiction is only effective insofar as the reader cares deeply what happens next, what takes place on the page he or she has yet to read. Tonight, though, we are here to discuss what happens next in mystery and suspense fiction. What trends have reached their peaks, and what trends are swelling just beyond the horizon."

She cleared her throat, took another sip of her drink. "Has the tough private eye passed his prime? Is the lineal descendant of Sam Spade and Philip Marlowe just a tedious outmoded macho sap?" She paused to smile pleasantly at Bart Halloran, who glowered back at her. "Conversely, has the American reader lost interest forever in the mannered English mystery? Are we ready to bid adieu to the body in the library, or—" she paused for an amiable nod at the slightly cockeyed Miss Trill "—the corpse in the formal gardens?

"Is the mystery, if you'll pardon the expression, *dead* as a literary genre? One of our number—" and a cheerless smile for Professor Porterfield "—would have us all turn to writing *Love's Saccharine Savagery* and *Penny Wyse, Stockyard Nurse*. Is the mystery bookshop, a store specializing in our brand of fiction, an idea whose time has come—and gone? And what do book publishers have to say on this subject? One of our number has worked for so many of them; she should be unusually qualified to comment."

Mavis certainly had the full attention of her fellow panelists. Now, to make sure she held the attention of the audience as well, she leaned forward, a particularly arresting move given the nature of the strapless, backless black number she was more or less wearing. Her hands tightened on the microphone.

"Please help me give our panel members full attention," she said, "as we turn the page to find out—" she paused dramatically "—What Happens Next!"

What happened next was that the lights went out. All of them, all at once, with a great crackling noise of electrical failure. Somebody screamed, and then so did somebody else, and then screaming became kind of popular. A shot rang out. There were more screams, and then another shot, and then everybody was shouting at once, and then some lights came on.

Guess who was dead.

That was Friday night. Tuesday afternoon, Haig was sitting back in his chair on his side of our huge old partners' desk. He didn't have his feet up—I'd broken him of that habit—but I could see he wanted to. Instead he contented himself with taking a pipe apart and putting it back together again. He had tried smoking pipes, thinking it a good mannerism for a detective, but it never took, so now he fiddles with them. It looks pretty dumb, but it's better than putting his feet up on the desk.

"I don't suppose you're wondering why I summoned you all here," he said.

They weren't wondering. They all knew, all of the panelists from the other night, plus two old friends of ours, a cop named Gregorio who wears clothes that could never be purchased on a policeman's salary, and another cop named Seidenwall, who wears clothes that could. They knew they'd been gathered together to watch Leo Haig pull a rabbit out of a hat, and it was going to be a neat trick because it looked as though he didn't even have the hat.

"We're here to clear up the mysterious circumstances of the death of Mavis Mallory. All of you assembled here, except for the two gentlemen of the law, had a motive for her murder. All of you had the opportunity. All of you thus exist under a cloud of suspicion. As a result, you should all be happy to learn that you have nothing to fear from my investigation. Mavis Mallory committed suicide."

"Suicide!" Gregorio exploded. "I've heard you make some ridiculous statements in your time, but that one grabs the gateau. You have the nerve to sit there like a toad on a lily pad and tell me the redheaded dame killed herself?"

"Nerve?" Haig mused. "Is nerve ever required to tell the truth?"

"Truth? You wouldn't recognize the truth if it dove into one of your fish tanks and swam around eating up all the brine shrimp. The Mallory woman got hit by everything short of tactical nuclear weapons. There were two bullets in her from different guns. She had a wavy-bladed knife stuck in her back and a short dagger in her chest, or maybe it was the other way around. The back of her skull was dented by a blow from a blunt instrument. There was enough rat poison in her system to put the Pied Piper out of business, and there were traces of curare, a South American arrow poison, in her martini glass. Did I leave something out?"

"Her heart had stopped beating," Haig said.

"Is that a fact? If you ask me, it had its reasons. And you sit there and call it suicide. That's some suicide."

Haig sat there and breathed, in and out, in and out, in the relaxed, connected breathing rhythm that Lori Schneiderman had taught him. Meanwhile they all watched him, and I in turn watched them. We had them arranged just the way they'd been on the panel, with Detective Vincent Gregorio sitting in the middle where Mavis Mallory had been. Reading left to right, I was looking at Bart Halloran, Dorothea Trill, Darrell Crenna, Gregorio, Lotte Benzler, Austin Porterfield, and Janice Cowan. Detective Wallace Seidenwall sat behind the others, sort of off to the side and next to the wall. If this were novel length I'd say what each of them was wearing and who scowled and who looked interested, but Haig says there's not enough plot here for a novel and that you have to be more concise in short stories, so just figure they were all feeling about the way you'd feel if you were sitting around watching a fat little detective practice rhythmic breathing.

"Some suicide," Haig said. "Indeed. Some years ago a reporter went to a remote county in Texas to investigate the death of a man who'd been trying to expose irregularities in election procedures. The coroner had recorded the death as suicide, and the reporter checked the autopsy and discovered that the deceased had been shot six times in the back with a high-powered rifle. He confronted the coroner with this fact and demanded to know how the man had dared call the death suicide.

" 'Yep,' drawled the coroner. 'Worst case of suicide I ever saw in my life.' "

Gregorio just stared at him.

"So it is with Miss Mallory," Haig continued. "Hers is the worst case of suicide in my experience. Miss Mallory was helplessly under the influence of her own unconscious death urge. She came to me, knowing that she was being drawn toward death, and yet she had not the slightest impulse to gain protection. She wished only that I contract to investigate her demise and see to its resolution. She deliberately assembled seven persons who had reason to rejoice in her death, and enacted a little drama in front of an audience. She—"

"Six persons," Gregorio said, gesturing to the three on either side of him. "Unless you're counting her, or unless all of a sudden I got to be a suspect."

Haig rang a little bell on his desk top, and that was Wong Fat's cue to usher in a skinny guy in a dark suit. "Mr. Abner Jenks," Haig announced. "Former editor of *Mallory's Mystery Magazine*, demoted to slush reader and part-time assistant."

"He passed the drinks," Dorothea Trill remembered. "So that's how she got the rat poison."

"I certainly didn't poison her," Jenks whined. "Nor did I shoot her or stab her or hit her over the head or—"

Haig held up a hand. There was a pipe stem in it, but it still silenced everybody. "You all had motives," he said. "None of you intended to act on them. None of you planned to make an attempt on Miss Mallory's life. Yet thought is creative and Mavis Mallory's thoughts were powerful. Some people attract money to them, or love, or fame. Miss Mallory attracted violent death."

"You're making a big deal out of nothing," Gregorio said. "You're saying she wanted to die, and that's fine, but it's still a crime to give her a hand with it, and that's what every single one of them did. What's that movie, something about the Orient Express, and they all stab the guy? That's what we got here, and I think what I gotta do is book 'em all on a conspiracy charge."

"That would be the act of a witling," Haig said. "First of all, there was no conspiracy. Perhaps more important, there was no murder."

"Just a suicide."

"Precisely," said Haig. *Huff*. "In a real sense, all death is suicide. As long as a man's life urge is stronger than his death urge, he is immortal and invulnerable. Once the balance shifts, he has an unbreakable appointment in Samarra. But Miss Mallory's death is suicide in a much stricter sense of the word. No one else tried to kill her, and no one else succeeded. She unquestionably created her own death."

"And shot herself?" Gregorio demanded. "And stuck knives in herself, and bopped herself over the head? And—"

"No," Haig said. *Huff*. "I could tell you that she drew the bullets and knives to herself by the force of her thoughts, but I would be wasting my—" *huff*! "—breath. The point is metaphysical, and in the present context immaterial. The bullets were not aimed at her, nor did they kill her. Neither did the stabbings, the blow to the head, the poison."

"Then what did?"

"The stopping of her heart."

"Well, that's what kills everyone," Gregorio said, as if explaining something to a child. "That's how you know someone's dead. The heart stops."

Haig sighed heavily, and I don't know if it was circular breathing or resignation. Then he started telling them how it happened.

"Miss Mallory's death urge created a powerful impulse toward violence," he said. "All seven of you, the six panelists and Mr. Jenks, had motives for killing the woman. But you are not murderous people, and you had no intention of committing acts of violence. Quite without conscious intent, you found yourselves bringing weapons to the Town Hall event. Perhaps you thought to display them to an audience of mystery fans. Perhaps you felt a need for a self-defense capability. It hardly matters what went through your minds.

"All of you, as I said, had reason to hate Miss Mallory. In addition, each of you had reason to hate one or more of your fellow panel members. Miss Benzler and Mr. Crenna are rival booksellers; their cordial loathing for one another is legendary. Mr. Halloran was romantically involved with the panel's female members, while Mr. Porterfield and Mr. Jenks were briefly, uh, closeted together in friendship. Miss Trill had been very harshly dealt with in some writings of Mr. Porterfield. Miss Cowan had bought books by Mr. Halloran and Miss Trill, then left the books stranded when she moved on to another employer. I could go on, but what's the point? Each and every one of you may be said to have had a sound desire to murder each and every one of your fellows, but in the ordinary course of things nothing would have come of any of these desires. We all commit dozens of mental murders a day, yet few of us ever dream of acting on any of them."

"I'm sure there's a point to this," Austin Porterfield said.

"Indeed there is, sir, and I am fast approaching it. Miss Mallory leaned forward, grasping her microphone, pausing for full dramatic value, and the lights went out. And it was then that knives and guns and blunt instruments and poison came into play."

The office lights dimmed as Wong Fat operated a wall switch. There was a sharp intake of breath, although the room didn't get all that dark, and there was a balancing *huff* from Haig. "The room went dark," he said. "That was Miss Mallory's doing. She chose the moment, not just unconsciously, but with knowing purpose. She wanted to make a dramatic point, and she succeeded beyond her wildest dreams.

"As soon as those lights went out, everyone's murderous impulses, already stirred up by Mavis Mallory's death urge, were immeasurably augmented. Mr. Crenna drew a Malayan kris and moved to stab it into the heart of his competitor, Miss Benzler. At the same time, Miss Benzler drew a poniard of her own and circled around to direct it at Mr. Crenna's back. Neither could see. Neither was well oriented. And Mavis Mallory's unconscious death urge drew both blades to her own body, even as it drew the bullet Mr. Porterfield meant for Mr. Jenks, the deadly blow Mr. Halloran meant for Cowan, the bullet Miss Cowan intended for Miss Trill, and the curare Miss Trill had meant to place in Mr. Halloran's glass.

"Curare, incidentally, works only if introduced into the bloodstream; it would have been quite ineffective if ingested. The rat poison Miss Mallory did ingest was warfarin, which would ultimately have caused her death by internal bleeding; it was in the glass when Abner Jenks served it to her."

"Then Jenks tried to kill her," Gregorio said.

Haig shook his head. "Jenks did not put the poison in the glass," he said. "Miss Lotte Benzler had placed the poison in the glass before Miss Mallory picked it up."

"Then Miss Benzler—"

"Was not trying to kill Miss Mallory either," Haig said, "because she placed the poison in the glass she intended to take for herself. She had previously ingested a massive dose of Vitamin K, a coagulant which is the standard antidote for warfarin, and intended to survive a phony murder attempt on stage, both to publicize The Murder Store and to discredit her competitor, Mr. Crenna. At the time, of course, she'd had no conscious intention of sticking a poniard into the same Mr. Crenna, the very poniard that wound up in Miss Mallory."

"You're saying they all tried to kill each other," Gregorio said. "And they all killed her instead."

"But they didn't succeed."

"They didn't? How do you figure that? She's dead as a bent doornail."

"She was already dead."

"How?"

"Dead of electrocution," Haig told him. "Mavis Mallory put out all the lights in Town Hall by short-circuiting the microphone. She got more than she bargained for, although in a sense it was precisely what she'd bargained for. In the course of shorting out the building's electrical system, she herself was subjected to an electrical charge that induced immediate and permanent cardiac arrest. The warfarin had not yet had time to begin inducing fatal internal bleeding. The knives and bullets pierced the skin of a woman who was already dead. The bludgeon crushed a dead woman's skull. Miss Mallory killed herself."

Wong Fat brought the lights up. Gregorio blinked at the brightness. "That's a pretty uncertain way to do yourself in," he said. "It's not like she had her foot in a pail of water. You don't necessarily get a shock shorting out a line that way, and the shock's not necessarily a fatal one."

"The woman did not consciously plan her own death," Haig told him. "An official verdict of suicide would be of dubious validity. Accidental death, I suppose, is what the certificate would properly read." He huffed mightily. "Accidental death! As that Texas sheriff would say, it's quite the worst case of accidental death I've ever witnessed."

And that's what it went down as, accidental death. No charges were ever pressed against any of the seven, although it drove Gregorio crazy that they all walked out of there untouched. But what could you get them for? Mutilating a corpse? It would be hard to prove who did what, and it would be even harder to prove that they'd been trying to kill each other. As far as Haig was concerned, they were all acting under the influence of Mavis Mallory's death urge, and were only faintly responsible for their actions.

"The woman was ready to die, Chip," he said, "and die she did. She wanted me to solve her death and I've solved it, I trust to the satisfaction of the lawyers for her estate. And you've got a good case to write up. It won't make a novel, and there's not nearly enough sex in it to satisfy the book-buying public, but I shouldn't wonder that it will make a good short story. Perhaps for *Mallory's Mystery Magazine*, or a publication of equal stature."

He stood up. "I'm going uptown," he announced, "to get rebirthed. I suggest you come along. I think Wolfe must have been a devotee of rebirthing, and Archie as well."

I asked him how he figured that.

"Rebirthing reverses the aging process," he explained. "How else do you suppose the great detectives manage to endure for generations without getting a day older? Archie Goodwin was a brash young man in *Fer-de-lance* in nineteen thirty-four. He was still the same youthful wisenheimer forty years later. I told you once, Chip, that your association with me would make it possible for you to remain eighteen years old forever. Now it seems that I can lead you not only to the immortality of ink and paper but to genuine physical immortality. If you and I work to purge ourselves of the effects of birth trauma, and if we use our breath to cleanse our cells, and if we stamp out deathist thoughts once and forever—"

"Huh," I said. But wouldn't you know it? It came out *huff*.

As Dark as Christmas Gets

It was 9:54 in the morning when I got to the little bookshop on West Fifty-sixth Street. Before I went to work for Leo Haig I probably wouldn't have bothered to look at my watch, if I was even wearing one in the first place, and the best I'd have been able to say was it was around ten o'clock. But Haig wanted me to be his legs and eyes, and sometimes his ears, nose, and throat, and if he was going to play in Nero Wolfe's league, that meant I had to turn into Archie Goodwin, for Pete's sake, noticing everything and getting the details right and reporting conversations verbatim.

Well, forget that last part. My memory's getting better—Haig's right about that part—but what follows won't be word for word, because all I am is a human being. If you want a tape recorder, buy one.

There was a lot of fake snow in the window, and a Santa Claus doll in handcuffs, and some toy guns and knives, and a lot of mysteries with a Christmas theme, including the one by Fredric Brown where the murderer dresses up as a department store Santa. (Someone pulled that a year ago, put on a red suit and a white beard and shot a man at the corner of Broadway and Thirty-seventh, and I told Haig how ingenious I thought it was. He gave me a look, left the room, and came back with a book. I read it—that's what I do when Haig hands me a book—and found out Brown had had the idea fifty years earlier. Which doesn't mean that's where the killer got the idea. The book's long out of print—the one I read was a paperback, and falling apart, not like the handsome hardcover copy in the window. And how many killers get their ideas out of old books?)

Now if you're a detective yourself you'll have figured out two things by now—the bookshop specialized in mysteries, and it was the Christmas season. And if you'd noticed the sign in the window you'd have made one more deduction, i.e., that they were closed.

I went down the half flight of steps and poked the buzzer. When nothing happened I poked it again, and eventually the door was opened by a little man with white hair and a white beard—all he needed was padding and a red suit, and someone to teach him to be jolly. "I'm terribly sorry," he said, "but I'm afraid we're closed. It's Christmas morning, and it's not even ten o'clock."

"You called us," I said, "and it wasn't even nine o'clock."

He took a good look at me, and light dawned. "You're Harrison," he said. "And I know your first name, but I can't—"

"Chip," I supplied.

"Of course. But where's Haig? I know he thinks he's Nero Wolfe, but he's not gone housebound, has he? He's been here often enough in the past."

"Haig gets out and about," I agreed, "but Wolfe went all the way to Montana once, as far as that goes. What Wolfe refused to do was leave the house on business, and Haig's with him on that one. Besides, he just spawned some unspawnable cichlids from Lake Chad, and you'd think the aquarium was a television set and they were showing *Midnight Blue*."

"Fish." He sounded more reflective than contemptuous. "Well, at least you're here. That's something." He locked the door and led me up a spiral staircase to a room full of books, and full as well with the residue of a party. There were empty glasses here and there, hors d'oeuvres trays that held nothing but crumbs, and a cut-glass dish with a sole remaining cashew.

"Christmas," he said, and shuddered. "I had a houseful of people here last night. All of them eating, all of them drinking, and many of them actually singing." He made a face. "I didn't sing," he said, "but I certainly ate and drank. And eventually they all went home and I went upstairs to bed. I must have, because that's where I was when I woke up two hours ago."

"But you don't remember."

"Well, no," he said, "but then what would there be to remember? The guests leave and you're alone with vague feelings of sadness." His gaze turned inward. "If she'd stayed," he said, "I'd have remembered."

"She?"

"Never mind. I awoke this morning, alone in my own bed. I swallowed some aspirin and came downstairs. I went into the library."

"You mean this room?"

"This is the salesroom. These books are for sale."

"Well, I figured. I mean, this is a bookshop."

"You've never seen the library?" He didn't wait for an answer but turned to open a door and lead me down a hallway to another room twice the size of the first. It was lined with floor-to-ceiling hardwood shelves, and the shelves were filled with double rows of hardcover books. It was hard to identify the books, though, because all but one section was wrapped in plastic sheeting.

"This is my collection," he announced. "These books are not for sale. I'll only part with one if I've replaced it with a finer copy. Your employer doesn't collect, does he?"

"Haig? He's got thousands of books."

"Yes, and he's bought some of them from me. But he doesn't give a damn about first editions. He doesn't care what kind of shape a book is in, or even if it's got a dust jacket. He'd as soon have a Grosset reprint or a book-club edition or even a paperback."

"He just wants to read them."

"It takes all kinds, doesn't it?" He shook his head in wonder. "Last night's party filled this room as well as the salesroom. I put up plastic to keep the books from getting handled and possibly damaged. Or—how shall I put this?"

Any way you want, I thought. You're the client.

"Some of these books are extremely valuable," he said. "And my guests were all extremely reputable people, but many of them are good customers, and that means they're collectors. Ardent, even rabid collectors."

"And you didn't want them stealing the books."

"You're very direct," he said. "I suppose that's a useful quality in your line of work. But no, I didn't want to tempt anyone, especially when alcoholic indulgence might make temptation particularly difficult to resist."

"So you hung up plastic sheets."

"And came downstairs this morning to remove the plastic, and pick up some dirty glasses and clear some of the debris. I puttered around. I took down the plastic from this one section, as you can see. I did a bit of tidying. And then I saw it."

"Saw what?"

He pointed to a set of glassed-in shelves, on top of which stood a three-foot row of leather-bound volumes. "There," he said. "What do you see?"

"Leatherbound books, but—"

"Boxes," he corrected. "Wrapped in leather and stamped in gold, and each one holding a manuscript. They're fashioned to look like finely-bound books, but they're original manuscripts."

"Very nice," I said. "I suppose they must be very rare."

"They're unique."

"That too."

He made a face. "One of a kind. The author's original manuscript, with corrections in his own hand. Most are typed, but the Elmore Leonard is handwritten. The Westlake, of course, is typed on that famous Smith-Corona manual portable of his. The Paul Kavanagh is the author's first novel. He only wrote three, you know."

I didn't, but Haig would.

"They're very nice," I said politely. "And I don't suppose they're for sale."

"Of course not. They're in the library. They're part of the collection."

"Right," I said, and paused for him to continue. When he didn't I said, "Uh, I was thinking. Maybe you could tell me . . ."

"Why I summoned you here." He sighed. "Look at the boxed manuscript between the Westlake and the Kavanagh."

"Between them?"

"Yes."

"The Kavanagh is *Such Men Are Dangerous,*" I said, "and the Westlake is *Drowned Hopes*. But there's nothing at all between them but a three-inch gap."

"Exactly," he said.

"As Dark as *It Gets,*" I said. "By Cornell Woolrich."

Haig frowned. "I don't know the book," he said. "Not under that title, not with Woolrich's name on it, nor William Irish or George Hopley. Those were his pen names."

"I know," I said. "You don't know the book because it was never published. The manuscript was found among Woolrich's effects after his death."

"There was a posthumous book, Chip."

"*Into the Night,*" I said. "Another writer completed it, writing replacement scenes for some that had gone missing in the original. It wound up being publishable."

"It wound up being published," Haig said. "That's not necessarily the same thing. But this manuscript, *As Dark—*"

"*As It Gets*. It wasn't publishable, according to our client. Woolrich evidently worked on it over the years, and what survived him incorporated unresolved portions of several drafts. There are characters who die early on and then reappear with no explanation. There's supposed to be some great writing and plenty of Woolrich's trademark paranoid suspense, but it doesn't add up to a book, or even something that could be edited into a book. But to a collector—"

"Collectors," Haig said heavily.

"Yes, sir. I asked what the manuscript was worth. He said, 'Well, I paid five thousand dollars for it.' That's verbatim, but don't ask me if the thing's worth more or less than that, because I don't know if he was bragging that he was a big spender or a slick trader."

"It doesn't matter," Haig said. "The money's the least of it. He added it to his collection and he wants it back."

"And the person who stole it," I said, "is either a friend or a customer or both."

"And so he called us and not the police. The manuscript was there when the party started?"

"Yes."

"And gone this morning?"

"Yes."

"And there were how many in attendance?"

"Forty or fifty," I said, "including the caterer and her staff."

"If the party was catered," he mused, "why was the room a mess when you saw it? Wouldn't the catering staff have cleaned up at the party's end?"

"I asked him that question myself. The party lasted longer than the caterer had signed on for. She hung around herself for a while after her employees packed it in, but she stopped working and became a guest. Our client was hoping she would stay."

"But you just said she did."

"After everybody else went home. He lives upstairs from the bookshop, and he was hoping for a chance to show her his living quarters."

Haig shrugged. He's not quite the misogynist his idol is, but he hasn't been at it as long. Give him time. He said, "Chip, it's hopeless. Fifty suspects?"

"Six."

"How so?"

"By two o'clock," I said, "just about everybody had called it a night. The ones remaining got a reward."

"And what was that?"

"Some fifty-year-old Armagnac, served in Waterford pony glasses. We counted the glasses, and there were seven of them. Six guests and the host."

"And the manuscript?"

"Was still there at the time, and still sheathed in plastic. See, he'd covered all the boxed manuscripts, same as the books on the shelves. But the cut-glass ship's decanter was serving as a sort of bookend to the manuscript section, and he took off the plastic to get at it. And while he was at it he took out one of the manuscripts and showed it off to his guests."

"Not the Woolrich, I don't suppose."

"No, it was a Peter Straub novel, elegantly handwritten in a leatherbound journal. Straub collects Chandler, and our client had traded a couple of Chandler firsts for the manuscript, and he was proud of himself."

"I shouldn't wonder."

"But the Woolrich was present and accounted for when he took off the plastic wrap, and it may have been there when he put the Straub back. He didn't notice."

"And this morning it was gone."

"Yes."

"Six suspects," he said. "Name them."

I took out my notebook. "Jon and Jayne Corn-Wallace," I said. "He's a retired stockbroker, she's an actress in a daytime drama. That's a soap opera."

"Piffle."

"Yes, sir. They've been friends of our client for years, and customers for about as long. They were mystery fans, and he got them started on first editions."

"Including Woolrich?"

"He's a favorite of Jayne's. I gather Jon can take him or leave him."

"I wonder which he did last night. Do the Corn-Wallaces collect manuscripts?"

"Just books. First editions, though they're starting to get interested in fancy bindings and limited editions. The one with a special interest in manuscripts is Zoltan Mihalyi."

"The violinist?"

Trust Haig to know that. I'd never heard of him myself. "A big mystery fan," I said. "I guess reading passes the time on those long concert tours."

"I don't suppose a man can spend all his free hours with other men's wives," Haig said. "And who's to say that all the stories are true? He collects manuscripts, does he?"

"He was begging for a chance to buy the Straub, but our friend wouldn't sell."

"Which would make him a likely suspect. Who else?"

"Philip Perigord."

"The writer?"

"Right, and I didn't even know he was still alive. He hasn't written anything in years."

"Almost twenty years. *More Than Murder* was published in 1980."

Trust him to know that, too. "Anyway," I said, "he didn't die. He didn't even stop writing. He just quit writing books. He went to Hollywood and became a screenwriter."

"That's the same as stopping writing," Haig reflected. "It's very nearly the same as being dead. Does he collect books?"

"No."

"Manuscripts?"

"No."

"Perhaps he wanted the manuscripts for scrap paper," Haig said. "He could turn the pages over and write on their backs. Who else was present?"

"Edward Everett Stokes."

"The small-press publisher. Bought out his partner, Geoffrey Poges, to became sole owner of Stokes-Poges Press."

"They do limited editions, according to our client. Leather bindings, small runs, special tip-in sheets."

"All well and good," he said, "but what's useful about Stokes-Poges is that they issue a reasonably priced trade edition of each title as well, and publish works otherwise unavailable, including collections of short fiction from otherwise uncollected writers."

"Do they publish Woolrich?"

"All his work has been published by mainstream publishers, and all his stories collected. Is Stokes a collector himself?"

"Our client didn't say."

"No matter. How many is that? The Corn-Wallaces, Zoltan Mihalyi, Philip Perigord, E. E. Stokes. And the sixth is—"

"Harriet Quinlan."

He looked puzzled, then nodded in recognition. "The literary agent."

"She represents Perigord," I said, "or at least she would, if he ever went back to novel-writing. She's placed books with Stokes-Poges. And she may have left the party with Zoltan Mihalyi."

"I don't suppose her client list includes the Woolrich estate. Or that she's a rabid collector of books and manuscripts."

"He didn't say."

"No matter. You said six suspects, Chip. I count seven."

I ticked them off. "Jon Corn-Wallace. Jayne Corn-Wallace. Zoltan Mihalyi. Philip Perigord. Edward Everett Stokes. Harriet Quinlan. Isn't that six? Or do you want to include our client, the little man with the palindromic first name? That seems farfetched to me, but—"

"The caterer, Chip."

"Oh. Well, he says she was just there to do a job. No interest in books, no interest in manuscripts, no real interest in the world of mysteries. Certainly no interest in Cornell Woolrich."

"And she stayed when her staff went home."

"To have a drink and be sociable. He had hopes she'd spend the night, but it didn't happen. I suppose technically she's a suspect, but—"

"At the very least she's a witness," he said. "Bring her."

"Bring her?"

He nodded. "Bring them all."

It's a shame this is a short story. If it were a novel, now would be the time for me to give you a full description of the off-street carriage house on West Twentieth Street, which Leo Haig owns and where he occupies the top two floors, having rented out the lower two stories to Madam Juana and her All-Girl Enterprise. You'd hear how Haig had lived for years in two rooms in the Bronx, breeding tropical fish and reading detective stories, until a modest inheritance allowed him to set up shop as a poor man's Nero Wolfe.

He's quirky, God knows, and I could fill a few pleasant pages recounting his quirks, including his having hired me as much for my writing ability as for my potential value as a detective. I'm expected to write up his cases the same way Archie Goodwin writes up Wolfe's, and this case was a slam-dunk, really, and he says it wouldn't stretch into a novel, but that it should work nicely as a short story.

So all I'll say is this. Haig's best quirk is his unshakable belief that Nero Wolfe exists. Under another name, of course, to protect his inviolable privacy. And the legendary brownstone, with all its different fictitious street numbers, isn't on West 35th Street at all but in another part of town entirely.

And someday, if Leo Haig performs with sufficient brilliance as a private investigator, he hopes to get the ultimate reward—an invitation to dinner at Nero Wolfe's table.

Well, that gives you an idea. If you want more in the way of background, I can only refer you to my previous writings on the subject. There have been two novels so far, *Make Out With Murder* and *The Topless Tulip Caper*, and they're full of inside stuff about Leo Haig. (There were two earlier books from before I met Haig, *No Score* and *Chip Harrison Scores Again*, but they're not mysteries and Haig's not in them. All they do, really, is tell you more than you'd probably care to know about me.)

Well, end of commercial. Haig said I should put it in, and I generally do what he tells me. After all, the man pays my salary.

And, in his own quiet way, he's a genius. As you'll see.

"They'll never come here," I told him. "Not today. I know it will always live in your memory as The Day the Cichlids Spawned, but to everybody else it's Christmas, and they'll want to spend it in the bosoms of their families, and—"

"Not everyone has a family," he pointed out, "and not every family has a bosom."

"The Corn-Wallaces have a family. Zoltan Mihalyi doesn't, but he's probably got somebody with a bosom lined up to spend the day with. I don't know about the others, but—"

"Bring them," he said, "but not here. I want them all assembled at five o'clock this afternoon at the scene of the crime."

"The bookshop? You're willing to leave the house?"

"It's not entirely business," he said. "Our client is more than a client. He's a friend, and an important source of books. The reading copies he so disdains have enriched our own library immeasurably. And you know how important that is."

If there's anything you need to know, you can find it in the pages of a detective novel. That's Haig's personal conviction, and I'm beginning to believe he's right.

"I'll pay him a visit," he went on. "I'll arrive at 4:30 or so, and perhaps I'll come across a book or two that I'll want for our library. You'll arrange that they all arrive around five, and we'll clear up this little business." He frowned in thought. "I'll tell Wong we'll want Christmas dinner at eight tonight. That should give us more than enough time."

Again, if this were a novel, I'd spend a full chapter telling you what I went through getting them all present and accounted for. It was hard enough finding them, and then I had to sell them on coming. I pitched the event as a second stage of last night's party—their host had arranged, for their entertainment and edification, that they should be present while a real-life private detective solved an actual crime before their very eyes.

According to Haig, all we'd need to spin this yarn into a full-length book would be a dead body, although two would be better. If, say, our client had wandered into his library that morning to find a corpse seated in his favorite chair, *and* the Woolrich manuscript gone, then I could easily stretch all this to sixty thousand words. If the dead man had been wearing a deerstalker cap and holding a violin, we'd be especially well off; when the book came out, all the Sherlockian completists would be compelled to buy it.

Sorry. No murders, no Baker Street Irregulars, no dogs barking or not barking.

I had to get them all there, and I did, but don't ask me how. I can't take the time to tell you.

"Now," Zoltan Mihalyi said. "We are all here. So can someone please tell me *why* we are all here?" There was a twinkle in his dark eyes as he spoke, and the trace of a knowing smile on his lips. He wanted an answer, but he was going to remain charming while he got it. I could believe he swept a lot of women off their feet.

"First of all," Jeanne Botleigh said, "I think we should each have a glass of eggnog. It's festive, and it will help put us all in the spirit of the day."

She was the caterer, and she was some cupcake, all right. Close-cut brown hair framed her small oval face and set off a pair of China-blue eyes. She had an English accent, roughed up some by ten years in New York, and she was short and slender and curvy, and I could see why our client had hoped she would stick around.

And now she'd whipped up a batch of eggnog, and ladled out cups for each of us. I waited until someone else tasted it—after all the mystery novels Haig's forced on me, I've developed an imagination—but once the Corn-Wallaces had tossed off theirs with no apparent effect, I took a sip. It was smooth and delicious, and it had a kick like a mule. I looked over at Haig, who's not much of a drinker, and he was smacking his lips over it.

"Why are we here?" he said, echoing the violinist's question. "Well, sir, I shall tell you. We are here as friends and customers of our host, whom we may be able to assist in the solution of a puzzle. Last night all of us, with the exception of course of myself and my young assistant, were present in this room. Also present was the original manuscript of an unpublished novel by Cornell Woolrich. This morning we were all gone, and so was the manuscript. Now we have returned. The manuscript, alas, has not."

"Wait a minute," Jon Corn-Wallace said. "You're saying one of us took it?"

"I say only that it has gone, sir. It is possible that someone within this room was involved in its disappearance, but there are diverse other possibilities as well. What impels me, what has prompted me to summon you here, is the likelihood that one or more of you knows something that will shed light on the incident."

"But the only person who would know anything would be the person who took it," Harriet Quinlan said. She was what they call a woman of a certain age, which generally means a woman of an uncertain age. Her figure was a few pounds beyond girlish, and I had a hunch she dyed her hair and might have had her face lifted somewhere along the way, but whatever she'd done had paid off. She was probably old enough to be my mother's older sister, but that didn't keep me from having the sort of ideas a nephew's not supposed to have.

Haig told her anyone could have observed something, and not just the guilty party, and Philip Perigord started to ask a question, and Haig held up a hand and cut him off in mid-sentence. Most people probably would have finished what they were saying, but I guess Perigord was used to studio executives shutting him up at pitch meetings. He bit off his word in the middle of a syllable and stayed mute.

"It is a holiday," Haig said, "and we all have other things to do, so we'd best avoid distraction. Hence I will ask the questions and you will answer them. Mr. Corn-Wallace. You are a book collector. Have you given a thought to collecting manuscripts?"

"I've thought about it," Jon Corn-Wallace said. He was the best-dressed man in the room, looking remarkably comfortable in a dark blue suit and a striped tie. He wore bull and bear cufflinks and one of those watches that's worth $5000 if it's real or $25 if you bought it from a Nigerian street vendor. "He tried to get me interested," he said, with a nod toward our client. "But I was always the kind of trader who stuck to listed stocks."

"Meaning?"

"Meaning it's impossible to pinpoint the market value of a one-of-a-kind item like a manuscript. There's too much guesswork involved. I'm not buying books with an eye to selling them, that's something my heirs will have to worry about, but I do like to know what my collection is worth and whether or not it's been a good investment. It's part of the pleasure of collecting, as far as I'm concerned. So I've stayed away from manuscripts. They're too iffy."

"And had you had a look at *As Dark as It Gets?*"

"No. I'm not interested in manuscripts, and I don't care at all for Woolrich."

"Jon likes hard-boiled fiction," his wife put in, "but Woolrich is a little weird for his taste. I think he was a genius myself. Quirky and tormented, maybe, but what genius isn't?"

Haig, I thought. You couldn't call him tormented, but maybe he made up for it by exceeding the usual quota of quirkiness.

"Anyway," Jayne Corn-Wallace said, "I'm the Woolrich fan in the family. Though I agree with Jon as far as manuscripts are concerned. The value is pure speculation. And who wants to buy something and then have to get a box made for it? It's like buying an unframed canvas and having to get it framed."

"The Woolrich manuscript was already boxed," Haig pointed out.

"I mean generally, as an area for collecting. As a collector, I wasn't interested in *As Dark as It Gets*. If someone fixed it up and completed it, and if someone published it, I'd have been glad to buy it. I'd have bought two copies."

"Two copies, madam?"

She nodded. "One to read and one to own."

Haig's face darkened, and I thought he might offer his opinion of people who were afraid to damage their books by reading them. But he kept it to himself, and I was just as glad. Jayne Corn-Wallace was a tall, handsome woman, radiating self-confidence, and I sensed she'd give as good as she got in an exchange with Haig.

"You might have wanted to read the manuscript," Haig suggested.

She shook her head. "I like Woolrich," she said, "but as a stylist he was choppy enough *after* editing and polishing. I wouldn't want to try him in manuscript, let alone an unfinished manuscript like that one."

"Mr. Mihalyi," Haig said. "You collect manuscripts, don't you?"

"I do."

"And do you care for Woolrich?"

The violinist smiled. "If I had the chance to buy the original manuscript of *The Bride Wore Black*," he said, "I would leap at it. If it were close at hand, and if strong drink had undermined my moral fiber, I might even slip it under my coat and walk off with it." A wink showed us he was kidding. "Or at least I'd have been tempted. The work in question, however, tempted me not a whit."

"And why is that, sir?"

Mihalyi frowned. "There are people," he said, "who attend open rehearsals and make surreptitious recordings of the music. They treasure them and even bootleg them to other like-minded fans. I despise such people."

"Why?"

"They violate the artist's privacy," he said. "A rehearsal is a time when one refines one's approach to a piece of music. One takes chances, one uses the occasion as the equivalent of an artist's sketch pad. The person who records it is in essence spraying a rough sketch with fixative and hanging it on the wall of his personal museum. I find it unsettling enough that listeners record concert performances, making permanent what was supposed to be a transitory experience. But to record a rehearsal is an atrocity."

"And a manuscript?"

"A manuscript is the writer's completed work. It provides a record of how he arranged and revised his ideas, and how they were in turn adjusted for better or worse by an editor. But it is finished work. An unfinished manuscript . . ."

"Is a rehearsal?"

"That or something worse. I ask myself, What would Woolrich have wanted?"

"Another drink," Edward Everett Stokes said, and leaned forward to help himself to more eggnog. "I take your point, Mihalyi. And Woolrich might well have preferred to have his unfinished work destroyed upon his death, but he left no instructions to that effect, so how can we presume to guess his wishes? Perhaps, for all we know, there is a single scene in the book that meant as much to him as anything he'd written. Or less than a scene—a bit of dialogue, a paragraph of description, perhaps no more than a single sentence. Who are we to say it should not survive?"

"Perigord," Mihalyi said. "You are a writer. Would you care to have your unfinished work published after your death? Would you not recoil at that, or at having it completed by others?"

Philip Perigord cocked an eyebrow. "I'm the wrong person to ask," he said. "I've spent twenty years in Hollywood. Forget unfinished work. My *finished* work doesn't get published, or 'produced,' as they so revealingly term it. I get paid, and the work winds up on a shelf. And, when it comes to having one's work completed by others, in Hollywood you don't have to wait until you're dead. It happens during your lifetime, and you learn to live with it."

"We don't know the author's wishes," Harriet Quinlan put in, "and I wonder how relevant they are."

"But it's his work," Mihalyi pointed out.

"Is it, Zoltan? Or does it belong to the ages? Finished or not, the author has left it to us. Schubert did not finish one of his greatest symphonies. Would you have laid its two completed movements in the casket with him?"

"It has been argued that the work was complete, that he intended it to be but two movements long."

"That begs the question, Zoltan."

"It does, dear lady," he said with a wink. "I'd rather beg the question than be undone by it. Of course I'd keep the Unfinished Symphony in the repertoire. On the other hand, I'd hate to see some fool attempt to finish it."

"No one has, have they?"

"Not to my knowledge. But several writers have had the effrontery to finish *The Mystery of Edwin Drood*, and I do think Dickens would have been better served if the manuscript had gone in the box with his bones. And as for sequels, like those for *Pride and Prejudice* and *The Big Sleep*, or that young fellow who had the colossal gall to tread in Rex Stout's immortal footsteps . . ."

Now we were getting onto sensitive ground. As far as Leo Haig was concerned, Archie Goodwin had always written up Wolfe's cases, using the transparent pseudonym of Rex Stout. (Rex Stout = fat king, an allusion to Wolfe's own regal corpulence.) Robert Goldsborough, credited with the books written since the "death" of Stout, was, as Haig saw it, a ghostwriter employed by Goodwin, who was no longer up to the chore of hammering out the books. He'd relate them to Goldsborough, who transcribed them and polished them up. While they might not have all the narrative verve of Goodwin's own work, still they provided an important and accurate account of Wolfe's more recent cases.

See, Haig feels the great man's still alive and still raising orchids and nailing killers. Maybe somewhere on the Upper East Side. Maybe in Murray Hill, or just off Gramercy Park . . .

The discussion about Goldsborough, and about sequels in general, roused Haig from a torpor that Wolfe himself might have envied. "Enough," he said with authority. "There's no time for meandering literary conversations, nor would Chip have room for them in a short-story-length report. So let us get to it. One of you took the manuscript, box and all, from its place on the shelf. Mr. Mihalyi, you have the air of one who protests too much. You profess no interest in the manuscripts of unpublished novels, and I can accept that you did not yearn to possess *As Dark as It Gets*, but you wanted a look at it, didn't you?"

"I don't own a Woolrich manuscript," he said, "and of course I was interested in seeing what one looked like. How he typed, how he entered corrections . . ."

"So you took the manuscript from the shelf."

"Yes," the violinist agreed. "I went into the other room with it, opened the box, and flipped through the pages. You can taste the flavor of the man's work in the visual appearance of his manuscript pages. The words and phrases x'd out, the pencil notations, the crossovers, even the typographical errors. The computer age puts paid to all that, doesn't it? Imagine Chandler running Spel-Chek, or Hammett with justified margins." He sighed. "A few minutes with the script made me long to own one of Woolrich's. But not this one, for reasons I've already explained."

"You spent how long with the book?"

"Fifteen minutes at the most. Probably more like ten."

"And returned to this room?"

"Yes."

"And brought the manuscript with you?"

"Yes. I intended to return it to the shelf, but someone was standing in the way. It may have been you, Jon. It was someone tall, and you're the tallest person here." He turned to our client. "It wasn't you. But I think you may have been talking with Jon. Someone was, at any rate, and I'd have had to step between the two of you to put the box back, and that might have led to questions as to why I'd picked it up in the first place. So I put it down."

"Where?"

"On a table. That one, I think."

"It's not there now," Jon Corn-Wallace said.

"It's not," Haig agreed. "One of you took it from that table. I could, through an exhausting process of cross-questioning, establish who that person is. But it would save us all time if the person would simply recount what happened next."

There was a silence while they all looked at each other. "Well, I guess this is where I come in," Jayne Corn-Wallace said. "I was sitting in the red chair, where Phil Perigord is sitting now. And whoever I'd been talking to went to get another drink, and I looked around, and there it was on the table."

"The manuscript, madam?"

"Yes, but I didn't know that was what it was, not at first. I thought it was a finely bound limited edition. Because the manuscripts are all kept on that shelf, you know, and this one wasn't. And it hadn't been on the table a few minutes earlier, either. I knew that much. So I assumed it was a book someone had been leafing through, and I saw it was by Cornell Woolrich, and I didn't recognize the title, so I thought I'd try leafing through it myself."

"And you found it was a manuscript."

"Well, that didn't take too keen an eye, did it? I suppose I glanced at the first twenty pages, just riffled through them while the party went on around me. I stopped after a chapter or so. That was plenty."

"You didn't like what you read?"

"There were corrections," she said disdainfully. "Words and whole sentences crossed out, new words penciled in. I realize writers have to work that way, but when I read a book I like to believe it emerged from the writer's mind fully formed."

"Like Athena from the brow of What's-his-name," her husband said.

"Zeus. I don't want to know there was a writer at work, making decisions, putting words down, and then changing them. I want to forget about the writer entirely and lose myself in the story."

"Everybody wants to forget about the writer," Philip Perigord said, helping himself to more eggnog. "At the Oscars each year some ninny intones, 'In the beginning was the Word,' before he hands out the screenwriting awards. And you hear the usual crap about how they owe it all to chaps like me who put words in their mouths. They say it, but nobody believes it. Jack Warner called us schmucks with Underwoods. Well, we've come a long way. Now we're schmucks with Power Macs."

"Indeed," Haig said. "You looked at the manuscript, didn't you, Mr. Perigord?"

"I never read unpublished work. Can't risk leaving myself open to a plagiarism charge."

"Oh? But didn't you have a special interest in Woolrich? Didn't you once adapt a story of his?"

"How did you know about that? I was one of several who made a living off that particular piece of crap. It was never produced."

"And you looked at this manuscript in the hope that you might adapt it?"

The writer shook his head. "I'm through wasting myself out there."

"They're through with you," Harriet Quinlan said. "Nothing personal, Phil, but it's a town that uses up writers and throws them away. You couldn't get arrested out there. So you've come back east to write books."

"And you'll be representing him, madam?"

"I may, if he brings me something I can sell. I saw him paging through a manuscript and figured he was looking for something he could steal. Oh, don't look so outraged, Phil. Why not steal from Woolrich, for God's sake? He's not going to sue. He left everything to Columbia University, and you could knock off anything of his, published or unpublished, and they'd never know the difference. Ever since I saw you reading, I've been wondering. Did you come across anything worth stealing?"

"I don't steal," Perigord said. "Still, perfectly legitimate inspiration can result from a glance at another man's work—"

"I'll say it can. And did it?"

He shook his head. "If there was a strong idea anywhere in that manuscript, I couldn't find it in the few minutes I spent looking. What about you, Harriet? I know you had a look at it, because I saw you."

"I just wanted to see what it was you'd been so caught up in. And *I* wondered if the manuscript might be salvageable. One of my writers might be able to pull it off, and do a better job than the hack who finished *Into the Night*."

"Ah," Haig said. "And what did you determine, madam?"

"I didn't read enough to form a judgment. Anyway, *Into the Night* was no great commercial success, so why tag along in its wake?"

"So you put the manuscript . . ."

"Back in its box, and left it on the table where I'd found it."

Our client shook his head in wonder. "*Murder on the Orient Express*," he said. "Or in the Calais coach, depending on whether you're English or American. It's beginning to look as though *everyone* read that manuscript. And I never noticed a thing!"

"Well, you were hitting the sauce pretty good," Jon Corn-Wallace reminded him. "And you were, uh, concentrating all your social energy in one direction."

"How's that?"

Corn-Wallace nodded toward Jeanne Botleigh, who was refilling someone's cup. "As far as you were concerned, our lovely caterer was the only person in the room."

There was an awkward silence, with our host coloring and his caterer lowering her eyes demurely. Haig broke it. "To continue," he said abruptly. "Miss Quinlan returned the manuscript to its box and to its place upon the table. Then—"

"But she didn't," Perigord said. "Harriet, I wanted another look at Woolrich. Maybe I'd missed something. But first I saw you reading it, and when I looked a second time it was gone. You weren't reading it and it wasn't on the table, either."

"I put it back," the agent said.

"But not where you found it," said Edward Everett Stokes. "You set it down not on the table but on that revolving bookcase."

"Did I? I suppose it's possible. But how did you know that?"

"Because I saw you," said the small-press publisher. "And because I wanted a look at the manuscript myself. I knew about it, including the fact that it was not restorable in the fashion of *Into the Night.* That made it valueless to a commercial publisher, but the idea of a Woolrich novel going unpublished ate away at me. I mean, we're talking about Cornell Woolrich."

"And you thought—"

"I thought why not publish it as is, warts and all? I could do it, in an edition of two or three hundred copies, for collectors who'd happily accept inconsistencies and omissions for the sake of having something otherwise unobtainable. I wanted a few minutes' peace and quiet with the book, so I took it into the lavatory."

"And?"

"And I read it, or at least paged through it. I must have spent half an hour in there, or close to it."

"I remember you were gone a while," Jon Corn-Wallace said. "I thought you'd headed on home."

"I thought he was in the other room," Jayne said, "cavorting on the pile of coats with Harriet here. But I guess that must have been someone else."

"It was Zoltan," the agent said, "and we were hardly cavorting."

"Canoodling, then, but—"

"He was teaching me a yogic breathing technique, not that it's any of your business. Stokes, you took the manuscript into the john. I trust you brought it back?"

"Well, no."

"You took it home? You're the person responsible for its disappearance?"

"Certainly not. I didn't take it home, and I hope I'm not responsible for its disappearance. I left it in the lavatory."

"You just left it there?"

"In its box, on the shelf over the vanity. I set it down there while I washed my hands, and I'm afraid I forgot it. And no, it's not there now. I went and looked as soon as I realized what all this was about, and I'm afraid some other hands than mine must have moved it. I'll tell you this—when it does turn up, I definitely want to publish it."

"*If* it turns up," our client said darkly. "Once E.E. left it in the bathroom, anyone could have slipped it under his coat without being seen. And I'll probably never see it again."

"But that means one of us is a thief," somebody said.

"I know, and that's out of the question. You're all my friends. But we were all drinking last night, and drink can confuse a person. Suppose one of you did take it from the bathroom and carried it home as a joke, the kind of joke that can seem funny after a few drinks. If you could contrive to return it, perhaps in such a way that no one could know your identity . . . Haig, you ought to be able to work that out."

"I could," Haig agreed. "If that were how it happened. But it didn't."

"It didn't?"

"You forget the least obvious suspect."

"Me? Dammit, Haig, are you saying I stole my own manuscript?"

"I'm saying the butler did it," Haig said, "or the closest thing we have to a butler. Miss Botleigh, your upper lip has been trembling almost since we all sat down. You've been on the point of an admission throughout and haven't said a word. Have you in fact read the manuscript of *As Dark as It Gets?*"

"Yes."

The client gasped. "You have? When?"

"Last night."

"But—"

"I had to use the lavatory," she said, "and the book was there, although I could see it wasn't an ordinary bound book but pages in a box. I didn't think I would hurt it by looking at it. So I sat there and read the first two chapters."

"What did you think?" Haig asked her.

"It was very powerful. Parts of it were hard to follow, but the scenes were strong, and I got caught up in them."

"That's Woolrich," Jayne Corn-Wallace said. "He can grab you, all right."

"And then you took it with you when you went home," our client said. "You were so involved you couldn't bear to leave it unfinished, so you, uh, borrowed it." He reached to pat her hand. "Perfectly understandable," he said, "and perfectly innocent. You were going to bring it back once you'd finished it. So all this fuss has been over nothing."

"That's not what happened."

"It's not?"

"I read two chapters," she said, "and I thought I'd ask to borrow it some other time, or maybe not. But I put the pages back in the box and left them there."

"In the bathroom?"

"Yes."

"So you never did finish the book," our client said. "Well, if it ever turns up I'll be more than happy to lend it to you, but until then—"

"But perhaps Miss Botleigh has already finished the book," Haig suggested.

"How could she? She just told you she left it in the bathroom."

Haig said, "Miss Botleigh?"

"I finished the book," she said. "When everybody else went home, I stayed."

"My word," Zoltan Mihalyi said. "Woolrich never had a more devoted fan, or one half so beautiful."

"Not to finish the manuscript," she said, and turned to our host. "You asked me to stay," she said.

"I *wanted* you to stay," he agreed. "I wanted to *ask* you to stay. But I don't remember . . ."

"I guess you'd had quite a bit to drink," she said, "although you didn't show it. But you asked me to stay, and I'd been hoping you would ask me, because I wanted to stay."

"You must have had rather a lot to drink yourself," Harriet Quinlan murmured.

"Not that much," said the caterer. "I wanted to stay because he's a very attractive man."

Our client positively glowed, then turned red with embarrassment. "I knew I had a hole in my memory," he said, "but I didn't think anything significant could have fallen through it. So you actually stayed? God. What, uh, happened?"

"We went upstairs," Jeanne Botleigh said. "And we went to the bedroom, and we went to bed."

"Indeed," said Haig.

"And it was . . ."

"Quite wonderful," she said.

"And I don't remember. I think I'm going to kill myself."

"Not on Christmas Day," E.E. Stokes said. "And not with a mystery still unsolved. Haig, what became of the bloody manuscript?"

"Miss Botleigh?"

She looked at our host, then lowered her eyes. "You went to sleep afterward," she said, "and I felt entirely energized, and knew I couldn't sleep, and I thought I'd read for a while. And I remembered the manuscript, so I came down here and fetched it."

"And read it?"

"In bed. I thought you might wake up, in fact I was hoping you would. But you didn't."

"Damn it," our client said, with feeling.

"So I finished the manuscript and still didn't feel sleepy. And I got dressed and let myself out and went home."

There was a silence, broken at length by Zoltan Mihalyi, offering our client congratulations on his triumph and sympathy for the memory loss. "When you write your memoirs," he said, "you'll have to leave that chapter blank."

"Or have someone ghost it for you," Philip Perigord offered.

"The manuscript," Stokes said. "What became of it?"

"I don't know," the caterer said. "I finished it—"

"Which is more than Woolrich could say," Jayne Corn-Wallace said.

"—and I left it there."

"There?"

"In its box. On the bedside table, where you'd be sure to find it first thing in the morning. But I guess you didn't."

"The manuscript? Haig, you're telling me you want the *manuscript*?"

"You find my fee excessive?"

"But it wasn't even lost. No one took it. It was next to my bed. I'd have found it sooner or later."

"But you didn't," Haig said. "Not until you'd cost me and my young associate the better part of our holiday. You've been reading mysteries all your life. Now you got to see one solved in front of you, and in your own magnificent library."

He brightened. "It is a nice room, isn't it?"

"It's first-rate."

"Thanks. But Haig, listen to reason. You did solve the puzzle and recover the manuscript, but now you're demanding what you recovered as compensation. That's like rescuing a kidnap victim and insisting on adopting the child yourself."

"Nonsense. It's nothing like that."

"All right, then it's like recovering stolen jewels and demanding the jewels themselves as reward. It's just plain disproportionate. I hired you because I wanted the manuscript in my collection, and now you expect to wind up with it in *your* collection."

It did sound a little weird to me, but I kept my mouth shut. Haig had the ball, and I wanted to see where he'd go with it.

He put his fingertips together. "In *Black Orchids*," he said, "Wolfe's client was his friend Lewis Hewitt. As recompense for his work, Wolfe insisted on all of the black orchid plants Hewitt had bred. Not one. All of them."

"That always seemed greedy to me."

"If we were speaking of fish," Haig went on, "I might be similarly inclined. But books are of use to me only as reading material. I want to *read* that book, sir, and I want to have it close to hand if I need to refer to it." He shrugged. "But I don't need the original that you prize so highly. Make me a copy."

"A copy?"

"Indeed. Have the manuscript photocopied."

"You'd be content with a . . . a copy?"

"And a credit," I said quickly, before Haig could give away the store. We'd put in a full day, and he ought to get more than a few hours' reading out of it. "A two thousand dollar store credit," I added, "which Mr. Haig can use up as he sees fit."

"Buying paperbacks and book-club editions," our client said. "It should last you for years." He heaved a sigh. "A photocopy and a store credit. Well, if that makes you happy . . ."

And that pretty much wrapped it up. I ran straight home and sat down at the typewriter, and if the story seems a little hurried it's because I was in a rush when I wrote it. See, our client tried for a second date with Jeanne Botleigh, to refresh his memory, I suppose, but a woman tends to feel less than flattered when you forget having gone to bed with her, and she wasn't having any.

So I called her the minute I got home, and we talked about this and that, and we've got a date in an hour and a half. I'll tell you this much, if I get lucky, I'll remember. So wish me luck, huh?

And, by the way . . .

Merry Christmas!

Martin Ehrengraf

The Ehrengraf Defense

"And you are Mrs. Culhane," Martin Ehrengraf said. "Do sit down, yes, I think you will find that chair comfortable. And please pardon the disarray. It is the natural condition of my office. Chaos stimulates me. Order stifles me. It is absurd, is it not, but so then is life itself, eh?"

Dorothy Culhane sat, nodded. She studied the small, trimly built man who remained standing behind his extremely disorderly desk. Her eyes took in the narrow mustache, the thin lips, the deeply set dark eyes. If the man liked clutter in his surroundings, he certainly made up for it in his grooming and attire. He wore a starched white shirt, a perfectly tailored dove gray three-button suit, a narrow dark blue necktie.

Oh, but she did not want to think about neckties—

"Of course you are Clark Culhane's mother," Ehrengraf said. "I had it that you had already retained an attorney."

"Alan Farrell."

"A good man," Ehrengraf said. "An excellent reputation."

"I dismissed him this morning."

"Ah."

Mrs. Culhane took a deep breath. "He wanted Clark to plead guilty," she said. "Temporary insanity, something of the sort. He wanted my son to admit to killing that girl."

"And you did not wish him to do this."

"My son is innocent!" The words came in a rush, uncontrollably. She calmed herself. "My son is innocent," she repeated, levelly now. "He could never kill anyone. He can't admit to a crime he never committed in the first place."

"And when you said as much to Farrell—"

"He told me he was doubtful of his ability to conduct a successful defense based on a plea of innocent." She drew herself up. "So I decided to find someone who could."

"And you came to me."

"Yes."

The little lawyer had seated himself. Now he was doodling idly on a lined yellow scratch pad. "Do you know much about me, Mrs. Culhane?"

"Not very much. It's said that your methods are unorthodox—"

"Indeed."

"But that you get results."

"Results. Indeed, results." Martin Ehrengraf made a tent of his fingertips and, for the first time since she had entered his office, a smile bloomed briefly on his thin lips. "Indeed I get results. I *must* get results, my dear Mrs. Culhane, or else I do not get my dinner. And while my slimness might indicate otherwise, it is my custom to eat very well indeed. You see, I do something which no other criminal lawyer does, at least not to my knowledge. You have heard what this is?"

"I understand you operate on a contingency basis."

"A contingency basis." Ehrengraf was nodding emphatically. "Yes, that is precisely what I do. I operate on a contingency basis. My fees are high, Mrs. Culhane. They are extremely high. But they are due and payable only in the event that my efforts are crowned with success. If a client of mine is found guilty, then my work on his behalf costs him nothing."

The lawyer got to his feet again, stepped out from behind his desk. Light glinted on his highly polished black shoes. "This is common enough in negligence cases. The attorney gets a share in the settlement. If he loses he gets nothing. How much greater is his incentive to perform to the best of his ability, eh? But why limit this practice to negligence suits? Why not have all lawyers paid in this fashion? And doctors, for that matter. If the operation's a failure, why not let the doctor absorb some of the loss, eh? But such an arrangement would be a long time coming, I am afraid. Yet I have found it workable in my practice. And my clients have been pleased by the results."

"If you can get Clark acquitted—"

"Acquitted?" Ehrengraf rubbed his hands together. "Mrs. Culhane, in my most notable successes it is not even a question of acquittal. It is rather a matter of the case never even coming to trial. New evidence is discovered, the actual miscreant confesses or is brought to justice, and one way or another charges against my client are dropped. Courtroom pyrotechnics, wizardry in cross-examination—ah, I prefer to leave that to the Perry Masons of the world. It is not unfair to say, Mrs. Culhane, that I am more the detective than the lawyer. What is the saying? 'The best defense is a good offense.' Or perhaps it is the other way around, the best offense being a good defense, but it hardly matters. It is a saying in warfare and in the game of chess, I believe, and neither serves as the ideal metaphor for what concerns us. And what does concern us, Mrs. Culhane—" and he leaned toward her and the dark eyes flashed "—what concerns us is saving your son's life and securing his freedom and preserving his reputation. Yes?"

"Yes. Yes, of course."

"The evidence against your son is considerable, Mrs. Culhane. The dead girl, Althea Patton, was his former fiancée. It is said that she jilted him—"

"He broke the engagement."

"I don't doubt that for a moment, but the prosecution would have it otherwise. This Patton girl was strangled. Around her throat was found a necktie."

Mrs. Culhane's eyes went involuntarily to the lawyer's own blue tie, then slipped away.

"A particular necktie, Mrs. Culhane. A necktie made exclusively for and worn exclusively by members of the Caedmon Society at Oxford University. Your son attended Dartmouth, Mrs. Culhane, and after graduation he spent a year in advanced study in England."

"Yes."

"At Oxford University.

"Where he became a member of the Caedmon Society."

"Yes."

Ehrengraf breathed in through clenched teeth. "He owned a necktie of the Caedmon Society. He appears to be the only member of the society residing in this city and would thus presumably be the only person to own such a tie. He cannot produce that tie, nor can he provide a satisfactory alibi for the night in question."

"Someone must have stolen his tie."

"The murderer, of course."

"To frame him."

"Of course," Ehrengraf said soothingly. "There could be no other explanation, could there?" He breathed in, he breathed out, he set his chin decisively. "I will undertake your son's defense," he announced. "And on my usual terms."

"Oh, thank heavens."

"My fee will be seventy-five thousand dollars. That is a great deal of money, Mrs. Culhane, although you might very well have ended up paying Mr. Farrell that much or more by the time you'd gone through the tortuous processes of trial and appeal and so on, and after he'd presented an itemized accounting of his expenses. My fee includes any and all expenses which I might incur. No matter how much time and effort and money I spend on your son's behalf, the cost to you will be limited to the figure I named. And none of that will be payable unless your son is freed. Does that meet with your approval?"

She hardly had to hesitate but made herself take a moment before replying. "Yes," she said. "Yes, of course. The terms are satisfactory."

"Another point. If, ten minutes from now, the district attorney should decide of his own accord to drop all charges against your son, you nevertheless owe me seventy-five thousand dollars. Even though I should have done nothing to earn it."

"I don't see—"

The thin lips smiled. The dark eyes did not participate in the smile. "It is my policy, Mrs. Culhane. Most of my work, as I have said, is more the work of a detective than the work of a lawyer. I operate largely behind the scenes and in the shadows. Perhaps I set currents in motion. Often when the smoke clears it is hard to prove to what extent my client's victory is the fruit of my labor. Thus I do not attempt to prove anything of the sort. I merely share in the victory by collecting my fee in full whether I seem to have earned it or not. You understand?"

It did seem reasonable, even if the explanation was the slightest bit hazy. Perhaps the little man dabbled in bribery, perhaps he knew the right strings to pull but could scarcely disclose them after the fact. Well, it hardly mattered. All that mattered was Clark's freedom, Clark's good name.

"Yes," she said. "Yes, I understand. When Clark is released you'll be paid in full."

"Very good."

She frowned. "In the meantime you'll want a retainer, won't you? An advance of some sort?"

"You have a dollar?" She looked in her purse, drew out a dollar bill. "Give it to me, Mrs. Culhane. Very good, very good. An advance of one dollar against a fee of seventy-five thousand dollars. And I assure you, my dear Mrs. Culhane, that should this case not resolve itself in unqualified success I shall even return this dollar to you." The smile, and this time there was a twinkle in the eyes. "But that will not happen, Mrs. Culhane, because I do not intend to fail."

It was a little more than a month later when Dorothy Culhane made her second visit to Martin Ehrengraf's office. This time the little lawyer's suit was a navy blue pinstripe, his necktie maroon with a subdued below-the-knot design. His starched white shirt might have been the same one she had seen on her earlier visit. The shoes, black wing tips, were as highly polished as the other pair he'd been wearing.

His expression was changed slightly. There was something that might have been sorrow in the deep-set eyes, a look that suggested a continuing disappointment with human nature.

"It would seem quite clear," Ehrengraf said now. "Your son has been released. All charges have been dropped. He is a free man, free even to the extent that no shadow of suspicion hangs over him in the public mind."

"Yes," Mrs. Culhane said, "and that's wonderful, and I couldn't be happier about it. Of course it's terrible about the girls, I hate to think that Clark's happiness and my own happiness stem from their tragedy, or I suppose it's tragedies, isn't it, but all the same I feel—"

"Mrs. Culhane."

She bit off her words, let her eyes meet his.

"Mrs. Culhane, it's quite cut and dried, is it not? You owe me seventy-five thousand dollars."

"But—"

"We discussed this, Mrs. Culhane. I'm sure you recall our discussion. We went over the matter at length. Upon the successful resolution of this matter you were to pay me my fee, seventy-five thousand dollars. Less, of course, the sum of one dollar already paid over to me as a retainer."

"But—"

"Even if I did nothing. Even if the district attorney elected to drop charges before you'd even departed from these premises. That, I believe, was the example I gave at the time."

"Yes."

"And you agreed to those terms."

"Yes, but—"

"But what, Mrs. Culhane?"

She took a deep breath, set herself bravely. "Three girls," she said. "Strangled, all of them, just like Althea Patton. All of them the same physical type, slender blondes with high foreheads and prominent front teeth, two of them here in town and one across the river in Montclair, and around each of their throats—"

"A necktie."

"The same necktie."

"A necktie of the Caedmon Society of Oxford University."

"Yes." She drew another breath. "So it was obvious that there's a maniac at large," she went on, "And the last killing was in Montclair, so maybe he's leaving the area, and my God, I hope so, it's terrifying, the idea of a man just killing girls at random because they remind him of his mother—"

"I beg your pardon?"

"That's what somebody was saying on television last night. A psychiatrist. It was just a theory."

"Yes," Ehrengraf said. "Theories are interesting, aren't they? Speculation, guesswork, hypotheses, all very interesting."

"But the point is—"

"Yes?"

"I know what we agreed, Mr. Ehrengraf. I know all that. But on the other hand you made one visit to Clark in prison, that was just one brief visit, and then as far as I can see you did nothing at all, and just because the madman happened to strike again and kill the other girls in exactly the same manner and even use the same tie, well, you have to admit that seventy-five thousand dollars sounds like quite a windfall for you."

"A windfall."

"So I was discussing this with my own attorney—he's not a criminal lawyer, he handles my personal affairs—and he suggested that you might accept a reduced fee by way of settlement."

"He suggested this, eh?"

She avoided the man's eyes. "Yes, he did suggest it, and I must say it seems reasonable to me. Of course I would be glad to reimburse you for any expenses you incurred, although I can't honestly say that you could have run up much in the way of expenses, and he suggested that I might give you a fee on top of that of five thousand dollars, but I am grateful, Mr. Ehrengraf, and I'd be willing to make that ten thousand dollars, and you have to admit that's not a trifle, don't you? I have money, I'm comfortably set up financially, but no one can afford to pay out seventy-five thousand dollars for nothing at all, and—"

"Human beings," Ehrengraf said, and closed his eyes. "And the rich are the worst of all," he added, opening his eyes, fixing them upon Dorothy Culhane. "It is an unfortunate fact of life that only the rich can afford to pay high fees. Thus I must make my living acting on their behalf. The poor, they do not agree to an arrangement when they are desperate and go back on their word when they are in more reassuring circumstances."

"It's not so much that I'd go back on my word," Mrs. Culhane said. "It's just that—"

"Mrs. Culhane."

"Yes?"

"I am going to tell you something which I doubt will have any effect upon you, but at least I shall have tried. The best thing you could do, right at this moment, would be to take out your checkbook and write out a check to me for payment in full. You will probably not do this, and you will ultimately regret it."

"Is that . . . are you threatening me?"

A flicker of a smile. "Certainly not. I have given you not a threat but a prediction. You see, if you do not pay my fee, what I shall do is tell you something else which will lead you to pay me my fee after all."

"I don't understand."

"No," Martin Ehrengraf said. "No, I don't suppose you do. Mrs. Culhane, you spoke of expenses. You doubted I could have incurred significant expenses on your son's behalf. There are many things I could say, Mrs. Culhane, but I think it might be best for me to confine myself to a brisk accounting of a small portion of my expenses."

"I don't—"

"Please, my dear lady. Expenses. If I were listing my expenses, dear lady, I would begin by jotting down my train fare to New York City. Then taxi fare to Kennedy Airport, which comes to twenty dollars with tip and bridge tolls, isn't that exorbitant?"

"Mr. Ehrengraf—"

"*Please*. Then airfare to London and back. I always fly first class, it's an indulgence, but since I pay my own expenses out of my own pocket I feel I have the right to indulge myself. Next a rental car hired from Heathrow Airport and driven to Oxford and back. The price of gasoline is high enough over here, Mrs. Culhane, but in England they call it petrol and they charge the earth for it."

She stared at him. His hands were folded atop his disorderly desk and he went on talking in the calmest possible tone of voice and she felt her jaw dropping but could not seem to raise it back into place.

"In Oxford I had to visit five gentlemen's clothiers, Mrs. Culhane. One shop had no Caedmon Society cravats in stock at the moment. I purchased one necktie from each of the other shops. I felt it really wouldn't do to buy more than one tie in any one shop. A man prefers not to call attention to himself unnecessarily. The Caedmon Society necktie, Mrs. Culhane, is not unattractive. A navy blue field with a half-inch stripe of royal blue and two narrower flanking stripes, one of gold and the other of a rather bright green. I don't care for regimental stripes myself, Mrs. Culhane, preferring as I do a more subdued style in neckwear, but the Caedmon tie is a handsome one all the same."

"My God."

"There were other expenses, Mrs. Culhane, but as I pay them myself I don't honestly think there's any need for me to recount them to you, do you?"

"My God. Dear God in heaven."

"Indeed. It would have been better all around, as I said a few moments ago, had you decided to pay my fee without hearing what you've just heard. Ignorance in this case would have been, if not bliss, at least a good deal closer to bliss than what you're undoubtedly feeling at the moment."

"Clark didn't kill that girl."

"Of course he didn't, Mrs. Culhane. Of course he didn't. I'm sure some rotter stole his tie and framed him. But that would have been an enormous chore to prove and all a lawyer could have done was persuade a jury that there was room for doubt, and poor Clark would have had a cloud over him all the days of his life. Of course you and I know he's innocent—"

"He *is* innocent," she said. "He *is*."

"Of course he is, Mrs. Culhane. The killer was a homicidal maniac striking down young women who remind him of his mother. Or his sister, or God knows whom. You'll want to get out your checkbook, Mrs. Culhane, but don't try to write the check just yet. Your hands are trembling. Just sit there, that's the ticket, and I'll get you a glass of water. Everything's perfectly fine, Mrs. Culhane. That's what you must remember. Everything's perfectly fine and everything will continue to be perfectly fine. Here you are, a couple of ounces of water in a paper cup, just drink it down, there you are, *there* you are."

And when it was time to write out the check her hand did not shake a bit. Pay to the order of Martin H. Ehrengraf, seventy-five thousand dollars, signed Dorothy Rodgers Culhane. Signed with a ball-point pen, no need to blot it dry, and handed across the desk to the impeccably dressed little man.

"Yes, thank you, thank you very much, my dear lady. And here is your dollar, the retainer you gave me. Go ahead and take it, please."

She took the dollar.

"Very good. And you probably won't want to repeat this conversation to anyone. What would be the point?"

"No. No, I won't say anything."

"Of course not."

"Four neckties." He looked at her, raised his eyebrows a fraction of an inch. "You said you bought four of the neckties. There were—there were three girls killed."

"Indeed there were."

"What happened to the fourth necktie?"

"Why, it must be in my bureau drawer, don't you suppose? And perhaps they're all there, Mrs. Culhane. Perhaps all four neckties are in my bureau drawer, still in their original wrappings, and purchasing them was just a waste of time and money on my part. Perhaps that homicidal maniac had neckties of his own and the four in my drawer are just an interesting souvenir and a reminder of what might have been."

"Oh."

"And perhaps I've just told you a story out of the whole cloth, an interesting turn of phrase since we are speaking of silk neckties. Perhaps I never flew to London at all, never motored to Oxford, never purchased a single necktie of the Caedmon Society. Perhaps that was just something I trumped up on the spur of the moment to coax a fee out of you."

"But—"

"Ah, my dear lady," he said, moving to the side of her chair, taking her arm, helping her out of the chair, turning her, steering her toward the door. "We would do well, Mrs. Culhane, to believe that which it most pleases us to believe. I have my fee. You have your son. The police have another line of inquiry to pursue altogether. It would seem we've all come out of this well, wouldn't you say? Put your mind at rest, Mrs. Culhane, dear Mrs. Culhane. There's the elevator down the hall on your left. If you ever need my services you know where I am and how to reach me. And perhaps you'll recommend me to your friends. But discreetly, dear lady. Discreetly. Discretion is everything in matters of this sort."

She walked very carefully down the hall to the elevator and rang the bell and waited. And she did not look back. Not once.

The Ehrengraf Presumption

"Now let me get this straight," Alvin Gort said. "You actually accept criminal cases on a contingency basis. Even homicide cases."

"Especially homicide cases."

"If your client is acquitted he pays your fee. If he's found guilty, then your efforts on his behalf cost him nothing whatsoever. Except expenses, I assume."

"That's very nearly true," Martin Ehrengraf said. The little lawyer supplied a smile which blossomed briefly on his thin lips while leaving his eyes quite uninvolved. "Shall I explain in detail?"

"By all means."

"To take your last point first, I pay my own expenses and furnish no accounting of them to my client. My fees are thus all-inclusive. By the same token, should a client of mine be convicted he would owe me nothing. I would absorb such expenses as I might incur acting on his behalf."

"That's remarkable."

"It's surely unusual, if not unique. Now the rest of what you've said is essentially true. It's not uncommon for attorneys to take on negligence cases on a contingency basis, participating handsomely in the settlement when they win, sharing their clients' losses when they do not. The principle has always made eminent good sense to me. Why shouldn't a client give substantial value for value received? Why should he be simply charged for service, whether or not the service does him any good? When I pay out money, Mr. Gort, I like to get what I pay for. And I don't mind paying for what I get."

"It certainly makes sense to me," Alvin Gort said. He dug a cigarette from the pack in his shirt pocket, scratched a match, drew smoke into his lungs. This was his first experience in a jail cell and he'd been quite surprised to learn that he was allowed to have matches on his person, to wear his own clothes rather than prison garb, to keep money in his pocket and a watch on his wrist.

No doubt all this would change if he were convicted of murdering his wife. Then he'd be in an actual prison and the rules would most likely be more severe. Here they had taken his belt as a precaution against suicide, and they would have taken the laces from his shoes had he not been wearing loafers at the time of his arrest. But it could have been worse.

And unless Martin Ehrengraf pulled off a small miracle, it would be worse.

"Sometimes my clients never see the inside of a courtroom," Ehrengraf was saying now. "I'm always happiest when I can save my clients not merely from prison but from going to trial in the first place. So you should understand that whether or not I collect my fee hinges on your fate, on the disposition of your case—and not on how much work I put in or how much time it takes me to liberate you. In other words, from the moment you retain me I have an interest in your future, and the moment you are released and all charges dropped, my fee becomes due and payable in full."

"And your fee will be—?"

"One hundred thousand dollars," Ehrengraf said crisply.

Alvin Gort considered the sum, then nodded thoughtfully. It was not difficult to believe that the diminutive attorney commanded and received large fees. Alvin Gort recognized good clothing when he saw it, and the clothing Martin Ehrengraf wore was good indeed. The man was well turned out. His suit, a bronze sharkskin number with a nipped-in waist, was clearly not off the rack. His brown wing-tip shoes had been polished to a high gloss. His tie, a rich teak in hue with an unobtrusive below-the-knot design, bore the reasonably discreet trademark of a genuine countess. And his hair had received the attention of a good barber while his neatly trimmed mustache served as a focal point for a face otherwise devoid of any single dominating feature. The overall impression thus created was one of a man who could announce a six-figure fee and make you feel that such a sum was altogether fitting and proper.

"I'm reasonably well off," Gort said.

"I know. It's a commendable quality in clients."

"And I'd certainly be glad to pay one hundred thousand dollars for my freedom. On the other hand, if you don't get me off then I don't owe you a dime. Is that right?"

"Quite right."

Gort considered again, nodded again. "Then I've got no reservations," he said. "But—"

"Yes?"

Alvin Gort's eyes measured the lawyer. Gort was accustomed to making rapid decisions. He made one now.

"You might have reservations," he said. "There's one problem."

"Oh?"

"I did it," Gort said. "I killed her."

"I can see how you would think that," Martin Ehrengraf said. "The weight of circumstantial evidence piled up against you. Long-suppressed unconscious resentment of your wife, perhaps even a hidden desire to see her dead. All manner of guilt feelings stored up since early childhood. Plus, of course, the natural idea that things do not happen without a good reason for their occurrence. You are in prison, charged with murder; therefore it stands to reason that you did something to deserve all this, that you did in fact murder your wife."

"But I did," Gort said.

"Nonsense. Palpable nonsense."

"But I was there," Gort said. "I'm not making this up. For God's sake, man, I'm not a psychiatric basket case. Unless you're thinking about an insanity defense? I suppose I could go along with that, scream out hysterically in the middle of the night, strip naked and sit gibbering in the corner of my cell. I can't say I'd enjoy it but I'll go along with it if you think that's the answer. But—"

"Don't be ridiculous," Ehrengraf said, wrinkling his nose with distaste. "I mean to get you acquitted, Mr. Gort. Not committed to an asylum."

"I don't understand," Gort said. He frowned, looked around craftily. "You think the place is bugged," he whispered. "That's it, eh?"

"You can use your normal tone of voice. No, they don't employ hidden microphones in this jail. It's not only illegal but against policy as well."

"Then I don't understand. Look, I'm the guy who fastened the dynamite under the hood of Ginnie's Pontiac. I hooked up a cable to the starter. I set things up so that she would be blown into the next world. Now how do you propose to—"

"Mr. Gort." Ehrengraf held up a hand like a stop sign. "Please, Mr. Gort."

Alvin Gort subsided.

"Mr. Gort," Ehrengraf continued, "I defend the innocent and leave it to more clever men than myself to employ trickery in the cause of the guilty. And I find this very easy to do because all my clients are innocent. There is, you know, a legal principle involved."

"A legal principle?"

"The presumption of innocence."

"The presumption of—? Oh, you mean a man is presumed innocent until proven guilty."

"A tenet of Anglo-Saxon jurisprudence," Ehrengraf said. "The French presume guilt until innocence is proven. And the totalitarian countries, of course, presume guilt and do not *allow* innocence to be proved, taking it for granted that their police would not dream of wasting their time arresting the innocent in the first place. But I refer, Mr. Gort, to something more far-reaching than the legal presumption of innocence." Ehrengraf drew himself up to his full height, such as it was, and his back went ramrod straight. "I refer," he said, "to the Ehrengraf Presumption."

"The Ehrengraf Presumption?"

"Any client of Martin H. Ehrengraf," said Martin Ehrengraf, "is presumed by Ehrengraf to be innocent, which presumption is invariably confirmed in due course, the preconceptions of the client himself notwithstanding." The little lawyer smiled with his lips. "Now," he said, "shall we get down to business?"

Half an hour later Alvin Gort was still sitting on the edge of his cot. Martin Ehrengraf, however, was pacing briskly in the manner of a caged lion. With the thumb and forefinger of his right hand he smoothed the ends of his neat mustache. His left hand was at his side, its thumb hooked into his trouser pocket. He continued to pace while Gort smoked a cigarette almost to the filter. Then, as Gort ground the butt under his heel, Ehrengraf turned on his own heel and fixed his eyes on his client.

"The evidence is damning," he conceded. "A man of your description purchased dynamite and blasting caps from Tattersall Demolition Supply just ten days before your wife's death. Your signature is on the purchase order. A clerk remembers waiting on you and reports that you were nervous."

"Damn right I was nervous," Gort said. "I never killed anyone before."

"Please, Mr. Gort. If you must maintain the facade of having committed murder, at least keep your illusion to yourself. Don't share it with me. At the moment I'm concerned with evidence. We have your signature on the purchase order and we have you identified by the clerk. The man even remembers what you were wearing. Most customers come to Tattersall in work clothes, it would seem, while you wore a rather distinctive burgundy blazer and white flannel slacks. And tasseled loafers," he added, clearly not approving of them.

"It's hard to find casual loafers without tassels or braid these days."

"Hard, yes. But scarcely impossible. Now you say your wife had a lover—a Mr. Barry Lattimore."

"That toad Lattimore!"

"You knew of this affair and disapproved."

"Disapproved! I hated them. I wanted to strangle both of them. I wanted—"

"*Please*, Mr. Gort."

"I'm sorry."

Ehrengraf sighed. "Now your wife seems to have written a letter to her sister in New Mexico. She did in fact have a sister in New Mexico?"

"Her sister Grace. In Socorro."

"She posted the letter four days before her death. In it she stated that you knew about her affair with Lattimore."

"I'd known for weeks."

"She went on to say that she feared for her life. 'The situation is deteriorating and I don't know what to do. You know what a temper he has. I'm afraid he might be capable of anything, anything at all. I'm defenseless and I don't know what to do.' "

"Defenseless as a cobra," Gort muttered.

"No doubt. That was from memory but it's a fair approximation. Of course I'll have to examine the original. And I'll want specimens of your wife's handwriting."

"You can't think the letter's a forgery?"

"We never know, do we? But I'm sure you can tell me where I can get hold of samples. Now what other evidence do we have to contend with? There was a neighbor who saw you doing something under the hood of your wife's car some four or five hours before her death."

"Mrs. Boerland. Damned old crone. Vicious gossiping busybody."

"You seem to have been in the garage shortly before dawn. You had a light on and the garage door was open, and you had the hood of the car up and were doing something."

"Damned right I was doing something. I was—"

"Please, Mr. Gort. Between tasseled loafers and these constant interjections—"

"Won't happen again, Mr. Ehrengraf."

"Yes. Now just let me see. There were two cars in the garage, were there not? Your Buick and your wife's Pontiac. Your car was parked on the left-hand side, your wife's on the right."

"That was so that she could back straight out. When you're parked on the left side you have to back out in a sort of squiggly way. When Ginnie tried to do that she always ran over a corner of the lawn."

"Ah."

"Some people just don't give a damn about a lawn," Gort said, "and some people do."

"As with so many aspects of human endeavor, Mr. Gort. Now Mrs. Boerland observed you in the garage shortly before dawn, and the actual explosion which claimed your wife's life took place a few hours later while you were having your breakfast."

"Toasted English muffin and coffee. Years ago Ginnie made scrambled eggs and squeezed fresh orange juice for me. But with the passage of time—"

"Did she normally start her car at that hour?"

"No," Gort said. He sat up straight, frowned. "No, of course not. Dammit, why didn't *I* think of that? I figured she'd sit around the house until noon. I wanted to be well away from the place when it happened—"

"Mr. Gort."

"Well, I did. All of a sudden there was this shock wave and a thunderclap right on top of it and I'll tell you, Mr. Ehrengraf, I didn't even know what it was."

"Of course you didn't."

"I mean—"

"I wonder why your wife left the house at that hour. She said nothing to you?"

"No. There was a phone call and—"

"From whom?"

Gort frowned again. "Damned if I know. But she got the call just before she left. I wonder if there's a connection."

"I shouldn't doubt it." Ehrengraf continued to probe, then he asked who inherited Virginia Gort's money.

"Money?" Gort grinned. "Ginnie didn't have a dime. I was her legal heir just as she was mine, but I was the one who had the money. All she left was the jewelry and clothing that my money paid for."

"Any insurance?"

"Exactly enough to pay your fee," Gort said, and grinned this time rather like a shark. "Except that I won't see a penny of it. Fifty thousand dollars, double indemnity for accidental death, and I think the insurance companies call murder an accident, although it's always struck me as rather purposeful. That makes one hundred thousand dollars, your fee to the penny, but none of it'll come my way."

"It's true that one cannot profit financially from a crime," Ehrengraf said. "But if you're found innocent—"

Gort shook his head. "Doesn't make any difference," he said. "I just learned this the other day. About the same time I was buying the dynamite, she was changing her beneficiary. The change went through in plenty of time. The whole hundred thousand goes to that rotter Lattimore."

"Now that," said Martin Ehrengraf, "is very interesting."

Two weeks and three days later Alvin Gort sat in a surprisingly comfortable straight-backed chair in Martin Ehrengraf's exceptionally cluttered office. He balanced a checkbook on his knee and carefully made out a check. The fountain pen he used had cost him $65. The lawyer's services, for which the check he was writing represented payment in full, had cost him considerably more, yet Gort, a good judge of value, thought Ehrengraf's fee a bargain and the pen overpriced.

"One hundred thousand dollars," he said, waving the check in the air to dry its ink. "I've put today's date on it but I'll ask you to hold it until Monday morning before depositing it. I've instructed my broker to sell securities and transfer funds to my checking account. I don't normally maintain a balance sufficient to cover a check of this size."

"That's understandable."

"I'm glad something is. Because I'm damned if I can understand how you got me off the hook."

Ehrengraf allowed himself a smile. "My greatest obstacle was your own mental attitude," he said. "You honestly believed yourself to be guilty of your wife's death, didn't you?"

"But—"

"Ah, my dear Mr. Gort. You see, I *knew* you were innocent. The Ehrengraf Presumption assured me of that. I merely had to look for someone with the right sort of motive, and who should emerge but Mr. Barry Lattimore, your wife's lover and beneficiary, a man with a need for money and a man whose affair with your wife was reaching crisis proportions.

"It was clear to me that you were not the sort of man to commit murder in such an obvious fashion. Buying the dynamite openly, signing the purchase order with your own name—my dear Mr. Gort, you would never behave so foolishly! No, you had to have been framed, and clearly Lattimore was the man who had reason to frame you."

"And then they found things," Gort said.

"Indeed they did, once I was able to tell them where to look. Extraordinary what turned up! You would think Lattimore would have had the sense to get rid of all that, wouldn't you? But no, a burgundy blazer and a pair of white slacks, a costume identical to your own but tailored to Mr. Lattimore's frame, hung in the very back of his clothes closet. And in a drawer of his desk the police found half a dozen sheets of paper on which he'd practiced your signature until he was able to do quite a creditable job of writing it. By dressing like you and signing your name to the purchase order, he quite neatly put your neck in the noose."

"Incredible."

"He even copied your tasseled loafers. The police found a pair in his closet, and of course the man never habitually wore loafers of any sort. Of course he denied ever having seen the shoes before. Or the jacket, or the slacks, and of course he denied having practiced your signature."

Gort's eyes went involuntarily to Ehrengraf's own shoes. This time the lawyer was wearing black wing tips. His suit was dove gray and somewhat more sedately tailored than the brown one Gort had seen previously. His tie was maroon, his cuff links simple gold hexagons. The precision of Ehrengraf's dress and carriage contrasted sharply with the disarray of his office.

"And that letter from your wife to her sister Grace," Ehrengraf continued. "It turned out to be authentic, as it happens, but it also proved to be open to a second interpretation. The man of whom Virginia was afraid was never named, and a thoughtful reading showed he could as easily have been Lattimore as you. And then of course a second letter to Grace was found among your wife's effects. She evidently wrote it the night before her death and never had a chance to mail it. It's positively damning. She tells her sister how she changed the beneficiary of her insurance at Lattimore's insistence, how your knowledge of the affair was making Lattimore irrational and dangerous, and how she couldn't avoid the feeling that he planned to kill her. She goes on to say that she intended to change her insurance again, making Grace the beneficiary, and that she would so inform Lattimore in order to remove any financial motive for her murder.

"But even as she was writing those lines, he was preparing to put the dynamite in her car."

Ehrengraf went on explaining and Gort could only stare at him in wonder. Was it possible that his own memory could have departed so utterly from reality? Had the twin shocks of Ginnie's death and of arrest have caused him to fabricate a whole set of false memories?

Damn it, he *remembered* buying that dynamite! He *remembered* wiring it under the hood of her Pontiac! So how on earth—

The Ehrengraf Presumption, he thought. If Ehrengraf could presume Gort's innocence the way he did, why couldn't Gort presume his own innocence? Why not give himself the benefit of the doubt?

Because the alternative was terrifying. The letter, the practice sheets of his signature, the shoes and slacks and burgundy blazer—

"Mr. Gort? Are you all right?"

"I'm fine," Gort said.

"You looked pale for a moment. The strain, no doubt. Will you take a glass of water?"

"No, I don't think so." Gort lit a cigarette, inhaled deeply. "I'm fine," he said. "I feel good about everything. You know, not only am I in the clear but ultimately I don't think your fee will cost me anything."

"Oh?"

"Not if that rotter killed her. Lattimore can't profit from a murder he committed. And while she may have intended to make Grace her beneficiary, her unfulfilled intent has no legal weight. So her estate becomes the beneficiary of the insurance policy, and she never did get around to changing her will, so that means the money will wind up in my hands. Amazing, isn't it?"

"Amazing." The little lawyer rubbed his hands together briskly. "But you do know what they say about unhatched chickens, Mr. Gort. Mr. Lattimore hasn't been convicted of anything yet."

"You think he's got a chance of getting off?"

"That would depend," said Martin Ehrengraf, "on his choice of attorney."

This time Ehrengraf's suit was navy blue with a barely perceptible stripe in a lighter blue. His shirt, as usual, was white. His shoes were black loafers—no tassels or braid—and his tie had a half-inch stripe of royal blue flanked by two narrower stripes, one of gold and the other of a rather bright green, all on a navy field. The necktie was that of the Caedmon Society of Oxford University, an organization of which Mr. Ehrengraf was not a member. The tie was a souvenir of another case and the lawyer wore it now and then on especially auspicious occasions.

Such as this visit to the cell of Barry Pierce Lattimore.

"I'm innocent," Lattimore said. "But it's gotten to the point where I don't expect anyone to believe me. There's so much evidence against me."

"Circumstantial evidence."

"Yes, but that's often enough to hang a man, isn't it?" Lattimore winced at the thought. "I loved Ginnie. I wanted to marry her. I never even thought of killing her."

"I believe you."

"You do?"

Ehrengraf nodded solemnly. "Indeed I do," he said. "Otherwise I wouldn't be here. I only collect fees when I get results, Mr. Lattimore. If I can't get you acquitted of all charges, then I won't take a penny for my trouble."

"That's unusual, isn't it?"

"It is."

"My own lawyer thinks I'm crazy to hire you. He had several criminal lawyers he was prepared to recommend. But I know a little about you. I know you get results. And since I *am* innocent, I feel I want to be represented by someone with a vested interest in getting me free."

"Of course my fees are high, Mr. Lattimore."

"Well, there's a problem. I'm not a rich man."

"You're the beneficiary of a hundred-thousand-dollars insurance policy."

"But I can't collect that money."

"You can if you're found innocent."

"Oh," Lattimore said. "Oh."

"And otherwise you'll owe me nothing."

"Then I can't lose, can I?"

"So it would seem," Ehrengraf said. "Now shall we begin? It's quite clear you were framed, Mr. Lattimore. That blazer and those trousers did not find their way to your closet of their own accord. Those shoes did not walk in by themselves. The two letters to Mrs. Gort's sister, one mailed and one unmailed, must have been part of the scheme. Someone constructed an elaborate frame-up, Mr. Lattimore, with the object of implicating first Mr. Gort and then yourself. Now let's determine who would have a motive."

"Gort," said Lattimore.

"I think not."

"Who else? He had a reason to kill her. And he hated me, so who would have more reason to—"

"Mr. Lattimore, I'm afraid that's not a possibility. You see, Mr. Gort was a client of mine."

"Oh. Yes, I forgot."

"And I'm personally convinced of his innocence."

"I see."

"Just as I'm convinced of yours."

"I see."

"Now who else would have a motive? Was Mrs. Gort emotionally involved with anyone else? Did she have another lover? Had she had any other lovers before you came into the picture? And how about Mr. Gort? A former mistress who might have had a grudge against both him and his wife? Hmmm?" Ehrengraf smoothed the ends of his mustache. "Or perhaps, just perhaps, there was an elaborate plot hatched by *Mrs.* Gort."

"Ginnie?"

"It's not impossible. I'm afraid I reject the possibility of suicide. It's always tempting but in this instance I fear it just won't wash. But let's suppose, let's merely suppose, that Mrs. Gort decided to murder her husband and implicate you."

"Why would she do that?"

"I've no idea. But suppose she did, and suppose she intended to get her husband to drive her car and arranged the dynamite accordingly, and then when she left the house so hurriedly she forgot what she'd done, and of course the moment she turned the key in the ignition it all came back to her in a rather dramatic way."

"But I can't believe—"

"Oh, Mr. Lattimore, we believe what it pleases us to believe, don't you agree? The important thing is to recognize that you are innocent and to act on that recognition."

"But how can you be absolutely certain of my innocence?"

Martin Ehrengraf permitted himself a smile. "Mr. Lattimore," he said, "let me tell you about a principle of mine. I call it the Ehrengraf Presumption."

The Ehrengraf Experience

"Innocence," said Martin Ehrengraf. "There's the problem in a nutshell."

"Innocence is a problem?"

The little lawyer glanced around the prison cell, then turned to regard his client. "Precisely," he said. "If you weren't innocent you wouldn't be here."

"Oh, really?" Grantham Beale smiled, and while it was hardly worthy of inclusion in a toothpaste commercial, it was the first smile he'd managed since his conviction on first-degree murder charges just two weeks and four days earlier. "Then you're saying that innocent men go to prison while guilty men walk free. Is that what you're saying?"

"It happens that way more than you might care to believe," Ehrengraf said softly. "But no, it is not what I am saying."

"Oh?"

"I am not contrasting innocence and guilt, Mr. Beale. I know you are innocent of murder. That is almost beside the point. All clients of Martin Ehrengraf are innocent of the crimes of which they are charged, and this innocence always emerges in due course. Indeed, this is more than a presumption on my part. It is the manner in which I make my living. I set high fees, Mr. Beale, but I collect them only when my innocent clients emerge with their innocence a matter of public record. If my client goes to prison I collect nothing whatsoever, not even whatever expenses I incur on his behalf. So my clients are always innocent, Mr. Beale, just as you are innocent, in the sense that they are not guilty."

"Then why is my innocence a problem?"

"Ah, *your* innocence." Martin Ehrengraf smoothed the ends of his neatly trimmed mustache. His thin lips drew back in a smile, but the smile did not reach his deeply set dark eyes. He was, Grantham Beale noted, a superbly well-dressed little man, almost a dandy. He wore a Dartmouth green blazer with pearl buttons over a cream shirt with a tab collar. His slacks were flannel, modishly cuffed and pleated and the identical color of the shirt. His silk tie was a darker green than his jacket and sported a design in silver and bronze thread below the knot, a lion battling a unicorn. His cuff links matched his pearl blazer buttons. On his aristocratically small feet he wore highly polished seamless cordovan loafers, unadorned with tassels or braid, quite simple and quite elegant. Almost a dandy, Beale thought, but from what he'd heard the man had the skills to carry it off. He wasn't all front. He was said to get results.

"*Your* innocence," Ehrengraf said again. "Your innocence is not merely the innocence that is the opposite of guilt. It is the innocence that is the opposite of experience. Do you know Blake, Mr. Beale?"

"Blake?"

"William Blake, the poet. You wouldn't know him personally, of course. He's been dead for over a century. He wrote two groups of poems early in his career, *Songs of Innocence* and *Songs of Experience*. Each poem in the one book had a counterpart in the other. 'Tyger, tyger, burning bright, In the forests of the night, What immortal hand or eye, Could frame thy fearful symmetry?' Perhaps that poem is familiar to you, Mr. Beale."

"I think I studied it in school."

"It's not unlikely. Well, you don't need a poetry lesson from me, sir, not in these depressing surroundings. Let me move a little more directly to the point. Innocence versus experience, Mr. Beale. You found yourself accused of a murder, sir, and you knew only that you had not committed it. And, being innocent not only of the murder itself but in Blake's sense of the word, you simply engaged a competent attorney and assumed things would work themselves out in short order. We live in an enlightened democracy, Mr. Beale, and we grow up knowing that courts exist to free the innocent and punish the guilty, that no one gets away with murder."

"And that's all nonsense, eh?" Grantham Beale smiled his second smile since hearing the jury's verdict. If nothing else, he thought, the spiffy little lawyer improved a man's spirits.

"I wouldn't call it nonsense," Ehrengraf said. "But after all is said and done, you're in prison and the real murderer is not."

"Walker Murchison."

"I beg your pardon?"

"The real murderer," Beale said. "I'm in prison and Walker Gladstone Murchison is free."

"Precisely. Because it is not enough to be guiltless, Mr. Beale. One must also be able to convince a jury of one's guiltlessness. In short, had you been less innocent and more experienced, you could have taken steps early on to assure you would not find yourself in your present condition right now."

"And what could I have done?"

"What you *have* done, at long last," said Martin Ehrengraf. "You could have called me immediately."

"Albert Speldron," Ehrengraf said. "The murder victim, shot three times in the heart at close range. The murder weapon was an unregistered handgun, a thirty-eight-caliber revolver. It was subsequently located in the spare tire well of your automobile."

"It wasn't my gun. I never saw it in my life until the police showed it to me."

"Of course you didn't," Ehrengraf said soothingly. "To continue. Albert Speldron was a loan shark. Not, however, the sort of gruff-voiced neckless thug who lends ten or twenty dollars at a time to longshoremen and factory hands and breaks their legs with a baseball bat if they're late paying the vig."

"Paying the what?"

"Ah, sweet innocence," Ehrengraf said. "The vig. Short for vigorish. It's a term used by the criminal element to describe the ongoing interest payments which a debtor must make to maintain his status."

"I never heard the term," Beale said, "but I paid it well enough. I paid Speldron a thousand dollars a week and that didn't touch the principal."

"And you had borrowed how much?"

"Fifty thousand dollars."

"The jury apparently considered that a satisfactory motive for murder."

"Well, that's crazy," Beale said. "Why on earth would I want to kill Speldron? I didn't hate the man. He'd done me a service by lending me that money. I had a chance to buy a valuable stamp collection. That's my business, I buy and sell stamps, and I had an opportunity to get hold of an extraordinary collection, mostly U.S. and British Empire but a really exceptional lot of early German States as well, and there were also—well, before I get carried away, are you interested in stamps at all?"

"Only when I've a letter to mail."

"Oh. Well, this was a fine collection, let me say that much and leave it at that. The seller had to have all cash and the transaction had to go unrecorded. Taxes, you understand."

"Indeed I do. The system of taxation makes criminals of us all."

"I don't really think of it as criminal," Beale said.

"Few people do. But go on, sir."

"What more is there to say? I had to raise fifty thousand dollars on the quiet to close the deal on this fine lot of stamps. By dealing with Speldron, I was able to borrow the money without filling out a lot of forms or giving him anything but my word. I was quite confident I would triple my money by the time I broke up the collection and sold it in job lots to a variety of dealers and collectors. I'll probably take in a total of fifty thousand out of the U.S. issues alone, and I know a buyer who will salivate when he gets a look at the German States issues."

"So it didn't bother you to pay Speldron his thousand a week."

"Not a bit. I figured to have half the stamps sold within a couple of months, and the first thing I'd do would be to repay the fifty thousand dollars principal and close out the loan. I'd have paid eight or ten thousand dollars in interest, say, but what's that compared to a profit of fifty or a hundred thousand dollars? Speldron was doing me a favor and I appreciated it. Oh, he was doing himself a favor too, two percent interest per week didn't put him in the hardship category, but it was just good business for both of us, no question about it."

"You've dealt with him before?"

"Maybe a dozen times over the years. I've borrowed sums ranging between ten and seventy thousand dollars. I never heard the interest payments called vigorish before, but I always paid them promptly. And no one ever threatened to break my legs. We did business together, Speldron and I. And it always worked out very well for both of us."

"The prosecution argued that by killing Speldron you erased your debt to him. That's certainly a motive a jury can understand, Mr. Beale. In a world where men are commonly killed for the price of a bottle of whiskey, fifty thousand dollars does seem enough to kill a man over."

"But I'd be crazy to kill for that sum. I'm not a pauper. If I was having trouble paying Speldron all I had to do was sell the stamps."

"Suppose you had trouble selling them."

"Then I could have liquidated other merchandise from my stock. I could have mortgaged my home. Why, I could have raised enough on the house to pay Speldron off three times over. That car they found the gun in, that's an Antonelli Scorpion. The car alone is worth half of what I owed Speldron."

"Indeed," Martin Ehrengraf said. "But this Walker Murchison. How does he come into the picture?"

"He killed Speldron."

"How do we know this, Mr. Beale?"

Beale got to his feet. He'd been sitting on his iron cot, leaving the cell's one chair for the lawyer. Now he stood up, stretched, and walked to the rear of the cell. For a moment he stood regarding some graffito on the cell wall. Then he turned and looked at Ehrengraf.

"Speldron and Murchison were partners," he said. "I only dealt with Speldron because he was the only one who dealt in unsecured loans. And Murchison had an insurance business in which Speldron did not participate. Their joint ventures included real estate, investments, and other activities where large sums of money moved around quickly with few records kept of exactly what took place."

"Shady operations," Ehrengraf said.

"For the most part. Not always illegal, not *entirely* illegal, but, yes, I like your word. Shady."

"So they were partners, and it is not unheard of for one to kill one's partner. To dissolve a partnership by the most direct means available, as it were. But why this partnership? Why should Murchison kill Speldron?"

Beale shrugged. "Money," he suggested. "With all that cash floating around, you can bet Murchison made out handsomely on Speldron's death. I'll bet he put a lot more than fifty thousand unrecorded dollars into his pocket."

"That's your only reason for suspecting him?"

Beale shook his head. "The partnership had a secretary," he said. "Her name's Felicia. Young, long dark hair, flashing dark eyes, a body like a magazine centerfold, and a face like a Chanel ad. Both of the partners were sleeping with her."

"Perhaps this was not a source of enmity."

"But it was. Murchison's married to her."

"Ah."

"But there's an important reason why I know it was Murchison who killed Speldron." Beale stepped forward, stood over the seated attorney. "The gun was found in the boot of my car," he said. "Wrapped in a filthy towel and stuffed in the spare tire well. There were no fingerprints on the gun and it wasn't registered to me but there it was in my car."

"The Antonelli Scorpion?"

"Yes. What of it?"

"No matter."

Beale frowned momentarily, then drew a breath and plunged onward. "It was put there to frame me," he said.

"So it would seem."

"It had to be put there by somebody who knew I owed Speldron money. Somebody with inside information. The two of them were partners. I met Murchison any number of times when I went to the office to pay the interest, or vigorish as you called it. Why do they call it that?"

"I've no idea."

"Murchison knew I owed money. And Murchison and I never liked each other."

"Why?"

"We just didn't get along. The reason's not important. And there's more, I'm not just grasping at straws. It was Murchison who suggested I might have killed Speldron. A lot of men owed Speldron money and there were probably several of them who were in much stickier shape financially than I, but Murchison told the police I'd had a loud and bitter argument with Speldron two days before he was killed!"

"And had you?"

"*No!* Why, I never in my life argued with Speldron."

"Interesting." The little lawyer raised his hand to his mustache, smoothing its tips delicately. His nails were manicured, Grantham Beale noted, and was there colorless nail polish on them? No, he observed, there was not. The little man might be something of a dandy but he was evidently not a fop.

"Did you indeed meet with Mr. Speldron on the day in question?"

"Yes, as a matter of fact I did. I made the interest payment and we exchanged pleasantries. There was nothing anyone could mistake for an argument."

"Ah."

"And even if there had been, Murchison wouldn't have known about it. He wasn't even in the office."

"Still more interesting," Ehrengraf said thoughtfully.

"It certainly is. But how can you possibly prove that he murdered his partner and framed me for it? You can't trap him into confessing, can you?"

"Murderers do confess."

"Not Murchison. You could try tracing the gun to him, I suppose, but the police tried to trace it to me and found they couldn't trace it at all. I just don't see—"

"Mr. Beale."

"Yes?"

"Why don't you sit down, Mr. Beale. Here, take this chair, I'm sure it's more comfortable than the edge of the bed. I'll stand for a moment. Mr. Beale, do you have a dollar?"

"They don't let us have money here."

"Then take this. It's a dollar which I'm lending to you."

The lawyer's dark eyes glinted. "No interest, Mr. Beale. A personal loan, not a business transaction. Now, sir, please give me the dollar which I've just lent to you."

"Give it to you?"

"That's right. Thank you. You have retained me, Mr. Beale, to look after your interests. The day you are released unconditionally from this prison you will owe me a fee of ninety thousand dollars. The fee will be all inclusive. Any expenses will be mine to bear. Should I fail to secure your release you will owe me nothing."

"But—"

"Is that agreeable, sir?"

"But what are you going to do? Engage detectives? File an appeal? Try to get the case reopened?"

"When a man engages to save your life, Mr. Beale, do you require that he first outline his plans for you?"

"No, but—"

"Ninety thousand dollars. Payable only if I succeed. Are the terms agreeable?"

"Yes, but—"

"Mr. Beale, when next we meet you will owe me ninety thousand dollars plus whatever emotional gratitude comes naturally to you. Until then, sir, you owe me one dollar." The thin lips curled in a shadowy smile. " 'The cut worm forgives the plow,' Mr. Beale. William Blake, *The Marriage of Heaven and Hell.* 'The cut worm forgives the plow.' You might think about that, sir, until we meet again."

The second meeting of Martin Ehrengraf and Grantham Beale took place five weeks and four days later. On this occasion the lawyer wore a navy two-button suit with a subtle vertical stripe. His shoes were highly polished black wing tips, his shirt a pale blue broadcloth with contrasting white collar and cuffs. His necktie bore a half-inch wide stripe of royal blue flanked by two narrower strips, one gold and the other a rather bright green, all on a navy field.

And this time Ehrengraf's client was also rather nicely turned out, although his tweed jacket and baggy flannels were hardly a match for the lawyer's suit. But Beale's dress was a great improvement over the shapeless gray prison garb he had worn previously, just as his office, a room filled with jumbled books and boxes, a desk covered with books and albums and stamps in and out of glassine envelopes, two worn leather chairs, and a matching sagging sofa—just as all of this comfortable disarray was a vast improvement over the spartan prison cell which had been the site of their earlier meeting.

Beale, seated behind his desk, gazed thoughtfully at Ehrengraf, who stood ramrod straight, one hand on the desk top, the other at his side. "Ninety thousand dollars," Beale said levelly. "You must admit that's a bit rich, Mr. Ehrengraf."

"We agreed on the price."

"No argument. We did agree, and I'm a firm believer in the sanctity of verbal agreements. But it was my understanding that your fee would be payable if my liberty came about as a result of your efforts."

"You are free today."

"I am indeed, and I'll be free tomorrow, but I can't see how it was any of your doing."

"Ah," Ehrengraf said. His face bore an expression of infinite disappointment, a disappointment felt not so much with this particular client as with the entire human race. "You feel I did nothing for you."

"I wouldn't say that. Perhaps you were taking steps to file an appeal. Perhaps you engaged detectives or did some detective work of your own. Perhaps in due course you would have found a way to get me out of prison, but in the meantime the unexpected happened and your services turned out to be unnecessary."

"The unexpected happened?"

"Well, who could have possibly anticipated it?" Beale shook his head in wonder. "Just think of it. Murchison went and got an attack of conscience. The bounder didn't have enough of a conscience to step forward and admit what he'd done, but he got to wondering what would happen if he died suddenly and I had to go on serving a life sentence for a crime he had committed. He wouldn't do anything to jeopardize his liberty while he lived but he wanted to be able to make amends if and when he died."

"Yes."

"So he prepared a letter," Beale went on. "Typed out a long letter explaining just why he had wanted his partner dead and how the unregistered gun had actually belonged to Speldron in the first place, and how he'd shot him and wrapped the gun in a towel and planted it in my car. Then he'd made up a story about my having had a fight with Albert Speldron, and of course that got the police looking in my direction, and the next thing I knew I was in jail. I saw the letter Murchison wrote. The police let me look at it. He went into complete detail."

"Considerate of him."

"And then he did the usual thing. Gave the letter to a lawyer with instructions that it be kept in his safe and opened only in the event of his death." Beale found a pair of stamp tongs in the clutter atop his desk, used them to lift a stamp, frowned at it for a moment, then set it down and looked directly at Martin Ehrengraf. "Do you suppose he had a premonition? For God's sake, Murchison was a young man, his health was good, and why should he anticipate dying? Maybe he did have a premonition."

"I doubt it."

"Then it's certainly a remarkable coincidence. A matter of weeks after turning this letter over to a lawyer, Murchison lost control of his car on a curve. Smashed right through the guard rail, plunged a couple of hundred feet, exploded on impact. I don't suppose the man knew what had happened to him."

"I suspect you're right."

"He was always a safe driver," Beale mused. "Perhaps he'd been drinking."

"Perhaps."

"And if he hadn't been decent enough to write that letter, I might be spending the rest of my life behind bars."

"How fortunate for you things turned out as they did."

"Exactly," said Beale. "And so, although I truly appreciate what you've done on my behalf, whatever that may be, and although I don't doubt you could have secured my liberty in due course, although I'm sure I don't know how you might have managed it, nevertheless as far as your fee is concerned—"

"Mr. Beale."

"Yes?"

"Do you really believe that a detestable troll like W. G. Murchison would take pains to arrange for your liberty in the event of his death?"

"Well, perhaps I misjudged the man. Perhaps—"

"Murchison *hated* you, Mr. Beale. If he found he was dying his one source of satisfaction would have been the knowledge that you were in prison for a crime you hadn't committed. I told you that you were an innocent, Mr. Beale, and a few weeks in prison has not dented or dulled your innocence. You actually think Murchison wrote that note."

"You mean he didn't?"

"It was typed upon a machine in his office," the lawyer said. "His own stationery was used, and the signature at the bottom is one many an expert would swear is Murchison's own."

"But he didn't write it?"

"Of course not." Martin Ehrengraf's hands hovered in the air before him. They might have been poised over an invisible typewriter or they might merely be looming as the talons of a bird of prey.

Grantham Beale stared at the little lawyer's hands in fascination. "You typed that letter," he said.

Ehrengraf shrugged.

"You—but Murchison left it with a lawyer!"

"The lawyer was not one Murchison had used in the past. Murchison evidently selected a stranger from the Yellow Pages, as far as one can determine, and made contact with him over the telephone, explaining what he wanted the man to do for him. He then mailed the letter along with a postal money order to cover the attorney's fee and a covering note confirming the telephone conversation. It seems he did not use his own name in his discussions with his lawyer, and he signed an alias to his covering note and to the money order as well. The signature he wrote, though, does seem to be in his own handwriting."

Ehrengraf paused, and his right hand went to finger the knot of his necktie. This particular tie, rather more colorful than his usual choice, was that of the Caedmon Society of Oxford University, an organization to which Martin Ehrengraf did not belong. The tie was a souvenir of an earlier case and he tended to wear it on particularly happy occasions, moments of personal triumph.

"Murchison left careful instructions," he went on. "He would call the lawyer every Thursday, merely repeating the alias he had used. If ever a Thursday passed without a call, and if there was no call on Friday either, the lawyer was to open the letter and follow its instructions. For four Thursdays in a row the lawyer received a phone call, presumably from Murchison."

"Presumably," Beale said heavily.

"Indeed. On the Tuesday following the fourth Thursday, Murchison's car went off a cliff and he was killed instantly. The lawyer read of Walker Murchison's death but had no idea that was his client's true identity. Then Thursday came and went without a call, and when there was no telephone call Friday either, why the lawyer opened the letter and went forthwith to the police." Ehrengraf spread his hands, smiled broadly. "The rest," he said, "you know as well as I."

"Great Scott," Beale said.

"Now if you honestly feel I've done nothing to earn my money—"

"I'll have to liquidate some stock," Beale said. "It won't be a problem and there shouldn't be much time involved. I'll bring a check to your office in a week. Say ten days at the outside. Unless you'd prefer cash?"

"A check will be fine, Mr. Beale. So long as it's a good check." And he smiled his lips to show he was joking.

The smile chilled Beale.

A week later Grantham Beale remembered that smile when he passed a check across Martin Ehrengraf's heroically disorganized desk. "A good check," he said. "I'd never give *you* a bad check, Mr. Ehrengraf. You typed that letter, you made all those phone calls, you forged Murchison's false name to the money order, and then when the opportunity presented itself you sent his car hurtling off the cliff with him in it."

"One believes what one wishes," Ehrengraf said quietly.

"I've been thinking about all of this all week long. Murchison framed me for a murder he committed, then paid for the crime himself and liberated me in the process without knowing what he was doing. 'The cut worm forgives the plow.' "

"Indeed."

"Meaning that the end justifies the means."

"Is that what Blake meant by that line? I've long wondered."

"The end justifies the means. I'm innocent, and now I'm free, and Murchison's guilty, and now he's dead, and you've got the money, but that's all right, because I made out fine on those stamps, and of course I don't have to repay Speldron, poor man, because death did cancel that particular debt, and—"

"Mr. Beale."

"Yes?"

"I don't know if I should tell you this, but I fear I must. You are more of an innocent than you realize. You've paid me handsomely for my services, as indeed we agreed that you would, and I think perhaps I'll offer you a lagniappe in the form of some experience to offset your colossal innocence. I'll begin with some advice. Do not, under any circumstances, resume your affair with Felicia Murchison."

Beale stared.

"You should have told me that was why you and Murchison didn't get along," Ehrengraf said gently. "I had to discover it for myself. No matter. More to the point, one should not share a pillow with a woman who has so little regard for one as to frame one for murder. Mrs. Murchison—"

"Felicia framed me?"

"Of course, Mr. Beale. Mrs. Murchison had nothing against you. It was sufficient that she had nothing *for* you. She murdered Mr. Speldron, you see, for reasons which need hardly concern us. Then having done so she needed someone to be cast as the murderer.

"Her husband could hardly have told the police about your purported argument with Speldron. He wasn't around at the time. He didn't know the two of you had met, and if he went out on a limb and told them, and then you had an alibi for the time in question, why he'd wind up looking silly, wouldn't he? But *Mrs.* Murchison knew you'd met with Speldron, and she told her husband the two of you argued, and so he told the police in perfectly good faith what she had told him, and then they went and found the murder gun in your very own Antonelli

Scorpion. A stunning automobile, incidentally, and it's to your credit to own such a vehicle, Mr. Beale."

"Felicia killed Speldron."

"Yes."

"And framed me."

"Yes."

"But—why did you frame Murchison?"

"Did you expect me to try to convince the powers that be that she did it? And had pangs of conscience and left a letter with a lawyer? Women don't leave letters with lawyers, Mr. Beale, any more than they have consciences. One must deal with the materials at hand."

"But—"

"And the woman is young, with long dark hair, flashing dark eyes, a body like a magazine centerfold, and a face like a Chanel ad. She's also an excellent typist and most cooperative in any number of ways which we needn't discuss at the moment. Mr. Beale, would you like me to get you a glass of water?"

"I'm all right."

"I'm sure you'll be all right, Mr. Beale. I'm sure you will. Mr. Beale, I'm going to make a suggestion. I think you should seriously consider marrying and settling down. I think you'd be much happier that way. You're an innocent, Mr. Beale, and you've had the Ehrengraf Experience now, and it's rendered you considerably more experienced than you were, but your innocence is not the sort to be readily vanquished. Give the widow Murchison and all her tribe a wide berth, Mr. Beale. They're not for you. Find yourself an old-fashioned girl and lead a proper old-fashioned life. Buy and sell stamps. Cultivate a garden. Raise terriers. The West Highland White might be a good breed for you but that's your decision, certainly. Mr. Beale? Are you *sure* you won't have a glass of water?"

"I'm all right."

"Quite. I'll leave you with another thought of Blake's, Mr. Beale. 'Lilies that fester smell worse than weeds.' That's also from *The Marriage of Heaven and Hell*, another of what he calls Proverbs of Hell, and perhaps someday you'll be able to interpret it for me. I never quite know for sure what Blake's getting at, Mr. Beale, but his things do have a nice sound to them, don't they? Innocence and experience, Mr. Beale. That's the ticket, isn't it? Innocence and experience."

The Ehrengraf Appointment

Martin Ehrengraf was walking jauntily down the courthouse steps when a taller and bulkier man caught up with him. "Glorious day," the man said. "Simply a glorious day."

Ehrengraf nodded. It was indeed a glorious day, the sort of autumn afternoon that made men recall football weekends. Ehrengraf had just been thinking that he'd like a piece of hot apple pie with a slab of sharp cheddar on it. He rarely thought about apple pie and almost never wanted cheese on it, but it was that sort of day.

"I'm Cutliffe," the man said. "Hudson Cutliffe, of Marquardt, Stoner, and Cutliffe."

"Ehrengraf," said Ehrengraf.

"Yes, I know. Oh, believe me, I know." Cutliffe gave what he doubtless considered a hearty chuckle. "Imagine running into Martin Ehrengraf himself, standing in line for an IDC appointment just like everybody else."

"Every man is entitled to a proper defense," Ehrengraf said stiffly. "It's a guaranteed right in a free society."

"Yes, to be sure, but—"

"Indigent defendants have attorneys appointed by the court. Our system here calls for attorneys to make themselves available at specified intervals for such appointments, rather than entrust such cases to a public defender."

"I quite understand," Cutliffe said. "Why, I was just appointed to an IDC case myself, some luckless chap who stole a satchel full of meat from a supermarket. Choice cuts, too—lamb chops, filet mignon. You just about have to steal them these days, don't you?"

Ehrengraf, a recent convert to vegetarianism, offered a thin-lipped smile and thought about pie and cheese.

"But Martin Ehrengraf himself," Cutliffe went on. "One no more thinks of you in this context than one imagines a glamorous Hollywood actress going to the bathroom. Martin Ehrengraf, the dapper and debonair lawyer who hardly ever appears in court. The man who only collects a fee if he wins. Is that really true, by the way? You actually take murder cases on a contingency basis?"

"That's correct."

"Extraordinary. I don't see how you can possibly afford to operate that way."

"It's quite simple," Ehrengraf said.

"Oh?"

His smile was fuller than before. "I always win," he said. "It's simplicity itself."

"And yet you rarely appear in court."

"Sometimes one can work more effectively behind the scenes."

"And when your client wins his freedom—"

"I'm paid in full," Ehrengraf said.

"Your fees are high, I understand."

"Exceedingly high."

"And your clients almost always get off."

"They're always innocent," Ehrengraf said. "That does help."

Hudson Cutliffe laughed richly, as if to suggest that the idea of bringing guilt and innocence into a discussion of legal procedures was amusing. "Well, this will be a switch for you," he said at length. "You were assigned the Protter case, weren't you?"

"Mr. Protter is my client, yes."

"Hardly a typical Ehrengraf case, is it? Man gets drunk, beats his wife to death, passes out, and sleeps it off, then wakes up and sees what he's done and calls the police. Bit of luck for you, wouldn't you say?"

"Oh?"

"Won't take up too much of your time. You'll plead him guilty to manslaughter, possibly get a reduced sentence on grounds of his previous clean record, and then Protter'll do a year or two in prison while you go about your business."

"You think that's the course I'll pursue, Mr. Cutliffe?"

"It's what anyone would do."

"Almost anyone," said Ehrengraf.

"And there's no reason to make work for yourself, is there?" Cutliffe winked. "These IDC cases—I don't know why they pay us at all, as small as the fees are. A hundred and seventy-five dollars isn't much of an all-inclusive fee for a legal defense, is it? Wouldn't you say your average fee runs a bit higher than that?"

"Quite a bit higher."

"But there are compensations. It's the same hundred and seventy-five dollars whether you plead your client or stand trial, let alone win. A far cry from your usual system, eh, Ehrengraf? You don't have to win to get paid."

"I do," Ehrengraf said.

"How's that?"

"If I lose the case, I'll donate the fee to charity."

"*If* you lose? But you'll plead him to manslaughter, won't you?"

"Certainly not."

"Then what will you do?"

"I'll plead him innocent."

"Innocent?"

"Of course. The man never killed anyone."

"But—" Cutliffe inclined his head, dropped his voice. "You know the man? You have some special information about the case?"

"I've never met him and know only what I've read in the newspapers."

"Then how can you say he's innocent?"

"He's my client."

"So?"

"I do not represent the guilty," Ehrengraf said. "My clients are innocent, Mr. Cutliffe, and Arnold Protter is a client of mine, and I intend to earn my fee as his attorney, however inadequate that fee may be. I did not seek appointment, Mr. Cutliffe, but that appointment is a sacred trust, sir, and I shall justify that trust. Good day, Mr. Cutliffe."

"They said they'd get me a lawyer and it wouldn't cost me nothing," Arnold Protter said. "I guess you're it, huh?"

"Indeed," said Ehrengraf. He glanced around the sordid little jail cell, then cast an eye on his new client. Arnold Protter was a thickset round-shouldered man in his late thirties with the ample belly of a beer drinker and the red nose of a whiskey drinker. His pudgy face recalled the Pillsbury Dough Boy. His hands, too, were pudgy, and he held them out in front of his red nose and studied them in wonder.

"These were the hands that did it," he said.

"Nonsense."

"How's that?"

"Perhaps you'd better tell me what happened," Ehrengraf suggested. "The night your wife was killed."

"It's hard to remember," Protter said.

"I'm sure it is."

"What it was, it was an ordinary kind of a night. Me and Gretch had a beer or two during the afternoon, just passing time while we watched television. Then we ordered up a pizza and had a couple more with it, and then we settled in for the evening and started hitting the boilermakers. You know, a shot and a beer. First thing you know, we're having this argument."

"About what?"

Protter got up, paced, glared again at his hands. He lumbered about, Ehrengraf thought, like a caged bear. His chino pants were ragged at the cuffs and his plaid shirt was a tartan no Highlander would recognize. Ehrengraf, in contrast, sparkled in the drab cell like a diamond on a dustheap. His suit was a herringbone tweed the color of a well-smoked briar pipe, and beneath it he wore a suede doeskin vest over a cream broadcloth shirt with French cuffs and a tab collar. His cufflinks were simple gold hexagons, his tie a wool knit in the same brown as his suit. His shoes were shell cordovan loafers, quite simple and elegant and polished to a high sheen.

"The argument," Ehrengraf prompted.

"Oh, I don't know how it got started," Protter said. "One thing led to another, and pretty soon she's making a federal case over me and this woman who lives one flight down from us."

"What woman?"

"Her name's Agnes Mullane. Gretchen's giving me the business that me and Agnes got something going."

"And were you having an affair with Agnes Mullane?"

"Naw, 'course not. Maybe me and Agnes'd pass the time of day on the staircase, and maybe I had some thoughts on the subject, but nothing ever came of it. But she started in on the subject, Gretch did, and to get a little of my own back I started ragging her about this guy lives one flight up from us."

"And his name is—"

"Gates, Harry Gates."

"You thought your wife was having an affair with Gates?"

Protter shook his head. "Naw, 'course not. But he's an artist, Gates is, and I was accusing her of posing for him, you know. Naked. No clothes on."

"Nude."

"Yeah."

"And did your wife pose for Mr. Gates?"

"You kidding? You never met Gretchen, did you?"

Ehrengraf shook his head.

"Well, Gretch was all right, and the both of us was used to each other, if you know what I mean, but you wouldn't figure her for somebody who woulda been Miss America if she coulda found her way to Atlantic City. And Gates, what would he need with a model?"

"You said he was an artist."

"*He* says he's an artist," Protter said, "but you couldn't prove it by me. What he paints don't look like nothing. I went up there one time on account of his radio's cooking at full blast, you know, and I want to ask him to put a lid on it, and he's up on top of this stepladder dribbling paint on a canvas that he's got spread out all over the floor. All different colors of paint, and he's just throwing them down at the canvas like a little kid making a mess."

"Then he's an abstract expressionist," Ehrengraf said.

"Naw, he's a painter. I mean, people buy these pictures of his. Not enough to make him rich or he wouldn't be living in the same dump with me and Gretch, but he makes a living at it. Enough to keep him in beer and pizza and all, but what would he need with a model? Only reason he'd want Gretchen up there is to hold the ladder steady."

"An abstract expressionist," said Ehrengraf. "That's very interesting. He lives directly above you, Mr. Protter?"

"Right upstairs, yeah. That's why we could hear his radio clear as a bell."

"Was it playing the night you and your wife drank the boilermakers?"

"We drank boilermakers lots of the time," Protter said, puzzled. "Oh, you mean the night I killed her."

"The night she died."

"Same thing, ain't it?"

"Not at all," said Ehrengraf. "But let it go. Was Mr. Gates playing his radio that night?"

Protter scratched his head. "Hard to remember," he said. "One night's like another, know what I mean? Yeah, the radio was going that night. I remember now. He was playing country music on it. Usually he plays that rock and roll, and that stuff gives me a headache, but this time it was country music. Country music, it sort of soothes my nerves." He frowned. "But I never played it on my own radio."

"Why was that?"

"Gretch hated it. Couldn't stand it, said the singers all sounded like dogs that ate poisoned meat and was dying of it. Gretch didn't like any music much. What she liked was the television, and then we'd have Gates with his rock and roll at top volume, and sometimes you'd hear a little country music coming upstairs from Agnes's radio. She liked country music, but she never played it very loud. With the windows open on a hot day you'd hear it, but otherwise no. Of course what you hear most with the windows open is the Puerto Ricans on the street with their transistor radios."

Protter went on at some length about Puerto Ricans and transistor radios. When he paused for breath, Ehrengraf straightened up and smiled with his lips. "A pleasure," he said. "Mr. Protter, I believe in your innocence."

"Huh?"

"You've been the victim of an elaborate and diabolical frame-up, sir. But you're in good hands now. Maintain your silence and put your faith in me. Is there anything you need to make your stay here more comfortable?"

"It's not so bad."

"Well, you won't be here for long. I'll see to that. Perhaps I can arrange for a radio for you. You could listen to country music."

"Be real nice," Protter said. "Soothing is what it is. It soothes my nerves."

An hour after his interview with his client, Ehrengraf was seated on a scarred wooden bench at a similarly distressed oaken table. The restaurant in which he was dining ran to college pennants and German beer steins suspended from the exposed dark wood beams. Ehrengraf was eating hot apple pie topped with sharp cheddar, and at the side of his plate was a small glass of neat Calvados.

The little lawyer was just preparing to take his first sip of the tangy apple brandy when a familiar voice sounded beside him.

"Ehrengraf," Hudson Cutliffe boomed out. "Fancy finding you here. Twice in one day, eh?"

Ehrengraf looked up, smiled. "Excellent pie here," he said.

"Come here all the time," Cutliffe said. "My home away from home. Never seen you here before, I don't think."

"My first time."

"Pie with cheese. If I ate that I'd put on ten pounds." Unbidden, the hefty attorney drew back the bench opposite Ehrengraf and seated himself. When a waiter appeared, Cutliffe ordered a slice of prime rib and a spinach salad.

"Watching my weight," he said. "Protein, that's the ticket. Got to cut down on the nasty old carbs. Well, Ehrengraf, I suppose you've seen your wife-murderer by now, haven't you? Or are you still maintaining he's no murderer at all?"

"Protter's an innocent man."

Cutliffe chuckled. "Commendable attitude, I'm sure, but why don't you save it for the courtroom? The odd juryman may be impressed by that line of country. I'm not, myself. I've always found facts more convincing than attitudes."

"Indeed," said Ehrengraf. "Personally, I've always noticed the shadow as much as the substance. I suspect it's a difference of temperament, Mr. Cutliffe. I don't suppose you're much of a fan of poetry, are you?"

"Poetry? You mean rhymes and verses and all that?"

"More or less."

"Schoolboy stuff, eh? *Boy stood on the burning deck,* that the sort of thing you mean? Had a bellyful of that in school." He smiled suddenly. "Unless you're talking about limericks. I like the odd limerick now and then, I must say. Are you much of a hand for limericks?"

"Not really," said Ehrengraf.

Cutliffe delivered four limericks while Ehrengraf sat with a pained expression on his face. The first concerned a mathematician named Paul, the second a young harlot named Dinah, the third a man from Fort Ord, and the fourth an old woman from Truk.

"It's interesting," Ehrengraf said at length. "On the surface there's no similarity whatsoever between the limerick and abstract expressionist painting. They're not at all alike. And yet they are."

"I don't follow you."

"It's not important," Ehrengraf said. The waiter appeared, setting a plateful of rare beef in front of Cutliffe, who at once reached for his knife and fork. Ehrengraf looked at the meat. "You're going to eat that," he said.

"Of course. What else would I do with it?"

Ehrengraf took another small sip of the Calvados. Holding the glass aloft, he began an apparently aimless dissertation upon the innocence of his client. "If you were a reader of poetry," he found himself saying, "and if you did not systematically dull your sensibilities by consuming the flesh of beasts, Mr. Protter's innocence would be obvious to you."

"You're serious about defending him, then. You're really going to plead him innocent."

"How could I do otherwise?"

Cutliffe raised an eyebrow while lowering a fork. "You realize you're letting an idle whim jeopardize a man's liberty, Ehrengraf. Your Mr. Protter will surely receive a stiffer sentence after he's been found guilty by a jury, and—"

"But he won't be found guilty."

"Are you counting on some technicality to get him off the hook? Because I have a friend in the District Attorney's office, you know, and I went round there while you were visiting your client. He tells me the state's case is gilt-edged."

"The state is welcome to the gilt," Ehrengraf said grandly. "Mr. Protter has the innocence."

Cutliffe put down his fork, set his jaw. "Perhaps," he said, "perhaps you simply do not care. Perhaps, having no true financial stake in Arnold Protter's fate, you just don't give a damn what happens to him. Whereas, had you a substantial sum riding on the outcome of the case—"

"Oh, dear," said Ehrengraf. "You're not by any chance proposing a wager?"

Miss Agnes Mullane had had a permanent recently, and her copper-colored hair looked as though she'd stuck her big toe in an electric socket. She had a freckled face, a pug nose, and a body that would send whole shifts of construction workers plummeting from their scaffolds. She wore a hostess outfit of a silky green fabric, and her walk, Ehrengraf noted, was decidedly slinky.

"So terrible about the Protters," she said. "They were good neighbors, although I never became terribly close with either of them. She kept to herself, for the most part, but he always had a smile and a cheerful word for me when I would run into him on the stairs. Of course I've always gotten on better with men than with women, Mr. Ehrengraf, though I'm sure I couldn't tell you why."

"Indeed," said Ehrengraf.

"You'll have some more tea, Mr. Ehrengraf?"

"If I may."

She leaned forward, displaying an alluring portion of herself to Ehrengraf as she filled his cup from a Dresden teapot. Then she set the pot down and straightened up with a sigh.

"Poor Mrs. Protter," she said. "Death is so final."

"Given the present state of medical science."

"And poor *Mr.* Protter. Will he have to spend many years in prison, Mr. Ehrengraf?"

"Not with a proper defense. Tell me, Miss Mullane. Mrs. Protter accused her husband of having an affair with you. I wonder why she should have brought such an accusation."

"I'm sure I don't know."

"Of course you're a very attractive woman—"

"Do you really think so, Mr. Ehrengraf?"

"—and you live by yourself, and tongues will wag."

"I'm a respectable woman, Mr. Ehrengraf."

"I'm sure you are."

"And I would never have an affair with anyone who lived here in this building. Discretion, Mr. Ehrengraf, is very important to me."

"I sensed that, Miss Mullane." The little lawyer got to his feet, walked to the window. The afternoon was warm, and the strains of Latin music drifted up through the open window from the street below.

"Transistor radios," Agnes Mullane said. "They carry them everywhere."

"So they do. When Mrs. Protter made that accusation, Miss Mullane, her husband denied it."

"Why, I should hope so!"

"And he in turn accused her of carrying on with Mr. Gates. Have I said something funny, Miss Mullane?"

Agnes Mullane managed to control her laughter. "Mr. Gates is an artist," she said.

"A painter, I'm told. Would that canvas be one of his?"

"I'm afraid not. He paints abstracts. I prefer representational art myself, as you can see."

"And country music."

"I beg your pardon?"

"Nothing. You're sure Mr. Gates was not having an affair with Mrs. Protter?"

"Positive." Her brow clouded for an instant, then cleared completely. "No," she said, "Harry Gates would never have been involved with her. But what's the point, Mr. Ehrengraf? Are you trying to establish a defense of justifiable homicide? The unwritten law and all that?"

"Not exactly."

"Because I really don't think it would work, do you?"

"No," said Ehrengraf, "I don't suppose it would."

Miss Mullane leaned forward again, not to pour tea but with a similar effect. "It's so noble of you," she said, "donating your time for poor Mr. Protter."

"The court appointed me, Miss Mullane."

"Yes, but surely not all appointed attorneys work so hard on these cases, do they?"

"Perhaps not."

"That's what I thought." She ran her tongue over her lips. "Nobility is an attractive quality in a man," she said thoughtfully. "And I've always admired men who dress well, and who bear themselves elegantly."

Ehrengraf smiled. He was wearing a pale blue cashmere sport jacket over a Wedgwood blue shirt. His tie matched his jacket, with an intricate below-the-knot design in gold thread.

"A lovely jacket," Miss Mullane purred. She reached over, laid a hand on Ehrengraf's sleeve. "Cashmere," she said. "I love the feel of cashmere."

"Thank you."

"And gray flannel slacks. What a fine fabric. Come with me, Mr. Ehrengraf. I'll show you where to hang your things."

In the bedroom Miss Mullane paused to switch on the radio. Loretta Lynn was singing something about having been born a coal miner's daughter.

"My one weakness," Miss Mullane said, "or should I say one of my two weaknesses, along with a weakness for well-dressed men of noble character. I hope you don't mind country music, Mr. Ehrengraf?"

"Not at all," said Ehrengraf. "I find it soothing."

Several days later, when Arnold Protter was released from jail, Ehrengraf was there to meet him. "I want to shake your hand," he told him, extending his own.

"You're a free man now, Mr. Protter, I only regret I played no greater part in securing your freedom."

Protter pumped the lawyer's hand enthusiastically. "Hey, listen," he said, "you're ace-high with me, Mr. Ehrengraf. You believed in me when nobody else did, including me myself. I'm just now trying to take all of this in. I'll tell you, I never would have dreamed Agnes Mullane killed my wife."

"It's something neither of us suspected, Mr. Protter."

"It's the craziest thing I ever heard of. Let me see if I got the drift of it straight. My Gretchen was carrying on with Gates after all. I thought it was just a way to get in a dig at her, accusing her of carrying on with him, but actually it was happening all the time."

"So it would seem."

"And that's why she got so steamed when I brought it up." Protter nodded, wrapped up in thought. "Anyway, Gates also had something going with Agnes Mullane. You know something, Mr. Ehrengraf? He musta been nuts. Why would anybody who was getting next to Agnes want to bother with Gretchen?"

"Artists perceive the world differently from the rest of us, Mr. Protter."

"If that's a polite way of saying he was cockeyed, I sure gotta go along with you on that. So here he's getting it on with the both of them, and Agnes finds out and she's jealous. How do you figure she found out?"

"It's always possible Gates told her," Ehrengraf suggested. "Or perhaps she heard you accusing your wife of infidelity. You and Gretchen had both been drinking, and your argument may have been a loud one."

"Could be. A few boilermakers and I tend to raise my voice."

"Most people do. Or perhaps Miss Mullane saw some of Gates's sketches of your wife. I understand there were several found in his apartment. He may have been an abstract expressionist, but he seems to have been capable of realistic sketches of nudes. Of course he's denied they were his work, but he'd be likely to say that, wouldn't he?"

"I guess so," Protter said. "Naked pictures of Gretchen, gee, you never know, do you?"

"You never do," Ehrengraf agreed. "In any event, Miss Mullane had a key to your apartment. One was found among her effects. Perhaps it was Gates's key, perhaps Gretchen had given it to him and Agnes Mullane stole it. She let herself into your apartment, found you and your wife unconscious, and pounded your wife on the head with an empty beer bottle. Your wife was alive when Miss Mullane entered your apartment, Mr. Protter, and dead when she left it."

"So I didn't kill her after all."

"Indeed you did not." Ehrengraf smiled for a moment. Then his face turned grave. "Agnes Mullane was not cut out for murder," he said. "At heart she was a gentle soul. I realized that at once when I spoke with her."

"You went and talked to Agnes?"

The little lawyer nodded. "I suspect my interview with her may have driven her over the edge," he said. "Perhaps she sensed that I was suspicious of her. She wrote out a letter to the police, detailing what she had done. Then she must have gone upstairs to Mr. Gates's apartment, because she managed to secure a twenty-five caliber automatic pistol registered to him. She returned to her own apartment, put the weapon to her chest, and shot herself in the heart."

"She had some chest, too."

Ehrengraf did not comment.

"I'll tell you," Protter said, "the whole thing's a little too complicated for a simple guy like me to take it all in all at once. I can see why it was open and shut as far as the cops were concerned. There's me and the wife drinking, and there's me and the wife fighting, and the next thing you know she's dead and I'm sleeping it off. If it wasn't for you, I'd be doing time for killing her."

"I played a part," Ehrengraf said modestly. "But it's Agnes Mullane's conscience that saved you from prison."

"Poor Agnes."

"A tortured, tormented woman, Mr. Protter."

"I don't know about that," Protter said. "But she had some body on her, I'll say that for her." He drew a breath. "What about you, Mr. Ehrengraf? You did a real job for me. I wish I could pay you."

"Don't worry about it."

"I guess the court pays you something, huh?"

"There's a set fee of a hundred and seventy-five dollars," Ehrengraf said, "but I don't know that I'm eligible to receive it in this instance because of the disposition of the case. The argument may be raised that I didn't really perform any actions on your behalf, that charges were simply dropped."

"You mean you'll get gypped out of your fee? That's a hell of a note, Mr. Ehrengraf."

"Oh, don't worry about it," said Ehrengraf. "It's not important in the overall scheme of things."

Ehrengraf, his blue pinstripe suit setting off his Caedmon Society striped necktie, sipped daintily at a Calvados. It was Indian Summer this afternoon, far too balmy for hot apple pie with cheddar cheese. He was eating instead a piece of cold apple pie topped with vanilla ice cream, and had discovered that Calvados went every bit as nicely with that dish.

Across from him, Hudson Cutliffe sat with a plate of lamb stew. When Cutliffe had ordered the dish, Ehrengraf had refrained from commenting on the barbarity of slaughtering lambs and stewing them. He had decided to ignore the contents of Cutliffe's plate. Whatever he'd ordered, Ehrengraf intended that the man eat crow today.

"You," said Cutliffe, "are the most astonishingly fortunate lawyer who ever passed the bar."

" 'Dame Fortune is a fickle gypsy, And always blind, and often tipsy,' " Ehrengraf quoted. "Winthrop Mackworth Praed, born eighteen-oh-two, died eighteen thirty-nine. But you don't care for poetry, do you? Perhaps you'd prefer the elder

Pliny's observation upon the eruption of Vesuvius. He said that Fortune favors the brave."

"A cliché, isn't it?"

"Perhaps it was rather less a cliché when Pliny said it," Ehrengraf said gently. "But that's beside the point. My client was innocent, just as I told you—"

"How on earth could you have known it?"

"I didn't have to know it. I presumed it, Mr. Cutliffe, as I always presume my clients to be innocent, and as in time they are invariably proven to be. And, because you were so incautious as to insist upon a wager—"

"Insist!"

"It was indeed your suggestion," Ehrengraf said. "*I* did not seek *you* out, Mr. Cutliffe. *I* did not seat myself unbidden at *your* table."

"You came to this restaurant," Cutliffe said darkly. "You deliberately baited me, goaded me. You—"

"Oh, come now," Ehrengraf said. "You make me sound like what priests would call an occasion of sin or lawyers an attractive nuisance. I came here for apple pie with cheese, Mr. Cutliffe, and you proposed a wager. Now my client has been released and all charges dropped, and I believe you owe me money."

"It's not as if you got him off. Fate got him off."

Ehrengraf rolled his eyes. "Oh, please, Mr. Cutliffe," he said. "I've had clients take that stance, you know, and they always change their minds in the end. My agreement with them has always been that my fee is due and payable upon their release, whether the case comes to court or not, whether or not I have played any evident part in their salvation. I specified precisely those terms when we arranged our little wager."

"Of course gambling debts are not legally collectible in this state."

"Of course they are not, Mr. Cutliffe. Yours is purely a debt of honor, an attribute which you may or may not be said to possess in accordance with your willingness to write out a check. But I trust you are an honorable man, Mr. Cutliffe."

Their eyes met. After a long moment Cutliffe drew a checkbook from his pocket. "I feel I've been manipulated in some devious fashion," he said, "but at the same time I can't gloss over the fact that I owe you money." He opened the checkbook, uncapped a pen, and filled out the check quickly, signing it with a flourish. Ehrengraf smiled narrowly, placing the check in his own wallet without noting the amount. It was, let it be said, an impressive amount.

"An astonishing case," Cutliffe said, "even if you yourself had the smallest of parts in it. This morning's news was the most remarkable thing of all."

"Oh?"

"I'm referring to Gates's confession, of course."

"Gates's confession?"

"You haven't heard? Oh, this *is* rich. Harry Gates is in jail. He went to the police and confessed to murdering Gretchen Protter."

"Gates murdered Gretchen Protter?"

"No question about it. It seems he shot her, used the very same small-caliber automatic pistol that the Mullane woman stole and used to kill herself. He was having an affair with both the women, just as Agnes Mullane said in her suicide note. He heard Protter accuse his wife of infidelity and was afraid Agnes Mullane would find out he'd been carrying on with Gretchen Protter. So he went down there looking to clear the air, and he had the gun along for protection, and—are you sure you didn't know about this?"

"Keep talking," Ehrengraf urged.

"Well, he found the two of them out cold. At first he thought Gretchen was dead but he saw she was breathing, and he took a raw potato from the refrigerator and used it as a silencer, and he shot Gretchen in the heart. They never found the bullet during postmortem examination because they weren't looking for it, just assumed massive skull injuries had caused her death. But after he confessed they looked, and there was the bullet right where he said it should be, and Gates is in jail charged with her murder."

"Why on earth did he confess?"

"He was in love with Agnes Mullane," Cutliffe said. "That's why he killed Gretchen. Then Agnes Mullane killed herself, taking the blame for a crime Gates committed, and he cracked wide open. Figures her death was some sort of divine retribution, and he has to clear things by paying the price for the Protter woman's death. The D.A. thinks perhaps he killed them both, faked Agnes Mullane's confession note, and then couldn't win the battle with his own conscience. He insists he didn't, of course, just as he insists he didn't draw nude sketches of either of the women, but it seems there's some question now about the validity of Agnes Mullane's suicide note, so it may well turn out that Gates killed her, too. Because if Gates killed Gretchen, why would Agnes have committed suicide?"

"I'm sure there are any number of possible explanations," Ehrengraf said, his fingers worrying the tips of his neatly trimmed mustache. "Any number of explanations. Do you know the epitaph Andrew Marvell wrote for a lady?

"To say—she lived a virgin chaste
In this age loose and all unlaced;
Nor was, when vice is so allowed,
Of virtue or ashamed or proud;
That her soul was on Heaven so bent,
No minute but it came and went;
That, ready her last debt to pay,
She summed her life up every day;
Modest as morn, as mid-day bright,
Gentle as evening, cool as night:
—'Tis true; but all too weakly said;
'Twas more significant, she's dead.

"She's dead, Mr. Cutliffe, and we may leave her to heaven, as another poet has said. My client was innocent. That's the only truly relevant point. My client was innocent."

"As you somehow knew all along."

"As I knew all along, yes. Yes, indeed, as I knew all along." Ehrengraf's fingers drummed the tabletop. "Perhaps you could get our waiter's eye," he suggested. "I think I might enjoy another glass of Calvados."

The Ehrengraf Riposte

Martin Ehrengraf placed his hands on the top of his exceedingly cluttered desk and looked across its top. He was seated, while the man at whom he gazed was standing, and indeed looked incapable of remaining still, let alone seating himself on a chair. He was a large man, tall and quite stout, balding, florid of face, with a hawk's-bill nose and a jutting chin. His hair, combed straight back, was a rich and glossy dark-brown; his bushy eyebrows were salted with gray. His suit, while of a particular shade of blue that Ehrengraf would never have chosen for himself, was well tailored and expensive. It was logical to assume that the man within the suit was abundantly supplied with money, an assumption the little lawyer liked to be able to make about all his prospective clients.

Now he said, "Won't you take a seat, Mr. Crowe? You'll be more comfortable."

"I'd rather stand," Ethan Crowe said. "I'm too much on edge to sit still."

"Hmmm. There's something I've learned in my practice, Mr. Crowe, and that's the great advantage in acting *as if.* When I'm to defend a client who gives every indication of guilt, I act *as if* he were indeed innocent. And you know, Mr. Crowe, it's astonishing how often the client does in fact *prove* to be innocent, often to his own surprise."

Martin Ehrengraf flashed a smile that showed on his lips without altering the expression in his eyes. "All of which is all-important to me, since I collect a fee only if my client is judged to be innocent. Otherwise I go unpaid. Acting *as if*, Mr. Crowe, is uncannily helpful, and you might help us both by sitting in that chair and acting as if you were at peace with the world."

Ehrengraf paused, and when Crowe had seated himself he said, "You say you've been charged with murder. But homicide is not usually a bailable offense, so how does it happen that you are here in my office instead of locked in a cell?"

"I haven't been charged with murder."

"But you said—"

"I said I wanted you to defend me against a homicide charge. But I haven't been charged yet."

"I see. Whom have you killed? No, let me amend that. Whom are you supposed to have killed?"

"No one."

"Oh?"

Ethan Crowe thrust his head forward. "I'll be charged with the murder of Terence Reginald Mayhew," he said, pronouncing the name with a full measure of loathing. "But I haven't been charged yet because the rancid scut's not dead yet because I haven't killed him yet."

"Mr. Mayhew is alive."

"Yes."

"But you intend to kill him."

Crowe chose his words carefully. "I expect to be charged with his murder," he said at length.

"And you want to arrange your defense in advance."

"Yes."

"You show commendable foresight," Ehrengraf said admiringly. He got to his feet and stepped out from behind his desk. He was a muted symphony of brown. His jacket was a brown Harris tweed in a herringbone weave, his slacks were cocoa flannel, his shirt a buttery tan silk, his tie a perfect match for the slacks with a below-the-knot design of fleur-de-lis in silver thread. Ehrengraf hadn't been quite certain about the tie when he bought it but had since decided it was quite all right. On his small feet he wore highly polished seamless tan loafers, unadorned with braids or tassels.

"Foresight," he repeated. "An unusual quality in a client, Mr. Crowe, and I can only wish that I met with it more frequently." He put the tips of his fingers together and narrowed his eyes. "Just what is it you wish from me?"

"Your efforts on my behalf, of course."

"Indeed. Why do you want to kill Mr. Mayhew?"

"Because he's driving me crazy."

"How?"

"He's playing tricks on me."

"Tricks? What sort of tricks?"

"Childish tricks," Ethan Crowe said, and averted his eyes. "He makes phone calls. He orders things. Last week he called different florists and sent out hundreds of orders of flowers to different women all over the city. He's managed to get hold of my credit-card numbers and placed all these orders in my name and billed them to me. I was able to stop some of the orders, but by the time I got wind of what he'd done, most of them had already gone out."

"Surely you won't have to pay."

"It may be easier to pay than to go through the process of avoiding payment. I don't know. But that's just one example. Another time ambulances and limousines kept coming to my house. One after the other. And taxicabs, and I don't know what else. These vehicles kept arriving from various sources and I kept having to send them away."

"I see."

"And he fills out coupons and orders things C.O.D. for me. I have to cancel the orders and return the products. He's had me join book clubs and record clubs, he's subscribed me to every sort of magazine, he's put me on every sort of mailing list. Did you know, for example, that there's an outfit called the International Society for the Preservation of Wild Mustangs and Burros?"

"It so happens I'm a member."

"Well, I'm sure it's a worthwhile organization," Crowe said, "but the point is I'm not interested in wild mustangs and burros, or even tame ones, but Mayhew made me a member and pledged a hundred dollars on my behalf, or maybe it was a thousand dollars, I can't remember."

"The exact amount isn't important at the moment, Mr. Crowe."

"He's driving me crazy!"

"So it would seem. But to kill a man because of some practical jokes—"

"There's no end to them. He started doing this almost two years ago. At first it was completely maddening because I had no idea what was happening or who was doing this to me. From time to time he'll slack off and I'll think he's had his fun and has decided to leave me alone. Then he'll start up again."

"Have you spoken to him?"

"I can't. He laughs like the lunatic he is and hangs up on me."

"Have you confronted him?"

"I can't. He lives in an apartment downtown on Chippewa Street. He doesn't let visitors in and never seems to leave the place."

"And you've tried the police?"

"They can't seem to do anything. He just lies to them, denies all responsibility, tells them it must be someone else. A very nice policeman told me the only sensible thing I can do is wait him out. He'll get tired, he assured me, the man's madness will run its course. He'll decide he's had his revenge."

"And you tried to do that?"

"For a while. When it didn't work, I engaged a private detective. He obtained evidence of Mayhew's activities, evidence that will stand up in court. But my attorney convinced me not to press charges."

"Why, for heaven's sake?"

"The man's a cripple."

"Your attorney?"

"Certainly not. Mayhew's a cripple, he's confined to a wheelchair. I suppose that's why he never leaves his squalid little apartment. But my attorney said I could only charge him with malicious mischief, which is not the most serious crime in the book and which sounds rather less serious than it is because it has the connotation of a child's impish prank—"

"Yes."

"—and there we'd be in court, myself a large man in good physical condition and Mayhew a sniveling cripple in a wheelchair, and he'd get everyone's sympathy and undoubtedly be exonerated of all charges while I'd come off as a bully and a laughingstock. I couldn't make charges stand up in criminal court, and if I sued him I'd probably lose. And even if I won that, what could I get? The man doesn't have anything to start with."

Ehrengraf nodded thoughtfully. "He blames you for crippling him?"

"I don't know. I had never even heard of him before he started tormenting me, but who knows what a madman might think? He doesn't seem to want anything from me. I've called him up, asked him what he wanted, and he only laughs and hangs up on me."

"And so you've decided to kill him."

"I haven't said that."

Ehrengraf sighed. "We're not in court, Mr. Crowe, so that sort of technicality's not important between us. You've implied you intend to kill him."

"Perhaps."

"At any rate, that's the inference I've drawn. I can certainly understand your feelings, but isn't the remedy you propose an extreme one? The cure seems worse than the disease. To expose yourself to a murder trial—"

"But your clients rarely go to trial."

"Oh?"

Crowe hazarded a smile. It looked out of place on his large red face, and after a moment it withdrew. "I'm familiar with your methods, Mr. Ehrengraf," he said. "Your clients rarely go to trial. You hardly ever show up in a courtroom. You take a case and then something curious happens. The evidence changes, or new evidence is discovered, or someone else confesses, or the murder turns out to be an accident, after all, or—well, *something* always happens."

"Truth will out," Ehrengraf said.

"Truth or fiction, something happens. Now here I am, plagued by a maniac, and I've engaged you to undertake my defense whenever it should become necessary, and it seems to me that by so doing I may bring things to the point where it *won't* become necessary."

Ehrengraf looked at him. A man who would select a suit of that particular shade, he thought, was either color blind or capable of anything.

"Of course I don't know what might happen," Ethan Crowe went on. "Just as hypothesis, Terence Mayhew might die. Of course, if that happened I wouldn't have any reason to murder him, and so I wouldn't come to trial. But that's just an example. It's certainly not my business to tell you your business, is it?"

"Certainly not," said Martin Ehrengraf.

While Terence Reginald Mayhew's four-room apartment on Chippewa Street was scarcely luxurious, it was by no means the squalid pesthole Ehrengraf had been led to expect. The block, to be sure, was not far removed from slum status. The building itself had certainly seen better days. But the Mayhew apartment itself, occupying the fourth-floor front and looking northward over a group of two-story frame houses, was cozy and comfortable.

The little lawyer followed Mayhew's wheelchair down a short hallway and into a book-lined study. A log of wax and compressed sawdust burned in the fireplace. A clock ticked on the mantel. Mayhew turned his wheelchair around, eyed his visitor from head to toe, and made a brisk clucking sound with his tongue. "So you're his lawyer," he said. "Not the poor boob who called me a couple of months ago, though. That one kept coming up with threats and I couldn't help laughing at him. He must have turned purple. When you laugh in a man's face after he's made legal threats, he generally turns purple. That's been my experience. What's your name again?"

"Ehrengraf. Martin H. Ehrengraf."

"What's the H. stand for?"

"Harrod."

"Like the king in the Bible?"

"Like the London department store." Ehrengraf's middle name was not Harrod, or Herod either, for that matter. He simply found untruths useful now and then, particularly in response to impertinence.

"Martin Harrod Ehrengraf," said Terence Reginald Mayhew. "Well, you're quite the dandy, aren't you? Sorry the place isn't spiffier but the cleaning woman only comes in once a week and she's not due until the day after tomorrow. Not that she's any great shakes with a dustcloth. Lazy slattern, in my opinion. You want to sit down?"

"No."

"Probably scared to crease your pants."

Ehrengraf was wearing a navy suit, a pale-blue-velvet vest, a blue shirt, a navy knit tie, and a pair of cordovan loafers. Mayhew was wearing a disgraceful terrycloth robe and tatty bedroom slippers. He had a scrawny body, a volleyball-shaped head, big guileless blue eyes, and red straw for hair. He was not so much ugly as bizarre; he looked like a cartoonist's invention. Ehrengraf couldn't guess how old he was—thirty? forty? fifty?—but it didn't matter. The man was years from dying of old age.

"Well, aren't you going to threaten me?"

"No," Ehrengraf said.

"No threats? No hint of bodily harm? No pending lawsuits? No criminal prosecution?"

"Nothing of the sort."

"Well, you're an improvement on your predecessor," Mayhew said. "That's something. Why'd you come here, then? Not to see how the rich folks live. You slumming?"

"No."

"Because it may be a rundown neighborhood, but it's a good apartment. They'd get me out if they could. Rent control—I've been here for ages and my rent's a pittance. Never find anything like this for what I can afford to pay. I get checks every month, you see. Disability. Small trust fund. Doesn't add up to much, but I get by. Have the cleaning woman in once a week, pay the rent, eat decent food. Watch the

TV, read my books and magazines, play my chess games by mail. Neighborhood's gone down but I don't live in the neighborhood. I live in the apartment. All I get of the neighborhood is seeing it from my window, and if it's not fancy that's all right with me. I'm a cripple, I'm confined to these four rooms, so I don't care what the neighborhood's like. If I was blind I wouldn't care what color the walls were painted, would I? The more they take away from you, why, the less vulnerable you are."

That last was an interesting thought and Ehrengraf might have pursued it, but he had other things to pursue. "My client," he said. "Ethan Crowe."

"That warthog."

"You dislike him?"

"Stupid question, Mr. Lawyer. Of course I dislike him. I wouldn't keep putting the wind up him if I thought the world of him, would I now?"

"You blame him for—"

"For me being a cripple? He didn't do that to me. God did." The volleyball head bounced against the back of the wheelchair, the wide slash of mouth opened and a cackle of laughter spilled out. "God did it! I was born this way, you chowderhead. Ethan Crowe had nothing to do with it."

"Then—"

"I just hate the man," Mayhew said. "Who needs a reason? I saw a preacher on Sunday-morning television; he stared right into the camera every minute with those great big eyes, said no one has cause to hate his fellow man. At first it made me want to retch, but I thought about it, and I'll be an anthropoid ape if he's not right. No one has cause to hate his fellow man because no one *needs* cause to hate his fellow man. It's natural. And it comes natural for me to hate Ethan Crowe."

"Have you ever met him?"

"I don't have to meet him."

"You just—"

"I just hate him," Mayhew said, grinning fiercely, "and I love hating him, and I have heaps of *fun* hating him, and all I have to do is pick up that phone and make him pay and pay and pay for it."

"Pay for what?"

"For everything. For being Ethan Crowe. For the outstanding war debt. For the loaves and the fishes." The head bounced back and the insane laugh was repeated. "For Tippecanoe and Tyler, too. For Tippecanee and Tyler Three."

"You don't have very much money," Ehrengraf said. "A disability pension, a small income."

"I have enough. I don't eat much and I don't eat fancy. You probably spend more on clothes than I spend on everything put together."

Ehrengraf didn't doubt that for a moment. "My client might supplement that income of yours," he said thoughtfully.

"You think I'm a blackmailer?"

"I think you might profit by circumstances, Mr. Mayhew."

"Fie on it, sir. I'd have no truck with blackmail. The Mayhews have been whitemailers for generations."

The conversation continued, but not for long. It became quite clear to the diminutive attorney that his was a limited arsenal. He could neither threaten nor bribe to any purpose. Any number of things might happen to Mayhew, some of them fatal, but such action seemed wildly disproportionate. This housebound wretch, this malevolent cripple, had simply not done enough to warrant such a response. When a child thumbed his nose at you, you were not supposed to dash its brains out against the curb. An action ought to bring about a suitable reaction. A thrust should be countered by an appropriate riposte.

But how was one to deal with a nasty madman? A helpless, pathetic madman?

Ehrengraf, who was fond of poetry, sought his memory for an illuminating phrase. Thoughts of madmen recalled Christopher Smart, an eighteenth-century Londoner who was periodically confined to Bedlam where he wrote a long poem that was largely comprehensible only to himself and God.

Quoting Smart, Ehrengraf said, " 'Let Ross, house of Ross, rejoice with Obadiah, and the rankle-dankle fish with hands.' "

Terence Reginald Mayhew nodded. "Now that," he said, "is the first sensible thing you've said since you walked in here."

A dozen days later, while Martin Ehrengraf was enjoying a sonnet of Thomas Hood's, his telephone rang. He took it up, said hello, and heard himself called an unconscionable swine.

"Ah," he said. "Mr. Mayhew."

"You are a man with no heart. I'm a poor housebound cripple, Mr. Ehrengraf—"

"Indeed."

"—and you've taken my life away. Do you have any idea what I went through to make this phone call?"

"I have a fair idea."

"Do you have any idea what I've been going through?"

"A fair idea of that as well," Ehrengraf said. "Here's a pretty coincidence. Just as you called, I was reading this poem of Thomas Hood's—do you know him?"

"I don't know what you're talking about."

"A sonnet called *Silence*. I'll just read you the sextet—

"But in green ruins, in the desolate walls,
Of antique palaces, where Man hath been,
Though the dun fox or wild hyena calls,
And owls that flit continually between,
Shriek to the echo, and the low winds moan—
There the true silence is, self-conscious and alone.

"Don't you think that's marvelously evocative of what you've been going through, Mr. Mayhew?"

"You're a terrible man."

"Indeed. And you should never forget it."

"I won't."

"It could all happen again. In fact, it could happen over and over."

"What do I have to do?"

"You have to leave my client strictly alone."

"I was having so much fun."

"Don't whine, Mr. Mayhew. You can't play your nasty little tricks on Mr. Crowe. But there's a whole world of other victims out there just waiting for your attentions."

"You mean—"

"I'm sure I've said nothing that wouldn't have occurred to you in good time, sir. On the other hand, you never know what some other victim might do. He might even find his way to my office, and you know full well what the consequences of that would be. Indeed, you know that you *can't* know. So perhaps what you ought to do is grow up, Mr. Mayhew, and wrap the tattered scraps of your life around your wretched body, and make the best of it."

"I don't—"

"Think of Thomas Hood, sir. Think of the true silence."

"I can't—"

"Think of Ross, house of Ross, and the rankle-dankle fish with hands."

"I'm not—"

"And think of Mr. Crowe while you're at it. I suggest you call him, sir. Apologize to him. Assure him that his troubles are over."

"I don't want to call him."

"Make the call," Ehrengraf said, his voice smooth as steel. "Or your troubles, Mr. Mayhew, are just beginning."

"The most remarkable thing," Ethan Crowe said. "I had a call from that troll Mayhew. At first I didn't believe it was he. I didn't recognize his voice. He sounded so frightened, so unsure of himself."

"Indeed."

"He assured me I'd have no further trouble from him. No more limousines or taxis, no more flowers, none of his idiotic little pranks. He apologized profusely for all the trouble he'd caused me in the past and assured me it would never happen again. It's hard to know whether to take the word of a madman, but I think he meant what he said."

"I'm certain he did."

They were once again in Martin Ehrengraf's office, and as usual the lawyer's desk was as cluttered as his person was immaculate. He was wearing the navy suit again, as it happened, but he had left the light-blue vest at home. His tie bore a half inch diagonal stripe of royal-blue flanked by two narrower stripes, one of gold and the other of a rather bright green, all on a navy field. Crowe was wearing a three-piece suit, expensive and beautifully tailored but in a rather morose shade of brown. Ehrengraf had decided charitably to regard the man as color blind and let it go at that.

"What did you do, Ehrengraf?"

The little lawyer looked off into the middle distance. "I suppose I can tell you," he said after a moment's reflection. "I took his life away from him."

"That's what I thought you would do. Take his life, I mean. But he was certainly alive when I spoke to him."

"You misunderstand me. Mr. Crowe, your antagonist was a housebound cripple who had adjusted to his mean little life of isolation. He had an income sufficient to his meager needs. And I went around his house shutting things down."

"I don't understand."

"I speak metaphorically, of course. Well, there's no reason I can't tell you what I did in plain English. First of all, I went to the post office. I filled out a change-of-address card, signed it in his name, and filed it. From that moment on, all his mail was efficiently forwarded to the General Delivery window in Greeley, Colorado, where it's to be held until called for, which may take rather a long time."

"Good heavens."

"I notified the electric company that Mr. Mayhew had vacated the premises and ordered them to cut off service forthwith. I told the telephone company the same thing, so when he picked up the phone to complain about the lights being out I'm afraid he had a hard time getting a dial tone. I sent a notarized letter to the landlord—over Mr. Mayhew's signature, of course—announcing that he was moving and demanding that his lease be canceled. I got in touch with his cleaning woman and informed her that her services would no longer be required. I could go on, Mr. Crowe, but I believe you get the idea. I took his life away and shut it down and he didn't like it."

"Good grief."

"His only remaining contact with the world was what he saw through his windows, and that was nothing attractive. Nevertheless, I was going to have his windows painted black from the outside—I was in the process of making final arrangements. A chap was going to suspend a scaffold as if to wash the windows but he would have painted them instead. I saw it as a neat coup de grace, but Mayhew made that last touch unnecessary by throwing in the sponge. That's a mixed metaphor, from coup de grace to throwing in the sponge, but I hope you'll pardon it."

"You did to him what he'd done to me. Hoist him on his own petard."

"Let's say I hoisted him on a similar petard. He plagued you by introducing an infinity of unwanted elements into your life. But I reduced his life to the four rooms he lived in and even threatened his ability to retain those very rooms—that drove the lesson home to him in a way I doubt he'll ever forget."

"Simple and brilliant," Crowe said. "I wish I'd thought of it."

"I'm glad you didn't."

"Why?"

"Because you'd have saved yourself fifty thousand dollars."

Crowe gasped. "Fifty thousand—"

"Dollars. My fee."

"But that's an outrage. All you did was write some letters and make some phone calls."

"All I did, sir, was everything you asked me to do. I saved you from answering to a murder charge."

"I wouldn't have murdered him."

"Nonsense," Ehrengraf snapped. "You *tried* to murder him. You thought engaging me would have precisely that effect. Had I wrung the wretch's neck you'd pay my fee without a whimper, but because I accomplished the desired result with style and grace instead of brute force you resist paying me. It would be an immense act of folly, Mr. Crowe, if you were to do anything other than pay my fee in full at once."

"You don't think the amount is out of line?"

"I don't keep my fees in a line, Mr. Crowe." Ehrengraf's hand went to the knot of his tie. It was the official tie of the Caedmon Society of Oxford University. Ehrengraf had not attended Oxford and did not belong to the Caedmon Society any more than he belonged to the International Society for the Preservation of Wild Mustangs and Burros, but it was a tie he habitually wore on celebratory occasions. "I set my fees according to an intuitive process," he went on, "and they are never negotiable. Fifty thousand dollars, sir. Not a penny more, not a penny less. Ah, Mr. Crowe, Mr. Crowe—do you know why Mayhew chose to torment you?"

"I suppose he feels I've harmed him."

"And have you?"

"No, but—"

"Supposition is blunder's handmaiden, Mr. Crowe. Mayhew made your life miserable because he hated you. I don't know why he hated you. I don't believe Mayhew himself knows why he hated you. I think he selected you at random. He needed someone to hate and you were convenient. Ah, Mr. Crowe—" Ehrengraf smiled with his lips "—consider how much damage was done to you by an insane cripple with no reason to do you harm. And then consider, sir, how much more harm could be done you by someone infinitely more ruthless and resourceful than Terence Reginald Mayhew, someone who is neither a lunatic nor a cripple, someone who is supplied with fifty thousand excellent reasons to wish you ill."

Crowe stared. "That's a threat," he said slowly.

"I fear you've confused a threat and a caution, Mr. Crowe, though I warrant the distinction's a thin one. Are you fond of poetry, sir?"

"No."

"I'm not surprised. It's no criticism, sir. Some people have poetry in their souls and others do not. It's predetermined, I suspect, like color blindness. I could recommend Thomas Hood, sir, or Christopher Smart, but would you read them? Or profit by them? Fifty thousand dollars, Mr. Crowe, and a check will do nicely."

"I'm not afraid of you."

"Certainly not."

"And I won't be intimidated."

"Indeed you won't," Ehrengraf agreed. "But do you recall our initial interview, Mr. Crowe? I submit that you would do well to act *as if*—as if you were afraid of me, as if you *were* intimidated."

Ethan Crowe sat quite still for several seconds. A variety of expressions played over his generally unexpressive face. At length he drew a checkbook from the breast pocket of his morosely brown jacket and uncapped a silver fountain pen.

"Payable to?"

"Martin H. Ehrengraf."

The pen scratched away. Then, idly, "What's the H. stand for?"

"Herod."

"The store in England?"

"The king," said Ehrengraf. "The king in the Bible."

The Ehrengraf Obligation

William Telliford gave his head a tentative scratch, in part because it itched, in part out of puzzlement. It itched because he had been unable to wash his lank brown hair during the four days he'd thus far spent in jail. He was puzzled because this dapper man before him was proposing to get him out of jail.

"I don't understand," he said. "The court appointed an attorney for me. A younger man, I think he said his name was Trabner. You're not associated with him or anything, are you?"

"Certainly not."

"Your name is—"

"Martin Ehrengraf."

"Well, I appreciate your coming to see me, Mr. Ehrengraf, but I've already got a lawyer, this Mr. Trabner, and—"

"Are you satisfied with Mr. Trabner?"

Telliford lowered his eyes, focusing his gaze upon the little lawyer's shoes, a pair of highly polished black wing tips. "I suppose he's all right," he said slowly.

"But?"

"But he doesn't believe I'm innocent. I mean he seems to take it for granted I'm guilty and the best thing I can do is plead guilty to manslaughter or something. He's talking in terms of making some kind of deal with the district attorney, like it's a foregone conclusion that I have to go to prison and the only question is how long."

"Then you've answered my question," Ehrengraf said, a smile flickering on his thin lips. "You're unsatisfied with your lawyer. The court has appointed him. It remains for you to disappoint him, as it were, and to engage me in his stead. You have the right to do this, you know."

"But I don't have the money. Trabner was going to defend me for free, which is about as much as I can afford. I don't know what kind of fees you charge for something like this but I'll bet they're substantial. That suit of yours didn't come from the Salvation Army."

Ehrengraf beamed. His suit, charcoal gray flannel with a nipped-in waist, had been made for him by a most exclusive tailor. His shirt was pink, with a button-down collar. His vest was a tattersall check, red and black on a cream background, and his tie showed half-inch stripes of red and charcoal gray. "My fees are on the high side," he allowed. "To undertake your defense I would ordinarily set a fee of eighty thousand dollars."

"Eighty dollars would strain my budget," William Telliford said. "Eighty thousand, well, it might take me ten years to earn that much."

"But I propose to defend you free of charge, sir."

William Telliford stared, not least because he could not recall the last time anyone had thought to call him *sir*. He was, it must be said, a rather unprepossessing young man, tending to slouch and sprawl. His jeans needed patching at the knees. His plaid flannel shirt needed washing and ironing. His chukka boots needed soles and heels, and his socks needed replacement altogether.

"But—"

"But why?"

Telliford nodded.

"Because you are a poet," said Martin Ehrengraf.

"Poets," said Ehrengraf, "are the unacknowledged legislators of the universe."

"That's beautiful," Robin Littlefield said. She didn't know just what to make of this little man but he was certainly impressive. "Could you say that again? I want to remember it."

"Poets are the unacknowledged legislators of the universe. But don't credit me with the observation. Shelley said it first."

"Is she your wife?"

The lawyer's deeply set dark eyes narrowed perceptibly. "Percy Bysshe Shelley," he said gently. "Born 1792, died 1822. The poet."

"Oh."

"So your young man is one of the world's unacknowledged legislators. Or you might prefer the lines Arthur O'Shaughnessy wrote. 'We are the music makers, And we are the dreamers of dreams.' You know the poem?"

"I don't think so."

"I like the second stanza," said Ehrengraf, and tilted his head to one side and quoted it:

"With wonderful deathless ditties
We build up the world's greatest
  cities,
And out of a fabulous story
We fashion an empire's glory:
One man with a dream, at
  pleasure,
Shall go forth and conquer a crown;
And three with a new song's
  measure
Can trample an empire down."

"You have a wonderful way of speaking. But I, uh, I don't really know much about poetry."

"You reserve your enthusiasm for Mr. Telliford's poems, no doubt."

"Well, I like it when Bill reads them to me. I like the way they sound, but I'll have to admit I don't always know what he's getting at."

Ehrengraf beamed, spread his hands. "But they sound good, don't they? Miss Littlefield, dare we require more of a poem than it please our ears? I don't read much modern poetry, Miss Littlefield. I prefer the bards of an earlier and more innocent age. Their verses are often simpler, but I don't pretend to understand any number of my favorite poems. Half the time I don't know just what Blake's getting at, Miss Littlefield, but that doesn't keep me from enjoying his work. That sonnet of your young man's, that poem about riding a train across Kansas and looking at the moon. I'm sure you remember it."

"Sort of."

"He writes of the moon 'stroking desperate tides in the liquid land.' That's a lovely line, Miss Littlefield, and who cares whether the poem itself is fully comprehensible? Who'd raise such a niggling point? William Telliford is a poet and I'm under an obligation to defend him. I'm certain he couldn't have murdered that woman."

Robin gnawed a thumbnail. "The police are pretty sure he did it," she said. "The fire axe was missing from the hallway of our building and the glass case where it was kept was smashed open. And Janice Penrose, he used to live with her before he met me, well, they say he was still going around her place sometimes when I was working at the diner. And they never found the fire axe, but Bill came home with his jeans and shirt covered with blood and couldn't remember what happened. And he was seen in her neighborhood, and he'd been drinking, plus he smoked a lot of dope that afternoon and he was always taking pills. Ups and downs, like, plus some green capsules he stole from somebody's medicine chest and we were never quite sure what they were, but they do weird things to your head."

"The artist is so often the subject of his own experiment," Ehrengraf said sympathetically. "Think of De Quincey. Consider Coleridge, waking from an opium dream with all of 'Kubla Khan' fixed in his mind, just waiting for him to write it down. Of course he was interrupted by that dashed man from Porlock, but the lines he did manage to save are so wonderful. You know the poem, Miss Littlefield?"

"I think we had to read it in school."

"Perhaps."

"Or didn't he write something about an albatross? Some guy shot an albatross, something like that."

"Something like that."

"The thing is," William Telliford said, "the more I think about it, the more I come to the conclusion that I must have killed Jan. I mean, who else would kill her?"

"You're innocent," Ehrengraf told him.

"You really think so? I can't remember what happened that day. I was doing some drugs and hitting the wine pretty good, and then I found this bottle of bourbon that I didn't think we still had, and I started drinking that, and that's about the last thing I remember. I must have gone right into blackout and the next thing I knew I was walking around covered with blood. And I've got a way of being violent when I'm drunk. When I lived with Jan I beat her up a few times, and I did the same with Robin. That's one of the reasons her father hates me."

"Her father hates you?"

"Despises me. Oh, I can't really blame him. He's this self-made man with more money than God and I'm squeezing by on food stamps. There's not much of a living in poetry."

"It's an outrage."

"Right. When Robin and I moved in together, well, her old man had a fit. Up to then he was laying a pretty heavy check on her the first of every month, but as soon as she moved in with me that was the end of that song. No more money for her. Here's her little brother going to this fancy private school and her mother dripping in sables and emeralds and diamonds and mink, and here's Robin slinging hash in a greasy spoon because her father doesn't care for the company she's keeping."

"Interesting."

"The man really hates me. Some people take to me and some people don't, but he just couldn't stomach me. Thought I was the lowest of the low. It really grinds a person down, you know. All the pressure he was putting on Robin, and both of us being as broke as we were, I'll tell you, it reached the point where I couldn't get any writing done."

"That's terrible," Ehrengraf said, his face clouded with concern. "The poetry left you?"

"That's what happened. It just wouldn't come to me. I'd sit there all day staring at a blank sheet of paper, and finally I'd say the hell with it and fire up a joint or get into the wine, and there's another day down the old chute. And then finally I found that bottle of bourbon and the next thing I knew—" the poet managed a brave smile "—well, according to you, I'm innocent."

"Of course you are innocent, sir."

"I wish I was convinced of that, Mr. Ehrengraf. I don't even see how you can be convinced."

"Because you are a poet," the diminutive attorney said. "Because, further, you are a client of Martin H. Ehrengraf. My clients are always innocent. That is the Ehrengraf presumption. Indeed, my income depends upon the innocence of my clients."

"I don't follow you."

"It's simple enough. My fees, as we've said, are quite high. But I collect them only if my efforts are successful. If a client of mine goes to prison, Mr. Telliford, he pays me nothing. I'm not even reimbursed for my expenses."

"That's incredible," Telliford said. "I never heard of anything like that. Do many lawyers work that way?"

"I believe I'm the only one. It's a pity more don't take up the custom. Other professionals as well, for that matter. Consider how much higher the percentage of successful operations might be if surgeons were paid on the basis of their results."

"Isn't that the truth. Hey, you know what's ironic?"

"What?"

"Mr. Littlefield. Robin's father. He could pay you that eighty thousand out of petty cash and never miss it. That's the kind of money he's got. But the way he feels about me, he'd pay to *send* me to prison, not to keep me out of it. In other words, if you worked for him you'd only get paid if you lost your case. Don't you think that's ironic?"

"Yes," said Ehrengraf. "I do indeed."

When William Telliford stepped into Ehrengraf's office, the lawyer scarcely recognized him. The poet's beard was gone and his hair had received the attention of a fashionable barber. His jacket was black velvet, his trousers a cream-colored flannel. He was wearing a raw silk shirt and a bold paisley ascot.

He smiled broadly at Ehrengraf's reaction. "I guess I look different," he said.

"Different," Ehrengraf agreed.

"Well, I don't have to live like a slob now." The young man sat down in one of Ehrengraf's chairs, shot his cuff, and checked the time on an oversized gold watch. "Robin'll be coming by for me in half an hour," he said, "but I wanted to take the time to let you know how much I appreciated what you tried to do for me. You believed in my innocence when I didn't even have that much faith in myself. And I'm sure you would have been terrific in the courtroom if it had come to that."

"Fortunately it didn't."

"Right, but whoever would have guessed how it would turn out? Imagine old

Jasper Littlefield killing Jan to frame me and get me out of his daughter's life. That's really a tough one to swallow. But he came over looking for Robin, and he found me drunk, and then it was evidently just a matter of taking the fire axe out of the case and taking me along with him to Jan's place and killing her and smearing her blood all over me. I must have been in worse than a blackout when it happened. I must have been passed out cold for him to be sure I wouldn't remember any of it."

"So it would seem."

"The police never did find the fire axe, and I wondered about that at the time. What I'd done with it, I mean, because deep down inside I really figured I must have been guilty. But what happened was Mr. Littlefield took the axe along with him, and then when he went crazy it was there for him to use."

"And use it he did."

"He sure did," Telliford said. "According to some psychologist they interviewed for one of the papers, he must have been repressing his basic instincts all his life. When he killed Jan for the purpose of framing me, it set something off inside him, some undercurrent of violence he'd been smothering for years and years. And then finally he up and dug out the fire axe, and he did a job on his wife and his son, chopped them both to hell and gone, and then he made a phone call to the police and confessed what he'd done and told about murdering Jan at the same time."

"Considerate of him," said Ehrengraf, "to make that phone call."

"I'll have to give him that," the poet said. "And then, before the cops could get there and pick him up, he took the fire axe and chopped through the veins in his wrists and bled to death."

"And you're a free man."

"And glad of it," Telliford said. "I'll tell you, it looks to me as though I'm sitting on top of the world. Robin's crazy about me and I'm all she's got in the world—me and the couple of million bucks her father left her. With the rest of the family dead, she inherits every penny. No more slinging hash. No more starving in a garret. No more dressing like a slob. You like my new wardrobe?"

"It's quite a change," Ehrengraf said diplomatically.

"Well, I realize now that I was getting sick of the way I looked, the life I was leading. Now I can live the way I want. I've got the freedom to do as I please with my life."

"That's wonderful."

"And you're the man who believed in me when nobody else did, myself included." Telliford smiled with genuine warmth. "I can't tell you how grateful I am. I was talking with Robin, and I had the idea that we ought to pay you your fee. You didn't actually get me off, of course, but your system is that you get paid no matter how your client gets off, just so he doesn't wind up in jail. That's how you explained it, isn't it?"

"That's right."

"That's what I said to Robin. But she said we didn't have any agreement to pay you eighty thousand dollars, as a matter of fact we didn't have any agreement to pay you anything, because you volunteered your services. In fact I would have gotten off the same way with my court-appointed attorney. I said that wasn't the point, but Robin said after all it's her money and she didn't see the point of giving you an eighty-thousand-dollar handout, that you were obviously well off and didn't need charity."

"Her father's daughter, I'd say."

"Huh? Anyway, it's her money and her decision to make, but I got her to agree that we'd pay for any expenses you had. So if you can come up with a figure—"

Ehrengraf shook his head. "You don't owe me a cent," he insisted. "I took your case out of a sense of obligation. And your lady friend is quite correct—I am not a charity case. Furthermore, my expenses on your behalf were extremely low, and in any case I should be more than happy to stand the cost myself."

"Well, if you're absolutely certain—"

"Quite certain, thank you." Ehrengraf smiled. "I'm most satisfied with the outcome of the case. Of course I regret the loss of Miss Littlefield's mother and brother, but at least there's a happy ending to it all. You're out of prison, you have no worries about money, your future is assured, and you can return to the serious business of writing poetry."

"Yeah," Telliford said.

"Is something wrong?"

"Not really. Just what you said about poetry."

"Oh?"

"I suppose I'll get back to it sooner or later."

"Don't tell me your muse has deserted you?"

"Oh, I don't know," the young man said nervously. "It's just that, oh, I don't really seem to care much about poetry now, you know what I mean?"

"I'm not sure that I do."

"Well, I've got everything I want, you know? I've got the money to go all over the world and try all the things I've always wanted to try, and, oh, poetry just doesn't seem very important anymore." He laughed. "I remember what a kick I used to get when I'd check the mailbox and some little magazine would send me a check for one of my poems. Now what I usually got was fifty cents a line for poems, and that's from the magazines that paid anything, and most of them just gave you copies of the issue with the poem in it and that was that. That sonnet you liked, 'On a Train Through Kansas,' the magazine that took it paid me twenty-five cents a line. So I made three dollars and fifty cents for that poem, and by the time I submitted it here and there and everywhere, hell, my postage came to pretty nearly as much as I got for it."

"It's a scandal."

"But the thing is, when I didn't have any money, even a little check helped. Now, though, it's hard to take the whole thing seriously. But besides that, I just don't get poetic ideas anymore. And I just don't feel it." He forced a smile. "It's funny. Getting away from poetry hasn't been bothering me, but now that I'm talking with you about it I find myself feeling bad. As though by giving up poetry I'm letting you down or something."

"You're not letting *me* down," Ehrengraf said. "But to dismiss the talent you have, to let it languish—"

"Well, I just don't know if I've got it anymore," Telliford said. "That's the whole thing. I sit down and try to write a poem and it's just not there, you know what I mean? And Robin says why waste my time, that nobody really cares about poetry nowadays anyway, and I figure maybe she's right."

"Her father's daughter."

"Huh? Well, I'll tell you something that's ironic, anyway. I was having trouble writing poetry before I went to jail, what with the hassles from Robin's old man and all our problems and getting into the wine and the grass too much. And I'm having more troubles now, now that we've got plenty of money and Robin's father's out of our hair. But you know when I was really having no trouble at all?"

"When?"

"During the time I was in jail. There I was, stuck in that rotten cell with a lifetime in the penitentiary staring me in the face, and I swear I was averaging a poem every day. My mind was just clicking along. And I was writing good stuff, too." The young man drew an alligator billfold from the breast pocket of the velvet jacket, removed and unfolded a sheet of paper. "You liked the Kansas poem," he said, "so why don't you see what you think of this one?"

Ehrengraf read the poem. It seemed to be about birds, and included the line "Puppets dance from bloody strings." Ehrengraf wasn't sure what the poem meant but he knew he liked the sound of that line.

"It's very good," he said.

"Yeah, I thought you'd like it. And I wrote it in the jug, just wrote the words down like they were flowing out of a faucet, and now all I can write is checks. It's ironic, isn't it?"

"It certainly is."

It was a little over two weeks later when Ehrengraf met yet again with William Telliford. Once again, the meeting took place in the jail cell where the two had first made one another's acquaintance.

"Mr. Ehrengraf," the young man said. "Gee, I didn't know if you would show up. I figured you'd wash your hands of me."

"Why should I do that, sir?"

"Because they say I killed Robin. But I swear I didn't do it!"

"Of course you didn't."

"I could have killed Jan, for all I knew. Because I was unconscious at the time, or in a blackout, or whatever it was. So I didn't know what happened. But I was away from the apartment when Robin was killed, and I was awake. I hadn't even been drinking much."

"We'll simply prove where you were."

Telliford shook his head. "What we can't prove is that Robin was alive when I left the apartment. I know she was, but how are we going to prove it?"

"We'll find a way," Ehrengraf said soothingly. "*We* know you're innocent, don't we?"

"Right."

"Then there is nothing to worry about. Someone else must have gone to your house, taking that fire axe along for the express purpose of framing you for murder. Someone jealous of your success, perhaps. Someone who begrudged you your happiness."

"But who?"

"Leave that to me, sir. It's my job."

"Your job," Telliford said. "Well, this time you'll get well paid for your job, Mr. Ehrengraf. And your system is perfect for my case, let me tell you."

"How do you mean?"

"If I'm found innocent, I'll inherit all the money Robin inherited from her father. She made me her beneficiary. So I'll be able to pay you whatever you ask, eighty thousand dollars or even more."

"Eighty thousand will be satisfactory."

"And I'll pay it with pleasure. But if I'm found guilty, well, I won't get a dime."

"Because one cannot legally profit from a crime."

"Right. So if you'll take the case on your usual terms—"

"I work on no other terms," Ehrengraf said. "And I would trust no one else with your case." He took a deep breath and held it in his lungs for a moment before continuing. "Mr. Telliford," he said, "your case is going to be a difficult one. You must appreciate that."

"I do."

"Of course I'll do everything in my power on your behalf, acting always in your best interest. But you must recognize that the possibility exists that you will be convicted."

"And for a crime I didn't commit."

"Such miscarriages of justice do occasionally come to pass. It's tragic, I agree, but don't despair. Even if you're convicted, the appeal process is an exhaustive one. We can appeal your case again and again. You may have to serve some time in prison, Mr. Telliford, but there's always hope. And you know what Lovelace had to say on the subject."

"Lovelace?"

"Richard Lovelace. Born 1618, died 1657. 'To Althea, from Prison,' Mr. Telliford.

"Stone walls do not a prison make,
Nor iron bars a cage;
Minds innocent and quiet take
That for an hermitage.
If I have freedom in my love,

And in my soul am free,
Angels alone, that soar above,
Enjoy such liberty."

Telliford shuddered. " 'Stone walls and iron bars,' " he said.

"Have faith, sir."

"I'll try."

"At least you have your poetry. Are you sufficiently supplied with paper and pencil? I'll make sure your needs are seen to."

"Maybe it would help me to write some poetry. Maybe it would take my mind off things."

"Perhaps it would. And I'll devote myself wholeheartedly to your defense, sir, whether I ever see a penny for my troubles or not." He drew himself up to his full height. "After all," he said, "it's my obligation. 'I could not love thee, dear, so much, Loved I not Honour more.' That's also Lovelace, Mr. Tellford. 'To Lucasta, Going to the Wars.' Good day, Mr. Telliford. You have nothing to worry about."

The Ehrengraf Alternative

"What's most unfortunate," Ehrengraf said, "is that there seems to be a witness."

Evelyn Throop nodded in fervent agreement. "Mrs. Keppner," she said.

"Howard Bierstadt's housekeeper."

"She was devoted to him. She'd been with him for years."

"And she claims she saw you shoot him three times in the chest."

"I know," Evelyn Throop said. "I can't imagine why she would say something like that. It's completely untrue."

A thin smile turned up the corners of Martin Ehrengraf's mouth. Already he felt himself warming to his client, exhilarated by the prospect of acting in her defense. It was the little lawyer's great good fortune always to find himself representing innocent clients, but few of those clients were as single-minded as Miss Throop in proclaiming their innocence.

The woman sat on the edge of her iron cot with her shapely legs crossed at the ankle. She seemed so utterly in possession of herself that she might have been almost anywhere but in a jail cell, charged with the murder of her lover. Her age, according to the papers, was forty-six. Ehrengraf would have guessed her to be perhaps a dozen years younger. She was not rich—Ehrengraf, like most lawyers, did have a special fondness for wealthy clients—but she had excellent breeding. It was evident not only in her exquisite facial bones but in her positively ducal self-assurance.

"I'm sure we'll uncover the explanation of Mrs. Keppner's calumny," he said gently. "For now, why don't we go over what actually happened."

"Certainly. I was at my home that evening when Howard called. He was in a mood and wanted to see me. I drove over to his house. He made drinks for both of us and paced around a great deal. He was extremely agitated."

"Over what?"

"Leona wanted him to marry her. Leona Weybright."

"The cookbook writer?"

"Yes. Howard was not the sort of man to get married, or even to limit himself to a single relationship. He believed in a double standard and was quite open about it. He expected his women to be faithful while reserving the option of infidelity to himself. If one was going to be involved with Howard Bierstadt, one had to accept this."

"As you accepted it."

"As I accepted it," Evelyn Throop agreed. "Leona evidently pretended to accept it but could not, and Howard didn't know what to do about her. He wanted to break up with her but was afraid of the possible consequences. He thought she might turn suicidal and he didn't want her death on his conscience."

"And he discussed all of this with you."

"Oh, yes. He often confided in me about his relationship with Leona." Evelyn Throop permitted herself a smile. "I played a very important role in his life, Mr. Ehrengraf. I suppose he would have married me if there'd been any reason to do so. I was his true confidante. Leona was just one of a long string of mistresses."

Ehrengraf nodded. "According to the prosecution," he said carefully, "you were pressuring him to marry you."

"That's quite untrue."

"No doubt." He smiled. "Continue."

The woman sighed. "There's not much more to say. He went into the other room to freshen our drinks. There was the report of a gunshot."

"I believe there were three shots."

"Perhaps there were. I can only remember the volume of the noise. It was so startling. I rushed in immediately and saw him on the floor, the gun by his outstretched hand. I guess I bent over and picked up the gun. I don't remember doing so, but I must have done because the next thing I knew I was standing there holding the gun." Evelyn Throop closed her eyes, evidently overwhelmed by the memory. "Then Mrs. Keppner was there—I believe she screamed, and then she went off to call the police. I just stood there for a while and then I guess I sat down in a chair and waited for the police to come and tell me what to do."

"And they brought you here and put you in a cell."

"Yes. I was quite astonished. I couldn't imagine why they would do such a thing, and then it developed that Mrs. Keppner had sworn she saw me shoot Howard."

Ehrengraf was respectfully silent for a moment. Then he said, "It seems they found some corroboration for Mrs. Keppner's story."

"What do you mean?"

"The gun," Ehrengraf said. "A .32-caliber revolver. I believe it was registered to you, was it not?"

"It was my gun."

"How did Mr. Bierstadt happen to have it?"

"I brought it to him."

"At his request?"

"Yes. When we spoke on the telephone, he specifically asked me to bring the gun. He said something about wanting to protect himself from burglars. I never thought he would shoot himself."

"But he did."

"He must have done. He was upset about Leona. Perhaps he felt guilty, or that there was no way to avoid hurting her."

"Wasn't there a paraffin test?" Ehrengraf mused. "As I recall, there were no nitrite particles found in Mr. Bierstadt's hand, which would seem to indicate he had not fired a gun recently."

"I don't really understand those tests," Evelyn Throop said. "But I'm told they're not absolutely conclusive."

"And the police gave you a test as well," Ehrengraf went on. "Didn't they?"

"Yes."

"And found nitrite particles in your right hand."

"Of course," Evelyn Throop said. "I'd fired the gun that evening before I took it along to Howard's house. I hadn't used it in the longest time, since I first practiced with it at a pistol range, so I cleaned it and to make sure it was in good operating condition I test-fired it before I went to Howard's."

"At a pistol range?"

"That wouldn't have been convenient. I just stopped at a deserted spot along a country road and fired a few shots."

"I see."

"I told the police all of this, of course."

"Of course. Before they gave you the paraffin test?"

"After the test, as it happens. The incident had quite slipped my mind in the excitement of the moment, but they gave me the test and said it was evident I'd fired a gun, and at that point I recalled having stopped the car and firing off a couple of rounds before continuing on to Howard's."

"Where you gave Mr. Bierstadt the gun."

"Yes."

"Whereupon he in due course took it off into another room and fired three shots into his heart," Ehrengraf murmured. "Your Mr. Bierstadt would look to be one of the most determined suicides in human memory."

"You don't believe me."

"But I do believe you," he said. "Which is to say that I believe you did not shoot Mr. Bierstadt. Whether or not he did in fact die by his own hand is not, of course, something to which either you or I can testify."

"How else could he have died?" The woman's gaze narrowed. "Unless he really was genuinely afraid of burglars, and unless he did surprise one in the other room. But wouldn't I have heard sounds of a struggle? Of course, I was in another room a fair distance away, and there was music playing, and I did have things on my mind."

"I'm sure you did."

"And perhaps Mrs. Keppner saw the burglar shoot Howard, and then she fainted or something. I suppose that's possible, isn't it?"

"Eminently possible," Ehrengraf assured her.

"She might have come to when I had already entered the room and picked up the gun, and the whole incident could have been compressed in her mind. She wouldn't remember having fainted and so she might now actually believe she saw me kill Howard, while all along she saw something entirely different." Evelyn Throop had been looking off into the middle distance as she formulated her theory and now she focused her eyes upon the diminutive attorney. "It could have happened that way," she said, "couldn't it?"

"It could have happened precisely that way," Ehrengraf said. "It could have happened in any of innumerable ways. Ah, Miss Throop"—and now the lawyer rubbed his small hands together—"that's the whole beauty of it. There are any number of alternatives to the prosecution's argument, but of course they don't see them. Give the police a supposedly ironclad case and they look no further. It is not their task to examine alternatives. But it is our task, Miss Throop, to find not merely *an* alternative but the correct alternative, the ideal alternative. And in just that fashion we will make a free woman of you."

"You seem very confident, Mr. Ehrengraf."

"I am."

"And prepared to believe in my innocence."

"Unequivocally. Without question."

"I find that refreshing," Evelyn Throop said. "I even believe you'll get me acquitted."

"I fully expect to," Ehrengraf said. "Now let me see, is there anything else we have to discuss at present?"

"Yes."

"And what would that be?"

"Your fee," said Evelyn Throop.

Back in his office, seated behind a desk which he kept as untidy as he kept his own person immaculate, Martin H. Ehrengraf sat back and contemplated the many extraordinary qualities of his latest client. In his considerable experience, while clients were not invariably opposed to a discussion of his fees, they were certainly loath to raise the matter. But Evelyn Throop, possessor of dove-gray eyes and remarkable facial bones, had proved an exception.

"My fees are high," Ehrengraf had told her, "but they are payable only in the event that my clients are acquitted. If you don't emerge from this ordeal scot-free, you owe me nothing. Even my expenses will be at my expense."

"And if I get off?"

"Then you will owe me one hundred thousand dollars. And I must emphasize, Miss Throop, that the fee will be due me however you win your freedom. It is not inconceivable that neither of us will ever see the inside of a courtroom, that your release when it comes will appear not to have been the result of my efforts at all. I will, nevertheless, expect to be paid in full."

The gray eyes looked searchingly into the lawyer's own. "Yes," she said after a moment. "Yes, of course. Well, that seems fair. If I'm released I won't really care how the end was accomplished, will I?"

Ehrengraf said nothing. Clients often whistled a different tune at a later date, but one could burn that bridge when one came to it.

"One hundred thousand dollars seems reasonable," the woman continued. "I suppose any sum would seem reasonable when one's life and liberty hangs in the balance. Of course, you must know I have no money of my own."

"Perhaps your family—"

She shook her head. "I can trace my ancestors back to William the Conqueror," she said, "and there were Throops who made their fortune in whaling and the China trade, but I'm afraid the money's run out over the generations. However, I shouldn't have any problem paying your fee."

"Oh?"

"I'm Howard's chief beneficiary," she explained. "I've seen his will and it makes it unmistakably clear that I held first place in his affections. After a small cash bequest to Mrs. Keppner for her loyal years of service, and after leaving his art collection—which, I grant you, *is* substantial—to Leona, the remainder comes to me. There may be a couple of cash bequests to charities but nothing that amounts to much. So while I'll have to wait for the will to make its way through probate, I'm sure I can borrow on my expectations and pay you your fee within a matter of days of my release from jail, Mr. Ehrengraf."

"A day that should come in short order," Ehrengraf said.

"That's your department," Evelyn Throop said, and smiled serenely.

Ehrengraf smiled now, recalling her smile, and made a little tent of his fingertips on the desk top. An exceptional woman, he told himself, and one on whose behalf it would be an honor to extend himself.

It was difficult, of course. Shot with the woman's own gun, and a witness to swear that she'd shot him. Difficult, certainly, but scarcely impossible.

The little lawyer leaned back, closed his eyes, and considered alternatives.

Some days later, Ehrengraf was seated at his desk reading the poems of William Ernest Henley, who had written so confidently of being the master of one's fate and the captain of one's soul. The telephone rang. Ehrengraf set his book down, located the instrument amid the desk top clutter, and answered it.

"Ehrengraf," said Ehrengraf.

He listened for a moment, spoke briefly in reply, and replaced the receiver.

Smiling brightly, he started for the door, then paused to check his appearance in a mirror.

His tie was navy blue, with a demure below-the-knot pattern of embroidered rams' heads. For a moment Ehrengraf thought of stopping at his house and changing it for his Caedmon Society necktie, one he'd taken to wearing on triumphal occasions. He glanced at his watch and decided not to squander the time.

Later, recalling the decision, he wondered if it hinted at prescience.

"Quite remarkable," Evelyn Throop said. "Although I suppose I should have at least considered the possibility that Mrs. Keppner was lying. After all, I knew for a fact that she was testifying to something that didn't happen to be true. But for some reason I assumed it was an honest mistake on her part."

"One hesitates to believe the worst of people," Ehrengraf said.

"That's exactly it, of course. Besides, I rather took her for granted."

"So, it appears, did Mr. Bierstadt."

"And that was his mistake, wasn't it?" Evelyn Throop sighed. "Dora Keppner had been with him for years. Who would have guessed she'd been in love with him? Although I gather their relationship was physical at one point."

"There was a suggestion to that effect in the note she left."

"And I understand he wanted to get rid of her—to discharge her."

"The note seems to have indicated considerable mental disturbance," Ehrengraf said. "There were other jottings in a notebook found in Mrs. Keppner's attic bedroom. The impression seems to be that either she and her employer had been intimate in the past or that she entertained a fantasy to that effect. Her attitude in recent weeks apparently became less and less the sort proper to a servant, and either Mr. Bierstadt intended to let her go or she feared that he did and—well, we know what happened."

"She shot him." Evelyn Throop frowned. "She must have been in the room when he went to freshen the drinks. I thought he'd put the gun in his pocket but perhaps he still had it in his hand. He would have set it down when he made the drinks and she could have snatched it up and shot him and been out of the room before I got there." The gray eyes moved to encounter Ehrengraf's. "She didn't leave any fingerprints on the gun."

"She seems to have worn gloves. She was wearing a pair when she took her own life. A test indicated nitrite particles in the right glove."

"Couldn't they have gotten there when she committed suicide?"

"It's unlikely," Ehrengraf said. "She didn't shoot herself, you see. She took poison."

"How awful," Evelyn Throop said. "I hope it was quick."

"Mercifully so," said Ehrengraf. Clearly this woman was the captain of her soul, he thought, not to mention master of her fate. Or ought it to be mistress of her fate?

And yet, he realized abruptly, she was not entirely at ease.

"I've been released," she said, "as is of course quite obvious. All charges have been dropped. A man from the District Attorney's Office explained everything to me."

"That was considerate of him."

"He didn't seem altogether happy. I had the feeling he didn't really believe I was innocent after all."

"People believe what they wish to believe," Ehrengraf said smoothly. "The state's whole case collapses without their star witness, and after that witness has confessed to the crime herself and taken her life in the bargain, well, what does it matter what a stubborn district attorney chooses to believe?

"The important thing," Ehrengraf said, "is that you've been set free. You're innocent of all charges."

"Yes."

His eyes searched hers. "Is there a problem, Miss Throop?"

"There is, Mr. Ehrengraf."

"Dear lady," he began, "if you could just tell me—"

"The problem concerns your fee."

Ehrengraf's heart sank. Why did so many clients disappoint him in precisely this fashion? At the onset, with the sword of justice hanging over their throats, they agreed eagerly to whatever he proposed. Remove the sword and their agreeability went with it.

But that was not it at all.

"The most extraordinary thing," Evelyn Throop was saying. "I told you the terms of Howard's will. The paintings to Leona, a few thousand dollars here and there to various charities, a modest bequest to Mrs. Keppner—I suppose she won't get that now, will she?"

"Hardly."

"Well, that's something. Though it doesn't amount to much. At any rate, the balance is to go to me. The residue, after the bequests have been made and all debts settled and the state and federal taxes been paid, all that remains comes to me."

"So you explained."

"I intended to pay you out of what I received, Mr. Ehrengraf. Well, you're more than welcome to every cent I get. You can buy yourself a couple of hamburgers and a milkshake."

"I don't understand."

"It's the damned paintings," Evelyn Throop said. "They're worth an absolute fortune. I didn't realize how much he spent on them in the first place or how rapidly they appreciated in value. Nor did I have any idea how deeply mortgaged everything else he owned was. He had some investment reversals over the past few months and he'd taken out a second mortgage on his home and sold off stocks and other holdings. There's a little cash and a certain amount of equity in the real estate, but it'll take all of that to pay the estate taxes on the several million dollars' worth of paintings that go free and clear to that bitch Leona."

"You have to pay the taxes?"

"No question about it," she said bitterly. "The estate pays the taxes and settles the debts. Then all the paintings go straight to America's favorite cook. I hope she chokes on them." Evelyn Throop sighed heavily, collected herself. "Please forgive the dramatics, Mr. Ehrengraf."

"They're quite understandable, dear lady."

"I didn't intend to lose control of myself in that fashion. But I feel this deeply. I know Howard had no intention of disinheriting me and having that woman get everything. It was his unmistakable intention to leave me the greater portion, and a cruel trick of fate has thwarted him in that purpose. Mr. Ehrengraf, I owe you one hundred thousand dollars. That was our agreement and I consider myself bound by it."

Ehrengraf made no reply.

"But I don't know how I can possibly pay you. Oh, I'll pay what I can, as I can, but I'm a woman of modest means. I couldn't honestly expect to discharge the debt in full within my lifetime."

"My dear Miss Throop." Ehrengraf was moved, and his hand went involuntarily to the knot of his necktie. "My dear Miss Throop," he said again, "I beg you not to worry yourself. Do you know Henley, Miss Throop?"

"Henley?"

"The poet," said Ehrengraf, and quoted:

"In the fell clutch of circumstance,
I have not winced nor cried aloud:
Under the bludgeonings of chance
My head is bloody, but unbowed.

"William Ernest Henley, Miss Throop. Born 1849, died 1903. Bloody but unbowed, Miss Throop. 'I have not yet begun to fight.' That was John Paul Jones, Miss Throop, not a poet at all, a naval commander of the Revolutionary War, but the sentiment, dear lady, is worthy of a poet. 'Things are seldom what they seem, Skim milk masquerades as cream.' William Schwenk Gilbert, Miss Throop."

"I don't understand."

"Alternatives, Miss Throop. Alternatives!" The little lawyer was on his feet, pacing, gesticulating with precision. "I tell you only what I told you before. There are always alternatives available to us."

The gray eyes narrowed in thought. "I suppose you mean we could sue to overturn the will," she said. "That occurred to me, but I thought you only handled criminal cases."

"And so I do."

"I wonder if I could find another lawyer who would contest the will on a contingency basis. Perhaps you know someone—"

"Ah, Miss Throop," said Ehrengraf, sitting back down and placing his fingertips together. "Contest the will? Life is too short for litigation. An unlikely sentiment for an attorney to voice, I know, but nonetheless valid for it. Put lawsuits far from your mind. Let us first see if we cannot find"—a smile blossomed on his lips—"the Ehrengraf alternative."

Ehrengraf, a shine on his black wing-tip shoes and a white carnation on his lapel, strode briskly up the cinder path from his car to the center entrance of the Bierstadt house. In the crisp autumn air, the ivy-covered brick mansion in its spacious grounds took on an aura suggestive of a college campus. Ehrengraf noticed this and touched his tie, a distinctive specimen sporting a half-inch stripe of royal blue flanked by two narrower stripes, one of gold and the other of a particularly vivid green, all on a deep navy field. It was the tie he had very nearly worn to the meeting with his client some weeks earlier.

Now, he trusted, it would be rather more appropriate.

He eschewed the doorbell in favor of the heavy brass knocker, and in a matter of seconds the door swung inward. Evelyn Throop met him with a smile.

"Dear Mr. Ehrengraf," she said. "It's kind of you to meet me here. In poor Howard's home."

"Your home now," Ehrengraf murmured.

"Mine," she agreed. "Of course, there are legal processes to be gone through but I've been allowed to take possession. And I think I'm going to be able to keep the place. Now that the paintings are mine, I'll be able to sell some of them to pay the taxes and settle other claims against the estate. But let me show you around. This is the living room, of course, and here's the room where Howard and I were having drinks that night—"

"That fateful night," said Ehrengraf.

"And here's the room where Howard was killed. He was preparing drinks at the sideboard over there. He was lying here when I found him. And—"

Ehrengraf watched politely as his client pointed out where everything had taken place.

Then he followed her to another room where he accepted a small glass of Calvados.

For herself, Evelyn Throop poured a pony of Benedictine.

"What shall we drink to?" she asked him.

To your spectacular eyes, he thought, but suggested instead that she propose a toast.

"To the Ehrengraf alternative," she said.

They drank.

"The Ehrengraf alternative," she said again. "I didn't know what to expect when we last saw each other. I thought you must have had some sort of complicated legal maneuver in mind, perhaps some way around the extortionate tax burden the government levies upon even the most modest inheritance. I had no idea the whole circumstances of poor Howard's murder would wind up turned utterly upside down."

"It was quite extraordinary," Ehrengraf allowed.

"I had been astonished enough to learn that Mrs. Keppner had murdered Howard and then taken her own life. Imagine how I felt to learn that she *wasn't* a murderer and that she *hadn't* committed suicide but that she'd actually *herself* been murdered."

"Life keeps surprising us," Ehrengraf said.

"And Leona Weybright winds up hoist on her own soufflé. The funny thing is that I was right in the first place. Howard *was* afraid of Leona, and evidently he had every reason to be. He'd apparently written her a note, insisting that they stop seeing each other."

Ehrengraf nodded. "The police found the note when they searched her quarters. Of course, she insisted she had never seen it before."

"What else could she say?" Evelyn Throop took another delicate sip of Benedictine and Ehrengraf's heart thrilled at the sight of her pink tongue against the brim of the tiny glass. "But I don't see how she can expect anyone to believe her. She murdered Howard, didn't she?"

"It would be hard to establish that beyond a reasonable doubt," Ehrengraf said. "The supposition exists. However, Miss Weybright does have an alibi, and it might not be easily shaken. And the only witness to the murder, Mrs. Keppner, is no longer available to give testimony."

"Because Leona killed her."

Ehrengraf nodded. "And that," he said, "very likely can be established."

"Because Mrs. Keppner's suicide note was a forgery."

"So it would appear," Ehrengraf said. "An artful forgery, but a forgery nevertheless. And the police seem to have found earlier drafts of that very note in Miss Weybright's desk. One was typed on the very machine at which she prepares her cookbook manuscripts. Others were written with a pen found in her desk, and the ink matched that on the note Mrs. Keppner purportedly left behind. Some of the drafts are in an imitation of the dead woman's handwriting, one in a sort of mongrel cross between the two women's penmanship, and one—evidently she was just trying to get the wording to her liking—was in Miss Weybright's own unmistakable hand. Circumstantial evidence, all of it, but highly suggestive."

"And there was other evidence, wasn't there?"

"Indeed there was. When Mrs. Keppner's body was found, there was a glass on a nearby table, a glass with a residue of water in it. An analysis of the water indicated the presence of a deadly poison, and an autopsy indicated that Mrs. Keppner's death had been caused by ingesting that very substance. The police, combining two and two, concluded not illogically that Mrs. Keppner had drunk a glass of water with the poison in it."

"But that's not how it happened?"

"Apparently not. Because the autopsy also indicated that the deceased had had a piece of cake not long before she died."

"And the cake was poisoned?"

"I should think it must have been," Ehrengraf said carefully, "because police investigators happened to find a cake with one wedge missing, wrapped securely in aluminum foil and tucked away in Miss Weybright's freezer. And that cake, when thawed and subjected to chemical analysis, proved to have been laced with the very poison which caused the death of poor Mrs. Keppner."

Miss Throop looked thoughtful. "How did Leona try to get out of that one?"

"She denied she ever saw the cake before and insisted she had never baked it."

"And?"

"And it seems to have been prepared precisely according to an original recipe in her present cookbook-in-progress."

"I suppose the book will never be published now."

"On the contrary, I believe the publisher has tripled the initial print order."

Ehrengraf sighed. "As I understand it, the presumption is that Miss Weybright was desperate at the prospect of losing the unfortunate Mr. Bierstadt. She wanted him, and if she couldn't have him alive she wanted him dead. But she didn't want to be punished for his murder, nor did she want to lose out on whatever she stood to gain from his will. By framing you for his murder, she thought she could increase the portion due her. Actually, the language of the will probably would not have facilitated this, but she evidently didn't realize it, any more than she realized that by receiving the paintings she would have the lion's share of the estate. In any event, she must have been obsessed with the idea of killing her lover and seeing her rival pay for the crime."

"How did Mrs. Keppner get into the act?"

"We may never know for certain. Was the housekeeper in on the plot all along? Did she actually fire the fatal shots and then turn into a false witness? Or did Miss Weybright commit the murder and leave Mrs. Keppner to testify against you? Or did Mrs. Keppner see what she oughtn't to have seen and then, after lying about you, try her hand at blackmailing Miss Weybright? Whatever the actual circumstances, Miss Weybright realized that Mrs. Keppner represented either an immediate or a potential hazard."

"And so Leona killed her."

"And had no trouble doing so." One might call it a piece of cake, Ehrengraf forbore to say. "At that point it became worth her while to let Mrs. Keppner play the role of murderess. Perhaps Miss Weybright became acquainted with the nature of the will and the estate itself and realized that she would already be in line to receive the greater portion of the estate, that it was not necessary to frame you. Furthermore, she saw that you were not about to plead guilty to a reduced charge or to attempt a Frankie-and-Johnny defense, as it were. By shunting the blame onto a dead Mrs. Keppner, she forestalled the possibility of a detailed investigation which might have pointed the finger of guilt in her own direction."

"My goodness," Evelyn Throop said. "It's quite extraordinary, isn't it?"

"It is," Ehrengraf agreed.

"And Leona will stand trial?"

"For Mrs. Keppner's murder."

"Will she be convicted?"

"One never knows what a jury will do," Ehrengraf said. "That's one reason I much prefer to spare my own clients the indignity of a trial."

He thought for a moment. "The district attorney might or might not have enough evidence to secure a conviction. Of course, more evidence might come to light between now and the trial. For that matter, evidence in Miss Weybright's favor might turn up."

"If she has the right lawyer."

"An attorney can often make a difference," Ehrengraf allowed. "But I'm afraid the man Miss Weybright has engaged won't do her much good. I suspect she'll wind up convicted of first-degree manslaughter or something of the sort. A few years in confined quarters and she'll have been rehabilitated. Perhaps she'll emerge from the experience with a slew of new recipes."

"Poor Leona," Evelyn Throop said, and shuddered delicately.

"Ah, well," Ehrengraf said. " 'Life is bitter,' as Henley reminds us in a poem. It goes on to say:

> "Riches won but mock the old, unable years;
> Fame's a pearl that hides beneath a sea of tears;
> Love must wither, or must live alone and weep.
> In the sunshine, through the leaves, across the flowers,
> While we slumber, death approaches through the
> hours . . .
> Let me sleep.

"Riches, fame, love—and yet we seek them, do we not? That will be one hundred thousand dollars, Miss Throop, and—Ah, you have the check all drawn, have you?" He accepted it from her, folded it, and tucked it into a pocket.

"It is rare," he said, "to meet a woman so businesslike and yet so unequivocally feminine. And so attractive."

There was a small silence. Then: "Mr. Ehrengraf? Would you care to see the rest of the house?"

"I'd like that," said Ehrengraf, and smiled his little smile.

The Ehrengraf Nostrum

Gardner Bridgewater paced to and fro over Martin Ehrengraf's office carpet, reminding the little lawyer rather less of a caged jungle cat than—what? He doth bestride the narrow world like a Colossus, Ehrengraf thought, echoing Shakespeare's Cassius. But what, really, did a Colossus look like? Ehrengraf wasn't sure, but the alleged uxoricide was unquestionably colossal, and there he was, bestriding all over the place as if determined to wear holes in the rug.

"If I'd wanted to kill the woman," Bridgewater said, hitting one of his hands with the other, "I'd have damn well done it. By cracking her over the head with something heavy. A lamp base. A hammer. A fireplace poker."

An anvil, Ehrengraf thought. A stove. A Volkswagen.

"Or I might have wrung her neck," said Bridgewater, flexing his fingers. "Or I might have beaten her to death with my hands."

Ehrengraf thought of Longfellow's village blacksmith. " 'The smith, a mighty man is he, with large and sinewy hands,' " he murmured.

"I beg your pardon?"

"Nothing important," said Ehrengraf. "You're saying, I gather, that if murderous impulses had overwhelmed you, you would have put them into effect in a more spontaneous and direct manner."

"Well, I certainly wouldn't have poisoned her. Poison's sneaky. It's the weapon of the weak, the devious, the cowardly."

"And yet your wife was poisoned."

"That's what they say. After dinner Wednesday she complained of headache and nausea. She took a couple of pills and lay down for a nap. She got up feeling worse, couldn't breathe. I rushed her to the hospital. Her heart ceased beating before I'd managed to fill out the questionnaire about medical insurance."

"And the cause of death," Ehrengraf said, "was a rather unusual poison."

Bridgewater nodded. "Cydonex," he said. "A tasteless, odorless, crystalline substance, a toxic hydrocarbon developed serendipitously as a by-product in the extrusion-molding of plastic dashboard figurines. Alyssa's system contained enough Cydonex to kill a person twice her size."

"You had recently purchased an eight-ounce canister of Cydonex."

"I had," Bridgewater said. "We had squirrels in the attic and I couldn't get rid of the wretched little beasts. The branches of several of our trees are within leaping distance of our roof and attic windows, and squirrels have quite infested the premises. They're noisy and filthy creatures, and clever at avoiding traps and poisoned baits. Isn't it extraordinary that a civilization with the capacity to devise napalm and Agent Orange can't come up with something for the control of rodents in a man's attic?"

"So you decided to exterminate them with Cydonex?"

"I thought it was worth a try. I mixed it into peanut butter and put gobs of it here and there in the attic. Squirrels are mad for peanut butter, especially the crunchy kind. They'll eat the creamy, but the crunchy really gets them."

"And yet you discarded the Cydonex. Investigators found the almost full canister near the bottom of your garbage can."

"I was worried about the possible effects. I recently saw a neighbor's dog with a squirrel in his jaws, and it struck me that a poisoned squirrel, reeling from the effects of the Cydonex, might be easy prey for a neighborhood pet, who would in turn be the poison's victim. Besides, as I said, poison's a sneak's weapon. Even a squirrel deserves a more direct approach."

A narrow smile blossomed for an instant on Ehrengraf's thin lips. Then it was gone. "One wonders," he said, "how the Cydonex got into your wife's system."

"It's a mystery to me, Mr. Ehrengraf. Unless poor Alyssa ate some peanut butter off the attic floor, I'm damned if I know where she got it."

"Of course," Ehrengraf said gently, "the police have their own theory."

"The police."

"Indeed. They seem to believe that you mixed a lethal dose of Cydonex into your wife's wine at dinner. The poison, tasteless and odorless as it is, would have been undetectable in plain water, let alone wine. What sort of wine was it, if I may ask?"

"Nuits-St.-Georges."

"And the main course?"

"Veal, I think. What difference does it make?"

"Nuits-St.-Georges would have overpowered the veal," Ehrengraf said thoughtfully. "No doubt it would have overpowered the Cydonex as well. The police said the wineglasses had been washed out, although the rest of the dinner dishes remained undone."

"The wineglasses are Waterford. I always do them up by hand, while Alyssa put everything else in the dishwasher."

"Indeed." Ehrengraf straightened up behind his desk, his hand fastening upon the knot of his tie. It was a small precise knot, and the tie itself was a two-inch-wide silk knit the approximate color of a bottle of Nuits-St.-Georges. The little lawyer wore a white-on-white shirt with French cuffs and a spread collar, and his suit was navy with a barely perceptible scarlet stripe. "As your lawyer," he said, "I must raise some unpleasant points."

"Go right ahead."

"You have a mistress, a young woman who is expecting your child. You and your wife were not getting along. Your wife refused to give you a divorce. Your business, while extremely profitable, has been experiencing recent cash-flow problems. Your wife's life was insured in the amount of five hundred thousand dollars with yourself as beneficiary. In addition, you are her sole heir, and her estate after taxes will still be considerable. Is all of that correct?"

"It is," Bridgewater admitted. "The police found it significant."

"I'm not surprised."

Bridgewater leaned forward suddenly, placing his large and sinewy hands upon Ehrengraf's desk. He looked capable of yanking the top off it and dashing it against the wall. "Mr. Ehrengraf," he said, his voice barely above a whisper, "do you think I should plead guilty?"

"Of course not."

"I could plead to a reduced charge."

"But you're innocent," Ehrengraf said. "My clients are always innocent, Mr. Bridgewater. My fees are high, sir. One might even pronounce them towering. But I collect them only if I win an acquittal or if the charges against my client are peremptorily dismissed. I intend to demonstrate your innocence, Mr. Bridgewater, and my fee system provides me with the keenest incentive toward that end."

"I see."

"Now," said Ehrengraf, coming out from behind his desk and rubbing his small hands briskly together, "let us look at the possibilities. Your wife ate the same meal you did, is that correct?"

"It is."

"And drank the same wine?"

"Yes. The residue in the bottle was unpoisoned. But I could have put Cydonex directly into her glass."

"But you didn't, Mr. Bridgewater, so let us not weigh ourselves down with what you could have done. She became ill after the meal, I believe you said."

"Yes. She was headachy and nauseous."

"Headachy and nauseated, Mr. Bridgewater. That she was nauseous in the bargain would be a subjective conclusion of your own. She lay down for a nap?"

"Yes."

"But first she took something."

"Yes that's right."

"Aspirin, something of that sort?"

"I suppose it's mostly aspirin," Bridgewater said. "It's a patent medicine called Darnitol. Alyssa took it for everything from cramps to athlete's foot."

"Darnitol," Ehrengraf said. "An analgesic?"

"An analgesic, an anodyne, an antispasmodic, a panacea, a catholicon, a cure-all, a nostrum. Alyssa believed in it, Mr. Ehrengraf, and my guess would be that her belief was responsible for much of the preparation's efficacy. I don't take pills, never have, and my headaches seemed to pass as quickly as hers." He laughed shortly. "In any event, Darnitol proved an inadequate antidote for Cydonex."

"Hmm," said Ehrengraf.

"To think it was the Darnitol that killed her."

Five weeks had passed since their initial meeting, and events in the interim had done a great deal to improve both the circumstances and the spirit of Ehrengraf's client. Gardner Bridgewater was no longer charged with his wife's murder.

"It was one of the first things I thought of," Ehrengraf said. "The police had their vision clouded by the extraordinary coincidence of your purchase and use of Cydonex as a vehicle for the extermination of squirrels. But my view was based on the presumption of your innocence, and I was able to discard this coincidence as irrelevant. It wasn't until other innocent men and women began to die of Cydonex poisoning that a pattern began to emerge. A schoolteacher in Kenmore. A retired steelworker in Lackawanna. A young mother in Orchard Park."

"And more," Bridgewater said. "Eleven in all, weren't there?"

"Twelve," Ehrengraf said. "But for diabolical cleverness on the part of the poisoner, he could never have gotten away with it for so long."

"I don't understand how he managed it."

"By leaving no incriminating residue," Ehrengraf explained. "We've had poisoners of this sort before, tainting tablets of some nostrum or other. And there was a man in Boston, I believe it was, who stirred arsenic into the sugar in coffee-shop dispensers. With any random mass murder of that sort, sooner or later a pattern emerges. But this killer only tampered with a single capsule in each bottle of Darnitol. The victim might consume capsules with impunity until the one fatal pill was swallowed, whereupon there would be no evidence remaining in the bottle, no telltale leftover capsule to give the police a clue."

"Good heavens."

"Indeed. The police did in fact test as a matter of course the bottles of Darnitol which were invariably found among the victims' effects. But the pills invariably proved innocent. Finally, when the death toll mounted high enough, the fact that Darnitol was associated with every single death proved indismissable. The police seized drugstore stocks of the painkiller, and again and again bottles turned out to have a single tainted capsule in with the legitimate pills."

"And the actual killer—"

"Will be found, I shouldn't doubt, in the course of time." Ehrengraf straightened his tie, a stylish specimen showing a half-inch stripe of royal blue flanked by two narrower stripes, one of gold and the other of a vivid green, all displayed on a field of navy. The tie was that of the Caedmon Society, and it brought back memories. "Some disgruntled employee of the Darnitol manufacturer, I shouldn't wonder," said Ehrengraf carelessly. "That's usually the case in this sort of affair. Or some unbalanced chap who took the pill himself and was unhappy with the results. Twelve dead, plus your wife of course, and a company on the verge of ruin, because I shouldn't think too many people are rushing down to their local pharmacy and purchasing Extra-Strength Darnitol."

"There's a joke going round," Bridgewater said, flexing his large and sinewy hands. "Patient calls his doctor, says he's got a headache, an upset stomach, whatever. Doctor says, 'Take two Darnitol and call me in the Hereafter.' "

"Indeed."

Bridgewater sighed. "I suppose," he said, "the real killer may never be found."

"Oh, I suspect he will," Ehrengraf said. "In the interests of rounding things out, you know. And, speaking of rounding things out, sir, if you've your checkbook with you—"

"Ah, yes," said Bridgewater. He made his check payable to Martin H. Ehrengraf and filled in the sum, which was a large one. He paused then, his pen hovering over the space for his signature. Perhaps he reflected for a moment on the curious business of paying so great an amount to a person who, on the face of it, had taken no concrete action on his behalf.

But who is to say what thoughts go through a man's mind? Bridgewater signed the check, tore it from the checkbook, and presented it with a flourish.

"What would you drink with veal?" he demanded.

"I beg your pardon?"

"You said the Nuits-St.-Georges would be overpowering with veal. What would you choose?"

"I shouldn't choose veal in the first place. I don't eat meat."

"Don't eat meat?" Bridgewater, who looked as though he might cheerfully consume a whole lamb at a sitting, was incredulous. "What *do* you eat?"

"Tonight I'm having a nut-and-soybean casserole," the little lawyer said. He blew on the check to dry the ink, folded it, and put it away. "Nuit-St.-Georges should do nicely with it," he said. "Or perhaps a good bottle of Chambertin."

The Chambertin and the nut-and-soybean casserole that it had so superbly complemented were but a memory four days later when a uniformed guard ushered the little lawyer into the cell where Evans Wheeler awaited him. The lawyer, neatly turned out in a charcoal-gray-flannel suit with a nipped-in waist, a Wedgwood-blue shirt, and a navy tie with a below-the-knot design, contrasted sharply in appearance with his prospective client. Wheeler, as awkwardly tall and thin as a young Lincoln, wore striped overalls and a denim shirt. His footwear consisted of a pair of chain-store running shoes. The lawyer wore highly polished cordovan loafers.

And yet, Ehrengraf noted, the young man was poised enough in his casual costume. It suited him, even to the stains and chemical burns on the overalls and the ragged patch on one elbow of the workshirt.

"Mr. Ehrengraf," said Wheeler, extending a bony hand. "Pardon the uncomfortable surroundings. They don't go out of their way to make suspected mass murderers comfortable." He smiled ruefully. "The newspapers are calling it the crime of the century."

"That's nonsense," said Ehrengraf. "The century's not over yet. But the crime's unarguably a monumental one, sir, and the evidence against you would seem to be particularly damning."

"That's why I want you on my side, Mr. Ehrengraf."

"Well," said Ehrengraf.

"I know your reputation, sir. You're a miracle worker, and it looks as though that's what I need."

"What you very likely need," Ehrengraf said, "is a master of delaying tactics. Someone who can stall your case for as long as possible to let some of the heat of the moment be discharged. Then, when public opinion has lost some of its fury, he can arrange for you to plead guilty to homicide while of unsound mind. Some sort of insanity defense might work, or might at least reduce the severity of your sentence."

"But I'm innocent, Mr. Ehrengraf."

"I wouldn't presume to say otherwise, Mr. Wheeler, but I don't know that I'd be the right person to undertake your defense. I charge high fees, you see, which I collect only in the event that my clients are entirely exonerated. This tends to limit the nature of my clients."

"To those who can afford you."

"I've defended paupers. I've defended the poor as a court-appointed attorney and I volunteered my services on behalf of a penniless poet. But in the ordinary course of things, my clients seem to have two things in common. They can afford my high fees. And, of course, they're innocent."

"I'm innocent."

"Indeed."

"And I'm a long way from being a pauper, Mr. Ehrengraf. You know that I used to work for Triage Corporation, the manufacturer of Darnitol."

"So I understand."

"You know that I resigned six months ago."

"After a dispute with your employer."

"Not a dispute," Wheeler said. "I told him where he could resituate a couple of test tubes. You see, I was in a position to make the suggestion, although I don't know that he was in a position to follow it. On my own time I'd developed a process for extenuating lapiform polymers so as to produce a variable-stress oxypolymer capable of withstanding—"

Wheeler went on to explain just what the oxypolymer was capable of withstanding, and Ehrengraf wondered what the young man was talking about. He tuned in again to hear him say, "And so my royalty on the process in the first year will be in excess of six hundred fifty thousand dollars, and I'm told that's only the beginning."

"Only the beginning," said Ehrengraf.

"I haven't sought other employment because there doesn't seem to be much point in it, and I haven't changed my lifestyle because I'm happy as I am. But I don't want to spend the rest of my life in prison, Mr. Ehrengraf, nor do I want to escape on some technicality and be loathed by my neighbors for the remainder of my days. I want to be exonerated and I don't care what it costs me."

"Of course you do," said Ehrengraf, drawing himself stiffly erect. "Of course you do. After all, son, you're innocent."

"Exactly."

"Although," Ehrengraf said with a sigh, "your innocence may be rather tricky to prove. The evidence—"

"Is overpowering."

"Like Nuits-St.-Georges with veal. A search of your workroom revealed a half-full container of Cydonex. You denied ever having seen it before."

"Absolutely."

Ehrengraf frowned. "I wonder if you mightn't have purchased it as an aid to pest control. Rats are troublesome. One is always being plagued by rats in one's cellar, mice in one's pantry, squirrels in one's attic—"

"And bats in one's belfry, I suppose, but my house has always been comfortingly free of vermin. I keep a cat. I suppose that helps."

"I'm sure it must, but I don't know that it helps your case. You seem to have purchased Cydonex from a chemical-supply house on North Division Street, where your signature appears in the poison-control ledger."

"A forgery."

"No doubt, but a convincing one. Bottles of Darnitol, some unopened, others with a single Cydonex-filled capsule added, were found on a closet shelf in your home. They seem to be from the same lot as those used to murder thirteen people."

"I was framed, Mr. Ehrengraf."

"And cleverly so, it would seem."

"I never bought Cydonex. I never heard of Cydonex—not until people started dying of it."

"Oh? You worked for the plastics company that discovered the substance. That was before you took employment with the Darnitol people."

"It was also before Cydonex was invented. You know those dogs people mount on their dashboards and the head bobs up and down when you drive?"

"Not when I drive," Ehrengraf said.

"Nor I either, but you know what I mean. My job was finding a way to make the dogs' eyes more realistic. If you had a dog bobbing on your dashboard, would you even *want* the eyes to be more realistic?"

"Well," said Ehrengraf.

"Exactly. I quit that job and went to work for the Darnitol folks, and then my previous employer found a better way to kill rats, and so it looks as though I'm tied into the murders in two different ways. But actually I've never had anything to do with Cydonex and I've never so much as swallowed a Darnitol, let alone paid good money for that worthless snake oil."

"*Someone* bought those pills."

"Yes, but it wasn't—"

"And someone purchased that Cydonex. And forged your name to the ledger."

"Yes."

"And planted the bottles of Darnitol on drugstore and supermarket shelves after fatally tampering with their contents."

"Yes."

"And waited for the random victims to buy the pills, to work their way through the bottle until they ingested the deadly capsule, and to die in agony. And planted evidence to incriminate you."

"Yes."

"And made an anonymous call to the police to put them on your trail." Ehrengraf permitted himself a slight smile, one that did not quite reach his eyes. "And there he made his mistake," he said. "He could have waited for nature to take its course, just as he had already waited for the Darnitol to do its deadly work. The police were checking on ex-employees of Triage Corporation. They'd have gotten to you sooner or later. But he wanted to hurry matters along, and that proves you were framed, sir, because who but the man who framed you would ever think to have called the police?"

"So the very phone call that got me on the hook serves to get me off the hook?"

"Ah," said Ehrengraf, "would that it were that easy."

Unlike Gardner Bridgewater, young Evans Wheeler proved a model of repose. Instead of pacing back and forth across Ehrengraf's carpet, the chemist sat in Ehrengraf's overstuffed leather chair, one long leg crossed over the other. His costume was virtually identical to the garb he had worn in prison, although an eye as sharp as Ehrengraf's could detect a different pattern to the stains and acid burns that gave character to the striped overalls. And this denim shirt, Ehrengraf noted, had no patch upon its elbow. Yet.

Ehrengraf, seated at his desk, wore a Dartmouth-green blazer over tan flannel slacks. As was his custom on such occasions, his tie was once again the distinctive Caedmon Society cravat.

"Ms. Joanna Pellatrice," Ehrengraf said. "A teacher of seventh- and eighth-grade social studies at Kenmore Junior High School. Unmarried, twenty-eight years of age, and living alone in three rooms on Deerhurst Avenue."

"One of the killer's first victims."

"That she was. The very first victim, in point of fact, although Ms. Pellatrice was not the first to die. Her murderer took one of the capsules from her bottle of Darnitol, pried it open, disposed of the innocent if ineffectual powder within, and replaced it with the lethal Cydonex. Then he put it back in her bottle, returned the bottle to her medicine cabinet or purse, and waited for the unfortunate woman to get a headache or cramps or whatever impelled her to swallow the capsules."

"Whatever it was," Wheeler said, "they wouldn't work."

"This one did, when she finally got to it. In the meantime, her intended murderer had already commenced spreading little bottles of joy all over the metropolitan area, one capsule to each bottle. There was danger in doing so, in that the toxic nature of Darnitol might come to light before Ms. Pellatrice took her pill and went to that big classroom in the sky. But he reasoned, correctly it would seem, that a great many persons would die before Darnitol was seen to be the cause of death. And indeed this proved to be the case. Ms. Pellatrice was the fourth victim, and there were to be many more."

"And the killer—"

"Refused to leave well enough alone. His name is George Grodek, and he'd had an affair with Ms. Pellatrice, although married to another teacher all the while. The affair evidently meant rather more to Mr. Grodek than it did to Ms. Pellatrice. He had made scenes, once at her apartment, once at her school during a midterm examination. The newspapers describe him as a disappointed suitor, and I suppose the term's as apt as any."

"You say he refused to leave well enough alone."

"Indeed," said Ehrengraf. "If he'd been content with depopulating the area and sinking Triage Corporation, I'm sure he'd have gotten away with it. The police would have had their hands full checking people with a grudge against Triage, known malcontents and mental cases, and the sort of chaps who get themselves into messes of that variety. But he has a neat sort of mind, has Mr. Grodek, and so he managed to learn of your existence and decided to frame you for the chain of murders."

Ehrengraf brushed a piece of lint from his lapel. "He did a workmanlike job," he said, "but it broke down on close examination. That signature in the poison-control book did turn out to be a forgery, and matching forgeries of your name—

trials, if you will—turned up in a notebook hidden away in a dresser drawer in his house."

"That must have been hard for him to explain."

"So were the bottles of Darnitol in another drawer of the dresser. So was the Cydonex, and so was the little machine for filling and closing the capsules, and a whole batch of broken capsules which evidently represented unsuccessful attempts at pill-making."

"Funny he didn't flush it all down the toilet."

"Successful criminals become arrogant," Ehrengraf explained. "They believe themselves to be untouchable. Grodek's arrogance did him in. It led him to frame you, and to tip the police to you."

"And your investigation did what no police investigation could do."

"It did," said Ehrengraf, "because mine started from the premise of your innocence. If you were innocent, someone else was guilty. If someone else was guilty and had framed you, that someone must have had a motive for the crime. If the crime had a motive, the murderer must have had a reason to kill one of the specific victims. And if that was the case, one had only to look to the victims to find the killer."

"You make it sound so simple," said Wheeler. "And yet if I hadn't had the good fortune to engage your services, I'd be spending the rest of my life in prison."

"I'm glad you see it that way," Ehrengraf said, "because the size of my fee might otherwise seem excessive." He named a figure, whereupon the chemist promptly uncapped a pen and wrote out a check.

"I've never written a check for so large a sum," he said reflectively.

"Few people have."

"Nor have I ever gotten greater value for my money. How fortunate I am that you believed in me, in my innocence."

"I never doubted it for a moment."

"You know who else claims to be innocent? Poor Grodek. I understand the madman's screaming in his cell, shouting to the world that he never killed anyone." Wheeler flashed a mischevious smile. "Perhaps he should hire you, Mr. Ehrengraf."

"Oh, dear," said Ehrengraf. "No, I think not. I can sometimes work miracles, Mr. Wheeler, or what have the appearance of miracles, but I can work them only on behalf of the innocent. And I don't think the power exists to persuade me of poor Mr. Grodek's innocence. No, I fear the man is guilty, and I'm afraid he'll be forced to pay for what he's done." The little lawyer shook his head. "Do you know Longfellow, Mr. Wheeler?"

"Old Henry Wadsworth, you mean? 'By the shores of Gitche Gumee, by the something Big-Sea-Water'? That Longfellow?"

"The shining Big-Sea-Water," said Ehrengraf. "Another client reminded me of 'The Village Blacksmith,' and I've been looking into Longfellow lately. Do you care for poetry, Mr. Wheeler?"

"Not too much."

" 'In the world's broad field of battle,' " Ehrengraf said,
" 'In the bivouac of Life,
" 'Be not like dumb, driven cattle!
" 'Be a hero in the strife!' "

"Well," said Evans Wheeler, "I suppose that's good advice, isn't it?"

"None better, sir. 'Let us then be up and doing, with a heart for any fate; still achieving, still pursuing, learn to labor and to wait.' "

"Ah, yes," said Wheeler.

" 'Learn to labor and to wait,' " said Ehrengraf. "That's the ticket, eh? 'To labor and to wait.' Longfellow, Mr. Wheeler. Listen to the poets, Mr. Wheeler. The poets have the answers, haven't they?" And Ehrengraf smiled, with his lips and with his eyes.

The Ehrengraf Affirmation

"I've been giving this a lot of thought," Dale McCandless said. "Actually, there's not much you can do around here but think."

Ehrengraf glanced around the cell, wondering to what extent it was conducive to thought. There were, it seemed to him, no end of other activities to which the little room would lend itself. There was a bed on which you could sleep, a chair in which you could read, a desk at which you might write the Great American Jailhouse Novel. There was enough floor space to permit pushups or situps or running in place, and, high overhead, there was the pipe that supported the light fixture, and that would as easily support you, should you contrive to braid strips of bedsheet into a rope and hang yourself.

Ehrengraf rather hoped the young man wouldn't attempt the last-named pursuit. He was, after all, innocent of the crimes of which he stood accused. All you had to do was look at him to know as much, and the little lawyer had not even needed to do that. He'd been convinced of his client's innocence the instant the young man had become a client. No client of Martin H. Ehrengraf could ever be other than innocent. This was more than a presumption for Ehrengraf. It was an article of faith.

"What I think would work for me," young McCandless continued, "is the good old Abuse Excuse."

"The Abuse Excuse?"

"Like those rich kids in California," McCandless said. "My father was all the time beating up on me and making me do stuff, and I was in fear for my life, blah blah blah, so what else could I do?"

"Your only recourse was to whip out a semiautomatic assault rifle," Ehrengraf said, "and empty a clip into the man."

"Those clips empty out in no time at all. You touch the trigger and the next thing you know the gun's empty and there's fifteen bullets in the target."

"Fortunately, however, you had another clip."

"For Mom," McCandless agreed. "Hey, she was as abusive as he was."

"And you were afraid of her."

"Sure."

"Your mother was in a wheelchair," Ehrengraf said gently. "She suffered from multiple sclerosis. Your father walked with a cane as the result of a series of small strokes. You're a big, strapping lad. Hulking, one might even say. It might be difficult to convince a jury that you were in fear for your life."

"That's a point."

"If you'd been living with your parents," Ehrengraf added, "people might wonder why you didn't just move out. But you had in fact moved out some time ago, hadn't you? You have your own home on the other side of town."

Dale McCandless nodded thoughtfully. "I guess the only thing to do," he said, "is play the Race Card."

"The Race Card?"

"Racist cops framed me," he said. "They planted the evidence."

"The evidence?"

"The assault rifle with my prints on it. The blood spatters on my clothes. The gloves."

"The gloves?"

"They found a pair of gloves on the scene," McCandless said. "But I'll tell you something nobody else knows. If I were to try on those gloves, you'd see that they're actually a size too small for me. I couldn't get my hands into them."

"And racist cops planted them."

"You bet."

Ehrengraf put the tips of his fingers together. "It's a little difficult for me to see the racial angle here," he said gently. "You're white, Mr. McCandless."

"Yeah, right."

"And both your parents were white. And all of the police officers involved in the investigation are white. All of your parents' known associates are white, and everyone living in that neighborhood is white. If there were a woodpile at the scene, I've no doubt we'd find a Caucasian in it. This is an all-white case, Mr. McCandless, and I just don't see a race card for us to play."

"Rats," Dale McCandless said. "If the Abuse Excuse is out and there's no way to play the Race Card, I don't know how I'm going to get out of this. The only thing left is the Rough Sex defense, and I suppose you've got some objection to that, too."

"I think it would be a hard sell," Ehrengraf said.

"I was afraid you'd say that."

"It seems to me you're trying to draw inspiration from some high-profile cases that don't fit the present circumstances. But there is one case that does."

"What's that?"

"Miss Elizabeth Borden," Ehrengraf said.

McCandless frowned in thought. "Elizabeth Borden," he said. "I know Elsie Borden, she's married to Elmer and she gives condensed milk. Even if Elsie's short for Elizabeth, I don't see how—"

"Lizzie," Ehrengraf pointed out, "is also short for Elizabeth."

"Lizzie Borden," McCandless said, and his eyes lit up. "Oh, yeah. A long time ago, right? Took an axe and gave her mother forty whacks?"

"So they say."

" 'And when she saw what she had done, she gave her father forty-one.' I remember the poem."

"Everybody remembers the poem," Ehrengraf said. "What everyone forgets is that Miss Borden was innocent."

"You're kidding. She got off?"

"Of course she did," Ehrengraf said. "The jury returned a verdict of Not Guilty. And how could they do otherwise, Mr. McCandless? The woman was innocent." He allowed himself a small smile. "Even as you and I," he said.

"Innocent," Dale McCandless said. "What a concept."

"All my clients are innocent," Ehrengraf told him. "That's what makes my work so gratifying. That and the fees, of course."

"Speaking of which," McCandless said, "you can set your mind to rest on that score. Even if they wind up finding me guilty and that keeps me from inheriting from my parents, I've still got more than enough to cover whatever you charge me. See, I came into a nice piece of change when my grandmother passed away."

"Is that what enabled you to buy a house of your own?"

"It set me up pretty good. I've got the house and I've got money in the bank. See, I was her sole heir, so when she took a tumble on the back staircase, everything she had came to me."

"She fell down the stairs?"

McCandless nodded. "They ought to do something about that staircase," he said. "Three months earlier, my grandfather fell down those same stairs and broke his neck."

"And left all his money to your grandmother," Ehrengraf said.

"Right."

"Who in turn left it to you."

"Yeah. Handy, huh?"

"Indeed," said Ehrengraf. "It must have been a frightening thing for an old woman, tumbling down a flight of stairs."

"Maybe not," McCandless said. "According to the autopsy, she was already dead when she fell. So what probably happened is she had a heart attack while she was standing at the top of the stairs and never felt a thing."

"A heart attack."

"Or a stroke or something," McCandless said carefully. "Or maybe she was sleeping and a pillow got stuck over her face and suffocated her."

"The pillow just got stuck on top of her face?"

"Well, she was old," McCandless said. "Who knows what could happen?"

"And then, after the pillow smothered her, how do you suppose she got from her bed to the staircase?"

"Sleepwalking," McCandless said.

"Of course," said Ehrengraf. "I should have thought of that."

"My parents lived in this ranch house," McCandless said. "Big sprawling thing, lots of square footage but all of it on one level. No basement and no attic." He sighed. "In other words, no stairs." He shook his head ruefully. "Point is, there was never any problem about my grandparents' death, so I've got some money of my own. So you don't have to worry about your fee."

Ehrengraf drew himself up straight. He was a small man, but his perfect posture and impeccably tailored raw silk suit lent him stature beyond his height. "There will be no fee," he said, "unless you are found innocent."

"Huh?"

"My longstanding policy, Mr. McCandless. My fees are quite considerable, but they are payable only in the event that my client is exonerated. As it happens, I rarely see the inside of a courtroom. My clients are innocent, and their innocence always wins out in the long run. I do what I can toward that end, often working behind the scenes. And, when charges are dropped, when the real killer confesses, when my client's innocence has been demonstrated to the satisfaction of the legal system, then and only then do I profit from my efforts on his behalf."

McCandless was silent for a long moment. At length he fixed his eyes on the little lawyer. "We got ourselves a problem," he said. "See, just between you and me, I did it."

"With stairs," young McCandless was saying, "it might have been entirely different. Especially with Mom in the wheelchair. Good steep flight of stairs and it's a piece of cake. Instead I went out and got the gun, and then I bought the gloves."

"Gloves?"

"A size too small," McCandless said. "To leave at the crime scene. I thought—well, never mind what I thought. I guess I wasn't thinking too clearly. Hey, that reminds me. You think maybe a Dim Cap defense would turn the trick?"

"Innocent by reason of diminished capacity?"

"Yeah. See, I did a couple of lines of DTT before I went out and bought the gloves."

"Do you mean DDT? The insecticide?"

"Naw, DTT. It's short for di-tetra thiazole, it's a tranquilizer for circus animals, but if you snort it it sort of mellows you out. What I could do, though, is I could forget about the DTT and tell people I ate a Twinkie."

Court TV, Ehrengraf thought, had a lot to answer for. "You got the gun," he prompted his client, "and you bought the gloves . . ."

"And I went over there and did what I had to do. But of course I don't remember that part."

"You don't?"

McCandless shook his head. "Not a thing, from the time I parked the car in their driveway until I woke up hours later in my own bed. See, I never remember. I don't remember doing my grandparents, either. It's all because of the EKG."

"I'm not sure I follow you," said Ehrengraf, rather understating the matter. "You had an electrocardiogram?"

"That's for your heart, isn't it? My heart's fine. No, EKG's this powder, you roll it up and smoke it. I couldn't tell you what the initials stand for, but it was originally developed as a fertilizer for African violets. They had to take it off the market when they found out what it did to people."

"What does it do?"

"I guess it gets you high," McCandless said, "but I don't know for sure. See, what happens is you take it and you black out. It's the same story every time I smoke it. I light up, I take the first puff, and the next thing I remember I'm waking up in my own bed hours later. So I couldn't tell you what it feels like. All I know is what it lets me do while I'm operating behind it. And so far it's let me do my grandparents and my mother and father."

"I knew it," Ehrengraf said.

"How's that?"

"I knew you were innocent," he said. "I knew it. Mr. McCandless, you have no memory whatsoever of any of those killings, is that what you're telling me?"

"Yeah, but—"

"You may have intended to do those persons harm. But it was so much against your nature that you had to ingest a dangerous controlled substance in order to gird yourself for the task. Is that correct?"

"Well, more or less, but—"

"And you have no recollection of committing any crimes whatsoever. You believe yourself to be guilty, and as a result you are in a jail cell charged with a hideous crime. Do you see the problem, sir? The problem is not what you have done, because in fact you have done nothing. The problem is what you believe."

McCandless looked at him.

"If you don't believe in your own innocence," Ehrengraf demanded, "how can the rest of the world believe in it? Your thoughts are powerful, Mr. McCandless. And right now your own negative thoughts are damning you as a murderer."

"But—"

"You must affirm your innocence, sir."

"Okay," McCandless agreed. " 'I'm innocent.' How's that?"

"It's a start," Ehrengraf said. He opened his briefcase, drew out a yellow legal pad, produced a pen. "But it takes more than a simple declaration to change your own thoughts on the matter. What I want you to do is affirm your innocence in writing."

"Just write 'I'm innocent' over and over?"

"It's a little more complicated than that." Ehrengraf uncapped the pen and drew a vertical line down the center of the page. "Here's what you do," he said. "Over here on the left you write 'I am completely innocent.' Then on the right you immediately write down the first negative response to that sentence that pops into your mind."

"Fair enough." McCandless took the pad and pen. *I am completely innocent,* he wrote in the left-hand column. *What a load of crap,* he wrote at once on the right.

"Excellent," Ehrengraf assured him. "Now keep going, but with a different response each time."

"Just keep going?"

"Until you get to the bottom of the page," Ehrengraf said.

The pen raced over the paper, as McCandless no sooner proclaimed his complete innocence than he dashed off a repudiation of it. When he'd reached the bottom of the page, Ehrengraf took the pad from him. *I am completely innocent. / I murdered both my parents . . . I am completely innocent. / Killed Grandma and Grampa . . . I am completely innocent. / I deserve the gas chamber . . . I am completely innocent. / I'm guilty as sin . . . I am completely innocent. / They ought to hang me . . . I am completely innocent. / I'm a murderer . . . I am completely innocent. / I killed a girl last year and there wasn't even any money in it for me . . . I am completely innocent. / I'm a born killer . . . I am completely innocent / I am bad, bad, bad!*

"Excellent," Ehrengraf said.

"You think so? If the District Attorney got a hold of that . . ."

"Ah, but he won't, will he?" Ehrengraf crumpled the paper, stuffed it into a pocket, handed the legal pad back to his client. "All of those negative thoughts," he explained, "have been festering in your mind and soul, preventing you from believing in your own untarnished innocence. By letting them surface this way, we can stamp them out and affirm your own true nature."

"My own true nature's nothing to brag about," McCandless said.

"That's your negativity talking," Ehrengraf told him. "At heart you're an innocent child of God." He pointed to the legal pad, made scribbling motions in the air. "You've got work to do," he said.

"I hope you got another of those yellow pads there," Dale McCandless said. "It's a funny thing. I was never much of a writer, and in school it was torture for me to write a two-page composition for English class. You know, 'How I Spent My Summer Vacation'?"

Ehrengraf, who could well imagine how a young McCandless might have spent his summer vacation, was diplomatically silent.

"But this time around," McCandless said, "I've been writing up a storm. What's it been, five days since you got me started? Well, I ran through that pad you gave me, and I got one of the guards to bring me this little notebook, but I like the pads better. Here, look at what I wrote this morning."

Ehrengraf unfolded a sheet of unlined white paper. McCandless had drawn a line down its center, writing his affirmation over and over again in the left-hand column, jotting down his responses to the right. *I am completely innocent. / I've been in trouble all my life . . . I am completely innocent. / Maybe it wasn't always my fault . . . I am completely innocent. / I don't remember doing anything bad . . . I am completely innocent. / In my heart I am . . . I am completely innocent. / How great it would be if it was true!*

"You've come a long way," Ehrengraf told his client. "You see how the nature of your responses is changing."

"It seems like magic," McCandless said.

"The magic of affirmation."

"All along, I would just write down the first thing that popped into my head. But the old bad stuff just stopped popping in."

"You cleared it away."

"I don't know what I did," McCandless said. "Maybe I just wore it out. But it got to the point where it didn't seem natural to write that I was a born killer."

"Because you're not."

"I guess."

"And how do you feel now, Mr. McCandless? Without a pen in your hand, just talking face-to-face? Are you innocent of the crimes of which you stand accused?"

"Maybe."

"Maybe?"

"It's almost too much to hope for," the young man said, "but maybe I am. I could be, couldn't I? I really could be."

Ehrengraf beamed. "Indeed you are," he said, "and it's my job to prove it. And yours—" he opened his briefcase, provided his client with a fresh legal pad "—yours to further affirm that innocence until there is no room in your consciousness for doubt and negativity. You've got work to do, Mr. McCandless. Are you up for it?"

Eagerly, McCandless reached for the pad.

"Little Bobby Bickerstaff," McCandless said, shaking his head in wonder.

Ehrengraf's hand went to the knot of his necktie, adjusting it imperceptibly. The tie was that of the Caedmon Society, and Ehrengraf was not entitled to wear it, never having been a member of that organization. It was, however, his invariable choice for occasions of triumph, and this was just such an occasion.

"I never would have dreamed it," McCandless said. "Not in a million years."

"You knew him, then?"

"We went to grade school together. In fact we were in the same class until I got held back. You know something? *That's* hard to believe, too."

"That you'd be held back? I must say I find it hard to believe myself. You're an intelligent young man."

"Oh, it wasn't for that. It was for deportment. You know, talking in class, throwing chalk."

"High spirits," Ehrengraf said.

"Setting fires," McCandless went on. "Breaking windows. Doing cars."

"Doing cars?"

"Teachers' cars," the young man explained. "Icepicking the tires, or sugaring the gas tank, or keying the paint job. Or doing the windows."

"Bricking them," Ehrengraf suggested.

"I suppose you could call it that. That's what's hard to believe, Mr. Ehrengraf. That I did those things."

"I see."

"I used to be like that," he said, and frowned in thought. "Or maybe I just used to *think* I was that way, and that's why I did bad things."

"Ah," Ehrengraf said.

"All along I was innocent," McCandless said, groping for the truth. "But I didn't know it, I had this belief I was bad, and when I was a little kid it made me do bad things."

"Precisely."

"And I got in trouble, and they blamed me even when I didn't do anything bad, and that convinced me I was really bad, bad clear to the bone. And . . . and . . ."

The youth put his head in his hands and sobbed. "There, there," Ehrengraf said softly, and clapped him on the shoulder. After a moment McCandless got hold of himself and said, "But little Bobby Bickerstaff. I can't get over it."

"He killed your parents," Ehrengraf said.

"It's so hard to believe. I always thought of him as a little goody-goody."

"A nice quiet boy," Ehrengraf said.

"Yeah, well, those are the ones who lose it, aren't they? They pop off one day and the neighbors can't believe it, same as I can't believe it myself about Bobby. What was the name of the couple he killed?"

"Roger and Sheila Capstone."

"I didn't know them," McCandless said, "but they lived in the same neighborhood as my folks, in the same kind of house. And was she in a wheelchair the same as my mom?"

"It was Mr. Capstone who was wheelchair-bound," Ehrengraf said. "He'd been crippled in an automobile accident."

"Poor guy. And little Bobby Bickerstaff emptied a clip into him, and another into his wife."

"So it seems."

"Meek little Bobby. Whacked them both, then went into the bathroom and wrote something on the mirror."

"It was Mrs. Capstone's dressing table mirror," Ehrengraf said. "And he used her lipstick to write his last message."

" 'This is the last time. God forgive me.' "

"His very words."

"And then he put on the woman's underwear," McCandless said, "or maybe he put it on before, who knows, and then he popped a fresh clip in his gun and stuck the business end in his mouth and got off a burst. Must have made some mess."

"I imagine it did."

McCandless shook his head in amazement. "Little Bobby," he said. "Mr. Straight Arrow. Cops searched his place afterward, house he grew up in, what did they find? All these guns and knives and dirty magazines and stuff."

"It happens all the time," Ehrengraf said.

"Other stuff, too. Some things that must have been stolen from my parents' house, not that anybody had even noticed they were missing. Some jewelry of my mom's and a sterling silver flask with my dad's initials engraved on it. I don't think I ever even knew he had a flask, but how many are you going to find engraved W. R. McC.?"

"It must have been his."

"Well, sure. But what really wrapped it up was the diary. From what I heard, most of it was sketchy, just weird stuff that was going through his mind. But the entry the day after my parents died, that was something else."

"It was a little vague as well," Ehrengraf said, "but quite conclusive all the same. He told how he'd gone to your parents' home and found you passed out in a chair."

"From the EKG, it must have been."

"He thought about killing all three of you. Instead he gunned down both your parents, making sure that you and your clothes were spattered with their blood, then wiped his prints off the empty gun and pressed it into your hands."

"Bobby's mom was crippled," McCandless remembered. "I remember kids used to say we ought to be friends because of it. Like him and me were in the same boat."

"But you weren't friends."

"Are you kidding? A hood like me team up with a goody-goody like Bobby Bickerstaff?" His expression turned thoughtful. "Except it turns out I was innocent all along, so I wasn't such a hood after all. And Bobby wasn't such a goody-goody."

"No."

"In fact," McCandless said, "he might have had something to do with his own parents' death. Bobby was still a kid at the time. They weren't too clear on what happened, whether it was a suicide pact or the old man committed a mercy killing and then killed himself afterward. I guess everybody figured it amounted to the same thing. But now . . ."

"Now there's suspicion that Bobby may have done it."

"I suppose he could have. There's a pattern, isn't there? His mom was crippled, my mom was in a wheelchair, and this Mr. Capstone was more of the same. Maybe the shock of what happened to his folks drove him around the bend, or maybe he was the one responsible for what happened to them to start with, and the other two murders were just a way of reenacting the crime. I wonder which it was."

"I doubt we'll ever know," Ehrengraf said gently.

"I guess not," McCandless said. "What we do know is *I* didn't kill anybody, and I already knew that, thanks to you. Bobby killed my parents, and my grandparents both had simple accidents. That's what the police decided at the time, and it was only my own negative thoughts about myself that led me to believe I had anything to do with their deaths."

"That's it," Ehrengraf said, delighted. "You're absolutely right."

"I'll tell you, Mr. Ehrengraf, this business with affirmations is pretty amazing stuff. I mean, I did some bad things over the years. Let's face it, I pulled some mean stuff. But do you know why?"

"Tell me, Dale."

"I did it because I thought I was bad. I mean, if you're a bad person, what do you do? You do bad things. I thought I was bad, so I did some bad things."

" 'Give a dog a bad name—' "

"And he'll bite you," McCandless said. "And I did, in a manner of speaking, but I never killed anybody. And now that I know I'm innocent, I'll be a changed human being entirely."

"A productive member of society."

"Well, I don't know about productive," McCandless said. "I mean, face it, I'm a rich man. Between what I had from my grandmother and what I stand to inherit from my parents, I can live a life of ease." He grinned. "Even after I pay your fee, I'm still set for life."

"An enviable position to be in."

"So I may not knock myself out being productive," McCandless went on. "I may just focus on having fun."

"Boys will be boys," said Ehrengraf.

"You said it. I'll work on my suntan, I'll see that the bar's well stocked, I'll round up a couple of totally choice babes. Get some good drugs, plenty of tasty food in case anybody gets the munchies, and next thing you know—"

"Drugs," Ehrengraf said.

"Hey, it's like you said, Mr. Ehrengraf. Boys will be boys."

"Suppose you got hold of some of that EKG."

"Suppose I did? I'm innocent, Mr. Ehrengraf. You're the one showed me how to see that. Anything I do, drunk or sober, straight or loaded, it's going to be innocent. So what have I got to worry about?"

He grinned disarmingly, but Ehrengraf was not disarmed. "I'm not sure EKG is a good idea for you," he said carefully.

"You could be right. But sooner or later it'll be around, and I won't be able to resist it. But so what? I can handle it."

Ehrengraf reached for the yellow legal pad, turned to a clean sheet, drew a line down the center of the page. "Here," he said, handing the pad to McCandless. "This time I'd like you to work with a different affirmation."

"How about 'I am a perfect child of God'? I sort of like the sound of that one."

"Let's try something a little more specific," Ehrengraf suggested. "Write, 'I am through with EKG, now and forever.' "

McCandless frowned, shrugged, took the pad, and started writing. Ehrengraf, watching over his shoulder, read the responses as his client wrote them. *I am through with EKG, now and forever. / You must be kidding . . . I am through with EKG, now and forever. / I love the way it makes me crazy . . . I am through with EKG, now and forever. / I'll never give it up . . . I am through with EKG, now and forever. / What harm does it do? . . . I am through with EKG, now and forever. / I couldn't resist it.*

"We have our work cut out for us," Ehrengraf said. "But that only shows how deep the thought goes. Look at the self-image you had earlier, and look how you managed to turn it around."

"I know I'm innocent."

"And the world has changed to reflect the change in your own mental landscape. Once you became clear on your innocence, proof of it began to manifest in the world around you."

"I think I see what you mean."

Ehrengraf handed the legal pad back to his client. The process would work, he assured himself. Soon the mere thought of ingesting EKG would be anathema to young Dale McCandless.

And that, Ehrengraf thought, would be all to the good. Because he had a feeling the world would be a kinder and gentler place for all if the innocent Mr. McCandless never ingested that particular chemical again.

The Ehrengraf Reverse

"I didn't do it," Blaine Starkey said.

"Of course you didn't."

"Everyone thinks I did it," Starkey went on, "and I guess I can understand why. But I'm innocent."

"Of course you are."

"I'm not a murderer."

"Of course you're not."

"Not this time," the man said. "Mr. Ehrengraf, it's not supposed to matter whether a lawyer thinks his client is guilty or innocent. But it matters to me. I really am innocent, and it's important that you believe me."

"I do."

"I don't know why it's so important," Starkey said, "but it just is, and—" He paused, and seemed to register for the first time what Ehrengraf had been saying all along. His big open face showed puzzlement. "You do?"

"Yes."

"You believe I'm innocent."

"Absolutely."

"That's pretty amazing, Mr. Ehrengraf. Nobody else believes me."

Ehrengraf regarded his client. Indeed, if you looked at the man's record you could hardly avoid presuming him guilty. But once you turned your gaze into his cornflower-blue eyes, how could you fail to recognize the innocence gleaming there?

Even if you didn't believe the man, how would you have the nerve to tell him so? Blaine Starkey's was, to say the least, an imposing presence. When you saw him on the television screen, catching a pass and racing downfield, breaking tackles as effortlessly as a politician breaks his word, you didn't appreciate the sheer size of him. All the men on the field were huge, and your eye learned to see them as normal.

In a jail cell, across a little pine table, you began to realize just how massive a man Blaine Starkey was. He stood as many inches over six feet as Ehrengraf stood under it, and was big in the shoulders and narrow in the waist, with thighs like tree trunks and arms like—well, words failed Ehrengraf. The man was enormous.

"The whole world thinks I killed Claureen," Starkey said, "and it's not hard to see why. I mean, look at my stats."

His stats? Thousands of yards gained rushing. Hundreds of passes caught. No end of touchdowns scored. Ehrengraf, who was more interested in watching the action on the field than in crunching the numbers, knew nevertheless that the big man's statistics were impressive.

He also knew Starkey meant another set of stats.

"I mean," the man said, "it's not like this never happened before. Three women, three coffins. Hell, Mr. Ehrengraf, if I was a hockey player they'd call it the hat trick."

"But it's not hockey," Ehrengraf assured him, "and it's not football, either. You're an innocent man, and there's no reason you should have to pay for a crime you didn't commit."

"You really think I'm innocent," Starkey said.

"Absolutely."

"That's what everybody's supposed to presume, until it's proved otherwise. Is that what you mean? That I'm innocent for the time being, far as the law's concerned?"

Ehrengraf shook his head. "That's not what I mean."

"You mean innocent no matter what the jury says."

"I mean exactly what you meant earlier," the little lawyer said. "You didn't kill your wife. You're entirely innocent of her death, and the jury should never be in a position to say anything on the subject, because you should never be brought to trial. You're an innocent man, Mr. Starkey."

The football player took a deep breath, and Ehrengraf was surprised that there was any air left in the cell. "That's just so hard for me to believe."

"That you're innocent?"

"Hell, I *know* I'm innocent," Starkey said. "What's hard to believe is that *you* believe it."

But how could Ehrengraf believe otherwise? He fingered the knot in his deep blue necktie and reflected on the presumption of innocence—not the one which had long served as a cardinal precept of Anglo-American jurisprudence, but a higher, more personal principle. The Ehrengraf presumption. Any client of Martin H. Ehrengraf's was innocent. Not until proven guilty, but until the end of time.

But he didn't want to get into a philosophical discussion with Blaine Starkey. He kept it simple, explaining that he only represented the innocent.

The football player took this in. His face fell. "Then if you change your mind," he said, "you'll drop me like a hot rock. Is that about right?"

"I won't change my mind."

"If you get to thinking I'm guilty—"

"I'll never think that."

"But—"

"We're wasting time," Ehrengraf told him. "We both know you're innocent. Why dispute a point on which we're already in agreement?"

"I guess I really found the one man who believes me," Starkey said. "Now where are we gonna find twelve more?"

"It's my earnest hope we won't have to," Ehrengraf said. "I rarely see the inside of a courtroom, Mr. Starkey. My fees are very high, but I have to earn them in order to receive them."

Starkey scratched his head "That's what I'm not too clear on."

"It's simple enough. I take cases on a contingency basis. I don't get paid unless and until you walk free."

"I've heard of that in civil cases," Starkey said, "but I didn't know there were any criminal lawyers who operated that way."

"As far as I know," Ehrengraf said, "I am the only one. And I don't depend on courtroom pyrotechnics. I represent the innocent, and through my efforts their innocence becomes undeniably clear to all concerned. Then and only then do I collect my fee."

And what would that be? Ehrengraf named a number.

"Whole lot of zeroes at the end of it," the football player said, "but it's nothing to the check I wrote out for the Proud Crowd. Five of them, and they spent close to a year on the case, hiring experts and doing studies and surveys and I don't know what else. A man can make a lot of money if he can run the ball and catch a pass now and then. I guess I can afford your fee, plus whatever the costs and expenses come to."

"The fee is all-inclusive," Ehrengraf said.

"If that's so," Starkey said, "I'd say it's a bargain. And I only pay if I get off?"

"And you will, sir."

"If I do, I don't guess I'll begrudge you your fee. And if I don't, do I get my retainer back? Not that I'd have a great use for it, but—"

"There'll be no retainer," Ehrengraf said smoothly. "I like to earn my money before I receive it."

"I never heard of anybody like you, Mr. Ehrengraf."

"There isn't anyone like me," Ehrengraf said. "I've thrilled to watch you play, and I don't believe there's anyone like you, either. We're both unique."

"Well," Starkey said.

"And yet you're charged with killing your wife," Ehrengraf said smoothly. "Hard to believe, but there it is."

"Not so hard to believe. I've been tried twice for murder and got off both times. How many times can a man kill his wife and get away with it?"

It was a good question, but Ehrengraf chose not to address it. "The first woman wasn't your wife," he said.

"My girlfriend. Kate Waldecker. I was in my junior year at Texas State." He looked at his hands. "We were in bed together, and one way or another my hands got around her neck."

"You engaged Joel Daggett as your attorney, if I remember correctly."

"The Bulldog," Starkey said fondly. "He came up with this rough sex defense. Brought in witnesses to testify that Kate liked to be hurt while she was making love, liked to be choked half to death. Made her out to be real kinky, and a tramp in the bargain. I have to say I felt sorry for her folks. They were in tears through the trial." He sighed. "But what else could he do? I mean, I got out of bed and called the cops, told everybody I did it. Daggett got the confession suppressed, but there was still plenty of evidence that I did it. He had to find a way to keep it from being murder."

"And he was successful. You were found not guilty."

"Yeah, but that was bullshit. Kate didn't like it rough. Fact, she was always telling me to slow down, to be gentler with her." He frowned. "Hard to say what happened that night. We'd been arguing earlier, but I thought I was over being mad about that. Next thing I knew she was dead and I was unhooking my hands from around her throat. I always figured the steroids I was taking might have had something to do with it, but maybe not. Maybe I just got carried away and killed her. Anyway, Daggett saw to it that I got away with it."

"You didn't go back for your senior year."

"No, I turned pro right after the trial. I would have liked to get my degree, but I didn't figure they'd cheer as hard for me after I'd killed a fellow student. Besides, I had a big legal bill to pay, and that's where the signing bonus went."

"You went with the Wranglers."

"I was their first-round draft choice and I was with them for four seasons. Born in Texas, went to school in Texas, and I thought I'd play my whole career in Texas. Married a Texas girl, too. Jacey was beautiful, even if she was hell on wheels. High-strung, you know? Threw a glass ashtray at me once, hit me right here on the cheekbone. Another inch and I might have lost an eye." He shook his head. "I figured we'd get divorced sooner or later. I just wanted to stay married to her until I got tired of, you know, goin' to bed with her. But I never did get tired of her that way, or divorced from her, either, and then the next thing I knew she was dead."

"She killed herself."

"They found her in bed, with bruises on her neck. And they picked me up at the country club, where I was sitting by myself in the bar, hitting the bourbon pretty good. They hauled me downtown and charged me with murder."

"You didn't give a statement."

"Didn't say a word. I knew that much from my first trial. Of course I couldn't get the Bulldog this time, on account of he was dead. Lee Waldecker walked up to him in a restaurant in Austin about a year after my acquittal, shot him in front of a whole roomful of people. I guess he never got over the job Daggett did on his sister's reputation. He said he could almost forgive me, because all I did was kill Kate, but what Daggett did to her was worse than murder."

"He's still serving his sentence, isn't he?"

"Life without parole. A jury might have cut him loose, or slapped him on the wrist with a short sentence, but he went and pleaded guilty. Said he did it in front of witnesses on purpose, so he wouldn't have some lawyer twisting the truth."

"So you got a whole team of lawyers," Ehrengraf said. "The press made up a name for them."

"The Proud Crowd. Each one thought he was the hottest thing going, and they spent a lot of time just cutting each other apart. And they sure weren't shy about charging for their services. But I'd made a lot of money all those years, and I figured to make a lot more if I kept on playing, and the Wranglers wanted to make sure I had the best possible defense."

"Not rough sex this time."

"No, I don't guess you can get by with that more than once. What's funny is that Jacey *did* like it rough. Matter of fact, there weren't too many ways she didn't like it. If the Bulldog was around, and if I hadn't already used that defense once already, rough sex would have had me home free. Jacey was everything Daggett tried to make Kate look like, and there would have been dozens of people willing to swear to it."

"As it turned out," Ehrengraf said, "it was suicide, wasn't it? And the police tampered with the evidence?"

"That was the line the Proud Crowd took. There were impressions on her neck from a large pair of hands, but they dug up a forensics expert who testified that they'd been inflicted after death, like somebody'd strangled her after she'd already been dead for some time. And they had another expert testify that there were rope marks on her neck, underneath the hand prints, suggesting she'd hanged herself and been cut down. There were fibers found on and near the corpse, and another defense expert matched them to a rope that had been retrieved from a Dumpster. And they found residue of talcum powder on the rope, and another expert testified that it was the same kind of talcum powder Jacey used, and had used the day of her death."

"So many experts," Ehrengraf murmured.

"And every damn one of 'em sent in a bill," Starkey said, "but I can't complain, because they earned their money. According to the Proud Crowd, Jacey hanged herself. I came home, saw her like that, and just couldn't deal with it. I cut her down and tried to revive her, then lost it and went to the club to brace myself with a few drinks while I figured out what to do next. Meantime, a neighbor called the cops, and as far as they were concerned I was this old boy who made a couple million dollars a year playing a kid's game, and already put one wife in the ground and got away with it. So they made sure I wouldn't get away with it a second time by taking the rope and losing it in a Dumpster, and pressing their hands into her neck to make it look like manual strangulation."

"And is that how it happened?"

Starkey rolled his eyes. "How it happened," he said, "is we were having an argument, and I took this hunk of rope and put it around her neck and strangled the life out of her."

Ehrengraf winced.

"Don't worry," his client went on. "Nobody can hear us, and what I tell you's privileged anyway, and besides it'd be double jeopardy, because twelve people already decided they believed the Proud Crowd's version. But they must have been the only twelve people in the country who bought it, because the rest of the world figured out that I did it. And got away with it again."

"You were acquitted."

"I was and I wasn't," he said. "Legally I was off the hook, but that didn't mean I got my old life back. The Wranglers put out this press release about how glad they were that justice was served and an innocent man exonerated, but nobody would look me in the eye. First chance they got, they traded me."

"And you've been with the Mastodons ever since."

"And I love it here," he said. "I don't even mind the winters. Back when I played for the Wranglers I hated coming up here for late-season games, but I got so I liked the cold weather. You get used to it."

Ehrengraf, a native, had never had to get used to the climate. But he nodded anyway.

"At first," Starkey said, "I thought about quitting. But I owed all this money to the Proud Crowd, and how was I going to earn big money off a football field? I lost my endorsements, you know. I had this one commercial, I don't know if you remember it, where Minnie Mouse is sitting on my lap and sort of flirting with me."

"You were selling a toilet-bowl cleaner," Ehrengraf recalled.

"Yeah, and when they dropped me I figured that meant I wasn't good enough to clean toilets. But what choice did they have? People were saying things like you could just about see the marks on Minnie's neck. Long story short, no more commercials. So what was I gonna do but play?"

"Of course."

"Besides, I was in my mid-twenties and I loved the game. Now it's ten years later and I still love it. I got Cletis Braden breathing down my neck, trying to take my job away, but I figure it's gonna be a few more years before he can do it. Love the city, live here year round, wouldn't want to live anywhere else. Love the house I bought. Love the people, even love the winters. Snow? What's so bad about snow?"

"It's pretty," Ehrengraf said.

"Damn pretty. It's around for a while and then it melts. And then it's gone." He made a fist, opened it, looked at his palm. "Gone, like everything else. Like my career. Like my damn life."

For a moment Ehrengraf thought the big man might burst into tears, and rather hoped he would not. The moment passed, and the little lawyer suggested they talk about the late Mrs. Starkey.

"Which one? No, I know you mean Claureen. Local girl, born and bred here. Went away to college and got on the cheerleading squad. I guess she got to know the players pretty good." He rolled his eyes. "Came back home, went to work teaching school, but she found a way to hang around football players. I'd been here a couple of years by then, and the Mastodons don't lack for feminine companionship, so I was doing okay in that department. But it was time to get married, and I figured she was the one."

Romeo and Juliet, Ehrengraf thought. Tristan and Isolde. Blaine and Claureen.

"And it was okay," Starkey said. "No kids, and that was disappointing, but we had a good life and we got along okay. I never ran around on her here in town, and what you do on the road don't count. Everybody knows that."

"And the day she died?"

"We had a home game coming up with the Leopards. I went out for a couple of beers after practice, but I left early because Clete Braden showed up and joined us and I can tire of his company pretty quick. I drove around for an hour or two. Went over to Boulevard Mall to see what was playing at the multiplex. They had twelve movies, but nothing I wanted to see. I thought I'd walk around the mall, maybe buy something, but I can't go anywhere without people recognizing me, and sometimes I just don't want to deal with that. I drove around some more and went home."

"And discovered her body."

"In the living room, crumpled up on the rug next to the fireplace, bareass naked and stone cold dead. First thing I thought was she'd had a fainting spell. She'd get light-headed if she went too long between meals, and she'd been trying to drop a few pounds. Don't ask me why, she looked fine to me, but you know women."

"Nobody does," Ehrengraf said.

"Well, that's the damn truth, but you know what I mean. Anyway, I knelt down and touched her, and right away I knew she was dead. And then I saw her head was all bloody, and I thought, well, here we go again."

"You called the police."

"Last thing I wanted to do. Wanted to get in the car and just drive, but I knew not to do that. And I wanted to pour a stiff drink and I didn't let myself do that, either. I called 911 and I sat in a chair, and when the cops came I let 'em in. I didn't answer any of their questions. I barely heard them. I just kept my mouth shut, and they brought me here, and I wound up calling you."

"And it's good you did," Ehrengraf told him. "You're innocent, and soon the whole world will know it."

Three days later the two men faced one another in the same cell across the same little table. Blaine Starkey looked weary. Part of it was the listless sallowness one saw in imprisoned men, but Ehrengraf noted as well the sag of the shoulders, the lines around the mouth. He was wearing the same clothes he'd worn at their previous meeting. Ehrengraf, in a three-piece suit with a banker's stripe and a tie striped like a coral snake, wondered not for the first time if he ought to dress down on such occasions, to put his client at ease. As always, he decided that dressing down was not his sort of thing.

"I've done some investigation," he reported. "Your wife's blood sugar was low."

"Well, she wasn't eating. I told you that."

"The medical examiner estimated the time of death at two to four hours before you reported discovering her body."

"I said she felt cold to the touch."

"She died," Ehrengraf said, "sometime after football practice was over for the day. The prosecution is going to contend that you had time before you met your teammates for drinks—"

"To race home, hit Claureen upside the head, and then rush out to grab a beer?"

"—or afterward, during the time you were driving around and trying to decide on a movie."

"I had the time then," Starkey allowed, "but that's not how I spent it."

"I know that. When you got home, was the door locked?"

"Sure. We keep it so it locks when you pull it shut."

"Did you use your key?"

"Easier than ringing the bell and waiting. Her car was there, so I knew she was home. I let myself in and keyed in the code so the burglar alarm wouldn't go off, and then I walked into the living room, and you know the rest."

"She died," Ehrengraf said, "as a result of massive trauma to the skull. There were two blows, one to the temple, the other to the back of the head. The first may have resulted from her fall, when she struck herself upon the sharp corner of the fireplace surround. The second blow was almost certainly inflicted by a massive bronze statue of a horse."

"She picked it out," Starkey said. "It was French, about a hundred and fifty years old. I didn't think it looked like any horse a reasonable man would want to place a bet on, but she fell in love with it and said it'd be perfect on the mantel."

Ehrengraf fingered the knot of his tie. "Your wife was nude," he said.

"Maybe she just got out of the shower," the big man said. "Or you know what I bet it was? She was on her way *to* the shower."

"By way of the living room?"

"If she was on the stair machine, which was what she would do when she decided she was getting fat. An apple for breakfast and an enema for lunch, and hopping on and off the stair machine all day long. She'd exercise naked if she was warm, or if she wore a sweat suit she'd leave it there in the exercise room and parade through the house naked."

"Then it all falls into place," Ehrengraf said. "She wasn't eating enough and was exercising excessively. She completed an ill-advised session on the stair climber, shed her exercise clothes if in fact she'd been wearing any in the first place, and walked through the living room on her way to the shower."

"She'd do that, all right."

"Her blood sugar was dangerously low. She got dizzy, and felt faint. She started to fall, and reached out to steady herself, grabbing the bronze horse. Then she lost consciousness and fell, dragging the horse from its perch on the mantelpiece as she did so. She went down hard, hitting her forehead on the bricks, and the horse came down hard as well, striking her on the head. And, alone in the house, the unfortunate woman died an accidental death."

"That's got to be it," Starkey said. "I couldn't put it together. All I knew was I didn't kill her. You can push that argument, right? You can get me off?"

But Ehrengraf was shaking his head. "If you had spent the twelve hours preceding her death in the company of an archbishop and a Supreme Court justice," he said, "and if both of those worthies were at your side when you discovered your wife's body, then it might be possible to advance that theory successfully in court."

"But—"

"The whole world thinks of you as a man who got away with murder twice already. Do you think a jury is going to let you get away with it a third time?"

"The prosecution can't introduce either of those earlier cases as evidence, can they?"

"They can't even mention them," Ehrengraf said, "or it's immediate grounds for a mistrial. But why mention them when everyone already knows all about them? If they didn't know to begin with, they're reading the full story every day in the newspaper and watching clips of your two trials on television."

"Then it's hopeless."

"Only if you go to trial."

"What else can I do? I could try fleeing the country, but where would I hide? What would I do, play professional football in Iraq or North Korea? And I can't even try, because they won't let me out on bail."

Ehrengraf put the tips of his fingers together. "I've no intention of letting this case go to trial," he said. "I don't much care for the whole idea of leaving a man's fate in the hands of twelve people, not one of them clever enough to get out of jury duty."

Puzzlement showed in Starkey's face.

"I remember a run you made against the Jackals," Ehrengraf said. "The quarterback gave the ball to that other fellow—"

"Clete Braden," Starkey said heavily.

"—and he began running to his right, and you were running toward him, and he handed the ball to you, and you swept around to the left, after all the Jackals had shifted over to stop Braden's run to the right."

Starkey brightened. "I remember the play," he said. "The reverse. When it works, it's one of the prettiest plays in football."

"It worked against the Jackals."

"I ran it in. Better than sixty yards from scrimmage, and once I was past midfield no one had a shot at me."

Ehrengraf beamed. "Ah, yes. The reverse. It is something to see, the reverse."

It was a new Blaine Starkey that walked into Martin Ehrengraf's office. He was dressed differently, for one thing, his double-breasted tan suit clearly the work of an accomplished tailor, his maroon silk shirt open at its flowing collar, his cordovan wing tips buffed to a high sheen. His skin had thrown off the jailhouse pallor and glowed with the ruddy health of a life lived outdoors. There was a sparkle in his eyes, a spring in his step, a set to his shoulders. It did the little lawyer's heart good to see him.

He was holding a football, passing it from hand to hand as he approached Ehrengraf's desk. How small it looked, Ehrengraf thought, in those big hands. And with what ease could those hands encircle a throat . . .

Ehrengraf pushed the thought aside, and his hand went to his necktie. It was his Caedmon Society tie, his inevitable choice on triumphant occasions, and a nice complement to his cocoa-brown blazer and fawn slacks.

"The game ball," Starkey announced, reaching to place it on the one clear spot on the little lawyer's cluttered desk. "They gave it to me after Sunday's game with the Ocelots. See, all the players signed it. All but Cletis Braden, but I don't guess he'll be signing too many game balls from here on."

"I shouldn't think so."

"And here's where I wrote something myself," he said, pointing.

Ehrengraf read: *To Marty Ehrengraf, who made it all possible. From your buddy, Blaine Starkey.*

"Marty," Ehrengraf said.

Starkey lowered his eyes. "I didn't know about that," he admitted. "If people called you Marty or Martin or what. I mean, all I ever called you was 'Mr. Ehrengraf.' But with sports memorabilia, people generally like it to look like, you know, like them and the athlete are good buddies. Do they call you Marty?"

They never had, but Ehrengraf merely smiled at the question and took the ball in his hands. "I shall treasure this," he said simply.

"Here's something else to treasure," Starkey said. "It's autographed, too."

"Ah," Ehrengraf said, and took the check, and raised his eyebrows at the amount. It was not the sum he had mentioned at their initial meeting. This had happened before, when a client's gratitude gave way to innate penuriousness, and Ehrengraf routinely made short work of such attempts to reduce his fee. But this check was for more than he had demanded, and that had *not* happened before.

"It's a bonus," Starkey said, anticipating the question. "I don't know if there's such a thing in your profession. We get them all the time in the NFL. It's not insulting, is it? Like tipping the owner of the restaurant? Because I surely didn't intend it that way."

Ehrengraf, nonplussed, shook his head. "Money is only insulting," he managed, "when there's too little of it." He beamed, and stowed the check in his wallet.

"I'll tell you," Starkey said, "writing checks isn't generally my favorite thing in the whole world, but I couldn't have been happier when I was writing out that one. Couple of weeks ago I was the worst thing since Jack the Ripper, and now I'm everybody's hero. Who was it said there's no second half in the game of life?"

"Scott Fitzgerald wrote something along those lines," Ehrengraf said, "but I believe he phrased it a little differently."

"Well, he was wrong," Starkey said, "and you proved it. And who would have dreamed it would turn out this way?"

Ehrengraf smiled.

"Clete Braden," Starkey said. "I knew the son of a bitch was after my job, but who'd have guessed he was after my wife, too? I swear I never had a clue those two were slipping around behind my back. It's still hard to believe Claureen was cheating on me when I wasn't even on a road trip."

"They must have been very clever in their deceit."

"But stupid at the same time," Starkey said. "Taking her to a motel and signing in as Mr. and Mrs. Cleveland Brassman. Same initials, plus he used his own handwriting on the registration card. Made up a fake address but used his real license plate number, just switching two digits around." He rolled his eyes. "And then leaving a pair of her panties in the room. Where was it they found them? Wedged under the chair cushion or some such?"

"I believe so."

"All that time and the maids never found them. I guess they don't knock themselves out cleaning the rooms in a place like that, but I'd still have to call it a piece of luck the panties were still there."

"Luck," Ehrengraf agreed.

"And no question they were hers, either. Matched the ones in her dresser drawer, and had her DNA all over 'em. It's a wonderful thing, DNA."

"A miracle of modern forensic science."

"Why'd they even go to a motel in the first place? Why not take her to his place? He wasn't married, he had women in and out of his apartment all the time."

"Perhaps he didn't want to be seen with her."

"Long as I wasn't the one doing the seeing, what difference could it make?"

"None," Ehrengraf said, "unless he was afraid of what people might remember afterward."

Starkey thought about that. Then his eyes widened. "He planned it all along," he said.

"It certainly seems that way."

"Wanted to make damn sure he got my job, by seeing to it that I wasn't around to compete for it. He didn't just lose his temper when he smashed her head with that horse. It was all part of the plan—kill her and frame me for it."

"Diabolical," Ehrengraf said.

"That explains what he wrote on that note," Starkey said. "The one they found at the very back of her underwear drawer, arranging to meet that last day after practice. 'Make sure you burn this,' he wrote. And he didn't even sign it. But it was in his handwriting."

"So the experts say."

"And on a piece of his stationery. The top part was torn off, with his name and address on it, but it was the same brand of bond paper. It would have been nice if they could have found the piece he tore off and matched them up, but I guess you can't have everything."

"Perhaps they haven't looked hard enough," Ehrengraf murmured. "There was another note as well, as I recall. One that she wrote."

"On one of the printed memo slips with her name on it. A little love note from her to him, and he didn't have the sense to throw it out. Carried it around in his wallet."

"It was probably from early in their relationship," Ehrengraf said, "and very likely he'd forgotten it was there."

"He must have. It surprised the hell out of him when the cops went through his wallet and there it was."

"I imagine it did."

"He must have gone to my house straight from practice. Wouldn't have been a trick to get her out of her clothes, seeing as he'd been managing that all along. 'My, Claureen, isn't that a cute little horse.' 'Yes, it's French, it's over a hundred years old.' 'Is that right? Let me just get the feel of it.' And that's the end of Claureen. A shame he didn't leave a fingerprint or two on the horse just for good measure."

"You can't have everything," Ehrengraf said. "Wiping his prints off the horse would seem to be one of the few intelligent things Mr. Braden managed. But they can make a good case against him without it. Of course much depends on his choice of an attorney."

"Maybe he'll call you," Starkey said with a wink. "But I guess that wouldn't do him any good, seeing as you only represent the innocent. What I hear, he's fixing to put together a Proud Crowd of his own. Figure they'll get him off?"

"It may be difficult to convict him," Ehrengraf allowed, "but he's already been tried and found guilty in the court of public opinion."

"The league suspended him, and of course he's off the Mastodons' roster. But what's really amazing is the way everybody's turned around as far as I'm concerned. Before, I was a man who got away with killing two women, but they could live with that as long as I could put it all together on the field. Then I killed a third woman, and they flat out hated me, and then it turns out I *didn't* kill Claureen, I was an innocent man framed for it, and they did a full-scale turnaround, and the talk is maybe I really *was* innocent those other two times, just the way the two juries decided I was. All of a sudden there's a whole lot of people telling each other the system works and feeling real good about it."

"As well they might," said Ehrengraf.

"They cheer you when you catch a pass," Starkey said philosophically, "and they boo you when you drop one. Except for you, Mr. Ehrengraf, there wasn't a person around who believed I didn't do it. But you did, and you figured out how the evidence showed Claureen's death was accidental. Low blood sugar, too much exercise, and she got dizzy and fell and pulled the horse down on top of her."

"Yes."

"And then you figured out they'd never buy that, true or false. So you dug deeper."

"It was the only chance," Ehrengraf said modestly.

"And they might not buy that Claureen killed herself by accident, but they loved the idea that she was cheating on me and Clete killed her so I'd be nailed for it."

"The Ehrengraf reverse."

"How's that?"

"The Ehrengraf reverse. When the evidence is all running one way, you hand off the ball and sweep around the other end." He spread his hands. "And streak down the sideline and into the end zone."

"Touchdown," Starkey said. "We win, and Braden's the goat and I'm the hero."

"As you clearly were on Sunday."

"I guess I had a pretty decent game."

"Eight pass receptions, almost two hundred yards rushing—yes, I'd say you had a good game."

"Say, were those seats okay?"

"Row M on the fifty-yard line? They were the best seats in the stadium."

"It was a beautiful day for it, too, wasn't it? And I couldn't do a thing wrong. Oh, next week I'll probably fumble three times and run into my own blockers a lot, but I'll have this one to remember."

Ehrengraf took the game ball in his hands. "And so will I," he said.

"Well, I wanted you to have a souvenir. And the bonus, well, I got more money coming in these days than I ever figured to see. Every time the phone rings it's another product endorsement coming my way, and I don't have to wait too long between rings, either. Hey, speaking of the reverse, how'd you like the one we ran Sunday?"

"Beautiful," Ehrengraf said fervently. "A work of art."

"You know, I was thinking of you when they called it in the huddle. Fact, when the defense was on the field I asked the coach if we couldn't run that play. Would have served me right if I'd been dumped for a loss, but that's not what happened."

"You gained forty yards," Ehrengraf said, "and if that one man hadn't missed a downfield block, you'd have had another touchdown."

"Well, it's a pretty play," Blaine Starkey said. "There's really nothing like the reverse."

Bernie Rhodenbarr

Like a Thief in the Night

At 11:30 the television anchorman counseled her to stay tuned for the late show, a vintage Hitchcock film starring Cary Grant. For a moment she was tempted. Then she crossed the room and switched off the set.

There was a last cup of coffee in the pot. She poured it and stood at the window with it, a tall and slender woman, attractive, dressed in the suit and silk blouse she'd worn that day at the office. A woman who could look at once efficient and elegant, and who stood now sipping black coffee from a bone-china cup and gazing south and west.

Her apartment was on the twenty-second floor of a building located at the corner of Lexington Avenue and Seventy-sixth Street, and her vista was quite spectacular. A midtown skyscraper blocked her view of the building where Tavistock Corp. did its business, but she fancied she could see right through it with x-ray vision.

The cleaning crew would be finishing up now, she knew, returning their mops and buckets to the cupboards and changing into street clothes, preparing to go off-shift at midnight. They would leave a couple of lights on in Tavistock's seventeenth floor suite as well as elsewhere throughout the building. And the halls would remain lighted, and here and there in the building someone would be working all night, and—

She liked Hitchcock movies, especially the early ones, and she was in love with Cary Grant. But she also liked good clothes and bone-china cups and the view from her apartment and the comfortable, well-appointed apartment itself. And so she rinsed the cup in the sink and put on a coat and took the elevator to the lobby, where the florid-faced doorman made a great show of hailing her a cab.

There would be other nights, and other movies.

The taxi dropped her in front of an office building in the West Thirties. She pushed through the revolving door and her footsteps on the marble floor sounded impossibly loud to her. The security guard, seated at a small table by the bank of elevators, looked up from his magazine at her approach. She said, "Hello, Eddie," and gave him a quick smile.

"Hey, how ya doin'," he said, and she bent to sign herself in as his attention returned to his magazine. In the appropriate spaces she scribbled *Elaine Halder, Tavistock, 1704,* and, after a glance at her watch, *12:15.*

She got into a waiting elevator and the doors closed without a sound.

She'd be alone up there, she thought. She'd glanced at the record sheet while signing it, and no one had signed in for Tavistock or any other office on seventeen.

Well, she wouldn't be long.

When the elevator doors opened she stepped out and stood for a moment in the corridor, getting her bearings. She took a key from her purse and stared at it for a moment as if it were an artifact from some unfamiliar civilization. Then she turned and began walking the length of the freshly mopped corridor, hearing nothing but the echo of her boisterous footsteps.

1704. An oak door, a square of frosted glass, unmarked but for the suite number and the name of the company. She took another thoughtful glance at the key before fitting it carefully into the lock.

It turned easily. She pushed the door inward and stepped inside, letting the door swing shut behind her.

And gasped.

There was a man not a dozen yards from her.

"Hello," he said.

He was standing beside a rosewood-topped desk, the center drawer of which was open, and there was a spark in his eyes and a tentative smile on his lips. He was wearing a gray suit patterned in a windowpane check. His shirt collar was buttoned down, his narrow tie neatly knotted. He was two or three years older than she, she supposed, and perhaps that many inches taller.

Her hand was pressed to her breast, as if to still a pounding heart. But her heart wasn't really pounding. She managed a smile. "You startled me," she said. "I didn't know anyone would be here."

"We're even."

"I beg your pardon?"

"I wasn't expecting company."

He had nice white even teeth, she noticed. She was apt to notice teeth. And he had an open and friendly face, which was also something she was inclined to notice, and why was she suddenly thinking of Cary Grant? The movie she hadn't seen, of course, that plus this Hollywood meet-cute opening, with the two of them encountering each other unexpectedly in this silent tomb of an office, and—

And he was wearing rubber gloves.

Her face must have registered something because he frowned, puzzled. Then he raised his hands and flexed his fingers. "Oh, these," he said. "Would it help if I spoke of an eczema brought on by exposure to the night air?"

"There's a lot of that going around."

"I knew you'd understand."

"You're a prowler."

"The word has the nastiest connotations," he objected. "One imagines a lot of lurking in shrubbery. There's no shrubbery here beyond the odd rubber plant and I wouldn't lurk in it if there were."

"A thief, then."

"A thief, yes. More specifically, a burglar. I might have stripped the gloves off when you stuck your key in the lock but I'd been so busy listening to your footsteps and hoping they'd lead to another office that I quite forgot I was wearing these things. Not that it would have made much difference. Another minute and you'd have realized that you've never set eyes on me before, and at that point you'd have wondered what I was doing here."

"What *are* you doing here?"

"My kid brother needs an operation."

"I thought that might be it. Surgery for his eczema."

He nodded. "Without it he'll never play the trumpet again. May I be permitted an observation?"

"I don't see why not."

"I observe that you're afraid of me."

"And here I thought I was doing such a super job of hiding it."

"You were, but I'm an incredibly perceptive human being. You're afraid I'll do something violent, that he who is capable of theft is equally capable of mayhem."

"Are you?"

"Not even in fantasy. I'm your basic pacifist. When I was a kid my favorite book was *Ferdinand the Bull*."

"I remember him. He didn't want to fight. He just wanted to smell the flowers."

"Can you blame him?" He smiled again, and the adverb that came to her was *disarmingly*. More like Alan Alda than Cary Grant, she decided. Well, that was all right. There was nothing wrong with Alan Alda.

"*You're* afraid of *me*," she said suddenly.

"How'd you figure that? A slight quiver in the old upper lip?"

"No. It just came to me. But why? What could I do to you?"

"You could call the, uh, cops."

"I wouldn't do that."

"And I wouldn't hurt you."

"I know you wouldn't."

"Well," he said, and sighed theatrically. "Aren't you glad we got all that out of the way?"

She was, rather. It was good to know that neither of them had anything to fear from the other. As if in recognition of this change in their relationship she took off her coat and hung it on the pipe rack, where a checked topcoat was already hanging. His, she assumed. How readily he made himself at home!

She turned to find he was making himself further at home, rummaging deliberately in the drawers of the desk. What cheek, she thought, and felt herself beginning to smile.

She asked him what he was doing.

"Foraging," he said, then drew himself up sharply. "This isn't your desk, is it?"

"No."

"Thank heaven for that."

"What were you looking for, anyway?"

He thought for a moment, then shook his head. "Nope," he said. "You'd think I could come up with a decent story but I can't. I'm looking for something to steal."

"Nothing specific?"

"I like to keep an open mind. I didn't come here to cart off the IBM Selectrics. But you'd be surprised how many people leave cash in their desks."

"And you just take what you find?"

He hung his head. "I know," he said. "It's a moral failing. You don't have to tell me."

"Do people really leave cash in an unlocked desk drawer?"

"Sometimes. And sometimes they lock the drawers, but that doesn't make them all that much harder to open."

"You can pick locks?"

"A limited and eccentric talent," he allowed, "but it's all I know."

"How did you get in here? I suppose you picked the office lock."

"Hardly a great challenge."

"But how did you get past Eddie?"

"Eddie? Oh, you must be talking about the chap in the lobby. He's not quite as formidable as the Berlin Wall, you know. I got here around eight. They tend to be less suspicious at an earlier hour. I scrawled a name on the sheet and walked on by. Then I found an empty office that they'd already finished cleaning and curled up on the couch for a nap."

"You're kidding."

"Have I ever lied to you in the past? The cleaning crew leaves at midnight. At about that time I let myself out of Mr. Higginbotham's office—that's where I've taken to napping, he's a patent attorney with the most comfortable old leather couch. And then I make my rounds."

She looked at him. "You've come to this building before."

"I stop by every little once in a while."

"You make it sound like a vending machine route."

"There are similarities, aren't there? I never looked at it that way."

"And then you make your rounds. You break into offices—"

"I never break anything. Let's say I let myself into offices."

"And you steal money from desks—"

"Also jewelry, when I run across it. Anything valuable and portable. Sometimes there's a safe. That saves a lot of looking around. You know right away that's where they keep the good stuff."

"And you can open safes?"

"Not every safe," he said modestly, "and not every single time, but—" he switched to a Cockney accent "—I has the touch, mum."

"And then what do you do? Wait until morning to leave?"

"What for? I'm well-dressed. I look respectable. Besides, security guards are posted to keep unauthorized persons out of a building, not to prevent them from leaving. It might be different if I tried rolling a Xerox machine through the lobby, but I don't steal anything that won't fit in my pockets or my attaché case. And I don't wear my rubber gloves when I saunter past the guard. That wouldn't do."

"I don't suppose it would. What do I call you?"

" 'That damned burglar,' I suppose. That's what everybody calls me. But you—" he extended a rubber-covered forefinger "—you may call me Bernie."

"Bernie the Burglar."

"And what shall I call you?"

"Elaine'll do."

"Elaine," he said. "Elaine, Elaine. Not Elaine Halder, by any chance?"

"How did you—?"

"Elaine Halder," he said. "And that explains what brings you to these offices in the middle of the night. You look startled. I can't imagine why. 'You know my methods, Watson.' What's the matter?"

"Nothing."

"Don't be frightened, for God's sake. Knowing your name doesn't give me mystical powers over your destiny. I just have a good memory and your name stuck in it." He crooked a thumb at a closed door on the far side of the room. "I've already been in the boss's office. I saw your note on his desk. I'm afraid I'll have to admit I read it. I'm a snoop. It's a serious character defect, I know."

"Like larceny."

"Something along those lines. Let's see now. Elaine Halder leaves the office, having placed on her boss's desk a letter of resignation. Elaine Halder returns in the small hours of the morning. A subtle pattern begins to emerge, my dear."

"Oh?"

"Of course. You've had second thoughts and you want to retrieve the letter before himself gets a chance to read it. Not a bad idea, given some of the choice things you had to say about him. Just let me open up for you, all right? I'm the tidy type and I locked up after I was through in there."

"Did you find anything to steal?"

"Eighty-five bucks and a pair of gold cuff links." He bent over the lock, probing its innards with a splinter of spring steel. "Nothing to write home about, but every little bit helps. I'm sure you have a key that fits this door—you had to in order to leave the resignation in the first place, didn't you? But how many chances do I get to show off? Not that a lock like this one presents much of a challenge, not to the nimble digits of Bernie the Burglar, and—ah, *there* we are!"

"Extraordinary."

"It's so seldom I have an audience."

He stood aside, held the door for her. On the threshold she was struck by the notion that there would be a dead body in the private office. George Tavistock himself, slumped over his desk with the figured hilt of a letter opener protruding from his back.

But of course there was no such thing. The office was devoid of clutter, let alone corpses, nor was there any sign that it had been lately burglarized.

A single sheet of paper lay on top of the desk blotter. She walked over, picked it up. Her eyes scanned its half dozen sentences as if she were reading them for the first time, then dropped to the elaborately styled signature, a far cry from the loose scrawl with which she'd signed the register in the lobby.

She read the note through again, then put it back where it had been.

"Not changing your mind again?"

She shook her head. "I never changed it in the first place. That's not why I came back here tonight."

"You couldn't have dropped in just for the pleasure of my company."

"I might have, if I'd known you were going to be here. No, I came back because—" She paused, drew a deliberate breath. "You might say I wanted to clean out my desk."

"Didn't you already do that? Isn't your desk right across there? The one with your name plate on it? Forward of me, I know, but I already had a peek, and the drawers bore a striking resemblance to the cupboard of one Ms. Hubbard."

"You went through my desk."

He spread his hands apologetically. "I meant nothing personal," he said. "At the time, I didn't even know you."

"That's a point."

"And searching an empty desk isn't that great a violation of privacy, is it? Nothing to be seen beyond paper clips and rubber bands and the odd felt-tipped pen. So if you've come to clean out that lot—"

"I meant it metaphorically," she explained. "There are things in this office that belong to me. Projects I worked on that I ought to have copies of to show to prospective employers."

"And won't Mr. Tavistock see to it that you get copies?"

She laughed sharply. "You don't know the man," she said.

"And thank God for that. I couldn't rob someone I knew."

"He would think I intended to divulge corporate secrets to the competition. The minute he reads my letter of resignation I'll be persona non grata in this office. I probably won't even be able to get into the building. I didn't even realize any of this until I'd gotten home tonight, and I didn't really know what to do, and then—"

"Then you decided to try a little burglary."

"Hardly that."

"Oh?"

"I have a key."

"And I have a cunning little piece of spring steel, and they both perform the signal function of admitting us where we have no right to be."

"But I work here!"

"Worked."

"My resignation hasn't been accepted yet. I'm still an employee."

"Technically. Still, you've come like a thief in the night. You may have signed in downstairs and let yourself in with a key, and you're not wearing gloves or padding around in crepe-soled shoes, but we're not all that different, you and I, are we?"

She set her jaw. "I have a right to the fruits of my labor," she said.

"And so have I, and heaven help the person whose property rights get in our way."

She walked around him to the three-drawer filing cabinet to the right of Tavistock's desk. It was locked.

She turned, but Bernie was already at her elbow. "Allow me," he said, and in no time at all he had tickled the locking mechanism and was drawing the top drawer open.

"Thank you," she said.

"Oh, don't thank me," he said. "Professional courtesy. No thanks required."

She was busy for the next thirty minutes, selecting documents from the filing cabinet and from Tavistock's desk, as well as a few items from the unlocked cabinets in the outer office. She ran everything through the Xerox copier and replaced the originals where she'd found them. While she was doing all this, her burglar friend worked his way through the office's remaining desks. He was in no evident hurry, and it struck her that he was deliberately dawdling so as not to finish before her.

Now and then she would look up from what she was doing to observe him at his work. Once she caught him looking at her, and when their eyes met he winked and smiled, and she felt her cheeks burning.

He was attractive, certainly. And unquestionably likable, and in no way intimidating. Nor did he come across like a criminal. His speech was that of an educated person, he had an eye for clothes, his manners were impeccable—

What on earth was she thinking of?

By the time she had finished she had an inch-thick sheaf of paper in a manila file folder. She slipped her coat on, tucked the folder under her arm.

"You're certainly neat," he said. "A place for everything and everything right back in its place. I like that."

"Well, you're that way yourself, aren't you? You even take the trouble to lock up after yourself."

"It's not that much trouble. And there's a point to it. If one doesn't leave a mess, sometimes it takes them weeks to realize they've been robbed. The longer it takes, the less chance anybody'll figure out whodunit."

"And here I thought you were just naturally neat."

"As it happens I am, but it's a professional asset. Of course your neatness has much the same purpose, doesn't it? They'll never know you've been here tonight, especially since you haven't actually taken anything away with you. Just copies."

"That's right."

"Speaking of which, would you care to put them in my attaché case? So that you aren't noticed leaving the building with them in hand? I'll grant you the chap downstairs wouldn't notice an earthquake if it registered less than seven-point-four on the Richter scale, but it's that seemingly pointless attention to detail that enables me to persist in my chosen occupation instead of making license plates and sewing mail sacks as a guest of the governor. Are you ready, Elaine? Or would you like to take one last look around for auld lang syne?"

"I've had my last look around. And I'm not much on auld lang syne."

He held the door for her, switched off the overhead lights, drew the door shut. While she locked it with her key he stripped off his rubber gloves and put them in the attaché case where her papers reposed. Then, side by side, they walked the length of the corridor to the elevator. Her footsteps echoed. His, cushioned by his crepe soles, were quite soundless.

Hers stopped, too, when they reached the elevator, and they waited in silence. They had met, she thought, as thieves in the night, and now they were going to pass like ships in the night.

The elevator came, floated them down to the lobby. The lobby guard looked up at them, neither recognition nor interest showing in his eyes. She said, "Hi, Eddie. Everything going all right?"

"Hey, how ya doin'," he said.

There were only three entries below hers on the register sheet, three persons who'd arrived after her. She signed herself out, listing the time after a glance at her watch: 1:56. She'd been upstairs for better than an hour and a half.

Outside, the wind had an edge to it. She turned to him, glanced at his attaché case, suddenly remembered the first school boy who'd carried her books. She could surely have carried her own books, just as she could have safely carried the folder of papers past Eagle-eye Eddie.

Still, it was not unpleasant to have one's books carried.

"Well," she began, "I'd better take my papers, and—"

"Where are you headed?"

"Seventy-sixth Street."

"East or west?"

"East. But—"

"We'll share a cab," he said. "Compliments of petty cash." And he was at the curb, a hand raised, and a cab appeared as if conjured up and then he was holding the door for her.

She got in.

"Seventy-sixth," he told the driver. "And what?"

"Lexington," she said.

"Lexington," he said.

Her mind raced during the taxi ride. It was all over the place and she couldn't keep up with it. She felt in turn like a schoolgirl, like a damsel in peril, like Grace Kelly in a Hitchcock film. When the cab reached her corner she indicated her building, and he leaned forward to relay the information to the driver.

"Would you like to come up for coffee?"

The line had run through her mind like a mantra in the course of the ride. Yet she couldn't believe she was actually speaking the words.

"Yes," he said. "I'd like that."

She steeled herself as they approached her doorman, but the man was discretion personified. He didn't even greet her by name, merely holding the door for her and her escort and wishing them a good night. Upstairs, she thought of demanding that Bernie open her door without the keys, but decided she didn't want any demonstrations just then of her essential vulnerability. She unlocked the several locks herself.

"I'll make coffee," she said. "Or would you just as soon have a drink?"

"Sounds good."

"Scotch? Or cognac?"

"Cognac."

While she was pouring the drinks he walked around her living room, looking at the pictures on the walls and the books on the shelves. Guests did this sort of thing all the time, but this particular guest was a criminal, after all, and so she imagined him taking a burglar's inventory of her possessions. That Chagall aquatint he was studying—she'd paid five hundred for it at auction and it was probably worth close to three times that by now.

Surely he'd have better luck foraging in her apartment than in a suite of deserted offices.

Surely he'd realize as much himself.

She handed him his brandy. "To criminal enterprise," he said, and she raised her glass in response.

"I'll give you those papers. Before I forget."

"All right."

He opened the attaché case, handed them over. She placed the folder on the LaVerne coffee table and carried her brandy across to the window. The deep carpet muffled her footsteps as effectively as if she'd been wearing crepe-soled shoes.

You have nothing to be afraid of, she told herself. *And you're not afraid, and—*

"An impressive view," he said, close behind her.

"Yes."

"You could see your office from here. If that building weren't in the way."

"I was thinking that earlier."

"Beautiful," he said, softly, and then his arms were encircling her from behind and his lips were on the nape of her neck.

" 'Elaine the fair, Elaine the lovable,' " he quoted. " 'Elaine, the lily maid of Astolat.' " His lips nuzzled her ear. "But you must hear that all the time."

She smiled. "Oh, not so often," she said. "Less often than you'd think."

The sky was just growing light when he left. She lay alone for a few minutes, then went to lock up after him.

And laughed aloud when she found that he'd locked up after himself, without a key.

It was late but she didn't think she'd ever been less tired. She put up a fresh pot of coffee, poured a cup when it was ready, and sat at the kitchen table reading through the papers she'd taken from the office. She wouldn't have had half of them without Bernie's assistance, she realized. She could never have opened the file cabinet in Tavistock's office.

"*Elaine the fair, Elaine the lovable. Elaine, the lily maid of Astolat.*"

She smiled.

A few minutes after nine, when she was sure Jennings Colliard would be at his desk, she dialed his private number.

"It's Andrea," she told him. "I succeeded beyond our wildest dreams. I've got copies of Tavistock's complete marketing plan for fall and winter, along with a couple of dozen test and survey reports and a lot of other documents you'll want a chance to analyze. And I put all the originals back where they came from, so nobody at Tavistock'll ever know what happened."

"Remarkable."

"I thought you'd approve. Having a key to their office helped, and knowing the doorman's name didn't hurt any. Oh, and I also have some news that's worth knowing. I don't know if George Tavistock is in his office yet, but if so he's reading a letter of resignation even as we speak. The Lily Maid of Astolat has had it."

"What are you talking about, Andrea?"

"Elaine Halder. She cleaned out her desk and left him a note saying bye-bye. I thought you'd like to be the first kid on your block to know that."

"And of course you're right."

"I'd come in now but I'm exhausted. Do you want to send a messenger over?"

"Right away. And you get some sleep."

"I intend to."

"You've done spectacularly well, Andrea. There will be something extra in your stocking."

"I thought there might be," she said.

She hung up the phone and stood once again at the window, looking out at the city, reviewing the night's events. It had been quite perfect, she decided, and if there was the slightest flaw it was that she'd missed the Cary Grant movie.

But it would be on again soon. They ran it frequently. People evidently liked that sort of thing.

The Burglar Who Dropped In on Elvis

"I know who you are," she said. "Your name is Bernie Rhodenbarr. You're a burglar."

I glanced around, glad that the store was empty save for the two of us. It often is, but I'm not usually glad about it.

"Was," I said.

"Was?"

"Was. Past tense. I had a criminal past, and while I'd as soon keep it a secret I can't deny it. But I'm an antiquarian bookseller now, Miss Uh—"

"Danahy," she supplied. "Holly Danahy."

"Miss Danahy. A dealer in the wisdom of the ages. The errors of my youth are to be regretted, even deplored, but they're over and done with."

She gazed thoughtfully at me. She was a lovely creature, slender, pert, bright of eye and inquisitive of nose, and she wore a tailored suit and flowing bow tie that made her look at once yieldingly feminine and as coolly competent as a Luger.

"I think you're lying," she said. "I certainly hope so. Because an antiquarian bookseller is no good at all to me. What I need is a burglar."

"I wish I could help you."

"You can." She laid a cool-fingered hand on mine. "It's almost closing time. Why don't you lock up? I'll buy you a drink and tell you how you can qualify for an all-expenses-paid trip to Memphis. And possibly a whole lot more."

"You're not trying to sell me a time-share in a thriving lakeside resort community, are you?"

"Not hardly."

"Then what have I got to lose? The thing is, I usually have a drink after work with—"

"Carolyn Kaiser," she cut in. "Your best friend, she washes dogs two doors down the street at the Poodle Factory. You can call her and cancel."

My turn to gaze thoughtfully. "You seem to know a lot about me," I said.

"Sweetie," she said, "that's my *job*."

"I'm a reporter," she said. "For the *Weekly Galaxy*. If you don't know the paper, you must never get to the supermarket."

"I know it," I said. "But I have to admit I'm not what you'd call one of your regular readers."

"Well, I should hope not, Bernie. Our readers move their lips when they think. Our readers write letters in crayon because they're not allowed to have anything sharp. Our readers make the *Enquirer's* readers look like Rhodes scholars. Our readers, face it, are D-U-M."

"Then why would they want to know about me?"

"They wouldn't, unless an extraterrestrial made you pregnant. That happen to you?"

"No, but Bigfoot ate my car."

She shook her head. "We already did that story. Last August, I think it was. The car was an AMC Gremlin with a hundred and ninety-two thousand miles on it."

"I suppose its time had come."

"That's what the owner said. He's got a new BMW now, thanks to the *Galaxy*. He can't spell it, but he can drive it like crazy."

I looked at her over the brim of my glass. "If you don't want to write about me," I said, "what do you need me for?"

"Ah, Bernie," she said. "Bernie the burglar. Sweetie pie, you're my ticket to Elvis."

"The best possible picture," I told Carolyn, "would be a shot of Elvis in his coffin. The *Galaxy* loves shots like that but in this case it would be counterproductive in the long run, because it might kill their big story, the one they run month after month."

"Which is that he's still alive."

"Right. Now the second-best possible picture, and better for their purposes overall, would be a shot of him alive, singing 'Love Me Tender' to a visitor from another planet. They get a chance at that picture every couple of days, and it's always some Elvis impersonator. Do you know how many full-time professional Elvis Presley impersonators there are in America today?"

"No."

"Neither do I, but I have a feeling Holly Danahy could probably supply a figure, and that it would be an impressive one. Anyway, the third-best possible picture, and the one she seems to want almost more than life itself, is a shot of the King's bedroom."

"At Graceland?"

"That's the one. Six thousand people visit Graceland every day. Two million of them walked through it last year."

"And none of them brought a camera?"

"Don't ask me how many cameras they brought, or how many rolls of film they shot. Or how many souvenir ashtrays and paintings on black velvet they bought and took home with them. But how many of them got above the first floor?"

"How many?"

"None. Nobody gets to go upstairs at Graceland. The staff isn't allowed up there, and people who've worked there for years have never set foot above the ground floor. And you can't bribe your way up there, either, according to Holly, and she knows because she tried, and she had all the *Galaxy*'s resources to play with. Two million people a year go to Graceland, and they'd all love to know what it looks like upstairs, and the *Weekly Galaxy* would just love to show them."

"Enter a burglar."

"That's it. That's Holly's masterstroke, the one designed to win her a bonus and a promotion. Enter an expert at illegal entry, i.e., a burglar. *Le* burglar, *c'est moi.* Name your price, she told me."

"And what did you tell her?"

"Twenty-five thousand dollars. You know why? All I could think of was that it sounded like a job for Nick Velvet. You remember him, the thief in the Ed Hoch stories who'll only steal worthless objects." I sighed. "When I think of all the worthless objects I've stolen over the years, and never once has anyone offered to pay me a fee of twenty-five grand for my troubles. Anyway, that was the price that popped into my head, so I tried it out on her. And she didn't even try to haggle."

"I think Nick Velvet raised his rates," Carolyn said. "I think his price went up in the last story or two."

I shook my head. "You see what happens? You fall behind on your reading and it costs you money."

Holly and I flew first class from JFK to Memphis. The meal was still airline food, but the seats were so comfortable and the stewardess so attentive that I kept forgetting this.

"At the *Weekly Galaxy*," Holly said, sipping an after-dinner something-or-other, "everything's first class. Except the paper itself, of course."

We got our luggage, and a hotel courtesy car whisked us to the Howard Johnson's on Elvis Presley Boulevard, where we had adjoining rooms reserved. I was just about unpacked when Holly knocked on the door separating the two rooms. I unlocked it for her and she came in carrying a bottle of scotch and a full ice bucket.

"I wanted to stay at the Peabody," she said. "That's the great old downtown hotel and it's supposed to be wonderful, but here we're only a couple of blocks from Graceland, and I thought it would be more convenient."

"Makes sense," I agreed.

"But I wanted to see the ducks," she said. She explained that ducks were the symbol of the Peabody, or the mascot, or something. Every day the hotel's guests could watch the hotel's ducks waddle across the red carpet to the fountain in the middle of the lobby.

"Tell me something," she said. "How does a guy like you get into a business like this?"

"Bookselling?"

"Get real, honey. How'd you get to be a burglar? Not for the edification of our readers, because they couldn't care less. But to satisfy my own curiosity."

I sipped a drink while I told her the story of my misspent life, or as much of it as I felt like telling. She heard me out and put away four stiff scotches in the process, but if they had any effect on her I couldn't see it.

"And how about you?" I said after a while. "How did a nice girl like you—"

"Oh, Gawd," she said. "We'll save that for another evening, okay?" And then she was in my arms, smelling and feeling better than a body had a right to, and just as quickly she was out of them again and on her way to the door.

"You don't have to go," I said.

"Ah, but I do, Bernie. We've got a big day tomorrow. We're going to see Elvis, remember?"

She took the scotch with her. I poured out what remained of my own drink, finished unpacking, took a shower. I got into bed, and after fifteen or twenty minutes I got up and tried the door between our two rooms, but she had locked it on her side. I went back to bed.

Our tour guide's name was Stacy. She wore the standard Graceland uniform, a blue-and-white-striped shirt over navy chinos, and she looked like someone who'd been unable to decide whether to become a stewardess or a cheerleader. Cleverly, she'd chosen a job that combined both professions.

"There were generally a dozen guests crowded around this dining table," she told us. "Dinner was served nightly between nine and ten P.M., and Elvis always sat right there at the head of the table. Not because he was head of the family but because it gave him the best view of the big color TV. Now that's one of fourteen TV sets here at Graceland, so you know how much Elvis liked to watch TV."

"Was that the regular china?" someone wanted to know.

"Yes, ma'am, and the name of the pattern is Buckingham. Isn't it pretty?"

I could run down the whole tour for you, but what's the point? Either you've been there yourself or you're planning to go or you don't care, and at the rate people are signing up for the tours, I don't think there are many of you in the last group. Elvis was a good pool player, and his favorite game was rotation. Elvis ate his breakfast in the Jungle Room, off a cypress coffee table. Elvis's own favorite singer was Dean Martin. Elvis liked peacocks, and at one time over a dozen of them roamed the grounds of Graceland. Then they started eating the paint off the cars, which Elvis liked even more than he liked peacocks, so he donated them to the Memphis Zoo. The peacocks, not the cars.

There was a gold rope across the mirrored staircase, and what looked like an electric eye a couple of stairs up. "We don't allow tourists into the upstairs," our guide chirped. "Remember, Graceland is a private home and Elvis's aunt Miss Delta Biggs still lives here. Now I can tell you what's upstairs. Elvis's bedroom is located directly above the living room and music room. His office is also upstairs, and there's Lisa Marie's bedroom, and dressing rooms and bathrooms as well."

"And does his aunt live up there?" someone asked.

"No, sir. She lives downstairs, through that door over to your left. None of us have ever been upstairs. Nobody goes there anymore."

"I bet he's up there now," Holly said. "In a La-Z-Boy with his feet up, eating one of his famous peanut-butter and banana sandwiches and watching three television sets at once."

"And listening to Dean Martin," I said. "What do you really think?"

"What do I really think? I think he's down in Paraguay playing three-handed pinochle with James Dean and Adolf Hitler. Did you know that Hitler masterminded Argentina's invasion of the Falkland Islands? We ran that story but it didn't do as well as we hoped."

"Your readers didn't remember Hitler?"

"Hitler was no problem for them. But they didn't know what the Falklands were. Seriously, where do I think Elvis is? I think he's in the grave we just looked at, surrounded by his nearest and dearest. Unfortunately, 'Elvis Still Dead' is not a headline that sells papers."

"I guess not."

We were back in my room at the HoJo, eating a lunch Holly had ordered from room service. It reminded me of our in-flight meal the day before, luxurious but not terribly good.

"Well," she said brightly, "have you figured out how we're going to get in?"

"You saw the place," I said. "They've got gates and guards and alarm systems everywhere. I don't know what's upstairs, but it's a more closely guarded secret than Zsa Zsa Gabor's true age."

"That'd be easy to find out," Holly said. "We could just hire somebody to marry her."

"Graceland is impregnable," I went on, hoping we could drop the analogy right there. "It's almost as bad as Fort Knox."

Her face fell. "I was sure you could find a way in."

"Maybe I can."

"But—"

"For one. Not for two. It'd be too risky for you, and you don't have the skills for it. Could you shinny down a gutterspout?"

"If I had to."

"Well, you won't have to, because you won't be going in." I paused for thought. "You'd have a lot of work to do," I said. "On the outside, coordinating things."

"I can handle it."

"And there would be expenses, plenty of them."

"No problem."

"I'd need a camera that can take pictures in full dark. I can't risk a flash."

"That's easy. We can handle that."

"I'll need to rent a helicopter, and I'll have to pay the pilot enough to guarantee his silence."

"A cinch."

"I'll need a diversion. Something fairly dramatic."

"I can create a diversion. With all the resources of the *Galaxy* at my disposal, I could divert a river."

"That shouldn't be necessary. But all of this is going to cost money."

"Money," she said, "is no object."

"So you're a friend of Carolyn's," Lucian Leeds said. "She's wonderful, isn't she? You know, she and I are the next-closest thing to blood kin."

"Oh?"

"A former lover of hers and a former lover of mine were brother and sister. Well, sister and brother, actually. So that makes Carolyn my something-in-law, doesn't it?"

"I guess it must."

"Of course," he said, "by the same token, I must be related to half the known world. Still, I'm real fond of our Carolyn. And if I can help you—"

I told him what I needed. Lucian Leeds was an interior decorator and a dealer in art and antiques. "Of course I've been to Graceland," he said. "Probably a dozen times, because whenever a friend or relative visits that's where one has to take them. It's an experience that somehow never palls."

"I don't suppose you've ever been on the second floor."

"No, nor have I been presented at court. Of the two, I suppose I'd prefer the second floor at Graceland. One can't help wondering, can one?" He closed his eyes, concentrating. "My imagination is beginning to work," he announced.

"Give it free rein."

"I know just the house, too. It's off Route 51 across the state line, just this side of Hernando, Mississippi. Oh, and I know someone with an Egyptian piece that would be perfect. How soon would everything have to be ready?"

"Tomorrow night?"

"Impossible. The day after tomorrow is barely possible. Just barely. I really ought to have a week to do it right."

"Well, do it as right as you can."

"I'll need trucks and schleppers, of course. I'll have rental charges to pay, of course, and I'll have to give something to the old girl who owns the house. First I'll have to sweet-talk her, but there'll have to be something tangible in it for her as well, I'm afraid. But all of this is going to cost you money."

That had a familiar ring to it. I almost got caught up in the rhythm of it and told him money was no object, but I managed to restrain myself. If money wasn't the object, what was I doing in Memphis?

"Here's the camera," Holly said. "It's all loaded with infrared film. No flash, and you can take pictures with it at the bottom of a coal mine."

"That's good," I said, "because that's probably where I'll wind up if they catch me. We'll do it the day after tomorrow. Today's what, Wednesday? I'll go in Friday."

"I should be able to give you a terrific diversion."

"I hope so," I said. "I'll probably need it."

Thursday morning I found my helicopter pilot. "Yeah, I could do it," he said. "Cost you two hundred dollars, though."

"I'll give you five hundred."

He shook his head. "One thing I never do," he said, "is get to haggling over prices. I said two hundred, and—wait a darn minute."

"Take all the time you need."

"You weren't haggling me down," he said. "You were haggling me up. I never heard tell of such a thing."

"I'm willing to pay extra," I said, "so that you'll tell people the right story afterward. If anybody asks."

"What do you want me to tell 'em?"

"That somebody you never met before in your life paid you to fly over Graceland, hover over the mansion, lower your rope ladder, raise the ladder, and then fly away."

He thought about this for a full minute. "But that's what you said you wanted me to do," he said.

"I know."

"So you're fixing to pay me an extra three hundred dollars just to tell people the truth."

"If anybody should ask."

"You figure they will?"

"They might," I said. "It would be best if you said it in such a way that they thought you were lying."

"Nothing to it," he said. "Nobody ever believes a word I say. I'm a pretty honest guy, but I guess I don't look it."

"You don't," I said. "That's why I picked you."

That night Holly and I dressed up and took a cab downtown to the Peabody. The restaurant there was named Dux, and they had *canard aux cerises* on the menu, but it seemed curiously sacrilegious to have it there. We both ordered the blackened redfish. She had two dry Rob Roys first, most of the dinner wine, and a

Stinger afterward. I had a Bloody Mary for openers, and my after-dinner drink was a cup of coffee. I felt like a cheap date.

Afterward we went back to my room and she worked on the scotch while we discussed strategy. From time to time she would put her drink down and kiss me, but as soon as things threatened to get interesting she'd draw away and cross her legs and pick up her pencil and notepad and reach for her drink.

"You're a tease," I said.

"I am not," she insisted. "But I want to, you know, save it."

"For the wedding?"

"For the celebration. After we get the pictures, after we carry the day. You'll be the conquering hero and I'll throw roses at your feet."

"Roses?"

"And myself. I figured we could take a suite at the Peabody and never leave the room except to see the ducks. You know, we never did see the ducks do their famous walk. Can't you just picture them waddling across the red carpet and quacking their heads off?"

"Can't you just picture what they go through cleaning that carpet?"

She pretended not to have heard me. "I'm glad we didn't have duckling," she said. "It would have seemed cannibalistic." She fixed her eyes on me. She'd had enough booze to induce coma in a six-hundred-pound gorilla, but her eyes looked as clear as ever. "Actually," she said, "I'm very strongly attracted to you, Bernie. But I want to wait. You can understand that, can't you?"

"I could," I said gravely, "if I knew I was coming back."

"What do you mean?"

"It would be great to be the conquering hero," I said, "and find you and the roses at my feet, but suppose I come home on my shield instead? I could get killed out there."

"Are you serious?"

"Think of me as a kid who enlisted the day after Pearl Harbor, Holly. And you're his girlfriend, asking him to wait until the war's over. Holly, what if that kid doesn't come home? What if he leaves his bones bleaching on some little hellhole in the South Pacific?"

"Oh my God," she said. "I never thought of that." She put down her pencil and notebook. "You're right, dammit. I *am* a tease. I'm worse than that." She uncrossed her legs. "I'm thoughtless and heartless. Oh, Bernie!"

"There, there," I said.

Graceland closes every evening at six. At precisely five-thirty Friday afternoon, a girl named Moira Beth Calloway detached herself from her tour group. "I'm coming, Elvis!" she cried, and she lowered her head and ran full speed for the staircase. She was over the gold rope and on the sixth step before the first guard laid a hand on her.

Bells rang, sirens squealed, and all hell broke loose. "Elvis is calling me," Moira

Beth insisted, her eyes rolling wildly. "He needs me, he wants me, he loves me tender. Get your hands off me. Elvis! I'm coming, Elvis!"

I.D. in Moira Beth's purse supplied her name and indicated that she was seventeen years old, and a student at Mount St. Joseph Academy in Millington, Tennessee. This was not strictly true, in that she was actually twenty-two years old, a member of Actors Equity, and a resident of Brooklyn Heights. Her name was not Moira Beth Calloway, either. It was (and still is) Rona Jellicoe. I think it may have been something else in the dim dark past before it became Rona Jellicoe, but who cares?

While a variety of people, many of them wearing navy chinos and blue-and-white-striped shirts, did what they could to calm down Moira Beth, a middle-aged couple in the Pool Room went into their act. "Air!" the man cried, clutching at his throat. "Air! I can't breathe!" And he fell down, flailing at the wall, where Stacy had told us some 750 yards of pleated fabric had been installed.

"Help him," cried his wife. "He can't breathe! He's dying! He needs *air*!" And she ran to the nearest window and heaved it open, setting off whatever alarms hadn't already been shrieking over Moira Beth's assault on the staircase.

Meanwhile, in the TV room, done in the exact shades of yellow and blue used in Cub Scout uniforms, a gray squirrel had raced across the rug and was now perched on top of the jukebox. "Look at that awful squirrel!" a woman was screaming. "Somebody get that squirrel! He's gonna kill us all!"

Her fear would have been harder to credit if people had known that the poor rodent had entered Graceland in her handbag, and that she'd been able to release it without being seen because of the commotion in the other room. Her fear was contagious, though, and the people who caught it weren't putting on an act.

In the Jungle Room, where Elvis's *Moody Blue* album had actually been recorded, a woman fainted. She'd been hired to do just that, but other unpaid fainters were dropping like flies all over the mansion. And, while all of this activity was hitting its absolute peak, a helicopter made its noisy way through the sky over Graceland, hovering for several long minutes over the roof.

The security staff at Graceland couldn't have been better. Almost immediately two men emerged from a shed carrying an extension ladder, and in no time at all they had it propped against the side of the building. One of them held it while the other scrambled up it to the roof.

By the time he got there, the helicopter was going *pocketa-pocketa-pocketa*, and disappearing off to the west. The security man raced around the roof but didn't see anyone. Within the next ten minutes, two others joined him on the roof and searched it thoroughly. They found a tennis sneaker, but that was all they found.

At a quarter to five the next morning I let myself into my room at the Howard Johnson's and knocked on the door to Holly's room. There was no response. I knocked again, louder, then gave up and used the phone. I could hear it ringing in her room, but evidently she couldn't.

So I used the skills God gave me and opened her door. She was sprawled out on the bed, with her clothes scattered where she had flung them. The trail of clothing began at the scotch bottle on top of the television set. The set was on, and some guy with a sport jacket and an Ipana smile was explaining how you could get cash advances on your credit cards and buy penny stocks, an enterprise that struck me as a lot riskier than burglarizing mansions by helicopter.

Holly didn't want to wake up, but when I got past the veil of sleep she came to as if transistorized. One moment she was comatose and the next she was sitting up, eyes bright, an expectant look on her face. "Well?" she demanded.

"I shot the whole roll."

"You got in."

"Uh-huh."

"And you got out."

"Right again."

"And you got the pictures." She clapped her hands, giddy with glee. "I knew it," she said. "I was a positive genius to think of you. Oh, they ought to give me a bonus, a raise, a promotion, oh, I bet I get a company Cadillac next year instead of a lousy Chevy, oh, I'm on a roll, Bernie, I swear I'm on a roll!"

"That's great."

"You're limping," she said. "Why are you limping? Because you've only got one shoe on, that's why. What happened to your other shoe?"

"I lost it on the roof."

"God," she said. She got off the bed and began picking up her clothes from the floor and putting them on, following the trail back to the scotch bottle, which evidently had one drink left in it. "Ahhhh," she said, putting it down empty. "You know, when I saw them race up the ladder I thought you were finished. How did you get away from them?"

"It wasn't easy."

"I bet. And you managed to get down onto the second floor? And into his bedroom? What's it like?"

"I don't know."

"You don't *know*? Weren't you in there?"

"Not until it was pitch-dark. I hid in a hall closet and locked myself in. They gave the place a pretty thorough search but nobody had a key to the closet. I don't think there is one, I locked it by picking it. I let myself out somewhere around two in the morning and found my way into the bedroom. There was enough light to keep from bumping into things but not enough to tell what it was I wasn't bumping into. I just walked around pointing the camera and shooting."

She wanted more details, but I don't think she paid very much attention to them. I was in the middle of a sentence when she picked up the phone and made a plane reservation to Miami.

"They've got me on a ten-twenty flight," she said. "I'll get these right into the office and we'll get a check out to you as soon as they're developed. What's the matter?"

"I don't think I want a check," I said. "And I don't want to give you the film without getting paid."

"Oh, come on," she said. "You can trust us, for God's sake."

"Why don't you trust me instead?"

"You mean pay you without seeing what we're paying for? Bernie, you're a burglar. How can I trust you?"

"You're the *Weekly Galaxy*," I said. "*Nobody* can trust you."

"You've got a point," she said.

"We'll get the film developed here," I said. "I'm sure there are some good commercial photo labs in Memphis and that they can handle infrared film. First you'll call your office and have them wire cash here or set up an interbank transfer, and as soon as you see what's on the film you can hand over the money. You can even fax them one of the prints first to get approval, if you think that'll make a difference."

"Oh, they'll love that," she said. "My boss loves it when I fax him stuff."

"And that's what happened," I told Carolyn. "The pictures came out really beautifully. I don't know how Lucian Leeds turned up all those Egyptian pieces, but they looked great next to the 1940s Wurlitzer jukebox and the seven-foot statue of Mickey Mouse. I thought Holly was going to die of happiness when she realized the thing next to Mickey was a sarcophagus. She couldn't decide which tack to take—that he's mummified and they're keeping him in it or he's alive and really weird and uses it for a bed."

"Maybe they can have a reader poll. Call a nine hundred number and vote."

"You wouldn't believe how loud helicopters are when you're inside them. I just dropped the ladder and pulled it back in again. And tossed an extra sneaker on the roof."

"And wore its mate when you saw Holly."

"Yeah, I thought a little verisimilitude wouldn't hurt. The chopper pilot dropped me back at the hangar and I caught a ride down to the Burrell house in Mississippi, I walked around the room Lucian decorated for the occasion, admired everything, then turned out all the lights and took my pictures. They'll be running the best ones in the *Galaxy*."

"And you got paid."

"Twenty-five grand, and everybody's happy, and I didn't cheat anybody or steal anything. The *Galaxy* got some great pictures that'll sell a lot of copies of their horrible paper. The readers get a peek at a room no one has ever seen before."

"And the folks at Graceland?"

"They get a good security drill," I said. "Holly created a peach of a diversion to hide my entering the building. What it hid, of course, was my not entering the building, and that fact should stay hidden forever. Most of the Graceland people have never seen Elvis's bedroom, so they'll think the photos are legit. The few who know better will just figure my pictures didn't come out, or that they weren't exciting enough so the *Galaxy* decided to run fakes instead. Everybody with any sense figures the whole paper's a fake anyway, so what difference does it make?"

"Was Holly a fake?"

"Not really. I'd say she's an authentic specimen of what she is. Of course her little fantasy about a hot weekend watching the ducks blew away with the morning mist. All she wanted to do was get back to Florida and collect her bonus."

"So it's just as well you got your bonus ahead of time. You'll hear from her again the next time the *Galaxy* needs a burglar."

"Well, I'd do it again," I said. "My mother was always hoping I'd go into journalism. I wouldn't have waited so long if I'd known it would be so much fun."

"Yeah," she said.

"What's the matter?"

"Nothing, Bern."

"Come on. What is it?"

"Oh, I don't know. I just wish, you know, that you'd gone in there and got the real pictures. He could be in there, Bern. I mean, why else would they make such a big thing out of keeping people out of there? Did you ever stop to ask yourself that?"

"Carolyn—"

"I know," she said. "You think I'm nuts. But there are a lot of people like me, Bern."

"It's a good thing," I told her. "Where would the *Galaxy* be without you?"

The Burglar Who Smelled Smoke

(with Lynne Wood Block)

I was gearing up to poke the bell a second time when the door opened. I'd been expecting Karl Bellermann, and instead I found myself facing a woman with soft blonde hair framing an otherwise severe, high-cheekboned face. She looked as if she'd been repeatedly disappointed in life but was damned if she would let it get to her.

I gave my name and she nodded in recognition. "Yes, Mr. Rhodenbarr," she said. "Karl is expecting you. I can't disturb him now as he's in the library with his books. If you'll come into the sitting room I'll bring you some coffee, and Karl will be with you in—" she consulted her watch "—in just twelve minutes."

In twelve minutes it would be noon, which was when Karl had told me to arrive. I'd taken a train from New York and a cab from the train station, and good connections had got me there twelve minutes early, and evidently I could damn well cool my heels for all twelve of those minutes.

I was faintly miffed, but I wasn't much surprised. Karl Bellermann, arguably the country's leading collector of crime fiction, had taken a cue from one of the genre's greatest creations, Rex Stout's incomparable Nero Wolfe. Wolfe, an orchid fancier, spent an inviolate two hours in the morning and two hours in the afternoon with his plants, and would brook no disturbance at such times. Bellermann, no more flexible in real life than Wolfe was in fiction, scheduled even longer sessions with his books, and would neither greet visitors nor take phone calls while communing with them.

The sitting room where the blonde woman led me was nicely appointed, and the chair where she planted me was comfortable enough. The coffee she poured was superb, rich and dark and winy. I picked up the latest issue of *Ellery Queen* and was halfway through a new Peter Lovesey story and just finishing my second cup of coffee when the door opened and Karl Bellermann strode in.

"Bernie," he said. "Bernie Rhodenbarr."

"Karl."

"So good of you to come. You had no trouble finding us?"

"I took a taxi from the train station. The driver knew the house."

He laughed. "I'll bet he did. And I'll bet I know what he called it. 'Bellermann's Folly,' yes?"

"Well," I said.

"Please, don't spare my feelings. That's what all the local rustics call it. They hold in contempt that which they fail to understand. To their eyes, the architecture is overly ornate, and too much a mixture of styles, at once a Rhenish castle and an alpine chalet. And the library dwarfs the rest of the house, like the tail that wags the dog. Your driver is very likely a man who owns a single book, the Bible given to him for Confirmation and unopened ever since. That a man might choose to devote to his books the greater portion of his house—and, indeed, the greater portion of his life—could not fail to strike him as an instance of remarkable eccentricity." His eyes twinkled. "Although he might phrase it differently."

Indeed he had. "The guy's a nut case," the driver had reported confidently. "One look at his house and you'll see for yourself. He's only eating with one chopstick."

A few minutes later I sat down to lunch with Karl Bellermann, and there were no chopsticks in evidence. He ate with a fork, and he was every bit as agile with it as the fictional orchid fancier. Our meal consisted of a crown loin of pork with roasted potatoes and braised cauliflower, and Bellermann put away a second helping of everything.

I don't know where he put it. He was a long lean gentleman in his mid-fifties, with a full head of iron-gray hair and a mustache a little darker than the hair on his head. He'd dressed rather elaborately for a day at home with his books—a tie, a vest, a Donegal tweed jacket—and I didn't flatter myself that it was on my account. I had a feeling he chose a similar get-up seven days a week, and I wouldn't have been surprised to learn he put on a black tie every night for dinner.

He carried most of the lunchtime conversation, talking about books he'd read, arguing the relative merits of Hammett and Chandler, musing on the likelihood that female private eyes in fiction had come to outnumber their real-life counterparts. I didn't feel called upon to contribute much, and Mrs. Bellermann never uttered a word except to offer dessert (*apfelküchen*, lighter than air and sweeter than revenge) and coffee (the mixture as before but a fresh pot of it, and seemingly richer and darker and stronger and winier this time around). Karl and I both turned down a second piece of the cake and said yes to a second cup of coffee, and then Karl turned significantly to his wife and gave her a formal nod.

"Thank you, Eva," he said. And she rose, all but curtseyed, and left the room.

"She leaves us to our brandy and cigars," he said, "but it's too early in the day for spirits, and no one smokes in Schloss Bellermann."

"Schloss Bellermann?"

"A joke of mine. If the world calls it Bellermann's Folly, why shouldn't Bellermann call it his castle? Eh?"

"Why not?"

He looked at his watch. "But let me show you my library," he said, "and then you can show me what you've brought me."

Diagonal mullions divided the library door into a few dozen diamond-shaped sections, each set with a mirrored pane of glass. The effect was unusual, and I asked if they were one-way mirrors.

"Like the ones in police stations?" He raised an eyebrow. "Your past is showing, eh, Bernie? But no, it is even more of a trick than the police play on criminals. On the other side of the mirror—" he clicked a fingernail against a pane "—is solid steel an inch and a half thick. The library walls themselves are reinforced with steel sheeting. The exterior walls are concrete, reinforced with steel rods. And look at this lock."

It was a Poulard, its mechanism intricate beyond description, its key one that not a locksmith in ten thousand could duplicate.

"Pickproof," he said. "They guarantee it."

"So I understand."

He slipped the irreproducible key into the impregnable lock and opened the unbreachable door. Inside was a room two full stories tall, with a system of ladders leading to the upper levels. The library, as tall as the house itself, had an eighteen-foot ceiling paneled in light and dark wood in a sunburst pattern. Wall-to-wall carpet covered the floor, and oriental rugs in turn covered most of the broadloom. The walls, predictably enough, were given over to floor-to-ceiling bookshelves, with the shelves themselves devoted entirely to books. There were no paintings, no Chinese ginger jars, no bronze animals, no sets of armor, no cigar humidors, no framed photographs of family members, no hand-colored engravings of Victoria Falls, no hunting trophies, no Lalique figurines, no Limoges boxes. Nothing but books, sometimes embraced by bronze bookends, but mostly extending without interruption from one end of a section of shelving to the other.

"Books," he said reverently—and, I thought, unnecessarily. I own a bookstore, I can recognize books when I see them.

"Books," I affirmed.

"I believe they are happy."

"Happy?"

"You are surprised? Why should objects lack feelings, especially objects of such a sensitive nature as books? And, if a book can have feelings, these books ought to be happy. They are owned and tended by a man who cares deeply for them. And they are housed in a room perfectly designed for their safety and comfort."

"It certainly looks that way."

He nodded. "Two windows only, on the north wall, of course, so that no direct sunlight ever enters the room. Sunlight fades book spines, bleaches the ink of a dust jacket. It is a book's enemy, and it cannot gain entry here."

"That's good," I said. "My store faces south, and the building across the street blocks some of the sunlight, but a little gets through. I have to make sure I don't keep any of the better volumes where the light can get at them."

"You should paint the windows black," he said, "or hang thick curtains. Or both."

"Well, I like to keep an eye on the street," I said. "And my cat likes to sleep in the sunlit window."

He made a face. "A cat? In a room full of books?"

"He'd be safe," I said, "even in a room full of rocking chairs. He's a Manx. And he's an honest working cat. I used to have mice damaging the books, and that stopped the day he moved in."

"No mice can get in here," Bellermann said, "and neither can cats, with their hair and their odor. Mold cannot attack my books, or mildew. You feel the air?"

"The air?"

"A constant sixty-four degrees Fahrenheit," he said. "On the cool side, but perfect for my books. I put on a jacket and I am perfectly comfortable. And, as you can see, most of them are already wearing their jackets. Dust jackets! Ha ha!"

"Ha ha," I agreed.

"The humidity is sixty percent," he went on. "It never varies. Too dry and the glue dries out. Too damp and the pages rot. Neither can happen here."

"That's reassuring."

"I would say so. The air is filtered regularly, with not only air-conditioning but special filters to remove pollutants that are truly microscopic. No book could ask for a safer or more comfortable environment."

I sniffed the air. It was cool, and neither too moist nor too dry, and as immaculate as modern science could make it. My nose wrinkled, and I picked up a whiff of something.

"What about fire?" I wondered.

"Steel walls, steel doors, triple-glazed windows with heat-resistant bulletproof glass. Special insulation in the walls and ceiling and floor. The whole house could burn to the ground, Bernie, and this room and its contents would remain unaffected. It is one enormous fire-safe."

"But if the fire broke out in here . . ."

"How? I don't smoke, or play with matches. There are no cupboards holding piles of oily rags, no bales of moldering hay to burst into spontaneous combustion."

"No, but—"

"And even if there were a fire," he said, "it would be extinguished almost before it had begun." He gestured and I looked up and saw round metal gadgets spotted here and there in the walls and ceiling.

I said, "A sprinkler system? Somebody tried to sell me one at the store once and I threw him out on his ear. Fire's rough on books, but water's sheer disaster. And those things are like smoke alarms, they can go off for no good reason, and then where are you? Karl, I can't believe—"

"Please," he said, holding up a hand. "Do you take me for an idiot?"

"No, but—"

"Do you honestly think I would use water to forestall fire? Credit me with a little sense, my friend."

"I do, but—"

"There will be no fire here, and no flood, either. A book in my library will be, ah, what is the expression? Snug as a slug in a rug."

"A bug," I said.

"I beg your pardon?"

"A bug in a rug," I said. "I think that's the expression."

His response was a shrug, the sort you'd get, I suppose, from a slug in a rug. "But we have no time for language lessons," he said. "From two to six I must be in the library with my books, and it is already one-fifty."

"You're already in the library."

"Alone," he said. "With only my books for company. So. What have you brought me?"

I opened my briefcase, withdrew the padded mailer, reached into that like Little Jack Horner, and brought forth a plum indeed. I looked up in time to catch an unguarded glimpse of Bellermann's face, and it was a study. How often do you get to see a man salivate less than an hour after a big lunch?

He extended his hands and I placed the book in them. *"Fer-de-Lance,"* he said reverently. "Nero Wolfe's debut, the rarest and most desirable book in the entire canon. Hardly the best of the novels, I wouldn't say. It took Stout several books fully to refine the character of Wolfe and to hone the narrative edge of Archie Goodwin. But the brilliance was present from the beginning, and the book is a prize."

He turned the volume over in his hands, inspected the dust jacket fore and aft. "Of course I own a copy," he said. "A first edition in dust wrapper. This dust wrapper is nicer than the one I have."

"It's pretty cherry," I said.

"Pristine," he allowed, "or very nearly so. Mine has a couple of chips and an unfortunate tear mended quite expertly with tape. This does look virtually perfect."

"Yes."

"But the jacket's the least of it, is it not? This is a special copy."

"It is."

He opened it, and his large hands could not have been gentler had he been repotting orchids. He found the title page and read, " 'For Franklin Roosevelt, with the earnest hope of a brighter tomorrow. Best regards from Rex Todhunter Stout.' " He ran his forefinger over the inscription. "It's Stout's writing," he announced. "He didn't inscribe many books, but I have enough signed copies to know his hand. And this is the ultimate association copy, isn't it?"

"You could say that."

"I just did. Stout was a liberal Democrat, ultimately a World Federalist. FDR, like the present incumbent, was a great fan of detective stories. It always seems to be the Democratic presidents who relish a good mystery. Eisenhower preferred Westerns, Nixon liked history and biography, and I don't know that Reagan read at all."

He sighed and closed the book. "Mr. Gulbenkian must regret the loss of this copy," he said.

"I suppose he must."

"A year ago," he said, "when I learned he'd been burglarized and some of his best volumes stolen, I wondered what sort of burglar could possibly know what books to take. And of course I thought of you."

I didn't say anything.

"Tell me your price again, Bernie. Refresh my memory."

I named a figure.

"It's high," he said.

"The book's unique," I pointed out.

"I know that. I know, too, that I can never show it off. I cannot tell anyone I have it. You and I alone will know that it is in my possession."

"It'll be our little secret, Karl."

"Our little secret. I can't even insure it. At least Gulbenkian was insured, eh? But he can never replace the book. Why didn't you sell it back to him?"

"I might," I said, "if you decide you don't want it."

"But of course I want it!" He might have said more but a glance at his watch reminded him of the time. "Two o'clock," he said, motioning me toward the door. "Eva will have my afternoon coffee ready. And you will excuse me, I am sure, while I spend the afternoon with my books, including this latest specimen."

"Be careful with it," I said.

"Bernie! I'm not going to *read* it. I have plenty of reading copies, should I care to renew my acquaintance with *Fer-de-Lance*. I want to hold it, to be with it. And then at six o'clock we will conclude our business, and I will give you a dinner every bit as good as the lunch you just had. And then you can return to the city."

He ushered me out, and moments later he disappeared into the library again, carrying a tray with coffee in one of those silver pots they used to give you on trains. There was a cup on the tray as well, and a sugar bowl and creamer, along with a plate of shortbread cookies. I stood in the hall and watched the library door swing shut, heard the lock turn and the bolt slide home. Then I turned, and there was Karl's wife, Eva.

"I guess he's really going to spend the next four hours in there," I said.

"He always does."

"I'd go for a drive," I said, "but I don't have a car. I suppose I could go for a walk. It's a beautiful day, bright and sunny. Of course your husband doesn't allow sunlight into the library, but I suppose he lets it go where it wants in the rest of the neighborhood."

That drew a smile from her.

"If I'd thought ahead," I said, "I'd have brought something to read. Not that there aren't a few thousand books in the house, but they're all locked away with Karl."

"Not all of them," she said. "My husband's collection is limited to books published before 1975, along with the more recent work of a few of his very favorite authors. But he buys other contemporary crime novels as well, and keeps them here and there around the house. The bookcase in the guest room is well stocked."

"That's good news. As far as that goes, I was in the middle of a magazine story."

"In *Ellery Queen*, wasn't it? Come with me, Mr. Rhodenbarr, and I'll—"

"Bernie."

"Bernie," she said, and colored slightly, those dangerous cheekbones turning from ivory to the pink you find inside a seashell. "I'll show you where the guest room is, Bernie, and then I'll bring you your magazine."

The guest room was on the second floor, and its glassed-in bookcase was indeed jam-packed with recent crime fiction. I was just getting drawn into the opening of one of Jeremiah Healy's Cuddy novels when Eva Bellermann knocked on the half-open door and came in with a tray quite like the one she'd brought her husband. Coffee in a silver pot, a gold-rimmed bone china cup and saucer, a matching plate holding shortbread cookies. And, keeping them company, the issue of *EQMM* I'd been reading earlier.

"This is awfully nice of you," I said. "But you should have brought a second cup so you could join me."

"I've had too much coffee already," she said. "But I could keep you company for a few minutes if you don't mind."

"I'd like that."

"So would I," she said, skirting my chair and sitting on the edge of the narrow captain's bed. "I don't get much company. The people in the village keep their distance. And Karl has his books."

"And he's locked away with them . . ."

"Three hours in the morning and four in the afternoon. Then in the evening he deals with correspondence and returns phone calls. He's retired, as you know, but he has investment decisions to make and business matters to deal with. And books, of course. He's always buying more of them." She sighed. "I'm afraid he doesn't have much time left for me."

"It must be difficult for you."

"It's lonely," she said.

"I can imagine."

"We have so little in common," she said. "I sometimes wonder why he married me. The books are his whole life."

"And they don't interest you at all?"

She shook her head. "I haven't the brain for it," she said. "Clues and timetables and elaborate murder methods. It is like working a crossword puzzle without a pencil. Or worse—like assembling a jigsaw puzzle in the dark."

"With gloves on," I suggested.

"Oh, that's funny!" She laughed more than the line warranted and laid a hand on my arm. "But I should not make jokes about the books. You are a bookseller yourself. Perhaps books are your whole life, too."

"Not my whole life," I said.

"Oh? What else interests you?"

"Beautiful women," I said recklessly.

"Beautiful women?"

"Like you," I said.

Believe me, I hadn't planned on any of this. I'd figured on finishing the Lovesey story, then curling up with the Healy book until Karl Bellermann emerged from his lair, saw his shadow, and paid me a lot of money for the book he thought I had stolen.

In point of fact, the *Fer-de-Lance* I'd brought him was legitimately mine to sell—or very nearly so. I would never have entertained the notion of breaking into Nizar Gulbenkian's fieldstone house in Riverdale. Gulbenkian was a friend as well as a valued customer, and I'd rushed to call him when I learned of his loss. I would keep an ear cocked and an eye open, I assured him, and I would let him know if any of his treasures turned up on the gray or black market.

"That's kind of you, Bernie," he'd said. "We will have to talk of this one day."

And, months later, we talked—and I learned there had been no burglary. Gulbenkian had gouged his own front door with a chisel, looted his own well-insured library of its greatest treasures, and tucked them out of sight (if not out of mind) before reporting the offense—and pocketing the payoff from the insurance company.

He'd needed money, of course, and this had seemed a good way to get it without parting with his precious volumes. But now he needed more money, as one so often does, and he had a carton full of books he no longer legally owned and could not even show off to his friends, let alone display to the public. He couldn't offer them for sale, either, but someone else could. Someone who might be presumed to have stolen them. Someone rather like me.

"It will be the simplest thing in the world for you, Bernie," old Nizar said. "You won't have to do any breaking or entering. You won't even have to come to Riverdale. All you'll do is sell the books, and I will gladly pay you ten percent of the proceeds."

"Half," I said.

We settled on a third, after protracted negotiations, and later over drinks he allowed that he'd have gone as high as forty percent, while I admitted I'd have taken twenty. He brought me the books, and I knew which one to offer first, and to whom.

The FDR *Fer-de-Lance* was the prize of the lot, and the most readily identifiable. Karl Bellermann was likely to pay the highest price for it, and to be most sanguine about its unorthodox provenance.

You hear it said of a man now and then that he'd rather steal a dollar than earn ten. (It's been said, not entirely without justification, of me.) Karl Bellermann was a man who'd rather buy a stolen book for a thousand dollars than pay half that through legitimate channels. I'd sold him things in the past, some stolen, some not, and it was the volume with a dubious history that really got him going.

So, as far as he was concerned, I'd lifted *Fer-de-Lance* from its rightful owner, who would turn purple if he knew where it was. But I knew better—Gulbenkian would cheerfully pocket two-thirds of whatever I pried out of Bellermann, and would know exactly where the book had wound up and just how it got there.

In a sense, then, I was putting one over on Karl Bellermann, but that didn't constitute a breach of my admittedly elastic moral code. It was something else entirely, though, to abuse the man's hospitality by putting the moves on his gorgeous young wife.

Well, what can I say? Nobody's perfect.

Afterward I lay back with my head on a pillow and tried to figure out what would make a man choose a leather chair and room full of books over a comfortable bed with a hot blonde in it. I marveled at the vagaries of human nature, and Eva stroked my chest and urged a cup of coffee on me.

It was great coffee, and no less welcome after our little interlude. The cookies were good, too. Eva took one, but passed on the coffee. If she drank it after lunchtime, she said, she had trouble sleeping nights.

"It never keeps me awake," I said. "In fact, this stuff seems to be having just the opposite effect. The more I drink, the sleepier I get."

"Maybe it is I who have made you sleepy."

"Could be."

She snuggled close, letting interesting parts of her body press against mine. "Perhaps we should close our eyes for a few minutes," she said.

The next thing I knew she had a hand on my shoulder and was shaking me awake. "Bernie," she said. "We fell asleep!"

"We did?"

"And look at the time! It is almost six o'clock. Karl will be coming out of the library any minute."

"Uh-oh."

She was out of bed, diving into her clothes. "I'll go downstairs," she said. "You can take your time dressing, as long as we are not together." And, before I could say anything, she swept out of the room.

I had the urge to close my eyes and drift right off again. Instead I forced myself out of bed, took a quick shower to clear the cobwebs, then got dressed. I stood for a moment at the head of the stairs, listening for conversation and hoping I wouldn't hear any voices raised in anger. I didn't hear any voices, angry or otherwise, or anything else.

It's quiet out there, I thought, like so many supporting characters in so many Westerns. And the thought came back, as it had from so many heroes in those same Westerns: *Yeah . . . too quiet.*

I descended the flight of stairs, turned a corner, and bumped into Eva. "He hasn't come out," she said. "Bernie, I'm worried."

"Maybe he lost track of the time."

"Never. He's like a Swiss watch, and he *has* a Swiss watch and checks it constantly. He comes out every day at six on the dot. It is ten minutes past the hour and where is he?"

"Maybe he came out and—"

"Yes?"

"I don't know. Drove into town to buy a paper."

"He never does that. And the car is in the garage."

"He could have gone for a walk."

"He hates to walk. Bernie, he is still in there."

"Well, I suppose he's got the right. It's his room and his books. If he wants to hang around—"

"I'm afraid something has happened to him. Bernie, I knocked on the door. I knocked loud. Perhaps you heard the sound upstairs?"

"No, but I probably wouldn't. I was all the way upstairs, and I had the shower on for a while there. I take it he didn't answer."

"No."

"Well, I gather it's pretty well soundproofed in there. Maybe he didn't hear you."

"I have knocked before. And he has heard me before."

"Maybe he heard you this time and decided to ignore you." Why was I raising so many objections? Perhaps because I didn't want to let myself think there was any great cause for alarm.

"Bernie," she said, "what if he is ill? What if he has had a heart attack?"

"I suppose it's possible, but—"

"I think I should call the police."

I suppose it's my special perspective, but I almost never think that's a great idea. I wasn't mad about it now, either, being in the possession of stolen property and a criminal record, not to mention the guilty conscience that I'd earned a couple of hours ago in the upstairs guest room.

"Not the police," I said. "Not yet. First let's make sure he's not just taking a nap, or all caught up in his reading."

"But how? The door is locked."

"Isn't there an extra key?"

"If there is, he's never told me where he keeps it. He's the only one with access to his precious books."

"The window," I said.

"It can't be opened. It is this triple pane of bulletproof glass, and—"

"And you couldn't budge it with a battering ram," I said. "He told me all about it. You can still see through it, though, can't you?"

"He's in there," I announced. "At least his feet are."

"His feet?"

"There's a big leather chair with its back to the window," I said, "and he's sitting in it. I can't see the rest of him, but I can see his feet."

"What are they doing?"

"They're sticking out in front of the chair," I said, "and they're wearing shoes, and that's about it. Feet aren't terribly expressive, are they?"

I made a fist and reached up to bang on the window. I don't know what I expected the feet to do in response, but they stayed right where they were.

"The police," Eva said. "I'd better call them."

"Not just yet," I said.

The Poulard is a terrific lock, no question about it. State-of-the-art and all that. But I don't know where they get off calling it pickproof. When I first came across the word in one of their ads I knew how Alexander felt when he heard about the Gordian knot. Pickproof, eh? We'll see about that!

The lock on the library door put up a good fight, but I'd brought the little set of picks and probes I never leave home without, and I put them (and my God-given talent) to the task.

And opened the door.

"Bernie," Eva said, gaping. "Where did you learn how to do that?"

"In the Boy Scouts," I said. "They give you a merit badge for it if you apply yourself. Karl? Karl, are you all right?"

He was in his chair, and now we could see more than his well-shod feet. His hands were in his lap, holding a book by William Campbell Gault. His head was back, his eyes closed. He looked for all the world like a man who'd dozed off over a book.

We stood looking at him, and I took a moment to sniff the air. I'd smelled something on my first visit to this remarkable room, but I couldn't catch a whiff of it now.

"Bernie—"

I looked down, scanned the floor, running my eyes over the maroon broadloom and the carpets that covered most of it. I dropped to one knee alongside one small Persian—a Tabriz, if I had to guess, but I know less than a good burglar should about the subject. I took a close look at this one and Eva asked me what I was doing.

"Just helping out," I said. "Didn't you drop a contact lens?"

"I don't wear contact lenses."

"My mistake," I said, and got to my feet. I went over to the big leather chair and went through the formality of laying a hand on Karl Bellermann's brow. It was predictably cool to the touch.

"Is he—"

I nodded. "You'd better call the cops," I said.

Elmer Crittenden, the officer in charge, was a stocky fellow in a khaki windbreaker. He kept glancing warily at the walls of books, as if he feared being called upon to sit down and read them one after the other. My guess is that he'd had less experience with them than with dead bodies.

"Most likely turn out to be his heart," he said of the deceased. "Usually is when they go like this. He complain any of chest pains? Shooting pains up and down his left arm? Any of that?"

Eva said he hadn't.

"Might have had 'em without saying anything," Crittenden said. "Or it could be he didn't get any advance warning. Way he's sitting and all, I'd say it was quick. Could be he closed his eyes for a little nap and died in his sleep."

"Just so he didn't suffer," Eva said.

Crittenden lifted Karl's eyelid, squinted, touched the corpse here and there. "What it almost looks like," he said, "is that he was smothered, but I don't suppose some great speckled bird flew in a window and held a pillow over his face. It'll turn out to be a heart attack, unless I miss my guess."

Could I just let it go? I looked at Crittenden, at Eva, at the sunburst pattern on the high ceiling up above, at the putative Tabriz carpet below. Then I looked at Karl, the consummate bibliophile, with FDR's *Fer-de-Lance* on the table beside his chair. He was my customer, and he'd died within arm's reach of the book I'd brought him. Should I let him *requiescat* in relative *pace*? Or did I have an active role to play?

"I think you were right," I told Crittenden. "I think he was smothered."

"What would make you say that, sir? You didn't even get a good look at his eyeballs."

"I'll trust your eyeballs," I said. "And I don't think it was a great speckled bird that did it, either."

"Oh?"

"It's classic," I said, "and it would have appealed to Karl, given his passion for crime fiction. If he had to die, he'd probably have wanted it to happen in a locked room. And not just any locked room, either, but one secured by a pickproof Poulard, with steel-lined walls and windows that don't open."

"He was locked up tighter than Fort Knox," Crittenden said.

"He was," I said. "And, all the same, he was murdered."

"Smothered," I said. "When the lab checks him out, tell them to look for halon gas. I think it'll show up, but not unless they're looking for it."

"I never heard of it," Crittenden said.

"Most people haven't," I said. "It was in the news a while ago when they installed it in subway toll booths. There'd been a few incendiary attacks on booth attendants—a spritz of something flammable and they got turned into crispy critters. The halon gas was there to smother a fire before it got started."

"How's it work?"

"It displaces the oxygen in the room," I said. "I'm not enough of a scientist to know how it manages it, but the net effect is about the same as that great speckled bird you were talking about. The one with the pillows."

"That'd be consistent with the physical evidence," Crittenden said. "But how would you get this halon in here?"

"It was already here," I said. I pointed to the jets on the walls and ceiling. "When I first saw them, I thought Bellermann had put in a conventional sprinkler system, and I couldn't believe it. Water's harder than fire on rare books, and a lot of libraries have been totaled when a sprinkler system went off by accident. I said something to that effect to Karl, and he just about bit my head off, making it clear he wouldn't expose his precious treasures to water damage.

"So I got the picture. The jets were designed to deliver gas, not liquid, and it went without saying that the gas would be halon. I understand they're equipping the better research libraries with it these days, although Karl's the only person I know of who installed it in his personal library."

Crittenden was halfway up a ladder, having a look at one of the outlets. "Just like a sprinkler head," he said, "which is what I took it for. How's it know when to go off? Heat sensor?"

"That's right."

"You said murder. That'd mean somebody set it off."

"Yes."

"By starting a fire in here? Be a neater trick than sending in the great speckled bird."

"All you'd have to do," I said, "is heat the sensor enough to trigger the response."

"How?"

"When I was in here earlier," I said, "I caught a whiff of smoke. It was faint, but it was absolutely there. I think that's what made me ask Karl about fire in the first place."

"And?"

"When Mrs. Bellermann and I came in and discovered the body, the smell was gone. But there was a discolored spot on the carpet that I'd noticed before, and I bent down for a closer look at it." I pointed to the Tabriz (which, now that I think about it, may very well have been an Isfahan). "Right there," I said.

Crittenden knelt where I pointed, rubbed two fingers on the spot, brought them to his nose. "Scorched," he reported. "But just the least bit. Take a whole lot more than that to set off a sensor way up there."

"I know. That was a test."

"A test?"

"Of the murder method. How do you raise the temperature of a room you can't enter? You can't unlock the door and you can't open the window. How can you get enough heat in to set off the gas?"

"How?"

I turned to Eva. "Tell him how you did it," I said.

"I don't know what you're talking about," she said. "You must be crazy."

"You wouldn't need a fire," I said. "You wouldn't even need a whole lot of heat. All you'd have to do is deliver enough heat directly to the sensor to trigger a response. If you could manage that in a highly localized fashion, you wouldn't even raise the overall room temperature appreciably."

"Keep talking," Crittenden said.

I picked up an ivory-handled magnifier, one of several placed strategically around the room. "When I was a Boy Scout," I said, "they didn't really teach me how to open locks. But they were big on starting fires. Flint and steel, fire by friction—and that old standby, focusing the sun's rays though a magnifying glass and delivering a concentrated pinpoint of intense heat onto something with a low kindling point."

"The window," Crittenden said.

I nodded. "It faces north," I said, "so the sun never comes in on its own. But you can stand a few feet from the window and catch the sunlight with a mirror, and you can tilt the mirror so the light is reflected through your magnifying glass and on through the window. And you can beam it onto an object in the room."

"The heat sensor, that'd be."

"Eventually," I said. "First, though, you'd want to make sure it would work. You couldn't try it out ahead of time on the sensor, because you wouldn't know it was working until you set it off. Until then, you couldn't be sure the thickness of the window glass wasn't disrupting the process. So you'd want to test it."

"That explains the scorched rug, doesn't it?" Crittenden stooped for another look at it, then glanced up at the window. "Soon as you saw a wisp of smoke or a trace of scorching, you'd know it was working. And you'd have an idea how long it would take to raise the temperature enough. If you could make it hot enough to scorch wool, you could set off a heat-sensitive alarm."

"My God," Eva cried, adjusting quickly to new realities. "I thought you must be crazy, but now I can see how it was done. But who could have done such a thing?"

"Oh, I don't know," I said. "I suppose it would have to be somebody who lived here, somebody who was familiar with the library and knew about the halon, somebody who stood to gain financially by Karl Bellermann's death. Somebody, say, who felt neglected by a husband who treated her like a housekeeper, somebody who might see poetic justice in killing him while he was locked away with his precious books."

"You can't mean me, Bernie."

"Well, now that you mention it . . ."

"But I was with you! Karl was with us at lunch. Then he went into the library and I showed you to the guest room."

"You showed me, all right."

"And we were together," she said, lowering her eyes modestly. "It shames me to say it with my husband tragically dead, but we were in bed together until almost six o'clock, when we came down here to discover the body. You can testify to that, can't you, Bernie?"

"I can swear we went to bed together," I said, "And I can swear that *I* was there until six, unless I went sleepwalking. But I was out cold, Eva."

"So was I."

"I don't think so," I said. "You stayed away from the coffee, saying how it kept you awake. Well, it sure didn't keep *me* awake. I think there was something in it to make me sleep, and that's why you didn't want any. I think there was more of the same in the pot you gave Karl to bring in here with him, so he'd be dozing peacefully while you set off the halon. You waited until I was asleep, went outside with a mirror and a magnifier, heated the sensor and set off the gas, and then came back to bed. The halon would do its work in minutes, and without warning even if Karl wasn't sleeping all that soundly. Halon's odorless and colorless, and the air-cleaning system would whisk it all away in less than an hour. But I think there'll be traces in his system, along with traces of the same sedative they'll find in the residue in both the coffee pots. And I think that'll be enough to put you away."

Crittenden thought so, too.

When I got back to the city there was a message on the machine to call Nizar Gulbenkian. It was late, but it sounded urgent.

"Bad news," I told him. "I had the book just about sold. Then he locked himself in his library to commune with the ghosts of Rex Stout and Franklin Delano Roosevelt, and next thing he knew they were all hanging out together."

"You don't mean he died?"

"His wife killed him," I said, and I went on to tell him the whole story. "So that's the bad news, though it's not as bad for us as it is for the Bellermanns. I've got the book back, and I'm sure I can find a customer for it."

"Ah," he said. "Well, Bernie, I'm sorry about Bellermann. He was a true bookman."

"He was that, all right."

"But otherwise your bad news is good news."

"It is?"

"Yes. Because I changed my mind about the book."

"You don't want to sell it?"

"I can't sell it," he said. "It would be like tearing out my soul. And now, thank God, I don't have to sell it."

"Oh?"

"More good news," he said. "A business transaction, a long shot with a handsome return. I won't bore you with the details, but the outcome was very good indeed. If you'd been successful in selling the book, I'd now be begging you to buy it back."

"I see."

"Bernie," he said, I'm a collector, as passionate about the pursuit as poor Bellermann. I don't ever want to sell. I want to add to my holdings." He let out a sigh, clearly pleased at the prospect. "So I'll want the book back. But of course I'll pay you your commission all the same."

"I couldn't accept it."

"So you had all that work for nothing?"

"Not exactly," I said.

"Oh?"

"I guess Bellermann's library will go on the auction block eventually," I said. "Eva can't inherit, but there'll be some niece or nephew to wind up with a nice piece of change. And there'll be some wonderful books in that sale."

"There certainly will."

"But a few of the most desirable items won't be included," I said, "because they somehow found their way into my briefcase, along with *Fer-de-Lance*."

"You managed that, Bernie? With a dead body in the room, and a murderer in custody, and a cop right there on the scene?"

"Bellermann had shown me his choicest treasures," I said, "so I knew just what to grab and where to find it. And Crittenden didn't care what I did with the books. I told him I needed something to read on the train and he waited patiently while I picked out eight or ten volumes. Well, it's a long train ride, and I guess he must think I'm a fast reader."

"Bring them over," he said. "Now."

"Nizar, I'm bushed," I said, "and you're all the way up in Riverdale. First thing in the morning, okay? And while I'm there you can teach me how to tell a Tabriz from an Isfahan."

"They're not at all alike, Bernie. How could anyone confuse them?"

"You'll clear it up for me tomorrow. Okay?"

"Well, all right," he said. "But I hate to wait."

Collectors! Don't you just love them?

Keller

Answers to Soldier

Keller flew United to Portland. He read a magazine on the leg from JFK to O'Hare, ate lunch on the ground, and watched the movie on the nonstop flight from Chicago to Portland. It was a quarter to three local time when he carried his hand luggage off the plane, and then he had only an hour's wait before his connecting flight to Roseburg.

But when he got a look at the size of the plane he walked over to the Hertz desk and told them he wanted a car for a few days. He showed them a driver's license and a credit card and they let him have a Ford Taurus with thirty-two hundred miles on the clock. He didn't bother trying to refund his Portland-to-Roseburg ticket.

The Hertz clerk showed him how to get on I-5. He pointed the Taurus in the right direction and set the cruise control three miles over the posted speed limit. Everybody else was going a few miles an hour faster than that but he was in no hurry, and he didn't want to invite a close look at his driver's license. It was probably all right, but why ask for trouble?

It was still light out when he took the off-ramp for the second Roseburg exit. He had a reservation at the Douglas Inn, a Best Western on Stephens Street. He found it without any trouble. They had him in a ground-floor room in the front, and he had them change it to one in the rear, and a flight up.

He unpacked, showered. The phone book had a street map of downtown Roseburg and he studied it, getting his bearings, then tearing it out and taking it with him when he went out for a walk. The little print shop was only a few blocks away on Jackson, two doors in from the corner between a tobacconist and a photographer with his window full of wedding pictures. A sign in Quik-Print's window offered a special on wedding invitations, perhaps to catch the eye of bridal couples making arrangements with the photographer.

Quik-Print was closed, of course, as were the tobacconist and the photographer and the credit jeweler next door to the photographer and, as far as Keller could tell, everybody in the neighborhood. Keller didn't stick around long. Two blocks away he found a Mexican restaurant that looked dingy enough to be authentic. He bought a local paper from the coin box out front and read it while he ate his chicken enchiladas. The food was good, and ridiculously inexpensive. If the place were in New York, he thought, everything would be three and four times as much and there'd be a line in front.

The waitress was a slender blonde, not Mexican at all. She had short hair and granny glasses and an overbite, and she sported an engagement ring on the appropriate finger, a diamond solitaire with a tiny stone. Maybe she and her fiancé had picked it out at the credit jeweler's, Keller thought. Maybe the photographer next door would take their wedding pictures. Maybe they'd get Burt Engleman to print their wedding invitations. Quality printing, reasonable rates, service you can count on.

In the morning he returned to Quik-Print and looked in the window. A woman with brown hair was sitting at a gray metal desk, talking on the telephone. A man in shirtsleeves stood at a copying machine. He wore horn-rimmed glasses with round lenses, and his hair was cropped short on his egg-shaped head. He was balding, and this made him look older, but Keller knew he was only thirty-eight.

Keller stood in front of the jeweler's and pictured the waitress and her fiancé picking out rings. They'd have a double-ring ceremony, of course, and there would be something engraved on the inside of each of their wedding bands, something no one else would ever see. Would they live in an apartment? For a while, he decided, until they saved the down payment for a starter home. That was the phrase you saw in real estate ads and Keller liked it. A starter home, something to practice on until you got the hang of it.

At a drugstore on the next block he bought an unlined paper tablet and a black felt-tipped pen. He used four sheets of paper before he was pleased with the result. Back at Quik-Print, he showed his work to the brown-haired woman.

"My dog ran off," he explained. "I thought I'd get some flyers printed, post them around town."

LOST DOG, he'd printed. *Part Ger. Shepherd. Answers to Soldier. Call 765-1904.*

"I hope you get him back," the woman said. "Is it a him? Soldier sounds like a male dog, but it doesn't say."

"It's a male," Keller said. "Maybe I should have specified."

"It's probably not important. Did you want to offer a reward? People usually do, although I don't know if it makes any difference. If I found somebody's dog I wouldn't care about a reward, I'd just want to get him back with his owner."

"Everybody's not as decent as you are," Keller said. "Maybe I should say something about a reward. I didn't even think of that." He put his palms on the desk and leaned forward, looking down at the sheet of paper. "I don't know," he said. "It looks kind of homemade, doesn't it? Maybe I should have you set it in type, do it right. What do you think?"

"I don't know," she said. "Ed? Would you come and take a look at this, please?"

The man in the horn rims came over and said he thought a hand-lettered look was best for a lost-dog notice. "It makes it more personal," he said. "I could do it in type for you, but I think people would respond to it better as it is. Assuming somebody finds the dog, that is."

"I don't suppose it's a matter of national importance anyway," Keller said. "My wife's attached to the animal and I'd like to recover him if it's possible, but I've a feeling he's not to be found. My name's Gordon, by the way. Al Gordon."

"Ed Vandermeer," the man said. "And this is my wife, Betty."

"A pleasure," Keller said. "I guess fifty of these ought to be enough. More than enough, but I'll take fifty. Will it take you long to run them?"

"I'll do it right now. Take about three minutes, cost you three-fifty."

"Can't beat that," Keller said. He uncapped the felt-tipped pen. "Just let me put in something about a reward," he said.

Back in his motel room he put through a call to a number in White Plains. When a woman answered he said, "Dot, let me speak to him, will you?" It took a few minutes, and then he said, "Yeah, I got here. It's him, all right. He's calling himself Vandermeer now. His wife's still going by Betty."

The man in White Plains asked when he'd be back.

"What's today, Tuesday? I've got a flight booked Friday but I might take a little longer. No point rushing things. I found a good place to eat. Mexican joint, and the motel set gets HBO. I figure I'll take my time, do it right. Engleman's not going anywhere."

He had lunch at the Mexican café. This time he ordered the combination plate. The waitress asked if he wanted the red or the green chili.

"Whichever's hotter," he said.

Maybe a mobile home, he thought. You could buy one cheap, a nice doublewide, make a nice starter home for her and her fellow. Or maybe the best thing for them was to buy a duplex and rent out half, then rent out the other half when they were ready for something nicer for themselves. No time at all you're in real estate, making a nice return, watching your holdings appreciate. No more waiting on tables for her, and pretty soon her husband can quit slaving at the lumber mill, quit worrying about layoffs when the industry hits one of its slumps.

How you do go on, he thought.

He spent the afternoon walking around town. In a gun shop the proprietor, a man named McLarendon, took some rifles and shotguns off the wall and let him get the feel of them. A sign on the wall said, GUNS DON'T KILL PEOPLE UNLESS YOU

AIM REAL GOOD. Keller talked politics with McLarendon, and socioeconomics. It wasn't that tricky to figure out McLarendon's position and to adopt it as one's own.

"What I really been meaning to buy," Keller said, "is a handgun."

"You want to protect yourself and your property," McLarendon said.

"That's the idea."

"And your loved ones."

"Sure."

He let the man sell him a gun. There was, locally, a cooling-off period. You picked out your gun, filled out a form, and four days later you could come back and pick it up.

"You a hothead?" McLarendon asked him. "You fixing to lean out the car window, shoot a state trooper on your way home?"

"It doesn't seem likely."

"Then I'll show you a trick. We just backdate this form and you've already had your cooling-off period. I'd say you look cool enough to me."

"You're a good judge of character."

The man grinned. "This business," he said, "a man's got to be."

It was nice, a town that size. You got in your car and drove for ten minutes and you were way out in the country.

Keller stopped the Taurus at the side of the road, cut the ignition, rolled down the window. He took the gun from one pocket and the box of shells from the other. The gun—McLarendon kept calling it a weapon—was a .38-caliber revolver with a two-inch barrel. McLarendon would have liked to sell him something heavier and more powerful. If Keller had wanted, McLarendon probably would have been thrilled to sell him a bazooka.

He loaded the gun and got out of the car. There was a beer can lying on its side perhaps twenty yards off. Keller aimed at it, holding the gun in one hand. A few years ago they started firing two-handed in cop shows on TV, and nowadays that was all you saw, television cops leaping through doorways and spinning around corners, gun gripped rigidly in both hands, held out in front of their bodies like a fire hose. Keller thought it looked silly. He'd feel self-conscious, holding a gun like that.

He squeezed the trigger. The gun bucked in his hand, and he missed the beer can by several feet. The report of the gunshot echoed for a long time.

He took aim at other things—at a tree, at a flower, at a white rock the size of a clenched fist. But he couldn't bring himself to fire the gun again, to break the stillness with another gunshot. What was the point, anyway? If he used the gun he'd be too close to miss. You got in close, you pointed, you fired. It wasn't rocket science, for God's sake. It wasn't neurosurgery. Anyone could do it.

He replaced the spent cartridge and put the loaded gun in the car's glove compartment. He spilled the rest of the shells into his hand and walked a few yards from the road's edge, then hurled them with a sweeping sidearm motion. He gave the empty box a toss and got back in the car.

Traveling light, he thought.

Back in town, he drove past Quik-Print to make sure they were still open. Then, following the route he'd traced on the map, he found his way to 1411 Cowslip, a Dutch colonial house on the north edge of town. The lawn was neatly trimmed and fiercely green, and there was a bed of rosebushes on either side of the path leading from the sidewalk to the front door.

One of the leaflets at the motel told how roses were a local specialty. But the town had been named not for the flower but for Aaron Rose, a local settler.

He wondered if Engleman knew that.

He circled the block, parked two doors away on the other side of the street from the Engleman residence. *Vandermeer Edward,* the White Pages listing had read. It struck Keller as an unusual alias. He wondered if Engleman had picked it out himself, or if the feds had selected it for him. Probably the latter, he decided. "Here's your new name," they would tell you, "and here's where you're going to live, and who you're going to be." There was an arbitrariness about it that somehow appealed to Keller, as if they relieved you of the burden of decision. Here's your new name, and here's your new driver's license with your new name already on it. You like scalloped potatoes in your new life, and you're allergic to bee stings, and your favorite color is blue.

Betty Engleman was now Betty Vandermeer. Keller wondered why her first name hadn't changed. Didn't they trust Engleman to get it right? Did they figure him for a bumbler, apt to blurt out "Betty" at an inopportune moment? Or was it sheer coincidence, or sloppiness on their part?

Around six-thirty the Englemans came home from work. They rode in a Honda Civic hatchback with local plates. They had evidently stopped to shop for groceries on the way home. Engleman parked in the driveway while his wife got a bag of groceries from the back. Then he put the car in the garage and followed her into the house.

Keller watched lights go on inside the house. He stayed where he was. It was starting to get dark by the time he drove back to the Douglas Inn.

On HBO, Keller watched a movie about a gang of criminals who have come to a small town in Texas to rob the bank. One of the criminals was a woman, married to one of the other gang members and having an affair with another. Keller thought that was a pretty good recipe for disaster. There was a prolonged shoot-out at the end, with everybody dying in slow motion.

When the movie ended he went over to switch off the set. His eye was caught by the stack of flyers Engleman had run off for him. LOST DOG. *Part Ger. Shepherd. Answers to Soldier. Call 765-1904.* REWARD.

Excellent watchdog, he thought. Good with children.

A little later he turned the set back on again. He didn't get to sleep until late, didn't get up until almost noon. He went to the Mexican place and ordered *huevos rancheros* and put a lot of hot sauce on them.

He watched the waitress's hands as she served the food and again when she took his empty plate away. Light glinted off the little diamond. Maybe she and her husband would wind up on Cowslip Lane, he thought. Not right away, of course, they'd have to start out in the duplex, but that's what they could aspire to. A Dutch colonial with that odd kind of pitched roof. What did they call it, anyway? Was that a mansard roof or did that word describe something else? Was it a gambrel, maybe?

He thought he ought to learn these things sometime. You saw the words and didn't know what they meant, saw the houses and couldn't describe them properly.

He had bought a paper on his way into the café, and now he turned to the classified ads and read through the real estate listings. Houses seemed very inexpensive. You could actually buy a low-priced home here for twice what he would be paid for the week's work.

There was a safe-deposit box no one knew about rented under a name he'd never used for another purpose, and in it he had enough cash to buy a nice home here for cash. Assuming you could still do that. People were funny about cash these days, leery of letting themselves be used to launder drug money.

Anyway, what difference did it make? He wasn't going to live here. The waitress could live here, in a nice little house with mansards and gambrels.

Engleman was leaning over his wife's desk when Keller walked into Quik-Print. "Why, hello," he said. "Have you had any luck finding Soldier?"

He remembered the name, Keller noticed.

"As a matter of fact," he said, "the dog came back on his own. I guess he wanted the reward."

Betty Engleman laughed.

"You see how fast your flyers worked," he went on. "They brought the dog back even before I got the chance to post them. I'll get some use out of them eventually, though. Old Soldier's got itchy feet, he'll take off again one of these days."

"Just so he keeps coming back," she said.

"Reason I stopped by," Keller said, "I'm new in town, as you might have gathered, and I've got a business venture I'm getting ready to kick into gear. I'm going to need a printer, and I thought maybe we could sit down and talk. You got time for a cup of coffee?"

Engleman's eyes were hard to read behind the glasses. "Sure," he said. "Why not?"

They walked down to the corner, Keller talking about what a nice afternoon it was, Engleman saying little beyond agreeing with him. At the corner Keller said, "Well, Burt, where should we go for coffee?"

Engleman just froze. Then he said, "I knew."

"I know you did, I could tell the minute I walked in there. How?"

"The phone number on the flyer. I tried it last night. They never heard of a Mr. Gordon."

"So you knew last night. Of course, you could have made a mistake on the number."

Engleman shook his head. "I wasn't going on memory. I ran an extra flyer and dialed the number right off it. No Mr. Gordon and no lost dog. Anyway, I think I knew before then. I think I knew the minute you walked in the door."

"Let's get that coffee," Keller said.

They went into a place called the Rainbow Diner and had coffee at a table on the side. Engleman added artificial sweetener to his and stirred it long enough to dissolve marble chips. He had been an accountant back East, working for the man Keller had called in White Plains. When the feds were trying to make a RICO case against Engleman's boss, Engleman was a logical place to apply pressure. He wasn't really a criminal, he hadn't done much of anything, and they told him he was going to prison unless he rolled over and testified. If he did what they said, they'd give him a new name and move him someplace safe. If not, he could talk to his wife once a month through a wire screen, and have ten years to get used to it.

"How did you find me?" he wanted to know. "Somebody leaked it in Washington?"

Keller shook his head. "Freak thing," he said. "Somebody saw you on the street, recognized you, followed you home."

"Here in Roseburg?"

"I don't think so. Were you out of town a week or so ago?"

"Oh, God," Engleman said. "We went down to San Francisco for the weekend."

"That sounds right."

"I thought it was safe. I don't even know anybody in San Francisco, I was never there in my life. It was her birthday, we figured nothing could be safer. I don't know a soul there."

"Somebody knew you."

"And followed me back here?"

"I don't even know. Maybe they got your plate and had somebody run it. Maybe they checked your registration at the hotel. What's the difference?"

"No difference."

He picked up his coffee and stared into the cup. Keller said, "You knew last night. Did you call someone?"

"Who?"

"I don't know. You're in the witness-protection program. Isn't there somebody you can call when this happens?"

"There's somebody I can call," Engleman said. He put his cup back down again. "It's not that great a program," he said. "It's great when they're telling you about it, but the execution leaves a lot to be desired."

"I've heard that," Keller said.

"Anyway, I didn't call anybody. What are they going to do? Say they stake my place out, the house and the print shop, and they pick you up. Even if they make something stick against you, what good does it do me? We have to move again because the guy'll just send somebody else, right?"

"I suppose so."

"Well, I'm not moving anymore. They moved us three times and I don't even know why. I think it's automatic, part of the program, they move you a few times during the first year or two. This is the first place we really settled into since we left, and we're starting to make money at Quik-Print, and I like it. I like the town and I like the business. I don't want to move."

"The town seems nice."

"It is," Engleman said. "It's better than I thought it would be."

"And you didn't want to develop an accounting practice?"

"Never," Engleman said. "I had enough of that, believe me. Look what it got me."

"You wouldn't necessarily have to work for crooks."

"How do you know who's a crook and who isn't? Anyway, I don't want any kind of work where I'm always looking at the inside of somebody else's business. I'd rather have my own little business work, there side by side with my wife, we're right there on the street and you can look in the front window and see us. You need stationery, you need business cards, you need invoice forms, I'll print 'em for you."

"How did you learn the business?"

"It's a franchise kind of a thing, a turn-key operation. Anybody could learn it in twenty minutes."

"No kidding," Keller said.

"Oh, yeah. Anybody."

Keller drank some of his coffee. He asked if Engleman had said anything to his wife, learned that he hadn't. "That's good," he said. "Don't say anything. I'm this guy, weighing some business ventures, needs a printer, has to have, you know, arrangements so there's no cash-flow problem. And I'm shy talking business in front of women, so the two of us go off and have coffee from time to time."

"Whatever you say," Engleman said.

Poor scared bastard, Keller thought. He said, "See, I don't want to hurt you, Burt. I wanted to, we wouldn't be having this conversation. I'd put a gun to your head, do what I'm supposed to do. You see a gun?"

"No."

"The thing is, I don't do it, they send somebody else. I come back empty, they want to know why. What I have to do, I have to figure something out. You don't want to run."

"No. The hell with running."

"Well, I'll figure something out," Keller said. "I've got a few days. I'll think of something."

After breakfast the next morning Keller drove to the office of one of the realtors whose ads he'd been reading. A woman about the same age as Betty Engleman took him around and showed him three houses. They were modest homes but decent and comfortable, and they ranged between forty and sixty thousand dollars.

He could buy any of them out of his safe-deposit box.

"Here's your kitchen," the woman said. "Here's your half-bath. Here's your fenced yard."

"I'll be in touch," he told her, taking her card. "I have a business deal pending and a lot depends on the outcome."

He and Engleman had lunch the next day. They went to the Mexican place and Engleman wanted everything very mild. "Remember," he told Keller, "I used to be an accountant."

"You're a printer now," Keller said. "Printers can handle hot food."

"Not this printer. Not this printer's stomach."

They each drank a bottle of Carta Blanca with the meal. Keller had another bottle afterward. Engleman had a cup of coffee.

"If I had a house with a fenced yard," Keller said, "I could have a dog and not worry about him running off."

"I guess you could," Engleman said.

"I had a dog when I was a kid," Keller said. "Just the once, I had him for about two years when I was eleven, twelve years old. His name was Soldier."

"I was wondering about that."

"He wasn't part shepherd. He was a little thing, I suppose he was some kind of terrier cross."

"Did he run off?"

"No, he got hit by a car. He was stupid about cars, he just ran out in the street. The driver couldn't help it."

"How did you happen to call him Soldier?"

"I forget. Then when I did the flyer, I don't know, I had to put *answers to something*. All I could think of were names like Fido and Rover and Spot. Like signing John Smith on a hotel register, you know? Then it came to me, Soldier. Been years since I thought about that dog."

After lunch Engleman went back to the shop and Keller returned to the motel for his car. He drove out of town on the same road he'd taken the day he bought the gun. This time he rode a few miles farther before pulling over and cutting the engine.

He got the gun from the glove box and opened the cylinder, spilling the shells out into his palm. He tossed them underhand, then weighed the gun in his hand for a moment before hurling it into a patch of brush.

McLarendon would be horrified, he thought. Mistreating a weapon in that fashion. Showed what a judge of character the man was.

He got back in his car and drove back to town.

He called White Plains. When the woman answered he said, "You don't have to disturb him, Dot. Just tell him I didn't make my flight today. I changed the reservation, I moved it ahead to Tuesday. Tell him everything's okay, only it's taking a little longer, like I thought it might." She asked how the weather was. "It's real nice," he said. "Very pleasant. Listen, don't you think that's part of it? If it was raining I'd probably have it taken care of, I'd be home by now."

Quik-Print was closed Saturdays and Sundays. Saturday afternoon Keller called Engleman at home and asked him if he felt like going for a ride. "I'll pick you up," he offered.

When he got there Engleman was waiting out in front. He got in and fastened his seat belt. "Nice car," he said.

"It's a rental."

"I didn't figure you drove your own car all the way out here. You know, it gave me a turn. When you said how about going for a ride. You know, going for a ride. Like there's a connotation."

"Actually," Keller said, "we probably should have taken your car. I figured you could show me the area."

"You like it here, huh?"

"Very much," Keller said. "I've been thinking. Suppose I just stayed here."

"Wouldn't he send somebody?"

"You think he would? I don't know. He wasn't killing himself trying to find you. At first, sure, but then he forgot about it. Then some eager beaver in San Francisco happens to spot you and sure, he tells me to go out and handle it. But if I just don't come back—"

"Caught up in the lure of Roseburg," Engleman said.

"I don't know, Burt, it's not a bad place. You know, I'm going to stop that."

"What?"

"Calling you Burt. Your name's Ed now, so why don't I call you Ed? What do you think, Ed? That sound good to you, Ed, old buddy?"

"And what do I call you?"

"Al's fine. What should I do, take a left here?"

"No, go another block or two," Engleman said. "There's a nice road, leads through some very pretty scenery."

A while later Keller said, "You miss it much, Ed?"

"Working for him, you mean?"

"No, not that. The city."

"New York? I never lived in the city, not really. We were up in Westchester."

"Still, the whole area. You miss it?"

"No."

"I wonder if I would." They fell silent, and after perhaps five minutes he said, "My father was a soldier, he was killed in the war when I was just a baby. That's why I named the dog Soldier."

Engleman didn't say anything.

"Except I think my mother was lying," he went on. "I don't think she was married, and I have a feeling she didn't know who my father was. But I didn't know that when I named the dog. When you think about it, it's a stupid name anyway for a dog, Soldier. It's probably stupid to name a dog after your father, as far as that goes."

Sunday he stayed in the room and watched sports on television. The Mexican place was closed; he had lunch at Wendy's and dinner at a Pizza Hut. Monday at noon he was back at the Mexican café. He had the newspaper with him, and he ordered the same thing he'd ordered the first time, the chicken enchiladas.

When the waitress brought coffee afterward, he asked her, "When's the wedding?"

She looked utterly blank. "The wedding," he repeated, and pointed at the ring on her finger.

"Oh," she said. "Oh, I'm not engaged or anything. The ring was my mom's from her first marriage. She never wears it, so I asked could I wear it, and she said it was all right. I used to wear it on the other hand but it fits better here."

He felt curiously angry, as though she'd betrayed the fantasy he'd spun out about her. He left the same tip he always left and took a long walk around town, gazing in windows, wandering up one street and down the next.

He thought, Well, you could marry her. She's already got the engagement ring. Ed'll print your wedding invitations, except who would you invite?

And the two of you could get a house with a fenced yard, and buy a dog.

Ridiculous, he thought. The whole thing was ridiculous.

At dinnertime he didn't know what to do. He didn't want to go back to the Mexican café but he felt perversely disinclined to go anywhere else. One more Mexican meal, he thought, and I'll wish I had that gun back so I could kill myself.

He called Engleman at home. "Look," he said, "this is important. Could you meet me at your shop?"

"When?"

"As soon as you can."

"We just sat down to dinner."

"Well, don't ruin your meal," Keller said. "What is it, seven-thirty? How about if you meet me in an hour."

He was waiting in the photographer's doorway when Engleman parked the Honda in front of his shop. "I didn't want to disturb you," he said, "but I had an idea. Can you open up? I want to see something inside."

Engleman unlocked the door and they went in. Keller kept talking to him, saying how he'd figured out a way he could stay in Roseburg and not worry about the man in White Plains. "This machine you've got," he said, pointing to one of the copiers. "How does this work?"

"How does it work?"

"What does that switch do?"

"This one?"

Engleman leaned forward, and Keller got the loop of wire out of his pocket and dropped it around the other man's neck. The garrote was fast, silent, deadly. Keller made sure Engleman's body was where it couldn't be seen from the street, made sure to wipe his prints off any surfaces he might have touched. He turned off the lights, closed the door behind him.

He had already checked out of the Douglas Inn, and now he drove straight to Portland, with the Ford's cruise control set just below the speed limit. He drove half an hour in silence, then turned on the radio and tried to find a station he could stand. Nothing pleased him and he gave up and switched it off.

Somewhere north of Eugene he said, "Jesus, Ed, what else was I going to do?"

He drove straight through to Portland and got a room at the ExecuLodge near the airport. In the morning he turned in the Hertz car and dawdled over coffee until his flight was called.

He called White Plains as soon as he was on the ground at JFK. "It's all taken care of," he said. "I'll come by sometime tomorrow. Right now I just want to get home, get some sleep."

The following afternoon in White Plains Dot asked him how he'd liked Roseburg.

"Really nice," he said. "Pretty town, nice people. I wanted to stay there."

"Oh, Keller," she said. "What did you do, look at houses?"

"Not exactly."

"Every place you go," she said, "you want to live there."

"It's nice," he insisted. "And living's cheap compared to here. A person could have a decent life."

"For a week," she said. "Then you'd go nuts."

"You really think so?"

"Come *on*," she said. "Roseburg, Oregon? Come on."

"I guess you're right," he said. "I guess a week's about as much as I could handle."

A few days later he was going through his pockets before taking some clothes to the cleaners. He found the Roseburg street map and went over it, remembering where everything was. Quik-Print, the Douglas Inn, the house on Cowslip. The Mexican café, the other places he'd eaten. The gun shop. The houses he'd looked at.

He folded the map and put it in his dresser drawer. A month later he came across it, and for a moment he couldn't place it. Then he laughed. And tore it in half, and in half again, and put it in the trash.

Keller's Therapy

"I had this dream," Keller said. "Matter of fact I wrote it down, as you suggested."

"Good."

Before getting on the couch Keller had removed his jacket and hung it on the back of a chair. He moved from the couch to retrieve his notebook from the jacket's inside breast pocket, then sat on the couch and found the page with the dream on it. He read through his notes rapidly, closed the book, and sat there, uncertain how to proceed.

"As you prefer," said Breen. "Sitting up or lying down, whichever is more comfortable."

"It doesn't matter?"

"Not to me."

And which was more comfortable? A seated posture seemed more natural for conversation, while lying down on the couch had the weight of tradition on its side. Keller, who felt driven to give this his best shot, decided to go with tradition. He stretched out, put his feet up.

He said, "I'm living in a house, except it's almost like a castle. Endless passageways and dozens of rooms."

"Is it your house?"

"No, I just live here. In fact I'm a kind of servant for the family that owns the house. They're almost like royalty."

"And you are a servant."

"Except I have very little to do, and I'm treated like an equal. I play tennis with members of the family. There's this tennis court in back of the house."

"And this is your job? To play tennis with them?"

"No, that's an example of how they treat me as an equal. And I eat at the same table with them, instead of eating downstairs with the servants. My job is the mice."

"The mice?"

"The house is infested with mice. I'm having dinner with the family, I've got a plate piled high with good food, and a waiter in black tie comes in and presents a covered dish. I lift the cover and there's a note on it, and it says, 'Mice.' "

"Just the single word?"

"That's all. I get up from the table and I follow the servant down a long hallway, and I wind up in an unfinished room in the attic. There are tiny mice all over the room, there must be twenty or thirty of them, and I have to kill them."

"How?"

"By crushing them underfoot. That's the quickest and most humane way, but it bothers me and I don't want to do it. But the sooner I finish, the sooner I can get back to my dinner, and I'm very hungry."

"So you kill the mice?"

"Yes," Keller said. "One almost gets away but I stomp on it just as it's getting out the door. And then I'm back at the dinner table and everybody's eating and drinking and laughing, and my plate's been cleared away. Then there's a big fuss, and finally they bring my plate back from the kitchen, but it's not the same food as before. It's . . ."

"Yes?"

"Mice," Keller said. "They're skinned and cooked, but it's a plateful of mice."

"And you eat them?"

"That's when I woke up," Keller said. "And not a moment too soon, I'd have to say."

"Ah," Breen said. He was a tall man, long-limbed and gawky, wearing chinos and a dark green shirt and a brown corduroy jacket. He looked to Keller like someone who had been a nerd in high school, and who now managed to look distinguished, in an eccentric sort of way. He said "Ah" again, and folded his hands, and asked Keller what he thought the dream meant.

"You're the doctor," Keller said.

"You think it means that I am the doctor?"

"No, I think you're the one who can say what it means. Maybe it just means I shouldn't eat Rocky Road ice cream right before I go to bed."

"Tell me what you think the dream might mean."

"Maybe I see myself as a cat."

"Or as an exterminator?"

Keller didn't say anything.

"Let us work with this dream on a very superficial level," Breen said. "You're employed as a corporate troubleshooter, except that you used another word for it."

"They tend to call us expediters," Keller said, "but troubleshooter is what it amounts to."

"Most of the time there is nothing for you to do. You have considerable opportunity for recreation, for living the good life. For tennis, as it were, and for nourishing yourself at the table of the rich and powerful. Then mice are discovered, and it is at once clear that you are a servant with a job to do."

"I get it," Keller said.

"Go on, then. Explain it to me."

"Well, it's obvious, isn't it? There's a problem and I'm called in and I have to drop what I'm doing and go and deal with it. I have to take abrupt arbitrary action, and that can involve firing people and closing out whole departments. I have to do it, but it's like stepping on mice. And when I'm back at the table and I want my food—I suppose that's my salary?"

"Your compensation, yes."

"And I get a plate of mice." He made a face. "In other words, what? My compensation comes from the destruction of the people I have to cut adrift. My sustenance comes at their expense. So it's a guilt dream?"

"What do you think?"

"I think it's guilt. My profit derives from the misfortunes of others, from the grief I bring to others. That's it, isn't it?"

"On the surface, yes. When we go deeper, perhaps we will begin to discover other connections. With your having chosen this job in the first place, perhaps, and with some aspects of your childhood." He interlaced his fingers and sat back in his chair. "Everything is of a piece, you know. Nothing exists alone and nothing is accidental. Even your name."

"My name?"

"Peter Stone. Think about it, why don't you, between now and our next session."

"Think about my name?"

"About your name and how it suits you. And"—a reflexive glance at his wristwatch—"I'm afraid our hour is up."

Jerrold Breen's office was on Central Park West at Ninety-fourth Street. Keller walked to Columbus Avenue, rode a bus five blocks, crossed the street, and hailed a taxi. He had the driver go through Central Park, and by the time he got out of the cab at Fiftieth Street he was reasonably certain he hadn't been followed. He bought coffee in a deli and stood on the sidewalk, keeping an eye open while he drank it. Then he walked to the building where he lived, on First Avenue between Forty-eighth and Forty-ninth. It was a prewar high-rise, with an Art Deco lobby and an attended elevator. "Ah, Mr. Keller," the attendant said. "A beautiful day, yes?"

"Beautiful," Keller agreed.

Keller had a one-bedroom apartment on the nineteenth floor. He could look out his window and see the UN building, the East River, the borough of Queens. On the first Sunday in November he could watch the runners streaming across the Queensboro Bridge, just a couple of miles past the midpoint of the New York marathon.

It was a spectacle Keller tried not to miss. He would sit at his window for hours while thousands of them passed through his field of vision, first the world-class runners, then the middle-of-the-pack plodders, and finally the slowest of the slow, some walking, some hobbling. They started in Staten Island and finished in Central Park, and all he saw was a few hundred yards of their ordeal as they made their way over the bridge into Manhattan. Sooner or later the sight always moved him to tears, although he could not have said why.

Maybe it was something to talk about with Breen.

It was a woman who had led him to the therapist's couch, an aerobics instructor named Donna. Keller had met her at the gym. They'd had a couple of dates, and had been to bed a couple of times, enough to establish their sexual incompatibility. Keller still went to the same gym two or three times a week to raise and lower heavy metal objects, and when he ran into her they were friendly.

One time, just back from a trip somewhere, he must have rattled on about what a nice town it was. "Keller," she said, "if there was ever a born New Yorker, you're it. You know that, don't you?"

"I suppose so."

"But you've always got this fantasy, living the good life in Elephant, Montana. Every place you go, you dream up a whole life to go with it."

"Is that bad?"

"Who's saying it's bad? But I bet you could have fun with it in therapy."

"You think I need to be in therapy?"

"I think you'd get a lot out of therapy," she said. "Look, you come here, right? You climb the Stair Monster, you use the Nautilus."

"Mostly free weights."

"Whatever. You don't do this because you're a physical wreck."

"I do it to stay in shape."

"And because it makes you feel good."

"So?"

"So I see you as all closed in and trying to reach out," she said. "Going all over the country and getting real estate agents to show you houses you're not going to buy."

"That was only a couple of times. And what's so bad about it, anyway? It passes the time."

"You do these things and don't know why," she said. "You know what therapy is? It's an adventure, it's a voyage of discovery. And it's like going to the gym. It's . . . look, forget it. The whole thing's pointless anyway unless you're interested."

"Maybe I'm interested," he said.

Donna, not surprisingly, was in therapy herself. But her therapist was a woman, and they agreed he'd be more comfortable working with a man. Her ex-husband had been very fond of his therapist, a West Side psychologist named Breen. Donna had never met the man herself, and she wasn't on the best of terms with her ex, but—

"That's all right," he said. "I'll call him myself."

He'd called Breen, using Donna's ex-husband's name as a reference. "But I doubt that he even knows me by name," he said. "We got to talking a while back at a party and I haven't seen him since. But something he said struck a chord with me, and, well, I thought I ought to explore it."

"Intuition is a powerful teacher," Breen said.

Keller made an appointment, giving his name as Peter Stone. In his first session he talked some about his work for a large and unnamed conglomerate. "They're a little old-fashioned when it comes to psychotherapy," he told Breen. "So I'm not going to give you an address or telephone number, and I'll pay for each session in cash."

"Your life is filled with secrets," Breen said.

"I'm afraid it is. My work demands it."

"This is a place where you can be honest and open. The idea is to uncover those secrets you've been keeping from yourself. Here you are protected by the sanctity of the confessional, but it's not my task to grant you absolution. Ultimately, you absolve yourself."

"Well," Keller said.

"Meanwhile, you have secrets to keep. I can respect that. I won't need your address or telephone number unless I'm forced to cancel an appointment. I suggest you call in to confirm your sessions an hour or two ahead of time, or you can take the chance of an occasional wasted trip. If you have to cancel an appointment, be sure to give me twenty-four hours' notice. Or I'll have to charge for the missed session."

"That's fair," Keller said.

He went twice a week, Mondays and Thursdays, at two in the afternoon. It was hard to tell what they were accomplishing. Sometimes Keller relaxed completely on the sofa, talking freely and honestly about his childhood. Other times he experienced the fifty-minute session as a balancing act; he was tugged in two directions at once, yearning to tell everything, compelled to keep it all a secret.

No one knew he was doing this. Once when he ran into Donna she asked if he'd ever given the shrink a call, and he'd shrugged sheepishly and said he hadn't. "I thought about it," he said, "but then somebody told me about this masseuse, she does a combination of Swedish and shiatsu, and I've got to tell you, I think it does me more good than somebody poking and probing at the inside of my head."

"Oh, Keller," she'd said, not without affection. "Don't ever change."

It was on a Monday that he recounted the dream about the mice. Wednesday morning his phone rang, and it was Dot. "He wants to see you," she said.

"Be right out," he said.

He put on a tie and jacket and caught a cab to Grand Central and a train to White Plains. There he caught another cab and told the driver to head out Washington Boulevard and let him off at the corner of Norwalk. After the cab drove off he walked up Norwalk to Taunton Place and turned left. The second house on the right was a big old Victorian with a wraparound porch. He rang the bell and Dot let him in.

"The upstairs den," she said. "He's expecting you."

He went upstairs, and forty minutes later he came down again. A young man named Louis drove him back to the station, and on the way they chatted about a recent boxing match they'd both seen on ESPN. "What I wish," Louis said, "I wish they had like a mute button on the remote, except what it would do is it would mute the announcers but you'd still hear the crowd noise and the punches landing. What you wouldn't have is the constant yammer-yammer-yammer in your ear." Keller wondered if they could do that. "I don't see why not," Louis said. "They can do everything else. If you can put a man on the moon, you ought to be able to shut up Al Bernstein."

Keller took the train back to New York and walked to his apartment. He made a couple of phone calls and packed a bag. At 3:30 he went downstairs, walked half a block, and hailed a cab to JFK, where he picked up his boarding pass for American's 6:10 flight to Tucson.

In the departure lounge he remembered his appointment with Breen. He called and canceled the Thursday session. Since it was less than twenty-four hours away, Breen said, he'd have to charge him for the missed session, unless he was able to book someone else into the slot.

"Don't worry about it," Keller told him. "I hope I'll be back in time for my Monday appointment, but it's always hard to know how long these things are going to take. If I can't make it I should at least be able to give you the twenty-four hours' notice."

He changed planes in Dallas and got to Tucson shortly before midnight. He had no luggage aside from the piece he was carrying, but he went to the baggage claim area anyway. A rail-thin man with a broad-brimmed straw hat stood there holding a hand-lettered sign that read NOSCAASI. Keller watched the man for a few minutes, and observed that no one else was watching him. He went up to him and said, "You know, I was figuring it out the whole way to Dallas. What I came up with, it's *Isaacson* spelled backwards."

"That's it," the man said. "That's exactly it." He seemed impressed, as if Keller had cracked the Japanese naval code. He said, "You didn't check a bag, did you? I didn't think so. Car's this way."

In the car the man showed him three photographs, all of the same man, heavy-set, dark, with glossy black hair and a greedy pig face. Bushy mustache, bushy eyebrows. Enlarged pores on his nose.

"That's Rollie Vasquez," the man said. "Son of a bitch wouldn't exactly win a beauty contest, would he?"

"I guess not."

"Let's go," the man said. "Show you where he lives, where he eats, where he gets his ashes hauled. Rollie Vasquez, this is your life."

Two hours later the man dropped him at a Ramada Inn and gave him a room key and a car key. "You're all checked in," he said. "Car's parked at the foot of the staircase closest to your room. She's a Mitsubishi Eclipse, pretty decent transportation. Color's supposed to be silver-blue, but she says gray on the papers. Registration's in the glove box."

"There was supposed to be something else."

"That's in the glove box, too. Locked, of course, but the one key fits the ignition and the glove box. And the doors and the trunk, too. And if you turn the key upside down it'll still fit, 'cause there's no up and down to it. You really got to hand it to those Japs."

"What'll they think of next?"

"Well, it may not seem like much," the man said, "but all the time you waste making sure you got the right key, then making sure you got it right side up."

"It adds up."

"It does," the man said. "Now, you got a full tank of gas. It takes regular, but what's in there's enough to take you upwards of four hundred miles."

"How're the tires? Never mind. Just a joke."

"And a good one," the man said. " 'How're the tires?' I like that."

The car was where it was supposed to be, and the glove box held the car's registration and a semiautomatic pistol, a .22-caliber Horstmann Sun Dog, fully loaded, with a spare clip lying alongside it. Keller slipped the gun and the spare clip into his carry-on, locked the car, and went to his room without passing the desk.

After a shower, he sat down and put his feet up on the coffee table. It was all arranged, and that made it simpler, but sometimes he liked it better the other way, when all he had was a name and address and no one on hand to smooth the way for him. This was simple, all right, but who knew what traces were being left? Who knew what kind of history the gun had, or what the string bean with the NOSCAASI sign would say if the police picked him up and shook him?

All the more reason to do it quickly. He watched enough of an old movie on cable to ready him for sleep, then slept until he woke up. When he went out to the car he had his bag with him. He expected to return to the room, but if he didn't he'd be leaving nothing behind, not even a fingerprint.

He stopped at Denny's for breakfast. Around one he had lunch at a Mexican place on Figueroa. In the late afternoon he drove up into the hills north of the city, and he was still there when the sun went down. Then he drove back to the Ramada.

That was Thursday. Friday morning the phone rang while he was shaving. He let it ring. It rang again just as he was ready to leave. He didn't answer it this time, either, but went around wiping surfaces a second time with a hand towel. Then he went out to the car.

At two that afternoon he followed Rolando Vasquez into the men's room of the Saguaro Lanes bowling alley and shot him three times in the head. The little gun didn't make much noise, not even in the confines of the tiled lavatory. Earlier he had fashioned an improvised suppressor by wrapping the barrel of the gun with a space-age insulating material that muffled most of the gun's report without adding much in the way of weight or bulk. If you could do that, he thought, you ought to be able to shut up Al Bernstein.

He left Vasquez propped in a stall, left the gun in a storm drain half a mile away, left the car in the long-term lot at the airport.

Flying home, he wondered why they had needed him in the first place. They'd supplied the car and the gun and the finger man. Why not do it all themselves? Did they really need to bring him all the way from New York to step on the mouse?

"You said to think about my name," he told Breen. "The significance of it. But I don't see how it could have any significance. It's not as if I chose it myself."

"Let me suggest something," Breen said. "There is a metaphysical principle which holds that we choose everything about our lives, that in fact we select the very parents we are born to, that everything which happens in our lives is a manifestation of our will. Thus there are no accidents, no coincidences."

"I don't know if I believe that."

"You don't have to. We'll just take it for the moment as a postulate. So, assuming that you chose the name Peter Stone, what does your choice tell us?"

Keller, stretched full length upon the couch, was not enjoying this. "Well, a peter's a penis," he said reluctantly. "A stone peter would be an erection, wouldn't it?"

"Would it?"

"So I suppose a guy who decides to call himself Peter Stone would have something to prove. Anxiety about his virility. Is that what you want me to say?"

"I want you to say whatever you wish," Breen said. "Are you anxious about your virility?"

"I never thought I was," Keller said. "Of course it's hard to say how much anxiety I might have had back before I was born, around the time I was picking my parents and deciding what name they should choose for me. At that age I probably had a certain amount of difficulty maintaining an erection, so I guess I had a lot to be anxious about."

"And now?"

"I don't have a performance problem, if that's the question. I'm not the way I was in my teens, ready to go three or four times a night, but then who in his right mind would want to? I can generally get the job done."

"You get the job done."

"Right."

"You perform."

"Is there something wrong with that?"

"What do you think?"

"Don't do that," Keller said. "Don't answer a question with a question. If I ask a question and you don't want to respond, just leave it alone. But don't turn it back on me. It's irritating."

Breen said, "You perform, you get the job done. But what do you feel, Mr. Peter Stone?"

"Feel?"

"It is unquestionably true that *peter* is a colloquialism for the penis, but it has an earlier meaning. Do you recall Christ's words to the first Peter? 'Thou art Peter, and upon this rock I shall build my church.' Because Peter *means* rock. Our Lord was making a pun. So your first name means rock and your last name is Stone. What does that give us? Rock and stone. Hard, unyielding, obdurate. Insensitive. Unfeeling."

"Stop," Keller said.

"In the dream, when you kill the mice, what do you feel?"

"Nothing. I just want to get the job done."

"Do you feel their pain? Do you feel pride in your accomplishment, satisfaction in a job well done? Do you feel a thrill, a sexual pleasure, in their death?"

"Nothing," Keller said. "I feel nothing. Could we stop for a moment?"

"What do you feel right now?"

"Just a little sick to my stomach, that's all."

"Do you want to use the bathroom? Shall I get you a glass of water?"

"No, I'm all right. It's better when I sit up. It'll pass. It's passing already."

Sitting at his window, watching not marathoners but cars streaming over the Queensboro Bridge, Keller thought about names. What was particularly annoying, he thought, was that he didn't need to be under the care of a board-certified metaphysician to acknowledge the implications of the name Peter Stone. He had very obviously chosen it, and not in the manner of a soul deciding what parents to be born to and planting names in their heads. He had picked the name himself when he called to make his initial appointment with Jerrold Breen. *Name?* Breen had demanded. *Stone,* he had replied. *Peter Stone.*

Thing is, he wasn't stupid. Cold, unyielding, insensitive, but not stupid. If you wanted to play the name game, you didn't have to limit yourself to the alias he had selected. You could have plenty of fun with the name he'd borne all his life.

His full name was John Paul Keller, but no one called him anything but Keller, and few people even knew his first or middle names. His apartment lease and most of the cards in his wallet showed his names as J. P. Keller. Just Plain Keller was what people called him, men and women alike. ("The upstairs den, Keller. He's expecting you." "Oh, Keller, don't ever change." "I don't know how to say this, Keller, but I'm just not getting my needs met in this relationship.")

Keller. In German it meant *cellar,* or *tavern.* But the hell with that, you didn't need to know what it meant in a foreign language. Just change a vowel. Keller = Killer.

Clear enough, wasn't it?

On the couch, eyes closed, Keller said, "I guess the therapy's working."

"Why do you say that?"

"I met a girl last night, bought her a couple of drinks, went home with her. We went to bed and I couldn't do anything."

"You couldn't do anything."

"Well, if you want to be technical, there were things I could have done. I could have typed a letter, sent out for a pizza. I could have sung 'Melancholy Baby.' But I couldn't do what we'd both been hoping I would do, which was have sex with her."

"You were impotent."

"You know, you're very sharp. You never miss a trick."

"You blame me for your impotence," Breen said.

"Do I? I don't know about that. I'm not sure I even blame myself. To tell you the truth, I was more amused than devastated by the experience. And she wasn't upset, perhaps out of relief that I wasn't upset. But just so nothing like this ever happens again, I've decided I'm changing my name to Dick Hardin."

"What was your father's name?"

"My father," Keller said. "Jesus, what a question. Where did that come from?"

Breen didn't say anything.

Neither, for several minutes, did Keller. Then, eyes closed, he said, "I never knew my father. He was a soldier. He was killed in action before I was born. Or he was shipped overseas before I was born and killed when I was a few months old. Or possibly he was home when I was born, or came home on leave when I was very small, and he held me on his knee and told me he was proud of me."

"You have such a memory?"

"I have no memory," Keller said. "The only memory I have is of my mother telling me about him, and that's the source of the confusion, because she told me different things at different times. Either he was killed before I was born or shortly after, and either he died without seeing me or he saw me one time and sat me on his knee. She was a good woman but she was vague about a lot of things. The one thing she was completely clear on, he was a soldier. And he got killed over there."

"And his name—"

Was Keller, he thought. "Same as mine," he said. "But forget the name, this is more important than the name. Listen to this. She had a picture of him, a head-and-shoulders shot, this good-looking young soldier in a uniform and wearing a cap, the kind that folds flat when you take it off. The picture was in a gold frame on her dresser when I was a little kid, and she would tell me how that was my father.

"And then one day the picture wasn't there anymore. 'It's gone,' she said. And that was all she would say on the subject. I was older then, I must have been seven or eight years old.

"Couple of years later I got a dog. I named him Soldier, I called him that after my father. Years after that two things occurred to me. One, Soldier's a funny thing to call a dog. Two, whoever heard of naming a dog after your father? But at the time it didn't seem the least bit unusual to me."

"What happened to the dog?"

"He became impotent. Shut up, will you? What I'm getting to's a lot more important than the dog. When I was fourteen, fifteen years old, I used to work afternoons after school helping out this guy who did odd jobs in the neighborhood. Cleaning out basements and attics, hauling trash, that sort of thing. One time this notions store went out of business, the owner must have died, and we were cleaning out the basement for the new tenant. Boxes of junk all over the place, and we had to go through everything, because part of how this guy made his money was selling off the stuff he got paid to haul. But you couldn't go through all this crap too thoroughly or you were wasting time.

"I was checking out this one box, and what do I pull out but a framed picture of my father. The very same picture that sat on my mother's dresser, him in his uniform and his military cap, the picture that disappeared, it's even in the same frame, and what's it doing here?"

Not a word from Breen.

"I can still remember how I felt. Like stunned, like *Twilight Zone* time. Then I reach back in the box and pull out the first thing I touch, and it's the same picture in the same frame.

"The whole box is framed pictures. About half of them are the soldier and the others are a fresh-faced blonde with her hair in a page boy and a big smile on her face. What it was, it was a box of frames. They used to package inexpensive frames that way, with a photo in it for display. For all I know they still do. So what my mother must have done, she must have bought a frame in a five-and-dime and told me it was my father. Then when I got a little older she got rid of it.

"I took one of the framed photos home with me. I didn't say anything to her, I didn't show it to her, but I kept it around for a while. I found out the photo dated from World War Two. In other words, it couldn't have been a picture of my father, because he would have been wearing a different uniform.

"By this time I think I already knew that the story she told me about my father was, well, a story. I don't believe she knew who my father was. I think she got drunk and went with somebody, or maybe there were several different men. What difference does it make? She moved to another town, she told people she was married, that her husband was in the service or that he was dead, whatever she told them."

"How do you feel about it?"

"How do I feel about it?" Keller shook his head. "If I slammed my hand in a cab door, you'd ask me how I felt about it."

"And you'd be stuck for an answer," Breen said. "Here's a question for you. Who was your father?"

"I just told you—"

"But someone fathered you. Whether or not you knew him, whether or not your mother knew who he was, there was a particular man who planted the seed that grew into you. Unless you believe yourself to be the second coming of Christ."

"No," Keller said. "That's one delusion I've been spared."

"So tell me who he was, this man who spawned you. Not on the basis of what you were told or what you've managed to figure out. I'm not asking this question of the part of you that thinks and reasons. I'm asking that part of you that simply knows. Who was your father? What was your father?"

"He was a soldier," Keller said.

Keller, walking uptown on Second Avenue, found himself standing in front of a pet shop, watching a couple of puppies cavorting in the window.

He went inside. One whole wall was given over to stacked cages of puppies and kittens. Keller felt his spirits sinking as he looked into the cages. Waves of sadness rocked him.

He turned away and looked at the other pets. Birds in cages, gerbils and snakes in dry aquariums, tanks of tropical fish. He was all right with them. It was the puppies that he couldn't bear to look at.

He left the store. The next day he went to an animal shelter and walked past cages of dogs waiting to be adopted. This time the sadness was overwhelming, and he felt it physically as pressure against his chest. Something must have shown on his face, because the young woman in charge asked him if he was all right.

"Just a dizzy spell," he said.

In the office she told him that they could probably accommodate him if he was especially interested in a particular breed. They could keep his name on file, and when a specimen of that breed became available—

"I don't think I can have a pet," he said. "I travel too much. I can't handle the responsibility." The woman didn't respond, and Keller's words echoed in her silence. "But I want to make a donation," he said. "I want to support the work you do."

He got out his wallet, pulled bills from it, handed them to her without counting them. "An anonymous donation," he said. "I don't want a receipt. I'm sorry for taking your time. I'm sorry I can't adopt a dog. Thank you. Thank you very much."

She was saying something, but he didn't listen. He hurried out of there.

" 'I want to support the work you do.' That's what I told her, and then I rushed out of there because I didn't want her thanking me. Or asking me questions."

"What would she ask?"

"I don't know," Keller said. He rolled over on the couch, facing away from Breen, facing the wall. " 'I want to support your work.' But I don't even know what their work is. They find homes for some animals, and what do they do with the others? Put them to sleep?"

"Perhaps."

"What do I want to support? The placement or the killing?"

"You tell me."

"I tell you too much as it is," Keller said.

"Or not enough."

Keller didn't say anything.

"Why did it sadden you to see the dogs in their cages?"

"I felt their sadness."

"One feels only one's own sadness. Why is it sad to you, a dog in a cage? Are you in a cage?"

"No."

"Your dog, Soldier. Tell me about him."

"All right," Keller said. "I guess I could do that."

A session or two later, Breen said, "You have never been married."

"No."

"I was married."

"Oh?"

"For eight years. She was my receptionist, she booked my appointments, showed clients to the waiting room until I was ready for them. Now I have no receptionist. A machine answers the phone. I check the machine between appointments, and take and return calls at that time. If I had had a machine in the first place I'd have been spared a lot of agony."

"It wasn't a good marriage?"

Breen didn't seem to have heard the question. "I wanted children. She had three abortions in eight years and never told me. Never said a word. Then one day she threw it in my face. I'd been to a doctor, I'd had tests, and all indications were that I was fertile, with a high sperm count and extremely motile sperm. So I wanted her to see a doctor. 'You fool, I've killed three of your babies already, why don't you leave me alone?' I told her I wanted a divorce. She said it would cost me."

"And?"

"We were married eight years. We've been divorced for nine. Every month I write an alimony check and put it in the mail. If it was up to me I'd rather burn the money."

Breen fell silent. After a moment Keller said, "Why are you telling me all this?"

"No reason."

"Is it supposed to relate to something in my psyche? Am I supposed to make a connection, clap my hand to my forehead, say, 'Of course, of course! I've been so blind!' "

"You confide in me," Breen said. "It seems only fitting that I confide in you."

A couple of days later Dot called. Keller took a train to White Plains, where Louis met him at the station and drove him to the house on Taunton Place. Later Louis drove him back to the train station and he returned to the city. He timed his call to Breen so that he got the man's machine. "This is Peter Stone," he said. "I'm flying to San Diego on business. I'll have to miss my next appointment, and possibly the one after that. I'll try to let you know."

Was there anything else to tell Breen? He couldn't think of anything. He hung up, packed a bag, and rode Amtrak to Philadelphia.

No one met his train. The man in White Plains had shown him a photograph and given him a slip of paper with a name and address on it. The man in question managed an adult bookstore a few blocks from Independence Hall. There was a tavern across the street, a perfect vantage point, but one look inside made it clear to Keller that he couldn't spend time there without calling attention to himself, not unless he first got rid of his tie and jacket and spent twenty minutes rolling around in the gutter.

Down the street Keller found a diner, and if he sat at the far end he could keep an eye on the bookstore's mirrored front windows. He had a cup of coffee, then walked across the street to the bookstore, where there were two men on duty. One was a dark and sad-eyed youth from India or Pakistan, the other the jowly, slightly exophthalmic fellow in the photo Keller had seen in White Plains.

Keller walked past a whole wall of videocassettes and leafed through a display of magazines. He had been there for about fifteen minutes when the kid said he was going for his dinner. The older man said, "Oh, it's that time already, huh? Okay, but make sure you're back by seven for a change, will you?"

Keller looked at his watch. It was six o'clock. The only other customers were closeted in video booths in the back. Still, the kid had had a look at him, and what was the big hurry, anyway?

He grabbed a couple of magazines at random and paid for them. The jowly man bagged them and sealed the bag with a strip of tape. Keller stowed his purchase in his carry-on and went to find himself a hotel room.

The next day he went to a museum and a movie, arriving at the bookstore at ten minutes after six. The young clerk was gone, presumably having a plate of curry somewhere. The jowly man was behind the counter, and there were three customers in the store, two checking the video selections, one looking at magazines.

Keller browsed, hoping they would decide to clear out. At one point he was standing in front of a whole wall of videocassettes and it turned into a wall of caged puppies. It was momentary, and he couldn't tell if it was a genuine hallucination or just some sort of mental flashback. Whatever it was, he didn't like it.

One customer left, but the other two lingered, and then someone new came in off the street. And in half an hour the Indian kid was due back, and who knew if he would take his full hour, anyway?

He approached the counter, trying to look a little more nervous than he felt. Shifty eyes, furtive glances. Pitching his voice low, he said, "Talk to you in private?"

"About what?"

Eyes down, shoulders drawn in, he said, "Something special."

"If it's got to do with little kids," the man said, "no disrespect intended, but I don't know nothing about it, I don't want to know nothing about it, and I wouldn't even know where to steer you."

"Nothing like that," Keller said.

They went into a room in back. The jowly man closed the door, and as he was turning around Keller hit him with the edge of his hand at the juncture of neck and shoulder. The man's knees buckled, and in an instant Keller had a loop of wire around his neck. In another minute he was out the door, and within the hour he was on the northbound Metroliner.

When he got home he realized he still had the magazines in his bag. That was sloppy, he should have discarded them the previous night, but he'd simply forgotten them altogether and never even unsealed the package.

Nor could he find a reason to unseal it now. He carried it down the hall, dropped it unopened into the incinerator. Back in his apartment, he fixed himself a weak scotch and water and watched a documentary on the Discovery Channel. The vanishing rain forest, one more goddam thing to worry about.

"Oedipus," Jerrold Breen said, holding his hands in front of his chest, his fingertips pressed together. "I presume you know the story. Unwittingly, he killed his father and married his mother."

"Two pitfalls I've thus far managed to avoid."

"Indeed," Breen said. "But have you? When you fly off somewhere in your official capacity as corporate expediter, when you shoot trouble, as it were, what exactly are you doing? You fire people, you cashier entire divisions, close plants, rearrange human lives. Is that a fair description?"

"I suppose so."

"There's an implied violence. Firing a man, terminating his career, is the symbolic equivalent of killing him. And he's a stranger, and I shouldn't doubt that the more important of these men are more often than not older than you, isn't that so?"

"What's the point?"

"When you do what you do, it's as if you are seeking out and killing your unknown father."

"I don't know," Keller said. "Isn't that a little far-fetched?"

"And your relationships with women," Breen went on, "have a strong Oedipal component. Your mother was a vague and unfocused woman, incompletely present in her own life, incapable of connection with others. Your own relationships with women are likewise blurred and out of focus. Your problems with impotence—"

"Once!"

"—are a natural consequence of this confusion. Your mother herself is dead now, isn't that so?"

"Yes."

"And your father is not to be found, and almost certainly deceased. What's called for, Peter, is an act specifically designed to reverse this entire pattern on a symbolic level."

"I don't follow you."

"It's a subtle point," Breen admitted. He crossed his legs, propped an elbow on a knee, extended his thumb, and rested his bony chin on it. Keller thought, not for the first time, that Breen must have been a stork in a prior life. "If there were a male figure in your life," Breen went on, "preferably at least a few years your senior, someone playing a faintly paternal role vis-à-vis yourself, someone to whom you turn for advice and direction."

Keller thought of the man in White Plains.

"Instead of killing this man," Breen said, "symbolically, I need hardly say—I am speaking symbolically throughout—but instead of killing him as you have done with father figures in the past, it seems to me that you might do something to nourish this man."

Cook a meal for the man in White Plains? Buy him a hamburger? Toss him a salad?

"Perhaps you could think of a way to use your particular talents to this man's benefit instead of his detriment," Breen went on. He drew a handkerchief from his breast pocket and mopped his forehead. "Perhaps there is a woman in his life—your mother, symbolically—and perhaps she is a source of great pain to your father. So, instead of making love to her and slaying him, like Oedipus, you might reverse the usual course of things by, uh, showing love to him and, uh, slaying her."

"Oh," Keller said.

"Symbolically, that is to say."

"Symbolically," Keller said.

A week later Breen handed him a photograph. "This is called the Thematic Apperception Test," Breen said. "You look at the photograph and make up a story about it."

"What kind of story?"

"Any kind at all," Breen said. "This is an exercise in imagination. You look at the subject of the photograph and imagine what sort of woman she is and what she is doing."

The photo was in color, and showed a rather elegant brunette dressed in tailored clothing. She had a dog on a leash. The dog was medium size, with a chunky body and an alert expression in its eyes. It was that color which dog people call blue, and which everyone else calls gray.

"It's a woman and a dog," Keller said.

"Very good."

Keller took a breath. "The dog can talk," he said, "but he won't do it in front of other people. The woman made a fool of herself once when she tried to show him off. Now she knows better. When they're alone he talks a blue streak, and the son of a bitch has an opinion on everything. He tells her everything from the real cause of the Thirty Years' War to the best recipe for lasagna."

"He's quite a dog," Breen said.

"Yes, and now the woman doesn't want other people to know he can talk, because she's afraid they might take him away from her. In this picture they're in the park. It looks like Central Park."

"Or perhaps Washington Square."

"It could be Washington Square," Keller agreed. "The woman is crazy about the dog. The dog's not so sure about the woman."

"And what do you think about the woman?"

"She's attractive," Keller said.

"On the surface," Breen said. "Underneath it's another story, believe me. Where do you suppose she lives?"

Keller gave it some thought. "Cleveland," he said.

"Cleveland? Why Cleveland, for God's sake?"

"Everybody's got to be someplace."

"If I were taking this test," Breen said, "I'd probably imagine the woman living at the foot of Fifth Avenue, at Washington Square. I'd have her living at number one Fifth Avenue, perhaps because I'm familiar with that particular building. You see, I once lived there."

"Oh?"

"In a spacious apartment on a high floor. And once a month," he continued, "I write out an enormous check and mail it to that address, which used to be mine. So it's only natural that I would have this particular building in mind, especially when I look at this particular photograph." His eyes met Keller's. "You have a question, don't you? Go ahead and ask it."

"What breed is the dog?"

"The dog?"

"I just wondered," Keller said.

"As it happens," Breen said, "it's an Australian cattle dog. Looks like a mongrel, doesn't it? Believe me, it doesn't talk. But why don't you hang on to that photograph?"

"All right."

"You're making really fine progress in therapy," Breen said. "I want to acknowledge you for the work you're doing. And I just know you'll do the right thing."

A few days later Keller was sitting on a park bench in Washington Square. He folded his newspaper and walked over to a dark-haired woman wearing a blazer and a beret. "Excuse me," he said, "but isn't that an Australian cattle dog?"

"That's right," she said.

"It's a handsome animal," he said. "You don't see many of them."

"Most people think he's a mutt. It's such an esoteric breed. Do you own one yourself?"

"I did. My ex-wife got custody."

"How sad for you."

"Sadder still for the dog. His name was Soldier. *Is* Soldier, unless she's gone and changed it."

"This fellow's name is Nelson. That's his call name. Of course the name on his papers is a real mouthful."

"Do you show him?"

"He's seen it all," she said. "You can't show him a thing."

"I went down to the Village last week," Keller said, "and the damnedest thing happened. I met a woman in the park."

"Is that the damnedest thing?"

"Well, it's unusual for me. I meet women at bars and parties, or someone introduces us. But we met and talked, and then I happened to run into her the following morning. I bought her a cappuccino."

"You just happened to run into her on two successive days."

"Yes."

"In the Village."

"It's where I live."

Breen frowned. "You shouldn't be seen with her, should you?"

"Why not?"

"Don't you think it's dangerous?"

"All it's cost me so far," Keller said, "is the price of a cappuccino."

"I thought we had an understanding."

"An understanding?"

"You don't live in the Village," Breen said. "I know where you live. Don't look so surprised. The first time you left here I watched you from the window. You behaved as though you were trying to avoid being followed. So I bided my time, and when you stopped taking precautions, that's when I followed you. It wasn't that difficult."

"Why follow me?"

"To find out who you were. Your name is Keller, you live at 865 First Avenue. I already knew *what* you were. Anybody might have known just from listening to your dreams. And paying in cash, and all of these sudden business trips. I still don't know who employs you, the crime bosses or the government, but then what difference does it make? Have you been to bed with my wife?"

"Your ex-wife."

"Answer the question."

"Yes, I have."

"Christ. And were you able to perform?"

"Yes."

"Why the smile?"

"I was just thinking," Keller said, "that it was quite a performance."

Breen was silent for a long moment, his eyes fixed on a spot above and to the right of Keller's shoulder. Then he said, "This is profoundly disappointing. I had hoped you would find the strength to transcend the Oedipal myth, not merely reenact it. You've had fun, haven't you? What a naughty little boy you've been! What a triumph you've scored over your symbolic father! You've taken his woman to bed. No doubt you have visions of getting her pregnant, so that she can give you what she so cruelly denied him. Eh?"

"Never occurred to me."

"It would, sooner or later." Breen leaned forward, concern showing on his face. "I hate to see you sabotaging your own therapeutic process this way," he said. "You were doing so *well*."

From the bedroom window you could look down at Washington Square Park. There were plenty of dogs there now, but none of them were Australian cattle dogs.

"Some view," Keller said. "Some apartment."

"Believe me," she said, "I earned it. You're getting dressed. Going somewhere?"

"Just feeling a little restless. Okay if I take Nelson for a walk?"

"You're spoiling him," she said. "You're spoiling both of us."

On a Wednesday morning, Keller took a cab to La Guardia and a plane to St. Louis. He had a cup of coffee with an associate of the man in White Plains and caught an evening flight back to New York. He caught another cab and went directly to the apartment building at the foot of Fifth Avenue.

"I'm Peter Stone," he told the doorman. "I believe Mrs. Breen is expecting me."

The doorman stared.

"Mrs. Breen," Keller said. "In Seventeen-J."

"I guess you haven't heard," the doorman said. "I wish it wasn't me that had to tell you."

"You killed her," he said.

"That's ridiculous," Breen told him. "She killed herself. She threw herself out the window. If you want my professional opinion, she was suffering from depression."

"If you want *my* professional opinion," Keller said, "she had help."

"I wouldn't advance that argument if I were you," Breen said. "If the police were to look for a murderer, they might look long and hard at Mr. Stone-hyphen-Keller, the stone killer. And I might have to tell them how the usual process of transference went awry, how you became obsessed with me and my personal life, how I couldn't seem to dissuade you from some inane plan to reverse the Oedipal complex. And then they might ask you why you employ aliases, and just how you make your living, and . . . do you see why it might be best to let sleeping dogs lie?"

As if on cue, the dog stepped out from behind the desk. He caught sight of Keller and his tail began to wag.

"Sit," Breen said. "You see? He's well trained. You might take a seat yourself."

"I'll stand. You killed her, and then you walked off with the dog, and—"

Breen sighed. "The police found the dog in the apartment, whimpering in front of the open window. After I went down and identified the body and told them about her previous suicide attempts, I volunteered to take the dog home with me. There was no one else to look after it."

"I would have taken him," Keller said.

"But that won't be necessary, will it? You won't be called upon to walk my dog or make love to my wife or bed down in my apartment. Your services are no longer required." Breen seemed to recoil at the harshness of his own words. His face softened. "You'll be able to get back to the far more important business of therapy. In fact"—he indicated the couch—"why not stretch out right now?"

"That's not a bad idea. First, though, could you put the dog in the other room?"

"Not afraid he'll interrupt, are you? Just a little joke. He can wait for us in the outer office. There you go, Nelson. Good dog . . . Oh, no. How dare you bring a gun to this office? Put that down immediately."

"I don't think so."

"For God's sake, why kill me? I'm not your father. I'm your therapist. It makes no sense for you to kill me. You've got nothing to gain and everything to lose. It's completely irrational. It's worse than that, it's neurotically self-destructive."

"I guess I'm not cured yet."

"What's that, gallows humor? But it happens to be true. You're a long way from cured, my friend. As a matter of fact, I would say you're approaching a psychotherapeutic crisis. How will you get through it if you shoot me?"

Keller went to the window, flung it wide open. "I'm not going to shoot you," he said.

"I've never been the least bit suicidal," Breen said, pressing his back against a wall of bookshelves. "Never."

"You've grown despondent over the death of your ex-wife."

"That's sickening, just sickening. And who would believe it?"

"We'll see," Keller told him. "As far as the therapeutic crisis is concerned, well, we'll see about that, too. I'll think of something."

The woman at the animal shelter said, "Talk about coincidence. One day you come in and put your name down for an Australian cattle dog. You know, that's a very uncommon breed in this country."

"You don't see many of them."

"And what came in this morning? A perfectly lovely Australian cattle dog. You could have knocked me over with a sledgehammer. Isn't he a beauty?"

"He certainly is."

"He's been whimpering ever since he got here. It's very sad, his owner died and there was nobody to keep him. My goodness, look how he went right to you! I think he likes you."

"I'd say we were made for each other."

"I can almost believe it. His name is Nelson, but of course you can change it."

"Nelson," he said. The dog's ears perked up. Keller reached to give him a scratch. "No, I don't think I'll have to change it. Who was Nelson, anyway? Some kind of English hero, wasn't he? A famous general or something?"

"I think an admiral. Commander of the British fleet, if I remember correctly. Remember? The Battle of Trafalgar Square?"

"It rings a muted bell," he said. "Not a soldier but a sailor. Well, that's close enough, wouldn't you say? Now I suppose there's an adoption fee to pay, and some papers to fill out."

When they'd handled that part she said, "I still can't get over it. The coincidence and all."

"I knew a man once," Keller said, "who insisted there was no such thing as a coincidence or an accident."

"Well, I wonder how he'd explain this."

"I'd like to hear him try," Keller said. "Let's go, Nelson. Good boy."

Keller on the Spot

Keller, drink in hand, agreed with the woman in the pink dress that it was a lovely evening. He threaded his way through a crowd of young marrieds on what he supposed you would call the patio. A waitress passed carrying a tray of drinks in stemmed glasses and he traded in his own for a fresh one. He sipped as he walked along, wondering what he was drinking. Some sort of vodka sour, he decided, and decided as well that he didn't need to narrow it down any further than that. He figured he'd have this one and one more, but he could have ten more if he wanted, because he wasn't working tonight. He could relax and cut back and have a good time.

Well, almost. He couldn't relax completely, couldn't cut back altogether. Because, while this might not be work, neither was it entirely recreational. The garden party this evening was a heaven-sent opportunity for reconnaissance, and he would use it to get a close look at his quarry. He had been handed a picture in the old man's study back in White Plains, and he had brought that picture with him to Dallas, but even the best photo wasn't the same as a glimpse of the fellow in the flesh, and in his native habitat.

And a lush habitat it was. Keller hadn't been inside the house yet, but it was clearly immense, a sprawling multilevel affair of innumerable large rooms. The grounds sprawled as well, covering an acre or two, with enough plants and shrubbery to stock an arboretum. Keller didn't know anything about flowers, but five minutes in a garden like this one had him thinking he ought to know more about the subject. Maybe they had evening classes at Hunter or NYU, maybe they'd take you on field trips to the Brooklyn Botanical Gardens. Maybe his life would be richer if he knew the names of the flowers, and whether they were annuals or perennials, and whatever else there was to know about them. Their soil requirements, say, and what bug killer to spray on their leaves, or what fertilizer to spread at their roots.

He walked along a brick path, smiling at this stranger, nodding at that one, and wound up standing alongside the swimming pool. Some twelve or fifteen people sat at poolside tables, talking and drinking, the volume of their conversation rising as they drank. In the enormous pool, a young boy swam back and forth, back and forth.

Keller felt a curious kinship with the kid. He was standing instead of swimming, but he felt as distant as the kid from everybody else around. There were two parties going on, he decided. There was the hearty social whirl of everybody else, and there was the solitude he felt in the midst of it all, identical to the solitude of the swimming boy.

Huge pool. The boy was swimming its width, but that dimension was still greater than the length of your typical backyard pool. Keller didn't know whether this was an Olympic pool, he wasn't quite sure how big that would have to be, but he figured you could just call it enormous and let it go at that.

Ages ago he'd heard about some college-boy stunt, filling a swimming pool with Jell-O, and he'd wondered how many little boxes of the gelatin dessert it would have required, and how the college boys could have afforded it. It would cost a fortune, he decided, to fill *this* pool with Jell-O—but if you could afford the pool in the first place, he supposed the Jell-O would be the least of your worries.

There were cut flowers on all the tables, and the blooms looked like ones Keller had seen in the garden. It stood to reason. If you grew all these flowers, you wouldn't have to order from the florist. You could cut your own.

What good would it do, he wondered, to know the names of all the shrubs and flowers? Wouldn't it just leave you wanting to dig in the soil and grow your own? And he didn't want to get into all that, for God's sake. His apartment was all he needed or wanted, and it was no place for a garden. He hadn't even tried growing an avocado pit there, and he didn't intend to. He was the only living thing in the apartment, and that was the way he wanted to keep it. The day that changed was the day he'd call the exterminator.

So maybe he'd just forget about evening classes at Hunter, and field trips to Brooklyn. If he wanted to get close to nature he could walk in Central Park, and if he didn't know the names of the flowers he would just hold off on introducing himself to them. And if—

Where was the kid?

The boy, the swimmer. Keller's companion in solitude. Where the hell did he go?

The pool was empty, its surface still. Keller saw a ripple toward the far end, saw a brace of bubbles break the surface.

He didn't react without thinking. That was how he'd always heard that sort of thing described, but that wasn't what happened, because the thoughts were there, loud and clear. *He's down there. He's in trouble. He's drowning.* And, echoing in his head in a voice that might have been Dot's, sour with exasperation: *Keller, for Christ's sake, do something!*

He set his glass on a table, shucked his coat, kicked off his shoes, dropped his pants and stepped out of them. Ages ago he'd earned a Red Cross lifesaving certificate, and the first thing they taught you was to strip before you hit the water. The six or seven seconds you spent peeling off your clothes would be repaid many times over in quickness and mobility.

But the strip show did not go unnoticed. Everybody at poolside had a comment, one more hilarious than the next. He barely heard them. In no time at all he was down to his underwear, and then he was out of range of their cleverness, hitting the water's surface in a flat racing dive, churning the water till he reached the spot where he'd seen the bubbles, then diving, eyes wide, barely noticing the burn of the chlorine.

Searching for the boy. Groping, searching, then finding him, reaching to grab hold of him. And pushing off against the bottom, lungs bursting, racing to reach the surface.

People were saying things to Keller, thanking him, congratulating him, but it wasn't really registering. A man clapped him on the back, a woman handed him a glass of brandy. He heard the word "hero" and realized that people were saying it all over the place, and applying it to him.

Hell of a note.

Keller sipped the brandy. It gave him heartburn, which assured him of its quality; good cognac always gave him heartburn. He turned to look at the boy. He was just a little fellow, twelve or thirteen years old, his hair lightened and his skin lightly bronzed by the summer sun. He was sitting up now, Keller saw, and looking none the worse for his near-death experience.

"Timothy," a woman said, "this is the man who saved your life. Do you have something to say to him?"

"Thanks," Timothy said, predictably.

"Is that all you have to say, young man?"

"It's enough," Keller said, and smiled. To the boy he said, "There's something I've always wondered. Did your whole life actually flash before your eyes?"

Timothy shook his head. "I got this cramp," he said, "and it was like my whole body turned into one big knot, and there wasn't anything I could do to untie it. And I didn't even think about drowning. I was just fighting the cramp, 'cause it hurt, and just about the next thing I knew I was up here coughing and puking up water." He made a face. "I must have swallowed half the pool. All I have to do is think about it and I can taste vomit and chlorine."

"Timothy," the woman said, and rolled her eyes.

"Something to be said for plain speech," an older man said. He had a mane of white hair and a pair of prominent white eyebrows, and his eyes were a vivid blue. He was holding a glass of brandy in one hand and a bottle in the other, and he reached with the bottle to fill Keller's glass to the brim. " 'Claret for boys, port for men,' " he said, " 'but he who would be a hero must drink brandy.' That's Samuel Johnson, although I may have gotten a word wrong."

The young woman patted his hand. "If you did, Daddy, I'm sure you just improved Mr. Johnson's wording."

"Dr. Johnson," he said, "and one could hardly do that. Improve the man's wording, that is. 'Being in a ship is being in a jail, with the chance of being drowned.' He said that as well, and I defy anyone to comment more trenchantly on the experience, or to say it better." He beamed at Keller. "I owe you more than a glass of brandy and a well-turned Johnsonian phrase. This little rascal whose life you've saved is my grandson, and the apple—nay, sir, the very nectarine—of my eye. And we'd have all stood around drinking and laughing while he drowned. You observed, and you acted, and God bless you for it."

What did you say to that? Keller wondered. *It was nothing? Well, shucks?* There had to be an apt phrase, and maybe Samuel Johnson could have found it, but he couldn't. So he said nothing, and just tried not to look po-faced.

"I don't even know your name," the white-haired man went on. "That's not remarkable in and of itself. I don't know half the people here, and I'm content to remain in my ignorance. But I ought to know your name, wouldn't you agree?"

Keller might have picked a name out of the air, but the one that leaped to mind was Boswell, and he couldn't say that to a man who quoted Samuel Johnson. So he supplied the name he'd traveled under, the one he'd signed when he checked into the hotel, the one on the driver's license and credit cards in his wallet.

"It's Michael Soderholm," he said, "and I can't even tell you the name of the fellow who brought me here. We met over drinks in the hotel bar and he said he was going to a party and it would be perfectly all right if I came along. I felt a little funny about it, but—"

"Please," the man said. "You can't possibly propose to apologize for your presence here. It's kept my grandson from a watery if chlorinated grave. And I've just told you I don't know half my guests, but that doesn't make them any the less welcome." He took a deep drink of his brandy and topped up both glasses. "Michael Soderholm," he said. "Swedish?"

"A mixture of everything," Keller said, improvising. "My great-grandfather Soderholm came over from Sweden, but my other ancestors came from all over Europe, plus I'm something like a sixteenth American Indian."

"Oh? Which tribe?"

"Cherokee," Keller said, thinking of the jazz tune.

"I'm an eighth Comanche," the man said. "So I'm afraid we're not tribal blood-brothers. The rest's British Isles, a mix of Scots and Irish and English. Old Texas stock. But you're not Texan yourself."

"No."

"Well, it can't be helped, as the saying goes. Unless you decide to move here, and who's to say that you won't? It's a fine place for a man to live."

"Daddy thinks everybody should love Texas the way he does," the woman said.

"Everybody should," her father said. "The only thing wrong with Texans is we're a long-winded lot. Look at the time it's taking me to introduce myself! Mr. Soderholm, Mr. Michael Soderholm, my name's Garrity, Wallace Penrose Garrity, and I'm your grateful host this evening."

No kidding, thought Keller.

The party, lifesaving and all, took place on Saturday night. The next day Keller sat in his hotel room and watched the Cowboys beat the Vikings with a field goal in the last three minutes of double overtime. The game had seesawed back and forth, with interceptions and runbacks, and the announcers kept telling each other what a great game it was.

Keller supposed they were right. It had all the ingredients, and it wasn't the players' fault that he himself was entirely unmoved by their performance. He could watch sports, and often did, but he almost never got caught up in it. He had occasionally wondered if his work might have something to do with it. On one level, when your job involved dealing regularly with life and death, how could you care if some overpaid steroid abuser had a touchdown run called back? And, on another level, you saw unorthodox solutions to a team's problems on the field. When Emmitt Smith kept crashing through the Minnesota line, Keller found himself wondering why they didn't deputize someone to shoot the son of a bitch in the back of the neck, right below his star-covered helmet.

Still, it was better than watching golf, say, which in turn had to be better than playing golf. And he couldn't get out and work, because there was nothing for him to do. Last night's reconnaissance mission had been both better and worse than he could have hoped, and what was he supposed to do now, park his rented Ford across the street from the Garrity mansion and clock the comings and goings?

No need for that. He could bide his time, just so he got there in time for Sunday dinner.

"Some more potatoes, Mr. Soderholm?"

"They're delicious," Keller said. "But I'm full. Really."

"And we can't keep calling you Mr. Soderholm," Garrity said. "I've only held off this long for not knowing whether you prefer Mike or Michael."

"Mike's fine," Keller said.

"Then Mike it is. And I'm Wally, Mike, or W.P., though there are those who call me 'The Walrus.' "

Timmy laughed, and clapped both hands over his mouth.

"Though never to his face," said the woman who'd offered Keller more potatoes. She was Ellen Garrity, Timmy's aunt and Garrity's daughter-in-law, and Keller was now instructed to call her Ellie. Her husband, a big-shouldered fellow who seemed to be smiling bravely through the heartbreak of male-pattern baldness, was Garrity's son, Hank.

Keller remembered Timothy's mother from the night before, but hadn't got her name at the time, or her relationship to Garrity. She was Rhonda Sue Butler, as it turned out, and everybody called her Rhonda Sue, except for her husband, who called her Ronnie. His name was Doak Butler, and he looked like a college jock who'd been too light for pro ball, although he now seemed to be closing the gap.

Hank and Ellie, Doak and Rhonda Sue. And, at the far end of the table, Vanessa, who was married to Wally but who was clearly not the mother of Hank or Rhonda Sue, or anyone else. Keller supposed you could describe her as Wally's trophy wife, a sign of his success. She was young, no older than Wally's kids, and she looked to be well-bred and elegant, and she even had the good grace to hide the boredom Keller was sure she felt.

And that was the lot of them. Wally and Vanessa, Hank and Ellen, Doak and Rhonda Sue. And Timothy, who he was assured had been swimming that very afternoon, the aquatic equivalent of getting right back on the horse. He'd had no cramps this time, but he'd had an attentive eye kept on him throughout.

Seven of them, then. And Keller . . . also known as Mike.

"So you're here on business," Wally said. "And stuck here over the weekend, which is the worst part of a business trip, as far as I'm concerned. More trouble than it's worth to fly back to Chicago?"

The two of them were in Wally's den, a fine room paneled in knotty pecan and trimmed out in red leather, with western doodads on the walls—here a branding iron, there a longhorn skull. Keller had accepted a brandy and declined a cigar, and the aroma of Wally's Havana was giving him second thoughts. Keller didn't smoke, but from the smell of it the cigar wasn't a mere matter of smoking. It was more along the lines of a religious experience.

"Seemed that way," Keller said. He'd supplied Chicago as Michael Soderholm's home base, though Soderholm's license placed him in Southern California. "By the time I fly there and back . . ."

"You've spent your weekend on airplanes. Well, it's our good fortune you decided to stay. Now what I'd like to do is find a way to make it your good fortune as well."

"You've already done that," Keller told him. "I crashed a great party last night and actually got to feel like a hero for a few minutes. And tonight I sit down to a fine dinner with nice people and get to top it off with a glass of outstanding brandy."

The heartburn told him how outstanding it was.

"What I had in mind," Wally said smoothly, "was to get you to work for me."

Whom did he want him to kill? Keller almost blurted out the question until he remembered that Garrity didn't know what he did for a living.

"You won't say who you work for," Garrity went on.

"I can't."

"Because the job's hush-hush for now. Well, I can respect that, and from the hints you've dropped I gather you're here scouting out something in the way of mergers and acquisitions."

"That's close."

"And I'm sure it's well paid, and you must like the work or I don't think you'd stay with it. So what do I have to do to get you to switch horses and come work for me? I'll tell you one thing—Chicago's a real nice place, but nobody who ever moved from there to Big D went around with a sour face about it. I don't know you well yet, but I can tell you're our kind of people and Dallas'll be your kind of town. And I don't know what they're paying you, but I suspect I can top it, and offer you a stake in a growing company with all sorts of attractive possibilities."

Keller listened, nodded judiciously, sipped a little brandy. It was amazing, he thought, the way things came along when you weren't looking for them. It was straight out of Horatio Alger, for God's sake—Ragged Dick stops the runaway horse and saves the daughter of the captain of industry, and the next thing you know he's president of IBM with rising expectations.

"Maybe I'll have that cigar after all," he said.

"Now, come on, Keller," Dot said. "You know the rules. I can't tell you that."

"It's sort of important," he said.

"One of the things the client buys," she said, "is confidentiality. That's what he wants and it's what we provide. Even if the agent in place—"

"The agent in place?"

"That's you," she said. "You're the agent, and Dallas is the place. Even if you get caught red-handed, the confidentiality of the client remains uncompromised. And do you know why?"

"Because the agent in place knows how to keep mum."

"Mum's the word," she agreed, "and there's no question you're the strong, silent type, but even if your lip loosens you can't sink a ship if you don't know when it's sailing."

Keller thought that over. "You lost me," he said.

"Yeah, it came out a little abstruse, didn't it? Point is you can't tell what you don't know, Keller, which is why the agent doesn't get to know the client's name."

"Dot," he said, trying to sound injured. "Dot, how long have you known me?"

"Ages, Keller. Many lifetimes."

"Many lifetimes?"

"We were in Atlantis together. Look, I know nobody's going to catch you red-handed, and I know you wouldn't blab if they did. But I can't tell what I don't know."

"Oh."

"Right. I think the spies call it a double cutout. The client made arrangements with somebody we know, and that person called us. But he didn't give us the client's name, and why should he? And, come to think of it, Keller, why do you have to know, anyway?"

He had his answer ready. "It might not be a single," he said.

"Oh?"

"The target's always got people around him," he said, "and the best way to do it might be a sort of group plan, if you follow me."

"Two for the price of one."

"Or three or four," he said. "But if one of those innocent bystanders turned out to be the client, it might make things a little awkward."

"Well, I can see where we might have trouble collecting the final payment."

"If we knew for a fact that the client was fishing for trout in Montana," he said, "it's no problem. But if he's here in Dallas—"

"It would help to know his name." She sighed. "Give me an hour or two, huh? Then call me back."

If he knew who the client was, the client could have an accident.

It would have to be an artful accident too. It would have to look good not only to the police but to whoever was aware of the client's own intentions. The local go-between, the helpful fellow who'd hooked up the client to the old man in White Plains, and thus to Keller, could be expected to cast a cold eye on any suspicious death. So it would have to be a damn good accident, but Keller had managed a few of those in his day. It took a little planning, but it wasn't brain surgery. You just figured out a method and took your best shot.

It might take some doing. If, as he rather hoped, the client was some business rival in Houston or Denver or San Diego, he'd have to slip off to that city without anyone noting his absence. Then, having induced a quick attack of accidental death, he'd fly back to Dallas and hang around until someone called him off the case. He'd need different ID for Houston or Denver or San Diego—it wouldn't do to overexpose Michael Soderholm—and he'd need to mask his actions from all concerned—Garrity, his homicidal rival, and, perhaps most important, Dot and the old man.

All told, it was a great deal more complicated (if easier to stomach) than the alternative.

Which was to carry out the assignment professionally and kill Wallace Penrose Garrity the first good chance he got.

And he really didn't want to do that. He'd eaten at the man's table, he'd drunk the man's brandy, he'd smoked the man's cigars. He'd been offered not merely a job but a well-paid executive position with a future, and, later that night, lightheaded from alcohol and nicotine, he'd had fantasies of taking Wally up on it.

Hell, why not? He could live out his days as Michael Soderholm, doing whatever unspecified tasks Garrity was hiring him to perform. He probably lacked the requisite experience, but how hard could it be to pick up the skills he needed as he went along? Whatever he had to do, it would be easier than flying from town to town killing people. He could learn on the job. He could pull it off.

The fantasy had about as much substance as a dream, and, like a dream, it was gone when he awoke the next morning. No one would put him on the payroll without some sort of background check, and the most cursory scan would knock him out of the box. Michael Soderholm had no more substance than the fake ID in his wallet.

Even if he somehow finessed a background check, even if the old man in White Plains let him walk out of one life and into another, he knew he couldn't really make it work. He already had a life. Misshapen though it was, it fit him like a glove.

Other lives made tempting fantasies. Running a print shop in Roseburg, Oregon, living in a cute little house with a mansard roof—it was something to tease yourself with while you went on being the person you had no choice but to be. This latest fantasy was just more of the same.

He went out for a sandwich and a cup of coffee. He got back in his car and drove around for a while. Then he found a pay phone and called White Plains.

"Do a single," Dot said.

"How's that?"

"No added extras, no free dividends. Just do what they signed on for."

"Because the client's here in town," he said. "Well, I could work around that if I knew his name. I could make sure he was out of it."

"Forget it," Dot said. "The client wants a long and happy life for everybody but the designated vic. Maybe the DV's close associates are near and dear to the client. That's just a guess, but all that really matters is that nobody else gets hurt. Capeesh?"

" 'Capeesh'?"

"It's Italian, it means—"

"I know what it means. It just sounded odd from your lips, that's all. But yes, I understand." He took a breath. "Whole thing may take a little time," he said.

"Then here comes the good news," she said. "Time's not of the essence. They don't care how long it takes, just so you get it right."

"I understand W.P. offered you a job," Vanessa said. "I know he hopes you'll take him up on it."

"I think he was just being generous," Keller told her. "I was in the right place at the right time, and he'd like to do me a favor, but I don't think he really expects me to come to work for him."

"He'd like it if you did," she said, "or he never would have made the offer. He'd have just given you money, or a car, or something like that. And as far as what he expects, well, W.P. generally expects to get whatever he wants. Because that's the way things usually work out."

And had she been saving up her pennies to get things to work out a little differently? You had to wonder. Was she truly under Garrity's spell, in awe of his power, as she seemed to be? Or was she only in it for the money, and was there a sharp edge of irony under her worshipful remarks?

Hard to say. Hard to tell about any of them. Was Hank the loyal son he appeared to be, content to live in the old man's shadow and take what got tossed his way? Or was he secretly resentful and ambitious?

What about the son-in-law, Doak? On the surface, he looked to be delighted with the aftermath of his college football career—his work for his father-in-law consisted largely of playing golf with business associates and drinking with them afterward. But did he seethe inside, sure he was fit for greater things?

How about Hank's wife, Ellie? She struck Keller as an unlikely Lady Macbeth. Keller could fabricate scenarios in which she or Rhonda Sue had a reason for wanting Wally dead, but they were the sort of thing you dreamed up while watching reruns of *Dallas* and trying to guess who shot J.R. Maybe one of their marriages was in trouble. Maybe Garrity had put the moves on his daughter-in-law, or maybe a little too much brandy had led him into his daughter's bedroom now and then. Maybe Doak or Hank was playing footsie with Vanessa. Maybe . . .

Pointless to speculate, he decided. You could go around and around like that and it didn't get you anywhere. Even if he managed to dope out which of them was the client, then what? Having saved young Timothy, and thus feeling obligated to spare his doting grandfather, what was he going to do? Kill the boy's father? Or mother or aunt or uncle?

Of course he could just go home. He could even explain the situation to the old man. Nobody loved it when you took yourself off a contract for personal reasons, but it wasn't something they could talk you out of, either. If you made a habit of that sort of thing, well, that was different, but that wasn't the case with Keller. He was a solid pro. Quirky perhaps, even whimsical, but a pro all the way. You told him what to do and he did it.

So, if he had a personal reason to bow out, you honored it. You let him come home and sit on the porch and drink iced tea with Dot.

And you picked up the phone and sent somebody else to Dallas.

Because either way the job was going to be done. If a hit man had a change of heart, it would be followed in short order by a change of hit man. If Keller didn't pull the trigger, somebody else would.

His mistake, Keller thought savagely, was to jump in the goddam pool in the first place. All he'd had to do was look the other way and let the little bastard drown. A few days later he could have taken Garrity out, possibly making it look like suicide, a natural consequence of despondency over the boy's tragic accident.

But no, he thought, glaring at himself in the mirror. No, you had to go and get involved. You had to be a hero, for God's sake. Had to strip down to your skivvies and prove you deserved that junior lifesaving certificate the Red Cross gave you all those years ago.

He wondered whatever happened to that certificate.

It was gone, of course, like everything he'd ever owned in his childhood and youth. Gone like his high school diploma, like his Boy Scout merit badge sash, like his stamp collection and his sack of marbles and his stack of baseball cards. He didn't mind that these things were gone, didn't waste time wishing he had them any more than he wanted those years back.

But he wondered what physically became of them. The lifesaving certificate, for instance. Someone might have thrown out his baseball cards, or sold his stamp collection to a dealer. A certificate, though, wasn't something you threw out, nor was it something anyone else would want.

Maybe it was buried in a landfill, or in a stack of paper ephemera in the back of some thrift shop. Maybe some pack rat had rescued it, and maybe it was now part of an extensive collection of junior lifesaving certificates, housed in an album and cherished as living history, the pride and joy of a collector ten times as quirky and whimsical as Keller could ever dream of being.

He wondered how he felt about that. His certificate, his small achievement, living on in some eccentric's collection. On the one hand, it was a kind of immortality, wasn't it? On the other hand, well, whose certificate was it, anyway? He'd been the one to earn it, breaking the instructor's choke hold, spinning him and grabbing him in a cross-chest carry, towing the big lug to the side of the pool. It was his accomplishment and it had his name on it, so didn't it belong on his own wall or nowhere?

All in all, he couldn't say he felt strongly either way. The certificate, when all was said and done, was only a piece of paper. What was important was the skill itself, and what was truly remarkable was that he'd retained it.

Because of it, Timothy Butler was alive and well. Which was all well and good for the boy, and a great big headache for Keller.

Later, sitting with a cup of coffee, Keller thought some more about Wallace Penrose Garrity, a man who increasingly seemed to have not an enemy in the world.

Suppose Keller had let the kid drown. Suppose he just plain hadn't noticed the boy's disappearance beneath the water, just as everyone else had failed to notice it. Garrity would have been despondent. It was his party, his pool, his failure to provide supervision. He'd probably have blamed himself for the boy's death.

When Keller took him out, it would have been the kindest thing he could have done for him.

He caught the waiter's eye and signaled for more coffee. He'd just given himself something to think about.

"Mike," Garrity said, coming toward him with a hand outstretched. "Sorry to keep you waiting. Had a phone call from a fellow with a hankering to buy a little five-acre lot of mine on the south edge of town. Thing is, I don't want to sell it to him."

"I see."

"But there's ten acres on the other side of town I'd be perfectly happy to sell to him, but he'll only want it if he thinks of it himself. So that left me on the phone longer than I would have liked. Now what would you say to a glass of brandy?"

"Maybe a small one."

Garrity led the way to the den, poured drinks for both of them. "You should have come earlier," he said. "In time for dinner. I hope you know you don't need an invitation. There'll always be a place for you at our table."

"Well," Keller said.

"I know you can't talk about it," Garrity said, "but I hope your project here in town is shaping up nicely."

"Slow but sure," Keller said.

"Some things can't be hurried," Garrity allowed, and sipped brandy, and winced. If Keller hadn't been looking for it, he might have missed the shadow that crossed his host's face.

Gently he said, "Is the pain bad, Wally?"

"How's that, Mike?"

Keller put his glass on the table. "I spoke to Dr. Jacklin," he said. "I know what you're going through."

"That son of a bitch," Garrity said, "was supposed to keep his mouth shut."

"Well, he thought it was all right to talk to me," Keller said. "He thought I was Dr. Edward Fishman from the Mayo Clinic."

"Calling for a consultation."

"Something like that."

"I did go to Mayo," Garrity said, "but they didn't need to call Harold Jacklin to double-check their results. They just confirmed his diagnosis and told me not to buy any long-playing records." He looked to one side. "They said they couldn't say for sure how much time I had left, but that the pain would be manageable for a while. And then it wouldn't."

"I see."

"And I'd have all my faculties for a while," he said. "And then I wouldn't."

Keller didn't say anything.

"Well, hell," Garrity said. "A man wants to take the bull by the horns, doesn't he? I decided I'd go out for a walk with a shotgun and have a little hunting accident. Or I'd be cleaning a handgun here at my desk and have it go off. But it turned out I just couldn't tolerate the idea of killing myself. Don't know why, can't explain it, but that seems to be the way I'm made."

He picked up his glass and looked at the brandy. "Funny how we hang on to life," he said. "Something else Sam Johnson said, said there wasn't a week of his life he'd voluntarily live through again. I've had more good times than bad, Mike, and even the bad times haven't been that godawful, but I think I know what he was getting at. I wouldn't want to repeat any of it, but that doesn't mean there's a minute of it I'd have been willing to miss. I don't want to miss whatever's coming next, either, and I don't guess Dr. Johnson did either. That's what keeps us going, isn't it? Wanting to find out what's around the next bend in the river."

"I guess so."

"I thought that would make the end easier to face," he said. "Not knowing when it was coming, or how or where. And I recalled that years ago a fellow told me to let him know if I ever needed to have somebody killed. 'You just let me know,' he said, and I laughed, and that was the last said on the subject. A month or so ago I looked up his number and called him, and he gave me another number to call."

"And you put out a contract."

"Is that the expression? Then that's what I did."

"Suicide by proxy," Keller said.

"And I guess you're holding my proxy," Garrity said, and drank some brandy. "You know, the thought flashed across my mind that first night, talking with you after you pulled my grandson out of the pool. I got this little glimmer, but I told myself I was being ridiculous. A hired killer doesn't turn up and save somebody's life."

"It's out of character," Keller agreed.

"Besides, what would you be doing at the party in the first place? Wouldn't you stay out of sight and wait until you could get me alone?"

"If I'd been thinking straight," Keller said. "I told myself it wouldn't hurt to have a look around. And this joker from the hotel bar assured me I had nothing to worry about. 'Half the town'll be at Wally's tonight,' he said."

"Half the town was. You wouldn't have tried anything that night, would you?"

"God, no."

"I remember thinking, I hope he's not here. I hope it's not tonight. Because I was enjoying the party and I didn't want to miss anything. But you *were* there, and a good thing, wasn't it?"

"Yes."

"Saved the boy from drowning. According to the Chinese, you save somebody's life, you're responsible for him for the rest of your life. Because you've interfered with the natural order of things. That make sense to you?"

"Not really."

"Or me either. You can't beat them for whipping up a meal or laundering a shirt, but they've got some queer ideas on other subjects. Of course they'd probably say the same for some of my notions."

"Probably."

Garrity looked at his glass. "You called my doctor," he said. "Must have been to confirm a suspicion you already had. What tipped you off? Is it starting to show in my face, or the way I move around?"

Keller shook his head. "I couldn't find anybody else with a motive," he said, "or a grudge against you. You were the only one left. And then I remembered seeing you wince once or twice, and try to hide it. I barely noticed it at the time, but then I started to think about it."

"I thought it would be easier than doing it myself," Garrity said. "I thought I'd just let a professional take me by surprise. I'd be like an old bull elk on a hillside, never expecting the bullet that takes him out in his prime."

"It makes sense."

"No, it doesn't. Because the elk didn't arrange for the hunter to be there. Far as the elk knows, he's all alone there. He's not wondering every damn day if today's the day. He's not bracing himself, trying to sense the crosshairs centering on his shoulder."

"I never thought of that."

"Neither did I," said Garrity. "Or I never would have called that fellow in the first place. Mike, what the hell are you doing here tonight? Don't tell me you came over to kill me."

"I came to tell you I can't."

"Because we've come to know each other."

Keller nodded.

"I grew up on a farm," Garrity said. "One of those vanishing family farms you hear about, and of course it's vanished, and I say good riddance. But we raised our own beef and pork, you know, and we kept a milk cow and a flock of laying hens. And we never named the animals we were going to wind up eating. The milk cow had a name, but not the bull calf she dropped. The breeder sow's name was Elsie, but we never named her piglets."

"Makes sense," Keller said.

"I guess it doesn't take a Chinaman to see how you can't kill me once you've hauled Timmy out of the drink. Let alone after you've sat at my table and smoked my cigars. Reminds me, you care for a cigar?"

"No, thank you."

"Well, where do we go from here, Mike? I have to say I'm relieved. I feel like I've been bracing myself for a bullet for weeks now. All of a sudden I've got a new lease on life. I'd say this calls for a drink except we're already having one, and you've scarcely touched yours."

"There is one thing," Keller said.

He left the den while Garrity made his phone call. Timothy was in the living room, puzzling over a chessboard. Keller played a game with him and lost badly. "Can't win 'em all," he said, and tipped over his king.

"I was going to checkmate you," the boy said. "In a few more moves."

"I could see it coming," Keller told him.

He went back to the den. Garrity was selecting a cigar from his humidor. "Sit down," he said. "I'm fixing to smoke one of these things. If you won't kill me, maybe it will."

"You never know."

"I made the call, Mike, and it's all taken care of. Be a while before the word filters up and down the chain of command, but sooner or later they'll call you up and tell you the client changed his mind. He paid in full and called off the job."

They talked some, then sat a while in silence. At length Keller said he ought to get going. "I should be at my hotel," he said, "in case they call."

"Be a couple of days, won't it?"

"Probably," he said, "but you never know. If everyone involved makes a phone call right away, the word could get to me in a couple of hours."

"Calling you off, telling you to come home. Be glad to get home, I bet."

"It's nice here," he said, "but yes, I'll be glad to get home."

"Wherever it is, they say there's no place like it." Garrity leaned back, then allowed himself to wince at the pain that came over him. "If it never hurts worse than this," he said, "then I can stand it. But of course it will get worse. And I'll decide I can stand *that,* and then it'll get worse again."

There was nothing to say to that.

"I guess I'll know when it's time to do something," Garrity said. "And who knows? Maybe my heart'll cut out on me out of the blue. Or I'll get hit by a bus, or I don't know what. Struck by lightning?"

"It could happen."

"Anything can happen," Garrity agreed. He got to his feet. "Mike," he said, "I guess we won't be seeing any more of each other, and I have to say I'm a little bit sorry about that. I've truly enjoyed our time together."

"So have I, Wally."

"I wondered, you know, what he'd be like. The man they'd send to do this kind of work. I don't know what I expected, but you're not it."

He stuck out his hand, and Keller gripped it. "Take care," Garrity said. "Be well, Mike."

Back at his hotel, Keller took a hot bath and got a good night's sleep. In the morning he went out for breakfast, and when he got back there was a message at the desk for him: *Mr. Soderholm—please call your office.*

He called from a pay phone, even though it didn't matter, and he was careful not to overreact when Dot told him to come home, the mission was aborted.

"You told me I had all the time in the world," he said. "If I'd known the guy was in such a rush—"

"Keller," she said, "it's a good thing you waited. What he did, he changed his mind."

"He changed his mind?"

"It used to be a woman's prerogative," Dot said, "but now we've got equality between the sexes, so that means anyone can do it. It works out fine because we're getting paid in full. So kick the dust of Texas off your feet and come on home."

"I'll do that," he said, "but I may hang out here for a few more days."

"Oh?"

"Or even a week," he said. "It's a pretty nice town."

"Don't tell me you're itching to move there, Keller. We've been through this before."

"Nothing like that," he said, "but there's this girl I met."

"Oh, Keller."

"Well, she's nice," he said. "And if I'm off the job there's no reason not to have a date or two with her, is there?"

"As long as you don't decide to move in."

"She's not that nice," he said, and Dot laughed and told him not to change.

He hung up and drove around and found a movie he'd been meaning to see. The next morning he packed and checked out of his hotel.

He drove across town and got a room on the motel strip, paying cash for four nights in advance and registering as J. D. Smith from Los Angeles.

There was no girl he'd met, no girl he wanted to meet. But it wasn't time to go home yet.

He had unfinished business, and four days should give him time to do it. Time for Wallace Garrity to get used to the idea of not feeling those imaginary crosshairs on his shoulder blades.

But not so much time that the pain would be too much to bear.

And, sometime in those four days, Keller would give him a gift. If he could, he'd make it look natural—a heart attack, say, or an accident. In any event it would be swift and without warning, and as close as he could make it to painless.

And it would be unexpected. Garrity would never see it coming.

Keller frowned, trying to figure out how he would manage it. It would be a lot trickier than the task that had drawn him to town originally, but he'd brought it on himself. Getting involved, fishing the boy out of the pool. He'd interfered with the natural order of things. He was under an obligation.

It was the least he could do.

Keller's Horoscope

Keller got out of the taxi at Bleecker and Broadway because that was easier than trying to tell the Haitian cabdriver how to find Crosby Street. He walked to Maggie's building, a former warehouse with a forbidding exterior, and rode up to her fifth-floor loft. She was waiting for him, wearing a black canvas coat of the sort you saw in western movies. It was called a duster, probably because it was cut long to keep the dust off. Maggie was a small woman—*elfin,* he had decided, was a good word for her—and this particular duster reached clear to the floor.

"Surprise," she said, and flung it open, and there was nothing under it but her.

Keller, who'd met Maggie Griscomb at an art gallery, had been keeping infrequent company with her for a while now. Just the other day a chance remark of his had led Dot to ask if he was seeing anybody, and he'd been stuck for an answer. Was he? It was hard to say.

"It's a superficial relationship," he'd explained.

"Keller, what other kind is there?"

"The thing is," he said, "she wants it that way. We get together once a week, if that. And we go to bed."

"Don't you at least go out for dinner first?"

"I've given up suggesting it. She's tiny, she probably doesn't eat much. Maybe eating is something she can only do in private."

"You'd be surprised how many people feel that way about sex," Dot said. "But I'd have to say she sounds like the proverbial sailor's dream. Does she own a liquor store?"

She was a failed painter who'd reinvented herself as a jewelry maker. "You bought earrings for the last woman in your life," Dot reminded him. "This one makes her own. What are you going to buy for her?"

"Nothing."

"That's economical. Between not giving her gifts and not taking her out to dinner, I can't see this one putting much of a strain on your budget. Can you at least send the woman flowers?"

"I already did."

"Well, it's something you can do more than once, Keller. That's one of the nice things about flowers. The little buggers die, so you get to throw them out and make room for fresh ones."

"She liked the flowers," he said, "but she told me once was enough. Don't do it again, she said."

"Because she wants to keep things superficial."

"That's the idea."

"Keller," she said, "I've got to hand it to you. You don't find that many of them, but you sure pick the strange ones."

"Now that was intense," Maggie said. "Was it just my imagination, or was that a major earth-shaking experience?"

"High up there on the Richter scale," he said.

"I thought tonight would be special. Full moon tomorrow."

"Does that mean we should have waited?"

"In my experience," she said, "it's the day *before* the full moon that I feel it the strongest."

"Feel what?"

"The moon."

"But what is it you feel? What effect does it have on you?"

"Makes me restless. Heightens my moods. Sort of intensifies things. Same as everybody else, I guess. What about you, Keller? What does the moon do for you?"

As far as Keller could tell, all the moon did for him was light up the sky a little. Living in the city, where there were plenty of streetlights to take up the slack, he paid little attention to the moon, and might not have noticed if someone took it away. New moon, half moon, full moon—only when he caught an occasional glimpse of it between the buildings did he know what phase it was in.

Maggie evidently paid more attention to the moon, and attached more significance to it. Well, if the moon had had anything to do with the pleasure they'd just shared, he was grateful to it, and glad to have it around.

"Besides," she was saying, "my horoscope says I'm going through a very sexy time."

"Your horoscope."

"Uh-huh."

"What do you do, read it every morning?"

"You mean in the newspaper? Well, I'm not saying I never look, but I wouldn't rely on a newspaper horoscope for advice and counsel any more than I'd need Ann Landers to tell me if I have to pet to be popular."

"On that subject," he said, "I'd say you don't absolutely have to, but what could it hurt?"

"And who knows," she said, reaching out for him. "I might even enjoy it."

A while later she said, "Newspaper astrology columns are fun, like *Peanuts* and *Doonesbury*, but they're not very accurate. But I got my chart done, and I go in once a year for a tune-up. So I'll have an idea what to expect over the coming twelve months."

"You believe in all that?"

"Astrology? Well, it's like gravity, isn't it?"

"It keeps things from flying off in space?"

"It works whether I believe in it or not," she said. "So I might as well. Besides, I believe in everything."

"Like Santa Claus?"

"And the Tooth Fairy. No, all the occult stuff, like tarot and numerology and palmistry and phrenology and—"

"What's that?"

"Head bumps," she said, and capped his skull with her hand. "You've got some."

"I've got head bumps?"

"Uh-huh, but don't ask me what they mean. I've never even been to a phrenologist."

"Would you?"

"Go to one? Sure, if somebody steered me to a good one. In all of these areas, some practitioners are better than others. There are the storefront gypsies who are really just running a scam, but after that you've still got different levels of proficiency. Some people have a knack and some just hack away at it. But that's true in every line of work, isn't it?"

It was certainly true in his.

"What I don't get," he said, "is how any of it works. What difference does it make where the stars are when you're born? What has that got to do with anything?"

"I don't know how anything works," she said, "or why it should. Why does the light go on when I throw the switch? Why do I get wet when you touch me? It's all a mystery."

"But head bumps, for Christ's sake. Tarot cards."

"Sometimes it's just a way for a person to access her intuition," she said. "I used to know a woman who could read shoes."

"The labels? I don't follow you."

"She'd look at a pair of shoes that you'd owned for a while, and she could tell you things about yourself."

" 'You need half-soles.' "

"No, like you eat too much starchy food, and you need to express the feminine side of your personality, and the relationship you're in is stifling your creativity. Things like that."

"All by looking at your shoes. And that makes sense to you?"

"Does sense make sense? Look, do you know what holism is?"

"Like eating brown rice?"

"No, that's whole foods. Holism is like with holograms, the principle's that any cell in the body represents the entire life in microcosm. That's why I can rub your feet and make your headache go away."

"You can?"

"Well, not me personally, but a foot reflexologist could. That's why a palmist can look at your hand and see evidence of physical conditions that have nothing to do with your hands. They show up there, and in the irises of your eyes, and the bumps on your head."

"And the heels of your shoes," Keller said. "I had my palm read once."

"Oh?"

"A year or two ago. I was at this party, and they had a palmist for entertainment."

"Probably not a very good one, if she was hiring out for parties. How good a reading did she give you?"

"She didn't."

"I thought you said you had your palm read."

"I was willing. She wasn't. I sat down at the table with her and gave her my hand, and she took a good look and gave it back to me."

"That's awful. You must have been terrified."

"Of what?"

"That she saw imminent death in your hand."

"It crossed my mind," he admitted. "But I figured she was just a performer, and this was part of the performance. I was a little edgy the next time I got on a plane—"

"I'll bet."

"—but it was a routine flight, and time passed and nothing happened, and I forgot about it. I couldn't tell you the last time I even thought about it."

She reached out a hand. "Gimme."

"Huh?"

"Give me your hand. Let's see what got the bitch in a tizzy."

"You can read palms?"

"Not quite, but I can claim a smattering of ignorance on the subject. Let's see now, I don't want to know too much, because it might jeopardize the superficiality of our relationship. There's your head line, there's your heart line, there's your life line. And no marriage lines. Well, you said you've never been married, and your hand says you were telling the truth. I can't say I can see anything here that would make me tell you not to buy any long-playing records."

"That's a relief."

"So I bet I know what spooked her. You've got a murderer's thumb."

Keller, working on his stamp collection, kept interrupting himself to look at his thumb. There it was, teaming up with his forefinger to grip a pair of tongs, to pick up a glassine envelope, to hold a magnifying glass. There it was, his own personal mark of Cain. His murderer's thumb.

"It's the particular way your thumb is configured," Maggie had told him. "See how it goes here? And look at my thumb, or your left thumb, as far as that goes. See the difference?"

She was able to recognize the murderer's thumb, he learned, because a childhood friend of hers, a perfectly gentle and nonviolent person, had one just like it. A palmist had told her friend it was a murderer's thumb, and the two of them had looked it up in a book on the subject. And there it was, pictured lifesize and in color, the Murderer's Thumb, and it was just like her friend Jacqui's thumb, and, now, just like Keller's.

"But she never should have given you your hand back the way she did," Maggie had assured him. "I don't know if anybody's keeping statistics, but I'm sure most of the murderers walking around have two perfectly normal thumbs, while most people who do happen to have a murderer's thumb have never killed anybody in their life, and never will."

"That's a comfort."

"How many people have you killed, Keller?"

"None, for God's sake."

"And do you sense a burst of homicidal rage in your future?"

"Not really."

"Then I'd say you can relax. You may have a murderer's thumb, but I don't think you have to worry about it."

He wasn't worried, not exactly. But he would have to say he was puzzled. How could a man have a murderer's thumb all his life and be unaware of it? And, when all was said and done, what did it mean?

He had certainly never paid any particular attention to his thumb. He had been aware that his two thumbs were not identical, that there was something slightly atypical about his right thumb, but it was not eye-catchingly idiosyncratic, not the sort of thing other kids would notice, much less taunt you about. He'd given it about as much thought over the years as he gave to the nail on the big toe of his left foot, which was marked with ridges.

Hit man's toe, he thought.

He was poring over a price list, France & Colonies, wrestling with some of the little decisions a stamp collector was called upon to make, when the phone rang. He picked it up, and it was Dot.

He made the usual round trip by train, Grand Central to White Plains and back again, He packed a bag before he went to bed that night, and in the morning he caught a cab to JFK and a plane to Tampa. He rented a Ford Escort and drove to Indian Rocks Beach, which sounded more like a headline in *Variety* than a place to live. But that's what it was, and, though he didn't see any Indians or rocks, it would have been hard to miss the beach. It was a beauty, and he could see why they had all these condos on it, and vacation time-shares.

The man Keller was looking for, an Ohioan named Stillman, had just moved in for a week's stay in a beachfront apartment on the fourth floor of Gulf Water Towers. There was an attendant in the lobby, Keller noticed, but he didn't figure to be as hard to get past as the Maginot Line.

But would he even need to find out? Stillman had just arrived from sunless Cincinnati, and how much time was he going to spend inside? No more than he had to, Keller figured. He'd want to get out there and soak up some rays, maybe splash in the Gulf a little, then zone out some more in the sun.

Keller's packing had included swim trunks, and he found a men's room and put them on. He didn't have a towel to lie on—he hadn't taken a room yet—but he could always lie on the sand.

It turned out he didn't have to. As he was walking along the public beach, he saw a woman approach a man, her hands cupped. She was holding water, and she threw it on the man, who sprang to his feet. They laughed joyously as he chased her into the surf. There they frolicked, perfect examples of young hormone-driven energy, and Keller figured they'd be frolicking for a while. They'd left two towels on the sand, anonymous unidentifiable white beach towels, and Keller decided one was all they needed. It would easily accommodate the two of them when they tired of splashing and ducking one another.

He picked up the other towel and walked off with it. He spread it out on the sand at the private beach for Gulf Water Towers residents. A glance left and right revealed no one who in any way resembled George Stillman, so Keller stretched out on his back and closed his eyes. The sun, a real stranger to New York of late, was evidently wholly at home in Florida, and felt wonderful on his skin. If it took a while to find Stillman, that was okay with him.

But it didn't.

Keller opened his eyes after half an hour or so. He sat up and looked around, feeling a little like Punxsutawney Phil on Groundhog Day. When he failed to see either Stillman or his own shadow, he lay down and closed his eyes again.

The next time he opened them was when he heard a man cursing. He sat up, and not twenty yards away was a barrel-chested man, balding and jowly, calling his right hand every name in the book.

How could the fellow be that mad at his own hand? Of course he might have a murderer's thumb, but what if he did? Keller had one himself, and had never felt the need to talk to it in those terms.

Oh, hell, of course. The man was on a cell phone. And, by God, he was Stillman. The face had barely registered on Keller at first, his attention held by the angry voice and the keg-shaped torso thickly pelted with black hair. None of that had been visible in the head-and-shoulders shot Dot had shown him, and it was what you noticed, but it was the same face, and here he was, and wasn't that handy?

While Stillman took the sun, Keller did the same. When Stillman got up and walked to the water's edge, so did Keller. When Stillman waded in, to test his mettle in the surf, Keller followed in his wake.

When Keller came ashore, Stillman stayed behind. And by the time Keller left the beach, carrying two towels and a cellular phone, Stillman had still not emerged from the water.

Why a thumb?

Keller, back in New York, pondered the question. He couldn't see what a thumb had to do with murder. When you used a gun, it was your index finger that gave the trigger a squeeze. When you used a knife, you held it in your palm with your fingers curled around the handle. Your thumb might press the hilt, as a sort of guide, but a man could have no thumbs at all and still get the business end of a knife to go where he wanted it.

Did you use your thumbs when you garroted somebody? He mimed the motion, letting his hands remember, and he didn't see where the thumbs had much of a part to play. Manual strangulation, now that was different, and you did use your thumbs, you used all of both hands, and would have a hard time otherwise.

Still, why a murderer's *thumb*?

"Here's what I don't get," Dot said. "You go off to some half-a-horse town at the ass end of nowhere special and you poke around for a week or two. Then you go to a vacation paradise in the middle of a New York winter and you're back the same day. The same day!"

"I had an opening and I took it," he said. "I wait and maybe I never get that good a shot at him again."

"I realize that, Keller, and God knows I'm not complaining. It just seems like a shame, that's all. Here you are, the two of you, fresh off a couple of planes from the frozen North, and before either one of you gets the chill out of your bones, you're on a flight to New York and he's rapidly approaching room temperature."

"Water temperature."

"I stand corrected."

"And it was like a bathtub."

"That's nice," she said. "He could have opened his veins in it, but after you held his head underwater for a few minutes he no longer felt the need to. But couldn't you have waited a few days? You'd have come home with a tan and he'd have gone into the ground with one. You meet your Maker, you want to look your best."

"Sure," he said. "Dot, have you ever noticed anything odd about my thumb?"

"Your thumb?"

"This one. Does it look strange to you?"

"You know," she said, "I've got to hand it to you, Keller. That's the most complete change of subject I've ever encountered in my life. I'd be hard put to remember what we were talking about before we started talking about your thumb."

"Well?"

"Don't tell me you're serious? Let me see. I'd have to say it looks like a plain old thumb to me, but you know what they say. You've seen one thumb . . ."

"But look, Dot. That's the whole point, that they're not identical. See how this one goes?"

"Oh, right. It's got that little . . ."

"Uh-huh."

"Are mine both the same? Like two peas in a pod, as far as I can make out. This one's got a little scar at the base, but don't ask me how I got it because I can't remember. Keller, you made your point. You've got an unusual thumb."

"Do you believe in destiny, Dot?"

"Whoa! Keller, you just switched channels again. I thought we were discussing thumbs."

"I was thinking about Louisville."

"I'm going to take the remote control away from you, Keller. It's not safe in your hands. Louisville?"

"You remember when I went there."

"Vividly. Kids playing basketball, guy in a garage, and, if I remember correctly, the subtle magic of carbon monoxide."

"Right."

"So?"

"Remember how I had a bad feeling about it, and then a couple got killed in my old room, and—"

"I remember the whole business, Keller. What about it?"

"I guess I've just been wondering how much of life is destined and preordained. How much choice do people really have?"

"If we had a choice," she said, "we could be having some other conversation."

"I never set out to be what I've become. It's not like I took an aptitude test in high school and my guidance counselor took me aside and recommended a career as a killer for hire."

"You drifted into it, didn't you?"

"That's what I always thought. That's certainly what it felt like. But suppose I was just fulfilling my destiny?"

"I don't know," she said, cocking her head. "Shouldn't there be music playing in the background? There always is when they have conversations like this in one of my soap operas."

"Dot, I've got a murderer's thumb."

"Oh, for the love of God, we're back to your thumb. How did you manage that, and what in the hell are you talking about?"

"Palmistry," he said. "In palmistry, a thumb like mine is called a murderer's thumb."

"In palmistry."

"Right."

"I grant you it's an unusual-looking thumb," she said, "although I never noticed it in all the years I've known you, and never would have noticed it if you hadn't pointed it out. But where does the murderer part come in? What do you do, kill people by running your thumb across their lifeline?"

"I don't think you actually do anything with your thumb."

"I don't see what you *could* do, aside from hitching a ride. Or making a rude gesture."

"All I know," he said, "is I had a murderer's thumb and I grew up to be a murderer."

" 'His Thumb Made Him Do It.' "

"Or was it the other way around? Maybe my thumb was normal at birth, and it changed as my character changed."

"That sounds crazy," she said, "but you ought to be able to clear it up, because you've been carrying that thumb around all your life. *Was* it always like that?"

"How do I know? I never paid much attention to it."

"Keller, it's your thumb."

"But did I notice it was different from other thumbs? I don't know, Dot. Maybe I should see somebody."

"That's not necessarily a bad idea," she said, "but I'd think twice before I let them put me on any medication."

"That's not what I mean," he said.

The astrologer was not what he'd expected.

Hard to say just what he'd been expecting. Someone with a lot of eye makeup, say, and long hair bound up in a scarf, and big hoop earrings—some sort of cross between a Gypsy fortune-teller and a hippie chick. What he got in Louise Carpenter was a pleasant woman in her forties who had thrown in the towel in the long battle to retain a girlish figure. She had big blue-green eyes and a low-maintenance haircut, and she lived in an apartment on West End Avenue full of comfortable furniture, and she wore loose clothing and read romance novels and ate chocolate, all of which seemed to agree with her.

"It would help," she told Keller, "if we knew the precise time of your birth."

"I don't think there's any way to find out."

"Your mother has passed?"

Passed. It might be more accurate, he thought, to say that she'd failed. He said, "She died a long time ago."

"And your father . . ."

"Died before I was born," Keller said, wondering if it was true. "You asked me over the phone if there was anyone who might remember. I'm the only one who's still around, and I don't remember a thing."

"There are ways to recover a lot of early memory," she said, and popped a chocolate into her mouth. "All the way back to birth, in some instances, and I've known people who claim they can remember their own conception. But I don't know how much to credit all of that. Is it memory or is it Memorex? Besides, you probably weren't wearing a watch at the time."

"I've been thinking," he said. "I don't know the doctor's name, and he might be dead himself by this time, but I've got a copy of my birth certificate. It doesn't have the time of birth, just the date, but do you suppose the Bureau of Vital Statistics would have the information on file somewhere?"

"Possibly," she said, "but don't worry about it. I can check it."

"On the Internet? Something like that?"

She laughed. "No, not that. You said your mother mentioned getting up early in the morning to go to the hospital."

"That's what she said."

"And you were a fairly easy birth."

"Once her labor started, I came right out."

"You wanted to be here. Now you happen to be a Gemini, John, and . . . shall I call you John?"

"If you want."

"Well, what do people generally call you?"

"Keller."

"Very well, Mr. Keller. I'm comfortable keeping it formal if you prefer it that way, and—"

"Not Mr. Keller," he said. "Just plain Keller."

"Oh."

"That's what people generally call me."

"I see. Well, Keller . . . no, I don't think that's going to work. I'm going to have to call you John."

"Okay."

"In high school kids used to call each other by their last names. It was a way to feel grown up. 'Hey, Carpenter, you finish the algebra homework?' I can't call you Keller."

"Don't worry about it."

"I'm being neurotic, I realize that, but—"

"John is fine."

"Well then," she said, and rearranged herself in the chair. "You're a Gemini, John, as I'm sure you know. A late Gemini, June nineteenth, which puts you right on the cusp of Cancer."

"Is that good?"

"Nothing's necessarily good or bad in astrology, John. But it's good in that I enjoy working with Geminis. I find it to be an extremely interesting sign."

"How so?"

"The duality. Gemini is the sign of the twins, you see." She went on talking about the properties of the sign, and he nodded, agreeing but not really taking it all in. And then she was saying, "I suppose the most interesting thing about Geminis is their relationship to the truth. Geminis are naturally duplicitous, yet they have an inner reverence for the truth that echoes their opposite number across the Zodiac. That's Sagittarius, of course, and your typical Sadge couldn't tell a lie to save his soul. Gemini can lie without a second thought, while being occasionally capable of this startling Sagittarian candor."

"I see."

He was influenced as well by Cancer, she continued, having his sun on its cusp, along with a couple of planets in that sign. And he had a Taurus moon, she told him, and that was the best possible place for the moon to be. "The moon is exalted in Taurus," she said. "Have you noticed in the course of your life how things generally turn out all right for you, even when they don't? And don't you have an inner core, a sort of bedrock stability that lets you always know who you are?"

"I don't know about that last part," he said. "I'm here, aren't I?"

"Maybe it's your Taurus moon that got you here." She reached for another chocolate. "Your time of birth determines your rising sign, and that's important in any number of ways, but in the absence of available information I'm willing to make the determination intuitively. My discipline is astrology, John, but it's not the only tool I use. I'm psychic, I sense things. My intuition tells me you have Cancer rising."

"If you say so."

"And I prepared a chart for you on that basis. I could tell you a lot of technical things about your chart, but I can't believe you're interested in all that, are you?"

"You're psychic, all right."

"So instead of nattering on about trines and squares and oppositions, let me just say it's an interesting chart. You're an extremely gentle person, John."

"Oh?"

"But there's so much violence in your life."

"Oh."

"That's the famous Gemini duality," she was saying. "On the one hand, you're thoughtful and sensitive and calm, exceedingly calm. John, do you ever get angry?"

"Not very often."

"No, and I don't think you stifle your anger, either. I get that it's just not a part of the equation. But there's violence all around you, isn't there?"

"It's a violent world we live in."

"There's been violence swirling around you all your life. You're very much a part of it, and yet you're somehow untouched by it." She tapped the sheet of paper, with his stars and planets all marked out. "You don't have an easy chart," she said.

"I don't?"

"Actually, that's something to be grateful for. I've seen charts of people who came into the world with no serious oppositions, no difficult aspects. And they wind up with lives where nothing much happens. They're never challenged, they never have to draw upon inner resources, and so they wind up leading reasonably comfortable lives and holding secure jobs and raising their kids in a nice safe clean suburb. And they never make anything terribly interesting of themselves."

"I haven't made much of myself," he said. "I've never married or fathered a child. Or started a business, or run for office, or planted a garden, or written a play, or . . . or . . ."

"Yes?"

"I'm sorry," he said. "I never expected to get . . ."

"Emotional?"

"Yes."

"It happens all the time."

"Oh."

"Just the other day I told a woman she's got Jupiter squaring her sun, but that her Jupiter and Mars are trined, and she burst into tears."

"I don't even know what that means."

"Neither did she."

"Oh."

"I see so much in your chart, John. This is a difficult time for you, isn't it?"

"I guess it must be."

"Not financially. Your Jupiter—well, you're not rich, and you're never going to be rich, but the money always seems to be there when you need it, doesn't it?"

"It's never been a problem."

"No, and it won't be. You've found ways to spend it in the past couple of years—" Stamps, he thought. "—and that's good, because now you're getting some pleasure out of your money. But you won't overspend, and you'll always be able to get more."

"That's good."

"But you didn't come here because you were concerned about money."

"No."

"You don't care that much about it. You always liked to get it and now you like to spend it, but you never cared deeply about it."

"No."

"I've prepared a solar return," she said, "to give you an idea what to expect in the next twelve months. Some astrologers are very specific—'July seventeenth is the perfect time to start a new project, and don't even think about being on water on the fifth of September.' My approach is more general, and . . . John? Why are you holding your right hand like that?"

"I beg your pardon?"

"With the thumb tucked inside. Is there something about your thumb that bothers you?"

"Not really."

"I've already seen your thumb, John."

"Oh."

"Did someone once tell you something about your thumb?"

"Yes."

"That it's a murderer's thumb?" She rolled her eyes. "Palmistry," she said heavily.

"You don't believe in it?"

"Of course I believe in it, but it does lend itself to some gross oversimplification." She reached out and took his hand in both of hers. Hers were soft, he noted, and pudgy, but not unpleasantly so. She ran a fingertip over his thumb, his homicidal thumb.

"To take a single anatomical characteristic," she said, "and fasten such a dramatic name to it. No one's thumb ever made him kill a fellow human being."

"Then why do they call it that?"

"I'm afraid I haven't studied the history of palmistry. I suppose someone spotted the peculiarity in a few notorious murderers and spread the word. I'm not even certain it's statistically more common among murderers than the general population. I doubt anyone really knows. John, it's an insignificant phenomenon and not worth noticing."

"But you noticed it," he said.

"I happened to see it."

"And you recognized it. You didn't say anything until you noticed me hiding it in my fist. That was unconscious, I didn't even know I was doing it."

"I see."

"So it must mean something," he said, "or why would it stay in your mind?"

She was still holding his hand. Keller had noticed that this was one of the ways a woman let you know she was interested in you. Women touched you a lot in completely innocent ways, on the hand or the arm or the shoulder, or held your hand longer than they had to. If a man did that it was sexual harassment, but it was a woman's way of letting you know she wouldn't mind being harassed herself.

But this was different. There was no sexual charge with this woman. If he'd been made of chocolate he might have had something to worry about, but mere flesh and blood was safe in her presence.

"John," she said, "I was looking for it."

"For . . ."

"The thumb. Or anything else that might confirm what I already knew about you."

She was gazing into his eyes as she spoke, and he wondered how much shock registered in them. He tried not to react, but how did you keep what you felt from showing up in your eyes?

"And what's that, Louise?"

"That I know about you?"

He nodded.

"That your life has been filled with violence, but I think I already mentioned that."

"You said I was gentle and not full of anger."

"But you've had to kill people, John."

"Who told you that?" She was no longer holding his hand. Had she released it? Or had he taken it away from her?

"Who told me?"

Maggie, he thought. Who else could it have been? Maggie was the only person they knew in common. But how did Maggie know? In her eyes he was a corporate suburbanite, even if he lived alone in the heart of the city.

"Actually," she was saying, "I had several informants."

His heart was hammering. What was she saying? How could it be true?

"Let me see, John. There was Saturn, and Mars, and we don't want to forget

Mercury." Her tone was soft, her gaze so gentle. "John," she said, "it's in your chart."

"My chart."

"I picked up on it right away. I got a very strong hit while I was working on your chart, and when you rang the bell I knew I would be opening the door to a man who had done a great deal of killing."

"I'm surprised you didn't cancel the appointment."

"I considered it. Something told me not to."

"A little bird?"

"An inner prompting. Or maybe it was curiosity. I wanted to see what you looked like."

"And?"

"Well, I knew right away I hadn't made a mistake with your chart."

"Because of my thumb?"

"No, though it was interesting to have that extra bit of confirmation. And the most revealing thing about your thumb was the effort you made to conceal it. But the vibration I picked up from you was far more revealing than anything about your thumb."

"The vibration."

"I don't know a better way to put it. Sometimes the intuitive part of the mind picks up things the five senses are blind and deaf to. Sometimes a person just knows something."

"Yes."

"I knew you were . . ."

"A killer," he supplied.

"Well, a man who has killed. And in a very dispassionate way, too. It's not personal for you, is it, John?"

"Sometimes a personal element comes into it."

"But not often."

"No."

"It's business."

"Yes."

"John? You don't have to be afraid of me."

Could she read his mind? He hoped not. Because what came to him now was that he was not afraid of her, but of what he might have to do to her.

And he didn't want to. She was a nice woman, and he sensed she would be able to tell him things it would be good for him to hear.

"You don't have to fear that I'll do anything, or say anything to anyone. You don't even need to fear my disapproval."

"Oh?"

"I don't make many moral judgments, John. The more I see, the less I'm sure I know what's right and what's wrong. Once I accepted myself"—she reached, grinning, for a chocolate—"I found it easier to accept other people. Thumbs and all."

He looked at his thumb, then raised his eyes to meet hers.

"Besides," she said, very gently, "I think you've done wonderfully in life, John." She tapped his chart. "I know what you started with. I think you've turned out just fine."

He tried to say something, but the words got stuck in his throat.

"It's all right," she said. "Go right ahead and cry. Never be ashamed to cry, John. It's all right."

And she drew his head to her breast and held him while, astonished, he sobbed his heart out.

"Well, that's a first," he said. "I don't know what I expected from astrology, but it wasn't tears."

"They wanted to come out. You've had them stored up for a while, haven't you?"

"Forever. I was in therapy for a while and never even got choked up."

"That would have been when? Three years ago?"

"How did you . . . It's in my chart?"

"Not therapy per se, but I saw there was a period when you were ready for self-exploration. But I don't believe you stayed with it for very long."

"A few months I got a lot of insight out of it, but in the end I felt I had to put an end to it."

Dr. Breen, the therapist, had had his own agenda, and it had conflicted seriously with Keller's. The therapy had come to an abrupt end, and so, not coincidentally, had the doctor.

He wouldn't let that happen with Louise Carpenter.

"This isn't therapy," she told him now, "but it can be a powerful experience. As you just found out."

"I'll say. But we must have used up our fifty minutes." He looked at his watch. "We went way over. I'm sorry. I didn't realize."

"I told you it's not therapy, John. We don't worry about the clock. And I never book more than two clients a day, one in the morning and one in the afternoon. We have all the time we need."

"Oh."

"And we need to talk about what you're going through. This is a difficult time for you, isn't it?"

Was it?

"I'm afraid the coming twelve months will continue to be difficult," she went on, "as long as Saturn's where it is. Difficult and dangerous. But I suppose danger is something you've learned to live with."

"It's not that dangerous," he said. "What I do."

"Really?"

Dangerous to others, he thought. "Not to me," he said. "Not particularly.

There's always a risk, and you have to keep your guard up, but it's not as though you have to be on edge all the time."

"What, John?"

"I beg your pardon?"

"You had a thought, it just flashed across your face."

"I'm surprised you can't tell me what it was."

"If I had to guess," she said, "I'd say you thought of something that contradicted the sentence you just spoke. About not having to be on edge all the time."

"That's what it was, all right."

"This would have been fairly recent."

"You can really tell all that? I'm sorry, I keep doing that. Yes, it was recent. A few months ago."

"Because the period of danger would have begun during the fall."

"That's when it was." And, without getting into specifics at all, he talked about his trip to Louisville, and how everything had seemed to be going wrong. "And there was a knock on the door of my room," he said, "and I panicked, which is not like me at all."

"No."

"I grabbed something"—a gun—"and stood next to the door, and my heart was hammering, and it was nothing but some drunk who couldn't find his friend. I was all set to kill him in self-defense, and all he did was knock on the wrong door."

"It must have been upsetting."

"The most upsetting part was seeing how upset I got. That didn't get my pulse racing like the knock on the door did, but the effects lasted longer. It still bothers me, to tell the truth."

"Because the reaction was unwarranted. But maybe you really were in danger, John. Not from the drunk, but from something invisible."

"Like what, anthrax spores?"

"Invisible to you, but not necessarily to the naked eye. Some unknown adversary, some secret enemy."

"That's how it felt. But it doesn't make any sense."

"Do you want to tell me about it?"

Did he?

"I changed my room," he said.

"Because of the drunk who knocked on your door?"

"No, why would I do that? But a couple of nights later I couldn't sleep because of noise from the people upstairs. I had to keep my room that night, the place was full, but I let them put me in a new room first thing the next morning. And that night . . ."

"Yes?"

"Two people checked into my old room. A man and a woman. They were murdered."

"In the room you'd just moved out of."

"It was her husband. She was there with somebody else, and the husband must have followed them. Shot them both. But I couldn't get past the fact that it was my room. Like if I hadn't changed my room, her husband would have come after me."

"But he wasn't anyone you knew."

"No, far from it."

"And yet you felt as though you'd had a narrow escape."

"But of course that's ridiculous."

She shook her head. "You could have been killed, John."

"How? I kept thinking the same thing myself, but it's just not true. The only reason the killer came to the room was because of the two people who were in it. They were what drew him, not the room itself. So how could he have ever been a danger to me?"

"There was a danger, though."

"The chart tells you that?"

She nodded solemnly, holding up one hand with the thumb and forefinger half an inch apart. "You and Death," she said, "came this close to one another."

"That's how it *felt*! But—"

"Forget the husband, forget what happened in that room. The woman's husband was never a threat to you, but someone else was. You were out there where the ice was very thin, John, and that's a good metaphor, because a skater never realizes the ice is thin until it cracks."

"But—"

"But it didn't," she said. "Whatever endangered you, the danger passed. Then those two people were killed, and that got your attention."

"Like ice cracking," he said, "but on another pond. I'll have to think about this."

"I'm sure you will."

He cleared his throat. "Louise? Is it all written in the stars, and do we just walk through it down here on earth?"

"No."

"You can look at that piece of paper," he said, "and you can say, 'Well, you'll come very close to death on such and such a day, but you'll get through it safe and sound.' "

"Only the first part. 'You'll come very close to death'—I could have looked at this and told you that much. But I wouldn't have been able to tell you that you'd survive. The stars show propensities and dictate probabilities, but the future is never entirely predictable. And we do have free will."

"If those people hadn't been killed, and if I'd just gone on home—"

"Yes?"

"Well, I'd be here having this conversation, and you'd tell me what a close shave I'd had, and I'd figure it for just so much starshine. I'd had a feeling, but I would have forgotten all about it. So I'd look at you and say, 'Yeah, right,' and turn the page."

"You can be grateful to the man and woman."

"And to the guy who shot them, as far as that goes. And to the bikers who made all the noise in the first place. And to Ralph."

"Who was Ralph?"

"The drunk's friend, the one he was looking for in all the wrong places. I can be grateful to the drunk, too, except I don't know his name. But then I don't know any of their names, except for Ralph."

"Maybe the names aren't important."

"I used to know the name of the man and woman, and of the man who shot them, the husband. I can't remember them now. You're right, the names aren't important."

"No."

He looked at her. "The next year . . ."

"Will be dangerous."

"What do I have to worry about? Should I think twice before I get on an airplane? Put on an extra sweater on windy days? Can you tell me where the threat's coming from?"

She hesitated, then said, "You have an enemy, John."

"An enemy?"

"An enemy. There's someone out there who wants to kill you."

"I don't know," he told Dot.

"You don't know? Keller, what's to know? What could be simpler? It's in Boston, for God's sake, not on the dark side of the moon. You take a cab to La Guardia, you hop on the Delta shuttle, you don't even need a reservation, and half an hour later you're on the ground at Logan. You take a cab into the city, you do the thing you do best, and you're on the shuttle again before the day is over, and back in your own apartment in plenty of time for Jay Leno. The money's right, the client's strictly blue-chip, and the job's a piece of cake."

"I understand all that, Dot."

"But?"

"I don't know."

"Keller," she said, "clearly I'm missing something. Help me out here. What part of 'I don't know' don't I understand?"

I don't know, he very nearly answered, but caught himself in time. In high school, a teacher had taken the class to task for those very words. "The way you use it," she said, " 'I don't know' is a lie. It's not what you mean at all. What you mean is 'I don't want to say' or 'I'm afraid to tell you.' "

"Hey, Keller," one of the other boys had called out. "What's the capital of South Dakota?"

"I'm afraid to tell you," he'd replied.

And what was he afraid to tell Dot? That the Boston job just wasn't in the stars? That the day the client had selected as ideal, this coming Wednesday, was a day specifically noted by his astrologer—his astrologer!—as a day fraught with danger, a day when he would be at extreme risk.

("So what do I do on those days?" he'd asked her. "Stay in bed with the door locked? Order all my meals delivered?" "The first part's not a terrible idea," she'd advised him, "but I'd be careful who was on the other side of the door before I opened it. And I'd be careful what I ate, too." The kid from the Chinese restaurant could be a Ninja assassin, he thought. The beef with oyster sauce could be laced with cyanide.)

"Keller?"

"The thing is, Wednesday's not the best day for me. There was something I'd planned on doing."

"What have you got, tickets to a matinee?"

"No."

"No, of course not. It's a stamp auction, isn't it? The thing is, Wednesday's the day the subject goes to his girlfriend's apartment in Back Bay, and he has to sneak over there, so he leaves his security people behind. Which makes it far and away the easiest time to get next to him."

"And she's part of the package, the girlfriend?"

"Your call, whatever you want. She's in or she's out, whatever works."

"And it doesn't matter how? Doesn't have to be an accident, doesn't have to look like an execution?"

"Anything you want. You can plunge the son of a bitch into a vat of lanolin and soften him to death. Anything at all, just so he doesn't have a pulse when you're through with him."

Hard job to say no to, he thought. Hard job to say *I don't know* to.

"I suppose the following Wednesday might work," Dot said. "The client would rather not wait, but my guess is he will if he has to. He said I was the first person he called, but I don't believe it. He's the type of guy's not that comfortable doing business with a woman. Our kind of business, anyway. So I think I was more like the third or fourth person he called, and I think he'll wait a week if I tell him he has to. Do you want me to see?"

Was he really going to lie in bed waiting for the bogeyman to get him?

"No, don't do that," he said. "This Wednesday's fine."

"Are you sure?"

"I'm sure," he said. He wasn't sure, he was miles short of sure, but it had a much better ring to it than *I don't know*.

Tuesday, the day before he was supposed to go to Boston, Keller had a strong urge to call Louise Carpenter. It had been a couple of weeks since she'd gone over his chart with him, and he wouldn't be seeing her again for a year. He'd thought it might turn out to be like therapy, with weekly appointments, and he gathered that there were some clients who dropped in frequently for an astrological tune-up and oil change, but he gathered that astrology was a sort of hobby for them. He already had a hobby, and Louise seemed to think an annual checkup was sufficient, and that was fine with him.

So he'd see her in a year's time. If he was still alive.

The forecast for Wednesday was rain and more rain, and when he woke up he saw they weren't kidding. It was a bleak, gray day, and the rain was coming down hard. An apologetic announcer on New York One said the downpour was expected to continue throughout the day and evening, accompanied by high winds and low temperatures. The way he was carrying on, you'd have thought it was his fault.

Keller put on a suit and tie, good protective coloration in a formal kind of city like Boston, and the standard uniform on the air shuttle. He got his trench coat out of the closet, put it on, and wasn't crazy about what he saw in the mirror. The salesman had called it olive, and maybe it was, at least in the store under their fluorescent lights. In the cold, damp light of a rainy morning, however, the damn thing looked green.

Not shamrock green, not Kelly green, not even putting green. But it was green, all right. You could slip into it on St. Patrick's Day and march up Fifth Avenue, and no one would mistake you for an Orangeman. No question about it, the sucker was green.

In the ordinary course of things, the coat's color wouldn't have bothered him. It wasn't so green as to bring on stares and catcalls, just green enough to draw the occasional appreciative glance. And there was a certain convenience in having a coat that didn't look like every other coat on the rack. You knew it on sight, and you could point it out to the cloakroom attendant when you couldn't find the check. "Right there, a little to your left," you'd say. "The green one."

But when you were flying up to Boston to kill a man, you didn't want to stand out in a crowd. You wanted to blend right in, to look like everybody else. Keller, in his unremarkable suit and tie, looked pretty much like everybody else.

In his coat, no question, he stood out.

Could he skip the coat? No, it was cold outside, and it would be colder in Boston. Wear his other topcoat, unobtrusively beige? No, it was porous, and he'd get soaked. He'd take an umbrella, but that wouldn't help much, not with a strong wind driving the rain.

What if he bought another coat?

But that was ridiculous. He'd have to wait for the stores to open, and then he'd spend an hour picking out the new coat and dropping off the old one at his apartment. And for what? There weren't going to be any witnesses in Boston, and anyone who did happen to see him go into the building would only remember the coat.

And maybe that was a plus. Like putting on a postman's uniform or a priest's collar, or dressing up as Santa Claus. People remembered what you were wearing, but that was all they remembered. Nobody noticed anything else about you that might be distinctive. Your thumb, for instance. And once you took off the uniform or the collar or the red suit and the beard, you became invisible.

Ordinarily he wouldn't have had to think twice. But this was an ominous day, one of the days his motherly astrologer had warned him about, and that made every little detail something to worry about.

And wasn't that silly? He had an enemy, and this enemy was trying to kill him, and on this particular day he was particularly at risk. And he had an assignment to kill a man, and that task inevitably carried risks of its own.

And, with all that going on, he was worrying about the coat he was wearing? That it was too discernibly green, for God's sake?

Get over it, he told himself.

A cab took him to La Guardia and a plane took him to Logan, and another cab dropped him in front of the Ritz-Carlton Hotel. He walked through the lobby, came out on Newbury Street, and walked along looking for a sporting goods store. He walked awhile without seeing one, and wasn't sure Newbury Street was the place for it. Antiques, leather goods, designer clothes, Limoges boxes—that was what you bought here, not Polartec sweats and climbing gear.

Or hunting knives. If you could find such an article here in Back Bay, it would probably have an ivory handle and a sterling silver blade, along with a three-figure price tag. He was sure it would be a beautiful object, and worth every penny, but how would he feel about tossing it down a storm drain when he was done with it?

Anyway, was it a good idea to buy a hunting knife in the middle of a big city on a rainy spring day in the middle of the week? Deer season was, what, seven or eight months off? How many hunting knives would be sold in Boston today? How many of them would be bought by men in green trench coats?

In a stationery store he browsed among the desk accessories and picked out a letter opener with a sturdy chrome-plated steel blade and an inlaid onyx handle. The salesgirl put it in a gift box without asking. It evidently didn't occur to her that anyone might buy an item like that for himself.

And in a sense Keller hadn't. He'd bought it for Alvin Thurnauer, and now it was time to deliver it.

That was the subject's name, Alvin Thurnauer, and Keller had seen a photograph of a big, outdoorsy guy with a full head of light brown hair. Along with the photo, the client had supplied an address on Emerson Street and a set of keys, one for the front door and one for the second-floor apartment where Thurnauer and his girlfriend would be playing Thank God It's Wednesday.

Thurnauer generally showed up around two, Dot had told him, and Keller was planted in a doorway across the street by half past one. The air was a little colder in Boston, and the wind a little stiffer, but the rain was about the same as it had been in New York. Keller's coat was waterproof, and his umbrella had not yet been blown inside out, but he still didn't stay a hundred percent dry. You couldn't, not when the rain came at you like God was pitching sidearm.

Maybe that was the risk. On a fateful day, you stood in the rain in Boston and caught your death of cold.

He toughed it out, and shortly before two a cab pulled up and a man got out, bundled up anonymously enough in a hat and coat, neither of them green. Keller's heart quickened. It could have been Thurnauer—it could have been anybody—and the fellow did stand looking across at the right house for a long moment before turning and heading off down the street. Keller gave up watching him when he got a couple of houses away. He retreated into the shadows, waiting for Thurnauer.

Who showed up right on time. Two on the button on Keller's watch, and there was the man himself, easy to spot as he got out of his cab because he wasn't wearing a hat. The mop of brown hair was a perfect field mark, identifiable at a glance.

Do it now?

It was doable. Just because he had keys didn't mean he had to use them. He could dart across the street and catch up with Thurnauer before the man had the front door open. Do him on the spot, shove him into the vestibule where the whole world wouldn't see him, and be out of sight himself in seconds.

That way he wouldn't have to worry about the girlfriend. But there might be other witnesses, people passing on the street, some moody citizen staring out the window at the rain. And he'd be awfully visible racing across the street in his green coat. And the letter opener was still in its box, so he'd have to use his hands.

And by the time he'd weighed all these considerations the moment had passed and Thurnauer was inside the house.

Just as well. If a roll in the hay was going to cost Thurnauer his life, let him at least have a chance to enjoy it. That was better than rushing in and doing a slapdash job. Thurnauer could have an extra thirty or forty minutes of life, and Keller could get out of the goddam rain and have a cup of coffee.

At the lunch counter, feeling only a little like one of the lonely guys in his Edward Hopper poster, Keller remembered that he hadn't eaten all day. He'd somehow missed breakfast, which was unusual for him.

Well, it was a high-risk day, wasn't it? Pneumonia, starvation—there were a lot of hazards out there.

Eating would have to wait. He didn't have the time, and he never liked to work on a full stomach. It made you sluggish, slowed your reflexes, spoiled your judgment. Better to wait and have a proper meal afterward.

While his coffee was cooling he went to the men's room and took the letter opener out of its gift box, which he discarded. He put the letter opener in his jacket pocket where he could reach it in a hurry. You couldn't cut with it, the blade's edge was rounded, but it came to a good sharp point. But was it sharp enough to penetrate several layers of cloth? Just as well he hadn't acted on the spur of the moment. Wait for Thurnauer to get out of his coat and jacket and shirt, and then the letter opener would have an easier time of it.

He drank his coffee, donned his green coat, picked up his umbrella, and went back to finish the job.

Nothing to it, really.

The keys worked. He didn't run into anybody in the entryway or on the stairs. He listened at the door of the second-floor apartment, heard music playing and water running, and let himself in.

He closed his umbrella, took off his coat, slipped off his shoes, and made his way in silence through the living room and along a hallway to the bedroom door. That was where the music was coming from, and it was where the woman, a slender dishwater blonde with almost translucent white skin, was sitting cross-legged on the edge of an unmade bed, smoking a cigarette.

She looked frighteningly vulnerable, and Keller hoped he wouldn't have to hurt her. If he could get Thurnauer alone, if he could do the man and get out without being seen, then he could let her live. If she saw him, well, then all bets were off.

The shower stopped running, and a moment later the bathroom door opened. A man emerged with a dark green towel around his waist. The guy was completely bald, and Keller wondered how the hell he'd managed to wind up in the wrong apartment. Then he realized it was Thurnauer after all. The guy had taken off his hair before he got in the shower.

Thurnauer walked over to the bed, made a face, and reached to take the cigarette away from the girl, stubbing it out in an ashtray. "I wish to God you'd quit," he said.

"And I wish you'd quit wishing I would quit," she said. "I've tried. I can't quit, all right? Not everybody's got your goddam willpower."

"There's the gum," he said.

"I started smoking to get out of the habit of chewing gum. I hate how it looks, grown women chewing gum, like a herd of cows."

"Or the patch," he said. "Why can't you wear a patch?"

"That was my last cigarette," she said.

"You know, you've said that before, and much as I'd like to believe it—"

"No, you moron," she snapped. "It was the last one I've got with me, not the last one I'm ever going to smoke. If you had to play the stern daddy and take a cigarette away from me, did it have to be my last one?"

"You can buy more."

"No kidding," she said. "You're damn right I can buy more."

"Go take a shower," Thurnauer said.

"I don't want to take a shower."

"You'll cool off and feel better."

"You mean I'll cool off and *you'll* feel better. Anyway, you just took a shower and you came out grumpy as a bear with a sore foot. The hell with taking a shower."

"Take one."

"Why? What's the matter, do I stink? Or do you just want to get me out of the room so you can make a phone call?"

"Mavis, for Christ's sake . . ."

"You can call some other girl who doesn't smoke and doesn't sweat and—"

"Mavis—"

"Oh, go to hell," Mavis said. "I'm gonna go take a shower. And put your hair on, will you? You look like a damn cue ball."

The shower was running and Thurnauer was hunched over her makeup mirror, adjusting his hairpiece, when Keller got a hand over his mouth and plunged the letter opener into his back, fitting it deftly between two ribs and driving it home into his heart. The big man had no time to struggle; by the time he knew what was happening, it had already happened. His body convulsed once, then went slack, and Keller lowered him to the floor.

The shower was still running. Keller could be out the door before she was out of the shower. But as soon as she did come out she would see Thurnauer, and she'd know at a glance that he was dead, and she'd scream and yell and carry on and call 911, and who needed that?

Besides, the pity he'd felt for her had dried up during her argument with her lover. He'd responded to a sense of her vulnerability, a fragile quality that he'd since decided was conveyed by that see-through skin of hers. She was actually a whining, sniping, carping nag of a woman, and about as fragile as an army boot.

So, when she stepped out of the bathroom, he took her from behind and broke her neck. He left her where she fell, just as he'd left Thurnauer on the bedroom floor. You could try to set a scene, make it look as though she had stabbed him and then broken her neck in a fall, but it would never fool anybody, so why bother? The client had merely stipulated that the man be dead, and that's what Keller had delivered.

It was sort of a shame about the girl, but it wasn't all that much of a shame. She was no Mother Teresa. And you couldn't let sentiment get in the way. That was always a bad idea, and especially on a high-risk day.

There were good restaurants in Boston, and Keller thought about going to Locke-Ober's, say, and treating himself to a really good meal. But the timing was wrong. It was just after three, too late for lunch and too early for dinner. If he went someplace decent they would just stare at him.

He could kill a couple of hours. He hadn't brought his catalog, so there was no point making the rounds of the stamp shops, but he could see a movie, or go to a museum. It couldn't be that hard to find a way to get through an afternoon, not in a city like Boston, for God's sake.

On a nicer day he'd have been happy enough just walking around Back Bay or

Beacon Hill. Boston was a good city for walking, not as good as New York, but better than most cities. With the rain still coming down, though, walking was no pleasure, and cabs were hard to come by.

Keller, back on Newbury Street, walked until he found an upscale coffee shop that looked okay. It wasn't going to remind anybody of Locke-Ober, but it was here and they would serve him now, and he was too hungry to wait.

The waitress wanted to know what the problem was. "It's my coat," Keller told her.

"What happened to your coat?"

"Well, that's the problem," he said. "I hung it on the hook over there, and it's gone."

"You sure it's not there?"

"Positive."

"Because coats tend to look alike, and there's coats hanging there, and—"

"Mine is green."

"Green green? Or more like an olive green?"

What difference did it make? There were three coats over there, all of them shades of beige, none at all like his. "The salesman called it olive," he said, "but it was pretty green. And it's not here."

"Are you sure you had it when you came in?"

Keller pointed at the window. "It's been like that all day," he said. "What kind of an idiot would go out without a coat?"

"Maybe you left it somewhere else."

Was it possible? He'd shucked the coat in the Emerson Street living room. Could he have left it there?

No, not a chance. He remembered putting it on, remembered opening his umbrella when he hit the street, remembered hanging both coat and umbrella on the peg before he slid into the booth and reached for the menu. And where was the umbrella? Gone, just like the coat.

"I didn't leave it anywhere else," he said firmly. "I was wearing the coat when I came in, and I hung it up right there, and it's not there now. And neither is my umbrella."

"Somebody must of taken it by mistake."

"How? It's green."

"Maybe they're color-blind," she suggested. "Or they have a green coat at home, and they forgot they were wearing the tan one today, so they took yours by mistake. When they bring it back—"

"Nobody's going to bring it back. Somebody stole my coat."

"Why would anybody steal a coat?"

"Probably because he didn't have a coat of his own," Keller said patiently, "and it's pouring out there, and he didn't want to get wet any more than I do. The three coats on the wall belong to your three other customers, and I'm not going to steal a coat from one of them, and the guy who stole my coat's not going to bring it back, so what am I supposed to do?"

"We're not responsible," she said, and pointed to a sign that agreed with her. Keller wasn't convinced the sign was enough to get the restaurant off the hook, but it didn't matter. He wasn't about to sue them.

"If you want me to call the police so you can report it . . ."

"I just want to get out of here," he said. "I need a cab, but I could drown out there waiting for an empty one to come along."

She brightened, able at last to suggest something. "Right over there," she said. "The hotel? There's a canopy'll keep you dry, and there's cabs pulling up and dropping people off all day long. And you know what? I'll bet Angela at the register's got an umbrella you can take. People leave them here all the time, and unless it's raining they never think to come back for them."

The girl at the cash register supplied a black folding umbrella, flimsy but serviceable. "I remember that coat," she said. "Green. I saw it come in and I saw it go out, but I never realized it was two different people coming and going. It was what you would call a very distinctive garment. Do you think you'll be able to replace it?"

"It won't be easy," he said.

"You didn't want to do this one," Dot said, "and I couldn't figure out why. It looked like a walk in the park, and it turns out that's exactly what it was."

"A walk in the rain," he said. "I had my coat stolen."

"And your umbrella. Well, there are some unscrupulous people out there, Keller, even in a decent town like Boston. You can buy a new coat."

"I never should have bought that one in the first place."

"It was green, you said."

"Too green."

"What were you doing, waiting for it to ripen?"

"It's somebody else's problem now," he said. "The next one's going to be beige."

"You can't go wrong with beige," she said. "Not too light, though, or it shows everything. My advice would be to lean toward the tan end of the spectrum."

"Whatever." He looked at her television set. "I wonder what they're talking about."

"Nothing as interesting as raincoats, would be my guess. I could unmute the thing, but I think we're better off wondering."

"You're probably right. I wonder if that was it. Losing the raincoat, I mean."

"You wonder if it was what?"

"The feeling I had."

"You did have a feeling about Boston, didn't you? It wasn't a stamp auction. You didn't want to take the job."

"I took it, didn't I?"

"But you didn't want to. Tell me more about this feeling, Keller."

"It was just a feeling," he said. He wasn't ready to tell her about his horoscope. He could imagine how she'd react, and he didn't want to hear it.

"You had a feeling another time," she said. "In Louisville."

"That was a little different."

"And both times the jobs went fine."

"That's true."

"So where do you suppose these feelings are coming from? Any idea?"

"Not really. It wasn't that strong a feeling this time, anyway. And I took the job, and I did it."

"And it went smooth as silk."

"More or less," he said.

"More or less?"

"I used a letter opener."

"What for? Sorry, dumb question. What did you do, pick it up off his desk?"

"Bought it on the way there."

"In Boston?"

"Well, I didn't want to take it through the metal detector. I bought it in Boston, and I took it with me when I left."

"Naturally. And chucked it in a Dumpster or down a sewer. Except you didn't or you wouldn't have brought up the subject. Oh, for Christ's sake, Keller. The coat pocket?"

"Along with the keys."

"What keys? Oh, hell, the keys to the apartment. A set of keys and a murder weapon and you're carrying them around in your coat pocket."

"They were going down a storm drain before I went to the airport," he said, "but first I wanted to get something to eat, and the next thing I knew my coat was gone."

"And the thief got more than just a coat."

"And an umbrella."

"Forget the umbrella, will you? Besides the coat he got keys and a letter opener. There's no little tag on the keys, tells the address, or is there?"

"Just two keys on a plain wire ring."

"And I hope you didn't let them engrave your initials on the letter opener."

"No, and I wiped it clean," he said. "But still."

"Nothing to lead to you."

"No."

"But still," she said.

"That's what I said. 'But still.' "

Back in the city, Keller picked up the Boston papers. Both covered the murder in detail. Alvin Thurnauer, it turned out, was a prominent local businessman with connections to local political interests and, the papers hinted, to less savory elements as well. That he'd died violently in a Back Bay love nest, along with a blonde to whom he was not married, did nothing to diminish the news value of his death.

Both papers assured him that the police were pursuing various leads. Keller, reading between the lines, concluded that they didn't have a clue. They might guess that someone had contracted to have Thurnauer hit, and they might be able to guess who that someone was, but they wouldn't be able to go anywhere with it. There were no witnesses, no useful physical evidence.

He almost missed the second murder.

The *Globe* didn't have it. But there it was in the *Herald*, a small story on a back page, a man found dead on Boston Common, shot twice in the head with a small-caliber weapon.

Keller could picture the poor bastard, lying facedown on the grass, the rain washing relentlessly down on him. He could picture the dead man's coat, too. The *Herald* didn't say anything about a coat, but that didn't matter. Keller could picture it all the same.

Green as the grass.

He stared hard at his thumb, then looked in a drawer for the copy of his chart Louise had given him. It looked even more impressive now, if no less incomprehensible. He put it back in the drawer.

Later, when the sky was dark, he went outside and looked up at the stars.

Keller's Designated Hitter

Keller, a beer in one hand and a hot dog in the other, walked up a flight and a half of concrete steps and found his way to his seat. In front of him, two men were discussing the ramifications of a recent trade the Tarpons had made, sending two minor-league prospects to the Florida Marlins in return for a left-handed reliever and a player to be named later. Keller figured he hadn't missed anything, as they'd been talking about the same subject when he left. He figured the player in question would have been long since named by the time these two were done speculating about him.

Keller took a bite of his hot dog, drew a sip of his beer. The fellow on his left said, "You didn't bring me one."

Huh? He'd told the guy he'd be back in a minute, might have mentioned he was going to the refreshment stand, but had he missed something the man had said in return?

"What didn't I bring you? A hot dog or a beer?"

"Either one," the man said.

"Was I supposed to?"

"Nope," the man said. "Hey, don't mind me. I'm just jerking your chain a little."

"Oh," Keller said.

The fellow started to say something else, but broke it off after a word or two as he and everybody else in the stadium turned their attention to home plate, where the Tarpons' cleanup hitter had just dropped to the dirt to avoid getting hit by a high inside fastball. The Yankee pitcher, a burly Japanese with a herky-jerky windup, seemed unfazed by the boos, and Keller wondered if he even knew they were for him. He caught the return throw from the catcher, set himself, and went into his pitching motion.

"Taguchi likes to pitch inside," said the man who'd been jerking Keller's chain, "and Vollmer likes to crowd the plate. So every once in a while Vollmer has to hit the dirt or take one for the team."

Keller took another bite of his hot dog, wondering if he ought to offer a bite to his new friend. That he even considered it seemed to indicate that his chain had been jerked successfully. He was glad he didn't have to share the hot dog, because he wanted every bite of it for himself. And, when it was gone, he had a feeling he might go back for another.

Which was strange, because he never ate hot dogs. A few years back he'd read a political essay on the back page of a news magazine that likened legislation to sausage. You were better off not knowing how it was made, the writer observed, and Keller, who had heretofore never cared how laws were passed or sausages produced, found himself more conscious of the whole business. The legislative aspect didn't change his life, but, without making any conscious decision on the matter, he found he'd lost his taste for sausage.

Being at a ballpark somehow made it different. He had a hunch the hot dogs they sold here at Tarpon Stadium were if anything more dubious in their composition than your average supermarket frankfurter, but that seemed to be beside the point. A ballpark hot dog was just part of the baseball experience, along with listening to some flannel-mouthed fan shouting instructions to a ballplayer dozens of yards away who couldn't possibly hear him, or booing a pitcher who couldn't care less, or having one's chain jerked by a total stranger. All part of the Great American Pastime.

He took a bite, chewed, sipped his beer. Taguchi went to three and two on Vollmer, who fouled off four pitches before he got one he liked. He drove it to the 396-foot mark in left center field, where Bernie Williams hauled it in. There had been runners on first and second, and they trotted back to their respective bases when the ball was caught.

"One out," said Keller's new friend, the chain jerker.

Keller ate his hot dog, sipped his beer. The next batter swung furiously and topped a roller that dribbled out toward the mound. Taguchi pounced on it, but his only play was to first, and the runners advanced. Men on second and third, two out.

The Tarpon third baseman was next, and the crowd booed lustily when the Yankees elected to walk him intentionally. "They always do that," Keller said.

"Always," the man said. "It's strategy, and nobody minds when their own team does it. But when your guy's up and the other side won't pitch to him, you tend to see it as a sign of cowardice."

"Seems like a smart move, though."

"Unless Turnbull shows 'em up with a grand slam, and God knows he's hit a few of 'em in the past."

"I saw one of them," Keller recalled. "In Wrigley Field, before they had the lights. He was with the Cubs. I forget who they were playing."

"That would have had to be before the lights came in, if he was with the Cubs. Been all around, hasn't he? But he's been slumping lately, and you got to go with the percentages. Walk him and you put on a .320 hitter to get at a .280 hitter, plus you got a force play at any base."

"It's a game of percentages," Keller said.

"A game of inches, a game of percentages, a game of woulda-coulda-shoulda," the man said, and Keller was suddenly more than ordinarily grateful that he was an American. He'd never been to a soccer match, but somehow he doubted they ever supplied you with a conversation like this one.

"Batting seventh for the Tarpons," the stadium announcer intoned. "Number 17, the designated hitter, Floyd Turnbull."

"He's a designated hitter," Dot had said, on the porch of the big old house on Taunton Place. "Whatever that means."

"It means he's in the lineup on offense only," Keller told her. "He bats for the pitcher."

"Why can't the pitcher bat for himself? Is it some kind of union regulation?"

"That's close enough," said Keller, who didn't want to get into it. He had once tried to explain the infield fly rule to a stewardess, and he was never going to make that sort of mistake again. He wasn't a sexist about it, he knew plenty of women who understood this stuff, but the ones who didn't were going to have to learn it from somebody else.

"I saw him play a few times," he told her, stirring his glass of iced tea. "Floyd Turnbull."

"On television?"

"Dozens of times on TV," he said. "I was thinking of seeing him in person. Once at Wrigley Field, when he was with the Cubs and I happened to be in Chicago."

"You just happened to be there?"

"Well," Keller said. "I don't ever just happen to be anyplace. It was business. Anyway, I had a free afternoon and I went to a game."

"Nowadays you'd go to a stamp dealer."

"Games are mostly at night nowadays," he said, "but I still go every once in a while. I saw Turnbull a couple of times in New York, too. Out at Shea, when he was with the Cubs and they were in town for a series with the Mets. Or maybe he was already with the Astros when I saw him. It's hard to remember."

"And not exactly crucial that you get it right."

"I think I saw him at Yankee Stadium, too. But you're right, it's not important."

"In fact," Dot said, "it would be fine with me if you'd never seen him at all, up close or on TV. Does this complicate things, Keller? Because I can always call the guy back and tell him we pass."

"You don't have to do that."

"Well, I hate to, since they already paid half. I can turn down jobs every day and twice on Sundays, but there's something about giving back money once I've got it in my hands that makes me sick to my stomach. I wonder why that is?"

"A bird in the hand," Keller suggested.

"When I've got a bird in my hand," she said, "I hate like hell to let go of it. But you saw this guy play. That's not gonna make it tough for you to take him out?"

Keller thought about it, shook his head. "I don't see why it should," he said. "It's what I do."

"Right," Dot said. "Same as Turnbull, when you think about it. You're a designated hitter yourself, aren't you, Keller?"

"Designated hitter," Keller said, as Floyd Turnbull took a called second strike. "Whoever thought that one up?"

"Some marketing genius," his new friend said. "Some dipstick who came up with research to prove that fans wanted to see more hits and home runs. So they lowered the pitching mound and told the umpires to quit calling the high strike, and then they juiced up the baseball and brought in the fences in the new ballparks, and the ballplayers started lifting weights and swinging lighter bats, and now you've got baseball games with scores like football games. Last week the Tigers beat the A's fourteen to thirteen. First thing I thought, Jeez, who missed the extra point?"

"At least the National League still lets pitchers hit."

"And at least nobody in the pros uses those aluminum bats. They show college baseball on ESPN and I can't watch it. I can't stand the sound the ball makes when you hit it. Not to mention it travels too goddam far."

The next pitch was in the dirt. Posada couldn't find it, but the third base coach, suspicious, held the runner. The fans booed, though it was hard to tell who they were booing, or why. The two in front of Keller joined in the booing, and Keller and the man next to him exchanged knowing glances.

"Fans," the man said, and rolled his eyes.

The next pitch was belt-high, and Turnbull connected solidly with it. The stadium held its collective breath and the ball sailed toward the left field corner, hooking foul at the last moment. The crowd heaved a sigh and the runners trotted back to their bases. Turnbull, looking not at all happy, dug in again at the plate.

He swung at the next pitch, which looked like ball four to Keller, and popped to right. O'Neill floated under it and gathered it in and the inning was over.

"Top of the order for the Yanks," said Keller's friend. "About time they broke this thing wide open, wouldn't you say?"

With two out in the Tarpons' half of the eighth inning, with the Yankees ahead by five runs, Floyd Turnbull got all of a Mike Stanton fastball and hit it into the upper deck. Keller watched as he jogged around the bases, getting a good hand from what remained of the crowd.

"Career home run number 393 for the old warhorse," said the man on Keller's left. "And all those people missed it because they had to beat the traffic."

"Number 393?"

"Leaves him seven shy of four hundred. And, in the hits department, you just saw number 2988."

"You've got those stats at your fingertips?"

"My fingers won't quite reach," the fellow said, and pointed to the scoreboard, where the information he'd cited was posted. "Just twelve hits to go before he joins the magic circle, the Three Thousand Hits club. That's the only thing to be said for the DH rule—it lets a guy like Floyd Turnbull stick around a couple of extra years, long enough to post the kind of numbers that get you into Cooperstown. And he can still do a team some good. He can't run the bases, he can't chase after fly balls, but the son of a bitch hasn't forgotten how to hit a baseball."

The Yankees got the run back in the top of the ninth on a walk to Jeter and a home run by Bernie Williams, and the Tarpons went in order in the bottom of the ninth, with Rivera striking out the first two batters and getting the third to pop to short.

"Too bad there was nobody on when Turnbull got his homer," said Keller's friend, "but that's usually the way it is. He's still good with a stick, but he hits 'em with nobody on, and usually when the team's too far behind or out in front for it to make any difference."

The two men walked down a succession of ramps and out of the stadium. "I'd like to see old Floyd get the numbers he needs," the man said, "but I wish he'd get 'em on some other team. What they need for a shot at the flag's a decent left-handed starter and some help in the bullpen, not an old man with bad knees who hits it out when you don't need it."

"You think they should trade him?"

"They'd love to, but who'd trade for him? He can help a team, but not enough to justify paying him the big bucks. He's got three years left on his contract, three years at six-point-five million a year. There are teams that could use him, but nobody can use him six-point-five worth. And the Tarps can't release him and go out and *buy* the pitching they need, not while they've got Turnbull's salary to pay."

"Tricky business," Keller said.

"And a business is what it is. Well, I'm parked over on Pentland Avenue, so this is where I get off. Nice talking with you."

And off the fellow went, while Keller turned and walked off in the opposite direction. He didn't know the name of the man he had talked to, and would probably never see him again, and that was fine. In fact it was one of the real pleasures of going to a game, the intense conversations you had with strangers whom you then allowed to remain strangers. The man had been good company, and at the end he'd provided some useful information.

Because now Keller had an idea why he'd been hired.

"The Tarpons are stuck with Turnbull," he told Dot. "He draws this huge salary, and they have to pay it whether they play him or not. And I guess that's where I come in."

"I don't know," she said. "Are you sure about this, Keller? That's a pretty extreme form of corporate downsizing. All that just to keep from paying a man his salary? How much could it amount to?"

He told her.

"That much," she said, impressed. "That's a lot to pay a man to hit a ball with a stick, especially when he doesn't have to go out and stand around in the hot sun. He just sits on the bench until it's his turn to bat, right?"

"Right."

"Well, I think you might be on to something," she said. "I don't know who hired us or why, but your guess makes more sense than anything I could come up with off the top of my head. But I feel myself getting a little nervous, Keller."

"Why?"

"Because this is just the kind of thing that could set your milk to curdling, isn't it?"

"What milk? What are you talking about?"

"I've known you a long time, Keller. And I can just see you deciding that this is a hell of a way to treat a faithful employee after long years of service, and how can you allow this to happen, di dah di dah di dah. Am I coming through loud and clear?"

"The di dah part makes more sense than the rest of it," he said. "Dot, as far as who hired us and why, all I am is curious. Curiosity's a long way from righteous indignation."

"Didn't do much for the cat, as I remember."

"Well," he said, "I'm not *that* curious."

"So I've got nothing to worry about?"

"Not a thing," he said. "The guy's a dead man hitting."

The Tarpons closed out the series with the Yankees—and a twelve-game home stand—the following afternoon. They got a good outing from their ace right-hander, who scattered six hits and held the New Yorkers to one run, a bases-empty homer by Brosius. The Tarps won, 3–1, with no help from their designated hitter, who struck out twice, flied to center, and hit a hard liner right at the first baseman.

Keller watched from a good seat on the third base side, then checked out of his hotel and drove to the airport. He turned in his rental car and flew to Milwaukee, where the Brewers would host the Tarps for a three-game series. He picked up a fresh rental and checked in at a motel half a mile from the Marriott where the Tarpons always stayed.

The Brewers won the first game, 5–2. Floyd Turnbull had a good night at bat, going three for five with two singles and a double, but he didn't do anything to affect the outcome; there was nobody on base when he got his hits, and nobody behind him in the order could drive him in.

The next night the Tarps got to the Brewers' rookie southpaw early and blew the game open, scoring six runs in the first inning and winding up with a 13–4 victory. Turnbull's homer was part of the big first inning, and he collected another hit in the seventh when he doubled into the gap and was thrown out trying to stretch it into a triple.

"Why'd he do that?" the bald guy next to Keller wondered. "Two out and he tries for third? Don't make the third out at third base, isn't that what they say?"

"When you're up by nine runs," Keller said, "I don't suppose it matters much one way or the other."

"Still," the man said, "it's what's wrong with that prick. Always for himself his whole career. He wanted one more triple in the record book, that's what he wanted. And forget about the team."

After the game Keller went to a German restaurant south of the city on the lake. The place dripped atmosphere, with beer steins hanging from the hand-hewn oak beams, an oompah band in lederhosen, and fifteen different beers on tap. Keller couldn't tell the waitresses apart, they all looked like grown-up versions of Heidi, and evidently Floyd Turnbull had the same problem; he called them all Gretchen and ran his hand up under their skirts whenever they came within reach.

Keller was there because he'd learned the Tarpons favored the place, but the sauerbraten was reason enough to make the trip. He made his beer last until he'd cleaned his plate, then turned down the waitress's suggestion of a refill and asked for a cup of coffee instead. By the time she brought it, several more fans had crossed the room to beg autographs from the Tarpons.

"They all want their menus signed," Keller told the waitress. "You people are going to run out of menus."

"It happens all the time," she said. "Not that we run out of menus, because we never do, but players coming here and our other customers asking for autographs. All the athletes like to come here."

"Well, the food's great," he said.

"And it's free. For the players, I mean. It brings in other customers, so it's worth it to the owner, plus he just likes having his restaurant full of jocks. About it being free for them, I'm not supposed to tell you that."

"It'll be our little secret."

"You can tell the whole world, for all I care. Tonight's my last night. I mean, what do I need with jerks like Floyd Turnbull? I want a pelvic exam, I'll go to my gynecologist, if it's all the same to you."

"I noticed he was a little free with his hands."

"And close with everything else. They eat and drink free, but most of them at least leave tips. Not good tips, ballplayers are cheap bastards, but they leave something. Turnbull always leaves exactly twenty percent."

"Twenty percent's not that bad, is it?"

"It is when it's twenty percent of nothing."

"Oh."

"He said he got a home run tonight, too."

"Number 394 of his career," Keller said.

"Well, he's not getting to first base with me," she said. "The big jerk."

"Night before last," Keller said, "I was in a German restaurant in Milwaukee."

"Milwaukee, Keller?"

"Well, not exactly in Milwaukee. It was south of the city a few miles, on Lake Michigan."

"That's close enough," Dot said. "It's still a long way from Memphis, isn't it? Although if it's south of the city, I guess it's closer to Memphis than if it was actually inside of Milwaukee."

"Dot . . ."

"Before we get too deep into the geography of it," she said, "aren't you supposed to be in Memphis? Taking care of business?"

"As a matter of fact . . ."

"And don't tell me you already took care of business, because I would have heard. CNN would have had it, and they wouldn't even make me wait until Headline Sports at twenty minutes past the hour. You notice how they never say which hour?"

"That's because of different time zones."

"That's right, Keller, and what time zone are you in? Or don't you know?"

"I'm in Seattle," he said.

"That's Pacific time, isn't it? Three hours behind New York."

"Right."

"But ahead of us," she said, "in coffee. I'll bet you can explain, can't you?"

"They're on a road trip," he said. "They play half their games at home in Memphis, and half the time they're in other cities."

"And you've been tagging along after them."

"That's right. I want to take my time, pick my spot. If I have to spend a few dollars on airline tickets, I figure that's my business. Because nobody said anything about being in a hurry on this one."

"No," she admitted. "If time is of the essence, nobody told me about it. I just thought you were gallivanting around, going to stamp dealers and all. Taking your eye off the ball, so to speak."

"So to speak," Keller said.

"So how can they play ball in Seattle, Keller? Doesn't it rain all the time? Or is it one of those stadiums with a lid on it?"

"A dome," he said.

"I stand corrected. And here's another question. What's Memphis got to do with fish?"

"Huh?"

"Tarpons," she said. "Fish. And there's Memphis, in the middle of the desert."

"Actually, it's on the Mississippi River."

"Spot any tarpons in the Mississippi River, Keller?"

"No."

"And you won't," she said, "unless that's where you stick Turnbull when you finally close the deal. It's a saltwater fish, the tarpon, so why pick that name for the Memphis team? Why not call them the Gracelanders?"

"They moved," he explained.

"To Milwaukee," she said, "and then to Seattle, and God knows where they'll go next."

"No," he said. "The franchise moved. They started out as an expansion team, the Sarasota Tarpons, but they couldn't sell enough tickets, so a new owner took over and moved them to Memphis. Look at basketball, the Utah Jazz and the L.A. Lakers. What's Salt Lake City got to do with jazz, and when did Southern California get to be the Land of Ten Thousand Lakes?"

"The reason I don't follow sports," she said, "is it's too damn confusing. Isn't there a team called the Miami Heat? I hope they stay put. Imagine if they move to Buffalo."

Why had he called in the first place? Oh, right. "Dot," he said, "I was in the Tarpons' hotel earlier today, and I saw a guy."

"So?"

"A little guy," he said, "with a big nose, and one of those heads that look as though somebody put it in a vise."

"I heard about a guy once who used to do that to people."

"Well, I doubt that's what happened to this fellow, but that's the kind of face he had. He was sitting in the lobby reading a newspaper."

"Suspicious behavior like that, it's no wonder you noticed him."

"No, that's the thing," he said. "He's distinctive-looking, and he looked wrong. And I saw him just a couple of nights before in Milwaukee at this German restaurant."

"The famous German restaurant."

"I gather it is pretty famous, but that's not the point. He was in both places, and he was alone both times. I noticed him in Milwaukee because I was eating by myself, and feeling a little conspicuous about it, and I saw I wasn't the only lone diner, because there he was."

"You could have asked him to join you."

"He looked wrong there, too. He looked like a Broadway sharpie, out of an old movie. Looked like a weasel, wore a fedora. He could have been in *Guys and Dolls,* saying he's got the horse right here."

"I think I see where this is going."

"And what I think," he said, "is I'm not the only DH in the lineup . . . Hello? Dot?"

"I'm here," she said. "Just taking it all in. I don't know who the client is, the contract came through a broker, but what I do know is nobody seems to be getting antsy. So why would they hire somebody else? You're sure this guy's a hitter? Maybe he's a big fan, hates to miss a game, follows 'em all over the country."

"He looks wrong for the part, Dot."

"Could he be a private eye? Ballplayers cheat on their wives, don't they?"

"Everybody does, Dot."

"So some wife hired him, he's gathering divorce evidence."

"He looks too shady to be a private eye."

"I didn't know that was possible."

"He doesn't have that crooked-cop look private eyes have. He looks more like the kind of guy they used to arrest, and he'd bribe them to cut him loose. I think he's a hired gun, and not one from the A-list, either."

"Or he wouldn't look like that."

"Part of the job description," he said, "is you have to be able to pass in a crowd. And he's a real sore thumb."

"Maybe there's more than one person who wants our guy dead."

"Occurred to me."

"And maybe a second client hired a second hit man. You know, maybe taking your time's a good idea."

"Just what I was thinking."

"Because you could do something and find yourself in a mess because of the heat this ferret-faced joker stirs up. And if he's there with a job to do, and you stay in the background and let him do it, where's the harm? We collect no matter who pulls the trigger."

"So I'll bide my time."

"Why not? Drink some of that famous coffee, Keller. Get rained on by some of that famous rain. They have any stamp dealers in Seattle, Keller?"

"There must be. I know there's one in Tacoma."

"So go see him," she said. "Buy some stamps. Enjoy yourself."

"I collect worldwide, 1840 to 1949, and up to 1952 for British Commonwealth."

"In other words, the classics," said the dealer, a square-faced man who was wearing a striped tie with a plaid shirt. "The good stuff."

"But I've been thinking of adding a topic. Baseball."

"Good topic," the man said. "Most topics, you get bogged down in all these phony Olympics issues every little stamp-crazy country prints up to sell to collectors. Soccer's even worse, with the World Cup and all. There's less of that crap with baseball, on account of it's not an Olympic sport. I mean, what do they know about baseball in Guinea-Bissau?"

"I was at the game last night," Keller said.

"Mariners win for a change?"

"Beat the Tarpons."

"About time."

"Turnbull went two for four."

"Turnbull. He on the Mariners?"

"He's the Tarpons' DH."

"They brought in the DH," the man said, "I lost interest in the game. He went two for four, huh? Am I missing something here? Is that significant?"

"Well, I don't know that it's significant," Keller said, "but that puts him just five hits shy of three thousand, and he needs three home runs to reach the four hundred mark."

"You never know," the dealer said. "One of these days, St. Vincent–Grenadines may put his picture on a stamp. Well, what do you say? Do you want to see some baseball topicals?"

Keller shook his head. "I'll have to give it some more thought," he said, "before I start a whole new collection. How about Turkey? There's page after page of early issues where I've got nothing but spaces."

"You sit down," the dealer said, "and we'll see if we can't fill some of them for you."

From Seattle the Tarpons flew to Cleveland for three games at Jacobs Field, then down to Baltimore for four games in three days with the division-leading Orioles. Keller missed the last game against the Mariners and flew to Cleveland ahead of them, getting settled in and buying tickets for all three games. Jacobs Field was one of the new parks and an evident source of pride to the local fans, and the previous year they'd filled the stands more often than not, but this year the Indians weren't doing as well and Keller had no trouble getting good seats.

Floyd Turnbull managed only one hit against the Indians, a scratch single in the first game. He went oh for three with a walk in game two, and rode the bench in the third game, the only one the Tarpons won. His replacement, a skinny kid just up from the minors, had two hits and drove in three runs.

"New kid beat us," said Keller's conversational partner du jour. He was a Cleveland fan, and assumed Keller was, too. Keller, who'd bought an Indians cap for the series, had encouraged him in this belief. "Wish they'd stick with old Turnbull," the man went on.

"Close to three thousand hits," Keller said.

"Lots of hits and homers, but he never seems to beat you like this kid just did. Hits for the record book, not for the game—that's Floyd for you."

"Excuse me," Keller said. "I see somebody I better go say hello to."

It was the Broadway sharpie, wearing a Panama fedora with a bright red hatband. That made him easy to spot, but even without it he was hard to miss. Keller had picked him out of the crowd back in the third inning, checked now and then to make sure he was still in the same seat. But now the guy was in conversation with a woman, their heads close together, and she didn't look right for the part.

The instant camaraderie of baseball notwithstanding, a woman who looked like her didn't figure to be discussing the subtleties of the double steal with a guy who looked like him.

She was tall and slender, and she bore herself regally. She was wearing a suit, and at first glance you thought she'd come from the office, and then you decided she probably owned the company. If she belonged at a ballpark at all, it was in the sky boxes, not the general-admission seats.

What were they discussing with such urgency? Whatever it was, they were done talking about it before Keller could get close enough to listen in. They separated and headed off in different directions, and Keller tossed a mental coin and set out after the woman. He already knew where the man was staying, and what name he was using.

He tagged the woman to the Ritz-Carlton, which sort of figured. He'd gotten rid of his Indians cap en route, but he still wasn't dressed for the lobby of a five-star hotel, not in the khakis and polo shirt that were just fine for Jacobs Field.

Couldn't be helped. He went in, hoping to spot her in the lobby, but she wasn't there. Well, he could have a drink at the bar. Unless they had a dress code, he could nurse a beer and maybe keep an eye on the lobby without looking out of place. If she was settled in for the night he was out of luck, but maybe she'd just gone to her room to change, maybe she hadn't had dinner yet.

Better than that, as it turned out. He walked into the bar and there she was, all by herself at a corner table, smoking a cigarette in a holder—you didn't see that much anymore—and drinking what looked like a rust-colored cocktail in a stemmed glass. A Manhattan or a Rob Roy, he figured. Something like that. Classy, like the woman herself, and slightly out-of-date.

Keller stopped at the bar for a bottle of Tuborg, carried it to the woman's table. Her eyes widened briefly at his approach, but otherwise nothing much showed on her face. Keller drew a chair for himself and sat down as if there was no question that he was welcome.

"I'm with the guy," he said.

"I don't know what you're talking about."

"No names, all right? Straw hat with a red band on it. You were talking to him, what, twenty minutes ago? You want to pretend I'm talking Greek, or do you want to come with me?"

"Where?"

"He needs to see you."

"But he just saw me!"

"Look, there's a lot I don't understand here," Keller said, not untruthfully. "I'm just an errand boy. He coulda come himself, but is that what you want? To be seen in public in your own hotel with Slansky?"

"Slansky?"

"I made a mistake there," Keller said, "using that name, which you wouldn't know him by. Forget I said that, will you?"

"But . . ."

"Far as that goes, *we* shouldn't spend too much time together. I'm going to walk out, and you finish your drink and sign the tab and then follow me. I'll be waiting out front in a blue Honda Accord."

"But . . ."

"Five minutes," he told her, and left.

It took her more than five minutes, but under ten, and she got into the front seat of Honda without any hesitation. He pulled out of the hotel lot and hit the button to lock her door.

While they drove around, ostensibly heading for a meeting with the man in the Panama hat (whose name wasn't Slansky, but so what?), Keller learned that Floyd Turnbull, who'd had an affair with this woman, had sweet-talked her into investing in a real estate venture of his. The way it was set up, she couldn't get her money out without a lengthy and expensive lawsuit—unless Turnbull died, in which case the partnership was automatically dissolved. Keller didn't try to follow the legal part. He got the gist of it, and that was enough. The way she spoke about Turnbull, he got the feeling she'd pay a lot to see him dead, even if there was nothing in it for her.

Funny how people tended not to like the guy.

And now Slansky had all the money in advance, and in return for that she had his sworn promise that Turnbull wouldn't have a pulse by the time the team got back to Memphis. She'd been after him to get it done in Cleveland, but he'd stalled until he'd gotten her to pay him the entire fee up front, and it looked as though he wouldn't do it until they were in Baltimore, but it really better happen in Baltimore, because that was the last stop before the Tarpons returned to Memphis for a long home stand, and—

Jesus, suppose the guy tried to save himself a trip to Baltimore?

"Here we go," he said, and turned into a strip mall. All the stores were closed for the night, and the parking area was empty except for a delivery van and a Chevy that wouldn't go anywhere until somebody changed its right rear tire. Keller parked next to the Chevy and cut the engine.

"Around the back," he said, and opened the door for her and helped her out. He led her so that the Chevy screened them from the street. "It gets tricky here," he said, and took her arm.

The man he'd called Slansky was staying at a budget motel off an interchange of I-71, where he'd registered as John Carpenter. Keller went and knocked on his door, but that would have been too easy.

Hell.

The Tarpons were staying at a Marriott again, unless they were already on their way to Baltimore. But they'd just finished a night game, and they had a night game tomorrow, so maybe they'd stay over and fly out in the morning. He drove over to the Marriott and walked through the lobby to the bar, and on his way he spotted the shortstop and a middle reliever. So they were staying over, unless someone in the front office had cut those two players, and that seemed unlikely, as they didn't look depressed.

He found two more Tarpons in the bar, where he stayed long enough to drink a beer. One of the pair, the second-string catcher, gave Keller a nod of recognition, and that gave him a turn. Had he been hanging around enough for the players to think of him as a familiar face?

He finished his beer and left. As he was on his way out of the lobby, Floyd Turnbull was on his way in, and not looking very happy. And what did he have to be happy about? A stringbean named Anliot had taken his job away from him for the evening, and had won the game for the Tarpons in the process. No wonder Turnbull looked like he wanted to kick somebody's ass, and preferably Anliot's. He also looked to be headed for his room, and Keller figured the man was ready to call it a night.

Keller went back to the budget motel. When his knock again went unanswered, he found a pay phone and called the desk. A woman told him that Mr. Carpenter had checked out.

And gone where? He couldn't have caught a flight to Baltimore, not at this hour. Maybe he was driving. Keller had seen his car, and it looked too old and beat-up to be a rental. Maybe he owned it, and he'd drive all night, from Cleveland to Baltimore.

Keller flew to Baltimore and was in his seat at Camden Yards for the first pitch. Floyd Turnbull wasn't in the lineup, they'd benched him and had Graham Anliot slotted as DH. Anliot got two singles and a walk in his first three trips to the plate, and Keller didn't stick around to see how he ended the evening. He left with the Tarpons coming to bat in the top of the seventh, and leading by four runs.

The clerk at Ace Hardware rang Keller's purchases—a roll of picture-hanging wire, a packet of screw eyes, a packet of assorted picture hooks—and came to a logical conclusion. With a smile, he said, "Gonna hang a pitcher?"

"A DH," Keller said.

"Huh?"

"Sorry," he said, recovering. "I was thinking of something else. Yeah, right. Hang a picture."

In his motel room, Keller wished he'd bought a pair of wire-cutting pliers. In their absence, he measured out a three-foot length of the picture-hanging wire and bent it back on itself until the several strands frayed and broke. He fashioned a loop at each end, then put the unused portion of the wire back in its box, to be discarded down the next handy storm drain. He'd already rid himself of the screw eyes and the picture hooks.

He didn't know where Slansky was staying, hadn't seen him at the game the previous evening. But he knew the sort of motel the man favored, and figured he'd pick one near the ballpark. Would he use the same name when he signed in? Keller couldn't think of a reason why not, and evidently neither could Slansky; when he called the Sweet Dreams Motel on Key Highway, a pleasant young woman with a Gujarati accent told him that yes, they did have a guest named John Carpenter, and would he like her to ring the room?

"Don't bother," he said. "I want it to be a surprise."

And it was. When Slansky—Keller couldn't help it, he thought of the man as Slansky, even though it was a name he'd made up for the guy himself—when Slansky got in his car, there was Keller, sitting in the backseat.

The man stiffened just long enough for Keller to tell that his presence was known. Then, smoothly, he moved to fit the key in the ignition. Let him drive away? No, because Keller's own car was parked here at the Sweet Dreams, and he'd only have to walk all the way back.

And the longer Slansky was around, the more chances he had to reach for a gun or crash the car.

"Hold it right there, Slansky," he said.

"You got the wrong guy," the man said, his voice a mix of relief and desperation. "Whoever Slansky is, I ain't him."

"No time to explain," Keller said, because there wasn't, and why bother? Simpler to use the picture-hook wire as he'd used it so often in the past, simpler and easier. And if Slansky went out thinking he was being killed by mistake, well, maybe that would be a comfort to him.

Or maybe not. Keller, his hands through the loops in the wire, yanking hard, couldn't see that it made much difference.

"Awww, hell," said the fat guy a row behind Keller, as the Oriole center fielder came down from his leap with nothing in his glove but his own hand. On the mound, the Baltimore pitcher shook his head the way pitchers do at such a moment, and Floyd Turnbull rounded first base and settled into his home-run trot.

"I thought we caught a break when the new kid got hurt," the fat guy said, "on account of he was hotter'n a pistol, not that he won't cool down some when the rest of the league figures out how to pitch to him. He'll be out what, a couple of weeks?"

"That's what I hear," Keller said. "He broke a toe."

"Got his foot stepped on? Is that how it happened?"

"That's what they're saying," Keller said. "He was in a crowded elevator, and nobody knows exactly what happened, whether somebody stepped on his foot or he'd injured it earlier and only noticed it when he put a foot wrong. They figure he'll be good as new inside of a month."

"Well, he's not hurting us now," the man said, "but Turnbull's picking up the slack. He really got ahold of that one."

"Number 398," Keller said.

"That a fact? Two shy of four hundred, and he's getting close to the mark for base hits, isn't he?"

"Four more and he'll have three thousand."

"Well, the best of luck to the guy," the man said, "but does he have to get 'em here?"

"I figure he'll hit the mark at home in Memphis."

"Fine with me. Which one? Hits? Homers?"

"Maybe both," Keller said.

"You didn't bring me one," the man said.

It was the same fellow he'd sat next to the first time he saw the Tarpons play, and that somehow convinced Keller he was going to see history made. At his first at-bat in the second inning, Floyd Turnbull had hit a grounder that had eyes, somehow picking out a path between the first and second basemen. It had taken a while, the Tarpons were four games into their home stand, playing the first of three with the Yankees, and Turnbull, who'd been a disappointment against Tampa Bay, was nevertheless closing in on the elusive numbers. He had 399 home runs, and that scratch single in the second inning was hit number 2999.

"I got the last hot dog," Keller said, "and I'd offer to share it with you, but I never share."

"I don't blame you," the fellow said. "It's a selfish world."

Turnbull walked in the bottom of the fourth and struck out on three pitches two innings later, but Keller didn't care. It was a perfect night to watch a ballgame, and he enjoyed the banter with his companion as much as the drama on the field. The game was a close one, seesawing back and forth, and the Tarpons were two runs down when Turnbull came up in the bottom of the ninth with runners on first and third.

On the first pitch, the man on first broke for second. The throw was high and he slid in under the tag.

"Shit," Keller's friend said. "Puts the tying run in scoring position, so you got to do it, but it takes the bat out of Turnbull's hands, because now they have to put him on, set up the double play."

And if the Yankees walked Turnbull, the Tarpon manager would lift him for a pinch runner.

"I was hoping we'd see history made," the man said, "but it looks like we'll have to wait a night or two. . . Well, what do you know? Torre's letting Rivera pitch to him."

But the Yankee closer only had to throw one pitch. The instant Turnbull swung, you knew the ball was gone. So did Bernie Williams, who just turned and watched the ball sail past him into the upper deck, and Turnbull, who watched from the batter's box, then jumped into the air, pumping both fists in triumph, before setting out on his circuit of the bases. The whole stadium knew, and the stands erupted with cheers.

Four hundred homers, three thousand hits—and the game was over, and the Tarps had won.

"Storybook finish," Keller's friend said, and Keller couldn't have put it better.

"Try that tea," Dot said. "See if it's all right."

Keller took a sip of iced tea and sat back in the slat-backed rocking chair. "It's fine," he said.

"I was beginning to wonder," she said, "if I was ever going to see you again. The last time I heard from you there was another hitter on the case, or at least that's what you thought. I started thinking maybe you were the one he was after, and maybe he took you out."

"It was the other way around," Keller said.

"Oh?"

"I didn't want him getting in the way," he explained, "and I figured the woman who hired him was a loose cannon. So she slipped and fell and broke her neck in a strip mall parking lot in Cleveland, and the guy she hired—"

"Got his head caught in a vise?"

"That was before I met him. He got all tangled up in some picture wire in Baltimore."

"And Floyd Turnbull died of natural causes," Dot said. "Had the biggest night of his life, and it turned out to be the last night of his life."

"Ironic," Keller said.

"That's the word Peter Jennings used. Celebrated, drank too much, went to bed, and choked to death on his own vomit. They had a medical expert on who explained how that happens more often than you'd think. You pass out, and you get nauseated and vomit without recovering consciousness, and if you're sleeping on your back, you aspirate the stuff and choke on it."

"And never know what hit you."

"Of course not," Dot said, "or you'd do something about it. But I never believe in natural causes, Keller, when you're in the picture. Except to the extent that you're a natural cause of death all by yourself."

"Well," he said.

"How'd you do it?"

"I just helped nature a little," he said. "I didn't have to get him drunk, he did that by himself. I followed him home, and he was all over the road. I was afraid he was going to have an accident."

"So?"

"Well, suppose he just gets banged around a little? And winds up in the hospital? Anyway, he made it home all right. I gave him time to go to sleep, and he didn't make it all the way to bed, just passed out on the couch." He shrugged. "I held a rag over his mouth, and I induced vomiting, and—"

"How? You made him drink warm soapy water?"

"Put a knee in his stomach. It worked, and the vomit didn't have anywhere to go, because his mouth was covered. Are you sure you want to hear all this?"

"Not as sure as I was a minute ago, but don't worry about it. He breathed it in and choked on it, end of story. And then?"

"And then I got out of there. What do you mean, 'and then'?"

"That was a few days ago."

"Oh," he said. "Well, I went to see a few stamp dealers. Memphis is a good city for stamps. And I wanted to see the rest of the series with the Yankees. The Tarpons all wore black armbands for Turnbull, but it didn't do them any good. The Yankees won the last two games."

"Hurray for our side," she said. "You want to tell me about it, Keller?"

"Tell you about it? I just told you about it."

"You were gone a month," she said, "doing what you could have done in two days, and I thought you might want to explain it to me."

"The other hitter," he began, but she was shaking her head.

"Don't give me 'the other hitter.' You could have closed the sale before the other hitter ever turned up."

"You're right," he admitted. "Dot, it was the numbers."

"The numbers?"

"Four hundred home runs," he said. "Three thousand hits. I wanted him to do it."

"Cooperstown," she said.

"I don't even know if the numbers'll get him into the Hall of Fame," he said, "and I don't really care about that part of it. I wanted him to get in the record books, four hundred homers and three thousand hits, and I wanted to be able to say I'd been there to see him do it."

"And to put him away."

"Well," he said, "I don't have to think about that part of it."

She didn't say anything for a while. Then she asked him if he wanted more iced tea, and he said he was fine, and she asked him if he'd bought some nice stamps for his collection.

"I got quite a few from Turkey," he said. "That was a weak spot in my collection, and now it's a good deal stronger."

"I guess that's important."

"I don't know," he said. "It gets harder and harder to say what's important and what isn't. Dot, I spent a month watching baseball. There are worse ways to spend your time."

"I'm sure there are, Keller," she said. "And sooner or later I'm sure you'll find them."

Matthew Scudder

Out the Window

There was nothing special about her last day. She seemed a little jittery, preoccupied with something or with nothing at all. But this was nothing new for Paula.

She was never much of a waitress in the three months she spent at Armstrong's. She'd forget some orders and mix up others, and when you wanted the check or another round of drinks you could go crazy trying to attract her attention. There were days when she walked through her shift like a ghost through walls, and it was as though she had perfected some arcane technique of astral projection, sending her mind out for a walk while her long lean body went on serving food and drinks and wiping down empty tables.

She did make an effort, though. She damn well tried. She could always manage a smile. Sometimes it was the brave smile of the walking wounded and other times it was a tight-jawed, brittle grin with a couple tabs of amphetamine behind it, but you take what you can to get through the days and any smile is better than none at all. She knew most of Armstrong's regulars by name and her greeting always made you feel as though you'd come home. When that's all the home you have, you tend to appreciate that sort of thing.

And if the career wasn't perfect for her, well, it certainly hadn't been what she'd had in mind when she came to New York in the first place. You no more set out to be a waitress in a Ninth Avenue gin mill than you intentionally become an ex-cop coasting through the months on bourbon and coffee. We have that sort of greatness thrust upon us. When you're as young as Paula Wittlauer you hang in there, knowing things are going to get better. When you're my age you just hope they don't get too much worse.

She worked the early shift, noon to eight, Tuesday through Saturday. Trina came on at six so there were two girls on the floor during the dinner rush. At eight Paula would go wherever she went and Trina would keep on bringing cups of coffee and glasses of bourbon for another six hours or so.

Paula's last day was a Thursday in late September. The heat of the summer was starting to break up. There was a cooling rain that morning and the sun never did show its face. I wandered in around four in the afternoon with a copy of the *Post* and read through it while I had my first drink of the day. At eight o'clock I was talking with a couple of nurses from Roosevelt Hospital who wanted to grouse about a resident surgeon with a Messiah complex. I was making sympathetic noises when Paula swept past our table and told me to have a good evening.

I said, "You too, kid." Did I look up? Did we smile at each other? Hell, I don't remember.

"See you tomorrow, Matt."

"Right," I said. "God willing."

But He evidently wasn't. Around three Justin closed up and I went around the block to my hotel. It didn't take long for the coffee and bourbon to cancel each other out. I got into bed and slept.

My hotel is on Fifty-seventh Street between Eighth and Ninth. It's on the uptown side of the block and my window is on the street side looking south. I can see the World Trade Center at the tip of Manhattan from my window.

I can also see Paula's building. It's on the other side of Fifty-seventh Street a hundred yards or so to the east, a towering high-rise that, had it been directly across from me, would have blocked my view of the trade center.

She lived on the seventeenth floor. Sometime after four she went out a high window. She swung out past the sidewalk and landed in the street a few feet from the curb, touching down between a couple of parked cars.

In high school physics they teach you that falling bodies accelerate at a speed of thirty-two feet per second. So she would have fallen thirty-two feet in the first second, another sixty-four feet the next second, then ninety-six feet in the third. Since she fell something like two hundred feet, I don't suppose she could have spent more than four seconds in the actual act of falling.

It must have seemed a lot longer than that.

I got up around ten, ten-thirty. When I stopped at the desk for my mail Vinnie told me they'd had a jumper across the street during the night. "A dame," he said, which is a word you don't hear much anymore. "She went out without a stitch on. You could catch your death that way."

I looked at him.

"Landed in the street, just missed somebody's Caddy. How'd you like to find something like that for a hood ornament? I wonder if your insurance would cover that. What do you call it, act of God?" He came out from behind the desk and walked with me to the door. "Over there," he said, pointing. "The florist's van there is covering the spot where she flopped. Nothing to see anyway. They scooped her up with a spatula and a sponge and then they hosed it all down. By the time I came on duty there wasn't a trace left."

"Who was she?"

"Who knows?"

I had things to do that morning, and as I did them I thought from time to time of the jumper. They're not that rare and they usually do the deed in the hours before dawn. They say it's always darkest then.

Sometime in the early afternoon I was passing Armstrong's and stopped in for a short one. I stood at the bar and looked around to say hello to Paula but she wasn't there. A doughy redhead named Rita was taking her shift.

Dean was behind the bar. I asked him where Paula was. "She skipping school today?"

"You didn't hear?"

"Jimmy fired her?"

He shook his head, and before I could venture any further guesses he told me.

I drank my drink. I had an appointment to see somebody about something, but suddenly it ceased to seem important. I put a dime in the phone and canceled my appointment and came back and had another drink. My hand was trembling slightly when I picked up the glass. It was a little steadier when I set it down.

I crossed Ninth Avenue and sat in St. Paul's for a while. Ten, twenty minutes. Something like that. I lit a candle for Paula and a few other candles for a few other corpses, and I sat there and thought about life and death and high windows. Around the time I left the police force I discovered that churches were very good places for thinking about that sort of thing.

After a while I walked over to her building and stood on the pavement in front of it. The florist's truck had moved on and I examined the street where she'd landed. There was, as Vinnie had assured me, no trace of what had happened. I tilted my head back and looked up, wondering what window she might have fallen from, and then I looked down at the pavement and then up again, and a sudden rush of vertigo made my head spin. In the course of all this I managed to attract the attention of the building's doorman and he came out to the curb anxious to talk about the former tenant. He was a black man about my age and he looked as proud of his uniform as the guy in the Marine Corps recruiting poster. It was a good-looking uniform, shades of brown, epaulets, gleaming brass buttons.

"Terrible thing," he said. "A young girl like that with her whole life ahead of her."

"Did you know her well?"

He shook his head. "She would give me a smile, always say hello, always call me by name. Always in a hurry, rushing in, rushing out again. You wouldn't think she had a care in the world. But you never know."

"You never do."

"She lived on the seventeenth floor. I wouldn't live that high above the ground if you gave me the place rent-free."

"Heights bother you?"

I don't know if he heard the question. "I live up one flight of stairs. That's just fine for me. No elevator and no, no high window." His brow clouded and he looked on the verge of saying something else, but then someone started to enter his building's lobby and he moved to intercept him. I looked up again, trying to count windows to the seventeenth floor, but the vertigo returned and I gave it up.

"Are you Matthew Scudder?"

I looked up. The girl who'd asked the question was very young, with long straight brown hair and enormous light brown eyes. Her face was open and defenseless and her lower lip was quivering. I said I was Matthew Scudder and pointed at the chair opposite mine. She remained on her feet.

"I'm Ruth Wittlauer," she said.

The name didn't register until she said, "Paula's sister." Then I nodded and studied her face for signs of a family resemblance. If they were there I couldn't find them. It was ten in the evening and Paula Wittlauer had been dead for eighteen hours and her sister was standing expectantly before me, her face a curious blend of determination and uncertainty.

I said, "I'm sorry. Won't you sit down? And will you have something to drink?"

"I don't drink."

"Coffee?"

"I've been drinking coffee all day. I'm shaky from all the damn coffee. Do I *have* to order something?"

She was on the edge, all right. I said, "No, of course not. You don't have to order anything." And I caught Trina's eye and warned her off and she nodded shortly and let us alone. I sipped my own coffee and watched Ruth Wittlauer over the brim of the cup.

"You knew my sister, Mr. Scudder."

"In a superficial way, as a customer knows a waitress."

"The police say she killed herself."

"And you don't think so?"

"I know she didn't."

I watched her eyes while she spoke and I was willing to believe she meant what she said. She didn't believe that Paula went out the window of her own accord, not for a moment. Of course, that didn't mean she was right.

"What do you think happened?"

"She was murdered." She made the statement quite matter-of-factly. "I know she was murdered. I think I know who did it."

"Who?"

"Cary McCloud."

"I don't know him."

"But it may have been somebody else," she went on. She lit a cigarette, smoked for a few moments in silence. "I'm pretty sure it was Cary," she said.

"Why?"

"They were living together." She frowned, as if in recognition of the fact that cohabitation was small evidence of murder. "He could do it," she said carefully. "That's why I think he did. I don't think just anyone could commit murder. In the heat of the moment, sure, I guess people fly off the handle, but to do it deliberately and throw someone out of a, out of a, to just deliberately throw someone out of a—"

I put my hand on top of hers. She had long small-boned hands and her skin was cool and dry to the touch. I thought she was going to cry or break or something but she didn't. It was just not going to be possible for her to say the word *window* and she would stall every time she came to it.

"What do the police say?"

"Suicide. They say she killed herself." She drew on the cigarette. "But they don't know her, they never knew her. If Paula wanted to kill herself she would have taken pills. She liked pills."

"I figured she took ups."

"Ups, tranquilizers, ludes, barbiturates. And she liked grass and she liked to drink." She lowered her eyes. My hand was still on top of hers and she looked at our two hands and I removed mine. "I don't do any of those things. I drink coffee, that's my one vice, and I don't even do that much because it makes me jittery. It's the coffee that's making me nervous tonight. Not . . . all of this."

"Okay."

"She was twenty-four. I'm twenty. Baby sister, square baby sister, except that was always how she *wanted* me to be. She did all these things and at the same time she told me not to do them, that it was a bad scene. I think she kept me straight. I really do. Not so much because of what she was saying as that I looked at the way she was living and what it was doing to her and I didn't want that for myself. I thought it was crazy, what she was doing to herself, but at the same time I guess I worshiped her, she was always my heroine. I loved her, God, I really did, I'm just starting to realize how much, and she's dead and he killed her, I *know* he killed her, I just know it."

After a while I asked her what she wanted me to do.

"You're a detective."

"Not in an official sense. I used to be a cop."

"Could you . . . find out what happened?"

"I don't know."

"I tried talking to the police. It was like talking to the wall. I can't just turn around and do nothing. Do you understand me?"

"I think so. Suppose I look into it and it still looks like suicide?"

"She didn't kill herself."

"Well, suppose I wind up thinking that she did."

She thought it over. "I still wouldn't have to believe it."

"No," I agreed. "We get to choose what we believe."

"I have some money." She put her purse on the table. "I'm the straight sister, I have an office job, I save money. I have five hundred dollars with me."

"That's too much to carry in this neighborhood."

"Is it enough to hire you?"

I didn't want to take her money. She had five hundred dollars and a dead sister, and parting with one wouldn't bring the other back to life. I'd have worked for nothing but that wouldn't have been good because neither of us would have taken it seriously enough.

And I have rent to pay and two sons to support, and Armstrong's charges for the coffee and the bourbon. I took four fifty-dollar bills from her and told her I'd do my best to earn them.

After Paula Wittlauer hit the pavement, a black-and-white from the Eighteenth Precinct caught the squeal and took charge of the case. One of the cops in the car was a guy named Guzik. I hadn't known him when I was on the force but we'd met since then. I didn't like him and I don't think he cared for me either, but he was reasonably honest and had struck me as competent. I got him on the phone the next morning and offered to buy him a lunch.

We met at an Italian place on Fifty-sixth Street. He had veal and peppers and a couple glasses of red wine. I wasn't hungry but I made myself eat a small steak.

Between bites of veal he said, "The kid sister, huh? I talked to her, you know. She's so clean and so pretty it could break your heart if you let it. And of course she don't want to believe sis did the Dutch act. I asked is she Catholic because then there's the religious angle but that wasn't it. Anyway your average priest'll stretch a point. They're the best lawyers going, the hell, two thousand years of practice, they oughta be good. I took that attitude myself. I said, 'Look, there's all these pills. Let's say your sister had herself some pills and drank a little wine and smoked a little pot and then she went to the window for some fresh air. So she got a little dizzy and maybe she blacked out and most likely she never knew what was happening.' Because there's no question of insurance, Matt, so if she wants to think it's an accident I'm not gonna shout suicide in her ear. But that's what it says in the file."

"You close it out?"

"Sure. No question."

"She thinks murder."

He nodded. "Tell me something I don't know. She says this McCloud killed sis. McCloud's the boyfriend. Thing is he was at an after-hours club at Fifty-third and Twelfth about the time sis was going skydiving."

"You confirm that?"

He shrugged. "It ain't airtight. He was in and out of the place, he coulda doubled back and all, but there was the whole business with the door."

"What business?"

"She didn't tell you? Paula Wittlauer's apartment was locked and the chain bolt was on. The super unlocked the door for us but we had to send him back to the basement for a bolt cutter so's we could get through the chain bolt. You can only fasten the chain bolt from inside and you can only open the door a few inches with it on, so either Wittlauer launched her own self out the window or she was shoved out by Plastic Man, and then he went and slithered out the door without unhooking the chain bolt."

"Or the killer never left the apartment."

"Huh?"

"Did you search the apartment after the super came back and cut the chain for you?"

"We looked around, of course. There was an open window, there was a pile of clothes next to it. You know she went out naked, don't you?"

"Uh-huh."

"There was no burly killer crouching in the shrubbery, if that's what you're getting at."

"You checked the place carefully?"

"We did our job."

"Uh-huh. Look under the bed?"

"It was a platform bed. No crawl space under it."

"Closets?"

He drank some wine, put the glass down hard, glared at me. "What the hell are you getting at? You got reason to believe there was somebody in the apartment when we went in there?"

"Just exploring the possibilities."

"Jesus. You honestly think somebody's gonna be stupid enough to stay in the apartment after shoving her out of it? She musta been on the street ten minutes before we hit the building. If somebody did kill her, which never happened, but if they did they coulda been halfway to Texas by the time we hit the door, and don't that make more sense than jumping in the closet and hiding behind the coats?"

"Unless the killer didn't want to pass the doorman."

"So he's still got the whole building to hide in. Just the one man on the front door is the only security the building's got, anyway, and what does he amount to? And suppose he hides in the apartment and we happen to spot him. Then where is he? With his neck in the noose, that's where he is."

"Except you didn't spot him."

"Because he wasn't there, and when I start seeing little men who aren't there is when I put in my papers and quit the department."

There was an unvoiced challenge in his words. I had quit the department, but not because I'd seen little men. One night some years ago I broke up a bar holdup and went into the street after the pair who'd killed the bartender. One of my shots went wide and a little girl died, and after that I didn't see little men or hear voices, not exactly, but I did leave my wife and kids and quit the force and start drinking on a more serious level. But maybe it all would have happened just that way even if I'd never killed Estrellita Rivera. People go through changes and life does the damnedest things to us all.

"It was just a thought," I said. "The sister thinks it's murder so I was looking for a way for her to be right."

"Forget it."

"I suppose. I wonder why she did it."

"Do they even need a reason? I went in the bathroom and she had a medicine cabinet like a drugstore. Ups, downs, sideways. Maybe she was so stoned she thought she could fly. That would explain her being naked. You don't fly with your clothes on. Everybody knows that."

I nodded. "They find drugs in her system?"

"Drugs in her . . . oh, Jesus, Matt. She came down seventeen flights and she came down fast."

"Under four seconds."

"Huh?"

"Nothing," I said. I didn't bother telling him about high school physics and falling bodies. "No autopsy?"

"Of course not. You've seen jumpers. You were in the department a lot of years, you know what a person looks like after a drop like that. You want to be technical, there coulda been a bullet in her and nobody was gonna go and look for it. Cause of death was falling from a great height. That's what it says and that's what it was, and don't ask me was she stoned or was she pregnant or any of those questions because who the hell knows and who the hell cares, right?"

"How'd you even know it was her?"

"We got a positive ID from the sister."

I shook my head. "I mean how did you know what apartment to go to? She was naked so she didn't have any identification on her. Did the doorman recognize her?"

"You kidding? He wouldn't go close enough to look. He was alongside the building throwing up a few pints of cheap wine. He couldn't have identified his own ass."

"Then how'd you know who she was?"

"The window." I looked at him. "Hers was the only window that was open more than a couple of inches, Matt. Plus her lights were on. That made it easy."

"I didn't think of that."

"Yeah, well, I was there, and we just looked up and there was an open window and a light behind it, and that was the first place we went to. You'da thought of it if you were there."

"I suppose."

He finished his wine, burped delicately against the back of his hand. "It's suicide," he said. "You can tell the sister as much."

"I will. Okay if I look at the apartment?"

"Wittlauer's apartment? We didn't seal it, if that's what you mean. You oughta be able to con the super out of a key."

"Ruth Wittlauer gave me a key."

"Then there you go. There's no department seal on the door. You want to look around?"

"So I can tell the sister I was there."

"Yeah. Maybe you'll come across a suicide note. That's what I was looking for, a note. You turn up something like that and it clears up doubts for the friends and relatives. If it was up to me I'd get a law passed. No suicide without a note."

"Be hard to enforce."

"Simple," he said. "If you don't leave a note you gotta come back and be alive again." He laughed. "That'd start 'em scribbling away. Count on it."

The doorman was the same man I'd talked to the day before. It never occurred to him to ask me my business. I rode up in the elevator and walked along the corridor to 17G. The key Ruth Wittlauer had given me opened the door. There was just the one lock. That's the way it usually is in high-rises. A doorman, however slipshod he may be, endows tenants with a sense of security. The residents of unserviced walk-ups affix three or four extra locks to their doors and still cower behind them.

The apartment had an unfinished air about it, and I sensed that Paula had lived there for a few months without ever making the place her own. There were no rugs on the wood parquet floor. The walls were decorated with a few unframed posters held up by scraps of red Mystik tape. The apartment was an L-shaped studio with a platform bed occupying the foot of the L. There were newspapers and magazines scattered around the place but no books. I noticed copies of *Variety* and *Rolling Stone* and *People* and *The Village Voice*.

The television set was a tiny Sony perched on top of a chest of drawers. There was no stereo, but there were a few dozen records, mostly classical with a sprinkling of folk music, Pete Seeger and Joan Baez and Dave Van Ronk. There was a dust-free rectangle on top of the dresser next to the Sony.

I looked through the drawers and closets. A lot of Paula's clothes. I recognized some of the outfits, or thought I did.

Someone had closed the window. There were two windows that opened, one in the sleeping alcove, the other in the living room section, but a row of undisturbed potted plants in front of the bedroom window made it evident she'd gone out of the other one. I wondered why anyone had bothered to close it. In case of rain, I supposed. That was only sensible. But I suspect the gesture must have been less calculated than that, a reflexive act akin to tugging a sheet over the face of a corpse.

I went into the bathroom. A killer could have hidden in the stall shower. If there'd been a killer.

Why was I still thinking in terms of a killer?

I checked the medicine cabinet. There were little tubes and vials of cosmetics, though only a handful compared with the array on one of the bedside tables. Here were containers of aspirin and other headache remedies, a tube of antibiotic ointment, several prescriptions and nonprescription hay fever preparations, a cardboard packet of Band-Aids, a roll of adhesive tape, a box of gauze pads. Some Q-tips, a hairbrush, a couple of combs. A toothbrush in the holder.

There were no footprints on the floor of the stall shower. Of course he could have been barefoot. Or he could have run water and washed away the traces of his presence before he left.

I went over and examined the windowsill. I hadn't asked Guzik if they'd dusted for prints and I was reasonably certain no one had bothered. I wouldn't have taken the trouble in their position. I couldn't learn anything looking at the sill. I opened the window a foot or so and stuck my head out, but when I looked down the vertigo was extremely unpleasant and I drew my head back inside at once. I left the window open, though. The room could stand a change of air.

There were four folding chairs in the room, two of them closed and leaning against a wall, one near the bed, the fourth alongside the window. They were royal blue and made of high-impact plastic. The one by the window had her clothes piled on it. I went through the stack. She'd placed them deliberately on the chair but hadn't bothered folding them.

You never know what suicides will do. One man will put on a tuxedo before blowing his brains out. Another one will take off everything. Naked I came into the world and naked will I go out of it, something like that.

A skirt. Beneath it a pair of panty hose. Then a blouse, and under it a bra with two small, lightly padded cups, I put the clothing back as I had found it, feeling like a violator of the dead.

The bed was unmade. I sat on the edge of it and looked across the room at a poster of Mick Jagger. I don't know how long I sat there. Ten minutes, maybe.

On the way out I looked at the chain bolt. I hadn't even noticed it when I came in. The chain had been neatly severed. Half of it was still in the slot on the door while the other half hung from its mounting on the jamb. I closed the door and fitted the two halves together, then released them and let them dangle. Then I touched their ends together again. I unhooked the end of the chain from the slot and went to the bathroom for the roll of adhesive tape. I brought the tape back with me, tore off a piece, and used it to fasten the chain back together again. Then I let myself out of the apartment and tried to engage the chain bolt from outside, but the tape slipped whenever I put any pressure on it.

I went inside again and studied the chain bolt. I decided I was behaving erratically, that Paula Wittlauer had gone out the window of her own accord. I looked at the windowsill again. The light dusting of soot didn't tell me anything one way or the other. New York's air is filthy and the accumulation of soot could have been deposited in a couple of hours, even with the window shut. It didn't mean anything.

I looked at the heap of clothes on the chair, and I looked again at the chain bolt, and I rode the elevator to the basement and found either the superintendent or one of his assistants. I asked to borrow a screwdriver. He gave me a long screwdriver with an amber plastic grip. He didn't ask me who I was or what I wanted it for.

I returned to Paula Wittlauer's apartment and removed the chain bolt from its moorings on the door and jamb. I left the building and walked around the corner to a hardware store on Ninth Avenue. They had a good selection of chain bolts but

I wanted one identical to the one I'd removed and I had to walk down Ninth Avenue as far as Fiftieth Street and check four stores before I found what I was looking for.

Back in Paula's apartment I mounted the new chain bolt, using the holes in which the original had been mounted. I tightened the screws with the super's screwdriver and stood out in the corridor and played with the chain. My hands are large and not terribly skillful, but even so I was able to lock and unlock the chain bolt from outside the apartment.

I don't know who put it up, Paula or a previous tenant or someone on the building staff, but that chain bolt had been as much protection as the Sanitized wrapper on a motel toilet seat. As evidence that Paula'd been alone when she went out the window, well, it wasn't worth a thing.

I replaced the original chain bolt, put the new one in my pocket, returned to the elevator, and gave back the screwdriver. The man I returned it to seemed surprised to get it back.

It took me a couple of hours to find Cary McCloud. I'd learned that he tended bar evenings at a club in the West Village called The Spider's Web. I got down there around five. The guy behind the bar had knobby wrists and an underslung jaw and he wasn't Cary McCloud. "He don't come on till eight," he told me, "and he's off tonight anyway." I asked where I could find McCloud. "Sometimes he's here afternoons but he ain't been in today. As far as where you could look for him, that I couldn't tell you."

A lot of people couldn't tell me but eventually I ran across someone who could. You can quit the police force but you can't stop looking and sounding like a cop, and while that's a hindrance in some situations it's a help in others. Ultimately I found a man in a bar down the block from The Spider's Web who'd learned it was best to cooperate with the police if it didn't cost you anything. He gave me an address on Barrow Street and told me which bell to ring.

I went to the building but I rang several other bells until somebody buzzed me through the downstairs door. I didn't want Cary to know he had company coming. I climbed two flights of stairs to the apartment he was supposed to be occupying. The bell downstairs hadn't had his name on it. It hadn't had any name at all.

Loud rock music was coming through his door. I stood in front of it for a minute, then hammered on it loud enough to make myself heard over the electric guitars. After a moment the music dropped in volume. I pounded on the door again and a male voice asked who I was.

I said, "Police. Open up." That's a misdemeanor but I didn't expect to get in trouble for it.

"What's it about?"

"Open up, McCloud."

"Oh, Jesus," he said. He sounded tired, aggravated. "How did you find me, anyway? Give me a minute, huh? I want to put some clothes on."

Sometimes that's what they say while they're putting a clip into an automatic. Then they pump a handful of shots through the door and into you if you're still standing behind it. But his voice didn't have that kind of edge to it and I couldn't summon up enough anxiety to get out of the way. Instead I put my ear against the door and heard whispering within. I couldn't make out what they were whispering about or get any sense of the person who was with him. The music was down in volume but there was still enough of it to cover their conversation.

The door opened. He was tall and thin, with hollow cheeks and prominent eyebrows and a worn, wasted look to him. He must have been in his early thirties and he didn't really look much older than that but you sensed that in another ten years he'd look twenty years older. If he lived that long. He wore patched jeans and a T-shirt with The Spider's Web silkscreened on it. Beneath the legend there was a sketch of a web. A macho spider stood at one end of it, grinning, extending two of his eight arms to welcome a hesitant girlish fly.

He noticed me noticing the shirt and managed a grin. "Place where I work," he said.

"I know."

"So come into my parlor. It ain't much but it's home."

I followed him inside, drew the door shut after me. The room was about fifteen feet square and held nothing you could call furniture. There was a mattress on the floor in one corner and a couple of cardboard cartons alongside it. The music was coming from a stereo, turntable and tuner and two speakers all in a row along the far wall. There was a closed door over on the right. I figured it led to the bathroom, and that there was a woman on the other side of it.

"I guess this is about Paula," he said. I nodded. "I been over this with you guys," he said. "I was nowhere near there when it happened. The last I saw her was five, six hours before she killed herself. I was working at the Web and she came down and sat at the bar. I gave her a couple of drinks and she split."

"And you went on working."

"Until I closed up. I kicked everybody out a little after three and it was close to four by the time I had the place swept up and the garbage on the street and the window gates locked. Then I came over here and picked up Sunny and we went up to the place on Fifty-third."

"And you got there when?"

"Hell, I don't know. I wear a watch but I don't look at it every damn minute. I suppose it took five minutes to walk here and then Sunny and I hopped right in a cab and we were at Patsy's in ten minutes at the outside, that's the after-hours place, I told you people all of this, I really wish you would talk to each other and leave me the hell alone."

"Why doesn't Sunny come out and tell me about it?" I nodded at the bathroom door. "Maybe she can remember the time a little more clearly."

"Sunny? She stepped out a little while ago."

"She's not in the bathroom?"

"Nope. Nobody's in the bathroom."

"Mind if I see for myself?"

"Not if you can show me a warrant."

We looked at each other. I told him I figured I could take his word for it. He said he could always be trusted to tell the truth. I said I sensed as much about him.

He said, "What's the hassle, huh? I know you guys got forms to fill out, but why not give me a break? She killed herself and I wasn't anywhere near her when it happened."

He could have been. The times were vague, and whoever Sunny turned out to be, the odds were good that she'd have no more time sense than a koala bear. There were any number of ways he could have found a few minutes to go up to Fifty-seventh Street and heave Paula out a window, but it didn't add up that way and he just didn't feel like a killer to me. I knew what Ruth meant and I agreed with her that he was capable of murder but I don't think he'd been capable of this particular murder.

I said, "When did you go back to the apartment?"

"Who said I did?"

"You picked up your clothes, Cary."

"That was yesterday afternoon. The hell, I needed my clothes and stuff."

"How long were you living there?"

He hedged. "I wasn't exactly living there."

"Where were you exactly living?"

"I wasn't exactly living anywhere. I kept most of my stuff at Paula's place and I stayed with her most of the time but it wasn't as serious as actual living together. We were both too loose for anything like that. Anyway, the thing with Paula, it was pretty much winding itself down. She was a little too crazy for me." He smiled with his mouth. "They have to be a little crazy," he said, "but when they're too crazy it gets to be too much of a hassle."

Oh, he could have killed her. He could kill anyone if he had to, if someone was making too much of a hassle. But if he were to kill cleverly, faking the suicide in such an artful fashion, fastening the chain bolt on his way out, he'd pick a time when he had a solid alibi. He was not the sort to be so precise and so slipshod all at the same time.

"So you went and picked up your stuff."

"Right."

"Including the stereo and records."

"The stereo was mine. The records, I left the folk music and the classical shit because that belonged to Paula. I just took my records."

"And the stereo."

"Right."

"You got a bill of sale for it, I suppose."

"Who keeps that crap?"

"What if I said Paula kept the bill of sale? What if I said it was in with her papers and canceled checks?"

"You're fishing."

"You sure of that?"

"Nope. But if you did say that, I suppose I'd say the stereo was a gift from her to me. You're not really gonna charge me with stealing a stereo, are you?"

"Why should I? Robbing the dead's a sacred tradition. You took the drugs, too, didn't you? Her medicine cabinet used to look like a drugstore but there was nothing stronger than Excedrin when I took a look. That's why Sunny's in the bathroom. If I hit the door all the pretty little pills go down the toilet."

"I guess you can think that if you want."

"And I can come back with a warrant if I want."

"That's the idea."

"I ought to rap on the door just to do you out of the drugs but it doesn't seem worth the trouble. That's Paula Wittlauer's stereo. I suppose it's worth a couple hundred dollars. And you're not her heir. Unplug that thing and wrap it up, McCloud. I'm taking it with me."

"The hell you are."

"The hell I'm not."

"You want to take anything but your own ass out of here, you come back with a warrant. Then we'll talk about it."

"I don't need a warrant."

"You can't—"

"I don't need a warrant because I'm not a cop. I'm a detective, McCloud, I'm private, and I'm working for Ruth Wittlauer, and that's who's getting the stereo. I don't know if she wants it or not, but that's her problem. She doesn't want Paula's pills so you can pop them yourself or give them to your girlfriend. You can shove 'em up your ass for all I care. But I'm walking out of here with that stereo and I'll walk through you if I have to, and don't think I wouldn't enjoy it."

"You're not even a cop."

"Right."

"You got no authority at all." He spoke in tones of wonder. "You said you were a cop."

"You can always sue me."

"You can't take that stereo. You can't even be in this room."

"That's right." I was itching for him. I could feel my blood in my veins. "I'm bigger than you," I said, "and I'm a whole lot harder, and I'd get a certain amount of satisfaction in beating the crap out of you. I don't like you. It bothers me that you didn't kill her because somebody did and it would be a pleasure to hang it on you. But you didn't do it. Unplug the stereo and pack it up so I can carry it or I'm going to take you apart."

I meant it and he realized as much. He thought about taking a shot at me and he decided it wasn't worth it. Maybe it wasn't all that much of a stereo. While he was unhooking it I dumped a carton of his clothes on the floor and we packed the stereo in it. On my way out the door he said he could always go to the cops and tell them what I'd done.

"I don't think you want to do that," I said.

"You said somebody killed her."

"That's right."

"You just making noise?"

"No."

"You're serious?" I nodded. "She didn't kill herself? I thought it was open and shut, from what the cops said. It's interesting. In a way, I guess you could say it's a load off my mind."

"How do you figure that?"

He shrugged. "I thought, you know, maybe she was upset it wasn't working out between us. At the Web the vibes were on the heavy side, if you follow me. Our thing was falling apart and I was seeing Sunny and she was seeing other guys and I thought maybe that was what did it for her. I suppose I blamed myself, like."

"I can see it was eating away at you."

"I just said it was on my mind."

I didn't say anything.

"Man," he said, "*nothing* eats away at me. You let things get to you that way and it's death."

I shouldered the carton and headed on down the stairs.

Ruth Wittlauer had supplied me with an Irving Place address and a GRamercy 5 telephone number. I called the number and didn't get an answer, so I walked over to Hudson and caught a northbound cab. There were no messages for me at the hotel desk. I put Paula's stereo in my room, tried Ruth's number again, then walked over to the Eighteenth Precinct. Guzik had gone off duty but the desk man told me to try a restaurant around the corner, and I found him there drinking draft Heinekens with another cop, named Birnbaum. I sat at their table and ordered bourbon for myself and another round for the two of them.

I said, "I have a favor to ask. I'd like you to seal Paula Wittlauer's apartment."

"We closed that out," Guzik reminded me.

"I know, and the boyfriend closed out the dead girl's stereo." I told him how I'd reclaimed the unit from Cary McCloud. "I'm working for Ruth, Paula's sister. The least I can do is make sure she gets what's coming to her. She's not up to cleaning out the apartment now and it's rented through the first of October. McCloud's got a key and God knows how many other people have keys. If you slap a seal on the door it'd keep the grave robbers away."

"I guess we can do that. Tomorrow all right?"

"Tonight would be better."

"What's there to steal? You got the stereo out of there and I didn't see anything else around that was worth much."

"Things have a sentimental value."

He eyed me, frowned. "I'll make a phone call," he said. He went to the booth in the back and I jawed with Birnbaum until he came back and told me it was all taken care of.

I said, "Another thing I was wondering. You must have had a photographer on the scene. Somebody to take pictures of the body and all that."

"Sure. That's routine."

"Did he go up to the apartment while he was at it? Take a roll of interior shots?"

"Yeah. Why?"

"I thought maybe I could have a look at them."

"What for?"

"You never know. The reason I knew it was Paula's stereo in McCloud's apartment was I could see the pattern in the dust on top of the dresser where it had been. If you've got interior pictures maybe I'll see something else that's not there anymore and I can lean on McCloud a little and recover it for my client."

"And that's why you'd like to see the pictures."

"Right."

He gave me a look. "That door was bolted from the inside, Matt. With a chain bolt."

"I know."

"And there was no one in the apartment when we went in there."

"I know that, too."

"You're still barking up the murder tree, aren't you? Jesus, the case is closed and the reason it's closed is the ditzy broad killed herself. What are you making waves for?"

"I'm not. I just wanted to see the pictures."

"To see if somebody stole her diaphragm or something."

"Something like that." I drank what remained of my drink. "You need a new hat anyway, Guzik. The weather's turning and a fellow like you needs a hat for fall."

"If I had the price of a hat, maybe I'd go out and get one."

"You got it," I said.

He nodded and we told Birnbaum we wouldn't be long. I walked with Guzik around the corner to the Eighteenth. On the way I palmed him two tens and a five, twenty-five dollars, the price of a hat in police parlance. He made the bills disappear.

I waited at his desk while he pulled the Paula Wittlauer file. There were about a dozen black-and-white prints, eight by tens, high-contrast glossies. Perhaps half of them showed Paula's corpse from various angles. I had no interest in these but I made myself look at them as a sort of reinforcement, so I wouldn't forget what I was doing on the case.

The other pictures were interior shots of the L-shaped apartment. I noted the wide-open window, the dresser with the stereo sitting on it, the chair with her clothing piled haphazardly upon it. I separated the interior pictures from the ones showing the corpse and told Guzik I wanted to keep them for the time being. He didn't mind.

He cocked his head and looked at me. "You got something, Matt?"

"Nothing worth talking about."

"If you ever do, I'll want to hear about it."

"Sure."

"You like the life you're leading? Working private, scuffling around?"

"It seems to suit me."

He thought it over, nodded. Then he started for the stairs and I followed after him.

Later that evening I managed to reach Ruth Wittlauer. I bundled the stereo into a cab and took it to her place. She lived in a well-kept brownstone a block and a half from Gramercy Park. Her apartment was inexpensively furnished but the pieces looked to have been chosen with care. The place was clean and neat. Her clock radio was tuned to an FM station that was playing chamber music. She had coffee made and I accepted a cup and sipped it while I told her about recovering the stereo from Cary McCloud.

"I wasn't sure whether you could use it," I said, "but I couldn't see any reason why he should keep it. You can always sell it."

"No, I'll keep it. I just have a twenty-dollar record player that I bought on Fourteenth Street. Paula's stereo cost a couple of hundred dollars." She managed a smile. "So you've already more than earned what I gave you. Did he kill her?"

"No."

"You're sure of that?"

I nodded. "He'd kill if he had a reason but I don't think he did. And if he did kill her he'd never have taken the stereo or the drugs, and he wouldn't have acted the way he did. There was never a moment when I had the feeling that he'd killed her. And you have to follow your instincts in this kind of situation. Once they point things out to you, then you can usually find the facts to go with them."

"And you're sure my sister killed herself?"

"No. I'm pretty sure someone gave her a hand."

Her eyes widened.

I said, "It's mostly intuition. But there are a few facts to support it." I told her about the chain bolt, how it had proved to the police that Paula'd killed herself, how my experiment had shown it could have been fastened from the corridor. Ruth got very excited at this but I explained that it didn't prove anything in and of itself, only that suicide remained a theoretical possibility.

Then I showed her the pictures I'd obtained from Guzik. I selected one shot which showed the chair with Paula's clothing without showing too much of the window. I didn't want to make Ruth look at the window.

"The chair," I said, pointing to it. "I noticed this when I was in your sister's apartment. I wanted to see a photograph taken at the time to make sure things hadn't been rearranged by the cops or McCloud or somebody else. But that clothing's exactly the way it was when I saw it."

"I don't understand."

"The supposition is that Paula got undressed, put her clothes on the chair, then went to the window and jumped." Her lip was trembling but she was holding herself together and I went right on talking. "Or she'd taken her clothes off earlier and maybe she took a shower or a nap and then came back and jumped. But look at the chair. She didn't fold her clothes neatly, she didn't put them away. And she didn't just drop them on the floor, either. I'm no authority on the way women get undressed but I don't think many people would do it that way."

Ruth nodded. Her face was thoughtful.

"That wouldn't mean very much by itself. If she were upset or stoned or confused she might have thrown things on the chair as she took them off. But that's not what happened. The order of the clothing is all wrong. The bra's underneath the blouse, the panty hose is underneath the skirt. She took her bra off after she took her blouse off, obviously, so it should have wound up on top of the blouse, not under it."

"Of course."

I held up a hand. "It's nothing like proof, Ruth. There are any number of other explanations. Maybe she knocked the stuff onto the floor and then picked it up and the order of the garments got switched around. Maybe one of the cops went through the clothing before the photographer came around with his camera. I don't really have anything terribly strong to go on."

"But you think she was murdered."

"Yes, I guess I do."

"That's what I thought all along. Of course I had a reason to think so."

"Maybe I've got one, too. I don't know."

"What are you going to do now?"

"I think I'll poke around a little. I don't know much about Paula's life. I'll have to learn more if I'm going to find out who killed her. But it's up to you to decide whether you want me to stay with it."

"Of course I do. Why wouldn't I?"

"Because it probably won't lead anywhere. Suppose she was upset after her conversation with McCloud and she picked up a stranger and took him home with her and he killed her. If that's the case we'll never know who he was."

"You're going to stay with it, aren't you?"

"I suppose I want to."

"It'll be complicated, though. It'll take you some time. I suppose you'll want more money." Her gaze was very direct. "I gave you two hundred dollars. I have three hundred more that I can afford to pay. I don't mind paying it, Mr. Scudder. I already got . . . I got my money's worth for the first two hundred, didn't I? The stereo. When the three hundred runs out, well, you can tell me if you think it's worth staying with the case. I couldn't afford more cash right away, but I could arrange to pay you later on or something like that."

I shook my head. "It won't come to more than that," I said. "No matter how much time I spend on it. And you keep the three hundred for the time being, all right? I'll take it from you later on. If I need it, and if I've earned it."

"That doesn't seem right."

"It seems right to me," I said. "And don't make the mistake of thinking I'm being charitable."

"But your time's valuable."

I shook my head. "Not to me it isn't."

I spent the next five days picking the scabs off Paula Wittlauer's life. It kept turning out to be a waste of time but the time's always gone before you realize you've wasted it. And I'd been telling the truth when I said my time wasn't valuable. I had nothing better to do, and my peeks into the corners of Paula's world kept me busy.

Her life involved more than a saloon on Ninth Avenue and an apartment on Fifty-seventh Street, more than serving drinks and sharing a bed with Cary McCloud. She did other things. She went one evening a week to group therapy on West Seventy-ninth Street. She took voice lessons every Tuesday morning on Amsterdam Avenue. She had an ex-boyfriend she saw once in a while. She hung out in a couple of bars in the neighborhood and a couple of others in the Village. She did this, she did that, she went here, she went there, and I kept busy dragging myself around town and talking to all sorts of people, and I managed to learn quite a bit about the person she'd been and the life she'd led without learning anything at all about the person who'd put her on the pavement.

At the same time, I tried to track her movements on the final night of her life. She'd evidently gone more or less directly to The Spider's Web after finishing her shift at Armstrong's. Maybe she'd stopped at her apartment for a shower and a change of clothes, but without further ado she'd headed downtown. Somewhere around ten she left the Web, and I traced her from there to a couple of other Village bars. She hadn't stayed at either of them long, taking a quick drink or two and moving on. She'd left alone as far as anyone seemed to remember. This didn't prove a thing because she could have stopped elsewhere before continuing uptown, or she could have picked someone up on the street, which I'd learned was something she'd done more than once in her young life. She could have found her killer loitering on a street corner or she could have phoned him and arranged to meet him at her apartment.

Her apartment. The doormen changed off at midnight, but it was impossible to determine whether she'd returned before or after the changing of the guard. She'd lived there, she was a regular tenant, and when she entered or left the building it was not a noteworthy occasion. It was something she did every night, so when she came home for the final time the man at the door had no reason to know it was the final time and thus no reason to take mental notes.

Had she come in alone or with a companion? No one could say, which did suggest that she'd come in alone. If she'd been with someone her entrance would have been a shade more memorable. But this also proved nothing, because I stood on the other side of Fifty-seventh Street one night and watched the doorway of her building, and the doorman didn't take the pride in his position that the afternoon doorman had shown. He was away from the door almost as often as he was on it.

She could have walked in flanked by six Turkish sailors and there was a chance no one would have seen her.

The doorman who'd been on duty when she went out the window was a rheumy-eyed Irishman with liver-spotted hands. He hadn't actually seen her land. He'd been in the lobby, keeping himself out of the wind, and then he came rushing out when he heard the impact of the body on the street.

He couldn't get over the sound she made.

"All of a sudden there was this noise," he said. "Just out of the blue there was this noise and it must be it's my imagination but I swear I felt it in my feet. I swear she shook the earth. I had no idea what it was, and then I came rushing out, and Jesus God, there she was."

"Didn't you hear a scream?"

"Street was empty just then. This side, anyway. Nobody around to scream."

"Didn't *she* scream on the way down?"

"Did somebody say she screamed? I never heard it."

Do people scream as they fall? They generally do in films and on television. During my days on the force I saw several of them after they jumped, and by the time I got to them there were no screams echoing in the air. And a few times I'd been on hand while they talked someone in off a ledge, but in each instance the talking was successful and I didn't have to watch a falling body accelerate according to the immutable laws of physics.

Could you get much of a scream out in four seconds?

I stood in the street where she'd fallen and I looked up toward her window. I counted off four seconds in my mind. A voice shrieked in my brain. It was Thursday night, actually Friday morning, one o'clock. Time I got myself around the corner to Armstrong's, because in another couple of hours Justin would be closing for the night and I'd want to be drunk enough to sleep.

And an hour or so after that she'd be one week dead.

I'd worked myself into a reasonably bleak mood by the time I got to Armstrong's. I skipped the coffee and crawled straight into the bourbon bottle, and before long it began to do what it was supposed to do. It blurred the corners of the mind so I couldn't see the bad dark things that lurked there.

When Trina finished for the night she joined me and I bought her a couple of drinks. I don't remember what we talked about. Some but by no means all of our conversation touched upon Paula Wittlauer. Trina hadn't known Paula terribly well—their contact had been largely limited to the two hours a day when their shift overlapped—but she knew a little about the sort of life Paula had been leading. There'd been a year or two when her own life had not been terribly different from Paula's. Now she had things more or less under control, and maybe there would have come a time when Paula would have taken charge of her life, but that was something we'd never know now.

I suppose it was close to three when I walked Trina home. Our conversation had turned thoughtful and reflective. On the street she said it was a lousy night for being alone. I thought of high windows and evil shapes in dark corners and took her hand in mine.

She lives on Fifty-sixth between Ninth and Tenth. While we waited for the light to change at Fifty-seventh Street I looked over at Paula's building. We were far enough away to look at the high floors. Only a couple of windows were lighted.

That was when I got it.

I've never understood how people think of things, how little perceptions trigger greater insights. Thoughts just seem to come to me. I had it now, and something clicked within me and a source of tension unwound itself.

I said something to that effect to Trina.

"You know who killed her?"

"Not exactly," I said. "But I know how to find out. And it can wait until tomorrow."

The light changed and we crossed the street.

She was still sleeping when I left. I got out of bed and dressed in silence, then let myself out of her apartment. I had some coffee and a toasted English muffin at the Red Flame. Then I went across the street to Paula's building. I started on the tenth floor and worked my way up, checking the three or four possible apartments on each floor. A lot of people weren't home. I worked my way clear to the top floor, the twenty-fourth, and by the time I was done I had three possibles listed in my notebook and a list of over a dozen apartments I'd have to check that evening.

At eight-thirty that night I rang the bell of Apartment 21G. It was directly in line with Paula's apartment and four flights above it. The man who answered the bell wore a pair of Lee corduroy slacks and a shirt with a blue vertical stripe on a white background. His socks were dark blue and he wasn't wearing shoes.

I said, "I want to talk with you about Paula Wittlauer."

His face fell apart and I forgot my three possibles forever because he was the man I wanted. He just stood there. I pushed the door open and stepped forward and he moved back automatically to make room for me. I drew the door shut after me and walked around him, crossing the room to the window. There wasn't a speck of dust or soot on the sill. It was immaculate, as well-scrubbed as Lady Macbeth's hands.

I turned to him. His name was Lane Posmantur and I suppose he was around forty, thickening at the waist, his dark hair starting to go thin on top. His glasses were thick and it was hard to read his eyes through them but it didn't matter. I didn't need to see his eyes.

"She went out this window," I said. "Didn't she?"

"I don't know what you're talking about."

"Do you want to know what triggered it for me, Mr. Posmantur? I was thinking of all the things nobody noticed. No one saw her enter the building. Neither doorman remembered it because it wasn't something they'd be likely to remember. Nobody saw her go out the window. The cops had to look for an open window in order to know who the hell she was. They backtracked her from the window she fell out of.

"And nobody saw the killer leave the building. Now that's the one thing that would have been noticed, and that's the point that occurred to me. It wasn't that significant by itself but it made me dig a little deeper. The doorman was alert once her body hit the street. He'd remember who went in or out of the building from that point on. So it occurred to me that maybe the killer was still inside the building, and then I got the idea that she was killed by someone who *lived* in the building, and from that point on it was just a question of finding you because all of a sudden it all made sense."

I told him about the clothes on the chair. "She didn't take them off and pile them up like that. Her killer put her clothes like that, and he dumped them on the chair so that it would look as though she undressed in her apartment, and so that it would be assumed she'd gone out of her own window.

"But she went out of your window, didn't she?"

He looked at me. After a moment he said he thought he'd better sit down. He went to an armchair and sat in it. I stayed on my feet.

I said, "She came here. I guess she took off her clothes and you went to bed with her. Is that right?"

He hesitated, then nodded.

"What made you decide to kill her?"

"I didn't."

I looked at him. He looked away, then met my gaze, then avoided my eyes again. "Tell me about it," I suggested. He looked away again and a minute went by and then he started to talk.

It was about what I'd figured. She was living with Cary McCloud but she and Lane Posmantur would get together now and then for a quickie. He was a lab technician at Roosevelt and he brought home drugs from time to time and perhaps that was part of his attraction for her. She'd turned up that night a little after two and they went to bed. She was really flying, he said, and he'd been taking pills himself, it was something he'd begun doing lately, maybe seeing her had something to do with it.

They went to bed and did the dirty deed, and then maybe they slept for an hour, something like that, and then she was awake and coming unglued, getting really hysterical, and he tried to settle her down and he gave her a couple of slaps to bring her around, except they didn't bring her around, and she was staggering and she tripped over the coffee table and fell funny, and by the time he sorted himself out and went to her she was lying with her head at a crazy angle and he knew her neck was broken and when he tried for a pulse there was no pulse to be found.

"All I could think of was she was dead in my apartment and full of drugs and I was in trouble."

"So you put her out the window."

"I was going to take her back to her own apartment. I started to dress her but it was impossible. And even with her clothes on I couldn't risk running into somebody in the hallway or on the elevator. It was crazy.

"I left her here and went to her apartment. I thought maybe Cary would help me. I rang the bell and nobody answered and I used her key and the chain bolt was on. Then I remembered she used to fasten it from outside. She'd showed me how she could do that. I tried with mine but it was installed properly and there's not enough play in the chain. I unhooked her bolt and went inside.

"Then I got the idea. I went back to my apartment and got her clothes and I rushed back and put them on her chair. I opened her window wide. On my way out the door I put her lights on and hooked the chain bolt again.

"I came back here to my own apartment. I took her pulse again and she was dead, she hadn't moved or anything, and I couldn't do anything for her, all I could do was stay out of it, and I, I turned off the lights here, and I opened my own window and dragged her body over to it, and, oh, God in heaven, God, I almost couldn't make myself do it but it was an accident that she was dead and I was so damned *afraid*—"

"And you dropped her out and closed the window." He nodded. "And if her neck was broken it was something that happened in the fall. And whatever drugs were in her system was just something she'd taken by herself, and they'd never do an autopsy anyway. And you were home free."

"I didn't hurt her," he said. "I was just protecting myself."

"Do you really believe that, Lane?"

"What do you mean?"

"You're not a doctor. Maybe she was dead when you threw her out the window. Maybe she wasn't."

"There was no pulse!"

"You couldn't find a pulse. That doesn't mean there wasn't any. Did you try artificial respiration? Do you know if there was any brain activity? No, of course not. All you know was that you looked for a pulse and you couldn't find one."

"Her neck was broken."

"Maybe. How many broken necks have you had occasion to diagnose? And people sometimes break their necks and live anyway. The point is that you couldn't have known she was dead and you were too worried about your own skin to do what you should have done. You should have phoned for an ambulance. You know that's what you should have done and you knew it at the time but you wanted to stay out of it. I've known junkies who left their buddies to die of overdoses because they didn't want to get involved. You went them one better. You put her out a window and let her fall twenty-one stories so that you wouldn't get involved, and for all you know she was alive when you let go of her."

"No," he said. "No. She was dead."

I'd told Ruth Wittlauer she could wind up believing whatever she wanted. People believe what they want to believe. It was just as true for Lane Posmantur.

"Maybe she was dead," I said. "Maybe that's your fault, too."

"What do you mean?"

"You said you slapped her to bring her around. What kind of a slap, Lane?"

"I just tapped her on the face."

"Just a brisk slap to straighten her out."

"That's right."

"Oh, hell, Lane. Who knows how hard you hit her? Who knows whether you may not have given her a shove? She wasn't the only one on pills. You said she was flying. Well, I think maybe you were doing a little flying yourself. And you'd been sleepy and you were groggy and she was buzzing around the room and being a general pain in the ass, and you gave her a slap and a shove and another slap and another shove and—"

"No!"

"And she fell down."

"It was an accident."

"It always is."

"I didn't hurt her. I liked her. She was a good kid, we got on fine, I didn't hurt her, I—"

"Put your shoes on, Lane."

"What for?"

"I'm taking you to the police station. It's a few blocks from here, not very far at all."

"Am I under arrest?"

"I'm not a policeman." I'd never gotten around to saying who I was and he'd never thought to ask. "My name's Scudder, I'm working for Paula's sister. I suppose you're under citizen's arrest. I want you to come to the precinct house with me. There's a cop named Guzik there and you can talk to him."

"I don't have to say anything," he said. He thought for a moment. "You're not a cop."

"No."

"What I said to you doesn't mean a thing." He took a breath, straightened up a little in his chair. "You can't prove a thing," he said. "Not a thing."

"Maybe I can and maybe I can't. You probably left prints in Paula's apartment. I had them seal the place a while ago and maybe they'll find traces of your presence. I don't know if Paula left any prints here or not. You probably scrubbed them up. But there may be neighbors who know you were sleeping with her, and someone may have noticed you scampering back and forth between the apartments that night, and it's even possible a neighbor heard the two of you struggling in here just before she went out the window. When the cops know what to look for, Lane, they usually find it sooner or later. It's knowing what you're after that's the hard part.

"But that's not even the point. Put your shoes on, Lane. That's right. Now we're going to go see Guzik, that's his name, and he's going to advise you of your rights. He'll tell you that you have a right to remain silent, and that's the truth, Lane, that's a right that you have. And if you remain silent and if you get a decent lawyer and do what he tells you I think you can beat this charge, Lane. I really do."

"Why are you telling me this?"

"Why?" I was starting to feel tired, drained, but I kept on with it. "Because the worst thing you could do is remain silent, Lane. Believe me, that's the worst thing you could do. If you're smart you'll tell Guzik everything you remember. You'll make a complete voluntary statement and you'll read it over when they type it up and you'll sign your name on the bottom.

"Because you're not really a killer, Lane. It doesn't come easily to you. If Cary McCloud had killed her he'd never lose a night's sleep over it. But you're not a psychopath. You were drugged and half-crazy and terrified and you did something wrong and it's eating you up. Your face fell apart the minute I walked in here tonight. You could play it cute and beat this charge, Lane, but all you'd wind up doing is beating yourself.

"Because you live on a high floor, Lane, and the ground's only four seconds away. And if you squirm off the hook you'll never get it out of your head, you'll never be able to mark it Paid in Full, and one day or night you'll open the window and you'll go out of it, Lane. You'll remember the sound her body made when she hit the street—"

"*No!*"

I took his arm. "Come on," I said. "We'll go see Guzik."

A Candle for the Bag Lady

He was a thin young man in a blue pinstripe suit. His shirt was white with a button-down collar. His glasses had oval lenses in brown tortoiseshell frames. His hair was a dark brown, short but not severely so, neatly combed, parted on the right. I saw him come in and watched him ask a question at the bar. Billie was working afternoons that week. I watched as he nodded at the young man, then swung his sleepy eyes over in my direction. I lowered my own eyes and looked at a cup of coffee laced with bourbon while the fellow walked over to my table.

"Matthew Scudder?" I looked up at him, nodded. "I'm Aaron Creighton. I looked for you at your hotel. The fellow on the desk told me I might find you here."

Here was Armstrong's, a Ninth Avenue saloon around the corner from my Fifty-seventh Street hotel. The lunch crowd was gone except for a couple of stragglers in front whose voices were starting to thicken with alcohol. The streets outside were full of May sunshine. The winter had been cold and deep and long. I couldn't recall a more welcome spring.

"I called you a couple times last week, Mr. Scudder. I guess you didn't get my messages."

I'd gotten two of them and ignored them, not knowing who he was or what he wanted and unwilling to spend a dime for the answer. But I went along with the fiction. "It's a cheap hotel," I said. "They're not always too good about messages."

"I can imagine. Uh. Is there someplace we can talk?"

"How about right here?"

He looked around. I don't suppose he was used to conducting his business in bars but he evidently decided it would be all right to make an exception. He set his briefcase on the floor and seated himself across the table from me. Angela, the new day-shift waitress, hurried over to get his order. He glanced at my cup and said he'd have coffee, too.

"I'm an attorney," he said. My first thought was that he didn't look like a lawyer, but then I realized he probably dealt with civil cases. My experience as a cop had given me a lot of experience with criminal lawyers. The breed ran to several types, none of them his.

I waited for him to tell me why he wanted to hire me. But he crossed me up.

"I'm handling an estate," he said, and paused, and gave what seemed a calculated if well-intentioned smile. "It's my pleasant duty to tell you you've come into a small legacy, Mr. Scudder."

"Someone's left me money?"

"Twelve hundred dollars."

Who could have died? I'd lost touch long since with any of my relatives. My parents went years ago and we'd never been close with the rest of the family.

I said, "Who—?"

"Mary Alice Redfield."

I repeated the name aloud. It was not entirely unfamiliar but I had no idea who Mary Alice Redfield might be. I looked at Aaron Creighton. I couldn't make out his eyes behind the glasses but there was a smile's ghost on his thin lips, as if my reaction was not unexpected.

"She's dead?"

"Almost three months ago."

"I didn't know her."

"She knew you. You probably knew her, Mr. Scudder. Perhaps you didn't know her by name." His smile deepened. Angela had brought his coffee. He stirred milk and sugar into it, took a careful sip, nodded his approval. "Miss Redfield was murdered." He said this as if he'd had practice uttering a phrase which did not come naturally to him. "She was killed quite brutally in late February for no apparent reason, another innocent victim of street crime."

"She lived in New York?"

"Oh, yes. In this neighborhood."

"And she was killed around here?"

"On West Fifty-fifth Street between Ninth and Tenth avenues. Her body was found in an alleyway. She'd been stabbed repeatedly and strangled with the scarf she had been wearing."

Late February. Mary Alice Redfield. West Fifty-fifth between Ninth and Tenth. Murder most foul. Stabbed and strangled, a dead woman in an alleyway. I usually kept track of murders, perhaps out of a vestige of professionalism, perhaps because I couldn't cease to be fascinated by man's inhumanity to man. Mary Alice Redfield had willed me twelve hundred dollars. And someone had knifed and strangled her, and—

"Oh, Jesus," I said. "The shopping bag lady."

Aaron Creighton nodded.

New York is full of them. East Side, West Side, each neighborhood has its own supply of bag women. Some of them are alcoholic but most of them have gone mad without any help from drink. They walk the streets, huddle on stoops or in doorways. They find sermons in stones and treasures in trash cans. They talk to themselves, to passersby, to God. Sometimes they mumble. Now and then they shriek.

They carry things around with them, the bag women. The shopping bags supply their generic name and their chief common denominator. Most of them seem to be paranoid, and their madness convinces them that their possessions are very valuable, that their enemies covet them. So their shopping bags are never out of their sight.

There used to be a colony of these ladies who lived in Grand Central Station. They would sit up all night in the waiting room, taking turns waddling off to the lavatory from time to time. They rarely talked to each other but some herd instinct made them comfortable with one another. But they were not comfortable enough to trust their precious bags to one another's safekeeping, and each sad crazy lady always toted her shopping bags to and from the ladies' room.

Mary Alice Redfield had been a shopping bag lady. I don't know when she set up shop in the neighborhood. I'd been living in the same hotel ever since I resigned from the NYPD and separated from my wife and sons, and that was getting to be quite a few years now. Had Miss Redfield been on the scene that long ago? I couldn't remember her first appearance. Like so many of the neighborhood fixtures, she had been part of the scenery. Had her death not been violent and abrupt I might never have noticed she was gone.

I'd never known her name. But she had evidently known mine, and had felt something for me that prompted her to leave money to me. How had she come to have money to leave?

She'd had a business of sorts. She would sit on a wooden soft drink case, surrounded by three or four shopping bags, and she would sell newspapers. There's an all-night newsstand at the corner of Fifty-seventh and Eighth, and she would buy a few dozen papers there, carry them a block west to the corner of Ninth, and set up shop in a doorway. She sold the papers at retail, though I suppose some people tipped her a few cents. I could remember a few occasions when I'd bought a paper and waved away change from a dollar bill. Bread upon the waters, perhaps, if that was what had moved her to leave me the money.

I closed my eyes, brought her image into focus. A thick-set woman, stocky rather than fat. Five-three or -four. Dressed usually in shapeless clothing, colorless gray and black garments, layers of clothing that varied with the season. I remembered that she would sometimes wear a hat, an old straw affair with paper and plastic flowers poked into it. And I remembered her eyes, large guileless blue eyes that were many years younger than the rest of her.

Mary Alice Redfield.

"Family money," Aaron Creighton was saying. "She wasn't wealthy but she had come from a family that was comfortably fixed. A bank in Baltimore handled her funds. That's where she was from originally, Baltimore, though she'd lived in New York for as long as anyone can remember. The bank sent her a check every month. Not very much, a couple of hundred dollars, but she hardly spent anything. She paid her rent—"

"I thought she lived on the street."

"No, she had a furnished room a few doors down the street from where she was killed. She lived in another rooming house on Tenth Avenue before that but moved when the building was sold. That was six or seven years ago and she lived on Fifty-fifth Street from then until her death. Her room cost her eighty dollars a month. She spent a few dollars on food. I don't know what she did with the rest. The only money in her room was a coffee can full of pennies. I've been checking the banks and there's no record of a savings account. I suppose she may have spent it or lost it or given it away. She wasn't very firmly grounded in reality."

"No, I don't suppose she was."

He sipped at his coffee. "She probably belonged in an institution," he said. "At least that's what people would say, but she got along in the outside world, she functioned well enough. I don't know if she kept herself clean and I don't know anything about how her mind worked but I think she must have been happier than she would have been in an institution. Don't you think?"

"Probably."

"Of course she wasn't safe, not as it turned out, but anybody can get killed on the streets of New York." He frowned briefly, caught up in a private thought. Then he said, "She came to our office ten years ago. That was before my time." He told me the name of his firm, a string of Anglo-Saxon surnames. "She wanted to draw a will. The original will was a very simple document leaving everything to her sister. Then over the years she would come in from time to time to add codicils leaving specific sums to various persons. She had made a total of thirty-two bequests by the time she died. One was for twenty dollars—that was to a man named John Johnson whom we haven't been able to locate. The remainder all ranged from five hundred to two thousand dollars." He smiled. "I've been given the task of running down the heirs."

"When did she put me into her will?"

"Two years ago in April."

I tried to think what I might have done for her then, how I might have brushed her life with mine. Nothing.

"Of course the will could be contested, Mr. Scudder. It would be easy to challenge Miss Redfield's competence and any relative could almost certainly get it set aside. But no one wishes to challenge it. The total amount involved is slightly in excess of a quarter of a million dollars—"

"That much."

"Yes. Miss Redfield received substantially less than the income which her holdings drew over the years, so the principal kept growing during her lifetime. Now the specific bequests she made total thirty-eight thousand dollars, give or take a few hundred, and the residue goes to Miss Redfield's sister. The sister—her name is Mrs. Palmer—is a widow with grown children. She's hospitalized with cancer and heart trouble and I believe diabetic complications and she hasn't long to live. Her children would like to see the estate settled before their mother dies, and they have enough local prominence to hurry the will through probate. So I'm authorized to tender checks for the full amount of the specific bequests on the condition that the legatees sign quit-claims acknowledging that this payment discharges in full the estate's indebtedness to them."

There was more legalese of less importance. Then he gave me papers to sign and the whole procedure ended with a check on the table. It was payable to me and in the amount of twelve hundred dollars and no cents.

I told Creighton I'd pay for his coffee.

I had time to buy myself another drink and still get to my bank before the windows closed. I put a little of Mary Alice Redfield's legacy in my savings account, took some in cash, and sent a money order to Anita and my sons. I stopped at my hotel to check for messages. There weren't any. I had a drink at McGovern's and crossed the street to have another at Polly's Cage. It wasn't five o'clock yet but the bar was doing good business already.

It turned into a funny night. I had dinner at the Greek place and read the *Post*, spent a little time at Joey Farrell's on Fifty-eighth Street, then wound up getting to Armstrong's around ten-thirty or thereabouts. I spent part of the evening alone at my usual table and part of it in conversation at the bar. I made a point of stretching my drinks, mixing my bourbon with coffee, making a cup last a while, taking a glass of plain water from time to time.

But that never really works. If you're going to get drunk you'll manage it somehow. The obstacles I placed in my path just kept me up later. By two-thirty I'd done what I had set out to do. I'd made my load and I could go home and sleep it off.

I woke around ten with less of a hangover than I'd earned and no memory of anything after I'd left Armstrong's. I was in my own bed in my own hotel room. And my clothes were hung neatly in the closet, always a good sign on a morning after. So I must have been in fairly good shape. But a certain amount of time was lost to memory, blacked out, gone.

When that first started happening I tended to worry about it. But it's the sort of thing you can get used to.

It was the money, the twelve hundred bucks. I couldn't understand the money. I had done nothing to deserve it. It had been left to me by a poor little rich woman whose name I'd not even known.

It had never occurred to me to refuse the dough. Very early in my career as a cop I'd learned an important precept. When someone put money in your hand you closed your fingers around it and put it in your pocket. I learned that lesson well and never had cause to regret its application. I didn't walk around with my hand out and I never took drug or homicide money but I certainly grabbed all the clean graft that came my way and a certain amount that wouldn't have stood a white glove inspection. If Mary Alice thought I merited twelve hundred dollars, who was I to argue?

Ah, but it didn't quite work that way. Because somehow the money gnawed at me.

After breakfast I went to St. Paul's but there was a service going on, a priest saying Mass, so I didn't stay. I walked down to St. Benedict the Moor's on Fifty-third Street and sat for a few minutes in a pew at the rear. I go to churches to try to think, and I gave it a shot but my mind didn't know where to go.

I slipped six twenties into the poor box. I tithe. It's a habit I got into after I left the department and I still don't know why I do it. God knows. Or maybe He's as mystified as I am. This time, though, there was a certain balance in the act. Mary Alice Redfield had given me twelve hundred dollars for no reason I could comprehend. I was passing on a ten percent commission to the church for no better reason.

I stopped on the way out and lit a couple of candles for various people who weren't alive anymore. One of them was for the bag lady. I didn't see how it could do her any good, but I couldn't imagine how it could harm her, either.

I had read some press coverage of the killing when it happened. I generally keep up with crime stories. Part of me evidently never stopped being a policeman. Now I went down to the Forty-second Street library to refresh my memory.

The *Times* had run a pair of brief back-page items, the first a report of the killing of an unidentified female derelict, the second a follow-up giving her name and age. She'd been forty-seven, I learned. This surprised me, and then I realized that any specific number would have come as a surprise. Bums and bag ladies are ageless. Mary Alice Redfield could have been thirty or sixty or anywhere in between.

The *News* had run a more extended article than the *Times*, enumerating the stab wounds—twenty-six of them—and described the scarf wound about her throat—blue and white, a designer print, but tattered at its edges and evidently somebody's castoff. It was this article that I remembered having read.

But the *Post* had really played the story. It had appeared shortly after the new owner took over the paper and the editors were going all out for human interest, which always translates out as sex and violence. The brutal killing of a woman touches both of those bases, and this had the added kick that she was a character. If they'd ever learned she was an heiress it would have been page three material, but even without that knowledge they did all right by her.

The first story they ran was straight news reporting, albeit embellished with reports on the blood, the clothes she was wearing, the litter in the alley where she was found, and all that sort of thing. The next day a reporter pushed the pathos button and tapped out a story featuring capsule interviews with people in the neighborhood. Only a few of them were identified by name and I came away with the feeling that he'd made up some peachy quotes and attributed them to unnamed nonexistent hangers-on. As a sidebar to that story, another reporter speculated on the possibility of a whole string of bag lady murders, a speculation which happily had turned out to be off the mark. The clown had presumably gone around the West Side asking shopping bag ladies if they were afraid of being the killer's next victim. I hope he faked the piece and let the ladies alone.

And that was about it. When the killer failed to strike again the newspapers hung up on the story. Good news is no news.

I walked back from the library. It was fine weather. The winds had blown all the crap out of the sky and there was nothing but blue overhead. The air actually had some air in it for a change. I walked west on Forty-second Street and north on Broadway, and I started noticing the number of street people, the drunks and the crazies and the unclassifiable derelicts. By the time I got within a few blocks of Fifty-seventh Street I was recognizing a large percentage of them. Each mini-neighborhood has its own human flotsam and jetsam and they're a lot more noticeable come springtime. Winter sends some of them south and others to shelter, and there's a certain percentage who die of exposure, but when the sun warms the pavement it brings most of them out again.

When I stopped for a paper at the corner of Eighth Avenue I got the bag lady into the conversation. The newsie clucked his tongue and shook his head. "The damnedest thing. Just the damnedest thing."

"Murder never makes much sense."

"The hell with murder. You know what she did? You know Eddie, works for me midnight to eight? Guy with the one droopy eyelid? Now he wasn't the guy used to sell her the stack of papers. Matter of fact that was usually me. She'd come by during the late morning or early afternoon and she'd take fifteen or twenty papers and pay me for 'em, and then she'd sit on her crate down the next corner and she'd sell as many as she could, and then she'd bring 'em back and I'd give her a refund on what she didn't sell."

"What did she pay for them?"

"Full price. And that's what she sold 'em for. The hell, I can't discount on papers. You know the margin we got. I'm not even supposed to take 'em back, but what difference does it make? It gave the poor woman something to do is my theory. She was important, she was a businesswoman. Sits there charging a quarter for something she just paid a quarter for, it's no way to get rich, but you know something? She had money. Lived like a pig but she had money."

"So I understand."

"She left Eddie seven-twenty. You believe that? Seven hundred and twenty dollars, she willed it to him, there was this lawyer come around two, three weeks ago with a check. Eddie Halloran. Pay to the order of. You believe that? She never had dealings with him. I sold her the papers, I bought 'em back from her. Not that I'm complaining, not that I want the woman's money, but I ask you this: Why Eddie? He don't know her. He can't believe she knows his name, Eddie Halloran. Why'd she leave it to him? He tells this lawyer, he says maybe she's got some other Eddie Halloran in mind. It's a common Irish name and the neighborhood's full of the Irish. I'm thinking to myself, Eddie, schmuck, take the money and shut up, but it's him all right because it says in the will. Eddie Halloran the newsdealer is what it says. So that's him, right? But why Eddie?"

Why me? "Maybe she liked the way he smiled."

"Yeah, maybe. Or the way he combed his hair. Listen, it's money in his pocket. I worried he'd go on a toot, drink it up, but he says money's no temptation. He says he's always got the price of a drink in his jeans and there's a bar on every block but he can walk right past 'em, so why worry about a few hundred dollars? You know something? That crazy woman, I'll tell you something, I miss her. She'd come, crazy hat on her head, spacy look in her eyes, she'd buy her stack of papers and waddle off all businesslike, then she'd bring the leftovers and cash 'em in, and I'd make a joke about her when she was out of earshot, but I miss her."

"I know what you mean."

"She never hurt nobody," he said. "She never hurt a soul."

"Mary Alice Redfield. Yeah, the multiple stabbing and strangulation." He shifted a cud-sized wad of gum from one side of his mouth to the other, pushed a lock of hair off his forehead, and yawned. "What have you got, some new information?"

"Nothing. I wanted to find out what you had."

"Yeah, right."

He worked on the chewing gum. He was a patrolman named Andersen who worked out of the Eighteenth. Another cop, a detective named Guzik, had learned that Andersen had caught the Redfield case and had taken the trouble to introduce the two of us. I hadn't known Andersen when I was on the force. He was younger than I, but then most people are nowadays.

He said, "Thing is, Scudder, we more or less put that one out of the way. It's in an open file. You know how it works. If we get new information, fine, but in the meantime I don't sit up nights thinking about it."

"I just wanted to see what you had."

"Well, I'm kind of tight for time, if you know what I mean. My own personal time, I set a certain store by my own time."

"I can understand that."

"You probably got some relative of the deceased for a client. Wants to find out who'd do such a terrible thing to poor old Cousin Mary. Naturally you're interested because it's a chance to make a buck and a man's gotta make a living. Whether a man's a cop or a civilian he's gotta make a buck, right?"

Uh-huh. I seem to remember that we were subtler in my day, but perhaps that's just age talking. I thought of telling him that I didn't have a client but why should he believe me? He didn't know me. If there was nothing in it for him, why should he bother?

So I said, "You know, we're just a couple weeks away from Memorial Day."

"Yeah, I'll buy a poppy from a Legionnaire. So what else is new?"

"Memorial Day's when women start wearing white shoes and men put straw hats on their heads. You got a new hat for the summer season, Andersen? Because you could use one."

"A man can always use a new hat," he said.

A hat is cop talk for twenty-five dollars. By the time I left the precinct house Andersen had two tens and a five of Mary Alice Redfield's bequest to me and I had all the data that had turned up to date.

I think Andersen won that one. I now knew that the murder weapon had been a kitchen knife with a blade approximately seven and a half inches long. That one of the stab wounds had found the heart and had probably caused death instantaneously. That it was impossible to determine whether strangulation had taken place before or after death. That should have been possible to determine—maybe the medical examiner hadn't wasted too much time checking her out, or maybe he had been reluctant to commit himself. She'd been dead a few hours when they found her—the estimate was that she'd died around midnight and the body wasn't reported until half-past five. That wouldn't have ripened her all that much, not in winter weather, but most likely her personal hygiene was nothing to boast about, and she was just a shopping bag lady and you couldn't bring her back to life, so why knock yourself out running tests on her malodorous corpse?

I learned a few other things. The landlady's name. The name of the off-duty bartender, heading home after a nightcap at the neighborhood after-hours joint, who'd happened on the body and who had been drunk enough or sober enough to take the trouble to report it. And I learned the sort of negative facts that turn up in a police report when the case is headed for an open file—the handful of non-leads that led nowhere, the witnesses who had nothing to contribute, the routine matters routinely handled. They hadn't knocked themselves out, Andersen and his partner, but would I have handled it any differently? Why knock yourself out chasing a murderer you didn't stand much chance of catching?

In the theater, SRO is good news. It means a sellout performance, standing room only. But once you get out of the theater district it means single room occupancy, and the designation is invariably applied to a hotel or apartment house which has seen better days.

Mary Alice Redfield's home for the last six or seven years of her life had started out as an old Rent Law tenement, built around the turn of the century, six stories tall, faced in red-brown brick, with four apartments to the floor. Now all of those little apartments had been carved into single rooms as if they were election districts gerrymandered by a maniac. There was a communal bathroom on each floor and you didn't need a map to find it.

The manager was a Mrs. Larkin. Her blue eyes had lost most of their color and half her hair had gone from black to gray but she was still pert. If she's reincarnated as a bird she'll be a house wren.

She said, "Oh, poor Mary. We're none of us safe, are we, with the streets full of monsters? I was born in this neighborhood and I'll die in it, but please God that'll be of natural causes. Poor Mary. There's some said she should have been locked up, but Jesus, she got along. She lived her life. And she had her check coming in every month and paid her rent on time. She had her own money, you know. She wasn't living off the public like some I could name but won't."

"I know."

"Do you want to see her room? I rented it twice since then. The first one was a young man and he didn't stay. He looked all right but when he left me I was just as glad. He said he was a sailor off a ship and when he left he said he'd got on with another ship and was on his way to Hong Kong or some such place, but I've had no end of sailors and he didn't walk like a sailor so I don't know what he was after doing. Then I could have rented it twelve times but didn't because I won't rent to colored or Spanish. I've nothing against them but I won't have them in the house. The owner says to me, Mrs. Larkin he says, my instructions are to rent to anybody regardless of race or creed or color, but if you was to use your own judgment I wouldn't have to know about it. In other words he don't want them either but he's after covering himself."

"I suppose he has to."

"Oh, with all the laws, but I've had no trouble." She laid a forefinger alongside her nose. It's a gesture you don't see too much these days. "Then I rented poor Mary's room two weeks ago to a very nice woman, a widow. She likes her beer, she does, but why shouldn't she have it? I keep my eye on her and she's making no trouble, and if she wants an old jar now and then whose business is it but her own?" She fixed her blue-gray eyes on me. "You like your drink," she said.

"Is it on my breath?"

"No, but I can see it in your face. Larkin liked his drink and there's some say it killed him but he liked it and a man has a right to live what life he wants. And he was never a hard man when he drank, never cursed or fought or beat a woman as some I could name but won't. Mrs. Shepard's out now. That's the one took poor Mary's room, and I'll show it to you if you want."

So I saw the room. It was kept neat.

"She keeps it tidier than poor Mary," Mrs. Larkin said. "Now Mary wasn't dirty, you understand, but she had all her belongings. Her shopping bags and other things that she kept in her room. She made a mare's nest of the place, and all the years she lived here, you see, it wasn't tidy. I would keep her bed made but she didn't want me touching her things and so I let it be cluttered as she wanted it. She paid her rent on time and made no trouble otherwise. She had money, you know."

"Yes, I know."

"She left some to a woman on the fourth floor. A much younger woman, she'd only moved here three months before Mary was killed, and if she exchanged a word with Mary I couldn't swear to it, but Mary left her almost a thousand dollars. Now Mrs. Klein across the hall lived here since before Mary ever moved in and the two old things always had a good word for each other, and all Mrs. Klein has is the welfare and she could have made good use of a couple of dollars, but Mary left her money instead to Miss Strom." She raised her eyebrows to show bewilderment. "Now Mrs. Klein said nothing, and I don't even know if she's had the thought that Mary might have mentioned her in her will, but Miss Strom said she didn't know what to make of it. She just couldn't understand it at all, and what I told her was you can't figure out a woman like poor Mary who never had both her feet on the pavement. Troubled as she was, daft as she was, who's to say what she might have had on her mind?"

"Could I see Miss Strom?"

"That would be for her to say, but she's not home from work yet. She works part-time in the afternoons. She's a close one, not that she hasn't the right to be, and she's never said what it is that she does. But she's a decent sort. This is a decent house."

"I'm sure it is."

"It's single rooms and they don't cost much so you know you're not at the Ritz Hotel, but there's decent people here and I keep it as clean as a person can. When there's not but one toilet on the floor it's a struggle. But it's decent."

"Yes."

"Poor Mary. Why'd anyone kill her? Was it sex, do you know? Not that you could imagine anyone wanting her, the old thing, but try to figure out a madman and you'll go mad your own self. Was she molested?"

"No."

"Just killed, then. Oh, God save us all. I gave her a home for almost seven years. Which it was no more than my job to do, not making it out to be charity on my part. But I had her here all that time and of course I never knew her, you couldn't get to know a poor old soul like that, but I got used to her. Do you know what I mean?"

"I think so."

"I got used to having her about. I might say Hello and Good morning and Isn't it a nice day and not get a look in reply, but even on those days she was someone familiar to say something to. And she's gone now and we're all of us older, aren't we?"

"We are."

"The poor old thing. How could anyone do it, will you tell me that? How could anyone murder her?"

I don't think she expected an answer. Just as well. I didn't have one.

After dinner I returned for a few minutes of conversation with Genevieve Strom. She had no idea why Miss Redfield had left her the money. She'd received $880 and she was glad to get it because she could use it, but the whole thing puzzled her. "I hardly knew her," she said more than once. "I keep thinking I ought to do something special with the money, but what?"

I made the bars that night but drinking didn't have the urgency it had possessed the night before. I was able to keep it in proportion and to know that I'd wake up the next morning with my memory intact. In the course of things I dropped over to the newsstand a little past midnight and talked with Eddie Halloran. He was looking good and I said as much. I remembered him when he'd gone to work for Sid three years ago. He'd been drawn then, and shaky, and his eyes always moved off to the side of whatever he was looking at. Now there was confidence in his stance and he looked years younger. It hadn't all come back to him and maybe some of it was lost forever. I guess the booze had him pretty good before he kicked it once and for all.

We talked about the bag lady. He said, "Know what I think it is? Somebody's sweeping the streets."

"I don't follow you."

"A cleanup campaign. Few years back, Matt, there was this gang of kids found a new way to amuse theirselves. Pick up a can of gasoline, find some bum down on the Bowery, pour the gas on him, and throw a lit match at him. You remember?"

"Yeah, I remember."

"Those kids thought they were patriots. Thought they deserved a medal. They were cleaning up the neighborhood, getting drunken bums off the streets. You know, Matt, people don't like to look at a derelict. That building up the block, the Towers? There's this grating there where the heating system's vented. You remember how the guys would sleep there in the winter. It was warm, it was comfortable, it was free, and two or three guys would be there every night catching some Z's and getting warm. Remember?"

"Uh-huh. Then they fenced it."

"Right. Because the tenants complained. It didn't hurt them any, it was just the local bums sleeping it off, but the tenants pay a lot of rent and they don't like to look at bums on their way in or out of their building. The bums were outside and not bothering anybody but it was the sight of them, you know, so the owners went to the expense of putting up cyclone fencing around where they used to sleep. It looks ugly as hell and all it does is keep the bums out but that's all it's supposed to do."

"That's human beings for you."

He nodded, then turned aside to sell somebody a *Daily News* and a *Racing Form*. Then he said, "I don't know what it is exactly. I was a bum, Matt. I got pretty far down. You probably don't know how far. I got as far as the Bowery. I panhandled, I slept in my clothes on a bench or in a doorway. You look at men like that and you think they're just waiting to die, and they are, but some of them come back. And you can't tell for sure who's gonna come back and who's not. Somebody coulda poured gas on me, set me on fire. Sweet Jesus."

"The shopping bag lady—"

"You'll look at a bum and you'll say to yourself, 'Maybe I could get like that and I don't wanta think about it.' Or you'll look at somebody like the shopping bag lady and say, 'I could go nutsy like her so get her out of my sight.' And you get people who think like Nazis. You know, take all the cripples and the lunatics and the retarded kids and all and give 'em an injection and Good-bye, Charlie."

"You think that's what happened to her?"

"What else?"

"But whoever did it stopped at one, Eddie."

He frowned. "Don't make sense," he said. "Unless he did the one job and the next day he got run down by a Ninth Avenue bus, and it couldn't happen to a nicer guy. Or he got scared. All that blood and it was more than he figured on. Or he left town. Could be anything like that."

"Could be."

"There's no other reason, is there? She musta been killed because she was a bag lady, right?"

"I don't know."

"Well, Jesus Christ, Matt. What other reason would anybody have for killing her?"

The law firm where Aaron Creighton worked had offices on the seventh floor of the Flatiron Building. In addition to the four partners, eleven other lawyers had their names painted on the frosted glass door. Aaron Creighton's came second from the bottom. Well, he was young.

He was also surprised to see me, and when I told him what I wanted he said it was irregular.

"Matter of public record, isn't it?"

"Well, yes," he said. "That means you can find the information. It doesn't mean we're obliged to furnish it to you."

For an instant I thought I was back at the Eighteenth Precinct and a cop was trying to hustle me for the price of a new hat. But Creighton's reservations were ethical. I wanted a list of Mary Alice Redfield's beneficiaries, including the amounts they'd received and the dates they'd been added to her will. He wasn't sure where his duty lay.

"I'd like to be helpful," he said. "Perhaps you could tell me just what your interest is."

"I'm not sure."

"I beg your pardon?"

"I don't know why I'm playing with this one. I used to be a cop, Mr. Creighton. Now I'm a sort of unofficial detective. I don't carry a license but I do things for people and I wind up making enough that way to keep a roof overhead."

His eyes were wary. I guess he was trying to guess how I intended to earn myself a fee out of this.

"I got twelve hundred dollars out of the blue. It was left to me by a woman I didn't really know and who didn't really know me. I can't seem to slough off the feeling that I got the money for a reason. That I've been paid in advance."

"Paid for what?"

"To try and find out who killed her."

"Oh," he said. "*Oh.*"

"I don't want to get the heirs together to challenge the will, if that was what was bothering you. And I can't quite make myself suspect that one of her beneficiaries killed her for the money she was leaving him. For one thing, she doesn't seem to have told people they were named in her will. She never said anything to me or to the two people I've spoken with thus far. For another, it wasn't the sort of murder that gets committed for gain. It was deliberately brutal."

"Then why do you want to know who the other beneficiaries are?"

"I don't know. Part of it's cop training. When you've got any specific leads, any hard facts, you run them down before you cast a wider net. That's only part of it. I suppose I want to get more of a sense of the woman. That's probably all I can realistically hope to get, anyway. I don't stand much chance of tracking her killer."

"The police don't seem to have gotten very far."

I nodded. "I don't think they tried too hard. And I don't think they knew she had an estate. I talked to one of the cops on the case and if he had known that he'd have mentioned it to me. There was nothing in her file. My guess is they waited for her killer to run a string of murders so they'd have something more concrete to work with. It's the kind of senseless crime that usually gets repeated." I closed my eyes for a moment, reaching for an errant thought. "But he didn't repeat," I said. "So they put it on a back burner and then they took it off the stove altogether."

"I don't know much about police work. I'm involved largely with estates and trusts." He tried a smile. "Most of my clients die of natural causes. Murder's an exception."

"It generally is. I'll probably never find him. I certainly don't expect to find him. Just killing her and moving on, hell, and it was all those months ago. He could have been a sailor off a ship, got tanked up and went nuts and he's in Macao or Port-au-Prince by now. No witnesses and no clues and no suspects and the trail's three months cold by now, and it's a fair bet the killer doesn't remember what he did. So many murders take place in blackout, you know."

"Blackout?" He frowned. "You don't mean in the dark?"

"Alcoholic blackout. The prisons are full of men who got drunk and shot their wives or their best friends. Now they're serving twenty-to-life for something they don't remember. No recollection at all."

The idea unsettled him, and he looked especially young now. "That's frightening," he said. "Really terrifying."

"Yes."

"I originally gave some thought to criminal law. My Uncle Jack talked me out of it. He said you either starve or you spend your time helping professional criminals beat the system. He said that was the only way you made good money out of a criminal practice and what you wound up doing was unpleasant and basically immoral. Of course there are a couple of superstar criminal lawyers, the hotshots everybody knows, but the other ninety-nine percent fit what Uncle Jack said."

"I would think so, yes."

"I guess I made the right decision." He took his glasses off, inspected them, decided they were clean, put them back on again. "Sometimes I'm not so sure," he said. "Sometimes I wonder. I'll get that list for you. I should probably check with someone to make sure it's all right but I'm not going to bother. You know lawyers. If you ask them whether it's all right to do something they'll automatically say no. Because inaction is always safer than action and they can't get in trouble for giving you bad advice if they tell you to sit on your hands and do nothing. I'm going overboard. Most of the time I like what I do and I'm proud of my profession. This'll take me a few minutes. Do you want some coffee in the meantime?"

His girl brought me a cup, black, no sugar. No bourbon, either. By the time I was done with the coffee he had the list ready.

"If there's anything else I can do—"

I told him I'd let him know. He walked out to the elevator with me, waited for the cage to come wheezing up, shook my hand. I watched him turn and head back to his office and I had the feeling he'd have preferred to come along with me. In a day or so he'd change his mind, but right now he didn't seem too crazy about his job.

The next week was a curious one. I worked my way through the list Aaron Creighton had given me, knowing what I was doing was essentially purposeless but compulsive about doing it all the same.

There were thirty-two names on the list. I checked off my own and Eddie Halloran and Genevieve Strom. I put additional check marks next to six people who lived outside of New York. Then I had a go at the remaining twenty-three names. Creighton had done most of the spadework for me, finding addresses to match most of the names. He'd included the date each of the thirty-two codicils had been drawn, and that enabled me to attack the list in reverse chronological order, starting with those persons who'd been made beneficiaries most recently. If this was a method, there was madness to it; it was based on the notion that a person added recently to the will would be more likely to commit homicide for gain, and I'd already decided this wasn't that kind of a killing to begin with.

Well, it gave me something to do. And it led to some interesting conversations. If the people Mary Alice Redfield had chosen to remember ran to any type, my mind wasn't subtle enough to discern it. They ranged in age, in ethnic background, in gender and sexual orientation, in economic status. Most of them were as mystified as Eddie and Genevieve and I about the bag lady's largesse, but once in a while I'd encounter someone who attributed it to some act of kindness he'd performed, and there was a young man named Jerry Forgash who was in no doubt whatsoever. He was some form of Jesus freak and he'd given poor Mary a couple of tracts and a Get Smart—Get Saved button, presumably a twin to the one he wore on the breast pocket of his chambray shirt. I suppose she put his gifts in one of her shopping bags.

"I told her Jesus loved her," he said, "and I suppose it won her soul for Christ. So of course she was grateful. Cast your bread upon the waters, Mr. Scudder. Brother Matthew. You know there was a disciple of Christ named Matthew."

"I know."

He told me Jesus loved me and that I should get smart and get saved. I managed not to get a button but I had to take a couple of tracts from him. I didn't have a shopping bag so I stuck them in my pocket, and a couple of nights later I read them before I went to bed. They didn't win my soul for Christ but you never know.

I didn't run the whole list. People were hard to find and I wasn't in any big rush to find them. It wasn't that kind of a case. It wasn't a case at all, really, merely an obsession, and there was surely no need to race the clock. Or the calendar. If anything, I was probably reluctant to finish up the names on the list. Once I ran out of them I'd have to find some other way to approach the woman's murder and I was damned if I knew where to start.

While I was doing all this, an odd thing happened. The word got around that I was investigating the woman's death, and the whole neighborhood became very much aware of Mary Alice Redfield. People began to seek me out. Ostensibly they had information to give me or theories to advance, but neither the information nor the theories ever seemed to amount to anything substantial, and I came to see that they were merely there as a prelude to conversation. Someone would start off by saying he'd seen Mary selling the *Post* the afternoon before she was killed, and that would serve as the opening wedge of a discussion of the bag woman, or bag women in general, or various qualities of the neighborhood, or violence in American life, or whatever.

A lot of people started off talking about the bag lady and wound up talking about themselves. I guess most conversations work out that way.

A nurse from Roosevelt said she never saw a shopping bag lady without hearing an inner voice say *There but for the grace of God.* And she was not the only woman who confessed she worried about ending up that way. I guess it's a specter that haunts women who live alone, just as the vision of the Bowery derelict clouds the peripheral vision of hard-drinking men.

Genevieve Strom turned up at Armstrong's one night. We talked briefly about the bag lady. Two nights later she came back again and we took turns spending our inheritances on rounds of drinks. The drinks hit her with some force and a little past midnight she decided it was time to go. I said I'd see her home. At the corner of Fifty-seventh Street she stopped in her tracks and said, "No men in the room. That's one of Mrs. Larkin's rules."

"Old-fashioned, isn't she?"

"She runs a daycent establishment." Her mock-Irish accent was heavier than the landlady's. Her eyes, hard to read in the lamplight, raised to meet mine. "Take me someplace."

I took her to my hotel, a less decent establishment than Mrs. Larkin's. We did each other little good but no harm, and it beat being alone.

Another night I ran into Barry Mosedale at Polly's Cage. He told me there was a singer at Kid Gloves who was doing a number about the bag lady. "I can find out how you can reach him," he offered.

"Is he there now?"

He nodded and checked his watch. "He goes on in fifteen minutes. But you don't want to go there, do you?"

"Why not?"

"Hardly your sort of crowd, Matt."

"Cops go anywhere."

"Indeed they do, and they're welcome wherever they go, aren't they? Just let me drink this and I'll accompany you, if that's all right. You need someone to lend you immoral support."

Kid Gloves is a gay bar on Fifty-sixth west of Ninth. The decor is just a little aggressively gay lib. There's a small raised stage, a scattering of tables, a piano, a loud jukebox. Barry Mosedale and I stood at the bar. I'd been there before and knew better than to order their coffee. I had straight bourbon. Barry had his on ice with a splash of soda.

Halfway through the drink Gordon Lurie was introduced. He wore tight jeans and a flowered shirt, sat on stage on a folding chair, sang ballads he'd written himself with his own guitar for accompaniment. I don't know if he was any good or not. It sounded to me as though all the songs had the same melody, but that may just have been a similarity of style. I don't have much of an ear.

After a song about a summer romance in Amsterdam, Gordon Lurie announced that the next number was dedicated to the memory of Mary Alice Redfield. Then he sang:

"She's a shopping bag lady who lives on
the sidewalks of Broadway
Wearing all of her clothes and her years
on her back

Toting dead dreams in an old paper sack
Searching the trash cans for something she
lost here on Broadway—
Shopping bag lady . . .

"You'd never know but she once was an
actress on Broadway
Speaking the words that they stuffed in
her head
Reciting the lines of the life that she led
Thrilling her fans and her friends and her
lovers on Broadway—
Shopping bag lady . . .

"There are demons who lurk in the corners
of minds and of Broadway
And after the omens and portents and
signs
Came the day she forgot to remember her
lines
Put her life on a leash and took it out
walking on Broadway—
Shopping bag lady . . ."

There were a couple more verses and the shopping bag lady in the song wound up murdered in a doorway, dying in defense of the "tattered old treasures she mined in the trash cans of Broadway." The song went over well and got a bigger hand than any of the ones that had preceded it.

I asked Barry who Gordon Lurie was.

"You know very nearly as much as I," he said. "He started here Tuesday. I find him whelming, personally. Neither overwhelming nor underwhelming but somewhere in the middle."

"Mary Alice never spent much time on Broadway. I never saw her more than a block from Ninth Avenue."

"Poetic license, I'm sure. The song would lack a certain something if you substituted Ninth Avenue for Broadway. As it stands it sounds a little like 'Rhinestone Cowboy.' "

"Lurie live around here?"

"I don't know where he lives. I have the feeling he's Canadian. So many people are nowadays. It used to be that no one was Canadian and now simply everybody is. I'm sure it must be a virus."

We listened to the rest of Gordon Lurie's act. Then Barry leaned forward and chatted with the bartender to find out how I could get backstage. I found my way to what passed for a dressing room at Kid Gloves. It must have been a ladies' lavatory in a prior incarnation.

I went in there thinking I'd made a breakthrough, that Lurie had killed her and now he was dealing with his guilt by singing about her. I don't think I really believed this but it supplied me with direction and momentum.

I told him my name and that I was interested in his act. He wanted to know if I was from a record company. "Am I on the threshold of a great opportunity? Am I about to become an overnight success after years of travail?"

We got out of the tiny room and left the club through a side door. Three doors down the block we sat in a cramped booth at a coffee shop. He ordered a Greek salad and we both had coffee.

I told him I was interested in his song about the bag lady.

He brightened. "Oh, do you like it? Personally I think it's the best thing I've written. I just wrote it a couple of days ago. I opened next door Tuesday night. I got to New York three weeks ago and I had a two-week booking in the West Village. A place called David's Table. Do you know it?"

"I don't think so."

"Another stop on the K-Y circuit. Either there aren't any straight people in New York or they don't go to nightclubs. But I was there two weeks, and then I opened at Kid Gloves, and afterward I was sitting and drinking with some people and somebody was talking about the shopping bag lady and I had had enough Amaretto to be maudlin on the subject. I woke up Wednesday morning with a splitting headache and the first verse of the song buzzing in my splitting head, and I sat up immediately and wrote it down, and as I was writing one verse the next would come bubbling to the surface, and before I knew it I had all six verses." He took a cigarette, then paused in the act of lighting it to fix his eyes on me. "You told me your name," he said, "but I don't remember it."

"Matthew Scudder."

"Yes. You're the person investigating her murder."

"I'm not sure that's the right word. I've been talking to people, seeing what I can come up with. Did you know her before she was killed?"

He shook his head. "I was never even in this neighborhood before. *Oh*. I'm not a suspect, am I? Because I haven't been in New York since the fall. I haven't bothered to figure out where I was when she was killed but I was in California at Christmastime and I'd gotten as far east as Chicago in early March, so I do have a fairly solid alibi."

"I never really suspected you. I think I just wanted to hear your song." I sipped some coffee. "Where did you get the facts of her life? Was she an actress?"

"I don't think so. Was she? It wasn't really *about* her, you know. It was inspired by her story but I didn't know her and I never knew anything about her. The past few days I've been paying a lot of attention to bag ladies, though. And other street people."

"I know what you mean."

"Are there more of them in New York or is it just that they're so much more visible here? In California everybody drives, you don't see people on the street. I'm from Canada, rural Ontario, and the first city I ever spent much time in was Toronto, and there are crazy people on the streets there but it's nothing like New York. Does the city drive them crazy or does it just tend to draw crazy people?"

"I don't know."

"Maybe they're not crazy. Maybe they just hear a different drummer. I wonder who killed her."

"We'll probably never know."

"What I really wonder is *why* she was killed. In my song I made up some reason. That somebody wanted what was in her bags. I think it works as a song that way but I don't think there's much chance that it happened like that. Why would anyone kill the poor thing?"

"I don't know."

"They say she left people money. People she hardly knew. Is that the truth?" I nodded. "And she left me a song. I don't even feel that I wrote it. I woke up with it. I never set eyes on her and she touched my life. That's strange, isn't it?"

Everything was strange. The strangest part of all was the way it ended.

It was a Monday night. The Mets were at Shea and I'd taken my sons to a game. The Dodgers were in for a three-game series which they eventually swept as they'd been sweeping everything lately. The boys and I got to watch them knock Jon Matlack out of the box and go on to shell his several replacements. The final count was something like 13–4. We stayed in our seats until the last out. Then I saw them home and caught a train back to the city.

So it was past midnight when I reached Armstrong's. Trina brought me a large double and a mug of coffee without being asked. I knocked back half of the bourbon and was dumping the rest into my coffee when she told me somebody'd been looking for me earlier. "He was in three times in the past two hours," she said. "A wiry guy, high forehead, bushy eyebrows, sort of a bulldog jaw. I guess the word for it is underslung."

"Perfectly good word."

"I said you'd probably get here sooner or later."

"I always do. Sooner or later."

"Uh-huh. You okay, Matt?"

"The Mets lost a close one."

"I heard it was thirteen to four."

"That's close for them these days. Did he say what it was about?"

He hadn't, but within the half hour he came in again and I was there to be found. I recognized him from Trina's description as soon as he came through the door. He looked faintly familiar but he was nobody I knew. I suppose I'd seen him around the neighborhood.

Evidently he knew me by sight because he found his way to my table without asking directions and took a chair without being invited to sit. He didn't say anything for a while and neither did I. I had a fresh bourbon and coffee in front of me and I took a sip and looked him over.

He was under thirty. His cheeks were hollow and the flesh of his face was stretched over his skull like leather that had shrunk upon drying. He wore a forest green work shirt and a pair of khaki pants. He needed a shave.

Finally he pointed at my cup and asked me what I was drinking. When I told him he said all he drank was beer.

"They have beer here," I said.

"Maybe I'll have what you're drinking." He turned in his chair and waved for Trina. When she came over he said he'd have bourbon and coffee, the same as I was having. He didn't say anything more until she brought the drink. Then, after he had spent quite some time stirring it, he took a sip. "Well," he said, "that's not so bad. That's okay."

"Glad you like it."

"I don't know if I'd order it again, but at least now I know what it's like."

"That's something."

"I seen you around. Matt Scudder. Used to be a cop, private eye now, blah blah blah. Right?"

"Close enough."

"My name's Floyd. I never liked it but I'm stuck with it, right? I could change it but who'm I kidding? Right?"

"If you say so."

"If I don't somebody else will. Floyd Karp, that's the full name. I didn't tell you my last name, did I? That's it, Floyd Karp."

"Okay."

"Okay, okay, okay." He pursed his lips, blew out air in a silent whistle. "What do we do now, Matt? Huh? That's what I want to know."

"I'm not sure what you mean, Floyd."

"Oh, you know what I'm getting at, driving at, getting at. You know, don't you?"

By this time I suppose I did.

"I killed that old lady. Took her life, stabbed her with my knife." He flashed the saddest smile. "Steee-rangled her with her skeeee-arf. Hoist her with her own whatchacallit, petard. What's a petard, Matt?"

"I don't know, Floyd. Why'd you kill her?"

He looked at me, he looked at his coffee, he looked at me again.

He said, "Had to."

"Why?"

"Same as the bourbon and coffee. Had to *see*. Had to taste it and find out what it was like." His eyes met mine. His were very large, hollow, empty. I fancied I could see right through them to the blackness at the back of his skull. "I couldn't get my mind away from murder," he said. His voice was more sober now, the mocking playful quality gone from it. "I tried. I just couldn't do it. It was on my mind all the time and I was afraid of what I might do. I couldn't function, I couldn't think, I just saw blood and death all the time. I was afraid to close my eyes for fear of what I might see. I would just stay up, days it seemed, and then I'd be tired enough to pass out the minute I closed my eyes. I stopped eating. I used to be fairly heavy and the weight just fell off of me."

"When did all this happen, Floyd?"

"I don't know. All winter. And I thought if I went and did it once I would know if I was a man or a monster or what. And I got this knife, and I went out a couple nights but lost my nerve, and then one night—I don't want to talk about that part of it now."

"All right."

"I almost couldn't do it, but I couldn't not do it, and then I was doing it and it went on forever. It was *horrible*."

"Why didn't you stop?"

"I don't know. I think I was afraid to stop. That doesn't make any sense, does it? I just don't know. It was all crazy, insane, like being in a movie and being in the audience at the same time. Watching myself."

"No one saw you do it?"

"No. I threw the knife down a sewer. I went home. I put all my clothes in the incinerator, the ones I was wearing. I kept throwing up. All that night I would throw up even when my stomach was empty. Dry heaves, Department of Dry Heaves. And then I guess I fell asleep, I don't know when or how but I did, and the next day I woke up and thought I dreamed it. But of course I didn't."

"No."

"And what I did think was that it was over. I did it and I knew I'd never want to do it again. It was something crazy that happened and I could forget about it. And I thought that was what happened."

"That you managed to forget about it?"

A nod. "But I guess I didn't. And now everybody's talking about her. Mary Alice Redfield, I killed her without knowing her name. Nobody knew her name and now everybody knows it and it's all back in my mind. And I heard you were looking for me, and I guess, I guess . . ." He frowned, chasing a thought around in his mind like a dog trying to capture his tail. Then he gave it up and looked at me. "So here I am," he said. "So here I am."

"Yes."

"Now what happens?"

"I think you'd better tell the police about it, Floyd."

"Why?"

"I suppose for the same reason you told me."

He thought about it. After a long time he nodded. "All right," he said. "I can accept that. I'd never kill anybody again. I know that. But—you're right. I have to tell them. I don't know who to see or what to say or, hell, I just—"

"I'll go with you if you want."

"Yeah. I want you to."

"I'll have a drink and then we'll go. You want another?"

"No. I'm not much of a drinker."

I had it without the coffee this time. After Trina brought it I asked him how he'd picked his victim. Why the bag lady?

He started to cry. No sobs, just tears spilling from his deep-set eyes. After a while he wiped them on his sleeve.

"Because she didn't count," he said. "That's what I thought. She was nobody. Who cared if she died? Who'd miss her?" He closed his eyes tight. "Everybody misses her," he said. "Everybody."

So I took him in. I don't know what they'll do with him. It's not my problem.

It wasn't really a case and I didn't really solve it. As far as I can see I didn't do anything. It was the talk that drove Floyd Karp from cover, and no doubt I helped some of the talk get started, but some of it would have gotten around without me. All those legacies of Mary Alice Redfield's had made her a nine-day wonder in the neighborhood. It was one of those legacies that got me involved.

Maybe she caught her own killer. Maybe he caught himself, as everyone does. Maybe no man's an island and maybe everybody is.

All I know is I lit a candle for the woman, and I suspect I'm not the only one who did.

By the Dawn's Early Light

All this happened a long time ago.

Abe Beame was living in Gracie Mansion, though even he seemed to have trouble believing he was really the mayor of the city of New York. Ali was in his prime, and the Knicks still had a year or so left in Bradley and DeBusschere. I was still drinking in those days, of course, and at the time it seemed to be doing more for me than it was doing to me.

I had already left my wife and kids, my home in Syosset, and the NYPD. I was living in the hotel on West Fifty-seventh Street where I still live, and I was doing most of my drinking around the corner in Jimmy Armstrong's saloon. Billie was the nighttime bartender. A Filipino youth named Dennis was behind the stick most days.

And Tommy Tillary was one of the regulars.

He was big, probably 6'2", full in the chest, big in the belly, too. He rarely showed up in a suit but always wore a jacket and tie, usually a navy or burgundy blazer with gray-flannel slacks or white duck pants in warmer weather. He had a loud voice that boomed from his barrel chest, and a big, clean-shaven face that was innocent around the pouting mouth and knowing around the eyes. He was somewhere in his late forties and he drank a lot of top-shelf scotch. Chivas, as I remember it, but it could have been Johnnie Black. Whatever it was, his face was beginning to show it, with patches of permanent flush at the cheekbones and a tracery of broken capillaries across the bridge of the nose.

We were saloon friends. We didn't speak every time we ran into each other, but at the least we always acknowledged each other with a nod or a wave. He told a lot of dialect jokes and told them reasonably well, and I laughed at my share of them. Sometimes I was in a mood to reminisce about my days on the force, and when my stories were funny, his laugh was as loud as anyone's.

Sometimes he showed up alone, sometimes with male friends. About a third of the time, he was in the company of a short and curvy blonde named Carolyn. "Carolyn from the Caro-line" was the way he occasionally introduced her, and she did have a faint Southern accent that became more pronounced as the drink got to her.

Then, one morning, I picked up the *Daily News* and read that burglars had broken into a house on Colonial Road, in the Bay Ridge section of Brooklyn. They had stabbed to death the only occupant present, one Margaret Tillary. Her husband, Thomas J. Tillary, a salesman, was not at home at the time.

I hadn't known Tommy was a salesman or that he'd had a wife. He did wear a wide yellow-gold band on the appropriate finger, and it was clear that he wasn't married to Carolyn from the Caroline, and it now looked as though he was a widower. I felt vaguely sorry for him, vaguely sorry for the wife I'd never even known of, but that was the extent of it. I drank enough back then to avoid feeling any emotion very strongly.

And then, two or three nights later, I walked into Armstrong's and there was Carolyn. She didn't appear to be waiting for him or anyone else, nor did she look as though she'd just breezed in a few minutes ago. She had a stool by herself at the bar and she was drinking something dark from a lowball glass.

I took a seat a few stools down from her. I ordered two double shots of bourbon, drank one, and poured the other into the black coffee Billie brought me. I was sipping the coffee when a voice with a Piedmont softness said, "I forget your name."

I looked up.

"I believe we were introduced," she said, "but I don't recall your name."

"It's Matt," I said, "and you're right, Tommy introduced us. You're Carolyn."

"Carolyn Cheatham. Have you seen him?"

"Tommy? Not since it happened."

"Neither have I. Were you-all at the funeral?"

"No. When was it?"

"This afternoon. Neither was I. There. Whyn't you come sit next to me so's I don't have to shout. Please?"

She was drinking a sweet almond liqueur that she took on the rocks. It tastes like dessert, but it's as strong as whiskey.

"He told me not to come," she said. "To the funeral. He said it was a matter of respect for the dead." She picked up her glass and stared into it. I've never known what people hope to see there, though it's a gesture I've performed often enough myself.

"Respect," she said. "What's he care about respect? I would have just been part of the office crowd; we both work at Tannahill; far as anyone there knows, we're just friends. And all we ever were is friends, you know."

"Whatever you say."

"Oh, *shit*," she said. "I don't mean I wasn't fucking him, for the Lord's sake. I mean it was just laughs and good times. He was married and he went home to Mama every night and that was jes' fine, because who in her right mind'd want Tommy Tillary around by the dawn's early light? Christ in the foothills, did I spill this or drink it?"

We agreed she was drinking them a little too fast. It was this fancy New York sweet-drink shit, she maintained, not like the bourbon she'd grown up on. You knew where you stood with bourbon.

I told her I was a bourbon drinker myself, and it pleased her to learn this. Alliances have been forged on thinner bonds than that, and ours served to propel us out of Armstrong's, with a stop down the block for a fifth of Maker's Mark—her choice—and a four-block walk to her apartment. There were exposed brick walls, I remember, and candles stuck in straw-wrapped bottles, and several travel posters from Sabena, the Belgian airline.

We did what grown-ups do when they find themselves alone together. We drank our fair share of the Maker's Mark and went to bed. She made a lot of enthusiastic noises and more than a few skillful moves, and afterward she cried some.

A little later, she dropped off to sleep. I was tired myself, but I put on my clothes and sent myself home. Because who in her right mind'd want Matt Scudder around by the dawn's early light?

Over the next couple of days, I wondered every time I entered Armstrong's if I'd run into her, and each time I was more relieved than disappointed when I didn't. I didn't encounter Tommy, either, and that, too, was a relief and in no sense disappointing.

Then, one morning, I picked up the *News* and read that they'd arrested a pair of young Hispanics from Sunset Park for the Tillary burglary and homicide. The paper ran the usual photo—two skinny kids, their hair unruly, one of them trying to hide his face from the camera, the other smirking defiantly, and each of them handcuffed to a broad-shouldered, grim-faced Irishman in a suit. You didn't need the careful caption to tell the good guys from the bad guys.

Sometime in the middle of the afternoon, I went over to Armstrong's for a hamburger and drank a beer with it. The phone behind the bar rang and Dennis put down the glass he was wiping and answered it. "He was here a minute ago," he said. "I'll see if he stepped out." He covered the mouthpiece with his hand and looked quizzically at me. "Are you still here?" he asked. "Or did you slip away while my attention was diverted?"

"Who wants to know?"

"Tommy Tillary."

You never know what a woman will decide to tell a man or how a man will react to it. I didn't want to find out, but I was better off learning over the phone than face-to-face. I nodded and took the phone from Dennis.

I said, "Matt Scudder, Tommy. I was sorry to hear about your wife."

"Thanks, Matt. Jesus, it feels like it happened a year ago. It was what, a week?"

"At least they got the bastards."

There was a pause. Then he said, "Jesus. You haven't seen a paper, huh?"

"That's where I read about it. Two Spanish kids."

"You didn't happen to see this afternoon's *Post*."

"No. Why, what happened? They turn out to be clean?"

"The two spics. Clean? Shit, they're about as clean as the men's room in the Times Square subway station. The cops hit their place and found stuff from my house everywhere they looked. Jewelry they had descriptions of, a stereo that I gave them the serial number, everything. Monogrammed shit. I mean, that's how clean they were, for Christ's sake."

"So?"

"They admitted the burglary but not the murder."

"That's common, Tommy."

"Lemme finish, huh? They admitted the burglary, but according to them it was a put-up job. According to them, I hired them to hit my place. They could keep whatever they got and I'd have everything out and arranged for them, and in return I got to clean up on the insurance by overreporting the loss."

"What did the loss amount to?"

"Shit, *I* don't know. There were twice as many things turned up in their apartment as I ever listed when I made out a report. There's things I missed a few days after I filed the report and others I didn't know were gone until the cops found them. You don't notice everything right away, at least I didn't, and on top of it, how could I think straight with Peg dead? You know?"

"It hardly sounds like an insurance setup."

"No, of course it wasn't. How the hell could it be? All I had was a standard homeowner's policy. It covered maybe a third of what I lost. According to them, the place was empty when they hit it. Peg was out."

"And?"

"And I set them up. They hit the place, they carted everything away, and I came home with Peg and stabbed her six, eight times, whatever it was, and left her there so it'd look like it happened in a burglary."

"How could the burglars testify that you stabbed your wife?"

"They couldn't. All they said was they didn't and she wasn't home when they were there, and that I hired them to do the burglary. The cops pieced the rest of it together."

"What did they do, take you downtown?"

"No. They came over to the house, it was early, I don't know what time. It was the first I knew that the spics were arrested, let alone that they were trying to do a job on me. They just wanted to talk, the cops, and at first I talked to them, and then I started to get the drift of what they were trying to put on to me. So I said I wasn't saying anything more without my lawyer present, and I called him, and he left half his breakfast on the table and came over in a hurry, and he wouldn't let me say a word."

"And the cops didn't take you in or book you?"

"No."

"Did they buy your story?"

"No way. I didn't really tell 'em a story, because Kaplan wouldn't let me say anything. They didn't drag me in, because they don't have a case yet, but Kaplan says they're gonna be building one if they can. They told me not to leave town. You believe it? My wife's dead, the *Post* headline says, 'Quiz Husband in Burglary Murder,' and what the hell do they think I'm gonna do? Am I going fishing for fucking trout in Montana? 'Don't leave town.' You see this shit on television, you think nobody in real life talks this way. Maybe television's where they get it from."

I waited for him to tell me what he wanted from me. I didn't have long to wait.

"Why I called," he said, "is Kaplan wants to hire a detective. He figured maybe these guys talked around the neighborhood, maybe they bragged to their friends, maybe there's a way to prove they did the killing. He says the cops won't concentrate on that end if they're too busy nailing the lid shut on me."

I explained that I didn't have any official standing, that I had no license and filed no reports.

"That's okay," he insisted. "I told Kaplan what I want is somebody I can trust, somebody who'll do the job for me. I don't think they're gonna have any kind of a case at all, Matt, but the longer this drags on, the worse it is for me. I want it cleared up, I want it in the papers that these Spanish assholes did it all and I had nothing to do with anything. You name a fair fee and I'll pay it, me to you, and it can be cash in your hand if you don't like checks. What do you say?"

He wanted somebody he could trust. Had Carolyn from the Caroline told him how trustworthy I was?

What did I say? I said yes.

I met Tommy Tillary and his lawyer in Drew Kaplan's office on Court Street, a few blocks from Brooklyn's Borough Hall. There was a Syrian restaurant next door and, at the corner, a grocery store specializing in Middle Eastern imports stood next to an antique shop overflowing with stripped-oak furniture and brass lamps and bedsteads. Kaplan's office ran to wood paneling and leather chairs and oak file cabinets. His name and the names of two partners were painted on the frosted-glass door in old-fashioned gold-and-black lettering. Kaplan himself looked conservatively up-to-date, with a three-piece striped suit that was better cut than mine. Tommy wore his burgundy blazer and gray-flannel trousers and loafers. Strain showed at the corners of his blue eyes and around his mouth. His complexion was off, too.

"All we want you to do," Kaplan said, "is find a key in one of their pants pockets, Herrera's or Cruz's, and trace it to a locker in Penn Station, and in the locker there's a footlong knife with their prints and her blood on it."

"Is that what it's going to take?"

He smiled. "It wouldn't hurt. No, actually, we're not in such bad shape. They got some shaky testimony from a pair of Latins who've been in and out of trouble since they got weaned to Tropicana. They got what looks to them like a good motive on Tommy's part."

"Which is?"

I was looking at Tommy when I asked. His eyes slipped away from mine. Kaplan said, "A marital triangle, a case of the shorts, and a strong money motive. Margaret Tillary inherited a little over a quarter of a million dollars six or eight months ago. An aunt left a million two and it got cut up four ways. What they don't bother to notice is he loved his wife, and how many husbands cheat? What is it they say—ninety percent cheat and ten percent lie?"

"That's good odds."

"One of the killers, Angel Herrera, did some odd jobs at the Tillary house last March or April. Spring cleaning; he hauled stuff out of the basement and attic, a little donkeywork. According to Herrera, that's how Tommy knew him to contact him about the burglary. According to common sense, that's how Herrera and his buddy Cruz knew the house and what was in it and how to gain access."

"The case against Tommy sounds pretty thin."

"It is," Kaplan said. "The thing is, you go to court with something like this and you lose even if you win. For the rest of your life, everybody remembers you stood trial for murdering your wife, never mind that you won an acquittal.

"Besides," he said, "you never know which way a jury's going to jump. Tommy's alibi is he was with another lady at the time of the burglary. The woman's a colleague; they could see it as completely aboveboard, but who says they're going to? What they sometimes do, they decide they don't believe the alibi because it's his girlfriend lying for him, and at the same time they label him a scumbag for screwing around while his wife's getting killed."

"You keep it up," Tommy said, "I'll find myself guilty, the way you make it sound."

"Plus he's hard to get a sympathetic jury for. He's a big handsome guy, a sharp dresser, and you'd love him in a gin joint, but how much do you love him in a courtroom? He's a securities salesman, he's beautiful on the phone, and that means every clown who ever lost a hundred dollars on a stock tip or bought magazines over the phone is going to walk into the courtroom with a hard-on for him. I'm telling you, I want to stay the hell out of court. I'll *win* in court, I know that, or the worst that'll happen is I'll win on appeal, but who needs it? This is a case that shouldn't be in the first place, and I'd love to clear it up before they even go so far as presenting a bill to the grand jury."

"So from me you want—"

"Whatever you can find, Matt. Whatever discredits Cruz and Herrera. I don't know what's there to be found, but you were a cop and now you're private, and you can get down in the streets and nose around."

I nodded. I could do that. "One thing," I said. "Wouldn't you be better off with a Spanish-speaking detective? I know enough to buy a beer in a bodega, but I'm a long way from fluent."

Kaplan shook his head. "A personal relationship's worth more than a dime's worth of '*Me llamo Matteo y ¿como está usted?*' "

"That's the truth," Tommy Tillary said. "Matt, I know I can count on you."

I wanted to tell him all he could count on was his fingers. I didn't really see what I could expect to uncover that wouldn't turn up in a regular police investigation. But I'd spent enough time carrying a shield to know not to push away money when somebody wants to give it to you. I felt comfortable taking a fee. The man was inheriting a quarter of a million, plus whatever insurance his wife had carried. If he was willing to spread some of it around, I was willing to take it.

So I went to Sunset Park and spent some time in the streets and some more time in the bars. Sunset Park is in Brooklyn, of course, on the borough's western edge, above Bay Ridge and south and west of Green-Wood Cemetery. These days, there's a lot of brownstoning going on there, with young urban professionals renovating the old houses and gentrifying the neighborhood. Back then, the upwardly mobile young had not yet discovered Sunset Park, and the area was a mix of Latins and Scandinavians, most of the former Puerto Ricans, most of the latter Norwegians. The balance was gradually shifting from Europe to the islands, from light to dark, but this was a process that had been going on for ages and there was nothing hurried about it.

I talked to Herrera's landlord and Cruz's former employer and one of his recent girlfriends. I drank beer in bars and the back rooms of bodegas. I went to the local station house, I read the sheets on both of the burglars and drank coffee with the cops and picked up some of the stuff that doesn't get on the yellow sheets.

I found out that Miguelito Cruz had once killed a man in a tavern brawl over a woman. There were no charges pressed; a dozen witnesses reported that the dead man had gone after Cruz first with a broken bottle. Cruz had most likely been carrying the knife, but several witnesses insisted it had been tossed to him by an anonymous benefactor, and there hadn't been enough evidence to make a case of weapons possession, let alone homicide.

I learned that Herrera had three children living with their mother in Puerto Rico. He was divorced but wouldn't marry his current girlfriend because he regarded himself as still married to his ex-wife in the eyes of God. He sent money to his children when he had any to send.

I learned other things. They didn't seem terribly consequential then and they've faded from memory altogether by now, but I wrote them down in my pocket notebook as I learned them, and every day or so I duly reported my findings to Drew Kaplan. He always seemed pleased with what I told him.

I invariably managed a stop at Armstrong's before I called it a night. One night she was there, Carolyn Cheatham, drinking bourbon this time, her face frozen with stubborn old pain. It took her a blink or two to recognize me. Then tears started to form in the corners of her eyes, and she used the back of one hand to wipe them away.

I didn't approach her until she beckoned. She patted the stool beside hers and I eased myself onto it. I had coffee with bourbon in it and bought a refill for her. She was pretty drunk already, but that's never been enough reason to turn down a drink.

She talked about Tommy. He was being nice to her, she said. Calling up, sending flowers. But he wouldn't see her, because it wouldn't look right, not for a new widower, not for a man who'd been publicly accused of murder.

"He sends flowers with no card enclosed," she said. "He calls me from pay phones. The son of a bitch."

Billie called me aside. "I didn't want to put her out," he said, "a nice woman like that, shit-faced as she is. But I thought I was gonna have to. You'll see she gets home?"

I said I would.

I got her out of there and a cab came along and saved us the walk. At her place, I took the keys from her and unlocked the door. She half sat, half sprawled on the couch. I had to use the bathroom, and when I came back, her eyes were closed and she was snoring lightly.

I got her coat and shoes off, put her to bed, loosened her clothing, and covered her with a blanket. I was tired from all that and sat down on the couch for a minute, and I almost dozed off myself. Then I snapped awake and let myself out.

I went back to Sunset Park the next day. I learned that Cruz had been in trouble as a youth. With a gang of neighborhood kids, he used to go into the city and cruise Greenwich Village, looking for homosexuals to beat up. He'd had a dread of homosexuality, probably flowing as it generally does out of a fear of a part of himself, and he stifled that dread by fag-bashing.

"He still doan' like them," a woman told me. She had glossy black hair and opaque eyes, and she was letting me pay for her rum and orange juice. "He's pretty, you know, an' they come on to him, an' he doan' like it."

I called that item in, along with a few others equally earth-shaking. I bought myself a steak dinner at the Slate over on Tenth Avenue, then finished up at Armstrong's, not drinking very hard, just coasting along on bourbon and coffee.

Twice, the phone rang for me. Once, it was Tommy Tillary, telling me how much he appreciated what I was doing for him. It seemed to me that all I was doing was taking his money, but he had me believing that my loyalty and invaluable assistance were all he had to cling to.

The second call was from Carolyn. More praise. I was a gentleman, she assured me, and a hell of a fellow all around. And I should forget that she'd been badmouthing Tommy. Everything was going to be fine with them.

I took the next day off. I think I went to a movie, and it may have been *The Sting,* with Newman and Redford achieving vengeance through swindling.

The day after that, I did another tour of duty over in Brooklyn. And the day after that, I picked up the *News* first thing in the morning. The headline was nonspecific, something like KILL SUSPECT HANGS SELF IN CELL, but I knew it was my case before I turned to the story on page three.

Miguelito Cruz had torn his clothing into strips, knotted the strips together, stood his iron bedstead on its side, climbed onto it, looped his homemade rope around an overhead pipe, and jumped off the up-ended bedstead and into the next world.

That evening's six o'clock TV news had the rest of the story. Informed of his friend's death, Angel Herrera had recanted his original story and admitted that he and Cruz had conceived and executed the Tillary burglary on their own. It had been Miguelito who had stabbed the Tillary woman when she walked in on them. He'd picked up a kitchen knife while Herrera watched in horror. Miguelito always had a short temper, Herrera said, but they were friends, even cousins, and they had hatched their story to protect Miguelito. But now that he was dead, Herrera could admit what had really happened.

I was in Armstrong's that night, which was not remarkable. I had it in mind to get drunk, though I could not have told you why, and that was remarkable, if not unheard of. I got drunk a lot those days, but I rarely set out with that intention. I just wanted to feel a little better, a little more mellow, and somewhere along the way I'd wind up waxed.

I wasn't drinking particularly hard or fast, but I was working at it, and then somewhere around ten or eleven the door opened and I knew who it was before I turned around. Tommy Tillary, well dressed and freshly barbered, making his first appearance in Jimmy's place since his wife was killed.

"Hey, look who's here!" he called out, and grinned that big grin. People rushed over to shake his hand. Billie was behind the stick, and he'd no sooner set one up on the house for our hero than Tommy insisted on buying a round for the bar. It was an expensive gesture—there must have been thirty or forty people in there—but I don't think he cared if there were three hundred or four hundred.

I stayed where I was, letting the others mob him, but he worked his way over to me and got an arm around my shoulders. "This is the man," he announced. "Best fucking detective ever wore out a pair of shoes. This man's money," he told Billie, "is no good at all tonight. He can't buy a drink; he can't buy a cup of coffee; if you went and put in pay toilets since I was last here, he can't use his own dime."

"The john's still free," Billie said, "but don't give the boss any ideas."

"Oh, don't tell me he didn't already think of it," Tommy said. "Matt, my boy, I love you. I was in a tight spot, I didn't want to walk out of my house, and you came through for me."

What the hell had I done? I hadn't hanged Miguelito Cruz or coaxed a confession out of Angel Herrera. I hadn't even set eyes on either man. But he was buying the drinks, and I had a thirst, so who was I to argue?

I don't know how long we stayed there. Curiously, my drinking slowed down even as Tommy's picked up speed. Carolyn, I noticed, was not present, nor did her name find its way into the conversation. I wondered if she would walk in—it was, after all, her neighborhood bar, and she was apt to drop in on her own. I wondered what would happen if she did.

I guess there were a lot of things I wondered about, and perhaps that's what put the brakes on my own drinking. I didn't want any gaps in my memory, any gray patches in my awareness.

After a while, Tommy was hustling me out of Armstrong's. "This is celebration time," he told me. "We don't want to sit in one place till we grow roots. We want to bop a little."

He had a car, and I just went along with him without paying too much attention to exactly where we were. We went to a noisy Greek club on the East Side, I think, where the waiters looked like Mob hit men. We went to a couple of trendy singles joints. We wound up somewhere in the Village, in a dark, beery cave.

It was quiet there, and conversation was possible, and I found myself asking him what I'd done that was so praiseworthy. One man had killed himself and another had confessed, and where was my role in either incident?

"The stuff you came up with," he said.

"What stuff? I should have brought back fingernail parings, you could have had someone work voodoo on them."

"About Cruz and the fairies."

"He was up for murder. He didn't kill himself because he was afraid they'd get him for fag-bashing when he was a juvenile offender."

Tommy took a sip of scotch. He said, "Couple days ago, huge black guy comes up to Cruz in the chow line. 'Wait'll you get up to Green Haven,' he tells him. 'Every blood there's gonna have you for a girlfriend. Doctor gonna have to cut you a brand-new asshole, time you get outa there.' "

I didn't say anything.

"Kaplan," he said. "Drew talked to somebody who talked to somebody, and that did it. Cruz took a good look at the idea of playin' drop the soap for half the jigs in captivity, and the next thing you know, the murderous little bastard was dancing on air. And good riddance to him."

I couldn't seem to catch my breath. I worked on it while Tommy went to the bar for another round. I hadn't touched the drink in front of me, but I let him buy for both of us.

When he got back, I said, "Herrera."

"Changed his story. Made a full confession."

"And pinned the killing on Cruz."

"Why not? Cruz wasn't around to complain. Who knows which one of 'em did it, and for that matter, who cares? The thing is, you gave us the lever."

"For Cruz," I said. "To get him to kill himself."

"And for Herrera. Those kids of his in Santurce. Drew spoke to Herrera's lawyer and Herrera's lawyer spoke to Herrera, and the message was, 'Look, you're going up for burglary whatever you do, and probably for murder; but if you tell the right story, you'll draw shorter time, and on top of that, that nice Mr. Tillary's gonna let bygones be bygones and every month there's a nice check for your wife and kiddies back home in Puerto Rico.' "

At the bar, a couple of old men were reliving the Louis-Schmeling fight, the second one, where Louis punished the German champion. One of the old fellows was throwing roundhouse punches in the air, demonstrating.

I said, "Who killed your wife?"

"One or the other of them. If I had to bet, I'd say Cruz. He had those little beady eyes; you looked at him up close and you got that he was a killer."

"When did you look at him up close?"

"When they came and cleaned the house, the basement, and the attic. Not when they came and cleaned me out; that was the second time."

He smiled, but I kept looking at him until the smile lost its certainty. "That was Herrera who helped around the house," I said. "You never met Cruz."

"Cruz came along, gave him a hand."

"You never mentioned that before."

"Oh, sure I did, Matt. What difference does it make, anyway?"

"Who killed her, Tommy?"

"Hey, let it alone, huh?"

"Answer the question."

"I already answered it."

"You killed her, didn't you?"

"What are you, crazy? Cruz killed her and Herrera swore to it, isn't that enough for you?"

"Tell me you didn't kill her."

"I didn't kill her."

"Tell me again."

"I didn't fucking kill her. What's the matter with you?"

"I don't believe you."

"Oh, Jesus," he said. He closed his eyes, put his head in his hands. He sighed and looked up and said, "You know, it's a funny thing with me. Over the telephone, I'm the best salesman you could ever imagine. I swear I could sell sand to the Arabs, I could sell ice in the winter, but face-to-face I'm no good at all. Why do you figure that is?"

"You tell me."

"I don't know. I used to think it was my face, the eyes and the mouth; I don't know. It's easy over the phone. I'm talking to a stranger, I don't know who he is or what he looks like, and he's not lookin' at me, and it's a cinch. Face-to-face, especially with someone I know, it's a different story." He looked at me. "If we were doin' this over the phone, you'd buy the whole thing."

"It's possible."

"It's fucking certain. Word for word, you'd buy the package. Suppose I was to tell you I did kill her, Matt. You couldn't prove anything. Look, the both of us walked in there, the place was a mess from the burglary, we got in an argument, tempers flared, something happened."

"You set up the burglary. You planned the whole thing, just the way Cruz and Herrera accused you of doing. And now you wriggled out of it."

"And you helped me—don't forget that part of it."

"I won't."

"And I wouldn't have gone away for it anyway, Matt. Not a chance. I'da beat it in court, only this way I don't have to go to court. Look, this is just the booze talkin', and we can forget it in the morning, right? I didn't kill her, you didn't accuse me, we're still buddies, everything's fine. Right?"

Blackouts are never there when you want them. I woke up the next day and remembered all of it, and I found myself wishing I didn't. He'd killed his wife and he was getting away with it. And I'd helped him. I'd taken his money, and in return I'd shown him how to set one man up for suicide and pressure another into making a false confession.

And what was I going to do about it?

I couldn't think of a thing. Any story I carried to the police would be speedily denied by Tommy and his lawyer, and all I had was the thinnest of hearsay evidence, my own client's own words when he and I both had a skinful of booze. I went over it for a few days, looking for ways to shake something loose, and there was nothing. I could maybe interest a newspaper reporter, maybe get Tommy some press coverage that wouldn't make him happy, but why? And to what purpose?

It rankled. But I would just have a couple of drinks, and then it wouldn't rankle so much.

Angel Herrera pleaded guilty to burglary, and in return, the Brooklyn D.A.'s Office dropped all homicide charges. He went Upstate to serve five to ten.

And then I got a call in the middle of the night. I'd been sleeping a couple of hours, but the phone woke me and I groped for it. It took me a minute to recognize the voice on the other end.

It was Carolyn Cheatham.

"I had to call you," she said, "on account of you're a bourbon man and a gentleman. I owed it to you to call you."

"What's the matter?"

"He ditched me," she said, "and he got me fired out of Tannahill and Company so he won't have to look at me around the office. Once he didn't need me to back up his story, he let go of me, and do you know he did it over the phone?"

"Carolyn—"

"It's all in the note," she said. "I'm leaving a note."

"Look, don't do anything yet," I said. I was out of bed, fumbling for my clothes. "I'll be right over. We'll talk about it."

"You can't stop me, Matt."

"I won't try to stop you. We'll talk first, and then you can do anything you want."

The phone clicked in my ear.

I threw my clothes on, rushed over there, hoping it would be pills, something that took its time. I broke a small pane of glass in the downstairs door and let myself in, then used an old credit card to slip the bolt of her spring lock.

The room smelled of cordite. She was on the couch she'd passed out on the last time I saw her. The gun was still in her hand, limp at her side, and there was a black-rimmed hole in her temple.

There was a note, too. An empty bottle of Maker's Mark stood on the coffee table, an empty glass beside it. The booze showed in her handwriting and in the sullen phrasing of the suicide note.

I read the note. I stood there for a few minutes, not for very long, and then I got a dish towel from the Pullman kitchen and wiped the bottle and the glass. I took another matching glass, rinsed it out and wiped it, and put it in the drainboard of the sink.

I stuffed the note in my pocket. I took the gun from her fingers, checked routinely for a pulse, then wrapped a sofa pillow around the gun to muffle its report. I fired one round into her chest, another into her open mouth.

I dropped the gun into a pocket and left.

They found the gun in Tommy Tillary's house, stuffed between the cushions of the living-room sofa, clean of prints inside and out. Ballistics got a perfect match. I'd aimed for soft tissue with the round shot into her chest, because bullets can fragment on impact with bone. That was one reason I'd fired the extra shots. The other was to rule out the possibility of suicide.

After the story made the papers, I picked up the phone and called Drew Kaplan. "I don't understand it," I said. "He was free and clear; why the hell did he kill the girl?"

"Ask him yourself," Kaplan said. He did not sound happy. "You want my opinion, he's a lunatic. I honestly didn't think he was. I figured maybe he killed his wife, maybe he didn't. Not my job to try him. But I didn't figure he was a homicidal maniac."

"It's certain he killed the girl?"

"Not much question. The gun's pretty strong evidence. Talk about finding somebody with the smoking pistol in his hand, here it was in Tommy's couch. The idiot."

"Funny he kept it."

"Maybe he had other people he wanted to shoot. Go figure a crazy man. No, the gun's evidence, and there was a phone tip—a man called in the shooting, reported a man running out of there, and gave a description that fitted Tommy pretty well. Even had him wearing that red blazer he wears, tacky thing makes him look like an usher at the Paramount."

"It sounds tough to square."

"Well, somebody else'll have to try to do it," Kaplan said. "I told him I can't defend him this time. What it amounts to, I wash my hands of him."

I thought of that when I read that Angel Herrera got out just the other day. He served all ten years because he was as good at getting into trouble inside the walls as he'd been on the outside.

Somebody killed Tommy Tillary with a homemade knife after he'd served two years and three months of a manslaughter stretch. I wondered at the time if that was Herrera getting even, and I don't suppose I'll ever know. Maybe the checks stopped going to Santurce and Herrera took it the wrong way. Or maybe Tommy said the wrong thing to somebody else and said it face-to-face instead of over the phone.

I don't think I'd do it that way now. I don't drink anymore, and the impulse to play God seems to have evaporated with the booze.

But then, a lot of things have changed. Billie left Armstrong's not long after that, left New York, too; the last I heard he was off drink himself, living in Sausalito and making candles. I ran into Dennis the other day in a bookstore on lower Fifth Avenue full of odd volumes on yoga and spiritualism and holistic healing. And Armstrong's is scheduled to close the end of next month. The lease is up for renewal, and I suppose the next you know, the old joint'll be another Korean fruit market.

I still light a candle now and then for Carolyn Cheatham and Miguelito Cruz. Not often. Just every once in a while.

Batman's Helpers

Reliable's offices are in the Flatiron Building, at Broadway and Twenty-third. The receptionist, an elegant black girl with high cheekbones and processed hair, gave me a nod and a smile, and I went on down the hall to Wally Witt's office.

He was at his desk, a short stocky man with a bulldog jaw and gray hair cropped close to his head. Without rising he said, "Matt, good to see you, you're right on time. You know these guys? Matt Scudder, Jimmy diSalvo, Lee Trombauer." We shook hands all around. "We're waiting on Eddie Rankin. Then we can go out there and protect the integrity of the American merchandising system."

"Can't do that without Eddie," Jimmy diSalvo said.

"No, we need him," Wally said. "He's our pit bull. He's attack-trained, Eddie is."

He came through the door a few minutes later and I saw what they meant. Without looking alike, Jimmy and Wally and Lee all looked like ex-cops, as I suppose do I. Eddie Rankin looked like the kind of guy we used to have to bring in on a bad Saturday night. He was a big man, broad in the shoulders, narrow in the waist. His hair was blond, almost white, and he wore it short at the sides but long in back. It lay on his neck like a mane. He had a broad forehead and a pug nose. His complexion was very fair and his full lips were intensely red, almost artificially so. He looked like a roughneck, and you sensed that his response to any sort of stress was likely to be physical, and abrupt.

Wally Witt introduced him to me. The others already knew him. Eddie Rankin shook my hand and his left hand fastened on my shoulder and gave a squeeze. "Hey, Matt," he said. "Pleased to meetcha. Whattaya say, guys, we ready to come to the aid of the Caped Crusader?"

Jimmy diSalvo started whistling the theme from *Batman,* the old television show. Wally said, "Okay, who's packing? Is everybody packing?"

Lee Trombauer drew back his suit jacket to show a revolver in a shoulder rig. Eddie Rankin took out a large automatic and laid it on Wally's desk. "Batman's gun," he announced.

"Batman don't carry a gun," Jimmy told him.

"Then he better stay outta New York," Eddie said. "Or he'll get his ass shot off. Those revolvers, I wouldn't carry one of them on a bet."

"This shoots as straight as what you got," Lee said. "And it won't jam."

"This baby don't jam," Eddie said. He picked up the automatic and held it out for display. "You got a revolver," he said, "a .38, whatever you got—"

"A .38."

"—and a guy takes it away from you, all he's gotta do is point it and shoot it. Even if he never saw a gun before, he knows how to do that much. This monster, though"—and he demonstrated, flicking the safety, working the slide—"all this shit you gotta go through, before he can figure it out I got the gun away from him and I'm making him eat it."

"Nobody's taking my gun away from me," Lee said.

"What everybody says, but look at all the times it happens. Cop gets shot with his own gun, nine times out of ten it's a revolver."

"That's because that's all they carry," Lee said.

"Well, there you go."

Jimmy and I weren't carrying guns. Wally offered to equip us but we both declined. "Not that anybody's likely to have to show a piece, let alone use one, God forbid," Wally said. "But it can get nasty out there and it helps to have the feeling of authority. Well, let's go get 'em, huh? The Batmobile's waiting at the curb."

We rode down in the elevator, five grown men, three of us armed with handguns. Eddie Rankin had on a plaid sport jacket and khaki trousers. The rest of us wore suits and ties. We went out the Fifth Avenue exit and followed Wally to his car, a five-year-old Fleetwood Cadillac parked next to a hydrant. There were no tickets on the windshield; a PBA courtesy card had kept the traffic cops at bay.

Wally drove and Eddie Rankin sat in front with him. The rest of us rode in back. We cruised up Sixth to Fifty-fourth Street and turned right, and Wally parked next to a hydrant a few doors from Fifth. We walked together to the corner of Fifth and turned downtown. Near the middle of the block a trip of black men had set up shop as sidewalk vendors. One had a display of women's handbags and silk scarves, all arranged neatly on top of a folding card table. The other two were offering T-shirts and cassette tapes.

In an undertone Wally said, "Here we go. These three were here yesterday. Matt, why don't you and Lee check down the block, make sure those two down at the corner don't have what we're looking for. Then double back and we'll take these dudes off. Meanwhile I'll let the man sell me a shirt."

Lee and I walked down to the corner. The two vendors in question were selling books. We established this and headed back. "Real police work," I said.

"Be grateful we don't have to fill out a report, list the titles of the books."

"The alleged books."

When we rejoined the others Wally was holding an oversize T-shirt to his chest, modeling it for us. "What do you say?" he demanded. "Is it me? Do you think it's me?"

"I think it's the Joker," Jimmy diSalvo said.

"That's what I think," Wally said. He looked at the two Africans, who were smiling uncertainly. "I think it's a violation, is what I think. I think we got to confiscate all the Batman stuff. It's unauthorized, it's an illegal violation of copyright protection, it's unlicensed, and we got to take it in."

The two vendors had stopped smiling, but they didn't seem to have a very clear idea of what was going on. Off to the side, the third man, the fellow with the scarves and purses, was looking wary.

"You speak English?" Wally asked them.

"They speak numbers," Jimmy said. " 'Fi dollah, ten dollah, please, thank you.' That's what they speak."

"Where you from?" Wally demanded. "Senegal, right? Dakar. You from Dakar?"

They nodded, brightening at words they recognized. "Dakar," one of them echoed. Both of them were wearing Western clothes, but they looked faintly foreign—loose-fitting long-sleeved shirts with long pointed collars and a glossy finish, baggy pleated pants. Loafers with leather mesh tops.

"What do you speak?" Wally asked. "You speak French? Parley-voo *Français*?" The one who'd spoken before replied now in a torrent of French, and Wally backed away from him and shook his head. "I don't know why the hell I asked," he said. "Parley-voo's all I know of the fucking language." To the Africans he said,

"Police. You parley-voo that? Police. *Policia.* You capeesh?" He opened his wallet and showed them some sort of badge. "No sell Batman," he said, waving one of the shirts at them. "Batman no good. It's unauthorized, it's not made under a licensing agreement, and you can't sell it."

"No Batman," one of them said.

"Jesus, don't tell me I'm getting through to them. Right, no Batman. No, put your money away, I can't take a bribe, I'm not with the department no more. All I want's the Batman stuff. You can keep the rest."

All but a handful of their T-shirts were unauthorized Batman items. The rest showed Walt Disney characters, themselves almost certainly as unauthorized as the Batman merchandise, but Disney wasn't Reliable's client today so it was none of our concern. While we loaded up with Batman and the Joker, Eddie Rankin looked through the cassettes, then pawed through the silk scarves the third vendor had on display. He let the man keep the scarves, but he took a purse, snakeskin by the look of it. "No good," he told the man, who nodded, expressionless.

We trooped back to the Fleetwood and Wally popped the trunk. We deposited the confiscated T's between the spare tire and some loose fishing tackle. "Don't worry if the shit gets dirty," Wally said. "It's all gonna be destroyed anyway. Eddie, you start carrying a purse, people are gonna say things."

"Woman I know," he said, "she'll like this." He wrapped the purse in a Batman T-shirt and placed it in the trunk.

"Okay," Wally said. "That went real smooth. What we'll do now, Lee, you and Matt take the east side of Fifth and the rest of us'll stay on this side and we'll work our way down to Forty-second. I don't know if we'll get much, because even if they can't speak English they can sure get the word around fast, but we'll make sure there's no unlicensed Batcrap on the avenue before we move on. We'll maintain eye contact back and forth across the street, and if you hit anything give the high sign and we'll converge and take 'em down. Everybody got it?"

Everybody seemed to. We left the car with its trunkful of contraband and returned to Fifth Avenue. The two T-shirt vendors from Dakar had packed up and disappeared; they'd have to find something else to sell and someplace else to sell it. The man with the scarves and purses was still doing business. He froze when he caught sight of us.

"No Batman," Wally told him.

"No Batman," he echoed.

"I'll be a son of a bitch," Wally said. "The guy's learning English."

Lee and I crossed the street and worked our way downtown. There were vendors all over the place, offering clothing and tapes and small appliances and books and fast food. Most of them didn't have the peddler's license the law required, and periodically the city would sweep the streets, especially the main commercial avenues, rounding them up and fining them and confiscating their stock. Then after a week or so the cops would stop trying to enforce a basically unenforceable law, and the peddlers would be back in business again.

It was an apparently endless cycle, but the booksellers were exempt from it.

The court had decided that the First Amendment embodied in its protection of freedom of the press the right of anyone to sell printed matter on the street, so if you had books for sale you never got hassled. As a result, a lot of scholarly antiquarian booksellers offered their wares on the city streets. So did any number of illiterates hawking remaindered art books and stolen best-sellers, along with homeless street people who rescued old magazines from people's garbage cans and spread them out on the pavement, living in hope that someone would want to buy them.

In front of St. Patrick's Cathedral we found a Pakistani with T-shirts and sweatshirts. I asked him if he had any Batman merchandise and he went right through the piles himself and pulled out half a dozen items. We didn't bother signaling the cavalry across the street. Lee just showed the man a badge—Special Officer, it said—and I explained that we had to confiscate Batman items.

"He is the big seller, Batman," the man said. "I get Batman, I sell him fast as I can."

"Well, you better not sell him anymore," I said, "because it's against the law."

"Excuse, please," he said. "What is law? Why is Batman against law? Is my understanding Batman is *for* law. He is good guy, is it not so?"

I explained about copyright and trademarks and licensing agreements. It was a little bit like explaining the internal-combustion engine to a field mouse. He kept nodding his head, but I don't know how much of it he got. He understood the main point—that we were walking off with his stock, and he was stuck for whatever it cost him. He didn't like that part but there wasn't much he could do about it.

Lee tucked the shirts under his arm and we kept going. At Forty-seventh Street we crossed over in response to a signal from Wally. They'd found another pair of Senegalese with a big spread of Batman items—T's and sweatshirts and gimme caps and sun visors, some a direct knockoff of the copyrighted Bat signal, others a variation on the theme, but none of it authorized and all of it subject to confiscation. The two men—they looked like brothers, and were dressed identically in baggy beige trousers and sky-blue nylon shirts—couldn't understand what was wrong with their merchandise and couldn't believe we intended to haul it all away with us. But there were five of us, and we were large intimidating white men with an authoritarian manner, and what could they do about it?

"I'll get the car," Wally said. "No way we're gonna schlepp this crap seven blocks in this heat."

With the trunk almost full, we drove to Thirty-fourth and broke for lunch at a place Wally liked. We sat at a large round table. Ornate beer steins hung from the beams overhead. We had a round of drinks, then ordered sandwiches and fries and half-liter steins of dark beer. I had a Coke to start, another Coke with the food, and coffee afterward.

"You're not drinking," Lee Trombauer said.

"Not today."

"Not on duty," Jimmy said, and everybody laughed.

"What I want to know," Eddie Rankin said, "is why everybody wants a fucking Batman shirt in the first place."

"Not just shirts," somebody said.

"Shirts, sweaters, caps, lunch boxes, if you could print it on Tampax they'd be shoving 'em up their twats. Why Batman, for Christ's sake?"

"It's hot," Wally said.

" 'It's hot.' What the fuck does that mean?"

"It means it's hot. That's what it means. It's hot means it's hot. Everybody wants it because everybody else wants it, and that means it's hot."

"I seen the movie," Eddie said. "You see it?"

Two of us had, two of us hadn't.

"It's okay," he said. "Basically I'd say it's a kid's movie, but it's okay."

"So?"

"So how many T-shirts in extra large do you sell to kids? Everybody's buying this shit, and all you can tell me is it's hot because it's hot. I don't get it."

"You don't have to," Wally said. "It's the same as the niggers. You want to try explaining to them why they can't sell Batman unless there's a little copyright notice printed under the design? While you're at it, you can explain to me why the assholes counterfeiting the crap don't counterfeit the copyright notice while they're at it. The thing is, nobody has to do any explaining because nobody has to understand. The only message they have to get on the street is Batman no good, no sell Batman. If they learn that much we're doing our job right."

Wally paid for everybody's lunch. We stopped at the Flatiron Building long enough to empty the trunk and carry everything upstairs, then drove down to the Village and worked the sidewalk market on Sixth Avenue below Eighth Street. We made a few confiscations without incident. Then, near the subway entrance at West Third, we were taking a dozen shirts and about as many visors from a West Indian when another vendor decided to get into the act. He was wearing a dashiki and had his hair in Rastafarian dreadlocks, and he said, "You can't take the brother's wares, man. You can't do that."

"It's unlicensed merchandise produced in contravention of international copyright protection," Wally told him.

"Maybe so," the man said, "but that don't empower you to seize it. Where's your due process? Where's your authority? You aren't police." Poe-lease, he said, bearing down on the first syllable. "You can't come into a man's store, seize his wares."

"Store?" Eddie Rankin moved toward him, his hands hovering at his sides. "You see a store here? All I see's a lot of fucking shit in the middle of a fucking blanket."

"This is the man's store. This is the man's place of business."

"And what's this?" Eddie demanded. He walked over to the right, where the man with the dreadlocks had stick incense displayed for sale on a pair of upended orange crates. "This your store?"

"That's right. It's my store."

"You know what it looks like to me? It looks like you're selling drug paraphernalia. That's what it looks like."

"It's incense," the Rasta said. "For bad smells."

"Bad smells," Eddie said. One of the sticks of incense was smoldering, and Eddie picked it up and sniffed at it. "Whew," he said. "That's a bad smell, I'll give you that. Smells like the catbox caught on fire."

The Rasta snatched the incense from him. "It's a good smell," he said. "Smells like your mama."

Eddie smiled at him, his red lips parting to show stained teeth. He looked happy, and very dangerous. "Say I kick your store into the middle of the street," he said, "and you with it. How's that sound to you?"

Smoothly, easily, Wally Witt moved between them. "Eddie," he said softly, and Eddie backed off and let the smile fade on his lips. To the incense seller Wally said, "Look, you and I got no quarrel with each other. I got a job to do and you got your own business to run."

"The brother here's got a business to run, too."

"Well, he's gonna have to run it without Batman, because that's how the law reads. But if you want to *be* Batman, playing the dozens with my man here and pushing into what doesn't concern you, then I got no choice. You follow me?"

"All I'm saying, I'm saying you want to confiscate the man's merchandise, you need you a policeman and a court order, something to make it official."

"Fine," Wally said. "You're saying it and I hear you saying it, but what I'm saying is all I need to do it is to do it, official or not. Now if you want to get a cop to stop me, fine, go ahead and do it, but as soon as you do I'm going to press charges for selling drug paraphernalia and operating without a peddler's license—"

"This here ain't drug paraphernalia, man. We both know that."

"We both know you're just trying to be a hard-on, and we both know what it'll get you. That what you want?"

The incense seller stood there for a moment, then dropped his eyes. "Don't matter what I want," he said.

"Well, you got that right," Wally told him. "It don't matter what you want."

We tossed the shirts and visors into the trunk and got out of there. On the way over to Astor Place Eddie said, "You didn't have to jump in there. I wasn't about to lose it."

"Never said you were."

"That mama stuff doesn't bother me. It's just nigger talk, they all talk that shit."

"I know."

"They'd talk about their fathers, but they don't know who the fuck they are, so they're stuck with their mothers. Bad smells, I shoulda stuck that shit up his ass, get right where the bad smells are. I hate a guy sticks his nose in like that."

"Your basic sidewalk lawyer."

"Basic asshole's what he is. Maybe I'll go back, talk with him later."

"On your own time."

"On my own time is right."

Astor Place hosts a more freewheeling street market, with a lot of Bowery types offering a mix of salvaged trash and stolen goods. There was something especially curious about our role, as we passed over hot radios and typewriters and jewelry and sought only merchandise that had been legitimately purchased, albeit from illegitimate manufacturers. We didn't find much Batman ware on display, although a lot of people, buyers and sellers alike, were wearing the Caped Crusader. We weren't about to strip the shirt off anybody's person, nor did we look too hard for contraband merchandise; the place was teeming with crackheads and crazies, and it was no time to push our luck.

"Let's get out of here," Wally said. "I hate to leave the car in this neighborhood. We already gave the client his money's worth."

By four we were back in Wally's office and his desk was heaped high with the fruits of our labors. "Look at all this shit," he said. "Today's trash and tomorrow's treasures. Twenty years and they'll be auctioning this crap at Christie's. Not this particular crap, because I'll messenger it over to the client and he'll chuck it in the incinerator. Gentlemen, you did a good day's work." He took out his wallet and gave each of the four of us a hundred-dollar bill. He said, "Same time tomorrow? Except I think we'll make lunch Chinese tomorrow. Eddie, don't forget your purse."

"Don't worry."

"Thing is you don't want to carry it if you go back to see your Rastafarian friend. He might get the wrong idea."

"Fuck him," Eddie said. "I got no time for him. He wants that incense up his ass, he's gonna have to stick it there himself."

Lee and Jimmy and Eddie went out, laughing, joking, slapping backs. I started out after them, then doubled back and asked Wally if he had a minute.

"Sure," he said. "Jesus, I don't believe this. Look."

"It's a Batman shirt."

"No shit, Sherlock. And look what's printed right under the Bat signal."

"The copyright notice."

"Right, which makes it a legal shirt. We got any more of these? No, no, no, no. Wait a minute, here's one. Here's another. Jesus, this is amazing. There any more? I don't see any others, do you?"

We went through the pile without finding more of the shirts with the copyright notice.

"Three," he said. "Well, that's not so bad. A mere fraction." He balled up the three shirts, dropped them back on the pile. "You want one of these? It's legit, you can wear it without fear of confiscation."

"I don't think so."

"You got kids? Take something home for your kids."

"One's in college and the other's in the service. I don't think they'd be interested."

"Probably not." He stepped out from behind his desk. "Well, it went all right out there, don't you think? We had a good crew, worked well together."

"I guess."

"What's the matter, Matt?"

"Nothing, really. But I don't think I can make it tomorrow."

"No? Why's that?"

"Well, for openers, I've got a dentist appointment."

"Oh, yeah? What time?"

"Nine-fifteen."

"So how long can that take? Half an hour, an hour tops? Meet us here ten-thirty, that's good enough. The client doesn't have to know what time we hit the street."

"It's not just the dentist appointment, Wally."

"Oh?"

"I don't think I want to do this stuff anymore."

"What stuff? Copyright and trademark protection?"

"Yeah."

"What's the matter? It's beneath you? Doesn't make full use of your talents as a detective?"

"It's not that."

"Because it's not a bad deal for the money, seems to me. Hundred bucks for a short day, ten to four, hour and a half off for lunch with the lunch all paid for. You're a cheap lunch date, you don't drink, but even so. Call it a ten-dollar lunch, that's a hundred and ten dollars for what, four and a half hours' work?" He punched numbers on a desk top calculator. "That's $24.44 an hour. That's not bad wages. You want to take home better than that, you need either burglar's tools or a law degree, seems to me."

"The money's fine, Wally."

"Then what's the problem?"

I shook my head. "I just haven't got the heart for it," I said. "Hassling people who don't even speak the language, taking their goods from them because we're stronger than they are and there's nothing they can do about it."

"They can quit selling contraband, that's what they can do."

"How? They don't even know what's contraband."

"Well, that's where we come in. We're giving them an education. How they gonna learn if nobody teaches 'em?"

I'd loosened my tie earlier. Now I took it off, folded it, put it in my pocket.

He said, "Company owns a copyright, they got a right to control who uses it. Somebody else enters into a licensing agreement, pays money for the right to produce a particular item, they got a right to the exclusivity they paid for."

"I don't have a problem with that."

"So?"

"They don't even speak the language," I said.

He stood up straight. "Then who told 'em to come here?" he wanted to know. "Who fucking invited them? You can't walk a block in midtown without tripping over another super-salesman from Senegal. They swarm off that Air Afrique flight from Dakar and first thing you know they got an open-air store on world-famous Fifth Avenue. They don't pay rent, they don't pay taxes, they just spread a blanket on the concrete and rake in the dollars."

"They didn't look as though they were getting rich."

"They must do all right. Pay two bucks for a scarf and sell it for ten, they must come out okay. They stay at hotels like the Bryant, pack together like sardines, six or eight to the room. Sleep in shifts, cook their food on hot plates. Two, three months of that and it's back to fucking Dakar. They drop off the money, take a few minutes to get another baby started, then they're winging back to JFK to start all over again. You think we need that? Haven't we got enough spades of our own can't make a living, we got to fly in more of them?"

I sifted through the pile on his desk, picked up a sun visor with the Joker depicted on it. I wondered why anybody would want something like that. I said, "What do you figure it adds up to, the stuff we confiscated? A couple of hundred?"

"Jesus, I don't know. Figure ten for a T-shirt, and we got what, thirty or forty of them? Add in the sweatshirts, the rest of the shit, I bet it comes to close to a grand. Why?"

"I was just thinking. You paid us a hundred a man, plus whatever lunch came to."

"Eighty with the tip. What's the point?"

"You must have billed us to the client at what, fifty dollars an hour?"

"I haven't billed anything to anybody yet, I just walked in the door, but yes, that's the rate."

"How will you figure it, four men at eight hours a man?"

"Seven hours. We don't bill for lunchtime."

Seven hours seemed ample, considering that we'd worked four and a half. I said, "Seven times fifty times four of us is what? Fourteen hundred dollars? Plus your own time, of course, and you must bill yourself at more than regular operative's rates. A hundred an hour?"

"Seventy-five."

"For seven hours is what, five hundred?"

"Five and a quarter," he said evenly.

"Plus fourteen hundred is nineteen and a quarter. Call it two thousand dollars to the client. Is that about right?"

"What are you saying, Matt? The client pays too much or you're not getting a big enough piece of the pie?"

"Neither. But if he wants to load up on this garbage"—I waved a hand at the heap on the desk—"wouldn't he be better off buying retail? Get a lot more bang for the buck, wouldn't he?"

He just stared at me for a long moment. Then, abruptly, his hard face cracked and he started to laugh. I was laughing, too, and it took all the tension out of the air. "Jesus, you're right," he said. "Guy's paying way too much."

"I mean, if you wanted to handle it for him, you wouldn't need to hire me and the other guys."

"I could just go around and pay cash."

"Right."

"I could even pass up the street guys altogether, go straight to the wholesaler."

"Save a dollar that way."

"I love it," he said. "You know what it sounds like? Sounds like something the federal government would do, get cocaine off the streets by buying it straight from the Colombians. Wait a minute, didn't they actually do something like that once?"

"I think so, but I don't think it was cocaine."

"No, it was opium. It was some years ago, they bought the entire Turkish opium crop because it was supposed to be the cheapest way to keep it out of the country. Bought it and burned it, and that, boys and girls, that was the end of heroin addiction in America."

"Worked like a charm, didn't it?"

"Nothing works," he said. "First principle of modern law enforcement. Nothing ever works. Funny thing is, in this case the client's not getting a bad deal. You own a copyright or a trademark, you got to defend it. Otherwise you risk losing it. You got to be able to say on such-and-such a date you paid so many dollars to defend your interests, and investigators acting as your agents confiscated so many items from so many merchants. And it's worth what you budget for it. Believe me, these big companies, they wouldn't spend the money year in and year out if they didn't figure it was worth it."

"I believe it," I said. "Anyway, I wouldn't lose a whole lot of sleep over the client getting screwed a little."

"You just don't like the work."

"I'm afraid not."

He shrugged. "I don't blame you. It's chickenshit. But Jesus, Matt, most P.I. work is chickenshit. Was it that different in the department? Or on any police force? Most of what we did was chickenshit."

"And paperwork."

"And paperwork, you're absolutely right. Do some chickenshit and then write it up. And make copies."

"I can put up with a certain amount of chickenshit," I said. "But I honestly don't have the heart for what we did today. I felt like a bully."

"Listen, I'd rather be kicking in doors, taking down bad guys. That what you want?"

"Not really."

"Be Batman, tooling around Gotham City, righting wrongs. Do the whole thing not even carrying a gun. You know what they didn't have in the movie?"

"I haven't seen it yet."

"Robin, they didn't have Robin. Robin the Boy Wonder. He's not in the comic book anymore, either. Somebody told me they took a poll, had their readers call a nine-hundred number and vote, should they keep Robin or should they kill him. Like in ancient Rome, those fights, what do you call them?"

"Gladiators."

"Right. Thumbs-up or thumbs-down, and Robin got thumbs-down, so they killed him. Can you believe that?"

"I can believe anything."

"Yeah, you and me both. I always thought they were fags." I looked at him. "Batman and Robin, I mean. His *ward*, for Christ's sake. Playing dress-up, flying around, costumes, I figured it's gotta be some kind of fag S-and-M thing. Isn't that what you figured?"

"I never thought about it."

"Well, I never stayed up nights over it myself, but what else would it be? Anyway, he's dead now, Robin is. Died of AIDS, I suppose, but the family's denying it, like What'shisname. You know who I mean."

I didn't, but I nodded.

"You gotta make a living, you know. Gotta turn a buck, whether it's hassling Africans or squatting out there on a blanket your own self, selling tapes and scarves. Fi' dollah, ten dollah." He looked at me. "No good, huh?"

"I don't think so, Wally."

"Don't want to be one of Batman's helpers. Well, you can't do what you can't do. What the fuck do I know about it, anyway? You don't drink. I don't have a problem with it, myself. But if I couldn't put my feet up at the end of the day, have a few pops, who knows? Maybe I couldn't do it either. Matt, you're a good man. If you change your mind—"

"I know. Thanks, Wally."

"Hey," he said. "Don't mention it. We gotta look out for each other, you know what I mean? Here in Gotham City."

The Merciful Angel of Death

"People come here to die, Mr. Scudder. They check out of hospitals, give up their apartments, and come to Caritas. Because they know we'll keep them comfortable here. And they know we'll let them die."

Carl Orcott was long and lean, with a long sharp nose and a matching chin. Some gray showed in his fair hair and his strawberry-blond mustache. His facial skin was stretched tight over his skull, and there were hollows in his cheeks. He might have been naturally spare of flesh, or worn down by the demands of his job. Because he was a gay man in the last decade of a terrible century, another possibility suggested itself. That he was HIV-positive. That his immune system was compromised. That the virus that would one day kill him was already within him, waiting.

"Since an easy death is our whole reason for being," he was saying, "it seems a bit much to complain when it occurs. Death is not the enemy here. Death is a friend. Our people are in very bad shape by the time they come to us. You don't run to a hospice when you get the initial results from a blood test, or when the first purple K-S lesions show up. First you try everything, including denial, and everything works for a while, and finally nothing works, not the AZT, not the pentamidine, not the Louise Hay tapes, not the crystal healing. Not even the denial. When you're ready for it to be over, you come here and we see you out." He smiled thinly. "We hold the door for you. We don't boot you through it."

"But now you think—"

"I don't know what I think." He selected a briar pipe from a walnut stand that held eight of them, examined it, sniffed its bowl. "Grayson Lewes shouldn't have died," he said. "Not when he did. He was doing very well, relatively speaking. He was in agony, he had a CMV infection that was blinding him, but he was still strong. Of course he was dying, they're all dying, everybody's dying, but death certainly didn't appear to be imminent."

"What happened?"

"He died."

"What killed him?"

"I don't know." He breathed in the smell of the unlit pipe. "Someone went in and found him dead. There was no autopsy. There generally isn't. What would be the point? Doctors would just as soon not cut up AIDS patients anyway, not wanting the added risk of infection. Of course, most of our general staff are seropositive, but even so you try to avoid unnecessary additional exposure. Quantity could make a difference, and there could be multiple strains. The virus mutates, you see." He shook his head. "There's such a great deal we still don't know."

"There was no autopsy."

"No. I thought about ordering one."

"What stopped you?"

"The same thing that keeps people from getting the antibody test. Fear of what I might find."

"You think someone killed Lewes."

"I think it's possible."

"Because he died abruptly. But people do that, don't they? Even if they're not sick to begin with. They have strokes or heart attacks."

"That's true."

"This happened before, didn't it? Lewes wasn't the first."

He smiled ruefully. "You're good at this."

"It's what I do."

"Yes." His fingers were busy with the pipe. "There have been a few unexpected deaths. But there would be, as you've said. So there was no real cause for suspicion. There still isn't."

"But you're suspicious."

"Am I? I guess I am."

"Tell me the rest of it, Carl."

"I'm sorry," he said. "I'm making you drag it out of me, aren't I? Grayson Lewes had a visitor. She was in his room for twenty minutes, perhaps half an hour. She was the last person to see him alive. She may have been the first person to see him dead."

"Who is she?"

"I don't know. She's been coming here for months. She always brings flowers, something cheerful. She brought yellow freesias the last time. Nothing fancy, just a five-dollar bunch from the Korean on the corner, but they do brighten a room."

"Had she visited Lewes before?"

He shook his head. "Other people. Every week or so she would turn up, always asking for one of our residents by name. It's often the sickest of the sick that she comes to see."

"And then they die?"

"Not always. But often enough so that it's been remarked upon. Still, I never let myself think that she played a causative role. I thought she had some instinct that drew her to your side when you were circling the drain." He looked off to the side. "When she visited Lewes, someone joked that we'd probably have his room available soon. When you're on staff here, you become quite irreverent in private. Otherwise you'd go crazy."

"It was the same way on the police force."

"I'm not surprised. When one of us would cough or sneeze, another might say, 'Uh-oh, you might be in line for a visit from Mercy.' "

"Is that her name?"

"Nobody knows her name. It's what we call her among ourselves. The Merciful Angel of Death. Mercy, for short."

A man named Bobby sat up in bed in his fourth-floor room. He had short gray hair and a gray brush mustache and a gray complexion bruised purple here and there by Kaposi's Sarcoma. For all of the ravages of the disease, he had a heartbreakingly youthful face. He was a ruined cherub, the oldest boy in the world.

"She was here yesterday," he said.

"She visited you twice," Carl said.

"Twice?"

"Once last week and once three or four days ago."

"I thought it was one time. And I thought it was yesterday." He frowned. "It all seems like yesterday."

"What does, Bobby?"

"Everything. Camp Arrowhead. *I Love Lucy*. The moon shot. One enormous yesterday with everything crammed into it, like his closet. I don't remember his name but he was famous for his closet."

"Fibber McGee," Carl said.

"I don't know why I can't remember his name," Bobby said languidly. "It'll come to me. I'll think of it yesterday."

I said, "When she came to see you—"

"She was beautiful. Tall, slim, gorgeous eyes. A flowing dove-gray robe, a blood-red scarf at her throat. I wasn't sure if she was real or not. I thought she might be a vision."

"Did she tell you her name?"

"I don't remember. She said she was there to be with me. And mostly she just sat there, where Carl's sitting. She held my hand."

"What else did she say?"

"That I was safe. That no one could hurt me anymore. She said—"

"Yes?"

"That I was innocent," he said, and he sobbed and let his tears flow.

He wept freely for a few moments, then reached for a Kleenex. When he spoke again his voice was matter-of-fact, even detached. "She *was* here twice," he said. "I remember now. The second time I got snotty, I really had the rag on, and I told her she didn't have to hang around if she didn't want to. And she said *I* didn't have to hang around if *I* didn't want to.

"And I said, right, I can go tap-dancing down Broadway with a rose in my teeth. And she said, no, all I have to do is let go and my spirit will soar free. And I looked at her, and I knew what she meant."

"And?"

"She told me to let go, to give it all up, to just let go and go to the light. And I said—this is strange, you know?"

"What did you say, Bobby?"

"I said I couldn't see the light and I wasn't ready to go to it. And she said that was all right, that when I was ready the light would be there to guide me. She said I would know how to do it when the time came. And she talked about how to do it."

"How?"

"By letting go. By going to the light. I don't remember everything she said. I don't even know for sure if all of it happened, or if I dreamed part of it. I never know anymore. Sometimes I have dreams and later they feel like part of my personal history. And sometimes I look back at my life and most of it has a veil over it, as if I never lived it at all, as if it were nothing but a dream."

Back in his office Carl picked up another pipe and brought its blackened bowl to his nose. He said, "You asked why I called you instead of the police. Can you imagine putting Bobby through an official interrogation?"

"He seems to go in and out of lucidity."

He nodded. "The virus penetrates the blood-brain barrier. If you survive the

K-S and the opportunistic infections, the reward is dementia. Bobby is mostly clear, but some of his mental circuits are beginning to burn out. Or rust out, or clog up, or whatever it is that they do."

"There are cops who know how to take testimony from people like that."

"Even so. Can you see the tabloid headlines? MERCY KILLER STRIKES AIDS HOSPICE. We have a hard enough time getting by as it is. You know, whenever the press happens to mention how many dogs and cats the SPCA puts to sleep, donations drop to a trickle. Imagine what would happen to us."

"Some people would give you more."

He laughed. " 'Here's a thousand dollars—kill ten of 'em for me.' You could be right."

He sniffed at the pipe again. I said, "You know, as far as I'm concerned you can go ahead and smoke that thing."

He stared at me, then at the pipe, as if surprised to find it in his hand. "There's no smoking anywhere in the building," he said. "Anyway, I don't smoke."

"The pipes came with the office?"

He colored. "They were John's," he said. "We lived together. He died . . . God, it'll be two years in November. It doesn't seem that long."

"I'm sorry, Carl."

"I used to smoke cigarettes, Marlboros, but I quit ages ago. But I never minded his pipe smoke, though. I always liked the aroma. And now I'd rather smell one of his pipes than the AIDS smell. Do you know the smell I mean?"

"Yes."

"Not everyone with AIDS has it but a lot of them do, and most sickrooms reek of it. You must have smelled it in Bobby's room. It's an unholy musty smell, a smell like rotted leather. I can't stand the smell of leather anymore. I used to love leather, but now I can't help associating it with the stink of gay men wasting away in fetid airless rooms.

"And this whole building smells that way to me. There's the stench of disinfectant over everything. We use tons of it, spray and liquid. The virus is surprisingly frail, it doesn't last long outside the body, but we leave as little as possible to chance, and so the rooms and halls all smell of disinfectant. But underneath it, always, there's the smell of the disease itself."

He turned the pipe over in his hands. "His clothes were full of the smell. John's. I gave everything away. But his pipes held a scent I had always associated with him, and a pipe is such a personal thing, isn't it, with the smoker's toothmarks in the stem." He looked at me. His eyes were dry, his voice strong and steady. There was no grief in his tone, only in the words themselves. "Two years in November, though I swear it doesn't seem that long, and I use one smell to keep another at bay. And, I suppose, to bridge the gap of years, to keep him a little closer to me." He put the pipe down. "Back to cases. Will you take a careful but unofficial look at our Angel of Death?"

I said I would. He said I'd want a retainer, and opened the top drawer of his desk. I told him it wouldn't be necessary.

"But isn't that standard for private detectives?"

"I'm not one, not officially. I don't have a license."

"So you told me, but even so—"

"I'm not a lawyer, either," I went on, "but there's no reason why I can't do a little *pro bono* work once in a while. If it takes too much of my time I'll let you know, but for now let's call it a donation."

The hospice was in the Village, on Hudson Street. Rachel Bookspan lived five miles north in an Italianate brownstone on Claremont Avenue. Her husband, Paul, walked to work at Columbia University, where he was an associate professor of political science. Rachel was a free-lance copy editor, hired by several publishers to prepare manuscripts for publication. Her specialties were history and biography.

She told me all this over coffee in her book-lined living room. She talked about a manuscript she was working on, the biography of a woman who had founded a religious sect in the late nineteenth century. She talked about her children, two boys, who would be home from school in an hour or so. Finally she ran out of steam and I brought the conversation back to her brother, Arthur Fineberg, who had lived on Morton Street and worked downtown as a librarian for an investment firm. And who had died two weeks ago at the Caritas Hospice.

"How we cling to life," she said. "Even when it's awful. Even when we yearn for death."

"Did your brother want to die?"

"He prayed for it. Every day the disease took a little more from him, gnawing at him like a mouse, and after months and months and months of hell it finally took his will to live. He couldn't fight anymore. He had nothing to fight with, nothing to fight *for*. But he went on living all the same."

She looked at me, then looked away. "He begged me to kill him," she said.

I didn't say anything.

"How could I refuse him? But how could I help him? First I thought it wasn't right, but then I decided it was his life, and who had a better right to end it if he wanted to? But how could I do it? How?

"I thought of pills. We don't have anything in the house except Midol for cramps. I went to my doctor and said I had trouble sleeping. Well, that was true enough. He gave me a prescription for a dozen Valium. I didn't even bother getting it filled. I didn't want to give Artie a handful of tranquilizers. I wanted to give him one of those cyanide capsules the spies always had in World War Two movies. You bite down and you're gone. But where do you go to get something like that?"

She sat forward in her chair. "Do you remember that man in the Midwest who unhooked his kid from a respirator? The doctors wouldn't let the boy die and the father went into the hospital with a gun and held everybody at bay until his son was dead. I think that man was a hero."

"A lot of people thought so."

"God, I wanted to be a hero! I had fantasies. There's a Robinson Jeffers poem about a crippled hawk and the narrator puts it out of its misery. 'I gave him the lead gift,' he says. Meaning a bullet, a gift of lead. I wanted to give my brother that gift. I don't have a gun. I don't even believe in guns. At least I never did. I don't know what I believe in anymore.

"If I'd had a gun, could I have gone in there and shot him? I don't see how. I have a knife, I have a kitchen full of knives, and believe me, I thought of going in there with a knife in my purse and waiting until he dozed off and then slipping the knife between his ribs and into his heart. I visualized it, I went over every aspect of it, but I didn't do it. My God, I never even left the house with a knife in my bag."

She asked if I wanted more coffee. I said I didn't. I asked her if her brother had had other visitors, and if he might have made the same request of one of them.

"He had dozens of friends, men and women who loved him. And yes, he would have asked them. He told everybody he wanted to die. As hard as he fought to live, for all those months, that's how determined he became to die. Do you think someone helped him?"

"I think it's possible."

"God, I hope so," she said. "I just wish it had been me."

"I haven't had the test," Aldo said. "I'm a forty-four-year-old gay man who led an active sex life since I was fifteen. I don't *have* to take the test, Matthew. I assume I'm seropositive. I assume everybody is."

He was a plump teddy bear of a man, with curly black hair and a face as permanently buoyant as a smile button. We were sharing a small table at a coffeehouse on Bleecker, just two doors from the shop where he sold comic books and baseball cards to collectors.

"I may not develop the disease," he said. "I may die a perfectly respectable death due to overindulgence in food and drink. I may get hit by a bus or struck down by a mugger. If I do get sick I'll wait until it gets really bad, because I love this life, Matthew, I really do. But when the time comes I don't want to make local stops. I'm gonna catch an express train out of here."

"You sound like a man with his bags packed."

"No luggage. Travelin' light. You remember the song?"

"Of course."

He hummed a few bars of it, his foot tapping out the rhythm, our little marble-topped table shaking with the motion. He said, "I have pills enough to do the job. I also have a loaded handgun. And I think I have the nerve to do what I have to do, when I have to do it." He frowned, an uncharacteristic expression for him. "The danger lies in waiting too long. Winding up in a hospital bed too weak to do anything, too addled by brain fever to remember what it was you were supposed to do. Wanting to die but unable to manage it."

"I've heard there are people who'll help."

"You've heard that, have you?"

"One woman in particular."

"What are you after, Matthew?"

"You were a friend of Grayson Lewes. And of Arthur Fineberg. There's a woman who helps people who want to die. She may have helped them."

"And?"

"And you know how to get in touch with her."

"Who says?"

"I forget, Aldo."

The smile was back. "You're discreet, huh?"

"Very."

"I don't want to make trouble for her."

"Neither do I."

"Then why not leave her alone?"

"There's a hospice administrator who's afraid she's murdering people. He called me in rather than start an official police inquiry. But if I don't get anywhere—"

"He calls the cops." He found his address book, copied out a number for me. "Please don't make trouble for her," he said. "I might need her myself."

I called her that evening, met her the following afternoon at a cocktail lounge just off Washington Square. She was as described, even to the gray cape over a long gray dress. Her scarf today was canary yellow. She was drinking Perrier, and I ordered the same.

She said, "Tell me about your friend. You say he's very ill."

"He wants to die. He's been begging me to kill him but I can't do it."

"No, of course not."

"I was hoping you might be able to visit him."

"If you think it might help. Tell me something about him, why don't you."

I don't suppose she was more than forty-five, if that, but there was something ancient about her face. You didn't need much of a commitment to reincarnation to believe she had lived before. Her facial features were pronounced, her eyes a graying blue. Her voice was pitched low, and along with her height it raised doubts about her sexuality. She might have been a sex change, or a drag queen. But I didn't think so. There was an Eternal Female quality to her that didn't feel like parody.

I said, "I can't."

"Because there's no such person."

"I'm afraid there are plenty of them, but I don't have one in mind." I told her in a couple of sentences why I was there. When I'd finished she let the silence stretch, then asked me if I thought she could kill anyone. I told her it was hard to know what anyone could do.

She said, "I think you should see for yourself what it is that I do."

She stood up. I put some money on the table and followed her out to the street.

We took a cab to a four-story brick building on Twenty-second Street west of Ninth. We climbed two flights of stairs, and the door opened when she knocked on it. I could smell the disease before I was across the threshold. The young black man who opened the door was glad to see her and unsurprised by my presence. He didn't ask my name or tell me his.

"Kevin's so tired," he told us both. "It breaks my heart."

We walked through a neat, sparsely furnished living room and down a short hallway to a bedroom, where the smell was stronger. Kevin lay in a bed with its head cranked up. He looked like a famine victim, or someone liberated from Dachau. Terror filled his eyes.

She pulled a chair up to the side of his bed and sat in it. She took his hand in hers and used her free hand to stroke his forehead. "You're safe now," she told him. "You're safe, you don't have to hurt anymore, you did all the things you had to do. You can relax now, you can let go now, you can go to the light.

"You can do it," she told him. "Close your eyes, Kevin, and go inside yourself and find the part that's holding on. Somewhere within you there's a part of you that's like a clenched fist, and I want you to find that part and be with that part. And let go. Let the fist open its fingers. It's as if the fist is holding a little bird, and if you open up the hand the bird can fly free. Just let it happen, Kevin. Just let go."

He was straining to talk, but the best he could do was make a sort of cawing sound. She turned to the black man, who was standing in the doorway. "David," she said, "his parents aren't living, are they?"

"I believe they're both gone."

"Which one was he closest to?"

"I don't know. I believe they're both gone a long time now."

"Did he have a lover? Before you, I mean."

"Kevin and I were never lovers. I don't even know him that well. I'm here 'cause he hasn't got anybody else. He had a lover."

"Did his lover die? What was his name?"

"Martin."

"Kevin," she said, "you're going to be all right now. All you have to do is go to the light. Do you see the light? Your mother's there, Kevin, and your father, and Martin—"

"Mark!" David cried. "Oh, God, I'm sorry, I'm so stupid, it wasn't Martin, it was Mark, Mark, that was his name."

"That's all right, David."

"I'm so damn stupid—"

"Look into the light, Kevin," she said. "Mark is there, and your parents, and everyone who ever loved you. Matthew, take his other hand. Kevin, you don't have to stay here anymore, darling. You did everything you came here to do. You don't have to stay. You don't have to hold on. You can let go, Kevin. You can go to the light. Let go and reach out to the light—"

I don't know how long she talked to him. Fifteen, twenty minutes, I suppose. Several times he made the cawing sound, but for the most part he was silent. Nothing seemed to be happening, and then I realized that his terror was no longer a presence. She seemed to have talked it away. She went on talking to him, stroking his brow and holding his hand, and I held his other hand. I was no longer listening to what she was saying, just letting the words wash over me while my mind played with some tangled thought like a kitten with yarn.

Then something happened. The energy in the room shifted and I looked up, knowing that he was gone.

"Yes," she murmured. "Yes, Kevin. God bless you, God give you rest. Yes."

"Sometimes they're stuck," she said. "They want to go but they can't. They've been hanging on so long, you see, that they don't know how to stop."

"So you help them."

"If I can."

"What if you can't? Suppose you talk and talk and they still hold on?"

"Then they're not ready. They'll be ready another time. Sooner or later everybody lets go, everybody dies. With or without my help."

"And when they're not ready—"

"Sometimes I come back another time. And sometimes they're ready then."

"What about the ones who beg for help? The ones like Arthur Fineberg, who plead for death but aren't physically close enough to it to let go?"

"What do you want me to say?"

"The thing you want to say. The thing that's stuck in your throat, the way his own unwanted life was stuck in Kevin's throat. You're holding on to it."

"Just let it go, eh?"

"If you want."

We were walking somewhere in Chelsea, and we walked a full block now without either of us saying a word. Then she said, "I think there's a world of difference between assisting someone verbally and doing anything physical to hasten death."

"So do I."

"And that's where I draw the line. But sometimes, having drawn that line—"

"You step over it."

"Yes. The first time I swear I acted without conscious intent. I used a pillow, I held it over his face and—" She breathed deeply. "I swore it would never happen again. But then there was someone else, and he just needed help, you know, and—"

"And you helped him."

"Yes. Was I wrong?"

"I don't know what's right or wrong."

"Suffering is wrong," she said, "unless it's part of His plan, and how can I presume to decide if it is or not? Maybe people can't let go because there's one more lesson they have to learn before they move on. Who the hell am I to decide it's time for somebody's life to end? How dare I interfere?"

"And yet you do."

"Just once in a while, when I just don't see a way around it. Then I do what I have to do. I'm sure I must have a choice in the matter, but I swear it doesn't feel that way. It doesn't feel as though I have any choice at all." She stopped walking, turned to look at me. She said, "Now what happens?"

"Well, she's the Merciful Angel of Death," I told Carl Orcott. "She visits the sick and dying, almost always at somebody's invitation. A friend contacts her, or a relative."

"Do they pay her?"

"Sometimes they try to. She won't take any money. She even pays for the flowers herself." She'd taken Dutch iris to Kevin's apartment on Twenty-second Street. Blue, with yellow centers that matched her scarf.

"She does it *pro bono*," he said.

"And she talks to them. You heard what Bobby said. I got to see her in action. She talked the poor son of a bitch straight out of this world and into the next one. I suppose you could argue that what she does comes perilously close to hypnosis, that she hypnotizes people and convinces them to kill themselves psychically, but I can't imagine anybody trying to sell that to a jury."

"She just talks to them."

"Uh-huh. 'Let go, go to the light.' "

" 'And have a nice day.' "

"That's the idea."

"She's not killing people?"

"Nope. Just letting them die."

He picked up a pipe. "Well, hell," he said, "that's what we do. Maybe I ought to put her on staff." He sniffed the pipe bowl. "You have my thanks, Matthew. Are you sure you don't want some of our money to go with it? Just because Mercy works *pro bono* doesn't mean you should have to."

"That's all right."

"You're certain?"

I said, "You asked me the first day if I knew what AIDS smelled like."

"And you said you'd smelled it before. Oh."

I nodded. "I've lost friends to it. I'll lose more before it's over. In the meantime I'm grateful when I get the chance to do you a favor. Because I'm glad this place is here, so people have a place to come to."

Even I was glad she was around, the woman in gray, the Merciful Angel of Death. To hold the door for them, and show them the light on the other side. And, if they really needed it, to give them the least little push through it.

The Night and the Music

We left halfway through the curtain calls, threading our way up the aisle and across the lobby. Inside it had been winter in Paris, with *La Bohème*'s lovers shivering and starving; outside it was New York, with spring turning into summer.

We held hands and walked across the great courtyard, past the fountain shimmering under the lights, past Avery Fisher Hall. Our apartment is in the Parc Vendome, at Fifty-seventh and Ninth, and we headed in that direction and walked a block or so in silence.

Then Elaine said, "I don't want to go home."

"All right."

"I want to hear music. Can we do that?"

"We just did that."

"Different music. Not another opera."

"Good," I said, "because one a night is my limit."

"You old bear. One a night is one over your limit."

I shrugged. "I'm learning to like it."

"Well, one a night's my limit. You know something? I'm in a mood."

"Somehow I sensed as much."

"She always dies," she said.

"Mimi."

"Uh-huh. How many times do you suppose I've seen *La Bohème*? Six, seven times?"

"If you say so."

"At least. You know what? I could see it a hundred times and it's not going to change. She'll die every fucking time."

"Odds are."

"So I want to hear something different," she said, "before we call it a night."

"Something happy," I suggested.

"No, sad is fine. I don't mind sad. As a matter of fact I prefer it."

"But you want them all alive at the end."

"That's it," she said. "Sad as can be, so long as nobody dies."

We caught a cab to a new place I'd heard about on the ground floor of a high-rise on Amsterdam in the Nineties. The crowd was salt and pepper, white college kids and black strivers, blonde fashion models and black players. The group was mixed, too; the tenor man and the bass player were white, the pianist and the drummer black. The *maître d'* thought he recognized me and put us at a table near the bandstand. They were a few bars into "Satin Doll" when we sat down and they followed it with a tune I recognized but couldn't name. I think it was a Thelonious

Monk composition, but that's just a guess. I can hardly ever name the tune unless there's a lyric to it that sticks in my mind.

Aside from ordering drinks, we didn't say a word until the set ended. We sipped our cranberry juice and soda and listened to the music. She watched the musicians and I watched her watch them. When they took a break she reached for my hand. "Thanks," she said.

"You okay?"

"I was always okay. I do feel better now, though. You know what I was thinking?"

"The night we met."

Her eyes widened. "How'd you know that?"

"Well, it was in a room that looked and felt a lot like this one. You were at Danny Boy's table, and this is his kind of place."

"God, I was young. We were both so goddamned young."

"Youth is one of those things time cures."

"You were a cop and I was a hooker. But you'd been on the force longer than I'd been on the game."

"I already had a gold shield."

"And I was new enough to think the life was glamorous. Well, it was glamorous. Look at the places I went and the people I got to meet."

"Married cops."

"That's right, you were married then."

"I'm married now."

"To me. Jesus, the way things turn out, huh?"

"A club like this," I said, "and the same kind of music playing."

"Sad enough to break your heart, but nobody dies."

"You were the most beautiful woman in the room that night," I said. "And you still are."

"Ah, Pinocchio," she said, and squeezed my hand. "Lie to me."

We closed the place. Outside on the street she said, "God, I'm impossible. I don't want the night to end."

"It doesn't have to."

"In the old days," she said, "you knew all the after-hours joints. Remember when Condon's would stay open late for musicians, and they'd jam until dawn?"

"I remember Eddie Condon's hangover cure," I said. " 'Take the juice of two quarts of whiskey . . .' I forget what came after that."

"Oblivion?"

"You'd think so. Say, I know where we can go."

I flagged a cab and we rode down to Sheridan Square, where there's a basement joint with the same name as a long-gone Harlem jazz club. They start around midnight and stay open past dawn, and it's legal because they don't serve alcohol. I used to go to late joints for the booze, and I learned to like the music because I heard so much of it there, and because you could just about taste the alcohol in every flatted fifth. Nowadays I go for the music, and what I hear in the blue notes is not so much the booze as all the feelings the drink used to mask.

That night there were a lot of different musicians sitting in with what I guess was the house rhythm section. There was a tenor player who sounded a little like Johnny Griffin and a piano player who reminded me of Lennie Tristano. And as always there was a lot of music I barely heard, background music for my own unfocused thoughts.

The sky was light by the time we dragged ourselves out of there. "Look at that," Elaine said. "It's bright as day."

"And well it might be. It's morning."

"What a New York night, huh? You know, I loved our trip to Europe, and other places we've gone together, but when you come right down to it—"

"You're a New York kind of gal."

"You bet your ass. And what we heard tonight was New York music. I know all about the music coming up the river from New Orleans, all that crap, and I don't care. That was New York music."

"You're right."

"And nobody died," she said.

"That's right," I said. "Nobody died."

Looking for David

Elaine said, "You never stop working, do you?"

I looked at her. We were in Florence, sitting at a little tile-topped table in the Piazza di San Marco, sipping cappuccino every bit as good as the stuff they served at the Peacock on Greenwich Avenue. It was a bright day but the air was cool and crisp, the city bathed in October light. Elaine was wearing khakis and a tailored safari jacket, and looked like a glamorous foreign correspondent, or perhaps a spy. I was wearing khakis, too, and a polo shirt, and the blue blazer she called my Old Reliable.

We'd had five days in Venice. This was the second of five days in Florence, and then we'd have six days in Rome before Alitalia took us back home again.

I said, "Nice work if you can get it."

"Uh-uh," she said. "I caught you. You were scanning the area the way you always do."

"I was a cop for a lot of years."

"I know, and I guess it's a habit a person doesn't outgrow. And not a bad one, either. I have some New York street smarts myself, but I can't send my eyes around a room and pick up what you can. And you don't even think about it. You do it automatically."

"I guess. But I wouldn't call it working."

"When we're supposed to be basking in the beauties of Florence," she said, "and exclaiming over the classic beauty of the sculpture in the piazza, and instead you're staring at an old queen in a white linen jacket five tables over, trying to guess if he's got a yellow sheet and just what's written on it—wouldn't you call that working?"

"There's no guesswork required," I said. "I know what it says on his yellow sheet."

"You do?"

"His name is Horton Pollard," I said. "If it's the same man, and if I've been sending a lot of looks his way it's to make sure he's the man I think he is. It's well over twenty years since I've seen him. Probably more like twenty-five." I glanced over and watched the white-haired gentleman saying something to the waiter. He raised an eyebrow in a manner that was at once arrogant and apologetic. It was as good as a fingerprint. "It's him," I said. "Horton Pollard. I'm positive."

"Why don't you go over and say hello?"

"He might not want that."

"Twenty-five years ago you were still on the job. What did you do, arrest him?"

"Uh-huh."

"Honestly? What did *he* do? Art fraud? That's what comes to mind, sitting at an outdoor table in Florence, but he was probably just a stock swindler."

"Something white-collar, in other words."

"Something flowing-collar, from the looks of him. I give up. What did he do?"

I'd been looking his way, and our glances caught. I saw recognition come into his eyes, and his eyebrows went up again in that manner that was unmistakably his. He pushed his chair back, got to his feet.

"Here he comes," I said. "You can ask him yourself."

"Mr. Scudder," he said. "I want to say Martin, but I know that's not right. Help me out."

"Matthew, Mr. Pollard. And this is my wife, Elaine."

"How fortunate for you," he told me, and took the hand she extended. "I looked over here and thought, What a beautiful woman! Then I looked again and thought, I know that fellow. But then it took me a minute to place you. The name came first, or the surname, at any rate. His name's Scudder, but how do I know him? And then of course the rest of it came to me, all but your first name. I knew it wasn't Martin, but I couldn't sweep that name out of my mind and let Matthew come in." He sighed. "It's a curious muscle, the memory. Or aren't you old enough yet to have found it so?"

"My memory's still pretty good."

"Oh, mine's *good*," he said. "It's just capricious. Willful, I sometimes think."

At my invitation, he pulled up a chair from a nearby table and sat down. "But only for a moment," he said, and asked what brought us to Italy, and how long we'd be in Florence. He lived here, he told us. He'd lived here for quite a few years now. He knew our hotel, on the east bank of the Arno, and pronounced it charming and a good value. He mentioned a café just down the street from the hotel that we really ought to try.

"Although you certainly don't need to follow my recommendations," he said, "or Michelin's, either. You can't get a bad meal in Florence. Well, that's not *entirely* true. If you insist on going to high-priced restaurants, you'll encounter the occasional disappointment. But if you simply blunder into whatever humble trattoria is closest, you'll dine well every time."

"I think we've been dining a little too well," Elaine said.

"It's a danger," he acknowledged, "although the Florentines manage to stay quite slim themselves. I started to bulk up a bit when I first came here. How could one help it? Everything tasted so good. But I took off the pounds I gained and I've kept them off. Though I sometimes wonder why I bother. For God's sake, I'm seventy-six years old."

"You don't look it," she told him.

"I wouldn't care to look it. But why is that, do you suppose? No one else on God's earth gives a damn what I look like. Why should it matter to me?"

She said it was self-respect, and he mused on the difficulty of telling where self-respect left off and vanity began. Then he said he was staying too long at the fair, wasn't he, and got to his feet. "But you must visit me," he said. "My villa is not terribly grand, but it's quite nice and I'm proud enough of it to want to show it off. Please tell me you'll come for lunch tomorrow."

"Well . . ."

"It's settled, then," he said, and gave me his card. "Any cabdriver will know how to find it. Set the price in advance, though. Some of them will cheat you, although most are surprisingly honest. Shall we say one o'clock?" He leaned forward, placed his palms on the table. "I've thought of you often over the years, Matthew. Especially here, sipping *caffé nero* a few yards from Michelangelo's David. It's not the original, you know. That's in a museum, though even the museums are less than safe these days. You know the Uffizzi was bombed a few years ago?"

"I read about that."

"The Mafia. Back home they just kill each other. Here they blow up masterpieces. Still, it's a wonderfully civilized country, by and large. And I suppose I had to wind up here, near the David." He'd lost me, and I guess he knew it, because he frowned, annoyed at himself. "I just ramble," he said. "I suppose the one thing I'm short of here is people to talk to. And I always thought I could talk to you, Matthew. Circumstances prevented my so doing, of course, but over the years I regretted the lost opportunity." He straightened up. "Tomorrow, one o'clock. I look forward to it."

"Well, of course I'm dying to go," Elaine said. "I'd love to see what his place looks like. 'It's not terribly grand but it's quite nice.' I'll bet it's nice. I'll bet it's gorgeous."

"You'll find out tomorrow."

"I don't know. He wants to talk to you, and three might be a crowd for the kind of conversation he wants to have. It wasn't art theft you arrested him for, was it?"

"No."

"Did he kill someone?"

"His lover."

"Well, that's what each man does, isn't it? Kills the thing he loves, according to what'shisname."

"Oscar Wilde."

"Thanks, Mr. Memory. Actually, I knew that. Sometimes when a person says what'shisname or whatchamacallit it's not because she can't remember. It's just a conversational device."

"I see."

She gave me a searching look. "There was something about it," she said. "What?"

"It was brutal." My mind filled with a picture of the murder scene, and I blinked it away. "You see a lot on the job, and most of it's ugly, but this was pretty bad."

"He seems so gentle. I'd expect any murder he committed to be virtually non-violent."

"There aren't many non-violent murders."

"Well, bloodless, anyway."

"This was anything but."

"Well, don't keep me in suspense. What did he do?"

"He used a knife," I said.

"And stabbed him?"

"Carved him," I said. "His lover was younger than Pollard, and I guess he was a good-looking man, but you couldn't prove it by me. What I saw looked like what's left of the turkey the day after Thanksgiving."

"Well, that's vivid enough," she said. "I have to say I get the picture."

"I was first on the scene except for the two uniforms who caught the squeal, and they were young enough to strike a cynical pose."

"While you were old enough not to. Did you throw up?"

"No, after a few years you just don't. But it was as bad as anything I'd ever seen."

Horton Pollard's villa was north of the city, and if it wasn't grand it was nevertheless beautiful, a white stuccoed gem set on a hillside with a commanding view of the valley. He showed us through the rooms, answered Elaine's questions about the paintings and furnishings, and accepted her explanation of why she couldn't stay for lunch. Or appeared to—as she rode off in the taxi that had brought us, something in his expression suggested for an instant that he felt slighted by her departure.

"We'll dine on the terrace," he said. "But what's the matter with me? I haven't offered you a drink. What will you have, Matthew? The bar's well stocked, although I don't know that Paolo has a very extensive repertoire of cocktails."

I said that any kind of sparkling water would be fine. He said something in Italian to his house boy, then gave me an appraising glance and asked me if I would want wine with our lunch.

I said I wouldn't. "I'm glad I thought to ask," he said. "I was going to open a bottle and let it breathe, but now it can just go on holding its breath. You used to drink, if I remember correctly."

"Yes, I did."

"The night it all happened," he said. "It seems to me you told me I looked as though I needed a drink. And I got out a bottle, and you poured drinks for both of us. I remember being surprised you were allowed to drink on duty."

"I wasn't," I said, "but I didn't always let that stop me."

"And now you don't drink at all?"

"I don't, but that's no reason why you shouldn't have wine with lunch."

"But I never do," he said. "I couldn't while I was locked up, and when I was released I found I didn't care for it, the taste or the physical sensation. I drank the odd glass of wine anyway, for a while, because I thought one couldn't be entirely civilized without it. Then I realized I didn't care. That's quite the nicest thing about age, perhaps the only good thing to be said for it. Increasingly, one ceases to care about more and more things, particularly the opinions of others. Different for you, though, wasn't it? You stopped because you had to."

"Yes."

"Do you miss it?"

"Now and then."

"I don't, but, then, I was never that fond of it. There was a time when I could distinguish different châteaux in a blind tasting, but the truth of the matter was that I never cared for any of them all that much, and after-dinner cognac gave me heartburn. And now I drink mineral water with my meals, and coffee after them. *Acqua minerale.* There's a favorite trattoria of mine where the owner calls it *acqua miserabile.* But he'd as soon sell me it as anything else. He doesn't care, and *I* shouldn't care if he did."

Lunch was simple but elegant—a green salad, ravioli with butter and sage, and a nice piece of fish. Our conversation was mostly about Italy, and I was sorry Elaine hadn't stayed to hear it. He had a lot to say—about the way art permeated everyday Florentine life, about the longstanding enthusiasm of the British upper classes for the city—and I found it absorbing enough, but it would have held more interest for her than for me.

Afterward Paolo cleared our dishes and served espresso. We fell silent, and I sipped my coffee and looked out at the view of the valley and wondered how long it would take for the eye to tire of it.

"I thought I would grow accustomed to it," he said, reading my mind. "But I haven't yet, and I don't think I ever will."

"How long have you been here?"

"Almost fifteen years. I came on a visit as soon as I could after my release."

"And you've never been back?"

He shook his head. "I came intending to stay, and once here I managed to arrange the necessary resident visa. It's not difficult if there's money, and I was fortunate. There's still plenty of money, and there always will be. I live well, but not terribly high. Even if I live longer than anyone should, there will be money sufficient to see me out."

"That makes it easier."

"It does," he agreed. "It didn't make the years inside any easier, I have to say that, but if I hadn't had money I might have spent them someplace even worse. Not that the place they put me was a pleasure dome."

"I suppose you were at a mental hospital."

"A facility for the criminally insane," he said, pronouncing the words precisely. "The phrase has a ring to it, doesn't it? And yet it was entirely appropriate. The act I performed was unquestionably criminal, and altogether insane."

He helped himself to more espresso. "I brought you here so that I could talk about it," he said. "Selfish of me, but that's part of being old. One becomes more selfish, or perhaps less concerned about concealing one's selfishness from oneself and others." He sighed. "One also becomes more direct, but in this instance it's hard to know where to start."

"Wherever you want," I suggested.

"With David, I suppose. Not the statue, though. The man."

"Maybe my memory's not all I like to think it is," I said. "Was your lover's name David? Because I could have sworn it was Robert. Robert Naismith, and there was a middle name, but that wasn't David, either."

"It was Paul," he said. "His name was Robert Paul Naismith. He wanted to be called Rob. I called him David sometimes, but he didn't care for that. In my mind, though, he would always be David."

I didn't say anything. A fly buzzed in a corner, then went still. The silence stretched.

Then he began to talk.

"I grew up in Buffalo," he said. "I don't know if you've ever been there. A very beautiful city, at least in its nicer sections. Wide streets lined with elms. Some fine public buildings, some notable private homes. Of course the elms are all lost to Dutch Elm disease, and the mansions on Delaware Avenue now house law firms and dental clinics, but everything changes, doesn't it? I've come round to the belief that it's supposed to, but that doesn't mean one has to like it.

"Buffalo hosted the Pan-American Exposition, which was even before my time. It was held in 1901, if I remember correctly, and several of the buildings raised for the occasion remain to this day. One of the nicest, built alongside the city's principal park, has long been the home of the Buffalo Historical Society, and houses their museum collection.

"Are you wondering where this is leading? There was, and doubtless still is, a circular drive at the Historical Building's front, and in the midst of it stood a bronze copy of Michelangelo's David. It might conceivably be a casting, though I think we can safely assume it to be just a copy. It's life-size, at any rate—or I should say actual size, as Michelangelo's statue is itself considerably larger than life, unless the young David was built more along the lines of his adversary Goliath.

"You saw the statue yesterday—although, as I said, that too was a copy. I don't know how much attention you paid to it, but I wonder if you know what the sculptor is supposed to have said when asked how he managed to create such a masterpiece. It's such a wonderful line it would almost have to be apocryphal.

" 'I looked at the marble,' Michelangelo is said to have said, 'and I cut away the part that wasn't David.' That's almost as delicious as the young Mozart explaining that musical composition is the easiest thing in the world, you have merely to write down the music you hear in your head. Who cares, really, if either of them ever said any such thing? If they didn't, well, they ought to have done, wouldn't you say?

"I've known that statue all my life. I can't recall when I first saw it, but it must have been on my first visit to the Historical Building, and that would have been at a very early age. Our house was on Nottingham Terrace, not a ten-minute walk from the Historical Building, and I went there innumerable times as a boy. And it seems to me I always responded to the David. The stance, the attitude, the uncanny combination of strength and vulnerability, of fragility and confidence. And, of course, the sheer physical beauty of the David, the sexuality—but it was a while before I was aware of that aspect of it, or before I let myself acknowledge my awareness.

"When we all turned sixteen and got driver's licenses, David took on new meaning in our lives. The circular drive, you see, was the lovers' lane of choice for young couples who needed privacy. It was a pleasant, parklike setting in a good part of town, unlike the few available alternatives in nasty neighborhoods down by the waterfront. Consequently, 'going to see David' became a euphemism for parking and making out—which, now that I think of it, are euphemisms themselves, aren't they?

"I saw a lot of David in my late teens. The irony, of course, is that I was far more drawn to his young masculine form than to the generous curves of the young women who were my companions on those visits. I was gay, it seems to me, from birth, but I didn't let myself know that. At first I denied the impulses. Later, when I learned to act on them—in Front Park, in the men's room at the Greyhound station—I denied that they meant anything. It was, I assured myself, a stage I was going through."

He pursed his lips, shook his head, sighed. "A lengthy stage," he said, "as I seem still to be going through it. I was aided in my denial by the fact that whatever I did with other young men was just an adjunct to my real life, which was manifestly normal. I went off to a good school, I came home at Christmas and during the summer, and wherever I was I enjoyed the company of women.

"Lovemaking in those years was usually a rather incomplete affair. Girls made a real effort to remain virginal, at least in a strictly technical sense, if not until marriage then until they were in what we nowadays call a committed relationship. I don't remember what we called it then, but I suspect it was a somewhat less cumbersome phrase.

"Still, sometimes one went all the way, and on those occasions I acquitted myself well enough. None of my partners had cause to complain. I could do it, you see, and I enjoyed it, and if it was less thrilling than what I found with male partners, well, chalk it up to the lure of the forbidden. It didn't have to mean there was anything *wrong* with me. It didn't mean I was *different* in any fundamental way.

"I led a normal life, Matthew. I would say I was determined to lead a normal life, but it never seemed to require much in the way of determination. During my senior year at college I became engaged to a girl I'd known literally all my life. Our parents were friends and we'd grown up together. I graduated and we were married. I took an advanced degree. My field was art history, as you may remember, and I managed to get an appointment to the faculty of the University of Buffalo. SUNY Buffalo, they call it now, but that was years before it became a part of the state university. It was just plain UB, with most of its student body drawn from the city and environs.

"We lived at first in an apartment near the campus, but then both sets of parents ponied up and we moved to a small house on Hallam, just about equidistant between the houses each of us had grown up in.

"It wasn't far from the statue of David, either."

He led a normal life, he explained. Fathered two children. Took up golf and joined the country club. He came into some family money, and a textbook he authored brought in royalties that grew more substantial each year. As the years passed, it became increasingly easy to believe that his relations with other men had indeed been a stage, and one he had essentially outgrown.

"I still felt things," he said, "but the need to act on them seemed to have passed. I might be struck by the physical appearance of one of my students, say, but I'd never do anything about it, or even seriously consider doing anything about it. I told myself my admiration was aesthetic, a natural response to male beauty. In youth, hormone-driven as one is, I'd confused this with actual sexual desire. Now I could recognize it for the innocent and asexual phenomenon it was."

Which was not to say that he'd given up his little adventures entirely.

"I would be invited somewhere to attend a conference," he said, "or to give a guest lecture. I'd be in another city where I didn't know anyone and nobody knew me. And I would have had a few drinks, and I'd feel the urge for some excitement. And I could tell myself that, while a liaison with another woman would be a betrayal of my wife and a violation of my marital vows, the same could hardly be said for some innocent sport with another man. So I'd go to the sort of bar one goes to—they were never hard to find, even in those closeted days, even in provincial cities and college towns. And, once there, it was never hard to find someone."

He was silent for a moment, gazing off toward the horizon.

"Then I walked into a bar in Madison, Wisconsin," he said, "and there he was."

"Robert Paul Naismith."

"David," he said. "That's who *I* saw, that's the youth on whom my eyes fastened the instant I cleared the threshold. I can remember the moment, you see. I can see him now exactly as I saw him then. He was wearing a dark silk shirt and tan trousers and loafers without socks, which no one wore in those days. He was standing at the bar with a drink in his hand, and his physique and the way he stood, the stance, the attitude—he was Michelangelo's David. More than that, he was *my* David. He was my ideal, he was the object of a lifelong quest I hadn't even known I was on, and I drank him in with my eyes and I was lost."

"Just like that," I said.

"Oh, yes," he agreed. "Just like that."

He was silent, and I wondered if he was waiting for me to prompt him. I decided he was not. He seemed to be choosing to remain in the memory for a moment.

Then he said, "Quite simply, I had never been in love with anybody. I have come to believe that it is a form of insanity. Not to love, to care deeply for another. That seems to me to be quite sane, and even ennobling. I loved my parents, certainly, and in a somewhat different way I loved my wife.

"This was categorically different. This was obsessive. This was preoccupation. It was the collector's passion: I must have this painting, this statue, this postage stamp. I must embrace it, I must own it utterly. It and it alone will complete me. It will change my own nature. It will make me worthwhile.

"It wasn't sex, not really. I won't say sex had nothing to do with it. I was attracted to David as I'd never been attracted to anyone before. But at the same time I felt less driven sexually than I had on occasion in the past. I wanted to possess David. If I could do that, if I could make him entirely mine, it scarcely mattered if I had sex with him."

He fell silent, and this time I decided he was waiting to be prompted. I said, "What happened?"

"I threw my life over," he said. "On some flimsy pretext or other I stayed on in Madison for a week after the conference ended. Then I flew with David to New York and bought an apartment, the top floor of a brownstone in Turtle Bay. And then I flew back to Buffalo, alone, and told my wife I was leaving her."

He lowered his eyes. "I didn't want to hurt her," he said, "but of course I hurt her badly and deeply. She was not completely surprised, I don't believe, to learn there was a man involved. She'd inferred that much about me over the years, and probably saw it as part of the package, the downside of having a husband with an aesthetic sensibility.

"But she thought I cared for her, and I made it very clear that I did not. She was a woman who had never hurt anyone, and I caused her a good deal of pain, and I regret that and always will. It seems to me a far blacker sin than the one I served time for.

"Enough. I left her and moved to New York. Of course I resigned my tenured professorship at UB. I had connections throughout the academic world, to be sure, and a decent if not glorious reputation, so I might have found something at Columbia or NYU. But the scandal I'd created made that less likely, and anyway I no longer gave a damn for teaching. I just wanted to live, and enjoy my life.

"There was money enough to make that possible. We lived well. Too well, really. Not wisely but too well. Good restaurants every night, fine wines with dinner. Season tickets to the opera and the ballet. Summers in the Pines. Winters in Barbados or Bali. Trips to London and Paris and Rome. And the company, in town or abroad, of other rich queens."

"And?"

"And it went on like that," he said. He folded his hands in his lap, and a little smile played on his lips. "It went on, and then one day I picked up a knife and killed him. You know that part, Matthew. It's where you came in."

"Yes."

"But you don't know why."

"No, that never came out. Or if it did I missed it."

He shook his head. "It never came out. I didn't offer a defense, and I certainly didn't provide an explanation. But can you guess?"

"Why you killed him? I have no idea."

"But you must have come to know some of the reasons people have for killing other people? Why don't you humor an old sinner and try to guess. Prove to me that my motive was not unique after all."

"The reasons that come to mind are the obvious ones," I said, "and that probably rules them out. Let me see. He was leaving you. He was unfaithful to you. He had fallen in love with someone else."

"He would never have left," he said. "He adored the life we led and knew he could never live half so well with someone else. He would never fall in love with anyone else any more than he could have fallen in love with me. David was in love with himself. And of course he was unfaithful, and had been from the beginning, but I had never expected him to be otherwise."

"You realized you'd thrown your life away on him," I said, "and hated him for it."

"I *had* thrown my life away, but I didn't regret it. I'd been living a lie, and what loss to toss it aside? While jetting off to Paris for a weekend, does one long for the gentle pleasures of a classroom in Buffalo? Some may, for all I know. I never did."

I was ready to quit, but he insisted I come up with a few more guesses. They were all off the mark.

He said, "Give up? All right, I'll tell you. He changed."

"He changed?"

"When I met him," he said, "my David was the most beautiful creature I had ever set eyes on, the absolute embodiment of my lifelong ideal. He was slender but muscular, vulnerable yet strong. He was—well, go back to the San Marco piazza and look at the statue. Michelangelo got it just right. That's what he looked like."

"And then what? He got older?"

He set his jaw. "Everyone gets older," he said, "except for the ones who die young. It's unfair, but there's nothing for it. David didn't merely age. He coarsened. He thickened. He ate too much and drank too much and stayed up too late and took too many drugs. He put on weight. He got bloated. He grew jowly, and got pouchy under his eyes. His muscles wasted beneath their coating of fat and his flesh sagged.

"It didn't happen overnight. But that's how I experienced it, because the process was well along before I let myself see it. Finally I couldn't help but see it.

"I couldn't bear to look at him. Before I had been unable to take my eyes off him, and now I found myself averting my gaze. I felt betrayed. I fell in love with a Greek god, and watched as he turned into a Roman emperor."

"And you killed him for that?"

"I wasn't trying to kill him."

I looked at him.

"Oh, I suppose I was, really. I'd been drinking, we'd both been drinking, and we'd had an argument, and I was angry. I don't suppose I was too far gone to know that he'd be dead when I was done, and that I'd have killed him. But that wasn't the point."

"It wasn't?"

"He passed out," he said. "He was lying there, naked, reeking of the wine seeping out of his pores, this great expanse of bloated flesh as white as marble. I suppose I hated him for having thus transformed himself, and I know I hated myself for having been an agent of his transformation. And I decided to do something about it."

He shook his head, and sighed deeply. "I went into the kitchen," he said, "and I came back with a knife. And I thought of the boy I'd seen that first night in Madison, and I thought of Michelangelo. And I tried to be Michelangelo."

I must have looked puzzled. He said, "Don't you remember? I took the knife and cut away the part that wasn't David."

It was a few days later in Rome when I recounted all this to Elaine. We were at an outdoor café near the Spanish Steps. "All those years," I said, "I took it for granted he was trying to destroy his lover. That's what mutilation generally is, the expression of a desire to annihilate. But he wasn't trying to disfigure him, he was trying to *re*figure him."

"He was just a few years ahead of his time," she said. "Now they call it liposuction and charge the earth for it. I'll tell you one thing. As soon as we get back I'm going straight from the airport to the gym, before all this pasta becomes a permanent part of me. I'm not taking any chances."

"I don't think you've got anything to worry about."

"That's reassuring. How awful, though. How godawful for both of them."

"The things people do."

"You said it. Well, what do *you* want to do? We could sit around feeling sorry for two men and the mess they made of their lives, or we could go back to the hotel and do something life-affirming. You tell me."

"It's a tough one," I said. "How soon do you need my decision?"

Let's Get Lost

When the phone call came I was parked in front of the television set in the front room, nursing a glass of bourbon and watching the Yankees. It's funny what you remember and what you don't. I remember that Thurman Munson had just hit a long foul that missed being a home run by no more than a foot, but I don't remember who they were playing, or even what kind of a season they had that year.

I remember that the bourbon was J. W. Dant, and that I was drinking it on the rocks, but of course I would remember that. I always remembered what I was drinking, though I didn't always remember why.

The boys had stayed up to watch the opening innings with me, but tomorrow was a school day, and Anita took them upstairs and tucked them in while I freshened my drink and sat down again. The ice was mostly melted by the time Munson hit his long foul, and I was still shaking my head at that when the phone rang. I let it ring, and Anita answered it and came in to tell me it was for me. Somebody's secretary, she said.

I picked up the phone, and a woman's voice, crisply professional, said, "Mr. Scudder, I'm calling for Mr. Alan Herdig of Herdig and Crowell."

"I see," I said, and listened while she elaborated, and estimated just how much time it would take me to get to their offices. I hung up and made a face.

"You have to go in?"

I nodded. "It's about time we had a break in this one," I said. "I don't expect to get much sleep tonight, and I've got a court appearance tomorrow morning."

"I'll get you a clean shirt. Sit down. You've got time to finish your drink, don't you?"

I always had time for that.

Years ago, this was. Nixon was president, a couple of years into his first term. I was a detective with the NYPD, attached to the Sixth Precinct in Greenwich Village. I had a house on Long Island with two cars in the garage, a Ford wagon for Anita and a beat-up Plymouth Valiant for me.

Traffic was light on the LIE, and I didn't pay much attention to the speed limit.

I didn't know many cops who did. Nobody ever ticketed a brother officer. I made good time, and it must have been somewhere around a quarter to ten when I left the car at a bus stop on First Avenue. I had a card on the dashboard that would keep me safe from tickets and tow trucks.

The best thing about enforcing the laws is that you don't have to pay a lot of attention to them yourself.

Her doorman rang upstairs to announce me, and she met me at the door with a drink. I don't remember what she was wearing, but I'm sure she looked good in it. She always did.

She said, "I would never call you at home. But it's business."

"Yours or mine?"

"Maybe both. I got a call from a client. A Madison Avenue guy, maybe an agency vice-president. Suits from Tripler's, season tickets for the Rangers, house in Connecticut."

"And?"

"And didn't I say something about knowing a cop? Because he and some friends were having a friendly card game and something happened to one of them."

"Something happened? Something happens to a friend of yours, you take him to a hospital. Or was it too late for that?"

"He didn't say, but that's what I heard. It sounds to me as though somebody had an accident and they need somebody to make it disappear."

"And you thought of me."

"Well," she said.

She'd thought of me before, in a similar connection. Another client of hers, a Wall Street warrior, had had a heart attack in her bed one afternoon. Most men will tell you that's how they want to go, and perhaps it's as good a way as any, but it's not all that convenient for the people who have to clean up after them, especially when the bed in question belongs to some working girl.

When the equivalent happens in the heroin trade, it's good PR. One junkie checks out with an overdose and the first thing all his buddies want to know is where did he get the stuff and how can they cop some themselves. Because, hey, it must be good, right? A hooker, on the other hand, has less to gain from being listed as cause of death. And I suppose she felt a professional responsibility, if you want to call it that, to spare the guy and his family embarrassment. So I made him disappear, and left him fully dressed in an alley down in the financial district. I called it in anonymously and went back to her apartment to claim my reward.

"I've got the address," she said now. "Do you want to have a look? Or should I tell them I couldn't reach you?"

I kissed her, and we clung to each other for a long moment. When I came up for air I said, "It'd be a lie."

"I beg your pardon?"

"Telling them you couldn't reach me. You can always reach me."

"You're a sweetie."

"You better give me that address," I said.

I retrieved my car from the bus stop and left it in another one a dozen or so blocks uptown. The address I was looking for was a brownstone in the East Sixties. A shop with handbags and briefcases in the window occupied the storefront, flanked by a travel agent and a men's clothier. There were four doorbells in the vestibule, and I rang the third one and heard the intercom activated, but didn't hear anyone say anything. I was reaching to ring a second time when the buzzer sounded. I pushed the door open and walked up three flights of carpeted stairs.

Out of habit, I stood to the side when I knocked. I didn't really expect a bullet, and what came through the door was a voice, pitched low, asking who was there.

"Police," I said. "I understand you've got a situation here."

There was a pause. Then a voice—maybe the same one, maybe not—said, "I don't understand. Has there been a complaint, Officer?"

They wanted a cop, but not just any cop. "My name's Scudder," I said. "Elaine Mardell said you could use some help."

The lock turned and the door opened. Two men were standing there, dressed for the office in dark suits and white shirts and ties. I looked past them and saw two more men, one in a suit, the other in gray slacks and a blue blazer. They looked to be in their early to mid forties, which made them ten to fifteen years older than me.

I was what, thirty-two that year? Something like that.

"Come on in," one of them said. "Careful."

I didn't know what I was supposed to be careful of, but found out when I gave the door a shove and it stopped after a few inches. There was a body on the floor, a man, curled on his side. One arm was flung up over his head, the other bent at his side, the hand inches from the handle of the knife. It was an easy-open stiletto and it was buried hilt-deep in his chest.

I pushed the door shut and knelt down for a close look at him, and heard the bolt turn as one of them locked the door.

The dead man was around their age, and had been similarly dressed until he took off his suit jacket and loosened his tie. His hair was a little longer than theirs, perhaps because he was losing hair on the crown and wanted to conceal the bald spot. Everyone tries that, and it never works.

I didn't feel for a pulse. A touch of his forehead established that he was too cold to have one. And I hadn't really needed to touch him to know that he was dead. Hell, I knew that much before I parked the car.

Still, I took some time looking him over. Without looking up I asked what had happened. There was a pause while they decided who would reply, and then the same man who'd questioned me through the closed door said, "We don't really know."

"You came home and found him here?"

"Hardly that. We were playing a few hands of poker, the five of us. Then the doorbell rang and Phil went to see who it was."

I nodded at the dead man. "That's Phil there?"

Someone said it was. "He'd folded already," the man in the blazer added.

"And the rest of you fellows were still in the middle of a hand."

"That's right."

"So he—Phil?"

"Yes, Phil."

"Phil went to the door while you finished the hand."

"Yes."

"And?"

"And we didn't really see what happened," one of the suits said.

"We were in the middle of a hand," another explained, "and you can't really see much from where we were sitting."

"At the card table," I said.

"That's right."

The table was set up at the far end of the living room. It was a poker table, with a green baize top and wells for chips and glasses. I walked over and looked at it.

"Seats eight," I said.

"Yes."

"But there were only the five of you. Or were there other players as well?"

"No, just the five of us."

"The four of you and Phil."

"Yes."

"And Phil was clear across the room answering the door, and one or two of you would have had your backs to it, and all four of you would have been more interested in the way the hand was going than who was at the door." They nodded along, pleased at my ability to grasp all this. "But you must have heard something that made you look up."

"Yes," the blazer said. "Phil cried out."

"What did he say?"

" 'No!' or 'Stop!' or something like that. That got our attention, and we got out of our chairs and looked over there, but I don't think any of us got a look at the guy."

"The guy who . . ."

"Stabbed Phil."

"He must have been out the door before you had a chance to look at him."

"Yes."

"And pulled the door shut after him."

"Or Phil pushed it shut while he was falling."

I said, "Stuck out a hand to break his fall . . ."

"Right."

"And the door swung shut, and he went right on falling."

"Right."

I retraced my steps to the spot where the body lay. It was a nice apartment, I noted, spacious and comfortably furnished. It felt like a bachelor's full-time residence, not a married commuter's pied-à-terre. There were books on the bookshelves, framed prints on the walls, logs in the fireplace. Opposite the fireplace, a two-by-three throw rug looked out of place atop a large Oriental carpet. I had a hunch I knew what it was doing there.

But I walked past it and knelt down next to the corpse. "Stabbed in the heart," I noted. "Death must have been instantaneous, or the next thing to it. I don't suppose he had any last words."

"No."

"He crumpled up and hit the floor and never moved."

"That's right."

I got to my feet. "Must have been a shock."

"A terrible shock."

"How come you didn't call it in?"

"Call it in?"

"Call the police," I said. "Or an ambulance, get him to a hospital."

"A hospital couldn't do him any good," the blazer said. "I mean, you could tell he was dead."

"No pulse, no breathing."

"Right."

"Still, you must have known you're supposed to call the cops when something like this happens."

"Yes, of course."

"But you didn't."

They looked at each other. It might have been interesting to see what they came up with, but I made it easy for them.

"You must have been scared," I said.

"Well, of course."

"Guy goes to answer the door and the next thing you know he's dead on the floor. That's got to be an upsetting experience, especially taking into account that you don't know who killed him or why. Or do you have an idea?"

They didn't.

"I don't suppose this is Phil's apartment."

"No."

Of course not. If it was, they'd have long since gone their separate ways.

"Must be yours," I told the blazer, and enjoyed it when his eyes widened. He allowed that it was, and asked how I knew. I didn't tell him he was the one man in the room without a wedding ring, or that I figured he'd changed from a business suit to slightly more casual clothes on his return home, while the others were still wearing what they'd worn to the office that morning. I just muttered something about policemen developing certain instincts, and let him think I was a genius.

I asked if any of them had known Phil very well, and wasn't surprised to learn that they hadn't. He was a friend of a friend of a friend, someone said, and did something on Wall Street.

"So he wasn't a regular at the table."

"No."

"This wasn't his first time, was it?"

"His second," somebody said.

"First time was last week?"

"No, two weeks ago. He didn't play last week."

"Two weeks ago. How'd he do?"

Elaborate shrugs. The consensus seemed to be that he might have won a few dollars, but nobody had paid much attention.

"And this evening?"

"I think he was about even. If he was ahead it couldn't have been more than a few dollars."

"What kind of stakes do you play for?"

"It's a friendly game. One-two-five in stud games. In draw it's two dollars before the draw, five after."

"So you can win or lose what, a couple of hundred?"

"That would be a big loss."

"Or a big win," I said.

"Well, yes. Either way."

I knelt down next to the corpse and patted him down. Cards in his wallet identified him as Philip I. Ryman, with an address in Teaneck.

"Lived in Jersey," I said. "And you say he worked on Wall Street?"

"Somewhere downtown."

I picked up his left hand. His watch was Rolex, and I suppose it must have been a real one; this was before the profusion of fakes. He had what looked like a wedding band on the appropriate finger, but I saw that it was in fact a large silver or white-gold ring that had gotten turned around, so that the large part was on the palm side of his hand. It looked like an unfinished signet ring, waiting for an initial to be carved into its gleaming surface.

I straightened up. "Well," I said, "I'd say it's a good thing you called me."

"There are a couple of problems," I told them. "A couple of things that could pop up like a red flag for a responding officer or a medical examiner."

"Like . . ."

"Like the knife," I said. "Phil opened the door and the killer stabbed him once and left, was out the door and down the stairs before the body hit the carpet."

"Maybe not that fast," one of them said, "but it was pretty quick. Before we knew what had happened, certainly."

"I appreciate that," I said, "but the thing is it's an unusual MO. The killer didn't take time to make sure his victim was dead, and you can't take that for granted when you stick a knife in someone. And he left the knife in the wound."

"He wouldn't do that?"

"Well, it might be traced to him. All he has to do to avoid that chance is take it away with him. Besides, it's a weapon. Suppose someone comes chasing after him? He might need that knife again."

"Maybe he panicked."

"Maybe he did," I agreed. "There's another thing, and a medical examiner would notice this if a reporting officer didn't. The body's been moved."

Interesting the way their eyes jumped all over the place. They looked at each other, they looked at me, they looked at Phil on the floor.

"Blood pools in a corpse," I said. "Lividity's the word they use for it. It looks to me as though Phil fell forward and wound up face downward. He probably fell against the door as it was closing, and slid down and wound up on his face. So you couldn't get the door open, and you needed to, so eventually you moved him."

Eyes darted. The host, the one in the blazer, said, "We knew you'd have to come in."

"Right."

"And we couldn't have him lying against the door."

"Of course not," I agreed. "But all of that's going to be hard to explain. You didn't call the cops right away, and you did move the body. They'll have some questions for you."

"Maybe you could give us an idea what questions to expect."

"I might be able to do better than that," I said. "It's irregular, and I probably shouldn't, but I'm going to suggest an action we can take."

"Oh?"

"I'm going to suggest we stage something," I said. "As it stands, Phil was stabbed to death by an unknown person who escaped without anybody getting a look at him. He may never turn up, and if he doesn't, the cops are going to look hard at the four of you."

"Jesus," somebody said.

"It would be a lot easier on everybody," I said, "if Phil's death was an accident."

"An accident?"

"I don't know if Phil has a sheet or not," I said. "He looks vaguely familiar to me, but lots of people do. He's got a gambler's face, even in death, the kind of face you expect to see in an OTB parlor. He may have worked on Wall Street, it's possible, because cheating at cards isn't necessarily a full-time job."

"Cheating at cards?"

"That would be my guess. His ring's a mirror; turned around, it gives him a peek at what's coming off the bottom of the deck. It's just one way to cheat, and he probably had thirty or forty others. You think of this as a social event, a once-a-week friendly game, a five-dollar limit and, what, three raises maximum? The wins and losses pretty much average out over the course of a year, and nobody ever gets hurt too bad. Is that about right?"

"Yes."

"So you wouldn't expect to attract a mechanic, a card cheat, but he's not looking for the high rollers, he's looking for a game just like yours, where it's all good friends and nobody's got reason to get suspicious, and he can pick up two or three hundred dollars in a couple of hours without running any risks. I'm sure you're all decent poker players, but would you think to look for bottom dealing or a cold deck? Would you know if somebody was dealing seconds, even if you saw it in slow motion?"

"Probably not."

"Phil was probably doing a little cheating," I went on, "and that's probably what he did two weeks ago, and nobody spotted him. But he evidently crossed someone else somewhere along the line. Maybe he pulled the same tricks in a bigger game, or maybe he was just sleeping in the wrong bed, but someone knew he was coming here, turned up after the game was going, and rang the bell. He would have come in and called Phil out, but he didn't have to, because Phil answered the door."

"And the guy had a knife."

"Right," I said. "That's how it was, but it's another way an investigating officer might get confused. How did the guy know Phil was going to come to the door? Most times the host opens the door, and the rest of the time it's only one chance in five it'll be Phil. Would the guy be ready, knife in hand? And would Phil just open up without making sure who it was?"

I held up a hand. "I know, that's how it happened. But I think it might be worth your while to stage a more plausible scenario, something a lot easier for the cops to come to terms with. Suppose we forget the intruder. Suppose the story we tell is that Phil was cheating at cards and someone called him on it. Maybe some strong words were said and threats were exchanged. Phil went into his pocket and came out with a knife."

"That's . . ."

"You're going to say it's far-fetched," I said, "but he'd probably have some sort of weapon on him, something to intimidate anyone who did catch him cheating. He pulls the knife and you react. Say you turn the table over on him. The whole thing goes crashing to the floor and he winds up sticking his own knife in his chest."

I walked across the room. "We'll have to move the table," I went on. "There's not really room for that sort of struggle where you've got it set up, but suppose it was right in the middle of the room, under the light fixture? Actually that would be a logical place for it." I bent down, picked up the throw rug, tossed it aside. "You'd move the rug if you had the table here." I bent down, poked at a stain. "Looks like somebody had a nosebleed, and fairly recently, or you'd have had the carpet cleaned by now. That can fit right in, come to think of it. Phil wouldn't have bled much from a stab wound to the heart, but there'd have been a little blood loss, and I didn't spot any blood at all where the body's lying now. If we put him in the right spot, they'll most likely assume it's his blood, and it might even turn out to be the same blood type. I mean, there are only so many blood types, right?"

I looked at them one by one. "I think it'll work," I said. "To sweeten it, we'll tell them you're friends of mine. I play in this game now and then, although I wasn't here when Phil was. And when the accident happened the first thing you thought of was to call me, and that's why there was a delay reporting the incident. You'd reported it to me, and I was on my way here, and you figured that was enough." I stopped for breath, took a moment to look each of them in the eye. "We'll want things arranged just right, " I went on, "and it'll be a good idea to spread a little cash around. But I think this one'll go into the books as accidental death."

"They must have thought you were a genius," Elaine said.

"Or an idiot savant," I said. "Here I was, telling them to fake exactly what had in fact happened. At the beginning I think they may have thought I was blundering into an unwitting reconstruction of the incident, but by the end they probably figured out that I knew where I was going."

"But you never spelled it out."

"No, we maintained the fiction that some intruder stuck the knife in Ryman, and we were tampering with the evidence."

"When actually you were restoring it. What tipped you off?"

"The body blocking the door. The lividity pattern was wrong, but I was suspicious even before I confirmed that. It's just too cute, a body positioned where it'll keep a door from opening. And the table was in the wrong place, and the little rug had to be covering something, or why else would it be where it was? So I pictured the room the right way, and then everything sort of filled in. But it didn't take a genius. Any cop would have seen some wrong things, and he'd have asked a few hard questions, and the four of them would have caved in."

"And then what? Murder indictments?"

"Most likely, but they're respectable businessmen and the deceased was a scumbag, so they'd have been up on manslaughter charges and probably would have pleaded to a lesser charge. Still, a verdict of accidental death saves them a lot of aggravation."

"And that's what really happened?"

"I can't see any of those men packing a switch knife, or pulling it at a card table. Nor does it seem likely they could have taken it away from Ryman and killed him with it. I think he went ass over teakettle with the table coming down on top of him and maybe one or two of the guys falling on top of the table. And he was still holding the knife, and he stuck it in his own chest."

"And the cops who responded—"

"Well, I called it in for them, so I more or less selected the responding officers. I picked guys you can work with."

"And worked with them."

"Everybody came out okay," I said. "I collected a few dollars from the four players, and I laid off some of it where it would do the most good."

"Just to smooth things out."

"That's right."

"But you didn't lay off all of it."

"No," I said, "not quite all of it. Give me your hand. Here."

"What's this?"

"A finder's fee."

"Three hundred dollars?"

"Ten percent," I said.

"Gee," she said. "I didn't expect anything."

"What do you do when somebody gives you money?"

"I say thank you," she said, "and I put it someplace safe. This is great. You get them to tell the truth, and everybody gets paid. Do you have to go back to Syosset right away? Because Chet Baker's at Mikell's tonight."

"We could go hear him," I said, "and then we could come back here. I told Anita I'd probably have to stay over."

"Oh, goodie," she said. "Do you suppose he'll sing 'Let's Get Lost'?"

"I wouldn't be surprised," I said. "Not if you ask him nice."

I don't remember if he sang it or not, but I heard it again just the other day on the radio. He'd ended abruptly, that aging boy with the sweet voice and sweeter horn. He went out a hotel room window somewhere in Europe, and most people figured he'd had help. He'd crossed up a lot of people along the way and always got away with it, but then that's usually the way it works. You dodge all the bullets but the last one.

"Let's Get Lost." I heard the song, and not twenty-four hours later I picked up the *Times* and read an obit for a commodities trader named P. Gordon Fawcett, who'd succumbed to prostate cancer. The name rang a bell, but it took me hours to place it. He was the guy in the blazer, the man in whose apartment Phil Ryman stabbed himself.

Funny how things work out. It wasn't too long after that poker game that another incident precipitated my departure from the NYPD, and from my marriage. Elaine and I lost track of each other, and caught up with each other some years down the line, by which time I'd found a way to live without drinking. So we got lost and found—and now we're married. Who'd have guessed?

My life's vastly different these days, but I can imagine being called in on just that sort of emergency—a man dead on the carpet, a knife in his chest, in the company of four poker players who only wish he'd disappear. As I said, my life's different, and I suppose I'm different myself. So I'd almost certainly handle it differently now, and what I'd probably do is call it in immediately and let the cops deal with it.

Still, I always liked the way that one worked out. I walked in on a cover-up, and what I did was cover up the cover-up. And in the process I wound up with the truth. Or an approximation of it, at least, and isn't that as much as you can expect to get? Isn't that enough?

A Moment of Wrong Thinking

Monica said, "What kind of a gun? A man shoots himself in his living room, surrounded by his nearest and dearest, and you want to know what kind of a gun he used?"

"I just wondered," I said.

Monica rolled her eyes. She's one of Elaine's oldest friends. They were in high school together, in Rego Park, and they never lost touch over the years. Elaine spent a lot of years as a call girl, and Monica, who was never in the life herself, seemed to have no difficulty accepting that. Elaine, for her part, had no judgment on Monica's predilection for dating married men.

She was with the current one that evening. The four of us had gone to a revival of *Allegro*, the Rodgers and Hammerstein show that hadn't been a big hit the first time around. From there we went to Paris Green for a late supper. We talked about the show and speculated on reasons for its limited success. The songs were good, we agreed, and I was old enough to remember hearing "A Fellow Needs a Girl" on the radio. Elaine said she had a Lisa Kirk LP, and one of the cuts was "The Gentleman Is a Dope." That number, she said, had stopped the show during its initial run, and launched Lisa Kirk.

Monica said she'd love to hear it sometime. Elaine said all she had to do was find the record and then find something to play it on. Monica said she still had a turntable for LPs.

Monica's guy didn't say anything, and I had the feeling he didn't know who Lisa Kirk was, or why he had to go through all this just to get laid. His name was Doug Halley—like the comet, he'd said—and he did something in Wall Street. Whatever it was, he did well enough at it to keep his second wife and their kids in a house in Pound Ridge, in Westchester County, while he was putting the kids from his first marriage through college. He had a boy at Bowdoin, we'd learned, and a girl who'd just started at Colgate.

We got as much conversational mileage as we could out of Lisa Kirk, and the drinks came—Perrier for me, cranberry juice for Elaine and Monica, and a Stolichnaya martini for Halley. He'd hesitated for a beat before ordering it—Monica would surely have told him I was a sober alcoholic, and even if she hadn't he'd have noted that he was the only one drinking—and I could almost hear him think it through and decide the hell with it. I was just as glad he'd ordered the drink. He looked as though he needed it, and when it came he drank deep.

It was about then that Monica mentioned the fellow who'd shot himself. It had happened the night before, too late to make the morning papers, and Monica had seen the coverage that afternoon on New York One. A man in Inwood, in the course of a social evening at his own home, with friends and family members present, had drawn a gun, ranted about his financial situation and everything that was wrong with the world, and then stuck the gun in his mouth and blown his brains out.

"What kind of a gun," Monica said again. "It's a guy thing, isn't it? There's not a woman in the world who would ask that question."

"A woman would ask what he was wearing," Halley said.

"No," Elaine said. "Who cares what he was wearing? A woman would ask what his wife was wearing."

"A look of horror would be my guess," Monica said. "Can you imagine? You're having a nice evening with friends and your husband shoots himself in front of everybody?"

"They didn't show it, did they?"

"They didn't interview her on camera, but they did talk with some man who was there and saw the whole thing."

Halley said that it would have been a bigger story if they'd had the wife on camera, and we started talking about the media and how intrusive they'd become. And we stayed with that until they brought us our food.

When we got home Elaine said, "The man who shot himself. When you asked if they showed it, you didn't mean an interview with the wife. You wanted to know if they showed him doing it."

"These days," I said, "somebody's almost always got a camcorder running. But I didn't really think anybody had the act on tape."

"Because it would have been a bigger story."

"That's right. The play a story gets depends on what they've got to show you. It would have been a little bigger than it was if they'd managed to interview the wife, but it would have been everybody's lead story all day long if they could have actually shown him doing it."

"Still, you asked."

"Idly," I said. "Making conversation."

"Yeah, right. And you want to know what kind of gun he used. Just being a guy, and talking guy talk. Because you liked Doug so much, and wanted to bond with him."

"Oh, I was crazy about him. Where does she find them?"

"I don't know," she said, "but I think she's got radar. If there's a jerk out there, and if he's married, she homes in on him. What did you care what kind of gun it was?"

"What I was wondering," I said, "was whether it was a revolver or an automatic."

She thought about it. "And if they showed him doing it, you could look at the film and know what kind of a gun it was."

"Anybody could."

"I couldn't," she said. "Anyway, what difference does it make?"

"Probably none."

"Oh?"

"It reminded me of a case we had," I said. "Ages ago."

"Back when you were a cop, and I was a cop's girlfriend."

I shook my head. "Only the first half. I was on the force, but you and I hadn't met yet. I was still wearing a uniform, and it would be a while before I got my gold shield. And we hadn't moved to Long Island yet, we were still living in Brooklyn."

"You and Anita and the boys."

"Was Andy even born yet? No, he couldn't have been, because she was pregnant with him when we bought the house in Syosset. We probably had Mike by then, but what difference does it make? It wasn't about them. It was about the poor son of a bitch in Park Slope who shot himself."

"And did he use a revolver or an automatic?"

"An automatic. He was a World War Two vet, and this was the gun he'd brought home with him. It must have been a forty-five."

"And he stuck it in his mouth and—"

"Put it to his temple. Putting it in your mouth, I think it was cops who made that popular."

"Popular?"

"You know what I mean. The expression caught on, 'eating your gun,' and you started seeing more civilian suicides who took that route." I fell silent, remembering. "I was partnered with Vince Mahaffey. I've told you about him."

"He smoked those little cigars."

"Guinea-stinkers, he called them. DeNobilis was the brand name, and they were these nasty little things that looked as though they'd passed through the digestive system of a cat. I don't think they could have smelled any worse if they had. Vince smoked them all day long, and he ate like a pig and drank like a fish."

"The perfect role model."

"Vince was all right," I said. "I learned a hell of a lot from Vince."

"Are you gonna tell me the story?"

"You want to hear it?"

She got comfortable on the couch. "Sure," she said. "I like it when you tell me stories."

It was a week night, I remembered, and the moon was full. It seems to me it was in the spring, but I could be wrong about that part.

Mahaffey and I were in a radio car. I was driving when the call came in, and he rang in and said we'd take this one. It was in the Slope. I don't remember the address, but wherever it was we weren't far from it, and I drove there and we went in.

Park Slope's a very desirable area now, but this was before the gentrification process got underway, and the Slope was still a working-class neighborhood, and predominantly Irish. The house we were directed to was one of a row of identical brownstone houses, four stories tall, two apartments to a floor. The vestibule was a half-flight up from street level, and a man was standing in the doorway, waiting for us.

"You want the Conways," he said. "Two flights up and on your left."

"You're a neighbor?"

"Downstairs of them," he said. "It was me called it in. My wife's with her now, the poor woman. He was a bastard, that husband of hers."

"You didn't get along?"

"Why would you say that? He was a good neighbor."

"Then how did he get to be a bastard?"

"To do what he did," the man said darkly. "You want to kill yourself, Jesus, it's an unforgivable sin, but it's a man's own business, isn't it?" He shook his head. "But do it in private, for God's sake. Not with your wife looking on. As long as the poor woman lives, that's her last memory of her husband."

We climbed the stairs. The building was in good repair, but drab, and the stairwell smelled of cabbage and of mice. The cooking smells in tenements have changed over the years, with the ethnic makeup of their occupants. Cabbage was what you used to smell in Irish neighborhoods. I suppose it's still much in evidence in Greenpoint and Brighton Beach, where new arrivals from Poland and Russia reside. And I'm sure the smells are very different in the stairwells of buildings housing immigrants from Asia and Africa and Latin America, but I suspect the mouse smell is there, too.

Halfway up the second flight of stairs, we met a woman on her way down. "Mary Frances!" she called upstairs. "It's the police!" She turned to us. "She's in the back," she said, "with her kids, the poor darlings. It's just at the top of the stairs, on your left. You can walk right in."

The door of the Conway apartment was ajar. Mahaffey knocked on it, then pushed it open when the knock went unanswered. We walked in and there he was, a middle-aged man in dark blue trousers and a white cotton tank-top undershirt. He'd nicked himself shaving that morning, but that was the least of his problems.

He was sprawled in an easy chair facing the television set. He'd fallen over on his left side, and there was a large hole in his right temple, the skin scorched around the entry wound. His right hand lay in his lap, the fingers still holding the gun he'd brought back from the war.

"Jesus," Mahaffey said.

There was a picture of Jesus on the wall over the fireplace, and, similarly framed, another of John F. Kennedy. Other photos and holy pictures reposed here and there in the room—on tabletops, on walls, on top of the television set. I was looking at a small framed photo of a smiling young man in an army uniform and just beginning to realize it was a younger version of the dead man when his wife came into the room.

"I'm sorry," she said, "I never heard you come in. I was with the children. They're in a state, as you can imagine."

"You're Mrs. Conway?"

"Mrs. James Conway." She glanced at her late husband, but her eyes didn't stay on him for long. "He was talking and laughing," she said. "He was making jokes. And then he shot himself. Why would he do such a thing?"

"Had he been drinking, Mrs. Conway?"

"He'd had a drink or two," she said. "He liked his drink. But he wasn't drunk."

"Where'd the bottle go?"

She put her hands together. She was a small woman, with a pinched face and pale blue eyes, and she wore a cotton housedress with a floral pattern. "I put it away," she said. "I shouldn't have done that, should I?"

"Did you move anything else, ma'am?"

"Only the bottle," she said. "The bottle and the glass. I didn't want people saying he was drunk when he did it, because how would that be for the children?" Her face clouded. "Or is it better thinking it was the drink that made him do it? I don't know which is worse. What do you men think?"

"I think we could all use a drink," he said. "Yourself not least of all, ma'am."

She crossed the room and got a bottle of Schenley's from a mahogany cabinet. She brought it, along with three small glasses of cut crystal. Mahaffey poured drinks for all three of us and held his to the light. She took a tentative sip of hers while Mahaffey and I drank ours down. It was an ordinary blended whiskey, an honest workingman's drink. Nothing fancy about it, but it did the job.

Mahaffey raised his glass again and looked at the bare-bulb ceiling fixture through it. "These are fine glasses," he said.

"Waterford," she said. "There were eight, they were my mother's, and these three are all that's left." She glanced at the dead man. "He had his from a jelly glass. We don't use the Waterford for every day."

"Well, I'd call this a special occasion," Mahaffey said. "Drink that yourself, will you? It's good for you."

She braced herself, drank the whiskey down, shuddered slightly, then drew a deep breath. "Thank you," she said. "It *is* good for me, I'd have to say. No, no more for me. But have another for yourselves."

I passed. Vince poured himself a short one. He went over her story with her, jotting down notes from time to time in his notebook. At one point she began to calculate how she'd manage without poor Jim. He'd been out of work lately, but he was in the building trades, and when he worked he made decent money. And there'd be something from the Veterans Administration, wouldn't there? And Social Security?

"I'm sure there'll be something," Vince told her. "And insurance? Did he have insurance?"

There was a policy, she said. Twenty-five thousand dollars, he'd taken it out when the first child was born, and she'd seen to it that the premium was paid each month. But he'd killed himself, and wouldn't that keep them from paying?

"That's what everybody thinks," he told her, "but it's rarely the case. There's generally a clause, no payment for suicide during the first six months, the first year, maybe even the first two years. To keep you from taking out the policy on Monday and doing away with yourself on Tuesday. But you've had this for more than two years, haven't you?"

She was nodding eagerly. "How old is Patrick? Almost nine, and it was taken out just around the time he was born."

"Then I'd say you're in the clear," he said. "And it's only fair, if you think about it. The company's been taking a man's premiums all these years, why should a moment of wrong thinking get them off the hook?"

"I had the same notion myself," she said, "but I thought there was no hope. I thought that was just the way it was."

"Well," he said, "it's not."

"What did you call it? A moment of wrong thinking? But isn't that all it takes to keep him out of heaven? It's the sin of despair, you know." She addressed this last to me, guessing that Mahaffey was more aware of the theology of it than I. "And is that fair?" she demanded, turning to Mahaffey again. "Better to cheat a widow out of the money than to cheat James Conway into hell."

"Maybe the Lord's able to take a longer view of things."

"That's not what the fathers say."

"If he wasn't in his right mind at the time . . ."

"His right mind!" She stepped back, pressed her hand to her breast. "Who in his right mind ever did such a thing?"

"Well . . ."

"He was joking," she said. "And he put the gun to his head, and even then I wasn't frightened, because he seemed his usual self and there was nothing frightening about it. Except I had the thought that the gun might go off by accident, and I said as much."

"What did he say to that?"

"That we'd all be better off if it did, himself included. And I said not to say such a thing, that it was horrid and sinful, and he said it was only the truth, and then he looked at me, he *looked* at me."

"What kind of a look?"

"Like, See what I'm doing? Like, Are you watching me, Mary Frances? And then he shot himself."

"Maybe it was an accident," I suggested.

"I saw his face. I saw his finger tighten on the trigger. It was as if he did it to spite me. But he wasn't angry at me. For the love of God, why would he . . ."

Mahaffey clapped me on the shoulder. "Take Mrs. Conway into the other room," he said. "Let her freshen up her face and drink a glass of water, and make sure the kids are all right." I looked at him, and he gave my shoulder a squeeze. "Something I want to check," he said.

I went into the kitchen, where Mrs. Conway wet a dish towel and dabbed tentatively at her face, then filled a jelly glass with water and drank it down in a series of small sips. Then we went to check on the children, a boy of eight and a girl a couple of years younger. They were just sitting there, hands folded in their laps, as if someone had told them not to move.

Mrs. Conway fussed over them and assured them everything was going to be fine and told them to get ready for bed. We left them as we found them, sitting side by side, their hands still folded in their laps. I suppose they were in shock, and it seemed to me they had the right.

I brought the woman back to the living room, where Mahaffey was bent over the body of her husband. He straightened up as we entered the room. "Mrs. Conway," he said, "I have something important to tell you."

She waited to hear what it was.

"Your husband didn't kill himself," he announced.

Her eyes widened, and she looked at Mahaffey as if he'd gone suddenly mad. "But I saw him do it," she said.

He frowned, nodded. "Forgive me," he said. "I misspoke. What I meant to say was that the poor man did not commit suicide. He did kill himself, of course he killed himself—"

"I saw him do it."

"—and of course you did, and what a terrible thing for you, what a cruel thing. But it was not his intention, ma'am. It was an accident!"

"An accident."

"Yes."

"To put a gun to your head and pull the trigger. An accident?"

Mahaffey had a handkerchief in his hand. He turned his hand palm up to show what he was holding with it. It was the cartridge clip from the pistol.

"An accident," Mahaffey said. "You said he was joking, and that's what it was, a joke that went bad. Do you know what this is?"

"Something to do with the gun?"

"It's the clip, ma'am. Or the magazine, they call it that as well. It holds the cartridges."

"The bullets?"

"The bullets, yes. And do you know where I found it?"

"In the gun?"

"That's where I would have expected to find it," he said, "and that's where I looked for it, but it wasn't there. And then I patted his pants pockets, and there it was." And, still using the handkerchief to hold it, he tucked the cartridge clip into the man's right-hand pocket.

"You don't understand," he told the woman. "How about you, Matt? You see what happened?"

"I think so."

"He was playing a joke on you, ma'am. He took the clip out of the gun and put it in his pocket. Then he was going to hold the unloaded gun to his head and give you a scare. He'd give the trigger a squeeze, and there'd be that instant before the hammer clicked on an empty chamber, that instant where you'd think he'd really shot himself, and he'd get to see your reaction."

"But he did shoot himself," she said.

"Because the gun still had a round in the chamber. Once you've chambered a round, removing the clip won't unload the gun. He forgot about the round in the chamber, he thought he had an unloaded weapon in his hand, and when he squeezed the trigger he didn't even have time to be surprised."

"Christ have mercy," she said.

"Amen to that," Mahaffey said. "It's a horrible thing, ma'am, but it's not suicide. Your husband never meant to kill himself. It's a tragedy, a terrible tragedy, but it was an accident." He drew a breath. "It might cost him a bit of time in purgatory, playing a joke like that, but he's spared hellfire, and that's something, isn't it? And now I'll want to use your phone, ma'am, and call this in."

"That's why you wanted to know if it was a revolver or an automatic," Elaine said. "One has a clip and one doesn't."

"An automatic has a clip. A revolver has a cylinder."

"If he'd had a revolver he could have played Russian roulette. That's when you spin the cylinder, isn't it?"

"So I understand."

"How does it work? All but one chamber is empty? Or all but one chamber has a bullet in it?"

"I guess it depends what kind of odds you like."

She thought about it, shrugged. "These poor people in Brooklyn," she said. "What made Mahaffey think of looking for the clip?"

"Something felt off about the whole thing," I said, "and he remembered a case of a man who'd shot a friend with what he was sure was an unloaded gun, because he'd removed the clip. That was the defense at trial, he told me, and it hadn't gotten the guy anywhere, but it stayed in Mahaffey's mind. And as soon as he took a close look at the gun he saw the clip was missing, so it was just a matter of finding it."

"In the dead man's pocket."

"Right."

"Thus saving James Conway from an eternity in hell," she said. "Except he'd be off the hook with or without Mahaffey, wouldn't he? I mean, wouldn't God know where to send him without having some cop hold up a cartridge clip?"

"Don't ask me, honey. I'm not even Catholic."

"Goyim is goyim," she said. "You're supposed to know these things. Never mind, I get the point. It may not make a difference to God or to Conway, but it makes a real difference to Mary Frances. She can bury her husband in holy ground and know he'll be waiting for her when she gets to heaven her own self."

"Right."

"It's a terrible story, isn't it? I mean, it's a good story as a story, but it's terrible, the idea of a man killing himself that way. And his wife and kids witnessing it, and having to live with it."

"Terrible," I agreed.

"But there's more to it. Isn't there?"

"More?"

"Come on," she said. "You left something out."

"You know me too well."

"Damn right I do."

"So what's the part I didn't get to?"

She thought about it. "Drinking a glass of water," she said.

"How's that?"

"He sent you both out of the room," she said, "*before* he looked to see if the clip was there or not. So it was just Mahaffey, finding the clip all by himself."

"She was beside herself, and he figured it would do her good to splash a little water on her face. And we hadn't heard a peep out of those kids, and it made sense to have her check on them."

"And she had to have you along so she didn't get lost on the way to the bedroom."

I nodded. "It's convenient," I allowed, "making the discovery with no one around. He had plenty of time to pick up the gun, remove the clip, put the gun back in Conway's hand, and slip the clip into the man's pocket. That way he could do his good deed for the day, turning a suicide into an accidental death. It might not fool God, but it would be more than enough to fool the parish priest. Conway's body could be buried in holy ground, regardless of his soul's ultimate destination."

"And you think that's what he did?"

"It's certainly possible. But suppose you're Mahaffey, and you check the gun and the clip's still in it, and you do what we just said. Would you stand there with the clip in your hand waiting to tell the widow and your partner what you learned?"

"Why not?" she said, and then answered her own question. "No, of course not," she said. "If I'm going to make a discovery like that I'm going to do so in the presence of witnesses. What I do, I get the clip, I take it out, I slip it in his pocket, I put the gun back in his hand, and then I wait for the two of you to come back. And *then* I get a bright idea, and we examine the gun and find the clip missing, and one of us finds it in his pocket, where I know it is because that's where I stashed it a minute ago."

"A lot more convincing than his word on what he found when no one was around to see him find it."

"On the other hand," she said, "wouldn't he do that either way? Say I look at the gun and see the clip's missing. Why don't I wait until you come back before I even look for the clip?"

"Your curiosity's too great."

"So I can't wait a minute? But even so, suppose I look and I find the clip in his pocket. Why take it out?"

"To make sure it's what you think it is."

"And why not put it back?"

"Maybe it never occurs to you that anybody would doubt your word," I suggested. "Or maybe, wherever Mahaffey found the clip, in the gun or in Conway's pocket where he said he found it, maybe he would have put it back if he'd had enough time. But we came back in, and there he was with the clip in his hand."

"In his handkerchief, you said. On account of fingerprints?"

"Sure. You don't want to disturb existing prints or leave prints of your own. Not that the lab would have spent any time on this one. They might nowadays, but back in the early sixties? A man shoots himself in front of witnesses?"

She was silent for a long moment. Then she said, "So what happened?"

"What happened?"

"Yeah, your best guess. What really happened?"

"No reason it couldn't have been just the way he reconstructed it. Accidental death. A dumb accident, but an accident all the same."

"But?"

"But Vince had a soft heart," I said. "Houseful of holy pictures like that, he's got to figure it's important to the woman that her husband's got a shot at heaven. If he could fix that up, he wouldn't care a lot about the objective reality of it all."

"And he wouldn't mind tampering with evidence?"

"He wouldn't lose sleep over it. God knows I never did."

"Anybody you ever framed," she said, "was guilty."

"Of something," I agreed. "You want my best guess, it's that there's no way of telling. As soon as the gimmick occurred to Vince, that the clip might be missing, the whole scenario was set. Either Conway had removed the clip and we were going to find it, or he hadn't and we were going to remove it for him, and *then* find it."

" 'The Lady or the Tiger.' Except not really, because either way it comes out the same. It goes in the books as an accident, whether that's what it was or not."

"That's the idea."

"So it doesn't make any difference one way or the other."

"I suppose not," I said, "but I always hoped it was the way Mahaffey said it was."

"Because you wouldn't want to think ill of him? No, that's not it. You already said he was capable of tampering with evidence, and you wouldn't think ill of him for it, anyway. I give up. Why? Because you don't want Mr. Conway to be in hell?"

"I never met the man," I said, "and it would be presumptuous of me to care where he winds up. But I'd prefer it if the clip was in his pocket where Mahaffey said it was, because of what it would prove."

"That he hadn't meant to kill himself? I thought we just said . . ."

I shook my head. "That she didn't do it."

"Who? The wife?"

"Uh-huh."

"That she didn't do what? Kill him? You think *she* killed him?"

"It's possible."

"But he shot himself," she said. "In front of witnesses. Or did I miss something?"

"That's almost certainly what happened," I said, "but she was one of the witnesses, and the kids were the other witnesses, and who knows what they saw, or if they saw anything at all? Say he's on the couch, and they're all watching TV, and she takes his old war souvenir and puts one in his head, and she starts screaming. 'Ohmigod, look what your father has done! Oh, Jesus Mary and Joseph, Daddy has killed himself!' They were looking at the set, they didn't see dick, but they'll think they did by the time she stops carrying on."

"And they never said what they did or didn't see."

"They never said a word, because we didn't ask them anything. Look, I don't think she did it. The possibility didn't even occur to me until sometime later, and by then we'd closed the case, so what was the point? I never even mentioned the idea to Vince."

"And if you had?"

"He'd have said she wasn't the type for it, and he'd have been right. But you never know. If she didn't do it, he gave her peace of mind. If she did do it, she must have wondered how the cartridge clip migrated from the gun butt to her husband's pocket."

"She'd have realized Mahaffey put it there."

"Uh-huh. And she'd have had twenty-five thousand reasons to thank him for it."

"Huh?"

"The insurance," I said.

"But you said they'd have to pay anyway."

"Double indemnity," I said. "They'd have had to pay the face amount of the policy, but if it's an accident they'd have had to pay double. That's if there was a double-indemnity clause in the policy, and I have no way of knowing whether or not there was. But most policies sold around then, especially relatively small policies, had the clause. The companies liked to write them that way, and the policy holders usually went for them. A fraction more in premiums and twice the payoff? Why not go for it?"

We kicked it around a little. Then she asked about the current case, the one that had started the whole thing. I'd wondered about the gun, I explained, purely out of curiosity. If it was in fact an automatic, and if the clip was in fact in his pocket and not in the gun where you'd expect to find it, surely some cop would have determined as much by now, and it would all come out in the wash.

"That's some story," she said. "And it happened when, thirty-five years ago? And you never mentioned it before?"

"I never thought of it," I said, "not as a story worth telling. Because it's unresolved. There's no way to know what really happened."

"That's all right," she said. "It's still a good story."

The guy in Inwood, it turned out, had used a .38-caliber revolver, and he'd cleaned it and loaded it earlier that same day. No chance it was an accident.

And if I'd never told the story over the years, that's not to say it hadn't come occasionally to mind. Vince Mahaffey and I never really talked about the incident, and I've sometimes wished we had. It would have been nice to know what really happened.

Assuming that's possible, and I'm not sure it is. He had, after all, sent me out of the room before doing whatever it was he did. That suggested he hadn't wanted me to know, so why should I think he'd be quick to tell me after the fact?

No way of knowing. And, as the years pass, I find I like it better that way. I couldn't tell you why, but I do.

New Stories

Almost Perfect

He was already at the ballpark when I got there, and that was unusual for Tommy. Of course he was scheduled to pitch that afternoon, going up against the Bobcats in the last game of a three-game home stand, but even when he pitched he tended to show up a lot closer to game time. He'd make it in time to warm up properly, and he'd generally be there for the batting practice that Hairston makes his pitchers take along with everybody else, seeing as our league has escaped the goddam designated hitter rule. But he was basically a last-minute kind of guy, and I'm the opposite, like most catchers. So it was a surprise to walk in and see him already suited up.

But not a big surprise, because Tommy Willis was a southpaw, and it's true what you've heard about them. Pud Hairston was a pitcher himself for twelve years and has been a pitching coach for better than twenty, and he swears they're all knuckleballs, meaning you never know which way they're going to break. I don't know why it should be true, why you can predict a man'll have a wild hair on the basis of which arm he uses to throw the ball, or why it only seems to work that way with pitchers, while a left-handed outfielder or first baseman will be as regular as the next person, or at least the next ballplayer. A southpaw has an edge against left-handed batters and gives up the same edge to righties, and I can see why that would be, same as I or anybody else can see why he'd have an advantage throwing over to first. But what has all of this got to do with what goes on in his head? That makes no sense to me, but I've known enough of them and caught enough of them to be able to swear it's true.

I said he was early for a change, and he grinned that lazy grin of his. "Gotta get them Bobcats," he said. We went out and threw a few, and then he put on a jacket and sat down while I went and took my turn in the cage. I love batting practice. You just stand there and you hit. I'd do it all day if they let me.

Around the time the ground crew got to smoothing out the base paths, I checked the stands and spotted my wife sitting where she generally did. I waved, but she was deep in conversation with Sally Peres and didn't see me. There were rumors that we were looking to trade Reynaldo Peres, and for Kathy's sake I hoped they weren't true, as Sally was her closest friend among the wives. (Other hand, if I was the general manager, Peres would have been gone by now. He's always behind in the count, and that means every hitter's a struggle for him.)

"I don't see Colleen," I said to Tommy, and he said she wasn't coming.

"She gets tired of baseball," he said.

Anybody'll tire of baseball from time to time, even the men who play it, and I can see how a wife could get sick of it, especially if she wasn't too crazy about hanging out with the other wives. And the TV cameras pan those rows all the time, so you have to make sure you look interested, and that the camera doesn't catch you yawning, or picking your nose. Kathy doesn't come to every home game, not by any means. Still, a pitcher doesn't start but one game in five, so when he's up his wife's usually there to see him.

I didn't say anything, and he said, "Hard to believe. I mean, how could a human being get tired of baseball? But she does. She even gets tired of the Bobcats."

They were the defending world champions, and a good bet to repeat this year, and our attendance was never higher than when they came to town. So his remark was natural enough, but it had a little extra on it, and I wondered about that. But not for any length of time. We were just minutes away from the first pitch, which he'd be throwing and I'd be catching, and I was more interested in whether his fastball had a little extra on it, and how his curve was breaking.

Introductions went like they always do, with cheers for us and boos for the Bobcats, with the loudest round of boos for Wade Bemis. He had two strikes against him, as far as our fans were concerned. Number one, he was hitting .341, and neck and neck with Clipper DeYoung of the Orioles in the home-run race. Number two, he played for us for four years, jumping to the Bobcats as a free agent. That's fans for you. The better you are, the more they hate you, and it goes double if you used to play for their team. It never made sense to me, but there's not much about fans that does.

After Bemis was introduced, the boos dropped to a more cordial level, and Pud Hairston came over and asked how Tommy was throwing. "He should be fine," I told him.

But we both knew you could never tell for sure. Not until the game got started, and even then you might not know right away.

Early on, I thought fine was the one thing Tommy wasn't going to be that day. His first three pitches to their leadoff batter, Jeff Coleman, were all off the plate, all in the same spot, and each one a little farther from being a strike than the one before it. I was calling for inside pitches, and he was missing away, and that's not a good sign. The next one was right down the middle, with Coleman taking all the way.

If I'd been coaching the Bobcats I'd have had him take the next pitch, too, the way Tommy had started him off 3–0, but he swung at a bad pitch and popped to short.

Tommy went to 3–1 on the second batter. The biggest mistake a pitcher can make is to get behind in the count, and that's especially true for a hard-throwing kid like Tommy, who can have a problem with control. His next pitch caught the corner. The batter lined the next one, really got good wood on it, but it went straight into the third baseman's glove like it had eyes.

Tommy started the next hitter off with two balls, the second one in the dirt, and I dug it out and walked it back to the mound. Bemis was in the on-deck circle, looking eager, and he'd be batting from the right-hand side of the plate today, since Tommy was a southpaw. His on-base average was about the same lefty or righty, but he had more power as a right-hander.

"Let's get this guy," I told Tommy.

"Piece of pie," he said.

He'd say that, piece of pie, where other people'd say piece of cake. Other hand, he'd say something was easy as cake. I was never sure if he got the expressions mixed up accidentally or on purpose.

I went back and gave the sign—the hitter was McGinley, their left fielder, and the book on him was give him nothing but fastballs. The next two were straight heat, right where I wanted them, outside and down. The next pitch was in the same place, and I thought it got the corner, but it was ball three. The next one was down and in, probably off the plate but too close to take, and McGinley got a piece of it, but I got my glove up and held on to it, and we were out of the inning.

We went down one-two-three, with two of our outs coming on the first pitch. There was just enough time for Pud to ask me how Tommy was throwing. I said I thought he was settling in. Pud said he hoped so.

Wade Bemis led off, and he did everything but tip his hat to the fans who booed him. He stood in there like he was waiting for someone to take his picture, and maybe he was. Bemis likes to crowd the plate, and the only way to get him out is to pitch him inside. Tommy almost hit him with the first pitch. Bemis went into the dirt to get away from it, and he had a smug look on his face as he brushed off his uniform. I called for heat and Tommy gave it to him. Bemis took it for strike one, swung at the next one and missed it, and looked silly swinging at a splitter that bounced on the plate.

That got a hand from the crowd. They cheered some more when Tommy struck out the side.

I don't know just when it was I realized something special was going on.

Oh, I knew he had his stuff when he fanned Wade Bemis. His fastball was really popping, and his control just got sharper and sharper. It got so I'd just stick the mitt out and he'd hit it. And his curve was breaking real good, and his change had the Bobcat batters digging for balls in the dirt.

And we were in sync, too. He wasn't shaking off my signs hardly at all, and the few times he did I was already questioning the sign in my own mind. It was like we had our minds hooked up, and we were going over the batters together, figuring how to move them back off the plate, then get them to chase stuff they couldn't hit. When it's like that, I sometimes lose track in my own mind as to who's catching and who's pitching. It's like we're both part of the same machine, with the gears meshing just right.

Bemis led off the top of the fifth. We'd left the bases loaded in the bottom of the fourth, and you hate to see that, and Bemis had a cocky smile on his face when he stepped in. Like we'd had our chance, and blew it, and it was his turn now.

Tommy got the first one in—he was throwing nothing but first-pitch strikes by now. His next delivery was low, but didn't miss by much. Next was a curve, and Bemis swung late and fouled it back. I called for a fastball down and on the outside corner, and Tommy got it where I wanted it, but Kalman called it ball two. I'd swear it caught the corner, but my opinion doesn't count. It was too close to take with two strikes, but Bemis stood there and took it. He's got a good eye, but he was plain lucky to get the call.

He fouled off about four pitches, or it could have been five, and checked his swing on a curve that he couldn't have reached with a broom. I checked with the first base umpire, but he said he didn't go around. I'd have sworn he did, but you see what you want to see, and anyway no one was asking me.

Next pitch we challenged him with a fastball, high and tight, and he fouled it off. I called for another in the same spot, and he was just the least bit late in his swing, and that's what saved us, because he really tagged that one. But instead of pulling it he lifted it to the gap in right center, and Justo Chacón floated under it and took it at the warning track.

Bemis was halfway to second when the catch was made, and he turned and trotted back to the Bobcats' dugout. I happened to notice the expression on his face, and he didn't look frustrated or disappointed, mad at himself or at Tommy or Justo. He looked all pleased with himself, which wasn't what you'd expect from someone who was oh for two for the day.

Maybe it was the look on his face that made me turn around and look over to the stands, where the wives were sitting. Kathy was there, of course, and I caught her eye when I turned around, and she gave me a wave. I grinned back, happy because we'd just dodged a bullet, with Bemis's shot nothing but a long out, happy too because there was my wife waving at me.

I looked for Colleen, too, but of course she wasn't there, and I reminded myself that Tommy had said she wasn't coming. I hadn't exactly forgotten that, but Bemis's expression made me look for her even though I knew she wouldn't be there.

I'd heard the rumors, see. I guess everybody heard the rumors. But you hear stuff like that all the time. You don't pay any attention to it, or at least you try not to.

Once Bemis was out of the way, it only took us four pitches to get out of the inning. Tommy used three of them to strike out the number five hitter, two fastballs that he swung at and missed and a curve he held off on. It was right on the corner, and this time we got the call. Then the next Bobcat batter fouled off the first pitch and our first baseman made a nice running catch at the stands. Three up and three down.

And that was when it first hit me that what I'd just seen was fifteen up and fifteen down, that we'd played five innings without a single Bobcat making it to first base. No runs, no hits, no errors, no bases on balls, no nothing. Tommy Willis, who'd started out shaky, like he might walk the bases loaded, was past the halfway mark of throwing a perfect game.

That's what it was, but you have to keep in mind that it sounds like more than it is. Being halfway to a perfect game (or an ordinary no-hitter, for that matter, if there can be such a thing as an ordinary no-hitter) is a little like being ninety years old and saying you're halfway to a hundred and eighty. It's not as though you're an even-money shot to get there.

No-hitters are a funny thing. Some of the winningest pitchers in baseball have never had one, or even come close. They get out the guys they have to get out, they shut things down when they've got men in scoring position, and game after game they scatter a handful of hits and come out on top.

But to throw a no-hitter you have to be on top of every batter you face. And you need to be lucky, too, because you can have the best stuff in the world and some lifetime .220 hitter can lunge at the ball and knock a flute into shallow left. A no-hitter's like a soap bubble, it doesn't take much to burst it.

And a perfect game's all that and more, because not only can a lucky swing beat you, but a batter can get lucky by not swinging, and your too-close-to-take curveball turns out to be ball four. Your outfielder can misjudge what should have been a routine fly ball, your shortstop can bobble a grounder and then throw it into the stands. Not your fault, but there goes your perfect game.

There's a million superstitions in baseball, plus the private rituals some players go through. Maybe it's because there's so much in the game you can't control, so you try to get a handle on it by fastening and unfastening the snaps on your batting glove, or keeping a hitting streak alive by not shaving, or pounding your glove a certain number of times between pitches. No one could follow all the baseball superstitions, especially since some of them contradict each other, and anyway there's too many of them to remember. But one that just about everybody follows is what you do when a guy's throwing a no-hitter, and that's that you don't do anything. And what you especially don't do is mention it.

It used to be that radio and TV announcers wouldn't mention it, and some of them still won't, but plenty of them seem to figure that they're too far away to jinx it, and their viewers would have a fit if they wound up watching a no-hitter without realizing it.

But you don't mention it in the dugout or on the field. You sure as hell don't say a word to the pitcher, but you don't say anything to anybody else, either. And here's something interesting—if you're on the other team, doing everything you can to keep from having a no-hitter pitched against you, you still don't say a word about it.

I don't know why that is. There's no limit to what ballplayers'll say, trying to get a rise out of each other. You'll hear comments about a player's wife, or even his mother. But you won't hear anything about the no-hitter he's so many outs away from throwing. I thought it might be like countries at war not using poison gas, because if they do the other side might use it right back at them, but how would that work in baseball? The other team couldn't mention your no-hitter until you had one going, and it might be forever before that happened.

I guess it's just a feeling that mentioning it would be bush. Looking bush is something a ballplayer'll do a lot in order not to.

But the point is Tommy was twelve outs away from a perfect game, which is miles and miles away, but close enough to be aware of. And I wasn't saying anything, and neither was anybody else, but I would look around and catch another player's eye and I'd know he knew what was going on, and he'd know the same about me. And pretty soon everybody knew, and nobody said a word.

Except the one person I wasn't sure about was Tommy. I tried not to stare, but of course I was looking at him when he was out there and I was behind the plate, because how could I catch him properly without taking a lot of long looks at him? And when it was our turn at bat I couldn't help sneaking peeks at him, and it seemed to me he was just looking straight ahead and not seeing anything. He was in a zone, all right. He was off somewhere with his own private thoughts, and what those thoughts might be or where they were headed was something I didn't have a clue about. Maybe he was seeing the whole game, past and future, pitch by pitch, or maybe he was off in some world where there was no such thing as baseball. I could stare at him all I wanted and it wouldn't matter. He wouldn't know I was staring, and I wouldn't be able to tell what was going on in his head.

Tommy struck out the side in the top of the sixth.

Justo walked to lead off our half of the inning, and I laid down a bunt that was good enough to get him to second. But that was as far as he got. A pop-up and a ground ball and the inning was over.

In the top of the seventh, Tommy went to three and two on the leadoff batter. Then he shook off my signs until I called for a curveball that I didn't really want him to throw, and he hung it. The batter got all of it, and I thought it was gone, and it was, but it hooked at the last minute and was foul by a couple of feet.

The whole ballpark held its breath, and when the ball went out and the umpire called it foul, everybody in the place sighed at once. And there were cheers, real cheers, and as far as I know it's the first time anybody drew cheers for hitting a foul ball. The batter had only got a few steps toward first base, since he and everybody else knew right away it was either a home run or a foul ball, so there was no need to set any records getting down the line. He trotted back and picked up his bat and struck out on the next pitch.

The next batter tapped a grounder to first, and the inning ended with a foul pop. It was high enough so that I could imagine a hundred things going wrong in the time it took to come down, but it plopped in my mitt and stayed there, and we were out of the inning. Twenty-one up and twenty-one down, and six to go.

We scored two runs in the bottom of the seventh, and I'd say it was about time. The thing is, no matter how good a pitcher is, he can't win a game without runs. There was even a case once of a pitcher throwing nine no-hit innings and losing in extra innings. People don't believe it could happen, but it's right there in the book.

Anyway, with one out, Darnell Weeks doubled down the line, and Tommy was next in the order. Ordinarily that would have meant a pinch hitter, because Tommy's batting average is a lot less than his playing weight. He takes a decent cut at the ball, but more often than not he fans.

So, with the game on the line, he'd have been gone. And that would have been true even if we already had a lot of runs on the board. Tommy would hardly ever stay in for a whole nine innings. If we were behind he'd come out for a pinch hitter, and if we were ahead we'd have Freddie Olendorff close things out. But you don't lift a guy who's six outs away from a no-hitter, let alone a perfect game. Tommy picked up a bat and struck out on three pitches.

Pepper Foxwell was up next, and he ran the count to three and two, fouled off five or six pitches, and finally got one he liked. He's our leadoff batter and doesn't usually hit for power, but this time he swung hard and got all of it, and just like that Tommy had a two-run cushion.

I watched the ball go out, and as soon as it cleared the fence I looked over at Tommy. Everybody else was off the bench with the crack of the bat, climbing up the dugout steps to watch and then to cheer, but Tommy never moved. I don't even know if he saw what was happening, or paid any attention to it.

He was in a zone, and he might as well have been in a bubble. Between innings, nobody sat down next to him and nobody talked to him. That's part of not mentioning a no-hitter. You just leave the pitcher alone, you let him stay in his own space, and I guess that's where he was.

The next man up hit a long fly, and it looked for a minute like it was going out, too, but their center fielder gathered it in at the track, and that was the third out.

Wade Bemis led off the top of the eighth. He had a funny look on his face, not what you expect of someone whose team's getting shut out. Like there was a joke and he was in on it.

"Hey, Willis," he called out. "You're almost perfect."

Now I'd say the whole park went silent, but it pretty much already was. Because everybody in the stadium knew Tommy Willis was six outs away from putting a perfect game in the record book, and if that won't quiet a crowd down I don't know what will.

Quiet as it was, Bemis's words rang out loud and clear, and what followed them was a whole lot of silence. I was truly shocked, and the first thing I did was look at Tommy, but if his face showed any expression I couldn't read it.

In an undertone, so nobody but Bemis could hear it, I said, "Man, that was really bush."

He must have heard me, but he didn't react. "Just like Colleen," he said, loud and clear. "She's pretty close to perfect herself, Willis."

Now Tommy reacted, but not like you'd expect. He got this big grin on his face. He stood up there on the mound while Wade Bemis knocked the dirt out of his spikes and got into his stance. Bemis crowded the plate, the way he always did, but this time he was closer than ever. I called for a fastball on the inside corner and Tommy delivered it belt-high. It was a strike and Ev Kalman called it a strike, but at the same time it was almost the end of Tommy's perfect game, because it was that close to brushing Wade Bemis's uniform. It was over the plate, but even so it almost hit him. In fact I wasn't sure it didn't touch the cloth, and if it had that would have put him on first, even if it was in the strike zone.

Everything would have been different. The box score would have been the same, if you think about it, but everything would have been different.

As close as the pitch was, Bemis didn't turn a hair. He didn't make a remark, either. He stepped out of the box, picked up some dirt, gave his batting helmet a tug, and stepped in again. If anything, he was crowding the plate more than ever.

I called for a curve outside. It would break in toward a right-handed batter like Bemis, and if it worked right it would just catch the outside corner. It would be a tougher pitch for him to handle if Tommy could first move him off the plate by throwing high and tight, but I was afraid another inside pitch would get a piece of his uniform and he'd be on first and Tommy's perfect game would be out the window. I set up low, figuring if Tommy kept the ball down it would be a tough pitch for Bemis to handle, even if he was just about standing on the plate.

Well, everybody in the world saw the pitch Tommy threw. They showed it over and over on every news program in the country. I try not to look at it, but I still guess I must have seen it a hundred times, with Tommy going into his windup and throwing his fastball straight at Wade Bemis's head. Except it wasn't right at his head, it was behind his head, so that when Bemis saw it coming and tried to get away from it he just pulled right back into it.

Somebody had a radar gun clocking the pitch—somebody always does, these days—and the ball was going 102 miles an hour when it hit Bemis. Tommy threw it at his head and there was nothing the matter with his control. It got Bemis just above the ear, and I'll never forget the sound it made.

I suppose they could hear it in Cooperstown.

Bemis was wearing a batting helmet. You have to, and I think they even wear them in slo-pitch softball nowadays, and there's no question that they prevent a lot of injuries. But so do seat belts, and what good are they if your plane flies into the side of a mountain?

Everybody saw the pitch, and everybody saw what happened next, with Wade Bemis falling flat and lying still, and a whole stadium full of people catching their breath. And then, the next thing anybody knew, there were a dozen cops out on the field, all of them heading for the pitcher's mound. My first thought was that they were there to protect Tommy, to keep the Bobcats from taking a shot at him, but the Bobcats were in the same state we were, too shocked and stunned to do anything much but stand around. And the cops weren't protecting Tommy. What they were doing was putting cuffs on him and taking him into custody.

Wade Bemis left first. An ambulance drove in from the bullpen entrance and drove right across the infield, and they got him on a stretcher and loaded him on the ambulance and drove out the way they came, siren blazing away. They didn't need the siren, as it turned out, and they didn't even need the ambulance, because Bemis was dead on arrival at the hospital, and he was most likely dead when he hit the ground.

Just about everybody watched the ambulance leave, and most of the crowd missed Tommy's exit. He left in handcuffs, escorted by ten or a dozen cops, and they took him out through the dugout and the locker room so nobody really knew what was happening.

And then we finished the game.

There was some criticism later about that, some people arguing that the game should have been called on the spot, but how could you do that? For one thing, I think you'd have had a riot on your hands. You don't call off a game every time a batter gets hit by a pitch.

Some rookie, a skinny guy named Hector Ruiz, was announced as a pinch runner, and he was awarded first base. And our closer, Freddie Olendorff, came on in relief. He took his warmup throws, and I got a hunch and called for a pitchout on the first pitch, and sure enough, Hector Ruiz was off and running. I threw down to Pepper Foxwell at second and we had him out by four feet.

The next two batters grounded out, and that was it for the Bobcats in the top of the eighth. They brought in a new pitcher in the bottom of the ninth and he walked the bases loaded, and we scored two more runs before they managed to stop the bleeding. Then Freddie went out there and shut down the Bobcats one two three, on a pair of ground balls and a foul pop that I caught for the last out.

We were in the locker room and the crowd was out of the stadium and halfway home before we found out what had actually happened that afternoon. That Bemis was dead, which was what we were all afraid of, of course, but didn't know for a fact, not until the word filtered through to us. And that Tommy Willis was in a jail cell, charged with murder.

That was hard to believe. I think everybody knew it wasn't an accident, that he'd thrown that ball at Wade Bemis on purpose. And some of us knew he hadn't been trying to just brush him back, but that he meant to hit him.

And I knew just how intentional it was, because I knew what pitch I'd called and where I'd set up. And Tommy didn't even bother to shake off my sign. He nodded and went into his windup and threw the ball straight at Bemis.

But since when did you charge a pitcher with murder for hitting a batter? There've been pitchers fined for throwing intentional beanballs, and there have been some brief suspensions, but criminal charges? That's something I've never heard of.

But of course it wasn't Wade Bemis that Tommy was charged with murdering. It was Colleen.

That was why the cops were out on the field almost before Wade Bemis hit the ground. They'd been waiting since the fourth inning. It was around then that police officers went to the Willis house in Northbrook in response to a neighbor's complaint. They found Tommy's wife, Colleen, in the bedroom with a carving knife stuck in her chest.

A pair of detectives came straight to the ballpark, but they had the car radio tuned to the ballgame, so before they got there they knew Tommy was pitching, and that he hadn't allowed a hit. They got a lot of flak later on for not arresting him right away, and there's no question but that Wade Bemis would be alive if they had, but I can see why they did what they did.

On the one hand, there was no rush. Tommy wasn't going anywhere. All they had to do was wait until the game was over, or at least until he'd been yanked for a pinch hitter, and he could be taken into custody without making a public spectacle of the whole thing. That's what you'd have if you arrested him in the middle of any game, and it would be even worse given the game he was pitching. Can you imagine the crowd reaction if the police interrupted a no-hitter and led the pitcher off in handcuffs? And this wasn't just any no-hitter, it was a perfect game in the making.

You could easily have a riot on your hands.

And suppose Tommy turned out to be innocent? Suppose somebody else stuck the knife in her, and when it was all over he'd lost not only his beautiful wife but his chance for baseball immortality, all because a couple of eager-beaver cops couldn't wait a few innings?

And here's another thing. If they had the game on the radio, it probably means they were fans. And what kind of fan is going to screw up a perfect game?

The way it turned out, the way it goes in the record book, Tommy Willis and Freddie Olendorff combined to throw a no-hitter. That's rare enough, but this was a no-hitter where they only faced twenty-seven batters. The one man who did reach first—not on a hit, a walk, or an error, unless you call a hit batsman a pitcher's error—that one man was thrown out stealing. So you'd have to say the game the two of them pitched was the closest possible thing to a perfect game.

Some perfect game.

Colleen was having an affair with Wade Bemis, and Tommy found out. And they had a fight about it, and you know how it ended, with the carving knife stuck in her chest. And maybe if Bemis hadn't said what he said at his last at-bat, Tommy would have just hung in there and pitched to him. The way he was throwing, you've got to figure he'd have gotten him out, and five more after him, and completed his perfect game and got his cheers and gone off quietly with the arresting officers.

Or maybe Bemis would have gotten a hit, and, with the no-hitter out of reach, Tommy would have come out of there. Maybe the Bobcats would have rallied and broken things open and won the game. I mean, it's baseball.

Anything can happen in a baseball game.

Headaches and Bad Dreams

Three days of headaches, three nights of bad dreams. On the third night she woke twice before dawn, her heart racing, the bedding sweat-soaked. The second time she forced herself up and out of bed and into the shower. Before she'd toweled dry the headache had begun, starting at the base of the skull and radiating to the temples.

She took aspirin. She didn't like to take drugs of any sort, and her medicine cabinet contained nothing but a few herbal preparations—echinacea and golden seal for colds, gingko for memory, and a Chinese herbal tonic, its ingredients a mystery to her, which she ordered by mail from a firm in San Francisco. She took sage, too, because it seemed to her to help center her psychically and make her perceptions more acute, although she couldn't remember having read that it had that property. She grew sage in her garden, picked leaves periodically and dried them in the sun, and drank a cup of sage tea almost every evening.

There were herbs that were supposed to ease headaches, no end of different herbs for the many different kinds of headaches, but she'd never found one that worked. Aspirin, on the other hand, was reliable. It was a drug, and as such it probably had the effect of dulling her psychic abilities, but those abilities were of small value when your head was throbbing like Poe's telltale heart. And aspirin didn't slam shut the doors of perception, as something strong might do. Truth to tell, it was the nearest thing to an herb itself, obtained originally from willow bark. She didn't know how they made it nowadays, surely there weren't willow trees enough on the planet to cure the world's headaches, but still . . .

She heated a cup of spring water, added the juice of half a lemon. That was her breakfast. She sipped it in the garden, listening to the birds.

She knew what she had to do but she was afraid.

It was a small house, just two bedrooms, everything on one floor, with no basement and shallow crawl space for an attic. She slept in one bedroom and saw clients in the other. A beaded curtain hung in the doorway of the second bedroom, and within were all the pictures and talismans and power objects from which she drew strength. There were religious pictures and statues, a crucifix, a little bronze Buddha, African masks, quartz crystals. A pack of tarot cards shared a small table with a little malachite pyramid and a necklace of bear claws.

A worn oriental rug covered most of the floor, and was itself in part covered by a smaller rug on which she would lie when she went into trance. The rest of the time she would sit in the straight-backed armchair. There was a chaise as well, and that was where the client would sit.

She had only one appointment that day, but it was right smack in the middle of the day. The client, Claire Warburton, liked to come on her lunch hour. So Sylvia got through the morning by watching talk shows on television and paging through old magazines, taking more aspirin when the headache threatened to return. At 12:30 she opened the door for her client.

Claire Warburton was a regular, coming for a reading once every four or five weeks, upping the frequency of her visits in times of stress. She had a weight problem—that was one of the reasons she liked to come on her lunch hour, so as to spare herself a meal's worth of calories—and she was having a lingering affair with a married man. She had occasional problems at work as well, a conflict with a new supervisor, an awkward situation with a co-worker who disapproved of her love affair. There were always topics on which Claire needed counsel, and, assisted by the cards, the crystals, and her own inner resources, Sylvia always found something to tell her.

"Oh, before I forget," Claire said, "you were absolutely right about wheat. I cut it out and I felt the difference almost immediately."

"I thought you would. That came through loud and clear last time."

"I told Dr. Greenleaf. 'I think I may be allergic to wheat,' I said. He rolled his eyes."

"I'll bet he did. I hope you didn't tell him where the thought came from."

"Oh, sure. 'Sylvia Belgrave scanned my reflex centers with a green pyramid and picked up a wheat allergy.' Believe me, I know better than that. I don't know why I bothered to say anything to him in the first place. I suppose I was looking for male approval, but that's nothing new, is it?" They discussed the point, and then she said, "But it's so hard, you know. Staying away from wheat, I mean. It's everywhere."

"Yes."

"Bread, pasta. I wish I could cut it out completely, but I've managed to cut way down, and it helps. Sylvia? Are you all right?"

"A headache. It keeps coming back."

"Really? Well, I hate to say it, but do you think maybe you ought to see a doctor?"

She shook her head. "No," she said. "I know the cause, and I even know the cure. There's something I have to do."

When Sylvia was nineteen years old, she fell in love with a young man named Gordon Sawyer. He had just started dental school, and they had an understanding; after he had qualified as a dentist, they would get married. They were not officially engaged, she did not have a ring, but they had already reached the stage of talking about names for their children.

He drowned on a family canoe trip. A couple of hours after it happened, but long before anybody could get word to her, Sylvia awoke from a nightmare, bathed in perspiration. The details of the dream had fled, but she knew it had been awful, and that something terrible had happened to Gordon. She couldn't go back to sleep, and she had been up for hours with an unendurable headache when the doorbell rang and a cousin of Gordon's brought the bad news.

That was her first undeniable psychic experience. Before that she'd had feelings and hunches, twinges of perception that were easy to shrug off or blink away. Once a fortune-teller at a county fair had read her palm and told her she had psychic powers herself, powers she'd be well advised to develop. She and Gordon had laughed about it, and he'd offered to buy her a crystal ball for her birthday.

When Gordon died her life found a new direction. If Gordon had lived she'd have gone on working as a salesgirl until she became a full-time wife and mother. Instead she withdrew into herself and began following the promptings of an inner voice. She could walk into a bookstore and her feet would lead her to some arcane volume that would turn out to be just what she needed to study next. She would sit in her room in her parents' house, staring for hours at a candle flame, or at her own reflection in the mirror. Her parents were worried, but nobody did anything beyond urging her to get out more and meet people. She was upset over Gordon's death, they agreed, and that was understandable, and she would get over it.

"Twenty-five dollars," Claire Warburton said, handing over two tens and a five. "You know, I was reading about this woman in *People* magazine, she reads the cards for either Oprah or Madonna, don't ask me which. And do you know how much she gets for a session?"

"Probably more than twenty-five dollars," Sylvia said.

"They didn't say, but they showed the car she drives around in. It's got an Italian name that sounds like testosterone, and it's fire-engine red, naturally. Of course, that's California. People in this town think you'd have to be crazy to pay twenty-five dollars. I don't see how you get by, Sylvia. I swear I don't."

"There was what my mother left," she said. "And the insurance."

"And a good thing, but it won't last forever. Can't you—"

"What?"

"Well, look into the crystal and try to see the stock market? Or ask your spirit guides for investment advice?"

"It doesn't work that way."

"That's what I knew you'd say," Claire said. "I guess that's what everybody says. You can't use it for your own benefit or it doesn't work."

"That's as it should be," she said. "It's a gift, and the Universe doesn't necessarily give you what you want. But you have to keep it. No exchanges, no refunds."

She parked across the street from the police station, turned off the engine, and sat in the car for a few moments, gathering herself. Her car was not a red Testarossa but a six-year-old Ford Tempo. It ran well, got good mileage, and took her where she wanted to go. What more could you ask of a car?

Inside, she talked to two uniformed officers before she wound up on the other side of a desk from a balding man with gentle brown eyes that belied his jutting chin. He was a detective, and his name was Norman Jeffcote.

He looked at her card, then looked directly at her. Twenty years had passed since her psychic powers had awakened with her fiancé's death, and she knew that the years had not enhanced her outward appearance. Then she'd been a girl with regular features turned pretty by her vital energy, a petite and slender creature, and now she was a little brown-haired mouse, dumpy and dowdy.

" 'Psychic counseling,' " he read aloud. "What's that exactly, Ms. Belgrave?"

"Sometimes I sense things," she said.

"And you think you can help us with the Sporran kid?"

"That poor little girl," she said.

Melissa Sporran, six years old, only child of divorced parents, had disappeared eight days previously on her way home from school.

"The mother broke down on camera," Detective Jeffcote said, "and I guess it got to people, so much so that it made some of the national newscasts. That kind of coverage pulls people out of the woodwork. I got a woman on the phone from Chicago, telling me she just knows little Melissa's in a cave at the foot of a waterfall. She's alive, but in great danger. You're a local woman, Ms. Belgrave. You know any waterfalls within a hundred miles of here?"

"No."

"Neither do I. This woman in Chicago, she may have been a little fuzzy on the geography, but she was good at making sure I got her name spelled right. But I won't have a problem in your case, will I? Because your name's all written out on your card."

"You're not impressed with psychic phenomena," she said.

"I think you people got a pretty good racket going," he said, "and more power to you if you can find people who want to shell out for whatever it is you're selling. But I've got a murder investigation to run, and I don't appreciate a lot of people with four-leaf clovers and crystal balls."

"Maybe I shouldn't have come," she said.

"Well, that's not for me to say, Ms. Belgrave, but now that you bring it up—"

"No," she said. "I didn't have any choice. Detective, have you heard of Sir Isaac Newton?"

"Sure, but I probably don't know him as well as you do. Not if you're getting messages from him."

"He was the foremost scientific thinker of his time," she said, "and in his later years he became quite devoted to astrology, which you may take as evidence either of his openmindedness or of encroaching senility, as you prefer."

"I don't see what this has to—"

"A colleague chided him," she said, brooking no interruption, "and made light of his enthusiasm, and do you know what Newton said? 'Sir, I have investigated the subject. You have not. I do not propose to waste my time discussing it with you.' "

He looked at her and she returned his gaze. After a long moment he said, "All right, maybe you and Sir Isaac have a point. You got a hunch about the Sporran kid?"

"Not a hunch," she said, and explained the dreams, the headaches. "I believe I'm linked to her," she said, "however it works, and I don't begin to understand how it works. I think . . ."

"Yes?"

"I'm afraid I think she's dead."

"Yes," Jeffcote said heavily. "Well, I hate to say it, but you gain in credibility with that one, Ms. Belgrave. We think so, too."

"If I could put my hands on some object she owned, or a garment she wore . . ."

"You and the dogs." She looked at him. "There was a fellow with a pack of bloodhounds, needed something of hers to get the scent. Her mother gave us this little sunsuit, hadn't been laundered since she wore it last. The dogs got the scent good, but they couldn't pick it up anywhere. I think we still have it. You wait here."

He came back with the garment in a plastic bag, drew it out, and wrinkled his nose at it. "Smells of dog now," he said. "Does that ruin it for you?"

"The scent's immaterial," she said. "It shouldn't even matter if it's been laundered. May I?"

"You need anything special, Ms. Belgrave? The lights out, or candles lit, or—"

She shook her head, told him he could stay, motioned for him to sit down. She took the child's sunsuit in her hands and closed her eyes and began to breathe deeply, and almost at once her mind began to fill with images. She saw the girl, saw her face, and recognized it from dreams she thought she had forgotten.

She felt things, too. Fear, mostly, and pain, and more fear, and then, at the end, more pain.

"She's dead," she said softly, her eyes still closed. "He strangled her."

"He?"

"I can't see what he looks like. Just impressions." She waved a hand in the air, as if to dispel clouds, then extended her arm and pointed. "That direction," she said.

"You're pointing southeast."

"Out of town," she said. "There's a white church off by itself. Beyond that there's a farm." She could see it from on high, as if she were hovering overhead, like a bird making lazy circles in the sky. "I think it's abandoned. The barn's unpainted and deserted. The house has broken windows."

"There's the Baptist church on Reistertown Road. A plain white building with a little steeple. And out beyond it there's the Petty farm. She moved into town when the old man died."

"It's abandoned," she said, "but the fields don't seem to be overgrown. That's strange, isn't it?"

"Definitely the Petty farm," he said, his voice quickening. "She let the grazing when she moved."

"Is there a silo?"

"Seems to me they kept a dairy herd. There'd have be a silo."

"Look in the silo," she said.

She was studying Detective Jeffcote's palm when the call came. She had already told him he was worried about losing his hair, and that there was nothing he could do about it, that it was inevitable. The inevitability was written in his hand, although she'd sensed it the moment she saw him, just as she had at once sensed his concern. You didn't need to be psychic for that, though. It was immediately evident in the way he'd grown his remaining hair long and combed it to hide the bald spot.

"You should have it cut short," she said. "Very short. A crew cut, in fact."

"I do that," he said, "and everybody'll be able to see how thin it's getting."

"They won't notice," she told him. "The shorter it is, the less attention it draws. Short hair will empower you."

"Wasn't it the other way around with Samson?"

"It will strengthen you," she said. "Inside and out."

"And you can tell all that just looking at my hand?"

She could tell all that just looking at his head, but she only smiled and nodded. Then she noticed an interesting configuration in his palm and told him about it, making some dietary suggestions based on what she saw. She stopped talking when the phone rang, and he reached to answer it.

He listened for a long moment, then covered the mouthpiece with the very palm she'd been reading. "You were right," he said. "In the silo, covered up with old silage. They wouldn't have found her if they hadn't known to look for her. And the smell of the fermented silage masked the smell of the, uh, decomposition."

He put the phone to his ear, listened some more, spoke briefly, covered the mouthpiece again. "Marks on her neck," he said. "Hard to tell if she was strangled, not until there's a full autopsy, but it looks like a strong possibility."

"Teeth," she said suddenly.

"Teeth?"

She frowned, upset with herself. "That's all I can get when I try to see *him*."

"The man who—"

"Took her there, strangled her, killed her. I can't say if he was tall or short, fat or thin, old or young."

"Just that he had teeth."

"I guess that must have been what she noticed. Melissa. She must have been frightened of him because of the teeth."

"Did he bite her? Because if he did—"

"No," she said sharply. "Or I don't know, perhaps he did, but it was the appearance of the teeth that frightened her. He had bad teeth."

"Bad teeth?"

"Crooked, discolored, broken. They must have made a considerable impression on her."

"Jesus," he said, and into the mouthpiece he said, "You still there? What was the name of that son of a bitch, did some handyman work for the kid's mother? Henrich, Heinrich, something like that? Looked like a dentist's worst nightmare? Yeah, well, pick him up again."

He hung up the phone. "We questioned him," he said, "and we let him go. Big gangly overgrown kid, God made him as ugly as he could and then hit him in the mouth with a shovel. This time I think I'll talk to him myself. Ms. Belgrave? You all right?"

"Just exhausted, all of a sudden," she said. "I haven't been sleeping well these past few nights. And what we just did, it takes a lot out of you."

"I can imagine."

"But I'll be all right," she assured him. And, getting to her feet, she realized she wouldn't be needing any more aspirin. The headache was gone.

The handyman, whose name turned out to be Walter Hendrick, broke down under questioning and admitted the abduction and murder of Melissa Sporran. Sylvia saw his picture on television but turned off the set, unable to look at him. His mouth was closed, you couldn't see his teeth, but even so she couldn't bear the sight of him.

The phone rang, and it was a client she hadn't seen in months, calling to book a session. She made a note in her appointment calendar and went into the kitchen to make a cup of tea. She was finishing the tea and trying to decide if she wanted another when the phone rang again.

It was a new client, a Mrs. Huggins, eager to schedule a reading as soon as possible. Sylvia asked the usual questions and made sure she got the woman's date of birth right. Astrology wasn't her main focus, but it never hurt to have that data in hand before a client's first visit. It made it easier, often, to get a grasp on the personality.

"And who told you about me?" she asked, almost as an afterthought. Business always came through referrals, a satisfied client told a friend or relative or coworker, and she liked to know who was saying good things about her.

"Now who was it?" the woman wondered. "I've been meaning to call for such a long time, and I can't think who it was that originally told me about you."

She let it go at that. But, hanging up, she realized the woman had just lied to her. That was not exactly unheard of, although it was annoying when they lied about their date of birth, shaving a few years off their age and unwittingly providing her with an erroneous astrological profile in the process. But this woman had found something wholly unique to lie about, and she wondered why.

Within the hour the phone rang again, another old client of whom she'd lost track. "I'll bet you're booked solid," the woman said. "I just hope you can fit me in."

"Are you being ironic?"

"I beg your pardon?"

"Because you know it's a rare day when I see more than two people, and there are days when I don't see anyone at all."

"I don't know how many people you see," the woman said. "I do know that it's always been easy to get an appointment with you at short notice, but I imagine that's all changed now, hasn't it?"

"Why would it . . ."

"Now that you're famous."

Famous.

Of course she wasn't, not really. Someone did call her from Florida, wanting an interview for a national tabloid, and there was a certain amount of attention in the local press, and on area radio stations. But she was a quiet, retiring woman, hardly striking in appearance and decidedly undramatic in her responses. Her personal history was not interesting in and of itself, nor was she inclined to go into it. Her lifestyle was hardly colorful.

Had it been otherwise, she might have caught a wave of publicity and been nationally famous for her statutory fifteen minutes, reading Joey Buttafuoco's palm on *Hard Copy*, sharing herbal weight-loss secrets with Oprah.

Instead she had her picture in the local paper, seated in her garden. (She wouldn't allow them to photograph her in her studio, among the candles and crystals.) And that was enough to get her plenty of attention, not all of which she welcomed. No one actually crept across her lawn to stare in her window, but cars did slow or even stop in front of her house, and one man got out of his car and took pictures.

She got more attention than usual when she left the house, too. People who knew her congratulated her, hoping to hear a little more about the case and the manner in which she'd solved it. Strangers recognized her—on the street, in the supermarket. While their interest was not intrusive, she was uncomfortably aware of it.

But the biggest change, really, was in the number of people who suddenly found themselves in need of her services. She was bothered at first by the thought that they were coming to her for the wrong reason, and she wondered if she should refuse to accommodate such curiosity seekers. She meditated on the question, and the answer that came to her was that she was unequipped to judge the motivation of those who sought her out. How could she tell the real reason that brought some troubled soul to her door? And how could she determine, irrespective of motivation, what help she might be able to provide?

She decided that she ought to see everyone. If she found herself personally uncomfortable with a client's energy, then she wouldn't see that person anymore. That had been her policy all along. But she wouldn't prejudge any of them, wouldn't screen them in advance.

"But it's impossible to fit everyone in," she told Claire Warburton. "I'm just lucky I got a last-minute cancellation or I wouldn't have been able to schedule you until the end of next week."

"How does it feel to be an overnight success after all these years?"

"Is that what I am? A success? Sometimes I think I liked it better when I was a failure. No, I don't mean that, but no more do I like being booked as heavily as I am, I'll tell you that. The work is exhausting. I'm seeing four people a day, and yesterday I saw five, which I'll never do again. It drains you."

"I can imagine."

"But the gentleman was so persistent, and I thought, well, I do have the time. But by the time the day was over . . ."

"You were exhausted."

"I certainly was. And I hate to book appointments weeks in advance, or to refuse to book them at all. It bothers me to turn anyone away, because how do I know that I'm not turning away someone in genuine need? For years I had less business than I would have preferred, and now I have too much, and I swear I don't know what to do about it." She frowned. "And when I meditate on it, I don't get anywhere at all."

"For heaven's sake," Claire said. "You don't need to look in a crystal for this one. Just look at a balance sheet."

"I beg your pardon?"

"Sylvia," Claire said, "raise your damn rates."

"My rates?"

"For years you've been seeing a handful of people a week and charging them twenty-five dollars each, and wondering why you're poor as a churchmouse. Raise your rates and you'll increase your income to a decent level—*and* you'll keep yourself from being overbooked. The people who really need you will pay the higher price, and the curiosity seekers will think twice."

"But the people who've been coming to me for years—"

"You can grandfather them in," Claire said. "Confine the rate increase to new customers. But I wouldn't."

"You wouldn't?"

"No, and I'm costing my own self money by saying this, but I'll say it anyhow. People appreciate less what costs them less. That woman in California, drives the red Tosteroni? You think she'd treasure that car if somebody sold it to her for five thousand dollars? You think *People* magazine would print a picture of her standing next to it? Raise your rates and everybody'll think more of you, and pay more attention to the advice you give 'em."

"Well," she said, slowly, "I suppose I could go from twenty-five to thirty-five dollars . . ."

"Fifty," Claire said firmly. "Not a penny less."

In the end, she had to raise her fee three times. Doubling it initially had the paradoxical effect of increasing the volume of calls. A second increase, to seventy-five dollars, was a step in the right direction, slowing the flood of calls; she waited a few months, then took a deep breath and told a caller her price was one hundred dollars a session.

And there it stayed. She booked three appointments a day, five days a week, and pocketed fifteen hundred dollars a week for her efforts. She lost some old clients, including a few who had been coming to her out of habit, the way they went to get their hair done. But it seemed to her that the ones who stayed actually listened more intently to what she saw in the cards or crystal, or channeled while she lay in trance.

"Told you," Claire said. "You get what you pay for."

One afternoon there was a call from Detective Jeffcote. There was a case, she might have heard or read about it, and could she possibly help him with it? She had appointments scheduled, she said, but she could come to the police station as soon as her last client was finished, and—

"No, I'll come to you," he said. "Just tell me when's a good time."

He turned up on the dot. His hair was very short, she noticed, and he seemed more confident and self-possessed than when she'd seen him before. In the living room, he accepted a cup of tea and told her about the girl who'd gone missing, an eleventh-grader named Peggy Mae Turlock. "There hasn't been much publicity," he said, "because kids her age just go off sometimes, but she's an A student and sings in the church choir, and her parents are worried. And I just thought, well . . ."

She reminded him that she'd had three nights of nightmares and headaches when Melissa Sporran disappeared.

"As if the information was trying to get through," he said. "And you haven't had anything like that this time? Because I brought her sunglasses case, and a baseball jacket they tell me she wore all the time."

"We can try," she said.

She took him into her studio, lit two of the new scented candles, seated him on the chaise, and took the chair for herself. She draped Peggy Mae's jacket over her lap and held the green vinyl eyeglass case in both hands. She closed her eyes, breathed slowly and deeply.

After a while she said, "Pieces."

"Pieces?"

"I'm getting these horrible images," she said, "of dismemberment, but I don't know that it has anything to do with the girl. I don't know where it's coming from."

"You picking up any sense of where she might be, or of who might have put her there?"

She slowed her breathing, let herself go deep, deep.

"Down down down," she said.

"How's that, Ms. Belgrave?"

"Something in a well," she said. "And old rusty chain going down into a well, and something down there."

A search of wells all over the country divulged no end of curious debris, including a skeleton that turned out to be that of a large dog. No human remains were found, however, and the search was halted when Peggy Mae came home from Indianapolis. She'd gone there for an abortion, expecting to be back in a day or so, but there had been medical complications. She'd been in the hospital there for a week, never stopping to think that her parents were afraid for her life, or that the police were probing abandoned wells for her dismembered corpse.

Sylvia got a call when the girl turned up. "The important thing is she's all right," he said, "although I wouldn't be surprised if right about now she wishes she was dead. Point is you didn't let us down. You were trying to home in on something that wasn't there in the first place, since she was alive and well all along."

"I'm glad she's alive," she said, "but disappointed in myself. All of that business about wells."

"Maybe you were picking up something from fifty years ago," he said. "Who knows how many wells there are, boarded up and forgotten years ago? And who knows what secrets one or two of them might hold?"

"Perhaps you're right."

Perhaps he was. But all the same the few days when the police were looking in old wells was a professional high water mark for her. After the search was called off, after Peggy Mae came home in disgrace, it wasn't quite so hard to get an appointment with Sylvia Belgrave.

Three nights of nightmares and fitful sleep, three days of headaches. And, awake or asleep, a constant parade of hideous images.

It was hard to keep herself from running straight to the police. But she forced herself to wait, to let time take its time. And then on the morning after the third unbearable night she showered away the stale night sweat and put on a skirt and a blouse and a flowered hat. She sat in the garden with a cup of hot water and lemon juice, then rinsed it in the kitchen sink and went to her car.

The car was a Taurus, larger and sleeker and, certainly, newer than her old Tempo, but it did no more and no less than the Tempo had done. It conveyed her from one place to another. This morning it brought her to the police station, and her feet brought her the rest of the way—into the building, and through the corridors to Detective Norman Jeffcote's office.

"Ms. Belgrave," he said. "Have a seat, won't you?"

His hair was longer than it had been when he'd come to her house. He hadn't regrown it entirely, hadn't once again taken to combing it over the bald spot, but neither was it as flatteringly short as she'd advised him to keep it.

And there was something unsettling about his energy. Maybe it had been a mistake to come.

She sat down and winced, and he asked her if she was all right. "My head," she said, and pressed her fingertips to her temples.

"You've got a headache?"

"Endless headaches. And bad dreams, and all the rest of it."

"I see."

"I didn't want to come," she said. "I told myself not to intrude, not to be a nuisance. But it's just like the first time, when that girl disappeared."

"Melissa Sporran."

"And now there's a little boy gone missing," she said.

"Eric Ackerman."

"Yes, and his address is no more than half a mile from my house. Maybe that's why all these impressions have been so intense."

"Do you know where he is now, Ms. Belgrave?"

"I don't," she said, "but I do feel connected to him, and I have the strong sense that I might be able to help."

He nodded. "And your hunches usually pay off."

"Not always," she said. "That was confusing the year before last, sending you to look in wells."

"Well, nobody's perfect."

"Surely not."

He leaned forward, clasped his hands. "The Ackerman boy, Ms. Belgrave. You think he's all right?"

"Oh, I wish I could say yes."

"But you can't."

"The nightmares," she said, "and the headaches. If he were all right, the way the Turlock girl was all right—"

"There'd be no dreams."

"That's my fear, yes."

"So you think the boy is . . ."

"Dead," she said.

He looked at her for a long moment before he nodded. "I suppose you'd like some article connected with the boy," he said. "A piece of clothing, say."

"If you had something."

"How's this?" he said, and opened a drawer and brought out a teddy bear, its plush fur badly worn, the stitches showing where it had been ripped and mended. Her heart broke at the sight of it and she put her hand to her chest.

"We ought to have a record of this," he said, propping a tape recorder on the desk top, pressing a button to start it recording. "So that I don't miss any of the impressions you pick up. Because you can probably imagine how frantic the boy's parents are."

"Yes, of course."

"So do you want to state your name for the record?"

"My name?"

"Yes, for the record."

"My name is Sylvia Belgrave."

"And you're a psychic counselor?"

"Yes."

"And you're here voluntarily."

"Yes, of course."

"Why don't you take the teddy bear, then. And see what you can pick up from it."

She thought she'd braced herself, but she was unprepared for the flood of images that came when she took the little stuffed bear in her hands. They were more vivid than anything she'd experienced before. Perhaps she should have expected as much; the dreams, and the headaches, too, were worse than they'd been after Melissa Sporran's death, worse than years ago, when Gordon Sawyer drowned.

"Smothered," she managed to say. "A pillow or something like it over his face. He was struggling to breathe and . . . and he couldn't."

"And he's dead."

"Yes."

"And would you happen to know where, Ms. Belgrave?"

Her hands tightened on the teddy bear. The muscles in her arms and shoulders went rigid, bracing to keep the images at bay.

"A hole in the ground," she said.

"A hole in the ground?"

"A basement!" Her eyes were closed, her heart pounding. "A house, but they haven't finished building it yet. The outer walls are up but that's all."

"A building site."

"Yes."

"And the body's in the basement."

"Under a pile of rags," she said.

"Under a pile of rags. Any sense of where, Ms. Belgrave? There are a lot of houses under construction. It would help if we knew what part of town to search."

She tried to get her bearings, then realized she didn't need them. Her hand, of its own accord, found the direction and pointed.

"North and west," he said. "Let's see, where's there a house under construction, ideally one they stopped work on? Seems to me there's one just off Radbourne Road about a quarter of a mile past Six Mile Road. You think that might be the house, Ms. Belgrave?"

She opened her eyes. He was reaching across to take the teddy bear from her. She had to will her fingers to open to release it.

"We've got some witnesses," he said, his voice surprisingly gentle. "A teenager mowing a lawn who saw Eric Ackerman getting into a blue Taurus just like the one you've got parked across the street. He even noticed the license plate, but then it's the kind you notice, isn't it? 2ND SITE. Second sight, eh? Perfect for your line of work."

God, her head was throbbing.

"A woman in a passing car saw you carrying the boy to the house. She didn't spot the vanity plate, but she furnished a good description of the car, and of you, Ms. Belgrave. She thought it was odd, you see. The way you were carrying him, as if he was unconscious, or even dead. Was he dead by then?"

"Yes."

"You killed him first thing? Smothered him?"

"With a pillow," she said. "I wanted to do it right away, before he became afraid. And I didn't want him to suffer."

"Real considerate."

"He struggled," she said, "and then he was still. But I didn't realize just how much he suffered. It was over so quickly, you see, that I told myself he didn't really suffer a great deal at all."

"And?"

"And I was wrong," she said. "I found that out in the dreams. And just now, holding the bear . . ."

He was saying something but she couldn't hear it. She was trembling, and the headache was too much to be borne, and she couldn't follow his words. He brought her a glass of water and she drank it, and that helped a little.

"There were other witnesses, too," he said, "once we found the body, and knew about the car and the license plate. People who saw your car going to and from the construction site. The chief wanted to have you picked up right away, but I talked him into waiting. I figured you'd come in and tell us all about it yourself."

"And here I am," she heard herself say.

"And here you are. You want to tell me about it from the beginning?"

She told it all simply and directly, how she'd selected the boy, how she got him to come into the car with her, how she'd killed him and dumped the body in the spot she'd selected in advance. How she'd gone home, and washed her hands, and waited through three days and nights of headaches and bad dreams.

"Ever kill anybody before, Ms. Belgrave?"

"No," she said. "No, of course not."

"Ever have anything to do with Eric Ackerman or his parents?"

"No."

"Why, then?"

"Don't you know?"

"Tell me anyway."

"Second sight," she said.

"Second . . ."

"Second sight. Vanity plates. Vanity."

"Vanity?"

"All is vanity," she said, and closed her eyes for a moment. "I never made more than a hundred fifty dollars a week," she said, "and nobody knew me or paid me a moment's attention, but that was all right. And then Melissa Sporran was killed, and I was afraid to come in but I came in anyway. And everything changed."

"You got famous."

"For a little while," she said. "And my phone started ringing, and I raised my rates, and my phone rang even more. And I was able to help people, more people than I'd ever helped before, and they were making use of what I gave them, they were taking it seriously."

"And you bought a new car."

"I bought a new car," she said, "and I bought some other things, and I stopped being famous, and the ones who only came because they were curious stopped coming when they stopped being curious, and old customers came less often because they couldn't afford it, and . . ."

"And business dropped off."

"And I thought, I could help so many more people if, if it happened again."

"If a child died."

"Yes."

"And if you helped."

"Yes. And I waited, you know, for something to happen. And there were crimes, there are always crimes. There were even murders, but there was nothing that gave me the dreams and the headaches."

"So you decided to do it yourself."

"Yes."

"Because you'd be able to help so many more people."

"That's what I told myself," she said. "But I was just fooling myself. I did it because I'm having trouble making the payments on my new car, a car I didn't need in the first place. But I need the car now, and I need the phone ringing, and I need—" She frowned, put her head in her hands. "I need aspirin," she said. "That first time, when I told you about Melissa Sporran, the headache went away. But I've told you everything about Eric Ackerman, more than I ever planned to tell you, and the headache hasn't gone away. It's worse than ever."

He told her it would pass, but she shook her head. She knew it wouldn't, or the bad dreams, either. Some things you just knew.

Hit the Ball, Drag Fred

One rarely thought of golf as a waiting game. Oh, to be sure, it was a game of considerable preparation, a game even of contemplation. One spent untold hours on the driving range, additional hours on the putting green. And, before actually hitting the ball, one took time to judge the distance, to assess the wind direction and velocity, and thus to select the right club and to envision the ideal shot. Then one took the indispensable practice swing, and in the follow-through one watched the imaginary ball sail to its intended landing place. Then and only then did one address the ball and take a cut at it.

But one did not in the ordinary course of things spend a great deal of time standing around and waiting. If, as sometimes happened, one was stuck in a foursome of dullards who spent half their time knocking the ball into the rough and the other half looking for it, then a certain amount of waiting was inevitable. But Nicholson rarely found himself in such company. He generally avoided playing with men he didn't know. Better to go out by oneself and play through the duffers and dawdlers.

Today, though, waiting seemed inescapable. At the first tee, a man named Jason Hedrick was waiting for someone to play a round with him, and, a hundred yards away in his car, Roland Nicholson waited for Hedrick to get tired of waiting. There was a bad moment when a car pulled up and golfers piled out of it, but Nicholson relaxed when he saw there were four of them. Their group was complete, and they wouldn't be asking Hedrick to join them.

The four men teed off in turn while Hedrick went on practicing on the putting green. By the time they had disappeared down the fairway, another car pulled up and two golfers emerged, a man and a woman. Nicholson didn't think such a couple would invite a single man to join them, nor could Hedrick politely invite himself. Still, anything could happen on a golf course, so Nicholson held his breath until the two had teed off and left Jason Hedrick with his putter in his hand.

The man, Nicholson noted, teed off twice. He topped his first drive and sent a little dribbler fifty yards down the middle of the fairway, and promptly teed up a second ball, driving it just as straight but three or four times as far. He'd taken a mulligan, obviously rejecting (and not troubling to count) his first effort. You couldn't do that in a tournament, or in any halfway serious game of golf, but a disheartening number of players allowed themselves a mulligan in noncompetitive social play, especially off the first tee.

Not Roland Nicholson. He was a far cry from a scratch golfer, and it was no rare thing for him to top a grounder off the tee, or slice the ball into deep woods. As far as he was concerned, that was part of the game. You could take all the practice swings you wanted, but once you actually hit the ball, you went where it went—and hit it again. That, after all, was the game those funny-talking men in skirts had invented at St. Andrew's. If you weren't going to play it by the rules, why play it at all?

When a third car arrived, Nicholson thought the day was lost. Two men got out of it and strode toward the clubhouse. Hedrick, who had to be heartily sick of the putting green by now, would feel free to ask if he could join them, and they'd have no reason to turn him down.

Nicholson could invite himself along and make up a foursome, but why on earth would he do that? Better to play a round by himself, and he didn't much feel like that, either. Easier to turn the car around and go home.

But then the two men came around the clubhouse, each at the wheel of a motorized golf cart. Hedrick might rent a cart himself, desperation might drive him to it, but Nicholson had a hunch the man would hold out. Golfers like Jason Hedrick, and indeed like Nicholson himself, golfers who walked the course, were apt to regard the cart contingent with a raised eyebrow, if not with a curled lip, much as a hunter who tracked and stalked game might regard a man who shot wolves in the Arctic from a helicopter.

The two wheeled golfers dismounted, teed off—no mulligans, Nicholson was pleased to note—and hopped on their motorized steeds. Even as they vanished in the distance, Jason Hedrick walked off the putting green, had a word with the club pro, and headed for the first tee. His drive was straight and true, as good as any Nicholson had seen that morning. He bent to retrieve his tee, straightened up, returned his driver to his bag, and started walking.

Now was the critical moment. If anyone came along, a twosome or foursome, anyone at all . . .

Nicholson had to wait, had to give Hedrick time to finish the first hole and begin the second. Had to wait, while some unwitting clown in plaid pants came along and spoiled everything.

But no one did. Time crawled, certainly, but still it passed, and when he judged that enough of it had done so, Roland Nicholson fetched his bag of clubs from the trunk, had a word with the club pro, and teed off.

The first hole was a 340-yard par four, with a dogleg to the left around a stand of trees. If Tiger Woods were to play the Oak Hollow course, or John Daly, or any of the really long hitters, he might try to hit a controlled hook that would curve to the left after it cleared the trees. Such refinements were not part of Nicholson's game, and all he tried to do was keep the ball in the middle of the fairway and drive it as far as he could.

The result was satisfactory. He'd have liked more distance, but the ball flew straight as an arrow, and what more could you ask? He walked to the ball, took out his two iron, put it back, touched the big silvery head of one club, then drew his four wood. His shot, after a deliberate practice swing, was hole high but off to the left. He chipped onto the green, some forty feet from the pin. His first putt ran well past the hole—never up, never in, he told himself—but he steadied himself and sank a twelve-footer coming back, for a bogey five.

A good start.

It took Nicholson several more holes to catch up with Hedrick. He played quickly, but he didn't want to hurry his shots, knowing that would amount to a false economy—he'd hit the ball poorly, and consequently would have to hit it more often.

He bogeyed the second hole. The third hole was a par five, and he put together a good drive and a strong second shot and was at the edge of the green in three. Par seemed a good possibility but his putter let him down, and he wound up with a seven.

He wrote it on the scorecard.

On the fourth hole he put it all together. His drive carried the fairway bunkers, and he followed it with a five iron, a wedge, and a putt that found the center of the cup. Four for a par.

The fifth hole was the first par three, and as he reached the tee he could see Hedrick 190 yards away, kneeling down, trying to read the green. Nicholson teed up a ball, grabbed his three iron, addressed the ball without benefit of a practice swing, and took his best shot.

"Fore!" he cried.

The ball sailed straight at the green, straight at Hedrick, but carried beyond both and dropped into a sand trap on the far side of the green.

He called out an apology, grabbed his clubs, and hurried down the fairway.

"So damned sorry," he was saying. "I don't know what's the matter with me. I never even saw you there until I'd hit the ball, and for a change it went right where it was supposed to. I thought it was going to take your head off."

"I could see it was long," Hedrick said, "the moment I looked up. What did you use, a three iron?"

"A four," Nicholson said.

"Oh? Then you must have had your heart in it. I always use a four here myself, but I never carry the green."

"I should have got more loft," Nicholson said. "Look, I'm sorry. I'll be quiet while you putt out, and I'll be careful not to hit into you again."

"Prefer to play alone, do you?"

"The only thing I prefer it to," said Nicholson, "is not playing at all. Fellow I was supposed to play with couldn't make it. Ben Weymouth. Don't suppose you know him?"

"I'm afraid not."

"He canceled at the last minute. I'd been hoping I'd run into somebody at the first tee, but no such luck, and I couldn't afford to wait on the off chance someone would turn up. And Jimmy said I'd just missed a fellow who'd been looking for somebody to play with."

"That would have been me," Hedrick said. "I got tired of waiting, but it looks as though we found each other after all. It's your shot."

"Oh," Nicholson said, seemingly taken aback. "But I couldn't possibly horn in, not after the way I almost crowned you there."

"No harm done. So why not finish the round together? Unless you really don't want company."

"Company's exactly what I do want. If you're sure . . ."

"I'm sure," Hedrick said. "And you're away, and the lie you've got in the trap is the reason God invented the sand wedge."

He got a good shot from the trap and two-putted for a bogey four. Hedrick's putt lipped the cup, hesitated for a long moment, then dropped for a birdie. Nicholson complimented him on the putt and Hedrick turned it aside, saying it was the result of having so much time to think about it.

"Anyway," he said, "you've brought me luck. If I'd hit that putt straight off, it never would have dropped."

"Good luck for both of us," Nicholson replied.

On the next hole they both hit good drives, but to opposite sides of the broad fairway. They met on the green, each reaching it in three, each two-putting for a bogey.

On number seven, Hedrick hooked his drive into the tall grass to the left of the fairway. "Hell," he said.

"Shouldn't hurt you much," Nicholson told him. He teed up his own ball and sent it down the left edge of the fairway.

"Birds of a feather," he said, retrieving his tee, returning his club to the bag. His forefinger stroked the silvery head of the big driver before he hoisted his bag and stepped away from the tee. "Hit the ball, drag Fred," he said.

"How's that?"

"I love golf jokes," Nicholson said, as they headed down the fairway together. "Not as much as I love golf, but I do get a kick out of them. Of course they're all the same joke."

"All the same joke?"

"The point of every golf joke I ever heard," said Nicholson, "is the obsessive nature of the game. That's what they're all about, and that's what makes them funny. Like the funeral passing by."

"I must have missed a couple of strokes there," Hedrick said. "What's so funny about a funeral?"

"Two fellows are playing golf," Nicholson said. "And as they approach the tee for the seventh hole there's a long string of cars passing by."

"In the middle of a golf course?"

"There's a road edging the course," Nicholson said patiently, "and from the seventh tee, they're within chipping distance of the road. And there are all these cars passing at slow speed, and the first one's a hearse and the next two are black limousines, and they've all of them got their lights on, so you can tell it's a funeral cortege."

"On their way to the cemetery," Hedrick said.

"Evidently. So the one golfer, he immediately shoves his driver back into his bag, whips off his cap, and stands in reverent silence until the very last car has passed them and disappeared into the distance."

"Why?"

"Just what his partner was wondering. 'What a respectful thing to do!' he says. 'All the times we've played together, and it turns out there's a spiritual side to you I never saw before.'

"The first golfer shrugs and puts his cap back on. 'I figure it's the least I can do,' he says. 'After all, she was a good wife to me for twenty-seven years.' "

Hedrick found his ball, took his second shot, made a good recovery. Nicholson took his own second shot, and they finished the hole in silence. Coming off the green, Hedrick said, "She was his wife."

"Right."

"In the hearse. His wife died, and she was being buried, and he was out on the golf course instead of showing up for her funeral."

"Well, it's not as though it actually happened," Nicholson said. "It's just a joke."

"Oh, I realize that. I'm just looking at it *as* a joke. She was his wife and it was a successful marriage, but because golf is the way it is and because golfers are the way they are—"

"The way we are," Nicholson put in.

"Well, yes. Because of these factors, his idea of showing respect is standing for a couple of minutes with his cap off."

"When you explain it that way," Nicholson said, "it's not terribly funny, is it?"

"Oh, it's funny," Hedrick said. "I'm just sort of, oh, deconstructing it, you might say. And I think you said all golf jokes are essentially the same, all based on the same element of humor."

"I'd say so," Nicholson said. "Can you think of one that isn't't?"

Hedrick couldn't, and they played on in relative silence, their conversation limited to compliments on one another's shots as they played the next two holes. Both men bogeyed the par-three eighth hole. Hedrick scored par on nine, while Nicholson, whose second shot stopped within six feet of the pin, read the green, set himself, and sank the putt for a birdie.

It was, he realized, the first hole he'd won outright.

Approaching the next green, Hedrick said, "But I'm afraid I don't see where Fred comes into it."

Nicholson looked at him.

" 'Hit the ball, drag Fred.' Isn't that what you said? If Fred's anywhere in the joke about the wife's funeral, he must have been hiding behind a tree. I have to say I didn't spot him."

"It's another joke," Nicholson told him, "but in a sense it's the same joke. Man goes to play a round of golf with his best friend and business partner."

"Fred, I suppose."

"Right, Fred. And his wife's waiting dinner for him, and he's more than two hours late by the time he walks in the door, and the guy looks terrible. 'Honey,' she says, 'are you all right? Did you have a good afternoon?'

" 'I'm not all right,' he says. 'And I just had the worst afternoon of my life. I met Fred and we went out together, and everything was fine, it was a beautiful afternoon, and we were both hitting the ball well. And then Fred's playing his second shot on the sixth hole, he's set up nicely just to the right of the long fairway bunker, and he goes into his backswing and collapses. He drops dead, right there in the middle of the fairway.'

" 'Oh, my God,' says the wife. 'Honey, that's horrible! How awful for poor Fred, and it must have been perfectly terrible for you, too.'

" 'I'll say,' he says. 'That was the sixth hole, the long par five. So for twelve more holes it was hit the ball, drag Fred, hit the ball, drag Fred.' "

Hedrick didn't say anything at first. Then he said, "I see what you mean. It's the same joke. It's different, but it's the same."

"It's a golf joke," Nicholson said. "They're all the same."

"Are you married?"

"I was," Hedrick replied. "She died, and the funeral's this afternoon. I'll tell you, if the hearse passes us, I'm taking my cap off."

"You're not wearing a cap."

"Well, if I were. No, I'm not married. Why do you ask?"

"Ever been?"

"Briefly, years ago. It didn't work out, and I'm in no hurry to repeat the experiment."

"I'm married," Nicholson said.

"Oh?"

"Happily. Or so I've always thought."

"Oh."

"There I was," Nicholson said, "with a beautiful wife. And a best friend. Do you begin to get the picture?"

"I get a picture," Hedrick said, "but I don't know whether or not it's *the* picture."

"There's only one picture," Nicholson said, "and you got it a lot quicker than I did. It took me a while. The signs were there, but I didn't see them at first. Then I began to notice things. Facial expressions, eye movements. Something in the air. Nothing concrete, but there came a day when I just knew, and realized I'd known for a while. Known without knowing I knew, if you follow me."

"Perhaps you were mistaken."

"Just what I told myself. Then there came the day when my friend backed out of a foursome at the last minute. It wasn't the first time he'd done this, and for once I could guess the reason."

"So what happened? The three of you played without him?"

"The three of us teed off together," Nicholson said, "and the three of us played a couple of holes together, and then I pulled a muscle hitting a two iron and I was in agony. Or at least that's the show I put on for the two fellows I was with."

"You dropped out?"

"And left them to finish the round. I knew they wouldn't quit just because I'd torn up my shoulder. I mean, they're golfers, right? Hit the ball, drag Fred. Except in this instance Fred picked up his golf clubs and went home. Where I was not greatly surprised to find my friend's car in my driveway."

"It was definitely his car?"

"I suppose it could have been somebody else's green Olds Cutlass, and that it just happened to have a dented right rear fender, and a license plate reading UNDRPAR. No, I'm afraid it was his car."

"Still, there might have been an innocent explanation."

"There might," Nicholson agreed. "I pulled into the driveway and parked behind his car. Then I walked around to the rear of the house and looked in the bedroom window. Again, there could be a perfectly innocent explanation for what I saw. Perhaps, for instance, my best friend had somehow sprung a leak, and my wife was merely trying to reinflate him."

"Oh."

"Quite."

"What did you do? Burst in the door? Confront them?"

"Of course not."

"Oh."

"What I felt like doing," Nicholson said, "was driving straight back to the country club and catching up with the fellows I'd been playing with. But how could I do that after my imaginary shoulder injury? So what I did was go to a chiropractor and get a deep heat treatment."

"Even though there was nothing wrong with you?"

"You can always find someone happy to give you a deep heat treatment, and what harm can it do? It's not as though I was in danger of melting. It enabled me to make a miraculous recovery, and I was out on the course the next day."

"But not with your friend, I don't suppose."

"Why not? We'd been playing together for years."

"But wasn't it awkward?"

"Why should it be? He didn't know that I knew anything."

"And you could just act as though nothing had happened?"

"Not much acting required, is there? All I had to do was play golf and have the sort of cursory conversation one has on a golf course."

"And inside?"

"In the clubhouse, you mean?"

"Inside yourself."

"Inside myself," Nicholson said calmly, "I was filled with murderous rage."

"I can imagine. You must have wanted to kill them both."

"Certainly not. Why would I want to kill my wife?"

"But—"

"The woman's been an ideal wife since the day I married her. An ornament in public, a social asset, an impeccable homemaker, a splendid cook. More to the point, she's an excellent companion, and, in intimate moments, a spirited partner. I'd have to be out of my mind to want any harm to come to her."

"But she deceived you," Hedrick pointed out. "She slept with your best friend."

"I'm not sure that's the right word for it," Nicholson said thoughtfully. "From the look of things, sleep didn't play much of a role in the relationship. But yes, she deceived me, and with my closest friend. And, quite possibly, with others I don't know about."

"And you can accept that?"

"I can certainly forgive it. She's a woman, for heaven's sake. Remember your Bible? Eve ate the apple. It cost us all our tenancy in Paradise, but does it make you want to kill the poor woman? Certainly not."

"But—"

"She was a woman. She was tempted, she was powerless to resist. Not her fault. But as for the one who tempted her . . ."

"The serpent."

"The snake," said Nicholson, with feeling, "in the grass. The damned snake. He's the one you want to crush under your heel."

Nicholson held the honors, having won the previous hole. He took an unusually vicious practice swing.

"My best friend," he said. "Fred."

"His name can't really be Fred."

"It's as good a name as any. And we might as well call him something. He's the one who betrayed me. He's the one I want to kill."

He settled himself, addressed the ball. His swing was picture-perfect, and the ball sailed off down the fairway.

"And I'll do it, too," he said, and stooped to pick up his tee.

Hedrick sliced his own drive into the woods, and Nicholson could see the notion of a mulligan cross the man's mind. But Hedrick walked manfully after his ball, and Nicholson kept him company and helped him find it. The man tried to recover with a daring shot between two trees, but the ball caromed off one of them and he wound up worse than where he'd started. He played safe on the third shot and got out onto the fairway, but it still took him five strokes before he reached the green of the par-four hole.

"You and . . . Fred," he said along the way. "Is this where the two of you play?"

"We're both members at Ellicott Creek," Nicholson said. "That's where we generally play. I've been a member here myself for a little over a year now as well, that's one of the perks my firm extends when you make junior partner, and I've had Fred here a couple of times as my guest. But I doubt you'd know him."

"I was wondering," Hedrick admitted. They reached the green, and Hedrick, who was away, knelt down to read the green. He got up, stood over the ball. He said, "What you said before. That you intend to kill him. You were just saying that, weren't you?"

The question was delivered in a tone that suggested it might or might not be rhetorical. One could answer it or not, and Nicholson chose not to.

Hedrick four-putted for a quintuple bogey.

"That big silver club in your bag," Hedrick said. "Except of course it's not silver. Titanium or something like that, isn't it?"

"Some space-age alloy."

"If they can put a man on the moon," Hedrick said, "I suppose they ought to be able to add a few yards to a man's tee shot. That's the Big Brenda, isn't it? But you haven't been using it."

"Just at the driving range."

"And did it perform the way it says in the ads? Evidently not, or you'd be using it on the course."

"I don't like it," Nicholson said. "There's something wrong with the way it's balanced."

"I ought to try it on the hole coming up. Par five, 585 yards. A little extra distance wouldn't hurt."

"I think the club's defective," Nicholson said. "Something wrong with the shaft. I'm planning on taking it back, letting them look at it."

Hedrick chuckled. "Relax," he said. "I don't really want to borrow your Big Brenda. I know better than to try a new club in the middle of a round."

Hedrick, using his own driver, hit the ball long and straight. It outran Nicholson's drive by a good thirty yards. They walked down the fairway together, in silence at first. Then Nicholson said, "Over and over I've thought about killing him."

"Your best friend. Except it turns out he's no friend at all, so I don't know what to call him."

"I thought we had settled on Fred."

"Seems silly, calling him that. But no sillier than talking of killing him."

"People kill people all the time," Nicholson said.

"Yes, but—"

"You read the papers, listen to the news, it's just one murder after another."

"That's true, but—"

"A golf club," Nicholson said.

"How's that?"

"Be the best way to do it, don't you think? After all the golf we played together over the years? Bash his treacherous brains out with a golf club, then wrap the shaft around his neck."

"Can you bend a shaft like that?" Hedrick wondered. "Of course, once you'd bashed his head in, the question's largely academic, isn't it?"

They fell silent again when they reached Nicholson's ball. He sent it on its way with his two wood.

"Good shot."

"Good old brassie," he said. "A little left, though. I was afraid of that fairway trap, and I played it a little too safe."

"Better safe than sorry."

"So they say. I bought Big Brenda with the idea that I might use her on Fred."

"Her?"

"Well, it, of course, but since the club has a woman's name . . ."

"That alone makes it a good murder weapon," Hedrick said. "Thing lists for close to five hundred dollars, doesn't it?"

"Five forty-nine, but I got it for a third off."

"Pretty good discount."

"It's still a lot to pay for a club you're only going to swing once. But I couldn't use one of my own clubs, could I?"

"No, I guess not."

"Although," he said, "when you come right down to it, what difference would it make? No matter what I used or how I did it, the police would come straight at me."

"How do you figure that?"

"Because they'd look for someone with a motive to kill Fred," Nicholson said, "and they'd root around in his life and find out who he was sleeping with. And where would that lead?"

"I see what you mean."

"And I'm sure I'd break down the minute they started questioning me. I'm not much good at keeping things to myself." He clapped Hedrick on the shoulder. "I know what you're thinking," he said.

"You know what I'm thinking?"

"That we ought to trade murders. Like the Hitchcock film, where two fellows meet on a train, and they switch victims. You kill Fred while I'm out getting an ironclad alibi, and in return I kill your wife."

"I'm not married," Hedrick said.

"Your boss, then, or the person who stands between you and a huge inheritance. Look, it doesn't matter, because we're not going to do it."

"I should say not," Hedrick said.

"I couldn't kill a stranger for no reason," Nicholson said. "And I couldn't let you kill Fred, either. I mean, the whole thing's pointless unless I get to kill the son of a bitch myself."

Hedrick's second shot was almost as long as his first, and didn't stop rolling until it was within a few yards of the green, just to the right of the trap. "Brilliant," Nicholson told him. "You're a sure bet to win your honors back this hole. An easy chip and you're putting for a birdie."

"If I putt the way I did last hole . . ."

"Well, why leave anything to chance? Sink the chip for an eagle."

They walked to Nicholson's ball. He shaded his eyes, looked at the green. "What do you think? A seven iron?"

"Or an eight. Pin's way at the back of the green, though."

"Seven iron," Nicholson said, and drew it from his bag. He took a practice swing, and his eyes tracked the imaginary ball clear to the rear portion of the green.

"The way to get away with it," he said, "would be to make it look as though it wasn't about him."

"Wasn't about him? Who are we talking about?"

"Fred," Nicholson said. "Who else?"

"If a man gets killed," Hedrick said, "it has to be about him. Doesn't it?"

"Not if it's about something else."

"Like what?"

"Like golf," Nicholson said. "If he were killed with a golf club, like we said, and if his body was found on a golf course . . ."

"I'm not sure I see what difference that makes," Hedrick said, and then his jaw dropped and his eyes widened. "Jesus," he said, "it was in the papers last week, wasn't it? A fellow found in the deep rough at Burning Hills. The twelfth hole, wasn't it?"

"I believe it was the fourteenth."

"That's the one with the water hazard, isn't it? I didn't pay much attention to the story, but he was killed with a golf club, wasn't he?"

"Is that what happened?"

"My God," Hedrick said, "you actually did it. And got away with it, from the sound of it. But why would you tell me about it now?" He frowned, then shook his head and took a step back, grinning. "Jesus, what a setup," he said admiringly. "You had me going there for a moment, didn't you?"

"Did I?"

"The poor guy at Burning Hills was a college kid, wasn't he? A little too young to be your best friend and your wife's lover, I'd have to say. You set up that whole story to get me going, and I have to give you credit." He laughed. " 'Hit the ball, drag Fred.' The college boy, I don't suppose his name was Fred, was it?"

"He was somebody else," Nicholson said.

"Well, I guess he was, wasn't he? Hell of a thing, dying at that age. They haven't found out who killed him or why, have they?"

"No."

"Hard to make sense of, isn't it? Why kill a college kid on a golf course?"

Nicholson addressed his ball, breathed in and out, in and out. He swung the seven iron and got just the right amount of loft. The ball floated all the way to the back edge of the green, backed up, and trolled to within inches of the cup.

"Beautiful," Hedrick said.

"Thanks," Nicholson said. "And to answer your question, I'd guess the boy was killed to establish a pattern."

"A pattern? What kind of a pattern?"

"Oh, I don't know," Nicholson said. "Look, you know something about clubs. Take a look at this."

He drew the Big Brenda out of his bag. Hedrick's face showed first puzzlement, then concern. He started to say something, but Nicholson didn't wait to find out what it was. Instead he seized the club's silver-colored head in one hand and the shaft in the other and twisted. The club head came off in his hand, revealing the end of the shaft, honed to razor sharpness. "Just look at this," he said, and lobbed the club head underhand at Hedrick.

Hedrick reached for it with both hands. And Nicholson lunged at him, wielding the club shaft like a rapier. The sharpened end of the shaft sank into the man's chest. Hedrick's mouth opened, forming a perfect circle, but he was dead before he could utter a sound.

"Hit the ball, drag Fred," Nicholson said, to no one in particular, and took hold of the dead man by his hands and dragged him across the turf to a convenient sand trap. He went back for Hedrick's clubs and stretched them out alongside the corpse. With a cloth from his golf bag he wiped the shaft and head of the Big Brenda, and anything else he'd touched that might hold a print. He took one of Hedrick's golf balls and stuck it in the dead man's mouth, took four of his tees—two white, two yellow—and used them as plugs in the man's nostrils and ear holes. He'd found this part of the process a little distasteful at Burning Hills, but discovered it was less objectionable now. Evidently a person got used to it.

He retrieved his own clubs—minus the Big Brenda, of course—and went to the green. He left Hedrick's ball where it lay, thinking it was a shame the man hadn't had a chance to try chipping for his eagle. But he wouldn't have made it anyway, and, when all was said and done, what earthly difference did it make?

His own ball lay less than a foot from the cup, close enough to concede under ordinary circumstances, but in this case it was for a birdie, and you couldn't make a habit of conceding birdie putts to yourself, could you? He drew the flagstick, got his putter, knocked the ball in, retrieved it, replaced the stick. There was still no one in sight, and this way he felt a good deal more sanguine about entering a four for the hole on his scorecard.

No mulligans taken, no birdie putts conceded. If you were going to play the game, you might as well play it right.

He walked briskly to the next tee. One or two more, he thought, over the course of one or two more weeks, and the pattern would be sufficiently established.

Then it would be Fred's turn.

How Far It Could Go

She picked him out right away, the minute she walked into the restaurant. It was no great trick. There were only two men seated alone, and one was an elderly gentleman who already had a plate of food in front of him.

The other was thirty-five or forty, with a full head of dark hair and a strong jawline. He might have been an actor, she thought. An actor you'd cast as a thug. He was reading a book, though, which didn't entirely fit the picture.

Maybe it wasn't him, she thought. Maybe the weather had delayed him.

She checked her coat, then told the headwaiter she was meeting a Mr. Cutler. "Right this way," he said, and for an instant she fancied that he was going to show her to the elderly gentleman's table, but of course he led her over to the other man, who closed his book at her approach and got to his feet.

"Billy Cutler," he said. "And you're Dorothy Morgan. And you could probably use a drink. What would you like?"

"I don't know," she said. "What are you having?"

"Well," he said, touching his stemmed glass, "night like this, minute I sat down I ordered a martini, straight up and dry as a bone. And I'm about ready for another."

"Martinis are in, aren't they?"

"Far as I'm concerned, they were never out."

"I'll have one," she said.

While they waited for the drinks they talked about the weather. "It's treacherous out there," he said. "The main roads, the Jersey Turnpike and the Garden State, they get these chain collisions where fifty or a hundred cars slam into each other. Used to be a lawyer's dream before no-fault came in. I hope you didn't drive."

"No, I took the PATH train," she said, "and then a cab."

"Much better off."

"Well, I've been to Hoboken before," she said. "In fact we looked at houses here about a year and a half ago."

"You bought anything then, you'd be way ahead now," he said. "Prices are through the roof."

"We decided to stay in Manhattan." And then we decided to go our separate ways, she thought but didn't say. And thank God we didn't buy a house, or he'd be trying to steal it from me.

"I drove," he said, "and the fog's terrible, no question, but I took my time and I didn't have any trouble. Matter of fact, I couldn't remember if we said seven or seven-thirty, so I made sure I was here by seven."

"Then I kept you waiting," she said. "I wrote down seven-thirty, but—"

"I figured it was probably seven-thirty," he said. "I also figured I'd rather do the waiting myself than keep you waiting. Anyway—" he tapped the book "—I had a book to read, and I ordered a drink, and what more does a man need? Ah, here's Joe with our drinks."

Her martini, straight up and bone dry, was crisp and cold and just what she needed. She took a sip and said as much.

"Well, there's nothing like a martini," he said, "and they make a good one here. Matter of fact, it's a good restaurant altogether. They serve a good steak, a strip sirloin."

"Also coming back in style," she said. "Along with the martini."

He looked at her. He said, "So? You want to be right up with the latest trends? Should I order us a couple of steaks?"

"Oh, I don't think so," she said. "I really shouldn't stay that long."

"Whatever you say."

"I just thought we'd have a drink and—"

"And handle what we have to handle."

"That's right."

"Sure," he said. "That'll be fine."

Except it was hard to find a way into the topic that had brought her to Hoboken, to this restaurant, to this man's table. They both knew why she was here, but that didn't relieve her of the need to broach the subject. Looking for a way in, she went back to the weather, the fog. Even if the weather had been good, she told him, she would have come by train and taxi. Because she didn't have a car.

He said, "No car? Didn't Tommy say you had a weekend place up near him? You can't go back and forth on the bus."

"It's his car," she said.

"His car. Oh, the fella's."

"Howard Bellamy's," she said. Why not say his name? "His car, his weekend place in the country. His loft on Greene Street, as far as that goes."

He nodded, his expression thoughtful. "But you're not still living there," he said.

"No, of course not. And I don't have any of my stuff at the house in the country. And I gave back my set of car keys. All my keys, the car and both houses. I kept my old apartment on West Tenth Street all this time. I didn't even sublet it because I figured I might need it in a hurry. And I was right, wasn't I?"

"What's your beef with him exactly, if you don't mind me asking?"

"My beef," she said. "I never had one, far as I was concerned. We lived together three years, and the first two weren't too bad. Trust me, it was never Romeo and Juliet, but it was all right. And then the third year was bad, and it was time to bail out."

She reached for her drink and found the glass empty. Odd—she didn't remember finishing it. She looked across the table at him and he was waiting patiently, nothing showing in his dark eyes.

After a moment she said, "He says I owe him ten thousand dollars."

"Ten large."

"He says."

"Do you?"

She shook her head. "But he's got a piece of paper," she said. "A note I signed."

"For ten thousand dollars."

"Right."

"Like he loaned you the money."

"Right." She toyed with her empty glass. "But he didn't. Oh, he's got the paper I signed, and he's got a canceled check made out to me and deposited to my account. But it wasn't a loan. He gave me the money and I used it to pay for a cruise the two of us took."

"Where? The Caribbean?"

"The Far East. We flew into Singapore and cruised down to Bali."

"That sounds pretty exotic."

"I guess it was," she said. "This was while things were still good between us, or as good as they ever were."

"This paper you signed," he prompted.

"Something with taxes. So he could write it off, don't ask me how. Look, all the time we lived together I paid my own way. We split expenses right down the middle. The cruise was something else, it was on him. If he wanted me to sign a piece of paper so the government would pick up part of the tab—"

"Why not?"

"Exactly. And now he says it's a debt, and I should pay it, and I got a letter from his lawyer. Can you believe it? A letter from a lawyer?"

"He's not going to sue you."

"Who knows? That's what the lawyer letter says he's going to do."

He frowned. "He goes into court and you start testifying about a tax dodge—"

"But how can I, if I was a party to it?"

"Still, the idea of him suing you after you were living with him. Usually it's the other way around, isn't it? They got a word for it."

"Palimony."

"That's it, palimony. You're not trying for any, are you?"

"Are you kidding? I said I paid my own way."

"That's right, you said that."

"I paid my own way before I met him, the son of a bitch, and I paid my own way while I was with him, and I'll go on paying my own way now that I'm rid of him. The last time I took money from a man was when my Uncle Ralph lent me bus fare to New York when I was eighteen years old. He didn't call it a loan, and he sure as hell didn't give me a piece of paper to sign, but I paid him back all the same. I saved up the money and sent him a money order. I didn't even have a bank account. I got a money order at the post office and sent it to him."

"That's when you came here? When you were eighteen?"

"Fresh out of high school," she said. "And I've been on my own ever since, and paying my own way. I would have paid my own way to Singapore, as far as that goes, but that wasn't the deal. It was supposed to be a present. And he wants me to pay my way and his way, he wants the whole ten thousand plus interest, and—"

"He's looking to charge you interest?"

"Well, the note I signed. Ten thousand dollars plus interest at the rate of eight percent per annum."

"Interest," he said.

"He's pissed off," she said, "that I wanted to end the relationship. That's what this is about."

"I figured."

"And what I figured," she said, "is if a couple of the right sort of people had a talk with him, maybe he would change his mind."

"And that's what brings you here."

She nodded, toying with her empty glass. He pointed to the glass, raised his eyebrows questioningly. She nodded again, and he raised a hand, and caught the waiter's eye, and signaled for another round.

They were silent until the drinks came. Then he said, "A couple of boys could talk to him."

"That would be great. What would it cost me?"

"Five hundred dollars would do it."

"Well, that sounds good to me."

"The thing is, when you say talk, it'll have to be more than talk. You want to make an impression, situation like this, the implication is either he goes along with it or something physical is going to happen. Now, if you want to give that impression, you have to get physical at the beginning."

"So he knows you mean it?"

"So he's scared," he said. "Because otherwise what he gets is angry. Not right away, two tough-looking guys push him against a wall and tell him what he's gotta do. That makes him a little scared right away, but then they don't get physical and he goes home, and he starts to think about it, and he gets angry."

"I can see how that might happen."

"But if he gets knocked around a little the first time, enough so he's gonna feel it for the next four, five days, he's too scared to get angry. That's what you want."

"Okay."

He sipped his drink, looked at her over the brim. His eyes were appraising her, assessing her. "There's things I need to know about the guy."

"Like?"

"Like what kind of shape is he in?"

"He could stand to lose twenty pounds, but other than that he's okay."

"No heart condition, nothing like that?"

"No."

"He work out?"

"He belongs to a gym," she said, "and he went four times a week for the first month after he joined, and now if he goes twice a month it's a lot."

"Like everybody," he said. "That's how the gyms stay in business. If all their paid-up members showed up, you couldn't get in the door."

"You work out," she said.

"Well, yeah," he said. "Weights, mostly, a few times a week. I got in the habit. I won't tell you where I got in the habit."

"And I won't ask," she said, "but I could probably guess."

"You probably could," he said, grinning. He looked like a little boy for an instant, and then the grin faded and he was back to business.

"Martial arts," he said. "He ever get into any of that?"

"No."

"You're sure? Not lately, but maybe before the two of you started keeping company?"

"He never said anything," she said, "and he would. It's the kind of thing he'd brag about."

"Does he carry?"

"Carry?"

"A gun."

"God, no."

"You know this for a fact?"

"He doesn't even own a gun."

"Same question. Do you know this for a fact?"

She considered it. "Well, how would you know something like that for a fact? I mean, you could know for a fact that a person did own a gun, but how would you know that he didn't? I can say this much—I lived with him for three years and there was never anything I saw or heard that gave me the slightest reason to think he might own a gun. Until you asked the question just now it never entered my mind, and my guess is it never entered his mind, either."

"You'd be surprised how many people own guns," he said.

"I probably would."

"Sometimes it feels like half the country walks around strapped. There's more carrying than there are carry permits. A guy doesn't have a permit, he's likely to keep it to himself that he's carrying, or that he even owns a gun in the first place."

"I'm pretty sure he doesn't own a gun, let alone carry one."

"And you're probably right," he said, "but the thing is you never know. What you got to prepare for is he might have a gun, and he might be carrying it."

She nodded, uncertain.

"Here's what I've got to ask you," he said. "What you got to ask yourself, and come up with an answer. How far are you prepared for this to go?"

"I'm not sure what you mean."

"We already said it's gonna be physical. Manhandling him, and a couple of shots he'll feel for the better part of a week. Work the rib cage, say."

"All right."

"Well," he said, "that's great, if that's how it goes. But you got to recognize it could go farther."

"What do you mean?"

He made a tent of his fingertips. "I mean you can't necessarily decide where it stops. I don't know if you ever heard the expression, but it's like, uh, having relations with a gorilla. You don't stop when you decide. You stop when the gorilla decides."

"I never heard that before," she said. "It's cute, and I sort of get the point, or maybe I don't. Is Howard Bellamy the gorilla?"

"He's not the gorilla. The violence is the gorilla."

"Oh."

"You start something, you don't know where it goes. Does he fight back? If he does, then it goes a little farther than you planned. Does he keep coming back for more? As long as he keeps coming back for it, you got to keep dishing it out. You got no choice."

"I see."

"Plus there's the human factor. The boys themselves, they don't have an emotional stake. So you figure they're cool and professional about it."

"That's what I figured."

"But it's only true up to a point," he went on, "because they're human, you know? So they start out angry with the guy, they tell themselves how he's a lowlife piece of garbage, so it's easier for them to shove him around. Part of it's an act but part of it's not, and say he mouths off, or he fights back and gets in a good lick. Now they're really angry, and maybe they do more damage than they intended to."

She thought about it. "I can see how that could happen," she said.

"So it could go farther than anybody had in mind. He could wind up in the hospital."

"You mean like broken bones?"

"Or worse. Like a ruptured spleen, which I've known of cases. Or as far as that goes there's people who've died from a bare-knuckle punch in the stomach."

"I saw a movie where that happened."

"Well, I saw a movie where a guy spreads his arms and flies, but dying from a punch in the stomach, they didn't just make that up for the movies. It can happen."

"Now you've got me thinking," she said.

"Well, it's something you got to think about. Because you have to be prepared for this to go all the way, and by all the way I mean all the way. It probably won't, ninety-five times out of a hundred it won't."

"But it could."

"Right. It could."

"Jesus," she said. "He's a son of a bitch, but I don't want him dead. I want to be done with the son of a bitch. I don't want him on my conscience for the rest of my life."

"That's what I figured."

"But I don't want to pay him ten thousand dollars, either, the son of a bitch. This is getting complicated, isn't it?"

"Let me excuse myself for a minute," he said, rising. "And you think about it, and then we'll talk some more."

While he was away from the table she reached for his book and turned it so she could read the title. She looked at the author's photo, read a few lines of the flap copy, then put it as he had left it. She sipped her drink—she was nursing this one, making it last—and looked out the window. Cars rolled by, their headlights slightly eerie in the dense fog.

When he returned she said, "Well, I thought about it."

"And?"

"I think you just talked yourself out of five hundred dollars."

"That's what I figured."

"Because I certainly don't want him dead, and I don't even want him in the hospital. I have to admit I like the idea of him being scared, really scared bad. And hurt a little. But that's just because I'm angry."

"Anybody'd be angry."

"But when I get past the anger," she said, "all I really want is for him to forget this crap about ten thousand dollars. For Christ's sake, that's all the money I've got in the world. I don't want to give it to him."

"Maybe you don't have to."

"What do you mean?"

"I don't think it's about money," he said. "Not for him. It's about sticking it to you for dumping him, or whatever. So it's an emotional thing and it's easy for you to buy into it. But say it was a business thing. You're right and he's wrong, but it's more trouble than it's worth to fight it out. So you settle."

"Settle?"

"You always paid your own way," he said, "so it wouldn't be out of the question for you to pay half the cost of the cruise, would it?"

"No, but—"

"But it was supposed to be a present, from him to you. But forget that for the time being. You could pay half. Still, that's too much. What you do is you offer him two thousand dollars. I have a feeling he'll take it."

"God," she said. "I can't even talk to him. How am I going to offer him anything?"

"You'll have someone else make the offer."

"You mean like a lawyer?"

"Then you owe the lawyer. No, I was thinking I could do it."

"Are you serious?"

"I wouldn't have said it if I wasn't. I think if I was to make the offer he'd accept it. I wouldn't be threatening him, but there's a way to do it so a guy feels threatened."

"He'd feel threatened, all right."

"I'll have your check with me, two thousand dollars, payable to him. My guess is he'll take it, and if he does you won't hear any more from him on the subject of the ten grand."

"So I'm out of it for two thousand. And five hundred for you?"

"I wouldn't charge you anything."

"Why not?"

"All I'd be doing is having a conversation with a guy. I don't charge for conversations. I'm not a lawyer, I'm just a guy owns a couple of parking lots."

"And reads thick novels by young Indian writers."

"Oh, this? You read it?"

She shook her head.

"It's hard to keep the names straight," he said, "especially when you're not sure how to pronounce them in the first place. And it's like if you ask this guy what time it is he tells you how to make a watch. Or maybe a sun-dial. But it's pretty interesting."

"I never thought you'd be a reader."

"Billy Parking Lots," he said. "Guy who knows guys and can get things done. That's probably all Tommy said about me."

"Just about."

"Maybe that's all I am. Reading, well, it's an edge I got on just about everybody I know. It opens other worlds. I don't live in those worlds, but I get to visit them."

"And you just got in the habit of reading? The way you got in the habit of working out?"

He laughed. "Yeah, but reading's something I've done since I was a kid. I didn't have to go away to get in that particular habit."

"I was wondering about that."

"Anyway," he said, "it's hard to read there, harder than people think. It's noisy all the time."

"Really? I didn't realize. I always figured that's when I'd get to read *War and Peace,* when I got sent to prison. But if it's noisy, then the hell with it. I'm not going."

"You're something else," he said.

"Me?"

"Yeah, you. The way you look, of course, but beyond the looks. The only word I can think of is class, but it's a word that's mostly used by people that haven't got any themselves. Which is probably true enough."

"The hell with that," she said. "After the conversation we just had? Talking me out of doing something I could have regretted all my life, and figuring out how to get that son of a bitch off my back for two thousand dollars? I'd call that class."

"Well, you're seeing me at my best," he said.

"And you're seeing me at my worst," she said, "or close to it. Looking to hire a guy to beat up an ex-boyfriend. That's class, all right."

"That's not what I see. I see a woman who doesn't want to be pushed around. And if I can find a way that helps you get where you want to be, then I'm glad to do it. But when all's said and done, you're a lady and I'm a wiseguy."

"I don't know what you mean."

"Yes, you do."

"Yes, I guess I do."

He nodded. "Drink up," he said. "I'll run you back to the city."

"You don't have to do that. I can take the PATH train."

"I've got to go into the city anyway. It's not out of my way to take you wherever you're going."

"If you're sure."

"I'm sure," he said. "Or here's another idea. We both have to eat, and I told you they serve a good steak here. Let me buy you dinner, and then I'll run you home."

"Dinner," she said.

"A shrimp cocktail, a salad, a steak, a baked potato—"

"You're tempting me."

"So let yourself be tempted," he said. "It's just a meal."

She looked at him levelly. "No," she said. "It's more than that."

"It's more than that if you want it to be. Or it's just a meal, if that's what you want."

"But you can't know how far it might go," she said. "We're back to that again, aren't we? Like what you said about the gorilla, and you stop when the gorilla wants to stop."

"I guess I'm the gorilla, huh?"

"You said the violence was the gorilla. Well, in this case it's not violence, but it's not either of us, either. It's what's going on between us, and it's already going on, isn't it?"

"You tell me."

She looked down at her hands, then up at him. "A person has to eat," she said.

"You said it."

"And it's still foggy outside."

"Like pea soup. And who knows? There's a good chance the fog'll lift by the time we've had our meal."

"I wouldn't be a bit surprised," she said. "I think it's lifting already."

In for a Penny

Paul kept it very simple. That seemed to be the secret. You kept it simple, you drew firm lines and didn't cross them. You put one foot in front of the other, took it day by day, and let the days mount up.

The state didn't take an interest. They put you back on the street with a cheap suit and figured you'd be back inside before the pants got shiny. But other people cared. This one outfit, about two parts ex-cons to one part holy joes, had wised him up and helped him out. They'd found him a job and a place to live, and what more did he need?

The job wasn't much, frying eggs and flipping burgers in a diner at Twenty-third and Eighth. The room wasn't much, either, seven blocks south of the diner, four flights up from the street. It was small, and all you could see from its window was the back of another building. The furnishings were minimal—an iron bedstead, a beat-up dresser, a rickety chair—and the walls needed paint and the floor needed carpet. There was a sink in the room, a bathroom down the hall. No cooking, no pets, no overnight guests, the landlady told him. No kidding, he thought.

His shift was four to midnight, Monday through Friday. The first weekend he did nothing but go to the movies, and by Sunday night he was ready to climb the wall. Too much time to kill, too few ways to kill it that wouldn't get him in trouble. How many movies could you sit through? And a movie cost him two hours' pay, and if you spent the whole weekend dragging yourself from one movie house to another . . .

Weekends were dangerous, one of the ex-cons had told him. Weekends could put you back in the joint. There ought to be a law against weekends.

But he figured out a way around it. Walking home Tuesday night, after that first weekend of movie-going, he'd stopped at three diners on Seventh Avenue, nursing a cup of coffee and chatting with the guy behind the counter. The third time was the charm; he walked out of there with a weekend job. Saturday and Sunday, same hours, same wages, same work. And they'd pay him off the books, which made his weekend work tax-free.

Between what he was saving in taxes and what he wasn't spending on movies, he'd be a millionaire.

Well, maybe he'd never be a millionaire. Probably be dangerous to be a millionaire, a guy like him, with his ways, his habits. But he was earning an honest dollar, and he ate all he wanted on the job, seven days a week now, so it wasn't hard to put a few bucks aside. The weeks added up and so did the dollars, and the time came when he had enough cash socked away to buy himself a little television set. The cashier at his weekend job set it up and her boyfriend brought it over, so he figured it fell off a truck or walked out of somebody's apartment, but it got good reception and the price was right.

It was a lot easier to pass the time once he had the TV. He'd get up at ten or eleven in the morning, grab a shower in the bathroom down the hall, then pick up doughnuts and coffee at the corner deli. Then he'd watch a little TV until it was time to go to work.

After work he'd stop at the same deli for two bottles of cold beer and some cigarettes. He'd settle in with the TV, a beer bottle in one hand and a cigarette in the other and his eyes on the screen.

He didn't get cable, but he figured that was all to the good. He was better off staying away from some of the stuff they were allowed to show on cable TV. Just because you had cable didn't mean you had to watch it, but he knew himself, and if he had it right there in the house how could he keep himself from looking at it?

And that could get you started. Something as simple as late-night adult programming could put him on a train to the big house upstate. He'd been there. He didn't want to go back.

He would get through most of a pack of cigarettes by the time he turned off the light and went to bed. It was funny, during the day he hardly smoked at all, but back in his room at night he had a butt going just about all the time. If the smoking was heavy, well, the drinking was ultralight. He could make a bottle of Bud last an hour. More, even. The second bottle was always warm by the time he got to it, but he didn't mind, nor did he drink it any faster than he'd drunk the first one. What was the rush?

Two beers was enough. All it did was give him a little buzz, and when the second beer was gone he'd turn off the TV and sit at the window, smoking one cigarette after another, looking out at the city.

Then he'd go to bed. Then he'd get up and do it all over again.

The only problem was walking home.

And even that was no problem at first. He'd leave his rooming house around three in the afternoon. The diner was ten minutes away, and that left him time to eat before his shift started. Then he'd leave sometime between midnight and twelve-thirty—the guy who relieved him, a manic Albanian, had a habit of showing up ten to fifteen minutes late. Paul would retrace his earlier route, walking the seven blocks down Eighth Avenue to Sixteenth Street with a stop at the deli for cigarettes and beer.

The Rose of Singapore was the problem.

The first time he walked past the place, he didn't even notice it. By day it was just another seedy bar, but at night the neon glowed and the jukebox music poured out the door, along with the smell of spilled drinks and stale beer and something more, something unnamable, something elusive.

"If you don't want to slip," they'd told him, "stay out of slippery places."

He quickened his pace and walked on by.

The next afternoon the Rose of Singapore didn't carry the same feeling of danger. Not that he'd risk crossing the threshold, not at any hour of the day or night. He wasn't stupid. But it didn't lure him, and consequently it didn't make him uncomfortable.

Coming home was a different story.

He was thinking about it during his last hour on the job, and by the time he reached it he was walking all the way over at the edge of the sidewalk, as far from the building's entrance as he could get without stepping down into the street. He was like an acrophobe edging along a precipitous path, scared to look down, afraid of losing his balance and falling accidentally, afraid too of the impulse that might lead him to plunge purposefully into the void.

He kept walking, eyes forward, heart racing. Once he was past it he felt himself calming down, and he bought his two bottles of beer and his pack of cigarettes and went on home.

He'd get used to it, he told himself. It would get easier with time.

But, surprisingly enough, it didn't. Instead it got worse, but gradually, imperceptibly, and he learned to accommodate it. For one thing, he steered clear of the west side of Eighth Avenue, where the Rose of Singapore stood. Going to work and coming home, he kept to the opposite side of the street.

Even so, he found himself hugging the inner edge of the sidewalk, as if every inch closer to the street would put him that much closer to crossing it and being drawn mothlike into the tavern's neon flame. And, approaching the Rose of Singapore's block, he'd slow down or speed up his pace so that the traffic signal would allow him to cross the street as soon as he reached the corner. As if otherwise, stranded there, he might cross in the other direction instead, across Eighth Avenue and on into the Rose.

He knew it was ridiculous but he couldn't change the way it felt. When it didn't get better he found a way around it.

He took Seventh Avenue instead.

He did that on the weekends anyway because it was the shortest route. But during the week it added two long crosstown blocks to his pedestrian commute, four blocks a day, twenty blocks a week. That came to about three miles a week, maybe a hundred and fifty extra miles a year.

On good days he told himself he was lucky to be getting the exercise, that the extra blocks would help him stay in shape. On bad days he felt like an idiot, crippled by fear.

Then the Albanian got fired.

He was never clear on what happened. One waitress said the Albanian had popped off at the manager one time too many, and maybe that was what happened. All he knew was that one night his relief man was not the usual wild-eyed fellow with the droopy mustache but a stocky dude with a calculating air about him. His name was Dooley, and Paul made him at a glance as a man who'd done time. You could tell, but of course he didn't say anything, didn't drop any hints. And neither did Dooley.

But the night came when Dooley showed up, tied his apron, rolled up his sleeves, and said, "Give her my love, huh?" And, when Paul looked at him in puzzlement, he added, "Your girlfriend."

"Haven't got one," he said.

"You live on Eighth Avenue, right? That's what you told me. Eighth and Sixteenth, right? Yet every time you leave here you head over toward Seventh. Every single time."

"I like the exercise," he said.

"Exercise," Dooley said, and grinned. "Good word for it."

He let it go, but the next night Dooley made a similar comment. "I need to unwind when I come off work," Paul told him. "Sometimes I'll walk clear over to Sixth Avenue before I head downtown. Or even Fifth."

"That's nice," Dooley said. "Just do me a favor, will you? Ask her if she's got a sister."

"It's cold and it looks like rain," Paul said. "I'll be walking home on Eighth Avenue tonight, in case you're keeping track."

And when he left he did walk down Eighth Avenue—for one block. Then he cut over to Seventh and took what had become his usual route.

He began doing that all the time, and whenever he headed east on Twenty-second Street he found himself wondering why he'd let Dooley have such power over him. For that matter, how could he have let a seedy gin joint make him walk out of his way to the tune of a hundred and fifty miles a year?

He was supposed to be keeping it simple. Was this keeping it simple? Making up elaborate lies to explain the way he walked home? And walking extra blocks every night for fear that the Devil would reach out and drag him into a neon-lit hell?

Then came a night when it rained, and he walked all the way home on Eighth Avenue.

It was always a problem when it rained. Going to work he could catch a bus, although it wasn't terribly convenient. But coming home he didn't have the option, because traffic was one-way the wrong way.

So he walked home on Eighth Avenue, and he didn't turn left at Twenty-second Street, and didn't fall apart when he drew even with the Rose of Singapore. He breezed on by, bought his beer and cigarettes at the deli, and went home to watch television. But he turned the set off again after a few minutes and spent the hours until bedtime at the window, looking out at the rain, nursing the beers, smoking the cigarettes, and thinking long thoughts.

The next two nights were clear and mild, but he chose Eighth Avenue anyway. He wasn't uneasy, not going to work, not coming home, either. Then came the weekend, and then on Monday he took Eighth again, and this time on the way home he found himself on the west side of the street, the same side as the bar.

The door was open. Music, strident and bluesy, poured through it, along with all the sounds and smells you'd expect.

He walked right on by.

You're over it, he thought. He went home and didn't even turn on the TV, just sat and smoked and sipped his two longneck bottles of Bud.

Same story Tuesday, same story Wednesday.

Thursday night, steps from the tavern's open door, he thought, Why drag this out?

He walked in, found a stool at the bar. "Double scotch," he told the barmaid. "Straight up, beer chaser."

He'd tossed off the shot and was working on the beer when a woman slid onto the stool beside him. She put a cigarette between bright red lips, and he scratched a match and lit it for her.

Their eyes met, and he felt something click.

She lived over on Ninth and Seventeenth, on the third floor of a brownstone across the street from the projects. She said her name was Tiffany, and maybe it was. Her apartment was three little rooms. They sat on the couch in the front room and he kissed her a few times and got a little dizzy from it. He excused himself and went to the bathroom and looked at himself in the mirror over the sink.

You could go home now, he told the mirror image. Tell her anything, like you got a headache, you got malaria, you're really a Catholic priest or gay or both. Anything. Doesn't matter what you say or if she believes you. You could go home.

He looked into his own eyes in the mirror and knew it wasn't true.

Because he was stuck, he was committed, he was down for it. Had been from the moment he walked into the bar. No, longer than that. From the first rainy night when he walked home on Eighth Avenue. Or maybe before, maybe ever since Dooley's insinuation had led him to change his route.

And maybe it went back further than that. Maybe he was locked in from the jump, from the day they opened the gates and put him on the street. Hell, from the day he was born, even.

"Paul?"

"Just a minute," he said.

And he slipped into the kitchen. In for a penny, in for a pound, he thought, and he started opening drawers, looking for the one where she kept the knives.

Like a Bone in the Throat

Throughout the trial, Paul Dandridge did the same thing every day. He wore a suit and tie, and he occupied a seat toward the front of the courtroom, and his eyes, time and time again, returned to the man who had killed his sister.

He was never called upon to testify. The facts were virtually undisputed, the evidence overwhelming. The defendant, William Charles Croydon, had abducted Dandridge's sister at knifepoint as she walked from the college library to her off-campus apartment. He had taken her to an isolated and rather primitive cabin in the woods, where he had subjected her to repeated sexual assaults over a period of three days, at the conclusion of which he had caused her death by manual strangulation.

Croydon took the stand in his own defense. He was a handsome young man who'd spent his thirtieth birthday in a jail cell awaiting trial, and his preppy good looks had already brought him letters and photographs and even a few marriage proposals from women of all ages. (Paul Dandridge was twenty-seven at the time. His sister, Karen, had been twenty when she died. The trial ended just weeks before her twenty-first birthday.)

On the stand, William Croydon claimed that he had no recollection of choking the life out of Karen Dandridge, but allowed as how he had no choice but to believe he'd done it. According to his testimony, the young woman had willingly accompanied him to the remote cabin, and had been an enthusiastic sexual partner with a penchant for rough sex. She had also supplied some particularly strong marijuana with hallucinogenic properties and had insisted that he smoke it with her. At one point, after indulging heavily in the unfamiliar drug, he had lost consciousness and awakened later to find his partner beside him, dead.

His first thought, he'd told the court, was that someone had broken into the cabin while he was sleeping, had killed Karen, and might return to kill him. Accordingly he'd panicked and rushed out of there, abandoning Karen's corpse. Now, faced with all the evidence arrayed against him, he was compelled to believe he had somehow committed this awful crime, although he had no recollection of it whatsoever, and although it was utterly foreign to his nature.

The district attorney, prosecuting this case himself, tore Croydon apart on cross-examination. He cited the bite marks on the victim's breasts, the rope burns indicating prolonged restraint, the steps Croydon had taken in an attempt to conceal his presence in the cabin. "You must be right," Croydon would admit, with a shrug and a sad smile. "All I can say is that I don't remember any of it."

The jury was eleven-to-one for conviction right from the jump, but it took six hours to make it unanimous. *Mr. Foreman, have you reached a verdict? We have, Your Honor. On the sole count of the indictment, murder in the first degree, how do you find? We find the defendant, William Charles Croydon, guilty.*

One woman cried out. A couple of others sobbed. The DA accepted congratulations. The defense attorney put an arm around his client. Paul Dandridge, his jaw set, looked at Croydon.

Their eyes met, and Paul Dandridge tried to read the expression in the killer's eyes. But he couldn't make it out.

Two weeks later, at the sentencing hearing, Paul Dandridge got to testify.

He talked about his sister, and what a wonderful person she had been. He spoke of the brilliance of her intellect, the gentleness of her spirit, the promise of her young life. He spoke of the effect of her death upon him. They had lost both parents, he told the court, and Karen was all the family he'd had in the world. And now she was gone. In order for his sister to rest in peace, and in order for him to get on with his own life, he urged that her murderer be sentenced to death.

Croydon's attorney argued that the case did not meet the criteria for the death penalty, that while his client possessed a criminal record he had never been charged with a crime remotely of this nature, and that the rough-sex-and-drugs defense carried a strong implication of mitigating circumstances. Even if the jury had rejected the defense, surely the defendant ought to be spared the ultimate penalty, and justice would be best served if he were sentenced to life in prison.

The DA pushed hard for the death penalty, contending that the rough-sex defense was the cynical last-ditch stand of a remorseless killer, and that the jury had rightly seen that it was wholly without merit. Although her killer might well have taken drugs, there was no forensic evidence to indicate that Karen Dandridge herself had been under the influence of anything other than a powerful and ruthless murderer. Karen Dandridge needed to be avenged, he maintained, and society needed to be assured that her killer would never, ever, be able to do it again.

Paul Dandridge was looking at Croydon when the judge pronounced the sentence, hoping to see something in those cold blue eyes. But as the words were spoken—*death by lethal injection*—there was nothing for Paul to see. Croydon closed his eyes.

When he opened them a moment later, there was no expression to be seen in them.

They made you fairly comfortable on Death Row. Which was just as well, because in this state you could sit there for a long time. A guy serving a life sentence could make parole and be out on the street in a lot less time than a guy on Death Row could run out of appeals. In that joint alone, there were four men with more than ten years apiece on Death Row, and one who was closing in on twenty.

One of the things they'd let Billy Croydon have was a typewriter. He'd never learned to type properly, the way they taught you in typing class, but he was writing enough these days so that he was getting pretty good at it, just using two fingers on each hand. He wrote letters to his lawyer, and he wrote letters to the women who wrote to him. It wasn't too hard to keep them writing, but the trick lay in getting them to do what he wanted. They wrote plenty of letters, but he wanted them to write really hot letters, describing in detail what they'd done with other guys in the past, and what they'd do if by some miracle they could be in his cell with him now.

They sent pictures, too, and some of them were good-looking and some of them were not. "That's a great picture," he would write back, "but I wish I had one that showed more of your physical beauty." It turned out to be surprisingly easy to get most of them to send increasingly revealing pictures. Before long he had them buying Polaroid cameras with timers and posing in obedience to his elaborate instructions. They'd do anything, the bitches, and he was sure they got off on it, too.

Today, though, he didn't feel like writing to any of them. He rolled a sheet of paper into the typewriter and looked at it, and the image that came to him was the grim face of that hardass brother of Karen Dandridge's. What was his name, anyway? Paul, wasn't it?

"Dear Paul," he typed, and frowned for a moment in concentration. Then he started typing again.

"Sitting here in this cell waiting for the day to come when they put a needle in my arm and flush me down God's own toilet, I found myself thinking about your testimony in court. I remember how you said your sister was a goodhearted girl who spent her short life bringing pleasure to everyone who knew her. According to your testimony, knowing this helped you rejoice in her life at the same time that it made her death so hard to take.

"Well, Paul, in the interest of helping you rejoice some more, I thought I'd tell you just how much pleasure your little sister brought to me. I've got to tell you that in all my life I never got more pleasure from anybody. My first look at Karen brought me pleasure, just watching her walk across campus, just looking at those jiggling tits and that tight little ass and imagining the fun I was going to have with them.

"Then when I had her tied up in the backseat of the car with her mouth taped shut, I have to say she went on being a real source of pleasure. Just looking at her in the rear-view mirror was enjoyable, and from time to time I would stop the car and lean into the back to run my hands over her body. I don't think she liked it much, but I enjoyed it enough for the both of us.

"Tell me something, Paul. Did you ever fool around with Karen yourself? I bet you did. I can picture her when she was maybe eleven, twelve years old, with her little titties just beginning to bud out, and you'd have been seventeen or eighteen yourself, so how could you stay away from her? She's sleeping and you walk into her room and sit on the edge of her bed . . ."

He went on, describing the scene he imagined, and it excited him more than the pictures or letters from the women. He stopped and thought about relieving his excitement but decided to wait. He finished the scene as he imagined it and went on:

"Paul, old buddy, if you didn't get any of that you were missing a good thing. I can't tell you the pleasure I got out of your sweet little sister. Maybe I can give you some idea by describing our first time together." And he did, recalling it all to mind, savoring it in his memory, reliving it as he typed it out on the page.

"I suppose you know she was no virgin," he wrote, "but she was pretty new at it all the same. And then when I turned her facedown, well, I can tell you she'd never done *that* before. She didn't like it much, either. I had the tape off her mouth and I swear I thought she'd wake the neighbors, even though there weren't any. I guess it hurt her some, Paul, but that was just an example of your darling sister sacrificing everything to give pleasure to others, just like you said. And it worked, because I had a hell of a good time."

God, this was great. It really brought it all back.

"Here's the thing," he wrote. "The more we did it, the better it got. You'd think I would have grown tired of her, but I didn't. I wanted to keep on having her over and over again forever, but at the same time I felt this urgent need to finish it, because I knew that would be the best part.

"And I wasn't disappointed, Paul, because the most pleasure your sister ever gave anybody was right at the very end. I was on top of her, buried in her to the hilt, and I had my hands wrapped around her neck. And the ultimate pleasure came with me squeezing and looking into her eyes and squeezing harder and harder and going on looking into those eyes all the while and watching the life go right out of them."

He was too excited now. He had to stop and relieve himself. Afterward he read the letter and got excited all over again. A great letter, better than anything he could get any of his bitches to write to him, but he couldn't send it, not in a million years.

Not that it wouldn't be a pleasure to rub the brother's nose in it. Without the bastard's testimony, he might have stood a good chance to beat the death sentence. With it, he was sunk.

Still, you never knew. Appeals would take a long time. Maybe he could do himself a little good here.

He rolled a fresh sheet of paper in the typewriter. *Dear Mr. Dandridge,* he wrote. *I'm well aware that the last thing on earth you want to read is a letter from me. I know that in your place I would feel no different myself. But I cannot seem to stop myself from reaching out to you. Soon I'll be strapped down onto a gurney and given a lethal injection. That frightens me horribly, but I'd gladly die a thousand times over if only it would bring your sister back to life. I may not remember killing her, but I know I must have done it, and I would give anything to undo it. With all my heart, I wish she were alive today.*

Well, that last part was true, he thought. He wished to God she were alive, and right there in that cell with him, so that he could do her all over again, start to finish.

He went on and finished the letter, making it nothing but an apology, accepting responsibility, expressing remorse. It wasn't a letter that sought anything, not even forgiveness, and it struck him as a good opening shot. Probably nothing would ever come of it, but you never knew.

After he'd sent it off, he took out the first letter he'd written and read it through, relishing the feelings that coursed through him and strengthened him. He'd keep this, maybe even add to it from time to time. It was really great the way it brought it all back.

Paul destroyed the first letter.

He opened it, unaware of its source, and was a sentence or two into it before he realized what he was reading. It was, incredibly, a letter from the man who had killed his sister.

He felt a chill. He wanted to stop reading but he couldn't stop reading. He forced himself to stay with it all the way to the end.

The nerve of the man. The unadulterated gall.

Expressing remorse. Saying how sorry he was. Not asking for anything, not trying to justify himself, not attempting to disavow responsibility.

But there had been no remorse in the blue eyes, and Paul didn't believe there was a particle of genuine remorse in the letter, either. And what difference did it make if there was?

Karen was dead. Remorse wouldn't bring her back.

His lawyer had told him they had nothing to worry about, they were sure to get a stay of execution. The appeal process, always drawn out in capital cases, was in its early days. They'd get the stay in plenty of time, and the clock would start ticking all over again.

And it wasn't as though it got to the point where they were asking him what he wanted for a last meal. That happened sometimes, there was a guy three cells down who'd had his last meal twice already, but it didn't get that close for Billy Croydon. Two and a half weeks to go and the stay came through.

That was a relief, but at the same time he almost wished it had run out a little closer to the wire. Not for his benefit, but just to keep a couple of his correspondents on the edges of their chairs.

Two of them, actually. One was a fat girl who lived at home with her mother in Burns, Oregon, the other a sharp-jawed old maid employed as a corporate librarian in Philadelphia. Both had displayed a remarkable willingness to pose as he specified for their Polaroid cameras, doing interesting things and showing themselves in interesting ways. And, as the countdown had continued toward his date with death, both had proclaimed their willingness to join him in heaven.

No joy in that. In order for them to follow him to the grave, he'd have to be in it himself, wouldn't he? They could cop out and he'd never even know it.

Still, there was great power in knowing they'd even made the promise. And maybe there was something here he could work with.

He went to the typewriter. "My darling," he wrote. "The only thing that makes these last days bearable is the love we have for each other. Your pictures and letters sustain me, and the knowledge that we will be together in the next world draws much of the fear out of the abyss that yawns before me.

"Soon they will strap me down and fill my veins with poison, and I will awaken in the void. If only I could make that final journey knowing you would be waiting there for me! My angel, do you have the courage to make the trip ahead of me? Do you love me that much? I can't ask so great a sacrifice of you, and yet I am driven to ask it, because how dare I withhold from you something that is so important to me?"

He read it over, crossed out "sacrifice" and penciled in "proof of love." It wasn't quite right, and he'd have to work on it some more. Could either of the bitches possibly go for it? Could he possibly get them to do themselves for love?

And, even if they did, how would he know about it? Some hatchet-faced dame in Philly slashes her wrists in the bathtub, some fat girl hangs herself in Oregon, who's going to know to tell him so he can get off on it? *Darling, do it in front of a video cam, and have them send me the tape.* Be a kick, but it'd never happen.

Didn't Manson get his girls to cut Xs on their foreheads? Maybe he could get his to cut themselves a little, where it wouldn't show except in the Polaroids. Would they do it? Maybe, if he worded it right.

Meanwhile, he had other fish to fry.

"Dear Paul," he typed. "I've never called you anything but 'Mr. Dandridge,' but I've written you so many letters, some of them just in the privacy of my mind, that I'll permit myself this liberty. And for all I know you throw my letters away unread. If so, well, I'm still not sorry I've spent the time writing them. It's a great help to me to get my thoughts on paper in this manner.

"I suppose you already know that I got another stay of execution. I can imagine your exasperation at the news. Would it surprise you to know that my own reaction was much the same? I don't want to die, Paul, but I don't want to live like this either, while lawyers scurry around just trying to postpone the inevitable. Better for both of us if they'd just killed me right away.

"Though I suppose I should be grateful for this chance to make my peace, with you and with myself. I can't bring myself to ask for your forgiveness, and I certainly can't summon up whatever is required for me to forgive myself, but perhaps that will come with time. They seem to be giving me plenty of time, even if they do persist in doling it out to me bit by bit . . ."

When he found the letter, Paul Dandridge followed what had become standard practice for him. He set it aside while he opened and tended to the rest of his mail. Then he went into the kitchen and brewed himself a pot of coffee. He poured a cup and sat down with it and opened the letter from Croydon.

When the second letter came he'd read it through to the end, then crumpled it in his fist. He hadn't known whether to throw it in the garbage or burn it in the fireplace, and in the end he'd done neither. Instead he'd carefully unfolded it and smoothed out its creases and read it again before putting it away.

Since then he'd saved all the letters. It had been almost three years since sentence was pronounced on William Croydon, and longer than that since Karen had died at his hands. (Literally at his hands, he thought; the hands that typed the letter and folded it into its envelope had encircled Karen's neck and strangled her. The very hands.)

Now Croydon was thirty-three and Paul was thirty himself, and he had been receiving letters at the approximate rate of one every two months. This was the fifteenth, and it seemed to mark a new stage in their one-sided correspondence. Croydon had addressed him by his first name.

"Better for both of us if they'd just killed me right away." Ah. but they hadn't, had they? And they wouldn't, either. It would drag on and on and on. A lawyer he'd consulted had told him it would not be unrealistic to expect another ten years of delay. For God's sake, he'd be forty years old by the time the state got around to doing the job.

It occurred to him, not for the first time, that he and Croydon were fellow prisoners. He was not confined to a cell and not under a sentence of death, but it struck him that his life held only the illusion of freedom. He wouldn't really be free until Croydon's ordeal was over. Until then he was confined in a prison without walls, unable to get on with his life, unable to have a life, just marking time.

He went over to his desk, took out a sheet of letterhead, uncapped a pen. For a long moment he hesitated. Then he sighed gently and touched pen to paper.

"Dear Croydon," he wrote. "I don't know what to call you. I can't bear to address you by your first name or to call you 'Mr. Croydon.' Not that I ever expected to call you anything at all. I guess I thought you'd be dead by now. God knows I wished it . . ."

Once he got started, it was surprisingly easy to find the words.

An answer from Dandridge.

Unbelievable.

If he had a shot, Paul Dandridge was it. The stays and the appeals would only carry you so far. The chance that any court along the way would grant him a reversal and a new trial was remote at best. His only real hope was a commutation of his death sentence to life imprisonment.

Not that he wanted to spend the rest of his life in prison. In a sense, you lived better on Death Row than if you were doing life in general prison population. But in another sense the difference between a life sentence and a death sentence was, well, the difference between life and death. If he got his sentence commuted to life, that meant the day would come when he made parole and hit the street. They might not come right out and say that, but that was what it would amount to, especially if he worked the system right.

And Paul Dandridge was the key to getting his sentence commuted.

He remembered how the prick had testified at the presentencing hearing. If any single thing had ensured the death sentence, it was Dandridge's testimony. And, if anything could swing a commutation of sentence for him, it was a change of heart on the part of Karen Dandridge's brother.

Worth a shot.

"Dear Paul," he typed. "I can't possibly tell you the sense of peace that came over me when I realized the letter I was holding was from you . . ."

Paul Dandridge, seated at his desk, uncapped his pen and wrote the day's date at the top of a sheet of letterhead. He paused and looked at what he had written. It was, he realized, the fifth anniversary of his sister's death, and he hadn't been aware of that fact until he'd inscribed the date at the top of a letter to the man who'd killed her.

Another irony, he thought. They seemed to be infinite.

"Dear Billy," he wrote. "You'll appreciate this. It wasn't until I'd written the date on this letter that I realized its significance. It's been exactly five years since the day that changed both our lives forever."

He took a breath, considered his words. He wrote, "And I guess it's time to acknowledge formally something I've acknowledged in my heart some time ago. While I may never get over Karen's death, the bitter hatred that has burned in me for so long has finally cooled. And so I'd like to say that you have my forgiveness in full measure. And now I think it's time for you to forgive yourself . . ."

It was hard to sit still.

That was something he'd had no real trouble doing since the first day the cell door closed with him inside. You had to be able to sit still to do time, and it was never hard for him. Even during the several occasions when he'd been a few weeks away from an execution date, he'd never been one to pace the floor or climb the walls.

But today was the hearing. Today the board was hearing testimony from three individuals. One was a psychiatrist who would supply some professional arguments for commuting his sentence from death to life. Another was his fourth-grade teacher, who would tell the board how rough he'd had it in childhood and what a good little boy he was underneath it all. He wondered where they'd dug her up, and how she could possibly remember him. He didn't remember her at all.

The third witness, and the only really important one, was Paul Dandridge. Not only was he supplying the only testimony likely to carry much weight, but it was he who had spent money to locate Croydon's fourth-grade teacher, he who had enlisted the services of the shrink.

His buddy, Paul. A crusader, moving heaven and earth to save Billy Croydon's life.

Just the way he'd planned it.

He paced, back and forth, back and forth, and then he stopped and retrieved from his locker the letter that had started it all. The first letter to Paul Dandridge, the one he'd had the sense not to send. How many times had he reread it over the years, bringing the whole thing back into focus?

"When I turned her facedown, well, I can tell you she'd never done that before." Jesus, no, she hadn't liked it at all. He read and remembered, warmed by the memory.

What did he have these days but his memories? The women who'd been writing him had long since given it up. Even the ones who'd sworn to follow him to death had lost interest during the endless round of stays and appeals. He still had the letters and pictures they'd sent, but the pictures were unappealing, only serving to remind him what a bunch of pigs they all were, and the letters were sheer fantasy with no underpinning of reality. They described, and none too vividly, events that had never happened and events that would never happen. The sense of power to compel them to write those letters and pose for their pictures had faded over time. Now they only bored him and left him faintly disgusted.

Of his own memories, only that of Karen Dandridge held any real flavor. The other two girls, the ones he'd done before Karen, were almost impossible to recall. They were brief encounters, impulsive, unplanned, and over almost before they'd begun. He'd surprised one in a lonely part of the park, just pulled her skirt up and her panties down and went at her, hauling off and smacking her with a rock a couple of times when she wouldn't keep quiet. That shut her up, and when he finished he found out why. She was dead. He'd evidently cracked her skull and killed her, and he'd been thrusting away at dead meat.

Hardly a memory to stir the blood ten years later. The second one wasn't much better, either. He'd been about half drunk, and that had the effect of blurring the memory. He'd snapped her neck afterward, the little bitch, and he remembered that part, but he couldn't remember what it had felt like.

One good thing. Nobody ever found out about either of those two. If they had, he wouldn't have a prayer at today's hearing.

After the hearing, Paul managed to slip out before the press could catch up with him. Two days later, however, when the governor acted on the board's recommendation and commuted William Croydon's sentence to life imprisonment, one persistent reporter managed to get Paul in front of a video camera.

"For a long time I wanted vengeance," he admitted. "I honestly believed that I could only come to terms with the loss of my sister by seeing her killer put to death."

What changed that, the reporter wanted to know.

He stopped to consider his answer. "The dawning realization," he said, "that I could really only recover from Karen's death not by seeing Billy Croydon punished but by letting go of the need to punish. In the simplest terms, I had to forgive him."

And could he do that? Could he forgive the man who had brutally murdered his sister?

"Not overnight," he said. "It took time. I can't even swear I've forgiven him completely. But I've come far enough in the process to realize capital punishment is not only inhumane but pointless. Karen's death was wrong, but Billy Croydon's death would be another wrong, and two wrongs don't make a right. Now that his sentence has been lifted, I can get on with the process of complete forgiveness."

The reporter commented that it sounded as though Paul Dandridge had gone through some sort of religious conversion experience.

"I don't know about religion," Paul said, looking right at the camera. "I don't really consider myself a religious person. But something's happened, something transformational in nature, and I suppose you could call it spiritual."

With his sentence commuted, Billy Croydon drew a transfer to another penitentiary, where he was assigned a cell in general population. After years of waiting to die he was being given a chance to create a life for himself within the prison's walls. He had a job in the prison laundry, he had access to the library and exercise yard. He didn't have his freedom, but he had life.

On the sixteenth day of his new life, three hard-eyed lifers cornered him in the room where they stored the bed linen. He'd noticed one of the men earlier, had several times caught him staring at him a few times, looking at Croydon the way you'd look at a woman. He hadn't spotted the other two before, but they had the same look in their eyes as the one he recognized.

There wasn't a thing he could do.

They raped him, all three of them, and they weren't gentle about it, either. He fought at first but their response to that was savage and prompt, and he gasped at the pain and quit his struggling. He tried to disassociate himself from what was being done to him, tried to take his mind away to some private place. That was a way old cons had of doing time, getting through the hours on end of vacant boredom. This time it didn't really work.

They left him doubled up on the floor, warned him against saying anything to the hacks, and drove the point home with a boot to the ribs.

He managed to get back to his cell, and the following day he put in a request for a transfer to B Block, where you were locked down twenty-three hours a day. He was used to that on Death Row, so he knew he could live with it.

So much for making a life inside the walls. What he had to do was get out.

He still had his typewriter. He sat down, flexed his fingers. One of the rapists had bent his little finger back the day before, and it still hurt, but it wasn't one that he used for typing. He took a breath and started in.

"Dear Paul . . ."

"Dear Billy,

"As always, it was good to hear from you. I write not with news but just in the hope that I can lighten your spirits and build your resolve for the long road ahead. Winning your freedom won't be an easy task, but it's my conviction that working together we can make it happen . . .

"Yours, Paul."

"Dear Paul,

"Thanks for the books. I missed a lot, all those years when I never opened a book. It's funny—my life seems so much more spacious now, even though I'm spending all but one hour a day in a dreary little cell. But it's like that poem that starts, 'Stone walls do not a prison make / Nor iron bars a cage.' (I'd have to say, though, that the stone walls and iron bars around this place make a pretty solid prison.)

"I don't expect much from the parole board next month, but it's a start . . ."

"Dear Billy,

"I was deeply saddened by the parole board's decision, although everything I'd heard had led me to expect nothing else. Even though you've been locked up more than enough time to be eligible, the thinking evidently holds that Death Row time somehow counts less than regular prison time, and that the board wants to see how you do as a prisoner serving a life sentence before letting you return to the outside world. I'm not sure I understand the logic there . . .

"I'm glad you're taking it so well.

"Your friend, Paul."

"Dear Paul,

"Once again, thanks for the books. They're a healthy cut above what's available here. This joint prides itself in its library, but when you say 'Kierkegaard' to the prison librarian he looks at you funny, and you don't dare try him on Martin Buber.

"I shouldn't talk, because I'm having troubles of my own with both of those guys. I haven't got anybody else to bounce this off, so do you mind if I press you into service? Here's my take on Kierkegaard . . .

"Well, that's the latest from the Jailhouse Philosopher, who is pleased to be

"Your friend, Billy."

"Dear Billy,

"Well, once again it's time for the annual appearance before parole board—or the annual circus, as you call it with plenty of justification. Last year we thought maybe the third time was the charm, and it turned out we were wrong, but maybe it'll be different this year . . ."

"Dear Paul,

" 'Maybe it'll be different this time.' Isn't that what Charlie Brown tells himself before he tried to kick the football? And Lucy always snatches it away.

"Still, some of the deep thinkers I've been reading stress that hope is important even when it's unwarranted. And, although I'm a little scared to admit it, I have a good feeling this time.

"And if they never let me out, well, I've reached a point where I honestly don't mind. I've found an inner life here that's far superior to anything I had in my years as a free man. Between my books, my solitude, and my correspondence with you, I have a life I can live with. Of course I'm hoping for parole, but if they snatch the football away again, it ain't gonna kill me . . ."

"Dear Billy,

" . . . Just a thought, but maybe that's the line you should take with them. That you'd welcome parole, but you've made a life for yourself within the walls and you can stay there indefinitely if you have to.

"I don't know, maybe that's the wrong strategy altogether, but I think it might impress them . . ."

"Dear Paul,

"Who knows what's likely to impress them? On the other hand, what have I got to lose?"

Billy Croydon sat at the end of the long conference table, speaking when spoken to, uttering his replies in a low voice, giving pro forma responses to the same questions they asked him every year. At the end they asked him, as usual, if there was anything he wanted to say.

Well, what the hell, he thought. What did he have to lose?

"I'm sure it won't surprise you," he began, "to hear that I've come before you in the hope of being granted early release. I've had hearings before, and when I was turned down it was devastating. Well, I may not be doing myself any good by saying this, but this time around it won't destroy me if you decide to deny me parole. Almost in spite of myself, I've made a life for myself within prison walls. I've found an inner life, a life of the spirit, that's superior to anything I had as a free man . . ."

Were they buying it? Hard to tell. On the other hand, since it happened to be the truth, it didn't really matter whether they bought it or not.

He pushed on to the end. The chairman scanned the room, then looked at him and nodded shortly.

"Thank you, Mr. Croydon," he said. "I think that will be all for now."

"I think I speak for all of us," the chairman said, "when I say how much weight we attach to your appearance before this board. We're used to hearing the pleas of victims and their survivors, but almost invariably they come here to beseech us to deny parole. You're virtually unique, Mr. Dandridge, in appearing as the champion of the very man who . . ."

"Killed my sister," Paul said levelly.

"Yes. You've appeared before us on prior occasions, Mr. Dandridge, and while we were greatly impressed by your ability to forgive William Croydon and by the relationship you've forged with him, it seems to me that there's been a change in your own sentiments. Last year, I recall, while you pleaded on Mr. Croydon's behalf, we sensed that you did not wholeheartedly believe he was ready to be returned to society."

"Perhaps I had some hesitation."

"But this year . . ."

"Billy Croydon's a changed man. The process of change has been completed. I know that he's ready to get on with his life."

"There's no denying the power of your testimony, especially in light of its source." The chairman cleared his throat. "Thank you, Mr. Dandridge. I think that will be all for now."

"Well?" Paul said. "How do you feel?"

Billy considered the question. "Hard to say," he said. "Everything's a little unreal. Even being in a car. Last time I was in a moving vehicle was when I got my commutation and they transferred me from the other prison. It's not like Rip van Winkle, I know what everything looks like from television, cars included. Tell the truth, I feel a little shaky."

"I guess that's to be expected."

"I suppose." He tugged his seat belt to tighten it. "You want to know how I feel, I feel vulnerable. All those years I was locked down twenty-three hours out of twenty-four. I knew what to expect, I knew I was safe. Now I'm a free man, and it scares the crap out of me."

"Look in the glove compartment," Paul said.

"Jesus, Johnny Walker Black."

"I figured you might be feeling a little anxious. That ought to take the edge off."

"Yeah, Dutch courage," Billy said. "Why Dutch, do you happen to know? I've always wondered."

"No idea."

He weighed the bottle in his hand. "Been a long time," he said. "Haven't had a taste of anything since they locked me up."

"There was nothing available in prison?"

"Oh, there was stuff. The jungle juice cons made out of potatoes and raisins, and some good stuff that got smuggled in. But I wasn't in population, so I didn't have access. And anyway it seemed like more trouble than it was worth."

"Well, you're a free man now. Why don't you drink to it? I'm driving or I'd join you."

"Well . . ."

"Go ahead."

"Why not?" he said, and uncapped the bottle and held it to the light. "Pretty color, huh? Well, here's to freedom, huh?" He took a long drink, shuddered at the burn of the whisky. "Kicks like a mule," he said.

"You're not used to it."

"I'm not." He put the cap on the bottle and had a little trouble screwing it back on. "Hitting me hard," he reported. "Like I was a little kid getting his first taste of it. Whew."

"You'll be all right."

"Spinning," Billy said, and slumped in his seat.

Paul glanced over at him, looked at him again a minute later. Then, after checking the mirror, he pulled the car off the road and braked to a stop.

Billy was conscious for a little while before he opened his eyes. He tried to get his bearings first. The last thing he remembered was a wave of dizziness after the slug of scotch hit bottom. He was still sitting upright, but it didn't feel like a car seat, and he didn't sense any movement. No, he was in some sort of chair, and he seemed to be tied to it.

That didn't make any sense. A dream? He'd had lucid dreams before and knew how real they were, how you could be in them and wonder if you were dreaming and convince yourself you weren't. The way you broke the surface and got out of it was by opening your eyes. You had to force yourself, had to open your real eyes and not just your eyes in the dream, but it could be done . . . There!

He was in a chair, in a room he'd never seen before, looking out a window at a view he'd never seen before. An open field, woods behind it.

He turned his head to the left and saw a wall paneled in knotty cedar. He turned to the right and saw Paul Dandridge, wearing boots and jeans and a plaid flannel shirt and sitting in an easy chair with a book. He said, "Hey!" and Paul lowered the book and looked at him.

"Ah," Paul said. "You're awake."

"What's going on?"

"What do you think?"

"There was something in the whiskey."

"There was indeed," Paul agreed. "You started to stir just as we made the turn off the state road. I gave you a booster shot with a hypodermic needle."

"I don't remember."

"You never felt it. I was afraid for a minute there that I'd given you too much. That would have been ironic, wouldn't you say? 'Death by lethal injection.' The sentence carried out finally after all these years, and you wouldn't have even known it happened."

He couldn't take it in. "Paul," he said, "for God's sake, what's it all about?"

"What's it about?" Paul considered his response. "It's about time."

"Time?"

"It's the last act of the drama."

"Where are we?"

"A cabin in the woods. Not the cabin. That would be ironic, wouldn't it?"

"What do you mean?"

"If I killed you in the same cabin where you killed Karen. Ironic, but not really feasible. So this is a different cabin in different woods, but it will have to do."

"You're going to kill me?"

"Of course."

"For God's sake, why?"

"Because that's how it ends, Billy. That's the point of the whole game. That's how I planned it from the beginning."

"I can't believe this."

"Why is it so hard to believe? We conned each other, Billy. You pretended to repent and I pretended to believe you. You pretended to reform and I pretended to be on your side. Now we can both stop pretending."

Billy was silent for a moment. Then he said, "I was trying to con you at the beginning."

"No kidding."

"There was a point where it turned into something else, but it started out as a scam. It was the only way I could think of to stay alive. You saw through it?"

"Of course."

"But you pretended to go along with it. Why?"

"Is it that hard to figure out?"

"It doesn't make any sense. What do you gain by it? My death? If you wanted me dead all you had to do was tear up my letter. The state was all set to kill me."

"They'd have taken forever," Paul said bitterly. "Delay after delay, and always the possibility of a reversal and a retrial, always the possibility of a commutation of sentence."

"There wouldn't have been a reversal, and it took you working for me to get my sentence commuted. There would have been delays, but there'd already been a few of them before I got around to writing to you. It couldn't have lasted too many years longer, and it would have added up to a lot less than it has now, with all the time I spent serving life and waiting for the parole board to open the doors. If you'd just let it go, I'd be dead and buried by now."

"You'll be dead soon," Paul told him. "And buried. It won't be much longer. Your grave's already dug. I took care of that before I drove to the prison to pick you up."

"They'll come after you, Paul. When I don't show up for my initial appointment with my parole officer—"

"They'll get in touch, and I'll tell them we had a drink and shook hands and you went off on your own. It's not my fault if you decided to skip town and violate the terms of your parole."

He took a breath. He said, "Paul, don't do this."

"Why not?"

"Because I'm begging you. I don't want to die."

"Ah," Paul said. "*That's* why."

"What do you mean?"

"If I left it to the state," he said, "they'd have been killing a dead man. By the time the last appeal was denied and the last request for a stay of execution turned down, you'd have been resigned to the inevitable. They'd strap you to a gurney and give you a shot, and it would be just like going to sleep."

"That's what they say."

"But now you want to live. You adjusted to prison, you made a life for yourself in there, and then you finally made parole, icing on the cake, and now you genuinely want to live. You've really got a life now, Billy, and I'm going to take it away from you."

"You're serious about this."

"I've never been more serious about anything."

"You must have been planning this for years."

"From the very beginning."

"Jesus, it's the most thoroughly premeditated crime in the history of the world, isn't it? Nothing I can do about it, either. You've got me tied tight and the chair won't tip over. Is there anything I can say that'll make you change your mind?"

"Of course not."

"That's what I thought." He sighed. "Get it over with."

"I don't think so."

"Huh?"

"This won't be what the state hands out," Paul Dandridge said. "A minute ago you were begging me to let you live. Before it's over you'll be begging me to kill you."

"You're going to torture me."

"That's the idea."

"In fact you've already started, haven't you? This is the mental part."

"Very perceptive of you, Billy."

"For all the good it does me. This is all because of what I did to your sister, isn't it?"

"Obviously."

"I didn't do it, you know. It was another Billy Croydon that killed her, and I can barely remember what he was like."

"That doesn't matter."

"Not to you, evidently, and you're the one calling the shots. I'm sure Kierkegaard had something useful to say about this sort of situation, but I'm damned if I can call it to mind. You knew I was conning you, huh? Right from the jump?"

"Of course."

"I thought it was a pretty good letter I wrote you."

"It was a masterpiece, Billy. But that didn't mean it wasn't easy to see through."

"So now you dish it out and I take it," Billy Croydon said, "until you get bored and end it, and I wind up in the grave you've already dug for me. And that's the end of it. I wonder if there's a way to turn it around."

"Not a chance."

"Oh, I know I'm not getting out of here alive, Paul, but there's more than one way of turning something around. Let's see now. You know, the letter you got wasn't the first one I wrote to you."

"So?"

"The past is always with you, isn't it? I'm not the same man as the guy who killed your sister, but he's still there inside somewhere. Just a question of calling him up."

"What's that supposed to mean?"

"Just talking to myself, I guess. I was starting to tell you about that first letter. I never sent it, you know, but I kept it. For the longest time I held on to it and read it whenever I wanted to relive the experience. Then it stopped working, or maybe I stopped wanting to call up the past, but whatever it was I quit reading it. I still held on to it, and then one day I realized I didn't want to own it anymore. So I tore it up and got rid of it."

"That's fascinating."

"But I read it so many times I bet I can bring it back word for word." His eyes locked with Paul Dandridge's, and his lips turned up in the slightest suggestion of a smile. He said, " 'Dear Paul, Sitting here in this cell waiting for the day to come when they put a needle in my arm and flush me down God's own toilet, I found myself thinking about your testimony in court. I remember how you said your sister was a goodhearted girl who spent her short life bringing pleasure to everyone who knew her. According to your testimony, knowing this helped you rejoice in her life at the same time that it made her death so hard to take.

" 'Well, Paul, in the interest of helping you rejoice some more, I thought I'd tell you just how much pleasure your little sister brought to me. I've got to tell you that in all my life I never got more pleasure from anybody. My first look at Karen brought me pleasure, just watching her walk across campus, just looking at those jiggling tits and that tight little ass and imagining the fun I was going to have with them.' "

"Stop it, Croydon!"

"You don't want to miss this, Paulie. 'Then when I had her tied up in the backseat of the car with her mouth taped shut, I have to say she went on being a real source of pleasure. Just looking at her in the rear-view mirror was enjoyable, and from time to time I would stop the car and lean into the back to run my hands over her body. I don't think she liked it much, but I enjoyed it enough for the both of us.' "

"You're a son of a bitch."

"And you're an asshole. You should have let the state put me out of everybody's misery. Failing that, you should have let go of the hate and sent the new William Croydon off to rejoin society. There's a lot more to the letter, and I remember it perfectly." He tilted his head, resumed quoting from memory. " 'Tell me something, Paul. Did you ever fool around with Karen yourself? I bet you did. I can picture her when she was maybe eleven, twelve years old, with her little titties just beginning to bud out, and you'd have been seventeen or eighteen yourself, so how could you stay away from her? She's sleeping and you walk into her room and sit on the edge of her bed.' " He grinned. "I always liked that part. And there's lots more. You enjoying your revenge, Paulie? Is it as sweet as they say it is?"

Points

The Knicks were hosting a first-year expansion team at the Garden, and when the two men arrived, thirty minutes before game time, half the seats were empty. "I'm afraid it's not going to be much of a game," the younger man said, "and it looks as though I'm not alone in that opinion. Last time I was here the Lakers were in town, and there wasn't an empty seat."

"We're early," the older man said. "They won't sell out tonight, but they'll come closer than you might guess. Remember, this is New York. A lot of guys don't even leave their desks until seven-thirty for a game that starts at eight."

"That's me you're describing. Not tonight, but the Laker game? There were points on the board by the time I got to my seat. And it would have been the same story tonight if I hadn't put my foot down. Carrigan came into my office at half past six with something that had to be done and would only take me a minute, swear to God. 'Not tonight,' I told him. 'I'm meeting my dad.' "

Anyone looking at them would have suspected they were father and son. The resemblance was unmistakable, in their faces and in the easy loose-limbed grace with which they moved. The son was a younger version of the father, his hair darker, his features less emphatic. Both were tall men, standing several inches over six feet. Both had been slim in their youth, and both had thickened some around the middle with age, the father more than the son. The son was perhaps an inch taller than the father, a fact which had not gone unremarked at their meeting a few minutes earlier.

"You're taller," Richard Parmalee had said. "I don't suppose your pituitary gland kicked into overdrive when nobody was looking. Have you been taking growth hormone?"

The son, whose name was Kevin, shook his head and grinned.

"Then the odds are you're not taller," the father said. "So, unless you've got lifts in your shoes—"

"Just insoles, but they don't make you any taller."

"That's what I was afraid of. Well, where does logic inexorably lead us? I'm shrinking."

"You look the same to me."

"Hell, I'm not melting away like the Wicked Witch of the West. Everybody shrinks, starting around forty or forty-five, but it takes fifteen or twenty years before it's enough to notice. You're not even forty for another year and a half, so you've got a while before your cuffs start scraping the pavement."

"That hasn't happened to you."

"No, if I've lost half an inch that's a lot. It's enough to notice, but only just. And I only just noticed it myself within the past month or so. I knew it was something that happens to everybody, but I figured I was different, it wouldn't happen to me. Same as right now you're listening and nodding and telling yourself it won't happen to you."

The younger man laughed. "Got me. Exactly what I was telling myself."

"And who knows? You might be right. You've got a few years, and by then they may have something to prevent it. I wouldn't put it past them."

As Richard Parmalee had predicted, there were a lot of late arrivals, and most seats were occupied by game time. The Knicks, eleven-point favorites according to the line in the papers, jumped off to an early lead that opened up to twenty-two points at halftime. "Well, it's not much of a game," the son said. "I was afraid of that."

"No, but it's still fun to watch them. I remember coming here to see the Harlem Globetrotters when I was still in high school. They were playing an exhibition game against somebody, probably the Knicks. I couldn't believe the things they did. Now everybody does that, but without the clowning."

"They're still around, the Globetrotters."

"And they're probably as entertaining as ever, but less remarkable, because everybody plays like that. It's a completely different game than when I played it."

"It looks completely different to me," the son said, "so I can only imagine the difference from your point of view."

"In my day we played on our feet. Your generation played the game on your toes. And now it's a game played in the air."

"It's true."

"And I swear the rules are different."

"Well, the three-point shot—"

"Of course, but that's not what I mean. They routinely commit what would have been a traveling violation, but you never see it called. If a guy's driving to the basket it doesn't seem to matter how many steps he takes."

"I know. There's a rule, but I can't figure out what it is."

"And they'll turn the ball over when they're dribbling. Double dribble, that used to be, and you lost possession. Not anymore."

"I like the three-point shot, though," Kevin Parmalee said.

"Improves the game. No question. But only at the pro distance. The college three-pointer is too close."

"It's ridiculous. And yet the college game's more fun to watch. It's not as good a game, but it's more exciting."

They went on chatting comfortably until play resumed, then fell largely silent and watched the action on the court. The visitors narrowed the gap in the third quarter, and with three minutes to play only six points separated the two teams. Then the Knicks surged, and led by fourteen when the buzzer sounded.

On their way out the son said, "Well, they made a game of it. It was never close, but you wouldn't have known that from the fans."

"They beat the spread," the father said, "and that wasn't a foregone conclusion. It could have gone either way until the final seconds."

"You figure that many of the people here had money on the game?"

"Probably more than you'd think, but that's not the point. We're New Yorkers, Kev. When we root for a team, we don't just want to win the game. We want to beat the spread."

"And we did, so hoorah for our side."

"Amen. It was a good game."

"And God knows the price was right."

"You told me who gave you the tickets, but I forget. One of the senior partners?"

"No, one of Joe Levin's clients. He gave them to Joe, and Joe thought he could go and then couldn't, which was why the whole thing was as last-minute as it was."

"Terrific seats."

"Well, some corporation pays for them, and lists them as a business expense. So they didn't cost us anything, and they didn't cost anybody else anything, either."

"That's the way it ought to be," Richard Parmalee said. "I made a reservation at Keen's, not that I think we'll need one at this hour on a weeknight. That sound all right to you?"

"As long as it's on me."

"Not a chance."

"Hey, I asked you out, remember?"

"You got the tickets, I get the dinner check."

"The tickets were free, remember?"

"So's the dinner, as far as you're concerned. You're not going to win this argument, Kevin, so don't even try."

The headwaiter greeted the older man by name and showed them to a table in the grill room. Richard Parmalee ordered a single-malt scotch, neat, with water back. Kevin ordered a Mexican beer.

"I was reading an article on malt whisky," he said, "and halfway through I decided I owed it to myself to develop a taste for it. Then I remembered that I never liked hard booze, and I especially don't like the stuff you drink. Laphroiag?"

"No one ever mistook it for mother's milk," the older man conceded. He took a small sip and savored it, as if tasting it for the first time. "I'm not sure I like the taste myself," he said. "I appreciate it, but that's not the same thing, is it? All in all, I'd have to say you're better off with beer."

"I'd probably be better off with orange juice."

"Chock full of vitamin C. But you don't drink much, do you?"

"No."

"I have a drink every day, but it's an unusual day when I have a second. Which I guess makes this an unusual day, come to think of it, because I had one at my club this afternoon, and here I am having a second. Two drinks in one day, and only five or six hours apart at that."

"I'll call AA."

They ordered the same meal, steak and salad. The restaurant's ceiling was festooned with white clay pipes, each reserved for a particular patron, and over coffee the father said, "I almost asked him to bring my pipe."

"That's right, you have a pipe here, don't you? I have a faint memory of you smoking it after dinner."

"It must have been the first time I brought you here. After a game, I suppose."

"St. John's–Iona. St. John's won, and if I worked at it I could probably remember the score. I was fifteen, and I remember deciding that when I grew up I'd have a pipe of my own here."

"If you were fifteen then I would have been forty-one. So that may well have been the last time I smoked that pipe, because I was forty-two when I quit. Your grandfather was diagnosed with lung cancer, and I threw my cigarettes in the garbage. I had some pipes, although I rarely smoked them."

"I don't think I ever saw you smoke a pipe aside from that one time right here."

"As I said, I rarely did. But I threw them out along with the cigarettes. And I gave away all my lighters and cigarette cases, including a silver Ronson that my father had given me. I figured he'd given me plenty of other things, I didn't have to hang on to it for sentimental reasons. You've never smoked, have you?"

"Not tobacco."

"Then what . . . oh, marijuana. Do you use it?"

"I did in college, and for a year or two after. I was never into it that much. Mostly just at parties. I haven't smoked it in years, and I haven't even smelled it, except on the street. I don't go to that many parties, and when I do there's never anybody lighting up a joint in the corner."

"I suppose I assumed you tried it in college, although I can't remember giving much thought to the subject. It wasn't around when I was in college. Oh, it must have been, but I wasn't aware of it and certainly didn't know anybody who smoked it."

"So you never tried it."

"I didn't say that. Your mother and I both tried it a few times in, oh, it must have been 'sixty-seven or -eight."

"I was five years old. Were you and Mom hippies? You should have turned me on while you were at it."

"Hippies," the father said, and shook his head. "The first time we smoked nothing happened. Our friends, the people who turned us on, swore we were stoned, but if we were we didn't know it, so what good was it? The second time we both got high and it was very nice, though I can't say I remember what exactly was nice about it. But it was. And then we smoked once or twice after that, and one time your mother became very anxious, and when it wore off we agreed this wasn't something we wanted to waste our time on."

"Mom got paranoid?"

"That's as good a word for it as any, and how did we get on this? Pipes on the ceiling, we're a long way from pipes on the ceiling. But I had a hell of a time quitting cigarettes, so I don't think I'll call for my pipe and my bowl."

"Did you smoke when you were playing basketball?"

"Not while I was out on the court. But that's not what you meant. Sure, I smoked. I was a kid, and kids are stupid. I heard smoking would cut my wind, so I tried it, and I didn't see any difference, so I decided they were full of crap. What did I expect, that the first cigarette I smoked would add three seconds to my time in the hundred-yard dash? Still, I was never that heavy a smoker when I was playing. After I graduated, that's when the habit took off."

"Neither of the girls smokes," Kevin Parmalee said.

"As far as you know."

"Well, that goes without saying, doesn't it? There's no end of things they don't do as far as I know, and God only knows what they do that I *don't* know, and I don't want to think about it."

"Jennifer's more the athlete, isn't she?"

They talked about the girls, Kevin Parmalee's daughters, Richard's granddaughters. They agreed that Jennifer, the older of the two, had innate athletic ability, but lacked the desire to do anything with it. She had the height for basketball, the older man pointed out, and they talked about the emergence of that sport.

He said, "You know how the college kids play a more interesting game than the pros? Well, I'll tell you something. The women's game is better than the men's."

"College or pro?"

"Either one."

"I know what you mean. But . . ."

"But it's impossible to give a damn which team wins."

"I was about to say it was hard to get interested in it, but you just nailed it. That's exactly what it is. It's like watching golf, I get completely absorbed in it but I don't give a damn who wins. Why do you figure that is?"

"One of life's mysteries," Richard Parmalee said. "Here's another. Remember how the fans were cheering earlier, rooting for the Knicks to win by more than twelve points?"

"To beat the spread. Sure."

"It meant something to the fans, whether or not they had bets down. We talked about that earlier. But what did it mean to the players?"

"I'm not sure I follow you. What did it mean to them?"

"Why did they knock themselves out? They couldn't have played any harder if the game was nip and tuck."

"You think they had money on the game?"

"You wouldn't think they'd bother, the kind of salaries they make. Other hand,

I don't suppose it's entirely unheard of. But I can't believe they all bet on the game, and they were all playing their hearts out."

"They're pros," Kevin Parmalee said. "Playing all-out is what they do."

"They've been known to dog it from time to time. Maybe they were trying to beat the spread so it wouldn't look as though they were trying *not* to beat the spread."

"In other words, if they dog it somebody might think they're shaving points. You think that goes on in the NBA?"

"Shaving points? I don't know. Again, with their salaries, how could you bribe them? Kev, I think you're probably right. They weren't even aware of the spread, and they played hard because that's the way they play." He picked up his coffee cup, set it down. "When you played," he said, "were you ever approached?"

"Approached? Oh."

"Were you?"

"God, why would anyone come to me? I was lucky to be on the team."

"Don't sell yourself short. You were damn good."

"I would have been okay somewhere else. I know, Duke was all my idea, but I've never been sorry I went. Even if I did ride the bench for four years. I never had more than eight minutes of playing time, so there were never any guys with bent noses trying to get me to dump games."

"And your teammates were too busy trying to get into the NBA."

"Trying to get into the Final Four. They *knew* they were going to get into the NBA."

The waiter came, and Kevin Parmalee put his hand over his cup. "Just a half a cup for me," Richard Parmalee said, and was silent until the waiter withdrew. Then he said, "I was approached."

"Really?"

"Not by a guy with a bent nose. His nose was as straight as yours or mine, and you wouldn't have marked him as a gangster, not by his appearance or by his manner. Although I suppose that's exactly what he was."

"And he wanted you to dump games?"

"Not to dump games. 'I would never ask you to lose a game,' he said. It was fine with him if we beat the other team. Just so we didn't beat the spread."

"Did you report him?"

"No," Richard Parmalee said. "No, I didn't report him."

"Oh."

"I took the money," he said, and raised his eyes to meet his son's. "And did what I could to earn it."

"You shaved points."

"I shaved points. If we were favored, and if Harold gave me the word, I did my best to see that we didn't cover the spread."

"How did you do it? Miss shots that you could have made?"

"I missed shots. I don't know that I could have made them if I hadn't had a reason not to. Another way, I'd be wide open and I'd pass off instead of taking the shot. There are a million things you can do without being too obvious about it."

"I can imagine."

"I got five hundred dollars a game. And this was 1957 we're talking about. That was a lot of money in 1957."

"Sure, it must have been a fortune."

"When I graduated, my first job was as a management trainee with Kaiser & Ledbetter. Starting salary was five thousand dollars a year. And that wasn't bad money. That's what you paid a promising college graduate in a job with a future. So every time we didn't manage to beat the spread, I was making a tenth of a year's salary, and that's not counting taxes."

"I guess you didn't declare the money that—Harold?"

"Harold. I never knew his last name, and no, I didn't declare it. He paid me in cash and I didn't know what the hell to do with it. It's funny. I was doing it for the money, but I didn't do anything *with* the money. I kept it in a cigar box, and I kept moving the box around because I was afraid somebody would find it."

"You couldn't put it in the bank?"

"Kev, I didn't have a bank account. I lived at home with my parents. They gave me a scholarship to play basketball, but all that covered was tuition. I thought the extra money would come in handy, but I didn't spend a dime of it."

"You saved it in a cigar box. What did it add up to, do you remember?"

"Forty-five hundred dollars, and how could I forget? He always paid me in twenty-dollar bills. Twenty-five of them at a time, so what does that come to? Two hundred twenty-five? Is that right? Well, it's close enough. Not enough bills to fill the cigar box, but a good-sized handful."

"Nine games, that would have been."

"Nine games," the father said. "Nine college basketball games, and all I had to do was hold back a little bit, and how hard was that? And who did it hurt? I mean, who gave a damn if we beat St. Bonaventure's by ten points or three points? The fans didn't care. The only people who got hurt were the ones who bet on us, and they were breaking the law in the first place by gambling on a basketball game. What the hell did I owe them?"

"It's not as though your team lost."

"We did lose one game. We played Adelphi at home, and we were favored, and Harold gave me the word. And I did what I could to keep us from getting too far ahead, and then in the third quarter Adelphi started playing way over their heads, and before I knew it they were out in front, and we never did catch up. Would they have beaten us anyway? The way they were playing I'm tempted to say they would have beaten the Knicks that night, but I don't know. Maybe yes and maybe no."

"It must have been weird, watching the game slip away from you."

"It was awful. I never played harder in my life than in the last five minutes of that game. We were all knocking ourselves out. I remember one shot that went around the rim and out, and the look on the face of the kid who put it up. I'd had my suspicions about him, and his expression confirmed it."

"You know, I'd been thinking you were the only one doing it, but of course there must have been others."

"And I never knew how many, or who they were. That one boy, on the basis of the look on his face, but which of the others? Not that I spent a lot of time thinking about it. And I certainly didn't let myself think about the consequences."

"Of losing the game?"

"Of doing what I was doing and getting caught at it. It was a crime, you know."

"I guess it must have been."

"Oh, no question. There'd been some scandals a few years earlier. A fair number of young men had their lives ruined, and a few went to prison for it. I didn't worry about it, and it turned out there was nothing to worry about."

"What happened to the money?"

"Nothing for a couple of years. Then when your mother and I got married, we had expenses. Young couples always do. So the money came in handy after all."

"Did Mom know where it came from?"

"All she knew was that the bills got paid. Nobody knew that I shaved points. Until tonight, I never said a word about it to anyone."

"It's hard to believe," Kevin Parmalee said, after a moment. "Not that you never said anything, but that you did it. It seems—"

"What?"

"Out of character, I guess."

"It seemed that way to me at the time. I don't know that I can explain it. Maybe Harold was a persuasive guy, or maybe I was easily persuaded."

"How come—no, never mind."

"What?"

"I just wondered how come you decided to tell me."

"I hadn't planned on it."

"Really? Because I had the sense there was something."

"There was, but that wasn't it."

"Oh?"

"If I'd called for my pipe," Richard Parmalee said, "I could fuss with it, and tamp the tobacco down and relight it, and kill a surprising amount of time that way. Sometimes I think that was as much of an addiction as the nicotine. I went to the doctor about six weeks ago for my annual physical, which is a misnomer, because I'm doing well if I get around to it every other year. He called me two days later to tell me my PSA was a little high, if you know what that is."

"I don't."

"You probably will in a few years. I forget what it stands for, but it's a prostate test. A slight elevation could be the result of enlargement of the prostate, or a sign of the presence of a low-grade infection. Or it could be an indication of early-stage prostate cancer."

The two men looked at each other. "So he sent me to a urologist," Richard Parmalee went on, "and he did his own examination and his own test, and put me on an antibiotic for a week in case it was an infection that was causing the high reading. And a week later he took blood for another test, and the result was still the same, so he had me come in for a biopsy."

"Jesus."

"It's a goddam undignified procedure," he said, "but less painful than a sprained ankle, and you don't need an Ace bandage. You have blood in the urine for a few days afterward, and in the semen for up to a month. All of that's nothing compared to waiting for the lab results. I had the biopsy on a Tuesday and I didn't hear until the following Monday. Not to keep you in suspense, it came back negative. I haven't got cancer."

"Thank God."

"I suppose I could have said that right off," Richard Parmalee said, "but instead I let you wait and wonder for what, five minutes? If that. Well, that was to give you an idea. I had a full month to wait and wonder, and maybe you can imagine what that was like."

"You never said anything."

"There was nothing to say, not until I found out what I had or didn't have."

"Did Mom know?"

"I told her the morning I went in for the biopsy. If it was just an infection, or a false positive, why put her through it? By the time I was ready to go in for the procedure, I figured she ought to know. And I was worn out keeping it to myself."

"But you're all right?"

"I have to go in every six months," he said, "for a PSA, which just means they take some blood and send it to the lab. If there's no change, all I do is make another appointment. It's normal for the level to increase gradually with age. If that's all it does, that's fine. If there's a big increase, I get to have another biopsy."

"Every six months for how long?"

"For as long as possible."

"For as long as . . . oh, I get it. In other words, every six months for the rest of your life."

"And I hope that's a long time. That's one of the things I found out while I was waiting. I didn't want it to be over. If I have to get a needle in my arm twice a year, well, that's a pretty small price to pay to stick around."

"I'll say."

"But from this point on my life is different. All of a sudden I'm an old man."

"The hell you're an old man."

"I was a kid with a basketball, and the next thing I know I'm an old fart with a prostate. Well, what's the difference? Either way you dribble."

They laughed, the two of them, a little more heartily than the line warranted, and when the laughter stopped they were silent. Then the older man said, "I knew I wanted to tell you. I wasn't in a rush, but it was something you ought to know. Then you called to say you had Knicks tickets, and while I was making dinner reservations I decided it would be the right time and place for this conversation."

"I'll probably be a while taking it all in."

"Oh, I'm sure of that. Intimations of mortality, and your own as well as mine. I'm in damn good shape, I'm happy to say, but in a sense I feel a good deal more vulnerable than I did a couple of months ago. But there's something I can't quite figure out. What made me tell you about my little arrangement with Harold?"

"Maybe you were stalling."

"Stalling? Telling you the one thing to delay telling you the other? No, I don't think so. That would have been a reason for small talk, but I wasn't making small talk."

"No."

"And it's something I've been thinking about lately. Would my life have been different if I'd told Harold thanks but no thanks?"

"How?"

"That's what I've been wondering. I did something that wasn't honest, and I kept it a secret. How did that affect the choices I made in life?"

"Maybe it didn't."

"Maybe not," Richard Parmalee said, "but I'll never know, will I? The road not taken. Maybe it's made a difference, and maybe it hasn't."

"Phil Carrigan called me in two, three weeks ago," the son said. "I'd knocked myself out for him, and he wanted to let me know how much he appreciated it. 'Listen,' he said, 'I owe you a big one. And Lisa, I want to make up to her for the extra hours you put in. Here's what you do, Kevin. Take the lovely lady to Lutèce. You can bill the client.' "

"That's perfect."

"Isn't it? His eyes, he was being magnanimous. Giving me something to show his appreciation of what I did for him. So I had his permission to stick it to the client for a couple of hundred dollars. That's his idea of a grand gesture, and he really thought he was being generous. And maybe he was, because he could just as easily have taken his wife to Lutèce at the client's expense."

"That's interesting. I'm not sure it fits with what we were talking about, but I'm not sure it doesn't, either. How was the meal?"

"It was terrific, but I'm just as happy with a steak and salad, to tell you the truth."

"You're like your old man. And it's time your old man headed home."

He raised his hand for the check. "I wish you'd let me get this," the son said.

"Not a chance. I told you, you got the tickets."

"And *I* told *you* they didn't cost me a cent."

"And neither will dinner," Richard Parmalee said. "The hell, I'll bill it to a client."

"Oh, right," Kevin Parmalee said. "That's just what you'll do."

Sweet Little Hands

Lying there, it seemed to him that he could hear his own cries echoing off the room's blank walls. His heart was pounding, his skin glossy with sweat. Should he be afraid of this? Could a person actually die at climax?

When he spoke, he did so as if resuming a conversation. "I wonder how often it happens," he said.

"How often what happens?"

"I'm sorry," he said. "I'd been thinking, and I guess I assumed you could read my mind. And sometimes I think you can."

For answer, she laid a hand on his thigh. Sweet little hand, he thought.

"My heart's back to normal now," he said, "or close enough to it. But I was wondering how often men die like that. If a fellow had a weak heart . . ."

"My husband's heart is strong."

"I wasn't thinking of your husband."

"I was," she said. "From the moment we got in bed. Longer than that, actually. Since we got here. Since I got up this morning, knowing I was going to be with you this afternoon."

"You've been thinking of him."

"And of what you're going to do."

He didn't say anything.

"His heart is strong," she said. "In a physical sense, that is. In another sense, he has no heart."

"Do we have to talk about him?"

She rolled onto her side, let her hand find the middle of his chest, more or less over his heart. "Yes," she said. "Yes, we have to talk about him. Do you know what it does to me? Knowing what you're going to do to him?"

"Tell me."

"It thrills me," she said. "God, Jimmy, it gets me so hot I'm melting. I couldn't wait to see you, and then I couldn't wait to be in bed with you. We've always been hot for each other and it's always been good between us, but all of a sudden it's at a whole new level. You felt it, didn't you? Just now?"

"You get me so hot, Rita."

Her bunched fingers stroked his chest, moving in a little circle. "If I could get him hot," she said, "so hot his heart would burst, I'd do it."

"You hate him that much."

"He's ruining my life, Jimmy. He's draining me, he's sucking the life out of me. You know what he's done."

"And you can't just leave him."

"He told me what I'd get if I ever tried. Didn't I tell you?"

"You really think . . ."

" 'Acid in your face, Rita. Not in the eyes, because I'll want you to be able to see what you look like. Acid all over your tits, too, and between your legs, so nobody will ever want you, not even with a bag over your head.' "

"What a bastard."

"George is worse than that. He's a monster."

"I mean, to say a thing like that."

"And it's not just talk, either. He'd do it. He'd enjoy doing it."

He was silent for a moment. Then he said, "He deserves to die."

"Tonight, Jimmy."

"Tonight?"

"Baby, I can't wait for it to be over. And we have to do it before he finds out about you and me. I think he's starting to suspect something, and if he ever finds out for sure . . ."

"That wouldn't be good."

"It would be the end of everything. Acid for me, and God knows what for you. We can't afford to wait."

"I know."

"He'll be home tonight. I'll make sure he drinks a lot of wine with dinner. There's a baseball game on television and he'll want to watch it. He always watches, and he never stays awake past the third inning. He settles into his La-Z-Boy and puts his feet up, and he's out in no time at all."

Her hand moved idly as she went over the plan, working its way down his chest, down over his stomach, stroking, petting, eliciting a response.

"He'll be in the den," she was saying. "You remember where that is. On the first floor, the second window on the right-hand side. He'll have the alarm set, but I'll fix it so it's limited to the doors. There's a way to do that, in case you want to have a window open for ventilation. And I'll have the window in the den open a couple of inches. Even if there's a draft and he gets up and closes it, it won't be locked. You'll be able to open it without setting off the alarm. Jimmy? Is something the matter?"

He took hold of her wrist. "Just that you're setting off my alarm," he said.

"Don't you like what I'm doing?"

"I love it, but—"

"You'll come in through the window," she went on. "He'll be asleep in his chair. There's all this crap on the walls, swords and daggers, a ceremonial war club from some South Sea Island tribe. Stab him with a dagger or beat his head in with the club."

"It'll look spur-of-the-moment," he said. "Burglar breaks in, panics when the guy wakes up, then grabs whatever's closest and—Christ!"

"I just grabbed whatever was closest," she said innocently. "Jimmy, I can't help it. It gets me all excited thinking about it." Her lips brushed him. "We may have to stay away from each other for a while," she said, "while I do the Grieving Widow number." Her breath was warm on his flesh. "So I've got an idea, Jimmy. Suppose we have our victory celebration now?"

"A splendid dinner," George said, pushing back from the table. He was a large and physically imposing man, twenty years her senior. "But you didn't eat much, my dear."

"No appetite," she said.

"For food."

"Well . . ."

"I guess it's almost time," he said, "for me to adjourn to the library for brandy and cigars. Except it's a den, not a library, and brandy gives me heartburn, and I don't smoke cigars. But you know what I mean."

"Time for you to watch the ballgame. Who's playing?"

"The Cubs and the Astros."

"And is it an important game?"

"There's no such thing as an important game," he said. "Grown men trying to hit a ball with a stick. How important could that possibly be?"

"But you'll watch it."

"Wouldn't miss it for the world."

"Another cup of coffee first?"

"Another cup? Hmmm. Well, it is exceptionally good coffee. And I guess there's time."

This is crazy, he thought.

There was her house, and there, in the second window on the right-hand side, was the flickering glow of a television screen. The garage door was closed, and there were no cars parked in the driveway, or at the curb. Nobody walking around on the street.

Crazy . . .

He drove halfway around the block, found a parking place out of the reach of the streetlights. He left the car unlocked and circled the block on foot, his heartbeat quickening as he neared her house.

Anyone who saw him would see a man of medium height and build dressed in dark clothes. And he'd burn the clothes when this was over. He'd assume there were bloodstains, or some other sort of physical evidence, and he'd leave nothing to chance.

Impossible to believe he was actually going to do this. Going to kill a man, a man he'd never met. And would never meet, because with any luck at all he'd strike the fatal blow while the man slept.

Not a man, not really. A monster. Acid on that beautiful face, those perfect breasts . . .

A monster.

Was it murder when Beowulf slew Grendel? When St. George struck down the dragon? That was heroism, not homicide. It was what you had to do if you wanted to win the heart of the fair maiden.

Or he could go home right now and forget about her. There were plenty of women out there, and most of them never asked you to kill anybody. How hard would it be to find somebody else?

Not like her, though. Never anybody like her. Never had been, and he somehow knew there never would be.

Never an afternoon like the one he'd just spent. Never. Drained him, emptied him out—and, even so, just remembering it was getting him stirred up again.

He was at the window now. It was open a few inches, as she'd said it would be, and through it he could hear the voices of the baseball announcers, the crack of the bat, the subdued roar of the crowd. The mindless prattle of the commercial. "Bud." "Wei." "Ser."

He strained to hear more. Movement from the man. The husband.

The monster.

He got up on his toes, hooked his hands under the bottom edge of the window. He was standing in a bed of shrubbery, and it struck him that he was leaving footprints. Have to get rid of the shoes, too, he thought, along with the rest of his clothes.

Unless he gave it up and went home right now.

But how much better he'd feel if he went home in triumph, with the monster slain and the maiden won!

Besides, he realized, he *wanted* to do it. Wanted to thrust with the dagger, to flail away with the war club. God help him, he couldn't wait.

He took a full breath and eased the window all the way open.

She hadn't been able to eat. Now, upstairs in the bedroom she shared with her husband, she found herself unable to sit still. Her pulse was rapid, her mouth dry, her palms damp.

Any minute now . . .

She stripped to her skin, let her clothes lie where they fell. She sat up in bed and gazed down at her naked body, as if with a lover's eyes. And touched herself, as if with a lover's hands.

Remembering:

Crouching over him, she'd reached to probe with a finger, felt him stiffen and resist. Probed again, not to be denied, and felt him open up reluctantly to her. Unwilling to respond, unable to keep from responding . . .

Her own excitement was mounting now. He was at the window now, he had to be, she was sure of it. But she was stuck up here, unable to know what was happening downstairs in the den. His den, George's den, and her lover was at the window, must be at the window, had to be at the window . . .

She looked down at her hands, then closed her eyes, remembering:

"*God, Rita, what you do to me.*"

"*I had two fingers in you.*"

"*God.*"

"*First one and then two.*"

"I wasn't expecting that."

"You liked it."

"It was . . . interesting."

"You didn't want to like it, but you liked it."

"Well, the novelty."

"Not just the novelty. You liked it."

"Well."

"Next time I'll use my whole hand."

"Rita, for God's sake—"

She made a fist, opened it and closed it, opened it and closed it, watching the expression on his face.

"You'll like it," she said.

And he was down there now. She knew he was, she could tell, she could feel him there. She cupped her breasts, felt their weight, then let her hands slide lower. Let her fingers move, let her fantasies build, let her excitement mount . . .

She was close, very close. Hovering there, not wanting to go any further, wanting to stay there, right on the brink—

A shot rang out.

God!

She stayed there, stayed right there, right on the edge, right on the fucking edge, trembling, trembling, hot and wet and trembling, and waiting, God, waiting, Christ, waiting—

Another shot. No louder than the first, how could it be louder than the first, but God, it *seemed* louder—

She cried out with joy and fell back onto the bed.

She was wearing a blue satin robe. Her feet were bare. She stepped carefully into the den and gasped at the sight of the man lying there. He was dressed all in black and lay sprawled on his back like a rag doll discarded by a spoiled child. One hand was at his side, the fingers splayed. The other still gripped the hilt of a foot-long dagger.

She drew back involuntarily, then forced herself to take a closer look. "Yes," she said, turning from the corpse. "Yes, that's the man."

"James Beckwith," the detective said.

"Is that his name?"

"According to the ID in his wallet."

"I never knew his name," she said. "When I reported him to the police, I didn't have a name to give them. Because I never knew it."

"You gave them a good description," the detective said. "When I called in just now, they read it back to me, and it was all right on the money. Height, weight, age, hair color, everything down to the mole on his right cheek. That was what, four days ago that you reported him?"

She nodded. "Can we go in the other room now? Seeing him there like that . . ."

In the living room the detective said, "You did the right thing, filing the report. He was stalking you and you reported it. It's a shame we couldn't have done anything that might have prevented this, but—"

"You didn't have a name," her husband said. "You couldn't have him picked up, not if you didn't know who he was."

"No, but we could have staked out your house, and we would have if we'd had reason to believe he was planning anything like this. But we get so many complaints of this nature it's hard to know which ones to take seriously. So we wait and see if the guy takes it to a new level, and then we do something."

"It's a shame it came to this," her husband said. "Possibly, with professional help—"

The detective was shaking his head. "My opinion," he said, "a guy's got this particular kind of a screw loose, there's not a whole lot anybody can do for him. You can say it's a shame he got hurt, but the thing to focus on is nobody else got hurt, not you and not your wife. That dagger he was holding, in fact he's still holding it, well, I don't think he was planning on using it for a toothpick. It's a damn good thing you had the gun handy."

"It's usually locked in a desk drawer. Ever since Rita told me about this fellow, about the remarks and the threats—"

"And I believe he assaulted you physically, ma'am?"

"My breasts," she said, and lowered her eyes. "He ran up and took hold of my breasts. It was the most awful violation."

The detective shook his head. "You can call him a sick man," he said, "and say he was emotionally disturbed, but another way of looking at it is he got pretty much what he deserved."

"He's gone," she said.

"He's gone, and the rest of them are gone, and the body's gone."

"The body."

"And they took my gun, but your friend swears I'll get it back."

"My friend?"

"He'd certainly like to be your friend. He couldn't keep his eyes off you. When he wasn't trying for a glimpse of your tits he was looking at your little pink toes."

"I guess I should have put slippers on."

"And fastened the top button of your robe. But I think you were just fine the way you were. Quite fetching, and the detective thought so, too."

"And now he's gone, and we're alone. So tell me."

"Tell you what?"

"Tell me everything, George. I was going crazy, sitting up there and not knowing what was going on down here."

"As if you didn't know."

"How could I know? Maybe he'd chicken out. Maybe you actually would fall asleep—"

"Small chance of that."

"Tell me what happened, will you?"

"He opened the window and climbed over the sill. Clumsily, I'd have to say. I was afraid he'd make so much noise he'd frighten himself off and pop out again before I could do anything."

"But he didn't."

"Obviously not. I opened one eye just wide enough to get a glimpse of him, and as soon as he had both feet on the floor I opened both eyes and pointed the gun at him."

"And he'd already grabbed the dagger off the wall?"

"Of course not. That came later."

"He grabbed it later?"

"Do you want to hear this or do you want to keep on interrupting?"

"I'm sorry, George."

"He saw the gun, and his eyes widened, and he looked on the point of saying something. So I shot him."

"That was the first shot."

"Obviously. I shot him in the pit of the stomach, and—"

"Where? I couldn't really see anything. Where did the bullet enter? Around the navel?"

"Below the navel. I'd say about halfway between his navel and the place where you left your lipstick."

"The place where I left—"

"Just a joke, my dear. Halfway between his navel and his dick, that's where I shot the son of a bitch. It put him down and shut him up and I guess it hurt. Abdominal wounds are supposed to be the most painful."

"And then it was ages before the second shot."

"I doubt it was more than thirty seconds. Say a minute at the outside."

"Was that all? It seemed longer."

"For him as well, I'm sure. But I wanted a moment or so to tell him."

"To tell him."

"I didn't want him to die thinking something had gone horribly wrong. I wanted him to know everything was working out just the way it was supposed to, that he'd been set up and played for a sap. He didn't want to believe it."

"But you convinced him."

" 'A few hours ago,' I told him, 'she had two fingers up your ass. I hope you enjoyed it.' "

"You told him that?"

"It was a convincer."

"And then what? You shot him?"

"In the heart. To put him out of his misery, although he didn't look miserable so much as he looked embarrassed. You should have seen the look on his face."

"I wish I had. That was the one thing wrong."

"That you weren't there for it."

"Yes."

"Well, you could have been waiting in the living room. You could have popped in when you heard the first shot. But I don't suppose it was a total loss, was it? Being stuck upstairs?"

"What do you mean?"

"You had your hands full, didn't you?"

"Well," she said.

"Excited, were you?"

"You know I was."

"Yes, I know you were. My goodness, now that I think about it, those pretty little fingers have been a lot of places today, haven't they? I hope you washed them before you shook hands with the detective."

"Did I shake hands with him? I don't remember shaking hands with him."

"Maybe you didn't. But if you did, I bet *he* remembers."

"You think he liked me?"

"I'll bet he calls you."

"You really think so?"

"Oh, he'll have a pretext. He's not fool enough to call without a pretext. He'll have something to report on the disposition of the case, or he'll want to check on your state of mind. And if he doesn't get any encouragement from you he'll have the sense to let it drop."

"But if he does?" She nibbled her lower lip. "He's kind of cute," she said.

"I had a feeling you liked him."

"I just wanted him to go home. But he *is* kind of cute. You think?"

"What?"

"Well, we couldn't do things the same way we did with Jimmy, could we?"

"What, get him to crawl in the window and then blow him away? I don't think so."

"When he calls," she said, "*if* he calls—"

"He'll call."

"—I don't think I'll encourage him."

"Even if he is cute."

"There are lots of cute guys," she said, "and there ought to be a way to surprise them the way we surprised Jimmy."

"We'll think of something."

"And next time I'll be in the room when it happens."

"Sure."

"I mean it, I want to be there."

"You could even do it," he said.

"Really?"

"Look at you," he said. "You're something, aren't you?"

"Am I?"

"I'll say. But yes, you can be there, and maybe you can do it. We'll see."

"You're good to me, George. Good to me and good for me."

"I am, and don't you forget it."

"I won't. You know the one thing I regret?"

"That you weren't in the room to see it happen."

"Besides that."

"What?"

"Oh, it's silly," she said. "But I wish we'd put it off a day or two longer."

"To stretch out the anticipation?"

"That, but something else. Remember what I told him today? That next time I'd get my whole hand inside of him?"

"You're saying you would have liked to try."

"Well, yeah. It would have been interesting."

"Sweet little hands. Maybe you could do that to me."

"You'd let me?"

"And maybe I could do it to you."

"God," she said. "You've got such big hands."

"Yes, I do, don't I?"

"God," she said. "Can we go upstairs now? Can we?"

Terrible Tommy Terhune

"As every high school chemistry student knows," wrote sportswriter Garland Hewes, "the initials TNT stand for tri-nitro-toluene, and the compound so designated is an explosive one indeed. And, as every tennis fan is by now aware, the same initials stand as well for Thomas Norton Terhune, supremely gifted, immensely personable, and, as he showed us once again yesterday on the clay courts of Roland Garros, an unstable and violently explosive mixture if ever there was one, and a grave danger to himself and others."

The incident to which the venerable Hewes referred was one of many in Tommy Terhune's career in world-class tennis. In the French Open's early rounds, he dazzled players and spectators alike with the brilliance of his play. His serve was powerful and on-target, but it was his inspired all-around play that lifted him above the competition. He was quick as a cat, covering the whole court, making impossible returns look easy. His drop shots dropped, his lobs landed just out of his opponent's reach but just inside the white line.

But when the ball was out, or, more to the point, when the umpire declared it to be out, Tommy exploded.

In his quarterfinal match at Roland Garros, a shot of Terhune's, just eluding the outstretched racquet of his Montenegrin opponent, landed just inside the baseline.

The umpire called it out.

As the television replay would demonstrate, time and time again, the call was an error on the official's part. The ball did in fact land inside the line, by two or three inches. Thus Tommy Terhune was correct in believing that the point should be his, and he was understandably dismayed at the call.

His behavior was less understandable. He froze at the call, his racquet at shoulder height, his mouth open. While the crowd watched in anticipatory silence, he approached the umpire's raised platform. "Are you out of your mind?" he shouted. "Are you blind as a bat? What the hell is the matter with you, you pop-eyed frog?"

The umpire's response was inaudible, but was evidently uttered in support of his decision. Tommy paced to and fro at the foot of the platform, ranting, raving, and drawing whistles of disapproval from the fans. Then, after a tense moment, he returned to the baseline and prepared to serve.

Two games later in the same set, he let a desperate return of his opponent's drop. It was long, landing a full six inches beyond the white line. The umpire declared it in, and Tommy went berserk. He screamed, he shouted, he commented critically on the umpire's lineage and sexual predilections, and he underscored his remarks by gripping his racquet in both hands, then swinging it like an axe as if to chop down the wooden platform, perhaps as a first step to chopping down the official himself. He managed to land three ringing blows, the third of which shattered his graphite racquet, before another official stepped in to declare the match a forfeit, while security personnel took the American in hand and led him off the court.

The French had never seen the like, and, characteristically, their reaction combined distaste for Terhune's lack of savoir-faire with grudging respect for his spirit. Phrases like *enfant terrible* and *monstre sacré* turned up in their press coverage. Elsewhere in the world, fans and journalists said essentially the same thing. Terrible Tommy Terhune, the tennis world's most gifted and most temperamentally challenged player, had proven to be his own worst enemy, and had succeeded in ousting himself from a tournament he'd been favored to win. He had done it again.

The racquet Tommy shattered at the French Open was not the first one to go to pieces in his hands. His racquets had the life expectancy of a rock star's guitar, and he consequently had learned to travel with not one but two spares. Even so, he'd been forced to withdraw from one tournament in the semifinal round, when, after a second double fault, he held his racquet high overhead, then brought it down full-force upon the hardened playing surface. He had already sacrificed his other two racquets in earlier rounds, one destroyed in similar fashion to protest an official's decision, the other snapped over his knee in fury at himself for a missed opportunity at the net. He was now out of racquets, and unable to continue. His double fault had cost him a point; his ungovernable rage had cost him the tournament.

Such episodes notwithstanding, Tommy won his share of tournaments. He did not always blow up, and not every episode led to disqualification. In England, one confrontation with an official provoked a clamor in the press that he be refused future entry, not merely to Wimbledon, but to the entire United Kingdom; in response, Tommy somehow held himself in check long enough to breeze through the semifinals, and, in the final round, treated the fans to an exhibition of play unlike anything they'd seen before.

Playing against Roger MacReady, the rangy Australian who was the crowd's clear favorite, Tommy played center court at Wimbledon as Joe Dimaggio had once played center field at Yankee Stadium. He anticipated every move MacReady made, moving in response not at the impact of ball and racquet but somehow before it, as if he knew where MacReady was going to send the ball before the Australian knew it himself. He won the first two sets, lost the third in a tiebreaker, and soared to an easy victory in the fourth set, winning 6–1, and winning over the crowd in the process. By the time his last impossible backhand return had landed where MacReady couldn't get to it, the English fans were on their feet cheering for him.

A month later, the laurels of Wimbledon still figuratively draped around his shoulders, Terrible Tommy Terhune diagnosed an official as suffering severely from myopia, astigmatism, and tunnel vision, and recommended an unorthodox course of ophthalmological treatment consisting of the performance of two sexual acts, one incestuous, the other physically impossible. He then threw his racquet on the ground, stepped on its face, and pulled up on its handle until the thing snapped. He picked up the two pieces, sailed them into the crowd, and stalked off the court.

Morley Safer leaned forward. "If you were watching a tennis match," he began, "and saw someone behave as you yourself have so often behaved—"

"I'd be disgusted," Tommy told him. "I get sick to my stomach when I see myself on videotape. I can't watch. I have to turn off the set. Or leave the room."

"Or pick up a racquet and smash the set?"

Tommy laughed along with the TV newsman, then assured him that his displays of temper were confined to the tennis court. "That's the only place they happen," he said. "As to why they happen, well, I know what provokes them. I get mad at myself when I play poorly, of course, and that's led me to smash a racquet now and then. It's stupid and self-destructive, sure, but it's nothing compared to what happens when an official makes a bad call. That drives me out of my mind."

"And out of control?"

"I'm afraid so."

"And yet there are skeptics who think you're crazy like a fox," Safer said. "Look at the publicity you get. After all, you're the subject of this *60 Minutes* profile, not Vasco Barxi, not Roger MacReady. All over the world, people know your name."

"They know me as a maniac who can't control himself. That's not how I want to be known."

"And there are others who say you gain by intimidating officials," Safer went on. "You get them so they're afraid to call a close point against you."

"They seem to be dealing with their fears," Tommy said. "And wouldn't that be brilliant strategy on my part? Get tossed out of a Grand Slam tournament in order to unnerve an official?"

"So it's not calculated? In fact it's not something subject to your control?"

"Of course not."

"Well, what are you going to do about it? Are you getting help?"

"I'm working on it," he said grimly. "It's not that easy."

"It's rage," he told Diane Sawyer. "I don't know where it comes from. I know what triggers it, but that's not necessarily the same thing."

"A bad call."

"That's right."

"Or a good call," Sawyer said, "that you *think* is a bad call."

Tommy shook his head ruefully. "It's embarrassing enough to explode when the guy gets it wrong," he said. "The incident I think you're referring to, where the replay clearly showed he'd made the right call, well, I felt more ashamed of myself than ever. But even when I'm clearly right and the official's clearly wrong, there's no excuse for my behavior."

"You realize that."

"Of course I do. I may be crazy, but I'm not stupid."

"And if you *are* crazy, it's temporary insanity. As I think our viewers can see, you're perfectly sane when you don't have a tennis racquet in your hand."

"Well, they haven't asked me to pose for any mental health posters," he said with a grin. "But it's true I don't have to struggle to keep a lid on it. That only happens when I'm playing tennis."

"The court's where the struggle takes place."

"Yes."

"And when you honestly think a call has gone against you, that it's a bad call . . ."

"Sometimes I can keep myself in check. But other times I just lose it. I go into a zone, and, well, everybody knows what happens then."

"And there's nothing you can do about it."

"Not really."

"You've had professional help?"

"I've tried a few things," he said. "Different kinds of therapy to help me develop more insight into myself. I think it's been useful, I think I know myself a little better than I used to, but when some clown says one of my shots was out when I just plain know it was in—"

"You're helpless."

"Utterly," he said. "Everything goes out the window, all the insight, all the coping techniques. The only thing that's left is the rage."

"You have a life most women would envy," Barbara Walters told Jennifer Terhune. "You're young, you're beautiful, you've had success as a model and as an actress. And you're the wife of an enormously talented and successful athlete."

"I've been very fortunate."

"What's it like being married to a man like Tommy Terhune?"

"It's wonderful."

"The clothes, the travel, the VIP treatment . . ."

"That's all nice," Jennifer acknowledged, "but it's, like, the least of it. Just being with Tommy, sharing his life, that's what's truly wonderful."

"You love your husband."

"Of course I do."

"But I'm sure there are women in my audience," Walters said, "who wonder if you might not be the least bit afraid of your husband."

"Afraid of Tommy?"

Walters raised her eyebrows. "Mr. TNT? Terrible Tommy Terhune?"

"Oh, that."

" 'Oh, that.' You're married to a man with the most famously explosive temper in the world. Don't tell me you're never afraid that something you might do or say will set him of."

"Not really."

"What makes you so confident, Jennifer?"

"Tommy has a problem with rage," Jennifer said, "and I recognize it, and *he* recognizes it. He's been working on it, trying a lot of different things, like, to help him cope with it. I just know he'll be able to get a handle on it."

"And I'm sure our hopes are with him," Walters said, "but that doesn't address the question, does it? What about you, Jennifer? How do you know that terrible temper, that legendary rage, won't one day be aimed at you?"

"I'm not an umpire."

"In other words . . ."

"In other words, the only time Tommy loses it, the only time his temper is the least bit of a problem, is when an official makes a bad call against him on the tennis court. He never gets mad at an opponent. He doesn't go into the stands after fans who make insulting remarks, and I've heard some of them say some pretty outrageous things. But he takes that sort of thing in stride. It's only bad calls that set him off."

"And after an explosion?"

"He's contrite. And ashamed of himself."

"And angry?"

"Only during a match. Not afterward."

"So it's never directed at you?"

"Never."

"He's a perfect gentleman?"

"He's thoughtful and gentle and funny and smart," Jennifer said, "in addition to being the best tennis player in the world. I'm a lucky girl."

Later, watching herself on television, Jennifer thought the interview had gone rather well. She sounded a little ditsy, saying *like* often enough to sound like a Valley Girl, but outside of that she'd done fine. Her hair, which had caused her some concern, wound up looking great on camera, and the dress she'd worn had proved a good choice.

And her comments seemed okay, too. The *likes* notwithstanding, she came across not as an airhead but as a concerned and supportive life partner and helpmate. And, she told herself, that was fair enough. Everything she'd said had been the truth.

Though not, she had to admit, the whole truth. Because how could she have sat there and told Barbara Walters that Tommy's temper was one of the things that had attracted her to him in the first place? All of that intensity, when he served and volleyed and made impossible shots look easy, well, it was exciting enough. But all of that passion, when he roared and ranted and just plain lost it, was even more exciting. It stirred her up, it got her juices flowing. It made her, well, *hot*—and how could she say all that to Barbara Walters?

In fact, when you came right down to it, she was a little disappointed that Tommy never lost it except on the tennis court. It was a pity, in a way, that he never brought that famous temper home with him, that he never lost it in the bedroom.

Sometimes—and she would never admit this to anyone, on or off camera—sometimes she tried to provoke him. Sometimes she tried to make him mad. Even if he were to get physical, even if he were to slap her around a little, well, maybe it was kinky of her, but she thought she might like that.

But it was hopeless. On the court, with a racquet in his hand and an official to argue with, he was Mr. TNT, the notorious Terrible Tommy Terhune. At home, even in the bedchamber, he was what she'd said he was, the perfect gentleman.

Darn it . . .

"So we begin to make progress," the psychoanalyst said. "The need to win your father's approval. The approval sometimes granted, other times withheld, for reasons having nothing to do with your own behavior."

"It wasn't fair," Tommy said.

"And that is what so infuriates you about a bad call on the tennis court, is it not so? The unfairness of it all. You have done everything you were supposed to do, everything within your power, and still the approval of the man in authority is denied to you. Instead he sits high above you, remote and unreachable, and punishes you."

"That's exactly what happens."

"And it is unfair."

"Damn right it is."

"And you explode in rage, the rage you never let yourself feel as a child. But now you know its source. It's not the official, who of course cannot be expected to be right every time."

"They're only human."

"Exactly. It's your father you're truly enraged at, and he's dead, and out of reach of your anger, no longer available to approve or disapprove, to applaud or punish."

"That's it, all right."

"And now, armed with the insight you've developed here, you'll be able to master your rage, to dispel it, to rise above it."

"You know something?" Tommy said. "I feel better already."

In a first-round match two weeks later, an unreturnable passing shot by his unseeded opponent fell just outside the sideline marker. The umpire called it in.

"You blind bastard," Tommy screamed. "How much are they paying you to steal the match from me?"

"With every breath," the little man in the loincloth intoned, "you draw the anger up from the third chakra. Up up up, past the heart chakra, past the throat chakra, to the third eye. Then, as you breathe out, you let the anger flow in a stream out through the third eye, transformed into peaceful energizing white light. Breathe in and the anger is drawn upward from the solar plexus, where it is stored. Breathe out and you release it as white light. With every breath, your reserve of rage grows less and less."

"Om," Tommy said.

In his next tournament, the Virginia Slims Equal Opportunity Challenge (dubbed Men Deserve Cancer Too by one commentator), Tommy waltzed through the early rounds, breathing in and breathing out. Then, in the quarterfinals, he smashed his racquet after a service double fault.

He had a replacement racquet, and it wasn't until midway through the next game that he snapped it over his knee.

"Why put you on the couch for ten or twelve years," the doctor said, "when I can give you a little pill that'll fix what's wrong with you? If you had high blood pressure, you wouldn't probe your psyche to uncover the underlying reasons for it, would you? You might stroke out while you were still trying to remember your childhood. No, you'd take your medication. If you had diabetes, you'd watch your diet and take your insulin. I'm going to write you a prescription for a new tranquilizer, and I want you to take one first thing every morning. And you won't have to master your anger, or figure out where it comes from. Because it'll be gone."

"Neat," said Tommy.

"There's something curiously listless about Terhune's play," the television announcer reported. "He's performing well enough to win his early matches, but we're used to seeing him rush the net more often, and his reflexes seem the tiniest bit less sharp. We've heard rumors that he's been taking medication to help him with his emotional difficulties, and it looks to me as though whatever he's taking is slowing him down."

"But his temper's in check, Jim. When that call went against him in the first set, he barely noticed it."

"Oh, he noticed it. He stared over at the official, and he looked puzzled. But he didn't seem to care very much, and he lifted his racquet and played the next point without incident."

"If he's on something, it does seem to be working . . . Oh, what's this?"

"He thought Beckheim's return was out."

"But it was clearly in, Jim."

"Not the way Terhune saw it. Oh, there he goes. Oh, my."

"Your eyelids are very heavy," the hypnotist said. "You cannot keep them open. You are sleeping, you are in a deep sleep. From now on, you will be completely calm and unruffled on the tennis court. Nothing will disturb your composure. If anything upsetting occurs, you will stop what you are doing and count slowly to ten. When you reach the count of ten, all tension and anger will vanish, and you will once again be calm and unruffled. Now how will you be when you play tennis?"

"Calm," Tommy mumbled. "Calm and unruffled."

"And what will you do if something upsetting occurs?"

"Count to ten."

"And how will you feel when you reach the count of ten?"

"Calm and unruffled."

"Very good. When I reach the count of five, you will wake up feeling curiously refreshed, with no conscious recollection of this experience. One. Two. Three. Four. Five. How do you feel, Tommy?"

"Calm and unruffled," he said. "And curiously refreshed."

Looking neither calm nor unruffled, Tommy stalked over to where the official was perched. "One," he said, and swung his racquet at the platform. "Two," he said, and he continued his count, punctuating each number with a hammer blow to the base of the platform. The racquet shattered on the count of six, but he continued counting all the way to ten as he marched off the court.

"You have the chicken?" Atuele said. "Perfect white chicken. No dark feather, no blemish. Very good." He placed the chicken on the little altar, placed his hands gently on the bird, and gazed thoughtfully at it. After a long moment the chicken fell over and lay on its side.

"What happened to the chicken?" Tommy asked.

"It is dead."

"But, uh, how did it die?"

"As it was supposed to," Atuele said.

Tommy looked around. He was in a compound about a third the size of a football field, just a batch of mud huts strung around an open area that faced the altar, where the chicken was apparently still dead. He'd flown Air Afrique from New York to Dakar, then transferred to Air Gabon, whatever that was, for a harrowing flight to Lomé, the capital of Togo, wherever *that* was. He'd been granted an audience with this Sorbonne-educated witch doctor, who'd sent him off to buy a chicken. And now the chicken was dead, and he felt like an idiot. What did any of this have to do with tennis? What could it possibly have to do with Thomas Norton Terhune?

"I don't know what this guy does," a friend had told him, "and you feel like the world's prize jackass while he's doing it, but it's magic. And it works."

"Maybe if you believe in it . . ."

"Hell, I didn't believe in it. I thought it was pure-Dee ooga-booga horseshit. But it worked anyway. You want to know something? I *still* think it was ooga-booga horseshit. But now I believe in it."

How, he wondered, could you believe in something while still believing it to be horseshit? And how could it possibly work? And—

"You need a spirit," Atuele told him. "A spirit who will live within you, and who will have the job of keeping you serene while you are playing tennis."

"A spirit," Tommy said hollowly.

"A spirit. In order to give you this spirit, you require a ceremony. Go to your hotel. Return at sunset. And you must bring something."

"Another chicken?"

"No, not another chicken. A bottle of scotch whiskey and a box of cigars."

"That's easy enough. What are we going to do, get drunk and smoke cigars together?"

"No, they are for me. And bring five thousand dollars."

"Five thousand dollars?"

"For the ceremony," Atuele explained.

The ceremony turned out to be ridiculous. Six half-naked men pounded on drums, while two dozen young women danced around, heads thrown back, eyes rolling. Atuele broke an egg in a bowl, poured it onto Tommy's head, rubbed it into his scalp. He gave him a ball of ground-up grass and told him to eat it, then left him to sit in the circle, and eventually to shuffle around on the dance floor. After an hour or so of this Tommy got a taxi back to his hotel and went to bed.

In the morning he showered, packed, and went to the airport, knowing he'd wasted his money, hoping only that nothing had leaked to the press, that the world would never know the lengths to which he'd been driven or how utterly he'd been made a fool of. He flew to Dakar and on to JFK, then caught another flight to Phoenix for the Scottsdale Open.

Jennifer met him at the airport. "Waste of time," he told her. She knew only that he'd heard about a secret treatment, not where you went for it or what it consisted of, and he didn't feel like filling her in. "Lots of mumbo jumbo," he said. "It won't work."

But it did.

At Scottsdale, Tommy Terhune reached the final round of the tournament, losing to Roger MacReady in four sets. He used the same racquet for the entire tournament, and never hit anything with it but the ball. He didn't raise his voice, didn't once curse himself, his opponents, the largely hostile audience, or the officials, who made their share of inaccurate calls. He was, that is to say, a perfect gentleman.

And he managed all this with no effort whatsoever. He didn't take a pill, didn't count to ten, didn't clamp a lid on his anger, didn't chant or meditate. All he did was play tennis, and the moment he stepped onto the court each day, a curious calm settled over him. He still took notice when a call went unfairly against him, but he didn't mind, didn't take it personally. He stayed focused on his game, and his game had never been better.

Of course, he told himself, one tournament didn't necessarily prove anything. He'd gone through whole tournaments before without treating the crowd to a display of the famous Terhune temper, only to lose it a week or a month down the line. How could he be sure that wouldn't happen?

Somehow, though, he knew it wouldn't. Somehow he could tell that something had happened within that circle of mud huts in Togo. According to Atuele, he now had a spirit invested inside of him, a spirit who took control of his temper the moment he picked up a racquet and stepped onto a court. And that's just how it felt. One way or another, he'd morphed into a person who didn't have to control himself because he didn't experience any anger to begin with. He played his matches, won or lost, and went home feeling fine either way.

Calm and unruffled, you might say.

Tommy played brilliantly in his next tournament. He sailed serenely through the early rounds, fell behind in his quarterfinal match, then rallied to salvage a victory over his unseeded opponent. Then, in the third set of the semis, the audience fell silent when Tommy served, came to the net, and leaped high into the air to slam his opponent's return. The ball struck near the baseline, but everyone present could see it was clearly in.

Except the official, who declared it out.

Tommy took a step toward the platform. The official cowered, but Tommy didn't seem to notice. He said, "Was that ball out?"

The official nodded.

"Oh," Tommy said, and shrugged. "From here it looked good, but I guess you can see better from where you're sitting."

He went back to the baseline and served the next point. He went on to win the match and advance to the finals, in which he played brilliantly, beating Roger MacReady in straight sets.

"And here's Mrs. Tommy Terhune, the lovely Jennifer," said the TV reporter, sticking a mike in her face. "Your husband was really commanding out there, wasn't he?"

"He was," she agreed.

"He played brilliant tennis, and he seems to have triumphed in the inner game as well, wouldn't you say?"

"The inner game?"

"He didn't lose his temper at all."

"Oh, that," she said. "No, he didn't."

"I'll bet you're proud of him."

"Very proud."

"You've been quoted as saying he's always been a perfect gentleman off the court. Now he seems to be every bit the perfect gentleman on the court as well. That must be extremely gratifying to you."

"Yes," she said, smiling furiously. "Extremely gratifying."

It was in the U.S. Open that the extent of the change in Terrible Tommy Terhune became unmistakably evident. Earlier, prior to his still-secret visit to West Africa, some commentators had theorized that the brilliance of his play might be of a piece with the ungovernability of his temper. Passion, after all, was the common denominator. Put the one on a leash, they suggested, and the other might wind up hobbled in the bargain.

But this was clearly not the case. Tommy had an easy time of it in the early rounds at Flushing Meadows, winning every match in straight sets. In the quarter-finals, his Croatian opponent won a single game in the first set and none at all in the second and third, but the fellow's play was not as pathetic as the score suggested. Tommy was simply everywhere, getting to every ball, his returns always on target and, more often than not, unreturnable.

The calls, of course, did not always go his way. But his reaction was never greater than a shrug or a raised eyebrow. Spectators looked for him to be struggling with his emotions, but what was becoming clear was that there was no struggle, and no emotions.

In the semifinals, Tommy's opponent was the young Chinese-American Scott Chin, but most fans were looking past the semis to a final round that would see Tommy pitted once again with his Australian rival, Roger MacReady. But this was not to be—while Tommy moved easily past Chin, MacReady lost the fifth set to a previously unknown Belgian player named Claude Macquereau.

Two days later, after a women's final in which one player grunted while the other wept, Terhune and Macquereau met for the men's championship. If the fans had been disappointed by MacReady's absence, the young Belgian soon showed himself as a worthy opponent for Tommy. His serve was strong and accurate, his game at net and at the baseline a near mirror image of Tommy's. Macquereau won the first set 7–6, lost the second 7–5. Most games went to deuce, and most individual points consisted of long, wearying volleys marked by one impossible return after another.

By the third set, which Tommy won in a tiebreaker, the fans knew they were watching tennis history being made. Midway through the fourth set, won by Macquereau in an even more attenuated tiebreaker, the television commentators had run out of superlatives and the crowd had shouted itself hoarse. Both players, run ragged in the late-summer heat and humidity, looked exhausted, but both played as though they were fresh as daisies.

In the third game of the final set, a perfectly placed passing shot of Tommy's was called out. The audience drew its collective breath—they knew the ball was in—and Tommy approached the platform.

"Ball was out?" he said conversationally.

The official managed a nod. The man must have known he'd missed the call, and must have been tempted to reverse himself. But all he did was nod.

"Okay," Tommy said, and played the next point, while the audience released its collective breath in a great sigh that mingled relief with disappointment.

After ten games in the final set, they had taken turns breaking each other's service, and were tied 5–5. In the eleventh game, Tommy served and went to the net, and Macquereau's return flew past Tommy's outstretched racquet and landed just inside the sideline.

The official called it out.

It was close, certainly closer than the call that had gone against Tommy earlier in the set, but the ball was definitely in and, more to the point, Tommy Terhune knew it was in. The game had been tied at 15–all, and this point put Tommy ahead, 30–15.

His response was immediate. He went to the service line, hit two serves into the net to tie the score at 30–all, then deliberately double-faulted a second time, putting Macquereau a point ahead, as he would have been had the call been correct.

The act was uncommonly gracious, and all the more so for coming when it did. It is, as one reporter pointed out, easier to give back a questionable point when you're winning or losing by a considerable margin, but Tommy's unprecedented act of chivalry might well cost him the championship.

Not so. Trailing 40–30, he won the next point with a service ace, then won the game by playing brilliantly for the next two points. The final game was almost anticlimactic; Macquereau, serving, seemed to know how it was going to end, and scored only a single point while Tommy broke his service to take the game, the set, the match, and the United States Open championship.

All of which made the aftermath just that much more tragic.

The whole world knows the rest. How Tommy Terhune, flushed with triumph, accompanied by his curiously unemotional wife, returned to his hotel, racquet in hand. How Roger MacReady was waiting for them in the lobby, and accompanied them upstairs to their suite. How Jennifer explained haltingly that she and MacReady had fallen in love, that they had been, like, having an affair, and that she wanted Tommy to give her a divorce so that she and MacReady could be married.

She said all this calmly, expecting Tommy to take it every bit as calmly. Perhaps she thought it was a good time to tell him—riding high after his victory, he could presumably take a lost love in stride. In any event, Tommy had never shown much emotion off the court, and now was equally cool on it, so she knew she could count on him to be a gentleman about this. If he could be gallant enough to hand two points to Claude Macquereau through purposeful double faults, wouldn't he be equally gallant and self-sacrificing now?

As it happened, he would not.

He was clutching his tennis racquet when she told him all this. It was the racquet he had been using ever since his return from Togo, and it had lasted longer than any racquet he had previously owned, because he had not once swung it at anything harder than a tennis ball.

By the time he let go of it now, it was in pieces, and his wife and his rival were both dead. He smashed the edge of the racquet into Roger MacReady's head, striking him five times in all, fracturing his skull even as he smashed the racquet, and he went on swinging until all he had left in his hand was the jagged handle.

Which he continued to hold as he backed the terrified Jennifer into a corner, where he pinned her against the wall and drove the racquet handle into the hollow of her throat.

Then he picked up the phone and told the desk clerk to summon the police.

Everyone had a theory, of course, and one that got a lot of play held that Tommy's temper, no longer released periodically on the tennis court, didn't just disappear. Instead it got tamped down, compressed, so that the eventual inevitable explosion was that much greater and more disastrous.

One enterprising newsman found his way to Togo, where the enigmatic Atuele told him essentially the same thing. "I gave the man a spirit," he said, between puffs on a cheroot. "To help him when he played tennis. And it helped him, is it not so?"

"But off the court—"

"Off the court," Atuele said, "the man had no problem. So, when he was not playing tennis, the spirit's work was done. And the anger had to go somewhere, didn't it?"

Three in the Side Pocket

You'd think they would have a pool table. When you walked into a joint called the Side Pocket, you expected a pool table. Maybe something smaller than regulation, maybe one of those dinky coin-operated Bumper Pool deals. But something, surely, where you poked a ball with a stick and it went into a hole.

Not that he cared. Not that he played the game, or preferred the sound of balls striking one another as background music for his drinking. It was just a matter of unfulfilled expectations, really. You saw the neon, "The Side Pocket," and you walked in expecting a pool table, and they didn't have one.

Of course, that was one of the things he liked about his life. You never knew what to expect. Sometimes you saw things coming, but not always. You could never be sure.

He stood for a moment, enjoying the air-conditioning. It was hot out, and humid, and he'd enjoyed the tropical feel of the air as he'd walked here from his hotel, and now he was enjoying the cool dry air inside. Enjoy it all, he thought. That was the trick. Hot or cold, wet or dry. Dig it. If you hate it, then dig hating it. Whatever comes along, get into it and enjoy it.

Right.

He walked over to the bar. There were plenty of empty stools but he stood instead. He gazed at the light glinting off the shoulders of the bottles on the top row of the back bar, listened to the hum of conversation floating on the surface of soft jazz from the jukebox, felt the cool air on his skin. He was a big man, tall and thickly muscled, and the sun had bronzed his skin and bleached blond streaks in his brown hair.

Earlier he'd enjoyed being in the sun. Now he was enjoying being out of it.

Contrasts, he thought. Name of the game.

"Help you?"

He'd been standing, staring, and there was no telling how long the bartender had been right in front of him, waiting for him to order something. A big fellow, the bartender, sort of an overgrown kid, with one of those sleeveless T-shirts cut to show off the delts and biceps. Weightlifter's muscles. Get up around noon, pump some iron, then go lie in the sun. Spend the evening pouring drinks and flexing your muscles, go home with some vacationing schoolteacher or somebody's itchy wife.

He said, "Double Cuervo, neat, water back."

"You got it."

Why did they say that? And they said it all the time. *You got it*. And he didn't have it, that was the whole point, and he'd have it sooner if they didn't waste time assuring him that he did.

He didn't like the bartender. Fine, nothing wrong with that. He examined the feeling of dislike and let himself enjoy it. In his imagination he drove two stiffened fingers into the bartender's solar plexus, heard the pained intake of breath, followed with a chop to the windpipe. He entertained these thoughts and smiled easily, smiled with genuine enjoyment, as the fellow poured the drink.

"Run a tab?"

He shook his head and drew out his wallet. "Pay as you go," he said, riffling through a thick sheaf of bills. "Sound fiscal policy." He plucked one halfway out, saw it was a hundred, tucked it back. He rejected another hundred, then found a fifty and laid in on top of the bar. He drank the tequila while the bartender rang the sale and left his change on the bar in front of him, returning the wallet to his side pocket.

Maybe the bar's name had nothing to do with pool, he thought. Maybe the Side Pocket meant a pocket in a pair of pants, not the hip pocket but the side pocket, which could have made it an *un*hip pocket, but in fact made it a more difficult target for pickpockets.

They had a pool table there once, he decided, and the owner found it didn't pay for itself, took up space where he could seat paying customers. Or the bar changed hands and the first thing the new guy did was get rid of the table. Kept the name, though, because he liked it, or because the joint had a following. That made more sense than pants and pickpockets.

He kept his own wallet in his side pocket, but more for convenience than security. He wasn't much afraid of pickpockets. Draining the drink, he felt the tequila stirring him and imagined a hand slipping artfully into his pocket, groping almost imperceptibly for his fat wallet. Imagined his own hand taking hold of the smaller hand. Squeezing, breaking small bones, doing damage without looking, without even seeing the face of the person he was hurting.

He saw the bartender was down at the end of the bar, talking to somebody on the telephone, grinning a lazy grin. He waited until the kid looked his way, then crooked a finger and pointed at his empty glass. Get it? *You got it.*

A pair of double Cuervos gave you a nice base to work on, got the blood humming in your veins. When the second was gone he switched to India Pale Ale. It had a nice bite to it, a complicated flavor. Sat comfortably on top of tequila, too. Not so comfortably, though, that you didn't know it was there. You definitely knew it was there.

He was halfway through the second IPA when she came in. He didn't exactly sense her presence, but the energy in the place shifted when she walked through the door. Not that everybody turned to look at her. For all he knew, nobody turned to look at her. He certainly didn't. He just stood there, his hand wrapped around the base of the longneck bottle, ready to refill his glass. He felt the shift in energy and turned it over in his mind.

He caught sight of her in the back bar, watched out of the corner of his eye as she approached. One empty stool separated the two of them, but she showed no awareness of his presence, her attention directed at the bartender.

She said, "Hi, Kevin."

"Lori."

"It's an oven out there. Sweetie, tell me something. Can I run a tab?"

"You always run a tab," Kevin said. "Though I heard someone say Pay As You Go is a sound fiscal policy."

"I don't mean a tab like pay at the end of the evening. I mean like I'll pay you tomorrow."

"Oh," he said. "The thing is I'm not supposed to do that."

"See, the ATM was down," she said.

"Down? Down where?"

"Down as in not working. I stopped on the way here and it wouldn't take my card."

"Is Jerry meeting you here? Because he could—"

"Jerry's in Chicago," she said. "He's not due back until the day after tomorrow." She was wearing a wedding ring, and she fiddled with it. "If you took plastic," she said, "like every other place . . ."

"Yeah, well," Kevin said. "What can I tell you, Lori? If we took plastic the owner couldn't cook the books as much. He hates to pay taxes even more than he hates to bathe."

"A wonderful human being."

"A prince," Kevin agreed. "Look, I'd let you run a tab, the hell, I'd just as soon let you drink free, far as it goes, but he's on my ass so much these days . . ."

"No, I don't want to get you in trouble, Kevvie."

He'd been taking this all in, hanging on every word, admiring the shape of it even as he'd admired her shape, long and curvy, displayed to great advantage in the pale yellow cotton shift. He liked the way Kevin had quoted his pay-as-you-go remark, a sure way to draw him toward the conversation if not into it.

Now he said, "Kevin, suppose I buy the lady a drink. How will that sit with the owner?"

This brought a big grin from the bartender, a pro forma protest from Lori. Very nice, little lady, he thought, but you have done this before. "I insist," he said. "What are you drinking?"

"I'm not," she said. "That's the whole problem, and you, kind sir, are the solution. What am I drinking? Kevin, what was that drink you invented?"

"Hey, I didn't invent it," Kevin said. "Guy was drinking 'em in Key West and described it to me, and I improvised, and he says I got it right. But I never tasted the original, so maybe it's right and maybe it isn't." He shrugged. "I don't know what to call it. I was leaning toward Key Hopper or maybe Florida Sunset but I don't know."

"Well, I want one," Lori said.

He asked what was in it.

"Rum and tequila, mostly. A little OJ." Kevin grinned. "Couple of secret ingredients. Fix you one? Or are you all right with the IPA?"

"I'll try one."

"You got it," Kevin said.

During the first round of Key Hoppers she told him her name was Lori, which he knew, and that her husband's name was Jerry, which he also knew. He told her his name was Hank Dettweiler and that he was in town on business. He'd been married once, he told her, but he was long divorced. Too many business trips.

During the second round she said that she and Jerry weren't getting along too well. Too few business trips, she said. It was when they were together that things were bad. Jerry was too jealous and too possessive. Sometimes he was physically abusive.

"That's terrible," he told her. "You shouldn't have to put up with that."

"I've thought about leaving him," she said, "but I'm afraid of what he might do."

During the third round of Key Hoppers (or Florida Sunsets, or whatever you wanted to call them) he wondered what would happen if he reached down the front of her dress and grabbed hold of one of her breasts. What would she do? It was almost worth doing just to find out.

There was no fourth round, because midway through the third she suggested they might be more comfortable at her place.

They took her car and drove to her house. It was a one-story box built fifty years ago to house vets. No Down Payment to GIs, Why Rent When You Can Own? He figured it was a rental now. Her car was an Olds Brougham a year old and her house was a dump with Salvation Army furniture and nothing on the walls but a calendar from the dry cleaners. Why rent when you can own? He figured Lori and Jerry had their reasons.

He followed her into the kitchen, watched as she found an oldies station on the radio, then made them both drinks. She'd kissed him once in the car, and now she came into his arms again and rubbed her little body against him like a cat. Then she wriggled free and headed for the living room.

He went after her, drink in hand, caught up with her, and put his arm around her, reaching into the front of her dress and cupping her breast. It was the move he'd imagined earlier, but of course the context was different. It would have been shocking in a public place like the Side Pocket. Here it was still surprisingly abrupt, but not entirely unexpected.

"Oh, Hank," she said.

Not bad. She remembered the name, and acted as if his touch left her weak-kneed with passion. His hand tightened a little on her breast, and he wondered just how hard he could squeeze before fear and pain took the place of passion. They'd be more genuine emotions, certainly, and a lot more interesting.

People always got more interesting when you handed them something they didn't expect. Especially if it wasn't what they wanted. Especially if it was painful or frightening, or both.

He pulled her down onto the couch and began making love to her. His touch and his kisses were gentle, exploratory, but in his mind he hurt her, he forced her. That was interesting, too, a mental exercise he had performed before. She was vibrating to his touch, but she'd be screaming her lungs out if his actions matched the images in his mind.

Just something for his own private amusement, while they waited for Jerry.

But where was good old Jere? That was the question, and he could tell it had occurred to her as well, could tell by the way she worked to slow the pace. It wouldn't do if he got to nail her before the Jealous Husband burst through the door. The game worked best if he was caught on the verge, made doubly vulnerable by guilt and frustration, and awkward, too, with his pants down around his knees.

Happily, their goals were the same. And, when his pants were indeed around his knees and consummation appeared to be right around the corner, they both froze at the sound of a key in the lock.

"Oh my God!" she cried.

Enter Jerry. The door flew open and there he was. You looked at him and you wanted to laugh, because he was hardly the intimidating figure he was supposed to be. Traditionally, the outraged husband was big as a house and meaner than a snake, so that his physical presence alone would scare the crap out of you. Jerry wasn't a shrimp, but he was a middle-aged guy who stood five-ten in his shoes and looked like his main form of exercise was changing channels with the remote control. He wore glasses, he had a bald spot. He looked like a store clerk, night man at the 7-Eleven, maybe.

Which helped explain the gun in his hand. You take a guy five-four, eighty years old, weighs no more than a sack of flour, you put a gun in his hand, you've got a figure that commands respect.

Lori was whimpering, trying to explain. Hank got to his feet, turned from her, turned toward Jerry. He pulled up his pants, fastened them.

"You must be Jerry," he said. "Now look, just because you got a gun don't mean you get to jump the line. You gotta wait your turn, just like everybody else."

It was comical, because Jerry wasn't expecting that. He was expecting a load of begging and pleading, explanations and justifications, and instead he got something that didn't fit any of the slots available for it.

So he didn't know how to react, and while he was figuring it out Hank crossed the room, grabbed the gun in one hand, hit him with the other. His fist went right into the pit of Jerry's soft stomach, just about midway between the nuts and the navel, and that was the end of the war. You hit a person there just right, before he's had a chance to tense his stomach muscles, and if you put enough shoulder into the punch you can deliver a fatal blow.

Not instantly fatal, though. It can take a day or a week, and who has that kind of time?

So he let Jerry double up, clutching his belly with both hands, and he grabbed hold of him by the hair on his head and forced his head down hard, fast, and brought his own knee up hard, fast. He smashed Jerry's face, broke his nose.

Behind him, she was carrying on, going *No, no, no,* clutching at his clothing. He backhanded her without looking, concentrating his attention on Jerry, who was blubbering through the blood that coursed from his nose and mouth.

That was nice, that knee-in-the-face maneuver. His pants were already bloody at the knee, and it was a sure bet there was nothing in Jerry's closet that would fit him. That was the advantage of having the husband be a big bozo, the way the script called for it; after you were done with him, you could pick out something nice from his wardrobe.

But his pants were khakis, replaceable for thirty bucks at the nearest mall. And, since they were already ruined—

This time he cupped Jerry's head with both hands, brought it down, brought his knee up. The impact brought a great cry from Lori. He gave Jerry a shove and the man wound up sprawled against the wall, jaw slack, eyes glassy. Conscious? Unconscious? Hard to say.

And what did it matter? Eager to get on with it now, he went over to Jerry, put one hand under his chin and the other on the top of his head, and snapped his neck.

Hell of a sound it made. First a grinding noise like something you'd hear in a dentist's office, and then a real sharp crack. Left you in no doubt of what you'd just done.

He turned to Lori, relishing the look on her face. God, the look on her face!

"Honey," he said, "you see what I did? I just saved your life."

It was amusing, watching the play of emotions on her sharp little face. Like her head was transparent, like you could see the different thoughts zooming around in there. She had to come up with something that would leave her with a pulse at the evening's end, and the effort made her thoughts visible.

Thoughts caroming around like balls on a pool table . . .

She said, "He was going to kill me."

"Going to kill us both," he agreed. "Violent fellow, your husband. What do you figure makes a man like that?"

"The gun was pointed right at me," she said, improvising nicely. "I thought I was going to die."

"Did your whole life flash before your eyes?"

"You saved my life."

"You're probably wondering how to thank me," he said. He unfastened his pants, let them drop to the floor, stepped out of them. A shadow of alarm flashed on her face, then disappeared.

He reached for her.

It was interesting, he thought, how rapidly the woman adjusted to new realities. Her husband—well, her partner, anyway, and for all he knew her husband as well—her guy was down for the count, on his way to room temperature. And she wasn't wasting time mourning him. Off with the old, on with the new.

"Oh, baby," she said, and sighed theatrically, as if her passion had been real, her climax authentic. "I knew I was hot for you, Hank. I knew that the minute I saw you. But I didn't know—"

"That it could possibly be this good," he supplied.

"Yes."

"It's Jerry being dead that does it," he told her. "Lovemaking as an affirmation of our own aliveness. He's lunch meat and we're still hot to trot. Get it?"

Her eyes widened. Oh, she was beginning to get it, all right. She was on the edge, the brink, the goddamn verge.

"I liked the bit with the bartender," he said. "Kevin, right?"

"The bartender?"

"You got it," he said, and grinned. " 'Oh, Kevvie, I haven't got any money, so how am I going to get a little drinkie-poo?' "

"I don't—"

"He phoned you," he said, "after he got a peek at my wallet. He probably thought they were all fifties and hundreds, too."

"Honey," she said, "I think all that sweet love scrambled my brains. I can't follow what you're saying. Let me get us a couple of drinks and I'll—"

Where was she going? Jerry's gun was unloaded, he was sure of that, but that didn't mean there wasn't a loaded gun stashed somewhere in the place. Or she might just open the door and take off. She wasn't dressed for it, but he already knew she cared more for survival than propriety.

He grabbed her arm, yanked her back down again. She looked at him and got it. It was interesting, seeing the knowledge come into her eyes. Her mouth opened to say something but she couldn't think of anything that might work.

"The badger game," he said. "The cheating wife, the outraged husband. And the jerk with a lot of cash who buys his way out of a mess. How about you? Got any cash? Want to buy your way out?"

"Anything you want," she said.

"Where's the money?"

"I'll get it for you."

"You know," he said, "I think I'll have more fun looking for it myself. Make a game of it, you know? Like a treasure hunt. I'm pretty good at finding things, anyway. Got a sixth sense for it."

"Please," she said.

"Please?"

Something went out of her eyes. "You son of a bitch," she said. "It's not a game and I'm not a toy. Just do it and get it over with, you son of a bitch."

Interesting. Sooner or later they let you know who they are. The mask drops and you see inside.

His hands went around her throat. "Jerry got a broken neck," he said. "Strangulation's not as quick. How it works, the veins are blocked off but not the arteries, so the blood gets in but it can't get out. Remember those Roach Motel ads? Thing is, you won't be pretty, but here's the good news. You won't have to see it."

Jerry's gun was unloaded. No surprise there.

Jerry's wallet had a couple of hundred in it, and so did Lori's purse, which suggested the ATM wasn't down after all. And a cigar box on a shelf in the closet held more cash, but most of it was foreign. French 500-franc notes, some Canadian dollars and British pounds.

He showered before he left the house, but he was perspiring before he'd walked a block, and he turned around and went back for her car. Risky, maybe, but it beat walking, and the Olds was wonderfully comfortable with its factory air. He'd always liked the sound of that, factory air, like they made all that air in Detroit, stamped it out under sterile conditions.

He parked down the block from the Side Pocket, waited. He didn't move when Kevin let out his last customers and turned off most of the lights, gave him another five minutes to get well into the business of shutting down for the night.

He was a loose end, capable of furnishing a full description. So it was probably worthwhile to tie him off, but that was almost beside the point. Thing is, Kevin was a player. He was in the game, hell, he'd started the game, picking up the phone to kick things off. You knocked down Jerry and Lori, you couldn't walk away and leave him standing, could you?

Besides, he'd be expecting a visitor now, Lori or Jerry or both, showing up with his piece of the action. What kind of finder's fee would he get? As much as a third? That seemed high, given that he wasn't there when it hit the fan, but on the other hand there was no game if he wasn't there to deal the cards.

Maybe they told Kevin he was getting a third, and then cheated him.

Guy in Kevin's position, he'd probably expect to be cheated. Probably took it for granted, same way as Kevin's boss took it for granted that not all of the money that passed over the bar wound up in the till. Long as the bottom line was high enough, you probably didn't mind getting cheated a little, probably figured it was part of the deal.

Interesting. He got out of the car, headed for the front door. Maybe, if there was time, he'd ask Kevin how they worked the split. Good old Kevvie, with that big grin and all those muscles. While he was at it, why not ask him why they called it the Side Pocket? Just to see what he'd say.

You Don't Even Feel It

She found them at the gym, Darnell in sweatpants and sneakers, his chest bare, Marty in khakis and a shirt and tie, the shirt a blue button-down, the tie loose at the throat. Marty was holding a watch and Darnell was working the speed bag, his hands fast and certain.

She'd been ready to burst in, ready to interrupt whatever they were doing, but she'd seen them like this so many times over so many years, Darnell working the bag and Marty minding the time, that the sight of them stopped her in her tracks. It was familiar, and thus reassuring, although it should not have been reassuring.

She found a spot against the wall, out of his line of sight, and watched him train. He finished with the speed bag and moved on to the double end bag, a less predictable device than the speed bag, its balance such that it came back at you differently each time, and you had to react to its responses. Like a live opponent, she thought, adjusting to you as you adjusted to it, bobbing and weaving, trying not to get hit.

But not hitting back . . .

From the double end bag they moved to the heavy bag, and by then she was fairly certain they had sensed her presence. But they gave no sign, and she stayed where she was. She watched Darnell practice combinations, following a double jab with a left hook. That's how he'd won the title the first time, hooking the left to Roland Weymouth's rib cage, punishing the champion's body until his hands came down and a string of head shots sent the man to the canvas. He was up at eight, but he had nothing left in his tank, and Darnell would have decked him again if the ref hadn't stopped it.

"The winner, and . . . *new* junior middleweight champion of the world . . . Darnell Roberts!"

He'd moved up two weight classes since then. Junior middleweight was what, 154? And middleweight was 160, and he'd held the IBF title for two years, winning it when the previous titleholder had been forced to give it up for reasons she hadn't understood then and couldn't remember now. The sport was such a mess, it was all politics and backroom deals, but all of that went away when you got down to business. You sweated it out in the gym, and then you stepped into the ring, you and the other man, and you stood and hit each other, and all the conniving and manipulation disappeared. It was just two men in a pure sport, bringing nothing with them but their bodies and whatever they had on the inside.

He was a super middleweight these days. That meant he'd have to be under 168 when he weighed in the day before the fight, and seven to ten pounds more when he actually stepped into the ring. You wanted those extra pounds, she knew, because the more you weighed the harder you punched.

Of course your opponent had those extra pounds, too, and punched harder for them.

Darnell had run through his combinations, and now he was standing in and slugging, hitting the bag full force with measured blows that had all his weight behind them. And Marty was standing behind the bag, holding on to it, steadying it, while Darnell meted out punishment.

Marty saw her then. Their eyes met, and she didn't see surprise in his, which meant she'd been right in sensing he knew she was there.

Other hand, Marty hardly ever looked surprised.

She drew her eyes away from Marty's and watched Darnell as he hit the bag with measured lefts and rights. He weighed what, 185? 190? But he wouldn't have trouble making the weight. He had two months, and he was just starting to train. All he had to do was work off twelve or fifteen pounds. Rest was water, and you sweated it out before you stepped on the scales, then drank yourself back to your fighting weight.

She always used to love to see him hit the heavy bag. It was fun to watch him train, watch that fine body show what it could do, but this part was the best because you saw the muscles work beneath the skin, saw the blows land, heard the impact, felt the power.

Early days, watching this, she'd get wet. Young as she was back then, it didn't take much. And, young as she was, it embarrassed her, even if nobody knew.

Fifteen years. They'd been married for twelve years, together for three before that. Three daughters, the oldest eleven. So she didn't get wet pants every time she watched him work up a sweat. Still, she always liked the sight of him, digging in, setting himself, throwing those measured punches.

She wasn't liking it much today.

"Time," Marty said, but he went on holding the bag, knowing Darnell would throw another punch or two. Then, when his fighter's hands dropped, he let go of the bag and stepped out from behind it, smiling. "Look who's here," he said, and Darnell turned to face her, and he didn't look surprised, either.

"Baby," he said. "How I look just now? Not too rusty, was I?"

"I heard it on the news," she said.

"I was gonna tell you," he said, "but you was sleepin' when I left this morning, and I didn't have the heart to wake you."

"And I guess it was news to you this morning," she said, "even if you signed the papers yesterday afternoon."

"Well," he said.

"Last I heard," she said, "we were thinking about quitting."

"I been thinkin' on it," he said. "I not ready yet."

"Darnell . . ."

"This gone be an easy fight for me," he said. He had the training gloves off now and he was holding out his hands for Marty to unwind the cotton wraps. The fingers that emerged showed the effects of all the punches he'd landed, on the heavy bag and on the heads and bodies of other fighters, even as his face showed the effects of all the punches he'd taken.

Well, some of the effects. The visible effects.

"This guy," he said. "Rubén Molina? Man is made for me, baby. Man never been in against a body puncher like me. Style he got, I can find him all day with the left hook. Man has this pawing jab, I can fit a right to the ribs in under it, take his legs out from under him."

"Maybe you can beat him, but—"

"Ain't no maybe. And I won't just beat him, I'll knock him out. All I need, what you call a decisive win, an' then I get a title shot."

"And then?"

"Then I fight, probably for the WBO belt, or maybe the WBC. And I win, and that makes three belts in three different weight classes, and ain't too many can claim that." He beamed at her, and she saw the face she'd seen when they first met, saw the face of the boy he'd been before she ever met him. Under all the scar tissue, all the years of punishment.

"And then I hang 'em up," he said. "That what you want to hear?"

"I don't want to wait two more fights to hear it," she said. "I worry about you, Darnell."

"No call for you to worry."

"They had this show on television. Muhammad Ali? They showed talking before the Liston fight, and then they showed him like he is now."

"Man has got a condition. Like that actor, used to be on *Spin City*."

"That's Parkinson's disease," Marty said. "That Michael J. Fox has. What Ali has is Parkinson's syndrome."

"Whatever it is," she said, "he got it because he didn't know when to quit. Darnell, you want to wind up shuffling and mumbling?"

He grinned, did a little shuffle.

"That's not funny."

"Just jivin' you some," he said. "Keisha, I gonna be fine. All I's gonna do is win one fight and get a title shot, then win one more and get my third belt."

"And take how many punches in the process?"

"Molina can't punch worth a damn," he said. "Walk through his punches, all's I gotta do."

"You think Ali didn't say the same thing?"

"It may not have been the punches he took," Marty put in. "They can't prove that's what did it."

"And can you prove it isn't?" She turned to her husband. "And Floyd Patterson," she said. "You don't think he got the way he is from taking too many punches? And that Puerto Rican boy, collapsed in his third professional bout and never regained consciousness."

"That there was a freak thing," Darnell said. "Ring ropes was too loose, and he got knocked through 'em and hit his head when he fell. Like gettin' struck by lightin', you know what I'm sayin'? For all it had to do with bein' in a boxin' ring."

If the boy hadn't been in the ring, she thought, then he couldn't have got knocked out of it.

"You worry too much," Darnell said, and gathered her in his arms. "Part of bein' a woman, I guess. Part of bein' a man's gettin' the job done."

"I just don't want you hurt, Darnell."

"You just don't want to miss the lovin'," he said, "the whole last month of training. That's what it is, girl, innit?"

"Darnell—"

"All that doin' without," he said, "just make it sweeter afterward. You think about that, help you get through the waitin' time."

"Tell her," Darnell said. "Tell Keisha how it went."

"He had a brain scan and an MRI," Marty told her. "This was to make you happy, because he had a scan after his last fight and there was no medical reason for another one."

"He's been slurring his words," she said. "Don't you call that a reason?"

"He sounds the same as ever to me," Marty said.

"Maybe you don't listen."

"And maybe you listen too hard."

"Hey," Darnell said. "Maybe I gets a little mushmouth some of the time. Sometimes my lips be a little puffy." He tapped his head. "Don't mean anything's messed up inside."

"All the punches you've taken—"

"Let me tell you something about the punches," he said. "Gettin' hit upside the head? Nine times, you don't even feel it. It don't hurt. Body shots, a man keeps beating on your ribs, man, that's a different story. Hurts when he does it and hurts the next day and the day after. Head shots? Don't mean nothin' at all. Why you lookin' at me like that?"

"Nine times."

"Huh?"

" 'Nine times, you don't even feel it.' That's what you just said."

"So?"

"Nine times out of ten, you meant."

"What I said."

"No, you just said 'nine times.' "

"Well, shit," he said. "You tellin' me you didn't know what I meant?"

"I'm telling you what you said. You left out some words there."

"Man, *there's* a sign," he said heavily. "I must have brain damage, leavin' out 'out of ten' like that."

"It's cumulative, Darnell."

"What you talkin' now?"

"Punches to the head, the effect is cumulative. Even if you barely feel them—"

"Which I just said I don't."

"—they add up, and you reach a point where every punch you take does real damage. It's irreversible, you can't turn it back, and once you see signs—"

"Which there ain't yet."

"If you're slurring words," she said, "then we're seeing signs."

"What happens," he said, grinning, "my tongue gets in the way of my teeth an' I can't see what I'm sayin'. Why you lookin' at me like that?"

"Your tongue gets in the way of your eyeteeth," she said, "and you can't see what you're saying."

"What I just said."

"Except you left out 'eye,' " she said. "You said your tongue got in the way of your teeth, and that doesn't mean anything."

"But you know what I meant."

"And I also know what you said."

"Damn," he said. "We just *had* the tests. Didn't have to, had 'em strictly to keep you happy, and look at you. You ain't happy!"

Marty said, "What's that, a Coke? You want something stronger?"

"This is fine."

"Because you're not in training. You can have a real drink, if you want."

"No, I'm fine."

"Well, I want a drink," he said, and ordered vodka on the rocks. "I'll tell you," he said, "I won't pretend I wanted to be having this conversation, but we ought to have it. Because you really got to cut the guy some slack, Keisha."

"I've got to cut him some slack?"

"Molina's style is tailor-made for Darnell," Marty said, "just like he says it is. You look at tapes of his fights, that jumps right out at you. But that doesn't mean this is gonna be a walk in the park. Molina's ten years younger."

"Eleven. He's twenty-six and Darnell turned thirty-seven last month."

"Can we compromise? Call it ten and a half?" His smile was disarming.

"Keisha, what I'm getting at, he should have training on his mind and nothing else, and what he's got is you hammering away at him, telling him he's slurring his words. He's training hard, he's tired by the end of the day, and is it any wonder his speech might be the least bit blurry? Time the day's done, I'm slurring my own words, come to that."

"Just let him see a doctor," she said.

"Keisha, he saw one. He had a scan and an MRI, remember?"

"A doctor to test his speech," she said. "There's a specialist, I wrote the name down. All Darnell has to do is sit down and talk with him, and he can tell whether there's been any damage."

Marty was shaking his head. "We looked at the brain waves," he said, "and he got a clean bill of health. No evidence of damage."

"Or proof there hasn't been any."

"You can't prove a negative. There's no evidence of any organic brain damage, Keisha, and he's been pronounced okay to fight by experts. You sit him down, have some quack listen to his speech and measure how his tongue moves, and it's a judgment call on his part, got nothing to do with anything you can put your finger on. And if he gets it into his head that there's something wrong, the fight's off. Doesn't matter that your expert turns out to be full of crap. The fight's off and Darnell's chance at a third belt's down the toilet."

"He doesn't need a third belt."

"He wants it, Keisha."

"And you? What do you want, Marty?"

"I want him to have a shot."

She looked at him. "The money doesn't mean a thing to you," she said.

"Not as much as it means to Darnell," he said. "His fight with Molina's on the pay-per-view undercard. He's getting eighty thousand dollars for it, Keisha. He's had title bouts where he didn't get that."

"We don't need the money."

"That's not how he sees it. What he sees is he can stand in there for ten rounds and put eighty grand in his pocket."

"Minus your cut, and training camp expenses, and everything else that takes a bite out of his check."

"Including taxes, which gets a lot more of his money than I do, and a lot more of mine, too. But ten rounds is what, thirty-nine minutes, start to finish? You do the numbers, Keisha, you're the one's good at numbers, but it's better than anybody ever made bagging groceries at the Safeway."

She looked at him. He met her gaze, then picked up his drink and drained it.

"And if he gets past Molina," he said, "which he will, and it probably won't take all ten rounds, either, I can get him a title shot, prolly WBO but it could be WBC, and for that he'll make close to a million. And if he wins it, which there's no reason why he can't, then he's a man won three different belts in three different weight categories, and he's that much more desirable when it comes to endorsements and public appearances, because that's the only way you can make any money after you hang the gloves up. You show up at a dinner, you make a little speech—"

"How's he going to make a speech," she demanded, "if he can't talk straight?"

"He sounds fine to me," Marty said. "Maybe you got ears like a dog, hear things I don't, but he sounds perfectly fine to me. And nobody is gonna expect him to perform Shakespeare. All they want is for him to show up, three-time champion of the world, sign some autographs, and pose for some snapshots. Keisha, all this is beside the point. It's what he wants, this fight and the fight after. Then he'll quit winners and hang 'em up."

"Will he?"

"He'll have no choice," he said. "I'll insist on it. I'll tell him I'm quitting him, and he'll have to quit."

"You could do that now."

"There's no reason."

"I already told you the reason, Marty. His head's the reason. All those punches he's taken, aren't they enough of a reason?"

"The man's never been knocked down."

"That Cuban fighter, had all those tattoos—"

"You didn't let me finish. The man's never been down from a blow to the head. The Cuban kid, what the hell was his name, they coulda called him the Human Sketchpad—"

"Was it Vizcacho?"

"Vizcacho, yes, and he had a funny first name. Filomeno, something like that. That was a shot to the liver put Darnell down, and that's a punch'll floor anybody, it lands right, and what did he do, Darnell? Got up, took an eight count, and hit Vargas hard enough to erase half his tattoos. Knocked him out, remember?"

"I remember."

"He's lost four fights, Darnell, his entire career. One early decision, it was the other kid's hometown, no way on earth we were gonna get a decision there. You didn't see that fight, Keisha, it was before you were in the picture, but believe me, we got robbed." He shrugged. "It happens. It still pisses me off, but that's the kind of shit that happens. He lost that fight, and he lost a decision to Armando Chaco that could have gone either way, and he was stopped twice. Once was a head butt, the other fighter couldn't continue, and they went to the scorecards and two judges had the other kid ahead." He closed his eyes, shook his head. "The other was when he lost the 160-pound title, and you couldn't argue with it. Darnell was taking way too much punishment, and the ref was right to step in."

"That's not how you felt at the time."

"Darnell wanted to go on, and he's my fighter. I got to want what he wants. But we looked at the films afterward, and we both agreed it was the right thing, stopping it. Look, Keisha, do you have to make it harder for him? He's gonna have this fight, and one more for the title. He's got his hands full training for it. Why give him a hard time?"

"Gee, I don't know, Marty. Maybe because I love him."

"You think I don't? Keisha, don't be like that. Sit down, have another Coke, a real drink, whatever. Listen, Darnell's gonna be fine."

She started to say something, but what was there to say? She kept on walking.

She was seated at ringside when he fought Rubén Molina.

At first she hadn't intended to be there. "I can't watch," she told him. "I can't."

"But you always there," he said. "You my good luck, don't you know that? How'm I gonna get in the ring, my good luck charm ain't there?"

She didn't believe she brought him luck, wasn't sure she believed in luck at all. But if *he* believed it . . .

She kept opening and closing her eyes. She couldn't watch, couldn't not watch. Every time Molina landed to Darnell's head, she felt the impact in the pit of her stomach. Molina didn't have much of a jab, he just stuck it out and groped with it, but he had an overhand right that he sometimes led with, and he was able to land it effectively.

In the third round, one of those right-hand leads snapped Darnell's head back, and he grinned to show it hadn't hurt. Fighters did that all the time, she knew, and it always indicated the opposite of what they intended.

Darnell stayed with his fight plan, working the body, punishing Molina relentlessly with hooks to the rib cage. In time, she knew, the body blows would get to Molina, taking the spring out of his legs and the power out of his punches, but meanwhile he kept landing that right, and Keisha winced every time he threw it, whether it landed or not.

Couldn't watch, couldn't not watch . . .

Midway through the sixth round, Darnell double-jabbed, then missed with a big left hook. Molina hit him with a right hand and put him on the canvas. She gasped—the whole crowd gasped, it seemed like—and he was up almost before the referee started counting, insisting it was a slip. He was off balance, that much was true, but it was a punch that put him down, and he had to take a count of eight, had to meet the ref's eyes, had to assure the man that yes, he was fine, yes, he wanted to keep fighting. Hell, yes.

He kept his jab in Molina's face for the rest of the round, and hurt him with body shots, but Molina landed an uppercut during a rare clinch and it snapped Darnell's head back. And there was another right hand at the bell, caught Darnell flush, and she saw his eyes right before the ref sprang between the two fighters.

The doctor came over to the corner between rounds, said something to Darnell and to Marty, shined a flashlight in Darnell's eyes. The ref came over to listen in. Oh, stop it, she wanted to shout, but she knew they weren't going to stop it, and the doctor returned to his seat and the bell rang for the seventh round.

And the seventh round was all Darnell's. He was determined to make up for the knockdown, and he pressed his attack, throwing three- and four- and five-punch combinations. The bodywork brought Molina's hands down, and a right cross with thirty seconds left in the round sent the boy to the canvas.

Stay down, she prayed. But no, he was up at eight, and the bell ended the round before Darnell could get to him.

The round took a lot out of both fighters, and they both coasted through the eighth. Molina kept his jab in Darnell's face through most of the round and landed the right once or twice, with no apparent effect.

At the bell, Darnell stood still for a moment, and she caught a look at his eyes. Then he recovered and loped over to his corner, and she got to her feet and pushed her way through, reaching a hand through the ropes and tugging at the cuff of Marty's pants. He was busy, talking to Darnell, using the End-Swell to bring down a mouse under his right eye, holding the water bottle for him, holding the spit bucket for him. If he was aware of Keisha he gave no sign, but when the warning buzzer sounded and he came down out of the ring he didn't look surprised to see her there.

"You got to stop it," she told him. "He didn't know where he was, he couldn't find his corner."

"You don't know what you're talking about," he told her.

"Marty, his eyes aren't right."

"They looked fine to the doc. Keisha, he's winning the fucking fight. The other guy's got nothing left and Darnell's prolly gonna take him out this round, and if he doesn't that's fine because we're way ahead on points."

"He was knocked down."

"He swung and missed, and it was his momentum knocked him down more than anything else. Next round he came back and knocked the other guy down, and came this close to knocking him out. Another thirty seconds in the round and the fight'd be over and we could go home."

"Marty, he's hurt."

"I don't agree with you," he said. "And if I did, which I don't, and I tried to stop it? He'd kill me. He's winning the fight, he's winning impressively enough to get a title shot, and—Keisha, sit down, will you? I got work to do here, I got to concentrate."

Toward the end of the ninth round, Darnell caught Molina with a big left hook and dropped him. Molina got through the round, but in the tenth Darnell got to him early, putting him down with a body shot, then flooring him a second time with a hard right to the temple. The referee didn't even count but stopped it right there, and the place went wild.

On his way out of the ring, Darnell told the TV guy Molina was a tough kid, and no, he himself was never hurt, the knockdown was more of a slip than anything else. "He hit me a few shots," he allowed, "but he never hurt me. Man punches like that, hit me in the head all day long. You don't even feel it, you know what I'm sayin'?"

Later, when they replayed the interview, they pointed out that Darnell had slurred his words, that his speech was hard to make out.

In his dressing room, Darnell was grinning and laughing and hollering, along with everybody else. Until his eyes went glassy and he mumbled that he didn't feel so good. He collapsed, and was rushed to the hospital, where he died three hours later without having regained consciousness.

He was wearing khakis, she noted, and a shirt and tie, but he'd added a navy blazer with brass buttons, and brown loafers instead of his usual sneakers. He said, "Keisha, I don't know what to say. I tried to see you, I don't know how many times, but I was told you weren't seeing anybody."

"I had to be by myself."

"Believe me," he said, "I can understand that. I didn't know whether it was everybody you weren't seeing or if it was just me, and either way I could understand it. I left messages, I don't even know if you got them, but I don't blame you for not calling back." He looked away. "I was going to write a letter, but what can you say in a letter? Far as that goes, what can you say in person? I'm glad you called me, and here I am, and I still don't know what to say."

"Come in, Marty."

"Thank you. Keisha, I just feel so awful about the whole thing. I loved Darnell. It's no exaggeration to say he was like a son to me."

"Let me fix you a drink," she said. "What can I get you?"

"Anything, it doesn't matter. Whatever you've got."

"Vodka?"

"Sure, if you've got it."

She put him in the overstuffed chair in the living room, came back with his vodka and a Coke for herself. And sat down across from him and listened to him talk, or tried to look as though she was listening.

"Another drink, Marty?"

"I better not," he said. "That one hit me kinda hard." He yawned, covered his mouth with his hand. "Excuse me," he said. "I feel a little sleepy all of a sudden."

"Go ahead and close your eyes."

"No, I'll be fine. 'Sfunny, vodka never hit me so sudden."

He said something else, but she couldn't make out the words. Then his eyes closed and he sagged in his chair.

She was sitting across from him when his eyes opened. He blinked a few times, then frowned at her. "Keisha," he said. "What the hell happened?"

"You got sleepy."

"I had a drink. That's the last thing I remember."

He shifted position, or tried to, and it was only then that he realized he was immobilized, his hands cuffed behind him, his ankles cuffed to the front legs of the chair. She'd wound clothesline around his upper body and the back of the chair, with a last loop around his throat, so that he couldn't move his head more than an inch or two.

"Jesus," he said. "What's going on?"

She looked at him and let him work it out.

"Something in the vodka," he said. "Tasted all right, but there was something in it, wasn't there?"

She nodded.

"Why, Keisha?"

"I didn't figure you'd let me tie you up if you were wide awake."

"But why tie me up? What's this all about?"

That was a hard question, and she had to think about it. "Payback," she said. "I guess."

"Payback?"

"For Darnell."

"Keisha," he said, "you want to blame me, go ahead. Or blame boxing, or blame Darnell, or blame the Molina kid, who feels pretty terrible, believe me. Son of a bitch killed a man in the ring and didn't even win the fight. Keisha, it's a tragedy, but it's not anybody's fault."

"You could have stopped it."

"And if I had? You think it would have made a difference if I threw in the towel when you told me to? He didn't get hit more than a couple shots after that, and Molina didn't have anything left by then. The damage was already done by then. You know what would have happened if I tried to stop it then? Darnell would have had a fit, and he probably would have dropped dead right then and there instead of waiting until he was back in his dressing room."

"You could have stopped it after the knockdown."

"Was that my job? The ref looked at him and let him go on. The ringside physician looked at him, shined a light in his eyes, and didn't see any reason to call a halt."

He went on, reasoning with her, talking very sensibly, very calmly. She stopped listening to what he was saying, and when she realized that he was waiting for a response, an answer to some question she hadn't heard, she got up and crossed the room.

She picked up the newspaper and stood in front of his chair.

He said, "What's that? Something in the paper?"

She rolled up the newspaper. He frowned at her, puzzled, and she drew back her arm and struck him almost gently on the top of the head with the rolled newspaper.

"Hey," he said.

She looked at him, looked at the newspaper, then hit him again.

"What are you doing, trying to housebreak me?"

The newspaper was starting to unroll. She left him there, ignoring what he was saying, and went into the other room. When she returned the newspaper was secured with tape so that she wouldn't have to worry about it unrolling. She approached him again, raised the newspaper, and he tried to dodge the blow but couldn't.

He said, "Is this symbolic? Because I'm not sure I should say this, Keisha, but it doesn't hurt."

"In the ring," she said, "when a fighter tries to indicate that a punch didn't hurt him, what it means is it did."

"Yeah, of course, because otherwise he wouldn't bother. And they all know that because they notice it in other fighters, but they do it anyhow. It's automatic. A guy hurts you, you want to make him think he didn't."

She raised the newspaper, struck him with it.

"Ouch!" he said. "That really hurt!"

"No, it didn't."

"No, it didn't," he agreed. "Why are we doing this? What's the point?"

"You don't even feel it," she said. "That's what Darnell always said about blows to the head. Body shots hurt you, when they land and again after the fight's over, but not head shots. They may knock you out, but they don't really hurt."

She punctuated the speech with taps on the head, hitting him with the rolled newspaper, a little harder than before but not very hard, certainly not hard enough to cause pain.

"Okay," he said. "Cut it out, will you?"

She hit him again.

"Keisha, what the hell's the point? What are you trying to prove, anyway?"

"It's cumulative," she said.

"What are you talking about?"

"The same as it is in the ring," she said. "Rubén Molina didn't kill Darnell. It was all those punches over all those years, punches he didn't even feel, punches that added up and added up and added up."

"Could you quit hitting me while we're talking? I can't concentrate on what you're saying."

"Punch after punch after punch," she said, continuing to hit him as she talked. "Down all the years, from playground fights to amateur bouts to pro fights. And then there's training, all those rounds sparring, and yes, you wear headgear, but there's still impact. The brain gets knocked around, same as your brain's getting knocked around right now, even if you don't feel it. Over a period of years, well, you got time to recover, and for a while that's just what you do, you recover each time, and then there's a point where you start to show the damage, and from that point on every punch you take leaves its mark on you."

"Keisha, will you for Chrissake stop it?"

She hit him, harder, on the top of the head. She hit him, not quite so hard, on the side of the head. She hit him, hard, right on the top of the head.

"Keisha!"

She sat down the rolled-up newspaper, fetched the roll of duct tape, taped his mouth shut. "Don't want to listen to you," she said. "Not right now." And, with Marty silent, she was silent herself, and the only sound in the room was the impact of the length of newspaper on his head. She fell into an easy rhythm, matching the blows with her own breathing, raising the newspaper as she inhaled, bringing it down as she breathed out.

She beat him until her arm ached.

When she took the tape from his mouth he winced but didn't cry out. He looked at her and she looked at him and neither of them said anything.

Then he said, "How long are you going to do this?"

"Long as it takes."

"Long as it takes to do what? To kill me?"

She shook her head.

"Then what?"

She didn't answer.

"Keisha, I didn't hit him. And I didn't try to make him do anything he didn't want to do. Keisha, there was no damage showed up in the MRI, nothing in the brain scan."

"I said for you to let an expert examine him. Study his speech and all. But you wouldn't do it."

"And I told you why. You want me to tell you again?"

"No."

"Keisha, he had an aneurysm. A blood vessel in the brain, it just blew out. Maybe it was from the punches he took, but maybe it wasn't. He could have been a hundred miles away from Rubén Molina, lying in a Jacuzzi and eating a ham sandwich, and the blood vessel coulda popped anyway, right on schedule."

"You don't know that."

"And you don't know any different. Keisha, you want to let me up? I gotta go to the bathroom."

She shook her head.

"It's your chair. You want me to make a mess on it?"

"If you want."

"Keisha—"

"Some of them," she said, "the ones who took too many punches, they get so they can't control their bladders. But that's a long ways down the line. Slurred speech comes first, and you aren't even slurring your words yet."

He started to say something, but she was pressing the tape in place. He didn't resist, and this time when she picked up the rolled newspaper he didn't even attempt to dodge the blows.

Two Old Stories

It Took You Long Enough

When the telephone rang she was sitting on the couch in a flannel robe struggling with a double-acrostic. The television set was on but she wasn't paying any attention to it. She turned the volume down before she picked up the phone.

"Shari? This is Howard Messinger."

"And so it is," she said.

"Shari?"

"What a stroke of luck," she said. "You're probably the only person I know who can tell me who commanded the Austrian forces at the battle of Blenheim."

"Prince Eugene."

"I somehow knew you would know that."

"Did you? The reason I called . . ."

"Only it doesn't fit."

"It has to."

'Three words."

"Eugene of Savoy."

"Just a minute."

"Shari . . ."

"Just a minute. Ha! It fits."

"Shari?"

"Yes. The reason you called."

"I'd like to see you."

She took a breath. "I don't think so," she said.

"I know what you're thinking. But it's important. I have to talk to you."

"What about?"

"I don't want to go into it over the phone. Christ, I'm in a booth, it's noisy here . . ."

"You sound a little shaky, Howard."

"I *am* a little shaky. Please?"

"I suppose so."

"I can be at your apartment in ten minutes."

"Well, don't. Give me at least a half hour. Have a drink or something. Or is that a bad idea?"

"Huh? Oh, am I drunk? My dear, I am so sober that it hurts."

"Well, have a drink and give me a half hour. Oh, if you want something to drink here you'd better pick up a bottle. I only have things like crème de banana."

He gave her forty minutes, and she used almost all of them to dress and straighten the apartment. She put on a little makeup, decided against perfume.

This is Howard Messinger. Always the announcement, always his full name. As if she could fail to remember the voice.

He called her every now and then. The calls always surprised her, although by now she felt she ought not to be surprised. He was likely to call every three or four months, usually late at night, usually after he'd had a great deal to drink. He would talk with her for a few minutes and then hang up and it might be months before she heard from him again. This pattern had established itself over the past five years and she supposed that she should have grown used to it by now.

But he had never before asked to come up. And she had never before heard this urgency in his voice.

He buzzed from the vestibule. She buzzed back to unlatch the downstairs door. He climbed the stairs, knocked on her door. She opened it, stepped back and motioned him inside. He took off his coat and looked around for a place to put it. She took it from him and hung it in the closet.

He said, "Stand still a minute. Let me look at you. You look the same."

"The hell I do."

"You do. When did you cut your hair?"

"God! Years ago."

"I liked it better long."

"I don't even remember what made me cut it. You're looking very good yourself, incidentally."

And indeed he was. His face was drawn, but he had the sort of dark good looks that were enhanced by stress. He had lost a bit of hair in front and his face had a few new lines in it but there was no denying that she still found him attractive. She was both pleased and distressed to discover this.

"I picked up a bottle of scotch," he said. "I don't know what you're drinking these days."

"Scotch'll do. How do you want it? Rocks?"

"Fine."

She made drinks. He took his and sat down in an armchair. She seated herself on the couch. She thought of several cute things to say and left them unsaid.

He said, "Thanks, incidentally."

"For letting you come over? You didn't give me much choice."

"Thanks all the same. Well. The only way to say it is to say it. My marriage is over."

"Just like that?"

"Just like that."

"Well, that wasn't what I expected. I don't know what I did expect but certainly not that."

"You're not the only one."

"I don't suppose I am. Well, it took you long enough, Howard."

"Took me—oh. No, that's not the way it was, I'm afraid. I didn't do anything. It got done."

"Lynn left you?"

He smiled. "I suppose I should be flattered that it surprises you. Yeah, she went and walked. For better than a dozen years I did not quite leave her. I kept wanting to and kept not doing it, until I reached the point where I even stopped leaving the woman in fantasy. And now she has flown de coop."

"She'll be back."

"No."

"Of course she will."

He was shaking his head. "No. No way. Damn, this turns out to be hard to say. The old macho pride."

"Oh."

"Uh-uh. She didn't just leave me, she left me for another guy."

"Somebody you know?"

"No, thank God."

"Is he married?"

"Divorced. She met him through the fucking PTA, if you can believe that. I think I need another drink."

"I'll get it for you."

She stayed an extra moment in the kitchen after replenishing his drink. She scrutinized the palm of her left hand. A couple of years ago someone had taken her to a pricy restaurant on First Avenue where a palmist had given her a reading. "Your head rules your heart," the palmist had told her, among other things. She studied her hand and hoped the old woman had spoken the truth. Just now would be a very bad time to let her heart get the upper hand.

When she was seated again on the couch she said, "Then it's definitely over?"

"No question. She wants to marry him, he wants to marry her, and I think we should raise our glasses to the happy couple."

"How do you feel about it, Howard?"

"That's the question, all right."

"Do you have an answer to go with it?"

He shrugged. "I always thought I did. Before it ever happened. When I used to think about leaving her, and when I began to reach the point where I knew it was never going to happen, I managed to dream up a lovely little scenario in which she fell in love with somebody else and so informed me, and I manfully accepted my fate while secretly rejoicing."

"Because you knew that was the only way you would get out of it."

"Right."

"But now you're not secretly rejoicing."

"I'm still rejoicing, damn it. But I'm also, I don't know, a little shaky. I don't know how much of this is wounded male pride. I've tried to allow for that and I still seem to feel something else."

"Not a question of suddenly realizing you love her?"

"Christ, no. But a sense of loss. And what the hell did I lose? A bad marriage to a woman who bored me to tears? I'm lucky to be out of this."

"You don't need to convince me. I thought you should have left her years ago."

"Nine years ago."

She forced herself to meet his eyes. "Nine years ago," she said.

"I wonder if it would have worked."

"No."

"You're awfully positive, Shari."

"Uh-huh."

"How can you be so sure?"

She thought for a moment. Then she said, "Do you know the story about the violinist? Once upon a time there was a great violinist who held a concert, and after the concert a young man came backstage for advice. He explained that he was studying the violin, that he had been told he had great talent, but that before he committed himself to a life on the concert stage he wanted to know if he had the potential to become truly great, as he didn't want to waste his life if he was doomed to be second rate. So the great violinist listened to him play, and then he said to him, 'Young man, your technique is excellent, you play very pleasingly, but you will never be truly great because you lack the fire. You just do not have the fire.'

"So the young man was crushed but he bore up manfully, thanked the great violinist for his candor, and left. He put his violin in the closet and applied himself to the business world where he was very successful. Many years later he met the great violinist at a benefit concert and told him that he owed all his success to him.

" 'How can that be?' asked the great violinist. 'Because I once came to you and played for you, and you told me I didn't have the fire, and so I gave up music and went to work in the widget business.' 'Ah,' said the great violinist. 'But one thing I always wondered,' said the businessman. 'How could you tell that I didn't have the fire just by listening to me for a few minutes?'

"The old violinist shrugged. 'I could tell nothing,' he said. 'In fact I barely listened to you. Whenever a young person plays for me I tell him the same thing. I tell him he does not have the fire.'

"The businessman was stunned. 'But that's terrible! I could have been a concert performer, I could have been a virtuoso! All my material success, it's nothing to me compared to the life I dreamed of, and I could have had it except that I believed you!'

"The old man smiled a sad smile. 'But that is everything,' he said. 'Don't you see? I told you you did not have the fire. And you listened to me, you believed me. But if you *had* had the fire you would not have paid any attention to me.' "

She had kept her eyes upon Howard Messinger while she told the story, but as she approached the end she looked away. Now she forced herself to seek his eyes again.

"I get the point," he said.

"Uh-huh. I've always liked that story."

"I'll bet you have. I don't think it'll ever be one of my all-time favorites. If you and I really had something I would have left her then and there. And since I didn't, *we* didn't."

"Something like that." She got to her feet. "I'm going to have some coffee. Would you like some? Or would you rather have another drink?"

"No, I'd rather have coffee."

A little later she said, "I'm sure you must be seeing someone these days."

"Am I that predictable?"

"I can't believe you suddenly embraced fidelity. That might add poignancy to all of this but it seems wildly out of character."

"It's comforting to see you're still a bitch."

"You'd hate me if I weren't. You're seeing somebody?"

He nodded. "A dancer. Lives on Horatio Street. She's awfully young."

"Most people are these days. A question comes to mind."

"Why am I here and not on Horatio Street?"

"Something like that."

"Well, it's a good question. You are not the first person in this room to have thought of it."

"And?"

"I don't think I'll be seeing much more of her."

"Because Lynn left you."

"Right."

"The dancer was good enough for you while you were married, but not when you're single again."

"It's not that simple," he said. "But it amounts to pretty much the same thing. Let's say she's been a diversion, and now that I don't have anything to be diverted *from*—"

"Uh-huh."

She knew he was going to ask if he could stay the night. When he did she said she didn't think it was a good idea.

"I just don't want to be alone, Shari."

"And I just don't want us to sleep together."

"Let me stay on the couch, then."

"Oh, Howard."

"I mean it."

"I know you do."

"I really don't want to go back to that hotel room."

She put out a cigarette. She said, "Once a man has slept with a woman, he always believes he can have her again anytime he wants her."

"Come off it."

"Or so I've been led to believe."

"That's not it at all."

"You know what I wish? I wish I could figure out just what role I play in your personal mythology. Drunken midnight phone calls every few months. A visit when your marriage breaks up. Just what are we supposed to be to each other?"

"Very good friends?"

"Maybe."

"Or maybe I'm still in love with you."

"Oh, Howard," she said. "Now you don't believe that any more than I do, baby."

She let him sleep on the couch. She had known all along that she would. She brought him a pillow and a blanket. "Don't come knocking on my door," she said. "I mean that."

She lay awake for a long time before slipping into a light and tentative sleep. She was awake before the alarm could sound. She showered and dressed, and when she entered the living room he had gone. There was a note on the arm of the couch. *I didn't come knocking on your door. But not for lack of wanting to. Thanks for the couch and the coffee. And mostly for being you.*

She tore the note in quarters and put the scraps in a wastebasket. She had been waiting for that knock. She had lain awake hoping it would not come, but knowing that she would not be able to deny him. If she had played a curious role in his personal mythology, so surely had he in hers. For years she had not really wanted to speak to him on the telephone, yet whenever he'd called, she had conversed willingly. She had let him come to her apartment last night, she had let him sleep on her couch, and she would have taken him into her bed if he had persisted.

But he had not, and now he would never have that power over her again. She knew this with a sudden assurance, and the knowledge was as frightening as any fresh liberation. They might indeed become friends, it was not impossible, but they would never again be whatever it was they had been. It had taken her nine years to get over him and one uneventful night had made all the difference.

Later that day, sitting at her desk, she burst abruptly into tears. But she got control of herself almost immediately. No one noticed a thing.

You Can't Lose

Anyone who starves in this country deserves it. Really. Almost anybody who is dumb enough to want to work can get a job without any back-breaking effort. Blindies and crips haul in twenty-five bucks an hour bumming the Times Square district. And if you're like me—able-bodied and all, but you just don't like to work, all you got to do is use your head a little. It's simple.

Of course, before you all throw up your jobs, let me explain that this routine has its limitations. I don't eat caviar, and East Third Street is a long way from Sutton Place. But I never cared much for caviar, and the pad I have is a comfortable one. It's a tiny room a couple blocks off the Bowery, furnished with a mattress, a refrigerator, a stove, a chair, and a table. The cockroaches get me out of bed, dress me, and walk me down to the bathroom down the hall. Maybe you couldn't live in a place like that, but I sort of like it. There's no problem keeping it up, 'cause it couldn't get any worse.

My meals, like I said, are not caviar. For instance, in the refrigerator right now I have a sack of coffee, a dozen eggs, and part of a fifth of bourbon. Every morning I have two fried eggs and a cup of coffee. Every evening I have three fried eggs and two cups of coffee. I figure, you find something you like, you should stick with it.

And the whole thing is cheap. I pay twenty a month for the room, which is cheap anywhere and amazing in New York. And in this neighborhood food prices are pretty low, too.

All in all, I can live on ten bucks a week with no trouble. At the moment I have fifty bucks in my pocket, so I'm set for a month, maybe a little more. I haven't worked in four months, haven't had any income in three.

I live, more or less, by my wits. I hate to work. What the hell, what good are brains if you have to work for a living? A cat lives fifty, sixty, maybe seventy years, and that's not a long time. He might as well spend his time doing what he likes. Me, I like to walk around, see people, listen to music, read, drink, smoke, and get a dame. So that's what I do. Since nobody's paying people to walk around or read or anything, I pick up some gold when I can. There's always a way.

By this I don't mean that I'm a mugger or a burglar or anything like that. It might be tough for you to get what I'm saying, so let me explain.

I mentioned that I worked four months ago, but I didn't say that I only held the job for a day. It was at a drugstore on West Ninety-sixth Street. I got a job there as a stock and delivery boy on a Monday morning. It was easy enough getting the job. I reported for work with a couple of sandwiches in a beat-up gym bag. At four that afternoon I took out a delivery and forgot to come back. I had twenty shiny new Zippo lighters in the gym bag, and they brought anywhere from a buck to a buck-seventy-five at the Third Avenue hockshops. That was enough money for three weeks, and took me all of one day to earn it. No chance of him catching me, either. He's got a fake name and a fake address, and he probably didn't notice the lighters were missing for a while.

Dishonest? Obviously, but so what? The guy deserved it. He told me straight off the Puerto Ricans in the neighborhood were not the cleverest mathematicians in the world, and when I made a sale I should shortchange them and we'd split fifty-fifty. Why should I play things straight with a bum like that? He can afford the loss. Besides, I worked one day free for him, didn't I?

It's all a question of using your head. If you think things out carefully, decide just what you want, and find a smart way to get it, you come out ahead, time after time. Like the way I got out of going into the army.

The army, as far as I'm concerned, is strictly for the sparrows. I couldn't see it a year ago, and I still can't. When I got my notice I had to think fast. I didn't want to try faking the eye chart or anything like that, and I didn't think I would get away with a conscientious objector pitch. Anyway, those guys usually wind up in stir or working twice as hard as everybody else. When the idea came to me it seemed far too simple, but it worked. I got myself deferred for homosexuality.

It was a panic. After the physical I went in for the psychiatric, and I played the beginning fairly straight, only I acted generally hesitant.

Then the Doc asks, "Do you like girls?"

"Well," I blurt out, "only as friends."

"Have you ever gone with girls?"

"Oh, no!" I managed to sound somewhat appalled at the idea.

I hesitated for a minute or two, then admitted that I was homosexual. I was deferred, of course.

You'd think that everybody who really wanted to avoid the army would try this, but they won't. It's psychological. Men are afraid of being homosexual, or of having people think they're homosexual. They're even afraid of some skull doctor who never saw them before and never will see them again. So many people are so stupid, if you just act a little smart you can't miss. After the examination was over I spent some time with the whore who lives across the hall from me. No sense talking myself into anything. A cat doesn't watch out, he can be too smart, you know.

To get back to my story—the money from the Zippos lasted two weeks, and I was practically broke again. This didn't bother me, though. I just sat around the pad for a while, reading and smoking, and sure enough, I got another idea that I figured would be worth a few bucks. I showered and shaved, and made a half-hearted attempt at shining my shoes. I had some shoe polish from the drugstore. I had some room in the gym bag after the Zippos, so I stocked up on toothpaste, shoe polish, aspirins, and that kind of junk. Then I put on the suit that I keep clean for emergencies. I usually wear dungarees, but once a month I need a suit for something, so I always have it clean and ready. Then, with a tie on and my hair combed for a change, I looked almost human. I left the room, splurged fifteen cents for a bus ride, and got off at Third Avenue and Sixtieth Street. At the corner of Third and Fifty-ninth is a small semi-hockshop that I cased a few days before. They do more buying and selling than actual pawning, and there aren't too many competitors right in the neighborhood. Their stock is average—the more common and lower-priced musical instruments, radios, cameras, record players, and the cheap stuff—clocks, lighters, rings, watches, and so on. I got myself looking as stupid as possible and walked in.

There must be thousands of hockshops in New York, but there are only two types of clerks. The first is usually short, bald, and over forty. He wears suspenders, talks straight to the lower-class customers and kowtows to the others. Most of the guys farther downtown fit into this category. The other type is like the guy I drew: tall, thick black hair, light-colored suit, and a wide smile. He talks gentleman-to-gentleman with his upper-class customers and patronizingly to the bums. Of the two, he's usually more dangerous.

My man came on with the Johnny-on-the-spot pitch, ready and willing to serve. I hated him immediately.

"I'm looking for a guitar," I said, "preferably a good one. Do you have anything in stock at the moment?" I saw six or seven on the wall, but when you play it dumb, you play it dumb.

"Yes," he said. "Do you play guitar?" I didn't and told him so. No point in lying all the time. But, I added, I was going to learn.

He picked one off the wall and started plucking the strings. "This is an excellent one, and I can let you have it for only thirty-five dollars. Would you like to pay cash or take it on the installment plan?"

I must have been a good actor, because he was certainly playing me for a mark. The guitar was a Pelton, and it was in good shape, but it never cost more than forty bucks new, and he had a nerve asking more than twenty-five. Any minute now he might tell me that the last owner was an old lady who only played hymns on it. I held back the laugh and plunked the guitar like a nice little customer.

"I like the sound. And the price sounds about right to me."

"You'll never find a better bargain." Now this was laying it on with a trowel.

"Yes, I'll take it." He deserved it now. "I was just passing by, and I don't have much money with me. Could I make a down payment and pay the rest weekly?"

He probably would have skipped the down payment. "Surely," he said. For some reason I've always disliked guys who say "surely." No reason, really. "How much would you like to pay now?"

I told him I was really short at the moment, but could pay ten dollars a week. Could I just put a dollar down? He said I could, but in that case the price would have to be forty dollars, which is called putting the gouge on.

I hesitated a moment for luck, then agreed. When he asked for identification I pulled out my pride and joy.

In a wallet that I also copped from that drugstore I have the best identification in the world, all phony and all legal. Everything in it swears up and down that my name is Leonard Blake and I live on Riverside Drive. I have a baptismal certificate that I purchased from a sharp little entrepreneur at our high school back in the days when I needed proof of age to buy a drink. I have a Social Security card that can't be used for identification purposes but always is, and an unapproved application for a driver's license. To get one of these you just go to the Bureau of Motor Vehicles and fill it out. It isn't stamped, but no pawnbroker ever noticed that. Then there are membership cards in everything from the Captain Marvel Club to the NAACP. Of course he took my buck and I signed some papers.

I made it next to Louie's shop at Thirty-fifth and Third. Louie and I know each other, so there's no haggling. He gave me fifteen for the guitar, and I let him know it wouldn't be hot for at least ten days. That's the way I like to do business.

Fifteen bucks was a week and a half, and you see how easy it was. And it's fun to shaft a guy who deserves it, like that sharp clerk did. But when I got back to the pad and read some old magazines, I got another idea before I even had a chance to start spending the fifteen.

I was reading one of those magazines that are filled with really exciting information, like how to build a model of the Great Wall of China around your house, and I was wondering what kind of damn fool would want to build a wall around his house, much less a Great Wall of China type wall, when the idea hit me. Wouldn't a hell of a lot of the same type of people like a Sheffield steel dagger, twenty-five inches long, an authentic copy of a twelfth-century relic recently discovered in a Bergdorf castle? And all of this for only two bucks post-paid, no CODs? I figured they might.

This was a big idea, and I had to plan it just right. A classified in that type of magazine cost two dollars, a post office box cost about five for three months. I was in a hurry, so I forgot about lunch, and rushed across town to the Chelsea Station on Christopher Street, and Lennie Blake got himself a post office box. Then I fixed up the ad a little, changing "twenty-five inches" to "over two feet." And customers would please allow three weeks for delivery. I sent ads and money to three magazines, and took a deep breath. I was now president of Cornet Enterprises. Or Lennie Blake was. Who the hell cared?

For the next month and a half I stalled on the rent and ate as little as possible. The magazines hit the stands after two weeks, and I gave people time to send in. Then I went west again and picked up my mail.

A hell of a lot of people wanted swords. There were about two hundred envelopes, and after I finished throwing out the checks and requests for information, I wound up with $196 and sixty-seven three-cent stamps. Anybody want to buy a stamp?

See what I mean? The whole bit couldn't have been simpler. There's no way in the world they can trace me, and nobody in the post office could possible remember me. That's the beauty of New York—so many people. And how much time do you think the cops will waste looking for a two-bit swindler? I could even have made another pick-up at the post office, but greedy guys just don't last long in this game. And a federal rap I need like a broken ankle.

Right now I'm 100 percent in the clear. I haven't heard a rumble on the play yet, and already Lennie Blake is dead—burned to ashes and flushed down the toilet. Right now I'm busy establishing Warren Shaw. I sign the name, over and over, so that I'll never make a mistake and sign the wrong name sometime. One mistake is above par for the course.

Maybe you're like me. I don't mean with the same fingerprints and all, but the same general attitudes. Do you fit the following general description: smart, coldly logical, content with coffee and eggs in a cold-water walk-up, and ready to work like hell for an easy couple of bucks? If that's you, you're hired. Come right in and get to work. You can even have my room. I'm moving out tomorrow.

It's been kicks, but too much of the same general pattern and the law of averages gets you. I've been going a long time, and one pinch would end everything. Besides, I figure it's time I took a step or two up the social ladder.